Fundamental Structures of **ALGEBRA**

George D. Mostow
YALE UNIVERSITY

Joseph H. Sampson
THE JOHNS HOPKINS UNIVERSITY

Jean-Pierre Meyer
THE JOHNS HOPKINS UNIVERSITY

Fundamental Structures of ALGEBRA

McGRAW-HILL BOOK COMPANY *New York Toronto London*

FUNDAMENTAL STRUCTURES OF ALGEBRA

Library of Congress Catalog Card Number 63–13148

ISBN 07-043500-6
5678910 HDBP 7654321

Preface

The great evolution of the physical, engineering, and social sciences during the past half century has cast mathematics in a rôle quite different from its familiar one of a powerful but essentially passive instrument for computing answers. In fact that view of mathematics was never a correct one, but it has had a strong influence in determining the standard undergraduate mathematics curriculum. Its inadequacy is becoming increasingly apparent with the growing recognition that mathematics is at the very heart of many modern scientific theories—not merely as a calculating device, but much more fundamentally as the *sole language* in which the theories can be expressed. Thus mathematics plays an organic and creative part in science, as a limitless source of concepts which provide fruitful new ways of representing natural phenomena.

The view of mathematics as a calculating device, and the traditional pre-eminence of analytic geometry and calculus in the undergraduate mathematics curriculum, can be traced in part to the dominant influence of classical physics, especially mechanics, and to the almost ineradicable prejudice in favor of expressing the laws of Nature in the form of simple mechanical analogies. This "billiard-ball" conception of Nature still persists, but its limitations have been known for a long time; modern science cannot confine itself to that naïve conception, and that part of mathematics with which it is linked—though utterly indispensable—is nonetheless inadequate for science. An ability to deal fluently with abstract systems has become a necessity.

Yet algebra, the mathematics of abstract systems par excellence, has been commonly neglected in undergraduate curricula; indeed it is often omitted almost entirely from the mathematical education of science students, greatly to the detriment of their understanding of mathematics. The aim of this book is to acquaint students in the physical, engineering, and social sciences with the most important algebraic structures and with the mathematician's way of discussing them. The book contains material which is not usually given before the junior or senior year of college, and much of the subject matter covered here is not generally presented to science students at all. It may therefore seem surprising that the book was designed to enable the student to begin his study of algebra at a very early stage of his undergraduate career. A preliminary mimeographed version was used with gratifying success in a course given by the authors at Johns Hopkins University in 1960–1961. Among those who took the first half of the course were freshmen who contemplated more than one term of mathematics in college. (Entry of freshmen into the second half of the course was restricted to those in the top third of their class who studied linear algebra† simultaneously with a course in calculus.) Although the material was of a level usually considered rather advanced, it was our experience that it was understood and learned as readily by the freshmen as by those students who had taken the standard analytic geometry and calculus courses. The explanation for this appears to be that the lesser mathematical experience of the freshmen was more than compensated by their freedom from stubborn misconceptions and by their stimulation upon encountering something that was not just a prolongation of high school. Before the first term was over, we were able to communicate with them in the precise and lucid language of mathematics.

And it is in the language of mathematics that many pedagogical difficulties lie. Few persons have learned the precise use of even their native tongue properly; and the habits of precision are not easily acquired. That is a fortiori so in learning the unfamiliar language of mathematics. It is not until the student is really well acquainted with the mathematical idiom that simple mathematical statements become simple for *him*. In order to communicate the idiom we have first applied it to rather familiar situations, and, as it is established, new subject matter is presented at an increasing rate.

The second half of this book is devoted chiefly to a rather detailed account of linear algebra and some of its applications. A student who completes it will be well prepared for the use of linear algebra in science and engineering courses, as well as in advanced mathematics courses. Chapter 12 presents an application of linear algebra to the solution of differential equations. It should be mentioned that Chapters 4 and 5 in this book were included mainly for reference. By omitting most of those two chapters it is possible to put the rest of the material through Chapter 8 into one term. Chapter 15 contains a precise discussion of mappings, relations, and equivalence classes, as well as of several important constructions involving equivalence classes. The reader may find it profitable to refer to Chapter 15 several times during the course. Chapter 16 is concerned with tensor algebra, a special but important part of linear algebra. Although a typical one-year course may stop short of Chapter 16, the material in it should not present great difficulty to students who have absorbed the main ideas in the earlier part of the book.

† Cf. Instructor's Manual.

The authors have been guided by the pedagogic philosophy that general abstract concepts are not really assimilated until employed in particular situations. As a result, this book makes excursions into special topics that are not usually found in a beginner's book on the foundations of algebra. Accordingly, the chapter on integers devotes considerable space to elementary number theory; the chapter on polynomials contains the solution of cubic and biquadratic equations; the chapter on group theory contains the Sylow theorems. The special topics have been selected with two objectives in mind: (1) They impart important information. (2) They provide pedagogically valuable opportunities for the manipulation of general concepts.

In conclusion we should like to comment on the place of this book in the undergraduate program. As indicated above, our experience has been that a one-year algebra course, early in the curriculum, accelerates the student's mathematical development and enhances his ability to understand and learn mathematics. Moreover, it helps to provide a better-balanced preparation for scientific applications and for advanced mathematics courses. And it should be noted that linear algebra is usually required in science and engineering courses earlier than it is given in the standard mathematics curriculum. Beginning students *can* understand algebra at this level, and therefore it is both practical and desirable to replace the usual six-semester sequence of analytic geometry† and calculus by a two-semester algebra and four-semester calculus sequence. This plan has the very important advantage that the superior student can take algebra and calculus simultaneously in his first year, being thereby enabled to complete the basic mathematics requirements in two years instead of three.

We take this opportunity to express our gratitude to Mr. James Sauvé, S.J., for his many important suggestions, for his invaluable contribution in the preparation of the manuscript, and for helping us to avoid errors and ambiguities.

George D. Mostow
Joseph H. Sampson
Jean-Pierre Meyer

† Chapter 8 contains a considerable discussion of analytic geometry.

Contents

16. Tensors 514

List of special symbols

$\mathbf{J}$	the system of positive integers, p. 36
$\mathbf{Z}$	the ring of integers, p. 36
$\mathbf{Z}_m$	the ring of residue classes modulo m, p. 72
$\mathbf{Q}$	the field of rational numbers, p. 86
$\mathbf{R}$	the field of real numbers, p. 110
$\mathbf{C}$	the field of complex numbers, p. 119
$a^j{}_i$	matrix element in jth row and ith column, p. 229
$\mathbf{a}^j$	jth row of a matrix, p. 229
$\mathbf{a}_i$	ith column of a matrix, p. 229
${}^t\mathbf{a}$	the transpose of a matrix, p. 235
$\tilde{\mathbf{a}}$	the adjoint of a matrix, p. 314
$\delta^j{}_i$	Kronecker delta, p. 230
$\mathrm{Tr}\ \mathbf{a}$	trace of a matrix, p. 311
$\det \mathbf{a}$	determinant of a matrix, p. 308
$\mathrm{mat}_{B,B'}\ \mathbf{T}$	the matrix of a linear mapping with respect to a base pair B, B'
K^m, K_n, $K^m{}_n$	respectively the sets of $m \times 1$, $1 \times n$, and $m \times n$ matrices with coefficients in K, p. 229
$\mathrm{Ker}\ \mathbf{T}$, $\mathrm{Im}\ \mathbf{T}$	p. 218
$\mathrm{Hom}\ (U, V)$	p. 222
$f : S \to T$	mapping symbol, p. 2
$f \circ g$	composition of mappings, p. 3
$\langle \mathbf{f}, \mathbf{x} \rangle$	inner product, p. 223
$\mathbf{u} \times \mathbf{v}$	vector product, p. 482
$A \times B$	cartesian product, pp. 495, 514
$\mathbf{u} \wedge \mathbf{v}$	exterior product, p. 552
$\otimes$	tensor product symbol, p. 438 and Chap. 16
$\oplus$	direct sum, pp. 173, 382, 385
$*$	dual operator, p. 565
$\#E$	number of elements in the set E, p. 277
$H \cap K$	intersection, p. 279
$\cong$	isomorphism, pp. 17, 293

(a)	cyclic subgroup generated by a, p. 267
End V	algebra of endomorphisms of V, p. 342
$\mathbf{T}_1 \sim \mathbf{T}_2$	similarity, p. 408
$GL(U)$	general linear group, p. 532
$B[t]$	adjunction of t to a ring B, p. 133
$K(x)$	field of rational functions, p. 163
$[1, b]$	segment, p. 38
(a, b)	greatest common divisor, pp. 57, 142

Fundamental Structures of **ALGEBRA**

1

Binary operations and groups

1. Introduction

The axioms that we shall assume in this chapter are inspired by experience with ordinary numerical calculations—for example, addition and multiplication. Each of these operations associates with two given numbers another number, their *sum* in the case of addition and their *product* in the case of multiplication. Here we shall investigate the consequences of assuming that we have some kind of operation that associates with two objects (not necessarily numbers) another object. The operation will be assumed to obey certain rules, or *axioms*. In this chapter we shall set down two main axioms, and they will be the basis for the definition of a mathematical system called a *group*. The same axioms will occur repeatedly in later chapters. These axioms require some explanation, and they are discussed at length in the following sections.

2. Sets and mappings

We begin by mentioning some terminology which is constantly used in modern mathematics. The word *set* will be understood as synonymous with *collection*. A set is then a collection of certain objects, usually called the *elements* of the set. Sets and their elements will often be denoted by letters of the alphabet. If S denotes a set, such a phrase as "let x be an element of S" means the following: we wish to talk about an arbitrary element selected from S, an element to be considered as fixed throughout the discussion at hand. In order to be able to talk about it conveniently, we give it a temporary name x (or whatever other symbol happens to be convenient). Thus x here does not denote an element fixed once for all in S (unless stated otherwise), but rather a "variable" or "arbitrary" element; its meaning is fixed only for the discussion that one has in mind.

A part of a set S is of course itself a set. A part of S is also called a *subset* of S.

We illustrate with some very simple examples—indeed trite examples. They merely serve to illustrate how the language is used, and we shall not bother about great precision at this point.

EXAMPLE 1 Let S denote the set of all cards in an ordinary deck. Thus S contains 52 elements, and we can say that if x is an element of S, then x bears one of the symbols 2, 3, . . . , 9, J, Q, K, A, and one of the colors red or black. We can define a subset R of S by declaring that R shall consist of all elements x in S which are red. Here we have imposed a condition on x; it now stands for an arbitrarily selected red card in S. That is, the subset R consists of all hearts and diamonds. In turn we can define a subset W of R by the condition that an element y of R is in W if and only if y bears the number 3. In other words, W consists of the 3 of hearts and the 3 of diamonds. A further subset T of S is defined by the condition that T shall consist of all elements z in S such that z bears a black diamond. This condition is not *a priori* unreasonable, for someone who plays only *bêsigue* or roulette might well be unaware of the composition of a bridge deck. The reader will of course be aware that the subset T just defined contains no cards; for convenience of language we call T the *empty* subset of S.

EXAMPLE 2 Odd numbers form a subset U of the set N of whole numbers. Let V be the subset of U consisting of all elements n such that n^2 leaves a remainder of 3 upon division by 4. It is not hard to see that V is empty, but that is not quite so obvious as in the case of T in the preceding example.

One of the most basic notions occurring in mathematics is that of *mapping*. *A mapping of a set S to a set T is a rule, or an operation, which assigns to every element in S a definite element in T.* (The sets S and T need not be different.) Mappings are also called *functions* or, sometimes, *operators*. Mappings are customarily denoted by letters. If f denotes a mapping of S to T, then the element of T which f assigns to an element x of S is often denoted by $f(x)$; one says that the mapping f *sends* (or *maps*) the element x into the element $f(x)$, and $f(x)$ is called the *image* of x. The notation $f\colon S \to T$ is useful to indicate that f is a mapping from S to T.

Some further useful notation is as follows: B being a subset of S, $f(B)$ denotes the subset of T consisting of all $f(x)$ for which x is in B; $f(B)$ is called the *image* of B under f. C being a subset of T, $f^{-1}(C)$ denotes the subset of S consisting of all elements x such that $f(x)$ is in C.

EXAMPLE 3 Assigning to every card in a bridge deck S its suit defines a mapping of S to the set of four elements consisting of hearts, diamonds, clubs, spades.

Assigning to every card in S the king in the same suit defines a mapping f of S to itself. Thus $f(3\text{D}) = \text{KD}$, $f(4\text{D}) = \text{KD}$, etc.; and $f^{-1}(\text{KD})$ denotes the set of all 13 cards in the suit of diamonds. Observe that $f^{-1}(3\text{D})$ is the empty set. The mapping f can also be considered as a mapping of S to the subset K consisting of the four kings.

EXAMPLE 4 Assigning to every card in a bridge deck S the corresponding card in a second deck S' defines a mapping of S to S'.

EXAMPLE 5 Assigning to the radius of a circle the area of that circle defines a mapping of the set of positive numbers to itself.

A mapping f of a set S to a set T is called a *one-to-one* mapping, or correspondence, if the following conditions hold:

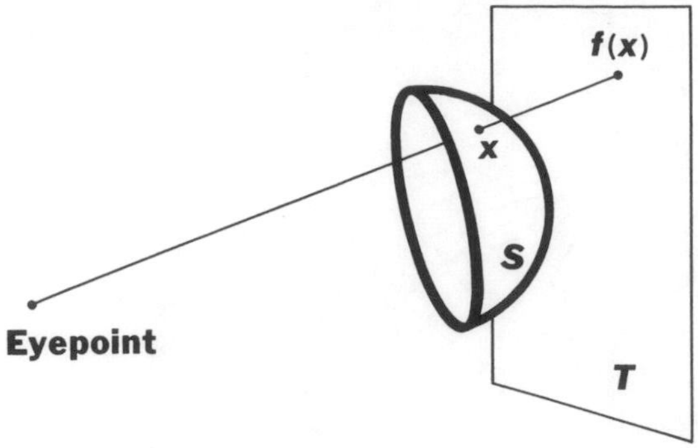

Figure 1

The projection, from the eyepoint, of the spherical zone S upon the plane T is a mapping f of S to T. If the plane T is tangent to the sphere, and the eyepoint lies at the end of the diameter through the point of tangency, such a mapping is called a *stereographic* projection.

(*a*) For every element y in T there is an element x in S such that $f(x) = y$.

(*b*) If x and x' are two *different* elements of S, then $f(x) \neq f(x')$.

The first condition asserts that for each element of T there is at least one element of S which is sent into it by f; and the second condition asserts that different elements of S are not sent by f into the same element of T. Thus, to every element in S there corresponds one and only one element in T, and vice versa.

The mappings of Example 3 are clearly not one-to-one; but the mapping of Example 4 is a one-to-one correspondence.

A one-to-one mapping of a set to itself is sometimes called a *permutation*. Thus the simple cryptographic codes obtained by scrambling the alphabet depend upon permutations, or one-to-one correspondences, of the letters of the alphabet.

If a mapping $f: S \to T$ is one-to-one, then we can define a mapping from T to S by assigning to each y of T the unique element x of S that f sends into y. This new mapping is usually denoted by f^{-1} and is called the *inverse* mapping of f. Clearly f^{-1} is also one-to-one.

EXAMPLE 6 Given any set S whatever, the mapping f from S to S that assigns each element of S to itself is certainly one-to-one. This mapping, as trivial as it seems, arises often enough to deserve a special name: it is called the *identity* mapping of S. In symbols it is characterized by $f(x) = x$ for all x in S.

Suppose now that we are given a mapping f of a set S to a set T and another mapping g of T to a set U. To every element x in S the first mapping assigns some element $f(x)$ in T; to every element y of T the second mapping g assigns an element $g(y)$ in U—in particular to $f(x)$ it assigns an element $g(f(x))$ in U. Therefore the operation that assigns to x in S the element $g(f(x))$ in U is a mapping from S to U. It is called the *composition* of f and g and is denoted by $g \circ f$, or simply by gf. Thus $g \circ f(x) = g(f(x))$.

For a "capsule" definition we can say simply that $g \circ f$ is the operation obtained by first applying f and then g.

EXAMPLE 7 If the first mapping assigns to every human being its last name, and the second assigns to every proper name its first letter, then the composition of the

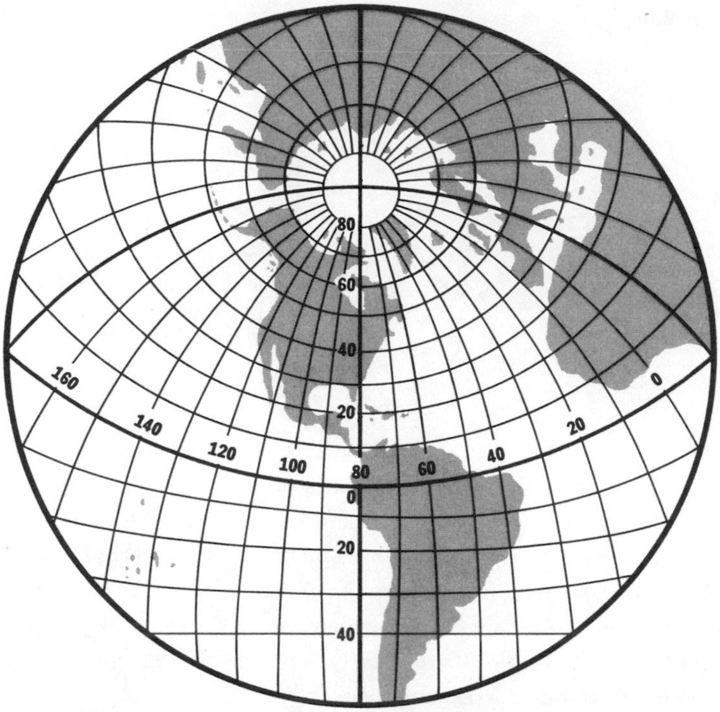

Figure 2 Stereographic projection sends circles on the sphere into circles on the plane, except for the great circles passing through the point of tangency; these great circles are mapped into straight lines.

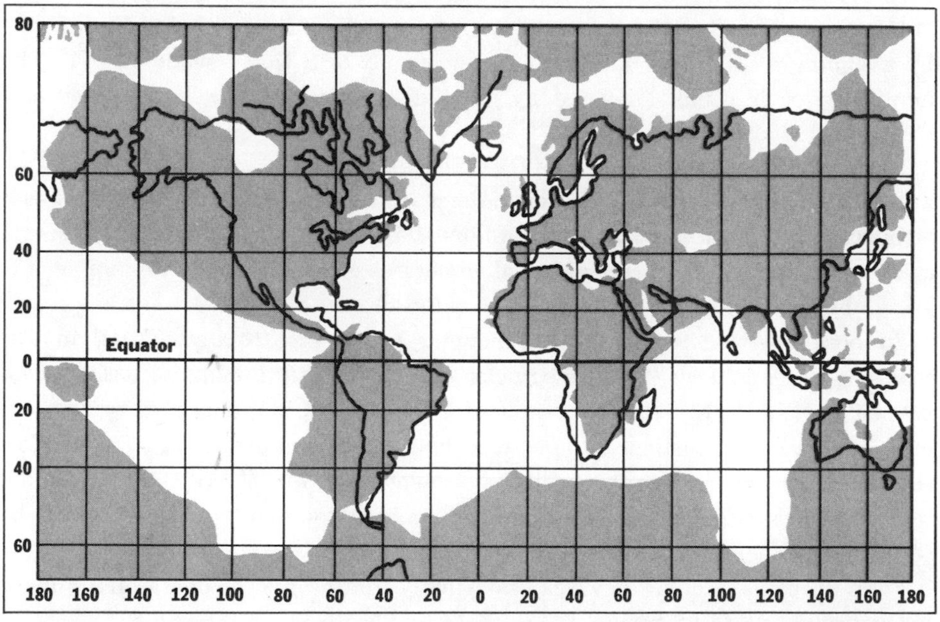

Figure 3 Mercator's projection from his World Map of 1569. Mercator's delineation of the land is shaded. This map, in common with all other geographical maps, provides a mapping of (a subset of) an idealized earth's surface.

given mappings is the mapping from the set of human beings to the alphabet which assigns to every human being his surname's initial.

Some of the examples of sets and mappings given above involve sets of real objects (cards, etc.). The sets that occur in mathematics always consist of elements of an abstract nature. And most often the real point of interest is not the nature of the elements in a given set but rather the relationships that happen to exist among the elements.

The notions of *set* and *mappings* lie at the very foundations of mathematics, and we wish to avoid completely any discussion of that aspect of things. For that reason we have limited ourselved here to explaining a few terms that are nearly indispensable. However some of these are taken up again briefly in Chap. 15.

EXERCISE

Let $h\colon S \to T$ be a one-to-one mapping, and let h^{-1} be its inverse. What are the composite mappings $h \circ h^{-1}$ and $h^{-1} \circ h$?

3. Binary operations

In this section we discuss a general kind of mathematical operation which includes as special cases the familiar operations of arithmetic, as well as many others that will be of importance later in the book.

DEFINITION 3.1 *A binary operation in a set S is a rule, or operation, which assigns to any pair of elements in S, taken in a definite order, another element in the same set S.*

For the present let us indicate such an operation by $*$. Thus, if a and b are elements of the set S, then the $*$ operation assigns to the pair a, b some element of S. We shall denote it by $a * b$. The operation also assigns to the pair b, a an element, namely $b * a$. Observe that the definition tells us nothing about the relation of $a * b$ to $b * a$. In fact, it tells us so little about $*$ that we could not expect to prove any very surprising theorems at this point.

Let us take time to point out some simple but important things about $*$. First of all, the symbol $*$ used to represent the operation is of no importance, and presently we shall use other symbols which are more convenient. Moreover, the same set S may be equipped with several different binary operations, as we shall soon see.

The adjective *binary* is used because the operation produces from a *pair* of elements S (taken in a specific order) some new element of S. If we select elements a, b, c of S (not necessarily different) there are various ways in which we can combine them by the operation $*$. For example, to the pair a, b our operation assigns the element $a * b$, and we can then use $*$ again to combine that element with c. We denote the result by $(a * b) * c$. To repeat, this symbol means the following: apply $*$ to the pair a, b obtaining $a * b$, and then apply $*$ to the pair

$a * b, c$. In like manner we can apply $*$ to the pair $a, b * c$, obtaining an element which we write as $a * (b * c)$. The parentheses are necessary to indicate just how the elements are to be grouped into pairs. It would make no sense to write down simply $a * b * c$ because $*$ can be applied only to *pairs* of elements. We shall soon see, however, that parentheses can be safely omitted under certain circumstances. Note that if we change the order of a, b, c in the foregoing we can write down still other combinations, for example, $b * (a * c)$. Similarly, if a, b, c, d are elements of S, we can form $a * (b * (c * d))$ or $(a * b) * (c * d)$ and many others.

Throughout this book the equality sign "$=$" is taken to mean "the same as." We take occasion here to point out some very important but very simple facts about $=$. Let a and b be elements of the set S we have been discussing, and suppose that $a = b$; that is, the letters a and b denote the same element of S, or in other words they are two *names* for the same element of S. It follows that if c is any element of S, then $a * c = b * c$, for the two sides of this equation are still simply two names of the same element of S. Similarly, if a, a', b, b' are elements of S such that $a * b = a' * b'$, then $a * b$ and $a' * b'$ are two names for the same element of S, and so it follows that $(a * b) * c = (a' * b') * c$ for any element c of S, and also $c * (a * b) = c * (a' * b')$. We might express this principle briefly by saying that "equals 'starred' with equals are equal." Observe, however, that this is a simple consequence of the meaning of equality and holds for all binary operations.

EXAMPLE 1 The following are binary operations: Addition of whole numbers; multiplication of whole numbers; subtraction of whole numbers (by which we mean the operation that assigns to a pair of numbers a, b their difference $a - b$).

EXAMPLE 2 Let S be a set and M be the set of all mappings of S to itself. The composition of mappings defines a binary operation in M, since the composition of two mappings of S to itself is again a mapping of S to itself.

The way in which $*$ operates upon pairs of elements of S can be written down in a "table"—at any rate if S does not have an unreasonably large number of elements. To give some concrete examples let us consider a set S consisting of elements represented by the letters p, q, r, s (these letters now stand for *fixed* elements of S, not for arbitrary elements, as with a, b, c above). The following tables† define binary operations which we denote by $\times$, $\diamondsuit$, $\circ$, $+$.

TABLE 1, FOR $\times$

	p	q	r	s
p	q	s	p	q
q	p	p	s	s
r	q	p	q	r
s	r	p	s	r

† These tables are for illustrative purposes and have no particular interest beyond that.

The table is to be read as follows: to find, say, $p \times q$ look for the element at the intersection of the p-row and q-column. According to the table, $p \times q = s$; similarly, $q \times p = p$, $r \times s = r$, and so on. Note that $p \times q$ and $q \times p$ are *different* elements.

TABLE 2, FOR $\diamond$

	p	q	r	s
p	q	q	q	q
q	q	q	q	q
r	q	q	q	q
s	q	q	q	q

Here $p \diamond q = r \diamond s = \cdots = q$.

TABLE 3, FOR $\circ$

	p	q	r	s
p	p	q	r	s
q	q	p	s	r
r	r	s	p	q
s	s	r	q	p

Note that, here, $x \circ y = y \circ x$ for any two elements x, y selected from p, q, r, s. A similar statement holds for the operation defined in the preceding table, as well as in the following.

TABLE 4, FOR $+$

	p	q	r	s
p	p	q	r	s
q	q	r	s	p
r	r	s	p	q
s	s	p	q	r

Note that, here, $p + x = x + p = x$ for any element x selected from p, q, r, s. An analogous statement holds for the preceding example. In both cases p is said to be an *identity* element for the particular binary operation $\circ$ or $+$ in question.

By now it should be fairly obvious that many other binary operations can be defined in the set S consisting of p, q, r, s. In fact, to define such an operation it is only necessary to fill the 16 blank spaces of a table with the letters p, q, r, s. Since there are four choices for each of the blank spaces, there are all together $4^{16} = 4{,}294{,}967{,}296$ possible binary operations in S. The reader will be heartened to learn that only two of these are of any real mathematical interest, namely the ones given in Tables 3 and 4. The operation defined by Table 2 is clearly very trivial in nature. The authors arrived at Table 1 by filling in the 16 spaces at random. Tables 3 and 4 are tables of groups, which we shall define presently.

The use of tables like those above becomes awkward and inconvenient for sets S containing many elements. Most of the sets of importance to us contain an infinite number of elements, and for such sets it is wholly impracticable to write down a table. We shall soon find other more convenient means of describing binary operations.

Referring back to the "identity" element p of Tables 3 and 4, we are led to make a general definition:

DEFINITION 3.2 *S being a set with a binary operation $*$, an element e of S is called an* identity *element for $*$ if $e * a = a$ and $a * e = a$ for every element a of S.*

An identity element in S (if there is one) plays a role analogous to that of zero for addition and of unity for multiplication. Indeed $0 + a = a + 0 = a$ for any integer a, and so 0 is the identity element for addition of integers. Similarly, $1 \cdot a = a \cdot 1 = a$, and 1 is the identity element for multiplication.

THEOREM 3.1 *Let S be a set with a binary operation $*$. If there is an identity element for $*$ in S, then there is only one.*

Proof. Suppose that e and e' are both identity elements in S. Then by Definition 3.2 we have $e * a = a$ for any element a of S. In particular, $e * e' = e'$. Similarly from Definition 3.2 we have $a * e' = a$ for any element a of S. In particular, $e * e' = e$. Hence, $e = e'$. Q.E.D.

EXERCISES

1. Compute the following expressions from each of the four tables above, where $*$ denotes, in each case, one of $\times$, $\diamond$, $\circ$, $+$:

(*a*) $p * p$, $q * r$, $p * s$, $p * q$.

(*b*) $((p * p) * (q * r)) * q$, $(p * (p * (q * r))) * q$, $(s * ((p * s) * q)) * (p * q)$.

2. How many binary operations can be defined in a set of two elements? In a set of seven elements? How many of these operations satisfy the *commutative* law: $x * y = y * x$?

3. Is there an identity element for the operation $\times$ of Table 1?

4. The associative axiom

DEFINITION 4.1 *Let S be a set with a binary operation $*$. The operation is said to be* associative *if, given any elements a, b, c, in S, the following equality holds:*

4.1 $$(a * b) * c = a * (b * c)$$

We also say that $*$ satisfies the *associative axiom*, or *law*, if (4.1) holds.

This is a very important axiom, and most of the binary operations which we shall encounter will satisfy it. Referring to the four tables of Sec. 3, the reader can verify that the last three define associative operations, in contrast with the

the first one, which does not: $(p \times q) \times r = s$ and $p \times (q \times r) = q$. To give another example, division of numbers is a binary operation which is not associative.

We can now prove a simple result which is not merely a restatement of the definition.

PROPOSITION 4.1 *If the operation $*$ is associative, then for any elements a, b, c, d in S we have*

$$((a * b) * c) * d = (a * b) * (c * d)$$

Proof. Denote $a * b$ temporarily by x. Then, since $*$ is associative, $(x * c) * d = x * (c * d)$. Replacing x by $a * b$ (another name for the same element!) we obtain the desired conclusion. It is of course necessary to enclose $a * b$ in parentheses, as explained in the preceding section.

An examination of Proposition 4.1 and Exercises 1 and 2 below discloses that the associative axiom permits us to shift parentheses in a step-by-step fashion and suggests the following very general result:

THEOREM 4.2 *Let S be a set with an associative binary operation $*$. Then if any combination of elements of S is formed by means of repeated application of the operation $*$, the result does not depend upon the grouping of the elements involved. In other words, the way in which parentheses appear in the combination does not affect the result.*

The assertion of this theorem is quite easily proved in any given special case where the number of elements involved is relatively small, and the truth of the theorem soon becomes rather obvious. A complete proof of the theorem, however, is rather involved and is not particularly instructive. Moreover it requires the use of *mathematical induction,* which will not be treated until the next chapter. We shall omit the proof of Theorem 4.2 in order to get on quickly with more interesting matters. Nonetheless the theorem is of great usefulness and permits an enormous simplification of notation. Thus, if a, b, c, d are any elements in S and if the operation $*$ is associative, then the expressions

$$((a * b) * c) * d \qquad (a * b) * (c * d) \qquad (a * (b * (c * d)))$$

all represent the same element (Proposition 4.1 and Exercise 1). Hence no ambiguity can arise if we denote that element simply by $a * b * c * d$. We can similarly omit parentheses in combinations of more elements. For the remainder of this chapter, however, we shall consistently retain parentheses in order to emphasize the use of the associative axiom.

At the end of Sec. 3 we defined what is meant by an *identity* element for a binary operation. Closely connected with that is the notion of *inverse* element:

DEFINITION 4.2 *Let S be a set with a binary operation $*$, and suppose that S contains an identity element e for that operation (e is necessarily unique, by Theorem 3.1).*

If a is an element of S and if there is an element a' in S such that $a * a' = e$ and $a' * a = e$, then a' is called an inverse *element of a.*

EXAMPLE Referring to Table 3, Sec. 3, p is the identity element; r has an inverse, namely, r itself. Similarly for q and s. For Table 4, p is again the identity; q has the inverse s, p has the inverse p.

THEOREM 4.3 *Let S and $*$ be as in Definition* 3.3, *and suppose furthermore that $*$ is associative. Then no element of S can have more than one inverse.*

Proof. Let a' and a'' be inverse elements for some element a of S. Then by definition we have $a * a' = a' * a = e$ and $a * a'' = a'' * a = e$. By the associative law, $(a'' * a) * a' = a'' * (a * a')$. Putting e for $a'' * a$ on the left and for $a * a'$ on the right, we get $e * a' = a'' * e$, and so $a' = a''$, by Definition 3.2. Q.E.D.

REMARK. In virtue of this theorem we can speak of *the* inverse element of a (if there is one and if $*$ is associative). For example, -5 is the inverse of 5 (and vice versa) if the binary operation is taken to be addition of numbers; one-fifth is the inverse of 5 if multiplication is the binary operation.

THEOREM 4.4 *Let S be a set with an associative binary operation $*$ and containing an identity element e for $*$. If a' is the inverse of an element a, then a is the inverse of a'. If further b' is the inverse of an element b, then $b' * a'$ is the inverse of $a * b$. Finally, e is its own inverse.*

Proof. The first assertion follows at once from the symmetry of Definition 4.2 and from Theorem 4.3. To prove the second assertion, we have (using the associative axiom)

$$(b' * a') * (a * b) = b' * ((a' * a) * b) = b' * (e * b) = b' * b = e$$

Similarly, $(a * b) * (b' * a') = e$, and so the element $b' * a'$ has the properties required by Definition 4.2. Therefore $b' * a'$ is the unique inverse of $a * b$, by Theorem 4.3. Finally, $e * e = e$, so that e is its own inverse, by Definition 4.2 and Theorem 4.3. Q.E.D.

THEOREM 4.5 **(Cancellation theorem)** *Let S be a set with an associative binary operation $*$ and containing an identity element e for $*$. Let c be an element of S which has an inverse. Then if $a * c = b * c$ or $c * a = c * b$ for elements a, b of S, it follows that $a = b$.*

Proof. Let c' be the inverse element of c. Thus $c * c' = c' * c = e$. Assuming now that $a * c = b * c$, we have, by "starring" with c' on both sides, $(a * c) * c' = (b * c) * c'$ (recall the discussion of equality in Sec. 3!). Using the associative law we get $a * (c * c') = b * (c * c')$, or $a * e = b * e$. Therefore $a = b$, by definition of identity element. The argument for the other case $c * a = c * b$ is similar. Q.E.D.

The theorem tells us that an element appearing on both sides of an equation can be "canceled out," provided that it has an inverse and provided that it occurs on both sides either on the extreme left or extreme right. Observe that Theorem 4.5 tells us nothing about the possibility of cancellation in such an equation as $a * c = c * b$. In some systems which we shall study later, cancellation is legitimate even for elements which do not have inverses.

EXERCISES

1. If the binary operation $*$ is associative, prove that

$$((a * b) * c) * d = a * (b * (c * d))$$

for any elements a, b, c, d.

2. Similarly, prove that

$$(((a * b) * c) * d) * e = a * ((b * c) * (d * e))$$

for any elements a, b, c, d, e.

3. Show that the associative axiom is satisfied by the operations $\diamondsuit$ and $\circ$ defined in Sec. 3.

4. Write out the definition of an associative binary operation entirely in words without the use of any symbols. (This exercise should convince almost anyone of the great utility of using letters to represent arbitrary, or variable, elements.)

5. Of the binary operations of Examples 1, 2, 3, Sec. 3, which are associative and which are not?

6. Write down the inverses for each of the elements p, q, r, s for the binary operations of Tables 3 and 4, Sec. 3. Do any of these elements have inverses for the operations of Tables 1 and 2?

7. Show by an example from Table 1, Sec. 3, that cancellation is not valid as a general rule in that system. What about the systems defined by Tables 2 and 3?

5. *The commutative axiom*

As we have just seen, the associative axiom allows us to omit parentheses in combinations of several elements of S. However, the *order* in which the elements occur is in general quite essential. For example, we will have in general $(a * b) * c \neq (b * a) * c$. Nevertheless many important binary operations are indifferent to the order in which the elements are written. More precisely, we give the following definition:

DEFINITION 5.1 *Let S be a set with a binary operation $*$. The operation is said to be* commutative *if, given any elements a, b in S, the following equality holds:*

5.1 $$a * b = b * a$$

We also say that $*$ satisfies the *commutative axiom,* or *law,* if (5.1) holds.

Note that this definition is completely independent of the associative axiom, discussed in Sec. 4 (cf. Exercise 3 at the end of this section).

EXAMPLE 1 Addition of whole numbers is a commutative binary operation.

EXAMPLE 2 Subtraction of whole numbers is not a commutative binary operation ($a - b \neq b - a$ in general).

We do not count the commutative axiom as one of the main axioms of this chapter, and we shall not assume that it is satisfied unless we explicitly say so.

Exercise 2 below and Theorem 4.2 suggest the following general theorem. The remarks concerning the proof of Theorem 4.2 are equally applicable here, and we shall omit the proof.

THEOREM 5.1 *Let S be a set with an associative and commutative binary operation $*$. Then if any combination of elements of S is formed by means of repeated application of $*$, the result depends neither upon the grouping of the elements involved nor upon their order.*

EXERCISES

1. Of the binary operations described in the examples and tables of Sec. 3, which are commutative and which are not?

2. Let the binary operation $*$ in a set S be associative and commutative, and let the letters in the following formulas denote elements of S. Prove the following formulas. (Do not omit parentheses; give complete proofs.)

(*a*) $a * (b * c) = b * (a * c)$ (*b*) $a * (b * c) = (b * a) * c$

(*c*) $c * (a * b) = b * (a * c)$ (*d*) $((a * b) * c) * d = (d * c) * (b * a)$

(*e*) $(a * b) * (c * d) = d * (c * (b * a))$

3. Find a commutative, but not associative, binary operation in a set consisting of two elements a and b. In this same set find an associative, but not commutative, binary operation.

***4.** Let $*$ be a binary operation with identity element in S. Prove that the operation is both associative and commutative if and only if it satisfies the so-called "commutassociative" law

$$(a * b) * (c * d) = (a * c) * (b * d)$$

for any elements a, b, c, d in S.†

6. *Groups*

We now come to the second main axiom of this chapter. By adding to the associative law one more simple axiom, (2) below, we arrive at the definition of the notion of *group*. Groups are mathematical systems of great importance, and they will be basic throughout the rest of the book.

DEFINITION 6.1 *A set G with a binary operation $*$ is called a* group *if*

(1) *The operation $*$ is associative.*

(2) *G contains an identity element for the binary operation; and every element in G has an inverse in G for the operation $*$.*

† Asterisks preceding exercise numbers indicate the more difficult exercises.

It is an easy matter to verify that the operations $\circ$ and $+$ given by Tables 3 and 4, Sec. 3, satisfy these two axioms, whereas $\times$ and $\diamond$ of Tables 1 and 2 do not. The set consisting of the elements p, q, r, s, together with either of the two binary operations $\circ$ or $+$, is a group; the two groups are clearly quite different.

As further examples we give below the tables for two groups based on a set of six elements p, q, r, s, t, u:

TABLE 5

	p	q	r	s	t	u
p	p	q	r	s	t	u
q	q	r	s	t	u	p
r	r	s	t	u	p	q
s	s	t	u	p	q	r
t	t	u	p	q	r	s
u	u	p	q	r	s	t

TABLE 6

	p	q	r	s	t	u
p	r	p	q	t	u	s
q	p	q	r	s	t	u
r	q	r	p	u	s	t
s	u	s	t	q	r	p
t	s	t	u	p	q	r
u	t	u	s	r	p	q

Returning to Definition 6.1, observe that a group involves a set of elements together with a binary operation satisfying the two axioms stated above. But we shall often use the same letter to denote both the set itself and the group. The binary operation is usually called the *group operation.*

From Theorem 3.1 it follows that the identity element of a group G is unique. From Theorem 4.3, the inverse of any element of G is unique. In this section we shall denote the identity element by e; the inverse of an arbitrary element a will be denoted by a^{-1}.

THEOREM 6.1 *Let G be a group, with binary operation $*$. If $a * c = a$ or $c * a = a$ for some element a in G, then c must be the identity element e of G. If $a * c = b * c$ or $c * a = c * b$ in G, then $a = b$. If $a * b = e$ or $b * a = e$, then a and b are inverses of each other.*

Proof. Let a^{-1} be the inverse element of a. If $a * c = a$, then clearly $a^{-1} * (a * c) = a^{-1} * a = e$, and so $(a^{-1} * a) * c = e$, whence $e * c = e$, or finally $c = e$. The arguments for the other assertions are similar.

Q.E.D.

THEOREM 6.2 *Let G be a group with operation $*$. For any two elements a and b of G the equations $a * x = b$ and $y * a = b$ have unique solutions for the unknowns x and y, namely $x = a^{-1} * b$ and $y = b * a^{-1}$.*

Proof. The solutions are necessarily unique. For if $a * x = b$ and $a * x' = b$, then $a * x = a * x'$, whence $x = x'$, by the preceding theorem. Similarly for the other equation. On the other hand, it is trivial to verify that the solutions given above are correct. For example, $a * (a^{-1} * b) = (a * a^{-1}) * b = e * b = b$, and similarly for the other. Q.E.D.

REMARK 1. If the operation $*$ satisfies the commutative axiom, then the two solutions x and y above are clearly identical.

The following theorem gives a very important source of groups:

THEOREM 6.3 *Let E be an arbitrary set, and let M denote the set of all one-to-one mappings of E to itself. Then M, with composition of mappings as a binary operation, is a group. Its identity element e is the identity mapping of E; the inverse of an element f of the group M is the inverse mapping f^{-1}.*

Proof. Let f, g be two elements of M, that is, two one-to-one mappings $E \to E$. By definition (Sec. 2), the composition $f \circ g$ is the mapping that sends an arbitrary x in E into the element $f(g(x))$. That is, $f \circ g(x) = f(g(x))$. It is obvious that $f \circ g$ is again a one-to-one mapping and therefore is an element of M. Consequently, composition of mappings is a binary operation in M. It is associative; for if f, g, h are in M, and if x is any element of E, then $f \circ (g \circ h)$ sends x into the element $f(g \circ h(x)) = f(g(h(x)))$, and $(f \circ g) \circ h$ sends x into $f \circ g(h(x)) = f(g(h(x)))$. Thus $f \circ (g \circ h) = (f \circ g) \circ h$. To verify axiom (2) of Definition 6.1, let e denote the identity mapping of E. That is, $e(x) = x$ for all x in E. Plainly e is an element of M, and for any f in M we have $f \circ e(x) = f(e(x)) = f(x)$ and $e \circ f(x) = e(f(x)) = f(x)$. Hence $e \circ f = f \circ e = f$, showing that e is the identity element for the binary operation in M. Finally, if f^{-1} is the inverse mapping of f, then by definition we have $f(f^{-1}(x)) = x$ and $f^{-1}(f(x)) = x$ for any x in E. Therefore, $f \circ f^{-1} = f^{-1} \circ f = e$, showing that f has an inverse for the binary operation in M. Q.E.D.

EXAMPLE Let E consist of three elements a, b, c. It is easily seen that there are precisely six one-to-one mappings of E to itself. Let q denote the identity mapping; let p denote the mapping of E represented by the symbol $\begin{pmatrix} a & b & c \\ c & a & b \end{pmatrix}$, by which we mean that p sends an element of the top row into the element of the bottom row directly beneath it. Thus $p(a) = c$, etc. Similarly put

$$r = \begin{pmatrix} a & b & c \\ b & c & a \end{pmatrix} \qquad s = \begin{pmatrix} a & b & c \\ b & a & c \end{pmatrix} \qquad t = \begin{pmatrix} a & b & c \\ a & c & b \end{pmatrix} \qquad u = \begin{pmatrix} a & b & c \\ c & b & a \end{pmatrix}$$

Then we have, for example, $r \circ t(a) = r(t(a)) = r(a) = b$, $r \circ t(b) = r(t(b)) = r(c) = a$, and $r \circ t(c) = r(t(c)) = r(b) = c$, showing that $r \circ t = s$. It is a routine matter to verify that the operation in the group M of permutations of E is given by Table 6 above.

It may happen that a certain subset of elements in a group is itself a group, and we now give a definition bearing on this situation.

DEFINITION 6.2 *Let G be a group with operation $*$, and let H be a non-empty subset of G. Then H is called a* subgroup *of G if for any elements a, b in H the elements a^{-1}, b^{-1} and $a * b$ are also in H.*

The definition requires that $*$ applied to a pair of elements of H must produce an element in H. Hence, $*$ gives a binary operation in H. Since H contains at least one element a, hence also a^{-1}, by assumption, it follows that H contains $a * a^{-1} = e$. It is easy to verify that H, with the operation $*$, is a group.

THEOREM 6.4 *Let H be a subgroup of a group G. Then G and H have the same identity element. Furthermore, the inverse of an element of H is the same, whether the element is considered as being in H or in the larger group G. The identity element of any group forms by itself a subgroup.*

Proof. The first two assertions follow from Theorem 6.1. The last assertion is trivial. Q.E.D.

Some examples of subgroups are readily found in the groups defined by Tables 3 and 4. The following indicate subgroups of the group given by Table 3:

	p
p	p

	p	q
p	p	q
q	q	p

	p	r
p	p	r
r	r	p

	p	s
p	p	s
s	s	p

The following indicate subgroups of the group given by Table 4:

	p
p	p

	p	r
p	p	r
r	r	p

As a further example, let E be any set and let E' be a subset. Let M be the group of all permutations (i.e., one-to-one mappings of E to itself), as in Theorem 6.3. Let M' denote the subset of M consisting of all mappings f such that $f(x) = x$ for every element x of E'. It is quickly seen that M' is a subgroup of M.

REMARK 2. G being a group, G itself should be counted among the subgroups of G, for it clearly satisfies Definition 6.2. In this context it is sometimes referred to as the *improper* subgroup, all other subgroups being called *proper*.

EXERCISES

1. Give an example of a group containing one element; give an example of a group containing three elements.

2. Let $\heartsuit$ denote the binary operation of Table 5. Solve the following equations for x and y:

$$r \heartsuit x = t \qquad y \heartsuit r = t$$
$$r \heartsuit x = r \qquad y \heartsuit r = r$$

Solve the same equations for the binary operation of Table 6. Are these operations commutative?

3. Find a rule permitting you to determine rapidly from examination of a table whether it defines a commutative binary operation.

4. The group of Table 6 contains a subgroup of one element and a subgroup of three elements. What are those subgroups? Find subgroups of one, two, and three elements of the group of Table 5.

5 Verify that the following is the table of a group:

	p	q	r
p	p	q	r
q	q	r	p
r	r	p	q

6. Let E be a set of two elements. Write out the table of the group M of one-to-one mappings $E \to E$ (see Theorem 6.3).

7. Let E be a set of four elements. Write out the table for the group M of one-to-one mappings of E to itself (as in Theorem 6.3). Find at least three proper subgroups of M, using the observation preceding Remark 2 above.

8. Let G be a group with operation $*$, and let H be a non-empty subset. Show that H is a subgroup of G if and only if $a^{-1} * b$ is in H whenever a, b are in H.

9. Let H, K be subgroups of a group G, and denote by $H \cap K$ the subset of G consisting of the elements in both H, K. Prove that $H \cap K$ is also a subgroup of G, as well as of H and K.

10. Let G be a group. Show that the set of elements common to any family of subgroups is itself a subgroup of G.

11. Let G be a group with operation $*$, and let c be a fixed element of G. Show that the mapping which sends an arbitrary element x of G into $c * x$ is a one-to-one mapping of G to itself (called *left translation* by c). Prove that right translation by c, defined by $x \to x * c$, is also a one-to-one mapping of G to itself.

12. Consider a square S in the plane, and let M denote the set of rotations which bring S into coincidence with itself. Show that M is a group of four elements (composition of mappings being the group operation), and write out its table. What do you get if S is replaced by an equilateral triangle?

***13.** Let T be a regular tetrahedron (four-sided solid). Let M denote the set of rotations which bring T into coincidence with itself. Show that M (with composition of rotations as operation) is a group containing 12 elements.

14. What are the identity elements for the groups of Tables 5 and 6? Write down the inverses for all six elements (for both tables).

7. *Isomorphisms and homomorphisms*

Let us return for a moment to the three subgroups

	p	q
p	p	q
q	q	p

	p	r
p	p	r
r	r	p

	p	s
p	p	s
s	s	p

of the group of Table 3. It is plain that these groups are essentially the same. Their elements are different, but their tables are the same, apart from the particular symbols used. The three groups are thus interchangeable, in much the same way that two automobiles of the same model, or two decks of cards, are interchangeable.

The groups above are said to be *isomorphic* (literally, of the same form). More generally, a group G and a group G' are isomorphic if the table for G is transformed into the table for G' by a suitable substitution of elements. For example, the substitution of r for q in the first table above transforms it into the second. Since we are about to abandon the use of tables, we formulate a definition which does not involve them.

DEFINITION 7.1 *Let G and G' be groups with group operations $*$ and $\diamond$, respectively. These groups are said to be* isomorphic, *in symbols $G \cong G'$, if there exists a one-to-one mapping f from G to G' such that*

7.1 $$f(a * b) = f(a) \diamond f(b)$$

for all a, b in G. Any such mapping is called an isomorphism.

In short, f is required to be "compatible" with the group operations, for (7.1) says that f sends $a * b$ into $a' \diamond b'$, where $a' = f(a)$ and $b' = f(b)$ are the elements of G' corresponding to a, b in G. Hence f, applied to every element in the table for G, simply carries the table for G into that for G'.

It is clear that the inverse mapping f^{-1} from G' to G has the same property. That is,

$$f^{-1}(a' \diamond b') = f^{-1}(a') * f^{-1}(b')$$

Therefore f^{-1} is an isomorphism from G' to G.

It may be possible to find many isomorphisms from one group to another, or from a group to itself.

REMARK. The groups of Tables 3 and 4 are not isomorphic, as can be seen by comparing their subgroups. For it is clear that an isomorphism from one group to another must carry subgroups of the first group into subgroups of the second.

Mappings which are compatible with group operations without necessarily being one-to-one are of great importance. They are called *homomorphisms:*

DEFINITION 7.2 *Let $f\colon G \to G'$ be a mapping of one group to another, with group operations $*$ and $\diamond$, respectively. Then f is called a* homomorphism *if*

7.2 $$f(a * b) = f(a) \diamond f(b)$$

for all a, b in G.

This differs from the preceding definition only in that the one-to-one requirement has been dropped. An isomorphism is thus a special kind of homomorphism.

EXAMPLE 1 The whole numbers (positive, negative, and zero) with the binary operation of addition form a group, and the mapping f defined by $f(a) = 2a$ is a homomorphism of that group to itself.

EXAMPLE 2 Let H be a subgroup of a group G, and define $f\colon H \to G$ by $f(x) = x$ for any x in H. Then f is a homomorphism.

EXAMPLE 3 If G, G' are groups, then the mapping that sends every element of G into the identity element of G' is a homomorphism.

The following two theorems about homomorphisms are basic:

THEOREM 7.1 *Let f be a homomorphism from a group G to a group G'. Then f maps the identity element of G into the identity of G'; and if f maps an element a into a', then it maps the inverse of a into the inverse of a'. In symbols,*

$$f(e) = e' = \text{identity of } G'$$
$$f(a^{-1}) = f(a)^{-1}$$

Proof. Denote the group operations in G, G' by $*$ and $\diamond$, respectively. For any element a in G we have $a = e * a$, whence $f(a) = f(e * a)$. Applying (7.2) to the right-hand side, we obtain $f(a) = f(e) \diamond f(a)$. From Theorem 6.1 applied to the elements $f(a)$, $f(e)$ in G', we conclude that $f(e) = e'$. To prove the second part, we have $a * a^{-1} = e$ in G, and so $f(a * a^{-1}) = f(e)$. Using (7.2) on the left and the result just obtained on the right, we get $f(a) \diamond f(a^{-1}) = e'$. From Theorem 6.1 in G' we see that $f(a^{-1})$ must be the inverse of $f(a)$. Q.E.D.

THEOREM 7.2 *Let f be a homomorphism from a group G to a group G'. If H is a subgroup of G, then $f(H)$ is a subgroup† of G'. If K is a subgroup of G', then $f^{-1}(K)$ is a subgroup of G.*

Proof. By definition, $f(H)$ consists of all elements $f(x)$ with x in H. Hence, if a' is in $f(H)$, then there is an element a in H such that $f(a) = a'$. But a^{-1} is also in H, by definition of subgroup, and so $f(a^{-1})$ is also in $f(H)$. By the preceding theorem, $f(a^{-1}) = a'^{-1}$. Therefore the inverse of any element in $f(H)$ is also in $f(H)$. If b' is a second element of $f(H)$, then there is a b in H such that $f(b) = b'$. Then $a * b$ is also in H (notation as above), since H is a subgroup, and so $f(a * b)$ is accordingly in $f(H)$. By (7.2), $f(a * b) = a' \diamond b'$. This proves that $f(H)$ satisfies Definition 6.2 in G'.

To prove the second part, recall that $f^{-1}(K)$ is the set of all x such that $f(x)$ is in K. Accordingly, if a is in $f^{-1}(K)$, then $f(a)$ is in K. Its inverse $f(a)^{-1}$ must also be in K, by definition of subgroup, and by the theorem above we have $f(a^{-1}) = f(a)^{-1}$. That is, $f(a^{-1})$ is in K, and so a^{-1} must be in the set $f^{-1}(K)$. Hence, the inverse of any element in $f^{-1}(K)$ is also in that set. Now if b is another element of $f^{-1}(K)$, then $f(b)$ is in K. There-

† This notation is explained in Sec. 2 and is recalled briefly in the course of the proof.

fore $f(a) \diamond f(b)$ is in K, since K is a subgroup of G'. From (7.2) it follows that $f(a * b)$ is in K; that is, $a * b$ is in $f^{-1}(K)$. Therefore, $f^{-1}(K)$ satisfies Definition 6.2 in G. Q.E.D.

REMARK. Taking $H = G$ in the theorem, we see that $f(G)$ is a subgroup of G'. It is called the *image* of f. Now the identity element e' of G' forms a subgroup of G'. Taking that for K in the theorem, we see that $f^{-1}(e')$ is a subgroup of G; it consists of all elements which are mapped into e' by f. The subgroup $f^{-1}(e')$ is called the *kernel* of f.

THEOREM 7.3 *Let f be a homomorphism from a group G to a group G'. Then f maps distinct elements of G into distinct elements of G' if and only if the kernel of f consists of the identity element alone.*

Proof. The kernel of f, being a subgroup of G, must certainly contain the identity element e of G. If the kernel contains another element a, then by definition we have $f(a) = e'$, and so $f(a) = f(e)$, showing that f does not map distinct elements of G into distinct elements of G'.

Suppose now that the kernel of f consists of e alone. That is, only e is mapped by f into e'. If $f(a) = f(b)$, then $f(a * b^{-1}) = e'$; for by (7.2) the left member here is equal to $f(a) \diamond f(b^{-1})$, which, by Theorem 7.1, is equal to $f(a) \diamond f(b)^{-1} = e'$. Then from our assumption it follows that $a * b^{-1} = e$, whence $a = b$. Q.E.D.

COROLLARY *A homomorphism $f\colon G \to G'$ of two groups is an isomorphism if and only if the image of f is equal to G' and the kernel of f consists solely of the identity element of G.*

For this is precisely the condition for f to be one-to-one.

EXERCISES

1. Find q^{-1}, $(s * t)^{-1}$, $(u^{-1} * s * t)^{-1}$, $u^{-1} * t^{-1}$ for the group defined by Table 5· Compute the same expressions for Table 6.

2. Let G be a group, and let f be the mapping of G to itself defined by $f(a) = a^{-1}$ (inverse of a). Show that f is one-to-one, and prove that it is an isomorphism if and only if† the group operation in G is commutative. Exhibit this isomorphism explicitly for the groups of Tables 4 and 5.

3. Let f be a homomorphism from a group G to a group G', and let g be a homomorphism from G' to a group G''. Prove that the composition gf is a homomorphism from G to G''.

4. Let f and g be homomorphisms of a group G to a group G'. Denoting the operation in G' by $\times$, define a mapping h of G to G' by $h(a) = f(a) \times g(a)$. Prove that h is a homomorphism if $\times$ is commutative.

† The expression "if and only if" means that the statements standing on either side of it are *equivalent*. Here you must show that, if f is an isomorphism, then the group operation is commutative. And, vice versa, you must show that, if the group operation is commutative, then f is an isomorphism.

5. Let a be an element of a group G with operation $*$, and let T_a denote the mapping of G to itself defined by $T_a(x) = a * x$ (called *left translation* by a; see Exercise 11, Sec. 6). Show that all such mappings T_a form a group G' with composition as group operation, and show that the mapping $G \to G'$ defined by $a \to T_a$ is an isomorphism.

8. *Restatement of the group axioms*

For convenience we repeat here the axioms for a group, and at the same time we introduce some less cumbersome notation. Namely, we shall indicate the group operation by writing simply ab instead of $a * b$ or $a \diamond b$, etc. The element ab is sometimes called the *product* of a and b.

A group G is a set equipped with an operation which assigns to each pair of elements a, b in G an element ab in G, subject to the following conditions:

8.1 $a(bc) = (ab)c$ *for any elements* a, b, c *in* G.

8.2 *G contains an element e such that* $ea = ae = a$ *for every element a in G.*

8.3 *For every element a in G there is an element in G, denoted by* a^{-1}, *such that* $aa^{-1} = a^{-1}a = e$.

If the group operation satisfies the commutative axiom

8.4 $ab = ba$ for any elements a, b in G

then the group is said to be *commutative*, or *abelian*.†

With the notation just introduced, the group is said to be written *multiplicatively*, or to be a *multiplicative* group. Naturally this has nothing to do with the group; it is merely a brief way of announcing the kind of notational conventions one is about to employ.

We point out the following important rules for inverses:

8.5
$$e^{-1} = e$$
$$(a^{-1})^{-1} = a \quad \text{for any } a \text{ in } G$$
$$(ab)^{-1} = b^{-1}a^{-1} \quad \text{for any } a, b \text{ in } G$$

These equations merely restate Theorem 4.4 applied to the case at hand.

If G and G' are two groups, both written multiplicatively, then a homomorphism f from G to G' is a mapping such that

8.6 $f(ab) = f(a)\, f(b)$

according to (7.2).

Instead of the multiplicative notation just described, the group operation in an *abelian* group is often indicated by $+$. When $a + b$ is used instead of ab, we say that the group is written *additively*, or that it is an *additive* group. In this case the identity element is customarily denoted by 0 instead of by e, and the inverse

† After the Norwegian mathematician N. H. Abel (1802–1829).

of an element a is denoted by $-a$ instead of a^{-1}. Equations (8.1) to (8.6) become the following in the additive notation:

8.7 $$a + (b + c) = (a + b) + c$$

8.8 $$a + 0 = a$$

8.9 $$a + (-a) = 0$$

8.10 $$a + b = b + a$$

8.11 $$\begin{cases} -0 = 0 \\ -(-a) = a \\ -(a + b) = -a + (-b) \end{cases}$$

8.12 $$f(a + b) = f(a) + f(b)$$

Finally, a combination $c + (-d)$ is written simply $c - d$. Equation (8.9) and the last equation of (8.11) can be written as

8.13 $$a - a = 0 \qquad -(a + b) = -a - b$$

The equations of Theorem 7.1 become

8.14 $$f(0) = 0 \qquad f(-a) = -f(a)$$

Many important theorems about groups depend upon certain properties of the integers. Groups will occur in all the chapters in connection with various mathematical systems. But in Chap. 10 we shall return briefly to the subject of groups considered by themselves, rather than as ingredients in more complex systems.

EXERCISES

1. Let G be an abelian group with the additive notation. Prove the following identities for elements in G:

(*a*) $-(-a - b) = a + b$ (*b*) $-(a - b) = -a + b = b - a$
(*c*) $a - 0 = a$ (*d*) $(c - b) + (b - a) = c - a$
(*e*) $(c - b) - (a - b) = c - a$

2. Rewrite all the identities above in the multiplicative notation. Do they depend upon the commutative law?

9.† *Systems with two binary operations: rings, integral domains, fields*

Whole numbers can be combined by means of the familiar operations of addition, subtraction, multiplication, and in certain cases, also by division. There appear to be four binary operations here, but we shall soon see that two of them (sub-

† This section consists of the material in Sec. 2, Chap. 2, and Sec. 2, Chap. 3; it is excerpted here for the convenience of readers who wish to pass directly to the study of linear algebra in Chap. 8.

traction and division) are easily defined in terms of the other two (addition and multiplication). We wish to investigate the relation between the latter two operations, and in order to achieve a setting which will also serve us for the rational-, real-, and complex-number systems, we shall begin by studying briefly abstract systems with two binary operations. In this and later chapters, we shall encounter many important examples of *rings*, which we now define.

DEFINITION 9.1 *A set A is called a* ring *if it is equipped with two binary operations $+$ and $\times$ such that the following axioms hold:*

(1) *A, with the operation $+$, is an abelian group.*

(2) *The operation $\times$ is associative.*

(3) *A contains an identity element e for the operation $\times$:*

$e \times a = a \times e = a$ *for any element a of A.*

(4) $a \times (b + c) = (a \times b) + (a \times c)$ *and* $(b + c) \times a = (b \times a) + (c \times a)$ *for any elements a, b, c of A (distributive axiom).*

We shall encounter many important examples of rings. The identity element e is often denoted by 1.

According to Definition 6.1, A must contain an identity element for the operation $+$. We will denote this identity element by 0; thus $a + 0 = a$. And every element a has an inverse $-a$ with the characteristic property $a + (-a) = 0$. Recall that $a - b$ stands for $a + (-b)$. We call $a + b$ the *sum* of a and b, $a - b$ their *difference*, and the operation $+$ *addition*.

For the present we do not require that the second operation $\times$ be commutative, although that assumption will soon be added. (If $\times$ happens to be commutative, then we call A a *commutative ring*.) We shall call the operation $\times$ *multiplication;* the element $a \times b$ will be called the *product* of a and b, and to simplify the notation we shall generally write it as $a \cdot b$ or ab. Axiom (3) states that A contains an identity element e for multiplication; e is usually called the *unit element* of the ring. Axiom (4) supplies the only connection between the two binary operations $+$ and $\times$.

Note that the introduction of the terms "addition" and "multiplication" for the operations of A is purely a matter of convenience. We do not mean to imply that the elements of A necessarily have any connection with numbers, or that the two operations $+$ and $\times$ have any connection with addition and multiplication of numbers, except insofar as axioms (1) to (4) hold in both cases.

NOTATION In order to minimize the use of cumbersome parentheses we shall adopt the following well-known convention: in any expression without parentheses involving combinations of elements of A by both $+$ and $\times$, we understand that the $\times$ operations are to be performed first, and then the $+$ operations. For example, $ab + c$ stands for $(ab) + c$ [not $a(b + c)$!]; $abc - a'b' + cd$ stands for $(abc) - (a'b') + (cd)$. Thus the distributive axiom can be written simply as

$$a(b + c) = ab + ac$$
$$(b + c)a = ba + ca$$

Since both $+$ and $\times$ are associative, we do not need parentheses to indicate grouping of terms, although we still need them of course if the order in which the operations are to be performed is not covered by the above convention, as in $a(b + c)$. The expression abc stands for either $a(bc)$ or $(ab)c$, as explained in Sec. 4. We now prove some very useful theorems which are true for any ring A.

THEOREM 9.1 *The unit element of a ring A is unique.*

This has already been proved in Theorem 3.1.

THEOREM 9.2 $a \cdot 0 = 0 \cdot a = 0$ *for any element a of A.*

Proof. For any element b in A we have $b + 0 = b$, and therefore $(b + 0) \cdot a = b \cdot a$. On the other hand, by axiom (4), $(b + 0) \cdot a = b \cdot a + 0 \cdot a$, and so $b \cdot a + 0 \cdot a = b \cdot a$. Adding $-(b \cdot a)$ to both sides, we obtain $0 \cdot a = 0$.

Similarly, $a \cdot (b + 0) = a \cdot b + a \cdot 0$ and $a \cdot (b + 0) = a \cdot b$; so $a \cdot b + a \cdot 0 = a \cdot b$. Adding $-(a \cdot b)$ to both sides, we obtain $a \cdot 0 = 0$.

THEOREM 9.3 $(-a) \cdot b = a \cdot (-b) = -(a \cdot b)$ *for any elements a, b of A.*

Proof. We have $a + (-a) = 0$. Taking the product with b on the right of both sides of this equality, we obtain $(a + (-a)) \cdot b = 0 \cdot b$. Using axiom (4) on the left-hand side and Theorem 9.2 on the right, we obtain $a \cdot b + (-a) \cdot b = 0$. Hence, by uniqueness of inverses, $(-a) \cdot b = -(a \cdot b)$.

The proof that $a \cdot (-b) = -(a \cdot b)$ is quite similar and is left as an exercise.

The results of Theorem 9.3, Exercise 2 and the rule $-(-a) = a$, obtained in Sec. 8, embody all the familiar rules of signs used in algebraic computations. These rules are thus seen to be necessary consequences of simple assumptions about the binary operations.

From Theorem 9.3 it follows that there is no ambiguity in writing $-ab$ for $-(ab)$, and we shall usually use that simpler notation.

DEFINITION 9.2 *A being a ring, let B be a subset of A. Then B is called a* subring *of A if*

(i) *B contains the unit element e of A.*

(ii) *For any two elements a, b of B the elements $a + b$, $a - b$ and ab are also in B.*

It is easy to verify that under these conditions the subset B, equipped with the two binary operations $+$ and $\times$ in A, is itself a ring.

Just as with groups in this chapter, we may study mappings of one ring to another which are "compatible" with the *two* operations.

DEFINITION 9.3 *A mapping f of one ring A to another ring A' is called a* homomorphism *(or, more precisely, a* ring-homomorphism*) if, for any elements a and b of A, the following equations hold:*

$$f(a + b) = f(a) + f(b)$$
$$f(ab) = f(a) \cdot f(b)$$

Let us compare this new notion of homomorphism to that already defined in Sec. 7. If we ignore the multiplication in the rings A and A', we may consider them as abelian groups. The first equation above is then precisely the requirement that f be a homomorphism of A to A' (considered as groups). Therefore, if 0 denotes the zero element of A, as well as that of A', we may conclude from equations (8.12) and (8.14) that

9.1
$$f(0) = 0$$
$$f(-a) = -f(a)$$
$$f(a - b) = f(a) - f(b)$$

Note that f does *not* necessarily satisfy $f(e) = e'$, where e' is the unit element of A'. Indeed the mapping defined by $f(a) = 0$ for every element a of A is a ring-homomorphism.

Many of the rings which we shall study have several additional properties, and it is convenient to introduce

DEFINITION 9.4 *A ring A is an* integral domain *if it satisfies the following axioms:*

(5) *The $\times$ operation is commutative.*

(6) *If a, b, c are any elements of A, with $c \neq 0$, and if $ac = bc$, then $a = b$.*

Axiom (6) is naturally called the *cancellation axiom*, or *law*.

Integral domains are clearly special cases of rings, since they are rings which satisfy certain additional conditions.

THEOREM 9.4 *A commutative ring A is an integral domain if and only if for any elements a, b of A we have $ab \neq 0$ unless $a = 0$ or $b = 0$.*

Proof. Suppose first that A is an integral domain, so that the cancellation law holds in A; and suppose that $ab = 0$, with say $a \neq 0$. We can write our equation as $ab = a \cdot 0$, and so from the cancellation law there follows $b = 0$.

Conversely, suppose that a product in A cannot be zero unless one of the two factors is zero. We show that the cancellation law holds. Namely, if $ac = bc$, then $ac - bc = 0$, or $(a - b) \cdot c = 0$. If $c \neq 0$, then by our assumption the first factor $a - b$ is zero. That is, $a = b$. Q.E.D.

EXERCISES

1. Prove that a ring contains only one unit element.
2. Prove that, if a, b, c, and d are elements of a ring A, then
   (*a*) $(-a) \cdot (-b) = a \cdot b$
   (*b*) $(-e) \cdot a = a \cdot (-e) = -a$
   (*c*) $(-a) \cdot (-b) \cdot (-c) = -(a \cdot b \cdot c)$
   (*d*) $(a + b) \cdot (c + d) = ac + bc + ad + bd$

3. Let A be a ring. A 2×2 *matrix* with coefficients in A consists of four elements a, b, c, d of A written in a square array

$$\begin{pmatrix} a & b \\ c & d \end{pmatrix}$$

Let M be the set of all such 2×2 matrices. We define two binary operations in M as follows:

$$\begin{pmatrix} a & b \\ c & d \end{pmatrix} + \begin{pmatrix} a' & b' \\ c' & d' \end{pmatrix} = \begin{pmatrix} a + a' & b + b' \\ c + c' & d + d' \end{pmatrix}$$

$$\begin{pmatrix} a & b \\ c & d \end{pmatrix} \times \begin{pmatrix} a' & b' \\ c' & d' \end{pmatrix} = \begin{pmatrix} aa' + bc' & ab' + bd' \\ ca' + dc' & cb' + dd' \end{pmatrix}$$

(A brief inspection shows that in the second equation each of the four entries in the right-hand side is obtained by combining a certain row of the first matrix with a certain column of the second, in the manner indicated.) Prove that M with these two operations is a ring. What are the zero and unit elements of M? Is M an integral domain? (M is an example of a *matrix algebra;* such systems are very important in many applications and will be studied in some detail in later chapters of this book.)

4. Let A be a ring, and let U be the subset of A consisting of all elements of A having inverses for the multiplication operation $\times$. Prove:

(*a*) If x, y are in U, so is xy.

(*b*) U, with the binary operation $\times$, is a group.

5. Let h be a ring-homomorphism of a ring A to an integral domain A'. Assume that h is not identically zero [that is, there is at least one element a in A such that $h(a) \neq 0$]. Prove that $h(e) = e'$, where e' is the unit element of A'.

6. Prove in detail that a subring of a ring (see Definition 9.2) is itself a ring.

7. Let h be a homomorphism from a ring A to a ring A', and let B be the subset consisting of all elements of A that are sent by h into the zero element of A'. Prove that B is closed under $+$ and $\times$.

DEFINITION 9.5 *A field K is an integral domain, containing more than one element, such that any element of K other than zero has an inverse with respect to multiplication.*

Thus if a is in K and $a \neq 0$, then there must be in K an element (we denote it as usual by a^{-1}) such that $aa^{-1} = 1$.† From Theorems 3.1 and 4.3 it follows that the unit element 1 of K is unique and the inverse a^{-1} of any element a is unique. In particular, we have $1^{-1} = 1$ and $(a^{-1})^{-1} = a$ for any element $a \neq 0$ and $(ab)^{-1} = a^{-1}b^{-1}$ for any elements $a, b \neq 0$. We observe furthermore that it is not necessary to assume the cancellation law for multiplication in K because it is a necessary consequence of the existence of inverses by Theorem 4.5. From Theorem 9.4 we recall that a product ab in K cannot be zero unless $a = 0$ or $b = 0$.

† We use the symbol 1 instead of e for the unit element of K.

EXAMPLE The rational-number system is a field (cf. Sec. 3, Chap. 3). The real-number system (cf. Chap. 4) and the complex-number system (cf. Chap. 5) are fields. For any prime number p, one can find fields with exactly p elements (cf. Sec. 10, Chap. 2).

Recall that *subtraction* in an abelian group is defined by $a - b = a + (-b)$, where $-b$ is the inverse of b for addition. In an entirely analogous way we can define *division* in a field K. Namely, if a and b are elements of K, with $b \neq 0$, then we put

9.2 $$\frac{a}{b} = ab^{-1} \qquad (b \neq 0)$$

(Sometimes $\frac{a}{b}$ is written a/b or $a \div b$ and is called the quotient of a by b. The operation is neither commutative nor associative in general.) Taking a or b to be 1 in (9.2) and recalling that $1^{-1} = 1$, we get

9.3 $$\frac{a}{1} = a \qquad \frac{1}{b} = b^{-1} \qquad \frac{a}{b} = a \cdot \frac{1}{b}$$

From (9.2) we have further $(ab^{-1}) \cdot b = a(b^{-1}b) = a$ and $c \cdot \frac{a}{b} = c(ab^{-1}) = (ca)b^{-1}$, and we get the elementary rules

9.4 $$\frac{a}{b} \cdot b = a \qquad c \cdot \frac{a}{b} = \frac{ca}{b} = a \cdot \frac{c}{b} \qquad \frac{b}{b} = 1$$

THEOREM 9.5 *If a and b are elements of a field K, with $b \neq 0$, then the element of K denoted by a/b is the unique solution of the equation $bx = a$.*

Proof. It is a solution of the equation, by (9.4), and it is unique by the cancellation law.

THEOREM 9.6 *Let a, b, a', b' be elements of a field K, with b and b' not zero. Then $a/b = a'/b'$ if and only if $ab' = a'b$; and that is so if and only if there is an element $c \neq 0$ in K such that $a' = ca$ and $b' = cb$.*

Proof. By definition $a/b = a'/b'$ means $ab^{-1} = a'b'^{-1}$. Multiplying by bb' and keeping in mind that multiplication in a field is commutative, we get $ab' = a'b$. Conversely, if $ab' = a'b$, then multiplying by $b^{-1}b'^{-1}$ yields $a/b = a'/b'$.

Now define $c = b'/b$. Then $cb = b'$, by Eq. (9.3), and $c \neq 0$. If $ab' = a'b$, then multiplying by b^{-1} we get $ab'b^{-1} = a'$. But $b'b^{-1} = c$, and so we have $a' = ca$. Conversely, if $a' = ca$ and $b' = cb$, then $a'b = cab$ and $ab' = cab$, whence $ab' = a'b$. Q.E.D.

THEOREM 9.7 *Let a, b, c, d be elements of a field K, with b and d not zero. Then*

$$\frac{a}{b} + \frac{c}{d} = \frac{ad + bc}{bd} \qquad \frac{a}{b} - \frac{c}{d} = \frac{ad - bc}{bd} \qquad \frac{a}{b} \cdot \frac{c}{d} = \frac{ac}{bd}$$

and if also $c \neq 0$, *then*

$$\frac{a}{b} \div \frac{c}{d} = \frac{ad}{bc} \quad \text{and} \quad \left(\frac{c}{d}\right)^{-1} = \frac{d}{c}$$

Proof. First note that $bd \neq 0$ because $b \neq 0$ and $d \neq 0$ (Theorem 9.4). To prove the first equality we have, using (9.2), (9.3), (9.4),

$$\begin{aligned} bd \cdot \left(\frac{a}{b} + \frac{c}{d}\right) &= bd \cdot \frac{a}{b} + bd \cdot \frac{c}{d} \\ &= da \cdot \frac{b}{b} + bc \cdot \frac{d}{d} = ad + bc \end{aligned}$$

But also

$$bd \cdot \left(\frac{ad + bc}{bd}\right) = ad + bc$$

Therefore both sides of the first equation are solutions of $bd \cdot x = ad + bc$. They are therefore equal, by Theorem 9.5. The other equations follow from similar arguments, and their proof is left as an exercise.

DEFINITION 9.6 *Let* A *be a subset of a field* K. *If* A, *equipped with the operations of* K, *is a ring, then* A *is called a* subring *of* K; *if a subring* A *happens to be a field, then it is called a* subfield *of* K.

EXERCISES

8. Show that the nonzero elements of a field K, with multiplication as binary operation, form an abelian group.

9. Show that the zero and unit elements of a subring A of a field K are the same as those of K. Show that if A is a subfield of K, then the inverse of a nonzero element in A (for either multiplication or addition) is the same as its inverse in K. Prove that a subring of a field is an integral domain.

10. If a, b, c, d are elements of a field with $a/b = c/d$, prove the following:

(*a*) $\dfrac{b}{a} = \dfrac{d}{c}$ (*b*) $\dfrac{a}{c} = \dfrac{b}{d}$

(*c*) $\dfrac{a + b}{b} = \dfrac{c + d}{d}$ (*d*) $\dfrac{a - b}{b} = \dfrac{c - d}{d}$

(*e*) $\dfrac{a + b}{a - b} = \dfrac{c + d}{c - d}$ (*f*) $\dfrac{a}{b} = \dfrac{a + c}{b + d}$

assuming of course that the various denominators are not zero.

2

Rings, integral domains, the integers

1. Introduction

The system of the natural numbers 1, 2, 3, etc., is unquestionably the most important mathematical system. It is also the most familiar one, and the beginning student may wonder what there is to say about it that he does not already know. Yet that system has such an extraordinarily rich and complex structure that it is still the source of some of the deepest and most challenging problems of mathematics. It must therefore be counted a singular fact that the natural-number system can be described with the utmost precision and brevity by a few simple axioms.

The simplest set of axioms for the natural-number system, and one of the first, was published in 1889 by the Italian mathematician and logician Giuseppe Peano. His axioms, five in number, are usually called Peano's postulates. Unfortunately the road from those postulates to the study of the properties of numbers is a rather lengthy one, and for the sake of brevity we shall give a slightly longer list of axioms which will lead us to our goal more quickly. Our axioms will describe the system of all integers 0, ± 1, ± 2, etc., rather than the positive integers, i.e., natural numbers. Several of these axioms will be very useful in describing other mathematical systems.

In order to understand the aim of this chapter and of some of the later ones, the student should try to answer the following questions: Just how does the natural-number system differ from the rational-number system (whole numbers and fractions), and how do these systems differ in turn from the real- and complex-number systems? What features do the four systems have in common? Reasonable answers to these apparently simple questions are in fact not so easy to give; one of our tasks will be to supply some of the answers.

2. Systems with two binary operations: rings and integral domains

Whole numbers can be combined by means of the familiar operations of addition, subtraction, multiplication, and in certain cases, also by division. There appear to be four binary operations here, but we shall soon see that two of them (subtraction and division) are easily defined in terms of the other two (addition and multiplication). We wish to investigate the relation between the latter two operations, and in order to achieve a setting which will also serve us for the rational-, real-, and complex-number systems, we shall begin by studying briefly abstract systems with two binary operations. In this and later chapters we shall encounter many important examples of *rings*, which we now define.

DEFINITION 2.1 *A set A is called a* ring† *if it is equipped with two binary operations $+$ and $\times$ such that the following axioms hold:*

(1) *A, with the operation $+$, is an abelian group.*

(2) *The operation $\times$ is associative.*

(3) *A contains an identity element e for the operation $\times$:*

$$e \times a = a \times e = a \qquad \text{for any element } a \text{ of } A.$$

(4) $a \times (b + c) = (a \times b) + (a \times c)$ *and* $(b + c) \times a = (b \times a) + (c \times a)$ *for any elements a, b, c of A (distributive axiom).*

We shall encounter many important examples of rings.

According to Definition 6.1, Chap. 1, A must contain an identity element for the operation $+$. We will denote this identity element by 0; thus $a + 0 = a$. And every element a has an inverse $-a$ with the characteristic property $a + (-a) = 0$. Recall that $a - b$ stands for $a + (-b)$. We call $a + b$ the *sum* of a and b, $a - b$ their *difference*, and the operation $+$ *addition*.

For the present we do not require that the second operation $\times$ be commutative, although that assumption will soon be added. (If $\times$ happens to be commutative, then we call A a *commutative ring*.) We shall call the operation $\times$ *multiplication;* the element $a \times b$ will be called the *product* of a and b, and to simplify the notation we shall generally write it as $a \cdot b$ or ab. Axiom (3) states that A contains an identity element e for multiplication; e is usually called the *unit element* of the ring. Axiom (4) supplies the only connection between the two binary operations $+$ and $\times$.

Note that the introduction of the terms "addition" and "multiplication" for the operations of A is purely a matter of convenience. We do not mean to imply that the elements of A necessarily have any connection with numbers, or that the two operations $+$ and $\times$ have any connection with addition and multiplication of numbers, except in so far as axioms (1) to (4) hold in both cases.

NOTATION In order to minimize the use of cumbersome parentheses we shall adopt the following well-known convention: in any expression without parentheses involving combinations of elements of A by both $+$ and $\times$, we understand that the $\times$ operations are to be performed first, and then the $+$ operations. For example, $ab + c$ stands for $(ab) + c$ [not $a(b + c)$!]; $abc - a'b' + cd$ stands for $(abc) - (a'b') + (cd)$. Thus the distributive axiom can be written simply as

† In some texts axiom (3) is not included in the definition of a ring. The rings of the type we consider, with axiom (3) in force, are sometimes called rings *with unit element*.

$$a(b + c) = ab + ac$$
$$(b + c)a = ba + ca$$

Since both $+$ and $\times$ are associative, we do not need parentheses to indicate grouping of terms, although we still need them of course if the order in which the operations are to be performed is not covered by the above convention, as in $a(b + c)$. The expression abc stands either for $a(bc)$ or $(ab)c$, as explained in Chap. 1. We now prove some very useful theorems which are true for any ring A.

THEOREM 2.1 *The unit element of a ring A is unique.*

This has already been proved in Theorem 3.1, Chap. 1.

THEOREM 2.2 $a \cdot 0 = 0 \cdot a = 0$ *for any element a of A.*

Proof. For any element b in A we have $b + 0 = b$, and therefore $(b + 0) \cdot a = b \cdot a$. On the other hand, by axiom (4), $(b + 0) \cdot a = b \cdot a + 0 \cdot a$, and so $b \cdot a + 0 \cdot a = b \cdot a$. Adding $-(b \cdot a)$ to both sides, we obtain $0 \cdot a = 0$.

Similarly, $a \cdot (b + 0) = a \cdot b + a \cdot 0$ and $a \cdot (b + 0) = a \cdot b$; so $a \cdot b + a \cdot 0 = a \cdot b$. Adding $-(a \cdot b)$ to both sides, we obtain $a \cdot 0 = 0$. (Naturally, if the operation $\times$ is commutative, the second part of this proof is unnecessary.)

THEOREM 2.3 $(-a) \cdot b = a \cdot (-b) = -(a \cdot b)$ *for any elements a, b of A.*

Proof. We have $a + (-a) = 0$. Taking the product with b on the right of both sides of this equality, we obtain $(a + (-a)) \cdot b = 0 \cdot b$. Using axiom (4) on the left-hand side and Theorem 2.2 on the right, we obtain $a \cdot b + (-a) \cdot b = 0$. Hence, by uniqueness of inverses, $(-a) \cdot b = -(a \cdot b)$.

The proof that $a \cdot (-b) = -(a \cdot b)$ is quite similar and is left as an exercise.

The results of Exercise 2, Theorem 2.3, and the rule $-(-a) = a$, obtained in Sec. 8, Chap. 1, embody all the familiar rules of signs used in algebraic computations. These rules are thus seen to be necessary consequences of simple assumptions about the binary operations.

From Theorem 2.3 it follows that there is no ambiguity in writing $-ab$ for $-(ab)$, and we shall usually use that simpler notation.

DEFINITION 2.2 *A being a ring, let B be a subset of A. Then B is called a* subring *of A if*

(i) *B contains the unit element e of A.*

(ii) *For any two elements a, b of B the elements* $a + b$, $a - b$ *and ab are also in B.*

It is easy to verify that under these conditions the subset B, equipped with the two binary operations $+$ and $\times$ in A, is itself a ring.

Just as with groups in Chap. 1, we may study mappings of one ring to another which are "compatible" with the *two* operations.

DEFINITION 2.3 *A mapping f of one ring A to another ring A′ is called a* homomorphism *(or, more precisely, a* ring-homomorphism*) if, for any elements a and b of A, the following equations hold:*

$$f(a + b) = f(a) + f(b)$$
$$f(ab) = f(a) \cdot f(b)$$

Let us compare this new notion of homomorphism to that already defined in Chap. 1. If we ignore the multiplication in the rings A and A', we may consider them as abelian groups. The first equation above is then precisely the requirement that f be a homomorphism of A to A' (considered as groups). Therefore, if 0 denotes the zero element of A, as well as that of A', we may conclude from Eqs. (8.12) and (8.14), Chap. 1, that

2.1
$$f(0) = 0$$
$$f(-a) = -f(a)$$
$$f(a - b) = f(a) - f(b)$$

Note that f does *not* necessarily satisfy $f(e) = e'$, where e' is the unit element of A'. Indeed the mapping defined by $f(a) = 0$ for every element a of A is a ring-homomorphism. A one-to-one homomorphism is called an *isomorphism* or, more precisely, a *ring-isomorphism.*

The following definition describes some special kinds of rings which will be our chief concern in this chapter.

DEFINITION 2.4 *A ring A is an* integral domain *if it satisfies the following axioms:*

(5) *The × operation is commutative.*

(6) *If a, b, c are any elements of A, with* $c \neq 0$, *and if* $ac = bc$, *then* $a = b$.

Axiom (6) is naturally called the *cancellation axiom* or *law.*

Integral domains are clearly special cases of rings, since they are rings which satisfy certain additional conditions.

THEOREM 2.4 *A commutative ring A is an integral domain if and only if for any elements a, b of A we have* $ab \neq 0$ *unless* $a = 0$ *or* $b = 0$.

Proof. Suppose first that A is an integral domain, so that the cancellation law holds in A; and suppose that $ab = 0$, with say $a \neq 0$. We can write our equation as $ab = a \cdot 0$, and so from the cancellation law there follows $b = 0$.

Conversely suppose that a product in A cannot be zero unless one of the two factors is zero. We show that the cancellation law holds. That is, if $ac = bc$, then $ac - bc = 0$, or $(a - b) \cdot c = 0$. If $c \neq 0$, then by our assumption the first factor $a - b$ is zero. That is, $a = b$. Q.E.D.

EXERCISES

1. Prove that a ring contains only one unit element.

2. Prove that if a, b, c, and d are elements of a ring A, then

(a) $(-a)\cdot(-b) = a\cdot b$

(b) $(-e)\cdot a = a\cdot(-e) = -a$

(c) $(-a)\cdot(-b)\cdot(-c) = -(a\cdot b\cdot c)$

(d) $(a+b)\cdot(c+d) = ac + bc + ad + bd$

3. Let A be a ring. A 2×2 *matrix* with coefficients in A consists of four elements a, b, c, d of A written in a square array

$$\begin{pmatrix} a & b \\ c & d \end{pmatrix}$$

Let M be the set of all such 2×2 matrices. We define two binary operations in M as follows:

$$\begin{pmatrix} a & b \\ c & d \end{pmatrix} + \begin{pmatrix} a' & b' \\ c' & d' \end{pmatrix} = \begin{pmatrix} a+a' & b+b' \\ c+c' & d+d' \end{pmatrix}$$

$$\begin{pmatrix} a & b \\ c & d \end{pmatrix} \times \begin{pmatrix} a' & b' \\ c' & d' \end{pmatrix} = \begin{pmatrix} aa'+bc' & ab'+bd' \\ ca'+dc' & cb'+dd' \end{pmatrix}$$

(A brief inspection shows that in the second equation each of the four entries in the right-hand side is obtained by combining a certain row of the first matrix with a certain column of the second, in the manner indicated.) Prove that M with these two operations is a ring. What are the zero and unit elements of M? Is M an integral domain? (M is an example of a *matrix algebra;* such systems are very important in many applications and will be studied in some detail in later chapters of this book.)

4. Let A be a ring, and let U be the subset of A consisting of all elements of A having inverses for the multiplication operation $\times$. Prove:

(a) If x, y are in U, so is xy.

(b) U, with the binary operation $\times$, is a group.

5. Let h be a ring-homomorphism of a ring A to an integral domain A'. Assume that h is not identically zero [i.e., there is at least one element a in A such that $h(a) \neq 0$]. Prove that $h(e) = e'$, where e' is the unit element of A'.

6. Prove in detail that a subring of a ring (see Definition 2.2) is itself a ring.

7. Let h be a homomorphism from a ring A to a ring A', and let B be the subset consisting of all elements of A that are sent by h into the zero element of A'. Prove that B satisfies axioms (1), (2), (4), Definition 2.1, with the same operations as in A (B is called the *kernel* of h).

3. *Ordered integral domains*

The nonzero whole numbers can be split into two sets, one consisting of the positive numbers and the other consisting of the negative numbers. Moreover the numbers can be ordered according to magnitude; for example, 3 is smaller than 7 (usually written $3 < 7$). In this section we shall investigate that kind of situation in a general framework which will also be of use in the study of the rational- and real-number systems.

DEFINITION 3.1 *An integral domain Z is called an* ordered *integral domain if its non-zero elements are split into two subsets J and J′ such that the following conditions hold:*

(1) *J' consists of the inverses (with respect to the + operation) of the elements of J.*

(2) *If a, b are any elements of J, then $a + b$ is also in J.*

(3) *If a, b are any elements of J, then ab is in J.*

Observe first of all that if J' consists of the inverses (for +) of the elements of J, as required by axiom (1), then reciprocally J consists of the inverses of elements of J', since $-(-x) = x$. The requirement of axiom (1) is therefore not altered if we interchange the roles of J and J'. Since inverses are unique, it follows moreover that the mapping that sends x into $-x$ establishes a one-to-one correspondence between J and J'.

Similarly axiom (2) is really symmetrical in J and J'. For let a, b be elements of J'. Then, as just noted, $-a$ and $-b$ are in J. Therefore $(-a) + (-b) = -(a + b)$ is in J, by axiom (2), and so the inverse element $a + b$ is in J', by axiom (1). Hence axiom (2) holds if J is replaced by J'. The situation is quite different with axiom (3), however. We shall in fact show that the product of two elements of J' is in J.

DEFINITION 3.2 *Z being as in Definition* 3.1, *the elements of J will be called* positive, *those of J′* negative. *If a, b are two elements of Z, then we say that a is* smaller *than b (or that b is* greater *than a) if the difference $b - a$ is in J, and in that case we write $a < b$, or $b > a$.*

With this notation we can rewrite axioms (2) and (3) in the more familiar form

(2′) *If* $a > 0$ *and* $b > 0$, *then* $a + b > 0$

(3′) *If* $a > 0$ *and* $b > 0$, *then* $ab > 0$

for $a > 0$ means that $a - 0 = a$ is in J, etc. (see Theorem 3.1). Observe that no meanings are to be attached to "positive," "less than," $<$, etc., other than those meanings just assigned to them.

In the following theorems we assume that Z, J, and J' satisfy the conditions of Definition 3.1.

THEOREM 3.1 *J consists of all elements x such that $x > 0$, and J' consists of all elements x such that $x < 0$.*

Proof. Since $x - 0 = x + (-0) = x + 0 = x$, x is in J if and only if $x - 0$ is in J. But $x - 0$ is in J, by definition, if and only if $x > 0$. Hence J consists of all elements x such that $x > 0$.

On the other hand, x is in J' if and only if $-x$ is in J. But $-x = 0 - x$, and so x is in J' if and only if $0 - x$ is in J, that is, $0 > x$.

COROLLARY *If x is in Z, then $x > 0$ if and only if $-x < 0$, and $x < 0$ if and only if $-x > 0$.*

Proof. By Theorem 3.1, $x > 0$ if and only if x is in J, and $-x < 0$ if and only if $-x$ is in J'. But, by axiom (1), x is in J if and only if $-x$ is in J'. The argument for the other case ($x < 0$) is similar.

THEOREM 3.2 *J and J' have no elements in common.*

Proof. Suppose that the element x is both in J and in J'. Then, by axiom (1), $x = -y$ for some y in J. By axiom (2), since x and y are in J, so is $x + y$, but $x + y = -y + y = 0$. This is a contradiction for J does not contain 0. Hence the original assumption that x is both in J and in J' is false, and the theorem is proved.

THEOREM 3.3 *If a, b are any elements of Z, then exactly one of the following relations must hold: $a < b$ or $a > b$* or *$a = b$.*

Proof. Consider the element $b - a$. If $b - a \neq 0$, then $b - a$ is in J or J', but cannot be in both, by Theorem 3.2. Hence the following cases exhaust all possibilities: $b - a$ is in J, $b - a$ is in J', or $b - a = 0$. These cases correspond, respectively, to the cases in the statement of the theorem, for if $b - a$ is in J', then $-(b - a) = a - b$ is in J and $a > b$.

This theorem is often called the *trichotomy* condition.

THEOREM 3.4 *If a, b, c are elements of Z such that $a < b$ and $b < c$, then $a < c$.*

Proof. If $a < b$, $b < c$, then $b - a$ and $c - b$ are in J. By axiom (2) so is their sum $(b - a) + (c - b) = c - a$. Hence $a < c$.

THEOREM 3.5 *If a, b are elements of Z such that $a < b$, then $a + c < b + c$ for any element c in Z.*

Proof. If $a < b$, then $b - a$ is in J. However, $b - a = (b + c) - (a + c)$, and so $(b + c) - (a + c)$ is in J. Hence $a + c < b + c$.

THEOREM 3.6 *If a, b are elements of Z such that $a < b$, and if $c > 0$, then $ca < cb$.*

Proof. If $a < b$ and $c > 0$, then $b - a$ and c are in J. By axiom (3), $c(b - a)$ is in J. But $c(b - a) = cb - ca$, and so $cb - ca$ is in J. Hence $ca < cb$.

THEOREM 3.7 *If a, b are elements of Z such that $a < 0$, $b < 0$, then $ab > 0$.*

Proof. By the corollary of Theorem 3.1, $-a > 0$ and $-b > 0$. So, by axiom (3), $(-a)(-b) > 0$. But $(-a)(-b) = ab$ by Exercise 2(*a*), Sec. 2; hence $ab > 0$.

This theorem says that the product of two elements of J' is in J, and so J and J' are not interchangeable in axiom (3).

THEOREM 3.8 *If $a \neq 0$, then $a \cdot a > 0$. Furthermore $e > 0$ provided Z contains more than one element.*

Proof. If $a \neq 0$, then either $a > 0$ or $a < 0$, by the trichotomy condition (Theorem 3.3). In either case, $a \cdot a > 0$, by axiom (2) or else by Theorem 3.7. If Z contains more than one element, then it certainly has an element $a \neq 0$. Since $e \cdot a = a$, it follows that $e \neq 0$, for $0 \cdot a = 0$ (Theorem 2.2). Hence by what has just been proved, $e \cdot e > 0$, and since $e \cdot e = e$, we have $e > 0$.

Thus the splitting of the nonzero elements of Z into J and J' satisfying the axioms of Definition 3.1 enables us in a very simple way to define an order relation $<$ among the elements of Z. And the preceding theorems show that $<$ obeys the familiar rules that we learn for the relation "less than" among numbers. The great advantage of the axiomatic treatment is that it shows us very clearly just what is involved in $<$ (namely, the axioms for an ordered integral domain) and it strips that relation of any vague and misleading philosophical connotations. Moreover we shall be able to apply our conclusions to other systems besides the system of integers (to be taken up in the next section).

EXERCISES †

All the exercises below refer to an ordered integral domain.

1. The notation $a \leq b$ means that either $a < b$ or $a = b$; similarly for $a \geq b$. Show that Theorems 3.3 to 3.6 remain valid if $<$, $>$ are replaced by $\leq$, $\geq$, respectively.

2. Prove that $a + b > a$ if $b > 0$; prove that $a + b < a$ if $b < 0$.

3. Prove that $a \leq b$ if and only if $a - b \leq 0$. Prove that $a \geq b$ if and only if $a - b \geq 0$.

4. Prove the following:

(*a*) If $a < b$ and $c < d$, then $a + c < b + d$.

(*b*) If $a < b$ and $c \leq d$, then $a + c < b + d$.

(*c*) If $a \leq b$ and $c \leq d$, then $a + c \leq b + d$.

5. Show that if $a < b$, then $c - a > c - b$ for any c; show that $-a > -b$.

6. For any element a in Z define the symbol $|a|$, the *absolute value* of a, as follows: $|a| = a$ if $a \geq 0$; $|a| = -a$ if $a < 0$. Prove the following properties:

(*a*) $|a| > 0$ unless $a = 0$

(*b*) $|a| = |-a|$

(*c*) $-|a| \leq a \leq |a|$

(*d*) $|a + b| \leq |a| + |b|$

(*e*) $|a + b + c| \leq |a| + |b| + |c|$

(*f*) $|a + b + c + d| \leq |a| + |b| + |c| + |d|$

(*g*) $|a| - |b| \leq |a + b|$

(*h*) $\big||a| - |b|\big| \leq |a + b|$

(*i*) $|ab| = |a| \cdot |b|$

[Relations of the types (*c*) to (*h*) are called *inequalities*. (*d*) is particularly important; it is sometimes called the *triangle* inequality.]

† You may use the theorems established above in working these exercises, rather than going back to the definitions.

7. Show that

(a) If $a < b$ and $c < 0$, then $ac > bc$.

(b) If $a < 0$, $b > 0$, then $ab < 0$.

(c) If $a < 0$, then $a \cdot a \cdot a < 0$; and if $a > 0$, then $a \cdot a \cdot a > 0$.

(d) If $ac < bc$ and $c > 0$, then $a < b$.

(e) If $0 \leq a < b$ and $0 \leq c < d$, then $ac < bd$.

(f) If $a > 0$ and $ab > 0$, then $b > 0$.

(g) If $a > 0$ and $ab < 0$, then $b < 0$.

8. Prove that if $a > e$ and $b > e$, then $ab > e$. Prove that if $0 \leq a < e$, $0 \leq b < e$, then $ab < e$.

9. Let a be a positive element of Z which has an inverse a^{-1} for the $\times$ operation. Show that $a^{-1} > 0$. Prove that if $a > e$, then $a^{-1} < e$; and if $a < e$, then $a^{-1} > e$.

*10. For any a, b in Z prove that

$$a \cdot a + b \cdot b \geq |ab| + |ab|$$

[Hint: Consider the product $(a - b) \cdot (a - b)$.]

11. Show that axiom (6) of Definition 2.4 is superfluous in the definition of an ordered integral domain. That is, show that the cancellation law follows from the other axioms. [Hint: Apply the trichotomy condition to $a - b$.]

12. Let Z be an integral domain and suppose there is defined a relation $<$ among the elements of Z satisfying the assertions of Theorems 3.3 to 3.6. Show that the nonzero elements of Z can then be split into two subsets J and J' satisfying axioms (1) to (3) of Definition 3.1.

*13. Given positive elements x and y in an ordered integral domain such that $xy = e$, show that $x + y \geq e + e$. Furthermore, $x + y = e + e$ if and only if $x = y = e$.

4. *The system of integers*

There are many mathematical systems which are ordered integral domains. Of greatest importance are the system of integers and the rational- and real-number systems. In this section we show that the system of integers can be distinguished from all other ordered integral domains by the addition of one new axiom. For convenience of reference we restate all the axioms here, and in the rest of this chapter we shall follow the new numbering given below. We also make some slight notational changes at this point: For the unit element e of our system we now write 1, and boldface letters **Z**, **J**, **J**$'$ will be used to prevent confusion with the notation of earlier sections.

AXIOMS FOR THE INTEGERS **Z** *is a set of elements equipped with two binary operations* $+$ *and* $\times$ *satisfying the following conditions:*

(1) **Z** *with the* $+$ *operation is an abelian group.*

(2) *The operation* $\times$ *is associative and commutative.*

(3) **Z** *contains an identity element* 1, *different from* 0, *for the* $\times$ *operation.*

(4) *The operations* $+$ *and* $\times$ *satisfy the distributive law*
$a \cdot (b + c) = ab + ac$ *for any elements* a, b, c *in* **Z**.

(5) *The nonzero elements of* **Z** *are divided into two subsets* **J** *and* **J**′ *such that* **J**′ *consists of the inverses (with respect to* $+$*) of the elements of* **J**.

(6) *If* a *and* b *are in* **J**, *then so are* $a + b$ *and* ab.

(7) *If* U *is a subset of* **J** *such that* 1 *is in* U *and such that* $x + 1$ *is in* U *whenever* x *is in* U, *then* $U =$ **J**.

As we have indicated above, there is essentially just one system which satisfies these axioms, and we shall take that system to be the system of integers, or whole numbers. We must of course give some kind of justification for doing so. That is, we must show that the system determined by axioms (1) to (7) somehow corresponds to our intuitive idea of the integers. Now (using the results of Sec. 3) the first six axioms simply say that our system has two operations ($+$ and $\times$) and an order relation ($<$)† which obey all the rules that we were obliged to memorize in elementary school. [The condition $1 \neq 0$ in axiom (3) merely means that **Z** must contain more than the single element 0.] Axiom (7) looks a little more complicated, but a brief examination of it discloses that the axiom merely expresses the intuitive idea that no part of **J** other than **J** itself can contain all the elements 1, $1 + 1$, $1 + 1 + 1$, etc. In other words, **J** consists precisely of all the elements 1, $1 + 1$, $1 + 1 + 1$, etc. That is clearly what we have in mind when we think of the positive integers. But we cannot state axiom (7) in that intuitively suggestive fashion because we would first have to give a precise meaning to "etc." (or some equivalent of it), and in the long run that would be more complicated than axiom (7). We shall return to this matter in Sec. 5.

It should be mentioned that the system of integers is an integral domain. The only axiom for an integral domain that is not explicitly contained in the axioms for the integers is the cancellation law, which we now prove. Accordingly, suppose that $ac = bc$ with $c \neq 0$. We want to prove that $a = b$. If $a \neq b$, then by axiom (5) either $a - b > 0$ or $b - a > 0$. For definiteness, say $a - b > 0$. Similarly either $c > 0$ or $-c > 0$, and for definiteness say $c > 0$. Then by axiom (6), $(a - b) \cdot c > 0$. But $(a - b) \cdot c = ac - bc = 0$—a contradiction. Thus $a = b$, and the same conclusion results if $-c > 0$.

In this section we establish some basic properties of **Z** and we state precisely what we mean when we say that the axioms above determine **Z** in an essentially unique way (Theorem 4.4). The proof (tedious but not really very difficult) is deferred until Sec. 11.

We recall first that the unit element 1 must be positive; that is, 1 must be in **J** (Theorem 3.8).

THEOREM 4.1 *If* x *is in* **J**, *then either* $x = 1$ *or* $x > 1$. *In other words,* 1 *is the smallest positive element of* **Z**.

† We continue with the definition of $<$ laid down in Sec. 3.

Proof. We define a subset U of **J** as follows: U consists of 1 itself and of all the elements of **J** which are greater than 1. Our proof will consist in showing that $U = \mathbf{J}$, and to achieve this, we will have to use axiom (7).

Let x be an element of U. Then either $x = 1$ or $x > 1$. We must show that $x + 1$ is an element of U. If $x = 1$, then $x + 1 = 1 + 1$ and $1 + 1 > 1$ (why?). On the other hand, if $x > 1$, then $x + 1 > 1 + 1$, by Theorem 3.4, and so $x + 1 > 1$, by Theorem 3.3. In either case $x + 1 > 1$, and therefore $x + 1$ is in U. Hence, by axiom (7), $U = \mathbf{J}$.

THEOREM 4.2 *If $x < y$, then $x + 1 \leq y$. In other words, there can be no element of* **Z** *between x and $x + 1$.*

Proof. If $x < y$, then $y - x$ is in **J**. By Theorem 4.1, $y - x \geq 1$ and so, by Theorem 3.5, $y \geq x + 1$.

THEOREM 4.3 *Let T be any subset of* **J** *containing at least one element. Then T contains a smallest element. That is, there is in T a unique element y such that $y < z$ for any other element z in T.*

Proof. If T contains 1, then 1 is clearly the smallest element in T, by Theorem 4.1. Suppose then that 1 is not in T. Let U be the subset of **J** consisting of all elements of **J** that are smaller than *every* element of T. Since 1 is not in T, 1 has that property and so 1 is in U.

Now let x be an element in U and consider $x + 1$. Let y be any element of T. By the definition of U, $x < y$ and therefore $x + 1 \leq y$, by Theorem 4.2. Suppose that $x + 1 = y$. We claim that then y must be the smallest element of T. Indeed, let z be any other element in T. Then by the above argument we have similarly $x + 1 \leq z$. But we cannot have $x + 1 = z$ for otherwise $y = z$. Hence $x + 1 < z$, showing that $y = x + 1$ is the smallest element in T. Suppose on the other hand that the following case occurs: for no x in U do we have $x + 1 = y$. Then $x + 1 < y$, and therefore $x + 1$ is in U whenever x is in U. Hence, by axiom (7), $U = \mathbf{J}$. But that is impossible unless T contains no elements at all. We have therefore arrived at a contradiction, showing that the last case considered is impossible. But in every other case T has a smallest element. Q.E.D.

The assertion of Theorem 4.3 is usually expressed by saying that **J** is *well-ordered*, meaning simply that every *non-empty subset* of **J** has a least element.

For some purposes it is convenient to introduce the term *segment*. Let a be an element of **J**. By the segment $[1, a]$ we mean the subset of **J** consisting of all elements x of **J** such that $x \leq a$. By Theorem 4.1, $1 \leq a$, and so 1 is in the segment $[1, a]$. Naturally $a \leq a$, and so a is also in the segment $[1, a]$. The segment $[1, 1]$ consists of 1 alone. The segment $[1, 1 + 1]$ consists of the elements $1, 1 + 1$ by Theorem 4.2.

We have already mentioned that axioms (1) to (7) determine the system of integers **Z** in an essentially unique way. A precise statement of this uniqueness theorem follows.

THEOREM 4.4 *Let* **Z** *and* $\bar{\mathbf{Z}}$ *be two systems satisfying axioms* (1) to (7). *Then there is one and only one ring-isomorphism of* **Z** *to* $\bar{\mathbf{Z}}$. *This isomorphism makes the zero and unit elements of* **Z** *and* $\bar{\mathbf{Z}}$ *correspond, and furthermore it preserves order.*

The proof will be given in Sec. 11.

EXERCISES

1. Let b be an element of **Z**, and let E be the set of all elements x of **Z** such that $x \geq b$. Prove that E is well-ordered.
2. Prove that if $xy = 1$, then $x = y = 1$ or $x = y = -1$.
3. Prove that the segment $[1, 1 + 1 + 1]$ consists of 1, $1 + 1$ and $1 + 1 + 1$.
4. Prove that, given two segments $[1, a]$ and $[1, b]$, one is wholly contained in the other.
5. Prove that $a + 1$ is the only element contained in $[1, a + 1]$ but not in $[1, a]$.
6. A non-empty subset T of **Z** is *bounded from above* if there is an element z such that $x < z$ for any element x of **Z**. Prove that, if T is bounded from above, it contains a greatest element y, that is $y \geq x$ for any element x of **Z**. Compare this result with Theorem 4.3.

5. *Some comments*

Theorem 4.4 states that any two systems satisfying axioms (1) to (7) have precisely the same structure; they are completely interchangeable. We henceforth suppose that one such system is fixed once and for all. We call it the *system of integers*, and we shall always denote it by **Z**. The elements of **Z** will of course be called *integers*. The set of positive elements in **Z** will be denoted by **J**, and its elements will also be called *natural numbers*. For elements of **J** we introduce the following notation:

$$1 + 1 = 2 \qquad 1 + 1 + 1 + 1 + 1 = 5$$
$$1 + 1 + 1 = 3 \qquad 1 + 1 + 1 + 1 + 1 + 1 = 6$$
$$1 + 1 + 1 + 1 = 4 \qquad 1 + 1 + 1 + 1 + 1 + 1 + 1 = 7$$

and so on in the familiar fashion. As explained earlier, axiom (7) states in effect that **J** consists of all the elements 1, 2, 3, etc.

We have stated that there cannot be two essentially different systems satisfying axioms (1) to (7), but we have not shown that there can exist even one such system. That is, we have not shown that our axiom set is free from internal inconsistencies. It is possible to do so, but we shall not enter into that matter here.

The reader may protest that **Z** is after all just the system of integers he studied in elementary school, and therefore the system must obviously exist! Are not integers—at least positive integers—essentially objects of Nature? And what is the point of going through all the axioms anyway?

Let us examine these rhethorical queries for a moment. It is certainly true that **Z** is just the system the student has studied in elementary school. And he may do well therefore to ask himself just what he learned there about the integers. Probably he learned to make numerical calculations, but very little beyond that. And the mere fact that one has studied something in elementary school is certainly no real guarantee that it is free from contradictions. Now what about the relation of integers to Nature? If you but look around you will find many instances of, say, the number 2—a pair of shoes, a pair of dice, etc. But you will not find the *number* 2, or any other number for that matter. The integer 2 and all the other integers are *concepts*, or constructions of the human intelligence. It may be worth noting that in some primitive societies there are no integers greater than 2. The integer 5 simply does not exist for the Hottentots, and there is no word for it in their language.

The numbers 2 and 5, etc., are abstract concepts and by that fact are rather far removed from Nature. It is of course true that they have counterparts in Nature; we can easily find many concrete instances of 2 or 5 about us, and we can even make experimental verifications of the rules of arithmetic for small numbers.

But the situation is rather different for very large numbers. For example, the integer 10^{5000} has no known counterpart whatever in Nature. Indeed that number is in all probability enormously larger than the total number of electrons, protons, and all other particles in the entire universe. It is not possible, even in principle—much less in practice—to find a concrete instance of 10^{5000}. But that fact in no way hinders us from thinking about 10^{5000}, from forming a concept of it, even from calculating with it. It would clearly be an extremely unsatisfactory solution to banish all very large numbers simply because they have no concrete realizations.

Integers are abstract concepts, and only relatively small integers have anything to do with Nature.† Therefore we cannot appeal to Nature for evidence of the existence of the abstract system of integers, nor can we infer any properties of the system from that source. Where then do we turn to find out about the system? As we have tried to make plain, the integers are, in an essential way, a product of the human mind, with all its frailties and inconsistencies. Can we then be sure that Tom, Dick, and Harry all have the same concept of the integers, the same understanding of that system? In all likelihood T, D, and H have only the haziest notion of the integers, derived chiefly from limited experience with elementary numerical computations. T, D, and H cannot help us much.

The easiest and most reasonable solution to this problem is obviously just to *say* what the system of integers is—to list its properties in a clear and unambiguous way. The attentive reader will be aware that that is precisely what we have done in axioms (1) to (7). We have listed the properties of the system **Z**, and we prove in Sec. 11 that its structure is thereby completely determined. Furthermore we

† That does not mean however that large numbers are useless in the study of Nature.

have been at pains to point out that our axioms reflect as closely as possible all the familiar properties that we expect the integers to have.

But there is an important point to be noted. For us, integers are elements of a set with certain operations—any elements at all. The individual natures of the elements of **Z** are of no interest to us whatever and have nothing at all to do with the structure of **Z**. That structure reposes ultimately in the operations + and ×, not in the peculiarities of the constituent elements. We have thus been able to divest integers of any philosophical connotations and any dependence on Nature. So to speak, we do not care what integers "are," in any philosophical sense, if indeed that implicit question has any meaning. The axiomatic method has therefore allowed us to ignore many very difficult, tiresome philosophical inquiries. That is a feature which is characteristic of the mathematical method. That method seeks to study only the structures of systems, not their ultimate constituents.

Before going on to prove some more theorems about integers, we shall make brief mention of Peano's postulates (they are axioms for the positive integers **J**, not for **Z**). They are listed below, but we have combined two of Peano's postulates into one, so that only four appear instead of the five mentioned in Sec. 1. In these postulates, **J** stands for a set of elements.

I. *To each element x of* **J** *there is assigned some element $S(x)$ of* **J** *(called the "successor" of x).*

II. *If $S(x) = S(y)$ for two elements x, y in* **J**, *then $x = y$.*

III. *There is an element in* **J**, *denoted by* 1, *which is not the successor of any element of* **J**.

IV. *If U is a part of* **J** *containing* 1 *such that for any element x in U the successor $S(x)$ is also in U, then necessarily $U =$* **J**.

These axioms are noteworthy for their simplicity, and in that respect they are logically more satisfactory than our axioms (1) to (7). It should be noted that IV looks very much like our axiom (7). Observe that Peano's postulates make no mention of addition or multiplication.

In order to show that these axioms determine a system with the properties that we expect of the positive integers, one proceeds as follows: One first shows that there can be essentially only one system satisfying the axioms. The proof is quite similar to our proof of Theorem 4.4 but is actually rather simpler because fewer things are involved. Next one shows that it is possible to construct in **J** a unique binary operation + which is associative and commutative and which satisfies the equation $S(x) = x + 1$ for all x in **J**. Then one shows in a similar way that it is possible to construct another unique binary operation × in **J** such that $1 \cdot x = x$ and $x \cdot (y + z) = xy + xz$ for any elements of **J**. Finally, one constructs from **J** a larger system **Z** containing **J** and satisfying our axioms (1) to (7).

EXERCISE

Prove that $2 \cdot 2 = 4$ and $2 \cdot 3 = 6$.

6. *Finite and countable sets*

We shall say that a set E is *finite* if its elements can be put into one-to-one correspondence with some segment $[1, n]$ in $\mathbf{J}$, n being of course a positive integer (segments are defined at the end of Sec. 4). We say then that E has n elements. The one-to-one correspondence between $[1, n]$ and E being regarded as fixed, we can then think of any element x in E as "labeled" by the corresponding integer in the segment—say j. We can write x_j for x, and in this way we can indicate all the elements of E by the indexed symbols $x_1, x_2, \ldots, x_n$, and we may speak of x_j as the jth element of E. This provides a very convenient and compact notation for a finite set, and it will often be used.

A set which is not finite is naturally called *infinite*. Among the infinite sets are those which are said to be *countable*, or *denumerable*.† A countable set E is one whose elements can be put into one-to-one correspondence with the elements of $\mathbf{J}$. (In particular, $\mathbf{J}$ itself is countable!) Some one-to-one correspondence between $\mathbf{J}$ and E being fixed, we can indicate the element of E corresponding to the positive integer j by some such symbol as x_j (or whatever other letter seems appropriate), and we can then indicate the elements of E by writing $x_1, x_2, x_3, \ldots$.

Now let X be any set, not necessarily countable. Suppose that we are given a fixed mapping f from the segment $[1, n]$ to X. Just as above, we can designate the element $f(j)$ of X corresponding to the integer j of the segment by some such symbol as x_j. The elements $f(1), f(2), \ldots, f(n)$ of X, which we can write as $x_1, x_2, \ldots, x_n$, are said to be an *ordered n-tuple* in X, often written simply as $(x_1, x_2, \ldots, x_n)$. The n-tuple is also called a *finite sequence* in X. Observe that f here is not required to be one-to-one, and so the n-tuple may very well contain repeated elements.

Similarly, if f is a mapping of $\mathbf{J}$ to the set X, then the elements $f(1), f(2), f(3), \ldots$ in X can be indicated (say) by $x_1, x_2, x_3, \ldots$, and we then speak of an *infinite sequence* of elements in X; $x_n = f(n)$ is called the "nth term" of the sequence. Again f need not be one-to-one, and so elements of X may be repeated in an infinite sequence.

EXAMPLE The integers $1 \cdot 2$, $2 \cdot 3$, $3 \cdot 4$, etc., form an infinite sequence whose nth term is $n \cdot (n + 1)$. The integers 1, $1 + 3$, $1 + 3 + 5$, $1 + 3 + 5 + 7$, etc., form an infinite sequence whose nth term is the sum of the first n odd integers (and is equal to n^2; see Exercise 2, Sec. 7).

† The real numbers constitute an infinite set which is not countable. See Theorem 4.2, Corollary, Chap. 4.

EXERCISES

1. Let E and E' be finite sets with no elements in common and containing, respectively, m and n elements. Let E'' be their *union*, that is, the set consisting of all elements in either E or E'. Show that E'' contains $m + n$ elements.

2. Let a, b be elements of **Z** with $b > a$. Let E consist of all integers x such that $a < x \leq b$. Show that E contains $b - a$ elements.

*3. Let E be a countable set and E' be a finite or a countable set. Show that the union of E and E' is a countable set.

*4. Let E be a countable set. Prove that any non-empty subset of E is either finite or countable.

*5. Let $E_1, E_2, \ldots$ be a finite or countable collection of sets, each of which is countable. Show that their union (set of all the elements in all the E_j) is countable.

6. If A is an infinite set, B a finite set, and f a mapping of A to B, show that there exist distinct elements a, a' in A such that $f(a) = f(a')$.

7. Show that any finite set of integers contains a smallest element and a greatest element, both unique.

*8. Show that the number of elements in a finite set E is uniquely defined; i.e., show that if there is a one-to-one mapping of a segment $[1, n]$ to E, then that is the only segment with a one-to-one mapping to E.

*9. Show that a non-empty subset of a finite set is itself finite.

7. *Mathematical induction and some of its applications*

7A. Axiom (7) of Sec. 4 is called the axiom of *complete induction* (also *finite* or *mathematical* induction). It is the basis of a very important method of proof which we now describe—proof by mathematical induction. Instead of using axiom (7) directly, however, we shall use Theorem 4.3. [It is an easy matter to see that axiom (7) and Theorem 4.3 are really equivalent, in the sense that we could have used the statement of Theorem 4.3 in place of axiom (7), then deducing the assertion of axiom (7) as a theorem.]

(I) *Let there be assigned to every positive integer n a statement P_n which may be either true or false. Suppose that P_1 is true and suppose that for each n the statement P_{n+1} is necessarily true whenever the preceding statements P_1, $P_2, \ldots, P_n$ are true. Then all the P_n are true.*

For let F be the set of all positive integers n for which P_n is false. By Theorem 4.3 the set F has a least element n_0 if it is not empty, and in that case $n_0 > 1$ because P_1 is true by assumption. Then $n = n_0 - 1$ is a positive integer, and by definition of F, *all* the statements $P_1, P_2, \ldots, P_n$ must be true. Therefore, by assumption, $P_{n+1} = P_{n_0}$ is also true—a contradiction. Hence F must be empty.

REMARK. Observe that there is nothing to prevent some of the P's from being true, irrespective of the truth or falsity of the preceding statements. Several examples of induction are given below.

We point out explicitly that (I) above does not have the status of a *theorem* because there are some rather vague things involved (e.g., what is meant by "statement"). Hence (I) should be regarded as a kind of "model" for induction proofs. Formulating the general principle of induction as we have done in (I) simply saves us a lot of needless repetition of a frequently used method of proof. In applications of (I), the "statements" P_n always have precise mathematical definitions, and when specific and exact mathematical statements are substituted for the P_n in (I) and the "proof" we have given for it, the result is of course a precise mathematical theorem. Frequently the actual procedure of writing out all the details of an induction proof is rather tiresome, and mathematicians often abbreviate the whole thing by simply writing "and so on," or some similar expression.

It sometimes happens that instead of having statements P_n for every positive integer n we have them for only a finite number of integers, say those in the segment $[1, r]$ consisting of all integers n such that $1 \leq n \leq r$. Mathematical induction can still be applied:

(II) *For each integer n in the segment $[1, r]$ let P_n be a statement which may be either true or false. Suppose that P_1 is true and that P_{n+1} is necessarily true (for $n < r$) whenever the preceding statements $P_1, P_2, \ldots, P_n$ are true. Then all the P_n are true, for $1 \leq n \leq r$.*

The argument is exactly the same as that given for (I).

7B. Before going on to give examples of mathematical induction proofs, we describe another equally important application of Theorem 4.3—*definition* by *induction*. Here the problem is one of defining certain mappings from the positive integers **J** to some set E.

Suppose that we wish to define a mapping f from **J** to a set E satisfying the following conditions:

7.1 *$f(1)$ is a given element x of E.*

7.2 *For each positive integer n there is given some rule, call it R_n, from which the element $f(n + 1)$ in E is uniquely determined by the elements $f(1), f(2), \ldots, f(n)$.*

For this situation we have a general "mapping principle" analogous to (I) above:

(III) *There is one and only one mapping f from **J** to E which satisfies the conditions* (7.1) and (7.2).

The idea behind this principle is almost obvious: (7.1) tells us what $f(1)$ is to be; then the rule R_1 tells how to determine $f(1 + 1) = f(2)$ from $f(1)$; the rule R_2 then tells how $f(2 + 1) = f(3)$ is to be determined from $f(1)$ and $f(2)$; knowing $f(1)$, $f(2)$, $f(3)$, we can then compute $f(4)$ by means of the rule R_3, and so on. The mapping f is said to be defined *inductively* by the given conditions (7.1) and (7.2). A precise demonstration of (III) involves some minor logical subtleties; we defer the demonstration until paragraph J below.

We shall give some examples of (III) presently. We first state a slightly modified version, analogous to (II) above: Suppose that we want to define a mapping f from some segment $[1, r]$ (rather than all of **J**) to a set E in such a way that the following conditions are satisfied:

7.3 *$f(1)$ is a given element x of E.*

7.4 *For each positive integer $n < r$ there is given some rule R_n from which the element $f(n + 1)$ in E is uniquely determined by the elements $f(1)$, $f(2)$, . . . , $f(n)$.*

The mapping principle for this case is

(IV) *There is one and only one mapping f from the segment $[1, r]$ to E which satisfies* (7.3) *and* (7.4).

Clearly the idea here is essentially the same as for (III) above.

In reference to the rules R_n mentioned above, we point out that R_n might flatly state what $f(n + 1)$ is to be, without any reference at all to $f(1)$, . . . , $f(n)$, or R_n might involve only some of the latter elements. These possibilities are illustrated in the examples below.

Just as with (I) and (II), the principles (III) and (IV) are not exactly theorems, because they involve the rather imprecise notion of a "rule" R_n. We could attempt to give a rigorous definition of that notion, but there is no great point to doing so. For, in specific applications of (III) or (IV), the rule R_n is given by a precise mathematical definition, and when that is done (III) and (IV) and their demonstration in paragraph J become precise mathematical statements.

7C. Here we give two simple examples of definition by induction. For the first example let it be required to find a mapping f from **J** to **J** satisfying the conditions

7.5
$$f(1) = 1$$
$$f(n + 1) = (n + 1) \cdot f(n) \qquad \text{for } n > 1$$

The rule R_n determining $f(n + 1)$ is particularly simple; it involves only $f(n)$. The mapping principle (III) declares that there is one and only one mapping f with these properties, and to write down a precise proof of that one has only to copy out the argument for (III) in paragraph J, putting in the mathematical condition

(7.5) for the unspecified rule R_n in (7.2). The mapping f defined inductively by (7.5) is of considerable importance. The integer $f(n)$ is usually indicated by $n!$ (read *n factorial*). From (7.5) one really sees that the first few values are $1! = 1$, $2! = 2$, $3! = 3 \cdot 2! = 6$, $4! = 4 \cdot 3! = 24$, etc. It is customary to define $0! = 1$.

Our second example is of no particular importance; it is merely intended as an illustration. Let it be required to define a mapping F from **J** to **J** satisfying the following conditions:

7.6
$$F(1) = 1 \qquad F(2) = 2 \qquad \text{and}$$
$$F(n+1) = (n+1) \cdot F(q) \qquad \text{for } n > 1, \text{ where } q \text{ is the greatest even integer not exceeding } n$$

Here the rule R_1 determining $F(2)$ is simply $F(2) = 2$. For $n > 1$ the rule R_n involves only $F(n)$ if n is even and only $F(n-1)$ if n is odd. The mapping principle (III) asserts that there is a unique mapping F satisfying these conditions. The first few values of F are as follows: $F(3) = 3 \cdot F(2) = 6$, $F(4) = 4 \cdot F(2) = 8$, $F(5) = 5 \cdot F(4) = 40$, $F(6) = 6 \cdot F(4) = 48$, etc.

7D. We now come to some very important applications of definition by induction, and in the course of working them out we shall also have some examples of proof by induction.

Let S be a set with an *associative* binary operation $*$. Let x be a fixed but arbitrary element of S. We wish to define a mapping, call it g, from **J** to S by the conditions

7.7
$$g(1) = x$$
$$g(n+1) = g(n) * x \qquad \text{for } n \geq 1$$

From (III) we know that there is a unique mapping g satisfying these requirements, and we have $g(2) = g(1) * x = x * x$, $g(3) = g(2) * x = x * x * x$, $g(4) = g(3) * x = x * x * x * x$, etc. (we omit parentheses because $*$ is supposed to be associative). In E and F below we shall develop some important special notation for the mapping g. First we prove the following basic fact:

7.8
$$g(m+n) = g(m) * g(n) \qquad \text{for any positive integers } m, n$$

Proof. We prove this by induction, assuming that m is fixed throughout the discussion. Then let P_n be the statement (7.8). P_1 is true, by (7.7) with m in place of n. We now show that P_{n+1} is true whenever P_n is true. We have $g(m+n+1) = g(m+n) * x$, by (7.7). If P_n is true, then $g(m+n) = g(m) * g(n)$, whence $g(m+n+1) = g(m) * g(n) * x$, by the preceding equation. Now $g(n) * x = g(n+1)$, by (7.7) again, and so we obtain $g(m+n+1) = g(m) * g(n+1)$, which is precisely the statement P_{n+1}. It follows from the principle (I) of mathematical induction that all the P_n are true. Hence (7.8) holds for all positive integers n. Since m was arbitrary, it also holds for all positive integers m. Q.E.D.

From (7.8) we note (interchanging m and n) that

7.9 $$g(m) * g(n) = g(n) * g(m) = g(m + n) \qquad \text{for any positive integers } m, n$$

7E. We now put our results in more familiar notation. If the binary operation in S is written in the usual product notation, xy instead of $x * y$, then the element $g(n)$ of (7.7) is denoted by x^n. This symbol is therefore defined for every element x in S and for every positive integer n. The Eqs. (7.7) can be written

7.10 $$\begin{aligned} x^1 &= x \\ x^{n+1} &= x^n * x \end{aligned}$$

Equation (7.1) becomes

7.11 $$x^m x^n = x^n x^m = x^{m+n} \qquad \text{for all positive integers } m, n$$

If the system S contains an identity element e for the binary operation, then it is customary to define

7.12 $$x^0 = e \qquad \text{for any } x \text{ in } S$$

The rules (7.11) hold for all m, $n \geq 0$.

Further, if x has an inverse, call it x^{-1}, for the binary operation under consideration, then we define

7.13 $$x^{-n} = (x^{-1})^n \qquad (n \geq 0)$$

Thus x^n is defined for all integers n, positive, negative, or zero. It is easy to verify that (7.11) remains valid for all integers m, n.

Another important rule for exponents is the following:

7.14 $$(x^n)^m = x^{nm} \qquad \text{for all positive integers } m, n$$

Proof. We use induction on m, the integer n being arbitrary but fixed. Let P_m be the statement (7.14). Then P_1 is true, since $y^1 = y$ for any y in S, in particular for $y = x^n$. Suppose that P_m is true for some m. We show that P_{m+1} must also be true. We have

$$(x^n)^{m+1} = (x^n)^m \cdot (x^n)$$

from (7.10) with x^n in place of x. By assumption, $(x^n)^m = x^{nm}$, and so the right-hand side above is equal to $x^{nm} \cdot x^n$, and this is equal to $x^{nm+n} = x^{n(m+1)}$, which is precisely the statement P_{m+1}. Therefore P_{m+1} is true if P_n is true. Since P_1 is true, as noted above, all the P_m are true, by (I). That is, (7.14) holds for all positive integers m, and also for all positive integers n, since n was arbitrary in the proof. Q.E.D.

It is clear that (7.14) holds if $m = 0$ or $n = 0$, assuming that S contains an identity element e for the operation. Using (7.13) one easily verifies that (7.14) holds for all integers m, n if x has an inverse.

As a further property of exponents we have

7.15 $(xy)^n = x^n y^n$ for all positive integers n, provided $xy = yx$

In order to prove this, we show first that

7.16 $xy^n = y^n x$ for all positive integers n, if $xy = yx$

Proof. The statement holds for $n = 1$, by assumption. If (7.16) holds for some n, then it holds for $n + 1$. Namely, we have $y^{n+1} = y \cdot y^n$, by (7.11), and so $xy^{n+1} = (xy)y^n = (yx)y^n = y(xy^n)$, since $xy = yx$. Since $xy^n = y^n x$, by assumption, there follows $xy^{n+1} = y(y^n x) = (yy^n)x = y^{n+1}x$, which is (7.16) with $n + 1$ in place of n. Hence (7.16) holds for all positive integers n, by mathematical induction. Q.E.D.

Proof of (7.15). The equation holds for $n = 1$, by assumption. Suppose now that it holds for some integer n. We show that it must also hold for $n + 1$. To do so we have $(xy)^{n+1} = (xy)^n(xy)$, by (7.10). By assumption, $(xy)^n = x^n y^n$. Therefore, $(xy)^{n+1} = x^n y^n xy$. By (7.16) this is equal to $x^n x y^n y = x^{n+1} y^{n+1}$. This shows that (7.15) holds for $n + 1$ if it holds for n. Therefore (since it holds for $n = 1$), (7.15) is true for all positive integers n, by mathematical induction. Q.E.D.

Obviously (7.15) and (7.16) hold for $n = 0$. Equation (7.16) is easily seen to hold for negative n if y has an inverse; (7.15) holds also for negative n if both x and y have inverses (assuming $xy = yx$). For example, we have $y^{-1}xy = y^{-1}yx$, whence $y^{-1}xy = x$. Therefore, $y^{-1}xyy^{-1} = xy^{-1}$, or finally $y^{-1}x = xy^{-1}$. Hence (7.16) holds with y^{-1} in place of y. Similarly, one shows that $x^{-1}y^{-1} = y^{-1}x^{-1}$, and therefore (7.15) is valid with x^{-1} in place of x and y^{-1} in place of y.

7F. A somewhat different notational convention is used in the case of additive notation. Consider then a set S equipped with an associative binary operation $+$. We shall assume that $+$ is commutative, since that symbol is rarely used otherwise. In this situation, the element $g(n)$ of (7.7) (with $+$ in place of $*$) is denoted by nx, or $n \cdot x$, instead of x^n. Equation (7.7) then reads

7.17
$$1 \cdot x = x$$
$$(n + 1)x = nx + x$$

If S contains an identity element for $+$, as we shall assume for simplicity, denoting it by 0, then we define

$$0 \cdot x = 0$$

the zero on the left being the integer zero, the zero on the right being the 0 in S. The equation is none other than (7.12) in the additive notation. Equation (7.11) transcribed into the new notation is

7.18 $$mx + nx = (m + n)x$$

this holding for all $m, n \geq 0$. If x has an inverse for the operation $+$, denote it by $-x$, then we define $(-n)x$ by

$$(-n)x = n(-x) \qquad (n \text{ a positive integer})$$

This equation is (7.13) in the additive notation. Equation (7.18) then holds for all integers m, n. Equation (7.14) becomes

7.19 $$m(nx) = (mn)x \qquad \text{for all integers } m, n \geq 0$$

and this is valid for all integers if x has an inverse.

Since $+$ is assumed to be commutative, Eq. (7.15) in the additive notation is

7.20 $$n(x + y) = nx + ny \qquad \text{for all } n \geq 0$$

It holds for $n < 0$ if x and y have inverses for the operation $+$.

As a particularly important application, suppose that S is a ring, hence is equipped with both a product and a sum operation. If x is any element of S, then x^n is defined for any integer $n \geq 0$ by (7.10) [or (7.12) for $n = 0$], and all the rules in paragraph E can be applied. Using the $+$ operation in S we can also define nx for any positive integer n, by (7.17). Since S is an abelian group with the operation $+$, the element nx is defined for all integers n, by the foregoing conventions, and all the rules of this paragraph hold. We mention the following rules, valid in any ring:

7.21 $$(nx)(my) = nm(xy) \qquad \text{for any integers } n, m$$

7.22 $$(nx)^m = n^m x^m \qquad \text{for any integer } n \text{ and any integer } m \geq 0$$

Their proofs are left as exercises in mathematical induction.

7G. Paragraphs *7D*, *7E*, and *7F* were concerned with the notation of applying a binary operation repeatedly to a single element x of S. Here we consider briefly the similar idea of applying the binary operation repeatedly to possibly different elements. We begin by considering an associative binary operation in a set S, and we use first the multiplicative notation.

Let $x_1, x_2, \ldots, x_n$ be an n-tuple of elements in S (see Sec. 6). We seek to define a mapping from the segment $[1, n]$ to S satisfying the conditions

7.23 $$\begin{aligned} f(1) &= x_1 \\ f(k + 1) &= f(k) \cdot x_{k+1} \qquad \text{for } 1 \leq k < n \end{aligned}$$

The mapping principle (IV) of paragraph *7B* assures us that there is exactly one mapping f satisfying these conditions. We have $f(2) = f(1) \cdot x_2 = x_1x_2$, $f(3) = f(2) \cdot x_3 = x_1x_2x_3$, etc. (we omit parentheses here because of the assumed associativity of the binary operation). It is natural to indicate $f(n)$ by $x_1x_2 \cdots x_n$, or some similar symbolism. The important point is that the symbol is given an unambiguous meaning by this definition. Comparing (7.10) and (7.23) one sees immediately that if $x_1, x_2, \ldots, x_n$ all happen to be the *same* element x of S, then $f(n) = x^n$. The new operation therefore includes that of (7.10), and we can write

7.24 $$x^n = xx \cdots x \qquad (n \text{ factors})$$

the right-hand side denoting the quantity $x_1x_2 \cdots x_n$ when all the factors are equal to x.

Comparing (7.5) and (7.23) we see that

7.25 $$n! = 1 \cdot 2 \cdots n$$

the right-hand side denoting the quantity $x_1x_2 \cdots x_n$ defined by (7.23) when x_k is the integer k ($k = 1, \ldots, n$), the operation being multiplication of integers.

Using mathematical induction it is easy to prove various rules for repeated operations. For example,

7.26 $$(x_1x_2 \cdots x_n)(x_{n+1}x_{n+2} \cdots x_{n+m}) = x_1x_2 \cdots x_{n+m}$$

for any $(n + m)$-tuple of elements in S. If the operation is commutative, then

7.27 $$x_{j_1}x_{j_2} \cdots x_{j_n} = x_1x_2 \cdots x_n$$

for any n-tuple of elements, where $j_1, j_2, \ldots, j_n$ denote the integers $1, 2, \ldots, n$ in some new order. We omit proofs of these statements.

Another useful symbolism for the repeated product of elements in S is defined by the following equation:

7.28 $$\prod_{j=1}^{n} x_j = x_1x_2 \cdots x_n$$

In regard to this notation, we point out that the particular choice of the "dummy" index j is a matter of indifference. Any other letter, i for example, can be used, provided that no confusion is produced thereby [for example, one would not use the letters x or n in place of j in (7.28), for obvious reasons].

In the case of a binary operation with additive notation $+$, we naturally write $x_1 + x_2 + \cdots + x_n$ instead of $x_1x_2 \cdots x_n$, and this quantity is also denoted by the symbol

7.29 $$\sum_{j=1}^{n} x_j$$

The remarks above concerning the dummy index j apply here, too. The additive version of Eq. (7.24) is

$$nx = x + x + \cdots + x \qquad (n \text{ terms})$$

In a ring both the symbols $x_1 + x_2 + \cdots + x_n$ and $x_1x_2 \cdots x_n$ are defined for any n-tuple $x_1, x_2, \ldots, x_n$ in the ring.

7H. We conclude with a few simple applications to rings. Let A be a ring (see Definition 2.1), and let $x_1, x_2, \ldots, x_n$ be an n-tuple of elements in A. Then

7.30 $$c \cdot (x_1 + x_2 + \cdots + x_n) = cx_1 + cx_2 + \cdots + cx_n$$

for any element c in A. (This is a generalized form of the distributive law.) The proof is easily obtained by induction (II). Namely, the equation $c \cdot (x_1 + \cdots + x_k) = cx_1 + \cdots + cx_k$ clearly holds for $k = 1$. If it holds for some k (with $k < n$), then it holds also for $k + 1$. For

$$\begin{aligned} c \cdot (x_1 + \cdots + x_{k+1}) &= c \cdot [(x_1 + \cdots + x_k) + x_{k+1}] \\ &= c \cdot (x_1 + \cdots + x_k) + cx_{k+1} \end{aligned}$$

by the distributive law. By assumption the right member is equal to $(cx_1 + \cdots + cx_k) + cx_{k+1}$, which in turn is equal to $cx_1 + \cdots + cx_{k+1}$, by Eq. (7.26) for the operation $+$. The induction principle (IV) then shows that the equation $c \cdot (x_1 + \cdots + x_k) = cx_1 + \cdots + cx_k$ holds for all $k = 1, \ldots, n$. In particular, it holds for $k = n$, which is (7.30).

In connection with induction proofs, we mention that they are frequently presented with only enough detail to convey the gist of the argument, the remaining details being left to the reader. A little experience with induction proofs will show how much detail is necessary to make the argument clear.

We give a useful application of (7.30): Let the unit element of our ring A be denoted by the symbol 1, and let b be any element of A, n any positive integer. Then

7.31 $$(1 - b)(1 + b + b^2 + \cdots + b^n) = 1 - b^{n+1}$$

For, by (7.30), the left-hand side is equal to

$$\begin{aligned} &(1 - b) + (b - b^2) + (b^2 - b^3) + \cdots + (b^{n+1} - b^n) \\ &\quad = 1 - b + b - b^2 + b^2 - b^3 + \cdots + b^{n-1} - b^n + b^n - b^{n+1} \\ &\quad = 1 - b^{n+1} \end{aligned}$$

As a final application, let A be an ordered integral domain (see Sec. 3), and let $x_1, x_2, \ldots, x_n$ be an n-tuple of elements in A. Then

7.32 $$|x_1 + x_2 + \cdots + x_n| \leq |x_1| + |x_2| + \cdots + |x_n|$$

The inequality is clearly correct for $n = 1$. Suppose that it holds for some integer n and for all n-tuples $x_1, \ldots, x_n$. Then it must hold for $n + 1$. For

$$
\begin{aligned}
|x_1 + x_2 + \cdots + x_{n+1}| \\
&= |(x_1 + \cdots + x_n) + x_{n+1}| \\
&\leq |x_1 + \cdots + x_n| + |x_{n+1}| && \text{(by Exercise 6, part (}d\text{), Sec. 3)} \\
&\leq |x_1| + \cdots + |x_n| + |x_{n+1}| && \text{(by assumption)}
\end{aligned}
$$

The theorem follows by induction (I).

7J. Proof of Definition by Induction (III) To prove (III) of paragraph *7B*, let U be the set of all positive integers k such that there is one and only one mapping, call it f_k, from the segment $[1, k]$ to E satisfying conditions (7.1), (7.2). That is,

$f_k(1) = x$;

7.33 *for* $1 \leq n < k$ *the element* $f_k(n + 1)$ *in* E *is determined by the given rule* R_n *from the elements* $f_k(1), f_k(2), \ldots, f_k(n)$.

We observe that if k and l are both in U, say with $k < l$, then

7.34 $f_k(n) = f_l(n) \qquad \text{for } 1 \leq n \leq k$

for f_l, applied only to elements of the shorter segment $[1, k]$, must satisfy the same conditions (7.33) as f_k, and by assumption those conditions determine f_k uniquely.

Now let T be the set of all positive integers not in U. If T is not empty, then it has a least element k_0, by Theorem 4.3. We show that this gives a contradiction. Clearly $k_0 > 1$ because the mapping of the segment $[1, 1]$ to E is uniquely prescribed by the condition that 1 be sent into x. Then $k = k_0 - 1$ is a positive integer in U, and so by definition of U there is one and only one mapping f_k from $[1, k]$ to E satisfying (7.33). We want to show that there is one and only one mapping f_{k0} from $[1, k_0]$ to E satisfying (7.33). Now the segment $[1, k_0]$ has only one element not already in $[1, k]$, namely, $k_0 = k + 1$. There cannot be two different mappings f_{k0}, f'_{k0} from $[1, k_0]$ to E meeting the requirements, for both of them applied to integers in $[1, k]$ must satisfy the same conditions as f_k and therefore (by the uniqueness of f_k) must coincide with f_k in the shorter segment. That is, $f_{k0}(n) = f'_{k0}(n) = f_k(n)$ for $1 \leq n \leq k$. But then condition (7.33) says that both $f_{k0}(k + 1)$ and $f'_{k0}(k + 1)$ are uniquely determined by the rule R_k from certain of the elements $f_k(1), f_k(2), \ldots, f_k(k)$, and so $f_{k0}(k + 1) = f'_{k0}(k + 1)$, whence $f_{k0} = f'_{k0}$. Hence, f_{k0} is unique, and it clearly exists, for we have only to put $f_{k0}(n) = f_k(n)$ for $1 \leq n \leq k$, then determining $f_{k0}(k + 1)$ from those elements by the rule R_k. This shows that k_0 is also in U, contradicting the definition of k_0. Hence T must be empty, and so $U = \mathbf{J}$.

Therefore for every positive integer k there is one and only one mapping f_k from the segment $[1, k]$ to E satisfying (7.33). Now for any positive integer n we define $f(n)$ by

$$f(n) = f_n(n)$$

This defines $f(n)$ uniquely for any positive integer n, and so f is a mapping from $\mathbf{J}$ to E; and f satisfies (7.1) and (7.2), as follows easily from (7.34). Furthermore, f is unique, since for the integers in any segment $[1, k]$ it satisfies the same conditions as f_k and must therefore coincide with f_k for every n in the segment $[1, k]$.

Q.E.D.

The mapping principle (IV) follows from (III) by simply taking R_n to be the rule $f(n + 1) = x_0$ for $n \geq r$, x_0 being any fixed element of E.

EXERCISES

1. Let x and y be elements of a group (written multiplicatively) such that $xy = yx$. Prove that $x^m y^n = y^n x^m$ for all integers m, n.

2. If n is any positive integer, then $2n - 1$ is the nth *odd* integer. Prove by induction that the sum $1 + 3 + \cdots + (2n - 1)$ of the first n odd integers is equal to n^2. What is the sum of the first n even integers (the nth *even* integer being $2n$)?

3. Let $E_1, E_2, \ldots, E_n$ be n sets, and suppose that E_j contains m_j elements, for $j = 1, 2, \ldots, n$. Assuming that no two of the given sets have any elements in common, prove that their union (that is, set of all the elements in all the E_j) contains $m_1 + m_2 + \cdots + m_n$ elements. (Use the definition of Sec. 6 and the result of Exercise 1, Sec. 6.)

4. Let A be a ring (see Definition 2.1), and let b be any element of A. Let B denote the subset consisting of the unit element of A and all finite sums of elements $m \cdot b^n$, where m is any integer and where n is any positive integer (see E and F above). Prove that B is a *commutative* subring of A (see Definition 2.2). (B is called the subring of A *generated* by b.)

5. Prove formula (7.31) by induction.

6. For any positive integer n prove that

$$2 \cdot (1 + 2 + \cdots + n) = n \cdot (n + 1)$$

7. Let a and d be elements of a ring A. Prove that

$$2 \cdot [a + (a + d) + (a + 2d) + \cdots + (a + nd)] = (n + 1)(2a + nd)$$

for any positive integer n.

8. Prove that

$$3 \cdot [1^2 + 3^2 + 5^2 + \cdots + (2n - 1)^2] = n(2n - 1)(2n + 1)$$

for any positive integer n.

9. Prove that

$$4 \cdot [1^3 + 2^3 + 3^3 + \cdots + n^3] = n^2(n + 1)^2$$

for any positive integer n.

10. Prove that

$$6 \cdot (1^2 + 2^2 + 3^2 + \cdots + n^2) = n(n + 1)(2n + 1)$$

for any positive integer n.

11. If $1 + b \geq 0$ in an ordered integral domain (1 being the unit element), prove that $(1 + b)^n \geq 1 + nb$ for any positive integer n.

12. If $x_1, x_2, \ldots, x_n$ are elements of an ordered integral domain such that

$$\prod_{i=1}^{n} x_i = 1 \qquad \text{then } \sum_{i=1}^{n} |x_i| \geq n$$

13. Show that $\sum_{i=1}^{n} i \cdot i! = (n+1)! - 1$.

8. Some elementary number theory

In the following paragraphs we are going to prove some of the basic theorems of arithmetic, theorems that are the core of the part of mathematics called elementary number theory.† That theory is primarily concerned with questions of divisibility of integers, and we now define that concept. Remember that we always deal with the system **Z** defined by axioms (1) to (7) of Sec. 4.

DEFINITION 8.1 *An integer $m \neq 0$ is said to* divide *another integer n (or to be a* divisor *of n) if there is an integer q such that $n = mq$. If that is so, then we write $m \mid n$ and we call q the* quotient *of n by m (it is uniquely determined, for if also $n = mq'$, then $mq = mq'$ and so $q = q'$, by the cancellation law). If m does not divide n, then we write $m \nmid n$.*

As a trivial example, $2 \mid 6$ and the quotient is 3. However $2 \nmid 7$.

We make some simple observations concerning the definition. First observe that 0 is divisible by any integer $m \neq 0$, for $m \cdot 0 = 0$. In the definition we have excluded $m = 0$, for (if $n \neq 0$) there is no number q such that $n = 0 \cdot q$.‡ Since the number 0 presents some trivial but annoying exceptions, we shall generally exclude it in the following.

Both 1 and -1 divide every integer n, and if $n \neq 0$, then n is divisible by n and $-n$, the quotients being 1 and -1, respectively. Some other simple consequences of the definition are brought out in

PROPOSITION 8.1 *(a) If $m \mid n$, then also $m \mid -n$, $-m \mid n$, and $-m \mid -n$. (b) If $k \mid m$ and $m \mid n$, then $k \mid n$. (c) If $m \mid n$ and $m \mid n'$, then $m \mid (n \pm n')$. (d) If $m \mid n$, then $m \mid kn$ for any integer k. (e) The integers 1 and -1 are divisible only by 1 and -1. (f) If $m \mid n$, then $|m| \leq |n|$. (g) If $m \mid n$ and $n \mid m$, then $m = \pm n$.*

Proof. All but (*e*), (*f*), and (*g*) follow very trivially from the definition; and (*e*) is an immediate consequence of Exercise 2, Sec. 4. To prove

† The term "elementary" does not necessarily mean "easy"; it refers to the nature of proofs and simply means that they do not use calculus, whose methods play an important part in more advanced investigations of number theory.

‡ The student may wonder about the possibility of putting a new element ∞ into the system **Z** and then defining the quotient of n by 0 to be ∞. There is nothing wrong with doing so, and in fact it is sometimes done. However it follows from Theorem 2.2 that it cannot be done in such a way as to give a ring. In other words, such a definition cannot be made without partially destroying the basic algebraic rules in the system. For most purposes that is too high a price to pay simply to be able to divide by 0.

(*f*) we have by definition $n = mq$, and so $|n| = |mq| = |m| \cdot |q|$, by Exercise 6, part (*i*), Sec. 3. Now $|q| \geq 1$, by Theorem 4.1, and so $|m| \cdot |q| \geq |m|$ (Theorem 3.6). Hence $|n| \geq |m|$.

To prove (*g*), it follows from (*f*) that if $m \mid n$ and $n \mid m$, then $|m| \leq |n|$ and $|n| \leq |m|$. Hence $|m| = |n|$ (by trichotomy), and so $m = \pm n$, by definition of absolute value.

DEFINITION 8.2 *An integer n is called a* prime number *if it is not equal to* 0, 1, *or* -1 *and if its only divisors are* ± 1 *and* $\pm n$.

The first few prime numbers are ± 2, ± 3, ± 5, ± 7, ± 11, ± 13, ± 17, ± 19, etc. It is the study of prime numbers that is the chief object of number theory. Later on we shall mention a few of the more advanced theorems concerning them.

REMARK. From (*a*) of Proposition 8.1 it follows that divisibility (or nondivisibility) of one integer by another is completely unaffected by a change of sign. Accordingly we shall usually restrict our attention to *positive* integers in the following. From now on when we refer to a *prime number* we shall always mean a *positive* prime—hence one of the integers 2, 3, 5, 7, 11, 13, etc. All the results we shall derive below will be applicable to negative integers, with transparent modifications.

PROPOSITION 8.2 *Every integer greater than* 1 *is divisible by a prime number.*

Proof. Let n be an integer greater than 1, and let T be the set of all integers greater than 1 which divide n. Since $n \mid n$ it is clear that T is not empty, for it certainly contains n. Therefore T has a least element m (Theorem 4.3); and m must be prime. For otherwise it would be divisible by a smaller integer $k > 1$. But then k would also divide n [Proposition 8.1 (*b*)] and therefore would have to be in T, a contradiction. Hence m is prime and $m \mid n$.

THEOREM 8.3 **(Euclid)** *There are infinitely many primes.*

Proof. Let $p_1, p_2, \ldots, p_r$ be any prime numbers. The integer $q = 1 + p_1p_2 \cdots p_r$ is divisible by some prime p_0, by the theorem above. But q is not divisible by the given primes $p_1, \ldots, p_r$. For suppose, for example, that $p_1 \mid q$. Clearly p_1 also divides $p_1p_2 \cdots p_r$, and so p_1 must divide $q - p_1p_2 \cdots p_r = 1$, by Proposition 8.1 (*c*). But that is impossible, by Proposition 8.1 (*e*). It follows then that p_0 does not appear among the primes $p_1, \ldots, p_r$; therefore no finite list of primes can exhaust the set of all primes.

The following theorem is central to our topic:

PROPOSITION 8.4 **(Division algorithm)** *Let m and n be any positive integers. Then there are two integers q and r such that*

$$n = qm + r \qquad \textit{and} \qquad 0 \leq r < m$$

Moreover q and r are thereby uniquely determined, and $q \geq 0$.

Proof. Let us prove the uniqueness first. Suppose then that there is a second pair of integers q' and r' satisfying the conditions. That is, $n = q'm + r'$ and $0 \leq r' < m$. We have $n = qm + r = q'm + r'$, and so $r - r' = (q' - q) \cdot m$, which shows that if $q = q'$, then also $r = r'$. Suppose that $q \neq q'$, say $q' > q$ for definiteness. Then $q' - q \geq 1$ (Theorem 4.1), and so $(q' - q) \cdot m \geq m$ (Theorem 3.6). From above there follows $r - r' \geq m$, or $r \geq m + r' \geq m$ (Theorem 3.5), a contradiction.

To show that q and r exist as claimed, let T be the set of all positive integers k for which $km > n$. T is not empty, for $n + 1$ itself is in T. Hence T contains a least element k_0 (Theorem 4.3). Accordingly we have $k_0 m > n$, but $(k_0 - 1) \cdot m \leq n$. Now define $q = k_0 - 1$. These last inequalities say $(q + 1) \cdot m > n$, but $qm \leq n$. If we subtract qm from both sides of these inequalities, we get $m > n - mq$ and $0 \leq n - mq$, by Theorem 3.5. Now define $r = n - mq$, and we are done.

REMARK. The uniquely determined numbers q and r are usually called *quotient* and *remainder*, respectively. Observe that to say m divides n means simply that $r = 0$. As simple numerical examples, if $n = 7$ and $m = 3$, then $q = 2$ and $r = 1$; if $n = 7$ and $m = 8$, then $q = 0$ and $r = 7$. The division algorithm is of course nothing but ordinary division with remainder, such as one learns in elementary school. The point here is that it has been stated precisely and has been deduced from the axioms characterizing the system $\mathbf{Z}$. The innocuous appearance of the theorem belies its far-reaching consequences, which we now begin to develop.

DEFINITION 8.3 *Let m and n be any two integers different from 0. An integer d is called the* greatest common divisor (g.c.d.) *of m and n if*

(1) $d > 0$

(2) *d divides m and n*

(3) *Any integer which divides both m and n also divides d*

More generally, if $n_1, n_2, \ldots, n_r$ are integers different from 0, then an integer d is called their greatest common divisor *if*

(1′) $d > 0$

(2′) *d divides $n_1, n_2, \ldots, n_r$*

(3′) *Any integer which divides $n_1, n_2, \ldots, n_r$ also divides d*

EXAMPLE 2 is the g.c.d. of 4 and 6; 3 is the g.c.d. of 6, 12, and 21; 1 is the g.c.d. of 4 and 15.

REMARK. Suppose that d and d' are two greatest common divisors of m and n. Then by (2) we have $d|d'$ and also $d'|d$. Consequently $d' = \pm d$, by Proposition 8.1(g). From condition (1) we conclude that $d' = d$. Therefore the g.c.d. of two numbers (we show below that it always exists) is *unique*. We shall denote the g.c.d. of m and n ($\neq 0$) by the symbol (m, n). From the definition it is readily verified that the following hold:

$$(m, n) > 0, \qquad (m, n) = (n, m) = (-m, n) = (m, -n) = (-m, -n);$$

8.1 $$(m, n) \leq |m| \quad \text{and} \quad (m, n) \leq |n|$$

The symbol $(n_1, n_2, \ldots, n_r)$ is similarly used to represent the g.c.d. of nonzero integers $n_1, n_2, \ldots, n_r$ (see Exercise 2 below).

THEOREM 8.5 (Euclidean algorithm) *Any two positive integers m and n have a unique greatest common divisor $d = (m, n)$. Moreover d can be calculated by the following method of successive divisions: Write a_0 for one of the given numbers m, n and a_1 for the other. Using the division algorithm (Proposition 8.4), divide a_0 by a_1, getting $a_0 = q_1a_1 + a_2$, a_2 being the remainder. If $a_2 = 0$, then $d = a_1$; if $a_2 \neq 0$, then divide a_1 by a_2, getting say $a_1 = q_2a_2 + a_3$, where a_3 is the remainder. If $a_3 = 0$, then $d = a_2$; if $a_3 \neq 0$, then divide a_2 by a_3, getting $a_2 = q_3a_3 + a_4$, and so on. The number d is equal to the last nonzero remainder obtained in this way.*

Proof. The uniqueness of d has already been shown. To prove that it exists and that the above process gives it, let us write the successive divisions down in an orderly fashion:

8.2 $$\begin{aligned} a_0 &= q_1a_1 + a_2 \\ a_1 &= q_2a_2 + a_3 \\ a_2 &= q_3a_3 + a_4 \\ &\cdots\cdots\cdots \\ a_{k-3} &= q_{k-2}a_{k-2} + a_{k-1} \\ a_{k-2} &= q_{k-1}a_{k-1} + a_k \\ a_{k-1} &= q_ka_k \end{aligned}$$

First of all from the division algorithm we have $a_2 < a_1$, $a_3 < a_2$, $a_4 < a_3$, etc. The successive remainders therefore decrease steadily, and it follows that the process must lead to a zero remainder after a finite number of steps—in fact after at most a_1 steps. We have assumed above that a zero remainder is first obtained on the kth step. We want to show that the last nonzero remainder, namely a_k, is the g.c.d. of the given integers a_0 and a_1. From the division algorithm all the remainders (including a_k) are positive, and so condition (1) of Definition 8.3 is clearly satisfied.

Now from the last equation above we have $a_k|a_{k-1}$. Therefore from the next to last equation we get $a_k|a_{k-2}$, because a_k divides both terms on the right. From the equation above, we conclude similarly that $a_k|a_{k-3}$. Continuing up the list we find that a_k divides all the preceding a's—in particular, a_0 and a_1. Hence condition (2) of Definition 8.3 is satisfied by a_k. To check condition (3), let b be any common divisor of a_0 and a_1. From the first equation of (8.2) it follows that $b|a_2$. Then, from the second equation, $b|a_3$ because b divides both a_1 and a_2. Therefore from the third equation we find that $b|a_4$. Continuing down the list we conclude that b divides all the a's—in particular a_k. This shows that condition (3) is verified, and so $a_k = (a_0, a_1)$.

EXAMPLE 1 Find the g.c.d. of 1426 and 343. Here we put $a_0 = 1426$ and $a_1 = 343$. The calculations are

$$
\begin{aligned}
1426 &= 4 \cdot 343 + 54 \\
343 &= 6 \cdot 54 \quad + 19 \\
54 &= 2 \cdot 19 \quad + 16 \\
19 &= 1 \cdot 16 \quad + 3 \\
16 &= 5 \cdot 3 \quad\; + 1 \\
3 &= 3 \cdot 1 \quad\; + 0
\end{aligned}
$$

Hence $(1426, 343) = 1$.

EXAMPLE 2 Find $(12, 148)$. The calculations are

$$
\begin{aligned}
148 &= 12 \cdot 12 + 4 \\
12 &= \;\;3 \cdot 4 \;\; + 0
\end{aligned}
$$

and so

$$(12, 148) = 4$$

REMARK. The proof of Theorem 8.5 contains some concealed uses of mathematical induction. Can you rewrite the proof in such a way as to put them in evidence?

From the euclidean algorithm there follows a very important corollary:

THEOREM 8.6 *If m and n are any positive integers, and if d is their g.c.d., then there exist two integers r and s such that $d = rm + sn$.*

Proof. Referring to Eq. (8.2) we see that $d = a_k$ can be expressed as a combination of a_{k-1}, a_{k-2}. Namely,

$$d = a_{k-2} - q_{k-1} \cdot a_{k-1}$$

From the equation immediately preceding, namely, $a_{k-3} = q_{k-2} \cdot a_{k-2} + a_{k-1}$, we have $a_{k-1} = a_{k-3} - q_{k-2} \cdot a_{k-2}$, and so

$$
\begin{aligned}
d &= a_{k-2} - q_{k-1}\,(a_{k-3} - q_{k-2} \cdot a_{k-2}) \\
&= (1 + q_{k-1} \cdot q_{k-2}) \cdot a_{k-2} - q_{k-1} \cdot a_{k-3}
\end{aligned}
$$

Continuing up the list in this way we can express a_{k-2} as a combination of a_{k-3} and a_{k-4}, and then we can express a_{k-3} as a combination of a_{k-4} and a_{k-5}, and so on until we finally arrive at an expression for d as a combination of a_0 and a_1. This is illustrated in the examples below.

REMARK. The integers r and s of Theorem 8.6 are not unique. In fact infinitely many pairs will work.

EXAMPLE 3 Referring to Example 1, we have $1 = 16 - 5 \cdot 3$ and $3 = 19 - 1 \cdot 16$, whence $1 = 16 - 5 \cdot (19 - 16) = 6 \cdot 16 - 5 \cdot 19$. From the third equation of Example 1, $16 = 54 - 2 \cdot 19$, and so $1 = 6 \cdot (54 - 2 \cdot 19) - 5 \cdot 19$, or $1 = 6 \cdot 54 - 17 \cdot 19$. From the second equation, $19 = 343 - 6 \cdot 54$, and so $1 = 6 \cdot 54 - 17 \cdot (343 - 6 \cdot 54) = 108 \cdot 54 - 17 \cdot 343$. From the first equation, $54 = 1426 - 4 \cdot 343$, and so $1 = 108 \cdot (1426 - 4 \cdot 343) - 17 \cdot 343 = 108 \cdot 1426 - 449 \cdot 343$. Therefore we can take $r = 108$ and $s = -449$.

EXAMPLE 4 Referring now to Example 2, we need only use the first equation, getting $4 = 148 - 12 \cdot 12$. In this example then we can take $r = 1$ and $s = -12$.

DEFINITION 8.4 *Two integers m and n, different from 0, are said to be* relatively prime, *or* coprime, *if their only common divisors are* 1 *and* -1.

PROPOSITION 8.7 *Two nonzero integers m and n are relatively prime if and only if $(m, n) = 1$. If m and n are relatively prime, then there are integers r and s such that $rm + sn = 1$.*

Proof. If m and n are relatively prime, according to Definition 8.4, then 1 is clearly their g.c.d., because 1 satisfies the conditions of Definition 8.3. Now suppose conversely that 1 is the g.c.d. of m and n. Let b be any common divisor of m and n. By condition (3) of Definition 8.3 the number b must then divide 1. By Proposition 8.1 (*e*) the only divisors of 1 are ± 1, and so $b = \pm 1$. The last assertion of our theorem follows from Theorem 8.6.

EXAMPLE The integers 1426 and 343 are coprime, by Example 1.

THEOREM 8.8 *Let p be a prime, and let m and n be two nonzero integers such that $p|mn$. Then $p|m$ or $p|n$.*

Proof. It clearly suffices to consider the case $m > 0$ and $n > 0$. Suppose then that $p \nmid m$. We must show that $p|n$. Now if p does not divide m, then m and p are coprime, because by definition p is divisible only by ± 1 and $\pm p$. Hence by Proposition 8.7 there are integers r and s such that $rp + sm = 1$. Multiply this by n: $rpn + smn = n$. Now p clearly divides the first term on the left, and by assumption it divides also the second term. It therefore divides their sum, which is n.

COROLLARY *Let $n_1, n_2, \ldots, n_r$ be integers different from zero, and let p be a prime which divides $n_1 n_2 \cdots n_r$. Then p must divide one of the factors $n_1, n_2, \ldots, n_r$.*

The proof is left as an exercise.

We now come to our main result:

THEOREM 8.9 **(Fundamental Theorem of Arithmetic)** *Any integer n greater than* 1 *can be expressed as a product*

8.3 $$n = p_1 p_2 \cdots p_r$$

of positive prime numbers, and this expression is unique apart from the order of the factors.

Proof. We first show that every integer $n > 1$ can be expressed in at least one way as a product of primes. To do so let T be the set of all integers > 1 that *cannot* be expressed as a product of a certain number of primes. We want to show that T is empty. If T is not empty, then it contains a least integer n_0. Now n_0 cannot be prime, for a prime number is already expressed in the required form (with just one factor of course). Now n_0 is divisible by some prime p, by Proposition 8.2, say $n_0 = p \cdot m$. Since $p > 1$, we have $m < n_0$. Hence m is not in the set T and can therefore be expressed as a product of primes, say $m = q_1 q_2 \cdots q_s$. But then $n_0 = p \cdot q_1 q_2 \cdots q_s$, which contradicts our assumption that n_0 cannot be so expressed. We conclude therefore that T is empty.

It remains to show that the expression (8.3) is unique (apart from the order of the factors). The proof is similar to the foregoing: If the assertion is false, then there is a *least* integer $n > 1$ for which it is false. For that n there must then be two essentially different expressions of the type (8.3), say

8.4 $$n = p_1 p_2 \cdots p_r = q_1 q_2 \cdots q_s$$

Since $p_1 | n$ we have $p_1 | (q_1 q_2 \cdots q_s)$. Therefore by the corollary to Theorem 8.8 it follows that p_1 must divide one of the primes $q_1, q_2, \ldots, q_s$. By rearranging the order of the factors on the right we can assume that $p_1 | q_1$. But then $p_1 = q_1$ since they are both (positive) primes. We can therefore cancel $p_1 = q_1$ on both sides above, getting

$$p_2 p_3 \cdots p_r = q_2 q_3 \cdots q_s$$

This integer is smaller than n, because $p_1 > 1$. But it is also greater than 1, for otherwise the original Eq. (8.4) would have to be simply $p_1 = q_1$. Now by assumption the theorem is true for the integer $p_2 p_3 \cdots p_r = q_2 q_3 \cdots q_s$, and therefore we must have $r = s$ and the primes $p_2, p_3, \ldots, p_r$ must coincide with $q_2, q_3, \ldots, q_r$ in some order. It follows that the two sides of (8.4) must be the same except for the order of the factors, and so the theorem is true for n. This contradicts our assumption concerning n and shows that the set of integers $n > 1$ for which the theorem is false must be empty. Q.E.D.

REMARK. The expression (8.3) is called the prime *decomposition* or *factorization* of n. The primes $p_1, p_2, \ldots, p_r$ are said to be "contained in n" or to be prime factors of n. In general a prime may appear more than once in the prime decomposition of an integer n. If we collect the repeated primes together, then we can rewrite (8.3) in the form

$$n = p_1^{e_1} p_2^{e_2} \cdots p_s^{e_s}$$

where $p_1, p_2, \ldots, p_s$ are now *distinct* primes and where the exponents $e_1, e_2, \ldots, e_s$ are positive integers. Simple examples are $3780 = 2^2 \cdot 3^3 \cdot 5 \cdot 7$ and $1728 = 3^3 \cdot 2^6$.

EXERCISES

1. Find the g.c.d. of the following pairs of integers and find integers r and s of Theorem 8.6 for each:

(*a*) 10324, 146 (*b*) 129, 27
(*c*) 3423, 21 (*d*) 1560, -125
(*e*) -78, -22

2. Prove that the g.c.d. of any finite set of nonzero integers $n_1, n_2, \ldots, n_r$ always exists, and give a method for finding it. Show that the g.c.d. can always be expressed as a combination $a_1n_1 + a_2n_2 + \cdots + a_rn_r$, where $a_1, a_2, \ldots, a_r$ are integers. Work this out for the following numerical cases:

(*a*) 215, 15, 325
(*b*) 1460, 122, 55, 12
(*c*) 17850, 1700, 2000, 55, 20

3. Let m and n be nonzero integers, and let U be the set of all integers of the form $am + bn$, where a and b are arbitrary integers. Show that U must contain positive elements, and show that the least positive integer in U is precisely (m, n). Show how this can be generalized for the case of r given nonzero integers $n_1, n_2, \ldots, n_r$.

4. Give the prime decompositions of the following integers: 1472, 176, 18365, 124648, 127.

5. Prove that if $a \mid bc$ and if a and b are relatively prime, then $a \mid c$ (here a, b, c stand for positive integers).

6. Prove the corollary to Theorem 8.8.

7. The *least common multiple* (l.c.m.) of two integers m, n different from 0 is defined to be an integer l such that

(*a*) $l > 0$.
(*b*) $m \mid l$ and $n \mid l$.
(*c*) If m and n both divide an integer h, then also l divides h.

Prove that the l.c.m. is unique and always exists. Assuming m, n positive, show that $d \cdot l = m \cdot n$, where d and l are their g.c.d. and l.c.m., respectively. Show how to determine the g.c.d. and l.c.m. from the prime decompositions of m and n. Generalize this to the case of more than two integers.

8. Let n be any positive integer, and let $\varphi(n)$ stand for the number of positive integers $\leq n$ which are relatively prime to n. Thus $\varphi(1) = 1$, $\varphi(2) = 1$, $\varphi(4) = 2$, etc. [$\varphi(n)$ is called the Euler function.] Calculate $\varphi(7)$, $\varphi(12)$, $\varphi(16)$, $\varphi(27)$, $\varphi(35)$. For any prime p show that $\varphi(p^e) = p^{e-1}(p - 1)$, where e is any positive integer.

*9. Let m and n be relatively prime positive integers. Show that $\varphi(m \cdot n) = \varphi(m) \cdot \varphi(n)$, where φ is defined in Example 8. Conclude from this that if n has the prime decomposition $n = p_1^{e_1}p_2^{e_2} \cdots p_r^{e_r}$, with distinct primes $p_1, p_2, \ldots, p_r$, then

$$\varphi(n) = p_1^{e_1-1}p_2^{e_2-1} \cdots p_r^{e_r-1} \cdot (p_1 - 1)(p_2 - 1) \cdots (p_r - 1)$$

10. Find the g.c.d. $(p_1^{a_1}p_2^{a_2} \cdots p_n^{a_n}, p_1^{b_1}p_2^{b_2} \cdots p_n^{b_n})$, where $p_1, p_2, \ldots, p_n$ are distinct primes and where the exponents are non-negative integers.

9. Notation for integers

Everyone is familiar with the usual notation for integers. In this paragraph we examine it briefly from the standpoint of what has been done in the foregoing sections. First let us recall that in ordinary numerical notation the symbol 67403 (for example) stands for

$$3 + 0 \cdot 10 + 4 \cdot 10^2 + 7 \cdot 10^3 + 6 \cdot 10^4$$

and in general if $a_0, a_1, \ldots, a_r$ represent integers between 0 and 9 (inclusive), then the symbol $a_ra_{r-1} \cdots a_2a_1a_0$ (we do not mean their product here!) stands for

$$a_0 + a_1 \cdot 10 + a_2 \cdot 10^2 + \cdots + a_{r-1} \cdot 10^{r-1} + a_r \cdot 10^r$$

Our purpose here is to understand the grounds for this mode of writing integers and to show that any integer $b > 1$ (instead of 10) can be used as a base for such a means of expressing integers.

The division algorithm (Proposition 8.4) affords the simplest approach to our problem. With minor modifications, the same method will be used in Chap. 3 to produce decimal expansions of fractions. We begin with two propositions which give us estimates on the magnitudes of expressions of the kind just mentioned.

PROPOSITION 9.1 *Let b be any integer. Then*

$$(b - 1)(1 + b + b^2 + \cdots b^r) < b^{r+1}$$

for any integer $r \geq 0$.

Proof. The assertion follows at once from the identity (7.31):
$(b - 1)(1 + b + b^2 + \cdots + b^r) = b^{r+1} - 1$
and from $b^{r+1} - 1 < b^{r+1}$ (Theorem 3.5).

COROLLARY *If $b > 1$, then $b^r > r$ for $r \geq 0$.*

Proof. Since $1 \leq b - 1$, by assumption and Theorem 4.2 we have $c \leq (b - 1) \cdot c$ for any positive integer c. Taking $c = 1 + b + b^2 + \cdots + b^r$ we obtain from this and Proposition 9.1

$$1 + b + b^2 + \cdots + b^r < b^{r+1}$$

Now every term on the left is ≥ 1, and there are $r + 1$ terms. It follows readily that the left-hand side here is greater than or equal to $r + 1$. We have therefore $r + 1 < b^{r+1}$ for $r \geq 0$. This proves the assertion of the corollary for $r \geq 1$, and the assertion is trivial for $r = 0$. Q.E.D.

PROPOSITION 9.2 *Let b be an integer greater than 1, and let $a_0, a_1, a_2, \ldots, a_r$ be integers between 0 and $b - 1$ inclusive, with $a_r \neq 0$. Put*

$$m = a_0 + a_1 b + a_2 b^2 + \cdots + a_r b^r$$

Then $b^r \leq m < b^{r+1}$.

Proof. Since all the numbers involved here are ≥ 0, it follows that $a_0 + a_1 b + \cdots + a_{r-1} b^{r-1} \geq 0$. Therefore by definition of $\leq$ we have $m \geq a_r b^r$. We have assumed that $a_r \geq 1$ and so $a_r b^r \geq b^r$ (Theorem 3.6), whence $m \geq b^r$. This proves the first inequality.

We now have also assumed that $a_k \leq b - 1$, and so $a_k b^k \leq (b - 1) \cdot b^k$ for $k = 0, 1, \ldots, r$. Hence

$$m \leq (b - 1) + (b - 1)b + (b - 1)b^2 + \cdots + (b - 1)b^r$$

or

$$m \leq (b - 1) \cdot (1 + b + b^2 + \cdots + b^r) < b^{r+1}$$

by Proposition 9.1. Q.E.D.

We now come to the main theorem of this section.

THEOREM 9.3 *Let m be a positive integer, and let b be an integer greater than 1. Then there are unique integers $a_0, a_1, \ldots, a_r$ such that*

9.1
$$m = a_0 + a_1 b + \cdots + a_r b^r \quad \text{and}$$
$$0 \leq a_j \leq b - 1 \quad \text{for } j = 0, \ldots, r, \text{ with } a_r \neq 0$$

Proof. Divide m by b, according to the division algorithm (Proposition 8.4). The result is $m = q_0 b + a_0$, where q_0 is the quotient and a_0 is the remainder. Next divide q_0 by b, say $q_0 = q_1 b + a_1$, where q_1 is the quotient and a_1 the remainder. Then divide q_1 by b, obtaining $q_1 = q_2 b + a_2$, and so on. In this way we define (definition by induction!) two sequences of numbers $q_0, q_1, q_2, \ldots$ and $a_0, a_1, a_2, \ldots$ connected by the equations

9.2
$$\begin{aligned} m &= q_0 b + a_0 \\ q_0 &= q_1 b + a_1 \\ q_1 &= q_2 b + a_2 \\ &\cdots\cdots\cdots \\ q_{k-1} &= q_k b + a_k \\ q_k &= q_{k+1} b + a_{k+1} \\ &\cdots\cdots\cdots \end{aligned}$$

Now substitute for q_0 in the first equation from the second. We get $m = a_0 + a_1b + q_1b^2$. Substituting for q_1 from the third equation we get $m = a_0 + a_1b + a_2b^2 + q_2b^3$. Substituting from the fourth equation for q_2, and so on (we are again using induction here), we obtain after k such steps the result

9.3 $$m = a_0 + a_1b + a_2b^2 + \cdots + a_{k-1}b^{k-1} + a_kb^k + q_kb^{k+1}$$

Observe first that $m \geq q_kb^{k+1}$, since all the terms on the right are ≥ 0. But $b^{k+1} \geq k + 1$ (Corollary to Prop. 9.1), and so we have $m \geq q_k(k + 1)$. This shows that $q_k = 0$ for $k > m$. Of course some of the earlier q's may also be zero. Let q_r be the first quotient which is zero. Then (9.3), with k replaced by r, is precisely in the required form (9.1), and all the a's lie between 0 and $b - 1$ (inclusive), by the division algorithm. Moreover, $a_r \neq 0$, since $a_r = q_{r-1}$ if $r > 0$, and $q_{r-1} \neq 0$, by definition of r. (If $r = 0$, then $a_0 = m$, by (9.2).)

It remains to show the uniqueness of the expression (9.1). Suppose then that $m = a'_0 + a'_1b + a'_2b^2 + \cdots + a'_sb^s$ is another such expression for m, with $0 \leq a'_j < b$ for $j = 1, \ldots, s$. Then clearly a'_0 is the remainder obtained upon division of m by b, and so $a'_0 = a_0$, by the uniqueness part of the division algorithm. And the quotient, namely $a'_1 + a'_2b + \cdots + a'_sb^{s-1}$, must be the same as q_0 in (9.2). The remainder upon division by b is a'_1, and this must be the same as the remainder upon division of q_0 by b. That is, $a'_1 = a_1$. Continuing in this way, one finds by a simple induction that the coefficients of like powers of b in the two expressions for m must be equal. Q.E.D.

DEFINITION 9.1 *The expression* (9.1) *for a positive integer* m *is called the* b-adic expansion *of* m.

REMARK. The b-adic expansion looks quite similar to the expressions in the first paragraph of this section. It should in fact be clear that the usual notation for integers is an abbreviated form of the 10-adic expansion (Example 1 below). The proof of Theorem 9.3 contains an effective method for computing the b-adic expansion of a given number, as the following examples show.

EXAMPLE 1 For $m = 159$ and $b = 10$ the equations (9.2) are

$$\begin{aligned} 159 &= 15 \cdot 10 + 9 \\ 15 &= 1 \cdot 10 + 5 \\ 1 &= 0 \cdot 10 + 1 \end{aligned}$$

etc.

all the q's here being zero beyond q_1. We find then, using (9.3) with $k = 2$, $159 = 9 + 5 \cdot 10 + 1 \cdot 10^2$, and this, as one might expect, is the 10-adic expansion of 159.

EXAMPLE 2 Take $m = 159$, $b = 4$. The equations (9.2) are

$$\begin{aligned} 159 &= 39 \cdot 4 + 3 \\ 39 &= 9 \cdot 4 + 3 \\ 9 &= 2 \cdot 4 + 1 \\ 2 &= 0 \cdot 4 + 2 \end{aligned}$$

the further equations of (9.2) being all the same as the last one here. The 4-adic expansion of 159 is therefore $159 = 3 + 3 \cdot 4 + 1 \cdot 4^2 + 2 \cdot 4^3$.

EXAMPLE 3 Take $m = 159$, $b = 2$. The equations (9.2) are

$$\begin{aligned} 159 &= 79 \cdot 2 + 1 \\ 79 &= 39 \cdot 2 + 1 \\ 39 &= 19 \cdot 2 + 1 \\ 19 &= 9 \cdot 2 + 1 \\ 9 &= 4 \cdot 2 + 1 \\ 4 &= 2 \cdot 2 + 0 \\ 2 &= 1 \cdot 2 + 0 \\ 1 &= 0 \cdot 1 + 1 \end{aligned}$$

with all further equations in (9.2) the same as the last one. The 2-adic expansion of 159 is therefore $159 = 1 + 2 + 2^2 + 2^3 + 2^4 + 2^7$.

Naturally it is possible to use the same kind of positional notation for any b-adic expansion that we use for the ordinary 10-adic case. For example, the 4-adic expansion of $m = 159$ can be abbreviated by the symbol 2133, by Example 2 above. Similarly its 2-adic expansion can be indicated by 10011111, as follows from Example 3.

In order to make calculations in some b-adic system of notation one must know the addition and multiplication tables for the integers $0, 1, \ldots, b - 1$ (these are the "digits" for the b-adic system). For $b = 5$ we have five digits, which we call 0, 1, 2, 3, 4. The tables for this case are as follows (omitting 0 from the addition table and both 0 and 1 from the multiplication table):

5-ADIC ADDITION TABLE

	1	2	3	4
1	2	3	4	10
2		4	10	11
3			11	12
4				13

5-ADIC MULTIPLICATION TABLE

	2	3	4
2	4	11	13
3		14	22
4			31

(Observe that in any b-adic system the symbol 10 always denotes the base number b.) Two sample 5-adic calculations are given below:

$$\begin{array}{r} 4\ 1\ 3\ 2 \\ +\ 2\ 1\ 2\ 4 \\ \hline 1\ 1\ 3\ 1\ 1 \end{array} \qquad \begin{array}{r} 1\ 4\ 3 \\ \times\ 2\ 4\ 0 \\ \hline 1\ 2\ 3\ 2\ 0 \\ 3\ 4\ 1\ \ \ \ \ \\ \hline 1\ 0\ 1\ 4\ 2\ 0 \end{array}$$

In recent years the 2-adic system (usually called the *binary* system) has come into great favor because it has only two digits, 0 and 1, and they can be represented by the "on" and "off" positions of some sort of electrical switch, making the binary system particularly suitable for digital computers. In ancient times the Babylonians used both the 10-adic and 60-adic (sexagesimal) systems, the former for the average citizen. Observe that the sexagesimal system requires 60 digits, and the usual symbols cannot be used beyond 9, because 10 in that system means 60, 11 means 61, and so on. In this book we use only the 10-adic notation, except for the examples and exercises here.

EXERCISES

1. Find the 2-, 3-, 7-, and 12-adic expansions of the (10-adic) numbers 12, 130, 876.

2. What integers are represented by the 9-adic symbols 17840 and 4031?

3. Write out the addition and multiplication tables for the 3-, 7-, and 12-adic systems.

4. Derive the rules for working out b-adic sums and products (i.e., the rules for "carrying" digits in b-adic additions and multiplications).

5. Understanding the symbols 1431 and 265 as 7-adic symbols, work out

$$\begin{array}{r} 1\ 4\ 3\ 1 \\ +\ 2\ 6\ 5 \\ \hline \end{array} \quad \text{and} \quad \begin{array}{r} 1\ 4\ 3\ 1 \\ \times\ 2\ 6\ 5 \\ \hline \end{array}$$

in the 7-adic system. Do the same, interpreting the given symbols as 12-adic. Check your results by putting everything in the 10-adic system.

10. More elementary number theory: congruences

The starting point for this paragraph is the following.

DEFINITION 10.1 *Let m be a positive integer, and let a and b be any two integers. Then a is said to be* congruent *to b* modulo *m if $a - b$ is divisible by m. If that is so, then we write $a \equiv b \pmod{m}$. If $a - b$ is not divisible by m, then we write $a \not\equiv b \pmod{m}$.*

EXAMPLES For $m = 6$ we have $2 \equiv 8 \pmod 6$, $1 \equiv 7 \pmod 6$, $-2 \equiv 4 \pmod 6$, $48 \equiv 0 \pmod 6$, $128 \equiv 8 \pmod 6$, etc.

If m divides $a - b$, then by Definition 8.1 we have $a - b = km$ for some integer k. Hence, $a \equiv b \pmod{m}$ if and only if $a = b + km$. All the integers that are congruent modulo m to a given integer b are obtained by adding multiples of m to b. For example, the integers that are congruent to 2 (mod 6) are the integers $2 + 6k$, where k is arbitrary. Those integers are

$$\cdots -22, -16, -10, -4, 2, 8, 14, 20, 26, 32, \ldots$$

The notion of congruence was first studied systematically by Gauss (1777–1855). Congruence has many properties in common with ordinary equality, as the following theorem shows.

PROPOSITION 10.1 *Let m be a positive integer.* (i) *If a and b are integers such that $a \equiv b \pmod{m}$, then $b \equiv a \pmod{m}$. If also $b \equiv c \pmod{m}$, then $a \equiv c \pmod{m}$.* (ii) *If $a \equiv a' \pmod{m}$ and $b \equiv b' \pmod{m}$, then $a + b \equiv a' + b' \pmod{m}$ and $a - b \equiv a' - b' \pmod{m}$ and $ab \equiv a'b' \pmod{m}$.* (iii) *If $a \equiv b \pmod{m}$, then $a^k \equiv b^k \pmod{m}$ for any positive integer k.* (iv) *If $ac \equiv bc \pmod{m}$ and if c and m are relatively prime, then $a \equiv b \pmod{m}$.*

Proof. Parts (i) and (ii) are trivial. For example to show that $ab \equiv a'b' \pmod{m}$ in (ii), we have by hypothesis $a' = a + km$ because $m \mid a' - a$, and similarly $b' = b + lm$, where k and l are integers. Then $a'b' = (a + km)(b + lm) = ab + m \cdot (al + bk + lm)$, which shows that $a'b' - ab$ is divisible by m.

We prove (iii) by induction. The assertion $a^k \equiv b^k \pmod{m}$ holds for $k = 1$, by hypothesis. Assuming that it holds for some positive integer k, we show that it must hold also for $k + 1$, hence for all positive integers. If $a^k \equiv b^k \pmod{m}$, then $a \cdot a^k \equiv b \cdot b^k \pmod{m}$ by the last part of (ii), proved above. That is, $a^{k+1} \equiv b^{k+1} \pmod{m}$.

To prove (iv) we must show that $m \mid (a - b)$. Now by assumption m divides $ac - bc = (a - b) \cdot c$, if $ac \equiv bc \pmod{m}$. Since m and c are relatively prime, we have $m \mid (a - b)$, by the result of Exercise 5, Sec. 8.

The theorem shows that $\equiv$ can be treated like $=$ except for cancellation. Part (iv) states that cancellation of a common factor in a congruence is permissible *provided* that factor is relatively prime to m. Cancellation may not be permissible otherwise. For example, $3 \cdot 11 \equiv 3 \cdot 7 \pmod{6}$ because 6 divides $3 \cdot 11 - 3 \cdot 7 = 3 \cdot 4 = 12$; but $11 \not\equiv 7 \pmod{6}$.

PROPOSITION 10.2 *Let m be a positive integer. Then any integer n is congruent* (mod m) *to one and only one of the integers* $0, 1, 2, \ldots, m - 1$.

Proof. Let n be any integer. We show first that n cannot be congruent (mod m) to two different integers a, b in the segment $0, 1, 2, \ldots, m - 1$. For if $n \equiv a \pmod{m}$ and $n \equiv b \pmod{m}$, then also $a \equiv b \pmod{m}$, by Proposition 10.1 (i) above. Supposing that $a > b$, we have $0 < a - b \leq m - 1$, and it is therefore impossible for m to divide $a - b$ [Proposition 8.1(f)], a contradiction.

If now $n = 0$, then obviously $n \equiv 0 \pmod{m}$. If $n > 0$, then by the division algorithm we have $n = qm + r$, where $0 \leq r < m - 1$ (Proposition 8.4), and so $n \equiv r \pmod{m}$. Finally, if $n < 0$, then $n + km > 0$ for some k ($k = -n + 1$, for example), and by what has just been shown $n + km$ is congruent (mod m) to some integer $0, 1, \ldots, m - 1$, say r. Since $n \equiv n + km \pmod{m}$, it follows that $n \equiv r \pmod{m}$. Q.E.D.

Proposition 10.2 tells us that the integers fall into m different classes—each class consisting of all the integers that are congruent modulo m to one of the integers $0, 1, 2, \ldots, m - 1$. These classes are called *residue classes modulo m*. The integers in a given residue class differ from each other by multiples of m—that is, they are congruent (mod m). Integers in different residue classes are not congruent (mod m).

EXAMPLE For $m = 4$ there are four residue classes, and they are

$$\begin{array}{l} \cdots -20, -16, -12, -8, -4, 0, 4, 8, 12, 16, 20, \ldots \\ \cdots -19, -15, -11, -7, -3, 1, 5, 9, 13, 17, 21, \ldots \\ \cdots -18, -14, -10, -6, -2, 2, 6, 10, 14, 18, 22, \ldots \\ \cdots -17, -13, -9, -5, -1, 3, 7, 11, 15, 19, 23, \ldots \end{array}$$

The usual way of counting hours on an ordinary clock amounts to reckoning modulo 12. A clock does not indicate a specific hour; it indicates a residue class modulo 12. The residue classes modulo 2 are simply the classes of even and odd integers.

DEFINITION 10.2 *Let m be a positive integer. A set of m integers $c_1, c_2, \ldots, c_m$ is called a* complete set of residues modulo m *if that set contains one integer from each of the m residue classes modulo m.*

EXAMPLE By Proposition 10.2 the integers $0, 1, 2, \ldots, m - 1$ form a complete set of residues (mod m). If we add m, say, to each one, then we get another complete set of residues (mod m), namely, $m, m + 1, m + 2, \ldots, 2m - 1$. For $m = 4$ the following are all complete sets of residues, as is easily seen from the example above: 0, 1, 2, 3; 4, 5, 6, 7; −4, −3, −2, −1; −20, 5, 14, −13, etc.

PROPOSITION 10.3 *Let m be a positive integer. Then a set of m integers $c_1, c_2, \ldots, c_m$ forms a complete set of residues modulo m if and only if no two of them are congruent* (mod m).

Proof. If $c_1, c_2, \ldots, c_m$ do form a complete set of residues, then by definition they are congruent modulo m, in some order, to the integers $0, 1, 2, \ldots, m - 1$, and therefore no two of the c's can be congruent (mod m) because no two of the integers $0, 1, \ldots, m - 1$ are congruent (mod m).

Conversely, suppose that no two of the c's are congruent (mod m). By Proposition 10.2 each of the c's is congruent (mod m) to exactly one of the integers $0, 1, 2, \ldots, m-1$; and two different c's cannot be congruent to the same one of these (mod m), for then those two c's would be congruent to each other (mod m). The assertion follows at once.

PROPOSITION 10.4 *Let m be a positive integer, and let a and b be any integers, with a relatively prime to m. Then if x runs through a complete set of residues* (mod m), *so does $ax + b$. In other words, if $c_1, c_2, \ldots, c_m$ form a complete set of residues* (mod m), *then so do $ac_1 + b, ac_2 + b, \ldots, ac_m + b$.*

Proof. From Proposition 10.3 we have only to show that no two of the latter are congruent (mod m). Suppose to the contrary that $ac_i + b \equiv ac_j + b \pmod{m}$, with $i \neq j$. Then $ac_i \equiv ac_j \pmod{m}$, by Proposition 10.1 (i). Since $(a, m) = 1$ by hypothesis, we can cancel the a, by Proposition 10.1 (iv), getting $c_i \equiv c_j \pmod{m}$, which contradicts the assumption that $c_1, c_2, \ldots, c_m$ form a complete set of residues (mod m).

EXAMPLE Take $m = 4$, $a = 7$, $b = -2$. If we let x run through the complete set of residues 0, 1, 2, 3, then $ax + b = 7x - 2$ runs through -2, 5, 12, 19, which is also a complete set of residues.

THEOREM 10.5 **(Fermat)** *Let p be a prime number, and let a be any integer not divisible by p. Then $a^{p-1} \equiv 1 \pmod{p}$.*

Proof. Consider the complete set of residues $0, 1, 2, \ldots, p-1$ modulo p. By Proposition 10.4 the integers $0 \cdot a, 1 \cdot a, 2 \cdot a, \ldots, (p-1) \cdot a$ also form a complete set of residues modulo p. Therefore each of the first set of numbers is congruent (mod p) to one of the second set, and conversely. Since 0 appears in both sets, it follows that each of the numbers $1, 2, \ldots, p-1$ is congruent (mod p) to exactly one of the numbers $1 \cdot a, 2 \cdot a, \ldots, (p-1) \cdot a$, and vice versa. By repeated application of Proposition 10.1 (ii) we conclude that $1 \cdot 2 \cdots (p-1) \equiv (1 \cdot a)(2 \cdot a) \cdots ((p-1) \cdot a) \pmod{p}$, or $(p-1)! \equiv a^{p-1} \cdot (p-1)! \pmod{p}$. Since $(p-1)!$ and p are relatively prime, we can cancel $(p-1)!$, by Proposition 10.1 (iv), obtaining $1 \equiv a^{p-1} \pmod{p}$.

EXAMPLE Take $p = 7$, $a = 2$. Our first complete set of residues is 0, 1, 2, 3, 4, 5, 6. The second set is $0 \cdot 2, 1 \cdot 2, 2 \cdot 2, \ldots, 6 \cdot 2$, or 0, 2, 4, 6, 8, 10, 12. We have $1 \equiv 8, 2 \equiv 2, 3 \equiv 10, 4 \equiv 4, 5 \equiv 12, 6 \equiv 6$, all modulo 7, and so $1 \cdot 2 \cdot 3 \cdot 4 \cdot 5 \cdot 6 \equiv 2 \cdot 4 \cdot 6 \cdot 8 \cdot 10 \cdot 12 \pmod{7}$, whence $6! \equiv 2^6 \cdot 6!$, or $1 \equiv 2^6 \pmod{7}$. This is easily verified, for $2^6 = 64 = 9 \cdot 7 + 1 \equiv 1 \pmod{7}$.

COROLLARY *For any integer a and any prime p, $a^p \equiv a \pmod{p}$.*

Proof. If $p \nmid a$, then this follows from the theorem above. If $p \mid a$, then both sides are congruent to 0 (mod p), hence are congruent to each other (mod p).

We mention here a somewhat more difficult theorem. Its proof will be given in Chap. 6.

THEOREM 10.6 **(Wilson)** *For any prime p we have* $(p - 1)! \equiv -1 \pmod{p}$.

EXAMPLE For $p = 7$, $(p - 1)! = 6! = 720 \equiv -1 \pmod{7}$. For $p = 2$, $(p - 1)! = 1$, and the assertion is correct, for $1 \equiv -1 \pmod{2}$.

Fermat's theorem has an important generalization. To get at it we recall the Euler function $\varphi(m)$ defined in Exercise 8, Sec. 8. $\varphi(m)$ is defined for any positive integer m to be the number of integers in the list $1, 2, 3, \ldots, m$ which are relatively prime to m. (m is prime to itself only when $m = 1$.) For example, if p is prime, then $\varphi(p) = p - 1$, because $1, 2, \ldots, p - 1$ are all relatively prime to p. It is possible to give a fairly simple formula for $\varphi(m)$ in general (see Exercise 9, Sec. 8), but that need not concern us here. We now make

DEFINITION 10.3 *Let m be a positive integer. A set of r integers* $c_1, c_2, \ldots c_r$ *is called a* reduced set of residues modulo m *if*

(1) *No two of the c's are congruent* (mod m).

(2) *Each* c_i *is relatively prime to m.*

(3) $r = \varphi(m)$.

The proofs of the following two theorems parallel very closely those of Proposition 10.4 and Theorem 10.5 and are relegated to the exercises.

PROPOSITION 10.7 *Let m be a positive integer, and let a be any integer which is relatively prime to m. If* $c_1, c_2, \ldots, c_r$ *form a reduced set of residues modulo m, then so do* $ac_1, ac_2, \ldots, ac_r$.

THEOREM 10.8 **(Fermat)** *Let m be a positive integer, and let a be an integer relatively prime to m. Then* $a^{\varphi(m)} \equiv 1 \pmod{m}$.

As noted above, if p is a prime, then $\varphi(p) = p - 1$, and so Theorem 10.5 is a special case of Theorem 10.8.

EXAMPLE Take $m = 12$, $a = 5$. Then $\varphi(12) = 4$, and so $a^{\varphi(m)} = 5^4 = 625 \equiv 1 \pmod{12}$.

We now turn our attention to the following problem: Given integers a and b and a positive integer m, can we solve the congruence

$$ax \equiv b \pmod{m}?$$

That is, can we find an integer x which makes this true? It is certainly not always possible, for $7x \equiv 1 \pmod{7}$ has no solution. Indeed the left-hand side is always congruent to zero (mod 7), whatever x. The congruence $2x \equiv 1 \pmod{6}$ has no solution, for 6 cannot divide $2x - 1$ for any choice of x.

On the other hand, the congruence $4x \equiv 3 \pmod{5}$ has a solution. For example, $x = 2$ works, and so do $x = 7, x = 12, x = 17, x = 22$, etc. The following theorem gives an answer to the problem under fairly general circumstances. It is not difficult to analyze the cases not covered by the theorem, but we shall not do so here.

THEOREM 10.9 *Let a, b, m be integers, with $m > 0$ and $(a, m) = 1$. Then the congruence $ax \equiv b \pmod{m}$ always has a solution x. Any two solutions are congruent $\pmod{m}$, and conversely if x is a solution, so is any integer which is congruent to x $\pmod{m}$. If m is a prime number, then $x = a^{m-2}b$ is a solution.*

Proof. If $(a, m) = 1$, as assumed, then there are integers r and s such that $ra + sm = 1$, by Proposition 8.7. Multiplying by b we get $bra + bsm = b$, whence $bra \equiv b \pmod{m}$. Putting $x = br$ we have then $ax \equiv b \pmod{m}$, as required.

Suppose now that x and x' are two solutions to the problem. Then $ax \equiv b \pmod{m}$ and $ax' \equiv b \pmod{m}$, and so $ax \equiv ax' \pmod{m}$. Therefore $x \equiv x' \pmod{m}$, by Proposition 10.1 (iv). Conversely, if x is a solution of the congruence, and if $x \equiv x' \pmod{m}$, then $ax \equiv ax' \pmod{m}$. By assumption $ax \equiv b \pmod{m}$, and so we get $ax' \equiv b \pmod{m}$, showing that x' is also a solution.

Finally, if m is prime, then $a^{m-1} \equiv 1 \pmod{m}$ by Fermat's theorem, and so $a \cdot a^{m-2} \cdot b \pmod{m}$, showing that $x = a^{m-2}b$ is a solution.

REMARK. From the generalized form of Fermat's theorem (Theorem 10.8) it follows that $x = a^{\varphi(m)-1}b$ is a solution of the congruence even if m is not prime.

EXAMPLE Solve $343x \equiv 15 \pmod{1426}$. From Example 3, Sec. 8, we have $108 \cdot 1426 - 449 \cdot 343 = 1$, and so $15 \cdot 108 \cdot 1426 - 15 \cdot 449 \cdot 343 = 15$, whence $-15 \cdot 449 \cdot 343 \equiv 15 \pmod{1426}$. One solution is therefore $x = -15 \cdot 449 = -6735$. To this we can add any multiple of 1426.

Solve $4x \equiv 5 \pmod{7}$. Here $m = 7$ is prime, and so one solution is $x = 5 \cdot 4^5 = 5 \cdot 1024 = 5120$. Any number congruent to 5120 (mod 7) is also a solution—for example, its remainder upon division by 7, namely, 3. This problem can also be solved of course by the method involving the determination of r and s such that $r \cdot 4 + s \cdot 7 = 1$. For example, we can take $r = -5$ and $s = 3$. Then from $-5 \cdot 4 + 3 \cdot 7 = 1$ we get $-5 \cdot 5 \cdot 4 + 5 \cdot 3 \cdot 7 = 5$, so that $-25 \cdot 4 \equiv 5 \pmod{7}$, showing that -25 is a solution.

REMARK. From Proposition 10.7 we see that a congruence $ax \equiv b \pmod{m}$, with a and m relatively prime, does not determine just one value of x; it determines an entire residue class modulo m. One solution x (and only one) will always be found among the integers $0, 1, 2, \ldots, m - 1$, and sometimes simple trial and error is the swiftest way to solve a congruence when m is small.

We have considered here only one kind of problem involving solution of congruences. Other kinds also arise. As a simple example we might consider two simultaneous congruences

$$ax + by \equiv c \pmod{m}$$
$$a'x + b'y \equiv c' \pmod{m}$$

for two unknowns x and y. Another type of problem arises if we try to solve two simultaneous congruences

$$ax \equiv b \pmod{m}$$
$$a'x \equiv b' \pmod{m'}$$

involving one unknown and two different moduli m and m'. Generalizations of this sort are not difficult to handle, but we shall not go into them here.

A deeper and much more difficult problem arises if the unknown x appears to a higher power than the first. Examples of such congruences are

$$3x^2 + 2x + 4 \equiv 0 \pmod{5}$$

and

$$x^5 + 2x^3 - 3x + 2 \equiv 0 \pmod{7}$$

etc. The integer $x = 4$ is a solution of the first [as well as any integer congruent to 4 (mod 5)]. But in general it is not possible to find integers which solve such congruences. We shall return to this topic briefly at the end of this chapter and then again later in Chap. 6.

We now return to residue classes. Let m be a fixed positive integer. As we have seen, all the integers then fall into m different residue classes modulo m. Integers in different residue classes are *not* congruent modulo m; integers in the same residue class are congruent modulo m. Each residue class contains exactly one of the integers $0, 1, 2, \ldots, m - 1$. Let us denote the corresponding residue classes by $\bar{0}, \bar{1}, \bar{2}, \ldots, \overline{m-1}$. We are going to regard these *classes* as elements of a new set, which we call $\mathbf{Z}_m$. Thus $\mathbf{Z}_m$ consists of exactly m elements, each of which is a residue class of integers modulo m.

In the set $\mathbf{Z}_m$ we proceed to define two binary operations as follows: Let $\bar{a}$ and $\bar{b}$ be two elements of $\mathbf{Z}_m$. Select in the class $\bar{a}$ a representative integer a, and select in the class $\bar{b}$ a representative integer b. We then define

10.1 $\bar{a} + \bar{b}$ = residue class (mod m) containing $a + b$
$\bar{a}\bar{b}$ = residue class (mod m) containing ab

First we observe that if we select different representatives a' and b' in the two residue classes $\bar{a}$ and $\bar{b}$, respectively, then $a \equiv a' \pmod{m}$ and $b \equiv b' \pmod{m}$. Hence $a' + b' \equiv a + b \pmod{m}$ and $a'b' \equiv ab \pmod{m}$. Therefore $a' + b'$ and $a + b$ are in the same residue class (mod m), and consequently the definition of $\bar{a} + \bar{b}$ above does not depend upon the particular choice of a and b. This same is true for $\bar{a}\bar{b}$.

REMARK. Observe that the meaning of the symbols $\bar{0}, \bar{1}, \bar{2}$, etc., depends upon m.

EXAMPLE Take $m = 5$. Then $\mathbf{Z}_5$ consists of five elements $\bar{0}, \bar{1}, \bar{2}, \bar{3}, \bar{4}$. By definition these elements are residue classes (mod 5). Specifically,

$\bar{0}$ consists of all multiples $5k$ of 5 (k any integer)
$\bar{1}$ consists of all integers $1 + 5k$
$\bar{2}$ consists of all integers $2 + 5k$
$\bar{3}$ consists of all integers $3 + 5k$
$\bar{4}$ consists of all integers $4 + 5k$

Let us now apply (10.1) to this example. To compute $\bar{2} + \bar{3}$ we select an integer in each of those classes, say 2 in $\bar{2}$ and 8 in $\bar{3}$. We add these numbers, getting $2 + 8 = 10$. Since $10 \equiv 0 \pmod 5$, the residue class containing $2 + 8$ is $\bar{0}$. Hence, by definition, $\bar{2} + \bar{3} = \bar{0}$. To compute $\bar{2} \cdot \bar{3}$ we multiply the representatives 2 and 8, getting 16, of course. Since $16 \equiv 1 \pmod 5$ we have $\bar{2} \cdot \bar{3} = \bar{1}$, by (10.1). If we had chosen other representative integers, e.g. -3 in $\bar{2}$ and 3 in $\bar{3}$, we would have got the same result. The complete addition and multiplication tables for $\mathbf{Z}_5$ are given below.

ADDITION IN $\mathbf{Z}_5$

	$\bar{0}$	$\bar{1}$	$\bar{2}$	$\bar{3}$	$\bar{4}$
$\bar{0}$	$\bar{0}$	$\bar{1}$	$\bar{2}$	$\bar{3}$	$\bar{4}$
$\bar{1}$	$\bar{1}$	$\bar{2}$	$\bar{3}$	$\bar{4}$	$\bar{0}$
$\bar{2}$	$\bar{2}$	$\bar{3}$	$\bar{4}$	$\bar{0}$	$\bar{1}$
$\bar{3}$	$\bar{3}$	$\bar{4}$	$\bar{0}$	$\bar{1}$	$\bar{2}$
$\bar{4}$	$\bar{4}$	$\bar{0}$	$\bar{1}$	$\bar{2}$	$\bar{3}$

MULTIPLICATION IN $\mathbf{Z}_5$

	$\bar{0}$	$\bar{1}$	$\bar{2}$	$\bar{3}$	$\bar{4}$
$\bar{0}$	$\bar{0}$	$\bar{0}$	$\bar{0}$	$\bar{0}$	$\bar{0}$
$\bar{1}$	$\bar{0}$	$\bar{1}$	$\bar{2}$	$\bar{3}$	$\bar{4}$
$\bar{2}$	$\bar{0}$	$\bar{2}$	$\bar{4}$	$\bar{1}$	$\bar{3}$
$\bar{3}$	$\bar{0}$	$\bar{3}$	$\bar{1}$	$\bar{4}$	$\bar{2}$
$\bar{4}$	$\bar{0}$	$\bar{4}$	$\bar{3}$	$\bar{2}$	$\bar{1}$

From the first table we observe that $\bar{0}$ is the identity element for addition in $\mathbf{Z}_5$. Since $\bar{1} + \bar{4} = \bar{0}$, we can write $\bar{4} = -\bar{1}$, or $\bar{1} = -\bar{4}$. Similarly $\bar{2} = -\bar{3}$ and $\bar{3} = -\bar{2}$. It is not hard to verify that the first table is the table of an abelian group. From the second table we see that $\bar{1}$ is the identity element for multiplication.

THEOREM 10.10 *Let m be a positive integer, and let $\mathbf{Z}_m$ be the set whose elements are the residue classes of integers modulo m. Then $\mathbf{Z}_m$ contains m elements. If addition and multiplication are defined in $\mathbf{Z}_m$ by* (10.1), *then $\mathbf{Z}_m$ is a commutative ring. For $m > 1$ the ring $\mathbf{Z}_m$ is an integral domain if and only if m is a prime, and when that is so, every element of $\mathbf{Z}_m$ except $\bar{0}$ has an inverse for multiplication. That is, if $\bar{a} \neq \bar{0}$, then there is an element $\bar{b}$ such that $\bar{a}\bar{b} = \bar{1}$.*

Proof. The verification that the ring axioms are satisfied is very straightforward and will be left as an exercise. One simply observes that first of all $\mathbf{Z}$ itself satisfies the ring axioms. By (10.1) calculations in $\mathbf{Z}_m$ are essentially calculations in $\mathbf{Z}$ ignoring multiples of m. Thus one easily sees that $\bar{0}$ is the identity for addition in $\mathbf{Z}_m$. The inverse (for addition) of $\bar{1}$ is $\overline{m-1}$, for $\bar{2}$ the inverse is $\overline{m-2}$, for $\bar{3}$ the inverse is $\overline{m-3}$, etc. In other words, $-\bar{1} = \overline{m-1}$, $-\bar{2} = \overline{m-2}$, $-\bar{3} = \overline{m-3}$, etc. The element $\bar{1}$ is the identity for multiplication.

If $m = 1$, then $\mathbf{Z}_1$ contains only one element. It is trivial to see that $\mathbf{Z}_1$

satisfies the axioms for an integral domain. Suppose now that m is not prime. Then there exist two positive integers a, b smaller than m such that $ab = m$. If we let $\bar{a}$ and $\bar{b}$ denote the residue classes containing a and b, respectively, then we have $\bar{a}\bar{b} = \bar{0}$, by (10.1). For according to (10.1), $\bar{a}\bar{b}$ is the residue class containing $ab = m$, and that class is $\bar{0}$. We conclude that $\mathbf{Z}_m$ cannot be an integral domain, by Theorem 2.4.

To prove that $\mathbf{Z}_m$ is an integral domain if m is a prime, we first prove the last part of the theorem—namely, that every element of $\mathbf{Z}_m$ except $\bar{0}$ has an inverse for multiplication. To see this let $\bar{a}$ be an element of $\mathbf{Z}_m$ different from $\bar{0}$, and choose a representative integer a in the class $\bar{a}$. Then $a \not\equiv 0 \pmod{m}$, and since m is prime it follows that $(a, m) = 1$. Consequently there exists an integer b such that $ab \equiv 1 \pmod{m}$, by Theorem 10.9. Let $\bar{b}$ be the residue class containing b. Then by (10.1) we have $\bar{a}\bar{b} = \bar{1}$, as required. It is now easy to see that $\mathbf{Z}_m$ is an integral domain. According to Theorem 2.4 we have only to show that if $\bar{a}$ and $\bar{c}$ are any two elements of $\mathbf{Z}_m$ different from $\bar{0}$, then $\bar{a}\bar{c} \neq \bar{0}$. To show this let $\bar{b}$ be, as above, the inverse of $\bar{a}$. That is, $\bar{a}\bar{b} = \bar{1}$. If we had $\bar{a}\bar{c} = \bar{0}$, then multiplying by $\bar{b}$ on both sides we get $\bar{b}\bar{a}\bar{c} = \bar{b}\bar{0}$, or $\bar{1}\bar{c} = \bar{0}$, or finally $\bar{c} = \bar{0}$, contradicting the assumption that $\bar{c} \neq \bar{0}$. Q.E.D.

SOME CONCLUDING REMARKS In this section and the preceding we have given only some of the most basic theorems of number theory. The reader who desires to pursue this beautiful topic further is referred to one of the standard treatises, for example, Hardy and Wright, "The Theory of Numbers," Oxford (1938).

As was said earlier, the prime numbers are the chief objects of number theory. We now mention briefly some of the more advanced aspects of the subject.

Let p be any prime number, and consider the congruence

$$ax^2 + 2bx + c \equiv 0 \pmod{p}$$

where a, b, c are given integers. The problem is to determine whether there is an integer x which makes this true. First of all we can suppose that $a \not\equiv 0 \pmod{p}$, for otherwise the first term could be struck out, reducing the problem to one already considered. Multiplying the congruence by a, we observe that it can be written $(ax + b)^2 \equiv b^2 - ac \pmod{p}$. If we put $y = ax + b$ and $c' = b^2 - ac$, then this becomes $y^2 \equiv c' \pmod{p}$. Therefore it suffices for the problem at hand to consider congruences of the simpler type

10.2 $$x^2 \equiv c \pmod{p}$$

It is clear that if x is a solution of this congruence, then so is any integer x' which is congruent to $x \pmod{p}$. Furthermore (10.2) is essentially unchanged if we replace c by any integer c' congruent to $c \pmod{p}$. Thus, if we want to do so, we can restrict ourselves to the complete set of residues $0, 1, 2, \ldots, p - 1$ modulo p.

In what follows we shall exclude the trivial case $c \equiv 0 \pmod{p}$, for which (10.2) always has the solution $x =$ any multiple of p (and those are the only solutions). We shall also exclude the case $p = 2$, and so p will always be odd (hence $p - 1$ even).

If we let x run through $1, 2, 3, \ldots, p - 1$, then x^2 runs through $1, 2^2, 3^2, \ldots, (p - 1)^2$. Since $-1 \equiv p - 1 \pmod{p}$, we have $1 \equiv (p - 1)^2 \pmod{p}$. Similarly, $-2 \equiv p - 2 \pmod{p}$, and so $2^2 \equiv (p - 2)^2 \pmod{p}$, and so on. It follows that only half the integers $1, 2, \ldots, p - 1$ can be congruent (mod p) to the square of an integer. [For example, if $p = 7$, then squares of 1, 2, 3, 4, 5, 6 are congruent (mod 7) to 1, 4, 2, 2, 4, 1, respectively. Therefore, for $p = 7$, the congruence (10.2) has a solution only if c is congruent (mod 7) to 1, 2, or 4.]

In general, if (10.2) has a solution, then c is called a *quadratic residue* (mod p), and this is indicated by writing $\left(\frac{c}{p}\right) = 1$. If (10.2) has no solution, then c is called a *quadratic nonresidue* (mod p), and this is indicated by writing $\left(\frac{c}{p}\right) = -1$. The symbol $\left(\frac{c}{p}\right)$ defined in this way (remember we assume that $p \nmid c$) is called the Legendre symbol.

If we let c run through $1, 2, \ldots, p - 1$, then as we have just observed, $\left(\frac{c}{p}\right) = +1$ for half of those values and $\left(\frac{c}{p}\right) = -1$ for the other half. The problem is, which half are quadratic residues $(+1)$ and which half are quadratic nonresidues (-1)? For any particular value of p it is very easy to find out, as we did above for $p = 7$. Our results there show that $\left(\frac{1}{p}\right) = 1$, $\left(\frac{4}{p}\right) = 1$, $\left(\frac{2}{p}\right) = 1$, $\left(\frac{3}{p}\right) = -1$, $\left(\frac{5}{p}\right) = -1$, $\left(\frac{6}{p}\right) = -1$. It is however not so easy to prove general results.

Legendre (1752–1833) discovered a very remarkable kind of reciprocity connecting quadratic residues for pairs of primes greater than 2. It can be stated briefly as follows. Let p and q be two primes greater than 2. Since they are odd we can write $p - 1 = 2k$ and $q - 1 = 2l$, where k and l are integers. Then the celebrated *law of quadratic reciprocity* states simply that

$$\left(\frac{p}{q}\right) = \left(\frac{q}{p}\right) \cdot (-1)^{kl}$$

For example, if $p = 5$, $q = 7$, then $\left(\frac{5}{7}\right) = -1$, as noted above, and $\left(\frac{7}{5}\right) = -1$, as is easily verified. In this case $k = 2$, $l = 3$. (The reader will find it a profitable exercise to write out the law of quadratic reciprocity in words.)

Legendre did not succeed in proving this simply stated but profound connection between pairs of primes. The first proof was given by Gauss at the age of nineteen. It was published in 1801 in his classical treatise *Disquisitiones arithmeticae*.

The way in which the prime numbers are distributed among the integers has long been an area of great mathematical interest. We conclude with two theorems concerning this question.

For any positive integer x let us define

10.3 $\pi(x) =$ number of primes not exceeding x

Thus $\pi(1) = 0$, $\pi(2) = 1$, $\pi(3) = 2$, $\pi(4) = 2$, etc.

Then $\pi(x)$ is approximated by $x/\log x$ for large values of x, in the sense that the ratio of the two quantities tends to 1 as x increases indefinitely (here $\log x$ stands for the natural logarithm of x). This result is known as the *prime-number theorem.* It was first proved in 1896 by Hadamard and de la Vallée Poussin.

Finally we mention the following theorem of Dirichlet (1805–1859): *If a is positive and if a and b are relatively prime integers, then there are infinitely many primes of the form $an + b$, where n stands for an arbitrary positive integer.*

EXERCISES

1. What integers are congruent
- (*a*) To 5 (mod 7)?
- (*b*) To 0 (mod 8)?
- (*c*) To -4 (mod 8)?

2. Give three different examples showing that $ac \equiv bc \pmod{m}$ does not always imply that $a \equiv b \pmod{m}$.

3. Give two different complete sets of residues modulo m for $m = 6$, $m = 11$, $m = 12$. For each of these values of m give three different *reduced* sets of residues.

4. Verify Fermat's theorem $a^{p-1} \equiv 1 \pmod{p}$ for $a = 4$, $p = 11$, and for $a = 6$, $p = 13$. Verify the generalized Fermat theorem $a^{\varphi(m)} \equiv 1 \pmod{m}$ for $a = 4$, $m = 15$. Show that the latter does not hold for $a = 10$ and explain why.

5. Let m be a positive integer, and let a be any integer. Let C stand for one of the m residue classes modulo m. Prove that if one integer in C is relatively prime to m, then every integer in C is relatively prime to m.

6. Prove Theorem 10.7.

7. Prove Theorem 10.8. [The proof is very similar to the proof of Theorem 10.5; one has merely to start out with a *reduced* set of residues (mod m)—in fact that is what we really used in Theorem 10.5, for when p is prime the numbers $1, 2, \ldots, p - 1$ form a reduced set of residues.]

8. Solve the following congruences:

(*a*) $3x \equiv 7 \pmod{4}$ (*b*) $-2x \equiv 12 \pmod{11}$
(*c*) $x - 6 \equiv 0 \pmod{12}$ (*d*) $87x \equiv 13 \pmod{5}$
(*e*) $10x - 146 \equiv 0 \pmod{12}$ (*f*) $2700x \equiv -12 \pmod{17}$
(*g*) $4x - 12 \equiv 0 \pmod{11}$

Show that $3x \equiv 7 \pmod{15}$ has no solution.

9. Let m be an odd integer. Prove that $m^2 \equiv 1 \pmod 4$.

10. Write out the verifications that were omitted in the proof of Theorem 10.10.

11. Write out the addition and multiplication tables for $\mathbf{Z}_7$ and $\mathbf{Z}_8$.

12. Prove that the only solutions of the congruence $x^2 \equiv 0 \pmod m$ are multiples of m, when m is prime. Show by an example that this need not be the case when m is not prime.

*13. Let p be a prime > 2. Show that if the congruence $x^2 \equiv c \pmod p$ has any solutions, then all possible solutions fill up precisely two residue classes (mod p). Show by an example that this need not be the case if p is not prime.

14. Find a solution of the simultaneous congruences

$$3x \equiv 5 \pmod 7$$
$$2x \equiv 12 \pmod 9$$

Describe the totality of all possible solutions.

*15. Let p be a prime greater than 2 and put $p - 1 = 2k$. Let c be any integer not divisible by p. Prove that $(c^k - 1)(c^k + 1) \equiv 0 \pmod p$ and deduce from this that either $c^k \equiv 1 \pmod p$ or $c^k \equiv -1 \pmod p$. Prove that if $\left(\frac{c}{p}\right) = 1$, then $c^k \equiv 1 \pmod p$, where $\left(\frac{c}{p}\right)$ is the Legendre symbol defined earlier. It can be shown that, conversely, if $c^k \equiv 1 \pmod p$, then $\left(\frac{c}{p}\right) = 1$. Consequently, $\left(\frac{c}{p}\right) \equiv c^k \pmod p$.

16. If the integer N is written as $a_n 10^n + \cdots + a_0 10^0$ in decimal notation, and $S = a_n + \cdots + a_0$ is the sum of its digits, show that $N \equiv S \pmod 9$. Use this fact to develop a fast method of partially verifying the accuracy of complicated arithmetical operations (the so-called "rule of nines").

17. Show that $6^n \equiv 6 \pmod{10}$ for any positive integer n. Use this fact to compute the last digit in the decimal expansion of the integers 6^{721}, 4^{100}.

18. Find the last digit in the decimal expansions of 3^{424} and 7^{101}.

19. Find the remainder of 4^{3691} upon division by 7.

20. Show that the sum of the third powers of three consecutive integers is divisible by 9.

21. Prove that the integers $2^{2^n} + 1$, $n = 0, 1, 2, \ldots$, are relatively prime in pairs; i.e., no two such integers have a (non-trivial) common factor. [Hint: If $a \mid 2^{2^n} + 1$, then $2^{2^n} \equiv -1 \pmod a$].

11. Proof of Theorem 4.4

THEOREM 4.4 *Let $\mathbf{Z}$ and $\bar{\mathbf{Z}}$ be two systems satisfying axioms* (1) to (7). *Then there is one and only one ring-isomorphism of $\mathbf{Z}$ to $\bar{\mathbf{Z}}$. This isomorphism makes the zero and unit elements of $\mathbf{Z}$ and $\bar{\mathbf{Z}}$ correspond, and furthermore it preserves order.*

Proof. By a ring-isomorphism we mean, of course, a ring-homomorphism (Definition 2.2) which is also a one-to-one correspondence.

As we saw in Sec. 2, such a homomorphism, call it t, satisfies $t(0) = \bar{0}$, $t(-a) = -t(a)$, $t(a - b) = t(a) - t(b)$, and also (Exercise 5, Sec. 2) $t(1) = \bar{1}$ where 0, 1 and $\bar{0}$, $\bar{1}$ denote, respectively, the zero and unit elements of $\mathbf{Z}$ and $\bar{\mathbf{Z}}$. Since t is one-to-one, the inverse mapping t^{-1} from $\bar{\mathbf{Z}}$ to $\mathbf{Z}$ is also defined and is one-to-one.

If a ring-isomorphism t of $\mathbf{Z}$ to $\bar{\mathbf{Z}}$ exists, we claim that the elements of $\mathbf{J}$ and $\bar{\mathbf{J}}$ (the set of positive elements of $\bar{\mathbf{Z}}$) correspond. Indeed, let U be the set of all elements x in $\mathbf{J}$ such that $t(x)$ is in $\bar{\mathbf{J}}$. Since $t(1) = \bar{1}$ and $\bar{1}$ is in $\bar{\mathbf{J}}$, by Theorem 3.8, it follows that 1 is in U. Let x be any element of U. Then $t(x + 1) = t(x) + t(1) = t(x) + \bar{1}$ which is in $\bar{\mathbf{J}}$ by axiom (6), since $t(x)$ and 1 are in $\bar{\mathbf{J}}$. Hence $x + 1$ is in U, and so by axiom (7), Sec. 4, $U = \mathbf{J}$, that is, for every x in $\mathbf{J}$, $t(x)$ is in $\bar{\mathbf{J}}$. Applying the same argument to t^{-1}, we see that every element of $\bar{\mathbf{J}}$ corresponds to an element of $\mathbf{J}$ and t establishes a one-to-one correspondence between $\mathbf{J}$ and $\bar{\mathbf{J}}$. Now let a, b be elements of $\mathbf{Z}$ such that $a < b$. Then $b - a$ is in $\mathbf{J}$, and therefore $t(b - a) = t(b) - t(a)$ is in $\bar{\mathbf{J}}$. This means that $t(a) < t(b)$. This is what we mean when we say that t preserves order or that it is compatible with the orders in $\mathbf{Z}$ and $\bar{\mathbf{Z}}$.

We have thus seen that, if an isomorphism exists, it has all the properties stated in the theorem. We now show that there cannot be two different isomorphisms. The final step of the proof will have to show of course that an isomorphism does exist.

Let then t and t' be two isomorphisms of $\mathbf{Z}$ to $\bar{\mathbf{Z}}$. We know that $t(1) = t'(1) = \bar{1}$. Let U denote the set of all elements x in $\mathbf{J}$ such that $t(x) = t'(x)$. Then 1 is in U. Let x be any element of U, that is, $t(x) = t'(x)$. Then $t(x + 1) = t(x) + t(1) = t'(x) + t'(1) = t'(x + 1)$ and so $x + 1$ is in U. Thus, by axiom (7), $U = \mathbf{J}$ and $t(x) = t'(x)$ for all x in $\mathbf{J}$, that is, t and t' are the same mapping for elements of $\mathbf{J}$. Let us compare t and t' for the other elements of $\mathbf{Z}$. Clearly $t(0) = t'(0)$ since they are both equal to the zero element of $\bar{\mathbf{Z}}$. Now let x be an element of $\mathbf{J}'$. Then $-x$ is in $\mathbf{J}$ and by the above $t(-x) = t'(-x)$. Hence $t(x) = -t(-x) = -t'(-x) = t'(x)$, and we conclude that t and t' are the same isomorphism of $\mathbf{Z}$ to $\bar{\mathbf{Z}}$.

The final step will consist of three parts. First we construct a mapping of $\mathbf{Z}$ to $\bar{\mathbf{Z}}$, then show that it is a ring-homomorphism; i.e., it satisfies the two equations of Definition 2.2; and finally we show that the mapping is a one-to-one correspondence.

As we have seen we have no choice but to put $t(0) = \bar{0}$ and $t(1) = \bar{1}$. We then define t for elements of $\mathbf{J}$ by induction, using the formula $t(x + 1) = t(x) + \bar{1}$. That is, the two conditions $t(1) = \bar{1}$ and $t(x + 1) = t(x) + \bar{1}$ for $x \geq 1$ determine a unique mapping t from $\mathbf{J}$ to $\bar{\mathbf{Z}}$, by Sec. 7 *B*. To define $t(x)$ for elements x of $\mathbf{J}'$ we put $t(x) = -t(-x)$, the right-hand side being already defined since $-x$ is in **J**. Note now that the equations $t(x) = -t(-x)$ and $t(x + 1) = t(x) + \bar{1}$ are true for *all* x in **Z**. We need prove only the first for $x \geq 0$ and the second for $x \leq 0$ [since the other cases are the definitions of $t(x)$ for $x < 0$ and $x > 0$, respectively]. In the first instance, since $x \geq 0$, then $-x \leq 0$ and $t(-x) = -t(-(-x)) = -t(x)$; so $t(x) = -t(-x)$. In the second instance, if $x = 0$, we have $t(x + 1) = t(0 + 1) = t(1) = \bar{1} = t(0) + \bar{1}$, since $t(0) = \bar{0}$. If $x < 0$, then $x + 1 \leq 0$, and so $-x - 1 \geq 0$. Therefore, from above, $t(-x - 1 + 1) = t(-x - 1) + \bar{1}$, or $t(-x) = t(-x - 1) + \bar{1}$. From what was just shown, this is the same as $-t(x) = -t(x + 1) + \bar{1}$, or $t(x + 1) = t(x) + \bar{1}$.

We now verify that the mapping t, defined in the preceding paragraph, satisfies $t(x + y) = t(x) + t(y)$ for all x, y in **Z**. The verification of $t(xy) = t(x)t(y)$ proceeds along similar lines and is left as an exercise. We first prove $t(x + y) = t(x) + t(y)$ for $x + y$ in **J**, using axiom (7). Let U be the set of all elements z in **J** such that $t(x + y) = t(x) + t(y)$ for all x, y in **Z** such that $x + y = z$.

We claim 1 is in U. Indeed, if $x + y = 1$, then $x = -y + 1$, $t(x) = t(-y + 1) = t(-y) + \bar{1} = -t(y) + \bar{1}$ and $t(x) + t(y) = \bar{1} = t(1) = t(x + y)$. Let now z be in U and $x + y = z + 1$. Then $x + y = (x - 1) + y + 1$ and $(x - 1) + y = z$. Thus, $t(x + y) = t((x - 1) + y + 1) = t(x - 1 + y) + \bar{1} = t(x - 1) + t(y) + \bar{1} = t(x - 1) + \bar{1} + t(y) = t(x) + t(y)$, so that $z + 1$ is in U, and $U = $ **J**.

The equation $t(x + y) = t(x) + t(y)$ must still be proved for $x + y \leq 0$. If $x + y = 0$, then $x = -y$, $t(x) = t(-y) = -t(y)$ and $t(x) + t(y) = \bar{0}$. If $x + y < 0$, then $-(x + y) = (-x) + (-y) > 0$, $t(-(x + y)) = t((-x) + (-y)) = t(-x) + t(-y) = -t(x) - t(y)$ and $t(x + y) = -t(-(x + y)) = -(-t(x) - t(y)) = t(x) + t(y)$.

We now prove that t is a one-to-one correspondence. According to the definition (Sec. 2, Chap. 1) we must prove:

(*a*) For every $\bar{x}$ in $\bar{\mathbf{Z}}$, there is an element x in **Z** such that $t(x) = \bar{x}$.

(*b*) If x, y are elements of **Z** such that $t(x) = t(y)$, then $x = y$.

To prove (*a*), let us first assume $\bar{x}$ is in $\bar{\mathbf{J}}$. Let U be the set of all elements $\bar{x}$ in $\bar{\mathbf{J}}$ such that there is an element x in **Z** with $t(x) = \bar{x}$. Since $t(1) = \bar{1}$, $\bar{1}$ is in U. Let now $\bar{x}$ be in U, so that there is an element x in **J** with $t(x) = \bar{x}$. Then $t(x + 1) = t(x) + \bar{1} = \bar{x} + \bar{1}$ and $\bar{x} + \bar{1}$ is in U. Hence $U = $ **J** and all elements of $\bar{\mathbf{J}}$ correspond to some element of **Z**. Let now $\bar{x} \leq \bar{0}$. If $\bar{x} = \bar{0}$, then $\bar{x} = t(0)$ and (*a*) is satisfied. If $\bar{x} < \bar{0}$, then $-\bar{x} > \bar{0}$ and there is an element y in **Z** with $t(y) = -\bar{x}$. Then $\bar{x} = -(-\bar{x}) = -t(y) = t(-y)$ and (*a*) is completely verified.

The proof of (*b*) is very similar to that of (*a*) and is left as an exercise. This finishes the proof of Theorem 4.4.

EXERCISES

1. Prove in detail that if t is a ring-isomorphism of $\mathbf{Z}$ to $\bar{\mathbf{Z}}$, then its inverse t^{-1} is itself a ring-isomorphism.

2. Prove in detail that $t(xy) = t(x)t(y)$ for all x, y in $\mathbf{Z}$. [Hint: Use the equation $xy - x = x(y - 1)$ and induction on one of the factors of xy.]

3. Prove in detail that if x, y are elements of $\mathbf{Z}$ such that $t(x) = t(y)$, then $x = y$. [Hint: Use the equation $t(x) + \bar{1} = t(x + 1)$ and use induction on the element $t(x)$ of $\bar{\mathbf{Z}}$.]

3

Fields, the rational numbers

1. *Introduction*

From Sec. 8, Chap. 2, we recall that an integer a is said to divide an integer b if there is a third integer x such that $ax = b$. That is so only for very special choices of a and b. For example, there is no integer x such that $3x = 2$. The present chapter is concerned with enlarging the system of integers **Z** in such a way that the equation $ax = b$ will always have a solution, provided that $a \neq 0$.

In the case of $3x = 2$ the "answer" is of course $x = 2/3$, and more generally the solution of $ax = b$ is well known to be b/a. Hence our problem is simply that of introducing fractions. The difficulty is that many fractions represent the same *number*. For example, $2/3$, $10/15$, $-4/-6$, etc., all denote the same number. What then is the number itself? A fraction being only a particular name for a number, it is not entirely obvious that it is possible to have a system of numbers representable by fractions and enjoying reasonable algebraic properties.

Just as in the case of the system of integers **Z**, we shall not try to say just what rational numbers "are." We shall instead lay down very simple axioms that characterize the rational-number system completely, in the same sense that axioms (1) to (7), Sec. 4, Chap. 2, determine the system **Z**. We begin with some more general considerations which will be useful to us in connection with other mathematical systems.

2. *Fields*

We recall from Chap. 2 that an integral domain is a set of elements, say D, with two associative and commutative binary operations (usually called addition and multiplication and denoted, respectively, by $a + b$ and ab for typical elements a, b of D). D with the operation $+$ is required to be an abelian group, and the operations are required to satisfy the distributive law $a(b + c) = ab + ac$ and the cancellation law: if $ac = bc$ and $c \neq 0$, then $a = b$. Finally D is supposed to contain an identity element for multiplication. We shall denote it by the symbol 1, noting however that it may have no connection with the integer 1.

DEFINITION 2.1 *A field K is an integral domain, containing more than one element, such that any element of K other than zero has an inverse with respect to multiplication.*

Thus if a is in K and $a \neq 0$, then there must be in K an element (we denote it as usual by a^{-1}) such that $aa^{-1} = 1$. From Theorems 3.1 and 4.3, Chap. 1, it follows that the unit element 1 of K is unique and the inverse a^{-1} of any element a is unique. In particular we have $1^{-1} = 1$ and $(a^{-1})^{-1} = a$ for any element $a \neq 0$, and $(ab)^{-1} = a^{-1}b^{-1}$ for any elements $a, b \neq 0$. We observe furthermore that it is not necessary to assume the cancellation law for multiplication in K because it is a necessary consequence of the existence of inverses, by Theorem 4.4, Chap. 1. From Theorem 2.4, Chap. 2, we recall that a product ab in K cannot be zero unless $a = 0$ or $b = 0$.

EXAMPLE From Sec. 10, Chap. 2 (Theorem 10.10), it follows that the set of residue classes $\mathbf{Z}_p$ of integers modulo a prime number p is a field containing p elements.

Recall that *subtraction* in an abelian group is defined by $a - b = a + (-b)$, where $-b$ is the inverse of b for addition. In an entirely analogous way we can define *division* in a field K. That is, if a and b are elements of K, with $b \neq 0$, then we put

2.1 $$\frac{a}{b} = ab^{-1} \qquad (b \neq 0)$$

(Sometimes $\frac{a}{b}$ is written a/b or $a \div b$ and is called the quotient of a by b; the operation is neither commutative nor associative in general.) Taking a or b to be 1 in (2.1) and recalling that $1^{-1} = 1$, we get

2.2 $$\frac{a}{1} = a \qquad \frac{1}{b} = b^{-1} \qquad \frac{a}{b} = a \cdot \frac{1}{b}$$

From (2.1) we have further $(ab^{-1})b = a(b^{-1}b) = a$, and $c(a/b) = c(ab^{-1}) = (ca) \cdot b^{-1}$, and we get the elementary rules

2.3 $$\frac{a}{b} \cdot b = a \qquad c \cdot \frac{a}{b} = \frac{ca}{b} = a \cdot \frac{c}{b} \qquad \frac{b}{b} = 1$$

PROPOSITION 2.1 *If a and b are elements of a field K, with $b \neq 0$, then the element of K denoted by a/b is the unique solution of the equation $bx = a$.*

Proof. It is a solution of the equation, by (2.2), and it is unique by the cancellation law.

PROPOSITION 2.2 *Let a, b, a', b' be elements of a field K, with b and b' not zero. Then $a/b = a'/b'$ if and only if $ab' = a'b$; and that is so if and only if there is an element $c \neq 0$ in K such that $a' = ca$ and $b' = cb$.*

Proof. By definition $a/b = a'/b'$ means $ab^{-1} = a'b'^{-1}$. Multiplying by bb' and keeping in mind that multiplication in a field is commutative, we get $ab' = a'b$. Conversely, if $ab' = a'b$, then multiplying by $b^{-1}b'^{-1}$ yields $a/b = a'/b'$.

Now define $c = b'/b$. Then $cb = b'$, by Eq. (2.2), and $c \neq 0$. If $ab' =$

$a'b$, then multiplying by b^{-1} we get $ab'b^{-1} = a'$. But $b'b^{-1} = c$, and so we have $a' = ca$. Conversely, if $a' = ca$ and $b' = cb$, then $a'b = cab$ and $ab' = cab$, whence $ab' = a'b$. Q.E.D.

PROPOSITION 2.3 *Let a, b, c, d be elements of a field K, with b and d not zero. Then*

$$\frac{a}{b} + \frac{c}{d} = \frac{ad + bc}{bd} \qquad \frac{a}{b} - \frac{c}{d} = \frac{ad - bc}{bd} \qquad \frac{a}{b} \cdot \frac{c}{d} = \frac{ac}{bd}$$

and if also $c \neq 0$, then

$$\frac{a}{b} \div \frac{c}{d} = \frac{ad}{bc} \qquad \text{and} \qquad \left(\frac{c}{d}\right)^{-1} = \frac{d}{c}$$

Proof. First note that $bd \neq 0$ because $b \neq 0$ and $d \neq 0$ (Theorem 2.4, Chap. 2). To prove the first equality we have, using (2.1), (2.2), (2.3),

$$bd \cdot \left(\frac{a}{b} + \frac{c}{d}\right) = bd \cdot \frac{a}{b} + bd \cdot \frac{c}{d}$$

$$= da \cdot \frac{b}{b} + bc \cdot \frac{d}{d} = ad + bc$$

But also

$$bd \cdot \left(\frac{ad + bc}{bd}\right) = ad + bc$$

Therefore both sides of the first equation are solutions of $bdx = ad + bc$. They are therefore equal, by Proposition 2.1; the other equations follow from similar arguments and their proof is left as an exercise.

DEFINITION 2.2 *Let A be a subset of a field K. If A, equipped with the operations of K, is a ring, then A is called a* subring *of K; if a subring A happens to be a field, then it is called a* subfield *of K.*

EXERCISES

1. Show that the nonzero elements of a field K, with multiplication as binary operation, form an abelian group.

2. Show that the zero and unit elements of a subring A of a field K are the same as those of K, provided that A contains more than one element. Show that if A is a subfield of K, then the inverse of a nonzero element in A (for either multiplication or addition) is the same as its inverse in K. Prove that a subring of a field is an integral domain.

3. If a, b, c, d are elements of a field with $a/b = c/d$, prove the following:

(a) $\dfrac{b}{a} = \dfrac{d}{c}$ (b) $\dfrac{a}{c} = \dfrac{b}{d}$

(c) $\dfrac{a + b}{b} = \dfrac{c + d}{d}$ (d) $\dfrac{a - b}{b} = \dfrac{c - d}{d}$

(e) $\dfrac{a + b}{a - b} = \dfrac{c + d}{c - d}$ (f) $\dfrac{a}{b} = \dfrac{a + c}{b + d}$

assuming of course that the various denominators are not zero.

4. If $\frac{a_1}{b_1} = \frac{a_2}{b_2} = \cdots = \frac{a_n}{b_n}$ in a field K, show that

$$\frac{c_1a_1{}^k + c_2a_2{}^k + \cdots + c_na_n{}^k}{c_1b_1{}^k + c_2b_2{}^k + \cdots + c_nb_n{}^k} = \frac{a_1{}^k}{b_1{}^k}$$

where $c_1, c_2, \ldots, c_n$ are arbitrary elements of K, not all zero, and where k is a positive integer.

***5.** Let D be an integral domain containing only a finite number of elements. Prove that D is a field. [Hint: For any $a \neq 0$ in D consider the elements a, a^2, a^3, etc.]

***6.** Let a be an element of a field K, $a \neq 0$. In Sec. 7, Chap. 2, it was shown how to define the element na of K for any integer n; for example, $3a = a + a + a$, etc. Now suppose that $na = 0$ for some integer $n \neq 0$. Prove that the smallest positive integer for which $na = 0$ must be a prime, say p, the same for all nonzero elements of K. [Hint: Consider the case $a = 1$ = unit element of K.] The prime p is called the *characteristic* of K. If $n \cdot 1 \neq 0$ for all positive integers n, then K is said to have characteristic zero.

7. Let A be a subring of a field K, containing more than one element. Let F be the subset of K consisting of all elements a/b, where a and b are in A and $b \neq 0$. Show that F is a subfield of K.

8. Write out the rules corresponding to (2.2), (2.3) for the operation $+$. Do the same for the rules $(a/b) \div (c/d) = ad/bc$ and $(c/d)^{-1} = d/c$.

9. Consider the following array

$$\begin{matrix} A & B & C \\ B & C & A \\ C & A & B \end{matrix}$$

This is a so-called *Latin square:* every letter A, B, C occurs once in every row and once in every column. Such squares are extremely useful in the design of statistical experiments. Suppose, as a specific example, that one wanted to study the relative yield of n kinds of seed. The simple-minded way would be to subdivide a field in n parcels and plant one kind of seed in each. The objection to this technique is that the fertility of the soil might well vary from point to point in the field, thus altering the results. If, however, one used a square field and subdivided it into n^2 squares, labeled by $A_1, A_2, \ldots, A_n$ according to an $n \times n$ Latin square, and planted the ith kind of seed in each square labeled A_i, then the effect of any variation in the soil would be greatly diminished.

Consider now a second array

$$\begin{matrix} a & b & c \\ c & a & b \\ b & c & a \end{matrix}$$

This is again a Latin square, and if we combine it with the first one we obtain the following array:

Aa	Bb	Cc
Bc	Ca	Ab
Cb	Ac	Ba

Note that in this combined array every possible combination of a capital and a lower-case letter occurs once exactly. We say that the two Latin squares are *orthogonal.* Such orthogonal Latin squares enable one to study simultaneously (and therefore economically) the effect of two different types of factors, each n in number (for example, seed and fertilizer). Unfortunately orthogonal $n \times n$ Latin squares do not exist for every integer n. A particularly simple method of constructing orthogonal Latin squares is the following:

Let K be a finite field containing n elements, $x_0 = 0, x_1, x_2, \ldots, x_{n-1}$. Then the addition table of K yields an $n \times n$ array T_1 whose (i, j) entry† is $x_i + x_j$. Let $1 \leq k \leq n - 1$ and consider the array T_k whose (i, j) entry is $x_k x_i + x_j$. Prove that T_k is a Latin square and that T_k, T_l $(k \neq l)$ are orthogonal. Construct four 5×5 Latin squares, which are pairwise-orthogonal. Can this procedure yield 6×6 Latin squares?

3. The field of rational numbers

The following theorem states in effect that an integral domain can always be embedded in a field in an essentially unique way.

THEOREM 3.1 *Given an integral domain D containing more than one element, there exists a field K containing D as a subring and such that every element of K can be expressed as the quotient of two elements of D. K is called the field of quotients of D. If K' is a second field satisfying the same conditions, then there is one and only one isomorphism from K to K' which sends elements of D into themselves.*

The existence of such a field K is proved in Chap. 15. The last part of the theorem says that K is essentially unique. The proof that there is a unique isomorphism as stated is very simple. We wish to define a one-to-one mapping f from K to K' such that $f(a) = a$ for any a in D and such that $f(a + b) = f(a) + f(b)$ and $f(ab) = f(a) \cdot f(b)$ for any a, b in K (cf. Sec. 2, Chap. 2). Now the theorem says that any element c of K can be expressed in the form $c = a/b$, where a, b are in D and of course $b \neq 0$. The same is true for K'. Now we simply map the element c of K into the element c' of K' represented by the same symbol a/b. Using Proposition 2.2 it is easy to see that the result is independent of the particular representation of c as a quotient of elements of D and that the mapping has all the required properties.

† Let the horizontal lines be called rows and the vertical ones columns; then the "(i, j) entry" is the symbol located at the intersection of the ith row and jth column.

Thus K and K' are interchangeable. It is convenient to think of D as having attached to it a particular field of quotients, and for that reason we speak of *the* field of quotients of D.

We now apply Theorem 3.1 to the integral domain $\mathbf{Z}$:

DEFINITION 3.1 *The field of quotients of the system of integers* $\mathbf{Z}$ *is called the* field of rational numbers *and is denoted by* $\mathbf{Q}$. *The elements of* $\mathbf{Q}$ *are called* rational numbers.

Thus $\mathbf{Z}$ is embedded in a larger set $\mathbf{Q}$ which is a field, and every rational number r, that is, element of $\mathbf{Q}$, can be expressed (in many ways) as the quotient $r = a/b$ of two integers.

THEOREM 3.2 *If K is a field containing the integers $\mathbf{Z}$ as a subring, then K contains a subfield F which can be identified with $\mathbf{Q}$—that is, is isomorphic to $\mathbf{Q}$ in one and only one way.*

Proof. Since K is a field, every integer $a \neq 0$ has an inverse a^{-1} in K. Let F be the set of all elements a/b in K, where a, b are integers, with $b \neq 0$. Then F is a subfield of K (cf. Exercise 7, Sec. 2). Since F satisfies the conditions of Theorem 3.1, it follows from that theorem that there is one and only one isomorphism from F to $\mathbf{Q}$ which sends elements of $\mathbf{Z}$ into themselves.

But in fact there can be no other isomorphisms at all. That is, there can be no isomorphism f from F to $\mathbf{Q}$ which does not send every integer into itself. For $f(1) = 1$, by Exercise 5, Sec. 2, Chap. 2. Then $f(2) = f(1 + 1) = f(1) + f(1) = 2$, etc. By induction we deduce that $f(n) = n$ for every positive integer n. By (2.1), Chap. 2, we have $f(-n) = -f(n) = -n$, and so f also sends negative integers into themselves. Q.E.D.

The theorem says in substance that any field K containing $\mathbf{Z}$ as a subring (i.e., the operations in $\mathbf{Z}$ are the same as in K) must contain a "copy" of the rational number field $\mathbf{Q}$. In this sense, $\mathbf{Q}$ can be thought of as the smallest field containing $\mathbf{Z}$.

The following proposition asserts the possibility of "reducing a fraction to lowest terms."

PROPOSITION 3.3 *Any rational number $r \neq 0$ can be expressed in one and only one way as a quotient $r = m/n$, with $n > 0$ and m, n relatively prime.*

Proof. By definition of $\mathbf{Q}$ the number r can be expressed as the quotient of two integers $r = a/b$, with $a, b \neq 0$. We can assume $b > 0$, for otherwise we have only to replace a, b by $-a$, $-b$. Now let $d = (a, b) =$ g.c.d. of a and b. Then we can write $a = md$ and $b = nd$. Since b, d are positive, we have $n > 0$, and $r = a/b = md/nd = m/n$, where now $(m, n) = 1$. The proof of uniqueness is left as an exercise.

$\mathbf{Z}$ is an *ordered* integral domain, and we now show that $\mathbf{Q}$ inherits an ordering from $\mathbf{Z}$.

DEFINITION 3.2 *A field K is called an* ordered field *if it is an ordered integral domain (Definition* 3.1, *Chap.* 2).

Thus it is required that the nonzero elements of K be split into two subsets, say F and F', such that F' consists of the negatives of elements of F and such that if a, b are in F, then so are $a + b$ and ab. We continue with the conventions of Sec. 3, Chap. 2, for the symbol $<$. Thus $a < b$ means that $b - a$ is in F.

THEOREM 3.4 *Let a, b, c, d be elements of an ordered field K, with b and d positive. Then $a/b < c/d$ if and only if $ad < bc$. In particular (taking $c = d = 1$), $a/b < 1$ if and only if $a < b$.*

Proof. By assumption, $bd > 0$. Therefore $a/b < c/d$ if and only if $(bd)(a/b) < (bd)(c/d)$, by Theorem 3.6, Chap. 2, and this is just $ad < bc$, by Eq. (2.3) above. Q.E.D.

DEFINITION 3.3 *Let r be a rational number different from zero, and let it be expressed as the quotient $r = a/b$ of two integers a, b. Then r is defined to be* positive ($r > 0$) *if the integer ab is positive, and r is defined to be* negative ($r < 0$) *if ab is negative.*

First of all we must show that the definition does not depend upon the particular fraction a/b. Suppose that $r = a'/b'$ also. We have then $ab' = a'b$ (by Proposition 2.2), and so $aba'b' = (a'b)^2$. The right-hand side is positive (Theorem 3.8, Chap. 2) and therefore ab and $a'b'$ must have the same sign (Exercise 7(b), Sec. 3, Chap. 2).

THEOREM 3.5 *The rational number field $\mathbf{Q}$ is an ordered field. Its ordering is compatible with that of $\mathbf{Z}$. That is, a positive integer is also a positive element of $\mathbf{Q}$.*

Proof. Let P be the set of positive rational numbers (according to Definition 3.3), and let P' be the set of negative rational numbers. Clearly P contains $\mathbf{J}$ (the set of positive integers), for any element n of $\mathbf{J}$ can be written as $n = n/1$, and then $n/1$ is positive by Definition 3.3. P and P' satisfy the requirements of Definition 3.1, Chap. 2, as is easily verified. Q.E.D.

The following theorem exhibits the great structural difference between the systems $\mathbf{Z}$ and $\mathbf{Q}$, for it shows that between any two rational numbers there is always another rational number.

PROPOSITION 3.6 *Let a and b be two rational numbers, with $a < b$. Then for the rational number $c = \frac{1}{2}(a + b)$ we have $a < c < b$. Furthermore $|c - a| = |c - b| = \frac{1}{2}(b - a)$.*

Proof. $c - a = \frac{1}{2}a + \frac{1}{2}b - a = \frac{1}{2}b + (\frac{1}{2} - 1)a = \frac{1}{2}(b - a)$. By assumption, $b - a > 0$, and so $c - a > 0$, or $c > a$. Furthermore, $|c - a| = |\frac{1}{2}(b - a)| = \frac{1}{2}(b - a)$. The argument for $c - b$ is similar. Q.E.D.

Taking $a = 0$, $b > 0$, the number c above is $\frac{1}{2}b$, and as the theorem shows, $0 < \frac{1}{2}b < b$. From this we conclude at once that *the set P of positive rational numbers has no least element.*

The following theorem shows that rational numbers are always "comparable in size" with integers.†

THEOREM 3.7 *For every rational number r there is a unique integer q such that $q \leq r < q + 1$.*

Proof. Suppose first that $r > 0$. Then we can write $r = m/n$, with m and n positive. Using the division algorithm, write $m = qn + a$, where $0 \leq a < n$ (Sec. 8, Chap. 2). Then $r = m/n = q + a/n$, and since $1 > a/n \geq 0$ (by Theorem 3.4) we have $r \geq q$ but $r < q + 1$. Hence $q \leq r < q + 1$. The proof for $r < 0$ is left as an exercise. Q.E.D.

EXERCISES

1. If a is an element of an ordered field, prove that $a > 0$ if and only if $1/a > 0$.

2. Let D be an ordered integral domain. Prove that the following three conditions on elements of D are equivalent:

$$|a - b| < c$$
$$b - c < a < b + c$$
$$a - c < b < a + c$$

3. Let a be a positive element of an ordered field. Show that $a > 1$ if and only if $1/a < 1$. If b, c are two other positive elements, prove that

$$\frac{a}{b} > \frac{a+c}{b+c} \quad \text{if } a > b \qquad \text{and} \qquad \frac{a}{b} < \frac{a+c}{b+c} \quad \text{if } a < o$$

4. Prove that any finite subset of an ordered field contains a least element and a greatest element.

5. Let $c_1, c_2, \ldots, c_n$ be positive elements of an ordered field K, and let $b_1, \ldots, b_n$ be any elements of K. Suppose that the elements $b_1/c_1, b_2/c_2, \ldots, b_n/c_n$ are not all equal. Prove that

$$\frac{b_1 + b_2 + \cdots + b_n}{c_1 + c_2 + \cdots + c_n}$$

lies between the largest and the smallest of the elements b_i/c_i.

6. Let r and b be two rational numbers greater than 1. Prove that there is a unique integer $n \geq 0$ such that $b^n \leq r < b^{n+1}$.

7. Prove that any ordered field K contains a subfield F which is isomorphic to $\mathbf{Q}$, the isomorphism $\mathbf{Q} \to F$ being compatible with the ordering. [Hint: Consider the elements $n \cdot 1$ of F, where $1 =$ unit element of F, n being any integer.]

† The point here is that one can find examples of ordered fields containing $\mathbf{Z}$ as a subring and containing elements which are greater than *every* integer.

8. Prove that $\mathbf{Q}$ is a *countable* set. [Hint: Consider the enumeration process indicated below.]

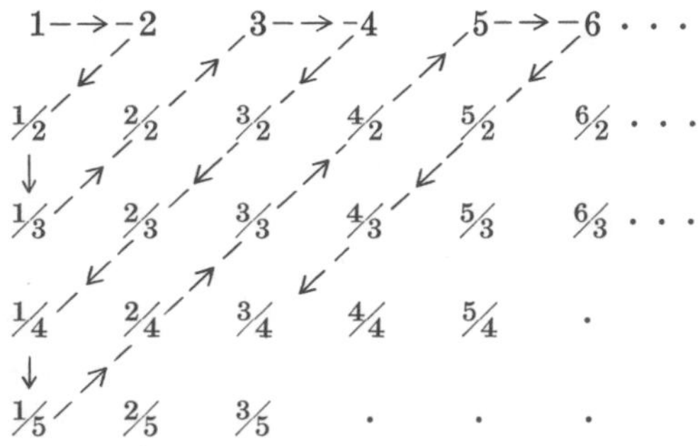

(This method of enumeration is called Cantor's first diagonal process.)

9. Let a, b, c, d be positive elements of an ordered integral domain, with $a < b$ and $c < d$. Prove that $ac < bd$. Prove that $a^n < b^n$ for every positive integer n. If $a < 1$, show that $a^m > a^n$ for any two positive integers with $m < n$.

10. Let r be a positive rational number, $r < 1$, and let c be a rational number such that $0 \leq c < r^n$ for every positive integer n. Show that $c = 0$. [Hint: Write r as a quotient of integers $r = p/q$. Show that $q > p$ and prove by induction that $q^n \geq p^n + n \cdot p^{n-1}$ for all positive integers n. Deduce from this that $r^n < p/(n + p)$, hence that $n < 1/c$, if $c \neq 0$. Then apply Theorem 3.7.]

11. Supply the proof of uniqueness in Proposition 3.3.

12. Let c be a positive rational number. Prove that if $c' = (2 + c)/(1 + c)$, then $|2 - c'^2| < |2 - c^2|$.

4. Decimals

In this paragraph we shall show how the familiar idea of decimal expansions is related to the foregoing theory. The discussion is very closely related to that of Sec. 9, Chap. 2. In order to avoid annoying minus signs, we shall generally confine our attention to *positive* rational numbers.

To fix ideas, consider (for example) the number 253.1402. We recall that the symbol stands for

$$253 + \frac{1}{10} + \frac{4}{10^2} + \frac{0}{10^3} + \frac{2}{10^4}$$

Of course 253 itself stands for $2 \cdot 10^2 + 5 \cdot 10 + 3$. Since we have already dealt with 10-adic expansions of integers in Sec. 9, Chap. 2, let us turn our attention to the decimal part $r = .1402$. The first decimal digit, namely 1 in this example, tells us that r lies in the range $1/10 \leq r < 2/10$. The second decimal digit 4 then tells us that r lies in the smaller range $1/10 + 4/100 \leq r < 1/10 + 5/100$. Similarly, the third digit 0 tells us then that r is in the yet smaller range $1/10 + 4/100 + 0/1000 \leq$

$r < 1/10 + 4/100 + 1/1000$, and so on. Hence the first decimal digit specifies our number within $1/10$; the second digit then specifies it within $1/100$, etc.

The slight difficulty that arises is that some numbers have unending decimal expansions. For example, $1/3 = .333 \cdots$. Now it would not make sense *prima facie* to write

$$\frac{1}{3} = \frac{3}{10} + \frac{3}{10^2} + \frac{3}{10^3} + \cdots$$

as we did with .1402 above, because that would indicate an infinite sum. But in a field (in particular the field **Q**) only finite sums are defined. It turns out that infinite sums can be defined under certain circumstances; this point will be taken up in the following chapter. For present purposes, this question can be avoided.

DEFINITION 4.1 A decimal *is an infinite sequence*† *of integers* a_0, a_1, a_2, a_3, *etc., satisfying the following conditions:*

$$a_0 \geq 0 \qquad \text{and} \qquad 0 \leq a_j < 10 \qquad \text{for } j = 1, 2, 3, \text{etc.}$$

The decimal is said to be a terminating *decimal if all the a_j are zero from some index on—say, $a_j = 0$ for all $j \geq N$. The decimal is said to be* recurrent, *or* periodic, *if there are two positive integers N and p such that $a_{j+p} = a_j$ for all $j \geq N$.*

Observe that if the decimal is recurrent, then $a_{N+p} = a_N$, $a_{N+2p} = a_{N+p} = a_N$, $a_{N+3p} = a_{N+3p} = a_N$, etc. The same is true for $a_{N+1+p} = a_{N+1}$, $a_{N+1+2p} = a_{N+1+p} = a_{N+1}$, etc. Therefore, starting with a_N, the numbers a_j simply repeat over and over again in blocks of length p. For example, 75.13421212121 $\cdots$ is recurrent. Here we can take $N = 4$ and $p = 2$. Note that a terminating decimal is recurrent.

A decimal is *not* a number; according to our definition it is simply an unending sequence of integers of which all but the first are required to be between 0 and 9. In Chap. 4 we shall see that a decimal can be interpreted as a number.

A decimal, as defined above, will be written $a_0.a_1a_2a_3a_4 \cdots$ and will sometimes be abbreviated by a single letter. For example, $A = a_0.a_1a_2a_3 \cdots$, $B = b_0.b_1b_2b_3 \cdots$, and so on. With the decimal $A = a_0.a_1a_2a_3 \cdots$, we associate the *rational number*

4.1 $$A_n = a_0 + \frac{a_1}{10} + \frac{a_2}{10^2} + \cdots + \frac{a_n}{10^n}$$

for any integer $n \geq 0$.

The following proposition shows how much A_n of (4.1) can change as n increases.

PROPOSITION 4.1 *n and k being positive integers, let $a_{n+1}, a_{n+2}, \ldots, a_{n+k}$ be integers between 0 and 9. Let r be the rational number*

$$r = \frac{a_{n+1}}{10^{n+1}} + \frac{a_{n+2}}{10^{n+2}} + \cdots + \frac{a_{n+k}}{10^{n+k}}$$

† For the definition of *infinite sequence*, see Sec. 6, Chap. 2.

Then

4.2 $$\frac{a_{n+1}}{10^{n+1}} \leq r < \frac{a_{n+1}+1}{10^{n+1}} \leq \frac{1}{10^n}$$

Proof. We have $10^{n+k} \cdot r = a_{n+1} \cdot 10^{k-1} + a_{n+2} \cdot 10^{k-2} + \cdots + a_{n+k}$, and so $a_{n+1} \cdot 10^{k-1} \leq 10^{n+k} \cdot r < (a_{n+1}+1) \cdot 10^{k-1}$, by Proposition 9.2, Chap. 2. The assertion follows at once. Q.E.D.

COROLLARY *Let $A = a_0.a_1a_2a_3 \cdots$ be a decimal, and let A_n be defined by* (4.1). *Then for any positive integer k we have*

4.3 $$A_n \leq A_{n+k} < A_n + \frac{1}{10^n}$$

DEFINITION 4.2 *A decimal $A = a_0.a_1a_2a_3 \cdots$ is called a* decimal expansion *of a rational number r if*

4.4 $$A_n \leq r \leq A_n + \frac{1}{10^n}$$

for all positive integers n, where A_n is the rational number defined by (4.1).

Since we have assumed that $a_0, a_1, a_2, \ldots$ are all ≥ 0, it follows that $A_n \geq 0$ and so $r \geq 0$, by (4.4). Our definition is thus limited to non-negative rational numbers. It is easily seen that *a decimal A cannot be the decimal expansion of two different rational numbers.* For the inequality (4.4) can be written $0 \leq r - A_n \leq 1/10^n$. If A were also *a decimal expansion of say* r_1, then we would have similarly $0 \leq r_1 - A_n \leq 1/10^n$. Hence, by a simple calculation, $|r - r_1| \leq 1/10^n$ for all $n = 1, 2, 3$, etc., and so $|r - r_1| = 0$, or $r = r_1$. For we have $1/10^n < 1/n$, by Proposition 9.1, Corollary, Chap. 2, and so $|r - r_1| < 1/n$ for all n. If $r \neq r_1$ this would give $n \leq 1/|r - r_1|$ for all n, an impossibility, by Theorem 3.7 (see Exercise 10, Sec. 3).

Suppose now that A is a terminating decimal, say $a_j = 0$ for $j \geq N$. It follows at once that all the numbers A_n derived from A by (4.1) are equal for large enough n, namely, for $n \geq N - 1$. Let their common value be r. It follows easily from Theorem 4.1 that A is a decimal expansion of r, in the sense of Definition 4.2.

If however A is a nonterminating decimal expansion of a rational number r, then the numbers A_n never equal r; but they approximate r with better and better accuracy as n increases.

The following theorem shows that every positive rational number has a decimal expansion. Moreover it shows how to compute it.

THEOREM 4.2 *Every (positive) rational number c has a decimal expansion, which is moreover recurrent.*

Proof. Write $c = a/b$, where a, b are positive integers. We use the division algorithm repeatedly (Proposition 8.4, Chap. 2). Namely, divide a by b, getting remainder r_0, say. Divide $10r_0$ by b, getting remainder r_1. Then divide $10r_1$ by b, and so forth. The calculation takes the form

4.5
$$\begin{aligned} a &= a_0 b + r_0 & 0 &\le r_0 < b \\ 10r_0 &= a_1 b + r_1 & 0 &\le r_1 < b \\ 10r_1 &= a_2 b + r_2 & 0 &\le r_2 < b \\ &\cdots\cdots & &\cdots \\ 10r_{n-1} &= a_n b + r_n & 0 &\le r_n < b \\ 10r_n &= a_{n+1} b + r_{n+1} & 0 &\le r_{n+1} < b \\ &\text{etc.} \end{aligned}$$

These operations produce two sequences of numbers a_0, a_1, a_2, etc., and r_0, r_1, r_2, etc. We show that the former is a decimal expansion of c. First of all, for the typical element a_n, with $n > 0$, we have $a_n b = 10r_{n-1} - r_n \le 10r_{n-1} < 10b$. Hence $a_n < 10$. Clearly all the a_j are integers ≥ 0, and so $A = a_0.a_1a_2a_3 \cdots$ indeed satisfies the definition of a decimal. Now from the equation above we get

$$\begin{aligned} c = \frac{a}{b} &= a_0 + \frac{r_0}{b} \\ &= a_0 + \frac{a_1}{10} + \frac{r_1}{10b} \\ &= a_0 + \frac{a_1}{10} + \frac{a_2}{10^2} + \frac{r_2}{10^2 b}, \text{ etc.} \end{aligned}$$

Using induction one easily shows that

$$c = \frac{a}{b} = a_0 + \frac{a_1}{10} + \frac{a_2}{10^2} + \cdots + \frac{a_n}{10^n} + \frac{r_n}{10^n \cdot b} \qquad (0 \le r_n < b)$$

for any positive integer n. Now the number A_n of (4.1) for our decimal A is just the first part of the expression above. That is, $c = A_n + \dfrac{r_n}{10^n \cdot b}$. Therefore $A_n \le c < A_n + \dfrac{1}{10^n}$, since $r_n/b < 1$, and so A is indeed a decimal expansion of c according to Definition 4.2.

To show that A is recurrent we note that all the remainders r_n satisfy $0 \le r_n < b$, and therefore r_n must be one of the b integers $0, 1, 2, \ldots, b - 1$. Hence after *at most* b steps in the computations (4.5) the remainder must be equal to one of the earlier remainders, and therefore the computations simply begin to repeat. Q.E.D.

EXAMPLE 1 For $c = 11941/4950$ the calculations are $11941 = 2 \cdot 4950 + 2041$, $20410 = 4 \cdot 4950 + 610$, $6100 = 1 \cdot 4950 + 1150$, $11500 = 2 \cdot 4950 + 1600$, $16000 = 3 \cdot 4950 + 1150$. Here we have arrived at a remainder obtained earlier, and so now the computations simply repeat. The desired decimal is $2.41232323 \cdots$.

THEOREM 4.3 *Let $A = a_0.a_1a_2a_3 \cdots$ be a recurrent decimal. Then A is a decimal expansion of a rational number r. In fact, if $a_{j+p} = a_j$ for all $j > k$, then*

$$r = \frac{10^p \cdot A_{k+p} - A_k}{10^p - 1}$$

It is not hard to see that, if the steps (4.5) are carried out, the result is precisely the decimal A, save in the case that the a_j are all equal to 9 from some point on, in which case (4.5) gives a terminating decimal. We omit the details since another proof is given in Proposition 2.8, Chap. 4.

EXAMPLE 2 The decimal $2.41232323 \cdots$ is recurrent, and here we can take $k = 2$, $p = 2$. According to the theorem,

$$r = \frac{10^2 \cdot A_4 - A_2}{99} = \frac{241.23 - 2.41}{99} = \frac{11941}{4950}$$

as in Example 1 above. For the decimal $0.3333 \cdots$ we have $k = 0$, $p = 1$, whence $r = (10A_1 - A_0)/9 = (3 - 0)/9 = 1/3$.

It is easily verified directly by referring to Definition 4.2 that the integer 1 has the two decimal expansions $1.0000 \cdots$ and $0.9999 \cdots$. The next theorem states that decimal expansions are unique except for this type of ambiguity.

THEOREM 4.4 *Let $A = a_0.a_1a_2a_3 \cdots$ and $B = b_0.b_1b_2b_3 \cdots$ be two different decimal expansions for the same rational number r. Then one of them, say A, must terminate: $a_j = 0$ for $j > N$, but $a_N \neq 0$. Then for B we must have $b_j = a_j$ for $j = 0, 1, \ldots, N - 1$ and $b_N = a_N - 1$, while $b_j = 9$ for $j > N$.*

Proof. Since A and B are different there must be a smallest j for which $a_j \neq b_j$, say $j = N$. Then $a_N \neq b_N$ but $a_j = b_j$ for $j < N$. Let us suppose, say, that $a_N > b_N$. For the numbers

$$A_n = a_0 + \frac{a_1}{10} + \cdots + \frac{a_n}{10^n}$$

$$B_n = b_0 + \frac{b_1}{10} + \cdots + \frac{b_n}{10^n}$$

we have by assumption $A_n \leq r \leq A_n + 1/10^n$, or $0 \leq r - A_n \leq 1/10^n$, and similarly $0 \leq r - B_n \leq 1/10^n$, for all $n = 1, 2, 3$, etc. It follows easily that $|A_n - B_n| \leq 1/10^n$. But for $n = N$ we have $A_N - B_N = (a_N - b_N)/10^N \geq 1/10^N$, since $a_N > b_N$ and $a_j = b_j$ for $j < N$. Since also $A_N - B_N \leq 1/10^N$, from above, there follows $A_N = B_N + 1/10^N$, whence $a_N = b_N + 1$, which is one of the things we wished to prove.

We claim now that $B_{N+k} < A_N$ for all k. Indeed $0 \leq B_{N+k} - B_N < 1/10^N$, by (4.3), and as we have just seen, $A_N - B_N = 1/10^N$. Hence $A_N - B_{N+k} = (A_N - B_N) - (B_{N+k} - B_N) > 0$. From this we conclude that $A_N = r$. For $0 \leq r - B_{N+k} \leq 1/10^{N+k}$, but $r - B_{N+k} = (r - A_N) + (A_N - B_{N+k}) > r - A_N$, and so $0 \leq r - A_N < 1/10^{N+k}$ for all $k = 1, 2, 3$, etc. Hence $r - A_N$ must be zero. Therefore the decimal A *must terminate* at N, for otherwise we would have $A_{N+k} > A_N = r$ for large enough k, which would contradict $0 \leq r - A_n < 1/10^n$ for all n.

It remains to show that $b_j = 9$ for $j > N$. Suppose then that $b_{N+l} < 9$ for some l. Taking $k > l$ we have

$$B_{N+k} - B_N = \frac{b_{N+1}}{10^{N+1}} + \cdots + \frac{b_{N+l}}{10^{N+l}} + \cdots + \frac{b_{N+k}}{10^{N+k}}$$

All the b's are ≤ 9, and we have assumed that $b_{N+l} < 9$. Hence

$$B_{N+k} - B_N \leq -\frac{1}{10^{N+l}} + \frac{9}{10^{N+1}} + \cdots + \frac{9}{10^{N+l}} + \cdots + \frac{9}{10^{N+k}}$$

Now from Eq. (7.31), Chap. 2, we have

$$\frac{9}{10^{N+1}} + \cdots + \frac{9}{10^{N+k}} = \frac{9}{10^{N+k}} \cdot (1 + 10 + \cdots + 10^{k-1})$$

$$= \frac{9}{10^{N+k}} \cdot \frac{10^k - 1}{9} = \frac{1 - 1/10^k}{10^N} < \frac{1}{10^N}$$

Therefore $B_{N+k} - B_N < 1/10^N - 1/10^{N+l}$ for all $k \geq l$. On the other hand we have from above $r - B_N = 1/10^N$ and $r - B_{N+k} \leq 1/10^{N+k}$, from which $B_{N+k} - B_N = (r - B_N) - (r - B_{N+k}) \geq 1/10^N - 1/10^{N+k}$. Comparing with above, $1/10^N - 1/10^{N+l} \geq 1/10^N - 1/10^{N+k}$, or $10^{N+k} \leq 10^{N+l}$ for all k, a contradiction. Q.E.D.

To sum up, every non-negative rational number has a decimal expansion, necessarily recurrent. Conversely, any recurrent decimal is an expansion of some rational number. Decimal expansions are unique except in the case of rational numbers with terminating decimal expansions. Such numbers have a second expansion differing from the terminating one in the manner described in Theorem 4.4. Observe that for such numbers the process (4.5) always yields the terminating expansion because the numbers A_n satisfy the sharper inequality $A_n \leq c < A_n + 1/10^n$. To include the case of negative rational numbers we simply allow minus signs before decimal expansions.

In the next chapter we shall see that the rational-number system **Q** can be enlarged to a system **R** in which nonrecurrent decimals will also be expansions of numbers.

EXERCISES

1. Find *all* decimal expansions of the following rational numbers:
$1/2$, $2/8$, $21/27$, 17, $1/6$, $1/13$, $4952/6531$, $9210/1425$, $17/100$, $3/4$

2. What rational numbers have the following decimal expansions:

(*a*) $25.21412121212 \cdots$ (*b*) $3.22300300300 \cdots$

(*c*) $4.19250000 \cdots$ (*d*) $2.714285714285 \cdots$

Verify your answers.

3. Give a criterion which will enable you to decide in advance whether a given fraction a/b has a terminating decimal expansion.

4. Referring to Sec. 9, Chap. 2, discuss the possibility of replacing 10 in the foregoing by another integer b.

5. *The binomial theorem*

Many useful formulas obtained from mathematical induction involve fractions, at least in appearance. The binomial theorem is a case in point, and that is why we have deferred discussion of it until now. The formula involves certain numbers, called *binomial coefficients*, which we now define.

For any integer $n \geq 0$ and for any integer k we denote by the symbol $\binom{n}{k}$ the rational number

5.1 $$\binom{n}{k} = \begin{cases} \dfrac{n!}{k!\,(n-k)!} & \text{if } 0 \leq k < n \\ 0 & \text{otherwise} \end{cases}$$

Recall that by definition $0! = 1$. Hence

5.2 $$\binom{n}{0} = \binom{n}{n} = 1 \qquad \binom{n}{1} = \binom{n}{n-1} = n$$

From (5.1) it is clear that

5.3 $$\binom{n}{k} = \binom{n}{n-k} \qquad \text{for all } k$$

Observe that by canceling out either $k!$ or $(n-k)!$ in (5.1) we get

5.4 $$\binom{n}{k} = \frac{n(n-1)\cdots(k+1)}{(n-k)!} = \frac{n(n-1)\cdots(n-k+1)}{k!} \qquad (0 \leq k \leq n)$$

The first few binomial coefficients are as follows

$$\binom{0}{0} = 1 \qquad \binom{1}{0} = \binom{1}{1} = 1 \qquad \binom{2}{0} = 1, \binom{2}{1} = 2, \binom{2}{2} = 1$$

$$\binom{3}{0} = 1, \binom{3}{1} = 3, \binom{3}{2} = 3, \binom{3}{3} = 1$$

$$\binom{4}{0} = 1, \binom{4}{1} = 4, \binom{4}{2} = 6, \binom{4}{3} = 4, \binom{4}{4} = 1$$

$$\binom{5}{k} = 1, 5, 10, 10, 5, 1$$

etc.

The binomial coefficients are connected by many identities. One that we require here is

5.5 $$\binom{n}{k-1} + \binom{n}{k} = \binom{n+1}{k} \qquad \text{for all } k$$

Proof. If $k = 0$, then (5.5) becomes $\binom{n}{-1} + \binom{n}{0} = \binom{n+1}{0}$, which is correct because $\binom{n}{-1} = 0$ and $\binom{n}{0} = \binom{n+1}{0} = 1$. For $k < 0$ all three terms in (5.2) are zero.

If $k = n + 1$, then (5.5) reads $\binom{n}{n} + \binom{n}{n+1} = \binom{n+1}{n+1}$, which is correct, by (5.2), since $\binom{n}{n+1} = 0$. If $k > n + 1$, then all three terms in (5.5) are zero.

We are then left with k in the range $1 \leq k \leq n$, and for such k all three terms of (5.5) are given by the first expression in (5.1). Thus the left-hand side of (5.5) now becomes

$$\frac{n!}{(k-1)!(n-k+1)!} + \frac{n!}{k!(n-k)!}$$

$$= \frac{n!}{(k-1)!(n-k)!} \cdot \left(\frac{1}{n-k+1} + \frac{1}{k}\right)$$

$$= \frac{n!}{(k-1)!(n-k)!} \cdot \frac{n+1}{k(n-k+1)}$$

$$= \frac{(n+1)!}{k!(n-k+1)!} = \binom{n+1}{k} \qquad \text{Q.E.D.}$$

From (5.5) we derive the following important theorem.

THEOREM 5.1 *The binomial coefficients* $\binom{n}{k}$ *are integers.*

Proof. We use induction on n. The assertion is clearly true for $n = 0$ and $n = 1$. Suppose now that for some n it is true that $\binom{n}{k}$ is an integer for *all* k. Then for any k the left-hand side of (5.5) is an integer, and so $\binom{n+1}{k}$ is also an integer for all k. Therefore the truth of the assertion for n implies its truth for $n + 1$, and so the assertion holds for all n (and k). Q.E.D.

THEOREM 5.2 **(Binomial theorem)** *Let a, b be two elements of a ring A, and suppose that $ab = ba$. Then, for any positive integer n,*

5.6 $$(a + b)^n = a^n + \binom{n}{1} a^{n-1}b + \binom{n}{2} a^{n-2}b^2 + \cdots + \binom{n}{n-1} ab^{n-1} + b^n$$

Proof. First of all, the right-hand side makes sense because $\binom{n}{k}$ is an integer, and therefore the expression $\binom{n}{k} c$ is defined for any element c in A; namely, it denotes the result of adding c to itself $\binom{n}{k}$ times (see Sec.

7F, Chap. 2). If we define $a^0 = b^0 =$ unit element of A, as usual, then (5.6) can be written in the more compact form

5.7 $$(a + b)^n = \sum_{k=0}^{n} \binom{n}{k} a^{n-k} b^k$$

We prove this formula by induction on n. For $n = 1$ it is true, for then (5.7) reduces to $(a + b)^1 = a + b$, which is certainly correct. Now supposing that (5.7) holds for some n we shall show that it must hold for $n + 1$, hence for all positive integers n, by mathematical induction. But first recall that if $ab = ba$, as assumed, then $a^k b^l = b^l a^k$ for any positive integers k, l (see Exercise 1, Sec. 7, Chap. 2). This fact is used in the calculations below:

Assuming that (5.7) holds for n, we have

$$(a + b)^{n+1} = (a + b) \cdot \sum_{k=0}^{n} \binom{n}{k} a^{n-k} b^k$$
$$= \sum_{k=0}^{n} \binom{n}{k} (a + b)\, a^{n-k} b^k$$

by the distributive law. Since $(a + b)a^{n-k}b^k = a^{n-k+1}b^k + ba^{n-k}b^k = a^{n-k+1}b^k + a^{n-k}b^{k+1}$, we get

$$(a + b)^{n+1} = \sum_{k=0}^{n} \binom{n}{k} a^{n-k+1}\, b^k + \sum_{k=0}^{n} \binom{n}{k} a^{n-k}\, b^{k+1}$$

Now put $k = j$ in the first sum and $k = j - 1$ in the second. There results

$$(a + b)^{n+1} = \sum_{j=0}^{n} \binom{n}{j} a^{n-j+1}\, b^j + \sum_{j=1}^{n+1} \binom{n}{j-1} a^{n-j+1}\, b^j$$

Since $\binom{n}{j} = 0$ if $j > n$ and $\binom{n}{j-1} = 0$ if $j < 1$, we can let both sums above run from $j = 0$ to $j = n + 1$, and then they can be combined to give

$$(a + b)^{n+1} = \sum_{j=0}^{n+1} \left\{ \binom{n}{j} + \binom{n}{j-1} \right\} a^{n-j+1}\, b^j$$
$$= \sum_{j=0}^{n+1} \binom{n+1}{j} a^{n+1-j}\, b^j \qquad \text{[by (5.5)]}$$

This is precisely Eq. (5.7) with n replaced by $n + 1$. Therefore (5.7) holds for all $n > 0$. Q.E.D.

EXAMPLE Applying this to **Z**, take $a = b = 1$, there results the formula

5.8 $$2^n = \sum_{k=0}^{n} \binom{n}{k}$$

The binomial coefficients arise frequently in certain types of counting problems. The following theorem is of great importance in this connection:

THEOREM 5.3 *Let E be a set containing n elements. Then the number of distinct subsets of E containing k elements is equal to $\binom{n}{k}$ for $1 \le k \le n$.*

Proof. We use induction on n. The assertion is clearly true for $n = 1$. Suppose that it holds for all n smaller than some integer n_0. We show that it must necessarily hold for n_0 also.

Let E be a set containing n_0 elements, and select a fixed element x in E. Now it is obvious that the assertion of the theorem holds here for $k = 1$ and for $k = n_0$, by (5.2). We therefore take k such that $2 \le k \le n_0 - 1$. The number of subsets of E containing k elements is equal to the sum of

A: the number of subsets of k elements including x

B: the number of subsets of k elements not including x

For A, $k - 1$ of the elements must be taken from among the $n_0 - 1$ elements different from x. By our induction assumption we have therefore $A = \binom{n_0 - 1}{k - 1}$. For B, all k of the elements must be taken from the $n_0 - 1$ elements different from x. Therefore, from our induction assumption, $B = \binom{n_0 - 1}{k}$. Hence $A + B = \binom{n_0}{k}$, by (5.5). We have shown that the assertion of the theorem must indeed be true for n_0. Hence it is true for all positive integers n, by mathematical induction. Q.E.D.

EXAMPLE The number of ways of choosing two elements from a set of four is equal to $\binom{4}{2} = 6$.

EXERCISES

1. Prove the identities $\binom{n}{k} = \binom{n}{n - k}$ and $\sum_{k=0}^{n} \binom{n}{k} \cdot (-1)^k = 0$.

2. Prove that $k!$ divides the product of any k consecutive positive integers.

3. For any prime p prove that p divides $\binom{p}{1}, \binom{p}{2}, \ldots, \binom{p}{p - 1}$.

4. Let p be a prime, and let $x, y, z, \ldots, w$ be any finite set of integers. Prove that $(x + y + z + \cdots + w)^p \equiv x^p + y^p + z^p + \cdots + w^p \pmod{p}$.

5. Let p be a prime, and let a, b, q be integers such that $0 < a \le b$ and $p \nmid q$. Prove that $m = \binom{p^b q}{p^a}$ is divisible by p^{b-a} but not by p^{b-a+1}. [Hint: Using (5.4) write m in the form

$$m = \frac{p^b q(p^b q - 1) \cdots (p^b q - k) \cdots (p^b q - p^a + 1)}{p^a(p^a - 1) \cdots (p^a - k) \cdots 1}$$

and show that $p^b q - k$ and $p^a - k$ are divisible by exactly the same power of p.]

6. Let a, b, c be elements of an integral domain. Prove that

$$(a + b + c)^n = \sum \frac{n!}{p!q!r!} a^p b^q c^r$$

where the sum is to be taken for all triples p, q, r of nonnegative integers such that $p + q + r = n$. (The numbers $n!/p!q!r!$ are called *trinomial* coefficients. Similar formulas can be proved for any number of terms a, b, c, etc.)

7. Prove that $\frac{1}{1 \cdot 2} + \frac{1}{2 \cdot 3} + \cdots + \frac{1}{n(n+1)} = \frac{n}{n+1}$.

8. For any positive integer n prove that $n^n > 1 \cdot 3 \cdot 5 \cdots (2n - 1)$.

9. Prove that $\frac{1}{1 \cdot 3} + \frac{1}{3 \cdot 5} + \cdots + \frac{1}{(2n-1)(2n+1)} = \frac{1}{2n+1}$.

10. Prove that $1^3 + 2^3 + \cdots + n^3 = \frac{1}{4} \cdot n^2 (n + 1)^2$.

***11.** Let K be a finite field of characteristic p (see Exercise 6, Sec. 2). Prove that the mapping of K to itself that sends any element x into x^p is an isomorphism.

12. Let E be a set containing n elements. What is the total number of distinct subsets of E?

13. Let E be a set of n elements, and let F be a set of m elements. How many distinct mappings from E to F are there?

4

The real-number system

1. Introduction

Consider for a moment some decimal $A = a_0.a_1a_2a_3 \ldots$, as defined in Chap. 3. With any such decimal we associated a certain sequence of rational numbers

1.1 $$A_n = a_0 + \frac{a_1}{10} + \frac{a_2}{10^2} + \cdots + \frac{a_n}{10^n} \qquad (n = 1, 2, 3, \ldots)$$

Now if A happens to be a decimal expansion of a rational number r (that is, if A is recurrent), then according to Definition 4.2, Chap. 3, the numbers A_n get closer and closer to r as n is made larger and larger. The number r can therefore be thought of as a "limiting value" of the approximations A_n. Now even if A is not a recurrent decimal the numbers A_n differ from each other very little for large n, for as was shown in Chap. 3 (Corollary of Proposition 4.1), $0 \leq A_{n+k} - A_n < 1/10^n$ for any positive integers n, k. In other words the numbers A_n, A_{n+1}, A_{n+2}, . . . differ from each other by less than $1/10^n$, and $1/10^n$ can be made as small as we wish by taking n large enough. Nonetheless there is no rational number which is approximated arbitrarily well by the A_n, in the sense of Definition 4.2, Chap. 3, because that is true only for recurrent decimals. This suggests that there are certain "gaps" in the rational-number system **Q**, and in this chapter we shall see how to go about filling them up.

This problem of gaps can be exhibited in an even more concrete way by another example: c being a rational number, consider the equation $x^2 = c$. For some numbers c this equation has a solution x in **Q**, and for some it does not. For example, if $c = 4$ then $x^2 = 4$ has two solutions in **Q**, namely 2 and -2. *But for $c = 2$, the equation has no solution in* **Q**. To prove this, suppose to the contrary that there is a rational number x whose square is 2. We can write $x = m/n$, where m and n are *relatively prime* integers (Proposition 3.3, Chap. 3). By assumption $(m/n)^2 = 2$, or $m^2 = 2n^2$. From this equation we see that if $n > 1$ then any prime factor p of n must divide m^2 and therefore must also divide m, by Theorem 8.8, Chap. 2. Hence m and n have the common factor p if $n > 1$, a contradiction. But if $n = 1$ our equation is $m^2 = 2$, and again we have a contradiction because clearly 2 is not the square of any integer, being a prime. *Thus there is no rational number whose square is* 2.

This negative conclusion need not deter us from trying to find rational numbers whose squares are very nearly equal to 2. Taking 1 as a first approximation, let us try to find a better one among the numbers 1.1, 1.2, . . . , 1.9. We have $(1.4)^2 = 1.96$ and $(1.5)^2 = 2.25$, and so let us take 1.4 as a second approximation. To improve this now try the numbers 1.41, 1.42, . . . , 1.49. We find $(1.41)^2 = 1.9881$ and $(1.42)^2 = 2.0164$. Therefore we take 1.41 as a third approximation. Continuing in this way we obtain a sequence of rational numbers

$$1,\ 1.4,\ 1.41,\ 1.414,\ 1.4142,\ \ldots$$

whose squares are

$$1,\ 1.96,\ 1.9881,\ 1.999396,\ 1.99996164,\ \ldots$$

It is rather obvious, and easy to prove, that by continuing this procedure we can obtain rational numbers whose squares are as close to 2 as we may desire. It is also clear that the procedure determines a certain decimal 1.414213 · · · .

These considerations naturally lead to the suggestion that it would be profitable to enlarge the rational-number system **Q** by including all decimals. We shall in fact do something very like that. But decimals themselves are very awkward for theoretical purposes, as the reader will quickly ascertain by trying to define the sum or product of two decimals in such a way as to get again a decimal. Moreover decimals provide only one rather special method of approximation, and there is no point in confining ourselves to it alone.

We mention briefly another type of approximation. The method leads to a rather interesting part of arithmetic, *continued fractions.* For the sake of brevity we limit ourselves to the problem of finding rational numbers whose squares are close to 2. For this special case the method is based upon the observation that if c is any positive rational number, and if $c' = (2 + c)/(1 + c)$, then c'^2 is closer to 2 than is c^2 (see Exercise 12, Sec. 3, Chap. 3). Taking $c = 1$ we get $c' = \frac{3}{2}$. Then taking $c = \frac{3}{2}$ we get $c' = \frac{7}{5}$, and so on. In this way we obtain a sequence of rational numbers

$$1,\ 3/2,\ 7/5,\ 17/12,\ 41/29,\ 99/70,\ 239/169,\ \ldots$$

and it is not hard to prove that their squares eventually get arbitrarily close to 2.

The central point of the foregoing, and indeed of the entire chapter, is the notion of approximation by rational numbers. The discerning reader may have observed a certain element of vagueness in the use of such terms as "near" and "close to" in the remarks above. In the following section we shall introduce terminology which will make it easy to deal with these concepts precisely.

EXERCISES

1. Prove that there is no rational number whose square is 3. Do the same for 5, 6, and 12.

2. Prove that no integer is the square of a rational number unless it is the square of an integer.

3. Prove that there is no rational number whose cube is 5.

4. k being a positive integer, prove that if n is an integer and $n = r^k$, where r is a rational number, then r must be an integer. What can you say about the prime decomposition of n if that is so? Prove that the integer 99,225,000 cannot be the kth power of any integer for any $k \geq 2$.

5. Let b be a positive integer. Devise a method for determining a decimal $A = a_0.a_1a_2a_3 \cdots$ such that the rational numbers A_n have squares that approach b as closely as desired. In other words, show that, once A_{n-1} is known, the digit a_n is determined by the condition of being the largest integer such that $a_n^2 + 2 \cdot 10^n A_{n-1} \cdot a_n \leq (b - A_{n-1}^2) \cdot 10^{2n}$.

2. Cauchy sequences and limits

The following definition is basic for the rest of this chapter.

DEFINITION 2.1 *Let $a_1, a_2, a_3, \ldots, a_n, \ldots$ be an infinite sequence of elements in an ordered field K. Then it is called a* Cauchy sequence† *if for every positive element e in K there exists an integer P (depending in general upon e) such that*

2.1 $$|a_n - a_m| < e \qquad \text{for all } m, n > P$$

The definition merely says that the elements in the sequence must all be close together provided that we go far enough out in the sequence. The point is that it gives to the informal notion "close together" a precise meaning that will stand up in any court. It might be expected that there is some connection with decimals. We prove

PROPOSITION 2.1 *Let $A = a_0.a_1a_2a_3 \cdots$ be any decimal, and let A_n be the rational number defined by Eq.* (1.1). *Then those numbers $A_1, A_2, A_3, \ldots$ form a Cauchy sequence in the rational field* **Q**.

Proof. Let e be any positive rational number. Our problem is to show that there is an integer P such that $|A_n - A_m| < e$ whenever $m, n > P$. This is very easy. For there is certainly a positive integer $P > 1/e$, by Theorem 3.7, Chap. 3. Since $10^P > P$ (Proposition 9.1, corollary, Chap. 2) we have then $10^P > 1/e$, or $e > 1/10^P$. Now suppose that m, $n > P$, with say $m < n$. By the Corollary of Proposition 4.1, Chap. 3, we then have $0 \leq A_n - A_m < 1/10^m < 1/10^P < e$. Q.E.D.

Some further examples of Cauchy sequences are given below.

EXAMPLE 1 $1, 2, 3, \ldots, n, \ldots$ is *not* a Cauchy sequence in **Q**.

For clearly $|a_n - a_m| = |n - m| \geq 1$ if $n \neq m$. If in Definition 2.1 we take $e = \frac{1}{2}$, say, then we can never have $|a_n - a_m| < \frac{1}{2}$ for all $n, m > P$, no matter how large we take P.

† After the French mathematician Augustin-Louis Cauchy (1789–1857).

EXAMPLE 2 For any rational number c the sequence $c, c, c, \ldots$ is a Cauchy sequence in $\mathbf{Q}$.

Indeed here we have $a_n = c$ for all n, and so $|a_n - a_m| = 0$, whatever m and n. Hence (2.1) is certainly satisfied. A Cauchy sequence of this trivial type is called a *constant* sequence.

EXAMPLE 3 The sequence $\frac{1}{2}, -\frac{1}{2}, \frac{1}{2}, -\frac{1}{2}$, etc., is *not* a Cauchy sequence in $\mathbf{Q}$.

Here $a_n = \pm\frac{1}{2}$, and $|a_n - a_m| = 1$ whenever $n - m$ is odd. Therefore condition (2.1) cannot be satisfied if we take, say, $e = \frac{99}{100}$.

EXAMPLE 4 $1, -\frac{1}{2}, \frac{1}{4}, -\frac{1}{8}, \frac{1}{16}$, etc., is a Cauchy sequence in $\mathbf{Q}$.

Here $a_n = \pm 1/2^n$, and so $a_n - a_m = \pm 1/2^n \pm 1/2^m$. Taking, say, $n \geq m$ we have then $|a_n - a_m| \leq 1/2^n + 1/2^m < 2/2^m$. Given now any positive rational number e there is an integer $P > 1/e$. Since $2^P > P$ there follows $e > 1/2^P$, and so $|a_n - a_m| < e$ if $m, n > P$.

EXAMPLE 5 $\frac{1}{2}, \frac{3}{4}, \frac{7}{8}, \ldots, (2^n - 1)/2^n, \ldots$ is a Cauchy sequence in $\mathbf{Q}$.

The proof is similar to that of Example 4.

Returning again to Definition 2.1, we point out that the condition stated must be fulfilled for *every* positive e, no matter how small. Hence by taking smaller and smaller values of e we see that (2.1) requires the elements of the sequence to be closer and closer together (provided that m and n are large enough).

We stress the fact that there is no general procedure for determining whether a given sequence is a Cauchy sequence or not. Each case must be studied individually, and frequently some rather ingenious tricks are required, as in the case of the following two sequences, which are discussed in any standard calculus text:

$$1,\ 1 + \frac{1}{2},\ 1 + \frac{1}{2} + \frac{1}{3}, \text{ etc.} \qquad \text{and} \qquad 1,\ 1 + \frac{1}{2^2},\ 1 + \frac{1}{2^2} + \frac{1}{3^2}, \text{ etc.}$$

The first of these is not a Cauchy sequence (in $\mathbf{Q}$), but the second is.

PROPOSITION 2.2 *If $a_1, a_2, a_3, \ldots$ is a Cauchy sequence in an ordered field K, then so is any sequence obtained from it by omitting any elements whatever (provided that what remains is still an infinite sequence) or by inserting any finite number of new elements.*

The proof is very trivial and is omitted.

The following proposition shows that the terms in a Cauchy sequence cannot become arbitrarily large.

PROPOSITION 2.3 *Let $a_1, a_2, a_3, \ldots$ be a Cauchy sequence in an ordered field K. Then there exists a positive element c in K such that $|a_n| < c$ for all n.*

Proof. Let e be any fixed positive element of K. By definition there is an integer P such that $|a_n - a_m| < e$ for all $n, m > P$. There follows in particular $|a_n - a_{P+1}| < e$ for all $n > P$. Hence $|a_n| < e + |a_{P+1}|$ for all $n > P$. Now put $c = e + |a_1| + \cdots + |a_P| + |a_{P+1}|$. Clearly $|a_n| < c$ for all n. Q.E.D.

PROPOSITION 2.4 *If $a_1, a_2, a_3, \ldots$ and $b_1, b_2, b_3, \ldots$ are Cauchy sequences in an ordered field K, then so are the sequences whose nth terms are, respectively, $a_n + b_n$, $a_n - b_n$, a_nb_n. Furthermore, if k is a positive integer, then $a_1^k, a_2^k, a_3^k, \ldots$ is a Cauchy sequence; and if there is a positive element b_0 such that $|b_n| \geq b_0$ for all $n = 1$, 2, 3, etc., then $1/b_1, 1/b_2, 1/b_3, \ldots$ is a Cauchy sequence.*

Proof. We prove the assertion only for the sequence $a_1b_1, a_2b_2, a_3b_3, \ldots$, leaving the others as exercises. We start with the trivial identity

$$a_nb_n - a_mb_m = (a_n - a_m) \cdot b_n + (b_n - b_m) \cdot a_m$$

From the triangle inequality (Exercise 6, Sec. 3, Chap. 2), we get

$$|a_nb_n - a_mb_m| \leq |a_n - a_m| \cdot |b_n| + |b_n - b_m| \cdot |a_m|$$

From Proposition 2.3 there exist fixed positive elements c_1, c_2 in K such that $|a_n| < c_1$ and $|b_n| < c_2$ for all n. Let c be the larger of c_1, c_2. Then we have

$$|a_nb_n - a_mb_m| \leq c \cdot |a_n - a_m| + c \cdot |b_n - b_m|$$

Now let e be any positive element in K, and put $e' = e/2c$. By Definition 2.1 there is an integer P_1 such that $|a_n - a_m| < e'$ for all n, $m > P_1$, and there is similarly an integer P_2 such that $|b_n - b_m| < e'$ for all n, $m > P_2$. Let P be the greater of P_1, P_2. Then for all n, $m > P$ we have $|a_n - a_m| < e'$ and $|b_n - b_m| < e'$, and so

$$|a_nb_n - a_mb_m| < c \cdot e' + ce' = 2ce' = e \qquad \text{Q.E.D.}$$

Therefore $a_1b_1, a_2b_2, \ldots$ is a Cauchy sequence. In particular, $a_1^2, a_2^2, a_3^2, \ldots$ is a Cauchy sequence, and by a simple induction one finds that $a_1^k, a_2^k, \ldots$ is a Cauchy sequence for any positive integer k.

DEFINITION 2.2 *Let $a_1, a_2, a_3, \ldots$ be any sequence in an ordered field K, and let a be an element in K. Then the sequence is said to have a as a* limit, *or, in symbols, $\lim_{n \to \infty} a_n = a$, if for every positive element e in K there exists an integer P (depending in general upon e) such that*

2.2 $\qquad |a_n - a| < e \qquad$ for all $n > P$

If this is true, then the sequence is also said to *converge* to a.

The definition merely expresses in precise terms the intuitive notion that the elements a_n get arbitrarily close to a if n is taken large enough. For example, if our field is **Q**, then we can take (say) $e = 10^{-6}$. The definition then says that a and a_n must differ by less than a millionth for large enough n. Replacing 10^{-6} by 10^{-12}, the definition says than a and a_n must differ by less than 10^{-12} for large enough n. In general, as e is made smaller the integer P will have to be made larger.

PROPOSITION 2.5 *A sequence $a_1, a_2, a_3, \ldots$ in K cannot have more than one limit.*

Proof. Suppose that a and a' are two different limits of the sequence. Then $|a - a'| > 0$, and by definition there is an integer P_1 such that $|a_n - a| < |a - a'|/2$ for all $n > P_1$.† Similarly, there is an integer P_2 such that $|a_n - a'| < |a - a'|/2$ for all $n > P_2$. But we have $|a - a'| = |(a - a_n) + (a_n - a')| \leq |a - a_n| + |a' - a_n|$, by the triangle inequality, and so $|a - a'| < |a - a'|/2 + |a - a'|/2 = |a - a'|$, a contradiction.

Q.E.D.

PROPOSITION 2.6 *If a sequence $a_1, a_2, a_3, \ldots$ in K has a limit a, then it must be a Cauchy sequence.*

Proof. Let e be a positive element in K, and let P be an integer such that $|a_n - a| < e/2$ for all $n > P$. Then $|a_n - a_m| = |a_n - a + a - a_m| \leq |a_n - a| + |a - a_m| < e/2 + e/2 = e$ for all $m, n > P$. Q.E.D.

The converse of this theorem is not true in general. That is, a Cauchy sequence may very well not have a limit.

PROPOSITION 2.7 *Let c be a rational number with $|c| < 1$. Then the numbers 1, $1 + c$, $1 + c + c^2$, $1 + c + c^2 + c^3$, etc., form a Cauchy sequence in $\mathbf{Q}$ and it has as a limit the number $1/(1 - c)$.*

Proof. Put $a_n = 1 + c + c^2 + \cdots + c^{n-1}$. Our problem is to show that $\lim_{n\to\infty} a_n = 1/(1 - c)$. Now $(1 - c) \cdot a_n = 1 - c^n$, by the identity proved in Chap. 2, (7.31), and so

$$a_n - \frac{1}{1-c} = \frac{1-c^n}{1-c} - \frac{1}{1-c} = -\frac{c^n}{1-c}$$

By Exercise 10, Sec. 3, Chap. 3, there is an integer P such that $|c|^n < e \cdot (1 - c)$ for all $n > P$, and so

$$\left|a_n - \frac{1}{1-c}\right| = \frac{|c|^n}{1-c} < e \qquad \text{for all } n > P$$

Q.E.D.

PROPOSITION 2.8 *Let $A = a_0.a_1a_2a_3 \cdots$ be a decimal. Then the sequence of numbers $A_1, A_2, A_3, \ldots$ defined by (1.1) has a limit r in $\mathbf{Q}$ if and only if the decimal is recurrent, and then A is a decimal expansion of r.*

Proof. Suppose that the sequence $A_1, A_2, A_3, \ldots$ has a limit r in $\mathbf{Q}$. Then $A_n \leq r$ for all n, because if, say, $A_k > r$, then for $n \geq k$ we have $A_n \geq A_k$ and so $A_n - r \geq A_k - r$, showing that Definition 2.2 is violated. Now fix some m and let e be any positive rational number. Since

† Here 2 stands for $1 + 1$, where 1 is the unit element of K.

$\lim_{n \to \infty} A_n = r$, it follows by definition that $|r - A_n| < e$ for all sufficiently large n, say for all n greater than some integer P. We have $r - A_m = r - A_n + A_n - A_m$, and so $r - A_m \leq e + A_n - A_m$ provided that $n > P$. But if $n \geq m$, as we may assume, then $0 \leq A_n - A_m < 1/10^m$, by the corollary of Proposition 4.1, Chap. 3. Recalling from above that $A_m \leq r$, we now have

$$0 \leq r - A_m < \frac{1}{10^m} + e$$

Then $r - A_m - 1/10^m < e$. Since e was an arbitrary positive number it follows that $r - A_m - 1/10^m \leq 0$. Hence we have finally $0 \leq r - A_m \leq 1/10^m$ for all m, showing that A is indeed a decimal expansion of r, according to Definition 4.2, Chap. 3. Therefore A must be a recurrent decimal, by the results of Sec. 4, Chap. 3.

To prove the converse, let A be a recurrent decimal, say with $a_{j+P} = a_j$ for all $j > k$, P therefore being the period of recurrence. Consider the sequence $b_1 = A_{k+P}$, $b_2 = A_{k+2P}$, . . . , $b_n = A_{k+nP}$, ... Then

$$b_{n+1} - b_n = \frac{a_{k+nP+1}}{10^{k+nP+1}} + \cdots + \frac{a_{k+(n+1)P}}{10^{k+(n+1)P}}$$

Since $a_{k+nP+1} = a_{k+1}$, etc., there follows

$$b_{n+1} - b_n = \frac{1}{10^{nP}} \cdot \left(\frac{a_{k+1}}{10^{k+1}} + \cdots + \frac{a_{k+P}}{10^{k+P}}\right) = \frac{1}{10^{nP}} \cdot (A_{k+P} - A_k)$$

Now $b_{n+1} = b_1 + (b_2 - b_1) + (b_3 - b_2) + \cdots + (b_{n+1} - b_n)$, and so by the formula just established we have

$$b_n = b_1 + (A_{k+P} - A_k) \cdot \left(\frac{1}{10^P} + \frac{1}{10^{2P}} + \cdots + \frac{1}{10^{nP}}\right)$$

Putting $b'_n = \dfrac{b_n - b_1}{A_{k+P} - A_k} \cdot 10^P = 1 + \dfrac{1}{10^P} + \cdots + \left(\dfrac{1}{10^P}\right)^{n-1}$ we see that the sequence b'_1, b'_2, b'_3, . . . has a limit, namely, $10^P/(10^P - 1)$, by Proposition 2.7. Since $b_n = b_1 + (A_{k+P} - A_k)/10^P \cdot b'_n$ it is easy to see that the sequence b_1, b_2, b_3, . . . also has a limit r, namely,

$$r = \lim_{n \to \infty} b_n = \lim_{n \to \infty} A_{k+nP} = b_1 + \frac{A_{k+P} - A_k}{10^P} \cdot \frac{10^P}{10^P - 1}$$

Since $b_1 = A_{k+P}$, we have

$$r = \frac{10^P A_{k+P} - A_k}{10^P - 1}$$

(cf. Theorem 4.3, Chap. 3). This shows that the sequence A_{k+P}, A_{k+2P}, A_{k+3P}, etc., has the limit r. It follows easily from the fact that $A_1 \leq$

$A_2 \leq A_3 \leq \cdots$ that the original sequence $A_1, A_2, A_3, \ldots$ also has the limit r. By what was shown above, A must be a decimal expansion of r.

Q.E.D.

The main idea of this section was to formulate a concept, namely, *Cauchy sequences*, which includes the notion of decimals (in the sense of Theorem 2.1) and is free from the cumbersome dependence on powers of $1/10$. For that reason they are far easier to deal with than decimals. Another advantage of Cauchy sequences is that they can be defined in systems in which decimals cannot be defined. As Proposition 2.8 shows, only certain Cauchy sequences in $\mathbf{Q}$ have limits, and in the next section we shall see that $\mathbf{Q}$ can be embedded in a larger ordered field $\mathbf{R}$ in which all Cauchy sequences have limits.

EXERCISES

1. Complete the proof of Proposition 2.4.

2. Let $a_1, a_2, a_3, \ldots$ be a Cauchy sequence in an ordered field, and let it have a limit a. Prove that any sequence obtained from the given one, either by omitting any terms whatever (but in such a way that what remains is still an infinite sequence), or by inserting any *finite* number of new terms, has the same limit a.

3. Let $a_1, a_2, a_3, \ldots$ and $b_1, b_2, b_3, \ldots$ be sequences in an ordered field having limits a, b, respectively. Prove the following:

(*a*) If $a_n < b_n$ for all but possibly a finite number of n, then $a \leq b$. (Give an example where equality holds.)

(*b*) $a \pm b = \lim\limits_{n \to \infty} (a_n \pm b_n)$.

(*c*) $ab = \lim\limits_{n \to \infty} a_n b_n$.

(*d*) If $b \neq 0$, then $a/b = \lim\limits_{n \to \infty} a_n/b_n$ (Show first that only a finite number of the b_n can be zero.)

(*e*) For any positive integer k, $ab = \lim\limits_{n \to \infty} a_n b_{n+k}$.

(*f*) For any positive integer k, $\lim\limits_{n \to \infty} a_n{}^k = a^k$.

(*g*) For any c_1, c_2 in K, $c_1 a + c_2 b = \lim\limits_{n \to \infty} (c_1 a_n + c_2 b_n)$.

4. Prove that $\lim\limits_{n \to \infty} \sum\limits_{k=1}^{n} \dfrac{1}{k \cdot (k+1)} = 1$. That is, prove that if $a_n = \dfrac{1}{1 \cdot 2} + \dfrac{1}{2 \cdot 3} + \cdots + \dfrac{1}{n \cdot (n+1)}$, then $\lim\limits_{n \to \infty} a_n = 1$. [Hint: Consider the expression $\dfrac{1}{k} - \dfrac{1}{k+1}$.]

5. Let r be a rational number with $r < 1$, and let a be any rational number. Prove that

$$\lim_{n \to \infty} \sum_{k=1}^{n} ar^k = \frac{ar}{1 - r}$$

6. Let $a_1, a_2, a_3, \ldots$ be a sequence of positive elements in an ordered field, and suppose that $a_1 \geq a_2 \geq a_3 \geq$, etc. Prove that the sequence whose nth term is $s_n = a_1 - a_2 + a_3 - + \cdots \pm a_n$ (alternating signs) is a Cauchy sequence.

3. The field of real numbers

Here we deal with the field of real numbers in much the same way we took up the rational-number system in Chap. 3, namely, by specifying its properties.

DEFINITION 3.1 *An ordered field K is said to be* complete *if every Cauchy sequence in K has a limit in K.*

DEFINITION 3.2 *A field R is called a* field of real numbers *if it is a complete ordered field containing the rational-number system* **Q** *as a subfield and if furthermore every element of R is the limit of some sequence of elements in* **Q**.

REMARK. A propos the requirement that **R** contain **Q**, one should realize that *any* ordered field contains a subfield *isomorphic* to **Q**. Cf. Exercise 7, Sec. 3, Chap. 3.

The intuitive idea of this last requirement is that every element of R can be approximated arbitrarily well by elements in **Q**. Of course the very notion of approximation here depends upon the notion of ordering of a field. Let us first observe that the ordering of R must necessarily be compatible with that already defined in **Q**. Recall that the square of a nonzero element in an ordered integral domain is always positive. Hence for the unit element 1 of R, which must be the same as the unit element of **Q**, namely, the integer 1, we have $1^2 = 1$; hence $1 > 0$ in R. By the ordering axioms, if $a > 0$ and $b > 0$ in R, then also $a + b > 0$ and $ab > 0$. In particular, $2 = 1 + 1 > 0$ in R. By a simple induction one finds that every positive integer n is also a positive element of R. Now let $r = m/n$ be a positive element of **Q**. By definition, $m \cdot n$ must be a positive integer; hence also a positive element of R. Since $1/n^2 = 1/n \cdot 1/n$ is positive in R, it follows that $(1/n^2)\, mn = r$ is positive in R. Hence positive elements of **Q** are also positive in R.

The following theorem, analogous to Theorem 3.7, Chap. 3, shows that elements of R are comparable in size to elements of **Z**. That is, there are no elements in R which are greater than all elements of **Z**.

THEOREM 3.1 *Let c be an element of a field of real numbers R. Then there is a unique integer q such that $q \leq c < q + 1$.*

Proof. By Definition 3.2 the element c is the limit of some sequence $c_1, c_2, c_3, \ldots$ in **Q**. Then, by Definition 2.2, there is an integer P such that $|c_n - c| < 1$ for all $n > P$. Fixing such a c_n (it is a rational number), there is an integer q' such that $q' \leq c_n < q' + 1$, by Theorem 3.7, Chap. 3. Since c_n and c differ by less than 1, we have $q' - 1 < c < q' + 2$. The assertion follows easily from this. Q.E.D.

COROLLARY 1 *If e is any positive element in R, then there is a positive integer n such that $1/n < e$.*

Proof. There is an integer $n > 1/e$ by the theorem above.

Thus for any positive element of R there is always a positive rational number which is smaller.

COROLLARY 2 *If c is any element of R and if e is any positive element of R, then there are rational numbers a, b such that $a < c < b$ and $c - a < e$, $b - c < e$.*

Proof. Let e' be a *rational* number with $0 < e' < \frac{1}{2}e$. Now by Definition 3.2 we have $c = \lim_{n \to \infty} c_n$, where $c_1, c_2, c_3, \ldots$ is a sequence of rational numbers. By Definition 2.2 there is an integer P such that $|c_n - c| < e'$ for all $n > P$. Fixing such a c_n simply put $a = c_n - e'$ and $b = c_n + e'$. Q.E.D.

COROLLARY 3 *A sequence $a_1, a_2, a_3, \ldots$ of rational numbers is a Cauchy sequence in R if and only if it is a Cauchy sequence in $\mathbf{Q}$.*

Proof. Let $a_1, a_2, a_3, \ldots$ be a Cauchy sequence in $\mathbf{Q}$, and let e be any positive element in R. Let e' be a positive *rational* number with $e' < e$. Such an e' exists by Corollary 1 above. By Definition 2.1, there exists an integer P such that $|a_n - a_m| < e'$ for all $n, m > P$. Therefore $|a_n - a_m| < e$ for all $n, m > P$, and consequently the sequence satisfies the requirements for a Cauchy sequence in R. The converse is trivial. Q.E.D.

The following theorem shows that there can be essentially just one field of real numbers.

THEOREM 3.2 *If R and R' are two fields of real numbers, then there is one and only one isomorphism f from R to R', and f must send every element of $\mathbf{Q}$ into itself.*

Proof. By Definition 2.3, Chap. 2, f is required to satisfy the conditions $f(a + b) = f(a) + f(b)$ and $f(ab) = f(a) \cdot f(b)$. Put $b = 1$ in the latter, obtaining $f(a) = f(a) \cdot f(1)$. This shows that if $f(1) = 0$, then f must map every element of R into 0. We assume then that $f(1) \neq 0$. Putting $a = 1$ in the equation above gives $f(1) = f(1) \cdot f(1)$, whence $f(1) \cdot [1 - f(1)] = 0$. It follows that $f(1) = 1$. Then $f(1 + 1) = f(1) + f(1) = 1 + 1$; that is, $f(2) = 2$. By a simple induction we find that $f(n) = n$ for every positive integer n. From (2.1), Chap. 2, we have $f(0) = 0$ and $f(-a) = -f(a)$. In particular, $f(-n) = -f(n) = -n$ for any positive integer n. This shows that f must map every element of $\mathbf{Z}$ into itself. Further, $1 = f(1) = f(n \cdot n^{-1}) = f(n) \cdot f(n^{-1}) = n \cdot f(n^{-1})$ for any positive integer n, and therefore $f(n^{-1}) = n^{-1}$. Hence $f(m/n) = f(m \cdot n^{-1}) = f(m) \cdot f(n^{-1}) = m \cdot n^{-1} = m/n$. We conclude that f must map every element of $\mathbf{Q}$ into itself.

To complete the proof we must borrow a result proved below (Theorem

4.3). It is entirely independent of the matter at hand. Namely, Theorem 4.3 shows that if x is a positive element of R, then there is an element y of R such that $y^2 = x$. Then $f(x) = f(y^2) = f(y \cdot y) = f(y) \cdot f(y)$, and so $f(x) \geq 0$, by Theorem 3.8, Chap. 2. Take a rational number r such that $0 < r < x$. By what we have just shown, $f(x - r) \geq 0$, since $x - r$ is positive. But $f(x - r) = f(x) - f(r) = f(x) - r$ (by the result proved above). Thus $f(x) - r \geq 0$, or $f(x) \geq r > 0$. Therefore $f(x)$ must be positive. Now if $b > a$ in R, then $b - a > 0$; by the result just established, $f(b - a) > 0$. But $f(b - a) = f(b) - f(a)$, and we conclude that $f(b) > f(a)$, so that f must preserve ordering.

Now let $c_1, c_2, c_3, \ldots$ be a Cauchy sequence of rational numbers. It is then a Cauchy sequence in both R and R', by Corollary 3 above. It therefore has a limit c in R and a limit c' in R', by Definition 3.2. We claim that $f(c) = c'$. For let e be a positive rational number. Then by definition of limit there is an integer P such that $|c - c_n| < e$ for all $n > P$. Since f preserves order, it follows that $|f(c) - f(c_n)| < f(e)$. Since c_n, e are rational, we have $f(c_n) = c_n$ and $f(e) = e$. Therefore $|f(c) - c_n| < e$ for $n > P$. Consequently $f(c)$ is the limit of the sequence $c_1, c_2, c_3, \ldots$ in R', and so $f(c) = c'$, by Theorem 2.5. It follows easily that f is one-to-one, although we merely assumed that f is a ring-homomorphism such that not every element of R is mapped into zero.

Now given R and R', this analysis shows us how to go about constructing a mapping f satisfying the requirements. Namely, we start by defining $f(a) = a$ for any rational number a. Then for any element c in R we select a Cauchy sequence $c_1, c_2, c_3, \ldots$ in **Q** having c as a limit (one exists, by Definition 3.2). The same sequence must have a limit c' in R', and we simply define $f(c) = c'$. It is easily verified that c' depends only on c and not on the particular Cauchy sequence selected, and therefore f is uniquely defined for all elements of R. It is a straightforward matter to verify that f is an isomorphism. Q.E.D.

Because of the essential uniqueness of a field of real numbers, as shown by the preceding theorem, we now suppose one such field is fixed once for all, and we denote it by **R**. Its elements are called *real numbers*. A real number is called *rational* if it is in the subfield **Q**, otherwise *irrational*.

The existence of such a field **R** is proved in Chap. 15. The idea of the construction is as follows: One simply takes the set S of *all* Cauchy sequences in **Q**, defining any two of them, say $a_1, a_2, a_3, \ldots$ and $a'_1, a'_2, a'_3, \ldots$, to be *equivalent* if $\lim_{n \to \infty} (a_n - a'_n) = 0$. This relation of equivalence partitions S into equivalence *classes*, and these classes are taken to be the elements of **R**. It is easy to define appropriate operations of addition and multiplication in the new set **R**.

EXERCISES

1. Let $a = \lim_{n\to\infty} a_n$ and let $b = \lim_{n\to\infty} b_n$. Prove that $a = b$ if and only if $\lim_{n\to\infty} (a_n - b_n) = 0$. Use this fact in both R and R' to show that the mapping f defined in the proof of Theorem 3.2 is well defined and one-to-one.

2. Prove that f of Theorem 3.2 is an isomorphism.

3. Let a, b be two real numbers, with $a < b$. Prove that there is a rational number c such that $a < c < b$.

4. Let L be a complete ordered field containing **Q** as a subfield and such that for any element c of L there is an integer $n > c$. Prove that L is a field of real numbers. [Hint: Show that for $e > 0$ in L there is a rational number a such that $|a - c| < e$. By taking smaller and smaller values of e, for example $1/n$, conclude that there is a sequence in **Q** having c as limit.]

4. *Some properties of* **R**

Consider the set S of all *rational* numbers r such that $r^2 \leq 2$. Since, for example, $(3/2)^2 > 2$, it follows that all elements of S are less than $3/2$. As we have seen in Sec. 1, there is no element in S whose square is 2, and S has no greatest element. We shall now show that this kind of situation does not occur in the field of real numbers **R**.

DEFINITION 4.1 *Let S be any set of real numbers. Then a real number b is called an* upper bound *of S if $b \geq a$ for every element a in S. A real number c is called the* least upper bound *(l.u.b.) of S if it is an upper bound and if $c \leq b$ for every upper bound b of S. [Lower bounds and the greatest lower bound (g.l.b.) are defined in an analogous fashion.]*

Observe that there cannot be two least upper bounds of S. For if c, c' are both l.u.b. of S, then by definition $c \leq c'$ and similarly $c' \leq c$, whence $c = c'$.

EXAMPLE 1 Let S be the set of all real numbers r such that $0 \leq r < 1$. Then 1 is an upper bound for S; so is 150,322,121.52. It is easily seen that 1 is the l.u.b. of S. Similarly -4000 is a lower bound for S; so is 0, and in fact 0 is the g.l.b. of S. Thus this S happens to contain its g.l.b. but not its l.u.b.

EXAMPLE 2 Let S be the set consisting of all positive integers n and their reciprocals $1/n$. Then S does not have an upper bound. But any number ≤ 0 is a lower bound for S, and 0 is easily seen to be its g.l.b. It is not in S.

THEOREM 4.1 *Let S be any non-empty set of real numbers. If S has an upper bound, then it must have a least upper bound.*

Proof. Let a be an element of S, and let b be an upper bound for S. Thus by definition $a \leq b$. By Theorem 3.1 there exist integers M and N such that $M < a$ and $b < N$. Now for each $k = 0, 1, 2, \ldots$ the integers n for which $n/10^k$ is *not* an upper bound of S form a non-empty set T_k (because $10^k \cdot M$ is in T_k) which contains no integers greater than $10^k N$. Therefore (by Exercise 6, Sec. 4, Chap. 2) T_k has a greatest element n_k. Thus n_k is the largest integer such that $n_k/10^k$ is not an upper bound of S.

We now show that the sequence n_0, $n_1/10$, $n_2/10^2$, . . . is a Cauchy sequence whose limit c is the least upper bound of S.

First of all, $n_k/10^k = (10^h \cdot n_k)/10^{k+h}$, and so by definition of n_{k+h} we have $10^h \cdot n_k \leq n_{k+h}$. But by definition of n_k the number $n_k + 1/10^k$ must be an upper bound of S, while $n_{k+h}/10^{k+n}$ is not, and so $n_{k+h}/10^{k+h} < (n_k + 1)/10^k$. Putting $l = k + h$ we have then all together

4.1 $$\frac{n_k}{10^k} \leq \frac{n_l}{10^l} < \frac{n_k + 1}{10^k} \qquad \text{for every } l \geq k$$

Therefore, if $l \geq k$,

4.2 $$0 \leq \frac{n_l}{10^l} - \frac{n_k}{10^k} < \frac{1}{10^k}$$

Now let e be any positive real number. Then there exists an integer P such that $1/P < e$ (by Corollary 1, Theorem 3.1). Then $1/10^P < 1/P < e$, and so there follows from (4.2)

$$\frac{n_l}{10^l} - \frac{n_k}{10^k} < e \qquad \text{for all } k, l > P$$

Thus the sequence n_0, $n_1/10$, $n_2/10^2$, . . . is indeed a Cauchy sequence in $\mathbf{R}$. Since $\mathbf{R}$ is complete, it has a limit $c = \lim_{k \to \infty} n_k/10^k$. Since the numbers $n_k/10^k$ increase with k, by (4.1), it follows that

$$\frac{n_k}{10^k} \leq c \qquad \text{for all } k = 0, 1, 2, \ldots$$

Suppose now that S contains an element $a > c$. Then we have also $a > n_k/10^k$ for all k, from just above. We show that this is impossible. For if $a - c > 0$, then there is an integer m such that $1/m < a - c$, whence $1/10^m < a - c$ (Corollary 1, Theorem 3.1). Then adding the inequalities $n_m/10^m \leq c$ and $1/10^m < a - c$ we get $(n_m + 1)/10^m < a$, showing that $(n_m + 1)/10^m$ is *not* an upper bound for S and therefore contradicting the definition of n_m. Hence we must have $a \leq c$ for every element of S, and so c is an upper bound for S.

Suppose now that c' is also an upper bound for S, with $c' < c$. Since $n_k/10^k$ is not an upper bound for S, there is an element of S which is greater than $n_k/10^k$. But it must be $\leq c'$, and so we have

$$\frac{n_k}{10^k} < c' < c$$

But then $c - n_k/10^k > c' - c$ for all k, contradicting the fact that $c = \lim_{n\to\infty} n_k/10^k$. Hence we must have $c \leq c'$, and therefore c is the l.u.b. of S.

Q.E.D.

The existence of a least upper bound of any subset S of **R** which has an upper bound is actually a characteristic property of **R**, in the sense that it could be used in place of completeness in Definition 3.2. See Exercise 5 below.

If we examine the foregoing proof carefully, it becomes evident that we have in effect produced a decimal expansion of c. For let us set

$$a_0 = n_0,\ a_1 = n_1 - 10n_0,\ \ldots,\ a_k = n_k - 10n_{k-1},\ \ldots$$

Then we have

$$a_0 + \frac{a_1}{10} + \cdots + \frac{a_k}{10^k}$$
$$= n_0 + \frac{n_1 - 10n_0}{10} + \frac{n_2 - 10n_1}{10^2} + \cdots + \frac{n_k - 10n_{k-1}}{10^k} = \frac{n_k}{10^k}$$

Furthermore, putting $l = k + 1$ in (4.1) we get $10n_k \leq n_{k+1} < 10n_k + 10$, or $0 \leq n_{k+1} - 10n_k < 10$. Therefore $0 \leq a_{k+1} \leq 9$ for $k \geq 0$, or $0 \leq a_k < 9$ for $k \geq 1$.

Now let us assume that $c > 0$. From (4.2) it follows readily that

4.3 $$0 \leq c - \frac{n_k}{10^k} \leq \frac{1}{10^k} \qquad \text{for } k = 0, 1, 2, \ldots$$

For otherwise we would have $c - n_k/10^k = 1/10^k + y$, where $y > 0$. But from (4.2)

$$c - \frac{n_k}{10^k} = c - \frac{n_l}{10^l} + \frac{n_l}{10^l} - \frac{n_k}{10^k} < c - \frac{n_l}{10^l} + \frac{1}{10^k}$$

this for all $l > k$. But then $1/10^k + y < c - n_l/10^l + 1/10^k$, whence $c - n_l/10^l > y$ for all $l > k$. This contradicts the fact that $c = \lim_{l\to\infty} n_l/10^l$ and therefore proves (4.3).

Putting $k = 0$ in (4.3) we get $0 \leq c - n_0 \leq 1$. Since we have assumed $c > 0$ and since n_0 is an integer, it follows that $m_0 = a_0 \geq 0$. Hence the numbers $a_0, a_1, a_2, \ldots$ defined above determine a decimal $A = a_0.a_1a_2a_3 \cdots$, and for this decimal we have from above

$$A_k = a_0 + \frac{a_1}{10} + \cdots + \frac{a_k}{10^k} = \frac{n_k}{10^k}$$

Then by definition of c we have $c = \lim_{k\to\infty} A_k$, and moreover, from (4.3) follows $0 \leq c - A_k \leq 1/10^k$. Hence if we carry over the definition of decimal expansion

(Definition 4.2, Chap. 3) to the real-number system **R**, then we have proved that A is a decimal expansion of the positive real number c.

Now given any positive real number c, it is obviously the l.u.b. of the set S consisting of c alone, and therefore the foregoing argument applies to any $c > 0$. Hence we have the following theorem:

THEOREM 4.2 *Every positive real number c has a decimal expansion $A = a_0.a_1a_2a_3 \cdots$. That is, for the rational numbers*

$$A_k = a_0 + \frac{a_1}{10} + \cdots + \frac{a_k}{10^k}$$

we have $0 \leq c - A_k \leq 1/10^k$ for $k = 1, 2, 3$, etc. Furthermore $c = \lim_{k \to \infty} A_k$.

It follows conversely that every decimal A is the expansion of some real number. For by Proposition 2.1 the numbers $A_1, A_2, A_3, \ldots$ form a Cauchy sequence, and it must have a limit c in **R**. The proof of Theorem 4.4, Chap. 3, holds good in **R** as is easily seen, and it shows that decimal expansions are unique except in the case of terminating decimals. Since only rational numbers have terminating decimals, it follows that the decimal expansion of any irrational number is unique.

COROLLARY *The set of real numbers* **R** *is uncountable.*

Proof. We show in fact that the set I of real numbers x such that $0 < x < 1$ is uncountable. Suppose to the contrary that the elements of I can be enumerated in some order, say a, b, c, d, etc. Represent these numbers by their decimal expansions A, B, C, D, etc. Now select a decimal $X = 0.x_1x_2x_3 \cdots$ as follows: Choose x_1 to be different from the first digit a_1 in A; choose x_2 to be different from the second digit b_2 of B; then choose x_3 to be different from the third digit c_3 of C; and so forth. This can certainly be done in such a way that X is not recurrent. Now X must represent some real number x in the set I. But X differs in at least one place from every one of the decimals A, B, C, D, etc., and therefore the number x cannot appear in the list $a, b, c, d, \ldots$, a contradiction.

Q.E.D.

We now return to the question raised in Sec. 1, the existence of roots.

THEOREM 4.3 *Let r be a positive real number, and let n be a positive integer. Then there is a unique positive real number x such that $x^n = r$.*

Proof. We first observe that it suffices to prove this for $r < 1$. For if $r > 1$, let k be an integer such than $k > r$. Then also $k^n > r$, and so $r' = r/k^n$ is less than 1. If now $x'^n = r'$, then for $x = kx'$ we have $x^n = k^n r' = r$.

Then, assuming $r < 1$, let S be the set of all numbers y such that $y^n \leq r$. Clearly 1 is an upper bound for S, and therefore S has a least upper bound x. We show that $x^n = r$.

To do so let a be a number such that $|a| < 1$. From the binomial theorem we have

$$\begin{aligned}(x + a)^n &= x^n + nx^{n-1}a + \cdots + nxa^{n-1} + a^n \\ &= x^n + a \cdot (nx^{n-1} + \cdots + nxa^{n-2} + a^{n-1})\end{aligned}$$

Since $|a| < 1$ it is clear that the expression in parentheses is smaller than what is obtained by replacing a by 1, namely

$$c = nx^{n-1} + \cdots + nx + 1$$

Therefore we have

$$|(x + a)^n - x^n| < c \cdot |a|$$

If now $x^n < r$, take $a = (r - x^n)/c$. Since $r < 1$, $c > 1$ it follows that $a < 1$, and we have

$$0 < (x + a)^n - x^n < c \cdot \frac{r - x^n}{c} = r - x^n$$

and so $(x + a)^n < r$. Therefore $x + a = x + (r - x^n)/c$ is in the set S and is bigger than x, a contradiction. Hence $x^n < r$ is impossible.

If $x^n > r$, take again $a = (r - x^n)/c$. Since 1 is an upper bound for S, we have $x \leq 1$, and so $-1 < a < 0$. Then $x + a < x$, and so $(x + a)^n < x^n$. Hence, from above, $|(x + a)^n - x^n| = x^n - (x + a)^n < c \cdot |a| = c \cdot x^n - r/c = x^n - r$, whence $-(x + a)^n < -r$, or $r < (x + a)^n$. Therefore $x + a = x + (r - x^n)/c$ is an upper bound for S but is smaller than x, a contradiction. Hence $x^n > r$ is also impossible, and so $x^n = r$. If $0 < x' < x$, then $x'^n < x^n = r$. If $0 < x < x'$, then $r = x^n < x'^n$. Hence x is the only positive number such that $x^n = r$. Q.E.D.

For any positive r the unique positive number x such that $x^n = r$ is usually denoted by $r^{1/n}$, or by $\sqrt[n]{r}$. We define

$$r^{m/n} = (r^{1/n})^m$$

for any integer m. Then

$$(r^{m/n})^n = (r^{1/n})^{mn} = (r^{1/n})^{nm} = ((r^{1/n})^n)^m = r^m$$

and so $r^{m/n} = (r^m)^{1/n}$, by uniqueness of positive nth roots. If $m/n = a/b$ (a, b integers, with $b > 0$), then $mb = na$. Therefore $(r^{a/b})^n = (r^{1/b})^{an} = (r^{1/b})^{bm} = r^m$, showing that $r^{a/b} = r^{m/n}$, again by uniqueness. Hence the symbol r^c is defined for any rational number c. It is easy to verify that the usual rules for exponents continue to hold for rational exponents.

We conclude this chapter with a brief mention of infinite series. Let c_0, c_1, c_2, c_3, etc., be real numbers. Our problem is to attach some meaning to an "infinite sum"

$$c_0 + c_1 + c_2 + c_3 + \cdots$$

or more compactly,

4.4 $$\sum_{k=0}^{\infty} c_k$$

This is easily done in many cases as follows: Consider the sequence

$$s_0 = c_0,\ s_1 = c_0 + c_1,\ s_2 = c_0 + c_1 + c_2,\ s_3 = c_0 + c_1 + c_2 + c_3, \text{ etc.}$$

These are called *partial sums* of the *infinite series* (4.4).

DEFINITION 4.2 *If the sequence of partial sums* $s_0, s_1, s_2, \ldots$ *is a Cauchy sequence, then the series* (4.4) *is said to* converge, *and its* sum *is defined to be* $\lim_{n\to\infty} s_n$.

Then we can write

$$\sum_{k=0}^{\infty} c_k = \lim_{n\to\infty} \sum_{k=0}^{n} c_k = \lim_{n\to\infty} (c_0 + c_1 + \cdots + c_n)$$

provided the conditions are fulfilled.

EXAMPLE 3 Let x be a real number such that $-1 < x < 1$, and for c_k above take x^k. Then

$$\sum_{k=0}^{\infty} x^k = \lim_{n\to\infty} (1 + x + x^2 + \cdots + x^n) = \lim_{n\to\infty} \frac{1 - x^n}{1 - x} = \frac{1}{1 - x}$$

The proof of this is the same as that of Proposition 2.7, save that the restriction to rational numbers is no longer necessary. The series does not converge if $|x| \geq 1$. The series is called the *geometric* series.

EXAMPLE 4 Let $A = a_0.a_1a_2a_3 \cdots$ be a decimal. Take $c_k = a_k/10^k$ in (4.4). The partial sum $c_0 + c_1 + \cdots c_n$ is what we have called A_n. Hence if r is the real number represented by the decimal A, then we have (Theorem 4.2)

$$\sum_{k=0}^{\infty} \frac{a_k}{10^k} = \lim_{n\to\infty} A_n = r$$

EXAMPLE 5 For any real number x the series

$$\sum_{k=0}^{\infty} \frac{x^k}{k!}$$

converges. The sum of the series is usually denoted by e^x. The operation $x \to e^x$ gives a mapping from **R** to itself, and it is called the *exponential function*. Taking $x = 1$, the number e^1, or simply e, plays an important role in mathematics. An approximate value for e is 2.71828.

EXAMPLE 6 The two series

$$\sum_{k=0}^{\infty} \frac{(-1)^k x^{2k}}{(2k)!} = 1 - \frac{x^2}{2!} + \frac{x^4}{4!} - + \cdots$$

and

$$\sum_{k=1}^{\infty} \frac{(-1)^{k-1}x^{2k-1}}{(2k-1)!} = x - \frac{x^3}{3!} + \frac{x^5}{5!} - + \cdots$$

converge for any real number x. The sum of the first one is $\cos x$, and the sum of the second is $\sin x$.

It is not difficult to prove that convergent infinite series can be manipulated in much the same way as ordinary finite sums. These matters are treated in any standard calculus text.

EXERCISES

1. Let r be a positive real number, and let a, b be rational numbers. Prove that $r^a \cdot r^b = r^{a+b}$ and $(r^a)^b = r^{ab}$.

2. Let a be a positive rational number. Show that if $0 < r < s$, then $r^a < s^a$.

3. Let a, b be rational numbers with $0 < a < b$. Show that $r^a < r^b$ if $r > 1$ and $r^a > r^b$ if $r < 1$.

4. Let $c_1, c_2, c_3, \ldots$ be a Cauchy sequence of rational numbers; let r be a positive real number. Show that $r^{c_1}, r^{c_2}, r^{c_3}, \ldots$ is a Cauchy sequence.

***5.** Let L be an ordered field containing **Q** as a subfield. Suppose that every non-empty subset of L which has an upper bound must have a least upper bound. Furthermore, suppose that L is *Archimedean;* i.e., that for any element c of L there is an integer $n > c$. Prove that L is a field of real numbers.

6. Let $a_1 \leq a_2 \leq a_3 \leq \cdots$ be a sequence of real numbers, and suppose that there is a number b such that $a_n < b$ for all n. Show that $a_1, a_2, a_3, \ldots$ is a Cauchy sequence.

7. Let S be a subset of **R** having a lower bound. Prove that S has a greatest lower bound.

8. Let m be a positive integer, and let $\mathbf{Q}(\sqrt{m})$ denote the set of all numbers $a + b\sqrt{m}$ in **R**, where a, b are rational. Prove that $\mathbf{Q}(\sqrt{m})$ is a subfield of **R**.

9. Analyze the method taught in high schools for extracting square roots. Devise a similar method for extracting cube roots.

10. Let S be an infinite set of real numbers, all lying between two fixed numbers a, b. Prove that S contains a Cauchy sequence. [This is the Bolzano-Weierstrass theorem. Hint: Divide the interval from a to b into two equal parts, then repeat that for each part, etc.]

***11.** Prove that the series $\sum_{k=0}^{\infty} \frac{x^k}{k!}$ converges for any x. [Hint: Let n be an integer $\geq |x|$, and show that $\frac{|x^k|}{k!} \leq \frac{n^n}{n!} \cdot \left(\frac{n}{n+1}\right)^{k-n}$ for large k. Then compare with the geometric series.]

5

The field of complex numbers

1. The square root of -1†

For any nonzero element x of an ordered integral domain, the element x^2 is always positive. In particular this is the case for any real number, and therefore the equation $x^2 = -1$ cannot have a solution in the field of real numbers. It was this deficiency that led to the introduction of complex numbers into mathematics. The present chapter is concerned with the problem of enlarging the real-number field in such a way that $x^2 = -1$ will have a solution.

DEFINITION 1.1 *A field C is called a* field of complex numbers *if*

(1) *C contains the field of real numbers* **R** *as a subfield.*

(2) *C contains an element, denoted by i, such that $i^2 = -1$.*

(3) *No subfield of C, other than C itself, contains both* **R** *and i.*

In Sec. 2 we shall see that it is very easy to build such a field C out of **R**. Another construction is given in Example 8, Sec. 4, Chap. 6. In this section we shall see that any two fields C and C' satisfying Definition 1.1 are interchangeable.

THEOREM 1.1 *C being a field of complex numbers, any element of C can be expressed uniquely in the form $a + bi$, where a and b are real numbers.*

Proof. Let F be the set of all elements $a + bi$ in C, where a, b are real. We show that F is a subfield of C. In fact, let u, v be any two elements of F. By definition of F we have

$$u = a + bi \qquad v = c + di \qquad \text{with } a, b, c, d \text{ real}$$

Then

$$u \pm v = (a + bi) \pm (c + di) = (a \pm c) + (b \pm d) \cdot i$$

Therefore $u + v$ and $u - v$ are elements of F. Furthermore,

$$\begin{aligned} uv = (a + bi)(c + di) &= ac + adi + bci + bdi^2 \\ &= (ac - bd) + (ad + bc) \cdot i \end{aligned}$$

Hence uv is in F. If $u \neq 0$, then

$$\frac{1}{u} = \frac{1}{a + bi} = \frac{1}{a + bi} \cdot \frac{a - bi}{a - bi} = \frac{a - bi}{a^2 + b^2} = \frac{a}{a^2 + b^2} - \frac{b}{a^2 + b^2} \cdot i$$

† Except for Sec. 4, the only fact needed about **R** is that it is an ordered field containing the (positive) nth root of any positive element.

and so the inverse of a nonzero element of F is also in F. It follows easily that F is a subfield of C. Furthermore F contains all elements $a + 0 \cdot i = a$, where a is real, and so F contains **R**. F also contains $0 + 1 \cdot i = i$, and therefore by (3) of Definition 1.1 we must have $F = C$. Hence every element of C can be expressed in the form $a + bi$, with a and b real. Now suppose that $a + bi = a' + b'i$, where a, a', b, b' are real. Subtracting the two we get $(a - a') + (b - b') \cdot i = 0$. Multiplying this by $(a - a') - (b - b') \cdot i$ we get

$$(a - a')^2 + (b - b')^2 = 0$$

and since $a - a'$ and $b - b'$ are real, it follows that $a = a'$, $b = b'$. Q.E.D.

Hence from $a + bi = a' + b'i$ we can conclude $a = a'$, $b = b'$, provided a, a', b, b', are *real.*

COROLLARY *The only elements in C whose squares are equal to -1 are i and $-i$.*

Proof. Let j be an element of C such that $j^2 = -1$. By the theorem we can write $j = a + bi$, where a, b are uniquely determined real numbers. Then $j^2 = -1 = (a + bi)^2 = (a^2 - b^2) + 2abi$. Since $-1 = -1 + 0 \cdot i$, it follows from the uniqueness that $a^2 - b^2 = -1$ and $2ab = 0$. From this we see that $a = 0$ and $b = \pm 1$. Q.E.D.

We shall call i and $-i$ *imaginary units* in C. Observe that Theorem 1.1 holds if we replace i by $-i$. For if $u = a + bi$, with a, b real, then also $u = a' + b'(-i)$, where $a' = a$, $b' = -b$.

The following theorem shows the essential uniqueness of fields of complex numbers.

THEOREM 1.2 *Let C and C' be two fields of complex numbers and let i and i' be imaginary units in C, C', respectively. Then there is one and only one isomorphism from C to C' which sends i into i' and sends real numbers into themselves.*

Proof. If f is an isomorphism with the required properties, then for any element $a + bi$ of C (with *real* a and b) we have $f(a + bi) = f(a) + f(bi) = f(a) + f(b) \cdot f(i) = a + b \cdot f(i) = a + bi'$. Hence there cannot be two such isomorphisms. Conversely if we define the mapping f from C to C' by $f(a + bi) = a + bi'$, then it is easily verified, using Theorem 1.1, that f is an isomorphism of the required kind. Q.E.D.

REMARK. There are many isomorphisms from C to C' (or from C to itself) which do not send every real number into itself.

As we have done with **Z**, **Q**, and **R**, we now suppose that some field of complex numbers is fixed once for all (for example the one constructed in Sec. 2). We denote it henceforth by **C**. Its elements will be called *complex numbers.*

If we take **C** for both C and C' in Theorem 1.2, and $-i$ for i', we get the following:

COROLLARY *There is one and only one isomorphism from* **C** *to itself which sends i into $-i$ and sends every real number into itself. Namely, if $u = a + bi$, where a and b are real, then the isomorphism sends u into $a - bi$.*

This isomorphism is very important. Some properties of it are listed below. First of all, if u is a complex number and if we write $u = a + bi$, where a and b are real, then a is called the *real* part of u, written Re $\{u\}$, and b is called the *imaginary* part of u, written Im $\{u\}$. If $b = 0$, then u is of course a real number; if $a = 0$, then u is said to be a *pure imaginary* number. The isomorphism of the corollary sends u into $a - bi$, and that number is called the *complex conjugate* of u, usually denoted by $\bar{u}$. We have

1.1 $\overline{a + bi} = a - bi$ *if a, b are real*

1.2 $\bar{i} = -i \qquad -\bar{i} = i$

1.3 $\bar{\bar{u}} = u$ *(that is, u is the conjugate of $\bar{u}$)*

1.4 $\bar{u} = u$ *if and only if u is real*

1.5 $\bar{u} = -u$ *if and only if u is pure imaginary*

1.6 $u + \bar{u} = 2a = 2\,\text{Re}\,\{u\} \qquad u - \bar{u} = 2bi = 2i\,\text{Im}\,\{u\}$

1.7 $u\bar{u} = a^2 + b^2$

The quantity

1.8 $|u| = \sqrt{u\bar{u}} = \sqrt{a^2 + b^2}$

is called the *absolute value*, or *modulus*, of u. Note that $|u| = 0$ if and only if $u = 0$. Clearly $|\bar{u}| = |u|$.

Since any isomorphism (in particular the isomorphism $u \to \bar{u}$) is by definition compatible with addition and multiplication, we have the following rules (easily verified directly):

1.9 $\overline{u \pm v} = \bar{u} \pm \bar{v}$

1.10 $\overline{uv} = \bar{u} \cdot \bar{v}$

Now $|uv|^2 = uv \cdot \overline{uv}$, by (1.8), and $uv \cdot \overline{uv} = uv \cdot \bar{u}\bar{v} = u\bar{u} \cdot v\bar{v} = |u|^2 \cdot |v|^2$, by (1.10); hence

1.11 $|uv| = |u| \cdot |v|$

Furthermore

1.12 $|u + v| \leq |u| + |v|$ (triangle inequality)

To prove this we have

$$|u + v|^2 = (u + v) \cdot \overline{(u + v)} = (u + v) \cdot (\bar{u} + \bar{v}) \quad \text{by (1.9)}$$
$$= u\bar{u} + v\bar{u} + u\bar{v} + v\bar{v}$$

Put $w = u\bar{v}$. Then $\bar{w} = \bar{u}v$, by (1.10) and (1.3). Therefore $u\bar{v} + v\bar{u} = w + \bar{w} = 2\,\mathrm{Re}\,\{w\}$, by (1.6). It is plain from (1.8) that $|\mathrm{Re}\,\{w\}| \leq |w|$. But by (1.11) we have $|w| = |u\bar{v}| = |u| \cdot |\bar{v}| = |u| \cdot |v|$. Therefore we get

$$|u + v|^2 \leq |u|^2 + 2|u| \cdot |v| + |v|^2 = (|u| + |v|)^2$$

from which (1.12) follows.

By a similar argument it is not hard to prove that

1.13 $$|u - v| \geq ||u| - |v||$$

THEOREM 1.3 *Let $a_0, a_1, a_2, \ldots, a_n$ be real numbers. If u is a complex number satisfying the equation*

$$a_0x^n + a_1x^{n-1} + \cdots + a_{n-1}x + a_n = 0$$

then so is $\bar{u}$.†

Proof. Set $w = a_0u^n + a_1u^{n-1} + \cdots + a_n$. By assumption, $w = 0$. But from (1.9), (1.10) we have $\bar{w} = \bar{a}_0\,\bar{u}^n + \bar{a}_1\,\bar{u}^{n-1} + \cdots + \bar{a}_n$. Since the a's are real and $\bar{w} = 0$, the assertion follows. Q.E.D.

The following theorem expresses a very remarkable property of the field **C**. The theorem is usually called the *fundamental theorem of algebra*. It is no longer considered to have that exalted status, but it is nonetheless very important. Its proof is beyond the scope of this book but can be found in any standard text on the theory of functions of a complex variable.

THEOREM 1.4 *Let $a_0, a_1, \ldots, a_n$ be any complex numbers, with $n > 0$ and $a_0 \neq 0$. Then the equation*

$$a_0x^n + a_1x^{n-1} + \cdots + a_{n-1}x + a_n = 0$$

has a solution in **C**.‡

As we shall see in the following chapter, it is easy to deduce from this that the equation has exactly n solutions (some of them possibly repeated). For this reason the field **C** is said to be *algebraically closed*. It can be shown that every field can be embedded as a subfield in an algebraically closed field.

The field **C** cannot be an ordered field, since $i^2 = -1 < 0$. Nonetheless it is possible to define a "distance" between any two elements u and v of **C**, namely, the real number $|u - v|$. A geometrical interpretation of this is given in Sec. 3. In Sec. 4 we show that it can be used to define Cauchy sequences in **C**.

† We mean that, if the equation becomes true when x is replaced by u, then it becomes true when x is replaced by the conjugate of u.

‡ That is, there is a number in **C** such that the equation becomes true when x is replaced by that number.

EXERCISES

1. Express the following complex numbers in the form $a + bi$, with a and b real:

(a) $(2 + 3i)^2$ (b) $(\frac{1}{2} + \frac{2}{3}i)(3 - i)$

(c) $1/i$ (d) $\dfrac{1}{1 + i}$

(e) $\left(\dfrac{1}{2} + \dfrac{\sqrt{3}}{2} i\right)^3$ (f) $\dfrac{1}{1 - i}$

(g) $\dfrac{7 - 6i}{2 + 3i}$ (h) $\dfrac{(5 + 2i)^3}{1 - i}$

(i) $\dfrac{1 + 2i}{(2 + i)^3}$ (j) $\left(\dfrac{1}{\sqrt{2}} + \dfrac{i}{\sqrt{2}}\right)^2$

2. Show that the set of all 2×2 matrices of the form

$$\begin{pmatrix} a & b \\ -b & a \end{pmatrix}$$

with a and b real numbers, is a field of complex numbers if multiplication and addition are defined as in Exercise 3, Sec. 2, Chap. 2.

3. Let a be a positive real number. Show that $\pm i \cdot \sqrt{a}$ are the only two solutions in **C** of the equation $x^2 + a = 0$.

4. Let m be a positive integer, and write $\sqrt{-m}$ for $i \cdot \sqrt{m}$ (see Example 3). Let **Q** $(\sqrt{-m})$ be the subset of **C** consisting of all numbers $a + b\sqrt{-m}$, where a, b are *rational* numbers. Prove that **Q** $(\sqrt{-m})$ is a subfield of **C**.

5. Find two solutions in **C** of the equation $x^2 + i = 0$.

6. Show that the fields **Q** and **R** are not algebraically closed.

2. *A construction of* **C**; *quaternions*

Here we shall give a very simple construction of a field of complex numbers from **R**. It can be taken for our fixed complex field **C**. The construction is very closely related to Exercise 2 above.

Let **C** denote the set of all ordered pairs of real numbers (a, b). We define two binary operations in the set **C** by the rules

2.1
$$\begin{aligned}(a, b) + (c, d) &= (a + c, b + d)\\ (a, b) \cdot (c, d) &= (ac - bd, ad + bc)\end{aligned}$$

where in the right-hand members are indicated operations in **R**. The two formulas above are not really very mysterious; the attentive reader will observe a great similarity between them and some of the calculations occuring in the proof of Theorem 1.1

It is a perfectly straightforward matter to verify that **C** with the two operations of (2.1) is a commutative ring. That is, it satisfies Definition 2.1, Chap. 2, and multiplication is commutative. The zero element of **C** is the pair $(0, 0)$; the inverse of an element (a, b) for addition is $(-a, -b)$. The unit element of **C** is the pair $(1, 0)$. But **C** is in fact a field, for if $(a, b) \neq (0, 0)$, then it is easily verified, using (2.1), that the element

$$\left(\frac{a}{a^2 + b^2}, \frac{-b}{a^2 + b^2}\right)$$

is the inverse of (a, b) for multiplication.

Now let R be the subset of **C** consisting of all pairs $(a, 0)$. From (2.1) we have $(a, 0) + (b, 0) = (a + b, 0)$ and $(a, 0) \cdot (b, 0) = (ab, 0)$. It follows readily that R is a subfield of **C** and that the mapping $\mathbf{R} \to R$ defined by $a \to (a, 0)$ is an isomorphism.

The field **C** just defined does not contain **R** itself, but it contains an isomorphic copy R of **R**, which is just as good. If we want to be very meticulous here we can simply replace each element $(a, 0)$ of **C** by a itself, and in that way we obtain a field which really contains the original **R** as a subfield. We shall not bother about this point.

Now in **C** we have $(0, 1)^2 = (0, 1) \cdot (0, 1) = (-1, 0)$, by (2.1), and $(-1, 0)$ is the same as $-(1, 0)$, being the inverse for addition of the unit element $(1, 0)$ of **C**. Therefore if we put $i = (0, 1)$, then we have $i^2 = -(1, 0)$, or simply $i^2 = -1$ if we agree to replace $(1, 0)$ by 1. Furthermore it follows from (2.1) that

$$(a, b) = (a, 0) + (b, 0) \cdot (0, 1)$$

or

$$(a, b) = (a, 0) + (b, 0) \cdot i$$

Again if we agree to replace $(a, 0)$ and $(b, 0)$ by a and b, this becomes $(a, b) = a + bi$. It follows easily that **C** satisfies Definition 1.1 and so is a field of complex numbers.

Let a, b be two real numbers. In **C** the expression $a^2 + b^2$ can be factored into a product of two terms containing only first powers, namely, $a^2 + b^2 = (a + bi)(a - bi)$. But in general $a^2 + b^2 + c^2$ or $a^2 + b^2 + c^2 + d^2$ cannot be factored in this way. By a procedure analogous to that above, one can construct a system U in which such expressions can be factored. Namely, let U be the set of all quadruples (a, b, c, d) of real numbers. Define addition in U by

$$(a, b, c, d) + (a', b', c', d') = (a + a', b + b', c + c', d + d')$$

entirely analogous to the first equation of (2.1). Multiplication in U is somewhat more complicated. A formula similar to the second one of (2.1) can be written down. Without actually doing that (it is rather lengthy) we can describe the result as follows: Write $e = (1, 0, 0, 0)$, $j = (0, 1, 0, 0)$, $k = (0, 0, 1, 0)$, and $l = (0, 0, 0, 1)$. Then the rule gives the following:

$$eu = ue = u$$

for any element $u = (a, b, c, d)$ in U. Hence e is the unit element in U. Further,

2.2
$$\begin{aligned} j^2 &= k^2 = l^2 = -e \\ jk &= l \qquad kj = -l \\ kl &= j \qquad lk = -j \\ lj &= k \qquad jl = -k \end{aligned}$$

and if $u = (a, b, c, d)$ is any element of U, then $(a, b, c, d) = (a, 0, 0, 0) + (b, 0, 0, 0) \cdot j + (c, 0, 0, 0) \cdot k + (d, 0, 0, 0) \cdot l$, and $vu = uv$ for any v of the type $v = (r, 0, 0, 0)$. It turns out furthermore that the distributive law holds. Then using these equations it is easy to calculate any product in U. It is not hard to verify that U is a ring and that the elements $(a, 0, 0, 0)$ form a subring which is isomorphic to **R**. For simplicity of notation let us therefore write a for $(a, 0, 0, 0)$. In particular instead of e we write simply 1. Then the last equation above is

$$(a, b, c, d) = a + bj + ck + dl$$

Then, for example, we have

$$(0, 3, 2, 0) \cdot (1, 1, 0, -1) = (3j + 2k) \cdot (1 + j - l)$$

Using the distributive law and the fact that any element $a = (a, 0, 0, 0)$ commutes with every element of U, we get

$$3j + 3j^2 - ejl + 2k + 2kj - 2kl$$

Using (2.2), this becomes $3j - 3 + 3k + 2k - 2l - 2j = -3 + j + 5k - 2l = (-3, 1, 5, -2)$. We have in general

$$\begin{aligned} (a, b, c, d) \cdot (a, -b, -c, -d) &= (a + bi + cj + dk)(a - bi - cj - dk) \\ &= a^2 + b^2 + c^2 + d^2 \end{aligned}$$

as is easily verified, and therefore $a^2 + b^2 + c^2 + d^2$ can be factored in U in the manner indicated. Moreover if $(a, b, c, d) \neq (0, 0, 0, 0)$, then from the equation above there follows

$$(a, b, c, d)^{-1} = \left(\frac{a}{r}, \frac{-b}{r}, \frac{-c}{r}, \frac{-d}{r}\right)$$

where

$$r = a^2 + b^2 + c^2 + d^2$$

Hence every nonzero element of U has an inverse for multiplication. Consequently U satisfies all the axioms for a field except one: Multiplication in U is not commutative in general. A system of this sort is called a *skew field* or a *division algebra*.

All the elements $(a, b, 0, 0) = a + bj$ in U form a subfield isomorphic to **C**; so do all the elements $(a, 0, b, 0)$ and also all the elements $(a, 0, 0, b)$. U is called the system of *quaternions*. It was discovered by K. F. Gauss (1777–1855) and, independently, by Sir William Rowan Hamilton (1805–1865).

We observe from (2.2) that -1 has more than two square roots in U, namely, $\pm j$, $\pm k$, $\pm l$. This is a consequence of the fact that multiplication in U is not commutative, as we shall see in the next chapter.

EXERCISE

Show that the set of all 2×2 complex matrices of the form

$$\begin{pmatrix} a + bi & c + di \\ -c + di & a - bi \end{pmatrix} \qquad a, b, c, d \text{ real}$$

form a system isomorphic to U, multiplication and addition being defined as in Example 3, Sec. 2, Chap. 2.

3. A geometric interpretation of addition and multiplication of complex numbers

In this section we shall depart temporarily from our axiomatic development. We shall borrow some simple results from geometry and trigonometry in order to show how operations with complex numbers can be represented pictorially.

If x and y are real numbers, then we can think of them as the coordinates of a point in the plane, and consequently we can represent the complex number $x + iy$ by that point. For example, the numbers 1, i, $2 + i$ and their conjugates $-i$, $2 - i$ are so represented in Fig. 1. In general we think of x in $x + iy$ as the horizontal coordinate and of y as the vertical coordinate.

If $z = x + iy$ and $w = u + iv$ are two complex numbers, with x, y, u, and v real, then $z + w = (x + u) + i(y + v)$, and it is easy to see that this corresponds to Fig. 2. Thus the point representing $z + w$ is obtained by completing the parallelogram whose first three vertices are 0, z, w.

Multiplication is a little more complicated. Recall that if $z = x + iy$ (x and y real), then $\bar{z} = x - iy$ and $|z| = \sqrt{z\bar{z}} = \sqrt{x^2 + y^2}$ (see Sec. 1). Consider Fig. 3 (in which we assume for simplicity that x, y are positive).

Figure 1

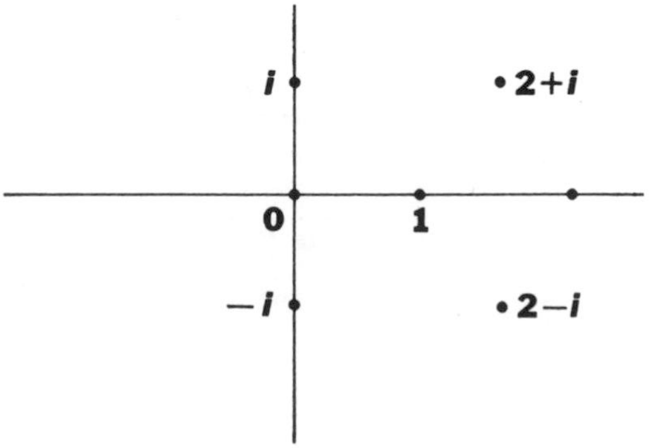

From trigonometry we have

3.1 $$x = r\cos\theta \qquad y = r\sin\theta \qquad r = \sqrt{x^2 + y^2} = |z|$$

The angle† θ (determined only up to multiples of 2π) is called the *argument* of z, denoted by arg z.

From (3.1) we observe that z can be written in the form

3.2 $$z = r(\cos\theta + i\sin\theta)$$

and we call this the *polar* form for z. For example, $z = -1$ has argument π, and its polar form is

$$-1 = 1 \cdot (\cos\pi + i\sin\pi)$$

The argument of $-\frac{1}{2} + i(\sqrt{3}/2)$ is $2\pi/3$, as is easily seen, and its absolute value is $\sqrt{(\frac{1}{4} + \frac{3}{4})} = 1$. Hence,

$$-\frac{1}{2} + i\frac{\sqrt{3}}{2} = \cos\frac{2\pi}{3} + i\sin\frac{2\pi}{3}$$

Similarly for the conjugate we have

$$-\frac{1}{2} - i\frac{\sqrt{3}}{2} = \cos\frac{4\pi}{3} + i\sin\frac{4\pi}{3}$$

Now let $z_1 = x_1 + iy_1$ and $z_2 = x_2 + iy_2$ be two complex numbers and write them in polar form:

$$z_1 = r_1(\cos\theta_1 + i\sin\theta_1) \qquad z_2 = r_2(\cos\theta_2 + i\sin\theta_2)$$

Then

$$z_1z_2 = r_1r_2[(\cos\theta_1\cos\theta_2 - \sin\theta_1\sin\theta_2) + i(\sin\theta_1\cos\theta_2 + \cos\theta_1\sin\theta_2)]$$

† We use only "radian measure" here. For example, 90° is $\pi/2$, etc.

Figure 2

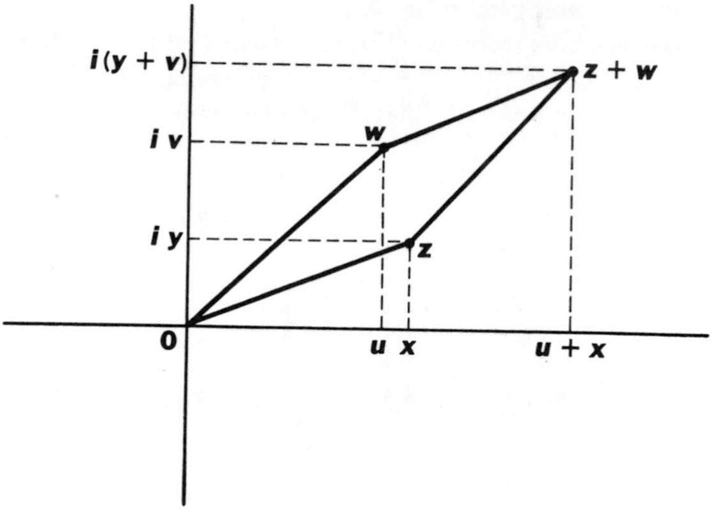

Figure 3

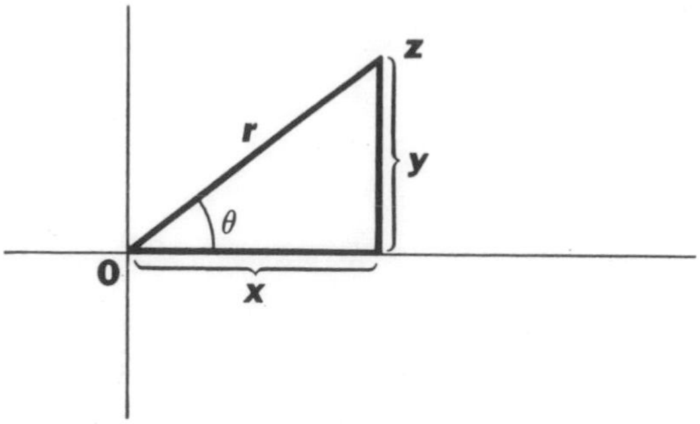

From the well-known formulas from trigonometry for $\cos(\theta_1 + \theta_2)$ and $\sin(\theta_1 + \theta_2)$ there follows

$$z_1 z_2 = r_1 r_2[\cos(\theta_1 + \theta_2) + i\sin(\theta_1 + \theta_2)]$$

Hence we have the following theorem.

THEOREM 3.1 *For any two complex numbers z_1 and z_2,*

$$|z_1 z_2| = |z_1| \cdot |z_2|$$

and

$$\arg(z_1 z_2) = \arg z_1 + \arg z_2$$

(The first equality was proved in Sec. 1.)

From this it is easily seen how to find the point representing $z_1 z_2$ geometrically: Just add the two angles and multiply the two absolute values.

THEOREM 3.2 **(De Moivre's theorem)** *For any integer n,*

$$(\cos\theta + i\sin\theta)^n = \cos n\theta + i\sin n\theta$$

Proof. For positive n this follows at once by induction from Theorem 3.1. For $n = 0$ it is trivial. For negative integers we proceed as follows: Put $z = \cos\theta + i\sin\theta$. Then $|z|^2 = \cos^2\theta + \sin^2\theta = 1$, and so $z\bar{z} = 1$. Thus $1/z = \bar{z}$, and so $1/z^n = \bar{z}^n$. If now n is a positive integer, then we have $z^{-n} = \bar{z}^n = (\cos\theta - i\sin\theta)^n = (\cos(-\theta) + i\sin(-\theta))^n$, and by what has already been shown, the latter is equal to $\cos(-n\theta) + i\sin(-n\theta)$. Q.E.D.

We point out again that we have departed from our axiomatic presentation in our use of some results of geometry and trigonometry—in particular the addition formulas for the sine and cosine. It is quite possible to give completely rigorous accounts of those subjects, and there is no doubt about the validity of our conclusions.

De Moivre's theorem has an important application: It tells us how to find nth roots of any complex number.

THEOREM 3.3 *Let $a = r(\cos\theta + i\sin\theta)$ be any complex number and n a positive integer. Then the numbers*

3.3 $$r^{1/n}\cdot\left(\cos\frac{\theta+2\pi k}{n} + i\sin\frac{\theta+2\pi k}{n}\right) \qquad (k = 0, 1, \ldots, n-1)$$

satisfy the equation $x^n = a$, and they are the only complex numbers that do satisfy it.

Proof. By De Moivre's theorem the nth power of (3.3) is $r(\cos(\theta + 2\pi k) + i\sin(\theta + 2\pi k))$, and this is just $r(\cos\theta + i\sin\theta)$ because $\cos(\theta + 2\pi k) = \cos\theta$ for any integer k, and $\sin(\theta + 2\pi k) = \sin\theta$. Observe that if $a \neq 0$, then (3.3) gives n different nth roots of a. If we plot these numbers in the plane, then they are represented by n points spaced equally round a circle of radius $r^{1/n}$. Now let $y = r_1(\cos\alpha + i\cos\alpha)$ be a number such that $y^n = a$. By De Moivre's theorem we have then $a = r(\cos\theta + i\sin\theta) = r_1^n(\cos n\alpha + i\sin n\alpha)$. Taking absolute values of both sides we get $r_1^n = r$. Since r_1 is assumed non-negative in the polar form, we must have $r_1 = r^{1/n}$. But then (if $a \neq 0$) we must have $\cos\theta = \cos n\alpha$ and $\sin\theta = \sin n\alpha$. It is easily seen from this that y must appear among the numbers (3.3). (In the next chapter we shall prove in general that $x^n = a$ cannot have more than n solutions in any field.) Q.E.D.

EXERCISES

1. Find all solutions in **C** of the following equations:

(*a*) $z^3 = 1$ (*b*) $z^5 = -1$

(*c*) $z^2 = i$ (*d*) $z^3 = i + \sqrt{3}$

2. Let n be a positive integer and put $w = \cos 2\pi/n + i\sin 2\pi/n$. Show that $1, w, w^2, \ldots, w^{n-1}$ are all solutions of $x^n = 1$.

3. Show that $1 + w + w^2 + \cdots + w^{n-1} = 0$, where w is defined in Exercise 2.

4. Show that if b is one solution of the equation $x^n = a$ (a any complex number), then the other solutions are $bw, bw^2, \ldots, bw^{n-1}$, where w is as in Exercise 2.

5. If $1, w, w^2$ are the solutions of $x^3 = 1$ ($n = 3$ in Exercise 2), then show that

(*a*) $(1 + w^2)^4 = w$

(*b*) $(1 - w + w^2)(1 + w - w^2) = 4$

(*c*) $(1 - w)(1 - w^2)(1 - w^4)(1 - w^5) = 9$

6. Give geometric proofs of the inequalities

$$|z_1 + z_2| \leq |z_1| + |z_2|$$
$$|z_1 - z_2| \geq \big||z_1| - |z_2|\big|$$

for any complex numbers z_1, z_2.

7. Give necessary and sufficient conditions for the equality

$$|z_1 + z_2| = |z_1| + |z_2|$$

8. What is the distance between the two points in the plane representing two complex numbers u and v?

9. Prove that $|z + z'|^2 + |z - z'|^2 = 2|z|^2 + 2|z'|^2$ for any complex numbers z, z'. What is the geometric interpretation of this identity?

10. Compute the sum $1 + 2\cos x + 2\cos 2x + \cdots + 2\cos nx$. [Hint: $\cos kx$ = real part of $(\cos x + i \sin x)^k$.]

11. Determine n complex numbers x such that $(x + i)^n + (x - i)^n = 0$.

4. Cauchy sequences and infinite series in **C**

The absolute value $|z|$ of a complex number z is a real number, positive unless $z = 0$. If z, w are two complex numbers, then the quantity $|z - w|$ can be interpreted as the "distance" between them, and from Sec. 3 this distance has a simple geometric meaning. By using it we can carry over bodily the definitions and main properties of Cauchy sequences as given in Chap. 4. For the sake of brevity we omit many minor details.

DEFINITION 4.1 *Let $c_1, c_2, c_3, \ldots$ be an infinite sequence of complex numbers. It is called a* Cauchy sequence *if for every real number $e > 0$ there is an integer P (depending in general upon e) such that*

$$|c_n - c_m| < e \qquad \text{for all } n, m > P$$

DEFINITION 4.2 *Let $c_1, c_2, c_3, \ldots$ be a sequence of complex numbers and let c be a complex number. Then the sequence is said to have c as a* limit, *in symbols $\lim_{n\to\infty} c_n = c$, if for every positive real number e there is an integer P such that*

$$|c - c_n| < e \qquad \text{for all } n > P$$

It is clear that if the c's happen to be real numbers, then these definitions coincide with those of Sec. 2, Chap. 4.

PROPOSITION 4.1 *Let $c_1, c_2, c_3, \ldots$ be a sequence of complex numbers, and write $c_n = a_n + b_n \cdot i$, where a_n and b_n are real. Then the given sequence $c_1, c_2, c_3, \ldots$ is a Cauchy sequence if and only if both $a_1, a_2, a_3, \ldots$ and $b_1, b_2, b_3, \ldots$ are Cauchy sequences.*

Proof. This is a straightforward consequence of the simple inequalities

$$|a_n - a_m|, |b_n - b_m| \le |c_n - c_m| \le |a_n - a_m| + |b_n - b_m|$$

COROLLARY *The sequence $c_1, c_2, c_3, \ldots$ has a limit c if and only if it is a Cauchy sequence, and c is unique.*

The proof follows easily from the proposition and is left as an exercise.

Just as in the case of the real numbers, these notions allow us to define infinite sums under certain circumstances.

DEFINITION 4.3 *Let $u_0, u_1, u_2, \ldots$ be a sequence of complex numbers. Then the infinite series $\sum_{n=1}^{\infty} u_n$ is said to* converge *if the sequence $s_0 = u_0$, $s_1 = u_0 + u_1$, $s_2 =$*

$u_0 + u_1 + u_2, \ldots, s_n = u_0 + u_1 + \cdots + u_n$, *etc. is a Cauchy sequence. If that is so, then the number* $\lim_{n\to\infty} s_n$ *is defined to be the sum of the series.*

Hence for brevity we can write

$$\sum_{n=0}^{\infty} u_n = \lim_{n\to\infty} \sum_{k=0}^{n} u_k = \lim_{n\to\infty}(u_0 + u_1 + \cdots + u_n)$$

provided that the series converges.

EXAMPLE 1 If z is any complex number with $|z| < 1$, then the series $\sum_{n=0}^{\infty} z^n$ converges and its sum is $1/(1 - z)$. (This series is called the *geometric* series.)

EXAMPLE 2 For every complex z the series

4.1 $$\sum_{n=0}^{\infty} \frac{z^n}{n!}$$

converges. Its value is denoted by e^z; it is called the *exponential* function. Then for two complex numbers z, w we have

$$e^{z+w} = \sum_{n=0}^{\infty} \frac{(z+w)^n}{n!}$$

By applying the binomial theorem to $(z + w)^n$, we get

$$\frac{(z+w)^n}{n!} = \sum_{k=0}^{n} \frac{1}{n!}\binom{n}{k} z^{n-k} w^k$$

$$= \sum_{k=0}^{n} \frac{z^{n-k}}{(n-k)!} \cdot \frac{w^k}{k!}$$

Using this it is not difficult to prove that

4.2 $$e^{z+w} = e^z \cdot e^w$$

EXAMPLE 3 For every complex number z the two series

4.3 $$\sum_{n=0}^{\infty} \frac{(-1)^n z^{2n}}{(2n)!} \qquad \sum_{n=0}^{\infty} (-1)^n \frac{z^{2n+1}}{(2n+1)!}$$

converge. The sum of the first one is denoted by $\cos z$ and the sum of the second by $\sin z$.

It is clear that if z happens to be a real number, then all the examples above coincide with those given at the end of Chap. 4.

If in the series $e^z = \sum_0^\infty \frac{z^n}{n!}$ we replace z by iz, then it is easy to see that the terms for even n are the same as the terms of the first series in (4.3); for odd n the terms are the same as the terms in the second series of (4.3), multiplied by i. From this it is simple to show that

4.4 $$e^{iz} = \cos z + i \sin z$$

Of course it is far from obvious that $\cos z$ and $\sin z$ as defined here have anything to do with the sine and cosine functions of elementary trigonometry. We refer to standard calculus texts for a proof that they are the same things when z is real. However it is easy to see that they have some of the correct properties. For example, from (4.3) it follows readily that $\cos(-z) = \cos z$ and $\sin(-z) = -\sin z$. Hence, by (4.4), $e^{-iz} = \cos z - i \sin z$. Then, using (4.2) and the fact that $e^0 = 1$ we get

$$1 = e^0 = e^{iz}e^{-iz} = (\cos z + i \sin z)(\cos z - i \sin z)$$

whence

4.5 $$\cos^2 z + \sin^2 z = 1 \qquad \text{for all } z$$

Now if z is real, then so are $\cos z$ and $\sin z$ because then all the terms in (4.3) are real. From (4.5) we conclude that

4.6 $$-1 \leq \cos z \leq 1 \qquad -1 \leq \sin z \leq 1 \qquad \text{if } z \text{ is real}$$

Furthermore, putting $z + w$ for z in (4.4) and using (4.2) we get $e^{i(z+w)} = e^{iz}e^{iw}$, or

$$\begin{aligned}\cos(z + w) + i \sin(z + w) &= (\cos z + i \sin z)(\cos w + i \sin w)\\ &= (\cos z \cos w - \sin z \sin w) + i(\sin z \cdot \cos w + \cos z \cdot \sin w)\end{aligned}$$

If z and w are real then all the quantities appearing here, except i, are real. Hence the real and imaginary parts of both sides must be equal, and we get

4.7 $$\begin{aligned}\cos(z + w) &= \cos z \cdot \cos w - \sin z \cdot \sin w\\ \sin(z + w) &= \sin z \cdot \cos w + \cos z \cdot \sin w\end{aligned}$$

These equations are also valid if z, w are not real. They are of course the usual addition formulas for the sine and cosine. From the series (4.3) themselves we cannot prove that $\cos \pi = -1$ or $\sin \pi = 0$, etc., for it is difficult to connect the two series with the number π.

The examples just cited are very important ones, and they serve to give some indication of the great power of Cauchy sequences, limits, and infinite series. These concepts are exploited very fully in the part of mathematics called *analysis*. We shall not have occasion to refer to them again except in Chap. 12.

EXERCISES

1. Let $\sum_{n=0}^{\infty} a_n$, $\sum_{n=0}^{\infty} b_n$ be two convergent series of complex numbers, and let c, d be any complex numbers. Prove that $\sum_{n=0}^{\infty} (ca_n + db_n)$ is convergent and that its sum is equal to

$$c \cdot \sum_{n=0}^{\infty} a_n + d \cdot \sum_{n=0}^{\infty} b_n$$

2. Let $\sum_{n=0}^{\infty} a_n$ be a convergent series of complex numbers. Prove that $\lim_{n\to\infty} a_n = 0$. Prove that the series $\sum_{n=k}^{\infty} a_n$ converges, for any positive integer k. Denoting its sum by c_k, prove that $\lim_{k\to\infty} c_k = 0$.

3. Prove that if $\sum_{n=0}^{\infty} a_n$ is a convergent series whose terms are all positive real numbers, then any series $\sum_{n=0}^{\infty} b_n$ such that $|b_n| \leq a_n$ for all n is also convergent.

4. Prove that $\sum_{n=0}^{\infty} a_n$ converges if the set of numbers $s_n = |a_0| + |a_1| + \cdots + |a_n|$ has an upper bound.

5. Give a complete proof of Theorem 4.1 and its corollary.

***6.** Show how to define Cauchy sequences and infinite sums in the system of quaternions.

6

Polynomials

1. *Introduction*

On several occasions we have had to deal with equations of the type

1.1 $$a_0x^n + a_1x^{n-1} + \cdots + a_{n-1}x + a_n = 0$$

in which $a_0, a_1, \ldots, a_n$ denote elements of some field and x denotes an "unknown." For example, at the beginning of Chap. 5 we pointed out that there is no real number satisfying the equation $x^2 + 1 = 0$. Here obviously x does *not* represent an element of the field **R** because there is no such element in **R**; x is merely a letter used to allow us to write out an equation which might or might not become true if x is replaced by some element of the system. Similar remarks apply to the equations occurring in Theorems 1.3 and 1.4, Chap. 5. It is sometimes convenient to be able to consider x as an element of an algebraic system, rather than as just a letter to be used for writing equations. The present chapter is concerned with showing how that can be done and with the algebraic systems that result.

2. *Indeterminates, or variables*

If $a_0, a_1, \ldots, a_n$ and t are any elements of a ring A, then a combination of the form

2.1 $$a_0 + a_1t + a_2t^2 + \cdots + a_nt^n$$

is called a *polynomial*, or more precisely a polynomial in t with coefficients in A

EXAMPLE 1 The quantity $1 + 3 \cdot 5^{1/2} + 4 \cdot 5 - 2 \cdot 5^{3/2} + 6 \cdot 5^4$ is a polynomial in $\sqrt{5}$ with coefficients in **Z**.

PROPOSITION 2.1 *Let A be a ring, B a subring, and t an element of A. Suppose that $bt = tb$ for every element b of B; and denote by $B[t]$ the set of all elements in A which can be expressed as polynomials in t with coefficients in B. Then $B[t]$ is a subring of A, and any subring of A which contains B and t must contain $B[t]$.*

Proof. We have only to show that the sum, difference, and product of any two elements a, b in $B[t]$ are also in $B[t]$. By assumption the elements can be expressed as polynomials $a = a_0 + a_1t + \cdots + a_mt^m$ and $b =$

$b_0 + b_1t + \cdots + b_nt^n$ with coefficients in B. Then $a + b = (a_0 + b_0) + (a_1 + b_1)t + (a_2 + b_2)t^2 +$ etc. This is a polynomial in t, and its coefficients $a_j + b_j$ are in B, since B is a subring. Therefore $a + b$ is in $B[t]$. The same is true for $a - b$. For the product we have

$$\begin{aligned} ab &= (a_0 + a_1t + \cdots + a_mt^m)(b_0 + b_1t + \cdots + b_nt^n) \\ &= a_0b_0 + a_0b_1t + a_1tb_0 + \cdots + a_jt^jb_kt^k + \cdots + a_mt^mb_nt^n \end{aligned}$$

We have assumed that $ct = tc$ for any c in B. Then, by a simple induction, $ct^k = t^kc$ for any positive integer k (see Sec. 7*E*, Chap. 2). Therefore the expression above for ab can be written

$$ab = a_0b_0 + (a_0b_1 + a_1b_0)t + (a_0b_2 + a_1b_1 + a_2b_0)t^2 + \cdots + a_mb_nt^{m+n}$$

which is a polynomial in t with coefficients in B. Hence ab is in $B[t]$, and $B[t]$ is a subring of A. If C is any subring of A containing both B and t, then it must contain t^2, t^3, etc. It follows at once that C contains every polynomial in t with coefficients in B, and so it contains $B[t]$. Q.E.D.

From the calculations just made it is clear that the coefficient c_k of t^k in the expression for ab is the quantity

2.2 $$c_k = a_0b_k + a_1b_{k-1} + a_2b_{k-2} + \cdots + a_{k-1}b_1 + a_kb_0$$

where it is understood that $a_j = 0$ if j exceeds m and $b_h = 0$ if h exceeds n.

It is obvious that $B[t]$ must be a commutative ring if B is commutative, assuming always that t commutes with every element of B.

DEFINITION 2.1 *The ring $B[t]$ of the preceding proposition is called the ring obtained by* adjoining t *to B.*

The following definition is fundamental:

DEFINITION 2.2 *Let A be a ring, let B be a subring, and let x be an element of A which commutes with every element of B. Then x is said to be an* indeterminate *over B (or to be* variable *over B, or* transcendental *over B) if no polynomial in x with coefficients in B is zero unless all the coefficients are zero. In the contrary case x is said to be* algebraic *over B, provided that B is an integral domain.*

In other words, the requirement for x to be variable over B is that $bx = xb$ for every b in B and that x should not satisfy any polynomial equation with coefficients in B, unless of course all the coefficients are zero. In the case that A is an integral domain, the assumption that x commutes with every element of B is superfluous, since multiplication in an integral domain is commutative, by definition.

EXAMPLE 2 The complex number $u = -(1/2) + (\sqrt{3}/2)i$ is algebraic over **Q** (also over **Z**, **R**) because $u^3 - 1 = 0$. The real number $a = -2 + \sqrt{2}$ is algebraic over **Q**, since $a^2 + 4a + 2 = 0$, as is easily verified. Complex numbers which are algebraic over **Q** are called *algebraic numbers*. All others are called *transcendental* *numbers.* It is known that the number π is transcendental. To repeat the definition, this means that if

$$a_0 + a_1\pi + a_2\pi^2 + \cdots + a_n\pi^n = 0$$

where the coefficients $a_0, a_1, \ldots, a_n$ are *rational,* then they must all be zero. In other words, π does not satisfy any polynomial equation with nonzero rational coefficients. The number e is also transcendental. In fact, "nearly all" real numbers are transcendental. For it can be shown fairly easily that all algebraic numbers in **R** form a countable subset, whereas **R** itself is uncountable. It is usually a very difficult problem to determine whether a given number is algebraic or transcendental.

By an *indeterminate,* or *variable,* over a ring B we shall mean an element of a ring containing B for which the conditions of Definition 2.2 are satisfied. Thus, if x is variable over B, then x must commute with every element of B. From the definition we have the following immediate consequence:

PROPOSITION 2.2 *Let x be a variable over a ring B. Then $B[x]$ is a ring, and every nonzero element of $B[x]$ can be expressed in one and only one way as a polynomial*

2.3 $$f(x) = a_0 + a_1x + \cdots + a_nx^n$$

with coefficients $a_0, a_1, \ldots, a_n$ in B and $a_n \neq 0$.†

Proof. $B[x]$ is a ring, by Proposition 2.1. Suppose that an element of $B[x]$ can be expressed in two different ways

$$a_0 + a_1x + \cdots + a_nx^n = b_0 + b_1x + \cdots + b_mx^m$$

and for definiteness suppose that $m \geq n$. Subtracting, we obtain

$$(a_0 - b_0) + (a_1 - b_1)x + \cdots + (a_n - b_n)x^n + b_{n+1}x^{n+1} + \cdots + b_mx^m = 0$$

From Definition 2.2, all the coefficients here must be zero. Thus $a_j = b_j$ for $j = 1, \ldots, n$, and $b_j = 0$ for $j > n$. The assertion follows at once.

Q.E.D.

The notation $f(x)$ of (2.3) is simply an abbreviation, of which frequent use will be made.

DEFINITION 2.3 *Let x be a variable over a ring B. Then $B[x]$ is called the* ring of polynomials *in x over B, or with coefficients in B. If $f(x) = a_0 + a_1x + \cdots + a_nx^n$ is an element of $B[x]$ and if $a_n \neq 0$ (the a_j are supposed to be in B), then n is called the* degree *of $f(x)$, denoted by* deg $f(x)$. *The coefficient a_n is called the* highest coefficient *of $f(x)$; if $a_n = 1$ (unit element of B), then $f(x)$ is called a* monic *polynomial.*

† Naturally any number of terms $0 \cdot x^{n+1} + 0 \cdot x^{n+2} +$, etc., can be added on; but then the uniqueness is destroyed.

Observe that no degree is assigned to the zero element of $B[x]$; we consider it to have any degree whatever in order to avoid annoying exceptions. For example, if we speak of all polynomials of degree 5, we understand that 0 is among them.

We shall show presently that there is always a variable element, or indeterminate, over any ring B. Therefore a polynomial ring over B always exists.

PROPOSITION 2.3 *Let $B[x]$ be a polynomial ring over a ring B, and let $f(x)$ and $g(x)$ be two nonzero elements of $B[x]$. Then* $\deg(f(x) + g(x)) \leq \max\{\deg f(x), \deg g(x)\}$.† *If B is an integral domain, then* $\deg(f(x) \cdot g(x)) = \deg f(x) + \deg g(x)$, *and $B[x]$ is an integral domain. If $f(x)$ and $g(x)$ are monic, then so is $f(x) \cdot g(x)$.*

Proof. Let $f(x)$ have degree m, with highest coefficient a_m, and let $g(x)$ have degree n, with highest coefficient b_n. It is plain that $f(x) + g(x)$ cannot have degree greater than both m and n, which is the first assertion. From (2.2) it follows at once that the highest power of x which can appear with nonzero coefficient in $f(x) \cdot g(x)$ is x^{m+n}, the coefficient being $a_m b_n$. By assumption, $a_m \neq 0$ and $b_m \neq 0$. If B is an integral domain, then $a_m b_n \neq 0$ (see Theorem 2.4, Chap. 2), and so $f(x) \cdot g(x)$ has degree $m + n$, the highest coefficient being $a_m b_n$. In particular, $f(x) \cdot g(x) \neq 0$. As we have already observed, if B is a commutative ring, then so is $B[x]$. Hence, if B is an integral domain, then $B[x]$ is a commutative ring in which the product of two nonzero elements is again nonzero. In other words, $B[x]$ is also an integral domain. The last assertion of the proposition is obvious. Q.E.D.

Again let x denote a variable element over a ring B, and let

2.4 $$f(x) = a_0 + a_1 x + \cdots + a_n x^n$$

be any element of the polynomial ring $B[x]$, the elements $a_0, \ldots, a_n$ being in B. Let t be any element of B, or of some ring containing B. Then we can form the element

2.5 $$f(t) = a_0 + a_1 t + \cdots + a_n t^n$$

simply replacing x in (2.4) by the element t. The following theorem concerns this substitution operation.

THEOREM 2.4 *Let x be an indeterminate over a ring B. Let t be any element of a ring containing B as a subring, and suppose that t commutes with every element of B. Then the operation that sends every polynomial $f(x)$ in $B[x]$ into $f(t)$ is a ring-homomorphism from $B[x]$ to $B[t]$.*

Proof. First of all, the operation defines a mapping from $B[x]$ to $B[t]$, since elements of $B[x]$ have unique expressions as polynomials (2.4), apart

† The symbol max $\{a, b\}$ denotes the larger of the numbers a, b or else their common value if they are equal.

from terms with coefficient zero. The theorem states that if $f(x)$ and $g(x)$ are any two elements of $B[x]$, then the results of forming $f(x) + g(x)$ and $f(x) \cdot g(x)$ and thereupon replacing x by t are $f(t) + g(t)$ and $f(t) \cdot g(t)$, respectively. The verification is perfectly trivial, since calculations with polynomials in x are the same as calculations with polynomials in t, both being as in the proof of Proposition 2.1 above. Observe, however, that the assumption that t (as well as x) commutes with every element of B is essential, since otherwise the calculation of the product in the proof of Proposition 2.1 is not correct.

As a special case, suppose that B is a commutative ring, and let t denote any element of B. It is clear that $B[t]$ is none other than B. The hypotheses of the theorem are fulfilled, and therefore substitution of t for x defines a homomorphism from $B[x]$ to B itself.

Homomorphisms of the sort just described will be called *substitution homomorphisms*, for obvious reasons. The whole point here is that an element $f(x)$ in the polynomial ring $B[x]$ has a *unique* expression as a polynomial with coefficients in B—unique, that is, apart from terms with zero coefficients. But the corresponding element $f(t)$ may have many different expressions as a polynomial in t with coefficients in B. That is, we may have $f(t) = g(t)$ but $f(x) \neq g(x)$. For example, let B be the ring of integers, and take $f(x) = x - 1$ and $g(x) = 2$ [hence $g(x)$ has degree zero]. We have $f(3) = g(3) = 2$, but $f(x) \neq g(x)$.

In this situation it is clear that trying to define an inverse mapping $B[t] \to B[x]$ by the rule $f(t) \to f(x)$ would be nonsense, since the same rule would send $g(t) = f(t)$ into $g(x) \neq f(x)$. In other words, the mapping would not be well defined. From Definition 2.2 it follows that every element of $B[t]$ has a unique expression as a polynomial in t with coefficients in B (apart from terms with coefficient zero) if and only if t is also variable over B (we continue with the assumption that t commutes with all elements of B). In this case the inverse mapping $f(t) \to f(x)$ does make sense. Applying the theorem above to it, we have the following corollary:

COROLLARY 1 *If t is also variable over B, then the mapping $f(x) \to f(t)$ is a ring-isomorphism from $B[x]$ to $B[t]$.*

For this mapping has an inverse and is therefore one-to-one.

EXAMPLE 3 If x is variable over B, then so is x^2 (in fact, every element of $B[x]$ not in B is variable over B). Hence, the substitution $x \to x^2$ determines an isomorphism from $B[x]$ to $B[x^2]$. The latter is a subring of $B[x]$.

COROLLARY 2 *Let $B[x]$ and $B[y]$ be two polynomial rings over a ring B. Then there is a unique isomorphism from $B[x]$ to $B[y]$ sending x into y and elements of B into themselves.*

For both x and y are variable elements over B, by definition of polynomial ring. The assertion follows from Corollary 1.

COROLLARY 3 *Let x be an indeterminate over a ring B. Any equation of polynomials in x with coefficients in B remains true if x is replaced by any element t of any ring containing B as a subring, provided t commutes with every element of B.*

The idea here is that an equation such as $(x - 3)(x + 2)(x^2 + 3x + 2) = x^4 + x^3 - 7x^2 - 20x - 12$, for example, which is correct in $B[x]$ remains true if x is replaced by t. Now that is exactly what Theorem 2.4 says; it simply states that sums and products can be performed either before or after substitution of t for x.

The following theorem shows that polynomial rings over a given ring B always exist:

THEOREM 2.5 *Let B be a ring. Then there exists a ring A containing B as a subring and containing an element x which is variable over B.*

Proof. The construction of A is very simple. Namely, we let A be the set of all infinite sequences $(a_0, a_1, a_2, \ldots)$ of elements of B such that *only finitely many elements a_j are nonzero.* Addition in A is defined by the rule

2.6 $$(a_0, a_1, a_2, \ldots) + (b_0, b_1, b_2, \ldots) = (a_0 + b_0, a_1 + b_1, a_2 + b_2, \ldots)$$

This operation gives again an element of A, because only finitely many of the elements $a_0 + b_0$, $a_1 + b_1$, etc., can be different from zero, since that is true of the two sequences on the left. It is a very straightforward matter to verify that A with this operation $+$ is an abelian group. Its zero element is $(0, 0, 0, \ldots)$, and the inverse of $(a_0, a_1, a_2, \ldots)$ for addition is the element $(-a_0, -a_1, -a_2, \ldots)$.

Multiplication in A is defined by the rule

2.7 $$(a_0, a_1, a_2, \ldots) \cdot (b_0, b_1, b_2, \ldots) = (c_0, c_1, c_2, \ldots)$$

where c_k is given (for any $k \geq 0$) by the formula

2.8 $$c_k = a_0b_k + a_1b_{k-1} + a_2b_{k-2} + \cdots + a_{k-2}b_2 + a_{k-1}b_1 + a_kb_0$$

which is the same as (2.2). By assumption, only finitely many of the a_i and b_j are different from zero, and so we shall have, say, $a_i = b_i = 0$ for all $i > p$. Then from (2.8) it is clear that $c_k = 0$ for $k > 2p$. Hence, only finitely many of the c_k can be different from zero, and therefore the right-hand side of (2.7) is indeed an element of A.

It is a straightforward matter to verify that A, with sum and product defined in this way, is a ring; its unit element is $(1, 0, 0, 0, \ldots)$, where 1 denotes the unit element of B. Now put $x = (0, 1, 0, 0, \ldots)$. From (2.7) and (2.8) a simple induction shows that $x^n = (0, 0, \ldots, 0, 1, 0, 0, \ldots)$ for any positive integer n, where 1 stands in the $(n + 1)$th place, all other entries being zero. Furthermore, from (2.7) and (2.8) it is easy to verify that

$$(a, 0, 0, 0, \ldots)x^n = (0, 0, \ldots, 0, a, 0, 0, \ldots)$$

where on the right the element a appears in the $(n + 1)$th place, zeros elsewhere. Then from the definition of addition in A it follows that for any element of A, say $(a_0, a_1, \ldots, a_n, 0, 0, 0, \ldots)$, we have

2.9 $$(a_0, a_1, \ldots, a_n, 0, 0, \ldots) = \sum_{k=0}^{n} (a_k, 0, 0, 0, \ldots) \cdot x^k$$

where as usual x^0 stands for the unit element $(1, 0, 0, \ldots)$ of A.

Now let B' be the subset of A consisting of all elements $(a, 0, 0, 0, \ldots)$ with zeros beyond the first place. For such elements the definitions above reduce to

$$(a, 0, 0, \ldots) + (b, 0, 0, \ldots) = (a + b, 0, 0, \ldots)$$

and

$$(a, 0, 0, \ldots) \cdot (b, 0, 0, \ldots) = (ab, 0, 0, \ldots)$$

Therefore B' is a subring of A. Let us write a' for the element $(a, 0, 0, \ldots)$ of B', so that (2.9) above can be written

2.10 $$(a_0, a_1, \ldots, a_n, 0, 0, \ldots) = \sum_{k=0}^{n} a_k' x^k$$

Since the zero element of A is $(0, 0, 0, \ldots)$, it follows from this that the right-hand side of (2.10) cannot be zero unless $a_0', a_1', a_2', \ldots$ are all zero. Since x commutes with every element of B', as is easily seen, it follows that x is *variable* over the subring B' of A. We observe that $A = B'[x]$.

Now A does not contain B, but it contains a subring B' which is isomorphic to B. Namely, the mapping $B \to B'$ defined in the obvious manner by $a \to (a, 0, 0, \ldots) = a'$ is an isomorphism. If we insist upon having the original B instead of the isomorphic copy B', then we can simply replace the elements of B' by the corresponding elements of B (retaining for them the operations defined in A for elements of B'). Q.E.D.

The theorem shows that, for any ring B, there always exists an element x which is variable over B, and therefore there always exists a polynomial ring $B[x]$ over B. Any two polynomial rings over B are isomorphic, by Corollary 2 of Theorem 2.4. And $B[x]$ is an integral domain if B is an integral domain. In the remainder of this chapter we shall deal only with integral domains.

We point out that the notion of a variable element depends very strongly on the ring in question. For example, if x is variable over B, it is certainly not variable over $B[x]$. The number π is variable over **Q**, as noted above; but it is not variable over **R**.

The terms *variable* and *indeterminate,* entirely synonymous here, are conventional terms; they have nothing to do with with something "varying" or being "undetermined."

EXERCISES

1. Carry out the verifications in the proof of Theorem 2.5.
2. Let B be a subring of a commutative ring A, and let t be an element of A, s an element of B. Show that $B[t] = B[t + s]$.
3. Let y be a variable element over a ring B. Prove that every element in $B[y]$ which is not in B is variable over B.
4. Let B be a subring of a field K, and let t be an element of K different from zero. Prove that t is variable over B if and only if t^{-1} is variable over B.
5. Prove that every element of the ring $\mathbf{Q}[\sqrt{2}]$ can be written uniquely in the form $a + b \cdot \sqrt{2}$, where a and b are rational numbers. Prove that this ring is a field. Do the same for $\mathbf{Q}[\sqrt{-2}]$.
6. Let B be an integral domain, and let x be an indeterminate over B. Prove that if an element u of $B[x]$ has an inverse in $B[x]$ (for multiplication), then u is an element of B which has an inverse in B.
7. Let w be the complex number $w = \cos(2\pi/n) + i \sin(2\pi/n)$, where n is a positive integer. Describe the ring $\mathbf{Q}[w]$. That is, show that every element can be written uniquely in the form $a_0 + a_1w + \cdots + a_{n-1}w^{n-1}$, where the a_j are rational numbers. (This ring is also a field.)
8. Let A be an ordered integral domain. Let J consist of all elements $a_nx^n + a_{n-1}x^{n-1} + \cdots + a_0$ of $A[x]$ with $a_n > 0$. Show that this makes $A[x]$ into an ordered integral domain. Note that $A[x]$ is *not* Archimedean: there are elements greater than any integer.
9. Show that $z^n + z^{-n}$ is a polynomial in $z + z^{-1}$, where z denotes an element in a field. [Hint: Use induction and consider separately the cases: n even and n odd.]

3. Factorization of polynomials

We now take up an investigation that parallels very closely the discussion of Sec. 8, Chap. 2. We begin with some general definitions.

DEFINITION 3.1 *Let D be an integral domain containing more than one element, and let a and b be two elements of D, with $a \neq 0$. Then a is said to* divide *b if there is an element c in D such that $ac = b$. An element which divides* 1 *is called* invertible. *An element $p \neq 0$ of D is called* prime *if it is not invertible and if the only elements of D which divide p are invertible elements and the elements up, where u is invertible.*

An invertible element u is simply one that has an inverse u^{-1} in D. Invertible elements are divisible only by invertible elements; for if u is invertible and if a divides u, then $u = ac$ for some c in D. Then $1 = a \cdot (cu^{-1})$, showing that a is invertible. Any element b is divisible by any invertible element u, for $b = u \cdot (u^{-1}b)$. If *a divides b and* if u, v are invertible, then ua divides vb. Therefore divisibility relationships are not affected by invertible factors. *If a divides b and b divides a, then $b = ua$, where u is invertible.* For by definition $b = ac$ and $a = bc'$ for some elements c, c' in D. But then $a = acc'$, and so from the cancellation law we have $1 = cc'$, showing that c and c' are invertible.

EXAMPLE 1 The only invertible elements in $\mathbf{Z}$ are 1 and -1. *Prime* elements of $\mathbf{Z}$ according to Definition 3.1 are just prime numbers, as defined in Sec. 8, Chap. 2.

Every nonzero element of a field K is invertible and is divisible by any other nonzero element.

DEFINITION 3.2 *Let $f_1, f_2, \ldots, f_n$ be elements of an integral domain D, not all zero. Then an element h of D is called a* greatest common divisor *(g.c.d.) of $f_1, f_2, \ldots, f_n$ if*

(1) *h divides $f_1, f_2, \ldots, f_n$.*

(2) *Any element of D which divides $f_1, \ldots, f_n$ must also divide h.*

If h, h' are two g.c.d. of $f_1, f_2, \ldots, f_n$, then by (1) and (2) they must divide each other. Therefore as pointed out above, $h' = u \cdot h$, where u is an invertible element of D. Conversely, if h satisfies (1) and (2), then clearly so does $u \cdot h$, for any invertible element u. Hence a greatest common divisor of a set of elements in D (if one exists) is unique apart from an arbitrary invertible factor. A greatest common divisor need not exist in general.

DEFINITION 3.3 *Elements $f_1, f_2, \ldots, f_n$ of an integral domain D are said to be* relatively prime, *or* coprime, *if 1 is a greatest common divisor of them.*

In this case any invertible element of D is also a g.c.d.

The definitions given above are clearly just straightforward extensions of definitions given in Sec. 8, Chap. 2. We now apply them to the case of a polynomial ring $K[x]$ over a field K.

First of all, suppose that f is an invertible element in $K[x]$. Then there is an element g in $K[x]$ such that $fg = 1$. That is, $g = f^{-1}$. Then $\deg(fg) = \deg f + \deg g = \deg 1 = 0$, and so $\deg f = \deg g = 0$. Therefore the invertible elements of $K[x]$ are precisely the nonzero elements of K. A prime element of $K[x]$ is usually called an *irreducible* polynomial. If $p(x)$ is irreducible, then, according to Definition 3.1, $p(x)$ must have positive degree and it cannot be expressed as a product $p(x) = f(x) \cdot g(x)$ of two polynomials of positive degree. *Clearly any polynomial of degree 1 is irreducible.*

EXAMPLE 2 The polynomial $x^2 - 2$ is irreducible in $\mathbf{Q}[x]$. For otherwise we would have $x^2 - 2 = f(x) \cdot g(x)$, with $\deg f > 0$ and $\deg g > 0$. The only possibility is then $\deg f = \deg g = 1$, and so we have, say, $x^2 - 2 = (ax + b)(cx + d)$, where

a, b, c, d are rational numbers. We have $ac = 1$, and so $a \neq 0$. By Theorem 2.4 (Corollary 3) the equation remains true if we replace x by $-b/a$ (or any other element of $\mathbf{Q}[x]$). We get then $(b/a)^2 - 2 = 0$, which is impossible, as we have seen in Sec. 1, Chap. 4. The polynomial $x^2 - 2$ is however *reducible* in $\mathbf{R}[x]$, for $x^2 - 2 = (x - \sqrt{2})(x + \sqrt{2})$, and both factors are in $\mathbf{R}[x]$. The polynomial $x^2 + 1$ is irreducible in $\mathbf{R}[x]$ (similar argument) but is reducible in $\mathbf{C}[x]$, namely, $x^2 + 1 = (x + i)(x - i)$.

Irreducible polynomials are analogous to prime numbers. But while it is relatively easy to determine whether a given integer is prime, it is often very difficult to decide whether a given polynomial is irreducible.

From the remarks following Definition 3.2 we see that the g.c.d. of two nonzero elements of $K[x]$ is unique apart from an arbitrary nonzero factor in K. (We shall show below that a g.c.d. always exists.) Then if $h(x)$ is a g.c.d. of $f(x)$ and $g(x)$, so is $ch(x)$ for any nonzero element c of K, and all g.c.d. of $f(x)$ and $g(x)$ are of this form. If b is the highest coefficient of $h(x)$, then $b^{-1} \cdot h(x)$ is a *monic* polynomial. We can assume that $h(x)$ is already monic, and it is then unique. We call it *the* greatest common divisor of f and g, denoted by (f, g). Thus,

3.1 $\quad (f, g) =$ the unique monic g.c.d. of $f(x)$ and $g(x)$

for any two nonzero polynomials. In particular, $(f, g) = 1$ if and only if f and g are relatively prime, by Definition 3.3.

THEOREM 3.1 *Any polynomial $f(x)$ in $K[x]$ of positive degree is divisible by an irreducible polynomial in $K[x]$.*

Proof. Suppose the assertion is false, and let $f(x)$ be a polynomial of least degree $n > 0$ which is not divisible by an irreducible polynomial. Then $f(x)$ cannot itself be irreducible because f divides f. Hence $f(x) = g(x) \cdot h(x)$, where g and h are polynomials of positive degree in $K[x]$. But then $\deg g = \deg f - \deg h < n$, and so $g(x)$ is divisible by an irreducible polynomial $p(x)$, by definition of n. Clearly $p(x)$ also divides $f(x)$, a contradiction. Q.E.D.

We recall that the key tool of Sec. 8, Chap. 2, was the division algorithm. A similar theorem holds for polynomials, and it has analogous consequences. The theorem simply asserts the possibility of "long division." Recall that K is supposed to be a field, so that every nonzero element c of K has an inverse c^{-1}.

PROPOSITION 3.2 **(Division algorithm)** *Let $f(x)$ and $g(x)$ be two nonzero elements of $K[x]$. Then there exist two polynomials $q(x)$ and $r(x)$ in $K[x]$ such that*

3.2 $\quad f(x) = q(x) \cdot g(x) + r(x)$ *and either* $r(x) = 0$ *or else*
$$\deg r(x) < \deg g(x)$$

Moreover $q(x)$ and $r(x)$ are uniquely determined by these conditions.

Proof. The uniqueness of q and r is very easily shown. For let $f(x) = q'(x) \cdot g(x) + r'(x)$, where either $r' = 0$ or else $\deg r' < \deg g$. Then we have $q(x) \cdot g(x) + r(x) = q'(x) \cdot g(x) + r'(x)$, whence $(q(x) - q'(x)) \cdot g(x) = r'(x) - r(x)$. If $q \neq q'$, then $\deg (q - q') \geq 0$. By Theorem 2.4 the degree of the left-hand side is $\geq \deg g$, while the degree of the right-hand side is $< \deg g$, a contradiction. Therefore, $q'(x) = q(x)$, and so $r'(x) = r(x)$.

To prove the existence of q and r we use induction on $n = \deg f(x)$. The process amounts to long division. If $\deg f = 0$, then the assertion is clearly true. For if $\deg g > 0$, then we just take $q(x) = 0$ and $r(x) = f(x)$. If $\deg g = 0$, then f and g are simply two elements of K, and we take then $r = 0$ and $q = f/g$.

Suppose then that the assertion holds if $\deg f \leq n$. We show that it must hold then if $\deg f = n + 1$. We have $f(x) = a_0 + a_1 x + \cdots + a_{n+1}x^{n+1}$, where $a_{n+1} \neq 0$, and, say, $g(x) = b_0 + b_1 x + \cdots + b_m x^m$, where $b_m \neq 0$. If $n + 1 < m$, then we put $q(x) = 0$, $r(x) = f(x)$ and we are done. If $n + 1 \geq m$, then the polynomial

$$f(x) - \frac{a_{n+1}}{b_m} \cdot x^{n+1-m} \cdot g(x)$$

has degree $\leq n$ clearly, and therefore by assumption it can be written in the form $q_1(x) \cdot g(x) + r(x)$, where either $r = 0$ or else $\deg r < \deg g$. We have then

$$f(x) = \left(q_1(x) + \frac{a_{n+1}}{b_m} \cdot x^{n+1-m}\right) \cdot g(x) + r(x)$$

and so the assertion that $q(x)$, $r(x)$ exist holds for $n + 1$. It follows by induction (Sec. 7A, Chap. 2) that the assertion is true for all n. Q.E.D.

The polynomial $q(x)$ of the theorem is called the *quotient* of $f(x)$ by $g(x)$; $r(x)$ is called the *remainder*. Clearly $g(x)$ divides $f(x)$ (Definition 3.1) if and only if $r(x) = 0$. Observe that if $g(x)$ is monic, then b_m above is 1 and so it is not necessary to assume the existence of inverses (for multiplication). That is, the proof works in this case if K is any integral domain.

THEOREM 3.3 (Euclidean algorithm) *Let $f(x)$ and $g(x)$ be two nonzero polynomials in $K[x]$. Then $f(x)$ and $g(x)$ have a greatest common divisor in $K[x]$, and it can be obtained by the following process† of successive division: write a_0 for one of the two given polynomials and a_1 for the other. Using the division algorithm divide a_0 by a_1, getting $a_0 = q_1a_1 + a_2$, where q_1 is the quotient and a_2 is the remainder. If $a_2 \neq 0$, then divide a_1 by a_2, getting $a_1 = q_2a_2 + a_3$, where q_2 is the quotient and a_3 the remainder, etc. Then the last nonzero remainder so obtained is a* g.c.d. *of $f(x)$ and $g(x)$.*

† The g.c.d. obtained in this way will not usually be monic.

Proof. The argument is essentially the same as for integers. The successive divisions produce a series of equations

3.3
$$\begin{aligned} a_0 &= q_1a_1 + a_2 \\ a_1 &= q_2a_2 + a_3 \\ a_2 &= q_3a_3 + a_4 \\ &\cdots\cdots\cdots\cdots \\ a_{k-2} &= q_{k-1}a_{k-1} + a_k \\ a_{k-1} &= q_ka_k + 0 \end{aligned}$$

Here we have assumed that a_k is the last nonzero remainder. Then $a_2, a_3, \ldots, a_{k-1}, a_k$ are all nonzero, and from Proposition 3.2 we have $\deg a_1 > \deg a_2 > \deg a_3 > \cdots > \deg a_{k-1} > \deg a_k$. [From this it is easy to see that the process (3.3) must terminate after a number of steps at most equal to $\deg a_1$.] From the last equation we see that a_k divides a_{k-1}. From the equation immediately above, a_k also divides a_{k-2}. Continuing up the list (an induction proof is really involved here) we conclude that a_k divides a_1 and a_0, that is, $f(x)$ and $g(x)$. Now suppose that $h(x)$ divides both $f(x)$ and $g(x)$, that is, a_0 and a_1. From the first equation of (3.3) it follows that $h(x)$ must divide a_2; hence, from the second equation, $h(x)$ divides a_3. Continuing down the list, we conclude that $h(x)$ divides a_k. Therefore a_k satisfies Definition 3.3. Q.E.D.

EXAMPLE 3 Find the g.c.d. of $f(x) = 3x^2 + 2x + 1$ and $g(x) = x^2 - x + 2$ in $\mathbf{Q}[x]$. The calculations (3.3) take the form

$$\begin{aligned} 3x^2 + 2x + 1 &= 3 \cdot (x^2 - x + 2) + (5x - 5) \\ x^2 - x + 2 &= \tfrac{1}{5}x \cdot (5x - 5) + 2 \\ 5x - 5 &= (\tfrac{5}{2}x - \tfrac{5}{2}) \cdot 2 + 0 \end{aligned}$$

Hence the last nonvanishing remainder is 2, and this is a g.c.d. of f and g. The *monic* polynomial obtained by dividing the polynomial 2 by its highest coefficient, namely 2, is 1. Hence $(3x^2 + 2x + 1, x^2 - x + 2) = 1$ according to (3.1), and the two polynomials are relatively prime.

EXAMPLE 4 Find the g.c.d. of $f(x) = x^5 - 1$ and $g(x) = x^4 - x^3 + 2x^2 + x - 3$ in $\mathbf{Q}[x]$. The calculations (3.3) are

$$\begin{aligned} x^5 - 1 &= (x + 1) \cdot (x^4 - x^3 + 2x^2 + x - 3) + (-x^3 - 3x^2 + 2x + 2) \\ x^4 - x^3 + 2x^2 + x - 3 &= (-x + 4) \cdot (-x^3 - 3x^2 + 2x + 2) \\ &\qquad + (16x^2 - 5x - 11) \\ -x^3 - 3x^2 + 2x + 2 &= -\frac{1}{16} \cdot \left(x + \frac{53}{16}\right) \cdot (16x^2 - 5x - 11) \\ &\qquad + \frac{71}{(16)^2} \cdot (x - 1) \\ 16x^2 - 5x - 11 &= \frac{(16)^2}{71} \cdot (16x + 11) \cdot \frac{71}{(16)^2} \cdot (x - 1) + 0 \end{aligned}$$

Hence $71/(16)^2 \cdot (x - 1)$ is a g.c.d. of f and g, and therefore so is $x - 1$, which is monic. We have then $(f, g) = x - 1$.

REMARK. The calculations involved in finding the g.c.d. can often be shortened by discarding constant factors along the way. Doing that will only alter the end result by a constant factor which does not matter anyway. For example, the second remainder $16x^2 - 5x - 11$ above could have been replaced by $x^2 - \frac{5}{16}x - \frac{11}{16}$, which would have avoided some of the denominators in the third equation. Or equally well the first remainder, where it appears in the third equation, could be multiplied by 16, etc.

From Theorem 3.3 we derive the following very important consequence:

THEOREM 3.4 *Let $f(x)$ and $g(x)$ be two nonzero polynomials in $K[x]$, and let $h(x)$ be their* g.c.d. *Then there exist polynomials $r(x)$ and $s(x)$ in $K[x]$ such that*

3.4 $$h(x) = r(x) \cdot f(x) + s(x) \cdot g(x)$$

Proof. From (3.3) we have $a_k = a_{k-2} - q_{k-1}a_{k-1}$. From the (unwritten) equation immediately proceeding we get $a_{k-1} = a_{k-3} - q_{k-2}a_{k-2}$, whence $a_k = a_{k-2} - q_{k-1}(a_{k-3} - q_{k-2}a_{k-2}) = (1 + q_{k-1}q_{k-2})a_{k-2} - q_{k-1}a_{k-3}$. Continuing up the list (3.3) we can successively get rid of a_{k-1}, etc., until we finally arrive at $a_k = p \cdot a_0 + q \cdot a_1$, where p and q are certain polynomials. Now a_k can differ from $h(x)$ by only a constant factor, say $a_k = c \cdot h(x)$. Then we get $h(x) = (p/c)a_0 + (q/c)a_1 = (p/c)f(x) + (q/c)g(x)$. Q.E.D.

There are infinitely many pairs of polynomials $r(x)$ and $s(x)$ which satisfy (3.4).

EXAMPLE 5 From Example 3 we have

$$\begin{aligned} 2 &= (x^2 - x + 2) - \tfrac{1}{5}x \cdot (5x - 5) \\ &= (x^2 - x + 2) - \tfrac{1}{5}x \cdot [(3x^2 + 2x + 1) - 3 \cdot (x^2 - x + 2)] \\ &= (\tfrac{3}{5}x + 1) \cdot (x^2 - x + 2) - \tfrac{1}{5}x \cdot (3x^2 + 2x + 1) \end{aligned}$$

Hence

$$1 = (f(x), g(x)) = (\tfrac{3}{10}x + \tfrac{1}{2}) \cdot g(x) - \tfrac{1}{10}x \cdot f(x)$$

Here

$$r(x) = -\tfrac{1}{10}x \qquad \text{and} \qquad s(x) = \tfrac{3}{10}x + \tfrac{1}{2}$$

EXAMPLE 6 The first three equations of Example 4 have the form $a_0 = q_1a_1 + a_2$, $a_1 = q_2a_2 + a_3$, and $a_2 = q_3a_3 + a_4$, where $a_4 = 71/(16)^2 \cdot (x - 1)$. Then $a_4 = a_2 - q_3a_3 = a_2 - q_3(a_1 - q_2a_2) = (1 + q_2q_3) \cdot a_2 - q_3a_1 = (1 + q_2q_3) \cdot (a_0 - q_1a_1) - q_3a_1 = (1 + q_2q_3) \cdot a_0 - [(1 + q_2q_3) \cdot q_1 + q_3] \cdot a_1$. Now $q_2 \cdot q_3 = (-x + 4) \cdot (-\frac{1}{16}) \cdot (x + \frac{53}{16}) = 1/(16)^2 \cdot (16x^2 - 11x - 212)$. Carrying out the calculations we get $(16)^2 \cdot a_4 = (16x^2 - 11x + 44) \cdot f(x) - (16x^3 +$

$5x^2 + 17x - 9) \cdot g(x)$. Then $x - 1 = r(x) \cdot f(x) + r(x) \cdot g(x)$, with $r(x) = \frac{1}{71} \cdot (16x^2 - 11x + 44)$ and $s(x) = -\frac{1}{71} \cdot (16x^3 + 5x^2 + 17x - 9)$.

The close analogy between the foregoing and Sec. 8, Chap. 2, should be apparent. Here we use the degree of a polynomial as a kind of measure of its "size." The proofs of the following two theorems are almost the same as the proofs of Theorems 8.8 and 8.9, Chap. 2, and are left as exercises.

THEOREM 3.5 *Let $f(x)$ and $g(x)$ be two nonzero elements of $K[x]$, and let $p(x)$ be an irreducible polynomial in $K[x]$. If $p(x)$ divides $f(x) \cdot g(x)$, then it must divide either $f(x)$ or $g(x)$.*

COROLLARY *If the irreducible polynomial divides a product $f_1(x)f_2(x) \cdots f_k(x)$ of nonzero elements of $K[x]$, then it must divide one of the factors.*

THEOREM 3.6 *Let $f(x)$ be a polynomial of degree greater than zero in $K[x]$. Then $f(x)$ can be expressed as a product*

3.5 $$f(x) = c \cdot p_1(x)p_2(x) \cdots p_r(x)$$

where c is an element of K and where $p_1(x), \ldots, p_r(x)$ are irreducible monic polynomials in $K[x]$. Furthermore the expression is unique apart from the order of the factors. Finally, any irreducible monic polynomial in $K[x]$ which divides $f(x)$ must coincide with one of the $p_i(x)$.

The expression on the right of (3.5) is called the prime decomposition, or factorization, of $f(x)$. Some of the factors $p_1, \ldots, p_r$ may be repeated, of course, and by collecting such factors we can write $f(x)$ in the form

$$f(x) = c \cdot p_1(x)^{e_1}p_2(x)^{e_2} \cdots p_k(x)^{e_k}$$

where now $p_1, p_2, \ldots, p_k$ are all different, the exponents being positive integers.

Sometimes it is convenient to allow zero exponents also. For example, let $p_1(x), p_2(x), \ldots, p_n(x)$ be *all* the irreducible monic polynomials appearing in the prime decompositions of two polynomials $f(x)$, $g(x)$ in $K[x]$ (of degree greater than zero). Then we can write

$$f(x) = c \cdot p_1(x)^{e_1}p_2(x)^{e_2} \cdots p_n(x)^{e_n}$$

and

$$g(x) = c' \cdot p_1(x)^{e'_1}p_2(x)^{e'_2} \cdots p_n(x)^{e'_n}$$

where now some of the exponents may be zero.

EXERCISES

1. Give complete proofs of Theorems 3.5, 3.6 and of the corollary to Theorem 3.5.

2. Let $f(x)$ and $g(x)$ be two nonzero elements of $K[x]$. Let B denote the set of all elements of the form $a(x) \cdot f(x) + b(x) \cdot g(x)$, where $a(x)$ and $b(x)$ are arbitrary polynomials in $K[x]$. Show that B is a subring of $K[x]$, and prove that if

$v(x)$ is in B, then so is $u(x) \cdot v(x)$ for any $u(x)$ in $K[x]$. Show that B contains a unique monic polynomial $h(x)$ of lowest degree, and prove that $h(x) = (f(x), g(x))$. [Hint: Apply the division algorithm to $h(x)$ and $f(x)$.]

3. Find the g.c.d. of the following polynomials in $\mathbf{Q}[x]$:

(*a*) $x^2 + 2x - 2$, $x^3 - 1$

(*b*) $x^3 + x^2 - 2x$, $x^7 + 2x^6 - x - 2$

(*c*) $x^3 - x^2 + x - 1$, $x^2 + x - 2$, $x^4 + 3x^3 - 3x^2 + 3x - 4$

For (*a*) and (*b*) find polynomials $r(x)$ and $s(x)$ satisfying (3.4).

4. If $f_1, f_2, \ldots, f_n$ are nonzero elements of $K[x]$, prove that they have a g.c.d. $h(x)$ in $K[x]$ and show that $h(x)$ is unique if it is required to be monic. Give a method for computing $h(x)$, and prove that there are elements $s_1, s_2, \ldots, s_n$ in $K[x]$ such that $h = s_1f_1 + s_2f_2 + \cdots + s_nf_n$.

5. Let h be the g.c.d. of two polynomials f, g of positive degree in $K[x]$. Show how to obtain the prime factorization of h from the prime factorizations of f and g.

6. With f, g, and h as in Example 5, show that $h^n = (f^n, g^n)$.

7. Let a, b, f, g be elements of an integral domain D, all nonzero, and let $af + bg = 1$. Prove that $(f, g) = 1$ and $(a, b) = 1$.

***8.** Let D be an integral domain, and let there be assigned to every *nonzero* element c of D an integer, denoted by $d(c)$, such that

(*a*) $d(c) \geq 0$ for any $c \neq 0$

(*b*) $d(ab) = d(a) + d(b)$ for any $a, b \neq 0$ in D

(*c*) $d(a + b) \leq \max\{d(a), d(b)\}$ for any $a, b \neq 0$

Prove that $d(1) = 0$ and that if c in D is invertible, then $d(c) = 0$. Suppose further that if a, b are any two nonzero elements of D, then there exist q and r in D such that $a = qb + r$ and either $r = 0$ or $d(r) < d(b)$. (D is then called a Euclidean ring.) Prove that if $d(c) = 0$, then c is invertible. Prove that every element a of D with $d(a) > 0$ can be expressed as a product $a = p_1p_2 \cdots p_n$ of prime elements in D, this expression being unique apart from invertible factors and the order.

9. Let $K[x]$ be a polynomial ring over a field K. Prove that $K[x]$ contains infinitely many monic irreducible polynomials. (This is trivial if K has infinitely many elements, for every polynomial $x + a$ of degree 1 is irreducible and monic.) Conclude that if K is a finite field, then $K[x]$ contains irreducible monic polynomials of arbitrarily large degree. [Hint: See Theorem 8.3, Chap. 2.]

10. Find the prime factorizations of the following polynomials:

(*a*) $x^3 - 1$ in $\mathbf{Q}[x]$ (*b*) $x^2 + 1$ in $\mathbf{C}[x]$

(*c*) $ax^2 + bx + c$ in $\mathbf{C}[x]$ (*d*) $x^2 + 1$ in $\mathbf{Q}[x]$

(*e*) $x^2 + x + 1$ in $\mathbf{C}[x]$ (*f*) $x^2 + \pi x - 3$ in $\mathbf{R}[x]$

11. Determine all irreducible polynomials of degree 2 and 3 in $\mathbf{Z}_2[x]$.

12. Determine all irreducible monic polynomials of degree 2 in $\mathbf{Z}_3[x]$.

13. Prove that the invertible elements in an integral domain form a group with multiplication as the binary operation.

4. Roots of polynomials

Let $f(x)$ be an element of a polynomial ring $K[x]$, where K is a field. Then $f(x)$ can be expressed in the form

$$f(x) = a_0 + a_1x + \cdots a_nx^n$$

and this expression is unique if $a_n \neq 0$. Now let c be an element of K (or of some larger ring containing K as a subring). Then we recall that $f(c)$ stands for

$$f(c) = a_0 + a_1c + \cdots + a_nc^n$$

If $\deg f(x) = 0$, that is, if $f(x) = a_0$, then $f(c) = a_0$ for any c. For this reason we sometimes refer to polynomials of degree zero, that is, elements of K, as *constants*. If $\deg f(x) > 0$, then of course $f(c)$ depends upon c.

DEFINITION 4.1 *Let $f(x)$ be a nonzero element of the polynomial ring $K[x]$, and let c be an element of K. Then c is called a* root *(or a* zero*) of $f(x)$ if $f(c) = 0$.*

Obviously $f(x)$ cannot have any roots if $\deg f = 0$. The following theorem is fundamental:

THEOREM 4.1 *Let $f(x)$ be a nonzero element of $K[x]$, and let c be a root of $f(x)$ in K. Then $x - c$ divides $f(x)$.*

Proof. By the division algorithm (Proposition 3.2) there exist polynomials $q(x)$ and $r(x)$ in $K[x]$ such that $f(x) = q(x) \cdot (x - c) + r(x)$, where either $r(x) = 0$ or $\deg r < \deg (x - c) = 1$. Hence r is an element of K. Now the equation remains true if we substitute c for x (Theorem 2.4, Corollary 3), and it becomes $0 = r(c)$. Therefore $r = 0$. Q.E.D.

COROLLARY *If $c_1, c_2, \ldots, c_k$ are distinct roots of $f(x)$ in K, then $f(x)$ is divisible by $(x - c_1)(x - c_2) \cdots (x - c_k)$. Therefore the number of distinct roots of $f(x)$ cannot exceed* $\deg f$.

All the irreducible polynomials $x - c_1, \ldots, x - c_k$ divide $f(x)$, by the theorem, and the corollary follows at once from Theorem 3.6 and Proposition 2.3. It can also be proved directly. For let $q(x)$ be the quotient of $f(x)$ by $x - c_1$. Then $f(x) = q(x) \cdot (x - c_1)$, and this equation remains true if we replace x by $c_2, \ldots, c_k$. Thus $0 = q(c_j) \cdot (c_j - c_1)$, and by assumption $c_j - c_1 \neq 0$ for $j = 2, \ldots, k$. Hence $c_2, c_3, \ldots, c_k$ are distinct roots of $q(x)$, and the argument can be repeated with $q(x)$ in place of $f(x)$. An induction is involved. We omit the details.

THEOREM 4.2 *Let $f(x)$ be a polynomial of degree $n > 0$ in $\mathbf{C}[x]$. Then $f(x)$ can be factored as a product*

$$f(x) = a(x - c_1)(x - c_2) \cdots (x - c_n) \qquad (4.1)$$

where $a, c_1, c_2, \ldots, c_n$ are complex numbers. In fact, a is the highest coefficient of $f(x)$. Moreover (4.1) is unique apart from the order of the factors. The irreducible polynomials in $\mathbf{C}[x]$ are the polynomials of degree 1.

Proof. The uniqueness of (4.1) follows from Theorem 3.6, and it is obvious that a is the coefficient of x^n. To prove the existence of such a factorization we use induction. For $n = 1$ the assertion is trivial. Suppose then that it is true for $n - 1$ (where $n > 1$). We show that it must be true for n. In fact, $f(x)$ has at least one root c_1 in $\mathbf{C}$, by Theorem 1.4, Chap. 5. By Theorem 4.1, $x - c_1$ divides $f(x)$, say, $f(x) = q(x) \cdot (x - c_1)$. Then $\deg q(x) = n - 1$, and by assumption $q(x)$ can be factored in the form (4.1), and therefore so can $f(x)$. Q.E.D.

Naturally some of the factors $x - c$ in (4.1) may appear several times. If $x - c$ appears exactly k times, then c is said to be a root of $f(x)$ of *multiplicity* k, or to be a k*-fold* root of $f(x)$.

COROLLARY *Let $f(x)$ be a polynomial of degree $n > 0$ in $\mathbf{R}[x]$. Then $f(x)$ can be expressed as a product*

4.2 $$f(x) = a \cdot p_1(x)p_2(x) \cdots p_r(x)$$

where $p_1(x), \ldots, p_r(x)$ are monic irreducible polynomials in $\mathbf{R}[x]$ of degree 1 or 2 and where a is the highest coefficient of $f(x)$. The factorization (4.2) is unique apart from the order of the factors. In particular, the irreducible polynomials in $\mathbf{R}[x]$ are those of degree 1 and certain polynomials of degree 2.

Proof. Uniqueness of (4.2) follows from Theorem 3.6. We use induction on n to prove the existence of such a factorization. For $n = 1$ this is trivial. Now let n be an integer < 1, and suppose that a factorization of the stated type is possible for all polynomials in $\mathbf{R}[x]$ of degree $< n$. We show that the same is true for degree n. Let $f(x)$ have degree n and factor $f(x)$ in the form (4.1). If all the roots $c_1, c_2, \ldots, c_n$ are *real*, then we are done. Otherwise let c_1, say, be a root which is not real. By Theorem 1.3, Chap. 5, its complex conjugate $\bar{c}_1$ is also a root. Hence $\bar{c}_1$ must appear among the numbers $c_2, c_3, \ldots, c_n$, and so the right-hand side of (4.1) must contain the product $(x - c_1)(x - \bar{c}_1)$. Call this polynomial $p(x)$. Then $p(x) = x^2 - (c_1 + \bar{c}_1)x + c_1\bar{c}_1$, and the coefficients here are *real*. Hence $p(x)$ is in $\mathbf{R}[x]$, and it is plainly irreducible in $\mathbf{R}[x]$. From (4.1) it is clear that $p(x)$ divides $f(x)$. That is, $f(x) = p(x) \cdot q(x)$, where $q(x)$ is the product of a and the $n - 2$ other factors different from $x - c_1$ and $x - \bar{c}_1$. The quotient $q(x)$ must have *real* coefficients. Apply the division algorithm to $f(x)$ and $p(x)$ in $\mathbf{R}[x]$, getting say $f(x) = p(x)q_1(x) + r(x)$, where q_1 and r have real coefficients, and either $r = 0$ or $\deg r < \deg q_1$. From the uniqueness part of Proposition 3.2 it follows that $q_1(x) = q(x)$ and $r(x) = 0$. Thus $q(x)$ is a polynomial in $\mathbf{R}[x]$ of degree $n - 2$. If $n = 2$, then it is a constant (namely, a), and we are done. If $n > 2$, then by assumption $q(x)$ has a factorization of the form (4.2), and therefore so does $f(x) = p(x) \cdot q(x)$. Hence the theorem holds for all $n > 0$, by mathematical induction. Q.E.D.

The corollary shows that complex roots of a real polynomial must occur in conjugate pairs. *If the polynomial has odd degree, it must then have at least one real root.*

EXAMPLE 1 The theorems above are often useful in determining prime factorizations of polynomials. Let us find the prime factorization of $x^4 + 1$ in $\mathbf{R}[x]$. This is not entirely trivial, and in fact it gave some trouble to as eminent a mathematician as G. W. Leibniz (1646–1716), one of the discoverers of calculus. Now the roots of the polynomial $x^4 + 1$ are just the 4th roots of -1. According to Theorem 3.3, Chap. 5, those roots in $\mathbf{C}$ can be found by writing -1 in polar form: $-1 = \cos \pi + i \sin \pi$. The 4th roots are then

$$\cos \frac{\pi + 2k\pi}{4} + i \sin \frac{\pi + 2k\pi}{4} \qquad (k = 0, 1, 2, 3)$$

These are easily seen to be the four numbers $\frac{1}{2}(\pm 1 \pm i)$. Therefore (using the corollary of Theorem 4.1) we get

$$\begin{aligned} x^4 + 1 &= \left(x - \frac{1+i}{2}\right)\left(x - \frac{1-i}{2}\right)\left(x + \frac{1+i}{2}\right)\left(x + \frac{1-i}{2}\right) \\ &= (x^2 - \sqrt{2}x + 1)(x^2 + \sqrt{2}x + 1) \end{aligned}$$

The first expression above is the prime factorization of $x^4 + 1$ in $\mathbf{C}[x]$; the second is its prime factorization in $\mathbf{R}[x]$. The polynomial $x^4 + 1$ is irreducible in $\mathbf{Q}[x]$, as is easily seen. The factorization above can also be obtained from the not entirely obvious observation that $x^4 + 1 = (x^2 + 1)^2 - 2x^2 = (x^2 + 1 + \sqrt{2}x)(x^2 + 1 - \sqrt{2}x)$.

Proof of Wilson's Theorem. As another application we now give a proof of Theorem 10.6, Chap. 2. We wish to show that if p is prime, then $(p - 1)! \equiv -1 \pmod{p}$. To do so we take for K the field $\mathbf{Z}_p$ of residue classes of integers modulo p (Sec. 10, Chap. 2). Since the theorem is easily verified for $p = 2$, we shall assume that $p > 2$; hence p is *odd*. Now let $\bar{c}$ denote any nonzero element of $\mathbf{Z}_p$. (Remember, $\bar{c}$ is a residue class of integers modulo p.) From Fermat's theorem (Theorem 10.5, Chap. 2) it follows at once that $\bar{c}^{p-1} = \bar{1}$, where $\bar{1}$ is the unit element of $\mathbf{Z}_p$. Hence every nonzero element of $\mathbf{Z}_p$ is a root of the polynomial $x^{p-1} - \bar{1}$ in $\mathbf{Z}_p[x]$. Letting $\bar{1}, \bar{2}, \ldots, \overline{p-1}$ denote the residue classes modulo p containing $1, 2, \ldots, p - 1$, respectively, we have from the corollary of Theorem 4.1

$$x^{p-1} - \bar{1} = (x - \bar{1})(x - \bar{2}) \cdots (x - \overline{p-1})$$

since $x^{p-1} - \bar{1}$ must be divisible by the right-hand side, and both sides have the same degree. Now put $\bar{0}$ for x in this equation ($\bar{0}$ being the zero element of $\mathbf{Z}_p$). We then get $-\bar{1} = (-\bar{1})(-\bar{2}) \ldots (-(\overline{p-1})) =$

$(-1)^{p-1} \cdot \bar{1} \cdot \bar{2} \cdots \overline{(p-1)} = \bar{1} \cdot \bar{2} \cdots \overline{(p-1)}$, since $p - 1$ is even. This equation means precisely that $-1 \equiv (p-1)! \pmod{p}$.

We mention another important theorem. It is a generalization of Theorem 3.3, Chap. 5.

THEOREM 4.3 *Let h be an isomorphism from a field K to a field K', and let x, y be variable quantities over K and K', respectively. Let $f(x)$ and $g(x)$ be two polynomials in $K[x]$, and let $f'(y)$, $g'(y)$ be the polynomials in $K[y]$ obtained by replacing x by y and by replacing each coefficient a by the corresponding element $h(a)$ in K'. If $g(x)$ divides $f(x)$, then also $g'(y)$ divides $f'(y)$.*

Proof. Consider the mapping h^* from $K[x]$ to $K'[y]$ defined as follows: If $a_0 + a_1x + \cdots + a_nx^n$ is any element of $K[x]$, then by definition it is sent by h^* into $a_0' + a_1'y + \cdots + a_n'y^n$, where $a_j' = h(a_j)$. Clearly for elements of K the mapping h^* is the same as the given mapping h; and the polynomials $f'(y)$, $g'(y)$ of the theorem are the result of applying h^* to $f(x)$ and $g(x)$. It is a very straightforward matter to verify that h^* is an isomorphism from $K[x]$ to $K'[y]$. If $f(x) = g(x) \cdot q(x)$, and if we let $q'(y)$ denote the result of applying h^* to $q(x)$, then $f'(y) = g'(y) \cdot q'(y)$, since h^* is an isomorphism, and so $g'(y)$ divides $f'(y)$. Q.E.D.

COROLLARY *If c is a root of $f(x)$ in K, then $c' = h(c)$ is a root of $f'(y)$ in K'.*

Proof. By Theorem 4.1, $x - c$ divides $f(x)$. Hence, by Theorem 4.3, $y - c'$ divides $f'(y)$. Q.E.D.

EXAMPLE 2 In particular, if we take $K = K' = \mathbf{C}$, $x = y$, and for h the isomorphism that sends every element of $\mathbf{C}$ into its complex conjugate, and if c is a root of a polynomial $f(x)$ with *real* coefficients, then from the corollary it follows that $\bar{c}$ is also a root of $f(x)$. This is Theorem 3.3, Chap. 5.

EXERCISES

1. Find the prime factorizations of the following polynomials in $\mathbf{Q}[x]$, $\mathbf{R}[x]$, and $\mathbf{C}[x]$:

(*a*) $x^2 - 2$ (*b*) $x^3 + 4x^2 + 5x + 2$

(*c*) $x^3 + 2x^2 - 1$ (*d*) $x^3 + 2x^2 + 2x + 1$

2. Let c be an element of a field K. Let S_c be the mapping $K[x] \to K$ that sends any element $f(x)$ in $K[x]$ into $f(c)$, the element of K obtained by substituting c for x. Let A denote the subset of $K[x]$ consisting of all elements which are sent by S_c into zero. Prove that A is a subring of $K[x]$. Give a simple criterion (not the one already given) for a polynomial to be in A.

3. Show that if c is any real number, then $x^2 - c^2$ divides $x^{2n} - c^{2n}$ for any positive integer n. Find the prime factorization in $\mathbf{R}[x]$ of $x^{2n} - c^{2n}$. [Hint: Use the method of Example 1.]

4. Let $f(x)$ and $g(x)$ be polynomials in $K[x]$, and suppose that they have a root c

in common in some field L containing K as a subfield. Prove that $f(x)$ and $g(x)$ then have a g.c.d. of positive degree in $K[x]$.

5. Consider the mapping D of a polynomial ring $K[x]$ to itself defined as follows: If $f(x) = a_0 + a_1x + a_2x^2 + \cdots + a_nx^n$, then $Df(x) = a_1 + 2a_2x + 3a_3x^2 + \cdots + na_nx^{n-1}$. [$Df(x)$ is called the *derivative* of $f(x)$.] Prove that $D(f(x) \pm g(x)) = Df(x) \pm Dg(x)$ and $D(f(x) \cdot g(x)) = Df(x) \cdot g(x) + f(x) \cdot Dg(x)$. Prove that an element $f(x)$ of $\mathbf{C}[x]$ has a repeated root if and only if $f(x)$ and $Df(x)$ are not relatively prime.

***6.** Let K be a subfield of a field L, and let c be an element of L which is a root of an irreducible polynomial $f(x)$ of degree n in $K[x]$. Prove that every element of $K[c]$ can be expressed in one and only one way in the form $a_0 + a_1c + \cdots + a_{n-1}c^{n-1}$, where $a_0, a_1, \ldots, a_{n-1}$ are in K (see Definition 2.1). Prove that $K[c]$ is a field. [Hint: If $g(x)$ is a nonzero polynomial of degree $<n$, show that there exist polynomials $r(x)$ and $s(x)$ in $K[x]$ such that $r(x) \cdot g(x) + s(x) \cdot f(x) = 1$.] If c' is another root of $f(x)$ in L, prove that $K[c]$ and $K[c']$ are isomorphic.

7. Let K be a subfield of a field L, and let c be an element of L which is *algebraic* over K (see Definition 2.2). Let A be the set of all polynomials in $K[x]$ having c as a root. Prove that A contains a unique monic polynomial $f(x)$ of lowest degree and that it divides every element of A. Prove that if c' is another element of L which is algebraic over K and that if A' is the similarly defined subset of $K[x]$, then $A = A'$ if and only c' is also a root of $f(x)$.

8. Let B be the set of all polynomials of degrees 0 and 1 in $\mathbf{R}[x]$. The sum of two elements of B is clearly again in B. Define a product $*$ in B as follows: If $f(x)$ and $g(x)$ are two elements of B, then $f(x) * g(x) =$ remainder of $f(x) \cdot g(x)$ upon division by $x^2 + 1$. The remainder must have degree < 2, and so $f(x) * g(x)$ is again in B. Prove that B with this product and its usual addition is a field of complex numbers (Definition 1.1, Chap. 5).

***9.** Let K be a field, and let $p(x)$ be an irreducible polynomial of degree n in $K[x]$. Let B consist of all polynomials in $K[x]$ of degree $<n$. For two elements $f(x)$, $g(x)$ in B define a product $*$ by $f(x) * g(x) =$ remainder of $f(x) \cdot g(x)$ upon division by $p(x)$. Prove that B with its usual addition and with the product $*$ is a field containing K as a subfield and containing a root of $p(x)$.

10. Let $f(x) = x^n + a_1x^{n-1} + \cdots + a_{n-1}x + a_n$ be a polynomial with coefficients in $\mathbf{Z}$. Prove that if $f(x)$ has a rational root r, then r must be an integer. Conclude then that the congruence $x^n + a_1x^{n-1} + \cdots + a_n \equiv 0 \pmod{m}$ has a solution in $\mathbf{Z}$ for every integer $m > 1$. From this prove that $x^3 - 8x + 6$ cannot have any rational roots (try $m = 5$; you only have to test five values of x). Show that $4x^3 + 2x - 3$ has no rational roots (multiply the equation by 2 and replace x by $y = 2x$).

11. Prove that $x^2 + x + 1$ divides $x^{3a} + x^{3b+1} + x^{3c+2}$ for any non-negative integers a, b, c. Can you find a generalization of this fact where the integer 3 is replaced by an arbitrary one?

12. Find the prime factorization of $(x + 1)^n + (x - 1)^n$ in $\mathbf{R}[x]$.

13. The polynomial $x^4 - x^3 - 2x^2 + 4x - 4$ has the root $1 + i$. Find the other three roots in $\mathbf{C}$.

14. Let $a_0, a_1, \ldots, a_n$ be distinct elements of a field K, and let $b_0, b_1, \ldots, b_n$ be arbitrary elements of K. Prove that there is one and only one polynomial $f(x)$ of degree n with coefficients in K such that $f(a_i) = b_i$ for $i = 1, \ldots, n$. Prove that $f(x)$ is given by the formula

$$f(x) = \sum_{j=0}^{n} b_j \cdot \frac{(x - a_0) \cdots (x - a_{j-1})(x - a_{j+1}) \cdots (x - a_n)}{(a_j - a_0) \cdots (a_j - a_{j-1})(a_j - a_{j+1}) \cdots (a_j - a_n)}$$

This is called Lagrange's interpolation formula. Find the polynomial f of degree 3 in $\mathbf{Q}[x]$ such that $f(1) = 1, f(2) = 3, f(3) = 6, f(4) = 10$.

***15.** For any sequence $\{a_i\} = \{a_0, a_1, a_2, a_3, \ldots\}$ of rational numbers, denote by $\Delta\{a_i\}$ the sequence of differences $\{a_1 - a_0, a_2 - a_1, a_3 - a_2, \ldots\}$. Define Δ^n inductively by $\Delta^n\{a_i\} = \Delta(\Delta^{n-1}\{a_i\})$. Thus $\Delta^2\{a_i\}$ is the sequence $\{a_2 - 2a_1 + a_0, a_3 - 2a_2 + a_1, a_4 - 2a_3 + a_2, \ldots\}$. Now let $f(x)$ be a polynomial of degree n with rational coefficients, and set $a_i = f(i)$ for $i = 0, 1, 2, \ldots$. Prove that $\Delta^r\{a_i\} = 0$ for $r > n$. Conversely, if $\{a_i\}$ is a sequence of rational numbers such that $\Delta^{n+1}\{a_i\} = 0$, prove that there is a polynomial $f(x)$ of degree at most n, with rational coefficients, such that $a_i = f(i)$ for $i = 0, 1, 2, \ldots$.

16. Using the results of the preceding exercise, prove that there is a unique polynomial $f(x)$ of degree $r + 1$, with rational coefficients, such that $f(n) = 1^r + 2^r + 3^r + \cdots + n^r$ for $n = 1, 2, 3, \ldots$.

5. *Polynomials in several variables*

We begin with some rather obvious generalizations of the definitions of Sec. 2; but for simplicity we shall restrict our considerations to integral domains, rather than arbitrary rings. Then let D be an integral domain, and let $t_1, t_2, \ldots, t_n$ be elements of D. Any (finite) sum of terms of the type

5.1 $\quad a \cdot t_1^{k_1} t_2^{k_2} \cdots t_n^{k_n} \qquad a$ in D; $k_1, \ldots, k_n$ integers ≥ 0

is called a *polynomial* in $t_1, t_2, \ldots, t_n$, with coefficients in D. A term of the type (5.1) is called a *monomial*; the integer $k_1 + k_2 + \cdots + k_n$ is its *degree*.

PROPOSITION 5.1 *Let D be a subring of an integral domain E, and let $t_1, t_2, \ldots, t_n$ be elements of E. Let $D[t_1, t_2, \ldots, t_n]$ denote the set of all elements in E which can be expressed as polynomials in $t_1, \ldots, t_n$ with coefficients in D. Then $D[t_1, t_2, \ldots, t_n]$ is a subring of E, and it is the smallest subring containing D and $t_1, t_2, \ldots, t_n$. Furthermore, if $k \leq n$ and if $D' = D[t_1, t_2, \ldots, t_k]$, then $D[t_1, t_2, \ldots, t_n] = D'[t_{k+1}, \ldots, t_n]$.*

The proof of the first part is essentially the same as the proof of Proposition 2.1 and is omitted. The last part simply says that a polynomial in $t_1, \ldots, t_n$ (with coefficients in D) can be considered as a polynomial in the last $n - k$ elements $t_{k+1}, \ldots, t_n$ with coefficients which are polynomials in $t_1, \ldots, t_k$, and vice versa. That is obvious.

DEFINITION 5.1 *Let D be a subring of an integral domain E, and let $x_1, x_2, \ldots, x_n$ be elements of E. Then they are said to be* independent variables (*or* independent indeterminates) *over D if no polynomial in $x_1, x_2, \ldots, x_n$ with coefficients in D is zero unless all the coefficients are zero. In that case, $D[x_1, x_2, \ldots, x_n]$ is called the* ring of polynomials *in $x_1, \ldots, x_n$ with coefficients in D.*

In other words, every element of $D[x_1, x_2, \ldots, x_n]$ can be expressed uniquely, apart from terms with zero coefficients, as a polynomial in $x_1, \ldots, x_n$ with coefficients in D. That is, two elements of $D[x_1, \ldots, x_n]$ are equal if and only if every monomial $x_1^{k_1}x_2^{k_2} \cdots x_n^{k_n}$ has the same coefficient in both elements. The *degree* of a polynomial is the greatest of the degrees of the monomials that occur in it with nonzero coefficients.

For brevity we shall say that elements $x_1, x_2, \ldots, x_n$ are independent variables over an integral domain D if they are elements in some integral domain containing D as a subring and if they satisfy the conditions of Definition 5.1. The ring $D[x_1, \ldots, x_n]$ is called the *ring of polynomials in $x_1, \ldots, x_n$ over D.*

Corresponding to Theorem 2.4 we have the following result:

THEOREM 5.2 *Let D be an integral domain and let $x_1, x_2, \ldots, x_n$ be independent variables over D. Let $t_1, t_2, \ldots, t_n$ be arbitrary elements of any integral domain containing D as a subring. Then the operation that sends every polynomial $f(x_1, x_2, \ldots, x_n)$ of $D[x_1, \ldots, x_n]$ into the element $f(t_1, t_2, \ldots, t_n)$ obtained by replacing each x_j by t_j $(j = 1, \ldots, n)$ is a ring-homomorphism from $D[x_1, \ldots, x_n]$ to $D[t_1, \ldots, t_n]$.*

The operation in question defines a mapping from $D[x_1, \ldots, x_n]$ to $D[t_1, \ldots, t_n]$, since every element of $D[x_1, \ldots, x_n]$ can be written as a sum of distinct monomials $a \cdot x_1^{k_1} \cdots x_n^{k_n}$ (a in D), and that representation is unique except for terms with coefficient zero. Therefore the element $f(t_1, \ldots, t_n)$ is uniquely determined by the element $f(x_1, \ldots, x_n)$ and does not depend upon the particular way in which the latter is written. The fact that the mapping so defined is a ring-homomorphism follows from the same argument as in the one-variable case of Theorem 2.4. We omit the details.

COROLLARY *If $t_1, \ldots, t_n$ are also independent variables over D, then the mapping $D[x, \ldots, x] \to D[t, \ldots, t]$ of Theorem 5.2 is an isomorphism.*

For then the mapping is clearly one-to-one, by Definition 5.1.

THEOREM 5.3 *Let D be an integral domain. Then there exists an integral domain E containing D as a subring and containing n independent variables $x_1, x_2, \ldots, x_n$ over D, where n is a given positive integer.*

By Theorem 2.5 there is an integral domain E_1 containing D as a subring and containing an independent variable x_1 over D. By the same theorem there is an integral domain E_2 containing E_1 as a subring and containing an independent variable x_2 over E_1. Then E_2 also contains D as a subring, and clearly x_1 and x_2 are independent variables over D. Continuing in this way one easily proves Theorem 5.3 by induction.

The theorem guarantees the existence of a polynomial ring $D[x_1, x_2, \ldots, x_n]$ in any number of independent variables.

Now let s denote a permutation of the integers $1, 2, \ldots, n$. That is, s is a one-to-one mapping of that set to itself. Then $x_{s(1)}, x_{s(2)}, \ldots, x_{s(n)}$ are the elements $x_1, x_2, \ldots, x_n$ in some other order (unless s is the identity permutation, of course). If in the corollary to Theorem 5.2 we take $t_1 = x_{s(1)}, \ldots, t_n = x_{s(n)}$, then it follows that the mapping from $D[x_1, \ldots, x_n]$ to itself obtained by applying the permutation s to $x_1, x_2, \ldots, x_n$ is an isomorphism.

EXAMPLE 1 Consider the case $n = 2$, and let the independent variables be x and y. Every element $f(x,y)$ of $D[x, y]$ can then be written in the form

$$f(x, y) = \sum_{k, l \geq 0} a_{kl} x^k y^l$$

where Σ indicates a finite sum and where the a_{kl} are elements of D. The only permutation of x and y other than the identity permutation is of course that one which interchanges x and y. From what has just been said above, the mapping that sends $f(x, y)$ into

$$f(y, x) = \Sigma a_{kl} y^k x^l$$

is an isomorphism from $D[x, y]$ to itself. For example it sends $x + 1$ into $y + 1$ and $x^3 + xy^2 - y^4 + x$ into $y^3 + yx^2 - x^4 + y$, etc.

DEFINITION 5.2 *Let $D[x_1, x_2, \ldots, x_n]$ be a ring of polynomials in $x_1, \ldots, x_n$ over an integral domain D. Then a polynomial $f(x_1, x_2, \ldots, x_n)$ in $D[x_1, \ldots, x_n]$ is called* symmetric *if $f(x_1, x_2, \ldots, x_n) = f(x_{s(1)}, x_{s(2)}, \ldots, x_{s(n)})$ for every permutation s of $1, 2, \ldots, n$.*

It is easily seen that the symmetric polynomials form a subring of $D[x_1, \ldots, x_n]$.

EXAMPLE 2 For two independent variables x and y the polynomials $x + y$, $x^2 + y^2$, xy, $x^2 + xy + y^2$ are symmetric.

For three independent variables x_1, x_2, x_3 the polynomials $(x_1 - x_2)^2(x_1 - x_3)^2(x_2 - x_3)^2$, $x_1x_2x_3$, $x_1 + x_2 + x_3$, $x_1x_2 + x_1x_3 + x_2x_3$ are all symmetric, but $(x_1 - x_2)(x_1 - x_3)(x_2 - x_3)$ is not symmetric,† for the permutation that interchanges 1 and 2 causes it to change sign, clearly.

† Except in the case of a coefficient domain D in which $1 = -1$, for example $\mathbf{Z}_2$.

For any elements $t_1, t_2, \ldots, t_n$ of an integral domain, we define the symbols $\sigma_1(t), \ldots, \sigma_n(t)$ by the formulas

5.2
$$\begin{aligned}
\sigma_1(t) &= t_1 + t_2 + \cdots + t_n = \Sigma t_i \\
\sigma_2(t) &= t_1t_2 + t_1t_3 + \cdots + t_1t_n + t_2t_3 + \cdots + t_{n-1}t_n = \sum_{i<j} t_it_j \\
\sigma_3(t) &= t_1t_2t_3 + t_1t_2t_4 + \cdots = \sum_{i<j<k} t_it_jt_k \\
&\cdots\cdots\cdots\cdots\cdots\cdots \\
\sigma_n(t) &= t_1t_2 \cdots t_n
\end{aligned}$$

In general, $\sigma_k(t)$ consists of the sum of all the different products of k of the elements $t_1, \ldots, t_n$ with different indices. The elements $\sigma_1(t), \ldots, \sigma_n(t)$ are called the *elementary symmetric functions* of $t_1, t_2, \ldots, t_n$. It is easily seen that if y is any element of the integral domain, then

5.3
$$(y - t_1)(y - t_2) \cdots (y - t_n) = y^n - \sigma_1(t) \cdot y^{n-1} + \sigma_2(t) \cdot y^{n-2} + \cdots + (-1)^n \cdot \sigma_n(t)$$

Hence, we have the following theorem:

THEOREM 5.4 *Let $f(x)$ be a monic polynomial of degree $n > 0$ in a polynomial ring $K[x]$, and suppose that $f(x)$ has n roots $c_1, c_2, \ldots, c_n$ in K. That is, suppose that $f(x)$ factors into*

$$f(x) = (x - c_1)(x - c_2) \cdots (x - c_n)$$

Then the coefficient of x^{n-k} in $f(x)$ is $(-1)^k \cdot \sigma_k(c)$.

The converse problem of expressing the roots of $f(x)$ in terms of the coefficients is discussed in Sec. 6.

The following theorem shows that if $x_1, x_2, \ldots, x_n$ are independent variables over an integral domain D, then every symmetric polynomial in $D[x_1, x_2, \ldots, x_n]$ can be expressed as a polynomial in the elementary symmetric functions $\sigma_1(x), \sigma_2(x), \ldots, \sigma_n(x)$. The proof is omitted.

THEOREM 5.5 *Let $D[x_1, x_2, \ldots, x_n]$ be a polynomial ring over an integral domain D. Then the set of symmetric polynomials in $D[x_1, \ldots, x_n]$ coincides with the subring $D[\sigma_1(x), \sigma_2(x), \ldots, \sigma_n(x)]$.*

EXAMPLE 3 For $n = 3$ the elementary symmetric functions $\sigma_1(x), \sigma_2(x), \sigma_3(x)$ are $x_1 + x_2 + x_3$, $x_1x_2 + x_1x_3 + x_2x_3$, and $x_1x_2x_3$. The polynomial $f(x_1, x_2, x_3) = x_1^2 + x_2^2 + x_3^2 + x_1 + x_2 + x_3 + 2$ is easily seen to be equal to $\sigma_1(x)^2 + \sigma_1(x) - 2\sigma_2(x) + 2$.

REMARK. If for any elements $t_1, t_2, \ldots, t_n$ we define

$$s_1(t) = t_1 + t_2 + \cdots + t_n$$

5.4 $$s_2(t) = t_1^2 + t_2^2 + \cdots + t_n^2$$

$$\cdots\cdots\cdots\cdots\cdots$$

$$s_n(t) = t_1^n + t_2^n + \cdots + t_n^n$$

then it can be shown that Theorem 5.5 holds with $s_1(x), s_2(x), \ldots, s_n(x)$ in place of $\sigma_1(x), \sigma_2(x), \ldots, \sigma_n(x)$ if D is a field of characteristic zero (cf. Exercise 6, Sec. 2, Chap. 3; see also Exercise 8 below). For example, in $D[x_1, x_2]$ we have $\sigma_1(x) = s_1(x)$, $\sigma_2(x) = \frac{1}{2}(s_1^2 - s_2)$.

Now let K be a field and consider a polynomial ring $K[x_1, x_2, \ldots, x_n]$ in n variables over K. This is an integral domain, and of course the definitions at the beginning of Sec. 3 apply. It is therefore reasonable to ask whether any analogue of Theorem 3.6 concerning unique factorization holds for polynomials in n variables. Such a theorem does indeed hold and is stated below. It can be proved fairly easily by induction, using Theorem 3.6, but we shall not give the proof here. In the case of polynomials in one variable, we were able to avoid annoying constant factors (nonzero elements of K) by "normalizing" the irreducible polynomials—i.e., by taking them to be monic. There is no very reasonable notion analogous to *monic* for polynomials in more than one variable, and therefore we shall not attempt to normalize irreducible polynomials for $n > 1$.

THEOREM 5.6 *Any nonconstant polynomial $f(x_1, \ldots, x_n)$ in $K[x_1, x_2, \ldots, x_n]$ can be expressed as a product*

$$f = p_1 p_2 \cdots p_r$$

where $p_1, p_2, \ldots, p_r$ are irreducible polynomials in $K[x_1, \ldots, x_n]$. The factorization is unique apart from constant factors and the order of the factors.

EXERCISES

1. Let x, y be independent variables over a field K. Prove that $x^2 \pm y$ and $ax + by$ are irreducible in $K[x, y]$ for any a, b in K not both zero. What is the g.c.d. (x, y)?

2. Prove that if n is an odd positive integer not divisible by 3, then $xy \cdot (x^2 + xy + y^2)$ divides $(x + y)^n - x^n - y^n$ in $K[x, y]$.

3. Prove that $(x + y)^7 - x^7 - y^7 = 7xy \cdot (x + y)(x^2 + xy + y^2)^2$.

4. Prove that there are elements X, Y in $\mathbf{R}[x_1, \ldots, x_n, y_1, \ldots, y_n]$ such that

$$\prod_{i=1}^{n} (x_i^2 + y_i^2) = X^2 + Y^2$$

where $x_1, \ldots, x_n, y_1, \ldots, y_n$ are independent variables.

5. Let $x^2 + ax + b$ be a polynomial in $\mathbf{C}[x]$, and let r_1, r_2 be its roots. Express $r_1^2 + r_2^2$ and $r_1^3 + r_2^3$ in terms of a and b.

6. Taking three independent variables x_1, x_2, x_3 express the polynomials $\sigma_1(x)$, $\sigma_2(x)$, $\sigma_3(x)$ of (5.2) as polynomials in $s_1(x)$, $s_2(x)$, $s_3(x)$ of (5.4), and vice versa. Express $x_1^4 + x_2^4 + x_3^4$ as a polynomial in σ_1, σ_2, σ_3.

7. Let $w_1, w_2, \ldots, w_n$ be the roots of $x^n = 1$ in $\mathbf{C}[x]$. Prove that $w_1 + w_2 + \cdots + w_n = 0$.

***8.** Prove the "Newton formulas" concerning the symmetric polynomials σ_i and s_i in the variables $x_1, x_2, \ldots, x_n$:

$$s_k - \sigma_1 s_{k-1} + \sigma_2 s_{k-2} + \cdots + (-1)^{k-1}\sigma_{k-1}s_1 + (-1)^k \sigma_k = 0 \qquad (k \leq n)$$

$$s_k - \sigma_1 s_{k-1} + \cdots + (-1)^n \sigma_n s_{k-n} = 0 \qquad (k > n)$$

Conclude that $K[\sigma_1, \ldots, \sigma_n] = K[s_1, \ldots, s_n]$ provided every element of K is divisible by $2, \ldots, n$. Compare with Theorem 5.5.

9. Let the roots of $f(x) = x^n + a_1x^{n-1} + \cdots + a_n$ be $x_1, x_2, \ldots, x_n$. Express $(x_1^2 + 1)(x_2^2 + 1) \cdots (x_n^2 + 1)$ in terms of $a_1, a_2, \ldots, a_n$. [Hint: Consider $f(j)f(-j)$.]

6. *Polynomials of degree less than 5*

Theorem 5.4 shows that the coefficients of a polynomial can be calculated very easily from the roots. The converse problem of finding a formula which gives the roots in terms of the coefficients is much more difficult. Indeed it is *unsolvable* in general by purely algebraic operations. In this section we shall show that such formulas do exist for polynomials of degree less than 5. We shall confine our attention to polynomials with complex coefficients. Since the roots of a polynomial are unaltered if we divide the polynomial by its highest coefficient, we can limit the discussion to *monic* polynomials. For polynomials of degree 1 the problem at hand is trivial, and we consider first the case of quadratic equations.

QUADRATIC EQUATIONS The problem in this case is to solve an equation of the type

6.1 $$x^2 + bx + c = 0$$

where b, c are any complex numbers. The answer of course is the well-known quadratic formula. It is instructive to carry out the steps, however. If in (6.1) we put $x = y - b/2$, then we get

$$y^2 + \left(c - \frac{b^2}{4}\right) = 0$$

as is easily seen. The point here is that we got rid of the term involving the first power of the unknown. To solve this last equation we simply have to find two square roots of the number $b^2/4 - c$, and we have seen how to do that in Theorem 3.3, Chap. 5. Calling one of them $\sqrt{b^2/4 - c}$, then the other is $-\sqrt{b^2/4 - c}$, and the solution is $y = \pm\sqrt{b^2/4 - c}$, or†

† The notation here is rather ambiguous: x is understood to be an indeterminate over $\mathbf{C}$, and therefore no such equation as (6.2) is possible. The "equation" should be interpreted as meaning that the numbers on the right are what must be put for x in (6.1) to get an equality.

6.2 $$x = -\frac{b}{2} \pm \frac{1}{2}\sqrt{b^2 - 4c}$$

CUBIC EQUATIONS Now let us take up equations of the type

6.3 $$x^3 + ax^2 + bx + c = 0$$

Just as in (6.1) we can make the second-degree term disappear by putting $x = y - a/3$. There results a new equation

6.4 $$y^3 + py + q = 0$$

in which p and q can easily be expressed in terms of a, b, c. The exact formulas are of no importance here.

To solve (6.4) we put $y = u + v$. Then

$$y^3 = u^3 + v^3 + 3uv \cdot (u + v) = u^3 + v^3 + 3uvy$$

and so (6.4) becomes

6.5 $$u^3 + v^3 + (3uv + p) \cdot y + q = 0$$

We now suppose that u and v satisfy the equation

6.6 $$3uv + p = 0$$

Then from (6.5) and (6.6) we get

6.7 $$u^3 + v^3 = -q \qquad u^3v^3 = -p^3/27$$

Therefore $(t - u^3)(t - v^3) = t^2 - (u^3 + v^3)t + u^3v^3 = t^2 + qt - p^3/27$. Hence u^3 and v^3 are roots of the quadratic equation

$$t^2 + qt - p^3/27 = 0$$

Hence, using (6.2),

6.8 $$u^3 = -\frac{q}{2} + \sqrt{\frac{q^2}{4} + \frac{p^3}{27}}$$
$$v^3 = -\frac{q}{2} - \sqrt{\frac{q^2}{4} + \frac{p^3}{27}}$$

Since $y = u + v$, we get for the roots of (6.4) the expression

6.9 $$\left[-\frac{q}{2} + \sqrt{\frac{q^2}{4} + \frac{p^3}{27}}\right]^{\frac{1}{3}} + \left[-\frac{q}{2} - \sqrt{\frac{q^2}{4} + \frac{p^3}{27}}\right]^{\frac{1}{3}}$$

A full discussion of this result would lead us too far afield; but a few words of explanation are necessary. The formula (6.9) yields in general nine different numbers, since every nonzero number has three distinct cube roots. The point is that the two cube roots (u and v) indicated in (6.9) must be chosen so as to satisfy (6.6).

EXAMPLE 1 Find the roots of $x^3 + 21x + 342$. This is already in the form (6.4). Putting $x = u + v$, Eq. (6.6) and (6.8) become

6.10 $$uv = -7 \qquad u^3 = 1 \qquad v^3 = -7^3$$

Taking $u = 1$, we must take $v = -7$, and so one root is $x = u + v = -6$. Let w be the number

$$w = \cos\frac{2\pi}{3} + i\sin\frac{2\pi}{3} = -\frac{1}{2} + \frac{i\sqrt{3}}{2}$$

Then $1, w, w^2$ are the three cube roots of 1. If we take $u = w$, then to satisfy (6.10) we must take $v = -7w^2$, and so $w - 7w^2$ is another root of our equation. Finally if we take $u = w^2$, then we must take $v = -7w$, getting for the third root the number $w^2 - 7w$. The three roots are, therefore, $-6,\ 3 \pm 4 \cdot \sqrt{3}i$.

BIQUADRATIC EQUATIONS Thus are called equations of degree 4:

6.11 $$x^4 + ax^3 + bx^2 + cx + d = 0$$

There are various methods for solving this equation. They are really equivalent and involve the solution of cubic and quadratic equations. The method we follow consists of adding $(ex + f)^2$ to both sides and choosing e and f in order to get a perfect square on the left. Adding $(ex + f)^2$ we get

6.12 $$x^4 + ax^3 + (b + e^2) \cdot x^2 + (c + 2ef) \cdot x + (d + f^2) = (ex + f)^2$$

Suppose the left-hand side is the square of, say, $x^2 + px + q$. Then we must have, equating coefficients,

$$2p = a \qquad p^2 + 2q = b + e^2 \qquad 2pq = c + 2ef \qquad q^2 = d + f^2$$

Rewrite the last three of these, squaring the third one:

$$e^2 = p^2 + 2q - b \qquad 4e^2f^2 = (2pq - c)^2 \qquad f^2 = q^2 - d$$

Substituting the first and third in the second we get

$$(2pq - c)^2 = 4(p^2 + 2q - b) \cdot (q^2 - d)$$

or (using $p = a/2$)

6.13 $$(aq - c)^2 = (a^2 + 8q - 4b) \cdot (q^2 - d)$$

This is a cubic equation for q, and it can be solved for q in terms of a, b, c, d by the method developed above. Once we have q, then e and f can be obtained from the preceding equations. Equation (6.12) becomes

$$(x^2 + px + q)^2 = (ex + f)^2$$

or

$$[x^2 + (p + e)x + (q + f)] \cdot [x^2 + (p - e)x + (q - f)] = 0$$

Then finally we are left with the two quadratic equations

$$x^2 + (p + e)x + (q + f) = 0$$
$$x^2 + (p - e)x + (q - f) = 0$$

to get the four roots of (6.11).

EXAMPLE 2 Solve $x^4 - 2x + 8x - 3 = 0$. For this Eq. (6.13) becomes $q^3 + q^2 + 3q - 5 = 0$, of which one root is $q = 1$ (we need only one). Then from the equations above we find $e^2 = 4$, $f^2 = 4$, $ef = -4$, whence $e = 2$, $f = -2$ (or vice versa). The last two quadratic equations are then $x^2 + 2x - 1 = 0$, $x^2 - 2x + 3 = 0$. Hence the roots are $-1 \pm \sqrt{2}$ and $1 \pm \sqrt{2}i$.

We observe that the foregoing solutions of equations of degrees 2, 3, and 4 involve extracting square and cube roots of certain numbers, along with ordinary algebraic manipulations. The question naturally arises as to the possibility of solving equations of higher degree by similar operations. For certain equations of degree > 4, such solutions are possible. For example, $x^n - a = 0$ can be solved for any positive integer n by simply extracting the nth root of a by the method given in Sec. 3, Chap. 5. The equation $x^6 - 2x^3 + 4 = 0$ can be solved by observing that it is a quadratic equation in x^3, and so $x = (1 \pm \sqrt{-3})^{1/3}$.

But in general, for equations of degree ≥ 5, it is *impossible* to obtain the roots by a series of operations of the kind encountered above—namely, operations in **C** (that is, $+$, $-$, $\times$, $\div$) and extraction of nth roots. Thus there is no formula (however complicated) for the roots of equations of degree ≥ 5 analogous to the quadratic formula.†

The thoughtful reader will, however, find this fact itself less remarkable than the possibility of *proving* it. That was first done, for equations of degree 5, by N. H. Abel (1802–1829). The general question of solvability of equations depends upon some deep relations among equations, fields, and groups, first fully explained by E. Galois (1811–1832) in a letter written on the thirtieth of May, 1832. The following morning he died in a duel over "*quelque coquette de bas étage.*" The algebraic theory that he sketched in his last few hours is called Galois theory.

With the concepts developed in Galois theory, it is an easy matter to dispose of some other famous problems, dating from antiquity. E.g., one can prove the impossibility of such ruler and compass constructions as trisecting the angle and duplicating the cube.

EXERCISES

1. Find a necessary and sufficient condition for the equation

$$a_0 + a_1x + \cdots + a_nx^n = 0$$

in order that the reciprocal of every root of it also be a root.

† This does not mean of course that it is impossible to compute roots of equations. There are several methods that enable one to calculate roots with any desired accuracy.

2. Find the roots of the following equations:

(*a*) $x^3 - 18x - 35 = 0$ (*b*) $2x^3 + 3x^2 + 3x + 1 = 0$

(*c*) $x^4 - 10x^2 - 20x - 16 = 0$ (*d*) $x^4 - 3x^2 - 6x - 2 = 0$

3. Prove that a polynomial $ax^2 + bx + c$ in $\mathbf{R}[x]$ with $a \neq 0$ is irreducible in $\mathbf{R}[x]$ if and only if $b^2 - 4ac < 0$.

4. Consider the polynomial $f(x) = ax^2 + bx + c$ in $\mathbf{R}[x]$, where $a > 0$ and $c > 0$. Suppose that $f(x)$ has two *distinct* real roots r_1 and r_2. Prove that if t is a number between r_1 and r_2, then $f(t) < 0$.

5. Let a, b, c be real numbers, with $a \geqslant 0, c \geqslant 0$. Prove that $at^2 + 2bt + c \geqslant 0$ for *all* real numbers t if and only if $b^2 \leqslant ac$.

***6.** Referring to (6.4), let $w = -\frac{1}{2} + i(\sqrt{3}/2)$. Prove that the formula (6.9) also gives the roots of the equations $y^3 + wpy + q = 0$ and $y^3 + w^2py + q = 0$.

7

Rational functions

1. Introduction

As we have seen in Chap. 6, the only invertible elements in a polynomial ring $K[x]$ over a field K are the nonzero elements of the coefficient field K. Thus the symbol $1/x$ has no meaning for $K[x]$; there is no such element in the system. The situation is similar to that which we encountered with $\mathbf{Z}$: the only invertible elements in $\mathbf{Z}$ are 1 and -1; the symbol $\frac{1}{2}$ has no meaning for $\mathbf{Z}$. Just as with the integers, it is often desirable to enlarge the system $K[x]$ in such a way that division is always possible (excluding division by zero, naturally). Now $K[x]$ is an integral domain, by definition, and Theorem 3.1, Chap. 3, shows that there exists a field E, essentially unique, containing $K[x]$ as a subring and such that every element of E can be expressed as a quotient of two elements of $K[x]$. That is our starting point.

2. Rational functions

DEFINITION 2.1 *Let K be a field, and let $x_1, x_2, \ldots, x_n$ be independent variables over K. Then the quotient field of the polynomial ring $K[x_1, x_2, \ldots, x_n]$ is called the* field of rational functions *in $x_1, x_2, \ldots, x_n$ over K; it is denoted by $K(x_1, x_2, \ldots, x_n)$.*

In this chapter we shall be concerned primarily with just one variable, say x. According to the definition, $K(x)$ stands for the quotient field of $K[x]$, and by Theorem 3.1, Chap. 3, every element of $K(x)$ can be expressed (in many ways) as the quotient $f(x)/g(x)$ of two polynomials in $K[x]$, with $g(x) \neq 0$. Thus every element of $K(x)$ can be written in the form

2.1 $$\frac{a_0 + a_1x + \cdots + a_nx^n}{b_0 + b_1x + \cdots + b_mx^m}$$

where $b_0, b_1, \ldots, b_m$ are not all zero. We shall usually denote elements of $K(x)$ by the same kind of symbols $f(x)$, $g(x)$, etc., we have used for polynomials.

Now let $f(x)$, $g(x)$, $f'(x)$, and $g'(x)$ be four polynomials (that is, elements of $K[x]$), with $g'(x)$ and $g(x)$ not zero. By Proposition 2.2, Chap. 3, we have then

$$\frac{f(x)}{g(x)} = \frac{f'(x)}{g'(x)} \qquad \text{if and only if} \qquad f(x) \cdot g'(x) = f'(x) \cdot g(x)$$

In particular, if $f(x) = 0$, then also $f'(x) = 0$, and conversely. If $f(x)$ is not zero, then its degree is defined, and from the equation above, $fg' = f'g$, we see that $\deg f - \deg g = \deg f' - \deg g'$. Therefore if for any nonzero element $f(x)/g(x)$ in $K(x)$ we define

2.2 $$\deg\left(\frac{f(x)}{g(x)}\right) = \deg f(x) - \deg g(x)$$

then the integer so obtained depends only on the element $f(x)/g(x)$, not upon its particular representation as a quotient of two polynomials $f(x)$ and $g(x)$. We do not assign any degree to the zero element of $K(x)$.

EXAMPLE 1 The rational functions $x/(x + 1)$ and $(2x^2 - x + 2)/(x^2 - 3)$ have degree zero; $1/x$ has degree -1 and so does $(3x + 1)/(x^2 + x + 1)$.

It is easily verified that for any nonzero elements $h_1(x)$, $h_2(x)$ in $K(x)$ we have

2.3 $$\deg (h_1(x) \cdot h_2(x)) = \deg h_1(x) + \deg h_2(x)$$

However it is not true in general that $\deg (h_1 + h_2) \leq \deg h_1 + \deg h_2$. That holds for polynomials, but for example

$$\deg\left(\frac{1}{x} + \frac{1}{x^2}\right) = \deg\left(\frac{x+1}{x^2}\right) = -1$$

which is *not* $\leq \deg (1/x) + \deg (1/x^2) = -3$. It is easily shown, however, that

2.4 $$\deg (h_1 + h_2) \leq \max [\deg h_1, \deg h_2]$$

where max indicates the greater of the two numbers (unless they are equal, in which case max indicates their common value).

The following theorem shows that every element of $K(x)$ can be expressed in "lowest terms."

THEOREM 2.1 *Let $h(x)$ be any element of $K(x)$. Then $h(x)$ can be expressed in one and only one way as a quotient*

$$h(x) = \frac{f(x)}{g(x)}$$

of relatively prime polynomials, with $g(x)$ monic.

Proof. By definition of $K(x)$ the element $h(x)$ can be expressed in some way as a quotient $f_1(x)/g_1(x)$ of polynomials, with $g_1 \neq 0$. Let $u(x)$ be the g.c.d. of $f_1(x)$ and $g_1(x)$ [see (3.1), Chap. 6]. Then we can write $f_1(x) = f_2(x) \cdot u(x)$ and $g_1(x) = g_2(x) \cdot u(x)$, where f_2 and g_2 are polynomials. Then $u \cdot (f_1g_2 - f_2g_1) = f_1g_1 - f_1g_1 = 0$, and therefore $f_1g_2 = f_2g_1$, since $u(x) \neq 0$. Hence, $h(x) = f_2(x)/g_2(x)$. Now let c be the highest coefficient of $g_2(x)$ and put $g(x) = (1/c)g_2(x)$, $f(x) = (1/c)f_2(x)$. Then $h(x) - f(x)/g(x)$, and $g(x)$ is monic and $(f, g) = 1$. The uniqueness is left as an exercise. (Theorem 3.6, Chap. 6, can also be used to prove this theorem.)

Q.E.D.

In Chap. 6 we saw that substitution of any element c of K for x in any polynomial $f(x)$ of $K[x]$ produces a homomorphism of $K[x]$ to K. This is no longer the case for the rational-function field $K(x)$. For example, 2 cannot be substituted for x in the rational function $1/(x - 2)$, obviously. See Exercise 2 below.

EXERCISES

1. Prove the uniqueness of $f(x)$ and $g(x)$ in Theorem 2.1.

2. Let c be an element of the field K, and let A denote the set of all elements $h(x)$ of $K(x)$ which can be expressed as quotients $h(x) = f(x)/g(x)$ of polynomials such that $g(c) \neq 0$. Show that if $h(c)$ is defined by $h(c) = f(c)/g(c)$, then the result does not depend upon the particular representation of $h(x)$ as a quotient of polynomials f/g, provided of course that $g(c) \neq 0$. Show that A is a subring of $K(x)$ and that the mapping $A \to K$ defined by $h(x) \to h(c)$ is a homomorphism.

3. Prove (2.3).

4. Let $p(x)$ and $q(x)$ be irreducible polynomials in $K[x]$. Prove that there exist polynomials $f(x)$, $g(x)$ such that in $K(x)$ we have

$$\frac{1}{pq} = \frac{f}{p} + \frac{g}{q} \qquad \text{and } \deg f < \deg p,\ \deg g < \deg q$$

3. Partial fractions

The remainder of this chapter is concerned with a particularly simple and useful method of expressing rational functions in $K(x)$, where K is again a field.

Any element of $K(x)$ can be expressed as a quotient $f(x)/g(x)$ of polynomials, with $g(x) \neq 0$. We can assume that $g(x)$ is *monic*, for otherwise we have only to divide $f(x)$ and $g(x)$ by the highest coefficient of $g(x)$. Then by Theorem 3.6, Chap. 6, the polynomial $g(x)$, if its degree is positive, has a prime decomposition

3.1 $$g(x) = p_1(x)^{e_1}p_2(x)^{e_2} \cdots p_n(x)^{e_n}$$

where $p_1, p_2, \ldots, p_n$ are *distinct* monic irreducible polynomials in $K[x]$, and where $e_1, e_2, \ldots, e_n$ are positive integers. Now let $q_j(x)$ denote the polynomial

3.2 $$q_j(x) = p_1^{e_1} \cdot p_2^{e_2} \cdots p_{j-1}^{e_{j-1}} \cdot p_{j+1}^{e_{j+1}} \cdots p_n^{e_n}$$

obtained by omitting the factor $p_j^{e_j}$ from (3.1). The polynomials $q_1, q_2, \ldots, q_n$ so obtained are relatively prime, for clearly none of the polynomials $p_1, p_2, \ldots, p_n$ divides all the q's. Therefore, by Exercise 4, Sec. 3, Chap. 6, there exist polynomials $s_1(x), s_2(x), \ldots, s_n(x)$ such that

$$1 = s_1q_1 + s_2q_2 + \cdots + s_nq_n$$

Multiplying by $f(x)/g(x)$ and using (3.1) and (3.2) we get

3.3 $$\frac{f}{g} = \frac{f \cdot s_1}{p_1^{e_1}} + \frac{f \cdot s_2}{p_2^{e_2}} + \cdots + \frac{f \cdot s_n}{p_n^{e_n}}$$

Applying the division algorithm (Proposition 3.2, Chap. 6) to $f \cdot s_j$ and $p_j^{e_j}$ we get

3.4 $$f \cdot s_j = h_j \cdot p_j^{e_j} + r_j \qquad \text{where } r_j = 0 \text{ or } \deg r_j < \deg p_j^{e_j}$$

h_j being of course the quotient and r_j the remainder. Putting this in (3.3) for each $j = 1, 2, \ldots, n$, we obtain finally

3.5 $$\frac{f(x)}{g(x)} = h(x) + \frac{r_1(x)}{p_1(x)^{e_1}} + \cdots + \frac{r_n(x)}{p_n(x)^{e_n}},$$

where $h(x)$ is the polynomial

$$h(x) = h_1(x) + h_2(x) + \cdots + h_n(x)$$

Now (3.5) can be simplified a little further if any of the exponents $e_1, \ldots, e_n$ exceed 1. Consider a typical term $r(x)/p(x)^e$ on the right of (3.5). We omit the index j temporarily. If $r = 0$, then of course there is nothing further to do. If $r \neq 0$, then by (3.4) we have $\deg r < \deg p^e$. If $e > 1$ we apply the division algorithm to $r(x)$ and $p(x)^{e-1}$, getting say

$$r = u_1 \cdot p^{e-1} + v_1 \qquad v_1 = 0 \text{ or } \deg v_1 < \deg p^{e-1}$$

If $e - 1 > 1$, then apply the division algorithm to v_1 and p^{e-2}, and so on. In this way we get a series of equations

$$\begin{array}{ll} v_1 = u_2 \cdot p^{e-2} + v_2 & v_2 = 0 \text{ or } \deg v_2 < \deg p^{e-2} \\ \cdots\cdots\cdots & \cdots\cdots\cdots \\ v_{e-3} = u_{e-2} \cdot p^2 + v_{e-2} & v_{e-2} = 0 \text{ or } \deg v_{e-2} < \deg p^2 \\ v_{e-2} = u_{e-1} \cdot p + v_{e-1} & v_{e-1} = 0 \text{ or } \deg v_{e-1} < \deg p \\ v_{e-1} = u_e \cdot 1 & \end{array}$$

From the first equation above we see that $\deg u_1 < \deg p$ because $\deg r < \deg p^e$. In a similar way it follows that $u_2, u_3, \ldots, u_{e-1}$ all have degree $< \deg p$ or else are zero. Combining these equations we get

$$r = u_1 \cdot p^{e-1} + u_2 \cdot p^{e-2} + \cdots + u_{e-1} \cdot p + u_e$$

and so

3.6 $$\frac{r}{p^e} = \frac{u_1}{p} + \frac{u_2}{p^2} + \cdots + \frac{u_e}{p^e}$$

where $u_j = 0$ or else $\deg u_j < \deg p$. We have therefore proved the following theorem.

THEOREM 3.1 *Let $f(x)/g(x)$ be any element in $K(x)$, where $f(x)$ and $g(x)$ are polynomials with $g(x) \neq 0$. Then $f(x)/g(x)$ can be expressed as a sum of terms of the following type: (1) a polynomial and (2) if $\deg g(x) > 0$ then for each factor $p(x)^e$ in the prime factorization of $g(x)$ a sum of terms $u_1/p + \cdots + u_e/p^e$, in which the u_j are polynomials such that if $u_j \neq 0$, then $\deg u_j < \deg p$.*

The decomposition of $f(x)/g(x)$ guaranteed by the theorem is called the *partial-fraction* decomposition of $f(x)/g(x)$. It is not hard to see that it is unique in the sense that in any two such decompositions the nonzero terms are identical. The result is particularly simple for $\mathbf{C}(x)$ because the irreducible polynomials in $\mathbf{C}[x]$ all have degree 1, and so the numerators u_j appearing in the theorem are all constants. In $\mathbf{R}[x]$ irreducible polynomials have degree 1 or 2 and therefore in that case the numerators all have degree at most 1. Several examples are worked out below. The proof of the theorem carries with it a method for making explicit computations, because each step of the proof simply involves use of the division algorithm. However in practice there are many short cuts which materially reduce the labor entailed.

EXAMPLE 1 Find the partial-fraction decomposition of

$$f(x) = \frac{3x^2 + 2x + 2}{x^3 + x^2 - 2x - 2} \qquad \text{in } \mathbf{Q}(x)$$

The denominator factors into $(x^2 - 2)(x + 1)$, and these factors are irreducible in $\mathbf{Q}[x]$. Hence

$$f(x) = h(x) + \frac{u}{x^2 - 2} + \frac{v}{x + 1}$$

where h, u, v are polynomials. The degree of $u(x)$ must be less than 2, and the degree of $v(x)$ must be less than 1. Hence u has the form $u(x) = ax + b$ and $v(x)$ has the form $v = c$, where a, b, c are constants. Now multiply the equation above by the denominator, getting

$$3x^2 + 2x + 2 = h(x)(x^2 - 1)(x + 1) + (ax + b)(x + 1) + c(x^2 - 2)$$

It is clear from this that $h(x) = 0$, for otherwise the right-hand side would have degree > 3. Multiplying out the factors we get then

$$3x^2 + 2x + 2 = (a + c)x^2 + (a + b)x + b - 2c$$

Therefore (Proposition 2.2, Chap. 6) we have $a + c = 3$, $a + b = 2$, $b - 2c = 2$. Solving these three simultaneous equations we get $a = 6$, $b = 4$, $c = -3$. Hence the desired decomposition is

$$f(x) = \frac{6x - 4}{x^2 - 2} - \frac{3}{x + 1}$$

Now in $\mathbf{R}[x]$ the polynomial $x^2 - 2$ is not irreducible. In fact $x^2 - 2 = (x - \sqrt{2})(x + \sqrt{2})$. Therefore, applying Theorem 3.1 to the first term above we get

$$\frac{6x - 4}{x^2 - 2} = h(x) + \frac{a'}{x - \sqrt{2}} + \frac{b}{x + \sqrt{2}}$$

where $h(x)$ is a polynomial and where a', b' are constants. Multiplying both sides by $x^2 - 2$, we see at once that $h(x) = 0$, and

$$6x - 4 = a'(x + \sqrt{2}) + b'(x - \sqrt{2})$$

whence $a' + b' = 6$, $(a' - b') \cdot \sqrt{2} = -4$. Solving these we get $a' = 3 - \sqrt{2}$, $b' = 3 + \sqrt{2}$. Hence the partial-fraction decomposition of $f(x)$ in $\mathbf{R}(x)$ is

$$f(x) = \frac{3 - \sqrt{2}}{x - \sqrt{2}} + \frac{3 + \sqrt{2}}{x + \sqrt{2}} - \frac{3}{x + 1}$$

REMARK. It is easily seen that if $\deg f < \deg g$ in Theorem 3.1, then the polynomial part (1) of the partial-fraction decomposition is zero. If $\deg f > \deg g$, then using the division algorithm we can write $f(x) = q(x) \cdot g(x) + f_1(x)$, where $\deg f_1 < \deg g$. Hence $f/g = q + f_1/g$, and so $q(x)$ is the polynomial part of the partial-fraction decomposition of f/g.

EXAMPLE 2 Find the partial-fraction decomposition in $\mathbf{Q}[x]$ of

$$f(x) = \frac{9x^2 + 10x - 2}{2x^3 - 7x^2 - 14x + 40}$$

Here the numerator has smaller degree than the denominator, and so the polynomial part is zero. The denominator factors into $(x - 2)(x - 4)(2x + 5)$, and so by Theorem 3.1 we have

3.7 $$f(x) = \frac{a}{x - 2} + \frac{b}{x - 4} + \frac{c}{2x + 5}$$

where a, b, c must be constants. Multiplying both sides of this equation by the denominator we get

$$9x^2 + 10x - 2 = a(x - 4)(2x + 5) + b(x - 2)(2x + 5) + c(x - 2)(x - 4)$$

Multiplying this out and equating coefficients we get

$$\begin{aligned} 2a + 2b + c &= 9 \\ -3a + b - 6c &= 10 \\ -20a - 10b + 8c &= -2 \end{aligned}$$

Solving these equations we get $a = -3$, $b = 7$, $c = 1$, and so

$$f(x) = \frac{-3}{x - 2} + \frac{7}{x - 4} + \frac{1}{2x + 5}$$

We now point out a useful short cut which applies in many cases; namely, multiply (3.7) by $x - 2$. There results

$$\frac{9x^2 + 10x - 2}{(x - 4)(2x + 5)} = a + b\,\frac{x - 2}{x + 4} + c\,\frac{x - 2}{2x + 5}$$

Put $x = 2$ in this, getting

$$\frac{54}{-18} = a$$

or $a = -3$. Both b and c can be found in the same way.

EXAMPLE 3 For the rational function $f(x) = (3x^2 + 15)/[(x + 1)^3(x - 2)]$ the theorem tells us that the partial-fraction decomposition has the form

3.8 $$\frac{3x^2 + 15}{(x + 1)^3(x - 2)} = \frac{a}{x + 1} + \frac{b}{(x + 1)^2} + \frac{c}{(x + 1)^3} + \frac{d}{x - 2}$$

where a, b, c, and d are constants. Multiplying through by $x - 2$ and putting 2 for x in the result, we get $d = 1$. Similarly, multiplying by $(x + 1)^3$ and putting $x = -1$, we find $c = -6$. But a and b cannot be found so simply. To determine them we proceed as in Examples 1 and 2: namely, multiply (3.8) by the total denominator, getting

$$3x^2 + 15 = a(x + 1)^2(x - 2) + b(x + 1)(x - 2) - 6(x - 2) + (x + 1)^3$$

Equating coefficients here we obtain

$$a + 1 = 0$$
$$b = 0$$
$$3a + b = -3$$
$$a + b = 1$$

Naturally only the first two equations are necessary, and we have $a = -1$, $b = 0$.

We mention here another device that is sometimes useful: namely, put $x + 1 = y$ in (3.8). It becomes

$$\frac{3(y - 1)^2 + 15}{y^3(y - 3)} = \frac{a}{y} + \frac{b}{y^2} + \frac{c}{y^3} + \frac{d}{y - 3}$$

Clearing out the denominator gives

$$3y^2 - 6y + 18 = (ay^2 + by + c)(y - 3) + dy^3$$

and it is very easy to equate coefficients here.

EXERCISES

1. Find the partial-fraction decomposition of each of the following, in both $\mathbf{Q}(x)$ and $\mathbf{C}(x)$.

(a) $\dfrac{13x + 41}{(x - 3)(x + 1)(x + 2)}$ (b) $\dfrac{3x^2 - 13x}{x^3 - 19x + 30}$

(c) $\dfrac{2x^3 + 1}{x^3 - 9x}$ (d) $\dfrac{1 - 8x^4}{x - 4x^3}$

(e) $\dfrac{2x^5 + 2x^4 + 5x^3 - 3x^2 - 2x}{(x^3 + 1)(x + 1)^3}$ (f) $\dfrac{9x^3 - 24x^2 + 48x}{(x - 2)^4(x + 1)}$

(g) $\dfrac{1 + 3x + 2x^2}{(1 - 2x)(1 - x^2)}$ (h) $\dfrac{x^5 + 2x + 1}{(x - 1)(x^2 + 1)}$

(i) $\dfrac{26x^2 + 208x}{(x^2 + 1)^2(x + 5)}$

2. A theorem analogous to Theorem 3.1 above holds for integers. Work it out. Express $259/540$ in the form $n + a/5 + b/2 + c/2^2 + d/3 + e/3^2 + f/3^3$, where $0 \leqslant a < 5$, $0 \leqslant b, c < 2$, $0 \leqslant d, e, f < 3$.

***3.** Prove that for any positive integer n

$$\frac{(x - 1)(x - 2) \cdots (x - n + 1)}{(x + 1)(x + 2) \cdots (x + n)} = \sum_{k=1}^{n} (-1)^{n+k} \cdot \binom{n - 1 + k}{k}\binom{n - 1}{k - 1}\frac{1}{x + k}$$

4. Find the partial-fractions decomposition of

$$\frac{1}{x^{2n} + 1}, \qquad \frac{x^{m-1}}{x^n - 1}$$

in $\mathbf{C}(x)$ and in $\mathbf{R}(x)$.

8

Vector spaces and affine spaces

1. Introduction

The subject of vector spaces, which sometimes goes under the alias "matrix algebra," is one of the most important parts of mathematics in applications to the natural sciences, and it is an indispensable tool in many parts of mathematics itself. In physical applications, the elements of a vector space are used to represent complex physical quantities. For example, forces and velocities are represented in mechanics by elements of a vector space; in quantum mechanics, the states of a system are represented by elements of a vector space; in modern electrical engineering, signals are represented by such elements; and so forth.

We do not intend here to study any of the various applications of vector spaces, and therefore we do not want to attach any unnecessary interpretations to them. We shall study vector spaces as abstract algebraic systems in order to discover the main consequences of the algebraic laws which are assumed to hold. Elements of vector spaces will often be called "vectors," but again we attach no physical meaning to that term.

2. The basic definitions

The main ingredients required are (1) a field K and (2) an abelian group V. The elements of the field K will be denoted by lowercase italic letters a, b, c, etc., and will frequently be called *scalars*. The elements of the abelian group V will be denoted by boldface letters $\mathbf{u}$, $\mathbf{v}$, $\mathbf{x}$, etc., and sometimes those elements will be called *vectors*.

First let us recall from Chap. 1 that an abelian group V is a set of elements with a binary operation (denoted here by $+$) such that the following axioms apply:

(1) *The operation* $+$ *assigns an element* $\mathbf{u} + \mathbf{v}$ *of* V *to every pair of elements* $\mathbf{u}, \mathbf{v}$ *in* V.

(2) $\mathbf{u} + (\mathbf{v} + \mathbf{w}) = (\mathbf{u} + \mathbf{v}) + \mathbf{w}$ *for any elements* $\mathbf{u}, \mathbf{v}, \mathbf{w}$ *of* V.

(3) $\mathbf{u} + \mathbf{v} = \mathbf{v} + \mathbf{u}$ *for any elements* $\mathbf{u}, \mathbf{v}$ *in* V.

(4) V *contains an "identity element"* $\mathbf{0}$ *(necessarily unique) such that* $\mathbf{u} + \mathbf{0} = \mathbf{u}$ *for every element* $\mathbf{u}$ *in* V.

(5) *For each element* $\mathbf{u}$ *in* V *there is a unique element in* V, *denoted by* $-\mathbf{u}$, *such that* $\mathbf{u} + (-\mathbf{u}) = \mathbf{0}$.

For the definition of a field we refer to Chap. 3.

Now V is said to be a *vector space* (or *linear space*) over the field K if, in addition to the various operations in K and V, there is given another operation, called *scalar multiplication*, satisfying the following new axioms.

(6) *For any element a in K and any element $\mathbf{u}$ in V, scalar multiplication assigns to the pair a, $\mathbf{u}$ another element of V, which we denote by $a \cdot \mathbf{u}$ or $a\mathbf{u}$. It is called the product of a and $\mathbf{u}$.*

(7) $(a \cdot b) \cdot \mathbf{u} = a \cdot (b \cdot \mathbf{u})$ *for any elements a, b in K and $\mathbf{u}$ in V.*

(8) $a \cdot (\mathbf{u} + \mathbf{v}) = (a \cdot \mathbf{u}) + (a \cdot \mathbf{v})$ *for any a in K and any elements $\mathbf{u}$, $\mathbf{v}$ in V.*

(9) $(a + b) \cdot \mathbf{u} = (a \cdot \mathbf{u}) + (b \cdot \mathbf{u})$ *for any a, b in K and any element $\mathbf{u}$ in V.*

(10) $1 \cdot \mathbf{u} = \mathbf{u}$ *for every element $\mathbf{u}$ in V, where 1 is the identity element for multiplication in K.*

These axioms say in effect that there is some way of "multiplying" elements of V by elements of K, giving again elements of V and satisfying reasonable rules of calculation. Axiom (7) above is a kind of associative law, and axioms (8) and (9) are distributive laws. When both + and scalar multiplication are involved in an expression we shall follow the usual conventions concerning omission of parentheses. For example, we write axioms (8) and (9) simply as $a(\mathbf{u} + \mathbf{v}) = a\mathbf{u} + a\mathbf{v}$ and $(a + b)\mathbf{u} = a\mathbf{u} + b\mathbf{u}$, respectively.

In most physical applications of vector spaces the field of scalars K is either the field of real numbers or the field of complex numbers. We shall give special attention to these cases later.

3. Some consequences of the axioms

Both K and V contain zero elements—i.e., the identity elements for their respective operations of addition. We denote the zero element of V by $\mathbf{0}$, that of K by 0 as usual.

PROPOSITION 3.1 *For any element $\mathbf{u}$ in V we have*

$$0 \cdot \mathbf{u} = \mathbf{0};$$

for any element c in K we have

$$c \cdot \mathbf{0} = \mathbf{0}$$

Proof. Since $1 + 0 = 1$ in K we have $1 \cdot \mathbf{u} = (1 + 0) \cdot \mathbf{u}$, whence $1 \cdot \mathbf{u} = 1 \cdot \mathbf{u} + 0 \cdot \mathbf{u}$, or $\mathbf{u} = \mathbf{u} + 0 \cdot \mathbf{u}$, by axioms (9) and (10). Adding $-\mathbf{u}$ to both sides we get $\mathbf{0} = \mathbf{0} + 0 \cdot \mathbf{u}$ [axiom (5)], and so $\mathbf{0} = 0 \cdot \mathbf{u}$, by axiom (4).

To prove the second part we start with $\mathbf{v} + \mathbf{0} = \mathbf{v}$ for any $\mathbf{v}$ in V [axiom (4)]. Then $c \cdot (\mathbf{v} + \mathbf{0}) = c \cdot \mathbf{v}$, and so from axiom (8) we have

$c \cdot \mathbf{v} + c \cdot \mathbf{0} = c \cdot \mathbf{v}$. Now $c \cdot \mathbf{v}$ is an element of V [axiom (6)] and so it has an inverse $-(c \cdot \mathbf{v})$ in V, by axiom (5). Adding that to both sides we get $c \cdot \mathbf{0} = \mathbf{0}$. Q.E.D.

PROPOSITION 3.2 *For any c in K and any $\mathbf{u}$ in V,*

$$(-c)\mathbf{u} = c(-\mathbf{u}) = -(c\mathbf{u})$$

The proof is left as an exercise (cf. Theorem 2.3, Chap. 2).

PROPOSITION 3.3 *Let c be any element of K, and let $\mathbf{u}_1, \mathbf{u}_2, \ldots, \mathbf{u}_r$ be any finite set of elements in V. Then*

$$c(\mathbf{u}_1 + \cdots + \mathbf{u}_r) = c\mathbf{u}_1 + \cdots + c\mathbf{u}_r$$

Similarly if $a_1, a_2, \ldots, a_s$ are any elements of K and $\mathbf{v}$ any element of V, then

$$(a_1 + \cdots + a_s) \cdot \mathbf{v} = a_1\mathbf{v} + \cdots + a_s\mathbf{v}$$

The proof is left as an exercise. The first part follows from axiom (8) by a simple induction, and the second assertion follows in the same way from axiom (9). Arguments of a very similar sort were given in Sec. 7, Chap. 2.

The theorems above, as well as the axioms themselves, are used constantly in what follows, and we shall usually not refer to them explicitly.

EXERCISES

1. Give complete proofs of Propositions 3.2 and 3.3.

2. Let V be a vector space over a field K, and let $\mathbf{v}_1$ and $\mathbf{v}_2$ be two fixed vectors in V. Let V' be the subset of V consisting of all elements $a\mathbf{v}_1 + b\mathbf{v}_2$, where a, b are arbitrary scalars. Show that the sum of two elements of V' is again in V'; show that the product of an element of K and an element of V' is again in V'. Finally show that V' satisfies the axioms for a vector space over K.

3. Let U and V be any two vector spaces over a field K. Let W be the set of all pairs $(\mathbf{u}, \mathbf{v})$ consisting of an element $\mathbf{u}$ in U and an element $\mathbf{v}$ in V. Define an operation $+$ in W by the rule $(\mathbf{u}, \mathbf{v}) + (\mathbf{u}', \mathbf{v}') = (\mathbf{u} + \mathbf{u}', \mathbf{v} + \mathbf{v}')$. Further define scalar multiplication in W by the rule $c \cdot (\mathbf{u}, \mathbf{v}) = (c\mathbf{u}, c\mathbf{v})$ for any c in K and any element $(\mathbf{u}, \mathbf{v})$ in W. Prove that W with these operations is also a vector space over K. (W is called the *direct sum* of U and V and is sometimes denoted by $U \oplus V$.)

4. Let $\mathbf{R}$ and $\mathbf{C}$ be the fields of real and complex numbers, respectively (see Chaps. 4 and 5). Show that $\mathbf{C}$ (with its usual operation of addition but with multiplication simply ignored) is a vector space over $\mathbf{R}$ if scalar multiplication is defined by the rule $c \cdot (a + bi) = ca + cb \cdot i$, where $a + bi$ is any complex number, a and b being real, and where c is any real number.

4. Some important examples

Here we define some special vector spaces which will be used frequently.

Let K be a field, and let n be a positive whole number. Denote by K_n the set of all n-tuples

$$\mathbf{a} = (a_1, a_2, \ldots, a_n)$$

consisting of n elements of K in a specific order. We make K_n into a vector space over K as follows:

4.1 *If* $\mathbf{a} = (a_1, a_2, \ldots, a_n)$ *and* $\mathbf{b} = (b_1, b_2, \ldots, b_n)$ *are any two elements of* K_n*, then we define*

$$\mathbf{a} + \mathbf{b} = (a_1 + b_1, a_2 + b_2, \ldots, a_n + b_n)$$

4.2 *If* $\mathbf{a} = (a_1, a_2, \ldots, a_n)$ *is any element of* K_n *and* c *any element of* K*, then we define*

$$c \cdot \mathbf{a} = (ca_1, ca_2, \ldots, ca_n)$$

It is easily verified (by using the axioms for K!) that addition as defined in (4.1) satisfies axioms (1) to (5), Sec. 2, and that scalar multiplication as defined by (4.2) satisfies axioms (6) to (10), Sec. 2. Therefore K_n with those operations is a vector space over K. The zero element of K_n is the n-tuple (0, 0, . . . , 0).

REMARK 1. If we take $n = 1$ in the foregoing, then K_1 is the same as K itself, save that in K_1 we ignore the multiplication of two elements. We shall not bother to distinguish between K and K_1.

Figure 1 Elements of a vector space are sometimes depicted by arrows. If one chooses a cartesian coordinate system in the plane, the element (a_1, a_2) of the vector space $\mathbf{R}_2$ is depicted by an arrow from the origin (0, 0) to the point with coordinates (a_1, a_2) for any a_1, a_2 in the field of real numbers $\mathbf{R}$. Vector addition is obtained by "completing the parallelogram" as shown in the figure.

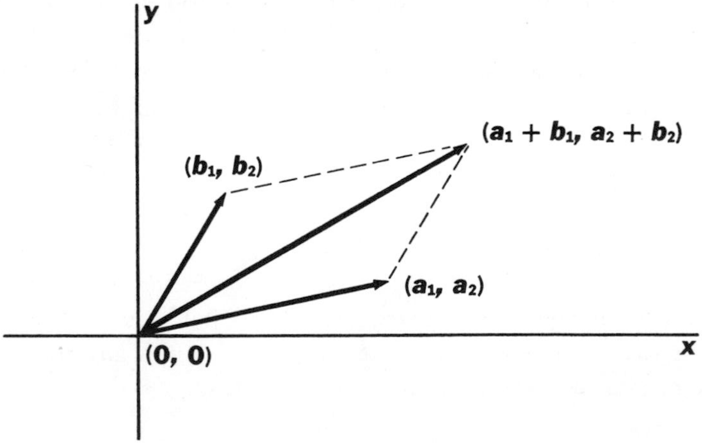

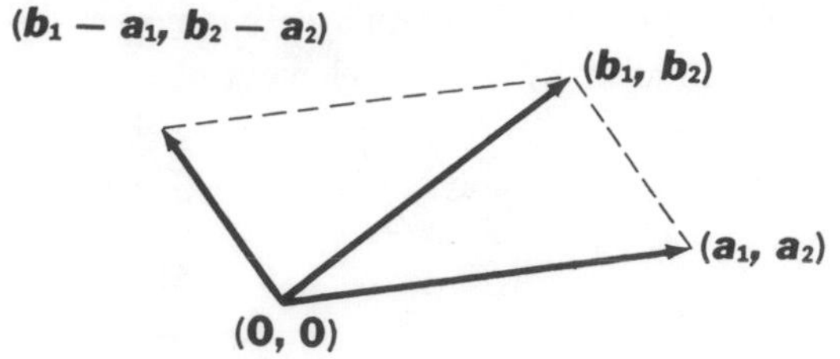

Figure 2

Subtraction in the vector space $\mathbf{R}_2$.

REMARK 2. Referring to Exercise 3, Sec. 3, we see that K_2 is nothing but the *direct sum* $K \oplus K$. More generally K_n can be considered as the direct sum $K \oplus K \oplus \cdots \oplus K$ of K with itself n times.

In the definition above, instead of using ordered n-tuples $(a_1, a_2, \ldots, a_n)$ of elements in K, we could equally well use *infinite sequences* of elements $(a_1, a_2, a_3, \ldots)$. Denoting the set of all such sequences by K_∞, it is easily verified that K_∞ can be made into a vector space over K by definitions analogous to (4.1) and (4.2).

In the definition of the notion of vector space in Sec. 2 only one binary operation $+$ was assumed in V; we did not assume that any kind of "multiplication" of two elements of V was defined. But as the example of K_1 shows, it may happen that a vector space V comes equipped with more than one binary operation. We shall encounter several important examples in which this is the case. If in V there is defined a second binary operation $\mathbf{u} \cdot \mathbf{v}$ such that V is a *ring* (see Sec. 2, Chap. 2), as well as a vector space over K, then V is called a K*-algebra* (or *hypercomplex system over* K) if the following new associative axiom is satisfied:

4.3 $$c(\mathbf{u} \cdot \mathbf{v}) = (c\mathbf{u}) \cdot \mathbf{v} = \mathbf{u} \cdot (c\mathbf{v}) \qquad \textit{for any } c \textit{ in } K \textit{ and any } \mathbf{u}, \mathbf{v} \textit{ in } V$$

For example, $\mathbf{C}$ is an $\mathbf{R}$-algebra (see Exercise 4, Sec. 3). Similarly the set of all 2×2 matrices

$$\begin{pmatrix} a & b \\ c & d \end{pmatrix}$$

with coefficients in K is an example of a K-algebra (see Exercise 3, Sec. 2, Chap. 2). Note that 2×2 matrices are simply quadruples of elements of K in a specific order, and therefore the set of all 2×2 matrices with coefficients in K can be identified with K_4 as defined above.

We mention some other important examples of vector spaces: K being a field, let $K[t]$ be the set of all polynomials in an indeterminate t with coefficients in K. Then with the usual definition of the sum of two polynomials and multiplication of polynomials by elements of K, it is easily verified that $K[t]$ is a vector space over K. $K[t]$ is in fact a K-algebra because an operation of multiplication of two elements of $K[t]$ is also defined, and it satisfies (4.3).

For any positive integer n, let $K[t]_n$ denote the set of polynomials in $K[t]$ of degree *less* than n. The sum of two such polynomials is again a polynomial of degree $<n$, and so is the product of a polynomial in $K[t]_n$ by an element of K. It is easily verified that $K[t]_n$ is a vector space over K. (But it is not a K-algebra, except for $n = 1$, because in general the product of two polynomials in $K[t]_n$ will not be in $K[t]_n$.)

EXERCISES

1. Perform the indicated operations in $\mathbf{Q}_3$, $\mathbf{Q}$ being the field of rational numbers:

$$3 \cdot (1, 0, 0) + 4 \cdot (0, 1, 0) - \tfrac{1}{2} \cdot (0, 0, 1), \qquad (4, 1, 2) - 5 \cdot (2, 1, 0)$$

and

$$3 \cdot (0, 1, 4) - (3, 1, 2) + \tfrac{1}{2} \cdot (4, 12, -2) + (1, 1, -1)$$

2. Prove that the only rational numbers a, b such that

$$a \cdot (2, 1, 3) + b \cdot (1, -1, 4) = 0$$

are $a = b = 0$.

3. Show that there are rational numbers a, b, c not all zero such that

$$a \cdot (1, 2, 2) + b \cdot (3, 0, 4) + c \cdot (5, -2, 6) = 0$$

Describe the set of all such triples (a, b, c).

4. Consider the vectors $\mathbf{u}_1 = (1, \sqrt{2})$ and $\mathbf{u}_2 = (\sqrt{3}, 2)$ in $\mathbf{R}_2$. Prove that the only real numbers a and b such that

$$a\mathbf{u}_1 + b\mathbf{u}_2 = 0$$

are $a = b = 0$. Let $\mathbf{v}$ be an arbitrary element of $\mathbf{R}_2$. Prove that there exist *uniquely* determined real numbers a and b such that

$$\mathbf{v} = a\mathbf{u}_1 + b\mathbf{u}_2$$

5. Let $\mathbf{e}_1 = (1, 0, 0)$, $\mathbf{e}_2 = (0, 1, 0)$, and $\mathbf{e}_3 = (0, 0, 1)$ be in $\mathbf{R}_3$. Let $\mathbf{v}$ be an arbitrary vector in $\mathbf{R}_3$. Prove that there exist uniquely determined real numbers x, y, z such that

$$\mathbf{v} = x\mathbf{e}_1 + y\mathbf{e}_2 + z\mathbf{e}_3$$

5. *Subspaces*

V being a vector space over a field K, it may happen that a part of V is also a vector space over K. The part is then called a *subspace* of V. For example, $K[t]_n$ (defined at the end of Sec. 4) is a subspace of $K[t]$. The formal definition is given below.

DEFINITION 5.1 *Let U be a subset of V. Then U is called a* subspace *of V if the following conditions are satisfied:*

(1) *U is not empty.*

(2) $\mathbf{u}$ *and* $\mathbf{v}$ *are any two elements of U, then* $\mathbf{u} + \mathbf{v}$ *is also in U.*

(3) *For any* $\mathbf{u}$ *in U and any c in K, the element* $c\mathbf{u}$ *is also in U.*

The last two conditions say simply that the vector-space operations in V, when applied to elements of the subset U, produce elements in U. It is easily verified from the axioms for V that if U is a subspace, as just defined, then U also satisfies the vector-space axioms when equipped with the operations defined in V, and U is therefore a vector space over K.

It is clear that V itself satisfies the conditions of Definition 5.1, and consequently V is to be counted as a subspace of V. *Observe that the zero element of V forms by itself a subspace of V,* as follows at once from Proposition 3.1.

EXAMPLES Let K be a field, and let K_3 be the vector space defined in Sec. 4. Then all elements of K_3 of the form $(a_1, a_2, 0)$ constitute a subspace U of K_3. Similarly all vectors in K_3 of the type $(a, 0, 0)$ form a subspace W of K_3. Moreover, W is also a subspace of U. The verifications are trivial.

As mentioned above, $K[t]_n$ is a subspace of $K[t]$. Furthermore, if $m < n$, then $K[t]_m$ is a subspace of $K[t]_n$.

The set V' defined in Exercise 2, Sec. 3, is a subspace of V. The following proposition is a generalization of that exercise.

PROPOSITION 5.1 *Let V be a vector space over a field K, and let $\mathbf{u}_1, \mathbf{u}_2, \ldots, \mathbf{u}_r$ be a set of r vectors in V $(r > 0)$. Let U be the set consisting of all elements $x_1\mathbf{u}_1 + x_2\mathbf{u}_2 + \cdots + x_r\mathbf{u}_r$, where $x_1, \ldots, x_r$ are arbitrary elements of K. Then U is a subspace of V (called the space* generated *or* spanned *by $\mathbf{u}_1, \ldots, \mathbf{u}_r$).*

The proof is left as an exercise.

DEFINITION 5.2 *Let V be a vector space, and let $U_1, \ldots, U_n$ be subspaces. Then V is said to be a direct sum of those subspaces if every element $\mathbf{v}$ in V can be expressed in one and only one way as a sum*

$$\mathbf{v} = \mathbf{u}_1 + \mathbf{u}_2 + \cdots + \mathbf{u}_n$$

where $\mathbf{u}_1$ is in U_1, $\mathbf{u}_2$ in U_2, $\ldots$, $\mathbf{u}_n$ in U_n.

In this situation we write $V = U_1 \oplus U_2 \oplus \cdots \oplus U_n$.

EXAMPLE K_n is the direct sum of the subspaces $U_1, \ldots, U_n$, where U_j consists of all elements in K_n of the type $(0, \ldots, a_j, \ldots, 0)$, in which the only nonzero element is the jth. As another example, K_4 is the direct sum of V_1 and V_2, where V_1 consists of all vectors of the form $(a_1, a_2, 0, 0)$ and V_2 consists of all vectors of the form $(0, 0, a_3, a_4)$. Etc.

Referring to Exercise 3, Sec. 3, it is easily verified that W is the direct sum of the subspaces U' and V' defined as follows: U' consists of all vectors of the type $(\mathbf{u}, \mathbf{0})$, and V' consists of all vectors of the type $(\mathbf{0}, \mathbf{u})$. It is clear moreover that U' is essentially the same as the original space U. More precisely, the mapping $\mathbf{u} \to (\mathbf{u}, \mathbf{0})$ of U to U' is a one-to-one correspondence which is an *isomorphism* (i.e., is compatible with the vector-space operations). Similarly V and V' are isomorphic. (The notion of isomorphism of vector spaces is analyzed more fully in Chap. 9.) Hence the direct sum as defined in Exercise 3, Sec. 3, is substantially the same as that of Definition 5.2.

EXERCISES

1. Prove Proposition 5.1.

2. Let U_1 and U_2 be two subspaces of a vector space V. Show that the set consisting of all elements common to both U_1 and U_2 is a subspace of V and is also a subspace of U_1 and of U_2.

3. Let V be a vector space, and let U_1 and U_2 be two subsets of V, with U_2 contained in U_1. Prove that if U_1 is a subspace of V and if U_2 is a subspace of U_1, then U_2 is a subspace of V. Prove that if U_1 and U_2 are subspaces of V, then U_2 is a subspace of U_1.

4. Let V be a vector space, and let $\{U_i\}$ be any family of subspaces, possibly infinite in number. Let W be the set of elements common to all the subspaces U_i in the family. Prove that W is a subspace of V.

5. Let V be a vector space over a field K, and let M be any subset of V containing at least one element. Let U be the subset of V consisting of all elements that can be expressed as finite sums of terms of the type $c \cdot \mathbf{u}$, where c is in K and $\mathbf{u}$ is in M. Prove that U is a subspace of V (it is called the subspace *generated*, or *spanned*, by M). If M consists of only a finite number of vectors $\mathbf{u}_1, \mathbf{u}_2, \ldots, \mathbf{u}_r$ in V, show that U as defined here is the same as the subspace U defined in Proposition 5.1.

6. K, V, M, and U being as in the preceding exercise, let U' be any subspace of V containing M. Prove that U must be a subspace of U'. (Thus U is the smallest subspace of V containing M.)

7. Let V be a vector space over a field K, and let $\mathbf{u}_1, \mathbf{u}_2, \ldots, \mathbf{u}_r$ be fixed vectors in V. Prove that all r-tuples $(x_1, x_2, \ldots, x_r)$ of elements in K such that $x_1\mathbf{u}_1 + x_2\mathbf{u}_2 + \cdots + x_r\mathbf{u}_r = 0$ form a subspace of K_r. Describe that subspace in the case where $\mathbf{u}_1, \mathbf{u}_2, \ldots$ are the following three vectors of K_4:

$$\mathbf{u}_1 = (1, 0, 0, 0) \qquad \mathbf{u}_2 = (1, 1, 0, 0) \qquad \mathbf{u}_3 = (0, -1, 0, 0)$$

8. Let V be a vector space, and let U_1 and U_2 be two subspaces. Prove that V is the direct sum of U_1 and U_2 if and only if the following hold: U_1 and U_2 have no element in common except $\mathbf{0}$; the elements of U_1 and U_2 generate V, in the sense of Exercise 5.

9. Let V be the direct sum of subspaces U_1, U_2, U_3. Let W be the subspace of V generated by the elements of U_2 and U_3. Prove that V is the direct sum of U_1 and W.

6. *Linear independence and dimension*

DEFINITION 6.1 *Let V be a vector space over a field K, and let $\mathbf{u}_1, \mathbf{u}_2, \ldots, \mathbf{u}_r$ be elements of V. Then they are said to be* linearly dependent *if there exist scalars $a_1, a_2, \ldots, a_r$ in K, not all zero, such that*

$$a_1\mathbf{u}_1 + a_2\mathbf{u}_2 + \cdots a_r\mathbf{u}_r = \mathbf{0}$$

In the contrary case the vectors $\mathbf{u}_1, \ldots, \mathbf{u}_r$ *are said to be* linearly independent.†

EXAMPLE The burden of Exercise 2, Sec. 4, is to show that (2, 1, 3) and (1, −1, 4) in $\mathbf{Q}_3$ are linearly independent. In Exercise 3 one is supposed to show that (1, 2, 2), (3, 0, 4), and (5, −2, 6) are linearly dependent.

Suppose now that given vectors $\mathbf{u}_1, \mathbf{u}_2, \ldots, \mathbf{u}_r$ in V are linearly *dependent*. Then according to the definition there are scalars $a_1, a_2, \ldots, a_r$, not all zero, such that $a_1\mathbf{u}_1 + a_2\mathbf{u}_2 + \cdots + a_r\mathbf{u}_r = 0$. Suppose, for example, that $a_1 \neq 0$. Then we can multiply the equation by $1/a_1$, getting

$$\mathbf{u}_1 = -\left(\frac{a_2}{a_1}\cdot \mathbf{u}_2 + \frac{a_3}{a_1}\cdot \mathbf{u}_3 + \cdots + \frac{a_r}{a_1}\cdot \mathbf{u}_r\right)$$

We conclude at once that $\mathbf{u}_1, \mathbf{u}_2, \ldots, \mathbf{u}_r$ *are linearly dependent if and only if one of them can be expressed as a linear combination of the remaining ones*, with coefficients in the field K. [Note: By a "linear combination of elements $\mathbf{w}_1, \mathbf{w}_2, \ldots, \mathbf{w}_n$ in V with coefficients in K" we mean an expression of the type $c_1\mathbf{w}_1 + c_2\mathbf{w}_2 + \cdots + c_n\mathbf{w}_n$, where $c_1, c_2, \ldots, c_n$ are elements of K. Such an expression stands on the right-hand side of the equation above for $\mathbf{u}_1$.]

The advantage of the formulation of linear dependence in Definition 6.1 is that it allows us to say that at least one of the vectors $\mathbf{v}_1, \mathbf{v}_2, \ldots, \mathbf{v}_r$ can be expressed as a linear combination of the others (with coefficients in K), without requiring us to say just which one(s) can be so expressed.

DEFINITION 6.2 *Let* $\mathbf{w}, \mathbf{u}_1, \mathbf{u}_2, \ldots, \mathbf{u}_r$ *be vectors in* V. *Then* $\mathbf{w}$ *is said to be linearly dependent on* $\mathbf{u}_1, \ldots, \mathbf{u}_r$ *if it can be expressed as a linear combination* $\mathbf{w} = c_1\mathbf{u}_1 + \cdots + c_r\mathbf{u}_r$.

The following proposition is used repeatedly. It is an immediate consequence of Definition 6.1, and its proof is left as an exercise.

PROPOSITION 6.1 *Let* $\mathbf{v}_1, \mathbf{v}_2, \ldots, \mathbf{v}_r$ *be linearly independent elements in a vector space* V *over a field* K. *Then an equation*

$$a_1\mathbf{v}_1 + a_2\mathbf{v}_2 + \cdots + a_r\mathbf{v}_r = b_1\mathbf{v}_1 + b_2\mathbf{v}_2 + \cdots + b_r\mathbf{v}_r$$

can hold (with $a_1, \ldots, a_r$ *and* $b_1, \ldots, b_r$ *in* K*) if and only if* $a_1 = b_1$, $a_2 = b_2$, $\ldots, a_r = b_r$.

DEFINITION 6.3 *Infinitely many elements* $\mathbf{v}_1, \mathbf{v}_2, \mathbf{v}_3, \ldots$ *in a vector space* V *are said to be* linearly dependent *if the vectors in some finite subset of them are linearly dependent. Otherwise the vectors* $\mathbf{v}_1, \mathbf{v}_2, \mathbf{v}_3$, etc., *are said to be* linearly independent.

† It often happens that a vector space V over a field K is also a vector space over another field K'. For example, a vector space V over $\mathbf{C}$ is also a vector space over $\mathbf{R}$ and $\mathbf{Q}$, as is easily seen. In this situation it is essential to be very explicit about which field is under consideration. One frequently uses such terms as "linearly dependent over K" to avoid any possible confusion.

DEFINITION 6.4 *Let V be a vector space over a field K. Then V is said to have* dimension n *(where n is an integer ≥ 0) if there exists in V a set of n linearly independent vectors and if there exists no set of more than n linearly independent vectors. In this case we write* $\dim V = n$. *If V contains a set of infinitely many linearly independent vectors, as defined above, then we write* $\dim V = \infty$.†

Observe that $\dim V = 0$ means that V must consist of the zero element alone.

The preceding definitions are very important, and they will be used constantly.

EXERCISES

1. Let $\mathbf{v}_1, \mathbf{v}_2, \ldots, \mathbf{v}_r$ and $\mathbf{w}_1, \mathbf{w}_2, \ldots, \mathbf{w}_s$ be elements in a vector space V. Prove that the subspace of V generated by $\mathbf{v}_1, \mathbf{v}_2, \ldots, \mathbf{v}_r$ is the same as the subspace generated by $\mathbf{v}_1, \mathbf{v}_2, \ldots, \mathbf{v}_r, \mathbf{w}_1, \mathbf{w}_2, \ldots, \mathbf{w}_s$ if and only if each of the $\mathbf{w}$'s is linearly dependent on $\mathbf{v}_1, \ldots, \mathbf{v}_r$.

2. K being a field, prove that $\dim K_n = n$ for $n = 1$ and $n = 2$ (the proof of this for all positive integers n is left for the next section). Prove that $\dim K_\infty = \infty$.

7. *A theorem on linear equations*

In order to prove some important theorems about the dimension of vector spaces we need the following auxiliary lemma:

LEMMA 7.1 *Let K be a field, and let*

7.1
$$\begin{aligned} a_{11}X_1 + a_{12}X_2 + \cdots + a_{1n}X_n &= 0 \\ a_{21}X_1 + a_{22}X_2 + \cdots + a_{2n}X_n &= 0 \\ \cdots\cdots\cdots\cdots\cdots\cdots\cdots\cdots \\ a_{m1}X_1 + a_{m2}X_2 + \cdots + a_{mn}X_n &= 0 \end{aligned}$$

be a set of m linear equations in the unknowns $X_1, X_2, \ldots, X_n$ with coefficients a_{11}, a_{12}, etc., in K.‡ If $n > m$, then there exist n elements $c_1, c_2, \ldots, c_n$ in K, not all zero, which satisfy the equations when substituted for $X_1, X_2, \ldots, X_n$, respectively.

REMARK. Obviously if we put 0 for $X_1, \ldots, X_n$, then Eqs. (7.1) will be satisfied. We call this the trivial solution. The theorem says that there is a nontrivial solution if $n > m$. Observe that if we put

$$\mathbf{a}_j = (a_{1j}, a_{2j}, \ldots, a_{mj})$$

for $j = 1, 2, \ldots, n$, then the $\mathbf{a}_j$ are vectors in K_m (see Sec. 4). The theorem says simply that there are elements $c_1, c_2, \ldots, c_n$ in K, not all zero, such that $c_1\mathbf{a}_1 + c_2\mathbf{a}_2 + \cdots + c_n\mathbf{a}_n = \mathbf{o}$, if $n > m$. In other words $\mathbf{a}_1, \mathbf{a}_2, \ldots, \mathbf{a}_n$ must be linearly *dependent* if $n > m$.

† If it is desirable to be explicit about the field of scalars involved, one speaks of the dimension of V *over* K, writing $\dim_K V$. For example $\dim_{\mathbf{R}} \mathbf{C} = 2$, as is easily seen, but $\dim_{\mathbf{Q}} \mathbf{C} = \infty$ (the latter is not so easy to prove).

‡ The double indices simply indicate the row and column in which the coefficient appears. This kind of notation is very convenient and will be used frequently.

Proof. We use mathematical induction to prove the theorem. In order to avoid a somewhat cumbersome double induction on both m and n, we observe that it suffices to prove the theorem for the largest possible value of m—namely, $n - 1$. For if $m < n - 1$ in (7.1), then we can simply add on more equations ($n - 1 - m$ of them) in which the coefficients are all zero, bringing the total number of equations up to $n - 1$. Writing that $m = n - 1$, or $n = m + 1$, in (7.1), that system is

$$\begin{aligned} a_{11}X_1 + a_{12}X_2 + \cdots + a_{1,m+1}X_{m+1} &= 0 \\ a_{21}X_1 + a_{22}X_2 + \cdots + a_{2,m+1}X_{m+1} &= 0 \\ \cdots\cdots\cdots\cdots\cdots\cdots\cdots\cdots\cdots &\cdots \\ a_{m1}X_1 + a_{m2}X_2 + \cdots + a_{m,m+1}X_{m+1} &= 0 \end{aligned} \tag{7.2}$$

We now use induction on m. The theorem is clearly true if $m = 1$, for then there is just one equation $a_{11}X_1 + a_{12}X_2 = 0$ in two unknowns. If a_{11} and a_{22} are both zero, then we can take any elements in K for X_1 and X_2. If a_{11}, a_{22} are not both zero, then we have merely to put $X_1 = a_{12}$ and $X_2 = -a_{11}$ to get a nontrivial solution.

We now assume that the theorem holds for some value m_0 of m, and we show that it must necessarily hold for the next value $m = m_0 + 1$. That will establish the theorem. Now if all the coefficients in (7.2) are zero, it is obvious that any values in K for $X_1, \ldots, X_{m+1}$ will satisfy the equations, and so the theorem is true in that case. If on the other hand not all the coefficients a_{ij} are zero in (7.2), then we can assume for simplicity (by renumbering the equations and unknowns if necessary) that the last coefficient $a_{m,m+1}$ is not zero. Then we can solve the last equation for X_{m+1}, getting (we write b for $a_{m,m+1}$)

$$X_{m+1} = -\frac{1}{b}\cdot(a_{m1}X_1 + \cdots + a_{mm}X_m) \qquad (b = a_{m,m+1}) \tag{7.3}$$

Now substitute this expression for X_{m+1} in the first $m - 1$ equations. Then, e.g., the ith equation becomes

$$\left(a_{i1} - \frac{a_{m1}}{b}\right)X_1 + \cdots + \left(a_{im} - \frac{a_{mm}}{b}\right)X_m = 0 \qquad (i = 1, \ldots, m - 1) \tag{7.4}$$

In this way we end up with $m - 1$ equations in the m unknowns $X_1, \ldots, X_m$. Therefore by our induction hypothesis Eqs. (7.4) have a nontrivial solution $X_1 = c_1, \ldots, X_m = c_m$ in K. Substituting these in (7.3) we get a value c_{m+1} for X_{m+1}, and it is immediate that the elements $c_1, c_2, \ldots, c_{m+1}$ of K so obtained satisfy the original Eqs. (7.2). Q.E.D.

EXERCISES

1. Take for K the field of rational numbers **Q**. Find a nontrivial solution c_1, c_2, c_3, c_4 in **Q** for the system

$$2X_1 - 3X_2 + X_3 - X_4 = 0$$
$$X_1 + 5X_2 - 2X_3 + 3X_4 = 0$$
$$X_2 + X_3 - 5X_4 = 0$$

2. Describe the set of all solutions (c_1, c_2, c_3, c_4) in **Q** of the system above. What happens if **Q** is replaced by **R**?

3. Prove that if K is any field and n any positive integer, then the vector space K_n defined in Sec. 4 has dimension n.

4. Prove that Lemma 7.1 is true if K is assumed to be an integral domain, not necessarily a field.

5. Referring to (7.1), prove that all n-tuples $(c_1, c_2, \ldots, c_n)$ of elements of K which are solutions of the system of equations form a subspace of K_n.

6. Prove that if the system

$$aX_1 + bX_2 = 0$$
$$cX_1 + dX_2 = 0$$

(with coefficients in a field K) has a nontrivial solution, then the vectors (a, b) and (c, d) in K_2 must be linearly dependent.

8. On the dimension of vector spaces

The main purpose for which we need Lemma 7.1 is the proof of the following theorem:

THEOREM 8.1 *Let* $\mathbf{v}_1, \mathbf{v}_2, \ldots, \mathbf{v}_r$ be *elements of a vector space V over a field K. Let U be the subspace of V generated by those vectors (see Proposition* 5.1). *Then* $\dim U \leqslant r$, *and equality holds if and only if* $\mathbf{v}_1, \ldots, \mathbf{v}_r$ *are linearly independent.*

Proof. We show that if $s > r$, then any s vectors $\mathbf{u}_1, \ldots, \mathbf{u}_s$ in U must be linearly dependent. It then follows from Definition 6.3 that $\dim U \leqslant r$.

First of all, according to Proposition 5.1, the subspace U consists of all elements

8.1 $$\mathbf{u} = a_1\mathbf{v}_1 + a_2\mathbf{v}_2 + \cdots + a_r\mathbf{v}_r$$

where $a_1, \ldots, a_r$ are arbitrary scalars. Hence, given s vectors $\mathbf{u}_1, \ldots, \mathbf{u}_s$ in U, each one of them can be expressed in this form, say

8.2 $$\mathbf{u}_i = a_{1i}\mathbf{v}_1 + a_{2i}\mathbf{v}_2 + \cdots + a_{ri}\mathbf{v}_r \qquad (i = 1, \ldots, s)$$

where a_{1i}, a_{2i}, etc., are in K. Now if $s > r$, then by Lemma 7.1 we can find elements $c_1, c_2, \ldots, c_s$ in K, not all zero, such that

8.3 $$\begin{aligned} a_{11}c_1 + a_{12}c_2 + \cdots + a_{1s}c_s &= 0 \\ a_{21}c_1 + a_{22}c_2 + \cdots + a_{2s}c_s &= 0 \\ \cdots\cdots\cdots\cdots\cdots\cdots \\ a_{r1}c_1 + a_{r2}c_2 + \cdots + a_{rs}c_s &= 0 \end{aligned}$$

But then from (8.2) we get

$$\begin{aligned} c_1\mathbf{u}_1 + \cdots + c_s\mathbf{u}_s &= c_1 \cdot (a_{11}\mathbf{v}_1 + \cdots + a_{r1}\mathbf{v}_r) + \cdots \\ &\qquad + c_s \cdot (a_{1s}\mathbf{v}_1 + \cdots + a_{rs}\mathbf{v}_r) \\ &= (a_{11}c_1 + \cdots + a_{1s}c_s) \cdot \mathbf{v}_1 + \cdots \\ &\qquad + (a_{r1}c_1 + \cdots + a_{rs}c_s) \cdot \mathbf{v}_r \\ &= \mathbf{0} \end{aligned}$$

by (8.3), showing that $\mathbf{u}_1, \ldots, \mathbf{u}_s$ are linearly dependent if $s > r$.

If $\mathbf{v}_1, \ldots, \mathbf{v}_r$ are linearly independent, then it follows at once from Definition 6.3 that $\dim U = r$. We now show that if $\mathbf{v}_1, \ldots, \mathbf{v}_r$ are linearly *dependent*, then $\dim U < r$, and that will complete the proof of the theorem. If the $\mathbf{v}$'s are linearly dependent, then one of them—for simplicity of notation say $\mathbf{v}_r$—can be expressed as a linear combination of the others $\mathbf{v}_1, \mathbf{v}_2, \ldots, \mathbf{v}_{r-1}$. But then $\mathbf{v}_1, \mathbf{v}_2, \ldots, \mathbf{v}_{r-1}$ generate the same subspace U as do $\mathbf{v}_1, \mathbf{v}_2, \ldots, \mathbf{v}_r$ (see Exercise 1, Sec. 6). By what has just been shown it follows that $\dim U \leqslant r - 1 < r$. Q.E.D.

EXERCISES

1. Let U be a subspace of a vector space V of finite dimension. Show that $\dim U \leqslant \dim V$, and show that equality holds if and only if $U = V$.

2. Show by an example that it is possible to have a subspace U of a vector space V such that $U \neq V$ but $\dim U = \dim V = \infty$.

3. What is the dimension of the subspace of K_3 defined at the end of Exercise 7, Sec. 5?

***4.** Let V be a vector space, and let U_1 and U_2 be subspaces. Let V' be the subspace of V generated by the elements of both U_1 and U_2 (see Exercise 5, Sec. 5), and let V'' be the set of elements common to both U_1 and U_2. Assuming that V' has finite dimension, prove that $\dim V' + \dim V'' = \dim U_1 + \dim U_2$.

9. *Base vectors*

Let V be a vector space of finite dimension n over a field K. The purpose of this paragraph is to show that in a certain sense the elements of V can be represented by elements of K—or more precisely, by n-tuples of scalars. This will provide us with a very important way of translating vector-space calculations into calculations with scalars.

By Definition 6.3, if $\dim V = n$, then there must exist in V a set of n linearly independent vectors, say $\mathbf{v}_1, \mathbf{v}_2, \ldots, \mathbf{v}_n$ (we shall soon see that there are in general infinitely many such sets). Now let $\mathbf{x}$ be any vector in V. The set $\mathbf{x}, \mathbf{v}_1, \ldots, \mathbf{v}_n$ then contains $n + 1$ vectors, and they must therefore be linearly independent (by definition of dimension), say

$$c_0\mathbf{x} + c_1\mathbf{v}_1 + c_2\mathbf{v}_2 + \cdots + c_n\mathbf{v}_n = \mathbf{0}$$

where $c_0, c_1, \ldots, c_n$ are elements of K, not all zero. Now c_0 cannot be zero, for otherwise this equation would imply that $\mathbf{v}_1, \ldots, \mathbf{v}_n$ are linearly dependent. Hence we can solve the equation for $\mathbf{x}$. Writing x_i for $-c_i/c_0$, we get

$$\mathbf{x} = x_1\mathbf{v}_1 + x_2\mathbf{v}_2 + \cdots + x_n\mathbf{v}_n$$

DEFINITION 9.1 *Let V be a vector space of finite dimension n over a field K. Then any ordered set of n linearly independent vectors $\mathbf{v}_1, \mathbf{v}_2, \ldots, \mathbf{v}_n$ in V is called a* base *for V.*

We shall often indicate a base $\mathbf{v}_1, \ldots, \mathbf{v}_n$ by a symbol such as $\{\mathbf{v}_i\}$.

From the remarks above we have at once the following theorem.

THEOREM 9.1 *If $\mathbf{v}_1, \mathbf{v}_2 \ldots, \mathbf{v}_n$ form a base for a vector space V over a field K, then any element in V can be expressed in one and only one way as a linear combination*

9.1 $$\mathbf{x} = x_1\mathbf{v}_1 + x_2\mathbf{v}_2 + \cdots + x_n\mathbf{v}_n$$

with $x_1, x_2, \ldots, x_n$ in K.

Uniqueness follows from Proposition 6.1.

DEFINITION 9.2 *The scalars $x_1, x_2, \ldots, x_n$ in (9.1) are called the* components *of $\mathbf{x}$ relative to the base $\{\mathbf{v}_i\} = \mathbf{v}_1, \ldots, \mathbf{v}_n$ of V.*

Theorem 9.1 tells us that once we select a base $\{\mathbf{v}_i\}$ in V, then for every vector $\mathbf{x}$ we get an n-tuple $(x_1, x_2, \ldots, x_n)$ of scalars, that is, the components of $\mathbf{x}$. The operation leading from $\mathbf{x}$ to its components is therefore a mapping from V to K_n. Calling the mapping $\mathbf{T}$, we have then by definition

9.2 $$\mathbf{T}(\mathbf{x}) = (x_1, \ldots, x_n) \qquad \text{if } \mathbf{x} = x_1\mathbf{v}_1 + \cdots + x_n\mathbf{v}_n$$

THEOREM 9.2 *The mapping $\mathbf{T}$ from V to K_n defined by (9.2) is a one-to-one mapping, and it is compatible with vector addition and scalar multiplication. That is,*

9.3 $$\mathbf{T}(\mathbf{x} + \mathbf{y}) = \mathbf{T}(\mathbf{x}) + \mathbf{T}(\mathbf{y}) \qquad \text{and} \qquad \mathbf{T}(c\mathbf{x}) = c \cdot \mathbf{T}(\mathbf{x})$$

for any vectors $\mathbf{x}$ and $\mathbf{y}$ in V and any scalar c in K.

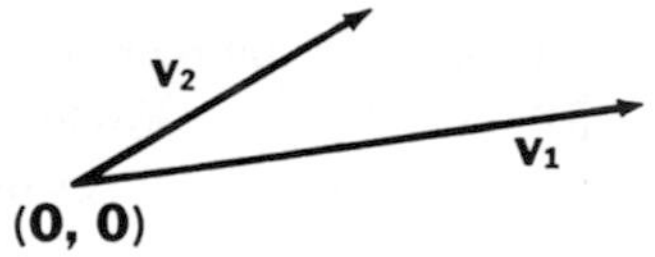

Figure 3a

$\mathbf{v}_1$, $\mathbf{v}_2$ form a base of $\mathbf{R}_2$.

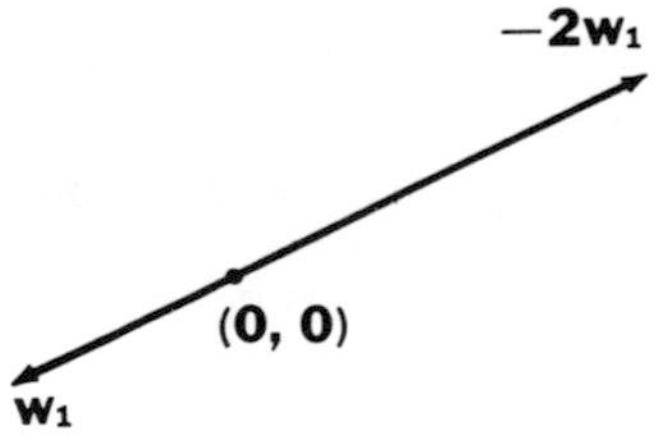

Figure 3b

$\mathbf{w}_1$, $-2\mathbf{w}_1$ do not form a base of $\mathbf{R}_2$.

Proof. First of all, if $(x_1, \ldots, x_n)$ is any element of K_n, then $\mathbf{x} = x_1\mathbf{v}_1 + \cdots + x_n\mathbf{v}_n$ is an element of V, by definition of a vector space, and for that vector $\mathbf{x}$ we have $\mathbf{T}(\mathbf{x}) = (x_1, \ldots, x_n)$. Therefore, given any element of K_n, there is at least one element of V which is sent into it by $\mathbf{T}$. But $\mathbf{T}$ cannot send two different elements $\mathbf{x}$, $\mathbf{y}$ of V into the same element of K_n. For if $\mathbf{T}(\mathbf{x}) = \mathbf{T}(\mathbf{y})$, then $\mathbf{x}$ and $\mathbf{y}$ must have the same components (relative to the given base in V), and so $\mathbf{x} = \mathbf{y}$, by Theorem 9.1.

To complete the proof we must verify the two equations (9.3). Suppose then that $\mathbf{x} = x_1\mathbf{v}_1 + \cdots + x_n\mathbf{v}_n$ and $\mathbf{y} = y_1\mathbf{v} + \cdots + y_n\mathbf{v}_n$. Then $\mathbf{x} + \mathbf{y} = (x_1 + y_1) \cdot \mathbf{v}_1 + \cdots + (x_n + y_n) \cdot \mathbf{v}_n$, and so by definition of $\mathbf{T}$ we have

$$\mathbf{T}(\mathbf{x} + \mathbf{y}) = (x_1 + y_1, \ldots, x_n + y_n)$$

By definition [Eq. (4.1), Sec. 4] the right-hand side is

$$(x_1, \ldots, x_n) + (y_1, \ldots, y_n) = \mathbf{T}(\mathbf{x}) + \mathbf{T}(\mathbf{y})$$

The second equation $\mathbf{T}(c\mathbf{x}) = c \cdot \mathbf{T}(\mathbf{x})$ is verified similarly. Q.E.D.

COROLLARY *Vectors* $\mathbf{u}_1, \ldots, \mathbf{u}_s$ *in* V *are linearly independent if and only if the corresponding vectors* $\mathbf{T}(\mathbf{u}_1), \ldots, \mathbf{T}(\mathbf{u}_s)$ *in* K_n *are so.*

Proof. If $c_1\mathbf{u}_1 + \cdots + c_s\mathbf{u}_s = \mathbf{0}$ for certain scalars $c_1, \ldots, c_s$ (not all zero), then (since $\mathbf{T}$ sends $\mathbf{0}$ in V into $\mathbf{0}$ in K_n) we have $\mathbf{T}(c_1\mathbf{u}_1 + \cdots + c_s\mathbf{u}_s) = \mathbf{0}$. Using (9.3) repeatedly, the left-hand side is equal to $\mathbf{T}(c_1\mathbf{u}_1) + \cdots + \mathbf{T}(c_s\mathbf{u}_s) = c_1 \cdot \mathbf{T}(\mathbf{u}_1) + \cdots + c_s \cdot \mathbf{T}(\mathbf{u}_s) = \mathbf{0}$, and so $\mathbf{T}(\mathbf{u}_1), \ldots, \mathbf{T}(\mathbf{u}_s)$ are linearly dependent. The converse is established by just reversing the argument.

REMARK 1. The mapping $\mathbf{T}$: $V \to K_n$ just discussed is called an *isomorphism* because it establishes a one-to-one correspondence between the two vector spaces which preserves vector-space operations. Isomorphisms of vector spaces will be discussed in detail in the next chapter.

Theorem 9.2 shows that V and K_n have precisely the same structure as vector spaces. Therefore K_n can be considered as a kind of model for all n-dimensional vector spaces over K.

Observe that the mapping $\mathbf{T}$ of Theorem 9.2 depends in an essential way upon the choice of base $\mathbf{v}_1, \ldots, \mathbf{v}_n$ in V (the effect of a change of base is calculated below). There are many possible choices of bases, and therefore the correspondence is in no way unique.

REMARK 2. Under certain circumstances it is possible to extend the concept of *base* to infinite dimensional spaces. This is of utmost importance for many practical applications of vector spaces. The question is discussed briefly in Chap. 14.

REMARK 3. The vectors $\mathbf{e}_1 = (1, 0, 0 \ldots, 0)$, $\mathbf{e}_2 = (0, 1, 0, \ldots, 0), \ldots, \mathbf{e}_n = (0, 0, \ldots, 0, 1)$ in K_n are easily seen to form a base. We shall call it the *canonical* base for K_n. If $\mathbf{x} = (x_1, \ldots, x_n)$ is any element of K_n, then $\mathbf{x} =$

$x_1 \cdot \mathbf{e}_1 + x_2 \cdot \mathbf{e}_2 + \cdots + x_n \cdot \mathbf{e}_n$. Thus the scalars $x_1, \ldots, x_n$ are precisely the components of $\mathbf{x}$ relative to the canonical base. In general there is no "preferred" base in a vector space, and K_n is exceptional in this respect.

The following theorem is sometimes useful:

THEOREM 9.3 *Let V be a vector space of finite dimension n, and let $\mathbf{v}_1, \mathbf{v}_2, \ldots, \mathbf{v}_r$ be linearly independent vectors in V. Then there exist $n - r$ vectors $\mathbf{v}_{r+1}, \ldots, \mathbf{v}_n$ in V such that the set $\mathbf{v}_1, \ldots, \mathbf{v}_n$ is a base for V.*

Proof. If $r < n$, then there is at least one vector $\mathbf{v}_{r+1}$ in V not in the subspace spanned by $\mathbf{v}_1, \ldots, \mathbf{v}_r$, by Theorem 8.1. Then $\mathbf{v}_1, \ldots, \mathbf{v}_r, \mathbf{v}_{r+1}$ must be linearly independent, clearly. If $r + 1 < n$, then we can find a vector $\mathbf{v}_{r+2}$ not in the subspace spanned by $\mathbf{v}_1, \ldots, \mathbf{v}_{r+1}$, and so on. (We are of course really using mathematical induction, abbreviated by "and so on.")

COROLLARY *V being as above, let U be an r-dimensional subspace, with $r < n$. Then there exists another subspace W of V, of dimension $n - r$, such that V is the direct sum $U \oplus W$ of U and W (see Definition* 5.2).

Proof. Choose a base $\mathbf{v}_1, \ldots, \mathbf{v}_r$ for U, and let $\mathbf{v}_{r+1}, \ldots, \mathbf{v}_n$ be as in the theorem. Let W be the subspace of V spanned by the latter. Then W has the required properties.

REMARK. The space W is not unique.

We conclude this section with a calculation showing the effect of a change of base in V upon the components of a vector. Let $\{\mathbf{v}_i\} = \mathbf{v}_1, \ldots, \mathbf{v}_n$ and $\{\mathbf{v}'_j\} = \mathbf{v}'_1, \ldots, \mathbf{v}'_n$ be two different bases in V. Then by Theorem 9.1 any vector in V can be expressed in terms of either base, say

9.4 $$\mathbf{x} = x_1\mathbf{v}_1 + \cdots + x_n\mathbf{v}_n = x'_1\mathbf{v}'_1 + \cdots + x'_n\mathbf{v}'_n.$$

In particular, the elements $\mathbf{v}'_1, \ldots, \mathbf{v}'_n$ can be so expressed in terms of the old base $\{\mathbf{v}_i\}$. Say

9.5 $$\mathbf{v}'_j = a_{j1}\mathbf{v}_1 + a_{j2}\mathbf{v}_2 + \cdots + a_{jn}\mathbf{v}_n \qquad (j = 1, \ldots, n)$$

Substituting this in (9.4) we get

$$\begin{aligned} \mathbf{x} &= x_1\mathbf{v}_1 + \cdots + x_n\mathbf{v}_n \\ &= x'_1 \cdot (a_{11}\mathbf{v}_1 + \cdots + a_{1n}\mathbf{v}_n) + \cdots + x'_n \cdot (a_{n1}\mathbf{v} + \cdots + a_{nn}\mathbf{v}_n) \\ &= (a_{11}x'_1 + \cdots + a_{n1}x'_n) \cdot \mathbf{v}_1 + \cdots + (a_{1n}x'_1 + \cdots + a_{nn}x'_n) \cdot \mathbf{v}_n \end{aligned}$$

Therefore, by Proposition 6.1, we have

9.6 $$x_i = a_{1i}x'_1 + a_{2i}x'_2 + \cdots + a_{ni}x'_n \qquad (i = 1, \ldots, n)$$

which shows how the components $(x_1, \ldots, x_n)$ and $(x'_1, \ldots, x'_n)$ of $\mathbf{x}$ relative to the two bases $\{\mathbf{v}_1\}$, $\{\mathbf{v}'_j\}$ are related. In Chap. 9 we shall develop some compact notation for handling such systems of equations.

EXERCISES

1. Let $\{\mathbf{v}_i\} = \mathbf{v}_1, \ldots, \mathbf{v}_n$ be a base for a vector space V. What are the components of the base vectors themselves relative to that base? That is, where does $\mathbf{T}$ of Theorem 9.2 send them?

2. Exhibit a base for the vector space K_n (K a field). Find a base for the space $K[t]_n$ defined at the end of Sec. 4.

3. Find a base for $\mathbf{Q}_2$ different from the one given in Remark 3, $\mathbf{Q}$ being the rational field. Write down the Eq. (9.5) connecting the two bases, and compute the components of the vector $(3, -2)$ relative to the bases. Verify (9.6) in this case.

4. The vectors $(1, 2, 0)$, $(-1, 1, 3)$, and $(0, 2, 4)$ form a base for $\mathbf{Q}_3$. Find the components of the vectors $(2, 4, 2)$ and $(6, 0, 1)$ relative to that base.

5. Let $\mathbf{v}_1, \ldots, \mathbf{v}_n$ be a base for V, and let U_j be the subspace of V generated by the vector $\mathbf{v}_j$ ($j = 1, \ldots, n$). Prove that V is the direct sum of $U_1, \ldots, U_n$.

6. Let V be a vector space of finite dimension, and let $U_1, \ldots, U_r$ be subspaces such that V is their direct sum. Prove that $\dim V = \dim U_1 + \cdots + \dim U_r$.

7. Let V be a vector space of finite dimension, and let U_1 and U_2 be two subspaces. Let V' be the subspace of V generated by all the elements of U_1 and U_2; let V'' be the set of elements common to U_1 and U_2. Prove that $\dim V' + \dim V'' = \dim U_1 + \dim U_2$.

8. Find a base for the complex number field $\mathbf{C}$ considered as a vector space over the real field $\mathbf{R}$.

9. Let V be a vector space of dimension 3 over a field K, and let $\mathbf{v}_1, \mathbf{v}_2, \mathbf{v}_3$ be a base. Let (b_1, b_2, b_2) be an element of K_3 different from $\mathbf{0}$. Let V' be the subset of V consisting of all vectors $\mathbf{x} = x_1\mathbf{v}_1 + x_2\mathbf{v}_2 + x_3\mathbf{v}_3$ whose components satisfy the equation $b_1x_1 + b_2x_2 + b_3x_3 = 0$. Prove that V' is a subspace of dimension 2.

***10.** Let K be a subfield of a field L. Show that L, with its given operation of addition, is a vector space over K if scalar multiplication $c \cdot x$ of an element c of K and an element x of L is defined by the product in L (see Exercise 4, Sec. 3). The dimension of L as vector space over K, if finite, is called the *degree* of L over K and is denoted by $[L:K]$. Now assume that L is in turn a subfield of a third field E such that E as vector space over L has finite dimension, denoted similarly by $[E:L]$. Since K is a subfield of E, the degree $[E:K]$ is also defined. Prove that $[E:K] = [E:L] \cdot [L:K]$. (The notion of *degree* defined here is of great importance in the study of fields.) What is $[\mathbf{C}:\mathbf{R}]$?

10. *Affine spaces*

Everyone is familiar with the idea of representing points in the plane by means of rectangular coordinates (x, y) or points in space by coordinates (x, y, z). Here x, y, and z stand for real numbers, and so (x, y) is an element of the vector space $\mathbf{R}_2$; (x, y, z) is an element of $\mathbf{R}_3$. Therefore the procedure of choosing coordinates can be thought of intuitively as temporarily "pasting" a copy of $\mathbf{R}_2$ onto the plane, or of $\mathbf{R}_3$ onto three-dimensional space. In order to achieve a workable formulation of these notions and their consequences, we must first give some account of what is meant by "the plane" and by "three-dimensional space."

Of course our physical insight gives us a rather clear idea of what those terms ought to imply. But just as in the case of the system of integers discussed in Chap. 2, it is desirable to avoid any reference to physical entities in making definitions. Therefore we propose to consider the plane and 3-space as abstract mathematical systems which in some sense reflect our intuitive apprehension of space but which are based upon an axiomatic foundation.

One procedure would be to take as the plane (or 3-space) the systems described by the axioms of euclidean geometry. Indeed that is the purpose for which those axioms were devised. However it is somewhat simpler for us to base our definitions of the plane and 3-space upon the real-number system $\mathbf{R}$. In that way it is also very easy to define analogous spaces of any number of dimensions.

One may wonder why we de not simply take the vector space $\mathbf{R}_3$ for 3-space, and similarly $\mathbf{R}_1$ and $\mathbf{R}_2$ for the line and plane, respectively. That is often done, but the procedure suffers from an awkward drawback: For ease of discussion let us designate by E_3 something that fits our intuitive notion of 3-space. Now $\mathbf{R}_3$, being a vector space, has an operation of addition. But of course we do not envisage any such operation upon the points of E_3; nor do we think of E_3 as having a distinguished point as "origin," like the zero element of $\mathbf{R}_3$. Hence, $\mathbf{R}_3$ possesses some features which do not agree with our idea of E_3. (Similar remarks apply to $\mathbf{R}_1$ and $\mathbf{R}_2$ as candidates for the line and plane, respectively.)

Now our idea of what E_3 should be does include a certain kind of operation—namely, rigid displacement—and it is by means of that notion that we shall be able to define E_3 from $\mathbf{R}_3$.

DEFINITION 10.1 *Let A be a set of elements, and let $T(A)$ be a set of one-to-one mappings of A to itself. Then the system consisting of A and $T(A)$ is called an* affine space *over a given field K if $T(A)$ satisfies the following conditions:*

(1) *For each ordered pair of elements p, q in A there is one and only one mapping in $T(A)$ which sends p into q.*

(2) *$T(A)$ with the binary operation of composition of mappings is an abelian group.*

(3) *For each element c of the field K and each element $\mathbf{t}$ of $T(A)$ there is assigned another element $c\mathbf{t}$ in $T(A)$.*

(4) *$T(A)$, with the operations of* (2) *and* (3) *is a vector space over K.*

The dimension *of A is defined to be the same as that of the vector space $T(A)$.*

One often speaks of A itself as an affine space, $T(A)$ being understood. But as the axioms show, the essential structure required is primarily in $T(A)$. A given

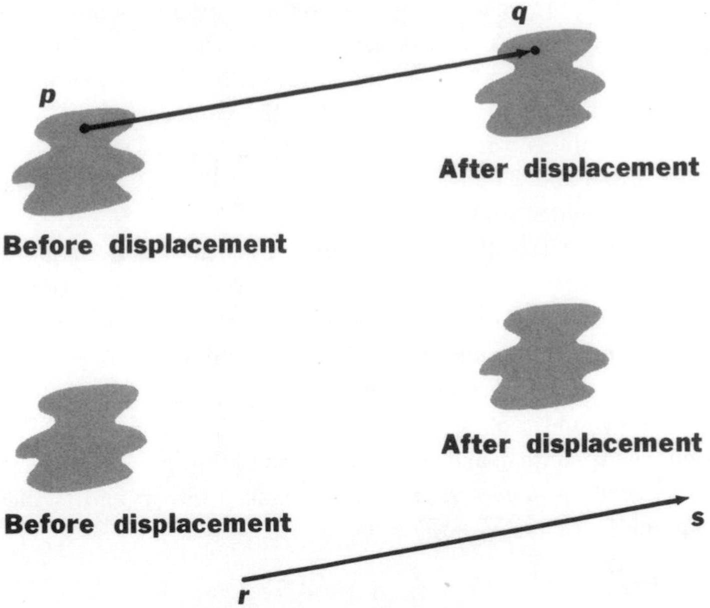

Figure 4 (*Top*) A rigid displacement of the plane E_2 can be described intuitively as the motion obtained upon regarding E_2 as a rigid solid and displacing it along the indicated arrow. Points p and q signify points in the plane; arrow signifies the rigid displacement from p to q. (*Bottom*) The rigid displacement of space from p to q yields the same outcome as the rigid displacement from r to s.

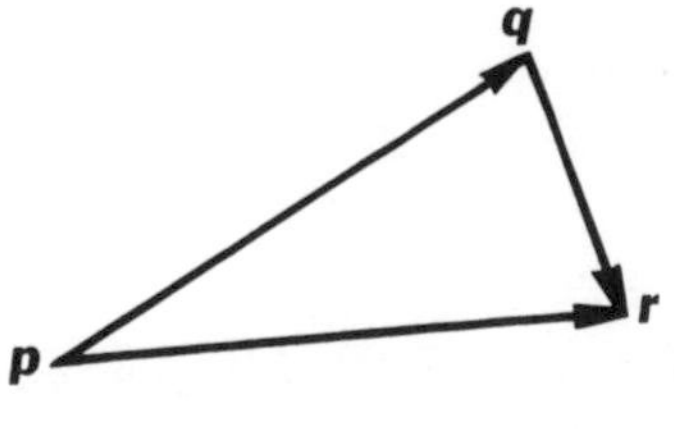

Figure 5

Composition of rigid displacements: the result of rigidly displacing E_2 from p to q and then from q to r is the rigid displacement from p to r; cf. Eq. (10.2).

set A may be made into an affine space in many ways by changing the choice of $T(A)$.

By axiom (2) the mappings in $T(A)$ form a subgroup of the total group—call it $M(A)$—of all one-to-one mappings of A to itself (see Theorem 6.3, Sec. 6, Chap. 1). Now $M(A)$ contains the identity mapping of A, and it is the (unique) identity element of $M(A)$. The identity element of the subgroup $T(A)$ is necessarily the same as that of $M(A)$, and so $T(A)$ must contain the identity mapping of A. The inverse of an element $\mathbf{t}$ of $T(A)$ is just the inverse mapping $\mathbf{t}^{-1}$.

The elements of A will be called *points*, and the elements of $T(A)$ will be called *translations* on A. We recall from Chap. 1 that if $\mathbf{t}_1$ and $\mathbf{t}_2$ are two translations, that is, elements of $T(A)$, then their composition $\mathbf{t}_1\mathbf{t}_2$ is defined by $\mathbf{t}_1\mathbf{t}_2(p) = \mathbf{t}_1(\mathbf{t}_2(p))$

for any point p of A. In general, composition of mappings is not a commutative operation, but in axiom (2) above we have assumed that it is so for the mappings in $T(A)$. Since we have used $+$ as the notation for the binary operation in a vector space, we shall now write $\mathbf{t}_1 + \mathbf{t}_2$ for the composition $\mathbf{t}_1\mathbf{t}_2 = \mathbf{t}_2\mathbf{t}_1$ of two translations. Accordingly, the inverse of a mapping $\mathbf{t}$ in $T(A)$ will now be denoted by $-\mathbf{t}$ instead of $\mathbf{t}^{-1}$, and the identity element of $T(A)$, that is, the identity mapping of A, will be denoted by $\mathbf{O}$.

If p and q are two points of A, then by axiom (1) there is a unique translation $\mathbf{t}$ in $T(A)$ such that $\mathbf{t}(p) = q$. It is sometimes convenient to denote that $\mathbf{t}$ by the symbol $\overrightarrow{pq}$; it is called *translation from p to q*. In particular, the symbol $\overrightarrow{pp}$ always represents the identity mapping $\mathbf{O}$ of A, for $\mathbf{O}$ certainly sends p into p, and by axiom (1) it is the only translation that does so.

For two points p and q of A we have two translations $\overrightarrow{pq}$ and $\overrightarrow{qp}$. The first (by definition) sends p into q, and the second sends q into p. Therefore the composition $\overrightarrow{qp} + \overrightarrow{pq}$ sends $p \to q \to p$; that is, it sends p into p and is therefore the identity mapping $\mathbf{O}$. Thus $\overrightarrow{qp} + \overrightarrow{pq} = \mathbf{O}$, or

10.1 $$\overrightarrow{qp} = -\overrightarrow{pq}$$

In other words, $\overrightarrow{qp}$ is the inverse mapping of $\overrightarrow{pq}$. If p, q, and r are any three points of A, then $\overrightarrow{pq} + \overrightarrow{qr}$ sends $p \to q \to r$, and so

10.2 $$\overrightarrow{pq} + \overrightarrow{qr} = \overrightarrow{pr}$$

Using (10.1) we get the alternate form of (10.2)

10.3 $$\overrightarrow{pq} - \overrightarrow{rq} = \overrightarrow{pr}$$

For four points p, q, r, s,

10.4 $$\overrightarrow{pq} = \overrightarrow{rs} \qquad \text{if and only if} \qquad \overrightarrow{pr} = \overrightarrow{qs}$$

Assuming the first equality we get from (10.3) $\overrightarrow{pr} = \overrightarrow{pq} + \overrightarrow{qr} = \overrightarrow{rs} + \overrightarrow{qr} = \overrightarrow{qs}$, which is the second equation. The converse is proved in the same way.

If $\mathbf{t}$ is any translation in $T(A)$, and p any point of A, then setting $q = \mathbf{t}(p)$ we have $\mathbf{t} = \overrightarrow{pq}$; q is uniquely determined by $\mathbf{t}$ (once p is fixed), and conversely. Hence any element of $T(A)$ can be written in the form $\overrightarrow{pq}$, and p can be arbitrarily chosen

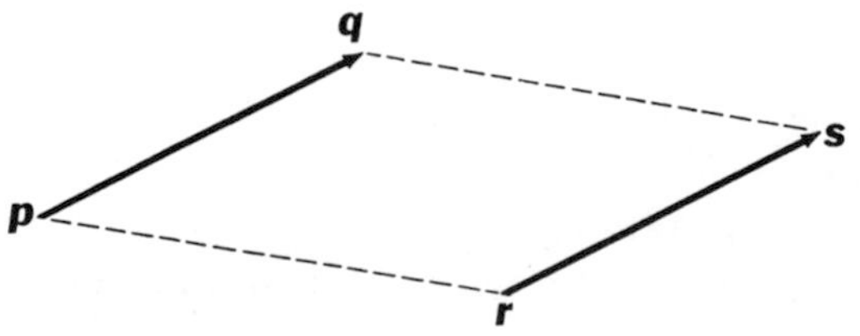

Figure 6

$\overrightarrow{pq} = \overrightarrow{rs}$. Geometrically, $\overrightarrow{pq} = \overrightarrow{rs}$ if and only if these translations have the same length and direction. Thus the interpretation of a vector as a translation of affine space puts the intuitive notion of "free vector" (by contrast with "bound vector") on a firm footing.

in advance. We shall often use this fact. From what has just been pointed out we have the following theorem:

THEOREM 10.1 *A and $T(A)$ being as in Definition* 10.1, *let p_0 be a point of A. Then the operation that assigns the translation $\overrightarrow{p_0q}$ to any point q of A is a one-to-one mapping of A to $T(A)$.*

The mapping just defined sends p_0 into $\overrightarrow{p_0p_0} = \mathbf{O}$.

EXAMPLE 1 Theorem 10.1 suggests a way of constructing an affine space from a vector space. Let V be a vector space over a field K. For A let us take the set V itself, without the vector-space operations; and for $T(A)$ again take V, this time with its vector-space operations. If now $\mathbf{x}$ is an element of $A(=V)$, and if $\mathbf{v}$ is an element of $T(A)(=V)$, then we define the translation of $\mathbf{x}$ by $\mathbf{v}$ to be the element $\mathbf{x} + \mathbf{v}$ of A. It is easily verified that the requirements of Definition 10.1 are satisfied.

Hence a vector space can always be regarded as an affine space. But an affine space cannot in general be regarded as a vector space. Roughly speaking, an affine space can be thought of as a vector space deprived of a fixed "origin." Theorem 10.1 shows that if we fix a point in A as origin, then we get a one-to-one correspondence between A and the vector space $T(A)$ which sends that point into the zero element of $T(A)$. In this way we can transfer questions concerning the set A into analogous questions concerning the vector space $T(A)$.

According to Definition 10.1, $\dim A = \dim T(A)$. Since a vector space of dimension zero contains only one element, it follows from Theorem 10.1 that an affine space of dimension zero consists of a single point. An affine space of dimension 1 is called a *line;* an affine space of dimension 2 is called a *plane.*

DEFINITION 10.2 *Let A and $T(A)$ be as in Definition* 10.1, *and let A' be a subset of A. Then A' is called an* affine subspace *of A if there is a subspace V of $T(A)$ and a point p_0 in A' such that q is in A' if and only if $\overrightarrow{p_0q}$ is in V. In other words, A' is the set of points obtained by applying to p_0 all the translations in V.*

Figure 7 The affine lines A' and B' are both associated with the vector space V.

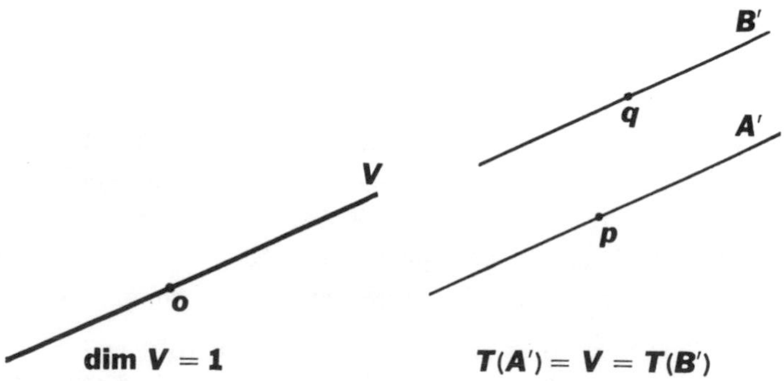

Any point p of A is an affine subspace (of dimension zero), corresponding to the subspace V of $T(A)$ consisting of the element $\mathbf{O}$ alone. And A is an affine subspace of itself, obtained by taking $V = T(A)$ in the definition.

Now let A' be as in the definition. We claim that every translation in V sends A' onto itself. For let q be any point of A', and let $\overrightarrow{qr}$ be any translation in V (it can be so written, by the remarks preceding Theorem 10.1). We must show that r is a point of A'. Now by assumption $\overrightarrow{p_0q}$ is in V, and therefore so is $\overrightarrow{p_0q} + \overrightarrow{qr} = \overrightarrow{p_0r}$ [using (10.2)], and so r is in A' by Definition 10.2.

Now let p be any point of A'. *Then $\overrightarrow{pq}$ is in V if and only if q is in A'.* For $\overrightarrow{pq} = \overrightarrow{p_0q} - \overrightarrow{p_0p}$, by (10.3), and $\overrightarrow{p_0p}$ is in V by assumption. Since V is a subspace of $T(A)$, it follows that $\overrightarrow{pq}$ is in V if and only if $\overrightarrow{p_0q}$ is in V, and that is so if and only if q is in A', by Definition 10.2. Therefore p_0 in Definition 10.2 can be replaced by any other point p of A'. And if we set $T(A') = V$, then A' and $T(A')$ satisfy† Definition 10.1. That is, an affine subspace of A is an affine space in its own right.

Let us apply these remarks to the problem of determining the *lines* in A (i.e., affine subspaces of dimension 1). Let p_0 and p_1 be any two distinct points of A. Then $\overrightarrow{p_0p_1}$ is a nonzero element of $T(A)$, and all the translations $x \cdot \overrightarrow{p_0p_1}$ (x an arbitary scalar in K) form a one-dimensional subspace V of $T(A)$. For each x there is a unique point q in A such that $\overrightarrow{p_0q} = x \cdot \overrightarrow{p_0p_1}$. According to Definition 10.2, all such points q form a line L in A, and by the remarks above, $T(L) = V$. We can thus describe L by the equation

10.5 $$\overrightarrow{p_0q} = x \cdot \overrightarrow{p_0p_1} \qquad (x \text{ an arbitrary scalar in } K)$$

The correspondence between q and x is one-to-one. That is, the points of L are in one-to-one correspondence with the elements of K. If conversely L is a line in A according to Definition 10.1, corresponding to some subspace V of $T(A)$, and if p_0 and p_1 are any two points of it, then by what was pointed out above the translation $\overrightarrow{p_0p_1}$ must be in V. If $p_0 \neq p_1$, then $\overrightarrow{p_0p_1}$ must be a base for V, since V is of dimension 1, by assumption. Therefore every element of V can be expressed uniquely in the form $x \cdot \overrightarrow{p_0p_1}$, where x is in K, and conversely every element of that form is in V. Therefore we arrive again at (10.5).

In a similar way we can determine the *planes* in A. Let p_0, p_1, and p_2 be three points in A, and assume they do not lie on a line in A. Then an equation of the type (10.5), with p_2 in place of q, is impossible, and consequently the two vectors $\overrightarrow{p_0p_1}$ and $\overrightarrow{p_0p_2}$ are linearly independent elements of $T(A)$. They span a subspace V of $T(A)$ of dimension 2, and the elements of V can be expressed uniquely in the form $x_1 \cdot \overrightarrow{p_0p_1} + x_2 \cdot \overrightarrow{p_0p_2}$, where x_1 and x_2 are scalars. For any choice of x_1 and x_2, that translation can be expressed uniquely in the form $\overrightarrow{p_0q}$, and conversely if $\overrightarrow{p_0q}$ is in V, then it can be expressed in the form $x_1 \cdot \overrightarrow{p_0p_1} + x_2 \cdot \overrightarrow{p_0p_2}$.

† The elements of V are translations on the larger set A. Strictly speaking, we should let $T(A')$ denote not V itself but the translations in V restricted to the smaller set A'. This distinction is necessary for logical precision, but no harm will come from overlooking it.

Figure 8a

The three vertices of a triangle in the plane are independent points if the triangle is not degenerate.

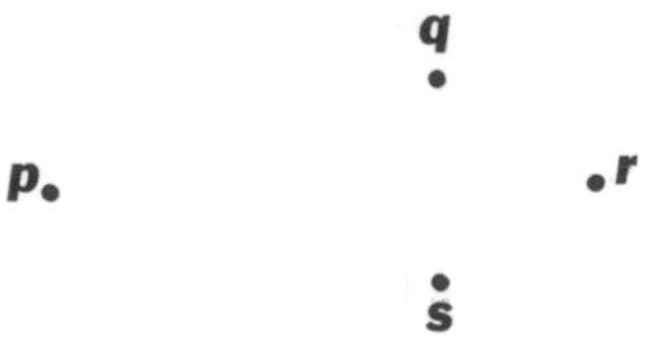

Figure 8b

Any four points in the plane are dependent, since any three vectors in $\mathbf{R}_2$ are linearly dependent.

According to Definition 10.2 all points q of A such that

10.6 $$\overrightarrow{p_0q} = x_1 \cdot \overrightarrow{p_0p_1} + x_2 \cdot \overrightarrow{p_0p_2} \qquad (x_1,\ x_2 \text{ elements of } K)$$

form a plane P in A. If on the other hand, P is a plane in A, corresponding to some subspace V of $T(A)$, and if p_0 is any point of P, then V has a base consisting of two linearly independent vectors $\overrightarrow{p_0p_1}$ and $\overrightarrow{p_0p_2}$, since by assumption V has dimension 2. Both p_1 and p_2 must also be in P, and every point q of P satisfies Eq. (10.6), and conversely if q satisfies (10.6) it must be a point of P.

Higher dimensional subspaces of A can be described in an analogous way. If A has finite dimension n, then A itself can be described in this way. We shall take that up in detail presently. We mention that a subspace of dimension $n - 1$ of A is sometimes called a *hyperplane*.

DEFINITION 10.3 *Let A and $T(A)$ be as in Definition* 10.1, *and let $p_0, p_1, \ldots, p_r$ be $r + 1$ points in A. Then they are said to be* independent *if the r vectors $\overrightarrow{p_0p_1}$, $\overrightarrow{p_0p_2}, \ldots, \overrightarrow{p_0p_r}$ in $T(A)$ are linearly independent. Otherwise the given points are said to be* dependent.

It is easy to see that it is immaterial which point is called p_0 in this definition. This follows from the theorem below but can also be proved directly.

THEOREM 10.2 *If $p_0, p_1, \ldots, p_r$ are independent points in the affine space A, then there is one and only one affine subspace A' of dimension r which contains them; and no affine subspace of smaller dimension can contain them. If however the points are dependent, there is an affine subspace of dimension less than r which contains them.*

Proof. Let V be the subspace of $T(A)$ spanned by the translations $\overrightarrow{p_0p_1}, \overrightarrow{p_0p_2}, \ldots, \overrightarrow{p_0p_r}$. Then clearly $\dim V = r$ if the points are independent, by Definition 10.3. Let A' be the affine subspace of A obtained (Definition 10.2) by applying all the translations in V to p_0. Then A' has dimension r, by Definition 10.1, and it contains $p_0, p_1, \ldots, p_r$. Now let A'' be any affine subspace of A which contains the $r + 1$ points. By Definition 10.2 and the remarks following it, all vectors of the form $\overrightarrow{p_0q}$, with q in A'', must constitute a subspace U of $T(A)$. Taking $q = p_1$,

. . . , p_r we find that U must contain the r translations $\overrightarrow{p_0p_1}, \ldots,$ $\overrightarrow{p_0p_r}$. Hence U must contain V, and so either dim $U > r$ or else $U = V$ and $A' = A''$. Finally, if the points are dependent, then dim $V < r$ and so dim $A' < r$. Q.E.D.

Two points p_0 and p_1 of A are independent if they are distinct, and they determine a line in A, as we have seen earlier. If three points p_0, p_1, p_2 are dependent, then they lie on a line, as the theorem shows. They are then said to be *collinear*. If they are independent, then they determine a plane in A, as we have seen above. If A has finite dimension n, then A contains a set of $n + 1$ independent points; but more than $n + 1$ points must be dependent.

We conclude this section by showing how the points of an affine space A of finite dimension n can be represented by coordinates. By definition the vector space $T(A)$ then has dimension n. Let us choose a base for it, say $\overrightarrow{p_0p_1}, \overrightarrow{p_0p_2}, \ldots,$ $\overrightarrow{p_0p_n}$, where p_0 is some selected point of A. If q is an arbitrary point of A, then the translation $\overrightarrow{p_0q}$ can be expressed uniquely in the form

10.7 $$\overrightarrow{p_0q} = x_1 \cdot \overrightarrow{p_0p_1} + x_2 \cdot \overrightarrow{p_0p_2} + \cdots + x_n \cdot \overrightarrow{p_0p_n}$$

where $x_1, x_2, \ldots, x_n$ are scalars in K. Combining Theorems 9.2 and 10.1 we see that the mapping

10.8 $$q \to (x_1, x_2, \ldots, x_n)$$

is a one-to-one mapping of A to K_n. A mapping obtained in this way is called a *cartesian coordinate system in* A *with origin* p_0; and $x_1, \ldots, x_n$ are called the *coordinates* of the point q. From (10.7) it is clear that the coordinates of p_0 are all zero because $\overrightarrow{p_0p_0} = \mathbf{O}$. It is obvious that (10.5) and (10.6) are special cases of (10.7).

Let us now determine how two different cartesian coordinate systems in A are related. Then let $\overrightarrow{s_0s_1}, \overrightarrow{s_0s_2}, \ldots, \overrightarrow{s_0s_n}$ be a new base for $T(A)$, and let the new coordinates of q be $y_1, y_2, \ldots, y_n$. That is,

10.9 $$\overrightarrow{s_0q} = y_1 \cdot \overrightarrow{s_0s_1} + \cdots + y_n \cdot \overrightarrow{s_0s_n}$$

Further, let the new origin have coordinates $b_1, \ldots, b_n$ in the old system. That is, from (10.7),

10.10 $$\overrightarrow{p_0s_0} = b_1 \cdot \overrightarrow{p_0p_1} + \cdots + b_n \cdot \overrightarrow{p_0p_n}$$

Subtracting this from (10.7) and taking account of the relation $\overrightarrow{p_0q} - \overrightarrow{p_0s_0} = \overrightarrow{s_0q}$ we get

10.11 $$\overrightarrow{s_0q} = (x_1 - b_1) \cdot \overrightarrow{p_0p_1} \cdots (x_n - b_n) \cdot \overrightarrow{p_0p_n}$$

We have the translation $\overrightarrow{s_0q}$ expressed in terms of two different bases in (10.9) and (10.11). As pointed out at the end of Sec. 9, the two bases for $T(A)$ are related by equations of the type (9.5), say

10.12 $\overrightarrow{s_0s_j} = a_{j1}\overrightarrow{p_0p_1} + \cdots + a_{jn}\overrightarrow{p_0p_n} \qquad (j = 1, \ldots, n)$

Then applying (9.6) to the translation $\overrightarrow{s_0q}$ we get

10.13 $x_i - b_i = a_{1i}y_1 + \cdots + a_{ni}y_n \qquad (i = 1, \ldots, n)$

from (10.9) and (10.11), or

10.14
$$\begin{aligned} x_1 &= b_1 + a_{11}y_1 + \cdots + a_{n1}y_n \\ &\cdots\cdots\cdots\cdots \\ x_n &= b_n + a_{1n}y_1 + \cdots + a_{nn}y_n \end{aligned}$$

A relation of this type connecting $(x_1, \ldots, x_n)$ and $(y_1, \ldots, y_n)$ is called an *affine transformation.* In Sec. 12 we shall have some specific examples. Observe that if the two origins p_0 and s_0 are the same, then the b's in (10.14) are all zero. On the other hand, if the two bases in $T(A)$ are the same, then (10.14) reduces to

$$x_1 = b_1 + y_1, \ldots, x_n = b_n + y_n$$

or

$$(x_1, \ldots, x_n) = (b_1, \ldots, b_n) + (y_1, \ldots, y_n)$$

The two coordinate systems are said to be related by a translation.

Let us now go back to the first coordinate system $x_1, \ldots, x_n$ of (10.7). Consider the one-dimensional subspace of $T(A)$ spanned by the base vector $\overrightarrow{p_0p_j}$. Every element in it can be expressed in the form $x \cdot \overrightarrow{p_0p_j}$, and each such translation applied to p_0 gives a point q such that $\overrightarrow{p_0q} = x \cdot \overrightarrow{p_0p_j}$. Referring to (10.5), all such points q fill up a line L_j in A. That is, L_j consists of all points q whose coordinates $x_1, \ldots, x_{j-1}, x_{j+1}, \ldots, x_n$ are all zero. The lines $L_1, L_2, \ldots, L_n$ are called the *coordinate axes* of the particular coordinate system.

Consider now the subspace V_j of $T(A)$ of dimension $n - 1$ spanned by $\overrightarrow{p_0p_1}, \ldots, \overrightarrow{p_0p_{j-1}}, \overrightarrow{p_0p_{j+1}}, \ldots, \overrightarrow{p_0p_n}$, that is, by all the base vectors *except* $\overrightarrow{p_0p_j}$. If we apply all the translations in V_j to the point p_0, we get an affine subspace A'_j,

Figure 9 The most general affine transformation of affine 3-space carries any set of coordinate axes into another. It sends lines into lines and, more generally, it sends affine subspaces into affine subspaces. The general affine transformation of euclidean space sends a cube into a parallelepiped.

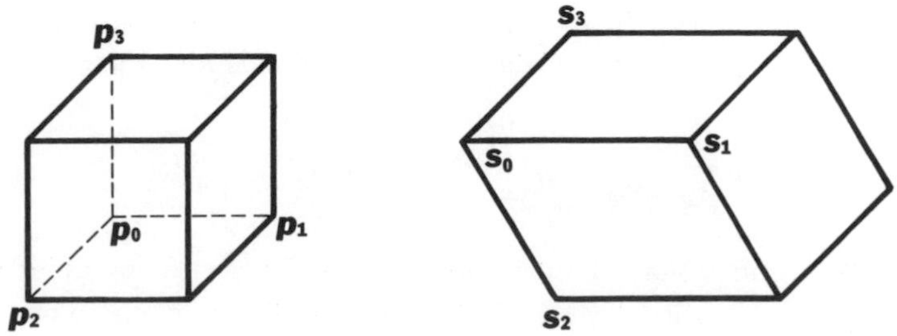

by Definition 10.2, and clearly it consists of all points q for which the jth coordinate x_j is zero. The n hyperplanes $A'_1, \ldots, A'_n$ obtained in this way are called the *coordinate hyperplanes* of the system $x_1, x_2, \ldots, x_n$. Observe that the coordinate axis L_j consists of all the points common to the $n - 1$ coordinate hyperplanes $A'_1, \ldots, A'_{j-1}, A'_{j+1}, \ldots, A'_n$.

More generally, if $c_0, c_1, \ldots, c_n$ are elements of K, of which the last n are not all zero, then the equation

10.15 $$c_0 + c_1x_1 + \cdots + c_nx_n = O$$

determines a hyperplane in A as follows: Let V be the $(n - 1)$-dimensional subspace of $T(A)$ consisting of all translations $u_1 \cdot \overrightarrow{p_0p_1} + \cdots + u_n \cdot \overrightarrow{p_0p_n}$ such that

10.16 $$c_1u_1 + \cdots + c_nu_n = O$$

Let q_0 be a point whose coordinates $x_1{}^0, \ldots, x_n{}^0$ satisfy Eq. (10.15), and let q be a point with coordinates $x_1, \ldots, x_n$. We have

$$\overrightarrow{q_0q} = \overrightarrow{p_0q} - \overrightarrow{p_0q_0} = (x_1 - x_1{}^0)\overrightarrow{p_0p_1} + \cdots + (x_n - x_n{}^0)\overrightarrow{p_0p_n}$$

using (10.7). Therefore, referring to (10.16), we see that $\overrightarrow{q_0q}$ is in the subspace V of $T(A)$ if and only if the coordinates $x_1, \ldots, x_n$ of q also satisfy Eq. (10.15). Hence, by Definition 10.2, all points q whose coordinates satisfy (10.15) form a hyperplane A' in A. If we specialize (10.15) by taking $c_j = 1$ and all the other c's equal to zero, then A' is the coordinate hyperplane A'_j.

Finally let us see how to represent the points of the affine subspace B of A determined by $r + 1$ independent points $q_0, q_1, \ldots, q_r$ (see Theorem 10.2). In the coordinate system (10.7) let q_j have coordinates $a_{j1}, a_{j2}, \ldots, a_{jn}$ $(j = 0, \ldots, r)$. By definition those scalars are the components of the vector $\overrightarrow{p_0q_j}$ with respect to the base $\overrightarrow{p_0p_1}, \ldots, \overrightarrow{p_0p_n}$. Then $\overrightarrow{q_0q_j} = \overrightarrow{p_0q_j} - \overrightarrow{p_0q_0} = (a_{j1} - a_{01})\overrightarrow{p_0p_1} + \cdots + (a_{jn} - a_{0n})\overrightarrow{p_0p_n}$. From the proof of Theorem 10.2 it is clear that a point q is in B if and only if $\overrightarrow{q_0q}$ is a linear combination of the independent vectors $\overrightarrow{q_0q_1}, \ldots, \overrightarrow{q_0q_r}$, say

$$\begin{aligned}\overrightarrow{q_0q} &= t_1 \cdot \overrightarrow{q_0q_1} + \cdots + t_r \cdot \overrightarrow{q_0q_r} \\ &= \sum_{j=1}^{r} t_j \cdot [(a_{j1} - a_{01}) \cdot \overrightarrow{p_0p_1} + \cdots + (a_{jn} - a_{0n}) \cdot \overrightarrow{p_0p_n}]\end{aligned}$$

If q has coordinates $x_1, \ldots, x_n$, then $\overrightarrow{q_0q} = (x_1 - a_{01}) \cdot \overrightarrow{p_0p_1} + \cdots + (x_n - a_{0n}) \cdot \overrightarrow{p_0p_n}$. Equating coefficients of $\overrightarrow{p_0p_k}$ in this and the preceding expression we obtain

10.17 $$x_k - a_{0k} = \sum_{j=1}^{r} t_j(a_{jk} - a_{0k}) \qquad (k = 1, \ldots, n)$$

As the t_j vary through the field of scalars K, the point q with coordinates $x_1, \ldots, x_n$ given by (10.17) varies through the subspace B, giving a one-to-one mapping of

B to K_r. In fact the correspondence $q \to (t_1, \ldots, t_r)$ is just a cartesian coordinate system in B. We can write (10.17) in a form which is not biased in favor of q_0 as follows: Put $t_0 = 1 - t_1 - t_2 - \cdots - t_r$. Then it is immediate that (10.17) is the same as

$$\textbf{10.18} \qquad x_k = t_0\, a_{0k} + \cdots + t_r\, a_{rk} \qquad \begin{cases} k = 1, \ldots, n \\ t_0 + t_1 + \cdots + t_r = 1 \end{cases}$$

As a special case, let q_0, q_1 be two distinct points of A. The subspace of A that they determine is a line L. If q_0 has coordinates $a_1, \ldots, a_n$ and if q_1 has coordinates $b_1, \ldots, b_n$, then (10.17) becomes

$$\textbf{10.19} \qquad x_k - a_k = t\,(b_k - a_k) \qquad (k = 1, \ldots, n)$$

These equations are called *parametric* equations of the line L; as t varies through K the point with coordinates $(x_1, \ldots, x_n)$ given by (10.19) varies through L. Equation (10.19) is just (10.5) written out in terms of vector components (with some minor changes of notation). If we put $t_1 = t$, $t_0 = 1 - t_1$, then (10.19) goes into the form (10.18):

$$\textbf{10.20} \qquad x_k = t_0 a_k + t_1 b_k \qquad (k = 1, \ldots, n,\ t_0 + t_1 = 1)$$

EXERCISES

1. Let A' be an affine subspace of an affine space A of finite dimension. Show that $\dim A' < \dim A$, with equality holding if and only if $A' = A$.

2. Let A' and A'' be two affine subspaces of an affine space A. Prove that the set of points common to both A' and A'' is either empty or else is an affine subspace of A. Prove that two distinct lines in A either have no points in common or else intersect in a single point. Prove that two distinct planes in A either have no points in common or else intersect in a point or a line.

3. Let A be an affine space of dimension n. Prove that, if $n = 3$, two distinct planes in A intersect in a line or else have no points in common. Show that, in general, two planes in A have no points in common if $n > 4$.

4. Let A be an affine plane (that is, $\dim A = 2$), and let x, y be a cartesian coordinate system in A. Prove that if a, b, and c are scalars with a and b not both zero, then the set of all points in A whose coordinates x, y satisfy the equation

$$ax + by + c = 0$$

is a line. Show conversely that every line in A can be obtained in this way by a suitable choice of a, b, c. Show how to determine a, b, c for the unique line passing through two distinct points p_0 and p_1, with coordinates (x_0, y_0) and (x_1, y_1), respectively.

5. Let A be an affine space of dimension n, and let $x_1, x_2, \ldots, x_n$ be a cartesian coordinate system in A. Prove that every hyperplane in A is determined by an equation of the type (10.15). Let A' and A'' be affine subspaces of dimensions r and $r - 1$, respectively. Show that there is a hyperplane in A such that A'' consists of all the points which that hyperplane has in common with A'. Use this result to prove by induction that A' is the intersection of $n - r$ hyperplanes in A.

6. Let A be an affine 3-space over the real field $\mathbf{R}$, and let (x, y, z) be a system of cartesian coordinates in A. Determine the line passing through the two points $(1, 0, 3)$ and $(-1, 2, 4)$; determine the plane passing through the points $(1, 0, 3)$, $(-1, 2, 4)$, and $(4, 1, 2)$. (We mean, determine the conditions that must be satisfied by the coordinates of a point in order for that point to be in the line or plane.)

11. Euclidean spaces

In general there is no way of defining lengths of vectors in a vector space, or angles between vectors. Similarly there is in general no way of defining distance between two points of an affine space, or of defining the angle between two intersecting lines. The axioms for vector and affine spaces simply do not provide any apparatus for making such definitions. We remark furthermore that it is quite possible for a vector space or an affine space to have only a finite number of points, even though the dimension is greater than zero. Indeed if the field of scalars K has only a finite number of elements, say r (as is the case with the fields $\mathbf{Z}_p$ of Chap. 2), then any vector or affine space of dimension n over K has just r^n elements, as is readily seen. It would be unreasonable to hope for a definition of angle or length in such a situation. We now turn our attention to a case where such definitions can be made—namely, to vector and affine spaces over the real number field $\mathbf{R}$. We begin with the following provisional definition; a more complete one is given in Chap. 14.

DEFINITION 11.1 *Let V be a vector space of finite dimension n over the real field $\mathbf{R}$. Then V is called a* euclidean vector space *if there is assigned to every element $\mathbf{x}$ of V a real number, denoted by $|\mathbf{x}|$, such that for at least one choice of base $\mathbf{e}_1, \ldots, \mathbf{e}_n$ in V we have*

11.1 $$|\mathbf{x}| = (x_1^2 + \cdots + x_n^2)^{\frac{1}{2}} \qquad \text{if} \qquad \mathbf{x} = x_1\mathbf{e}_1 + \cdots + x_n\mathbf{e}_n$$

It is clear that $|\mathbf{x}| \geq \mathbf{0}$ and $|\mathbf{x}| = 0$ if and only if $\mathbf{x} = \mathbf{0}$. The number $|\mathbf{x}|$ is called the *length* of the vector $\mathbf{x}$. Starting with any n-dimensional vector space V over $\mathbf{R}$ we can make it into a euclidean vector space by simply choosing any base in V and then defining $|\mathbf{x}|$ by the formula (11.1). We mention that the particular form of (11.1) is dictated by the fact that it makes the Pythagorean theorem true, as we shall see presently, and that would not be so if we had perversely decided to make the right-hand member of (11.1), say, $(x_1^4 + \cdots + x_n^4)^{\frac{1}{4}}$. However, the form chosen for (11.1) is not the only one which makes the Pythagorean theorem true.

According to Definition 11.1, the number $|\mathbf{x}|$ is assumed to be given, without reference to any base in V; it is merely required that there be some base for which (11.1) is valid. From it we deduce the equation

11.2 $|t\mathbf{x}|^2 = t^2|\mathbf{x}|^2$ (t any real number)

We now define the *inner product* $(\mathbf{x}, \mathbf{y})$ of any two elements $\mathbf{x}$ and $\mathbf{y}$ of V by the equation

11.3 $|\mathbf{x} + \mathbf{y}|^2 = |\mathbf{x}|^2 + 2(\mathbf{x}, \mathbf{y}) + |\mathbf{y}|^2$

Putting $\mathbf{x}$ for $\mathbf{y}$ here and using (11.2) we find for example that $(\mathbf{x}, \mathbf{x}) = |\mathbf{x}|^2$. Putting $\mathbf{O}$ for $\mathbf{y}$ we get $(\mathbf{x}, \mathbf{O}) = 0$. Clearly $(\mathbf{x}, \mathbf{y}) = (\mathbf{y}, \mathbf{x})$ for any two vectors. If $\mathbf{e}_1, \ldots, \mathbf{e}_n$ is a base for which (11.1) holds, and if $\mathbf{x} = x_1\mathbf{e}_1 + \cdots + x_n\mathbf{e}_n$ and $\mathbf{y} = y_1\mathbf{e}_1 + \cdots + y_n\mathbf{e}_n$, then it is easily seen from (11.1) and (11.3) that

11.4 $(\mathbf{x}, \mathbf{y}) = x_1y_1 + \cdots + x_ny_n$

From this formula it is clear that

11.5 $(t\mathbf{x}, \mathbf{y}) = t \cdot (\mathbf{x}, \mathbf{y})$ and $(\mathbf{x} + \mathbf{y}, \mathbf{z}) = (\mathbf{x}, \mathbf{z}) + (\mathbf{y}, \mathbf{z})$

for any vectors $\mathbf{x}$, $\mathbf{y}$, $\mathbf{z}$ and any real number t. Two vectors $\mathbf{x}$ and $\mathbf{y}$ are said to be *orthogonal* if $(\mathbf{x}, \mathbf{y}) = 0$. A vector of length 1 is called a *unit* vector. Applying (11.4) to the base vectors $\mathbf{e}_i$ we get at once

11.6 $$(\mathbf{e}_i, \mathbf{e}_j) = \begin{cases} 1 & \text{if } i = j \\ 0 & \text{if } i \neq j \end{cases}$$

Thus if (11.1) is valid for the base $\mathbf{e}_i$, then the vectors are all unit vectors and any two different vectors in the base are orthogonal. For this reason the base is said to be *orthonormal*. It is easy to see conversely that if a base for V is orthonormal, then (11.1) holds for that base.

THEOREM 11.1 **(Schwarz's inequality)** *For any two vectors* $\mathbf{x}$ *and* $\mathbf{y}$ *in* V,

11.7 $(\mathbf{x}, \mathbf{y})^2 \leq |\mathbf{x}|^2 \cdot |\mathbf{y}|^2$

Proof. Replace $\mathbf{x}$ in (11.3) by $t\mathbf{x}$, t being any real number. Using (11.2) and (11.5), we have $|t\mathbf{x} + \mathbf{y}|^2 = t^2|\mathbf{x}|^2 + 2t(\mathbf{x}, \mathbf{y}) + |\mathbf{y}|^2$. Temporarily write $a = |\mathbf{x}|^2$, $b = (\mathbf{x}, \mathbf{y})$, and $c = |\mathbf{y}|^2$. Since $|t\mathbf{x} + \mathbf{y}|^2 \geqslant 0$, we have then

$$at^2 + 2bt + c \geqslant 0$$

and this must hold for any real number t. Consequently this quadratic polynomial cannot have two distinct real roots, and therefore $b^2 \leq ac$, which is what we wanted to prove (see Exercise 5, Sec. 6, Chap. 6). Q.E.D.

Now let $\mathbf{x}$ and $\mathbf{y}$ be any two *nonzero* vectors in our euclidean vector space V. Taking square roots in the Schwarz inequality we get

$$|(\mathbf{x}, \mathbf{y})| \leqslant |\mathbf{x}| \cdot |\mathbf{y}| \qquad |(\mathbf{x}, \mathbf{y})| = \text{absolute value of } (\mathbf{x}, \mathbf{y})$$

Since $|\mathbf{x}| \neq 0$ and $|\mathbf{y}| \neq 0$, there follows

$$-1 \leq \frac{(\mathbf{x}, \mathbf{y})}{|\mathbf{x}| \cdot |\mathbf{y}|} \leq 1$$

Therefore there is a unique number θ between 0 and π (inclusive) such that

11.8 $$\cos \theta = \frac{(\mathbf{x}, \mathbf{y})}{|\mathbf{x}| \cdot |\mathbf{y}|}$$

We define θ to be the *angle* between $\mathbf{x}$ and $\mathbf{y}$, and we shall also denote it by

$$\theta = \measuredangle \mathbf{x}, \mathbf{y}$$

Observe that $\theta = \pi/2$ if $(\mathbf{x}, \mathbf{y}) = 0$. Therefore our earlier definition of orthogonality agrees with the definition of angle above. It is easily verified, using (11.2) and (11.5), that if a and b are any *positive* numbers, then the angle between $a\mathbf{x}$ and $b\mathbf{y}$ is the same as the angle between $\mathbf{x}$ and $\mathbf{y}$. Taking $\mathbf{x} = \mathbf{y}$ in (11.8) we get $\cos \theta = 1$; hence $\theta = 0$. This shows that θ has at least some of the properties we ought to expect of the definition of angle. Writing (11.8) as $(\mathbf{x}, \mathbf{y}) = |\mathbf{x}| \cdot |\mathbf{y}| \cos \theta$ and putting this in (11.3) we get

11.9 $$|\mathbf{x} \pm \mathbf{y}|^2 = |\mathbf{x}|^2 \pm 2|\mathbf{x}| \cdot |\mathbf{y}| \cos \theta + |\mathbf{y}|^2$$

which is a form of the law of cosines. From it there follows at once the triangle inequality

11.10 $$|\mathbf{x} \pm \mathbf{y}| \leq |\mathbf{x}| + |\mathbf{y}|$$

for the right-hand side of (11.9) cannot exceed $(|\mathbf{x}| + |\mathbf{y}|)^2$.

Now let $\mathbf{x}$ have components $x_1, \ldots, x_n$ with respect to an orthonormal base $\mathbf{e}_1, \ldots, \mathbf{e}_n$, so that $\mathbf{x} = x_1\mathbf{e}_1 + \cdots + x_n\mathbf{e}_n$. Since the components of $\mathbf{e}_j$ with respect to that base are all zero except the jth, which is 1, it follows at once from (11.4) and (11.8) that

11.11 $$(\mathbf{x}, \mathbf{e}_j) = x_j = |\mathbf{x}| \cos \alpha_j$$

where α_j denotes the angle between $\mathbf{x}$ and $\mathbf{e}_j$. In particular, if $\mathbf{x}$ is a *unit* vector, then its components with respect to the orthonormal base are the same as the cosines of the angles that $\mathbf{x}$ makes with the base vectors.

We now show how these definitions can be carried over into affine spaces.

DEFINITION 11.2 *An affine space E of finite dimension n over the real field* **R** *is called* a euclidean space *if its vector space of translations $T(E)$ has the structure of a euclidean vector space.*

It is simply required that there be assigned to every translation $\mathbf{t}$ in $T(E)$ a length $|\mathbf{t}|$ satisfying Definition 11.1; such a length can always be defined. Supposing then that E is a euclidean space, it is very easy to define the *distance* $|pq|$ between two of its points p and q: we put

11.12 $|pq| = |\overrightarrow{pq}|$

where on the right stands the length of the translation vector $\overrightarrow{pq}$. It is clear that $|pq| = |qp|$, from (11.12). From (10.2) we have $\overrightarrow{pq} + \overrightarrow{qr} = \overrightarrow{pr}$, and from (11.9) there follows the *law of cosines*

11.13 $|pr|^2 = |pq|^2 + |qr|^2 - 2|pq| \cdot |qr| \cdot \cos \theta$

where θ is the angle between $\overrightarrow{qp}$ and $\overrightarrow{qr}$. In particular, if those two vectors are orthogonal, then (11.13) reduces to the pythagorean theorem. From (11.10) we have the *triangle inequality*

11.14 $|pr| \leq |pq| + |qr|$

It is also very easy to define the angle between two lines L and L', but some preliminary remarks are necessary. If L is a line in E, then all the translations $\overrightarrow{pq}$ (p and q points of L) form the one-dimensional vector space $T(L)$. And since that space has dimension 1, it follows that there are exactly two *unit* vectors in it; if one of them is $\mathbf{u}$, then the other is $-\mathbf{u}$. By an *oriented* line L we shall mean a line along with one of the two unit vectors $\pm\mathbf{u}$. If then L and L' are two oriented lines, with associated unit vectors $\mathbf{u}$ and $\mathbf{u}'$, respectively, we define the angle between L and L' by

11.15 $\sphericalangle\, L, L' = \sphericalangle\, \mathbf{u}, \mathbf{u}'$

the right-hand side being of course defined by (11.8). If the orientations of the two lines are reversed (that is, if $\mathbf{u}, \mathbf{u}'$ are replaced by $-\mathbf{u}, -\mathbf{u}'$), then the angle between L and L' is not changed. If however the orientation of just one of the two lines is reversed, then the angle (11.15), call it θ, is replaced by $\pi - \theta$, as follows from (11.8). The two lines are said to be *parallel* if the angle between them is 0 or π; they are said to be *orthogonal* (or *perpendicular*) if the angle is $\pi/2$. In the latter case it is clear that the orientation is a matter of indifference. It is possible to define angles between affine subspaces of E of dimension greater than 1, but we shall not go into that here.

We point out that either of the vectors $\mathbf{u}$ or $-\mathbf{u}$ in $T(L)$ satisfies the conditions of Definition 11.1. For if $\mathbf{x}$ is any vector in $T(L)$, then $\mathbf{x} = x \cdot \mathbf{u}$ for some real number x, and $|\mathbf{x}|^2 = x^2 \cdot |\mathbf{u}| = x^2$, by (11.2), and this is just Eq. (11.1) for $n = 1$. Hence $T(L)$ is a euclidean vector space, and so L itself is a euclidean space, by Definition 11.2. It is not hard to show that any affine subspace of the euclidean space E is also a euclidean space. For example, let P be a plane in E. Then the vector space of translations $T(P)$ has dimension 2. Let $\mathbf{u}_1$ be any nonzero vector in $T(P)$. By multiplying $\mathbf{u}_1$ by a suitable number (namely, the reciprocal of its length) we obtain a unit vector. Therefore let us assume that $\mathbf{u}_1$ itself is a unit vector in $T(P)$. Since $\mathbf{u}_1$ does not span $T(P)$, there is a vector $\mathbf{w}$ in $T(P)$ which is not a multiple of $\mathbf{u}_1$. Put $\mathbf{w}' = \mathbf{w} - a\,\mathbf{u}_1$, where $a = (\mathbf{u}_1, \mathbf{w})$. From (11.5) we have $(\mathbf{u}_1, \mathbf{w}') = (\mathbf{u}_1, \mathbf{w} - a\,\mathbf{u}_1) = (\mathbf{u}_1, \mathbf{w}) - a \cdot (\mathbf{u}_1, \mathbf{u}_1) = a - a = 0$. Hence $\mathbf{u}_1$ and $\mathbf{w}'$ are orthogonal, and $\mathbf{w}' \neq 0$, for otherwise $\mathbf{w}$ would be a multiple of $\mathbf{u}_1$. Set finally $\mathbf{u}_2 = b\,\mathbf{w}'$, where $b = 1/|\mathbf{w}'|$. It is immediate that $\mathbf{u}_1$ and $\mathbf{u}_2$ form an orthonormal base for $T(P)$, which must therefore be a euclidean vector space. Hence P is a euclidean space, by Definition 11.2. A similar procedure can be used for affine subspaces of any dimension in E.

There is an important relation between lines and hyperplanes in E. Let L be a line, and let $\mathbf{u}$ be one of the two unit vectors in $T(L)$. Let V be the subset of $T(E)$ consisting of all translations which are orthogonal to $\mathbf{u}$. From (11.5) it is easy to verify that V is a subspace of $T(E)$. Furthermore, V has dimension $n - 1$. For there exist $n - 1$ vectors $\mathbf{w}_1, \ldots, \mathbf{w}_{n-1}$ in $T(E)$ such that $\mathbf{u}, \mathbf{w}_1, \ldots, \mathbf{w}_{n-1}$ span $T(E)$ (Theorem 9.3). Put $\mathbf{v}_j = \mathbf{w}_j - a_j \cdot \mathbf{u}$, where $a_j = (\mathbf{u}, \mathbf{w}_j)$. Then, as remarked above, the vectors $\mathbf{v}_j$ are all orthogonal to $\mathbf{u}$, and they form a base for V, as is quickly seen. Now let p_0 be any point. Then the set of all points q such that $\overrightarrow{p_0q}$ is in V is a hyperplane H in E, by Definition 10.2, and $T(H) = V$. Every element of $T(H)$ is orthogonal to every element of $T(L)$, since the latter is spanned by $\mathbf{u}$; and the line determined by any two points of H is orthogonal to L. For this reason we say that the affine subspaces L and H are orthogonal. H can be described briefly by

11.16 $$H = \text{set of all points } q \text{ such that } (\mathbf{u}, \overrightarrow{p_0q}) = 0$$

H is uniquely determined by L and p_0.

In a similar way, if we start off with a hyperplane H in E and let U be the set of all translations in $T(E)$ which are orthogonal to every translation in $T(H)$, then U is a one-dimensional subspace of $T(E)$ (see Exercise 4 below). Fixing some point p_0, the set of all points q such that $\overrightarrow{p_0q}$ is in U is a line L which is orthogonal to H.

It is not hard to generalize these considerations to affine subspaces of dimension r and $n - r$ in E, but we shall not go into that here. Observe that for $n = 3$ a hyperplane is just a plane; for $n = 2$ a hyperplane is a line.

We now take up the question of coordinate systems in E. Since $T(E)$ is a euclidean vector space, there must be an orthonormal base $\mathbf{e}_1, \mathbf{e}_2, \ldots, \mathbf{e}_n$ in $T(E)$, by Definition 11.1. Choosing a point p_0 in E as origin, then for any point q the vector $\overrightarrow{p_0q}$ can be expressed uniquely in the form

11.17 $$\overrightarrow{p_0q} = x_1\mathbf{e}_1 + \cdots + x_n\mathbf{e}_n$$

which is just (10.7) with minor changes of notation. By the definition of Sec. 10, the mapping $q \to (x_1, \ldots, x_n)$ is a cartesian coordinate system in E. We shall call it a *euclidean coordinate system* because of the additional assumption that the base vectors are orthonormal. If p is a point with coordinates $y_1, \ldots, y_n$, that is, if $\overrightarrow{p_0p} = y_1\mathbf{e}_1 + \cdots + y_n\mathbf{e}_n$, then $\overrightarrow{pq} = \overrightarrow{p_0q} - \overrightarrow{p_0p} = (x_1 - y_1) \cdot \mathbf{e}_1 + \cdots + (x_n - y_n) \cdot \mathbf{e}_n$, and so from (11.12) and (11.1) we get

11.18 $$|pq| = [(x_1 - y_1)^2 + \cdots + (x_n - y_n)^2]^{\frac{1}{2}}$$

It is to be emphasized that this distance formula holds only for euclidean coordinate systems and is not valid for other cartesian systems.

Recall that the jth coordinate axis L_j of the given coordinate system is the line consisting of all points whose coordinates are all zero except the jth. The vector space of translations $T(L_j)$ is spanned by $\mathbf{e}_j$, and we orient L_j by assigning to it that unit vector. There is a unique point p_j on L_j such that $\overrightarrow{p_0p_j} = \mathbf{e}_j$, and so $\mathbf{e}_j$ is represented by the pair of points consisting of the origin p_0 and the point p_j, which is at distance 1 from the origin. The jth coordinate hyperplane H_j consists of all points† $(x_1, x_2, \ldots, x_n)$ such that $x_j = 0$. It is clear that L_j and H_j are orthogonal.

Consider now an oriented line L in E, with associated unit translation $\mathbf{u}$. Let the components of $\mathbf{u}$ with respect to the base $\mathbf{e}_j$ be $u_1, \ldots, u_n$, and let α_j be the angle between L and the axis L_j. Then from (11.15) and (11.11) we have

11.19 $$u_j = (\mathbf{u}, \mathbf{e}_j) = \cos \alpha_j \qquad (j = 1, \ldots, n)$$

These numbers are sometimes called the *direction cosines* of the line L.

Let p_1 and q be two points of L, and let their coordinates be $a_1, \ldots, a_n$ and $x_1, \ldots, x_n$, respectively. Then $\overrightarrow{p_1q} = \overrightarrow{p_0q} - \overrightarrow{p_0p_1} = (x_1 - a_1) \cdot \mathbf{e}_1 + \cdots + (x_n - a_n) \cdot \mathbf{e}_n$. But $\overrightarrow{p_1q}$ is in the space spanned by the unit vector $\mathbf{u}$, and so $\overrightarrow{p_1q} = t\mathbf{u}$, for some real number t. In fact, from (11.2) it follows that $t = \pm|\overrightarrow{p_1q}|$. Now writing $\mathbf{u}$ out in terms of the base vectors and comparing the two expressions for $\overrightarrow{p_1q}$ we get $x_j - a_j = tu_j$, or

11.20 $$x_j = a_j + tu_j \qquad (j = 1, \ldots, n)$$

These equations are called *parametric equations* for L. They are the same as (10.19), with $b_j - a_j$ in place of u_j, save that in (10.19) the elements $b_j - a_j$ may not be the components of a unit vector, since it is impossible to define that notion in the case of an arbitrary field of scalars. As t varies over all real numbers, the point $(x_1, \ldots, x_n)$ defined by (11.20) varies over L. Because of this auxiliary role, t is called a *parameter*. If $b_1, \ldots, b_n$ and $v_1, \ldots, v_n$ are any real numbers, of which the last n are not all zero, and if we put

11.21 $$x_j = b_j + tv_j \qquad (j = 1, \ldots, n)$$

then the set of all points $(x_1, \ldots, x_n)$ obtained by letting t vary through $\mathbf{R}$ is a line L' in E. For put $\mathbf{v} = v_1\mathbf{e}_1 + \cdots + v_n\mathbf{e}_n$, and let q_1 be the point with coordinates $b_1, \ldots, b_n$. Then (11.20) is equivalent to $\overrightarrow{q_1q} = t\mathbf{v}$, and therefore L' consists of all points q such that $\overrightarrow{q_1q}$ is in the one-dimensional vector space spanned by $\mathbf{v}$ (of course $\mathbf{v}$ may not be a unit vector).

Returning to L above, let us now consider the hyperplane H that is orthogonal to L and contains p_1. Referring to (11.16), H consists of all points q such that $(\mathbf{u}, \overrightarrow{p_1q}) = 0$, and by (11.4) this is so if and only if

11.22 $$u_1 \cdot (x_1 - a_1) + \cdots + u_n \cdot (x_n - a_n) = 0$$

where again $x_1, \ldots, x_n$ are the coordinates of q. Hence Eq. (11.22) determines H completely, and it is called the equation of H. Putting $u_0 = -(u_1a_1 + \cdots + u_na_n)$ we can write (11.22) as

† In referring to a point it is often convenient to represent it by its coordinates. Thus such a phrase as "let $(x_1, \ldots, x_n)$ be a point of E" means "let us consider the point of E whose coordinates are $x_1, \ldots, x_n$."

11.23 $$u_0 + u_1x_1 + \cdots + u_nx_n = 0$$

Conversely, if $v_0, v_1, \ldots, v_n$ are any real numbers, of which the last n are not all zero, then the equation

11.24 $$v_0 + v_1x_1 + \cdots + v_nx_n = 0$$

determines a hyperplane H', and it is orthogonal to the line L' defined by (11.21). The argument is essentially that given at the end of Sec. 10 in connection with (10.15).

EXERCISES

1. Let V be a euclidean vector space of finite dimension n, and let $\mathbf{v}_1, \ldots, \mathbf{v}_n$ be a set of n orthonormal vectors in V. Prove that they form a base for V and that (11.1) holds for that base.

2. Let V be as above and let $\mathbf{w}_1, \ldots, \mathbf{w}_k$ be any set of linearly independent vectors in V. Define a new set of k vectors $\mathbf{v}_1, \ldots, \mathbf{v}_k$ by the equations $\mathbf{v}_1 = \mathbf{w}_1$, $\mathbf{v}_2 = \mathbf{w}_2 - a_{21}\mathbf{v}_1$, $\mathbf{v}_3 = \mathbf{w}_3 - a_{31}\mathbf{v}_1 - a_{32}\mathbf{v}_2$, $\mathbf{v}_4 = \mathbf{w}_4 - a_{41}\mathbf{v}_1 - a_{42}\mathbf{v}_2 - a_{43}\mathbf{v}_3, \ldots,$ $\mathbf{v}_k = \mathbf{w}_k - a_{k1}\mathbf{v}_1 - a_{k2}\mathbf{v}_2 - \cdots - a_{k,k-1}\mathbf{v}_{k-1}$, where the a_{ij} are real numbers. Prove that none of the $\mathbf{v}_j$ can be zero. Show that the numbers a_{ij} can be determined uniquely in such a way that the $\mathbf{v}_j$ are all orthogonal. (This method of obtaining orthogonal vectors is called the Schmidt orthogonalization process.)

3. Make $\mathbf{R}_3$ into a euclidean vector space by defining $|(x_1, x_2, x_3)|$ to be $(x_1^2 + x_2^2 + x_3^2)^{\frac{1}{2}}$. Apply the Schmidt process to the following set of three vectors: $(1, 0, 4)$, $(3, -1, 2)$, $(1, 1, 5)$. Find an orthonormal base for the subspace of $\mathbf{R}_3$ spanned by $(4, 1, -1)$ and $(1, -1, 2)$.

4. V being as in Exercise 1, let U be a subspace of dimension r. Show that U is a euclidean vector space if the length of a vector in U is taken to be the same as its length in V. Let W be the set of all vectors in V which are orthogonal to every vector in U. Prove that W is a subspace of dimension $n - r$ and that $V = U \oplus W$ (W is called the *orthogonal complement* of U in V).

5. Show that the line defined by (11.21) intersects the plane defined by (11.24) in exactly one point.

6. Let L, L', L'' be three lines in an n-dimensional euclidean space E, with L' and L'' parallel. Prove that L' and L'' can be oriented in such a way that $\measuredangle L, L' = \measuredangle L, L''$ for either orientation of L. Show that if L' and L'' are distinct, then they have no points in common. Show that if p is a point not on L, then there is one and only one line through p which is parallel to L. If $n = 2$ show that two distinct lines are parallel if and only if they have no points in common.

7. Let p, q, r be distinct points in a euclidean n-space E. Prove that the sum of the interior angles of the triangle they determine is equal to π. Prove the law of sines for the triangle.

8. Let P be a plane in a euclidean 3-space E_3. Let q be a point not in P. Prove that there is one and only one point p in P for which the distance $|pq|$ is a minimum, and show that the line determined by p and q is orthogonal to P.

12. Analytic geometry

As we have seen in Sec. 10, it is possible to introduce a cartesian coordinate system in any affine space of finite dimension. In this way it is possible to translate certain types of geometrical questions into algebraic problems, and vice versa. This is the whole point of analytic geometry, and we have already encountered some examples—for instance in (11.20) to (11.24), dealing with lines and hyperplanes, and in some of the exercises. Here we shall go into a little more detail in the special case of a two-dimensional euclidean space E_2. Everything to be discussed can be generalized without much difficulty to euclidean spaces of higher dimension. However it is rather cumbersome to do so without the use of matrices, discussed in Chap. 9.

According to Sec. 11 we obtain a *euclidean* coordinate system in E_2 by selecting a point p_0 as origin and an orthonormal base $\mathbf{e}_1$, $\mathbf{e}_2$ for the vector space of translations $T(E_2)$. Then for any point q the translation vector $\overrightarrow{p_0q}$ can be expressed uniquely in the form

12.1 $$\overrightarrow{p_0q} = x\mathbf{e}_1 + y\mathbf{e}_2$$

where x and y are real numbers. They are the coordinates of q for the particular system. If p is another point, having coordinates x_1, y_1, then the distance formula (11.18) becomes

12.2 $$|pq| = \sqrt{(x - x_1)^2 + (y - y_1)^2}$$

Now let p_1, p_2 be two distinct points of E_2, and let L be the line they determine. For any point q on L the translation vector $\overrightarrow{p_1q}$ must be in the space spanned by $\overrightarrow{p_1p_2}$ because $T(L)$ has dimension 1. Therefore $\overrightarrow{p_1q} = t \cdot \overrightarrow{p_1p_2}$ for some real number t. If the coordinates of p_1, p_2, q are, respectively, (x_1, y_1), (x_2, y_2), (x, y), then this vector equation is the same $(x - x_1) \cdot \mathbf{e}_1 + (y - y_1) \cdot \mathbf{e}_2 = t \cdot (x_2 - x_1) \cdot \mathbf{e}_1 + t \cdot (y_2 - y_1) \cdot \mathbf{e}_2$, from which we get

12.3 $$\begin{aligned} x &= x_1 + t(x_2 - x_1) \\ y &= y_1 + t(y_2 - y_1) \end{aligned}$$

As t varies through $\mathbf{R}$, all the points (x, y) obtained from (12.3) form the line L. These are *parametric* equations for L, special cases of (10.19) and (11.21).

Now let $\mathbf{u}$ be a unit vector in $T(L)$, say $\mathbf{u} = u_1\mathbf{e}_1 + u_2\mathbf{e}_2$. There are two unit vectors in $T(L)$, $\pm\mathbf{u}$, and we suppose $\mathbf{u}$ is the one for which $u_2 > 0$ (or else $u_1 > 0$ if $u_2 = 0$). We orient L by assigning to it that unit vector. The direction cosines of L [see (11.19)] are

$$u_1 = \cos\alpha_1 = (\mathbf{u}, \mathbf{e}_1) \qquad u_2 = \cos\alpha_2 = (\mathbf{u}, \mathbf{e}_2)$$

Since $u_1^2 + u_2^2 = 1$, we have $u_2^2 = 1 - u_1^2 = 1 - \cos^2\alpha_1 = \sin^2\alpha_1$. By assumption $u_2 \geqslant 0$ and $0 \leq \alpha_1 \leq \pi$. Hence $u_2 = \sin\alpha_1$. Let us therefore write α for α_1, so that

$$u_1 = \cos\alpha \qquad u_2 = \sin\alpha$$

Now $\overrightarrow{p_1p_2} = c \cdot \mathbf{u}$ for some number c, and in fact $c = \pm |p_1p_2|$. Hence

12.4 $x_2 - x_1 = c \cdot \cos \alpha \qquad y_2 - y_1 = c \cdot \sin \alpha$

Putting $s = ct$ we can write (12.3) in the form

12.5 $x = x_1 + s \cdot \cos \alpha \qquad y = y_1 + s \cdot \sin \alpha$

If L is not parallel to the y axis, that is, if $\alpha \neq \pi/2$, then $\cos \alpha \neq 0$. Set

12.6 $m = \tan \alpha$

The number m is called the *slope* of L. From (12.4), $m = (y_2 - y_1)/(x_2 - x_1)$. From (12.5), $m = (y - y_1)/(x - x_1)$. Hence we can get rid of the parameter s in (12.5) by writing

12.7 $y - y_1 = m(x - x_1)$

or

12.8 $$y - y_1 = \frac{(y_2 - y_1)}{(x_2 - x_1)} \cdot (x - x_1)$$

The situation is illustrated in Fig. 10.

Of course (12.7) and (12.8) do not make sense in the case of a line parallel to the y axis ($\alpha = \pi/2$). In that case (12.5) reduces to $x = x_1$ and $y = y_1 + s$. Since the parameter s can take on all values, so can y. Therefore the line L consists of all points satisfying the equation

12.9 $x = x_1$

Observe that (12.7) and (12.9) are special cases of the equation

12.10 $ax + by + c = 0$

For that is what (12.7) is if we put $a = m$, $b = -1$, $c = y_1 - mx_1$; and (12.9) is just (12.10) with $a = 1$, $b = 0$, $c = -x_1$. Hence the equation of any line in E_2

Figure 10

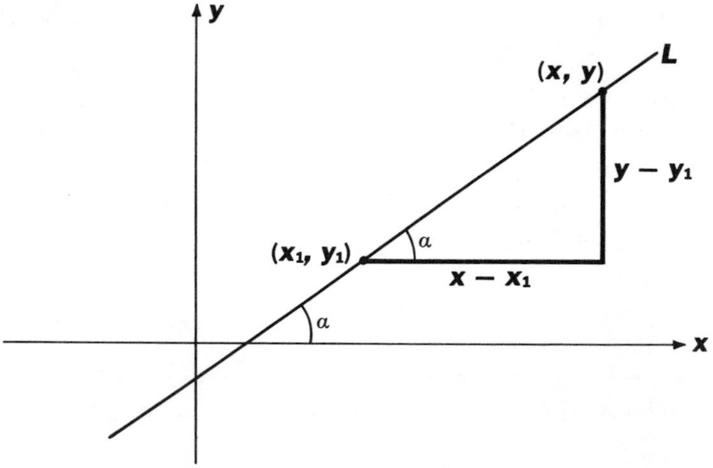

can be put in the form (12.10). Conversely, if a, b are not both zero, then (12.10) is the equation of a line. For if $b \neq 0$, then it can be written

$$y + \frac{c}{b} = -\frac{a}{b}x$$

which is the same as (12.7) with $m = -a/b$, $x_1 = 0$, and $y_1 = -c/b$. If $b = 0$, then (12.10) becomes $x = -c/a$, which is the same as (12.9) with $x_1 = -c/a$. Equation (12.10) is (10.15) for $n = 2$.

The equations above contain all the information that one could possibly need to know about lines in E_2, and we shall therefore leave the subject of lines with the following example: Find the equation of the line through (2, 1) and (4, 5). Putting these numbers in (12.8) we get $y - 1 = (x - 2)(5 - 1)/(4 - 2)$, or $y = 2x + 3$. The slope here is 2, and the angle α is approximately 63°. We have $\tan^2 \alpha = \sin^2 \alpha/(1 - \sin^2 \alpha) = 4$, or $5 \sin^2 \alpha = 4$, whence $\sin \alpha = 2/\sqrt{5}$ and $\cos \alpha = 1/\sqrt{5}$. The parametric equations (12.5) are

$$x = 2 + s/\sqrt{5} \qquad y = 1 + 2s/\sqrt{5}$$

Putting $s = 0$ gives the first point (2, 1); putting $s = 2\sqrt{5}$ gives the second point (4, 5); and $2\sqrt{5}$ is the distance between them. Since $\tan(\alpha + \pi/2) = -1/\tan \alpha$, the line *perpendicular* to the given line and passing through (a, b) has equation

$$y - b = -\tfrac{1}{2}(x - a)$$

by (12.7).

Lines in E_2 correspond to Eqs. (12.10) of the first degree. We now consider briefly some problems leading to second-degree equations. First of all let q_0 be a point of E_2 and let a be a positive number. The locus† C consisting of all points q such that $|q_0q| = a$ is by definition a circle of radius a and center q_0. If q_0 has coordinates x_0, y_0 and if q has coordinates x, y, then from (12.2) q is on C if and only if

12.11 $$(x - x_0)^2 + (y - y_0)^2 = a^2$$

This equation therefore determines C completely. We point out that any equation of the type

12.12 $$x^2 + dx + y^2 + ey + f = 0$$

can be put in the form (12.11) by simply adding $(d/2)^2 + (e/2)^2 - f$ to both sides. The result is

$$(x + d/2)^2 + (y + e/2)^2 = (d/2)^2 + (e/2)^2 - f$$

The left-hand side cannot be negative, and so there can be no points satisfying this equation unless $(d/2)^2 + (e/2)^2 - f \geqslant 0$. If that is the case, then (12.12) is the equation of a circle of radius $[(d/2)^2 + (e/2)^2 - f]^{\frac{1}{2}}$ and center $(-d/2, -e/2)$.

† The set of all points satisfying some specified conditions is sometimes called the *locus* satisfying those conditions.

Figure 11

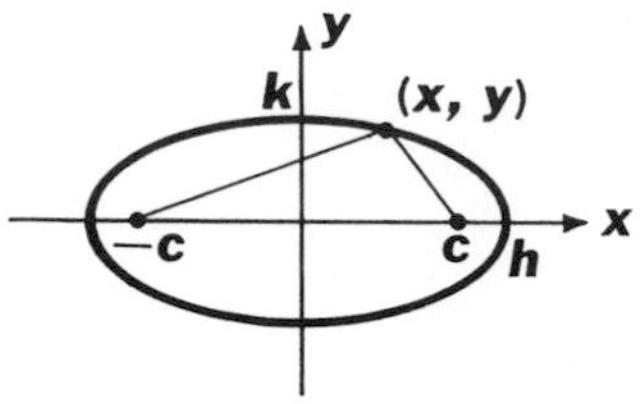

Now let us take up a somewhat more complicated problem. Let q_1, q_2 be two points of E_2, and consider the locus of all points q such that

12.13 $$|q_1q| + |q_2q| = 2h$$

where h is some positive number. From the triangle inequality (11.14) it is clear that there are no such points q unless $2h \geqslant |q_1q_2|$. If $2h = |q_1q_2|$, then it is easily seen that the locus consists of all points between q_1 and q_2 on the line joining them. We shall suppose that $2h > |q_1q_2|$. For simplicity let us assume that q_1 and q_2 are on the x axis, equidistant from the origin. Their coordinates will then be $(c, 0)$, $(-c, 0)$, where $c > 0$. The situation is illustrated in Fig. 11. We have $|q_1q_2| = 2c$, and we assume that $2h > 2c$, or $h > c$. If q has coordinates (x, y), then (12.13) becomes $[(x - c)^2 + y^2]^{\frac{1}{2}} + [(x + c)^2 + y^2]^{\frac{1}{2}} = 2h$. To simplify this, square both sides and transpose to obtain

$$(x - c)^2 + y^2 + (x + c)^2 + y^2 - 4h^2 = -2[(x - c)^2 + y^2]^{\frac{1}{2}} \cdot [(x + c)^2 + y^2]^{\frac{1}{2}}$$

Square again and collect terms. The result is

12.14 $$(h^2 - c^2)x^2 + h^2y^2 = h^2(h^2 - c^2)$$

We have assumed that $h > c$, and so $h^2 > c^2$. Put

12.15 $$k = \sqrt{h^2 - c^2}$$

Then (12.14) is

12.16 $$k^2x^2 + h^2y^2 = h^2k^2$$

Dividing by h^2k^2 we can write this in the so-called *normal form*

12.17 $$\frac{x^2}{h^2} + \frac{y^2}{k^2} = 1$$

The locus in question is of course called an *ellipse*, and the points on it are precisely the points whose coordinates satisfy (12.17). Putting $y = 0$ in it we get $x = \pm h$. Hence the locus cuts the x axis at $(\pm h, 0)$. Similarly it cuts the y axis at $(0, \pm k)$. The points q_1 and q_2 are called the *foci* of the ellipse, and h, k are its semimajor and semiminor axes, respectively.

Suppose now that instead of the sum of the two distances in (12.13) we take their difference—or more precisely its absolute value:

12.18 $||q_1q| - |q_2q|| = 2h$

First of all it is clear from the triangle inequality that there are no points q satisfying this condition unless $2h \leqslant 2c$, or $h \leqslant c$. Going through the calculations analogous to those for (12.13) we again arrive at (12.14), but now we have $c^2 \geqslant h^2$. We shall assume that $c > h > 0$ (the excluded cases are easy to analyze). This time we put

12.19 $k = \sqrt{c^2 - h^2}$

Then (12.14) becomes

12.20 $k^2x^2 - h^2y^2 = h^2k^2$

Since we have assumed $h > 0$, $k > 0$, we can divide through by h^2k^2 to put this in the *normal form*

12.21 $$\frac{x^2}{h^2} - \frac{y^2}{k^2} = 1$$

The locus is called a *hyperbola* and is shown in Fig. 12. The points q_1, q_2 are called its *foci*. Putting $y = 0$ in (12.21) we see that the locus intersects the x axis at $(\pm h, 0)$. However it does not intersect the y axis. The two lines $y = (k/h)x$ and $y = -(k/h)x$ shown in Fig. 12 are called the *asymptotes* of the hyperbola. If we write (12.21) in the form $(x/h - y/k) \cdot (x/h + y/k) = 1$, then for large $|x|$ one of

Figure 12

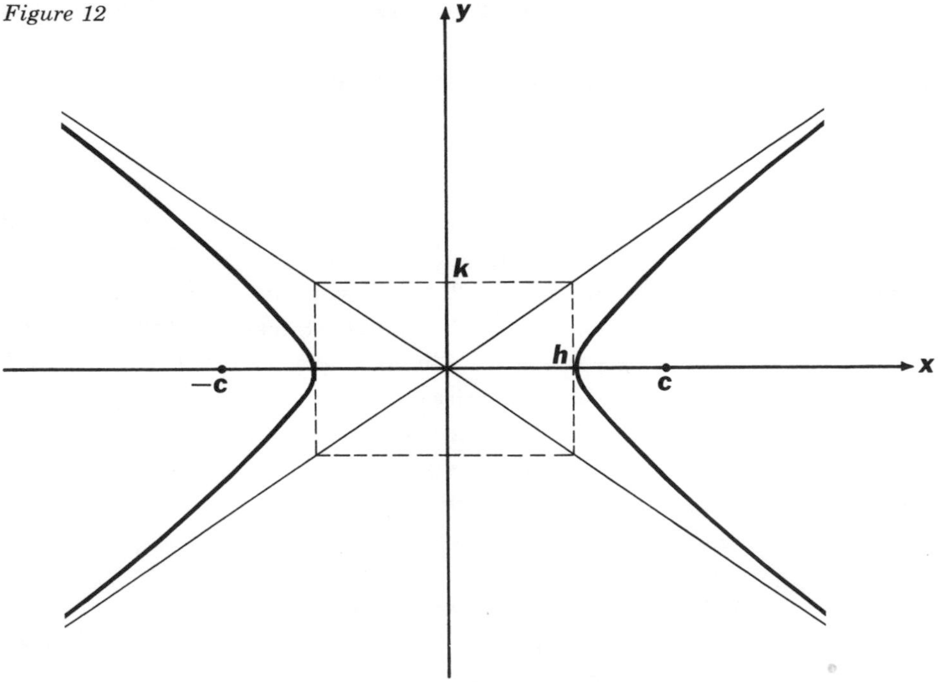

Figure 13

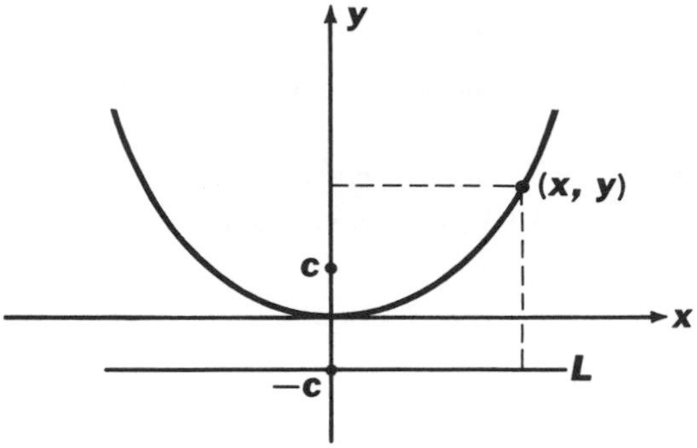

the two factors must be large. Hence the other one must be small. If for example the first factor is small, then y is approximately equal to $(k/h)x$. This shows roughly that the hyperbola is approximated by its asymptotes for large values of $|x|$.

Finally let us consider the locus consisting of all points q such that the distance from q to given point q_0 is equal to the distance from q to a given line L (i.e., the *perpendicular* distance). Let us take q_0 to be the point $(0, c)$ on the y axis, and let us take L to be the line $y = -c$ parallel to the x axis, as shown in Fig. 13. The condition here on the point (x, y) is $[x^2 + (y - c)^2]^{\frac{1}{2}} = y + c$. Squaring we get

12.22 $$x^2 = 4cy$$

The locus is called a *parabola*, the point $(0, c)$ is called its *focus*, and the line L is called its *directrix*.

Both (12.17) and (12.21) are special cases of equations of the type

12.23 $$ax^2 + by^2 = c$$

Conversely, with certain simple exceptions, this equation can be put in one of those two forms. We assume of course that a and b are not both zero here. If one of them is zero, say b, then the equation is $x^2 = c/a$. There are no points (x, y) satisfying this equation if $c/a < 0$. If $c/a \geqslant 0$, then the equation can be written $x = \pm\sqrt{c/a}$, and its locus therefore consists of two vertical lines (coinciding if $c = 0$). Similar remarks apply if $a = 0$, $b \neq 0$. Let us now assume that a, b are both different from zero. Consider first the case $c = 0$, so that our equation is $ax^2 + by^2 = 0$. If a and b have the same sign, then the only point satisfying the equation is $(0, 0)$. If a and b have opposite signs, say $a > 0$ and $b < 0$, then writing $b' = -b$, we can put the equation in the form $ax^2 - b'y^2 = (\sqrt{a}x + \sqrt{b'}y)(\sqrt{a}x - \sqrt{b'}y) = 0$. A point (x, y) satisfies this equation if and only if it is on one of the two lines $y = \sqrt{a/b'} \cdot x$ or $y = -\sqrt{a/b'} \cdot x$. Hence, *if one or more of the three numbers a, b, c in (12.23) is zero, then either there are no points (x, y) which satisfy the equation, or else $(0, 0)$ is the only point which satisfies it, or else the equation has a locus consisting of two lines, possibly coincident.*

Let us now assume that a, b, c are all different from zero. Then putting $a' = a/c$ and $b' = b/c$, we get $a'x^2 + b'y^2 = 1$. If a', b' are both negative, then there is no point (x, y) which satisfies the equation. If a', b' are both positive, then setting $h = 1/\sqrt{a'}$, $k = 1/\sqrt{b'}$ we get an equation of the type (12.17), and the locus is an ellipse. If $a' > 0$, $b' < 0$, then putting $h = 1/\sqrt{a'}$, $k = 1/\sqrt{-b'}$ we obtain an equation of the form (12.21), and the locus is a hyperbola. If $a' < 0$, $b' > 0$ then we get a hyperbola, with the x and y axes interchanged.

A locus of an equation of the type (12.22) or (12.23) is called a *conic section*, except for the case of a locus consisting of two distinct parallel lines. Now both (12.22) and (12.23) are special cases of the *general equation* of second degree in x, y:

12.24 $$ax^2 + 2bxy + cy^2 + dx + ey + f = 0$$

[We assume that a, b, c are not all zero here, for otherwise the equation reduces to one of the type (12.10).] The high point of many texts on analytic geometry is the observation that (12.24) can be put either in the form (12.22) or (12.23) by means of a suitable change of coordinate system in E_2. Consequently the locus of an equation of the type (12.24), unless empty, is always a conic section or else a pair of parallel lines.

First of all, if $b = 0$ in (12.24), the result can be achieved by means of a *translation*. For suppose that a, c are both different from zero. Adding $d^2/4a + e^2/4c$ to both sides we obtain

$$a(x + d/2a)^2 + c(y + e/2c)^2 = d^2/4a + e^2/4c - f$$

If we introduce new coordinates x', y' in E_2 by putting $x' = x + d/2a$, $y' = y + e/2c$, which corresponds to choosing $(d/2a, e/2c)$ as a new origin, then our equation becomes

$$ax'^2 + cy'^2 = g$$

where $g = d^2/4a + e^2/4c - f$, and this is indeed of the type (12.23).

If one of the numbers a, c is also zero, say $c = 0$, then by adding $d^2/4a$ to both sides of (12.24) we get

$$a(x + d/2a)^2 = f - ey + d^2/4a$$

Put $x' = x + d/2a$ and $y' = y - f/e - d^2/4ae$. Then our equation can be written

$$x'^2 = -\frac{e}{a}y'$$

which is of the type (12.22). Here we have simply translated coordinates by taking the point $(d/2a, -fe - d^2/4ae)$ as the new origin. Of course a similar reduction is possible if $a = 0$, $c \neq 0$.

Thus it is a simple matter to deal with (12.23) if the offending term $2bxy$ is absent. We shall now see how to make it disappear. Let us choose a new euclidean coordinate system (x', y') in E_2, with the same origin p_0 as in (12.1). To do so we must select another pair of orthonormal vectors $\mathbf{e}_1'$, $\mathbf{e}_2'$ in the space of translations $T(E_2)$. If q is any point of E_2, then $\overrightarrow{p_0q}$ can be expressed uniquely in the form

12.25 $$\overrightarrow{p_0q} = x' \cdot \mathbf{e}_1' + y' \cdot \mathbf{e}_2'$$

and x', y' are the new coordinates of q. Now both $\mathbf{e}_1'$, $\mathbf{e}_2'$ can similarly be expressed as linear combinations of $\mathbf{e}_1$, $\mathbf{e}_2$, say

$$\mathbf{e}_1' = a_1 \cdot \mathbf{e}_1 + a_2 \cdot \mathbf{e}_2$$
$$\mathbf{e}_2' = b_1 \cdot \mathbf{e}_1 + b_2 \cdot \mathbf{e}_2$$

By assumption $(\mathbf{e}_1', \mathbf{e}_1') = 1$, $(\mathbf{e}_1', \mathbf{e}_2') = 0$, and $(\mathbf{e}_2', \mathbf{e}_2') = 1$. By (11.4) there follows $a_1^2 + a_2^2 = 1$, $b_1^2 + b_2^2 = 1$, $a_1b_1 + a_2b_2 = 0$. From this it is easily seen that $a_1b_2 - a_2b_1 \neq 0$. We shall assume that $\mathbf{e}_1'$ and $\mathbf{e}_2'$ are so numbered that $a_1b_2 - a_2b_1 > 0$. Now from the foregoing relations on a_1, a_2, b_1, b_2 and this last assumption it follows easily that $b_2 = a_1$ and $b_1 = -a_2$. To simplify notation let us put $a_1 = u$ and $a_2 = v$. Then we have

12.26 $$\begin{aligned} \mathbf{e}_1' &= u\mathbf{e}_1 + v\mathbf{e}_2 \\ \mathbf{e}_2' &= -v\mathbf{e}_1 + u\mathbf{e}_2 \end{aligned} \qquad (u^2 + v^2 = 1)$$

Since $u = (\mathbf{e}_1, \mathbf{e}_1')$, we have $u = \cos\theta$, where θ is the angle between $\mathbf{e}_1$ and $\mathbf{e}_1'$. Hence $v = \pm \sin\theta$. (Recall that by definition $0 \leqslant \theta \leqslant \pi$, and so $\sin\theta \geqslant 0$.) Define φ as follows:

$$\varphi = \theta \quad \text{if } v \geqslant 0 \qquad \text{and} \qquad \varphi = 2\pi - \theta \quad \text{if } v < 0$$

Then

$$u = \cos\varphi \qquad v = \sin\varphi$$

We say therefore that the new coordinate system (x', y') is obtained from the original one by rotation through the angle φ.

Substituting (12.26) in (12.25) and comparing with (12.1) we get

12.27 $$\begin{aligned} x &= ux' - vy' \\ y &= vx' + uy' \end{aligned}$$

These are special cases of the general Eqs. (10.14).

Now set

12.28 $$Q = ax^2 + 2bxy + cy^2$$

which is the quadratic part of (12.24). Substituting (12.27) in this we get

12.29 $$Q = a'x'^2 + 2b'x'y' + c'y'^2$$

where

12.30 $$b' = -auv + b(u^2 - v^2) + cuv$$

and similar expressions for a', c'. Assuming that $b \neq 0$ we can make $b' = 0$ by choosing u and v so that $u^2 - v^2 = [(a - c)/b]uv$, or $\cos^2 \varphi - \sin^2 \varphi = [(a - c)/b] \sin \varphi \cos \varphi$, or

12.31 $$\cot 2\varphi = \frac{a - c}{2b}$$

That being done it follows that (12.24) in the new coordinate system is of the form

12.32 $$a'x'^2 + c'y'^2 + d'x' + e'y' + f' = 0$$

As pointed out above this can be reduced by a translation to one of the forms (12.23) or (12.22), or else (12.22) with the coordinates interchanged.

It is not hard to verify that

12.33 $$ac - b^2 = a'c' - b'^2$$

in (12.28) and (12.29), for any choice of φ. This quantity is called the *discriminant* of Q, and Q itself is called a *quadratic form*. If φ is chosen according to (12.31), then $b' = 0$, and so $ac - b^2 = a'c'$. It follows that the locus of (12.24) can be a parabola only if the discriminant is zero, an ellipse only if the discriminant is positive, and a hyperbola only if the discriminant is negative.

EXAMPLE 1 The most severe case of the presence of an xy term in (12.24) is the equation $xy = 1$. Here $a = c = 0$, $b = \frac{1}{2}$. According to (12.31) we take $\cot 2\varphi = 0$, and so $\varphi = \pi/4$. Then $\cos \varphi = \sin \varphi = 1/\sqrt{2}$. Equation (12.27) becomes $x = (x' - y')/\sqrt{2}$, $y = (x' + y')/\sqrt{2}$. Substituting these in $xy = 1$ we get $x'^2/2 - y'^2/2 = 1$; the locus is a hyperbola, with h and k of (12.21) equal to $\sqrt{2}$. By (12.19), $c = \sqrt{h^2 + k^2} = 2$; the asymptotes are the lines $y' = \pm x'$. Going back to the original coordinate system we see that the foci are at $(\sqrt{2}, \sqrt{2})$ and $(-\sqrt{2}, -\sqrt{2})$. The asymptotes are the x and y axes. The discriminant is $-\frac{1}{4}$.

EXAMPLE 2 Find the locus of the equation $21x^2 - 10\sqrt{3}xy + 31y^2 + (84 + 40\sqrt{3})x - (248 + 20\sqrt{3})y = -336 - 80\sqrt{3}$. Here $a = 21$, $b = -5\sqrt{3}$, $c = 31$. The discriminant is 576, and so, if there is a locus, it must be an ellipse. Using (12.31) we determine φ by

$$\cot 2\varphi = \frac{21 - 31}{-10\sqrt{3}} = \frac{1}{\sqrt{3}}$$

whence $2\varphi = \pi/3$, $\varphi = \pi/6$, and so $\cos \varphi = u = \sqrt{3/2}$, $\sin \varphi = v = \frac{1}{2}$. The rotation (12.27) is then $x = (\sqrt{3/2})x' - (\frac{1}{2})y'$ and $y = (\frac{1}{2})x' + (\sqrt{3/2})y'$. Put-

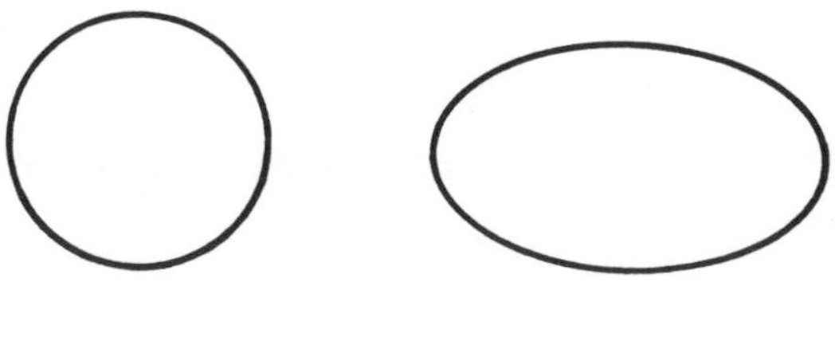

Figure 14

An affine transformation of E_2 carries any conic section into a conic section, thus sending a circle into an ellipse.

ting these in the given equation we get $16x'^2 + 36y'^2 + 32(\sqrt{3} - 2)x' - 72(1 + 2\sqrt{3})y' = -436 - 80\sqrt{3}$. By choosing a new origin we can get rid of the first-degree terms here. Namely, put $x'' = x' + \sqrt{3} - 2$ and $y'' = y' - 1 - 2\sqrt{3}$. Then the equation becomes

$$16x''^2 + 36y''^2 = 144 \qquad \text{or} \qquad \frac{x''^2}{9} + \frac{y''^2}{4} = 1$$

which is the equation of an ellipse with $h = 3$, $k = 2$, $c = \sqrt{5}$, in the notation of (12.15) and (12.17). The foci are at $(\pm\sqrt{5}, 0)$ in the x'', y'' system, and the ellipse cuts the axes at $(\pm 3, \pm 2)$. Using the equations above we can easily find the coordinates of these points in the original x, y system. For example, using

$$x = (\sqrt{3}/2)(x'' - \sqrt{3} + 2) - (\tfrac{1}{2})(y'' + 1 + 2\sqrt{3})$$

and putting in the x'', y'' coordinates of the foci, namely, $x'' = \pm\sqrt{5}$, $y'' = 0$, we get $x = (\tfrac{1}{2} \pm \sqrt{15} - 4)$ as the x coordinates of the foci.

To summarize, the problem of reducing (12.24) to a more agreeable form by means of a change of coordinate systems involves first a rotation, in order to banish the xy term, and then a translation in order to get rid of the first-degree terms (only one of them can be eliminated in general if the discriminant is zero). Problems of a similar nature arise in spaces of dimension greater than 2, and then rotations become quite complicated. In Chap. 14 we shall develop some methods which make it easy to deal with rotations in any number of dimensions.

We mention that there is no good reason for stopping with quadratic equations of the type (12.24). The problem of classifying the loci of equations of higher degree leads to some extremely interesting questions.

EXERCISES

1. Find the point on the line $2x + 3y - 1 = 0$ which is closest to the point (2, 7).

2. Derive a formula which gives the distance from a point (x_0, y_0) to the nearest point on the line $ax + by + c = 0$. (Here x, y are understood to be euclidean coordinates in E_2.)

3. Find the points at which the line $y = 4x + 1$ intersects the locus $y^2 - 4x^2 = 16$. Describe the latter locus, and draw an accurate diagram of it and the line.

4. Describe the following three loci and draw pictures of them, showing the coordinate axes and the foci.

(*a*) $2x^2 - xy + 4y^2 + 3x - 25 = 0$

(*b*) $4x^2 - 12xy + 9y^2 + 3x + y = 2$

(*c*) $4x^2 - 20xy + 9y^2 + 3x + y = 2$

5. Let x_1, x_2, x_3 be euclidean coordinates in a three-dimensional euclidean space E_3. Let C be the locus of the equation

$$x_1^2 + x_2^2 - x_3^2 = 0$$

Prove that the line through the origin and any other point of C lies entirely in C.

***6.** With the notation of Exercise 5, let E_2 be any plane in E_3. Let x, y be a system of euclidean coordinates in E_2. Prove that the intersection of E_2 with the cone C consists of all points in E_2 whose coordinates x, y satisfy an equation of the type (12.24).

9

Linear transformations and matrices

1. Introduction

Most applications of vector spaces involve certain kinds of mappings which assign to each vector of one vector space U another vector in another (or possibly the same) space V. The mappings of interest in this connection are called *linear mappings* (or *linear transformations,* or *operators*). In this chapter we shall find out how to obtain all such mappings for finite-dimensional spaces and how to calculate with them.

2. A notational convention

Let V be a vector space of finite dimension n over a field K, and let $\mathbf{v}_1, \ldots, \mathbf{v}_n$ be a set of base vectors in V. That is, the $\mathbf{v}_i$ are any n linearly independent vectors in V. Then, as we have seen in Chap. 8 (Theorem 9.1), any vector $\mathbf{x}$ in V can be written uniquely as a linear combination $\mathbf{x} = x_1\mathbf{v}_1 + \cdots + x_n\mathbf{v}_n$, with coefficients x_i in K. Recall that the x_i are called the *components* of $\mathbf{x}$ relative to the base $\{\mathbf{v}_i\}$. Now we are going to adopt the following rule: Indices on the components x_i will henceforth† be written as *superscripts* rather than subscripts: x^i instead of x_i. (Thus x^i does *not* mean x raised to the ith power; it means the ith one of the components $x^1, x^2, \ldots, x^n$!) Accordingly we now agree to write

$$\mathbf{x} = x^1\mathbf{v}_1 + \cdots + x^n\mathbf{v}_n$$

or

$$\mathbf{x} = \sum_{i=i}^{n} x^i\mathbf{v}_i$$

A considerable saving of space is achieved by simply omitting the summation sign, writing just

2.1 $$\mathbf{x} = x^i\mathbf{v}_i$$

† Some exceptions to this will be pointed out later. Namely, it is sometimes convenient to write the indices on the *base* vectors as superscripts, rather than those on the components (see Sec. 4).

and understanding that the expression is to be summed over all relevant values of the index i—in this case 1 up to n. This abbreviated notation was introduced by Einstein; the understanding that the expression is to be summed is called the Einstein *summation convention.* Its use and advantages will become clearer as we go along. Presently we shall encounter symbols with several indices, and the summation convention will be applied to them also. The general form of the summation convention is as follows: *In any "product" of symbols with upper and lower indices, summation over an index is understood if that index appears exactly once as a superscript and exactly once as a subscript; otherwise summation is not understood.* For example, the symbol $a^h_{ijk}b^ic^j_kd^k$ stands for

$$\sum_{i=1}^{n}\sum_{j=1}^{n} a^h_{ijk}b^ic^j_kd^k$$

assuming that the indices range from 1 to n. If it is desired to indicate summation over k or h also, then that must be done in the usual way.

As a final remark here, we note, referring to (2.1), that the symbols $x^i\mathbf{v}_i$, $x^j\mathbf{v}_j$, $x^k\mathbf{v}_k$, $x^l\mathbf{v}_l$, etc., all mean exactly the same thing, namely, $x^1\mathbf{v}_1 + \cdots + x^n\mathbf{v}_n$. Thus indices *which are summed* can be changed at will without altering the meaning of the symbol—provided of course that one does not infringe upon the rights of another index already present.

3. Linear mappings

The fundamental definition is the following:

DEFINITION 3.1 *A mapping* $\mathbf{T}: U \to V$ *of two vector spaces over a field* K *is called a* linear *mapping if*

(1) $\mathbf{T}(\mathbf{x} + \mathbf{y}) = \mathbf{T}(\mathbf{x}) + \mathbf{T}(\mathbf{y})$ *for any* $\mathbf{x}$ *and* $\mathbf{y}$ *in* U

(2) $\mathbf{T}(a\mathbf{x}) = a \cdot \mathbf{T}(\mathbf{x})$ *for any* $\mathbf{x}$ *in* U *and any* a *in* K

In the first of these two equations, $\mathbf{T}(\mathbf{x})$ and $\mathbf{T}(\mathbf{y})$ stand for vectors in the second space V, and the right-hand side of (1) means the sum of those two elements for the + operation in V. In the left-hand side of (1), $\mathbf{x} + \mathbf{y}$ denotes the sum of $\mathbf{x}$ and $\mathbf{y}$ with the + operation in U. Hence Eq. (1) says that $\mathbf{T}$ is compatible with the + operations in U and V. In other words, $\mathbf{T}$ is a homomorphism of the abelian groups U and V [cf. Definition 7.2, Chap. 1, and Theorem 7.1, Eq. (8.14)], and consequently $\mathbf{T}$ sends the zero of U into the zero of V and it sends $-\mathbf{x}$ into the inverse $-\mathbf{T}(\mathbf{x})$ of $\mathbf{T}(\mathbf{x})$. That is, $\mathbf{T}(\mathbf{0}) = \mathbf{0}$ and $\mathbf{T}(-\mathbf{x}) = -\mathbf{T}(\mathbf{x})$. In a similar way, Eq. (2) says that $\mathbf{T}$ is compatible with scalar multiplication. For $a\mathbf{x}$ on the left is scalar multiplication in U of $\mathbf{x}$ by a; and $a \cdot \mathbf{T}(\mathbf{x})$ on the right is scalar multiplication in V of $\mathbf{T}(\mathbf{x})$ by a.

Supposing still that $\mathbf{T}$ satisfies (1) and (2) above, let $\mathbf{x}$ and $\mathbf{y}$ be two vectors in U, and let a, b be two scalars in K. By (1) we have $\mathbf{T}(a\mathbf{x} + b\mathbf{y}) = \mathbf{T}(a\mathbf{x}) + \mathbf{T}(b\mathbf{y})$.

Applying (2) to both of these terms we get

3.1 $$\mathbf{T}(a\mathbf{x} + b\mathbf{y}) = a \cdot \mathbf{T}(\mathbf{x}) + b \cdot \mathbf{T}(\mathbf{y})$$

A very simple argument by mathematical induction allows us to deduce the more general formula

3.2 $$\mathbf{T}(a^1\mathbf{x}_1 + \cdots + a^r\mathbf{x}_r) = a^1 \cdot \mathbf{T}(\mathbf{x}_1) + \cdots + a^r \cdot \mathbf{T}(\mathbf{x}_r)$$

for any vectors $\mathbf{x}_1, \ldots, \mathbf{x}_r$ in U and scalars $a^1, a^2, \ldots, a^r$ in K. Equation (3.2) will be used constantly in this chapter. Using the Einstein summation convention we can put it in the shorter form

3.3 $$\mathbf{T}(a^i\mathbf{x}_i) = a^i \cdot \mathbf{T}(\mathbf{x}_i)$$

EXAMPLES K_n being the vector space defined in Sec. 4, Chap. 8, for any field K, let $\mathbf{T}$: $K_n \to K$ be defined by $\mathbf{T}(\mathbf{x}) = x_1$ for any vector $\mathbf{x} = (x_1, \ldots, x_n)$ in K_n. Then $\mathbf{T}$ is linear, as is very easily seen. More generally, if $k_1, k_2, \ldots, k_m$ are any integers between 1 and n (inclusive), then the mapping T: $K_n \to K_m$ defined by $\mathbf{T}(\mathbf{x}) = (x_{k_1}, x_{k_2}, \ldots, x_{k_m})$ for any $\mathbf{x} = (x_1, x_2, \ldots, x_n)$ is linear. The following mapping S: $K_2 \to K_2$ is linear: let a, b, c, d be any four scalars, and for any $\mathbf{x} = (x_1, x_2)$ put $\mathrm{S}(\mathbf{x}) = \mathbf{y} = (y_1, y_2)$, where $y_1 = ax_1 + bx_2$ and $y_2 = cx_1 + dx_2$. The mapping $\mathbf{T}$ of Theorem 9.2, Chap. 8, is linear.

DEFINITION 3.2 *Let* $\mathbf{T}$: $U \to V$ *be as in Definition* 3.1. *Then the* kernel *of* $\mathbf{T}$, *abbreviated* Ker $\mathbf{T}$, *is the set of all vectors in* U *that are mapped by* $\mathbf{T}$ *into the zero element of* V. *The* image *of* $\mathbf{T}$, *abbreviated* Im $\mathbf{T}$, *is the set of all vectors in* V *that are images under* $\mathbf{T}$ *of vectors in* U.

Hence an element $\mathbf{x}$ of U is in Ker $\mathbf{T}$ if and only if $\mathbf{T}(\mathbf{x}) = \mathbf{0}$. An element $\mathbf{y}$ of V is in Im $\mathbf{T}$ if and only if there is a vector $\mathbf{x}$ in U such that $\mathbf{T}(\mathbf{x}) = \mathbf{y}$. In other words, as $\mathbf{x}$ runs through all the elements of U, $\mathbf{T}(\mathbf{x})$ runs through all the elements of Im $\mathbf{T}$. In the first example $\mathbf{T}$: $K_n \to K$ mentioned above, Ker $\mathbf{T}$ consists of all vectors $\mathbf{x}$ of the form $\mathbf{x} = (0, x_2, \ldots, x_n)$ and those vectors form a subspace of K_n of dimension $n - 1$. In the same example, Im $\mathbf{T} = K$, because every element of K is the image under $\mathbf{T}$ of some $\mathbf{x}$ in K_n.

DEFINITION 3.3 *A linear mapping* $\mathbf{T}$: $U \to V$ *is called an* epimorphism *if* Im $\mathbf{T} = V$, *or in other words, if* $\mathbf{T}$ *maps* U *onto all of* V. $\mathbf{T}$ *is called a* monomorphism *if no two different elements of* U *are sent by* $\mathbf{T}$ *into the same element of* V. $\mathbf{T}$ *is called an* isomorphism *if it is both a monomorphism and an epimorphism—that is, if* $\mathbf{T}$ *is a one-to-one mapping.*

The "component" mapping $\mathbf{T}$ of Theorem 9.2, Chap. 8, is an isomorphism $V \to K_n$. The *identity* mapping $V \to V$ of any vector space is an isomorphism. We shall usually denote that mapping by $\mathbf{I}$. Thus $\mathbf{I}(\mathbf{x}) = \mathbf{x}$ for any $\mathbf{x}$ in V. The mapping $\mathbf{T}$: $K_n \to K$ discussed in the example above is an epimorphism; it is not a monomorphism except for $n = 1$.

A linear mapping $\mathbf{T}$: $V \to V$ of a space to itself is often called an *endomorphism*; an isomorphism $V \to V$ is also called an *automorphism*.

The following simple theorem will be used frequently.

PROPOSITION 3.1 *Let* $\mathbf{T}$: $U \to V$ *be a linear mapping of two vector spaces over a field* K. *Then* Ker $\mathbf{T}$ *is a subspace of* U, *and* $\mathbf{T}$ *is a monomorphism if and only if* Ker $\mathbf{T}$ *is the subspace consiting of the zero element of* U *alone.* Im $\mathbf{T}$ *is a subspace of* V; *and, more generally,* $\mathbf{T}$ *maps every subspace of* U *onto a subspace of* V. *If* $\mathbf{T}$ *is an isomorphism, then the inverse mapping* $\mathbf{T}^{-1}$: $V \to U$ *is also an isomorphism.*

The theorem follows very easily from the definitions, and its proof is left as an exercise. But let us show here, for example, that $\mathbf{T}$ maps any subspace U' of U onto a subspace of V (see Definition 5.1, Chap. 8). To do so let V' be the subset of V consisting of all vectors $\mathbf{T}(\mathbf{x})$, where $\mathbf{x}$ runs through U'. Take any two elements of V'. They can be written as $\mathbf{T}(\mathbf{x})$ and $\mathbf{T}(\mathbf{y})$, say, where $\mathbf{x}$, $\mathbf{y}$ are in U'. We want to show that their sum $\mathbf{T}(\mathbf{x}) + \mathbf{T}(\mathbf{y})$ is also in V'. By Definition 3.1 the last expression is equal to $\mathbf{T}(\mathbf{x} + \mathbf{y})$, and this is again an element of V', by definition of the latter, because $\mathbf{x} + \mathbf{y}$ is an element of U' (since U' is a subspace of U). Similarly, the product of any element of V' by a scalar c in K is again in V'. Write the given element of V' as $\mathbf{T}(\mathbf{x})$, with $\mathbf{x}$ in U'. Then $c \cdot \mathbf{T}(\mathbf{x}) = \mathbf{T}(c\mathbf{x})$, by Definition 3.1, and this is in V' because $c\mathbf{x}$ is in U'.

DEFINITION 3.4 *If* $\mathbf{T}$: $U \to V$ *is a linear mapping,* U *having finite dimension, then the dimension of the subspace* Ker $\mathbf{T}$ *of* U *is called the* nullity *of* $\mathbf{T}$. *The dimension of the subspace* Im $\mathbf{T}$ *of* V *is called the* rank *of* $\mathbf{T}$.

EXAMPLE The mapping $\mathbf{T}$: $K_4 \to K_2$ defined by $\mathbf{T}(x_1, x_2, x_3, x_4) = (x_1, x_2)$ for any (x_1, x_2, x_3, x_4) in K_4 is easily seen to be linear. Its kernel is plainly the set of all vectors of the type $(0, 0, x_3, x_4)$ in K_4, and so the nullity of $\mathbf{T}$ is 2. Clearly $\mathbf{T}$ maps K_4 onto all of K_2, hence is an epimorphism. The rank of $\mathbf{T}$ is 2.

The mapping $\mathbf{S}$: $K_2 \to K_4$ defined by $\mathbf{S}(x_1, x_2) = (0, x_1, x_2, 0)$ is linear. It is a monomorphism (hence of nullity zero), and its image is a two-dimensional subspace of K_4. Thus the rank of $\mathbf{S}$ is 2.

THEOREM 3.2 *Let* $\mathbf{T}$: $U \to V$ *be a linear mapping of two vector spaces over a field* K, *and suppose that* U *has finite dimension. Then*

$$\begin{aligned} \dim U &= \text{rank of } \mathbf{T} + \text{nullity of } \mathbf{T} \\ &= \dim \operatorname{Im} \mathbf{T} + \dim \operatorname{Ker} \mathbf{T} \end{aligned}$$

Proof. To fix notation, let $\dim U = n$, let rank $= r$ and nullity $= s$. We want to show that $n = r + s$. To do so select a base $\mathbf{u}_1, \ldots, \mathbf{u}_s$ for Ker $\mathbf{T}$. By Theorem 9.3, Chap. 8, this set can be enlarged to a base for U by adding on $n - s$ new vectors $\mathbf{v}_1, \ldots, \mathbf{v}_{n-s}$. Now let $\mathbf{y}$ be in Im $\mathbf{T}$. By definition there is a vector $\mathbf{x}$ in U such that $\mathbf{T}(\mathbf{x}) = \mathbf{y}$. Writing $\mathbf{x}$ in terms of our base in U we have, say,

$$\mathbf{x} = a^1\mathbf{u}_1 + \cdots + a^s\mathbf{u}_s + b^1\mathbf{v}_1 + \cdots + b^{n-s}\mathbf{v}_{n-s}$$

Applying **T** to **x** and recalling that $\mathbf{T}(\mathbf{u}_1) = \mathbf{0}, \ldots, \mathbf{T}(\mathbf{u}_s) = \mathbf{0}$, we get

$$\mathbf{T}(\mathbf{x}) = \mathbf{y} = b^1 \cdot \mathbf{T}(\mathbf{v}_1) + \cdots + b^{n-s} \cdot \mathbf{T}(\mathbf{v}_{n-s})$$

Therefore the $n - s$ vectors $\mathbf{T}(\mathbf{v}_1), \ldots, \mathbf{T}(\mathbf{v}_{n-s})$ span Im **T**. They are moreover linearly independent. For if $c^1 \cdot \mathbf{T}(\mathbf{v}_1) + \cdots + c^{n-s} \cdot \mathbf{T}(\mathbf{v}_{n-s}) = \mathbf{0}$ for certain scalars $c^1, \ldots, c^{n-s}$, then $\mathbf{T}(c^1\mathbf{v}_1 + \cdots + c^{n-s}\mathbf{v}_{n-s}) = \mathbf{0}$, and therefore $c^1\mathbf{v}_1 + \cdots + c^{n-s}\mathbf{v}_{n-s}$ is in Ker **T**, hence can be expressed as a linear combination of $\mathbf{u}_1, \ldots, \mathbf{u}_s$. But that would imply that the vectors $\mathbf{u}_1, \ldots, \mathbf{u}_s, \mathbf{v}_1, \ldots, \mathbf{v}_{n-s}$ are linearly dependent, contrary to hypothesis, unless the c^j are all zero. Hence $\mathbf{T}(\mathbf{v}_1), \cdots, \mathbf{T}(\mathbf{v}_{n-s})$ form a base for Im **T**, and so $r = n - s$. Q.E.D.

COROLLARY *Let* $\mathbf{T}$: $U \to V$ *be a linear mapping of two vector spaces of the same finite dimension* n. *If* **T** *is a monomorphism* (that is, Ker $\mathbf{T} = \mathbf{0}$), *then it must be an isomorphism.*

Proof. By assumption the nullity is zero, and so dim U = dim Im **T**. Therefore Im **T** is an n-dimensional subspace of the n-dimensional space V, whence Im $\mathbf{T} = V$ (cf. Exercise 1, Sec. 8, Chap. 8).

REMARK. This corollary is not true for spaces of infinite dimension. For example, let **T** be the mapping of K_∞ to itself defined as follows: $\mathbf{T}(x_1, x_2, x_3, x_4, \ldots) = (0, x_1, x_2, x_3, x_4, \ldots)$. Then **T** is obviously a monomorphism but not an epimorphism.

EXERCISES

1. Prove that a linear mapping $\mathbf{T}$: $U \to V$ is a monomorphism if and only if **T** sends every finite set of linearly independent vectors in U into such a set in V.

2. Let $\mathbf{C}[t]$ be the vector space of polynomials in an indeterminate t over the complex field (cf. Sec. 4, Chap. 8). Let $\mathbf{D}$: $\mathbf{C}[t] \to \mathbf{C}[t]$ be the mapping defined by the formula

$$\mathbf{D}(a_0 + a_1t + a_2t^2 + \cdots + a_rt^r) = a_1 + 2a_2t + 3a_3t^2 + \cdots + ra_rt^{r-1}$$

(The mapping **D** will occur later; we shall call it the *derivative* mapping.) Show that **D** is a linear mapping. Letting $\mathbf{C}[t]_n$ denote the subspace consisting of polynomials of degree $<n$, it is clear that **D** maps $\mathbf{C}[t]_n$ into itself. Let $\mathbf{D}_0$ denote the operation **D** restricted to the subspace $\mathbf{C}[t]_n$. Find the image and kernel of $\mathbf{D}_0$ and its rank and nullity. Work the same problem with **C** replaced by the finite field $\mathbf{Z}_5$ (see Sec. 10, Chap. 2), taking $n = 7$ and $n = 10$.

3. Let $\mathbf{T}$: $U \to V$ and $\mathbf{S}$: $V \to W$ be linear mappings of the indicated vector spaces. Prove that the composition $\mathbf{S} \circ \mathbf{T}$, mapping U to W, is a linear mapping. Prove that if **S** and **T** are monomorphisms; then so is $\mathbf{S} \circ \mathbf{T}$. Prove that if **S** and **T** are epimorphisms, then so is $\mathbf{S} \circ \mathbf{T}$.

4. Let $\mathbf{T}$: $\mathbf{Q}_3 \to \mathbf{Q}_3$ be the mapping defined as follows: If $\mathbf{x} = (x_1, x_2, x_3)$, then $\mathbf{T}(\mathbf{x}) = \mathbf{y} = (y_1, y_2, y_3)$, where $y_1 = 3x_1 - 2x_2 + x_3$, $y_2 = 2x_1 + x_2 - x_3$, and $y_3 =$

$2x_1 - 6x_2 + 4x_3$. Prove that **T** is an endomorphism of $\mathbf{Q}_3$, and determine bases for its kernel and image. Find the rank and nullity of **T**.

5. Let $\mathbf{T}$: $U \to V$ be a linear mapping of two vector spaces, and let V' be a subspace of V. Let U' consist of all elements of U which are mapped by **T** into V'. Prove that U' is a subspace of U.

4. *Operations on linear mappings*

It is possible to combine linear mappings in various ways to obtain new linear mappings. These operations are of great importance and will be used constantly in what follows.

First of all, if $\mathbf{T}$: $U \to V$ and $\mathbf{S}$: $V \to W$ are linear mappings of vector spaces over a field K, then their composition $\mathbf{S} \circ \mathbf{T}$ is a mapping from U to W. It is defined, as usual, by the formula

4.1 $$\mathbf{S} \circ \mathbf{T}(\mathbf{x}) = \mathbf{S}(\mathbf{T}(\mathbf{x})) \qquad \text{for any } \mathbf{x} \text{ in } U$$

It is immediate that $\mathbf{S} \circ \mathbf{T}$ is again a *linear* mapping (see Exercise 3 above). Hence, composition of linear mappings yields linear mappings. Furthermore, the operation is associative, for that is true of any mappings, linear or not. To put it in symbols, let $\mathbf{L}$: $W \to Z$ be another linear mapping of vector spaces over K. Then

4.2 $$\mathbf{L} \circ (\mathbf{S} \circ \mathbf{T}) = (\mathbf{L} \circ \mathbf{S}) \circ \mathbf{T}$$

To prove this it is only necessary to show that the mappings indicated on both sides of (4.2) send an arbitrary element of U into the same element of Z, and that follows trivially from (4.1).

We now define two other operations on linear mappings.

DEFINITION 4.1 *If* $\mathbf{T}$: $U \to V$ *is a linear mapping of two vector spaces over a field* K, *and if* a *is any element of* K, *then* $a\mathbf{T}$ *will denote the mapping of* U *to* V *that sends an arbitrary element* $\mathbf{x}$ *of* U *into* $a \cdot \mathbf{T}(\mathbf{x})$. *In symbols,*

4.3 $$(a\mathbf{T})(\mathbf{x}) = a \cdot \mathbf{T}(\mathbf{x}) \qquad \textit{for any } \mathbf{x} \textit{ in } U$$

If $\mathbf{T}'$: $U \to V$ *is a second linear mapping, then* $\mathbf{T} + \mathbf{T}'$ *will denote the mapping of* U *to* V *that sends an arbitrary element* $\mathbf{x}$ *of* U *into* $\mathbf{T}(\mathbf{x}) + \mathbf{T}'(\mathbf{x})$. *That is,*

4.4 $$(\mathbf{T} + \mathbf{T}')(\mathbf{x}) = \mathbf{T}(\mathbf{x}) + \mathbf{T}'(\mathbf{x}) \qquad \textit{for any } \mathbf{x} \textit{ in } U$$

It is a very simple matter to see that $a\mathbf{T}$ and $\mathbf{T} + \mathbf{T}'$ are again linear mappings of U to V. The operations defined above are connected by distributive laws, as the following proposition shows.

PROPOSITION 4.1 *Let* U, V, *and* W *be vector spaces over a field* K. *Let* $\mathbf{T}$, $\mathbf{T}'$ *be linear mappings of* U *to* V; *and let* $\mathbf{S}$, $\mathbf{S}'$ *be linear mappings of* V *to* W; *let* a *be any scalar. Then the following equations hold:*

4.5
$$\begin{aligned} \mathbf{S} \circ (\mathbf{T} + \mathbf{T}') &= \mathbf{S} \circ \mathbf{T} + \mathbf{S} \circ \mathbf{T}' \\ (\mathbf{S} + \mathbf{S}') \circ \mathbf{T} &= \mathbf{S} \circ \mathbf{T} + \mathbf{S}' \circ \mathbf{T} \\ a(\mathbf{T} + \mathbf{T}') &= a\mathbf{T} + a\mathbf{T}' \\ a(\mathbf{S} \circ \mathbf{T}) &= (a\mathbf{S}) \circ \mathbf{T} = \mathbf{S} \circ (a\mathbf{T}) \end{aligned}$$

Proof. We must show that the mappings standing on either side of any of the equations above send an arbitrary element $\mathbf{x}$ of U into the same thing. By (4.1) the mapping on the left of the first equation sends $\mathbf{x}$ into $\mathbf{S}[(\mathbf{T} + \mathbf{T}')(\mathbf{x})]$. By (4.4) this is equal to $\mathbf{S}[\mathbf{T}(\mathbf{x}) + \mathbf{T}'(\mathbf{x})]$. Since $\mathbf{S}$ is linear, this is the same as $\mathbf{S}(\mathbf{T}(\mathbf{x})) + \mathbf{S}(\mathbf{T}'(\mathbf{x}))$. On the other hand, the mapping on the right of the first Eq. (4.5) sends $\mathbf{x}$ into $\mathbf{S} \circ \mathbf{T}(\mathbf{x}) + \mathbf{S} \circ \mathbf{T}'(\mathbf{x})$, by (4.4), and this is equal to $\mathbf{S}(\mathbf{T}(\mathbf{x})) + \mathbf{S}(\mathbf{T}'(\mathbf{x}))$, by (4.1). The other equations are verified in a similar way.

In the set of all linear mappings $U \to V$ we have defined a binary operation $+$ in (4.4) and an operation of scalar multiplication, in (4.3). We now have the following proposition:

PROPOSITION 4.2 *Let U and V be two vector spaces over a field K. Then the set of all linear mappings of U to V, with the operations defined in* (4.3) *and* (4.4), *is itself a vector space over K. It is denoted by*† Hom (U, V).

It is an entirely straightforward matter to verify that the axioms of Sec. 2, Chap. 8, hold for Hom (U, V), and that is left as an exercise. We mention that the zero element of Hom (U, V) is the mapping of U to V that sends every element of U into the zero element of V. In general we shall not have much to do with Hom (U, V) itself, but the operations in it will occur frequently. For example, if $\mathbf{T}_1, \mathbf{T}_2, \ldots, \mathbf{T}_k$ are any linear mappings from U to V, and if $a_1, a_2, \ldots, a_k$ are any scalars in K, then $a_1\mathbf{T}_1 + \cdots + a_k\mathbf{T}_k$ is an element of Hom (U, V)—that is, a linear mapping from U to V. By (4.3) and (4.4) it sends any $\mathbf{x}$ in U into the vector

$$a_1\mathbf{T}_1(\mathbf{x}) + \cdots + a_k\mathbf{T}_k(\mathbf{x})$$

in V.

There are, however, two particularly important special cases of the foregoing, namely Hom (U, U) and Hom (U, K). Let us consider first Hom (U, U). It consists of all linear mappings of U to itself. If $\mathbf{S}$ and $\mathbf{T}$ are two such mappings of U, then so are the mappings $\mathbf{S} + \mathbf{T}$ and $\mathbf{S} \circ \mathbf{T}$ defined by (4.4) and (4.1) above. Hence sum and product operations are defined in Hom (U, U), which, with these operations, is a *ring*. We omit the verifications here but commend them to the reader as an exercise. For example, the distributive axiom for rings [axiom (4), Definition 2.1, Chap. 2] holds in Hom (U, U), by (4.5) above.

† Hom comes from *homomorphism*. A homomorphism of two vector spaces is the same thing as a linear mapping.

But Hom (U, U) is also a vector space over K, by Proposition 4.2. Referring now to Sec. 4, Chap. 8, there follows immediately the next theorem:

THEOREM 4.3 *Let U be a vector space over a field K, and let* Hom (U, U) *denote the set of all linear mappings of U to itself. Then that set, equipped with the operations defined in* (4.1), (4.3), *and* (4.4), *is a K-algebra.*

As pointed out above, the zero element of Hom (U, U) is the mapping that sends every element of U into $\mathbf{O}$. The unit element of the ring is the identity mapping $\mathbf{I}$ of U. If $\mathbf{T}$ is any element of Hom (U, U), then, as in any ring, we write $\mathbf{T}^2$ for $\mathbf{T} \circ \mathbf{T}$, $\mathbf{T}^3$ for $\mathbf{T} \circ \mathbf{T} \circ \mathbf{T}$, and so on. These are all linear mappings of U to itself, and therefore so is any linear combination of them with coefficients in K, say

4.6 $$a_0\mathbf{I} + a_1\mathbf{T} + a_2\mathbf{T}^2 + \cdots + a_n\mathbf{T}^n$$

where again $\mathbf{I}$ (we can also denote it by $\mathbf{T}^0$) is the identity mapping of U. Such polynomials are of crucial importance and will occur frequently later on.

It is to be noted that all the linear transformations $a\mathbf{I}$ of U (a any scalar) form a subring of Hom (U, U) which is isomorphic in an obvious way to the field K.

Now let us have a look at Hom (U, K). By our definition above this consists of all linear mappings of U to the field of scalars K. According to Proposition 4.2 it is a vector space over the field K. We shall denote Hom (U, K) by the symbol U^*. In the case of a finite-dimensional vector space U, the new space U^* is called the *dual* vector space of U.

If $\mathbf{f}$ is an element of U^*, then it is required to satisfy the following conditions:

4.7
$$\begin{aligned} &\mathbf{f}(\mathbf{x}) \text{ is an element of } K \text{ for every } \mathbf{x} \text{ in } U \\ &\mathbf{f}(\mathbf{x} + \mathbf{y}) = \mathbf{f}(\mathbf{x}) + \mathbf{f}(\mathbf{y}) \qquad \text{for any } \mathbf{x}, \mathbf{y} \text{ in } U \\ &\mathbf{f}(a\mathbf{x}) = a \cdot \mathbf{f}(\mathbf{x}) \qquad \text{for any } \mathbf{x} \text{ in } U \text{ and } a \text{ in } K \end{aligned}$$

The last two equations are simply the requirements of Definition 3.1. Instead of writing $\mathbf{f}(\mathbf{x})$, it is usually more convenient to introduce the notation

4.8 $$\mathbf{f}(\mathbf{x}) = <\mathbf{f}, \mathbf{x}>$$

which has the advantage of giving $\mathbf{f}$ and $\mathbf{x}$ a kind of equal status in the symbolism. The quantity (4.8) is called the *inner product* of $\mathbf{f}$ and $\mathbf{x}$. It is easy to verify that this inner product is *bilinear*, meaning that the following equations hold for any $\mathbf{f}$, $\mathbf{g}$ in U^*, for any $\mathbf{x}$, $\mathbf{y}$ in U, and for any c in K:

4.9
$$\begin{aligned} &<\mathbf{f}, \mathbf{x} + \mathbf{y}> = <\mathbf{f}, \mathbf{x}> + <\mathbf{f}, \mathbf{y}> \\ &<\mathbf{f} + \mathbf{g}, \mathbf{x}> = <\mathbf{f}, \mathbf{x}> + <\mathbf{g}, \mathbf{x}> \\ &<c\mathbf{f}, \mathbf{x}> = <\mathbf{f}, c\mathbf{x}> = c \cdot <\mathbf{f}, \mathbf{x}> \end{aligned}$$

In other words, the operation symbolized by $< \; , \; >$ is linear in its dependence upon both of the entries. The first equation in (4.9) is the same as the first equation of (4.7); the second equation in (4.9) is just (4.4) applied to $\mathbf{f}$ and $\mathbf{g}$; the third equation above combines (4.3) and the second equation of (4.7).

The space U^* will not play a great part until Chaps. 14 and 16, but we shall come across it from time to time.

THEOREM 4.4 *Let* $\mathbf{T}$: $U \to V$ *be a linear mapping of two vector spaces over a field* K. *Then there is a unique linear mapping* $\mathbf{T}^*$: $V^* \to U^*$ *such that* $<\mathbf{T}^*(\mathbf{g}), \mathbf{x}> = <\mathbf{g}, \mathbf{T}(\mathbf{x})>$ *for any* $\mathbf{g}$ *in* V^* *and any* $\mathbf{x}$ *in* U. *In fact,* $\mathbf{T}^*(\mathbf{g}) = \mathbf{g} \circ \mathbf{T}$.

Proof. Any $\mathbf{g}$ in V^* is by definition a linear mapping $V \to K$. Therefore the composition $\mathbf{g} \circ \mathbf{T}$ is a linear mapping of U to K, hence is an element of U^*. Therefore the operation $\mathbf{g} \to \mathbf{g} \circ \mathbf{T}$ is a mapping of V^* to U^*, which we denote by $\mathbf{T}^*$. Then $<\mathbf{T}^*(\mathbf{g}), \mathbf{x}> = <\mathbf{g} \circ \mathbf{T}, \mathbf{x}>$, and by (4.8) this is $\mathbf{g} \circ \mathbf{T}(\mathbf{x})$, which by (4.1) is the same as $\mathbf{g}(\mathbf{T}(\mathbf{x}))$. From (4.8) again, this is equal to $<\mathbf{g}, \mathbf{T}(\mathbf{x})>$. Therefore $\mathbf{T}^*$ satisfies the equations appearing in the theorem. $\mathbf{T}^*$ is linear. Let $\mathbf{h}$ be another element of V^*. We must show that $\mathbf{T}^*(\mathbf{g} + \mathbf{h}) = \mathbf{T}^*(\mathbf{g}) + \mathbf{T}^*(\mathbf{h})$. By definition of $\mathbf{T}^*$, the left member here is the same as $(\mathbf{g} + \mathbf{h}) \circ \mathbf{T}$, which, by (4.5), is equal to $\mathbf{g} \circ \mathbf{T} + \mathbf{h} \circ \mathbf{T}$, and this is in turn equal to $\mathbf{T}^*(\mathbf{g}) + \mathbf{T}^*(\mathbf{h})$, by definition of $\mathbf{T}^*$. Furthermore we must show that $\mathbf{T}^*(c\mathbf{g}) = c \cdot \mathbf{T}^*(\mathbf{g})$ for any $\mathbf{g}$ in V^* and any scalar c. But this equation is the same as $(c\mathbf{g}) \cdot \mathbf{T} = c(\mathbf{g} \cdot \mathbf{T})$, by definition of $\mathbf{T}^*$, and the equation is therefore true, by (4.5). Finally, $\mathbf{T}^*$ is unique: Let $\mathbf{T}_1^*$ be another linear mapping from V^* to U^* such that $<\mathbf{T}_1^*(\mathbf{g}), x> = <\mathbf{g}, \mathbf{T}(\mathbf{x})>$ for all $\mathbf{g}$, $\mathbf{x}$. Putting $\mathbf{S} = \mathbf{T}^* - \mathbf{T}_1^*$, we have $<\mathbf{S}(\mathbf{g}), \mathbf{x}> = <\mathbf{T}^*(\mathbf{g}) - \mathbf{T}_1^*(g), \mathbf{x}>$, by definition of $\mathbf{T}^* - \mathbf{T}_1^*$, that is, by (4.3) and (4.4). From (4.9) the last expression is equal to $<\mathbf{T}^*(\mathbf{g}), \mathbf{x}> - <\mathbf{T}_1^*(\mathbf{g}), \mathbf{x}>$, and by assumption this is $<\mathbf{g}, \mathbf{T}(\mathbf{x})> - <\mathbf{g}, \mathbf{T}(\mathbf{x})>$. Hence, $<\mathbf{S}(\mathbf{g}), \mathbf{x}> = \mathbf{0}$ for all $\mathbf{g}$ and $\mathbf{x}$. Then $\mathbf{S}(\mathbf{g})$ is the zero mapping of U to K, for any $\mathbf{g}$. That is, $\mathbf{S}(\mathbf{g})$ is the zero element of U^*. Therefore $\mathbf{S}$ maps all of V^* into the zero of U^*, and so $\mathbf{S} = \mathbf{0}$, or $\mathbf{T}^* = \mathbf{T}_1^*$. Q.E.D.

DEFINITION 4.2 *The mapping* $\mathbf{T}^*$ *of Theorem* 4.4 *is called the* transpose *of* $\mathbf{T}$.

EXERCISES

1. Let $\mathbf{T}$ be the endomorphism of $\mathbf{Q}_3$ defined in Exercise 4, Sec. 3. Where do the two mappings $\mathbf{I} + 4\mathbf{T}^2$ and $2\mathbf{I} - 3\mathbf{T} + 5\mathbf{T}^2 - \mathbf{T}^3$ send the vectors (1, 0, 2) and (2, −1, 1)? Determine the rank and nullity of the first of the two mappings.

2. Let $\mathbf{D}_0$ be the endormorphism of $\mathbf{C}[t]_n$ defined in Exercise 2, Sec. 3. What is the mapping $\mathbf{D}_0{}^n$? Find bases for the kernel and image of the operator $2\mathbf{I} - \mathbf{D}_0 + 3\mathbf{D}_0{}^2$.

3. Let W be a K-algebra, where K is a field. Let $\mathbf{T}$ be a linear mapping of W to itself, W being considered as a vector space over K (we do not assume that $\mathbf{T}$ is compatible with the product operation defined in W). Let $\mathbf{u}$ be an element of W, and define a new mapping $\mathbf{uT}$ of W to itself by the rule that $\mathbf{uT}$ sends an arbitrary element $\mathbf{x}$ of W into $\mathbf{u} \cdot \mathbf{T}(\mathbf{x})$. Show that $\mathbf{uT}$ is again a linear mapping of W [this operation generalizes (4.3)].

4. Let $\mathbf{D}$ be the derivative mapping of $\mathbf{C}[t]$ defined in Exercise 2, Sec. 3. If $f(t)$ is any polynomial in $\mathbf{C}[t]$, then $f(t)\mathbf{D}$, as defined in the preceding exercise, is a new linear mapping of $\mathbf{C}[t]$ to itself, that is, it maps an arbitrary polynomial $g(t)$ into the polynomial $f(t)\mathbf{D}[g(t)]$. A special instance of this is the operator $(1 - t^2)\mathbf{D}$. The composition of $\mathbf{D}$ and $(1 - t^2)\mathbf{D}$ is then the operator $\mathbf{D}(1 - t^2)\mathbf{D}$. It is of considerable importance in some applications, and we shall encounter it in later exercises. Where does it send the polynomials $2 - t + t^3$ and $1 - t + t^2 - t^3 + t^4 - t^5$? Show that the operator is the same as $(1 - t^2)\mathbf{D}^2 - 2t\mathbf{D}$.

5. Let $\mathbf{S}$ and $\mathbf{T}$ be two isomorphisms of a vector space U. Show that $(\mathbf{S} \circ \mathbf{T})^{-1} = \mathbf{T}^{-1} \circ \mathbf{S}^{-1}$.

6. Let $\mathbf{T}\colon\ U \to V$ and $\mathbf{S}\colon\ V \to W$ be linear mappings of vector spaces, and let $\mathbf{T}^*$ resp. $\mathbf{S}^*$ be their transposes. Prove that $(\mathbf{S} \circ \mathbf{T})^* = \mathbf{T}^* \circ \mathbf{S}^*$.

7. Let U and V be two vector spaces over a field K. Show that the operation that sends a linear mapping $\mathbf{T}$ of U to V into its transpose $\mathbf{T}^*$ is a linear mapping from Hom (U, V) to Hom (V^*, U^*). Show that if $\mathbf{T}$ is an epimorphism, then $\mathbf{T}^*$ is a monomorphism.

8. U being a vector space, let $GL(U)$ denote the set of all automorphisms of U. Prove that this set, with composition of mappings as binary operation, is a group (called the general *linear group* on U).

5. *Linear transformations and matrices*

We shall now show how to transcribe calculations with linear mappings into calculations with scalars. This is a very important step for many purposes, and it will lend an appearance of concreteness to some of the things we have been discussing. It is to be remarked, however, that many arguments involving linear mappings are most easily effected without the use of matrices.

PROPOSITION 5.1 *Let U and V be vector spaces over a field K, and suppose that U has finite dimension n. Let $\mathbf{u}_1, \ldots, \mathbf{u}_n$ be a base for U, and let $\mathbf{y}_1, \ldots, \mathbf{y}_n$ be arbitrary vectors in V. Then there is one and only one linear mapping $\mathbf{T}\colon\ U \to V$ such that*

$$\mathbf{T}(\mathbf{u}_1) = \mathbf{y}_1,\ \mathbf{T}(\mathbf{u}_2) = \mathbf{y}_2,\ \ldots,\ \mathbf{T}(\mathbf{u}_n) = \mathbf{y}_n$$

and every linear transformation $U \to V$ is determined in this way by a suitable choice of $\mathbf{y}_1, \ldots, \mathbf{y}_n$.

Proof. Since $\mathbf{u}_1, \ldots, \mathbf{u}_n$ form a base for U, every $\mathbf{x}$ in U can be expressed *uniquely* as a linear combination

5.1 $$\mathbf{x} = x^1\mathbf{v}_1 + \cdots + x^n\mathbf{v}_n$$

with $x^1, \ldots, x^n$ in K. Now $\mathbf{y}_1, \ldots, \mathbf{y}_n$ being given in V, we define $\mathbf{T}$ by the formula

5.2 $$\mathbf{T}(\mathbf{x}) = x^1\mathbf{y}_1 + \cdots + x^n\mathbf{y}_n$$

Since there is only one way to write $\mathbf{x}$ in the form (5.1), it is clear that $\mathbf{T}(\mathbf{x})$ as defined in this manner is uniquely determined by $\mathbf{x}$. It is a trivial matter to verify that $\mathbf{T}$ is indeed a linear mapping. If now we take $\mathbf{u}_1$, say, for $\mathbf{x}$, then (5.1) becomes

$$\mathbf{u}_1 = 1 \cdot \mathbf{u}_1 + 0 \cdot \mathbf{u}_2 + \cdots + 0 \cdot \mathbf{u}_n$$

and so (5.2) gives $\mathbf{T}(\mathbf{u}_1) = \mathbf{y}_1$. Similarly, $\mathbf{T}(\mathbf{u}_j) = \mathbf{y}_j$ for $j = 1, \ldots, n$.

On the other hand, if $\mathbf{T}$: $U \to V$ is any given linear mapping, and if we define $\mathbf{y}_j$ by $\mathbf{T}(\mathbf{u}_j) = \mathbf{y}_j$ $(j = 1, \ldots, n)$, then from (3.3) we get $\mathbf{T}(\mathbf{x}) = x^1\mathbf{y}_1 + \cdots + x^n\mathbf{y}_n$, which is the same as (5.2). This shows that our definition of $\mathbf{T}(\mathbf{x})$ by (5.2) is the only one possible. Q.E.D.

The proposition says simply that a linear transformation $U \to V$ is completely determined by its effect on a set of base vectors in U and that effect may be prescribed arbitrarily. As a simple application we have the following corollary:

COROLLARY *Let U be a vector space of finite dimension n over a field K. Then the dual vector space U^* also has dimension n.*

Proof. Let $\mathbf{u}_1, \ldots, \mathbf{u}_n$ be a base for U, and for each $j = 1, \ldots, n$ let $\mathbf{u}^j$ denote the linear mapping of U to K determined by the following conditions:

5.3 $$<\mathbf{u}^j, \mathbf{u}_i> = \begin{cases} 1 & \text{if } j = i \\ 0 & \text{if } j \neq i \end{cases} \qquad (i = 1, \ldots, n)$$

We recall that the left member of this equation stands for $\mathbf{u}^j(\mathbf{u}_i)$. According to Proposition 5.1, for given j there is one and only one linear mapping $U \to K$ for which (5.3) holds. Now let $\mathbf{f}$ be any element of U^*, and set $<\mathbf{f}, \mathbf{u}_i> = f_i$ $(i = 1, \ldots, n)$. Each $\mathbf{u}^j$ is an element of U^*, and therefore, by the general definitions given in Sec. 4, so is $f_1\mathbf{u}^1 + f_2\mathbf{u}^2 + \cdots + \mathbf{f}_n\mathbf{u}^n$. Furthermore, this mapping sends $\mathbf{u}_i$ into f_i, by (5.3). It therefore has precisely the same effect as $\mathbf{f}$ on the given base of U and consequently must coincide with $\mathbf{f}$, by the proposition above. Hence, using the Einstein summation convention, we have

$$\mathbf{f} = f_j\mathbf{u}^j$$

The elements $\mathbf{u}^1, \ldots, \mathbf{u}^n$ therefore span the space U^*. From (5.3) it is very easily seen that they are linearly independent and consequently form a base for U^*, which accordingly has dimension n. If $\mathbf{x} = x^i\mathbf{u}_i$ is an arbitrary element of U, then using (4.9) we get

$$<\mathbf{f}, \mathbf{x}> = <f_j\mathbf{u}^j, x^i\mathbf{u}_i> = f_jx^i <\mathbf{u}^j, \mathbf{u}_i>$$

and by (5.3) this reduces to

5.4 $$\langle \mathbf{f}, \mathbf{x} \rangle = f_i x^i$$

the summation convention being used throughout.

REMARK. In Sec. 2 it was mentioned that it is sometimes desirable to reverse the index convention. It is precisely in connection with the dual vector space that this situation arises. In the original space U we used lower indices on base vectors and upper indices on components. A brief examination of the foregoing shows that it is entirely natural to use upper indices on the base $\mathbf{u}^1, \ldots, \mathbf{u}^n$ that we found for U^* and lower indices for the components $f_1, \ldots, f_n$ of $\mathbf{f}$ relative to that base. The base defined by (5.3) for U^* is said to be *dual* to the given base in U.

Now let U and V be vector spaces over a field K of dimensions n and m, respectively. Let $\mathbf{T}$: $U \to V$ be a linear mapping. If $\mathbf{u}_1, \ldots, \mathbf{u}_n$ is a base for U, and if $\mathbf{v}_1, \ldots, \mathbf{v}_m$ is a base for V, then each element $\mathbf{T}(\mathbf{u}_i)$ can be expressed uniquely as a linear combination of the base elements in V, say

5.5 $$\mathbf{T}(\mathbf{u}_i) = t^1{}_i\mathbf{v}_1 + t^2{}_i\mathbf{v}_2 + \cdots + t^m{}_i\mathbf{v}_m = t^j{}_i\mathbf{v}_j \qquad (i = 1, \ldots, n)$$

where on the right we have used the summation convention. The coefficients $t^j{}_i$ are elements of the field K, and there are mn of them. It is very convenient to think of them as arranged in a rectangular array

5.6 $$\begin{pmatrix} t^1{}_1 & t^1{}_2 & \cdots & t^1{}_n \\ t^2{}_1 & t^2{}_2 & \cdots & t^2{}_n \\ \cdots & \cdots & \cdots & \cdots \\ t^m{}_1 & t^m{}_2 & \cdots & t^m{}_n \end{pmatrix}$$

Such an array is called an $m \times n$ *matrix*, and the entries $t^j{}_i$ are called its coefficients. Observe that the upper index j indicates the row containing $t^j{}_i$, and the lower index tells which column it is in. We shall sometimes abbreviate the matrix (5.6) by the symbol $(t^j{}_i)$ or by the boldface letter $\mathbf{t}$. (Naturally for different matrices we shall use different letters; the particular choice of indices is a matter of indifference, of course.)

DEFINITION 5.1 *The matrix* (5.6) *is called the matrix of* $\mathbf{T}$ *relative to the base pair* $\{\mathbf{u}_i\}$, $\{\mathbf{v}_j\}$ *in* U *and* V.

From the matrix $\mathbf{t}$ of the mapping $\mathbf{T}$ it is easy to calculate the components of $\mathbf{T}(\mathbf{x})$ for any $\mathbf{x}$ in U. To do so, let $\mathbf{x} = x^1\mathbf{u}_1 + x^2\mathbf{u}_2 + \cdots + x^n\mathbf{u}_n = x^i\mathbf{u}_i$. By (3.3) we have then

$$\mathbf{T}(\mathbf{x}) = \mathbf{T}(x^i\mathbf{u}_i) = x^i \cdot \mathbf{T}(\mathbf{u}_i)$$

Substituting (5.5) in the last expression, we get

$$\mathbf{T}(x) = x^i t^j{}_i \mathbf{v}_j$$

The coefficient of $\mathbf{v}_j$ here is $x^i t^j{}_i = x^1 t^j{}_1 + \cdots + x^n t^j{}_n$, which we prefer to write as $t^j{}_i x^i$.

THEOREM 5.2 *If $\mathbf{t} = (t^j{}_i)$ is the matrix of the linear mapping $\mathbf{T}\colon U \to V$ relative to the base pair $\{\mathbf{u}_i\}$, $\{\mathbf{v}_j\}$, and if $x^1, \ldots, x^n$ are the components of an element $\mathbf{x}$ of U relative to $\{\mathbf{u}_i\}$, then the components of $\mathbf{T}(\mathbf{x})$ relative to $\{\mathbf{v}_j\}$ are*

5.7 $$t^j{}_i x^i$$

EXAMPLE Let U, V be vector spaces of dimension 2 resp. 3 over the rational field $\mathbf{Q}$. Let $\mathbf{u}_1$, $\mathbf{u}_2$ and $\mathbf{v}_1$, $\mathbf{v}_2$, $\mathbf{v}_3$ be bases for them, and let $\mathbf{T}$ be the linear mapping of U to V for which

$$\mathbf{T}(\mathbf{u}_1) = 2\mathbf{v}_1 + 4\mathbf{v}_2 - \mathbf{v}_3$$
$$\mathbf{T}(\mathbf{u}_2) = \mathbf{v}_1 - 4\mathbf{v}_3$$

Then the corresponding matrix of $\mathbf{T}$ is the 3×2 matrix

$$\begin{pmatrix} 2 & 1 \\ 4 & 0 \\ -1 & -4 \end{pmatrix}$$

(It is important not to mix up the rows and columns!) For the vector $\mathbf{x} = 5\mathbf{u}_1 + 2\mathbf{u}_2$ in U, the components of $\mathbf{T}(\mathbf{x})$ are, by (5.7), $t^1{}_i x^i$, $t^2{}_i x^i$, $t^3{}_i x^i$, or $2 \cdot 5 + 1 \cdot 2$, $4 \cdot 5 + 0 \cdot 2$, $-1 \cdot 5 + (-4) \cdot 2$. Thus $\mathbf{T}(\mathbf{x}) = 12\mathbf{v}_1 + 20\mathbf{v}_2 - 13\mathbf{v}_3$. This is easily verified directly.

Equation (5.5) tells us how to calculate the effect of $\mathbf{T}$ on the base elements $\mathbf{u}_1, \ldots, \mathbf{u}_n$ from the matrix (5.6), and therefore $\mathbf{T}$ is completely determined by the matrix once the bases in U and V are given, by Proposition 5.1. A different choice of bases in U and V results in a different matrix (5.6) for $\mathbf{T}$. We shall soon see how different matrices for the same linear mapping are related.

REMARK. Any $m \times n$ matrix $(t^j{}_i)$ with coefficients in a field K is the matrix of some linear transformation. For we have only to take any two spaces of the proper dimension, for example, K_n and K_m, along with bases for each, say $\mathbf{u}_1, \ldots, \mathbf{u}_n$ and $\mathbf{v}_1, \ldots, \mathbf{v}_m$, respectively. If we then define $\mathbf{T}(\mathbf{u}_i)$ by Eq. (5.5), we shall automatically determine a linear transformation $\mathbf{T}$ of the two spaces, by Proposition 5.1; and clearly $(t^j{}_i)$ will be its matrix with respect to the base pair chosen.

Matrices of particular importance are those for which either m or n equals 1. A $1 \times n$ matrix consists of a single row of n scalars and therefore has the form

$$\mathbf{a} = (a_1, a_2, \ldots, a_n)$$

Matrices of this type are simply vectors in the space K_n of n-tuples. We shall call them *row vectors*.

On the other hand, an $m \times 1$ matrix consists of a single column of m scalars and has the form

$$\mathbf{b} = \begin{pmatrix} b^1 \\ b^2 \\ \cdot \\ \cdot \\ \cdot \\ b^m \end{pmatrix}$$

Matrices of this type will be called *column vectors*. All such column vectors with coefficients in K constitute a set which, apart from the notation, is the same as K_m. We shall call it K^m in order to indicate the vertical arrangement.

It is then natural to denote by $K^m{}_n$ the set of all $m \times n$ matrices with coefficients in the field K. Further, we denote by $\mathbf{t}^j$ the jth row of (5.6). It is an element of K_m. And we denote by $\mathbf{t}_i$ the ith column of (5.6). It is an element of K^m. Thus, if we want to consider the matrix (5.6) in terms of its columns, we can write it as

5.8 $$\mathbf{t} = (\mathbf{t}_1, \mathbf{t}_2, \ldots, \mathbf{t}_n)$$

If we want to express (5.6) in terms of its rows, we can write it as

5.9 $$\mathbf{t} = \begin{pmatrix} \mathbf{t}^1 \\ \mathbf{t}^2 \\ \cdot \\ \cdot \\ \cdot \\ \mathbf{t}^m \end{pmatrix}$$

To summarize, the general notational rules that we shall adopt are as follows:

5.10

$t^j{}_i$ denotes the element in the jth row and ith column of the matrix $\mathbf{t}$—or briefly, the (j, i) element of $\mathbf{t}$.
$\mathbf{t}^j$ denotes the jth row of the matrix $\mathbf{t}$.
$\mathbf{t}_i$ denotes the ith column of $\mathbf{t}$.
$K^m{}_n$ denotes the set of all $m \times n$ matrices with coefficients in the field K, except that we write K^m for $K^m{}_1$ and K_n for $K^1{}_n$.

Of course 1×1 matrices are just scalars, and boldface characters will not be used for them.

Observe that if $\mathbf{T} = \mathbf{0}$, that is, if $\mathbf{T}$ maps every element of U into the zero element of V, then all the coefficients $t^j{}_i$ in (5.6) must be zero. In this case $\mathbf{t}$ is said to be the $m \times n$ *zero matrix*, denoted simply by $\mathbf{0}$.

In Definition 5.1 two bases are involved, one for U and one for V. If the two spaces happen to be the same, then of course there is no necessity for two *different* bases. If the two bases are taken to be the same, say $\{\mathbf{u}_i\}$, $\{\mathbf{u}_i\}$, we shall simply call **t** the matrix of **T** relative to the base $\{\mathbf{u}_i\}$. Observe that in the case of an endomorphism, the matrix **t** will be $n \times n$. Such a matrix is called *square*.

Let us now determine the matrix of the identity mapping **I** of the space U. For the given base $\{\mathbf{u}_i\}$ we have

5.11 $$\mathbf{I}(\mathbf{u}_i) = \mathbf{u}_i = 0 \cdot \mathbf{u}_1 + 0 \cdot \mathbf{u}_2 + \cdots + 1 \cdot \mathbf{u}_i + \cdots + 0 \cdot \mathbf{u}_n$$

and from the general definition above it follows that the matrix of **I** relative to the base $\{\mathbf{u}_i\}$ is

5.12 $$\mathbf{I}_n = \begin{pmatrix} 1 & 0 & 0 & \cdots & 0 \\ 0 & 1 & 0 & \cdots & 0 \\ \cdot & \cdot & \cdot & \cdot & \cdot \\ 0 & 0 & 0 & \cdots & 1 \end{pmatrix}$$

where naturally 1 denotes the unit element of the field of scalars K. $\mathbf{I}_n$ is called the $n \times n$ *unit matrix*. We shall sometimes denote it simply by **I**. The matrices of the zero and the identity mappings $U \to U$ do not depend upon the particular choice of base in U. But for all other endomorphisms of U the matrix depends in an essential way on the choice of base.

It is often useful to have a symbol for the coefficients of the $n \times n$ unit matrix, and we shall indicate the element in the jth row and ith column of (5.12) by the symbol $\delta^j{}_i$.

5.13 $$\delta^j{}_i = \begin{cases} 1 & \text{if} \quad i = j \\ 0 & \text{if} \quad i \neq j \end{cases}$$

The symbol is called the Kronecker *delta*.

EXERCISES

1. Let U, V, W be vector spaces of dimensions 2, 3, 4, respectively, over **Q**. Let $\{\mathbf{u}_1, \mathbf{u}_2\}$, $\{\mathbf{v}_1, \mathbf{v}_2, \mathbf{v}_3\}$, and $\{\mathbf{w}_1, \mathbf{w}_2, \mathbf{w}_3, \mathbf{w}_4\}$ be bases for them. Let $\mathbf{T}$: $U \to V$ and $\mathbf{S}$: $V \to W$ be the mappings defined by

$$\begin{aligned} \mathbf{T}(\mathbf{u}_1) &= 3\mathbf{v}_1 - 2\mathbf{v}_2 + \mathbf{v}_3 \\ \mathbf{T}(\mathbf{u}_2) &= 4\mathbf{v}_1 + \mathbf{v}_2 \\ \mathbf{S}(\mathbf{v}_1) &= \mathbf{w}_1 + \mathbf{w}_2 + \mathbf{w}_3 - \mathbf{w}_4 \\ \mathbf{S}(\mathbf{v}_2) &= 2\mathbf{w}_1 - \mathbf{w}_2 + \mathbf{w}_3 \\ \mathbf{S}(\mathbf{v}_3) &= 2\mathbf{w}_1 - \mathbf{w}_3 + 4\mathbf{w}_4 \end{aligned}$$

Write down the corresponding matrices of **T**, **S**, and $\mathbf{S} \circ \mathbf{T}$.

2. With **S**, **T** as above, find the components of $\mathbf{S} \circ \mathbf{T}(\mathbf{x})$ relative to $\{\mathbf{w}_k\}$, where $\mathbf{x} = 5\mathbf{u}_1 - \mathbf{u}_2$.

3. Find bases for Ker **T**, Ker **S**, and Ker $(\mathbf{S} \circ \mathbf{T})$. What is the rank of $\mathbf{S} \circ \mathbf{T}$?

4. With **T** as in Exercise 1, write down the matrix of its transpose $\mathbf{T}^*$ relative to the dual base pair $\{\mathbf{v}^j\}$ and $\{\mathbf{u}^i\}$. Do the same for $\mathbf{S}^*$.

5. Referring to Exercise 2, Sec. 4, find a base for $\mathbf{C}[t]_n$ and give the matrix of $\mathbf{D}_0$ relative to that base. Give the matrix of $2\mathbf{I} - \mathbf{D}_0 + 3\mathbf{D}_0^2$ relative to that base.

6. Operations on matrices

We shall now see how the operations on linear transformations discussed in Sec. 4 can be expressed in terms of matrices. We start with the operation (4.1) of composition.

Let U, V, W be vector spaces of dimensions n, m, r, respectively, over a field K; and let $\mathbf{T}: U \to V$ and $\mathbf{S}: V \to W$ be linear mappings. Choose bases $\{\mathbf{u}_i\}$, $\{\mathbf{v}_j\}$, and $\{\mathbf{w}_k\}$ for the three spaces. Let $\mathbf{t}$ be the matrix of $\mathbf{T}$ relative to the base pair $\{\mathbf{u}_i\}$, $\{\mathbf{v}_j\}$; let $\mathbf{s}$ be the matrix of $\mathbf{S}$ relative to base pair $\{\mathbf{v}_j\}$, $\{\mathbf{w}_k\}$; and finally let $\mathbf{q}$ be matrix of $\mathbf{S} \circ \mathbf{T}$ relative to the base pair $\{\mathbf{u}_i\}$, $\{\mathbf{w}_k\}$. Then, according to Definition 5.1, we have

6.1
$$\begin{aligned} \mathbf{T}(\mathbf{u}_i) &= t^j{}_i\mathbf{v}_j = t^1{}_i\mathbf{v}_1 + \cdots + t^m{}_i\mathbf{v}_m \\ \mathbf{S}(\mathbf{v}_j) &= s^k{}_j\mathbf{w}_k = s^1{}_j\mathbf{w}_1 + \cdots + s^r{}_j\mathbf{w}_r \\ \mathbf{S} \circ \mathbf{T}(\mathbf{u}_i) &= q^k{}_i\mathbf{w}_k = q^1{}_i\mathbf{w}_1 + \cdots + q^r{}_i\mathbf{w}_r \end{aligned}$$

Apply $\mathbf{S}$ to the first of these equations. Using (3.3) we get

$$\mathbf{S} \circ \mathbf{T}(\mathbf{u}_i) = \mathbf{S}(t^j{}_i\mathbf{v}_j) = t^j{}_i\mathbf{S}(\mathbf{v}_j)$$

Substituting from the second equation we get†

6.2
$$\mathbf{S} \circ \mathbf{T}(\mathbf{u}_i) = t^j{}_is^k{}_j\mathbf{w}_k$$

The coefficient of $\mathbf{w}^k$ here is the sum $t^j{}_is^k{}_j$, which we prefer to write as $s^k{}_jt^j{}_i$ (legitimate because multiplication in K is commutative). Comparing (6.2) with the last equation of (6.1) we conclude (Proposition 6.1, Chap. 8) that

6.3
$$q^k{}_i = s^k{}_jt^j{}_i = s^k{}_1t^1{}_i + s^k{}_2t^2{}_i + \cdots + s^k{}_mt^m{}_i$$

We take this equation as the basis of the following definition:

DEFINITION 6.1 *Let* $\mathbf{s}$ *be an* $r \times m$ *matrix and let* $\mathbf{t}$ *be an* $m \times n$ *matrix, both with coefficients in a field* K. *Then the* $r \times n$ *matrix* $\mathbf{q}$ *whose coefficients are given by* (6.3) *is called the product* $\mathbf{st}$ *of* $\mathbf{s}$ *and* $\mathbf{t}$.

Hence, with this definition we can state the following: If $\mathbf{s}$ is the matrix of $\mathbf{S}: V \to W$ with respect to the base pair $\{\mathbf{v}_j\}$, $\{\mathbf{w}_k\}$, and if $\mathbf{t}$ is the matrix of $\mathbf{T}$: $U \to V$ with respect to the base pair $\{\mathbf{u}_i\}$, $\{\mathbf{v}_j\}$, then the product matrix $\mathbf{st}$ is the matrix of $\mathbf{S} \circ \mathbf{T}$ relative to the base pair $\{\mathbf{u}_i\}$, $\{\mathbf{w}_k\}$.

Observe that the element $q^k{}_i$ in the kth row and ith column of $\mathbf{st}$ is obtained from the kth row of $\mathbf{s}$ and the ith column of $\mathbf{t}$. *A matrix product is defined only when the number of columns in the first factor is equal to the number of rows in the second factor.*

EXAMPLE

$$\begin{pmatrix} 3 & 1 & 2 \\ 0 & 1 & 1 \\ 1 & 2 & 0 \end{pmatrix}\begin{pmatrix} 1 & 4 \\ 2 & 2 \\ 1 & 0 \end{pmatrix} = \begin{pmatrix} 7 & 14 \\ 3 & 2 \\ 5 & 8 \end{pmatrix}$$

In this case the factors on the left cannot be interchanged.

† We chose different indices i, j, k in (6.1) to avoid conflict in (6.2).

In the following example the factors on the left can be interchanged. We see that matrix multiplication is not commutative, in general, even when it makes sense to reverse the order of the factors:

$$\begin{pmatrix} 1 & 0 \\ 2 & 1 \end{pmatrix}\begin{pmatrix} 4 & 1 \\ -1 & 2 \end{pmatrix} = \begin{pmatrix} 4 & 1 \\ 7 & 4 \end{pmatrix}$$

$$\begin{pmatrix} 4 & 1 \\ -1 & 2 \end{pmatrix}\begin{pmatrix} 1 & 0 \\ 2 & 1 \end{pmatrix} = \begin{pmatrix} 6 & 1 \\ 3 & 2 \end{pmatrix}$$

However, matrix multiplication is associative whenever it is defined. More precisely, let **a**, **b**, **c** be matrices of sizes $m \times n$, $n \times r$, and $r \times s$, respectively.† Then, by Definition 6.1, **ab** is an $m \times r$ matrix, and so (**ab**)**c** is defined and is $m \times s$. Similarly, **bc** is an $n \times s$ matrix, and so **a**(**bc**) is defined and is $m \times s$. We have

6.4 $$\mathbf{a}(\mathbf{bc}) = (\mathbf{ab})\mathbf{c}$$

This follows easily from (4.2), of which it is the matricial form, but it can be proved directly without trouble from Definition 6.1.

We have further, for any $m \times n$ matrix **a**,

6.5 $$\mathbf{I}_m \cdot \mathbf{a} = \mathbf{a} \cdot \mathbf{I}_n = \mathbf{a}$$

where $\mathbf{I}_m$ and $\mathbf{I}_n$ are unit matrices (5.12). For example, the (k, i)-element of $\mathbf{I}_m a$ is

$$\delta^k{}_j a^j{}_i = \delta^k{}_1 a^1{}_i + \delta^k{}_2 a^2{}_i + \cdots + \delta^k{}_k a^k{}_i + \cdots + \delta^k{}_m a^m{}_i$$

by (6.3), and this sum is equal to $a^k{}_i$, by (5.13). Equation (6.5) has the following meaning: Let $\mathbf{A}$: $U \to V$ be a linear mapping of vector spaces, where dim $U = n$ and dim $V = m$. Let **a** be the matrix of **A** with respect to some base pair $\{\mathbf{u}_i\}$ $\{\mathbf{v}_j\}$. If **I** denotes the identity mapping of V, then $\mathbf{I} \circ \mathbf{A} = \mathbf{A}$, of course. The matrix of **I** relative to the base $\{\mathbf{v}_j\}$ is $\mathbf{I}_m$, and so the matrix of $\mathbf{I} \circ \mathbf{A}$ relative to the base pair $\{\mathbf{u}_i\}$, $\{\mathbf{v}_j\}$ is $\mathbf{I}_m \cdot \mathbf{a}$, which must be the same as **a**. Similarly, if $\mathbf{I}'$ denotes the identity mapping of U, then $\mathbf{A} \circ \mathbf{I}' = \mathbf{A}$. The matrix of $\mathbf{A} \circ \mathbf{I}$ relative to the base pair $\{\mathbf{u}_i\}$, $\{\mathbf{v}_j\}$ is $\mathbf{a} \cdot \mathbf{I}_n$, which must be equal to **a**.

Let us now consider matrix products involving row vectors and column vectors. It follows readily from Definition 6.1 that the product of two row vectors, or of two column vectors, is not defined unless at least one of them is a scalar (1×1 matrix). Let us then consider the product of a row vector $\mathbf{x} = (x_1, \ldots, x_m)$ in K_m and of a column vector

$$\mathbf{y} = \begin{pmatrix} y^1 \\ \cdot \\ \cdot \\ \cdot \\ y^n \end{pmatrix}$$

† With coefficients in the same field, naturally.

in K^n. The product **yx** is always defined and is the $n \times m$ matrix

$$\mathbf{yx} = \begin{pmatrix} y^1x_1 & \cdots & y^1x_m \\ \cdot & \cdots & \cdot \\ y^nx_1 & \cdots & y^nx_m \end{pmatrix}$$

But the product **xy** is not defined unless $m = n$, in which case it is a 1×1 matrix, that is, the scalar

6.6 $$\mathbf{xy} = x_iy^i = x_1y^1 + \cdots + x_my^m$$

With **x** in K_m and **y** in K^n, as above, let **a** be an element of $K^m{}_n$, that is, an $m \times n$ matrix with coefficients in K. Then **ay** is defined and is $m \times 1$, hence is again a column vector. Similarly, **xa** is defined and is $1 \times n$, a row vector.

If **b** is an element of $K^n{}_s$, then $\mathbf{c} = \mathbf{ab}$ is defined and is in $K^m{}_s$. With the foregoing remarks in view it is easy to verify the following rules, which summarize the relations between **a**, **b**, and **c**:

6.7 $$\begin{array}{lll} \mathbf{ab} = \mathbf{c} & a^k{}_jb^j{}_i = c^k{}_i & \\ \mathbf{ab}_i = \mathbf{c}_i & \mathbf{a}^k\mathbf{b} = \mathbf{c}^k & \mathbf{a}^k\mathbf{b}_i = c^k{}_i \end{array}$$

The first two equations are merely the definition of the product **ab**. The third equation says that the ith column of **c** is equal to **a** times the ith column of **b**. Similarly, the fourth equation states that the kth row of **c** is the product of the kth row of **a** with **b**. The fifth equation is (6.6) applied to $\mathbf{a}^k$ and $\mathbf{b}_i$.

We point out that (5.7) can be expressed as a matrix product. For let **x** be an element of the n-dimensional space U, **x** having components $x^1, x^2, \ldots, x^n$ relative to a base $\{\mathbf{u}_i\}$, so that $\mathbf{x} = x^i\mathbf{u}_i$. Because of our index convention we now consider the n-tuple formed of $x^1, x^2, \ldots, x^n$ as an element of K^n—a *column vector*. To prevent confusion with **x** we denote that column vector by $\mathbf{x}_c$,

6.8 $$\mathbf{x}_c = \begin{pmatrix} x^1 \\ x^2 \\ \cdot \\ \cdot \\ \cdot \\ x^n \end{pmatrix}$$

and we call it the *component vector* of **x** (relative to the given base). This being established, we have the following proposition:

PROPOSITION 6.1 *Let* $\mathbf{T}$: $U \to V$ *be a linear mapping of finite-dimensional vector spaces, and let* **t** *be its matrix relative to some base pair* $\{\mathbf{u}_i\}, \{\mathbf{v}_j\}$. *If* **x** *in* U *has component vector* $\mathbf{x}_c$ *relative to* $\{\mathbf{u}_i\}$, *then the component vector of* $\mathbf{T}(\mathbf{x})$ *relative to* $\{\mathbf{v}_j\}$ *is the matrix product* $\mathbf{tx}_c$.

This follows immediately from (5.7) and the definition of matrix multiplication. The proposition below is of a similar nature.

PROPOSITION 6.2 *K being a field, let* $\mathbf{a}$ *be an element of* $K^m{}_n$*, that is, an* $m \times n$ *matrix with coefficients in* K*. Then the operation that assigns to any vector* $\mathbf{x}$ *in* K^n *the new vector* $\mathbf{ax}$ *is a linear mapping* $\mathbf{A}$ *from* K^n *to* K^m*. Furthermore,* $\mathbf{a}$ *is the matrix of* $\mathbf{A}$ *relative to the canonical bases.*† *Similarly, the operation that sends any vector* $\mathbf{y}$ *in* K_m *into* $\mathbf{ya}$ *is a linear mapping from* K_m *to* K_n*, and* $\mathbf{a}$ *is its matrix relative to the canonical base pair. If* $\mathbf{B}$: $K^n \to K^m$ *is any linear mapping, and if its matrix relative to the canonical bases is denoted by* $\mathbf{b}$*, then* $\mathbf{B}(\mathbf{x}) = \mathbf{bx}$ *for any* $\mathbf{x}$ *in* K^n*. If* $\mathbf{B}'$: $K_m \to K_n$ *is a linear mapping, with matrix* $\mathbf{b}$ *relative to the canonical bases, then* $\mathbf{B}'(\mathbf{y}) = \mathbf{yb}$ *for any* $\mathbf{y}$ *in* K_m.

The verifications involved here are very simple and straightforward and are therefore omitted.

We observe that if $\mathbf{a}$ and $\mathbf{b}$ are two *square* matrices of the same size, say $n \times n$, then $\mathbf{ab}$ is also $n \times n$. Hence, matrix multiplication is a binary operation in $K^n{}_n$, the set of all $n \times n$ matrices with coefficients in K. The operation is associative, by (6.4). In particular, we can form $\mathbf{a}^2 = \mathbf{a} \cdot \mathbf{a}$, $\mathbf{a}^3 = \mathbf{a} \cdot \mathbf{a} \cdot \mathbf{a}$, etc., for any $\mathbf{a}$ in $K^n{}_n$ (we are using Sec. 7*E*, Chap. 2, here).

We now introduce two other very simple operations on matrices: If $\mathbf{a} = (a^j{}_i)$ is any element of $K^m{}_n$, and if p is any element of K, then we define $p\mathbf{a}$ by

6.9 $$p\mathbf{a} = (pa^j{}_i)$$

That is, $p\mathbf{a}$ is the $m \times n$ matrix whose (j, i) element is $pa^j{}_i$. If $\mathbf{b} = (b^j{}_i)$ is another matrix in $K^m{}_n$, then we define $\mathbf{a} \pm \mathbf{b}$ by

6.10 $$\mathbf{a} \pm \mathbf{b} = (a^j{}_i \pm \mathbf{b}^j{}_i)$$

Thus $\mathbf{a} \pm \mathbf{b}$ has $a^j{}_i \pm b^j{}_i$ as its (j, i) element. These definitions are obviously straightforward extensions of the operations defined in K_n in Sec. 4, Chap. 8. In fact they are the *same* definitions if one imagines the elements of an $m \times n$ matrix written out in a single row. It follows at once that $K^m{}_n$, with the operations (6.9) and (6.10), is a vector space of dimension mn over K.

These operations and matrix multiplication satisfy the following relations, whenever the indicated operations are defined (p denotes an arbitrary scalar; $\mathbf{a}$, $\mathbf{b}$, $\mathbf{c}$ denote arbitrary matrices with coefficients in K):

6.11
$$\begin{aligned}
\mathbf{a}(\mathbf{bc}) &= (\mathbf{ab})\mathbf{c} \\
(\mathbf{a} + \mathbf{b})\mathbf{c} &= \mathbf{ac} + \mathbf{bc} \\
\mathbf{c}(\mathbf{a} + \mathbf{b}) &= \mathbf{ca} + \mathbf{cb} \\
p(\mathbf{a} + \mathbf{b}) &= p\mathbf{a} + p\mathbf{b} \\
p(\mathbf{ab}) &= (p\mathbf{a})\mathbf{b} = \mathbf{a}(p\mathbf{b})
\end{aligned}$$

These rules of calculation are the matricial counterparts of (4.2) and (4.5). We have repeated (6.4). All the equations follow trivially from the definitions of the

† The *canonical base* of K^n consists of the n columns $\mathbf{e}_1, \mathbf{e}_2, \ldots, \mathbf{e}_n$ of the unit matrix $\mathbf{I}_n$. The canonical base of K_n consists of the n rows $\mathbf{e}^1, \mathbf{e}^2, \ldots, \mathbf{e}^n$ of $\mathbf{I}_n$. Cf. Remark 3, Sec. 9, Chap. 8.

operations and from the field axioms for K. It is quickly seen that $K^n{}_n$ is a K-algebra.

PROPOSITION 6.3 *Let U, V be vector spaces over a field K of dimensions n, m, respectively. Let $\{\mathbf{u}_i\}$ and $\{\mathbf{v}_j\}$ be bases for them. Then the operation that associates with any linear mapping $\mathbf{T}$: $U \to V$ its matrix $\mathbf{t}$ relative to the given base pair is an isomorphism of the vector space* Hom (U, V) *to* $K^m{}_n$.

This follows immediately from Definitions 4.1 and 6.1 and from (6.9) and (6.10). There is no operation of "product" defined for elements of Hom (U, V), in general, but there is one in Hom (U, U). We have the following theorem:

THEOREM 6.4 *Let U be a vector space of dimension n over K, and let $\{\mathbf{u}_i\}$ be a base for U. Then the operation that assigns to a linear mapping $\mathbf{T}$: $U \to U$ its matrix $\mathbf{t}$ relative to the base $\{\mathbf{u}_i\}$ is an isomorphism from the K-algebra* Hom (U, U) *to the K-algebra $K^n{}_n$.*

An isomorphism of K-algebras is a one-to-one mapping which is compatible with addition, multiplication, and *scalar* multiplication. That the mapping in question is compatible with addition and scalar multiplication is stated in Proposition 6.3. Its compatibility with the product follows from Definition 6.1 (see the remark following it).

These two theorems show that linear mappings of finite-dimensional vector spaces can be replaced by matrices. For purposes of calculation this is often essential.

We now introduce one more operation on matrices. It is a very trivial one, but it is often useful.

Let $\mathbf{a} = (a^j{}_i)$ be an element of $K^m{}_n$. Then the *transpose* of $\mathbf{a}$, denoted by ${}^t\mathbf{a}$, is the matrix $({}^ta^j{}_i)$ in $K^n{}_m$ such that

$${}^ta^j{}_i = a^i{}_j$$

That is, the (j, i) element of ${}^t\mathbf{a}$ is the same as the (i, j) element of $\mathbf{a}$.

EXAMPLE The transpose of

$$\begin{pmatrix} 2 & 1 \\ 3 & 4 \\ 1 & 2 \end{pmatrix} \quad \text{is} \quad \begin{pmatrix} 2 & 3 & 1 \\ 1 & 4 & 2 \end{pmatrix}$$

The transpose operation merely interchanges rows and columns of a matrix. It is clear that ${}^t({}^t\mathbf{a}) = \mathbf{a}$. That is, the transpose operation applied twice gives back the original matrix. The important properties of the transpose operations are as follows:

6.12
$$\begin{aligned} {}^t({}^t\mathbf{a}) &= \mathbf{a} \\ {}^t(\mathbf{a} + \mathbf{b}) &= {}^t\mathbf{a} + {}^t\mathbf{b} \\ {}^t(p\mathbf{a}) &= p \cdot {}^t\mathbf{a} \\ {}^t(\mathbf{ab}) &= {}^t\mathbf{b}\,{}^t\mathbf{a} \end{aligned}$$

The first three rules are completely trivial. The second and third allow us to conclude that transposition is an isomorphism from $K^m{}_n$ to $K^n{}_m$. To prove the last equation we have:

$$[(k,\ i) \text{ element of } {}^t(\mathbf{ab})] = [(i,\ k) \text{ element of } (\mathbf{ab})] = a^i{}_j b^j{}_k = b^j{}_k a^i{}_j = {}^t b^k{}_j {}^t a^j{}_i = [(k,\ i) \text{ element of } {}^t\mathbf{b}\,{}^t\mathbf{a}]$$

The equation is easily checked by numerical examples.

We mention here some terminology which is often used in connection with matrices.

Let $\mathbf{a} = (a^j{}_i)$ be any $m \times n$ matrix. Then the coefficients $a^1{}_1$, $a^2{}_2$, $a^3{}_3$, etc., are called the *diagonal* coefficients of $\mathbf{a}$ (the term is usually restricted to square matrices). The matrix $\mathbf{a}$ is called a *diagonal matrix* if all terms not on the diagonal are zero. For example, $\mathbf{I}_n$ is a diagonal matrix.

The matrix $\mathbf{a}$ is called *triangular* if all the entries below the diagonal are zero, that is, $a^i{}_j = 0$ if $i > j$. For example,

$$\begin{pmatrix} 2 & 1 & 3 & 4 \\ 0 & 1 & 1 & 2 \\ 0 & 0 & 3 & 1 \end{pmatrix}$$

is triangular. The term is usually restricted to square matrices.

A square matrix $\mathbf{a}$ is called *symmetric* if ${}^t\mathbf{a} = \mathbf{a}$, that is, if $a^j{}_i = a^i{}_j$ for all relevant i and j.

EXERCISES

1. Work out the products **ab** and **ba**, where

$$\mathbf{a} = \begin{pmatrix} 2 & 0 & 3 \\ 1 & -1 & 2 \\ 3 & 1 & 1 \\ 1 & -1 & 4 \end{pmatrix} \qquad \mathbf{b} = \begin{pmatrix} 1 & 4 & 2 & 0 \\ 5 & 5 & 0 & 6 \\ -1 & 2 & -1 & 3 \end{pmatrix}$$

2. Find a matrix $\mathbf{b}$ such that $\mathbf{ab} = \mathbf{I}_2$, where $\mathbf{a} = \begin{pmatrix} 1 & 2 \\ 3 & 4 \end{pmatrix}$. Compute **ba**. What happens if you take $\mathbf{a} = \begin{pmatrix} 2 & -1 \\ -6 & 3 \end{pmatrix}$?

3. Compute ${}^t\mathbf{b}\,{}^t\mathbf{a}$, where $\mathbf{a}$, $\mathbf{b}$ are the matrices of Exercise 1.

4. Let $\mathbf{a}$ be an element of $K^m{}_n$, and let $\mathbf{x}$, $\mathbf{y}$ be elements of K^n and K^m, respectively. Show that the equations

$$\mathbf{ax} = \mathbf{y}$$

$$x^1\mathbf{a}_1 + \cdots + x^n\mathbf{a}_n = \mathbf{y}$$

and

$$\begin{aligned} a^1{}_1x^1 + \cdots + a^1{}_nx^n &= y^1 \\ \cdots\cdots\cdots\cdots& \\ a^m{}_1x^1 + \cdots + a^m{}_nx^n &= y^m \end{aligned}$$

are all equivalent.

5. Referring to Exercise 4, write out the equation ${}^t\mathbf{x}{}^t\mathbf{a} = {}^t\mathbf{y}$, exhibiting the coefficients of the three matrices.

6. Let $\mathbf{a}$ be an element of $K^n{}_n$, and suppose that its columns are linearly independent vectors. Prove that there exists a unique vector $\mathbf{b}_j$ such that $\mathbf{a}\mathbf{b}_j = \mathbf{e}_j$, where $\mathbf{e}_j$ is the jth column of $\mathbf{I}_n$. Compute $\mathbf{ab}$, where $\mathbf{b}$ is the $n \times n$ matrix whose columns are $\mathbf{b}_1, \ldots, \mathbf{b}_n$.

7. Compute the following matrix product, where t is an indeterminate over $\mathbf{Q}$.

$$\begin{pmatrix} t^2 & 3t & 1 - \dfrac{1}{t} \\ 2 + t & 1 & -t \\ t^3 & t^4 & 0 \end{pmatrix} \cdot \begin{pmatrix} 1 \\ t^2 \\ t^{-2} \end{pmatrix}$$

8. Let $\mathbf{a}$, $\mathbf{b}$ be triangular matrices in $K^n{}_n$. Prove that $\mathbf{ab}$ is triangular.

*9. Let $\mathbf{a}$ be an element of $K^n{}_n$, and suppose that $\mathbf{ab} = \mathbf{ba}$ for every matrix $\mathbf{b}$ in $K^n{}_n$. Prove that $\mathbf{a} = a \cdot \mathbf{I}_n$, where a is a scalar. Matrices of this type are called *scalar* matrices. Prove that the set of all scalar matrices in $K^n{}_n$ is a subring which is isomorphic to K.

10. Prove that $K^m{}_n$ is a vector space of dimension mn over K.

11. Let $\mathbf{a}$ be a matrix in $K^n{}_n$ with $a^i{}_j = 0$ for $i \geqslant j$. Prove that $\mathbf{a}^n = \mathbf{0}$. [Hint: Experiment with a 3×3 matrix.]

*12. Let $\mathbf{a} = (a^i{}_j)$ be an $n \times n$ matrix. Show that the following two conditions on $\mathbf{a}$ are equivalent:

(*a*) The matrix $\mathbf{a}$ represents a linear mapping $\mathbf{A}\colon K_n \to K_n$ such that the matrix of $\mathbf{A}$ with respect to some base has form

$$\begin{pmatrix} \mathbf{b} & \mathbf{c} \\ \mathbf{0} & \mathbf{d} \end{pmatrix}$$

where $\mathbf{b}$, $\mathbf{d}$ are square matrices.

(*b*) The matrix $\mathbf{a}$ represents a linear mapping $\mathbf{A}\colon K_n \to K_n$ which possesses an invariant subspace L of dimension $<n$, that is, $\mathbf{A}(L) \subset L$. A matrix satisfying any of these conditions is called *reducible*; otherwise, it is *irreducible*.

*13. If $\mathbf{a} = (a^i{}_j)$ is an irreducible real $n \times n$ matrix and $a^i{}_j \geq 0$; then every entry of the matrix

$$(\mathbf{I} + \mathbf{a})^{n-1}$$

is positive.

[Hint: Prove that if $\mathbf{u}$ is a nonzero vector whose components are non-negative, then the vector $(\mathbf{I} + \mathbf{a})\mathbf{u}$ has fewer zero components than $\mathbf{u}$.]

14. An important aspect of recent mathematical economics is the study of the

"input-output" model of an economy.† The viewpoint implicit in this model is that an economy is a system where many different types of goods and services (called *commodities*) are produced and then used up in the production of still more commodities. Let $C_1, C_2, \ldots, C_n$ be the commodities produced in an economy and suppose that $\pi^i{}_j$ is the amount of C_i consumed to produce a unit of C_j and that $\varphi^i{}_j$ is the amount of C_i used (but *not* necessarily used up) in the production of a unit of C_j. Thus $\pi^{\text{flour}}{}_{\text{bread}} \neq 0$, $\pi^{\text{oven}}{}_{\text{bread}} = 0$, but $\varphi^{\text{oven}}{}_{\text{bread}} \neq 0$. Assuming that the price of a commodity is the sum of the price of the commodities used up in its production plus ρ (the "rate of profit," assumed constant for all commodities) times the price of the commodities used, write a matrix equation relating $\pi^i{}_j$, $\varphi^i{}_j$ and the prices of $C_1, C_2, \ldots, C_n$. The study of the required equation is an interesting problem, for the solution of which we refer to Schwartz's book. Let us merely mention here that a positive rate of profit ρ exists if and only if there is a program of production in the economy which yields a surplus, i.e., for which the amount of every commodity produced is greater than or equal to the amount consumed.

7. *Change of base*

In Sec. 9, Chap. 8, we have already considered briefly the matter of changing bases in vector spaces. The calculations involved can be expressed very compactly by the use of matrices.

Let U be an n-dimensional vector space over a field K, and let $\mathbf{u}_1, \ldots, \mathbf{u}_n$ and $\mathbf{u}'_1, \ldots, \mathbf{u}'_n$ be two bases for U. Then any element in one of the bases can be expressed uniquely as a linear combination of elements in the other base. Hence, the two bases will be related by equations of the following type [cf. Eq. (9.5), Chap. 8]:

7.1
$$\begin{aligned} \mathbf{u}'_i &= p^j{}_i\mathbf{u}_j = p^1{}_i\mathbf{u}_1 + \cdots + p^n{}_i\mathbf{u}_n \\ \mathbf{u}_j &= q^k{}_j\mathbf{u}'_k = q^1{}_j\mathbf{u}'_1 + \cdots + q^n{}_j\mathbf{u}'_n \end{aligned}$$

We have here two $n \times n$ matrices, $\mathbf{p} = (p^j{}_i)$ and $\mathbf{q} = (q^k{}_j)$.

Now let $\mathbf{x}$ be an element of U, and let $\mathbf{x}_c$, $\mathbf{x}'_c$ be its component vectors relative to the two bases. That is,

$$\mathbf{x}_c = \begin{pmatrix} x^1 \\ \cdot \\ \cdot \\ \cdot \\ x^n \end{pmatrix} \qquad \text{and} \qquad \mathbf{x} = \mathbf{x}^i\mathbf{u}_i$$

† See, for example, J. T. Schwartz, "Lectures on the Mathematical Method in Analytical Economics," from which we borrow the above considerations.

Similarly,

$$\mathbf{x}'_c = \begin{pmatrix} x'^1 \\ \cdot \\ \cdot \\ \cdot \\ x'^n \end{pmatrix} \qquad \text{and} \qquad \mathbf{x} = x'^i\mathbf{u}'_i$$

In the last equation substitute $\mathbf{u}'_i = p^j{}_i\mathbf{u}_j$ from (7.1). There results $\mathbf{x} = x'^i p^j{}_i\mathbf{u}_j$. The coefficient of $\mathbf{u}_j$ here is then $p^j{}_i x'^i$, and that must be the same as x^j. Thus $x^j = p^j{}_i x'^i$. Similarly, substituting $\mathbf{u}_j = q^k{}_j\mathbf{u}'_k$ into $\mathbf{x} = x^j\mathbf{u}_j$ we get $x'^k = q^k{}_j x^j$. From Definition 6.1 it follows that the two equations just derived can be expressed as matrix products. We have

7.2 $$\mathbf{x}_c = \mathbf{p}\mathbf{x}'_c \qquad \text{and} \qquad \mathbf{x}'_c = \mathbf{q}\mathbf{x}_c$$

[Cf. Eq. (9.6), Chap. 8].

The two matrices $\mathbf{p}$ and $\mathbf{q}$ of (7.1) are very intimately related. For ease of reference we shall call $\mathbf{p}$ the matrix from the base $\{\mathbf{u}_i\}$ to the base $\{\mathbf{u}'_i\}$, and $\mathbf{q}$ the matrix from $\{\mathbf{u}'_i\}$ to $\{\mathbf{u}_i\}$. We shall show that $\mathbf{pq} = \mathbf{qp} = \mathbf{I}_n$ ($n \times n$ unit matrix). In fact, substitute the second equation of (7.1) into the first, getting $\mathbf{u}'_i = p^j{}_i q^k{}_j\mathbf{u}'_k$. Equating coefficients on both sides (Proposition 6.1, Chap. 8), we see that $p^j{}_i q^k{}_j = q^k{}_j p^j{}_i$ must be zero if $k \neq i$ and 1 if $k = i$. Thus

$$q^k{}_j p^j{}_i = \delta^k{}_i = \begin{cases} 1 & \text{if } k = i \\ 0 & \text{if } k \neq i \end{cases}$$

Therefore, by (5.12), (5.13) and the definition of matrix multiplication, we have $\mathbf{qp} = \mathbf{I}_n$. In like manner we can substitute the first equation of (7.1) into the second. To do so we must first change i to k; and j in the first equation must be changed to some other letter, say h, in order to avoid conflict with the j in the second equation. We get $\mathbf{u}_j = q^k{}_j p^h{}_k\mathbf{u}_h$, from which we conclude that $p^h{}_k q^k{}_j = \delta^h{}_j$, just as above. By Definition 6.1, this is precisely the matrix equation $\mathbf{pq} = \mathbf{I}_n$.

Now $\mathbf{I}_n$ is the unit element of the ring $K^n{}_n$ of all $n \times n$ matrices with coefficients in K. From our general definition of inverses (Definition 4.2, Chap. 1) it follows that the matrices $\mathbf{p}$, $\mathbf{q}$ above are *inverses* of each other (i.e., with respect to the product operation). We therefore write $\mathbf{p} = \mathbf{q}^{-1}$ or $\mathbf{q} = \mathbf{p}^{-1}$.

We observe that $\mathbf{p}$ is none other than the matrix, with respect to the base $\{\mathbf{u}_i\}$ of the linear transformation $\mathbf{P}$: $U \to U$ that maps $\mathbf{u}_i$ into $\mathbf{v}_i$ for $i = 1, \ldots, n$. $\mathbf{P}$ is clearly an isomorphism. Thus any change of base in U can be described by an isomorphism from U to itself.

DEFINITION 7.1 *A matrix in* $K^n{}_n$ *is called* nonsingular *if it has an inverse; otherwise it is said to be* singular.

The following proposition shows that any nonsingular matrix can be used to define a change of base.

PROPOSITION 7.1 *Let U be an n-dimensional vector space over K, and let $\mathbf{u}_1, \ldots, \mathbf{u}_n$ be a base for U. If $\mathbf{p} = (p^i{}_i)$ is any nonsingular matrix in $K^n{}_n$, then the n elements $\mathbf{u}'_i = p^j{}_i\mathbf{u}_j$ $(i = 1, \ldots, n)$ form a base for U.*

Proof. If the $\mathbf{u}'_i$ were linearly dependent, then there would be a nonzero column vector $\mathbf{a} = (a^i)$ in K^n such that $a^i\mathbf{u}'_i = 0$. That is, $a^ip^j{}_i\mathbf{u}_j = 0$. From this we conclude that $p^j{}_ia^i = 0$ for $j = 1, \ldots, n$, because of the linear independence of $\mathbf{u}_1, \ldots, \mathbf{u}_n$. By Definition 6.1 we have then $\mathbf{pa} = 0$. By assumption, $\mathbf{p}$ has an inverse matrix $\mathbf{p}^{-1}$. Multiplying the last equation by it we get $\mathbf{p}^{-1}(\mathbf{pa}) = \mathbf{0}$, or $(\mathbf{p}^{-1}\mathbf{p})\mathbf{a} = \mathbf{0}$, or $\mathbf{I}_n\mathbf{a} = \mathbf{0}$, whence $\mathbf{a} = \mathbf{0}$ by (6.5), a contradiction. Q.E.D.

We can now calculate very easily the effect of a change of base on the matrix of a linear transformation.

THEOREM 7.2 *Let $\mathbf{T}$: $U \to V$ be a linear mapping of an n-dimensional vector space over K to an m-dimensional vector space over K. Let $\{\mathbf{u}_i\}$ and $\{\mathbf{u}'_i\}$ be two bases for U, and let $\mathbf{p}$ be the matrix from the former to the latter. Let $\{\mathbf{v}_j\}$ and $\{\mathbf{v}'_j\}$ be two bases for V, and let $\mathbf{q}$ be the matrix from $\{\mathbf{v}_j\}$ to $\{\mathbf{v}'_j\}$. Finally, let $\mathbf{t}$ be the matrix of $\mathbf{T}$ relative to the base pair $\{\mathbf{u}_i\}$, $\{\mathbf{v}_j\}$;* and let $\mathbf{t}'$ *be its matrix relative to the base pair $\{\mathbf{u}'_i\}$, $\{\mathbf{v}'_j\}$. Then*

7.3 $$\mathbf{t}' = \mathbf{q}^{-1}\mathbf{t}\mathbf{p}$$

Proof. By assumption we have $\mathbf{u}'_i = p^j{}_i\mathbf{u}_j$. Therefore $\mathbf{T}(\mathbf{u}'_i) = \mathbf{T}(p^j{}_i\mathbf{u}_j) = p^j{}_i\mathbf{T}(\mathbf{u}_j)$. By definition of $\mathbf{t}$, $\mathbf{T}(\mathbf{u}_j) = t^k{}_j\mathbf{v}_k$, and so we have $\mathbf{T}(\mathbf{u}'_i) = p^j{}_it^k{}_j\mathbf{v}_k$. By definition of $\mathbf{t}'$, $\mathbf{T}(\mathbf{u}'_i) = t'^h{}_i\mathbf{v}'_h$; and $\mathbf{v}'_h = q^k{}_h\mathbf{v}_k$, by definition of $\mathbf{q}$. Hence, $\mathbf{T}(\mathbf{u}'_i) = t'^h{}_iq^k{}_h\mathbf{v}_k$. Comparing the two expressions for $\mathbf{T}(\mathbf{u}'_i)$ we get $p^j{}_it^k{}_j\mathbf{v}_k = t'^h{}_iq^k{}_h\mathbf{v}_k$. The coefficients of $\mathbf{v}_k$ on both sides must be the same, and so† $t^k{}_jp^j{}_i = q^k{}_ht'^h{}_i$. From the definition of matrix multiplication this says that $\mathbf{tp} = \mathbf{qt}'$, from which (7.3) follows by multiplying both sides by $\mathbf{q}^{-1}$ on the left. Q.E.D.

In the special case of an endomorphism $\mathbf{T}$: $U \to U$, if $\mathbf{t}$ is its matrix relative to $\{\mathbf{u}_i\}$ and if $\mathbf{t}'$ is its matrix relative to $\{\mathbf{u}'_i\}$, then (7.3) reduces to

7.4 $$\mathbf{t}' = \mathbf{p}^{-1}\mathbf{t}\mathbf{p}$$

The following theorem shows that it is always possible to choose bases in U and V such that the matrix of a linear mapping $\mathbf{T}$: $U \to V$ is a *diagonal* matrix as defined at the end of Sec. 6.

THEOREM 7.3 *Let $\mathbf{T}$: $U \to V$ be a linear mapping of finite-dimensional vector spaces over a field K, and let $\mathbf{T}$ have rank r. Then there exist bases $\{\mathbf{u}_i\}$ and $\{\mathbf{v}_j\}$ of U and V for which the matrix $\mathbf{t}$ of $\mathbf{T}$ has the following form:*

† As on several earlier occasions we have reversed the order of the factors so that they will appear in the same order as in the matrix equations that follow.

7.5 $$t^i{}_i = 1 \quad \text{for } i = 1, \ldots, r \text{ (no summation on } i\text{)}$$
$$t^j{}_i = 0 \quad \text{otherwise}$$

Conversely, if the matrix $\mathbf{t}$ *has this form, then the mapping* $\mathbf{T}$ *has rank* r.

Proof. Let $n = \dim U$. Then $\dim \operatorname{Ker} \mathbf{T} = n - r$, by Theorem 3.2. Let $\mathbf{u}_{r+1}, \mathbf{u}_{r+2}, \ldots, \mathbf{u}_n$ be a base for Ker $\mathbf{T}$. By Theorem 9.3, Chap. 8, this set can be enlarged to a base for U by adding on r new vectors $\mathbf{u}_1, \mathbf{u}_2, \ldots, \mathbf{u}_r$. Set $\mathbf{v}_j = \mathbf{T}(\mathbf{u}_j)$ for $j = 1, \ldots, r$. Just as in the proof of Theorem 3.2, the vectors $\mathbf{v}_1, \ldots, \mathbf{v}_r$ form a base for Im $\mathbf{T}$. By Theorem 9.3, Chap. 8, again, this set can be enlarged to a base for V by adding on certain number of new elements $\mathbf{v}_{r+1}, \mathbf{v}_{r+2}$, etc. The matrix of $\mathbf{T}$ relative to the base pair $\{\mathbf{u}_i\}$, $\{\mathbf{v}_j\}$ has the form stated in (7.5). The last part of the theorem is trivial. Q.E.D.

Now a linear mapping $\mathbf{T}$ is usually specified by giving its matrix $\mathbf{t}$ relative to some base pair. In order to get its matrix in the form (7.5), it is necessary to change the bases in U and V. That is, it is necessary to choose $\mathbf{p}$ and $\mathbf{q}$ in (7.3) in such a way that $\mathbf{t}'$ has the form (7.5). In Sec. 9 we shall see how to do that effectively. A somewhat different problem arises in the case of endomorphisms, for then it is usual to define the matrix of a mapping in terms of a single base $\{\mathbf{u}_i\}$, rather than a pair of independent bases $\{\mathbf{u}_i\}$, $\{\mathbf{v}_j\}$. Then there is only one base to change in order to simplify the matrix. That is, we have only $\mathbf{p}$ at our disposal in (7.4), rather than both $\mathbf{p}$ and $\mathbf{q}$ in (7.3). It is to be expected that the problem of simplifying the matrix will be more difficult in this situation because of the decreased freedom. The problem is a very important one, and it will be discussed in detail in Chap. 13.

As a complement to Theorem 7.3 we have the following theorem:

THEOREM 7.4 *If the matrix* $\mathbf{t}$ *of a linear mapping* $\mathbf{T}\colon U \to V$ *has the form* (7.5) *relative to a base pair* $\{\mathbf{u}_i\}$, $\{\mathbf{u}_j\}$, *then* $\mathbf{u}_{r+1}, \mathbf{u}_{r+2}, \ldots, \mathbf{u}_n$ *form a base for* Ker $\mathbf{T}$ *and* $\mathbf{T}(\mathbf{u}_1), \ldots, \mathbf{T}(\mathbf{u}_r)$ *form a base for* Im $\mathbf{T}$.

The proof is very straightforward and is similar to that of Theorem 3.2.

EXERCISES

1. Let $\{\mathbf{u}_1, \mathbf{u}_2, \mathbf{u}_3\}$ and $\{\mathbf{v}_1, \mathbf{v}_2\}$ be bases for vector spaces U, V over $\mathbf{Q}$. Let $\mathbf{T}$ be the mapping from U to V defined by $\mathbf{T}(\mathbf{u}_1) = \mathbf{v}_1 + \mathbf{v}_2$, $\mathbf{T}(\mathbf{u}_2) = \mathbf{v}_1 - \mathbf{v}_2$, $\mathbf{T}(\mathbf{u}_3) = 3\mathbf{v}_2$. Let new bases $\{\mathbf{u}'_i\}$ and $\{\mathbf{v}'_j\}$ be defined by $\mathbf{u}'_1 = 2\mathbf{u}_1 - \mathbf{u}_2 + \mathbf{u}_3$, $\mathbf{u}'_2 = \mathbf{u}_1 + \mathbf{u}_2 - \mathbf{u}_3$, $\mathbf{u}'_3 = 2\mathbf{u}_1 - \mathbf{u}_3$ and $\mathbf{v}'_1 = \mathbf{v}_2$, $\mathbf{v}'_2 = \mathbf{v}_1 + \mathbf{v}_2$. Calculate the matrix of $\mathbf{T}$ relative to the new base pair, and verify (7.3).

2. Find new bases for U and V above such that the matrix of $\mathbf{T}$ has the form (7.5).

3. Let $\{\mathbf{u}_1, \mathbf{u}_2, \mathbf{u}_3\}$ be a base for a vector space U over $\mathbf{Q}$, and let $\mathbf{T}$ be the endomorphism defined by $\mathbf{T}(\mathbf{u}_1) = \mathbf{u}_1 + \mathbf{u}_2 + \mathbf{u}_3$, $\mathbf{T}(\mathbf{u}_2) = \mathbf{u}_2 - \mathbf{u}_3$, $\mathbf{T}(\mathbf{u}_3) = \mathbf{u}_1 - \mathbf{u}_3$. Let $\{\mathbf{u}'_i\}$ be the new base defined by $\mathbf{u}'_1 = 2\mathbf{u}_1 - \mathbf{u}_3$, $\mathbf{u}'_2 = \mathbf{u}_1 + \mathbf{u}_2 + 3\mathbf{u}_3$, $\mathbf{u}'_3 = \mathbf{u}_1$. Calculate the matrix of $\mathbf{T}$ relative to the new base, and verify (7.4).

4. Prove that a triangular matrix in $K^n{}_n$ is nonsingular if and only if its diagonal elements are all nonzero. Show that its inverse must also be triangular and show how to calculate it. [Hint: Consider the matrix as defining a change of base in a vector space.]

5. Prove that all nonsingular matrices in $K^n{}_n$ form a group, with matrix multiplication as the group operation. Show that the nonsingular triangular matrices form a subgroup.

6. Let $\{\mathbf{u}_i\}$, $\{\mathbf{v}_i\}$, and $\{\mathbf{w}_i\}$ be three bases in a vector space. Let $\mathbf{p}$ be the matrix from $\{\mathbf{u}_i\}$ to $\{\mathbf{v}_i\}$, and let $\mathbf{q}$ be the matrix from $\{\mathbf{v}_i\}$ to $\{\mathbf{w}_i\}$. Show that $\mathbf{pq}$ is the matrix from $\{\mathbf{u}_i\}$ to $\{\mathbf{w}_i\}$.

8. Rank of a matrix; linear equations; subspaces

K being a field, consider an $m \times n$ matrix $\mathbf{a} = (a^j{}_i)$ with coefficients in K. The columns $\mathbf{a}_1, \mathbf{a}_2, \ldots, \mathbf{a}_n$ of $\mathbf{a}$ are elements of K^m, and they span a certain subspace C of K^m. The dimension of C, that is, the maximum number of linearly independent column vectors in $\mathbf{a}$, is called the *column rank* of $\mathbf{a}$.

Similarly, the rows $\mathbf{a}^1, \mathbf{a}^2, \ldots, \mathbf{a}^m$ are elements of K_n, and they span a certain subspace R of K_n. The number dim R, that is, the maximum number of linearly independent row vectors in $\mathbf{a}$, is called the *row rank* of $\mathbf{a}$.

THEOREM 8.1 *For any matrix* $\mathbf{a}$ *in* $K^m{}_n$*, the row rank and column rank are equal. Their value is called the* rank *of* $\mathbf{a}$.

Proof. Let r be the column rank. By its definition there are r linearly independent columns in $\mathbf{a}$. Let us call them $\mathbf{a}'_1, \ldots, \mathbf{a}'_r$. They span C, and so each column of $\mathbf{a}$ can be expressed as a linear combination of them, say

$$\mathbf{a}_i = \sum_{j=1}^{r} p^j{}_i \mathbf{a}'_j \qquad (i = 1, \ldots, n)$$

Then

$$a^k{}_i = \sum_{j=1}^{r} p^j{}_i a'^k{}_j$$

where $a'^k{}_j$ is the kth element in the column called $\mathbf{a}'_j$. Now $(p^j{}_i)$ is an $r \times n$ matrix, and the last equation, written in terms of rows, is

$$\mathbf{a}^k = \sum_{j=1}^{r} a'^k{}_j \cdot \mathbf{p}^j \qquad (k = 1, \ldots, m)$$

This says that the rows of $\mathbf{a}$ are all in the subspace of K_n spanned by the r vectors $\mathbf{p}^1, \mathbf{p}^2, \ldots, \mathbf{p}^r$. That subspace therefore has dimension $\leq r$ (Theorem 8.1, Chap. 8). Hence we have row rank $\leq$ column rank. By applying the same argument to the transpose ${}^t\mathbf{a}$ of $\mathbf{a}$ we conclude similarly that column rank $\leq$ row rank. Q.E.D.

The next theorem connects the notions of rank of a matrix and rank of a linear mapping.

THEOREM 8.2 *Let* $\mathbf{T}$: $U \to V$ *be a linear mapping of two vector spaces of finite dimension, and let* $\mathbf{t}$ *be its matrix relative to some base pair. Then the rank of* $\mathbf{T}$ *is equal to the rank of* $\mathbf{t}$.

Proof. Let $\mathbf{u}_1, \ldots, \mathbf{u}_n$ and $\mathbf{v}_1, \ldots, \mathbf{v}_m$ be the base pair in question, so that $\mathbf{T}(\mathbf{u}_i) = t^j{}_i\mathbf{v}_j$. Let $c^1, \ldots, c^n$ be n scalars. Then $c^i \cdot \mathbf{T}(\mathbf{u}_i) = c^i t^j{}_i \mathbf{v}_j$, and this is zero if and only if $c^i t^j{}_i = 0$ for $j = 1, \ldots, m$, because of the linear independence of the $\mathbf{v}_j$, and that is so if and only if $c^i\mathbf{t}_i = 0$. Thus $c^1 \cdot \mathbf{T}(\mathbf{u}_1) + \cdots + c^n \cdot \mathbf{T}(\mathbf{u}_n) = 0$ if and only if $c^1\mathbf{t}_1 + \cdots + c^n\mathbf{t}_n = 0$. It follows readily from this that a certain number of the vectors $\mathbf{T}(\mathbf{u}_1), \ldots, \mathbf{T}(\mathbf{u}_n)$ are linearly independent if and only if the column vectors $\mathbf{t}_j$ with the *same* indices are linearly independent. The assertion of the theorem is an immediate consequence. Q.E.D.

THEOREM 8.3 *A matrix* $\mathbf{a}$ *in* $K^n{}_n$ *is nonsingular if and only if it has rank* n, *and that is so if and only if the mapping of* K^n *to itself that sends an arbitrary vector* $\mathbf{x}$ *into* $\mathbf{ax}$ *is an isomorphism.*

Proof. By Proposition 6.2 the mapping $\mathbf{A}$: $K^n \to K^n$ defined by $\mathbf{A}(\mathbf{x}) = \mathbf{ax}$ is a linear mapping whose matrix relative to the canonical base is $\mathbf{a}$. If $\mathbf{a}$ is nonsingular, let $\mathbf{b}$ be its inverse matrix, and let $\mathbf{B}$ be the mapping of K^n defined by $\mathbf{B}(\mathbf{x}) = \mathbf{bx}$. The mapping $\mathbf{AB}$ has matrix $\mathbf{ab} = \mathbf{I}_n$ (relative to the canonical base) and is therefore the identity mapping. Hence $\mathbf{A}$ must be one-to-one. Its rank is therefore n, and by the theorem above, n is also the rank of $\mathbf{a}$.

Conversely, if $\mathbf{a}$ has rank n, then so does $\mathbf{A}$. Hence $\mathbf{A}$ is an isomorphism, by Theorem 3.2 and its corollary. Let $\mathbf{A}^{-1}$ be its inverse mapping, and let $\mathbf{b}$ be the matrix of $\mathbf{A}^{-1}$ (relative to the canonical base).

Then the matrix of $\mathbf{AA}^{-1} = \mathbf{I}$ is $\mathbf{ab}$, which must accordingly be the unit matrix. Similarly, the matrix of $\mathbf{A}^{-1}\mathbf{A} = \mathbf{I}$ is $\mathbf{ba}$, whence also $\mathbf{ba} = \mathbf{I}_n$. Q.E.D.

Let $\mathbf{a}$ be any matrix. By a *submatrix* of $\mathbf{a}$ is meant any of the matrices that are obtained by striking out given rows or columns of $\mathbf{a}$.

COROLLARY *Let* $\mathbf{a}$ *be an* $m \times n$ *matrix with coefficients in* K, *and let* r *be its rank. Then* r *is equal to the size of the largest nonsingular square submatrix of* $\mathbf{a}$.

Proof. By assumption, some r rows of $\mathbf{a}$ are linearly independent. Fixing some such set of r rows, let $\mathbf{a}'$ be the $r \times n$ submatrix obtained by striking out the other $m - r$ rows of $\mathbf{a}$. The matrix $\mathbf{a}'$ has r linearly independent rows, and therefore r of its columns are linearly independent, by Theorem 8.1. Fixing such a set of r columns, let $\mathbf{a}''$ be the submatrix of $\mathbf{a}'$ obtained by striking out the other $n - r$ columns. Then $\mathbf{a}''$ clearly has rank r, and it is an $r \times r$ submatrix of $\mathbf{a}$; $\mathbf{a}''$ is nonsingular, by the preceding theorem. Conversely, if $\mathbf{b}$ is an $s \times s$ nonsingular submatrix of $\mathbf{a}$, then the rows of $\mathbf{b}$ are linearly independent, by the theorem above. The corresponding rows of $\mathbf{a}$ must be linearly independent, *a fortiori*, showing that $\mathbf{a}$ has rank $\geq s$. That is, $r \geq s$. Q.E.D.

REMARK. The inverse of a nonsingular matrix is unique, by Theorem 4.3, Chap. 1. But we can prove a stronger result. If $\mathbf{a}$ and $\mathbf{b}$ are elements of $K^n{}_n$, and if $\mathbf{ab} = \mathbf{I}_n$, then $\mathbf{a}$ and $\mathbf{b}$ are inverses of each other. In fact, this follows at once from the first part of the proof above. For then $\mathbf{AB} = \mathbf{I}$; hence also $\mathbf{BA} = \mathbf{I}$, obviously. The matrix of $\mathbf{BA}$ is $\mathbf{ba}$, and so $\mathbf{ba} = \mathbf{I}_n$.

THEOREM 8.4 *Let* $\mathbf{a}$ *be an element of* $K^m{}_n$. *Then the set of vectors* $\mathbf{x}$ in K^n *such that* $\mathbf{ax} = 0$ *is a subspace of dimension* $n - r$, *where* r *is the rank of* $\mathbf{a}$. *The set of all vectors* $\mathbf{ax}$ ($\mathbf{x}$ *arbitrary in* K^n) *is a subspace of* K^m *of dimension* r.

Proof. Let $\mathbf{A}$: $K^n \to K^m$ be the mapping defined by $\mathbf{A}(\mathbf{x}) = \mathbf{ax}$ (Proposition 6.2). Then the rank of $\mathbf{A}$ ($=$ dim Im $\mathbf{A}$) is r, by Theorem 8.2. The nullity of $\mathbf{A}$ ($=$ dim Ker $\mathbf{A}$) is $n - r$, by Theorem 3.2. Q.E.D.

From these theorems we can easily deduce the so-called *fundamental theorem on linear equations*. First of all, a system of linear equations

8.1
$$\begin{aligned} a^1{}_1x^1 + \cdots + a^1{}_nx^n &= y^1 \\ a^2{}_1x^1 + \cdots + a^2{}_nx^n &= y^2 \\ \cdots\cdots\cdots\cdots\cdots&\cdots \\ a^m{}_1x^1 + \cdots + a^m{}_nx^n &= y^m \end{aligned}$$

with coefficients in a field K is the same as the matrix equation

8.2 $$\mathbf{ax} = \mathbf{y}$$

where $\mathbf{a}$ is the $m \times n$ matrix $(a^i{}_j)$ and where $\mathbf{x}$ and $\mathbf{y}$ are the column vectors (x^i) and (y^i) in K^n and K^m, respectively. Equations (8.1) and (8.2) are also the same as the vector equation

8.3 $$x^1\mathbf{a}_1 + \cdots + x^n\mathbf{a}_n = \mathbf{y}$$

where, as usual, $\mathbf{a}_j$ denotes the jth column of $\mathbf{a}$. It is plain that two elements $\mathbf{x}$ and $\mathbf{x}'$ of K^n are solutions of (8.2) only if $\mathbf{a}(\mathbf{x} - \mathbf{x}') = 0$, that is, if and only if $\mathbf{x} - \mathbf{x}'$ is in the kernel of the linear mapping $\mathbf{A}$: $K^n \to K^m$ determined by $\mathbf{a}$ as in Proposition 6.2. Therefore all solutions of (8.2) [or (8.1), (8.3)] are obtained from any one of them by adding to it any vector $\mathbf{z}$ such that $\mathbf{az} = 0$. The solution of (8.2), if one exists, is unique if and only if Ker $\mathbf{A} = \mathbf{0}$, which is so if and only if $\mathbf{a}$ has rank $\mathbf{n}$, by Theorem 8.4.

From (8.3) it is clear that, for given $\mathbf{y}$, a solution $\mathbf{x}$ exists if and only if $\mathbf{y}$ is in the subspace C of K^m spanned by the columns of $\mathbf{a}$. If $\mathbf{a}$ has rank r, then, by definition, C has dimension r; and some r of the columns of $\mathbf{a}$ form a base for C. For simplicity of notation, suppose that $\mathbf{a}_1, \mathbf{a}_2, \ldots, \mathbf{a}_r$ are linearly independent. Rewrite (8.3) as

8.4 $$x^1\mathbf{a}_1 + \cdots + x^r\mathbf{a}_r = \mathbf{y} - (x^{r+1}\mathbf{a}_{r+1} + \cdots + x^n\mathbf{a}_n)$$

Since $\mathbf{a}_{r+1}, \ldots, \mathbf{a}_n$ are in the subspace C of K^m spanned by $\mathbf{a}_1, \ldots, \mathbf{a}_r$, it follows that the right-hand side of this equation is in C if and only if $\mathbf{y}$ is in C. If that is so, then for arbitrarily given elements $x^{r+1}, \ldots, x^n$ in K there are elements $x^1, \ldots, x^r$ in K for which (8.4) holds. The latter set is uniquely determined, because $\mathbf{a}_1, \ldots, \mathbf{a}_r$ form a base for C. We have proved

THEOREM 8.5 *Let r be the rank of the matrix $\mathbf{a}$ of the system* (8.1). *Then the system has a solution $\mathbf{x}$ for given $\mathbf{y}$ if and only if $\mathbf{y}$ is in the r-dimensional subspace of K^m spanned by the columns of $\mathbf{a}$. If that is so, then some $n - r$ of the x^i can be prescribed arbitrarily in K, and the remaining unknowns are then uniquely determined. All solutions of* (8.1) *are obtained from any one of them by adding to it an arbitrary vector $\mathbf{z}$ such that $\mathbf{az} = \mathbf{0}$.*

In Sec. 9 we shall develop an efficient method for solving systems of the type (8.1).

THEOREM 8.6 *Let $\mathbf{w}^1, \mathbf{w}^2, \ldots, \mathbf{w}^s$ be vectors in K_n, and let V be the set of all vectors $\mathbf{x}$ in K^n such that*† $\mathbf{w}^j\mathbf{x} = 0$ *for $j = 1, \ldots, s$. Then V is an $(n - r)$-dimensional subspace of K^n, where r is the rank of the matrix $\mathbf{w}$ whose rows are $\mathbf{w}^1, \ldots, \mathbf{w}^s$. Conversely, if V' is a q-dimensional subspace of K^n, then there exist $n - q$ linearly independent vectors $\mathbf{y}^1, \ldots, \mathbf{y}^{n-q}$ in K_n such that V' consists of all $\mathbf{x}$ for which* $\mathbf{y}^j\mathbf{x} = 0$ $(j = 1, \ldots, n - q)$.

Proof. Clearly the equations $\mathbf{w}^1\mathbf{x} = 0, \ldots, \mathbf{w}^s\mathbf{x} = 0$ are equivalent to the matrix equation $\mathbf{wx} = \mathbf{0}$, where $\mathbf{w}$ is the $s \times n$ matrix whose rows are $\mathbf{w}^1, \ldots, \mathbf{w}^s$. Hence V consists of all $\mathbf{x}$ such that $\mathbf{wx} = \mathbf{0}$, and therefore V is an $(n - r)$-dimensional subspace of K^n, by Theorem 8.4. To prove the remainder of the theorem, let $\mathbf{u}_1, \ldots, \mathbf{u}_q$ be a base for V'. By the argument just given, all vectors $\mathbf{y}$ in K_n such that $\mathbf{yu}_1 = 0, \ldots, \mathbf{yu}_q = 0$ form an $(n - q)$-dimensional subspace W' of K_n. If $\mathbf{y}^1, \ldots, \mathbf{y}^{n-q}$ is any base for W', then those vectors will have the properties stated, by what has already been shown. Q.E.D.

COROLLARY *Let U be an n-dimensional vector space over K, and let $\mathbf{u}_1, \ldots, \mathbf{u}_n$ be a base for U. Let $\mathbf{w}^1, \ldots, \mathbf{w}^{n-q}$ be linearly independent vectors in K_n. Then the set of all elements $\mathbf{x}$ in U whose component vectors $\mathbf{x}_c$ relative to the base $\{\mathbf{u}_i\}$ satisfy $\mathbf{w}^1\mathbf{x}_c = 0, \ldots, \mathbf{w}^{n-q}\mathbf{x}_c = 0$ form a q-dimensional subspace of U. Moreover, every q-dimensional subspace is obtained in this way by a suitable choice of $\mathbf{w}^1, \ldots, \mathbf{w}^{n-q}$.*

† $\mathbf{w}^j\mathbf{x}$ is a scalar. Cf. Eq. (6.6).

This follows at once from the theorem above and from the fact that the component mapping $\mathbf{x} \to \mathbf{x}_c$ is an isomorphism from U to K^n (Theorem 9.2, Chap. 8).

In particular, an $(n-1)$-dimensional subspace V of U is obtained by selecting a nonzero vector $\mathbf{w}$ in K_n. The corresponding V then consists of all $\mathbf{x}$ in U such that $\mathbf{w}\mathbf{x}_c = 0$, that is, such that

$$w_1x^1 + \cdot \cdot \cdot + w_nx^n = 0$$

This way of determining $(n-1)$-dimensional subspaces has already been used in connection with (10.15) of Chap. 8. A proof of the corollary is implicit in Exercise 5, Sec. 10, Chap. 8.

As an application of Theorem 8.6 we give a criterion for the solvability of (8.1).

THEOREM 8.7 *The system* (8.1) *has a solution if and only if* $\mathbf{zy} = 0$ *for every vector* $\mathbf{z}$ *in* K_m *such that* $\mathbf{za} = 0$.

Proof. If a solution $\mathbf{x}$ exists, and if $\mathbf{za} = \mathbf{0}$, then $\mathbf{zy} = \mathbf{z}(\mathbf{ax}) = (\mathbf{za})\mathbf{x} = 0$, whence the necessity of our condition. Recall that $\mathbf{ax} = \mathbf{y}$ has a solution if and only if $\mathbf{y}$ is in the r-dimensional subspace C of K^m spanned by the columns of $\mathbf{a}$. Now all vectors $\mathbf{z}$ in K_m such that $\mathbf{za} = \mathbf{0}$ form an $(m-r)$-dimensional subspace W of K_m, by Theorem 8.4. Let $\mathbf{w}^1, \ldots, \mathbf{w}^{m-r}$ be a base for W. Then it is clear that $\mathbf{zy} = 0$ for all $\mathbf{z}$ in W if and only if $\mathbf{w}^1\mathbf{y} = 0, \ldots, \mathbf{w}^{m-r}\mathbf{y} = 0$. But all $\mathbf{y}$ in K^m satisfying these last equations form an r-dimensional subspace of K^m, by Theorem 8.6, and, as pointed out above, that subspace must contain C, hence must coincide with C because they both have dimension r. Q.E.D.

EXERCISES

1. Fill in the details of the last part of the proof of Theorem 8.2.

2. Do the same for Theorem 8.7.

3. Prove that a matrix $\mathbf{a}$ in $K^n{}_n$ is singular if and only if there is a nonzero element $\mathbf{x}$ in K^n such that $\mathbf{ax} = 0$.

4. Let $\mathbf{a}$ be a matrix of rank r in $K^m{}_n$. Show that it is possible to strike out $n - r$ columns and $m - r$ rows in $\mathbf{a}$ in such a way that the remaining $r \times r$ matrix is nonsingular.

5. What is the form of an $n \times n$ matrix of rank 1?

6. Prove that an $n \times n$ matrix of rank r is the sum of r $n \times n$ matrices of rank 1.

9. Reduction to diagonal form

Let $\{\mathbf{u}_1, \ldots, \mathbf{u}_n\}$ and $\{\mathbf{v}_1, \ldots, \mathbf{v}_m\}$ be bases for vector spaces U and V over a field K, and let $\mathbf{a}$ be the matrix of a linear mapping $\mathbf{T}$: $U \to V$ relative to that base pair, so that $\mathbf{T}(\mathbf{u}_i) = a^j{}_i\mathbf{v}_j$. We shall now describe a procedure for finding new bases for U and V for which the matrix of $\mathbf{T}$ has the diagonal form (7.5). This will be accomplished by a series of simple base changes of three different types.

It will be convenient to denote bases by single letters, and we shall start off by writing A for $\{\mathbf{u}_i\}$ and B for $\{\mathbf{v}_j\}$. We say then that $\mathbf{a}$ is the matrix of $\mathbf{T}$ relative to (A, B).

The first type of base change that we consider consists simply of renumbering the elements in a base. For example, let $A' = \{\mathbf{u}'_1, \ldots, \mathbf{u}'_n\}$ denote the base for U defined as follows: $\mathbf{u}'_1 = \mathbf{u}_2$, $\mathbf{u}'_2 = \mathbf{u}_1$, $\mathbf{u}'_3 = \mathbf{u}_3, \ldots, \mathbf{u}'_n = \mathbf{u}_n$. That is, A' is obtained from A by reversing the numbering of $\mathbf{u}_1$ and $\mathbf{u}_2$. If $\mathbf{a}'$ denotes the matrix of $\mathbf{T}$ relative to (A', B), then $\mathbf{T}(\mathbf{u}'_1) = a'^j{}_1\mathbf{v}_j$. But $\mathbf{T}(\mathbf{u}'_1) = \mathbf{T}(\mathbf{u}_2) = a^j{}_2\mathbf{v}_j$. Hence, the column $\mathbf{a}'_1$ of $\mathbf{a}'$ is equal to the column $\mathbf{a}_2$ of $\mathbf{a}$. Similarly, $\mathbf{a}'_2 = \mathbf{a}_1$; and all the other columns in $\mathbf{a}'$ are the same as in $\mathbf{a}$. In general, it is easy to see that renumbering the base elements in U results in a permutation of the corresponding columns in the matrix $\mathbf{a}$. Similarly, renumbering the base elements in V is equivalent to a permutation of the corresponding rows of $\mathbf{a}$. We shall often use this observation in what follows in order to move elements in a matrix to more desirable locations.

Now take up the second type of base change which we require. Let $B_1 = \{\mathbf{v}'_j\}$ be the new base for V defined as follows:

9.1
$$\begin{aligned} \mathbf{v}'_j &= \mathbf{v}_j \qquad \text{if } j \neq k \qquad (k = \text{some fixed index}) \\ \mathbf{v}'_k &= \mathbf{v}_k + y^1\mathbf{v}_1 + \cdots + y^{k-1}\mathbf{v}_{k-1} + y^{k+1}\mathbf{v}_{k+1} + \cdots + y^m\mathbf{v}_m \end{aligned}$$

Here only the kth base element has been changed. Of course $y^1, \ldots, y^{k-1}, y^{k+1}, \ldots, y^m$ denote arbitrarily selected scalars. We must first ascertain that (9.1) really defines a change of base. But that is trivial, for (9.1) is clearly equivalent to

9.2
$$\begin{aligned} \mathbf{v}_j &= \mathbf{v}'_j \qquad \text{if } j \neq k \\ \mathbf{v}_k &= \mathbf{v}'_k - (y^1\mathbf{v}'_1 + \cdots + y^{k-1}\mathbf{v}'_{k-1} + y^{k+1}\mathbf{v}'_{k+1} + \cdots + y^m\mathbf{v}'_m) \end{aligned}$$

which shows that the $\mathbf{v}_j$ can be expressed in terms of the $\mathbf{v}'_j$. Hence the latter must span V. The matrix from $\{\mathbf{v}_j\}$ to $\{\mathbf{v}'_j\}$ is

9.3 $$(\mathbf{e}_1, \ldots, \mathbf{e}_{k-1}, \mathbf{y}, \mathbf{e}_{k+1}, \ldots, \mathbf{e}_m)$$

where the $\mathbf{e}_j$ are columns of $\mathbf{I}_m$ and where $\mathbf{y}$ is the column vector whose elements are $y^1, \ldots, y^{k-1}, 1, y^{k+1}, \ldots, y^m$. The matrix from $\{\mathbf{v}'_j\}$ to $\{\mathbf{v}_j\}$, that is, from B_1 to B, is

9.4 $$(\mathbf{e}_1, \ldots, \mathbf{e}_{k-1}, \mathbf{y}^*, \mathbf{e}_{k+1}, \ldots, \mathbf{e}_m)$$

where $\mathbf{y}^*$ denotes the column vector whose elements are $-y^1, \ldots, -y^{k-1}, 1, -y^{k+1}, \ldots, -y^m$. It is easily seen that (9.3) and (9.4) are inverse matrices.

Let us calculate the matrix of $\mathbf{T}$ relative to (A, B_1). Substituting from (9.2) in $\mathbf{T}(\mathbf{u}_i) = a^j{}_i\mathbf{v}_j$ we get

$$\begin{aligned} \mathbf{T}(\mathbf{u}_i) = a^1{}_i\mathbf{v}'_1 + \cdots + a_i^{k-1}\mathbf{v}'_{k-1} + a^k{}_i(\mathbf{v}'_k - y^1\mathbf{v}'_1 - \cdots - y^{k-1}\mathbf{v}'_{k-1} \\ - y^{k+1}\mathbf{v}'_{k+1} - \cdots - y^m\mathbf{v}'_m) + a_i^{k+1}\mathbf{v}'_{k+1} + \cdots + a^m{}_i\mathbf{v}'_m \end{aligned}$$

and so

$$\mathbf{T}(\mathbf{u}_i) = (a^1{}_i - y^1 a^k{}_i)\mathbf{v}'_1 + \cdots + (a^{k-1}_i - y^{k-1}a^k{}_i)\mathbf{v}'_{k-1} + a^k{}_i\mathbf{v}'_k$$
$$+ (a^{k+1}_i - y^{k+1}a^k{}_i)\mathbf{v}'_{k+1} + \cdots + (a^m{}_i - y^m a^k{}_i)\mathbf{v}'_m$$

Denoting the matrix of $\mathbf{T}$ relative to (A, B_1) by $\mathbf{b}$, we have the equation

$$b^j{}_i = a^j{}_i - y^j a^k{}_i \qquad (j \neq k)$$
$$b^k{}_i = a^k{}_i$$

Hence, for the rows of $\mathbf{b}$, we have

$$\mathbf{b}^j = \mathbf{a}^j - y^j \mathbf{a}^k \qquad (j \neq k)$$
$$\mathbf{b}^k = \mathbf{a}^k$$

We can therefore state the following rule:

(I) *For a change of base in V of the form* (9.1), *the new matrix of* $\mathbf{T}$ *is obtained from the old one by subtracting y^j times row k from row j $(j \neq k)$, leaving row k unaltered.*

Such an operation on a matrix is called an *elementary row operation.*

REMARK. The matrix (9.4) is obtained from $\mathbf{I}_m$ by the operation of rule (I).

In the applications which we shall make of the rule above, the elements y^j will be chosen as follows: Suppose that the element $a^k{}_k$ (no summation here!) is not zero and put

9.5
$$\mathbf{v}'_j = \mathbf{v}_j \qquad (j \neq k)$$
$$\mathbf{v}'_k = (1/a^k{}_k) \cdot \mathbf{T}(\mathbf{u}_k)$$

That is,

$$\mathbf{v}'_k = (a^1{}_k/a^k{}_k)\mathbf{v}_1 + \cdots + (a^{k-1}_k/a^k{}_k)\mathbf{v}_{k-1}$$
$$+ \mathbf{v}_k + (a^{k+1}_k/a^k{}_k)\mathbf{v}_{k+1} + \cdots + (a^m{}_k/a^k{}_k)\mathbf{v}_m$$

Here we have taken $y_j = a^j{}_k/a^k{}_k$. For this special case, rule (I) becomes

(I′) *For a change of base in V of the form* (9.5), *the new matrix of* $\mathbf{T}$ *is obtained from the old one by subtracting $a^j{}_k/a^k{}_k$ times row k from row j $(j \neq k)$, leaving row k unaltered.*

It is clear that in the new matrix all the elements in column k will be zero except the one in the (k, k) place, which will still be $a^k{}_k$. By repeated operations of this sort we shall obtain a base for V such that the matrix of $\mathbf{T}$ has as many zero coefficients as possible.

We now take up the question of operations on the columns of a matrix. The operations will be of the same sort as those just discussed, but they correspond to a somewhat different kind of base change—this time in U, rather than V.

Starting with a base pair $A = \{\mathbf{u}_i\}$ and $B = \{\mathbf{v}_j\}$, again let $\mathbf{a}$ be the corresponding matrix of $\mathbf{T}: U \to V$. Define a new base $A_1 = \{\mathbf{u}'_i\}$ in U by

9.6
$$\begin{aligned} \mathbf{u}'_k &= \mathbf{u}_k & &(k \textit{ fixed}) \\ \mathbf{u}'_i &= \mathbf{u}_i - x_i\mathbf{u}_k & &(i \neq k) \end{aligned}$$

where $x_1, \ldots, x_{k-1}, x_{k+1}, \ldots, x_n$ are arbitrarily given scalars. The equations of (9.6) are equivalent to

9.7
$$\begin{aligned} \mathbf{u}_k &= \mathbf{u}'_k \\ \mathbf{u}_i &= \mathbf{u}'_i + x_i\mathbf{u}'_k & &(i \neq k) \end{aligned}$$

showing that $\{\mathbf{u}'_k\}$ must span U and is consequently a base for U. From (9.6) the matrix from $\{\mathbf{u}_i\}$ to $\{\mathbf{u}'_i\}$ is

9.8
$$\begin{pmatrix} \mathbf{e}^1 \\ \cdot \\ \cdot \\ \cdot \\ \mathbf{e}^{k-1} \\ \mathbf{x}^* \\ \mathbf{e}^{k+1} \\ \cdot \\ \cdot \\ \cdot \\ \mathbf{e}^n \end{pmatrix}$$

where the $\mathbf{e}^j$ are rows of $\mathbf{I}_n$, and where $\mathbf{x}^* = (-x_1, \ldots, -x_{k-1}, 1, -x_{k+1}, \ldots, -x_n)$. From (9.7) the matrix from $\{\mathbf{u}'_i\}$ to $\{\mathbf{u}_i\}$ is

9.9
$$\begin{pmatrix} \mathbf{e}^1 \\ \cdot \\ \cdot \\ \cdot \\ \mathbf{e}^{k-1} \\ \mathbf{x} \\ \mathbf{e}^{k+1} \\ \cdot \\ \cdot \\ \cdot \\ \mathbf{e}^n \end{pmatrix}$$

where $\mathbf{x} = (x_1, \ldots, x_{k-1}, 1, x_{k+1}, \ldots, x_n)$. The transposes of these matrices are of the same type as (9.3) and (9.4). It is easily verified that (9.8) and (9.9) are inverse matrices.

Now let us compute the matrix of $\mathbf{T}$ relative to (A_1, B). From (9.6) we get

$$\mathbf{T}(\mathbf{u}'_k) = \mathbf{T}(\mathbf{u}_k) = a^j{}_k\mathbf{v}_j$$

and, for $i \neq k$,

$$\begin{aligned}\mathbf{T}(\mathbf{u}'_i) &= \mathbf{T}(\mathbf{u}_i - x_i\mathbf{u}_k)\\ &= \mathbf{T}(\mathbf{u}_i) - x_i\mathbf{T}(\mathbf{u}_k)\\ &= a^j{}_i\mathbf{v}_j - x_i a^j{}_k\mathbf{v}_j\end{aligned}$$

Letting **c** denote the matrix of **T** relative to (A_1, B), we have for the columns of **c**

$$\mathbf{c}_k = \mathbf{a}_k, \ \mathbf{c}_i = \mathbf{a}_i - x_i\mathbf{a}_k \qquad \text{for } i \neq k$$

We can state the following rule:

(II) *For a base change of the form* (9.6) *in* U, *the new matrix for* **T** *is obtained from the old one by subtracting* x_i *times column* k *from column* i ($i \neq k$), *leaving column* k *unaltered.*

Such an operation on a matrix is called an *elementary column operation.*

REMARK. The matrix (9.8) is obtained from the identity matrix $\mathbf{I}_n$ by the operation of rule (II).

In our applications of rule (II) we shall choose the scalars x_i as follows: Suppose that the element $a^k{}_k$ (no sum here) is not zero, and put $x_i = a^k{}_i/a^k{}_k$. That is, we take for (9.6) the equations

9.10
$$\begin{aligned}\mathbf{u}'_k &= \mathbf{u}_k && (k \text{ fixed})\\ \mathbf{u}'_i &= \mathbf{u}_i - (a^k{}_i/a^k{}_k)\mathbf{u}_k && (i \neq k)\end{aligned}$$

For this special choice rule (II) becomes rule (II′) as follows:

(II′) *For a change of base in* U *of the form* (9.10), *the new matrix of* **T** *is obtained from the old one by subtracting* $a^k{}_i/a^k{}_k$ *times column* k *from column* i ($i \neq k$), *leaving column* k *unaltered.*

In the resulting matrix all elements in the kth row will be zero except the element in the (k, k) place, which will still be $a^k{}_k$.

Now let us apply these operations to the matrix **a** of **T** relative to the base pair (A, B) in order to reduce it to a more agreeable form. We start with elementary row operations, that is, rule (I′). Let r denote the rank of **T**, hence also the rank of **a**, by Theorem 8.2. If $r = 0$, then $\mathbf{a} = 0$, and there is little more to be said. We suppose then that $r > 0$. At least one element of **a** must be different from zero; and by suitably renumbering the base elements—that is, by making a suitable permutation of rows and columns—we can get a nonzero element into the (1, 1) location. Thus we can assume that $a^1{}_1 \neq 0$.

We make a base change of the form (9.5), taking $k = 1$:

$$\begin{aligned}\mathbf{v}'_j &= \mathbf{v}_j && (j \neq 1)\\ \mathbf{v}_1 &= (1/a^1{}_1) \cdot \mathbf{T}(\mathbf{u}_1)\end{aligned}$$

Calling this new base B_1, it follows from rule (I′) that the matrix **b** of **T** relative to (A, B_1) has the form

$$\mathbf{b} = \begin{pmatrix} b^1{}_1 & * & \cdot & \cdot & \cdot & \cdot & * \\ 0 & * & \cdot & \cdot & \cdot & \cdot & * \\ \cdot & \cdot & \cdot & \cdot & \cdot & \cdot & \cdot \\ 0 & * & \cdot & \cdot & \cdot & \cdot & * \end{pmatrix} \qquad (b^1{}_1 = a^1{}_1)$$

where the $*$'s denote the elements obtained from **a** by (I′). By Theorem 8.2, **b** must have rank r. If $r = 1$, then all the rows below the first one must be zero. For they must be multiples of the first row, and the only multiple of $\mathbf{b}^1$ that has zero in the first entry is $0 \cdot \mathbf{b}^1 = \mathbf{0}$, since $b^1{}_1 \neq 0$.

If $r > 1$, then we can repeat the process. For there must be a nonzero element below the first row of **b**, and by suitably renumbering the base elements $\mathbf{u}_2, \ldots, \mathbf{u}_n$ and $\mathbf{v}'_2, \ldots, \mathbf{v}'_m$, if necessary (not $\mathbf{u}_1$ or $\mathbf{v}'_1$), we can put a nonzero element in the (2, 2) location without disturbing the first column. Therefore, if $r > 1$, we can assume that $b^2{}_2 \neq 0$. We now choose a new base $B_2 = \{\mathbf{v}''_j\}$ in V by setting

$$\begin{aligned} \mathbf{v}''_j &= \mathbf{v}'_j \qquad (j \neq 2) \\ \mathbf{v}''_2 &= (1/b^2{}_2) \cdot \mathbf{T}(\mathbf{u}_2) \end{aligned}$$

From (I′) it follows that the matrix of **T** relative to (A, B_2), call it **c**, has the form

$$\mathbf{c} = \begin{pmatrix} c^1{}_1 & 0 & * & \cdot & \cdot & \cdot & \cdot & * \\ 0 & c^2{}_2 & * & \cdot & \cdot & \cdot & \cdot & * \\ 0 & 0 & * & \cdot & \cdot & \cdot & \cdot & * \\ \cdot & \cdot & \cdot & \cdot & \cdot & \cdot & \cdot & \cdot \\ 0 & 0 & * & \cdot & \cdot & \cdot & \cdot & * \end{pmatrix}$$

where $c^1{}_1 = b^1{}_1$ and $c^2{}_2 = b^2{}_2$, whence $c^1{}_1$ and $c^2{}_2$ are not zero. Again the $*$'s indicate elements which we do not need to know explicitly.

The rank of **c** is the same as the rank of **T**, therefore is equal to r. If $r = 2$, then every row below the second in **c** must be zero. For the first two rows, $\mathbf{c}^1$ and $\mathbf{c}^2$ of **c** are obviously linearly independent. If the rank is 2, then all the other rows can be expressed as linear combinations $x\mathbf{c}^1 + y\mathbf{c}^2$ of the first two. But $x\mathbf{c}^1 + y\mathbf{c}^2$ cannot have zero in the first two places, as required, unless $x = y = 0$.

If $r > 2$, then there are nonzero elements below the second row of **c**, and we can assume that $c^3{}_3 \neq 0$. The process can be repeated again, resulting in a new matrix for **T** in which the first two columns are the same as above, the third column having all zeros except for $c^3{}_3$. If $r = 3$, then all the rows in this new matrix below the third must be zero. If $r > 3$, we can continue the process, arriving finally at a matrix for **T** of the following form:

9.11
$$\begin{pmatrix} p_1 & 0 & \cdots & 0 & * & \cdots & * \\ 0 & p_2 & \cdots & 0 & * & \cdots & * \\ \cdot & \cdot & \cdot & \cdot & \cdot & \cdot & \cdot \\ 0 & 0 & \cdots & p_r & * & \cdots & * \\ 0 & 0 & \cdots & 0 & 0 & \cdots & 0 \\ \cdot & \cdot & \cdot & \cdot & \cdot & \cdot & \cdot \\ 0 & 0 & \cdots & 0 & 0 & \cdots & 0 \end{pmatrix}$$

with an $r \times r$ diagonal matrix in the upper left-hand corner, the elements p_1, $p_2, \ldots, p_r$ being nonzero, and with all rows below the rth equal to zero. The matrix (9.11) is of the kind that we have earlier called *triangular*.

By means of some further base changes the elements indicated by $*$ can be made zero. Let us now define a new base $A_1 = \{\mathbf{u}_i\}$ in U by

$$\begin{aligned} \mathbf{u}_1' &= \mathbf{u}_1 \\ \mathbf{u}_i' &= \mathbf{u}_i - (p^1{}_i/p^1{}_1)\mathbf{u}_1 \qquad (i \neq 1) \end{aligned}$$

where $p^j{}_i$ denotes the (j, i) element of (9.11) (except that $p^1{}_1, \ldots, p^r{}_r$ will be written also as $p_1, \ldots, p_r$). If B^* denotes the final base obtained above for V, so that (9.11) is the matrix of $\mathbf{T}$ relative to (A, B^*), then from rule (II′) it follows that the matrix of $\mathbf{T}$ relative to (A_1, B^*) is the same as (9.11) except that the elements in its top row, other than p_1, are all zero.

We can repeat the same process in the second row by defining the new base $A_2 = \{\mathbf{u}_i''\}$ in U by

$$\begin{aligned} \mathbf{u}_2'' &= \mathbf{u}_2 \\ \mathbf{u}_i'' &= \mathbf{u}_i' - (p^2{}_i/p^2{}_2) \cdot \mathbf{u}_2' \qquad (i \neq 2) \end{aligned}$$

By (II′), the matrix of $\mathbf{T}$ relative to (A_2, B^*) is the same as the matrix of $\mathbf{T}$ relative to (A_1, B^*), save that all the elements in its second row, other than p_2, are zero.

Repeating this same process for rows $3, \ldots, r$, we arrive finally at a base A^* for U such that the matrix of $\mathbf{T}$ relative to (A^*, B^*) has the diagonal form

9.12
$$\begin{pmatrix} p_1 & 0 & \cdots & 0 & \cdots & 0 \\ 0 & p_2 & \cdots & 0 & \cdots & 0 \\ \cdot & \cdot & \cdots & \cdot & \cdots & \cdot \\ 0 & 0 & \cdots & p_r & \cdots & 0 \\ 0 & 0 & \cdots & 0 & \cdots & 0 \\ \cdot & \cdot & \cdots & \cdot & \cdots & \cdot \\ 0 & 0 & \cdots & 0 & \cdots & 0 \end{pmatrix}$$

As a last step we can replace the p_j by 1 by one further trivial base change. Namely, if $A^* = \{\mathbf{u}_i^*\}$ and $B_j^* = \{\mathbf{v}_j^*\}$, then (9.12) tells us that

$$\begin{aligned} \mathbf{T}(\mathbf{u}_i^*) &= p_i \cdot \mathbf{v}_i^* \qquad (i = 1, \ldots, r) \\ \mathbf{T}(\mathbf{u}_i^*) &= 0 \qquad (i > r) \end{aligned}$$

If $B^{**} = \{\mathbf{v}_j^{**}\}$ is defined by

$$\begin{aligned} \mathbf{v}_j^{**} &= p_j \mathbf{v}_j^* \qquad (j = 1, \ldots, r) \\ \mathbf{v}_j^{**} &= \mathbf{v}_j^* \qquad (j > r) \end{aligned}$$

then the matrix of $\mathbf{T}$ relative to (A^*, B^{**}) consists of the $r \times r$ unit matrix in the upper left-hand corner, zeros elsewhere. This last step is usually not necessary.

We carry this out in detail for a mapping $\mathbf{T}$ of a five-dimensional space U to a four-dimensional space V, the field of scalars being $\mathbf{Q}$. Suppose then that for a given base pair $A = \{\mathbf{u}_i\}$ and $B = \{\mathbf{v}_j\}$ the mapping $\mathbf{T}$ has matrix

$$\begin{pmatrix} 2 & 0 & -4 & -12 & 4 \\ 3 & 8 & -5 & -7 & -1 \\ 2 & 4 & -3 & -5 & 1 \\ -4 & -2 & 7 & 19 & -7 \end{pmatrix} \tag{9.13}$$

According to the foregoing, the first reduction step consists of introducing the new base† $B_\alpha = \{\mathbf{v}_j^\alpha\}$ defined by

$$\begin{aligned} \mathbf{v}_j^\alpha &= \mathbf{v}_j \qquad (j \neq 1) \\ \mathbf{v}_1^\alpha &= (\tfrac{1}{2}) \cdot \mathbf{T}(\mathbf{u}_1) = \tfrac{1}{2} \cdot (2\mathbf{v}_1 + 3\mathbf{v}_2 + 2\mathbf{v}_3 - 4\mathbf{v}_4) \end{aligned} \tag{9.14}$$

By rule (I′) the matrix of $\mathbf{T}$ relative to (A, B_α) is

$$\begin{pmatrix} 2 & 0 & -4 & -12 & 4 \\ 0 & 8 & 1 & 11 & -7 \\ 0 & 4 & 1 & 7 & -3 \\ 0 & -2 & -1 & -5 & 1 \end{pmatrix} \tag{9.15}$$

The (2, 2) element here is not zero, and we can repeat the process. However, we can spare ourselves some fractions here by interchanging columns 2 and 3. That step is scarcely necessary, but we shall do it to illustrate the operation. Switching columns 2 and 3 corresponds to reversing the numbering of $\mathbf{u}_2$ and $\mathbf{u}_3$. Therefore let $A_\alpha = \{\mathbf{u}_i^\alpha\}$ be the base for U defined by

$$\begin{aligned} \mathbf{u}_2^\alpha &= \mathbf{u}_3 \qquad \mathbf{u}_3^\alpha = \mathbf{u}_2 \\ \mathbf{u}_i^\alpha &= \mathbf{u}_i \qquad \textit{for } i \neq 2, 3 \end{aligned} \tag{9.16}$$

Then the matrix of $\mathbf{T}$ relative to (A_α, B_α) is

$$\begin{pmatrix} 2 & -4 & 0 & -12 & 4 \\ 0 & 1 & 8 & 11 & -7 \\ 0 & 1 & 4 & 7 & -3 \\ 0 & -1 & -2 & -5 & 1 \end{pmatrix} \tag{9.17}$$

Our next step is to apply rule (I′) to the second column here. For that purpose we define a new base $B_\beta = \{\mathbf{v}_j^\beta\}$ in V by

$$\begin{aligned} \mathbf{v}_j^\beta &= \mathbf{v}_j^\alpha \qquad \textit{for } j \neq 2 \\ \mathbf{v}_2^\beta &= \mathbf{T}(\mathbf{u}_2^\alpha) = -4\mathbf{v}_1^\alpha + \mathbf{v}_2^\alpha + \mathbf{v}_3^\alpha - \mathbf{v}_4^\alpha \end{aligned} \tag{9.18}$$

(remember that we have made a base change in U, which is why $\mathbf{u}_2^\alpha$ appears here instead of $\mathbf{u}_2$). By (I′) the matrix of $\mathbf{T}$ relative to (A_α, B_β), our most recent base pair, is

† We shall use Greek letters instead of primes to distinguish the various bases, for otherwise the symbolism becomes unwieldy.

9.19
$$\begin{pmatrix} 2 & 0 & 32 & 32 & -24 \\ 0 & 1 & 8 & 11 & -7 \\ 0 & 0 & -4 & -4 & 4 \\ 0 & 0 & 6 & 6 & -6 \end{pmatrix}$$

We now work on the third column. Let $B_\gamma = \{\mathbf{v}_j^\gamma\}$ be the base

9.20
$$\mathbf{v}_j^\gamma = \mathbf{v}_j^\beta \qquad (j \neq 3)$$
$$\mathbf{v}_3^\gamma = (-1/4) \cdot \mathbf{T}(\mathbf{u}_3^\alpha) = -1/4 \cdot (32\mathbf{v}_1^\beta + 8\mathbf{v}_2^\beta - 4\mathbf{v}_3^\beta + 6\mathbf{v}_4^\beta)$$

By (I′) the matrix of $\mathbf{T}$ for (A_α, B_γ) is

9.21
$$\begin{pmatrix} 2 & 0 & 0 & 0 & 8 \\ 0 & 1 & 0 & 3 & 1 \\ 0 & 0 & -4 & -4 & 4 \\ 0 & 0 & 0 & 0 & 0 \end{pmatrix}$$

We have achieved here the triangular form (9.11), and we conclude from it that the rank of $\mathbf{T}$ is 3, for the first three rows are obviously linearly independent. We point out that if we are interested only in finding the rank, then it is not necessary to keep track of the base changes.

Let us see how the final base B_γ in V is related to the original base B. We read this off from (9.14), (9.18), (9.20):

$$\mathbf{v}_1^\gamma = \mathbf{v}_1 + 3/2\,\mathbf{v}_2 + \mathbf{v}_3 - 2\mathbf{v}_4$$
$$\mathbf{v}_2^\gamma = -4\mathbf{v}_1 - 5\mathbf{v}_2 - 3\mathbf{v}_3 + 7\mathbf{v}_4$$
$$\mathbf{v}_3^\gamma = -2\mathbf{v}_2 - \mathbf{v}_3 + 1/2\,\mathbf{v}_4$$
$$\mathbf{v}_4^\gamma = \mathbf{v}_4$$

Hence the matrix from B to B_γ is

9.22
$$\mathbf{q} = \begin{pmatrix} 1 & -4 & 0 & 0 \\ 3/2 & -5 & -2 & 0 \\ 1 & -3 & -1 & 0 \\ -2 & 7 & 1/2 & 1 \end{pmatrix}$$

The base changes $B \to B_\alpha \to B_\beta \to B_\gamma$ are given by certain matrices

9.23
$$\mathbf{v}_i^\alpha = a^j{}_i\mathbf{v}_j \qquad \mathbf{v}_i^\beta = b^j{}_i\mathbf{v}_j^\alpha \qquad \mathbf{v}_i^\gamma = c^j{}_i\mathbf{v}_j^\beta$$

and from (9.14), (9.18), (9.20) they are

9.24
$$\mathbf{a} = \begin{pmatrix} 1 & 0 & 0 & 0 \\ 3/2 & 1 & 0 & 0 \\ 1 & 0 & 1 & 0 \\ -2 & 0 & 0 & 1 \end{pmatrix} \qquad \mathbf{b} = \begin{pmatrix} 1 & -4 & 0 & 0 \\ 0 & 1 & 0 & 0 \\ 0 & 1 & 1 & 0 \\ 0 & -1 & 0 & 1 \end{pmatrix}$$

$$\mathbf{c} = \begin{pmatrix} 1 & 0 & -8 & 0 \\ 0 & 1 & -2 & 0 \\ 0 & 0 & 1 & 0 \\ 0 & 0 & -3/2 & 1 \end{pmatrix}$$

These are all instances of (9.14), and their inverses are given by (9.15). Now $\mathbf{q} = \mathbf{abc}$ (see Exercise 6, Sec. 7), and so $\mathbf{q}^{-1}$ can be easily computed, since $\mathbf{q}^{-1} = \mathbf{c}^{-1}\mathbf{b}^{-1}\mathbf{a}^{-1}$, by the general rule for inverses. $\mathbf{q}^{-1}$ can also be obtained by solving the equations preceding (9.22) for $\mathbf{v}_1, \mathbf{v}_2, \mathbf{v}_3, \mathbf{v}_4$.

Returning to (9.21), let us now complete the reduction to diagonal form by applying (II′) in the manner described in connection with (9.11).

The first step is to replace the base A_α of U by $A_\beta = \{\mathbf{u}_i^\beta\}$ defined as follows:

9.25
$$\begin{aligned} \mathbf{u}_i^\beta &= \mathbf{u}_i^\alpha \qquad \text{for } i \neq 5 \\ \mathbf{u}_5^\beta &= \mathbf{u}_5^\alpha - 4\mathbf{u}_1^\alpha \end{aligned}$$

By (II) the effect of this is to subtract four times column 1 of (9.21) from column 5. Hence the matrix of $\mathbf{T}$ relative to (A_α, B_γ) is

9.26
$$\begin{pmatrix} 2 & 0 & 0 & 0 & 0 \\ 0 & 1 & 0 & 3 & 1 \\ 0 & 0 & -4 & -4 & 4 \\ 0 & 0 & 0 & 0 & 0 \end{pmatrix}$$

Now replace A_β by $A_\gamma = \{\mathbf{u}_i^\gamma\}$, where

9.27
$$\begin{aligned} \mathbf{u}_i^\gamma &= \mathbf{u}_i^\beta \qquad i \neq 4, 5 \\ \mathbf{u}_4^\gamma &= \mathbf{u}_4^\beta - 3\mathbf{u}_2^\beta \\ \mathbf{u}_5^\gamma &= \mathbf{u}_5^\beta - \mathbf{u}_2^\beta \end{aligned}$$

By (II) the effect of this is to subtract three times column 2 from column 4 and one times column 2 from column 5. Hence the matrix of $\mathbf{T}$ for (A_γ, B_γ) is

9.28
$$\begin{pmatrix} 2 & 0 & 0 & 0 & 0 \\ 0 & 1 & 0 & 0 & 0 \\ 0 & 0 & -4 & -4 & 4 \\ 0 & 0 & 0 & 0 & 0 \end{pmatrix}$$

Finally we change A_γ to $A_\mu = \{\mathbf{u}_i^\mu\}$ defined by

9.29
$$\begin{aligned} \mathbf{u}_i^\mu &= \mathbf{u}_i^\gamma \qquad \text{for } i \neq 4, 5 \\ \mathbf{u}_4^\mu &= \mathbf{u}_4^\gamma - \mathbf{u}_3^\gamma \\ \mathbf{u}_5^\mu &= \mathbf{u}_5^\gamma + \mathbf{u}_3^\gamma \end{aligned}$$

By (II) the matrix of **T** for (A_μ, B_γ) is

9.30
$$\begin{pmatrix} 2 & 0 & 0 & 0 & 0 \\ 0 & 1 & 0 & 0 & 0 \\ 0 & 0 & -4 & 0 & 0 \\ 0 & 0 & 0 & 0 & 0 \end{pmatrix}$$

which is indeed in diagonal form. As pointed out in relation to (9.13), if we replace the base $\{\mathbf{v}_j^\gamma\}$ in V by the new base $\{2\mathbf{v}_1^\gamma, \mathbf{v}_2^\gamma, -4\mathbf{v}_3^\gamma, \mathbf{v}_4^\gamma\}$, then the new matrix for **T** will have the 3×3 unit matrix in the upper left-hand corner. We shall not bother with this minor point.

Let us now see what information we can obtain from (9.30). That is the matrix of **T** relative to (A_μ, B_γ), and so we have

9.31
$$\begin{aligned} \mathbf{T}(\mathbf{u}_1^\mu) &= 2\mathbf{v}_1^\gamma \\ \mathbf{T}(\mathbf{u}_2^\mu) &= \mathbf{v}_2^\gamma \\ \mathbf{T}(\mathbf{u}_3^\mu) &= -4\mathbf{v}_3^\gamma \\ \mathbf{T}(\mathbf{u}_4^\mu) &= \mathbf{T}(\mathbf{u}_5^\mu) = \mathbf{0} \end{aligned}$$

From this it is clear (see Theorem 7.4) that Im **T** is spanned by $\mathbf{v}_1^\gamma, \mathbf{v}_2^\gamma, \mathbf{v}_3^\gamma$. That is, given $\mathbf{y}$ in V, the equation $\mathbf{T}(\mathbf{x}) = \mathbf{y}$ has a solution if and only if $\mathbf{y}$ is a linear combination of $\mathbf{v}_1^\gamma, \mathbf{v}_2^\gamma, \mathbf{v}_3^\gamma$. From the equations preceding (9.22) we see that, in terms of the original base B in V, the image of **T** has the following base:

9.32
$$\begin{aligned} &\mathbf{v}_1 + \tfrac{3}{2}\mathbf{v}_2 + \mathbf{v}_3 - 2\mathbf{v}_4 \\ -&4\mathbf{v}_1 - 5\mathbf{v}_2 + 3\mathbf{v}_3 + 7\mathbf{v}_4 \\ -&2\mathbf{v}_2 - \mathbf{v}_3 + \tfrac{1}{2}\mathbf{v}_4 \end{aligned}$$

From (9.30) we find furthermore that Ker **T** is spanned by $\mathbf{u}_4^\mu$ and $\mathbf{u}_5^\mu$. In order to express these in terms of the original base A in U we must find out how the bases A and A_μ are related. The base changes involved were $A \to A_\alpha \to A_\beta \to A_\gamma \to A_\mu$, given by (9.16), (9.25), (9.27), (9.29). By working backward it is easy to find A_μ in terms of A:

9.33
$$\begin{aligned} \mathbf{u}_1^\mu &= \mathbf{u}_1 \\ \mathbf{u}_2^\mu &= \mathbf{u}_3 \\ \mathbf{u}_3^\mu &= \mathbf{u}_2 \\ \mathbf{u}_4^\mu &= -\mathbf{u}_2 - 3\mathbf{u}_3 + \mathbf{u}_4 \\ \mathbf{u}_5^\mu &= -4\mathbf{u}_1 + \mathbf{u}_2 - \mathbf{u}_3 + \mathbf{u}_5 \end{aligned}$$

The matrix from A to A_μ is therefore

9.34
$$\mathbf{p} = \begin{pmatrix} 1 & 0 & 0 & 0 & -4 \\ 0 & 0 & 1 & -1 & 1 \\ 0 & 1 & 0 & -3 & -1 \\ 0 & 0 & 0 & 1 & 0 \\ 0 & 0 & 0 & 0 & 1 \end{pmatrix}$$

The last two elements in (9.33) span Ker **T**. Denoting (9.13) by **a** and (9.30) by **a**′, one verifies easily that $\mathbf{a}' = \mathbf{q}^{-1}\mathbf{ap}$, as required by Theorem 7.2.

EXERCISES

1. Compute $\mathbf{a}^{-1}$ for the matrix (9.22) and carry out the verification of the equation $\mathbf{a}' = \mathbf{q}^{-1}\mathbf{ap}$.

2. Compute the rank of the matrix

$$\begin{pmatrix} 1 & 0 & 4 & -3 & 2 & 0 \\ 4 & 0 & 2 & -1 & 1 & 2 \\ 2 & 3 & -2 & 5 & -4 & 1 \\ -1 & 2 & 3 & 0 & 0 & 2 \\ 6 & -2 & 2 & 3 & 1 & 4 \end{pmatrix}$$

3. Let a linear mapping $\mathbf{T}\colon U \to V$ have matrix

$$\begin{pmatrix} 2 & 0 & -2 & 4 \\ 1 & 0 & -2 & 3 \\ 0 & 4 & 2 & 1 \\ 6 & 4 & -4 & 13 \\ 2 & 4 & -2 & 7 \end{pmatrix}$$

with respect to a certain base pair $\{\mathbf{u}_i\}$, $\{\mathbf{v}_j\}$. Compute the rank, image, and kernel of **T**.

4. Given the system of linear equations

$$\begin{aligned} X_1 + 3X_2 - X_3 + X_5 &= Y_1 \\ 2X_1 - 2X_2 + X_4 - X_5 &= Y_2 \\ X_1 + 2X_3 + 2X_4 + 4X_5 &= Y_3 \\ 5X_2 + X_3 + X_4 + 6X_5 &= Y_4 \end{aligned}$$

determine what conditions must be satisfied by Y_1, Y_2, Y_3, Y_4 in order that this system have a solution for $X_1, \ldots, X_5$. Determine all solutions for $Y_1 = -8$, $Y_2 = 9$, $Y_3 = 12$, $Y_4 = -5$.

5. Let $\mathbf{a} = (a^j{}_i)$ be an $m \times n$ triangular matrix (that is, $a^j{}_i = 0$ if $i < j$) and suppose that $a^1{}_1, a^2{}_2, \ldots, a^r{}_r$ are different from zero. Prove that **a** has rank r if and only if every row below the rth is zero.

6. Compute the rank of

$$\begin{pmatrix} 2 & t^2 + 1 & (t+1)^2 \\ -3t + 3 & t^3 - 1 & (t-1)^3 \\ t^2 & t + 4 & t^3 + t + 4 \end{pmatrix}$$

where t is an indeterminate over **Q**.

7. Let $\mathbf{u}_1, \ldots, \mathbf{u}_n$ be a base for a vector space U over a field K, and let $\mathbf{c} = (c^j{}_i)$ be a triangular matrix in $K^n{}_n$. Prove that the vectors $\mathbf{v}_i = c^j{}_i\mathbf{u}_j$ form a base for U if and only if $c^1{}_1c^2{}_2 \cdots c^n{}_n \neq 0$.

8. Determine all solutions of the system

$$\begin{aligned} \bar{2}x + y - w + \bar{3}z &= \bar{3} \\ x - \bar{4}y + \bar{2}w + z &= \bar{3} \\ \bar{2}y + \bar{4}w - z &= -\bar{3} \end{aligned}$$

the field of scalars being $\mathbf{Z}_5$ (residue class notations as in Sec. 10, Chap. 2).

9. Let U be a four-dimensional vector space over the real field, and let $A = \mathbf{e}_1, \mathbf{e}_2, \mathbf{e}_3, \mathbf{e}_4$ be a base in U. Let $\mathbf{T}$ be the endomorphism of U whose matrix with respect to the base A is

$$\begin{pmatrix} 1 & 3 & -2 & 5 \\ -1 & 1 & -4 & 15 \\ 2 & 4 & -1 & 0 \\ 4 & 10 & -5 & 10 \end{pmatrix}$$

Find bases for the kernel and image of $\mathbf{T}$.

10. Quotient spaces

Let U be a vector space over a field K, and let V be a subspace. For any element $\mathbf{x}$ in V, we denote by

10.1 $\quad \mathbf{x} + V$

the set of all elements in U of the form $\mathbf{x} + \mathbf{v}$ with $\mathbf{v}$ an element in V. The subset (10.1) contains the element $\mathbf{x}$, since $\mathbf{x} = \mathbf{x} + \mathbf{0}$. The subset (10.1) is called a *V-coset* (or simply, a *coset*, when the subspace V is fixed in any given discussion).

10.2 *Every element of U is contained in one and only one V-coset.*

For suppose that $\mathbf{x}$ is also contained in a coset $\mathbf{x}' + V$. Then $\mathbf{x} = \mathbf{x}' + \mathbf{v}_1$, with $\mathbf{v}_1$ in V. We have $\mathbf{x} + \mathbf{v} = \mathbf{x}' + (\mathbf{v}_1 + \mathbf{v})$; and as $\mathbf{v}$ runs through all the elements of the subspace V, so does $\mathbf{v}_1 + \mathbf{v}$. Hence $\mathbf{x} + V = \mathbf{x}' + V$. From this we conclude that two cosets $\mathbf{x} + V$ and $\mathbf{x}' + V$ either have no elements in common, or else are identical, the latter being true if and only if $\mathbf{x} - \mathbf{x}'$ is in V.

We can thus describe the coset $\mathbf{x} + V$ as *the* unique V-coset containing $\mathbf{x}$.

Now let U/V denote the set whose elements are all the different cosets $\mathbf{x} + V$. Define addition in U/V by

10.3 $\quad (\mathbf{x} + V) + (\mathbf{y} + V) = (\mathbf{x} + \mathbf{y}) + V$

Define scalar multiplication by

10.4 $\quad c(\mathbf{x} + V) = (c\mathbf{x}) + V$

for any scalar c. These definitions make sense (despite the fact that they depend apparently on the arbitrary selection of the element $\mathbf{x}$ from its coset). For if we had expressed the cosets $\mathbf{x} + V$ and $\mathbf{y} + V$ as $\mathbf{x}' + V$ and $\mathbf{y}' + V$, respectively, we would have $\mathbf{x} = \mathbf{x}' + \mathbf{v}_1$ and $\mathbf{y} = \mathbf{y}' + \mathbf{v}_2$, with $\mathbf{v}_1$ and $\mathbf{v}_2$ in V. But then

$$(\mathbf{x} + \mathbf{y}) + V = (\mathbf{x}' + \mathbf{v}_1 + \mathbf{y}' + \mathbf{v}_2) + V = (\mathbf{x}' + \mathbf{y}') + (\mathbf{v}_1 + \mathbf{v}_2) + V$$
$$= (\mathbf{x}' + \mathbf{y}') + V$$

showing that (4.1) depends only on the cosets and not on the particular elements $\mathbf{x}$ and $\mathbf{y}$ used to represent the cosets. The same is true for (10.4). It is a routine matter to verify that U/V with these operations is a vector space over the same field of scalars as U.

The mapping

$$\mathbf{S}\colon \mathbf{x} \to \mathbf{x} + V$$

is called the *projection* of U onto U/V. The definitions (10.3) and (10.4) show that the projection $\mathbf{S}$ is a *linear* mapping; indeed $\mathbf{S}$ is an epimorphism.

Let $\mathbf{T}\colon U \to U$ be a linear mapping such that $\mathbf{T}$ sends V into V. In this situation, we call V a **T**-*stable subspace*. We denote by $\mathbf{T}_V$ the *restriction* of $\mathbf{T}$ to V; that is, $\mathbf{T}_V$ is the mapping of V to V given by

10.5 $\quad \mathbf{T}_V(\mathbf{x}) = \mathbf{T}(\mathbf{x})$

for any $\mathbf{x}$ in V. It is clear that $\mathbf{T}_V$ is a linear mapping; it is called the *V-part* of $\mathbf{T}$.

It is a simple matter to verify, by the reasoning used above, that the coset $\mathbf{T}(\mathbf{x}) + V$ remains unchanged if we replace $\mathbf{x}$ by $\mathbf{x} + \mathbf{v}_1$, with $\mathbf{v}_1$ in V. It follows at once that

10.6 $\quad \mathbf{T}_{U/V}\colon \mathbf{x} + V \to \mathbf{T}(\mathbf{x}) + V$

is a well-defined mapping of U/V into U/V. From the definitions (10.3) and (10.4), one sees at once that $\mathbf{T}_{U/V}$ is a linear mapping. It is called the *U/V-part* of $\mathbf{T}$. The relation of $\mathbf{T}_{U/V}$ to $\mathbf{T}$ is best summed up by the relation

10.7 $\quad \mathbf{T}_{U/V} \circ \mathbf{S} = \mathbf{S} \circ \mathbf{T}$

which is depicted in the diagram below.

$$\begin{array}{ccc} & \mathbf{T} & \\ U & \longrightarrow & U \\ \mathbf{S}\downarrow & & \downarrow \mathbf{S} \\ U/V & \longrightarrow & U/V \\ & \mathbf{T}_{U/V} & \end{array}$$

That is, the composition of the vertical and horizontal mappings yield a single result via either the upper or the lower circuit.

We shall now take up the matrix counterpart of the endomorphisms $\mathbf{T}_V$ and $\mathbf{T}_{U/V}$. As before, let $\mathbf{T}$ be an endomorphism of the vector space U, and let V be a $\mathbf{T}$-stable subspace. We assume that U is finite dimensional.

We select a base $B = \{\mathbf{e}_1, \mathbf{e}_2, \ldots, \mathbf{e}_n\}$ for U such that $\mathbf{e}_1, \mathbf{e}_2, \ldots, \mathbf{e}_r$ is a base for V. Let $\mathbf{a} = (a^j{}_i)$ denote the matrix of $\mathbf{T}$ with respect to the base B. Then

$$\mathbf{T}(\mathbf{e}_i) = \sum_{j=1}^{n} a^j{}_i \mathbf{e}_j \qquad (i = 1, \ldots, n)$$

The hypothesis that V is $\mathbf{T}$ stable implies that

$$\mathbf{T}(\mathbf{e}_i) = \sum_{j=1}^{r} a^j{}_i \mathbf{e}_j \qquad (i = 1, \ldots, r)$$

that is,

10.8 $\quad a^j{}_i = 0 \qquad \text{if } i = 1, \ldots, r \text{ and } j = r+1, \ldots, n$

Thus the matrix $\mathbf{a}$ has the *block* form

10.8′ $\quad \begin{pmatrix} \mathbf{a}' & \mathbf{b} \\ \mathbf{0} & \mathbf{a}'' \end{pmatrix}$

where $\mathbf{a}'$ and $\mathbf{a}''$ are square $r \times r$ and $(n - r) \times (n - r)$ matrices, respectively, $\mathbf{0}$ is an $(n - r) \times r$ matrix of zeros, and $\mathbf{b}$ is an $r \times (n - r)$ matrix. Let B' denote the subset $\{\mathbf{e}_1, \ldots, \mathbf{e}_r\}$ of V. Let B'' denote the subset $\{\mathbf{S}(\mathbf{e}_{r+1}), \ldots, \mathbf{S}(\mathbf{e}_n)\}$ of U/V.

It is clear that B' is a base of V and that $\mathbf{a}'$ is the matrix of the V part $\mathbf{T}_V$ with respect to B'.

What about the matrix $\mathbf{a}''$?

We observe first that B'' is a base of U/V. For if $c_{r+1}, \ldots, c_n$ are any scalars such that

$$\sum_{j=r+1}^{n} c_j \mathbf{S}(\mathbf{e}_j) = \mathbf{0} \qquad \text{then } \mathbf{0} = \mathbf{S}\left(\sum_{j=r+1}^{n} c_j \mathbf{e}_j\right)$$

and consequently $\sum_{j=r+1}^{n} c_j \mathbf{e}_j$ is in V, the kernel of $\mathbf{S}$. Inasmuch as $\mathbf{e}_1, \ldots, \mathbf{e}_r$ form a base of V, it follows immediately that $c_{r+1} = \cdots = c_n = 0$. Set

10.9 $\quad \mathbf{e}_i'' = \mathbf{S}(\mathbf{e}_i) \qquad (c = r+1, \ldots, n)$

From Eq. (10.7) we find

$$T_{U/V}(\mathbf{e}_i'') = \sum_{j=r+1}^{n} a^j{}_i \mathbf{e}_i''$$

Hence $\mathbf{a}''$ is the matrix of $\mathbf{T}_{U/V}$ with respect to the base B''.

EXERCISES

1. Prove that the sum and product of two matrices in the block form (10.8′) is again of the same block form. What is the corresponding assertion about the V part and U/V part of two endomorphisms?

*2. Continue the notation of Sec. 10. Under what condition on the endomorphism T can one find a base B so that the submatrix $\mathbf{b}$ in the block form (10.8′) consists entirely of zeros. Give an example of an endomorphism whose matrix has block form (10.8′) but for no base does its matrix have the form

$$\begin{pmatrix} \mathbf{a}' & 0 \\ 0 & \mathbf{a}'' \end{pmatrix}$$

where $\mathbf{a}'$ and $\mathbf{a}''$ have at least one row.

3. Let $\mathbf{T}$: $U \to W$ be a linear mapping, and let V be the kernel of $\mathbf{T}$. Let $\mathbf{S}$ denote the projection of U onto U/V. Prove that there is a monomorphism $\mathbf{T}^*$: $U/V \to W$ such that $\mathbf{T}^* \circ \mathbf{S} = \mathbf{T}$.

4. Let V be a subspace of the vector space U and let $\mathbf{S}$: $U \to U/V$ denote the projection of U onto U/V. Prove: There exist linear mappings: $\mathbf{R}''$: $U/V \to U$ and $\mathbf{R}'$: $U \to V$ such that

(*a*) $\mathbf{S} \circ \mathbf{R}'' = \mathbf{I}''$, the identity mapping of U/V

(*b*) $\mathbf{R}'' \circ \mathbf{S} + \mathbf{I}' \circ \mathbf{R}' = \mathbf{I}$, where $\mathbf{I}$ is the identity mapping of U and $\mathbf{I}'$: $V \to U$ is the mapping $v \to v$ of V into U.

5. Let $\mathbf{T}$ be an endomorphism of a vector space U, and let V be a $\mathbf{T}$-stable subspace. Prove: There exists a base B with respect to which the matrix of $\mathbf{T}$ has the block form

$$\begin{pmatrix} \mathbf{a}' & 0 \\ 0 & \mathbf{a}'' \end{pmatrix}$$

$\mathbf{a}'$ and $\mathbf{a}''$ being the matrices of $\mathbf{T}_V$ and $\mathbf{T}_{U/V}$, respectively, if and only if there is a linear mapping $\mathbf{R}''$: $U/V \to U$ satisfying

(*a*) $\mathbf{S} \circ \mathbf{R}'' = \mathbf{I}''$ the identity mapping of U/V

(*b*) $\mathbf{T} \circ \mathbf{R}'' = \mathbf{T}_{U/V} \circ \mathbf{S}$

11. Modules

If, in the definition of a vector space over a field K (cf. Sec. 2, Chap. 8), we replace the field K by a *ring* A, all the conditions continue to make sense. The resulting system might be called a "vector space over a ring." However, it is customary to use the term a *module over a ring* A or an *A-module*. Many, but not all, of the theorems for vector spaces carry over to modules. We enumerate in this section some of the basic properties of modules, which will be needed in later chapters.

To summarize the definition, a module M over a ring A is an additive abelian group admitting scalar multiplication by elements of the ring A and satisfying the conditions

$(a \cdot b) \cdot m = a \cdot (b \cdot m)$ for all a, b in A and m in M

$a \cdot (m + n) = a \cdot m + a \cdot n$ for all a in A and m, n in M

$(a + b) \quad m = a \cdot m + b \cdot m$ for all a, b in A and m in M

$1 \cdot m = m$ for all m in M

where 1 is the identity element for multiplication in the ring A. One often denotes the scalar product $a \cdot m$ simply by am, where a is an element of A and m an element of M.

A *submodule* N of the module M is a non-empty subset such that

(1) For any x and y in N, $x + y$ is in N.

(2) For any x in N and a in A, ax is in N.

A *homomorphism* of an A-module M into an A-module M_2 is a mapping $\mathbf{f}$ such that

(1) $\mathbf{f}(x + y) = \mathbf{f}(x) + \mathbf{f}(y)$ for all x, y in M

(2) $\mathbf{f}(ax) = a\mathbf{f}(x)$ for all a in A and x in M

The *kernel* of a homomorphism $\mathbf{f}$ is the set of elements which $\mathbf{f}$ sends into the zero element. A homomorphism $\mathbf{f}$ is a *monomorphism* (sending distinct elements into distinct elements) if and only if the kernel of $\mathbf{f}$ consists of zero alone. A *base* in the A-module M is a subset $\{m_1, m_2, \ldots, m_n, \ldots\}$ such that each element x of M can be expressed uniquely as a finite linear combination of base elements:

11.1 $$x = a_1m_1 + a_2m_2 + \cdots$$

each a_i being in the ring A. By contrast with vector spaces over fields, not all modules have a base.

EXAMPLE 1 Let G be an abelian group, the group operation being denoted by $+$. Then we can consider G as a module over the ring of integers $\mathbf{Z}$ upon defining scalar multiplication as: $a \cdot x =$ the ath multiple of x, for any integer a (cf. Sec. 7*F*, Chap. 2, for the definition of "multiple") Equations (7.23) to (7.25), Sec. 7*F*, Chap. 2, assert in effect that G is indeed a module over the ring $\mathbf{Z}$. A submodule is merely a subgroup in this case.

Suppose now that G is a finite abelian group. Then G cannot have a base as $\mathbf{Z}$-module. For if m_1 were a base element, the elements $1 \cdot m_1, 2 \cdot m_1, 3 \cdot m_1, \ldots, a \cdot m_1, \ldots$ would all be distinct—which is impossible.

Let M be a module over a ring A, and let N be a submodule. We define the *quotient module* M/N exactly as in the vector-space case of Sec. 10: an element of M/N is a *coset* $x + N$. Exactly as in the vector-space case, one sees that M/N is a module over the ring A. Furthermore, one defines the *projection* of M onto M/N as the mapping $x \to x + N$ which assigns to each element x of M the coset containing x. The projection of M onto M/N is seen to be a homomorphism whose kernel is N. If $\mathbf{T}$ is an *endomorphism* of M (i.e., a homomorphism of M into M) which sends N into N, we call N a $\mathbf{T}$-*stable* submodule. One defines the N part and M/N part of $\mathbf{T}$ by means of Eqs. (10.5) and (10.6). Both $\mathbf{T}_N$ and $\mathbf{T}_{M/N}$ are endomorphisms and we have

11.2 $$\mathbf{T}_{M/N} \circ \boldsymbol{\pi} = \boldsymbol{\pi} \circ \mathbf{T} \qquad (\boldsymbol{\pi} \text{ denotes the projection } M \to M/N)$$

More generally, let M_1 and M_2 be modules over a ring A; let $\mathbf{T}$ be a homomorphism of M_1 to M_2; and let N_1, N_2 be submodules of M_1, M_2, respectively, with $\mathbf{T}(N_1) \subset N_2$. Then the formula

$$\mathbf{T}''(x + N_1) = \mathbf{T}(x) + N_2$$

yields a well-defined homomorphism $\mathbf{T}''$ of the quotient module M_1/N_1 into M_2/N_2; $\mathbf{T}''$ is called the M_1/N_2 part of $\mathbf{T}$. Its relation to $\mathbf{T}$ is given in the diagram:

11.3

$$\begin{array}{ccc} & \mathbf{T} & \\ M_1 & \longrightarrow & M_2 \\ \pi_1 \downarrow & & \downarrow \pi_2 \\ M_1/N_1 & \longrightarrow & M_2/N_2 \\ & \mathbf{T}'' & \end{array}$$

that is, $\pi_2 \circ \mathbf{T} = \mathbf{T}'' \circ \pi_1$, where π_1, π_2 denote the projections of M_1, M_2 onto the corresponding quotient modules.

The significance of the quotient module M/N can best be explained by its following property:

11.4 *Let* $\mathbf{f}$: $M \to M_0$ *be a homomorphism and let* N *be a submodule contained in the kernel of* $\mathbf{f}$. *Then there is a unique homomorphism* $\mathbf{f}''$: $M\ /N \to M_0$ *such that*

$$\mathbf{f} = \mathbf{f}'' \cdot \pi$$

where π *is the projection of* M *onto* M/N.

Assertion (11.4) follows immediately from (11.3) with $N_2 = 0$. The assertion can be depicted by the diagram

$$\begin{array}{ccc} & \mathbf{f} & \\ M & \longrightarrow & M_0 \\ \pi \downarrow & \nearrow \mathbf{f}'' & \\ M/N & & \end{array}$$

There is one important special case of (11.4) deserving separate mention, namely, when N is the kernel of $\mathbf{f}$ and $\mathbf{f}$ is an onto-mapping. In this case the kernel of the homomorphism $\mathbf{f}''$ is seen to reduce to the zero coset alone. Hence $\mathbf{f}''$ is a monomorphism. Since the image of $\mathbf{f}''$ coincides with the image of $\mathbf{f}$, the mapping $\mathbf{f}''$ is a one-to-one mapping. Hence $\mathbf{f}''$ is an isomorphism. To sum up,

11.5 $\mathbf{f}''$ *is an isomorphism of* M *onto* M_0 *if* $\mathbf{f}$ *is an epimorphism with kernel* N.

EXAMPLE 2 Let $\mathbf{Z}$ be the additive group of integers considered as a $\mathbf{Z}$-module. Let $m\mathbf{Z}$ be the submodule consisting of all the multiples of the fixed positive integer m. Then an element of the quotient module is precisely a *residue class* modulo m (cf. Sec. 10, Chap. 2) and the quotient module is the $\mathbf{Z}$-module formed from the group $\mathbf{Z}_m$ of residue classes modulo m.

In view of the intimate similarity in the definition of modules and vector spaces, many of the theorems proved in Chap. 8 for vector spaces are also valid for modules. For example all the results in Secs. 3 to 5, Chap. 8. The results of Sec. 5

on the *direct sum* of submodules are valid. However, the results in Sec. 6, Chap. 2, on linear independence are definitely *not* true for modules in general.

The analogy between modules and vector spaces can be carried further for those special modules which have a base; such modules are called *free* modules.

EXAMPLE 3 Let A be a ring, and let A^n denote the set of all n-tuples $(a_1, \ldots, a_n)$ of elements of A. Defining addition and scalar multiplication componentwise [cf. (4.1) and (4.2) Chap. 8], we find that A^n is a module over the ring A. Let $\mathbf{e}_i$ denote the element of A^n whose ith component is 1 and whose other components are 0. Then $(a_1, a_2, \cdots, a_n) = b_1\mathbf{e}_1 + b_2\mathbf{e}_2 + \cdots + b_n\mathbf{e}_n$ if and only if $b_1 = a_1, b_2 = a_2, \ldots, b_n = a_n$. Hence $\mathbf{e}_1, \ldots, \mathbf{e}_n$ is a base of A^n and A^n is a free A-module. In the special case that $n = 1$, a submodule of A is called an *ideal* (or a *left ideal* in case A is not commutative). An ideal of the form $A\mathbf{x}$ with $\mathbf{x}$ a fixed element in A is called a *principal* ideal.

Given a homomorphism $\mathbf{f}\colon M \to N$ of a free module M into a free module N, one can associate with $\mathbf{f}$ a matrix exactly as in the case of vector spaces. Explicitly, if $\{\mathbf{x}_1, \ldots, \mathbf{x}_m\}$ and $\{\mathbf{y}_1, \ldots, \mathbf{y}_n\}$ are bases in M and N, respectively, then the matrix of $\mathbf{f}$ with respect to these bases is the matrix $\mathbf{a} = (a^j{}_i)$ given by

11.6 $$\mathbf{f}(\mathbf{x}_i) = \sum_{j=1}^{n} a^j{}_i \mathbf{y}_j \qquad (i = 1, \ldots, m)$$

In the special case that $M = N$ and the above bases are the same, we call $\mathbf{a}$ the matrix of $\mathbf{f}$ with respect to the base $\{\mathbf{x}_1, \ldots, \mathbf{x}_n\}$.

Let M be a free A-module with base $B = \{\mathbf{x}_1, \ldots, \mathbf{x}_n\}$. Then any homomorphism $\mathbf{f}\colon M \to N$ of M into a module N (not necessarily free) is determined entirely by the effect of the mapping $\mathbf{f}$ on the elements of the base $\mathbf{x}_1, \ldots, \mathbf{x}_n$. For given any element $\mathbf{x}$ in M, we can express $\mathbf{x}$ as a linear combination $\mathbf{x} = a_1\mathbf{x}_1 + \cdots + a_n\mathbf{x}_n$ in one and only one way, and therefore $\mathbf{f}(\mathbf{x}) = a_1\mathbf{f}(\mathbf{x}_1) + \cdots + a_n f(\mathbf{x})$ is uniquely determined by $\mathbf{f}(\mathbf{x}), \ldots, \mathbf{f}(\mathbf{x}_n)$. Moreover given arbitrary elements $\mathbf{v}_1, \ldots, \mathbf{v}_n$ in the A-module N, there exists a homomorphism $\mathbf{f}$ of M to N such that $f(\mathbf{x}_1) = \mathbf{y}_1, \ldots, \mathbf{f}(\mathbf{x}_n) = \mathbf{y}_n$; namely, define $\mathbf{f}$ by

$$\sum_{j=1}^{n} a^j\mathbf{x}_j \to \sum_{j=1}^{n} a^j\mathbf{f}(\mathbf{x}_j)$$

EXERCISES

1. Let A be a commutative ring. Define an A-module structure on Hom (M, N), the set of all homomorphisms of the A-module M into the A-module N.

2. Let V be a vector space over a field K, and set $A = \text{Hom}\ (V, V)$. Define an A-module structure on V.

3. Let A be a ring and let A' denote its *opposite*; that is, its elements are the elements of A but the multiplication $\cdot$ in the ring A' is given by $a \cdot b = ba$ for any

a, b in A'. Let M, N be A-modules and define scalar multiplication $a \cdot \mathbf{f}$ in Hom (M, N) by $(a \cdot \mathbf{f})(\mathbf{x}) = \mathbf{f}(a\mathbf{x})$ for any a in A and $\mathbf{f}$ in Hom (M, N).

(*a*) With this definition, does Hom (M, N) become a module over A if A is noncommutative?

(*b*) Prove that Hom (M, N) becomes a module over the opposite ring A'.

(*c*) Define scalar multiplication in A^n by

$$a \cdot (a_1, \ldots, a_n) = (a_1 a, \ldots, a_n a)$$

Prove that with this scalar product, A^n becomes an A'-module.

4. Prove that every module is isomorphic to a quotient module of a free module.

5. Let A be a ring. We regard $A = A'$ as an A-module as in Example 3. Prove that A is a free A-module.

6. Let A be a ring. Prove: If every ideal of A is a free submodule having a base with one element, then A satisfies the cancellation law.

7. Let A be a commutative ring. Prove: If every ideal in A is a free A-submodule, then A is an integral domain in which every ideal is principal.

8. Let $K[t]$ be the ring of polynomials in an indeterminate t with coefficients in the field K. Prove that every ideal in $K[t]$ is principal (cf. Exercise 2, Sec. 3, Chap. 6).

9. Let B be an ideal in the ring A. Prove: In the quotient module A/B, there is a unique multiplication such that the projection π: $A \to A/B$ becomes a *ring* homomorphism if and only if $\mathbf{x}B$ lies in B for every $\mathbf{x}$ in A (that is, B is a so-called right ideal as well as a left ideal). The ring A/B is called the *quotient ring*.

10. Let A be a commutative integral domain in which every ideal is principal. Prove that every submodule of a free A-module M is free. [Hint: Consider the homomorphism $M \to A$

$$\sum_j a_j \mathbf{e}_j \to a_1$$

of the module onto the coefficient of the first base element.]

11. Let $A = K[t]$ be the ring of polynomials in an indeterminate t, and let $q(t)$ be a polynomial in t of degree n. Let B be the principal ideal $Aq(t)$, and π: $A \to A/B$ denote the projection of A onto the quotient ring A/B. Prove: As a vector space over the field K, A/B has the base $\pi(1)$, $\pi(t)$, $\pi(t^2)$, . . . , $\pi(t^{n-1})$. [Hint: Consider the remainder of a polynomial after division by $q(t)$.]

10

Groups and permutations

1. *Introduction*

Groups have played a basic role in all the preceding chapters, but as parts of more complex systems. Here we shall briefly take up the study of groups for themselves in order to point out some of the fundamental facts concerning them. In particular, we shall see that the system of integers **Z** plays a fundamental part in the theory of groups. That theory is very extensive, and we shall be able to touch on only a few points here. The only part of this chapter required later is Sec. 3.

2. *Basic properties*

We recall from Chap. 1 that a group G is a set of elements with an associative binary operation, which we shall usually write here in the product notation, with the property that G contains an identity element e for the operation and G contains the inverse a^{-1} of every element a. We have $ea = ae = a$ for every element a in G, and $a^{-1}a = aa^{-1} = e$. The element e is unique, and the inverse a^{-1} is uniquely determined by a.

A *subgroup* of G is a non-empty subset, say H, such that if a and b are any elements of H, then ab, a^{-1}, b^{-1} are also elements of H (see Sec. 6, Chap. 1). It follows that H is itself a group, and it has the same identity element e as does G. The identity element e forms by itself a subgroup of G. If H is a subgroup of G and if H' is a subgroup of H, then H' is also a subgroup of G.

A mapping f from a group G to a group G' is called a *homomorphism* if $f(ab) = f(a) \cdot f(b)$ for any elements a, b of G. That is, if f sends a into a' and b into b', then it must send ab into $a'b'$. It follows that $f(e) = e' =$ identity of G'; and if $f(a) = a'$, then $f(a^{-1}) = a'^{-1}$ (Theorem 7.1, Chap. 1). If f is one-to-one, then it is called an *isomorphism*, and in that case f^{-1}, the inverse mapping from G' to G, is also an isomorphism. (If $G = G'$, then an isomorphism is also called an automorphism.)

The group consisting of the system of integers **Z** with the $+$ operation will occur frequently in what follows, and we shall call it the *additive group of integers*. It will be denoted by $\mathbf{Z}^+$ in order to distinguish it from **Z** considered as an integral domain. Similarly, for any positive integer m, we denote by $\mathbf{Z}_m{}^+$ the group consisting of the residue classes of integers modulo m, with addition as the group operation [Eq. (10.1), Chap. 2].

THEOREM 2.1 *Let H be a subgroup of the additive group of integers $\mathbf{Z}^+$. If $H \neq 0$, then there is a unique positive integer d in H such that H consists of all multiples qd of d ($q = 0, \pm 1, \pm 2$, etc.).* The mapping *of $\mathbf{Z}^+$ to H defined by $q \to qd$ is an isomorphism.*

Proof. If H does not consist of 0 alone, then it must contain positive integers. For if a is any nonzero element of H, then $-a$ is also in H, and one of the two is positive. Let d be the least positive integer in H (Theorem 4.2, Chap. 2). For any integer m the integer md is also in H, as follows from a simple induction. Now let n be any positive integer in H. By the division algorithm (Proposition 9.4, Chap. 2) there exist integers q and r such that $n = qd + r$ and $0 \leq r < d$. By the remark above, qd is in H, and therefore so is $n - qd = r$, since H is a subgroup of $\mathbf{Z}^+$. Therefore $r = 0$, by definition of d; and so we have $n = qd$. The rest of the theorem follows easily.

THEOREM 2.2 *Let a be an element of a group G (with group operation written multiplicatively). Then the mapping $\mathbf{Z}^+ \to G$ that sends an arbitrary integer n into a^n is a homomorphism. The set of all the elements a^n is an abelian subgroup of G, denoted by (a) and called the* cyclic *subgroup generated by a. If $a^m \neq a^n$ whenever $m \neq n$, then the mapping $n \to a^n$ is an isomorphism of $\mathbf{Z}^+$ to (a). In the contrary case, there is a unique positive integer d such that $a^d = e$ and such that $a^m = e$ if and only if m is divisible by d; and then (a) is isomorphic to $\mathbf{Z}_d{}^+$. The integer d is called the* order *of a.*

Proof. The mapping $n \to a^n$ was discussed in detail in Sec. 7*E*, Chap. 2. The fact that it is a homomorphism is the assertion of (7.11) of Chap. 2, and from the same equation† it follows that (a) is an abelian subgroup of G. If $a^m \neq a^n$ whenever $m \neq n$, then the mapping is a one-to-one homomorphism of $\mathbf{Z}^+$ to (a), that is, is an isomorphism. Suppose then that $a^m = a^n$ for two distinct integers m and n. There follows $a^{-m} \cdot a^m = a^{-m} \cdot a^n$, or $e = a^{n-m}$; and $n - m \neq 0$. Now all integers n such that $a^n = e$ form a subgroup H of $\mathbf{Z}^+$, as follows at once from (7.11), Chap. 2, and H cannot consist of 0 alone, as was just shown. By Theorem 2.1, H consists of all multiples of a uniquely determined positive integer d. That is, $a^m = e$ if and only if m is a multiple of d—that is, if and only if $d|m$. Therefore $a^m = a^n$ if and only if $d|n - m$, or, in other words, if and only if $m \equiv n \pmod{d}$. From this it is easy to see that (a) is isomorphic to $\mathbf{Z}_d{}^+$. Q.E.D.

REMARK. Observe that in the case just discussed the subgroup (a) consists of the *d distinct* elements $e, a, a^2, \ldots, a^{d-1}$.

† It is pointed out in Sec. 7*E*, Chap. 2, that (7.11) holds for all integers, not just for positive integers.

DEFINITION 2.1 *A group G is called a* cyclic *group if it is isomorphic to one of the groups* $\mathbf{Z}_m^+$ *for some m, or else to* $\mathbf{Z}^+$. *In the latter case G is called* infinite cyclic.

EXERCISES†

1. Let f be a homomorphism from a group G to a group G'. Let H be the subset of G consisting of all elements of G that are sent by f into the identity element e' of G' (H is called the *kernel* of f). Further, let H' be the subset of G' consisting of all elements $f(a)$, where a is an arbitrary element of G (H' is called the *image* of f). Prove that H is a subgroup of G and that H' is a subgroup of G'.

2. Let E be an arbitrary set of elements. Let S be the set of all one-to-one mappings of E to itself. Prove that S, with composition of mappings as the binary operation, is a group. What is its identity element? What is the inverse of an element of S?

3. Let c be an element of a group G. Prove that the mapping of G to itself that sends an arbitrary element x of G into $c^{-1}xc$ is an isomorphism. (The operation $x \to c^{-1}xc$ is called *conjugation* by c; the various isomorphisms of G to G obtained in this way are called *inner* automorphisms of G.)

4. Let G be a finite group (i.e., containing only finitely many elements). Let a be an element of G, and let H be the subset consisting of all the elements a, a^2, a^3, a^4, etc. Prove that H is a subgroup of G.

5. Let G be a group. In G define a new binary operation $*$ by the rule $a * b = ba$, the right-hand side denoting the operation in G. Prove that G with the operation $*$ is also a group (called the *opposite* group of G).

6. Let f be a homomorphism from a group G to a group G'. Let H be a subgroup of G, and let $f(H)$ denote the set of all elements $f(x)$, where x is in H. Prove that $f(H)$ is a subgroup of G'. Let K be a subgroup of G', and let $f^{-1}(K)$ denote the set of all elements x in G such that $f(x)$ is in K. Prove that $f^{-1}(K)$ is a subgroup of G.

3. *Permutations*

We now turn our attention to some special groups of great importance. First we recall that a *permutation* of a set E is a one-to-one mapping from E to itself. Let us write $S(E)$ for the set of all permutations of E. Referring to Theorem 6.3, Chap. 1, we state the following theorem:

THEOREM 3.1 *For any set E, all the permutations of E, with composition of mappings as binary operation, form a group S(E). Its identity element e is the identity mapping of E; and for any element s in S(E) the inverse group element is the inverse mapping* s^{-1} *of E. If E contains n elements, then S(E) contains n! elements.*

† Some of these have been repeated from the first chapter.

We recall again that composition of mappings is defined as follows:† If s and s' are any elements of $S(E)$, then ss' is the mapping that sends an arbitrary element x of E into $s(s'(x))$. That is,

3.1 $$ss'(x) = s(s'(x))$$

To verify the last part of the theorem, let $x_1, x_2, \ldots, x_n$ be the elements of E in some fixed order. If we try to define a one-to-one mapping s of E, then there are n possible choices for $s(x_1)$, since it may be any one of the elements $x_1, x_2, \ldots, x_n$. Making now some choice for $s(x_1)$ we see that there remain only $n - 1$ choices for $s(x_2)$, because s is to be one-to-one, and therefore we cannot allow $s(x_2)$ to be the same as $s(x_1)$. Fixing one of the $n - 1$ choices for $s(x_2)$, we have only $n - 2$ choices for $s(x_3)$, and so on. The total number of ways in which s can be defined is therefore $n(n - 1)(n - 2) \cdots 2 \cdot 1 = n!$ (the argument here contains a concealed induction).

To give a specific example, let E consist of just three elements, and let us label them simply 1, 2, 3. In this case $S(E)$ consists of the $3! = 6$ mappings listed below:

3.2
$$e = \begin{pmatrix} 1 & 2 & 3 \\ 1 & 2 & 3 \end{pmatrix} \qquad s_1 = \begin{pmatrix} 1 & 2 & 3 \\ 3 & 1 & 2 \end{pmatrix}$$
$$s_2 = \begin{pmatrix} 1 & 2 & 3 \\ 2 & 3 & 1 \end{pmatrix} \qquad s_3 = \begin{pmatrix} 1 & 2 & 3 \\ 2 & 1 & 3 \end{pmatrix}$$
$$s_4 = \begin{pmatrix} 1 & 2 & 3 \\ 3 & 2 & 1 \end{pmatrix} \qquad s_6 = \begin{pmatrix} 1 & 2 & 3 \\ 1 & 3 & 2 \end{pmatrix}$$

These are to be read as follows, taking s_2 for example: The symbol means that s_2 sends each element of the top row into the element directly beneath it in the bottom row. Thus s_2 sends 1 into 2, 2 into 3, and 3 into 1. That is, $s_2(1) = 2$, $s_2(2) = 3$, $s_2(3) = 1$. Similarly for the others. Observe that s_2 could be equally well represented by the symbols

$$\begin{pmatrix} 2 & 1 & 3 \\ 3 & 2 & 1 \end{pmatrix} \qquad \begin{pmatrix} 2 & 3 & 1 \\ 3 & 1 & 2 \end{pmatrix} \qquad \text{etc.}$$

(The particular numbering of the mappings $s_1, s_2, \ldots, s_5$ is of no importance; however we reserve the letter e for the identity mapping.) To illustrate the product of permutations we have, by (3.1), $s_3s_2(1) = s_3(s_2(1)) = s_3(2) = 1$; $s_3s_2(2) = s_3(s_2(2)) = s_3(3) = 3$; $s_3s_2(3) = s_3(1) = 2$. Thus s_3s_2 is represented by the symbol

$$\begin{pmatrix} 1 & 2 & 3 \\ 1 & 3 & 2 \end{pmatrix}$$

† In this section we shall use the notation ss' instead of $s \circ s'$ for the composition of two permutations.

and so $s_3s_2 = s_5$. Similarly, $s_4s_5 = s_1$, $s_5s_4 = s_2$, $s_1s_1 = s_2$, and so forth. Of course we have $es = se = s$ for any of the six permutations s; and $s_2^{-1} = s_1$, etc. It is easily verified that the "multiplication table" of this group is the same as Table 6, Sec. 6, Chap. 1.

The notation used above for a set of three elements can be used equally well for a set E containing any finite number of elements, say n. If we think of the elements of E as labeled in some fixed order by the numbers 1, 2, . . . , n, and if s is a permutation of E, then just as in (3.2) we can represent s by the symbol

3.3 $$s = \begin{pmatrix} 1 & 2 & \cdots & n \\ s(1) & s(2) & \cdots & s(n) \end{pmatrix}$$

or by any of the symbols derived from it by reordering the columns. In particular the identity permutation e is represented by

$$\begin{pmatrix} 1 & 2 & \cdots & n \\ 1 & 2 & \cdots & n \end{pmatrix}$$

and the inverse s^{-1} of s above can be represented by

3.4 $$s^{-1} = \begin{pmatrix} s(1) & s(2) & \cdots & s(n) \\ 1 & 2 & \cdots & n \end{pmatrix}$$

It is obvious that if E and E' are two sets of n objects each, then $S(E)$ and $S(E')$ are essentially the same. We can make this more precise as follows: Labeling the elements of both E and E' with the numbers 1, 2, . . . , n, we can represent the permutations of E and E' by symbols of the type (3.3). If we associate a permutation s of E with that permutation s' of E' represented by the same symbol, then we establish a one-to-one correspondence between $S(E)$ and $S(E')$ which is easily seen to be an isomorphism. Any such $S(E)$ is called the *symmetric group on n elements.*

We now develop a somewhat different way of describing permutations.

PROPOSITION 3.2 *Let s and s' be two permutations of a set E, and suppose that no element of E is moved by both s and s'. That is, suppose that if $s(x) \neq x$, then $s'(x) = x$, and vice versa. Then $s's = ss'$.*

The proof is trivial and is left as an exercise.

DEFINITION 3.1 *Let $x_1, x_2, \ldots, x_r$ be distinct elements of a set E. Then the symbol $(x_1, x_2, \ldots, x_r)$ will denote the permutation that sends x_1 into x_2, x_2 into x_3, . . . , x_{r-1} into x_r, and finally x_r into x_1, leaving all the other elements of E fixed. The permutation is called a* cycle of order *r.*

Observe that, according to our definition, the symbols $(x_1, x_2, \ldots, x_r)$, $(x_r, x_1, x_2, \ldots, x_{r-1})$, $(x_{r-1}, x_r, x_1, x_2, \ldots, x_{r-2})$, etc., all denote the same permutation.

EXAMPLE Let E consist of five elements 1, 2, 3, 4, 5. Then the symbols (2, 3, 1) and $\begin{pmatrix} 1 & 2 & 3 & 4 & 5 \\ 2 & 3 & 1 & 4 & 5 \end{pmatrix}$ both denote the same permutation. From the definition of the product of two permutations, (2, 3, 1)(4, 1) is the same as the permutation $\begin{pmatrix} 1 & 2 & 3 & 4 & 5 \\ 4 & 3 & 1 & 2 & 5 \end{pmatrix}$, as is easily verified. For example, (4, 1) sends 4 into 1, and (2, 3, 1) sends 1 into 2. Therefore (2, 3, 1)(4, 1) sends 4 into 2, etc.

Now let E be a set of n elements, and let s be a permutation of E. Select an element x in E and consider the list of elements†

3.5 $$x, s(x), s^2(x), s^3(x), \ldots, s^n(x), s^{n+1}(x), \ldots$$

obtained by applying s repeatedly. Since E has only n elements, it is clear that at least two of the elements above must be the same, say $s^j(x) = s^k(x)$, with $j < k$. Apply s^{-j} = inverse of s^j to this equation, getting $s^{-j}s^j(x) = s^{-j}s^k(x)$, or $x = s^{k-j}(x)$. Thus the element x must appear in the list (3.5) more than once. Let r be the least positive integer such that $s^r(x) = x$. Then $s^{r+1}(x) = s(s^r(x)) = s(x)$ and $s^{r+2}(x) = s(s^{r+1}(x)) = s^2(x)$, and so on; and it follows that (3.5) simply consists of the r elements $x, s(x), s^2(x), \ldots, s^{r-1}(x)$ repeated over and over again. Let us write x_1 for x, x_2 for $s(x)$, x_3 for $s^2(x)$, . . . , x_r for $s^{r-1}(x)$. Then s sends x_1 into x_2, x_2 into x_3, . . . , x_{r-1} into x_r, and finally x_r back to x_1. The set consisting of $x_1, x_2, \ldots, x_r$ is called the *s-orbit* of $x = x_1$, and s permutes these elements cyclically. Referring to Definition 3.1, we see that the cycle $(x_1, x_2, \ldots, x_r)$ has the same effect on the r elements as does s. It is clear moreover that all the elements $x_1, x_2, \ldots, x_r$ have the same s-orbit, namely, the set consisting of those r elements.

If $r = n$, then all the elements of E appear in the cycle $(x_1, x_2, \ldots, x_n)$, and in this case s is simply a cyclic permutation of E. If $r < n$, then there is at least one element y of E not in the cycle $(x_1, x_2, \ldots, x_r)$. Repeating the foregoing argument for the elements

$$y, s(y), s^2(y), s^3(y), \ldots$$

we obtain in the same way the s-orbit of y, consisting say of k elements $y_1 = y$, $y_2 = s(y), \ldots, y_k = s^{k-1}(y)$, where $s(y_k) = s^k(y) = y$. Corresponding to this orbit we have a cycle $(y_1, y_2, \ldots, y_k)$ of order k. This cycle has precisely the same effect on the k elements $y_1, y_2, \ldots, y_k$ as does s. The two cycles $(x_1, x_2, \ldots, x_r)$ and $(y_1, y_2, \ldots, y_k)$ cannot have any elements in common. For suppose that $x_i = y_j$, say. That is, $s^{i-1}(x) = s^{j-1}(y)$. Applying s^{k-j+1} to both sides we get $s^{k+i-j}(x) = s^k(y)$. But $s^k(y) = y$, from above, and so $s^{k+i-j}(x) = y$. Thus y is in the s-orbit of x, a contradiction.

If the two cycles $(x_1, x_2, \ldots, x_r)$ and $(y_1, y_2, \ldots, y_k)$ do not contain all the elements of E (that is, if $r + k < n$), then we can continue the process. But it must obviously stop after at most n steps. We arrive finally at a decomposition of E into

† Recall that $s^2 = ss$, $s^3 = sss$, etc. See Sec. 7E, Chap. 2.

a certain number of s-orbits, with corresponding cycles $(x_1, x_2, \ldots, x_r)$, $(y_1, y_2, \ldots, y_k)$, $\ldots$, $(w_1, w_2, \ldots, w_l)$. As just observed, no two of the orbits, and thus no two of the cycles, have any elements in common. For this reason we say that they are *disjoint*. The mapping s produces a cyclic permutation in each orbit, represented by the corresponding cycle, and therefore s cannot send an element of one orbit into another orbit. It follows readily that s is the product of the cycles corresponding to its orbits,

$$s = (x_1, \ldots, x_r)(y_1, \ldots, y_k) \cdots (w_1, \ldots, w_l)$$

We have therefore the following theorem:

THEOREM 3.3 *E being a finite set, any permutation s of E can be expressed as a product of disjoint cycles. The elements of the cycles form the s-orbits in E, and that representation of s is consequently unique, apart from the order of the factors.*

Note that since the cycles are disjoint the order in which they appear is immaterial, by Proposition 3.2. A cycle of order 1 stands for the identity permutation, and therefore such cycles can simply be omitted.

EXAMPLE Consider the permutation $s = \begin{pmatrix} 1 & 2 & 3 & 4 & 5 & 6 & 7 & 8 \\ 8 & 7 & 2 & 6 & 5 & 4 & 1 & 3 \end{pmatrix}$ of eight elements. Let us compute the s-orbit of, say, the element 1. The mapping sends $1 \to 8$, $8 \to 3$, $3 \to 2$, $2 \to 7$, $7 \to 1$, and so the s-orbit of 1 consists of 1, 8, 3, 2, 7. That set of five elements is also the s-orbit of 8, 3, 2, and 7, plainly. The s-orbit of 4 consists of the elements 4 and 6; the s-orbit of 5 consists of the single element 5. That exhausts the set of eight elements, and we have $s = (1, 8, 3, 2, 7)(4, 6)(5)$. As remarked above, the cycle (5) represents the identity permutation, and so we can also write $s = (1, 8, 3, 2, 7)(4, 6)$, or $s = (4, 6)(1, 8, 3, 2, 7)$.

DEFINITION 3.2 *Let s be a permutation of a finite set E, and suppose that s can be expressed as a product of h disjoint cycles, of orders $r_1, r_2, \ldots, r_h$, respectively. Then the number $I(s) = (r_1 - 1) + (r_2 - 1) + \cdots + (r_h - 1)$ is called the* index *of s. If $I(s)$ is even, then s is said to be an even permutation; if $I(s)$ is odd, then s is said to be odd.*

In this definition it is obviously immaterial whether cycles of order 1 are included or not. Since the decomposition of s into a product of *disjoint* cycles is unique, apart from order and from cycles of order 1, it follows that the index $I(s)$ is uniquely determined by s. In the example above, the permutation $(4, 6)(1, 8, 3, 2, 7)$ has index $1 + 4 = 5$ and is therefore odd. The identity permutation always has index zero and is therefore even.

THEOREM 3.4 *Any permutation s of a finite set E can be expressed as a product of cycles of order 2 (not necessarily disjoint and not unique).*

Proof. Consider a cycle $(x_1, \ldots, x_r)$. It follows from the definition of composition of mappings that

$$(x_1, \ldots, x_r) = (x_r, x_1)(x_{r-1}, x_1) \cdots (x_3, x_1)(x_2, x_1)$$

Therefore the assertion is true for cycles. Now if we express an arbitrary permutation s of E as a product of disjoint cycles and in turn express each of those cycles as a product of cycles of order 2, then we obtain an expression for s as a product of cycles of order 2. Q.E.D.

A cycle of order 2 is sometimes called a *transposition* because it simply interchanges two elements of E. The main results of this section are Theorem 3.4 and the following theorem:

THEOREM 3.5 *Let E be a finite set, and let $t_1, t_2, \ldots, t_m$ be transpositions of E, that is, cycles of order 2. Then the permutation $s = t_1t_2 \cdots t_m$ of E is even if m is even and is odd if m is odd.*

Proof. This can be shown directly by induction on m. However we give a somewhat different proof. Let n be the number of elements in E. If we replace the elements of E by the integers $1, 2, \ldots, n$ in some way, then every permutation s of E can be regarded as a permutation of $1, \ldots, n$. As usual, the effect of a permutation s on an integer j in that set will be denoted by $s(j)$, so that s can be represented by the symbol (3.3).

Now consider the ring $A = \mathbf{Z}[x_1, \ldots, x_n]$ of polynomials in n independent variables over the integers $\mathbf{Z}$ (see Sec. 5, Chap. 6). For any permutation s of $1, \ldots, n$ there is a unique isomorphism of A to itself—we call it s also—sending x_j into $x_{s(j)}$ for $j = 1, \ldots, n$ (Theorem 5.2, Corollary, Chap. 6). Denote simply by sf the image of a polynomial f under this isomorphism. That is, sf is the polynomial defined by $sf(x_1, \ldots, x_n) = f(x_{s(1)}, \ldots, x_{s(n)})$, obtained by permuting the variables in f according to s. In particular we have $sx_j = x_{s(j)}$ for the monomial x_j. If s' is another permutation of $1, \ldots, n$, then $s'(sx_j) = s'x_{s(j)} = x_{s'(s(j))} = x_{s's(j)}$, and so $s'(sx_j) = (s's)x_j$. From this it follows easily that, for any polynomial f in A,

3.6 $$s'(sf) = (s's)f$$

Consider now the special polynomial

3.7 $$h = \prod_{i<j} (x_i - x_j) = (x_1 - x_2)(x_1 - x_3) \cdots (x_{n-1} - x_n)$$

For example, for $n = 3$ we have $h = (x_1 - x_2)(x_1 - x_3)(x_2 - x_3)$. Now if t is any transposition of two integers in $1, \ldots, n$, it is easily seen that $th = -h$. Therefore, if $t_1, \ldots, t_m$ are all transpositions, then $(t_1t_2 \cdots t_m)h = (-1)^m h$, by repeated applications of (3.6). Hence, to prove the theorem, we merely have to show that $sh = h$ if s is an even permutation and $sh = -h$ if s is an odd permutation.

Write the arbitrary permutation s of $1, \ldots, n$ as a product $s =$

$s_1 s_2 \cdots s_k$ of disjoint cycles. If s_k is the cycle $(j_1, \ldots, j_r)$, say, then s_k can be expressed as a product of $r - 1$ transpositions, as in the proof of Theorem 3.4. From the remarks above it follows that $s_k h = (-1)^{r-1}h$, and $r - 1$ is precisely the index of s_k. By (3.6) we have $sh = (s_1 \cdots s_{k-1})s_k h) = (-1)^{r-1}(s_1 \cdots s_{k-1})h$. By repeated applications of the argument we arrive at $sh = (-1)^b h$, where b is the sum of the indices $I(s_1) + \cdots + I(s_k)$. By Definition 3.2 this number is the index of s. Hence we have $sh = (-1)^{I(s)}h$, which proves the theorem. Q.E.D.

THEOREM 3.6 *Let s and s' be two permutations of a finite set E. Then their product ss' is even if s and s' are both even or both odd; otherwise the product is an odd permutation. The even permutations in $S(E)$ form a subgroup† $A(E)$ containing $n!/2$ elements, if n is the number of elements in E.*

This follows immediately from Theorems 3.4 and 3.5.

EXERCISES

1. Let E be a set of n elements, and let E_1 and E_2 be two subsets, each containing r elements. Determine the number of permutations of E which send E_1 into E_2.

2. Write each of the following permutations as a product of disjoint cycles. Determine the indices of the permutations, and express each one as a product of transpositions:

(*a*) $\begin{pmatrix} 1 & 2 & 3 & 4 & 5 & 6 & 7 \\ 7 & 6 & 5 & 4 & 3 & 2 & 1 \end{pmatrix}$ (*b*) $\begin{pmatrix} 7 & 6 & 5 & 4 & 3 & 2 & 1 \\ 4 & 3 & 1 & 2 & 6 & 7 & 5 \end{pmatrix}$

(*c*) $\begin{pmatrix} 1 & 2 & 3 & 4 & 5 & 6 & 7 & 8 & 9 & 10 \\ 8 & 4 & 2 & 1 & 3 & 6 & 10 & 9 & 7 & 5 \end{pmatrix}$ (*d*) $\begin{pmatrix} 2 & 3 & 8 & 9 & 1 & 4 & 7 & 6 & 5 \\ 1 & 8 & 9 & 6 & 7 & 5 & 4 & 2 & 3 \end{pmatrix}$

3. Write the following permutations of a set of eight elements in the form (3.3), and determine whether they are odd or even. Write them also as products of transpositions.

(*a*) (1, 3, 5)(5, 4, 3, 2)(5, 6, 7, 8) (*b*) (4, 1, 2, 8, 7)(4, 1, 2, 3)

(*c*) (1, 2)(2, 4)(1, 7)(7, 6, 8) (*d*) (5, 4, 8, 6, 7, 1, 3, 2)

4. Let E be a set of n elements, and let E' be a subset of r elements. How many permutations of E send each element of E' into itself? Show that all such permutations form a subgroup of $S(E)$.

5. With E and E' as above, how many permutations of E map E' into itself? Show that all such permutations form a subgroup of $S(E)$.

***6.** Let E be a finite set, and let G be a *transitive* group of permutations of E generated by transpositions. That is, let G be a subgroup of $S(E)$ such that (1) for any pair of elements x, y in E there is an element of G which sends x into y and (2) every element of G can be expressed as a product of transpositions which are themselves elements of G. Prove that $G = S(E)$.

7. Consider permutations of $1, 2, \ldots, n$: Assuming $i < j$, show that the

† $A(E)$ is called the *alternating* group on n elements.

transposition (i, j) can be expressed as a product of transpositions of *adjacent* elements of $i, i + 1, \ldots, j$, necessarily an odd number of them.

4. Subgroups and quotient groups

We now return to a discussion of arbitrary groups. The definition of quotient groups given below is very closely connected with the definition of quotient spaces in Sec. 10, Chap. 9. We begin by defining two operations on the *subsets* of a group.

DEFINITION 4.1 *Let G be a group (multiplicative notation), and let A be a non-empty subset of G. Then A^{-1} will denote the set consisting of all the inverses of the elements in A. If B is a second non-empty subset, then AB will denote the set of all products ab, where a is an element of A and b is an element of B.*

From Definition 4.1 it is trivial to verify the rules

4.1 $$(AB)^{-1} = B^{-1}A^{-1} \qquad A(BC) = (AB)C$$

for subsets of G. The following fact is useful:

4.2 $$HH = H \quad \text{and} \quad H^{-1} = H \quad \text{if and only if } H \text{ is a subgroup of } G$$

If these equalities hold, and if a, b are elements of H, then from the first equality it follows that ab is in H, and from the second equality it follows that a^{-1} and b^{-1} are in H. Hence H is a subgroup of G. The converse is equally trivial to verify.

If H, K are subgroups of G, the set HK is not in general a subgroup. However we have

4.3 *If H, K are subgroups of G such that $HK = KH$, then HK is also a subgroup of G.*

For $(HK)^{-1} = K^{-1}H^{-1}$, and this is equal to KH, by (4.2), hence is equal to HK, by assumption. Thus $(HK)^{-1} = HK$. Similarly, $(HK)(HK) = H(KH)K = HHKK = HK$. Hence HK satisfies (4.2).

DEFINITION 4.2 *Let H be a subgroup of a group G. Then any set of the type aH (a an element of G) is called a* left coset *of H; any set of the type Ha is called a* right coset *of H.*

According to Definition 4.1 above, the left coset aH consists of all the elements ax, where x is an arbitrary element of H. Similarly, Ha consists of all elements xa. Since H contains the identity element e, it is clear that aH and Ha both contain a. Hence every element of G is contained in a left coset of H and in a right coset of H. It is plain that $eH = H$ and $He = H$, and so H itself appears among the cosets; $aH = Ha$ if the group G is *commutative.*

REMARK. In the case of an abelian group with the additive notation, we naturally write $A + B$ instead of AB in Definition 4.1. This operation among subsets of G is then commutative. If A, B are subgroups of G, then so is $A + B$. H being a subgroup of G, its (left) cosets are written $a + H$ instead of aH, and clearly $a + H = H + a$.

EXAMPLE 1 Let m be a positive integer, and let H be the subgroup of the additive group of integers $\mathbf{Z}^+$ consisting of all multiples $0, \pm m, \pm 2m, \pm 3m$, etc., of m. If a is any integer, then the coset $a + H$ consists of all the integers $a + km$ (k an arbitrary integer). In other words, $a + H$ consists of all integers which are congruent to a *modulo m*; that is, $a + H$ is the residue class *modulo m* that contains a.

THEOREM 4.1 *Let H be a subgroup of a group G, and let c be an element of G. Then $cH = H$ if and only if c is an element of H. Similarly, $Hc = H$ if and only if c is in H.*

Proof. $ce = c$ is an element of cH, hence must be an element of H if $cH = H$. Conversely, if c is in H and if x is in H, then cx is in H, since H is a subgroup, and so cH is certainly a subset of H. But, given any y in H, there is an element x in H such that $cx = y$, namely $x = c^{-1}y$. Therefore cH must be identical with H. The proof for Hc is quite similar. Q.E.D.

COROLLARY *Two elements a, b of G are in the same left coset of H if and only if $a^{-1}b$ is in H. Every element of G is in one and only one left coset of H.*

Proof. Suppose that a and b are both in the left coset cH. Then, by definition of the latter, there are elements x, y in H such that $a = cx$ and $b = cy$. From this there follows $a^{-1} = x^{-1}c^{-1}$, whence $a^{-1}b = x^{-1}y$, which is an element of H, since H is a subgroup of G. Conversely, if $a^{-1}b$ is in H, then $a^{-1}bH = H$, by the theorem above. Multiplying by a we get $bH = aH$. But bH contains $be = b$, and aH contains a; a and b are in the same left coset. Every element of G is in some left coset, since a is in aH. Suppose now that a is in another left coset bH. The latter contains b, and therefore $a^{-1}b$ is in H, and so $aH = bH$, as we have just seen; the two cosets are identical. Q.E.D.

REMARK. The corollary holds equally well for right cosets, save that $a^{-1}b$ in the statement must be replaced by ab^{-1}. In order to minimize repetition, we shall generally state and prove things for left cosets.

The corollary says that the subgroup H determines a decomposition of G into disjoint (i.e., nonoverlapping) subsets, namely, the left cosets of H. The number of distinct left cosets of H in G is called the *index* of H in G. This is the same as the number of distinct right cosets, as is easily seen. For $(aH)^{-1} = H^{-1}a^{-1} = Ha^{-1}$, by (4.1) and (4.2). That is, the set of inverses of elements in aH is precisely the right coset Ha^{-1}. In this way there is established a one-to-one correspondence between left and right cosets of H.

EXAMPLE 2 Let H be the subgroup of $\mathbf{Z}^+$ defined in Example 1. The cosets of H (left or right) are the residue classes of integers *modulo m*, and in Sec. 10, Chap. 2, it was shown that there are m of them. That is, the index of H in $\mathbf{Z}^+$ is m.

It will be convenient to use the symbol $\#E$ to denote the number of elements in an arbitrary (finite) set E. A group G is called *finite* if it consists of only a finite number of elements, and that number $\#G$ is called the *order* of G. If H is a subgroup of G, then $\#(aH) = \#H$ for any a in G. That is, any left coset of H contains the same number of elements as H. For the mapping $H \to aH$ defined by $x \to ax$ is a one-to-one mapping. Assuming that G is finite, put $n = \#G$, $m = \#H$, and let i denote the index of H in G (the number of distinct left cosets). From the corollary above we clearly have $n = mi$, for the left cosets of H decompose G into i disjoint sets of m elements each. We state this important result as

THEOREM 4.2 (Lagrange) *Let G be a group of order n, and let H be a subgroup of order m. Let i be the index of H in G. Then $n = m \cdot i$. In particular, m divides n. The order of any element a in G divides the order n of G, and $a^n = e$.*

We recall from Theorem 2.2 that the *order* of an element a is the least positive integer d such that $a^d = e$. In other words, d is the number of elements in the cyclic subgroup (a) generated by a. By what has been shown, d must divide n, say $n = dk$. Then $a^n = a^{dk} = (a^d)^k = e$.

COROLLARY *Let G be a group whose order is a prime p. Then G is a cyclic group, and it is generated by any of its elements a other than the identity. That is, G consists of the powers $e, a, a^2, \ldots, a^{p-1}$. In particular, G is abelian.*

Proof. The element a generates a cyclic subgroup (a), by Theorem 2.2. Since $a \neq e$, the order of this subgroup must be p, by the theorem above, and so $G = (a)$. Q.E.D.

Let H be a subgroup of a group G, and consider the set L whose elements are the various left cosets of H. Under certain circumstances L, with the operation of Definition 4.1, is itself a group. Now H itself appears among the left cosets of H, and so H is an element of L. Since $HH = H$, by (4.2), it follows that if L does happen to be a group with the operation of Definition 4.1, then H must be the identity element of L. Then $H(cH) = cH$, for any left coset cH. Now the set standing on the left of this equation must contain the subset $Hce = Hc$. Therefore, Hc is contained in cH. By the same argument applied to $c^{-1}H$, we find that Hc^{-1} is contained in $c^{-1}H$. Consequently $(Hc^{-1})^{-1}$ is contained in $(c^{-1}H)^{-1}$. That is, cH is contained in Hc [using (4.1) and (4.2)]. Therefore, if L is a group, then $cH = Hc$ for any element c in G.

DEFINITION 4.3 *A subgroup H of a group G is called a* normal *(or* invariant*) subgroup if $cH = Hc$ for every c in G, or what is the same thing, if $H = c^{-1}Hc$.*

REMARK. Let c be a fixed element of G. The mapping $G \to G$ that sends an arbitrary element x into $c^{-1}xc$ is an isomorphism of G to itself (cf. Exercise 3, Sec. 2). Isomorphisms obtained in this way are called *inner automorphisms* of G. According to Definition 4.3, a subgroup H is a normal subgroup if and only if H is mapped to itself by every inner automorphism of G.

The mapping $x \to c^{-1}xc$ takes any subgroup H into a new subgroup $c^{-1}Hc$. Any such subgroup is called a *conjugate* of H. (Taking $c = e$, we see that H is included amongst its conjugates.) Replacing c by c^{-1} we get a new conjugate cHc^{-1}. Thus we can write the conjugates of H either in the form $c^{-1}Hc$ or else cHc^{-1}. (However, the two conjugates indicated here are different, in general.)

Every group G has at least two normal subgroups, namely, G itself and the subgroup (e) consisting of the identity element. Every subgroup of an abelian group is a normal subgroup.

A normal subgroup H of G is simply one for which the left and right cosets are identical, and in this situation we can speak simply of the *cosets* of H, without specifying *left* or *right*.

THEOREM 4.3 *Let G be a group, and let H be a subgroup. If the left cosets of H form a group with the operation of Definition* 4.1, *then H is a normal subgroup of G. Conversely, if H is a normal subgroup, then the cosets of H form a group with the binary operation of Definition* 4.1. *That group is called the* quotient *group (or* factor *group) of G by H and is denoted by G/H. The product $(aH)(bH)$ of two elements of G/H is the coset abH; the inverse of aH is $a^{-1}H$; the identity element of G/H is the coset H. The mapping $G \to G/H$ defined by $a \to aH$ is a homomorphism (called the* canonical *homomorphism). Its kernel*† *is H.*

The first assertion has already been proved. If H is a normal subgroup, then $(aH)(bH) = a(Hb)H = a(bH)H = abHH = abH$, as claimed, by (4.2). The other verifications are entirely routine. For example, to show that H is the identity element of G/H, we have $H \cdot (aH) = (Ha)H = (aH)H = aHH = aH$, and $(aH) \cdot H = aHH = aH$. To show that $a^{-1}H$ is the inverse of aH, $(a^{-1}H)(aH) = a^{-1}(Ha)H = a^{-1}(aH)H = eHH = H$, and by the same reasoning $(aH)(a^{-1}H) = H$.

THEOREM 4.4 *Let f be a homomorphism from a group G to a group G', and let H be the kernel*† *of f. Then H is a normal subgroup of G, and all the elements in any coset of H are mapped by f into the same element of G'. The mapping $\bar{f}$: $G/H \to G'$ defined by $\bar{f}(aH) = f(a)$ is a homomorphism and in fact is an isomorphism between G/H and $f(G)$;*† *$\bar{f}$ is called the mapping* induced *by f.*

Proof. By definition, x is in H if and only if $f(x) = e' =$ identity of G'. Let c be any element of G, and let x be any element of H. Then $f(c^{-1}xc) = f(c^{-1})f(x)f(c) = f(c^{-1}) \cdot e' \cdot f(c) = f(c^{-1})f(c) = e'$, since $f(c^{-1}) = f(c)^{-1}$. Thus $c^{-1}xc$ is also in H. This shows that $c^{-1}Hc$ is contained in H. Replacing c by c^{-1} in this argument, we find similarly that cHc^{-1} is contained in H; hence $c^{-1}(cHc^{-1})c$ is contained in $c^{-1}Hc$; that is, H is contained in $c^{-1}Hc$. Therefore $H = c^{-1}Hc$; showing that H is a normal subgroup of G.

Now if a, b are in the same coset of H, then $a^{-1}b$ is in H, by the corollary

† See Exercise 1, Sec. 2.

of Theorem 4.1. Thus $f(a^{-1}b) = e'$, and so $f(b) = f(aa^{-1}b) = f(a)f(a^{-1}b) = f(a) \cdot e' = f(a)$. Therefore, f maps all the elements in any coset of H into the same element of G', and consequently the definition of $\bar{f}\colon G/H \to G'$ is consistent, for if $aH = bH$, then $f(a) = f(b)$. It is trivial to verify that $\bar{f}$ has the properties stated. Q.E.D.

THEOREM 4.5 *Let f be a homomorphism of a group G onto a group G' [that is, $f(G) = G'$]. Then f maps any normal subgroup of G onto a normal subgroup of G'.*

Proof. Let K be a normal subgroup of G, and let K' consist of all elements $f(a)$, with a in K. If a, b are in K, so are ab, a^{-1}, b^{-1}. Hence $f(ab) = f(a) \cdot f(b)$ and $f(a^{-1}) = f(a)^{-1}$, $f(b^{-1}) = f(b)^{-1}$ are also in K', showing that K' is a subgroup of G'. Now take any c' in G'. We want to show that $c'^{-1} \cdot K' \cdot c' = K'$. By assumption there is some c in G such that $f(c) = c'$. For any a in K the element $c^{-1}ac$ is in K, and so $f(c^{-1}ac) = f(c)^{-1}f(a)f(c) = c'^{-1} \cdot f(a) \cdot c'$ is in K'. Q.E.D.

The following two theorems are usually called the *first* and *second isomorphism theorems*, respectively.

THEOREM 4.6 *Let H, K be subgroups of a group G, and suppose that K is a normal subgroup. Let $f\colon G \to G/K$ be the canonical homomorphism. Then f maps H onto HK/K; and if h denotes the mapping f restricted to elements of H, then the kernel of h is $H \cap K$, the set of elements common to both H and K. $H \cap K$ is a normal subgroup of H, and the mapping $h\colon H/H \cap K \to G/K$ induced by h maps $H/H \cap K$ isomorphically* onto HK/K.

Proof. $HK = KH$, since K is a normal subgroup of G. Therefore HK is a subgroup of G, by (4.3), and it clearly contains K, since H contains e. Thus K is a subgroup of HK, and it is a normal subgroup, since $c^{-1}Kc = K$ for any c in G, hence a fortiori for any c in HK.

Any element in HK can be expressed in the form ac, with a in H and c in K. For the coset we have $(ac) \cdot K = a(cK) = aK$, by Theorem 4.1. Hence every coset of K in HK can be written in the form aK, with a in H. Now the canonical homomorphism f maps any a in G into the coset aK. In particular, this is so for elements a in H, and so f maps H onto the system of all cosets aK (a in H). As we have just seen, this is precisely HK/K.

Denoting by h the mapping $H \to G/K$ obtained by confining f to elements of H, we have $h(a) = aK$ for any a in H. And, as we have just seen, h maps H onto the subgroup HK/K of G/K. That is, $h(H) = HK/K$. The kernel of h consists of all elements of H which are mapped by h into the identity element of G/K. Now that identity element is the coset K. Hence, the kernel of h consists of all a in H such that $h(a) = K$, that is, such that $aK = K$. By Theorem 4.1 that is so if and only if a is in K. But a is also in H, and therefore the kernel of h is the set $H \cap K$ of all elements common to both H and K. Then $H \cap K$ is a normal subgroup of H, by Theorem 4.4; and by that same theorem (applied to h), the induced mapping $\bar{h}$: $H/H \cap K \to G/K$ maps the first group isomorphically onto $h(H) = HK/K$. Q.E.D.

Observe that $\bar{h}$ simply maps a coset $a(H \cap K)$ into the coset aK.

THEOREM 4.7 *Let K be a normal subgroup of a group G, and let f: $G \to \bar{G}$ be the canonical homomorphism of G onto the quotient group $\bar{G} = G/K$. Let $\bar{H}$ be a normal subgroup of $\bar{G}$, and denote by H the set of all elements in G which are mapped by f into $\bar{H}$. Then H is a normal subgroup of G, containing K, and the groups G/H and $\bar{G}/\bar{H}$ are isomorphic in a natural way.*

Proof. Let $\bar{g}$: $\bar{G} \to \bar{G}/\bar{H}$ be the canonical homomorphism. Then the composition $\bar{g}f$ is a homomorphism $G \to \bar{G}/\bar{H}$. The kernel of $\bar{g}f$ consists of all x in G such that $\bar{g}f(x) = \bar{H} =$ identity of $\bar{G}/\bar{H}$. Now by definition, $\bar{g}f(x) = \bar{g}(f(x)) = f(x) \cdot \bar{H}$, and this is equal to $\bar{H}$ if and only if $f(x)$ is in $\bar{H}$, which is so if and only if x is in H, by definition of H. Therefore H is the kernel of $\bar{g}f$ and accordingly is a normal subgroup of G (Theorem 4.4). The mapping $G/H \to \bar{G}/\bar{H}$ induced by $\bar{g}f$ is an isomorphism, by Theorem 4.4. Q.E.D.

EXERCISES

1. Let f: $G \to G'$ be a homomorphism of groups, and let H' be a normal subgroup of G'. Let H be the set of all x in G such that $f(x)$ is in H'. Prove that H is a normal subgroup of G. Prove that G/H is isomorphic to a subgroup of G'/H'.

2. Let H be a normal subgroup of a group G, and let H' be a normal subgroup of a group G'. Let f: $G \to G'$ be a homomorphism such that $f(x)$ is in H' whenever x is in H. Let g: $G \to G/H$ and g': $G \to G'/H'$ be the canonical homomorphisms. Prove that there is one and only one homomorphism $\bar{f}$: $G/H \to G'/H'$ such that $\bar{f}g = g'f$. (This $\bar{f}$ is called the homomorphism *induced* by f.)

***3.** Let G be a group. By a *commutator* of G is meant an element of the type $aba^{-1}b^{-1}$ (a, b in G, naturally). Let K denote the set of all elements in G which can be expressed as products of commutators. Prove that K is a normal subgroup of G and that G/K is abelian. [Hint: Show that conjugation $x \to c^{-1}xc$ by an element c sends a commutator into a commutator.] Prove that if f: $G \to G'$ is a homomorphism of G to an *abelian* group, then the kernel of f must contain K. (K is called the *commutator subgroup* of G.)

4. Let H be a subgroup of a group G. Let L consist of all x in G such that $xH = Hx$. Show that L is a subgroup of G and that H is a normal subgroup of L. Show that if K is any subgroup of G containing H and that if H is normal in K, then K is a subgroup of L. (L is called the *normalizer* of H in G.)

5. G being a group, let C denote the subset consisting of all elements c such that $cx = xc$ for all x in G. Show that C is a normal subgroup of G (called the *center* of G).

6. Let S_n denote the symmetric group of n elements, and let A_n denote the alternating subgroup (that is, consisting of all even permutations; cf. Sec. 3). Show that A_n is a normal subgroup of S_n and that S_n/A_n is a cyclic group of order 2.

7. Let H be a subgroup of index 2 in a group G. Prove that H is a normal subgroup.

8. Referring to Table 5, Sec. 6, Chap. 1, show that the subgroups $\{p, s\}$, $\{p, r, t\}$ are normal subgroups. Write out the cosets for both of them, and compute the multiplication tables for the corresponding quotient groups.

9. Let G be a group of prime order (that is, $\#G$ is a prime number). Show that G is abelian and that its only subgroups are G itself and the identity subgroup.

10. Let G be a group of order p^α, where p is a prime. Show that any subgroup has order p^β for some $\beta \leq \alpha$.

11. Let G be a group of order mk, and let H be a subgroup of order m. For any element a in G show that there is an integer h, with $1 \leq h \leq k$, such that a^h is in H. If H is normal, prove that a^k is in H for any a. [Hint: Consider the cosets H, aH, a^2H, etc.]

12. Let H be a subgroup of a group G, and let L be the normalizer of H (see Exercise 4). Prove that the number of distinct conjugates of H is equal to $\#H/\#L$.

***13.** Let E be a euclidean space (Sec. 11, Chap. 8), and let G be the set of all distance-preserving mappings $f\colon E \to E$. That is, the distance between $f(p)$ and $f(q)$ must be equal to the distance between p and q for any two points of E. Prove that G with composition of mappings as binary operation is a group. Prove that an element f of E is a translation if and only if $\overrightarrow{f(p)f(q)} = \overrightarrow{pq}$ for any two points p, q of E. Deduce that the set of all translations T of E is a normal subgroup of G. Prove that the quotient group G/T is isomorphic to the subgroup G_0 of G consisting of all f which leave a specified point p_0 fixed, that is, which map p_0 to itself. (Show that each coset of T contains one and only one mapping in G_0.)

14. In many primitive societies, the rules governing allowed marriages are quite complicated. As we will see, algebraic formalism may simplify the study of these marriage laws.† Suppose that, in a given society, there are n types of marriage, denoted by $M_1, M_2, \ldots, M_n$, subject to the following conditions:

(1) There is one and only one type of marriage allowed any person.

(2) The type of marriage allowed any person depends uniquely on his sex and on the type of marriage of his parents.

(3) A man may always marry the daughter of his mother's brother.

According to (2), we may write $m(M_i)$ for the type of marriage allowed a man whose parents' marriage was of type M_i, and $w(M_i)$ for the type allowed a woman

† Appendix by A. Weil, in "Les structures élémentaires de la parenté," by C. Lévi-Strauss.

of similar extraction. Condition (3) may be expressed as $w(m(M_i)) = m(w(M_i))$. We may assume that the functions m and w are permutations of the set M_1, $M_2, \ldots M_n$ (why?); thus, m and w are commuting elements of the permutation group on n objects. What can one say about the group generated by m and w? Discuss the special case where m and w generate a cyclic group. Classify, in this case, the possible types of marriages. Is it ever allowed, in such a society, that a man marry the daughter of his father's sister?

5. *Transformation groups; Sylow's theorems*

Let G be a group and a an element of G. The mapping $G \to G$ that sends an arbitrary element x into ax is called *left translation* by a. Denoting the mapping by L_a, we have then $L_a(x) = ax$. L_a is a one-to-one mapping, as is easily verified, hence is a permutation of the elements of G. In a similar way we define *right translation* by the element a to be the mapping R_a: $G \to G$ defined by $R_a(x) = xa$. It is also one-to-one. Observe that L_a and R_a are *not* homomorphisms of G unless a is the identity of G. Given a, b in G, we have

$$L_aL_b(x) = L_a(L_b(x)) = L_a(bx) = abx = L_{ab}(x)$$

Hence

5.1 $$L_aL_b = L_{ab}$$

Similarly,

$$R_bR_a = R_{ab}$$

If we denote by $S(G)$ the group of all permutations of the set G (see Sec. 3), then each left translation L_a is an element of $S(G)$, and (5.1) says that the mapping $G \to S(G)$ defined by $a \to L_a$ is a homomorphism. Since L_a is clearly not the identity mapping of G unless $a = e$, it follows that $a \to L_a$ maps G isomorphically onto a subgroup of $S(G)$.† In this way G can be thought of as a subgroup of the permutation group $S(G)$. In the older literature on groups it was customary to view all groups as groups of permutations.

It is useful to formulate a definition which includes the foregoing considerations.

DEFINITION 5.1 *Given a group G and a set E, G is said to* operate *on E as a* group of transformations *if to each a in G there is assigned a permutation T_a of E such that $T_aT_b = T_{ab}$ for any a, b in G.*‡

In other words, it is merely required that there be given a homomorphism $G \to$

† Similar considerations hold for right translations, except that $a \to R_a$ is an "antihomomorphism," since it sends ab into R_bR_a, not R_aR_b.

‡ More precisely, G is said to operate "from the left." If $T_bT_a = T_{ab}$, then G is said to operate from the right.

$S(E)$, where $S(E)$ is the group of one-to-one mappings of E with composition of mappings as group operation. Since a homomorphism sends identity into identity and inverses into inverses, it follows that T_e = identity map of E (where e = identity element of G), and $T_{a^{-1}} = T_a^{-1}$ = inverse mapping of T_a.

An an immediate example of Definition 5.1, a group G operates on itself by left translations, as was pointed out above. If H is a subgroup of G, then left translation (by an element of G) sends any left coset of H into another left coset. Hence G operates by left translation on the set of left cosets of H. We shall make use of this fact presently.

As a second example, if E is any set and if $S(E)$ is the group of permutations of E, then clearly $S(E)$ operates on E pursuant to Definition 5.1. Any subgroup of $S(E)$ also operates on E.

The group of permutations of the integers $1, \ldots, n$ operates on the polynomial ring $\mathbf{Z}[x_1, \ldots, x_n]$ in the manner described in the proof of Theorem 3.5.

Returning to Definition 5.1, instead of writing $T_a(x)$ for the result of T_a applied to an element x in E, it is easier just to write ax. In general this symbol does not denote a group product, since a is in G and x in E. In the case of left translations, however, E is the same as G, and ax is then indeed the product in G. In the abbreviated notation, the requirement $T_aT_b = T_{ab}$ becomes simply

5.2 $$a(bx) = (ab)x \qquad a, b \text{ in } G,\ x \text{ in } E$$

For the special case of left translations in G, this is just the associative law in G. As was pointed out above, T_e is the identity mapping of E, where e = identity of G. In the new notation this is simply

5.3 $$ex = x \qquad \text{for all } x \text{ in } E$$

We now embark upon some considerations similar to those involved in connection with Theorem 4.2.

We observe first that if G operates on E according to Definition 5.1, then any subgroup of G also operates on E as a transformation group, plainly.

DEFINITION 5.2 *Let G operate as a group of transformations on a set E. Let x be an element of E. The set of all elements ax (a an arbitrary element of G) is called the G-orbit of x, denoted by Gx.*

If H is a subgroup of G, then H also operates on E, as pointed out above, and therefore the H-orbit Hx of x is also defined by Definition 5.2. It consists of all bx, b here running through all elements of H, rather than G.

EXAMPLE 1 Let s be a permutation of a finite set E. The group of all permutations $S(E)$ is then finite, and consequently the sequence e, s, s^2, s^3, etc., must constitute a cyclic subgroup (s) of $S(E)$ (cf. Exercise 4, Sec. 2). Now $S(E)$ operates on E, and so does the cyclic subgroup (s). For x in E, the (s)-orbit, as just defined, is none other than the s-orbit of x as defined in Sec. 3.

EXAMPLE 2 Let G operate on itself by left translations, and let H be a subgroup of G, x an element of G. Then the H-orbit of x consists of all elements ax (a in H) and is precisely the coset Hx.

THEOREM 5.1 *Let a group G operate on a set E. Then every element of E is in one and only one G-orbit.*

Proof. Clearly x is in at least one G-orbit, namely Gx, for G contains the identity e, and $ex = x$, by (5.3). Now suppose that two orbits Gy and Gz have an element x in common. Then, by definition of orbit, there are group elements a, b such that $x = ay$ and $x = bz$. Therefore $y = a^{-1}x = a^{-1}(bz) = (a^{-1}b)z$, by (5.2). Hence $cy = (ca^{-1}b)z$ for any c in G, again using (5.2). This shows that Gy is a subset of Gz. By the same reasoning, Gz is a subset of Gy, whence $Gy = Gz$. Hence, if two orbits have a common element, then they are identical. Q.E.D.

This theorem includes the last part of the corollary of Theorem 4.1 (with right cosets in place of left cosets), as follows from Example 2 above. It also essentially includes Theorem 3.3, by the remark of Example 1.

DEFINITION 5.3 *Let G operate on a set E, and let x be an element of E. All elements a in G such that $ax = x$ form a subgroup of G, called the* stabilizer, *or* isotropy subgroup, *of x. We denote it by G_x.*

THEOREM 5.2 *Let a group G operate on a set E. If two elements x and y of E are in the same G-orbit, then their stabilizers G_x and G_y are conjugate subgroups. That is, there is an element c in G such that $G_y = cG_xc^{-1}$. In fact, there must be an element c in G such that $y = cx$, and for any such c we have $G_y = cG_xc^{-1}$. In particular, G_x and G_y have the same number of elements.*

Proof. From Theorem 5.1 it follows that y is in the orbit Gx (since x is there), and so $y = cx$ for some c in G. Now a group element b is in G_y if $by = y$, that is, if $bcx = cx$. This holds if and only if $c^{-1}bcx = x$. Therefore, b is in G_y if and only if $c^{-1}bc$ is in G_x. It follows easily that $G_x = c^{-1}G_yc$, or $G_y = cG_xc^{-1}$, and that the correspondence $b \to c^{-1}bc$ is a one-to-one mapping, in fact an isomorphism, from G_y to G_x. Q.E.D.

Now let us suppose that both G and E are finite. Consider an orbit Gx in E. If we assign to any group element a the point ax in the orbit, we obtain a mapping $G \to Gx$. Now $ax = bx$ if and only if $b^{-1}ax = x$, that is, if and only if $b^{-1}a$ is in the stabilizer G_x of x. From the corollary of Theorem 4.1, that is true if and only if the left cosets aG_x and bG_x are identical. Therefore our mapping $G \to Gx$ establishes a one-to-one correspondence between the *left cosets* of G_x in G and the elements in Gx. Hence, the number of elements in the orbit Gx is the same as the number of left cosets of G_x, and that number, we recall, is the *index* of G_x in G. Applying Theorem 4.2, we obtain the following conclusion:

THEOREM 5.3 *Let G operate on a set E, with both G and E finite. Then, for the number of elements in any orbit Gx,*

$$\#(Gx) = \#G/\#G_x$$

where G_x is the stabilizer of x.

Again consider some G-orbit in E; we call it M. To each point x in M is attached the stabilizer G_x, a subgroup of G. Now it may happen that different points of M have the same stabilizer. This is the case, for example, if G is abelian, for then all the stabilizers of elements of M, being conjugate, must be identical. We look into this question briefly.

Let us collect together into bunches all the elements of the orbit M having the same stabilizer. In this way we divide M into a certain number of subsets $U_1, \ldots, U_r$, two elements x, y of M being in the same U_i if and only if they have the same stabilizer. We want to show that all the U_i have the same number of elements. Select an x in U_1, and suppose that U_1 has s elements. Since $M = Gx$, we can write out the elements of U_1 in the form

5.4 $$x, c_2x, \ldots, c_sx$$

where $c_2, \ldots, c_s$ are all in G. From Theorem 5.2 we have $G_{c_jx} = c_jG_xc_j^{-1}$. By assumption, x and c_jx have the same stabilizer, whence

5.5 $$G_x = c_jG_xc_j^{-1} \qquad (j = 2, \ldots, s)$$

Now let y be an element in some other U_i, say U_2. Since it is in $M = Gx$, we have $y = ax$ for some a in G. Consider the elements

5.6 $$y = ax, ac_2x, \ldots, ac_sx$$

By Theorem 5.2, the stabilizer of ac_jx is

$$G_{ac_jx} = (ac_j)G_x(ac_j)^{-1} = ac_jG_xc_j^{-1}a^{-1}$$

By (5.5), this is

$$G_{ac_jx} = aG_xa^{-1}$$

But by Theorem 5.2 again,

$$G_y = G_{ax} = aG_xa^{-1}$$

Therefore all the elements (5.6) have the same stabilizer, hence are all in U_2 along with y. The elements (5.6) are all distinct, assuming that the elements (5.4) are distinct. Therefore, U_2 must contain at least s elements. Since U_1, U_2 were arbitrarily selected U's, it follows that they all contain s elements. Furthermore, referring to (5.6), any U_i can be mapped into any other U_j by applying a suitable operation of G. Observe that the number of elements in M is the sum of the number of elements in each U_i, hence is equal to rs. Finally, if cG_xc^{-1} is any conjugate of G_x, then by Theorem 5.2 it is the stabilizer of the element cx in the orbit M. Consequently, r is the number of distinct conjugates of G_x (including G_x, naturally).

THEOREM 5.4 *Let G be a finite group operating on a finite set E, and let M be any G-orbit in E. Let r denote the number of different subgroups appearing among the stabilizers of the elements of M. Then r is the number of distinct conjugates of any one of those subgroups. Each of the subgroups is the stabilizer of a certain number s of elements in M, the same number s for each of the r subgroups, and $\#M = rs$.*

We now give an application of the notions developed above. The following theorem is very important in the study of finite groups.

THEOREM 5.5 **(Sylow's three theorems)** *Let G be a group of finite order n. Let p be a prime, and suppose that p^α divides n (α a positive integer). Then (1) G contains a subgroup of order p^α; (2) if p^α is the highest power of p which divides n, then all the subgroups of order p^α are conjugate; (3) the number of them is congruent to 1 modulo p, and it divides n/p^α.*

Proof. Let E denote the set whose elements are the various subsets A, B, etc., of G containing each exactly p^α elements. The number of such sets is the binomial coefficient $\binom{n}{p^\alpha}$. That is, E has $\binom{n}{p^\alpha}$ elements. We require a simple fact about this number. Let p^β be the largest power of p which divides $n = \#G$, so that

$$n = p^\beta q \qquad \beta \geq \alpha$$

q being an integer not divisible by p. We claim that

5.7 *$\#E$ is divisible by $p^{\beta-\alpha}$ but not by $p^{\beta-\alpha+1}$.*

For

$$\#E = \binom{n}{p^\alpha} = \frac{n(n-1)\cdots(n-p^\alpha+1)}{p^\alpha(p^\alpha-1)\cdots 1} = \frac{p^\beta q}{p^\alpha}\cdot\prod_{k=1}^{p^\alpha-1}\frac{p^\beta q - k}{p^\alpha - k}$$

It is quickly seen that $p^\beta q - k$ and $p^\alpha - k$ are divisible by exactly the same power of p for $k = 1, \ldots, p^\alpha - 1$. Therefore the prime factorization of $\#E$ contains exactly the power $p^{\beta-\alpha}$ (see Exercise 5, Sec. 5, Chap. 3).

Now let A be an element of E, hence a subset of G consisting of p^α elements. If b is any element of G, then bA also has p^α elements and therefore is also an element of E. In this way G operates on E according to Definition 5.1. Consider the stabilizer G_A of some element A of E. That is, G_A consists of all b in G such that $bA = A$. We claim that

5.8 $\#G_A \leq p^\alpha$

For let $a_1, a_2, \ldots, a_{p^\alpha}$ be the elements constituting A. If b is in G_A, then ba_1 must appear in the list, say $ba_1 = a_k$. But then $b = a_k a_1^{-1}$, showing that there are at most p^α possibilities for b.

By Theorem 5.1, the operation of G in E decomposes the latter into a certain number of disjoint orbits, say M, M', M'', etc. Then

$$\#E = (\#M) + (\#M') + (\#M'') + \text{etc.}$$

From (5.7) it follows that not all the numbers on the right can be divisible by $p^{\beta-\alpha+1}$. Suppose that to be the case for the orbit M. Thus

5.9 *$\#M$ is not divisible by $p^{\beta-\alpha+1}$.*

We henceforth deal only with this orbit. Let A be one of its elements, so that $M = GA$, and let G_A be its stabilizer. By Theorem 5.3 we have

$$\#M = \#G/G_A = p^\beta q/\#G_A$$

From (5.9) we see that $\#G_A$ must contain at least the power p^α. Combining this with (5.8), we conclude that

5.10 $\#G_A = p^\alpha$

This proves Sylow's first theorem.

We now suppose that $\alpha = \beta$, that is, that p^α is the greatest power of p which divides n. Then from (5.9) we have now

5.11 *$\#M$ is not divisible by p.*

Let H be any subgroup of G of order p^α. Now G operates in the orbit M itself, clearly, and therefore so does H. Hence H decomposes M into certain H-orbits W, W', W'', etc. Since

$$\#M = (\#W) + (\#W') + (\#W'') + \text{etc.}$$

it follows from (5.11) that at least one of these H-orbits contains a number of elements *not* divisible by p, say the orbit W. Select an element in W, say B, so that $W = HB$, and let H_B be its stabilizer. By (5.4) again we have

5.12 $\#W = \#H/\#H_B = p^\alpha/\#H_B$

But $\#W$ is not divisible by p, and therefore the only possibility is that $\#H_B = p^\alpha$. In other words, $H = H_B$. But from (5.10), with B in place of A, we have $\#G_B = p^\alpha$, from which it follows that $H = G_B$. Thus

5.13 *Every subgroup of order p^α (maximum α) is the G-stabilizer of an element in the orbit M.*

It follows from Theorem 5.2 that all these subgroups (they are called *Sylow subgroups*) must be conjugate. This proves Sylow's second theorem.

Finally, let $H_1, H_2, \ldots, H_r$ be all the different Sylow subgroups (for the given prime p), that is, all the subgroups of order p^α. From (5.10) and (5.13), they are precisely the distinct stabilizers of the elements in M. Fix attention on one of the H_i, and call it simply H. It is the stabilizer of a certain number of elements in M, say $A_1, \ldots, A_s$. Each of these elements forms by itself an H-orbit in M. By (5.12) it follows that any other H-orbit contains a number of elements divisible by p. Now $\#M$ is the sum of the number of elements in the various H-orbits, hence is equal to s plus a multiple of p. That is,

5.14 $$\#M \equiv s \pmod p$$

By Theorem 5.4 we have $\#M = rs$, so that

5.15 $$s \equiv rs \pmod p$$

From (5.11) and (5.14) we have $s \not\equiv 0 \pmod p$. Therefore, from (5.15), it follows that

5.16 $$r \equiv 1 \pmod p$$

From above, $\#M = rs$. From (5.10) and the preceding equation, $\#M = n/p^\alpha$. Hence, r divides n/p^α. This completes the proof of Sylow's third theorem. Q.E.D.

EXAMPLE 3 Let G be a group of order $42 = 2 \cdot 3 \cdot 7$. By Sylow's first theorem, G contains a subgroup H of order 7. We claim it is a normal subgroup. By Sylow's third theorem, the number r of distinct conjugates aHa^{-1} of H divides $42/7 = 6$ and is congruent to 1 (mod 7). The only possibility is $r = 1$. Therefore H is equal to all its conjugates, hence is normal. The factor group G/H has order 6, and the same argument can be repeated for it.

The following theorem gives an example of an application of Sylow's theorems.

THEOREM 5.6 **(Sylow)** *If G is a group of order p^α (p a prime), then every subgroup of order $p^{\alpha-1}$ is a normal subgroup, and there is at least one such subgroup.*

Proof. By Sylow's first theorem, there is at least one subgroup H of order $p^{\alpha-1}$. Now let E denote the set of left cosets of H in G. By Theorem 4.2, E contains p elements. Now H operates on E by left translations. Thus, if a is an element of H (or G), and if bH is an element of E, then abH is a new element of E, and thus a produces a permutation of E. (It is easily seen that Definition 5.1 is satisfied.) By Theorem 5.1, the operation of H on E decomposes E into a certain number of disjoint H-orbits, say $M_1, M_2, \ldots, M_r$. We have then

5.17 $$p = \#E = (\#M_1) + \cdots + (\#M_r)$$

Now one of the orbits contains the coset H, say the orbit M_1. It is clear that M_1 must then consist of just that one coset H. It follows from (5.17) that $r > 1$.

Consider now any coset aH, and let M_i be the orbit of E that contains it. Thus M_i consists of all cosets caH, where c is in H. The stabilizer of aH therefore consists of all c in H such that $caH = aH$. That is so if and only if $ca = ax$ for some x in H, or $c = axa^{-1}$. Hence, the stabilizer of aH is the subgroup K consisting of all elements common to both H and aHa^{-1}.

Now any subgroup of H, in particular the stabilizer K, must contain p^β elements for some β, by Theorem 4.2. By Theorem 5.3, $\#M_i = \#H/\#K = p^{\alpha-1}/p^\beta$. From (5.17) and the fact that $r > 1$ we conclude that $\#M_i = 1$, for otherwise it would have to be at least p. Hence K contains the same number of elements as H, namely, p^α. Since aHa^{-1} also contains p^α elements, it follows that $H = aHa^{-1}$. Therefore H is the same as all its conjugates and consequently is normal. Q.E.D.

THEOREM 5.7 *Let p and q be primes with $p \geq q$ and $p \not\equiv 1 \pmod q$. Then any group of order pq is abelian.*

Proof. Let G have order pq. We want to show first that G contains two normal subgroups H, K of order p and q, respectively.

Case 1. $p \neq q$. By Sylow's first theorem G contains subgroups H, K of orders p, q, respectively. By Sylow's third theorem the number of conjugates of H must divide q and must be congruent to $1 \pmod p$. Since $q < p$, it follows that H must coincide with all its conjugates and is therefore normal. Similarly, the number of conjugates of K must divide p and must be congruent to $1 \pmod q$. By assumption, $p \not\equiv 1 \pmod q$, and therefore there is only one conjugate, K itself. Hence K is normal.

Case 2. $p = q$. By Theorem 5.6, G contains a subgroup H of order p, and any such subgroup is normal. Take an element c not in H. Then c has order p or p^2 (Theorem 4.2). In the latter case G is just the cyclic subgroup (c) generated by c, hence is abelian. We therefore assume that c has order p. It then generates a cyclic subgroup K containing p elements. K is a normal subgroup of G, by Theorem 5.6.

Thus in either case we have a subgroup H of order p and a subgroup K of order q, both of them normal. Furthermore, *they have only the identity element in common.* For the set of elements common to H and K is a subgroup L of both H and K. Its order must divide both p and q (Theorem 4.2). In case 1 ($p \neq q$) it follows that L must have order 1; hence $L = (e)$. The same conclusion holds for Case 2 ($p = q$), for otherwise

L would have order p and would therefore have to coincide with both H and K, contradicting the choice of c.

Consider now the left cosets aK of K with a in H. No two of them can be the same, for if $aK = a'K$ (a, a' in H), then $a^{-1}a'$ is in K (Theorem 4.1, Corollary); but $a^{-1}a'$ is also in H, since H is a subgroup of G. From the remarks above, $a^{-1}a' = e$, or $a = a'$. Therefore, since there are exactly p left cosets of K in G and since H contains p elements, it follows that the left cosets of K appear exactly once among the aK, with a in H. Every element of G is in one and only one left coset, and we conclude that every element of G can be expressed *uniquely* in the form

5.18 *ab, with a in H, b in K*

Now choose any a in H, b in K. Since H and K are normal, we have $bH = Hb$ and $Ka = aK$. It follows that $ba = a'b$ for some a' in H, and $ba = ab'$ for some b' in K. Thus $a'b = ab'$, and from the uniqueness of the expression (5.18) we conclude that $a' = a$, $b' = b$, whence $ab = ba$.

This shows that elements of H commute with elements of K. Consider now any two elements of G. They can be expressed in the form (5.18), say ab and a_1b_1. We have then $(ab)(a_1b_1) = a(ba_1)b_1 = a(a_1b)b_1 = (aa_1)(bb_1)$. But both H and K are cyclic, hence abelian (Theorem 4.2, Corollary). Hence $(ab)(a_1b_1) = (a_1a)(b_1b) = (a_1b_1)(ab)$, showing that G is commutative. Q.E.D.

For example, any group of order 4 must be abelian, or any group of order 15, etc. Groups of order 6 violate the condition $p \not\equiv 1 \pmod{q}$. The symmetric group S_3 on three elements has order 6 and is not abelian. In general, if $p \equiv 1 \pmod{q}$, then there are both abelian and non-abelian groups of order pq.

The two theorems above serve to illustrate some applications of Theorems 5.3 and 5.5 to the study of finite groups. There are a number of other important theorems closely related to the foregoing, but we shall not go into them here.

EXERCISES

1. Prove that any group of order 231 contains normal subgroups of orders 7 and 11.

2. Let G operate on a set E, and let M be a G-orbit. Let H be the stabilizer of an element in M. Let N be the normalizer of H (see Exercise 4, Sec. 4). Prove that the number of elements in M having H as stabilizer is equal to the index of H in N. Prove that the number of different subgroups appearing among the stabilizers of elements of M is equal to the index of N in G. Deduce from these facts a proof of Theorem 5.4.

3. Let a group G operate on a set E, both finite, and let H be a normal subgroup of G. Let M be a G-orbit in E. Prove that the H-orbits in M all contain the same number of elements. [Hint: Use Theorem 5.3.]

4. A group G is said to operate *transitively* on a set E if for every pair x, y in E there is an element a in G such that $ax = y$. Suppose now that G and E are finite and that G has at least as many elements as E. Assume further that there is some x in E which is not left fixed by any a in G other than the identity. Prove that G operates transitively on E.

5. Let $S(E)$ be the group of permutations of a set E. Prove that the stabilizers in $S(E)$ of any two elements of E are conjugate subgroups.

6. Let $B = \mathbf{Q}[x_1, \ldots, x_n]$ denote the ring of polynomials in n independent variables $x_1, \ldots, x_n$ over the rational field. Let S denote the group of permutations of the set $\{x_1, \ldots, x_n\}$. We make S operate on B as follows: If s is an element of S and $f(x_1, \ldots, x_n)$ any element of B, then we define $sf(x_1, \ldots, x_n)$ to be the polynomial $f(sx_1, \ldots, sx_n)$, where sx_i denotes the result of applying the permutation s to x_i. Show that each s determines in this way a ring isomorphism $B \to B$, and show that the requirements of Definition 5.1 are satisfied. Taking $n = 4$, what are the stabilizers of the elements $x_1 - x_2$, $2x_1 - x_2$, $x_1 + x_2 + x_3$, $x_1x_2x_3$? Describe the S-orbits of B, for arbitrary n. Which elements of B are left fixed by all elements of S?

7. Let p, q be primes, with $p > q$ and $p \not\equiv \pm 1 \pmod{q}$. Prove that any group of order p^2q must be abelian.

8. Give conditions on two primes p, q such that any group of order p^2q^2 is abelian. Prove your contention.

6. *The Jordan-Hölder theorem*

In order to understand the structure of a given group G there are two main devices available:

(1) Determining the subgroups of G, in the hope that some of them will turn out to be more or less familiar, for example, cyclic groups (any group contains some cyclic subgroups, by Theorem 2.2). In this way it is often possible to split G into simpler pieces. The subgroups of interest in this connection are the *normal* subgroups of G.

(2) Determining homomorphisms $f: G \to G'$, where G' is a group with which one feels at ease. For this purpose it is fruitful to take for G' the group of automorphisms (i.e., one-to-one linear mappings) of a vector space. The image $f(G)$ is a subgroup of G' which reflects some of the structure of G. As we have seen, a homomorphism f gives rise to a normal subgroup of G, namely, the kernel of f, and therefore this method is not entirely separated from that of (1) above.

The following definition singles out those groups which cannot be decomposed conveniently into simpler parts.

DEFINITION 6.1 *A group G is said to be* simple *if its only normal subgroups are the group G itself and the subgroup (e) consisting of the identity element alone.*

Thus, if G is simple and if $f: G \to G'$ is a homomorphism, then the kernel of f is either G or (e). Hence f either maps all of G into the identity of G', or else f maps G isomorphically onto a subgroup of G'.

EXAMPLE 1 Let G be abelian, so that every subgroup is normal. Let a be an element of G, $a \neq e$. Then the cyclic subgroup (a) generated by a is a normal subgroup. Hence, if G is simple, then $(a) = G$, and therefore G is cyclic. It cannot be infinite cyclic (i.e., isomorphic to $\mathbf{Z}^+$), for such a group contains infinitely many subgroups. Therefore a has finite order m. That is, (a) consists of $e, a, \ldots, a^{m-1}$, with $m > 1$, since $a \neq e$. We claim that m is a prime. For if $m = hk$ (h, k integers >1), then $b = a^h$ has order k, and the cyclic subgroup (b) is not equal to either (e) or G, contradicting the assumption that G is simple. It follows at once that *an abelian group is simple if and only if it is cyclic of prime order.*

We shall see presently that any finite group can be decomposed in a certain way into simple groups.

The following definition is closely connected with method (1) mentioned above, and it is analogous to Definition 5.2, Chap. 8.

DEFINITION 6.2 Let $H_1, \ldots, H_r$ be subgroups of a group G. Then G is said *to be their* direct sum (or direct product) *under the following conditions:*

(1) *If x_i is in H_i and x_j is in H_j, with $i \neq j$, then $x_ix_j = x_jx_i$.*

(2) *Any element x of G can be expressed in one and only one way as a product*†

$$x = x_1x_2 \cdots x_r$$

with x_i in H_i($(i = 1, 2, \ldots, r)$.

Observe that each H_i must then be a *normal subgroup* of G. For from (2) and repeated applications of (1) we have $H_ix = H_ix_1x_2 \cdots x_r = x_1H_ix_2 \cdots x_r = x_1x_2H_ix_3 \cdots x_r = \cdots = x_1x_2 \cdots x_rH_i = xH_i$.

From (2) it follows that if $x_1x_2 \cdots x_r = e(x_i \text{ in } H_i)$, then $x_i = e$ for $i = 1, \ldots, r$.

EXAMPLE 2 Consider the group G with the multiplication table

	e	a	b	c
e	e	a	b	c
a	a	e	c	b
b	b	c	e	a
c	c	b	a	e

The elements e, a form a subgroup H_1 and the elements e, b form a subgroup H_2. Every element of G occurs just once in the list ee, eb, ae, ab. Since G is abelian, condition (1) holds, and it follows that G is the direct sum of H_1 and H_2. Both

† If G is abelian, with additive notation, then naturally we speak of the *sum* $x_1 + x_2 + \cdots + x_r$. In this case (1) is superfluous.

H_1 and H_2 are cyclic of order 2, that is, isomorphic to $\mathbf{Z}_2^+$. The group G is sometimes called the Klein 4-group. Note that e, c form another cyclic subgroup of order 2.

EXAMPLE 3 Consider a group G of order pq, where p and q are primes satisfying the conditions of Theorem 5.7. From the proof of that theorem [cf. (5.17)] it is easily seen that G is the direct sum of the subgroups H, K of orders p, q, respectively, or else G is cyclic of order p^2. For example, a group of order 4 must be either the direct sum of two subgroups of order 2, hence isomorphic to the Klein 4-group of the preceding example, or it must be isomorphic to $\mathbf{Z}_4^+$.

EXAMPLE 4 Let $H_1, \ldots, H_r$ be given groups (multiplicative notation). Let G consist of all r-tuples $x = (x_1, \ldots, x_r)$, with x_i in H_i $(i = 1, \ldots, r)$. Define multiplication in G by $(x_1, \ldots, x_r) \cdot (y_1, \ldots, y_r) = (x_1y_1, x_2y_2, \ldots, x_ry_r)$. It is easily verified that G with this operation is a group. Furthermore, if H_i denotes the subset of G consisting of all elements $(e_1, \ldots, x_i, \ldots, e_r)$ in which the jth entry is e_j = identity of H_j, for $j \neq i$, the ith entry unrestricted, then H_i' is a subgroup of G, and it is isomorphic to H_i in a natural way. G is the direct sum of $H_i', \ldots, H_r'$. (This construction is analogous to that of Exercise 2, Sec. 3, Chap. 8, concerning vector spaces.) The group G constructed in the manner indicated from $H_1, \ldots, H_r$ is called the *direct sum* of the H_i.

If a group G is a direct sum of subgroups H_1 and H_2, then G/H_1 is isomorphic in a natural way to H_2. For write x in G in the form $x = x_1x_2$, with x_1 in H_1 and x_2 in H_2. Then x_1, x_2 are uniquely determined by x, and the assignment $x \to x_2$ defines a homomorphism $G \to H_2$ whose kernel is H_1. The assertion follows from Theorem 4.4.

More generally, let G be the direct sum of subgroups $H_1, \ldots, H_r$. From (1) of Definition 5.2 we have $H_iH_j = H_jH_i$. From this and (4.3) it follows that $H_{i+1}H_{i+2} \cdots H_r$ is a subgroup of G, call it G_i $(i = 0, 1, \ldots, r-1)$. Moreover G_i is the direct sum of $H_{i+1}, \ldots, H_r$, and it is a *normal* subgroup of G_{i-1} (in fact, of G), the argument being essentially that following Definition 5.2. Denoting by G_r the identity subgroup (e), we have then

6.1 $$G = G_0 \supset G_1 \supset \cdots \supset G_{r-1} \supset G_r = (e)$$

where the symbol $\supset$ stands for "contains." We have $G_{i-1} = H_iH_{i+1} \cdots H_r = H_iG_i$, by definition, and G_{i-1} is the direct sum of H_i and G_i. Consequently

6.2 $$G_0/G_1 \cong H_1, G_1/G_2 \cong H_2, \ldots, G_{r-1}/G_r \cong H_r$$

where the symbol $\cong$ stands for "is isomorphic to."

Hence, a decomposition of G into a direct sum gives rise to a descending sequence (5.1) of normal subgroups, and the quotient groups of the successive subgroup (5.2) are isomorphic to the H_i.

In general it is impossible to split a group into a direct sum, but for any finite group it is possible to achieve a situation of the type (6.1) for which the quotient groups (6.2) are *simple* groups, in the sense of Definition 6.1. We now look into this question.

DEFINITION 6.3 *Let G be a group and K a normal subgroup. Then K is said to be* maximal *if $K \neq G$ and if K is not contained in any larger normal subgroup of G other than G itself.*

THEOREM 6.1 *A normal subgroup K of a group G is maximal if and only if the quotient group G/K is simple and contains more than one element.*

Proof. Suppose K is maximal. Then, by definition, $K \neq G$ and so G/K contains more than one coset. G/K must be simple. For let $\bar{H}$ be a normal subgroup of G/K. By Theorem 4.6 there is a normal subgroup H of G which contains K and which is mapped onto $\bar{H}$ by the canonical homomorphism $G \to G/K$. Then, by Definition 6.3, either $H = K$ or $H = G$. Therefore either $\bar{H}$ is the identity subgroup of G/K or else coincides with G/K.

Conversely, suppose that G/K is simple and contains more than one element, so that $K \neq G$. Let H be a normal subgroup of G which contains K. By Theorem 4.5, the canonical homomorphism maps H onto a normal subgroup $\bar{H}$ of G/K, and by Theorem 4.6 we have $\bar{H} = HK/K$. Since H contains K, it follows that $HK = H$, and so $\bar{H} = H/K$. By assumption either $\bar{H} = G/K$ or else $\bar{H}$ is the identity subgroup of G/K. In the first case we have $H/K = G/K$, and we claim that $H = G$. For let x be an element of G. Then there is an element y in H such that $xK = yK$, and so $y^{-1}x$ is in K, hence in H. Therefore $y(y^{-1}x) = x$ is in H. In the second case, H/K is the identity subgroup of G/K, whence plainly $H = K$. Therefore there are no normal subgroups in G between K and G. Q.E.D.

THEOREM 6.2 *Let K be a normal subgroup of a finite group G, with $K \neq G$. Then K is contained in at least one maximal normal subgroup.*

Proof. If K is not already maximal, then there is a larger normal subgroup $K' \neq G$ containing K. If K' is not maximal, then there is a yet larger normal subgroup $K'' \neq G$ containing K', etc. Since G is finite, this process must lead after a finite number of steps to a maximal normal subgroup of G which contains K. Q.E.D.

THEOREM 6.3 *Let G be a finite group containing more than one element. Then there exists a series of subgroups $G_0, G_1, \ldots, G_r$ such that*

(1) *$G_0 = G$ and $G_r = (e) =$ identity subgroup.*

(2) *G_i is a maximal normal subgroup of G_{i-1} for $i = 1, \ldots, r$.*

Furthermore, if K is any normal subgroup of G, then a series of the above type can be found such that K is one of its members.

Proof. Take any normal subgroup $K \neq G$, possibly the identity subgroup (e). By Theorem 6.2, it is contained in a maximal normal subgroup G_1 of $G = G_0$. If $G_1 \neq K$, then again, by Theorem 6.2 applied to G_1, there is a maximal normal subgroup G_2 of G_1 which contains K. Continuing in this way we eventually arrive at K itself. If $K \neq (e)$, then we simply continue on with K in place of G, and we obviously obtain a series of the required sort. Q.E.D.

REMARK. The proofs of Theorems 6.2 and 6.3 contain ill-concealed induction arguments.

DEFINITION 6.4 *A series of subgroups satisfying conditions* (1) *and* (2) *of Theorem* 6.3 *is called a* composition series *for G. The factor groups $H_i = G_{i-1}/G_i$ are called the* factors of composition *of G. They are simple groups, by Theorem* 6.1.

From the proof of Theorem 6.3 it is clear that a composition series for G is in general far from unique. However, any two composition series are intimately related, and that is the subject of the Jordan-Hölder theorem below. It is an easy consequence of the following theorem:

THEOREM 6.4 *Let G_1 and G_1' be two distinct maximal normal subgroups of a group G, and let K be the set of elements common to both of them. Then K is a maximal normal subgroup of G_1 and G_1'. Furthermore the groups G/G_1' and G_1/K are isomorphic in a natural way, and similarly for the groups G/G_1 and G_1'/K.*

Proof. Since G_1 and G_1' are normal, we have $G_1G_1' = G_1'G_1$, and therefore G_1G_1' is a subgroup of G, by (4.3). It is a *normal* subgroup, for $a(G_1G_1') = (aG_1)G_1' = (G_1a)G_1' = G_1(aG_1') = (G_1G_1')a$ for any a in G. But G_1G_1' contains both G_1 and G_1'. Since $G_1 \neq G_1'$, we have $G_1G_1' \neq G_1$. Since G_1 is maximal, it follows that $G_1G_1' = G$.

Now by Theorem 4.6, the groups $G_1/G_1 \cap G_1'$ and G_1G_1'/G_1' are isomorphic in a natural way. That is, G_1/K and G/G_1' are isomorphic in a natural way. But G/G_1' is simple, by Theorem 6.1, and therefore so is G_1/K. Consequently, K is a maximal normal subgroup of G_1, again by Theorem 6.1. A similar argument applies to G_1'/K and G/G_1. Q.E.D.

THEOREM 6.5 **(Jordan-Hölder)** *Let G be a finite group containing more than one element, and let $G_0, G_1, \ldots, G_r$ and $G_0', G_1', \ldots, G_s'$ be two composition series for G. Then $r = s$, and the factors of composition G_{i-1}/G_i of the first series are isomorphic, in some order, to the factors of composition of the second series.*

Proof. We prove this by induction on the order n of G. For the smallest admissible value of n, namely, 2, the statement is true. For any group G of order 2 is a simple group, being cyclic of prime order.

A composition series for a simple group can consist only of the two terms G and (e).

Suppose then that the theorem holds for all groups of order $<n$, and let G have order n. Let K be the set of elements common to G_1 and G_1'. Either $K = (e)$, or by Theorem 6.3 we can find a composition series $K, K', K'', \ldots,$ for K, the last term of which is (e). It follows at once from Theorem 6.4 that the series

6.3 $G_1, K, K', K'', \ldots, (e)$

and

6.4 $G_1', K, K', K'', \ldots, (e)$

are composition series for G_1, G_1', respectively. By assumption,

6.5 $G_1, G_2, \ldots, G_r$

and

6.6 $G_1', G_2', \ldots, G_s'$

are also composition series for G_1, G_1', respectively. By induction assumption, the number of terms in (6.3) must be the same as the number of terms in (6.5). Similarly for (6.4) and (6.6). Hence $r = s$. By induction assumption again, the factors of composition

6.7 $G_1/K, K/K', K'/K''$, etc.

obtained from (6.3) must be isomorphic, in some order, to those obtained from (6.5):

6.8 $G_1/G_2, G_2/G_3, G_3/G_4$, etc.

Similarly for

6.9 $G_1'/K, K/K', K'/K''$, etc.

6.10 $G_1'/G_2', G_2'/G_3', G_3'/G_4'$, etc.

But G/G_1 is isomorphic to G_1'/K, by Theorem 6.4; and G/G_1' is isomorphic to G_1/K. Hence, the groups

$G/G_1, G_1/G_2, G_2/G_3$, etc.

must be isomorphic, in some order, to

$G/G_1', G_1'/G_2', G_2'/G_3'$, etc.

This completes the proof.

It is possible to give a rather more refined analysis of composition series, but we shall not pursue the matter further except in Sec. 7 for abelian groups.

The Jordan-Hölder theorem shows that with any finite group G we can associate, by means of any composition series, a sequence of *simple* groups H_1, H_2, . . . , H_r. These groups, apart from the order in which they appear, are uniquely determined by G up to isomorphism. In this sense they do not depend upon the particular composition series. The knowledge of these groups gives a considerable amount of information about the structure of G, but not enough to reconstruct G from the H_i, in general. Observe that if we construct the direct sum G' of $H_1, \ldots, H_r$ according to Example 4, then G' will have the same factors of composition as G, as follows easily from the discussion concerning (6.1) and (6.2). However G' may not be isomorphic to G.

DEFINITION 6.5 *A finite group G is called* solvable, *or* metacyclic, *if the factors of composition of G are all abelian.*

The factors of composition, being simple, must then be cyclic of prime order (see Example 1 above).

The notion introduced in the foregoing definition is of great importance. By means of *Galois* theory it is possible to attach to any irreducible polynomial

$$a_0x^n + a_1x^{n-1} + \cdots + a_{n-1}x + a_n$$

with coefficients in the rational field $\mathbf{Q}$,† a certain finite group G, called the *Galois group* of the polynomial. Roughly speaking, G describes the possible permutations of the set of roots of the polynomial in the complex field $\mathbf{C}$. Galois theory shows that the roots of the polynomial can be obtained from the coefficients a_i by ordinary field operations $(+, -, \times, \div)$ and root extractions if and only if the Galois group G is solvable. For polynomials of degree >4, that is not usually the case. In this way it can be shown that there is no "formula," analogous to the quadratic formula, for equations of degree >4 (cf. Sec. 6, Chap. 6).

THEOREM 6.6 *Any group of prime power order p^α is solvable.*

Proof. This follows at once from Theorem 5.6.

THEOREM 6.7 *The symmetric group S_n of all permutations of n objects is not solvable if $n > 4$.*

We omit the proof of this theorem, referring to the books cited in the Introduction for details. This theorem is closely connected with the reference to Galois theory above. For the Galois group of "most" polynomials of degree n is precisely S_n.

EXERCISES

1. Find a composition series for the symmetric group S_3.
2. Find a composition series for the symmetric group S_4.
3. Let f be a homomorphism of a group G onto a group G', and let $\{G_0, G_1,$

† With minor changes, $\mathbf{Q}$ can be replaced here by any field.

. . . , $G_r\}$ be a composition series for G. Analyze the series of subgroups $f(G_i)$ in G'.

4. Let G be the direct sum of cyclic subgroups H, K of orders m, n, respectively. If m, n are relatively prime, prove that G is cyclic.

5. Prove that any group of order 4 must be isomorphic either to $\mathbf{Z}_4^+$ or to the Klein 4-group (i.e., the direct sum of two copies of $\mathbf{Z}_2^+$).

6. Let $K_1, K_2, \ldots, K_t$ be distinct normal subgroups of a finite group G, with $K_1 \supset K_2 \supset \cdots \supset K_t$. Prove that there is a composition series for G which includes the K_i among its terms.

7. Let G be a group of order pq, where p and q are distinct primes. Prove that G is cyclic.

8. Prove that the order of each factor of composition of a finite group G must divide the order of G.

9. Determine the maximal subgroups of $\mathbf{Z}^+$.

10. Let G be the direct sum of subgroups $H_1, \ldots, H_r$ of orders $n_1, \ldots, n_r$, respectively. Prove that G has order $n_1 n_2 \cdots n_r$.

11. Let G be an abelian group, and let H, K be subgroups. Prove that G is their direct sum if and only if $H \cap K = (e)$ and $HK = G$.

12. Let a group G be a direct sum of subgroups $H_1, \ldots, H_r$. For $i = 1, \ldots, r$ let f_i be a homomorphism from H_i to an abelian group G'. Prove that there is a unique homomorphism $f\colon G \to G'$ such that $f(x) = f_i(x)$ whenever x is in H_i $(i = 1, \ldots, r)$.

7. *Finite abelian groups*

We close this introduction to group theory by showing that finite abelian groups can be split into direct sums of cyclic groups. This represents a considerable refinement over the mere existence of a composition series, as guaranteed by Theorem 6.3. We shall continue here with the multiplicative notation.

Let G be an abelian group of order n, and let q be a prime which divides n. Then

7.1 *G contains a subgroup of order q.*

This follows from Sylow's theorem (Theorem 5.5) but can be proved more simply as follows: Let $c_1, c_2, \ldots, c_n$ be all the elements in G, and let n_i be the order of c_i. That is, n_i is the least integer such that $c_i^{n_i} = e$. Consider the expression

7.2 $$c_1^{k_1} c_2^{k_2} \cdots c_n^{k_n} \qquad 0 \le k_i < n_i \qquad \text{for } i = 1, \ldots, n$$

It is easily seen, using the fact that G is abelian, that (7.2) represents every element of G (for suitable choices of the k_i) as many times as it represents the identity. There are $n_1 n_2 \cdots n_n$ choices of the n-tuple $(k_1, \ldots, k_n)$, and so that number must be divisible by n, hence also by q. Then q must divide some n_i, and the element $c' = c_i^{n_i/q}$ has order q. Hence the cyclic subgroup (c') of G has order q.

G being an abelian group of order n, let

7.3 $$n = p_1^{\alpha_1} \cdots p_r^{\alpha_r}$$

be the prime factorization of n (distinct p_i). For brevity set

7.4 $$m_i = p_i^{\alpha_i}$$

Define

7.5 H_i = *set of all elements x in G such that $x^{m_i} = e$.*

We observe first of all that H_i is a subgroup of G. For if a, b are in H_i, then $(ab)^{m_i} = a^{m_i}b^{m_i} = e$, since G is abelian, and so ab is in H_i. Clearly a^{-1}, b^{-1} are also in H_i.

7.6 *The order of H_i is a power of p_i.*

For otherwise the order of H_i would be divisible by some other prime q. By (7.1), H_i would contain a subgroup K of order q. Let b be an element of K different from e. We have $b^{m_i} = e$ and $b^q = e$ (Theorem 4.2). Since m_i and q are relatively prime, there are integers such that $m_ik + qh = 1$. Then $b = b^{m_ik+qh} = b^{m_ik}b^{qh} = e$, a contradiction.

THEOREM 7.1 *G is the direct sum of the subgroups $H_1, \ldots, H_r$ of* (7.3). *That is, every element a in G can be written in one and only one way in the form $a = a_1a_2 \cdots a_r$ with a_i in H_i.*

Proof. Suppose first that $a_1a_2 \cdots a_r = b_1b_2 \cdots b_r$, with a_i and b_i in H_i. Since G is abelian we have $a_1b_1^{-1} = (a_2^{-1}b_2) \ldots (a_r^{-1}b_r)$. The left-hand side is an element of H_1. The right-hand side is an element of $H_2 \cdots H_r$. Raise both sides to the power $n/m_1 = m_2 \cdots m_r$. On the right we get the identity, since $(a_jb_j^{-1})^{m_j} = e$. Hence $(a_1b_1^{-1})^{m_2 \ldots m_r} = e$. But by (7.6) and Theorem 4.2, the order of any element of H_1 is a power of p_1. Thus, if $x \neq e$ in H_1 and if $x^k = e$, then p_1 must divide k. Since p_1 does not divide $m_2 \cdots m_r$, it follows that $a_1b_1^{-1} = e$, or $a_1 = b_1$. Similarly, $a_j = b_j$ for $j = 1, \ldots, r$.

Now put $k_i = n/m_i$. The k_i are relatively prime, clearly, and therefore there exist integers h_i such that $h_1k_1 + \cdots + h_rk_r = 1$. For any a in G set

$$a_i = a^{h_ik_i} \qquad (i = 1, \ldots, r)$$

Then $a_i^{m_i} = a^{h_ik_im_i} = a^{h_in} = (a^n)^{h_k} = e$, by Theorem 4.2. Therefore a_i is in H_i. Furthermore,

$$a_1a_2 \cdots a_r = a^{h_1k_1} \cdots a^{h_rk_r} = a^{h_1k_1+\cdots+h_rk_r} = a$$ Q.E.D.

COROLLARY 1 *The subgroup H_i has order $m_i = p_i^{\alpha_i}$.*

Proof. From (7.6), H_i has some order $p_i^{\beta_i}$. Then $H_1H_2 \cdots H_r$ contains $p_1^{\beta_1} \cdots p_r^{\beta_r}$ elements, clearly. From Theorem 7.1 and (7.3) it follows that $\beta_i = \alpha_i$. Q.E.D.

COROLLARY 2 *If G is decomposed in any way into a direct sum of subgroups H'_1, . . . , H'_s whose orders are powers of distinct primes, then that decomposition is the same as the decomposition of Theorem* 7.1, *apart from the enumeration.*

Proof. Let H'_i have order $q_i^{\beta_1}$. By Theorem 4.2, $q_1^{\beta_1}$ must divide n, and so q_i must be the same as one of the p_j. We can renumber things so that $q_i = p_i$ $(i = 1, \ldots, s)$. It follows from the direct-sum assumption that the order of G is equal to $p_1^{\beta_1} \cdots p_s^{\beta_s}$. Hence, $s = r$ and $\beta_i = \alpha_i$. Then for any a in H'_i we have $a^{m_i} = e$, and so H'_i is contained in H_i, by definition of H_i. Therefore $H_i = H'_i$, by Corollary 1. Q.E.D.

To obtain a further decomposition of G we must now investigate groups of prime-power order.

THEOREM 7.2 *Let H be an abelian group of order p^α (p a prime). Then H is the direct sum of a certain number of cyclic subgroups.*

Proof. We use induction on α. For $\alpha = 1$ the assertion is clearly true, for then H is cyclic of order p and contains no subgroups other than itself and (e).

Now given $\alpha > 1$, we suppose that the theorem holds for all groups of order p^γ, with $\gamma < \alpha$. By Theorem 4.2, the order of every element of H is a power of p. Let a be an element of maximum order p^β, and let $K = (a)$ be the cyclic subgroup generated by a. If $\beta = \alpha$, then $K = H$, and so H itself is cyclic. Suppose then that $\beta < \alpha$. The quotient group H/K has order $p^{\alpha-\beta}$. By induction hypothesis, H/K is the direct sum of certain cyclic subgroups $\bar{H}_1, \ldots, \bar{H}_r$. Let the order of $\bar{H}_i$ be p^{γ_i}, and let $\bar{H}_i$ be generated by the coset c_iK. Then p^{γ_i} is the lowest power of c_i which is in K. To simplify notation, write c for c_i and γ for γ_i. Then c^{p^γ} is in K, hence is a power of a, say

$$c^{p^\gamma} = a^s$$

Now $c^{p^\beta} = e$, by definition of β, and so

$$c^{p^\beta} = (c^{p^\gamma})^{p^{\beta-\gamma}} = (a^s)^{p^{\beta-\gamma}} = a^{sp^{\beta-\gamma}} = e$$

Therefore $sp^{\beta-\gamma}$ must be a multiple of p^β, say

$$sp^{\beta-\gamma} = kp^\beta$$

or

$$s = kp^\gamma$$

Set

$$b = ca^{-k}$$

then

$$b^{p^\gamma} = c^{p^\gamma}a^{-kp^\gamma} = a^s a^{-s} = e$$

Restoring the index i, for each c_i we have produced an element b_i in the same coset of K and such that b_i has order precisely p^{γ_i}. Let $H_i = (b_i)$ denote the cyclic subgroup of H generated by b_i, and consider the subgroup

$$H' = KH_1H_2 \cdots H_r$$

of H. Let $x_0x_1 \cdots x_r$ and $y_0y_1 \cdots y_r$ be two of its elements, with x_0, y_0 in K and x_i, y_i in $H_i(x = 1, \ldots, r)$. If they are equal, then $x_0y_0^{-1} = (x_1^{-1}y_1) \cdots (x_r^{-1}y_r)$. The canonical homomorphism f: $H \to H/K$ carries the left-hand side into the identity of H/K; and it carries each element $x_i^{-1}y_i$ into an element of H_i. Since H/K is the direct sum of the $\bar{H}_i$, it follows that f must map each $x_i^{-1}y_i$ into the identity of H/K. In other words, each $x_i^{-1}y_i$ is in K. But the only element in both K and H_i is e (for the lowest power of b_i in K is $b_i^{p^{\gamma_i}} = e$). Hence $x_i = y_i$. It follows that H' contains precisely $p^\beta \cdot p^{\gamma_1} \cdots p^{\gamma_r} = p^\beta p^{\alpha-\beta} = p^\alpha$ elements. Hence $H' = H$, and therefore we have H expressed as a direct sum of cyclic subgroups. Q.E.D.

To establish some kind of uniqueness concerning the decomposition of an abelian group of order p^α into cyclic subgroups, we need the following simple result.

THEOREM 7.3 *Let H be a cyclic group of order p^α. Then the elements of order at most p^γ ($\gamma \leq \alpha$) in H form a subgroup of order p^γ.*

Proof. Let H be generated by a. An element a^k has $(a^k)^{p^\gamma} = e$ if and only if kp^γ is a multiple of p^β, or k a multiple of $p^{\beta-\gamma}$. There are p^γ integers in the range $0 \leq k < p^\beta$ which are multiples of $p^{\beta-\gamma}$. Q.E.D.

COROLLARY 1 *Let H be an abelian group of order p^α (p a prime), and let H be decomposed in any way into a direct sum of cyclic subgroups $H_1, \ldots, H_r$ of orders >1. Then the number of them r and their orders are completely determined by H.*

Proof. Let n_γ denote the number of elements x in H such that $x^{p^\gamma} = e$. Write $x = x_1x_2 \cdots x_r$, with x_i in H_i. Then $x^p = e$ if and only if each $x_i^p = e$, by the direct-sum assumption. By Theorem 7.3 each H_i contains p elements such that $x_i^p = e$. It follows readily that $n_1 = p^r$, showing that r depends only on H. In a similar way it is easily seen that if s of the H_i have order $\geq p^2$, then $n_2 - n_1 = p^{2s} - p^s$. Thus s depends only on H. Continuing in this way one finds that the number of H_i of order $\geq p^\gamma$ can be expressed in terms of the n_γ, hence is determined by H alone.

Q.E.D.

COROLLARY 2 *Let H be an abelian group of order p^α. Then H is cyclic if and only if the number of elements x in H such that $x^p = e$ is p.*

This follows at once from Corollary 1, since then $r = 1$.

Combining Theorem 7.1 and its Corollary 2 with Theorem 7.2 and its Corollary 1, we have the following theorem:

THEOREM 7.4 *Any finite abelian group G can be expressed as a direct sum of cyclic subgroups of prime power order. The number of the cyclic subgroups in the direct sum and their orders are completely determined by G. If G' is another abelian group for which the corresponding set of integers is the same as for G, then G and G' are isomorphic.*

The last assertion is easily proved as follows. Let $G = H_1H_2 \cdots H_r$ and $G' = H_1'H_2' \cdots H_r'$ be direct-sum decompositions, the H_i and H_i' being cyclic of prime-power order. From our assumption we can assume that the numbering is such that H_i and H_i' have the same order ($i = 1, \ldots, r$). Being cyclic, they must clearly be isomorphic. Let f_i: $H_i \to H_i'$ be any isomorphism. For x in G write $x = x_1 \cdots x_r$, with x_i in H_i. Define $f(x)$ by

$$f(x) = f_1(x_1) \cdots f_r(x_r)$$

It is easy to verify that this prescription defines an isomorphism from G to G' (cf. Exercise 12, Sec. 6).

THEOREM 7.5 *Let G be the direct sum of cyclic groups $H_1, \ldots, H_r$ of orders $m_1, \ldots, m_r$, respectively. If the m_i are relatively prime, then G is cyclic.*

Proof. Let H_i be generated by a_i, and put $a = a_1a_2 \cdots a_r$. Then $a^k = a_1{}^k a_2{}^k \cdots a_r{}^k$, and so $a^k = e$ if and only if $a_j{}^k = e$ for $j = 1, \ldots, r$. That is so if and only if k is divisible by $m_1, \ldots, m_r$, and thus k must be divisible by their product. The cyclic subgroup (a) therefore contains $m_1m_2 \cdots m_r$ elements, and that is the order of G. Hence $(a) = G$.

Q.E.D.

EXERCISES

1. Describe in detail how to decompose a cyclic group of order n into a direct sum of cyclic subgroups of prime-power order. Write out the subgroups for $n = 15$ and $n = 20$. To what extent are the subgroups unique?

2. Referring to the proof of Corollary 1, Theorem 7.3, show that $n_2 - n_1 = p^{2s} - p^s$, and work out the corresponding formula for $n_3 - n_2$.

3. Let G be a finite abelian group. By a *character* χ of G is meant a mapping $G \to \mathbf{C}$ (complex field) such that $\chi(ab) = \chi(a) \cdot \chi(b)$ for any a, b in G and such that χ does not map every element of G into zero. Show then that χ cannot map any element into zero and is therefore a homomorphism of G to the multiplicative group $\mathbf{C}^*$ of nonzero complex numbers. Prove that $\chi(a)$ must be a number of absolute value 1 for any a in G. Prove that all the characters of G form a group $\hat{G}$ if we define $\chi\chi'$ by the rule $(\chi\chi')(a) = \chi(a) \cdot \chi'(a)$ for any two characters and any a in G. $\hat{G}$ is called the *character group* of G.

4. Write out all the characters of $\mathbf{Z}_5{}^+$.

5. Referring to Exercise 3, show that

$$\sum_a \chi(a) = 0$$

for any character $\chi \neq \chi_0$, where χ_0 denotes the *principal character*, i.e., the unit element of G. [Hint: Replace a in $\chi(a)$ by ab, b being an arbitrary element of G.] Show that

$$\sum_\chi \chi(a) = 0$$

if a is not the unit element of G.

6. Show that a finite abelian group G and its character group $\hat{G}$ are isomorphic. [Hint: Use Theorem 7.4.]

7. Let G be a finite abelian group. Show that G is the direct sum of subgroups $G_1, \ldots, G_t$ such that the order n_i of G_i divides the order n_{i+1} of G_{i+1} for $i = 1, \ldots, t-1$. Show that the n_i are uniquely determined by G (they are called its *torsion coefficients*). [Hint: Write G as a direct sum of cyclic groups H_i of prime-power order and assemble the latter judiciously, taking note of Theorem 7.5.]

8. Suppose that the G can be expressed as the direct sum of subgroups of the following respective orders:

$2, 2, 2^3, 5, 5^2, 7^3, 7^3$.

What are the torsion coefficients of G?

11

Determinants

1. *Introduction*

The first part of this chapter is concerned with the problem of defining what is meant by the *determinant* of a square matrix. Before taking that up in the general case, it is helpful to review the special case of 2×2 matrices.

It is well known that the determinant of a 2×2 matrix $a = (a^j{}_i)$ with coefficients in a field K is the quantity

$$a^1{}_1a^2{}_2 - a^1{}_2a^2{}_1$$

again an element of K. For example, the determinant of

$$\begin{pmatrix} 2 & 1 \\ 3 & -1 \end{pmatrix}$$

is -5. The determinant is thus a function, or operation, which produces an element of K from any 2×2 matrix with coefficients in K. It is obvious that if the two columns (or else the two rows) of a 2×2 matrix are interchanged, then its determinant changes sign; the determinant is zero if the two columns (or two rows) are identical. Some other simple properties are the following: For the two matrices

$$\begin{pmatrix} a^1{}_1 & a^1{}_2 \\ a^2{}_1 & a^2{}_2 \end{pmatrix} \quad \text{and} \quad \begin{pmatrix} ca^1{}_1 & a^1{}_2 \\ ca^2{}_1 & a^2{}_2 \end{pmatrix}$$

the determinant of the second is equal to the determinant of the first multiplied by c (and similarly for a common factor in the second column, or else in one of the two rows). Further, the determinant of

$$\begin{pmatrix} a^1{}_1 + b^1 & a^1{}_2 \\ a^2{}_1 + b^2 & a^2{}_2 \end{pmatrix}$$

is $(a^1{}_1 + b^1)a^2{}_2 - (a^2{}_1 + b^2)a^1{}_2$, which is just the sum of the determinants of

$$\begin{pmatrix} a^1{}_1 & a^1{}_2 \\ a^2{}_1 & a^2{}_2 \end{pmatrix} \quad \text{and} \quad \begin{pmatrix} b^1 & a^1{}_2 \\ b^2 & a^2{}_2 \end{pmatrix}$$

(a similar statement holds if the b's are added to the second column, or else to one of the two rows). Clearly the determinant of the 2×2 unit matrix $\mathbf{I}_2$ is 1 (the unit element of the field K).

We shall see that these simple properties are characteristic of determinants, and we shall in effect take them as a definition of determinants. A geometrical interpretation of determinants is given in Sec. 6.

2. Axioms for determinants

We consider now $n \times n$ matrices with coefficients in a field K, both n and K being fixed for the present. According to the notation of Chap. 9, the set of all such matrices is denoted by $K^n{}_n$.

Suppose that in some way there is defined a mapping F from $K^n{}_n$ to K. That is, F assigns to each matrix $\mathbf{a}$ in $K^n{}_n$ a scalar $F(\mathbf{a})$. For our purposes it will be convenient to think of $\mathbf{a}$ in terms of its column vectors† $\mathbf{a}_1, \mathbf{a}_2, \ldots, \mathbf{a}_n$, and we shall frequently write $F(\mathbf{a}_1, \mathbf{a}_2, \ldots, \mathbf{a}_n)$, or other similar expressions, for $F(\mathbf{a})$. Suppose now that F satisfies the following hypotheses:

(1) *$F(\mathbf{a})$ changes sign if two adjacent columns of $\mathbf{a}$ are interchanged, and $F(\mathbf{a}) = 0$ if two adjacent columns of $\mathbf{a}$ are identical.*‡

(2) *F is linear as a function of the first column. That is,*

$$F(\mathbf{a}_1 + \mathbf{b}, \mathbf{a}_2, \ldots, \mathbf{a}_n) = F(\mathbf{a}_1, \mathbf{a}_2, \ldots, \mathbf{a}_n) + F(\mathbf{b}, \mathbf{a}_2, \ldots, \mathbf{a}_n);$$
$$F(c\mathbf{a}_1, \mathbf{a}_2, \ldots, \mathbf{a}_n) = c \cdot F(\mathbf{a}_1, \mathbf{a}_2, \ldots, \mathbf{a}_n)$$

for any $\mathbf{a}_1, \ldots, \mathbf{a}_n, \mathbf{b}$ in K^n and any c in K.

(3) $F(\mathbf{I}_n) = 1$.

Observe that these three hypotheses are straightforward extensions of the properties noted above for 2×2 matrices. Our aim is to show that there is one and only one mapping $F\colon K^n{}_n \to K$ which satisfies (1), (2), and (3), and $F(\mathbf{a})$ will then be defined as the determinant of $\mathbf{a}$. It is important to remark that (3) is not used until (2.7). In Propositions 2.1 and 2.2, F stands for an operation satisfying axioms (1) and (2).

PROPOSITION 2.1 *If $\mathbf{a}'$ is the matrix obtained from some matrix $\mathbf{a}$ by interchanging two columns, then $F(\mathbf{a}') = -F(\mathbf{a})$. If any two columns of $\mathbf{a}$ are identical, then $F(\mathbf{a}) = 0$. Finally, F is linear as a function of any of the columns. That is,*§

$$F(\ldots, \mathbf{a}_j + \mathbf{b}, \ldots) = F(\ldots, \mathbf{a}_j, \ldots) + F(\ldots, \overset{(j)}{\mathbf{b}}, \ldots)$$

2.1 $$F(\ldots, c\mathbf{a}_j, \ldots) = c \cdot F(\ldots, \mathbf{a}_j, \ldots)$$

† We could equally well use the row vectors.

‡ If two adjacent columns of a are identical, then a remains unaltered if they are permuted; but $F(\mathrm{a})$ must change sign, by the first assumption. Hence we have $F(\mathrm{a}) = -F(\mathrm{a})$, or $(1 + 1) \cdot F(\mathrm{a}) = 0$. If $1 + 1 \neq 0$, then we can conclude that $F(\mathrm{a}) = 0$, so that the second assumption is unnecessary. However, there exist fields in which $1 + 1 = 0$, and for such fields the conclusion that $F(\mathrm{a}) = 0$ is not valid. That is why it is explicitly included in our assumptions. An example of a field of *characteristic* 2 (i.e., in which $1 + 1 = 0$) is the field $\mathbf{Z}_2$ of Sec. 10, Chap. 2. It contains only two elements. A somewhat less trivial example is the rational function field $\mathbf{Z}_2(t)$ in an indeterminate t over $\mathbf{Z}_2$.

§ The notation of (2.1) is meant to indicate that only the jth column is in question. All other columns are arbitrary but fixed.

where $\mathbf{a}_j$ *and* $\mathbf{b}$ *are any two elements of* K_n *(column vectors) and where* $\mathbf{c}$ *is any element of* K.

Proof. First of all, let $\mathbf{a}'$ be the matrix obtained from $\mathbf{a}$ by interchanging the ith and $(i + k)$th columns of $\mathbf{a}(k > 0)$. The transposition $(i, i + k)$ is equal to the product

$$(i, i + 1) \cdots (i + k - 2, i + k - 1)(i + k, i + k - 1) \cdots (i + 2, i + 1)(i + 1, i)$$

which involves only permutations of adjacent indices, and there are $2k - 1$ factors (see Exercise 7, Sec. 3, Chap. 10). Hence the permutation of columns $\mathbf{a}_i$ and $\mathbf{a}_{i+k}$ can be achieved by a series of permutations of *adjacent* columns. Each such permutation results in a change of sign of F, by axiom (1), and since there are an odd number of them, namely, $2k - 1$, it follows that the net result is a change of sign: $F(\mathbf{a}') = -F(\mathbf{a})$.

Now suppose that two columns of $\mathbf{a}$ are identical, say the ith and $(i + k)$th. Let $\mathbf{a}'$ denote the matrix obtained from $\mathbf{a}$ by interchanging the ith column and the $(i + k - 1)$th column. Then $\mathbf{a}'$ has two adjacent columns which are identical, and therefore $F(\mathbf{a}') = 0$, by axiom (1). But, by what has just been shown, $F(\mathbf{a}') = -F(\mathbf{a})$, and so $F(\mathbf{a}) = 0$.

Finally, to prove that (2.1) holds, we have only to interchange the first and the jth columns in the expressions on the left. Then, applying axiom (2) to the result, we again interchange the first and jth columns. For example, to verify the second equation of (2.1), we have $F(\mathbf{a}_1, \ldots, c\mathbf{a}_j, \ldots) = -F(c\mathbf{a}_j, \ldots, \mathbf{a}_1, \ldots) = -c \cdot F(\mathbf{a}_j, \ldots, \mathbf{a}_1, \ldots)$, by axiom (2), and from the result established above this last expression is equal to $+c \cdot F(\mathbf{a}_1, \ldots, \mathbf{a}_j, \ldots)$. The first equation of (2.1) is verified similarly. Q.E.D.

COROLLARY 1 $F(\mathbf{a}) = 0$ *if any column of* $\mathbf{a}$ *is zero.*

Proof. Suppose the first column is zero. We have then $F(\mathbf{0}, \mathbf{a}_2, \ldots, \mathbf{a}_n) = F(0 \cdot \mathbf{0}, \mathbf{a}_2, \ldots, \mathbf{a}_n) = 0 \cdot F(\mathbf{0}, \mathbf{a}_2, \ldots, \mathbf{a}_n) = 0$, by (2.1). The same argument clearly holds for any column.

COROLLARY 2 *Let* $\mathbf{a}'$ *be the matrix obtained from a given matrix* $\mathbf{a}$ *by an arbitrary permutation* s *of the columns of* $\mathbf{a}$. *Then* $F(\mathbf{a}') = \pm F(\mathbf{a})$, *the plus sign holding if* s *is an even permutation and the minus sign holding if* s *is an odd permutation.*

This follows immediately from the first assertion of the theorem above and from Theorems 3.4 and 3.5, Chap. 10.

REMARK. Since F is linear in its dependence upon each of the n column vectors, it is called a *multilinear* function, or more specifically, an n-linear function. Because F changes sign if two columns are permuted, it is said to be *skew-symmetric*.

We recall that if $\mathbf{a}$ is any element of $K^n{}_n$ and if c is any scalar, then $c\mathbf{a}$ is the matrix obtained by multiplying each coefficient of **a** by c (see Sec. 6, Chap. 9). We have

2.2 $$F(c\mathbf{a}) = F(c\mathbf{a}_1, \ldots, c\mathbf{a}_n) = c^n F(\mathbf{a}_1, \ldots, \mathbf{a}_n) = c^n F(\mathbf{a})$$

as follows at once from (2.1). In particular,

2.3 $$F(-\mathbf{a}) = (-1)^n F(\mathbf{a})$$

PROPOSITION 2.2 *Let* $\mathbf{a}'$ *be obtained from a matrix* $\mathbf{a}$ *by adding* c *times the jth column of* $\mathbf{a}$ *to its ith column, where* $i \neq j$. *That is,* $\mathbf{a}'$ *has* $\mathbf{a}_i + c\mathbf{a}_j$ *as its ith column, all other columns being the same as in* $\mathbf{a}$. *Then* $F(\mathbf{a}') = F(\mathbf{a})$.

Proof. Assuming that $i < j$ we have $F(\mathbf{a}') = F(\ldots, \mathbf{a}_i + c\mathbf{a}_j, \ldots, \mathbf{a}_j, \ldots) = F(\ldots, \mathbf{a}_i, \ldots, \mathbf{a}_j, \ldots) + F(\ldots, c\mathbf{a}_j, \ldots, \mathbf{a}_j, \ldots)$, by (2.1). The last term here is zero, for the scalar c can be taken out, by the second equation of (2.1), leaving two identical columns. Q.E.D.

We now derive an explicit formula for $F(\mathbf{a})$. Let $\mathbf{e}_j$ denote the jth column of the $n \times n$ unit matrix $\mathbf{I}_n$, so that $\mathbf{I}_n = (\mathbf{e}_1, \mathbf{e}_2, \ldots, \mathbf{e}_n)$, and let $\mathbf{a} = (\mathbf{a}_1, \mathbf{a}_2, \ldots, \mathbf{a}_n)$ be any $n \times n$ matrix with coefficients in the field K. We have then

2.4 $$\mathbf{a}_i = a^1{}_i\mathbf{e}_1 + \cdots + a^n{}_i\mathbf{e}_n = a^j{}_i\mathbf{e}_j$$

using the summation convention on the right. In particular, $\mathbf{a}_1 = a_1{}^j\mathbf{e}_j$. Let us substitute this expansion in $F(\mathbf{a}_1, \ldots, \mathbf{a}_n)$. We get

$$F(\mathbf{a}_1, \mathbf{a}_2, \ldots, \mathbf{a}_n) = F(a^1{}_1\mathbf{e}_1 + \cdots + a^n{}_1\mathbf{e}_n, \mathbf{a}_2, \ldots, \mathbf{a}_n)$$

Applying the first equation of (2.1) repeatedly to the right-hand side, we get for it

$$F(a^1{}_1\mathbf{e}_1, \mathbf{a}_2, \ldots, \mathbf{a}_n) + \cdots + F(a^n{}_1\mathbf{e}_n, \mathbf{a}_2, \ldots, \mathbf{a}_n)$$

From the second equation of (2.1) we find that this is equal to

$$a^1{}_1 \cdot F(\mathbf{e}_1, \mathbf{a}_2, \ldots, \mathbf{a}_n) + \cdots + a^n{}_1 \cdot F(\mathbf{e}_n, \mathbf{a}_2, \ldots, \mathbf{a}_n)$$

Using the summation convention, we can condense the foregoing calculation into

$$F(\mathbf{a}_1, \mathbf{a}_2, \ldots, \mathbf{a}_n) = F(a^j{}_1\mathbf{e}_j, \mathbf{a}_2, \ldots, \mathbf{a}_n) = a^j{}_1 \cdot F(\mathbf{e}_j, \mathbf{a}_2, \ldots, \mathbf{a}_n)$$

In each term on the right we repeat this procedure, using the expansion (2.4) for $\mathbf{a}_2$. However, we must be careful to use a different summation index in order to avoid conflict with the j that is already there. To achieve a systematic notation we shall therefore replace j above by j_1, and we shall write $\mathbf{a}_2 = a_2^{j_2}\mathbf{e}_{j_2}$, etc. The equation above becomes

$$F(\mathbf{a}_1, \mathbf{a}_2, \ldots, \mathbf{a}_n) = a_1^{j_1}F(\mathbf{e}_{j_1}, \mathbf{a}_2, \ldots, \mathbf{a}_n)$$

For each term on the right we have

$$\begin{aligned} F(\mathbf{e}_{j_1}, \mathbf{a}_2, \ldots, \mathbf{a}_n) &= F(\mathbf{e}_{j_1}, a_2^{j_2}\mathbf{e}_{j_2}, \mathbf{a}_3, \ldots, \mathbf{a}_n) \\ &= a_2^{j_2}F(\mathbf{e}_{j_1}, \mathbf{e}_{j_2}, \mathbf{a}_3, \ldots, \mathbf{a}_n) \end{aligned}$$

where we have again used (2.1) repeatedly, just as above for $\mathbf{a}_1$. Substituting the last expression in the preceding equation we obtain

$$F(\mathbf{a}_1, \mathbf{a}_2, \ldots, \mathbf{a}_n) = a_1^{j_1}a_2^{j_2}F(\mathbf{e}_{j_1}, \mathbf{e}_{j_2}, \mathbf{a}_3, \ldots, \mathbf{a}_n)$$

Continuing in this way, replacing $\mathbf{a}_3$ by its expansion $a_3^{j_3}\mathbf{e}_{j_3}$, etc., we finally arrive at the formula

2.5 $$F(\mathbf{a}_1, \mathbf{a}_2, \ldots, \mathbf{a}_n) = a_1^{j_1}a_2^{j_2} \cdots a_n^{j_n}F(\mathbf{e}_{j_1}, \mathbf{e}_{j_2}, \ldots, \mathbf{e}_{j_n})$$

Now what is $F(\mathbf{e}_{j_1}, \mathbf{e}_{j_2}, \ldots, \mathbf{e}_{j_n})$? If two of the indices $j_1, \ldots, j_n$ happen to have equal values (they all range independently from 1 to n), then $F(\mathbf{e}_{j_1}, \ldots, \mathbf{e}_{j_n})$ is zero, by Proposition 2.1. The corresponding terms in the summation (2.5) can therefore be omitted. If on the other hand no two of the indices $j_1, \ldots, j_n$ have the same value, then $j_1, \ldots, j_n$ must be a permutation of $1, \ldots, n$. In that case the matrix $(\mathbf{e}_{j_1}, \ldots, \mathbf{e}_{j_n})$ is obtained from the unit matrix by the permutation

$$\begin{pmatrix} 1 & 2 & \cdots & n \\ j_1 & j_2 & \cdots & j_n \end{pmatrix}$$

of its columns. Hence,

$$F(\mathbf{e}_{j_1}, \ldots, \mathbf{e}_{j_n}) = \operatorname{sign}\begin{pmatrix} 1 & 2 & \cdots & n \\ j_1 & j_2 & \cdots & j_n \end{pmatrix} \cdot F(\mathbf{I}_n)$$

by Corollary 2, Proposition 2.1, where the symbol sign $(\cdots)$ stands for $+1$ if the permutation is even and for -1 if it is odd. Putting this in (2.5) we get the formula

2.6 $$F(\mathbf{a}) = F(\mathbf{I}_n) \cdot \sum \operatorname{sign}\begin{pmatrix} 1 & 2 & \cdots & n \\ j_1 & j_2 & \cdots & j_n \end{pmatrix} \cdot a_1^{j_1} a_2^{j_2} \cdots a_n^{j_n}$$

the summation being over all permutations of $1, 2, \ldots, n$. We recall that only axioms (1) and (2) were used in arriving at this formula. It shows that $F(\mathbf{a})$ is completely determined once $F(\mathbf{I}_n)$ is specified. If we now add axiom (3), $F(\mathbf{I}_n) = 1$, it follows that there cannot be two different functions F satisfying (1), (2), (3). The unique function satisfying the three axioms—we have not yet proved that it exists—is denoted by det rather than by F, and according to (2.6) it must be given by the formula

2.7 $$\det \mathbf{a} = \sum \operatorname{sign}\begin{pmatrix} 1 & 2 & \cdots & n \\ j_1 & j_2 & \cdots & j_n \end{pmatrix} \cdot a_1^{j_1} a_2^{j_2} \cdots a_n^{j_n}$$

But now it is easily seen that the right-hand side of (2.7) defines a function which satisfies axioms (1), (2), and (3). The details of the verification are left to the reader. Axioms (2) and (3) are very trivial to check; the verification of axiom (1) requires Theorem 3.6, Chap. 10. We indicate the argument briefly, taking columns 1 and 2 for simplicity. If those two columns are interchanged, then the right-hand side of (2.7) becomes

$$\sum \operatorname{sign}\begin{pmatrix}1 & 2 & \cdots & n\\ j_1 & j_2 & \cdots & j_n\end{pmatrix}\cdot a_2^{j_1}\, a_1^{j_2} \cdots a_n^{j_n}$$

Now this symbol has exactly the same meaning as

2.8 $$\sum \operatorname{sign}\begin{pmatrix}1 & 2 & \cdots & n\\ j_2 & j_1 & \cdots & j_n\end{pmatrix}\cdot a_2^{j_2}\, a_1^{j_1} \cdots a_n^{j_n}$$

since the particular choice of summation index is immaterial (provided always that no conflict results). The permutation indicated here can also be written $\begin{pmatrix}2 & 1 & \cdots & n\\ j_1 & j_2 & \cdots & j_n\end{pmatrix}$, and it is equal to the product of $\begin{pmatrix}1 & 2 & \cdots & n\\ j_1 & j_2 & \cdots & j_n\end{pmatrix}$ and the transposition (1, 2), in that order. Therefore, by Theorem 3.6, Chap. 10, the permutations

$$\begin{pmatrix}2 & 1 & \cdots & n\\ j_1 & j_2 & \cdots & j_n\end{pmatrix} \quad\text{and}\quad \begin{pmatrix}1 & 2 & \cdots & n\\ j_1 & j_2 & \cdots & j_n\end{pmatrix}$$

have opposite signs, and it follows that (2.8) is the negative of (2.7). From similar considerations it is easily seen that (2.7) is zero if columns 1 and 2 (or any other two adjacent columns) are equal (see footnote ‡, page 305). We point out here that an essential consideration in connection with (2.7) is the possibility of classifying permutations into even and odd categories. We state our results as the following theorem:

THEOREM 2.3 *There is one and only one mapping from $K^n{}_n$ to K which satisfies axioms* (1), (2), *and* (3) *above, and it is given by formula* (2.7).

Naturally Propositions 2.1 and 2.2, and Corollaries 1 and 2, Theorem 2.1, hold for det.

EXAMPLE For 2×2 matrices, (2.7) reduces to

$$\det \mathbf{a} = \sum \operatorname{sign}\begin{pmatrix}1 & 2\\ i & j\end{pmatrix}\cdot a_1^i a_2^j = a_1^1 a_2^2 - a_1^2 a_2^1$$

REMARK. For 1×1 matrices—i.e., scalars—axiom (1) does not apply. It is easily seen that axioms (2) and (3) lead simply to $\det(a) = a$ in this trivial case, and the same result is given by (2.7).

THEOREM 2.4 *For any $n \times n$ matrix* $\mathbf{a}$, $\det {}^t\mathbf{a} = \det \mathbf{a}$.

Proof. By definition of the transpose, the element in the jth row and the ith column of ${}^t\mathbf{a}$ is $a^i{}_j$. Consequently (2.7) becomes

$$\det {}^t\mathbf{a} = \sum \begin{pmatrix}1 & 2 & \cdots & n\\ j_1 & j_2 & \cdots & j_n\end{pmatrix}\cdot a_{j_1}^1\, a_{j_2}^2 \cdots a_{j_n}^n$$

Now let $\begin{pmatrix}1 & 2 & \cdots & n\\ k_1 & k_2 & \cdots & k_n\end{pmatrix}$ denote the inverse of the permutation

$$\begin{pmatrix}1 & 2 & \cdots & n\\ j_1 & j_2 & \cdots & j_n\end{pmatrix}$$

Applying that inverse to the n-tuple $a^1_{j_1}, a^2_{j_2}, \ldots, a^n_{j_n}$ rearranges it into $a^{k_1}{}_1, a^{k_2}{}_2, \ldots, a^{k_n}{}_n$, and so the sum above can also be written

$$\sum \operatorname{sign}\begin{pmatrix} 1 & 2 & \cdots & n \\ j_1 & j_2 & \cdots & j_n \end{pmatrix} \cdot a^{k_1}_1 \, a^{k_2}_2 \cdots a^{k_n}_n$$

But the sign of a permutation is the same as the sign of its inverse, and so this expression is equal to

$$\sum \operatorname{sign}\begin{pmatrix} 1 & 2 & \cdots & n \\ k_1 & k_2 & \cdots & k_n \end{pmatrix} \cdot a^{k_1}_1 \, a^{k_2}_2 \cdots a^{k_n}_n$$

which is det **a**, by (2.7). Q.E.D.

COROLLARY *Propositions* 2.1 *and* 2.2, *as well as axioms* (1) *and* (2), *hold if the word "column" is everywhere replaced by "row."*

THEOREM 2.5 *Let* **a** *and* **b** *be two* $n \times n$ *matrices with coefficients in* K. *Then* det (**ba**) = (det **b**)(det **a**).

Proof. If as usual we denote the columns of **a** by $\mathbf{a}_1, \ldots, \mathbf{a}_n$, then the columns of **ba** are the vectors $\mathbf{ba}_1, \ldots, \mathbf{ba}_n$. Now let us temporarily regard **b** as fixed and **a** as arbitrary. Define F by the formula $F(\mathbf{a}) = \det(\mathbf{ba})$. Then, in terms of columns, we have

$$F(\mathbf{a}_1, \ldots, \mathbf{a}_n) = \det(\mathbf{ba}_1, \ldots, \mathbf{ba}_n)$$

Since det satisfies axioms (1) and (2), it is easy to see that F defined in this way also satisfies (1) and (2). Therefore from (2.6) we have

$$\begin{aligned} F(\mathbf{a}) &= F(\mathbf{I}_n) \cdot \sum \operatorname{sign}\begin{pmatrix} 1 & 2 & \cdots & n \\ j_1 & j_2 & \cdots & j_n \end{pmatrix} \cdot a^{j_1}_1 \, a^{j_2}_2 \cdots a^{j_n}_n \\ &= F(\mathbf{I}_n) \cdot \det \mathbf{a} \end{aligned}$$

by (7.2). But $F(\mathbf{I}_n) = \det(\mathbf{bI}_n) = \det \mathbf{b}$, whence $F(\mathbf{a}) = \det(\mathbf{ba}) = \det \mathbf{b} \cdot \det \mathbf{a}$. Q.E.D.

EXERCISES

1. From (7.2) write out explicitly the formula for 3×3 determinants. Compute

$$\det\begin{pmatrix} 1 & 0 & 2 & 4 \\ -1 & 2 & 0 & 0 \\ 3 & 1 & -2 & 1 \\ 0 & 1 & 2 & 0 \end{pmatrix} \quad \text{and} \quad \det\begin{pmatrix} t-1 & 1 & 4 \\ 0 & t-2 & -1 \\ 3 & 2 & t-3 \end{pmatrix}$$

2. Let **a** be an $n \times n$ triangular matrix. That is, all the elements below the diagonal are zero: $a^j{}_i = 0$ if $i < j$. Show that

$$\det \mathbf{a} = a^1{}_1 a^2{}_2 \cdots a^n{}_n$$

3. Let **a** be an $n \times n$ *skew-symmetric* matrix, that is, $a^j{}_i = -a^i{}_j$, and suppose

that the field of scalars does not have characteristic 2 (see footnote ‡, page 305). Prove that $\det \mathbf{a} = 0$ if n is odd.

4. Let $\mathbf{a}$ be an $n \times n$ matrix, and let $\mathbf{c}$ be a nonsingular $n \times n$ matrix (Sec. 7, Chap. 9). Show that the determinant of $\mathbf{a}' = \mathbf{cac}^{-1}$ is equal to the determinant of $\mathbf{a}$. Show furthermore that $\operatorname{Tr} \mathbf{a} = \operatorname{Tr} \mathbf{a}'$, where $\operatorname{Tr} \mathbf{a}$ denotes the sum of the diagonal elements of $\mathbf{a}$, and similarly for $\mathbf{a}'$. That is, $\operatorname{Tr} \mathbf{a} = a^j{}_j$. (This quantity is called the *trace* of $\mathbf{a}$.)

3. *Some applications*

Determinants provide a very useful criterion for the linear dependence of vectors, as the following theorem shows.

THEOREM 3.1 *Let* $\mathbf{a}$ *be an* $n \times n$ *matrix with coefficients in a field* K. *Then* $\det \mathbf{a} = 0$ *if and only if the columns of* $\mathbf{a}$ *are linearly dependent.*

Proof. Suppose that the columns of $\mathbf{a}$ are linearly dependent. Then one of them—for simplicity suppose the first—can be expressed as a linear combination of the others, say $\mathbf{a}_1 = c_2\mathbf{a}_2 + \cdots + c_n\mathbf{a}_n$. By repeated applications of Proposition 2.2 we have

$$\begin{aligned}\det(\mathbf{a}_1, \ldots, \mathbf{a}_n) &= \det(\mathbf{a}_1 - c_2\mathbf{a}_2 - \cdots - c_n\mathbf{a}_n, \ldots, \mathbf{a}_n)\\ &= \det(\mathbf{0}, \mathbf{a}_2, \ldots, \mathbf{a}_n) = 0\end{aligned}$$

by Corollary 1 of Proposition 2.1. If, on the other hand, the columns of $\mathbf{a}$ are linearly independent, then $\mathbf{a}$ has an inverse $\mathbf{a}^{-1}$, by Theorem 8.3, Chap. 9.

Applying Theorem 2.5 to the equation $\mathbf{aa}^{-1} = \mathbf{I}_n$, we get $(\det \mathbf{a})(\det \mathbf{a}^{-1}) = 1$, which shows that $\det \mathbf{a} \neq 0$. Q.E.D.

COROLLARY 1 $\det \mathbf{a} = 0$ *if and only if the rows of* $\mathbf{a}$ *are linearly dependent;* $\mathbf{a}$ *has an inverse if and only if* $\det \mathbf{a} \neq 0$.

For the first assertion we have only to replace $\mathbf{a}$ in the theorem above by its transpose, taking account of Theorem 2.4. The second assertion follows from the foregoing and from Theorem 8.3, Chap. 9.

Now let $\mathbf{a}$ denote any $m \times n$ matrix with coefficients in K, and let $\mathbf{b}$ denote any one of the $r \times r$ submatrices of $\mathbf{a}$ which can be obtained by striking out $m - r$ rows and n $- r$ columns of $\mathbf{a}$ (naturally we assume that $r \leq m, n$). The quantity $\det \mathbf{b}$ is called an $r \times r$ *minor* of $\mathbf{a}$, or a minor of *order* r. We have

COROLLARY 2 *The rank of a matrix is equal to the largest integer* r *for which the matrix has a nonzero minor of order* r.

Proof. This follows at once from the theorem above and from the corollary of Theorem 8.3, Chap. 9.

We now show a method for calculating determinants which is often simpler than the formula (2.7). Again let **a** denote an $n \times n$ matrix with coefficients in a field K.

DEFINITION 3.1 *The $(n-1) \times (n-1)$ matrix obtained by striking out the kth row and jth column of the $n \times n$ matrix* **a** *is called the* minor *of the element $a^k{}_j$, and it is denoted by $\mathbf{A}^k{}_j$. The scalar*

$$A^k{}_j = (-1)^{k+j} \cdot \det \mathbf{A}^k{}_j$$

is called the cofactor *of the element $a^k{}_j$.*

Consider now the mapping $F\colon K^n{}_n \to K$ of $n \times n$ matrices to the field K defined by

$$F(\mathbf{a}) = a^k{}_1 A^k{}_1 + a^k{}_2 A^k{}_2 + \cdots + a^k{}_n A^k{}_n$$

the index k being arbitrary but fixed. We claim that F satisfies axioms (1), (2), (3) of Sec. 2 and must therefore be the same as det. To verify (1) let us consider the effect of interchanging the first two columns of **a**. That produces an interchange of the corresponding columns of all the minors $\mathbf{A}^k{}_j$ except $\mathbf{A}^k{}_1$ and $\mathbf{A}^k{}_2$, and consequently all the cofactors $A^k{}_j$ must change sign, except $A^k{}_1$ and $A^k{}_2$. But those two must also change sign; for the reversal of columns 1 and 2 interchanges the minors $\mathbf{A}^k{}_1$ and $\mathbf{A}^k{}_2$, hence produces a change of sign in the cofactors because of the factors $(-1)^{k+1}$ and $(-1)^{k+2}$ involved in their definition. It follows at once that $F(\mathbf{a})$ must change sign. If the first two columns of **a** are identical, then $F(\mathbf{a}) = 0$; for then all the minors $\mathbf{A}^k{}_j (j \neq 1, 2)$ have two identical columns, and therefore the corresponding cofactors are zero. Hence the expression above for $F(\mathbf{a})$ reduces to its first two terms, and they are identical except for sign. The same argument applies to any two adjacent columns of **a**, and therefore F satisfies axiom (1). The verification of axioms (2) and (3) is routine. We have the following theorem:

THEOREM 3.2 *For any $n \times n$ matrix with coefficients in K $(n > 1)$,*

$$\begin{aligned} \det \mathbf{a} &= a^k{}_1 A^k{}_1 + a^k{}_2 A^k{}_2 + \cdots + a^k{}_n A^k{}_n \\ &= a^1{}_h A^1{}_h + a^2{}_h A^2{}_h + \cdots + a^n{}_h A^n{}_h \end{aligned}$$

The first formula is often called the "expansion of det **a** by the kth row"; the second formula, expansion of det **a** by the hth column, follows from the first applied to the hth row of ${}^t\mathbf{a}$.

EXAMPLE 1 The following determinant is computed using expansion by the second row (determinants are often indicated by enclosing the matrix elements between vertical straight lines):

$$\begin{vmatrix} 3 & 1 & -2 \\ 4 & 2 & 5 \\ 1 & -3 & 0 \end{vmatrix} = -4 \begin{vmatrix} 1 & -2 \\ -3 & 0 \end{vmatrix} + 2 \begin{vmatrix} 3 & -2 \\ 1 & 0 \end{vmatrix} - 5 \begin{vmatrix} 3 & 1 \\ 1 & -3 \end{vmatrix}$$

$$= -4 \cdot (-6) + 2.2 - 5 \cdot (-9 - 1) = 78$$

In computing determinants by the method of Theorem 3.2 it is obviously advantageous to expand by a row or column containing as many zeros as possible.

EXAMPLE 2 The well-known Vandermonde determinant

$$\Delta_n = \begin{vmatrix} 1 & x_1 & x_1^2 & \cdots & x_1^{n-1} \\ 1 & x_2 & x_2^2 & \cdots & x_2^{n-1} \\ \cdots & \cdots & \cdots & \cdots & \cdots \\ 1 & x_n & x_n^2 & \cdots & x_n^{n-1} \end{vmatrix}$$

is equal to $\prod_{i>k} (x_i - x_k)$. (Superscripts here are exponents.)

This may be proved by induction, starting with $n = 2$, where both sides of the identity yield $x_2 - x_1$. Assume now the identity true for all positive integers smaller than n. Applying Proposition 2.2 repeatedly, we subtract from the nth column the $(n-1)$th column multiplied by x_1, then subtract from the $(n-1)$th column the $(n-2)$th column multiplied by x_1, etc. In this way, we obtain

$$\Delta_n = \begin{vmatrix} 1 & 0 & 0 & \cdots & 0 \\ 1 & x_2 - x_1 & x_2^2 - x_1x_2 & \cdots & x_2^{n-1} - x_1x_2^{n-2} \\ \cdots & \cdots & \cdots & \cdots & \cdots \\ 1 & x_n - x_1 & x_n^2 - x_1x_n & \cdots & x_n^{n-1} - x_1x_n^{n-2} \end{vmatrix}$$

We now apply the corollary of Theorem 2.4 and subtract the first row from the others, obtaining

$$\Delta_n = \begin{vmatrix} 1 & 0 & 0 & \cdots & 0 \\ 0 & x_2 - x_1 & x_2^2 - x_1x_2 & \cdots & x_2^{n-1} - x_1x_2^{n-2} \\ \cdots & \cdots & \cdots & \cdots & \cdots \\ 0 & x_n - x_1 & x_n^2 - x_1x_n & \cdots & x_n^{n-1} - x_1x_n^{n-2} \end{vmatrix}$$

By Proposition 2.1 and the corollary of Theorem 2.4, we may take the factors $x_2 - x_1, x_3 - x_1, \ldots, x_n - x_1$ out of the second, third, . . . , nth rows of Δ_n and

$$\Delta_n = \prod_{i=2}^{n} (x_i - x_1) \cdot \begin{vmatrix} 1 & 0 & 0 & \cdots & 0 \\ 0 & 1 & x_2 & \cdots & x_2^{n-2} \\ \cdots & \cdots & \cdots & \cdots & \cdots \\ 0 & 1 & x_n & \cdots & x_n^{n-2} \end{vmatrix}$$

If we now expand by the first row, we see that the remaining determinant is equal to the Vandermonde determinant Δ_{n-1} whose entries are powers of $x_2, x_3, \ldots, x_n$. The result now follows by induction, since

$$\prod_{n>i>k>1} (x_i - x_k) = \prod_{i=2}^{n} (x_i - x_1) \cdot \prod_{n>i>k>2} (x_i - x_k)$$

From the theorem above we derive two important corollaries:

COROLLARY 1 *If $j \neq k$, then*

$$a^j{}_1A^k{}_1 + a^j{}_2A^k{}_2 + \cdots + a^j{}_nA^k{}_n = 0$$

and

$$a^1{}_jA^1{}_k + a^2{}_jA^2{}_k + \cdots + a^n{}_jA^n{}_k = 0$$

Proof. Let $\mathbf{a}'$ be the matrix obtained by replacing the kth row of $\mathbf{a}$ by the jth row. Then the jth and kth rows of $\mathbf{a}'$ are identical, and so $\det \mathbf{a}' = 0$, by Proposition 2.1. Expanding $\det \mathbf{a}'$ by the kth row according to Theorem 3.2, we get the first equation of the corollary. The second equation follows similarly by using the columns of $\mathbf{a}$. Q.E.D.

COROLLARY 2 *Let $\tilde{\mathbf{a}} = {}^t(A^i{}_j)$ be the transpose of the matrix of cofactors of* $\mathbf{a}$. *Then* $\mathbf{a}\tilde{\mathbf{a}} = \tilde{\mathbf{a}}\mathbf{a} = (\det \mathbf{a}) \cdot \mathbf{I}_n$. *Hence, if* $\det \mathbf{a} \neq 0$, *we have*

$$\mathbf{a}^{-1} = \frac{1}{\det \mathbf{a}} \cdot \tilde{\mathbf{a}}$$

Proof. This follows immediately from the equations in Theorem 3.2 and Corollary 1 and from the definition of matrix multiplication.

DEFINITION 3.2 *The matrix $\tilde{\mathbf{a}}$ associated with* $\mathbf{a}$ *is called the* adjoint *of* $\mathbf{a}$.

EXAMPLE The adjoint of

$$\begin{pmatrix} 2 & 1 & 3 \\ 0 & 1 & 2 \\ 1 & 0 & -2 \end{pmatrix} \quad \text{is} \quad \begin{pmatrix} -2 & 2 & -1 \\ 2 & -7 & -4 \\ -1 & 1 & 2 \end{pmatrix}$$

We next show how determinants can be used to obtain a formula for the solution of a system of linear equations. Again let $\mathbf{a}$ be a matrix in $K^n{}_n$, and suppose that we want to solve the equation

$$\mathbf{ax} = \mathbf{y}$$

for the column vector $\mathbf{x}$, where $\mathbf{y}$ is a given vector in K^n. If $\det \mathbf{a} \neq 0$, then $\mathbf{a}^{-1}$ exists, and the answer is obtained by multiplying the equation by $\mathbf{a}^{-1}$:

$$\mathbf{x} = \mathbf{a}^{-1}\mathbf{y}$$

A somewhat different formula for $\mathbf{x}$ can be obtained as follows: The equations to be solved are

$$a^i{}_jx^j = y^i \qquad (i = 1, \ldots, n)$$

Multiply by the cofactor $A^i{}_k$ and sum over i:

$$\sum_{i,j} A^i{}_ka^i{}_jx^j = \sum_i A^i{}_ky^i$$

It follows at once from the second equations of Theorem 3.2 and of Corollary 1 above that this equation is simply

$$(\det \mathbf{a}) \cdot x^k = \sum_i A^i{}_k y^i$$

By Theorem 3.2 the right-hand side of this is the determinant of the matrix $(\mathbf{a}_1, \ldots, \mathbf{a}_{k-1}, \mathbf{y}, \mathbf{a}_{k+1}, \ldots, \mathbf{a}_n)$ obtained from $\mathbf{a}$ by replacing its kth column by $\mathbf{y}$. We have then the following theorem:

THEOREM 3.3 **(Cramer's rule)** *Let* $\mathbf{a}$ *be a nonsingular matrix in* $K^n{}_n$, *and let* $\mathbf{y}$ *be a column vector in* K^n. *Then the unique solution of the equation* $\mathbf{ax} = \mathbf{y}$ *is given by the formula*

$$x^k = \frac{\det (\mathbf{a}_1, \ldots, \overset{(k)}{\mathbf{y}}, \ldots, \mathbf{a}_n)}{\det \mathbf{a}} \qquad (k = 1, \ldots, n)$$

REMARK. The problem of computing determinants is one of considerable practical importance. The general formula (2.7) contains $n!$ terms. For example, for $n = 10$, a rather modest value, there are 3,628,800 terms to be added, each involving a product of 10 factors. It is plain that (2.7) does not afford a very practical method of computation. Many special procedures have been devised for diminishing the labor of computing determinants. Some of them refer to matrices whose entries occur in rather special patterns; others yield approximate values of determinants. For ordinary purposes the most practical general method of computation consists of reducing the matrix in question to triangular form by means of elementary row and column operations, as described in Sec. 9, Chap. 9. We recall that an elementary row operation involves adding multiples of one row in a matrix to the other rows; similarly for elementary column operations. It follows from Proposition 2.2 and the corollary of Theorem 2.4 that such operations do not alter the value of the determinant. In Sec. 9, Chap. 9, it was shown that any matrix can be reduced to triangular form by a series of elementary row operations, possibly with certain permutations of the rows or columns. The permutations, if required, do alter the sign of the determinant, but that does not pose a serious problem. For a triangular matrix it is trivial to compute the determinant (see Exercise 2, Sec. 2). If a (square) matrix contains several zero entries, it is sometimes possible to maneuver them into one corner so as to form a block of zeros. The following theorem is useful in that situation:

THEOREM 3.4 *Let* $\mathbf{a}$ *be an* $m \times m$ *matrix, let* $\mathbf{b}$ *be an* $n \times n$ *matrix, and let* $\mathbf{c}$ *be an* $m \times n$ *matrix, all with coefficients in a field* K. *Then the determinant of the* $(m + n) \times (m + n)$ *matrix*

3.1 $$\begin{pmatrix} \mathbf{a} & \mathbf{c} \\ \mathbf{0} & \mathbf{b} \end{pmatrix}$$

is equal to (det **a**)(det **b**).†

Proof. Temporarily regard **b** and **c** as fixed matrices and **a** as an arbitrary matrix. Denote the determinant of (3.1) by $F(\mathbf{a})$. Then it is trivial to see that $F(\mathbf{a})$ so defined satisfies axioms (1) and (2) of Sec. 2. Therefore, by (2.6) and (2.7) $F(\mathbf{a}) = F(\mathbf{I}_m) \cdot \det \mathbf{a}$. Now $F(\mathbf{I}_m)$ is the determinant of the matrix

$$\begin{pmatrix} \mathbf{I}_m & \mathbf{c} \\ \mathbf{0} & \mathbf{b} \end{pmatrix}$$

Denote this determinant by $G(\mathbf{b})$, regarding **c** as fixed. It is very simple to verify that $G(\mathbf{b})$ satisfies axioms (1) and (2) for the *rows* of **b**, rather than the columns. In other words, $G(\mathbf{b})$ satisfies axioms (1) and (2) for the *columns* of ${}^t\mathbf{b}$. Hence, by (2.6), (2.7), and Theorem 2.4, $G(\mathbf{b}) = G(\mathbf{I}_n) \cdot \det \mathbf{b}$. But $G(\mathbf{I}_n)$ is by definition equal to

$$\det \begin{pmatrix} \mathbf{I}_m & \mathbf{c} \\ \mathbf{0} & \mathbf{I}_n \end{pmatrix}$$

which is equal to 1, since the matrix is triangular and all its diagonal entries are 1. Since $F(\mathbf{I}_m)$ is the same as $G(\mathbf{b})$, the assertion follows at once.

Q.E.D.

Similar results can be proved if the block of zeros occurs in one of the other corners.

EXERCISES

1. Compute the following determinant in three ways, expanding by the first row, expanding by the second column, and reducing to triangular form.

$$\begin{vmatrix} 1 & -2 & 0 & 3 \\ 4 & 0 & 2 & -4 \\ 2 & 0 & 6 & 0 \\ 1 & -1 & 0 & 2 \end{vmatrix}$$

2. Compute the determinant of the following matrix. Compute the adjoint matrix and verify the equation $\mathbf{a}\tilde{\mathbf{a}} = (\det \mathbf{a}) \cdot \mathbf{I}$:

$$\begin{pmatrix} t-1 & 1 & 4 \\ 0 & t-2 & -1 \\ 3 & 2 & t-3 \end{pmatrix}$$

3. Compute the following determinant:

$$\begin{vmatrix} \mathbf{0} & \mathbf{I}_m \\ \mathbf{I}_n & \mathbf{0} \end{vmatrix}$$

(The zeros stand for zero matrices of the appropriate size.)

† The symbol **0** here denotes the $n \times m$ zero matrix.

4. Compute the determinant and the adjoint of the following matrix with coefficients in the field $\mathbf{Z}_5$. (See Sec. 10, Chap. 2. The residue class notation introduced there is used below.)

$$\begin{pmatrix} \bar{1} & \bar{2} & \bar{2} \\ -\bar{1} & \bar{3} & \bar{3} \\ \bar{2} & -\bar{2} & \bar{0} \end{pmatrix}$$

Verify Corollary 2 of Theorem 3.2 for this matrix.

5. Solve the following equations using Cramer's rule:

$$\begin{aligned} 3x^1 + 2x^2 &= 1 \\ x^1 - 2x^2 &= 2 \end{aligned} \qquad \begin{aligned} x + 2y \phantom{{}+z} &= 4 \\ x - 4y + z &= 1 \\ 2x + y - 3z &= 0 \end{aligned}$$

6. Let x_1, x_2, x_3 be coordinates in a three-dimensional euclidean affine space, and let $a^i{}_j x_i = b_j$ $(j = 1, 2, 3)$ be equations of three planes in that space. Prove that the intersection of these planes consists of a single point if and only if $\det \mathbf{a} \neq 0$.

7. If

$$D_n = \begin{vmatrix} a_1 & 1 & 0 & \cdot & \cdot & \cdot & \cdot & \cdot & \cdot \\ -1 & a_2 & 1 & 0 & & & \cdot & \cdot & \cdot \\ 0 & -1 & a_3 & 1 & 0 & & \cdot & \cdot & \cdot \\ \cdot & \cdot & \cdot & \cdot & \cdot & \cdot & \cdot & \cdot & \cdot \\ 0 & 0 & \cdot & \cdot & \cdot & \cdot & & -1 & a_n \end{vmatrix}$$

prove that $D_n = a_n D_{n-1} + D_{n-2}$.

4. *The characteristic polynomial*

Here we shall have occasion to consider matrices whose entries are polynomials (such matrices have already appeared in some of the exercises). In Chap. 6 (Theorem 2.5) it was shown that, starting with any field K (or more generally any integral domain), we can construct from it a new integral domain $K[t]$ whose elements are all the polynomials

$$f(t) = a_0 + a_1 t + a_2 t^2 + \cdots + a_n t^n$$

in a *variable* t, with coefficients in K. If a_n above is not zero, then the expression for $f(t)$ is unique, and n is called the *degree* of $f(t)$.

From the domain $K[t]$ we can furthermore construct a *field* $K(t)$ containing $K[t]$ as a subring, each element of $K(t)$ being a polynomial or else the quotient of two polynomials (Sec. 2, Chap. 7). Since $K(t)$ is a field, the foregoing discussion of determinants applies to matrices with coefficients in $K(t)$. For the most part our matrices will have polynomial entries (including of course polynomials of degree zero, i.e., elements of K). Taking K to be the field of rational numbers, two simple examples of matrices with coefficients in $\mathbf{Q}(t)$ are

$$\begin{pmatrix} 3t & \dfrac{t^2+1}{t} \\ \dfrac{1}{t} & 2 \end{pmatrix} \qquad \begin{pmatrix} 1 & 0 & 3t+1 \\ 2t & t^2 & 4+t^2 \\ 0 & t & t+1 \end{pmatrix}$$

In order to indicate that a matrix has coefficients which are polynomials in t, possibly but not necessarily of degree greater than zero, we shall sometimes use such notations as $\mathbf{a}(t)$, $\mathbf{b}(t)$, etc. It will be convenient to refer to elements of K as "constants." A matrix with constant coefficients is thus just a matrix with coefficients in K.

It follows from our earlier definitions (Sec. 6, Chap. 9) that the second matrix above is equal to

$$\begin{pmatrix} 1 & 0 & 1 \\ 0 & 0 & 4 \\ 0 & 0 & 1 \end{pmatrix} + t \cdot \begin{pmatrix} 0 & 0 & 3 \\ 2 & 0 & 0 \\ 0 & 1 & 1 \end{pmatrix} + t^2 \cdot \begin{pmatrix} 0 & 0 & 0 \\ 0 & 1 & 1 \\ 0 & 0 & 0 \end{pmatrix}$$

an expression in which all the matrices have constant entries. This observation leads at once to the following proposition:

PROPOSITION 4.1 *Let $\mathbf{a}(t)$ be a matrix with coefficients in $K[t]$ (that is, polynomials in t). Assuming that not all the entries are zero, let m be the greatest of their degrees. Then $\mathbf{a}(t)$ can be expressed in one and only one way in the form*

$$\mathbf{a}(t) = \mathbf{a}_0 + t\mathbf{a}_1 + t^2\mathbf{a}_2 + \cdots + t^m\mathbf{a}_m$$

where each $\mathbf{a}_i$ is a matrix [of the same size as $\mathbf{a}(t)$] with constant coefficients.

The proof is trivial.

Of particular importance to us are matrices of the type

$$t \cdot \mathbf{I}_n - \mathbf{a}$$

where $\mathbf{a}$ is an $n \times n$ matrix with *constant* coefficients. (When n is understood, we shall sometimes write $\mathbf{I}$ instead of $\mathbf{I}_n$ for the $n \times n$ unit matrix.)

EXAMPLE 1 For the matrix

$$\mathbf{a} = \begin{pmatrix} 1 & 3 & 2 \\ 0 & 1 & -1 \\ 0 & -1 & -2 \end{pmatrix}$$

we have

$$t\mathbf{I} - \mathbf{a} = t \cdot \begin{pmatrix} 1 & 0 & 0 \\ 0 & 1 & 0 \\ 0 & 0 & 1 \end{pmatrix} - \begin{pmatrix} 1 & 3 & 2 \\ 0 & 1 & -1 \\ 0 & -1 & -2 \end{pmatrix}$$

$$= \begin{pmatrix} t & 0 & 0 \\ 0 & t & 0 \\ 0 & 0 & t \end{pmatrix} - \begin{pmatrix} 1 & 3 & 2 \\ 0 & 1 & -1 \\ 0 & -1 & -2 \end{pmatrix} = \begin{pmatrix} t-1 & -3 & -2 \\ 0 & t-1 & 1 \\ 0 & 1 & t+2 \end{pmatrix}$$

THEOREM 4.2 *Let* $\mathbf{a}$ *be an* $n \times n$ *matrix with coefficients in the field* K. *Then the quantity* $\varphi(t) = \det(t\mathbf{I} - \mathbf{a})$ *is a polynomial of degree* n *in* t *with coefficients in* K. $\varphi(t)$ *is called the* characteristic polynomial *of the matrix* $\mathbf{a}$. *Its highest coefficient is* 1, *and its constant term is equal to* $(-1)^n \det \mathbf{a}$. *The negative of the coefficient of* t^{n-1} *in* $\varphi(t)$ *is equal to the sum of the diagonal elements of* $\mathbf{a}$.†

Proof. As usual let $a^j{}_k$ be the (j, k) entry of $\mathbf{a}$, and let $\delta^j{}_k$ be the (j, k) entry of $\mathbf{I}$. Then the (j, k) entry of $t\mathbf{I} - \mathbf{a}$ is by definition equal to $t\delta^j{}_k - a^j{}_k$. The determinant of this matrix is then, by (2.7), equal to

$$\begin{aligned}\varphi(t) &= \det(t\mathbf{I} - \mathbf{a})\\ &= \sum \operatorname{sign}\begin{pmatrix}1 & \cdots & n\\ j_1 & \cdots & j_n\end{pmatrix} \cdot (t\delta_1^{j_1} - a_1^{j_1}) \cdots (t\delta_n^{j_n} - a_n^{j_n})\end{aligned}$$

It is obvious from this that $\varphi(t)$ is a polynomial of degree at most n. Recall that $\delta_1^{j_1} = 0$ unless $j_1 = 1$, and so on. It follows that there can be only one term in the sum above containing t^n, namely, that term for which $j_1 = 1, j_2 = 2, \ldots, j_n = n$. The term is therefore equal to

$$(t - a^1{}_1)(t - a^2{}_2) \cdots (t - a^n{}_n) = t^n - (a^1{}_1 + a^2{}_2 + \cdots + a^n{}_n) \cdot t^{n-1} + \text{etc.}$$

This shows that the coefficient of t^n in the polynomial $\varphi(t)$ is 1, as claimed. Now for any permutation $j_1, \ldots, j_n$ of $1, \ldots, n$, if any one of $\delta_1^{j_1}$, $\delta_2^{j_2}, \ldots, \delta_n^{j_n}$ is zero, then another one must also be zero, and in that case

$$(t\delta_1^{j_1} - a_1^{j_1}) \cdots (t\delta_n^{j_n} - a_n^{j_n})$$

can have degree at most equal to $n - 2$. Hence the only term of degree $n - 1$ is the one written above, and the negative of the coefficient of t^{n-1} is indeed the trace of $\mathbf{a}$. Finally, the constant term of $\varphi(t)$ is simply $\varphi(0) = \det(0 \cdot \mathbf{I} - \mathbf{a}) = \det(-\mathbf{a}) = (-1)^n \det \mathbf{a}$. Q.E.D.

EXAMPLE 2 The characteristic polynomial of the matrix $\mathbf{a}$ of Example 1 is $t^3 - 4t + 3$.

We now come to an important theorem about characteristic polynomials. Let $\mathbf{a}$ again denote an $n \times n$ matrix with coefficients in the field K, and let

$$f(t) = c_0 + c_1 t + c_2 t^2 + \cdots + c_r t^r$$

be a polynomial, also with coefficients in K. We introduce the notation

$$f(\mathbf{a}) = c_0 \mathbf{I}_n + c_1 \mathbf{a} + c_2 \mathbf{a}^2 + \cdots + c_r \mathbf{a}^r$$

Thus $f(\mathbf{a})$ is an $n \times n$ *matrix* obtained by putting $\mathbf{a}$ for the indeterminate t (and the unit matrix for t^0). Similar notation has already occurred in Sec. 4, Chap. 9.

THEOREM 4.3 (Cayley-Hamilton) *Let* $\varphi(t)$ *be the characteristic polynomial of an* $n \times n$ *matrix* $\mathbf{a}$ *with coefficients in* K. *Then* $\varphi(\mathbf{a}) = \mathbf{0}$.

Proof. By definition, $\varphi(t) = \det(t\mathbf{I} - \mathbf{a})$. One might naïvely try to substitute $\mathbf{a}$ for t in this determinant. The result would be $\det(\mathbf{aI} - \mathbf{a}) =$

† The sum of the diagonal elements is called the *trace of* $\mathbf{a}$, denoted by Tr $\mathbf{a}$.

det $(\mathbf{a} - \mathbf{a}) = 0$, all right; but that has nothing at all to do with the theorem we want to prove, for the zero here is a scalar, whereas the theorem says that $\varphi(\mathbf{a})$ is the $n \times n$ matrix whose entries are all zero. That point being settled, we go on with the proof.

Let us write $\mathbf{b}(t)$ for $t\,\mathbf{I} - \mathbf{a}$. Then det $\mathbf{b}(t) = \varphi(t)$, of course. Now let $\tilde{\mathbf{b}}(t)$ denote the adjoint matrix of $\mathbf{b}(t)$ (Definition 3.2). The entries of $\tilde{\mathbf{b}}(t)$ are then the cofactors of the elements of $\mathbf{b}(t)$ (Definition 3.1), and it is readily seen from (2.7) that those entries are therefore polynomials in t of degree at most $n - 1$. Consequently we can write $\tilde{\mathbf{b}}(t)$ uniquely in the form

$$\tilde{\mathbf{b}}(t) = \tilde{\mathbf{b}}_0 + t\tilde{\mathbf{b}}_1 + \cdots + t^{n-1}\tilde{\mathbf{b}}_{n-1}$$

where the $\mathbf{b}_i$ are *constant* matrices (see Proposition 4.1). Now by Corollary 2 of Theorem 3.2 we have $\mathbf{b}(t) \cdot \tilde{\mathbf{b}}(t) = \det \mathbf{b}(t) \cdot \mathbf{I}$. That is,

4.1 $$(t\,\mathbf{I} - \mathbf{a}) \cdot (\tilde{\mathbf{b}}_0 + t\tilde{\mathbf{b}}_1 + \cdots + t^{n-1}\tilde{\mathbf{b}}_{n-1}) = \varphi(t) \cdot \mathbf{I}$$

Expanding the left side out [using the rules (6.11), Chap. 9] we get

4.2 $$-a\tilde{\mathbf{b}}_0 + t(\tilde{\mathbf{b}}_0 - \mathbf{a}\tilde{\mathbf{b}}_1) + \cdots + t^{n-1}(\tilde{\mathbf{b}}_{n-2} - \mathbf{a}\tilde{\mathbf{b}}_{n-1}) + t^n\tilde{\mathbf{b}}_{n-1} = \varphi(t) \cdot \mathbf{I}$$

By Proposition 4.1 this is an identity, meaning that the matrices on either side of the equation with a given power t^k of t must be the same. In other words, if say

$$\varphi(t) = c_0 + c_1t + c_2t^2 + \cdots + c_{n-1}t^{n-1} + t^n$$

then we must have

$$-\mathbf{a}\tilde{\mathbf{b}}_0 = c_0 \cdot \mathbf{I} \qquad \tilde{\mathbf{b}}_0 - \mathbf{a}\tilde{\mathbf{b}}_1 = c_1 \cdot \mathbf{I} \qquad \text{etc.}$$

Consequently, (4.2) *must remain true if we replace t by the matrix* **a**, or by any other $n \times n$ matrix. Now we would like to substitute **a** for t in (4.1). The left-hand side would clearly become zero, allowing us to conclude that $\varphi(\mathbf{a})$ must be zero. The trouble here is that the coefficients of t are matrices, not scalars, and there is no guarantee that a polynomial identity involving matrices remains true if we substitute a matrix for t, because matrix multiplication is not commutative in general. Hence, even though (4.2) does remain true if we substitute **a** for t, it does not follow automatically that (4.1) remains true under the same circumstances. To see what happens here, suppose we had first substituted some matrix **s** for the variable t in (4.1) and had then expanded out the left-hand side. We should have got

$$(\mathbf{s} - \mathbf{a})(\tilde{\mathbf{b}}_0 + \mathbf{s}\tilde{\mathbf{b}}_1 + \cdots + \mathbf{s}^{n-1}\tilde{\mathbf{b}}_{n-1}) = -\mathbf{a}\tilde{\mathbf{b}}_0 + (\mathbf{s}\tilde{\mathbf{b}}_0 - \mathbf{a}\mathbf{s}\tilde{\mathbf{b}}_1) + \cdots$$
$$+ (\mathbf{s}^{n-1}\tilde{\mathbf{b}}_{n-2} - \mathbf{a}\mathbf{s}^{n-1}\tilde{\mathbf{b}}_{n-1}) + \mathbf{s}^n\tilde{\mathbf{b}}_{n-1}$$

which is *not* the same as the result of substituting **s** for t in (4.2) unless $\mathbf{sa} = \mathbf{as}$. But for the special case $\mathbf{s} = \mathbf{a}$ that is certainly true, and therefore substitution of **a** for t in the left member of (4.1) gives the same result, namely, **0**, as substituting **a** for t in the left member of (4.2). And since the latter equation remains true with **a** in place of t, we conclude that $\varphi(\mathbf{a}) = \mathbf{0}$. Q.E.D.

EXAMPLE 3 For the matrix **a** of Example 1, we have $\mathbf{a}^3 - 4\mathbf{a} + 3\mathbf{I} = 0$ (cf. Example 2). This is easily verified directly.

The question of substituting a matrix for a variable, as in the foregoing proof, will arise from time to time, and we therefore insert the following theorem, which covers many cases of importance, although not the case with which we have just been occupied.

THEOREM 4.4 *Any identity among polynomials in t with coefficients in K remains true if t is replaced by any $n \times n$ matrix* **a** *with coefficients in K.*

The proof is quite trivial, essentially the same as the proof of Theorem 2.4, Chap. 6. The point is that the only matrices which will appear after the substitution are various powers of **a**, and they all commute with each other.

As an immediate application we have the following theorem:

THEOREM 4.5 *Let* **a** *be an $n \times n$ matrix with coefficients in K. Then any positive power of* **a** *can be expressed as a linear combination, with coefficients in K, of* $\mathbf{I}$, $\mathbf{a}$, $\mathbf{a}^2, \ldots, \mathbf{a}^{n-1}$. *If* $\det \mathbf{a} \neq 0$, *then any negative power of* **a** *can be expressed in the same way.*

Proof. Let m be a positive integer. By the division algorithm (Proposition 3.2, Chap. 6) there exist polynomials $q(t)$ and $r(t)$ in $K[t]$ such that $t^m = q(t) \cdot \varphi(t) + r(t)$, $\varphi(t)$ being the characteristic polynomial of **a**; and $\deg r < \deg \varphi$ or else $r = 0$. By the preceding theorem we can put **a** for t in this equation, getting $\mathbf{a}^m = q(\mathbf{a}) \cdot \varphi(\mathbf{a}) + r(\mathbf{a})$. By the Cayley-Hamilton theorem, $\varphi(\mathbf{a}) = \mathbf{0}$, and so $\mathbf{a}^m = r(\mathbf{a})$. The right-hand side is indeed a linear combination of powers of **a** not exceeding the $(n-1)$th power.

For negative powers, we recall that $\varphi(0) = (-1)^n \det \mathbf{a}$ (Theorem 4.2). Hence $\varphi(0) \neq 0$ if $\det \mathbf{a} \neq 0$, and then clearly $\varphi(t)$ is not divisible by the irreducible polynomial t (Theorem 4.1, Chap. 6). Hence t^m and $\varphi(t)$ are relatively prime, and so there exist polynomials $g(t)$ and $h(t)$ in $K[t]$ such that $1 = g(t) \cdot t^m + h(t) \cdot \varphi(t)$. We can assume moreover that $\deg g(t) < n$, for otherwise let $q(t)$ be the quotient and $r(t)$ the remainder upon division of $g(t)$ by $\varphi(t)$, so that $g(t) = q(t) \cdot \varphi(t) + r(t)$. Then we have $1 = r(t) \cdot t^m + [g(t) \cdot t^m + h(t)] \cdot \varphi(t)$. By Theorem 4.4, this equation remains valid upon substitution of **a** for t (and **I** for 1 on the left). Since $\varphi(\mathbf{a}) = \mathbf{0}$, we get $\mathbf{I} = r(\mathbf{a}) \cdot \mathbf{a}^m$. Multiplying by $\mathbf{a}^{-m}$ we obtain finally $\mathbf{a}^{-m} = r(\mathbf{a})$. Q.E.D.

REMARK. In many instances the methods just described for computing $\mathbf{a}^{\pm m}$ are quite useful; they replace matrix calculations in part by polynomial calculations. We point out here the following short cut for $\mathbf{a}^{-1}$: If the characteristic polynomial is $\varphi(t) = c_0 + c_1 t + \cdots + c_{n-1}t^{n-1} + t^n$, then we have (Theorem 4.3)

$$c_0\mathbf{I} + c_1\mathbf{a} + \cdots + c_{n-1}\mathbf{a}^{n-1} + \mathbf{a}^n = \mathbf{0}$$

and multiplication by $\mathbf{a}^{-1}$ gives us the formula

$$\mathbf{a}^{-1} = -\frac{1}{c_0}(c_1\mathbf{I} + \cdots + c_{n-1}\mathbf{a}^{n-2} + \mathbf{a}^{n-1})$$

Theorem 4.3 says that any $n \times n$ matrix $\mathbf{a}$ with coefficients in K satisfies a certain polynomial equation of degree n with coefficients in K. Now it may happen that there is a polynomial $f(t)$ in $K[t]$ of degree less than n such that $f(\mathbf{a}) = \mathbf{0}$. Among all the polynomials $f(t)$ of lowest possible degree such that $f(\mathbf{a}) = \mathbf{0}$ there is clearly a unique *monic* polynomial, say $\varphi_0(t)$. It is called the *minimal* polynomial of $\mathbf{a}$. There is a close connection between the characteristic and minimal polynomials, as the theorem below shows. They may indeed be identical. To give an example where they are not the same, we mention that the characteristic polynomial of the $n \times n$ unit matrix is $(t - 1)^n$; its minimal polynomial is $t - 1$. In Theorem 4.5 and its proof the characteristic polynomial can be replaced by the minimal polynomial.

THEOREM 4.6 *Let $\mathbf{a}$ be an $n \times n$ matrix with coefficients in K. Let $\varphi(t)$ and $\varphi_0(t)$ denote its characteristic and minimal polynomials, respectively. Then $\varphi_0(t)$ divides $\varphi(t)$, and $\varphi(t)$ divides $\varphi_0(t)^n$. The prime factorizations of $\varphi(t)$ and $\varphi_0(t)$ contain the same irreducible factors.*

Proof. From the division algorithm we can write $\varphi(t) = q(t) \cdot \varphi_0(t) + r(t)$, where q and r are certain polynomials such that $\deg r < \deg \varphi_0$ or else $r = 0$. Putting $\mathbf{a}$ for t in the equation, we get $r(\mathbf{a}) = \mathbf{0}$, using Theorems 4.3 and 4.4. Therefore $r(t) = 0$, by definition of $\varphi_0(t)$.

To prove that $\varphi(t) | \varphi_0(t)^n$ we use the following device: Let $\varphi_0(t) = t^r + c_1 t^{r-1} + \cdots + c_{r-1}t + c_r$. We define new matrices $\mathbf{w}_j$ by

$$\mathbf{w}_j = \mathbf{a}^j + c_1\mathbf{a}^{j-1} + \cdots + c_{j-1}\mathbf{a} + c_j\mathbf{I} \qquad (j = 0, 1, \ldots, r-1)$$

In particular, $\mathbf{w}_0 = \mathbf{I}$ and $\mathbf{w}_{r-1} = \mathbf{a}^{r-1} + c_1\mathbf{a}^{r-2} + \cdots + c_{r-1}\mathbf{I}$. Clearly $\mathbf{a}\mathbf{w}_j = \mathbf{w}_{j+1} - c_{j+1}\mathbf{I}$ for $j < r - 1$, and $\mathbf{a}\mathbf{w}_{r-1} = \varphi_0(\mathbf{a}) - c_r\mathbf{I} = -c_r\mathbf{I}$, since $\varphi_0(\mathbf{a}) = \mathbf{0}$. Now put

$$\mathbf{w}(t) = t^{r-1}\mathbf{w}_0 + t^{r-2}\mathbf{w}_1 + \cdots + t\mathbf{w}_{r-2} + \mathbf{w}_{r-1}$$

From the equations above we have

$$\begin{aligned}(t\mathbf{I} - \mathbf{a}) \cdot \mathbf{w}(t) &= t^r\mathbf{w}_0 + t^{r-1}\mathbf{w}_1 + \cdots + t^2\mathbf{w}_{r-2} \\ &\quad + t\mathbf{w}_{r-1} - t^{r-1}\mathbf{a}\mathbf{w}_0 - t^{r-2}\mathbf{a}\mathbf{w}_1 - \cdots \\ &\quad - t\mathbf{a}\mathbf{w}_{r-2} - \mathbf{a}\mathbf{w}_{r-1} \\ &= t^r\mathbf{I} + t^{r-1}w_1 + \cdots + t^2\mathbf{w}_{r-2} \\ &\quad + t\mathbf{w}_{r-1} - t^{r-1}(\mathbf{w}_1 - c_1\mathbf{I}) - \cdots \\ &\quad - t(\mathbf{w}_{r-1} - c_{r-1}\mathbf{I}) + c_r\mathbf{I} \\ &= \varphi_0(t) \cdot \mathbf{I}\end{aligned}$$

Taking determinants of both sides and using Theorem 2.5, we get $\varphi(t) \cdot \det \mathbf{w}(t) = \varphi_0(t)^n$. Since $\det \mathbf{w}(t)$ is a polynomial, the assertion is proved. If an *irreducible* polynomial $p(t)$ divides $\varphi(t)$, then it must divide $\varphi_0(t)^n$, hence also $\varphi_0(t)$ (Theorem 3.5, Chap. 6). It follows at once that $\varphi(t)$ and $\varphi_0(t)$ have the same irreducible factors.

COROLLARY *If $f(t)$ is any polynomial in $K[t]$, then the matrix $f(\mathbf{a})$ is nonsingular if and only if $f(t)$ and $\varphi(t)$ are relatively prime. If $g(t)$ is any polynomial of positive degree which divides $\varphi(t)$, then* $\det g(\mathbf{a}) = 0$.

Proof. Let $g(t)$ be the g.c.d. of $f(t)$ and $\varphi(t)$; and let $p(t)$ be an irreducible factor of $g(t)$, assuming that $\deg g(t) > 0$. Then, by the theorem just proved, $p(t)$ also divides the minimal polynomial $\varphi_0(\mathbf{t})$, say $\varphi_0(t) = q(t) \cdot p(t)$. Then $\varphi_0(\mathbf{a}) = q(\mathbf{a}) \cdot p(\mathbf{a}) = \mathbf{0}$. It follows that $\det p(\mathbf{a}) = 0$, for otherwise $p(\mathbf{a})$ would have an inverse and it would follow that $q(\mathbf{a}) = \mathbf{0}$, contradicting the definition of $\varphi_0(t)$. Since $p(t)$ divides $g(t)$, we have, say, $g(t) = q_1(t) \cdot p(t)$, and so $g(\mathbf{a}) = q_1(\mathbf{a}) \cdot p(\mathbf{a})$. Hence $\det g(\mathbf{a}) = \det q_1(\mathbf{a}) \cdot \det p(\mathbf{a}) = 0$. Similarly, $\det f(\mathbf{a}) = \mathbf{0}$.

From this it follows that if $f(t)$ and $\varphi(t)$ are not relatively prime, or if $g(t)$ divides $\varphi(t)$, then $\det f(\mathbf{a}) = \det g(\mathbf{a}) = 0$. If $f(t)$ and $\varphi(t)$ are relatively prime, then there exist polynomials $r(t)$, $s(t)$ such that $1 = r(t)f(t) + s(t)\varphi(t)$. From Theorems 4.3 and 4.4 we have then $\mathbf{I} = r(\mathbf{a}) \cdot f(\mathbf{a})$, showing that $f(\mathbf{a})$ is nonsingular. Q.E.D.

The important part played by the characteristic polynomial will be clarified in the following section and in Chap. 13.

EXERCISES

1. Use Theorem 4.5 to express $\mathbf{a}^8$ and $\mathbf{a}^{-4}$ as linear combinations of $\mathbf{I}$, $\mathbf{a}$, $\mathbf{a}^2$, where

$$\mathbf{a} = \begin{pmatrix} 1 & 0 & 2 \\ 2 & 1 & 1 \\ 0 & -1 & 4 \end{pmatrix}$$

2. Show how to compute the characteristic polynomial of a triangular matrix. If $\mathbf{a}$ is an $n \times n$ triangular matrix whose diagonal elements are all zero, prove that $\mathbf{a}^n = \mathbf{0}$.

3. Let $\mathbf{a}$ be an $n \times n$ matrix such that $\mathbf{a}^m = \mathbf{0}$ for some positive integer m. Prove that $(\mathbf{I} - \mathbf{a})^{-1} = \mathbf{I} + \mathbf{a} + \cdots + \mathbf{a}^{m-1}$.

4. Let $f(t) = c_0 + c_1 t + \cdots + c_{n-1}t^{n-1} + t^n$ be a polynomial in $K[t]$. Show that the characteristic polynomial of the matrix

$$\begin{pmatrix} 0 & 0 & 0 & . & . & . & 0 & -c_0 \\ 1 & 0 & 0 & . & . & . & 0 & -c_1 \\ 0 & 1 & 0 & . & . & . & 0 & -c_2 \\ \\ . & . & . & . & . & . & . & . \\ \\ 0 & 0 & . & . & . & 1 & 0 & -c_{n-2} \\ 0 & 0 & . & . & . & . & 1 & -c_{n-1} \end{pmatrix}$$

is $f(t)$. [Hint: Expand the required determinant by the first column and use induction on n.]

5. Show that a square matrix and its transpose have the same characteristic polynomial.

6. Write a matrix whose characteristic polynomial is $t^4 - t^2 + 1$ and verify it.

7. Determine the minimal and characteristic polynomials of the matrix

$$\begin{pmatrix} 0 & 1 & 2 & 0 \\ 0 & 0 & -3 & 4 \\ 0 & 0 & 0 & 5 \\ 0 & 0 & 0 & 0 \end{pmatrix}$$

8. If $\mathbf{a}$ is a nonsingular $n \times n$ matrix with characteristic polynomial $\varphi(t)$, show that $\mathbf{a}^{-1}$ has $(-1)^n \cdot (1/\det \mathbf{a}) \cdot t^n \varphi(1/t)$ as its characteristic polynomial. Verify this for the matrix of Example 1 above.

5. Eigenvalues and eigenvectors

One of the most commonly occurring problems involving vector spaces and linear mappings is the following: Given a linear mapping $\mathbf{T}$ of a vector space U to itself, does there exist a nonzero vector in U which is mapped by $\mathbf{T}$ into itself—or more generally, into some multiple of itself? That is, does the vector equation

$$\mathbf{T}(\mathbf{x}) = p\mathbf{x}$$

have a solution for p and $\mathbf{x}$ (other than zero)?

The importance of this problem, both in mathematics and its applications, can hardly be overstated. Indeed it would be fair to say that this problem and some of its ramifications constitute one of the most important applications of mathematics to science.

If the equation above holds, then we have $\mathbf{T}(a\mathbf{x}) = a \cdot \mathbf{T}(\mathbf{x}) = ap \cdot \mathbf{x}$ for any scalar a. Hence $\mathbf{T}$ maps the one-dimensional subspace of U spanned by $\mathbf{x}$ into itself. Therefore our problem can be stated as follows: Is there a one-dimensional subspace of U which is mapped into itself by **T**?

In the case of a euclidean vector space U (Sec. 11, Chap. 8) a nonzero vector **x** can be thought of as determining a direction. Then **x** and $p\mathbf{x}$ represent either the same direction or else opposite directions, for any scalar $p \neq 0$. Hence our problem, in geometrical terms, is that of determining whether there is some direction which is either unchanged by **T**, or else simply reversed.

In this section we shall discuss this so-called "eigenvalue problem" for finite-dimensional vector spaces. We begin by stating the Cayley-Hamilton theorem in a somewhat changed form. We require first the following theorem:

THEOREM 5.1 *Let* **a**, **b** *be two* $n \times n$ *matrices with coefficients in a field* K, *with* **b** *nonsingular. Then* **a** *and* $\mathbf{b}^{-1}\mathbf{ab}$ *have the same characteristic polynomial.*

Proof. $\mathbf{b}^{-1}(t\mathbf{I} - \mathbf{a})\mathbf{b} = t\mathbf{I} - \mathbf{b}^{-1}\mathbf{ab}$. Since $(\det \mathbf{b}^{-1}) \cdot (\det \mathbf{b}) = \det (\mathbf{b}^{-1}\mathbf{b}) = \det \mathbf{I} = 1$, we have $\det (t\mathbf{I} - \mathbf{a}) = \det [\mathbf{b}^{-1}(t\mathbf{I} - a)\mathbf{b}] = \det (t\mathbf{I} - \mathbf{b}^{-1}\mathbf{ab})$. Q.E.D.

COROLLARY *Let* $\mathbf{T}: U \to U$ *be a linear mapping of an n-dimensional*† *vector space over a field* K *to itself. Then the characteristic polynomial of the matrix of* **T** *relative to a base in* U *depends only on* **T** *and not on the particular choice of base.*

Proof. Let **a** be the matrix of **T** relative to a base $\{\mathbf{u}_i\}$, and let $\mathbf{a}'$ be its matrix relative to a second base $\{\mathbf{u}_i'\}$. If **b** is the matrix from $\{\mathbf{u}_i\}$ to $\{\mathbf{u}_i'\}$, then $\mathbf{a}' = \mathbf{b}^{-1}\mathbf{ab}$, by Theorem 7.2, Chap. 9 [see Eq. (7.4)]. The assertion then follows at once from the theorem above. Q.E.D.

The corollary shows that the characteristic polynomial is associated with **T** and not just with a particular matrix representing **T**. We make the following definition:

DEFINITION 5.1 *The characteristic polynomial of a linear mapping* $\mathbf{T}: U \to U$ *of an n-dimensional vector space is defined to be the characteristic polynomial* $\varphi(t)$ *of the matrix of* **T** *relative to any base* $\mathbf{u}_1, \ldots, \mathbf{u}_n$ *of* U. *The quantity* $(-1)^n \cdot \varphi(0)$ *is defined to be the* determinant *of* **T**.

Thus the determinant of **T** is just the determinant of the matrix of **T** relative to any base.

Theorem 4.3 can now be stated for linear mappings. We first introduce the following rather obvious notation: If $f(t) = c_0 + c_1 t + \cdots + c_r t^r$ is any polynomial with coefficients in a field K, and if $\mathbf{T}: U \to U$ is an endomorphism of a vector space over K, then by $f(\mathbf{T})$ we denote the linear mapping

$$f(\mathbf{T}) = c_0\mathbf{I} + c_1\mathbf{T} + \cdots + c_r\mathbf{T}^r$$

where **I** as usual denotes the identity mapping (cf. Sec. 4, Chap. 9).

† We naturally assume $n > 0$ to avoid trivialities.

THEOREM 5.2 **(Cayley-Hamilton)** *Let* **T** *be an endomorphism of a finite-dimensional vector space U, and let $\varphi(t)$ be its characteristic polynomial. Then* $\varphi(\mathbf{T}) = \mathbf{0}$.

Proof. Let **a** be the matrix of **T** relative to some base in U. Then the matrix of $\varphi(\mathbf{T})$ is $\varphi(\mathbf{a})$, by Theorem 6.4, Chap. 9. Hence the matrix of $\varphi(\mathbf{T})$ is **0**, by Theorem 4.3. That is, $\varphi(\mathbf{T})$ maps every vector in U into the zero vector. Q.E.D.

REMARK 1. By a similar argument, Theorem 4.5 holds with **T** in place of the matrix **a**. The definition of the *minimal* polynomial extends at once to endomorphisms **T** of finite-dimensional vector spaces; and it is easily seen that the minimal polynomial of **T**, that is, the monic polynomial $\varphi_0(t)$ of lowest degree, with coefficients in the field of scalars, such that $\varphi_0(\mathbf{T}) = \mathbf{0}$, is the same as the minimal polynomial of any matrix representing **T**. Theorem 4.6 and its corollary hold for **T**. In particular, we have the following theorem:

THEOREM 5.3 *Let* **T** *be an endomorphism of a finite-dimensional vector space U over a field K, and let $\varphi(t)$ be its characteristic polynomial. Then there exists a nonzero vector x in U such that*

5.1 $$\mathbf{T}(\mathbf{x}) = p\mathbf{x}$$

for a scalar p in K if and only if $\varphi(p) = 0$.

Proof. Equation (5.1) is the same as $(p\mathbf{I} - \mathbf{T})(\mathbf{x}) = \mathbf{0}$, by definition of $p\mathbf{I} - \mathbf{T}$, where **I** is the identity mapping. There is a nonzero vector **x** which is mapped into zero by $p\mathbf{I} - \mathbf{T}$ if and only if this operator has nullity > 0, and that is so if and only if its rank is $< n$ (Theorem 3.2, Chap. 9). If **a** is the matrix of **T** relative to some base, then $p\mathbf{I} - \mathbf{a}$ is the matrix of $p\mathbf{I} - \mathbf{T}$ relative to the same base, and the rank of $p\mathbf{I} - \mathbf{T}$ is the same as the rank of $p\mathbf{I} - \mathbf{a}$ (Theorem 8.2, Chap. 9). Hence (5.1) has a nonzero solution if and only if the matrix $p\mathbf{I} - \mathbf{a}$ has rank $< n$, which is the case if and only if its determinant is zero (corollary to Theorem 3.1 above). But $\det(p\mathbf{I} - \mathbf{a}) = \varphi(p)$. Q.E.D.

As a matrix version of the same theorem we have the following corollary:

COROLLARY *Let* **a** *be an $n \times n$ matrix with coefficients in a field K, and let p be an element of K. Then there is a nonzero column vector* **x** *in K^n such that* $\mathbf{ax} = p\mathbf{x}$ *if and only if* $\varphi(p) = 0$, *where φ is the characteristic polynomial of* **a**.

DEFINITION 5.2 **T** *being a linear mapping of a finite-dimensional vector space U to itself, the roots of the characteristic polynomial of* **T** *which are in the field of scalars are called the* eigenvalues *of* **T** *(or of the matrix of* **T** *relative to any base for U). If p is an eigenvalue of* **T**, *then any vector x in U such that* $\mathbf{T}(\mathbf{x}) = p\mathbf{x}$ *is called an* eigenvector *of* **T** *belonging to p.*

The term *characteristic root* is sometimes used instead of *eigenvalue.*

EXAMPLE 1 Consider the mapping of $\mathbf{Q}^2$ to itself that maps a column vector $\mathbf{x}$ into $\mathbf{ax}$, where

$$\mathbf{a} = \begin{pmatrix} 1 & 2 \\ 0 & 1 \end{pmatrix}$$

The characteristic polynomial here is

$$\varphi(t) = \begin{vmatrix} t-1 & -2 \\ 0 & t-1 \end{vmatrix} = (t-1)^2$$

Hence 1 is the only eigenvalue. According to Theorem 5.3, the equation $\mathbf{ax} = p\mathbf{x}$ has a nontrivial solution only if $p = 1$. Hence the equation to be solved is $\mathbf{ax} = \mathbf{x}$, or

$$\begin{aligned} x^1 + 2x^2 &= x^1 \\ x^2 &= x^2 \end{aligned}$$

or simply $x^2 = 0$. Hence the eigenvectors belonging to the root 1 are the vectors

$$\begin{pmatrix} x \\ 0 \end{pmatrix}$$

where x is an arbitrary element of $\mathbf{Q}$, and these are the only eigenvectors.

EXAMPLE 2 Consider the mapping $\mathbf{R}^2 \to \mathbf{R}^2$ that sends an arbitrary column vector $\mathbf{x}$ into $\mathbf{ax}$, where

$$\mathbf{a} = \begin{pmatrix} 0 & -1 \\ 1 & 0 \end{pmatrix}$$

The characteristic polynomial is $t^2 + 1$. There are no (real) eigenvalues. If we replace $\mathbf{R}$ by the complex field $\mathbf{C}$, then the eigenvalues are $\pm i$, and Eq. (5.1) becomes $\mathbf{ax} = i\mathbf{x}$ or $\mathbf{ax} = -i\mathbf{x}$. Taking the $+$ sign, our equation $\mathbf{ax} = i\mathbf{x}$ is

$$\begin{aligned} -x^2 &= ix^1 \\ x^1 &= ix^2 \end{aligned}$$

If we put $x^1 = c$, then $x^2 = -ic$, and it is quickly seen that the eigenvectors belonging to $+i$ are all the vectors

$$\begin{pmatrix} c \\ -ic \end{pmatrix} = c \cdot \begin{pmatrix} 1 \\ -i \end{pmatrix} \qquad (c \text{ any complex number})$$

Similarly, the eigenvectors belonging to $-i$ are all the vectors

$$\begin{pmatrix} c \\ ic \end{pmatrix} = c \begin{pmatrix} 1 \\ i \end{pmatrix}$$

REMARK 2. If p is an eigenvalue of a linear mapping $\mathbf{T} : U \to U$, then all the eigenvectors of $\mathbf{T}$ belonging to p form a *subspace* V of U. For V is simply the kernel of the mapping $p\mathbf{I} - \mathbf{T}$ (see proposition 3.1, Chap. 9). The dimension of V is called the *multiplicity* of the eigenvalue p. In Example 2 above, both i and $-i$ have multiplicity 1. In Example 1, the root 1 also has multiplicity 1, although it is a two-fold root of the characteristic polynomial. In general the multiplicity of an eigenvalue need not be the same as its multiplicity in the characteristic polynomial. A connection is established in a special case in Theorem 5.5.

EXAMPLE 3 Let U be a vector space of dimension n over a field K, and let $\mathbf{u}_1$, $\mathbf{u}_2, \ldots, \mathbf{u}_n$ be a base for U. Define a mapping $\mathbf{T}: U \to U$ by $\mathbf{T}(\mathbf{u}_i) = p_i\mathbf{u}_i$ $(i = 1, \ldots, n)$, where $p_1, p_2, \ldots, p_n$ are arbitrary scalars (Proposition 5.1, Chap. 9). Then the p_i are the eigenvalues of $\mathbf{T}$, for the matrix of $\mathbf{T}$ relative to the given base in the diagonal matrix whose diagonal elements are $p_1, \ldots, p_n$. Consider now one of the p's, and suppose it appears exactly k times in the given list, say as $p_1, p_2, \ldots, p_k$, for simplicity. It is then easily seen that the eigenvectors corresponding to that eigenvalue are precisely the vectors in the subspace of U spanned by $\mathbf{u}_1, \ldots, \mathbf{u}_k$, and so the eigenvalue in question has multiplicity k.

THEOREM 5.4 *Let $\mathbf{T}: U \to U$ be an endomorphism of a vector space U of dimension n over a field K, and let $p_1, p_2, \ldots, p_r$ be distinct eigenvalues of $\mathbf{T}$ (in the field K). Let $\mathbf{v}_1, \mathbf{v}_2, \ldots, \mathbf{v}_r$ be nonzero eigenvectors belonging to $p_1, p_2, \ldots, p_r$, respectively. Then those vectors are linearly independent.*

Proof. We show that $\mathbf{v}_1, \mathbf{v}_2, \ldots, \mathbf{v}_k$ are linearly independent for $k = 1, 2, \ldots, r$, by induction. The assertion that $\mathbf{v}_1, \mathbf{v}_2, \ldots, \mathbf{v}_k$ are independent is true for $k = 1$, since $\mathbf{v}_1 \neq 0$ by assumption. Suppose now that the assertion is true for some $k < r$, but false for $k + 1$. Then there are scalars $c_1, c_2, \ldots, c_{k+1}$, not all zero, such that $c_1\mathbf{v}_1 + c_2\mathbf{v}_2 + \cdots + c_{k+1}\mathbf{v}_{k+1} = \mathbf{0}$. Applying $\mathbf{T}$ to this equation and keeping in mind that $\mathbf{T}(\mathbf{v}_i) = p_i\mathbf{v}_i$, we get $c_1p_1\mathbf{v}_1 + c_2p_2\mathbf{v}_2 + \cdots + c_{k+1}p_{k+1}\mathbf{v}_{k+1} = \mathbf{0}$. Multiply the first equation by p_{k+1} and subtract the result from the second equation. We get

5.2 $$\sum_{i=1}^{k} c_i(p_i - p_{k+1})\mathbf{v}_i = \mathbf{0}$$

Now $p_i - p_{k+1} \neq 0$ $(i = 1, \ldots, k)$, because the p's are assumed distinct. Furthermore $c_1, c_2, \ldots, c_k$ cannot all be zero, for otherwise our first equation above would reduce to $c_{k+1}\mathbf{v}_{k+1} = \mathbf{0}$, with $c_{k+1} \neq 0$, and that is impossible because of our assumption that $\mathbf{v}_{k+1} \neq 0$. Therefore (5.2) shows that $\mathbf{v}_1, \ldots, \mathbf{v}_k$ are linearly dependent, a contradiction. Hence the assumption that $\mathbf{v}_1, \ldots, \mathbf{v}_{k+1}$ are linearly dependent is untenable.

Q.E.D.

THEOREM 5.5 *Let $\mathbf{T}: U \to U$ be an endomorphism of an n-dimensional vector space over a field K, and suppose that $\mathbf{T}$ has n distinct eigenvalues $p_1, p_2, \ldots, p_n$ (in K). If $\mathbf{v}_1, \mathbf{v}_2, \ldots, \mathbf{v}_n$ are nonzero eigenvectors of $\mathbf{T}$ belonging to $p_1, p_2, \ldots, p_n$, re-*

spectively, then they form a base for U; and the matrix of $\mathbf{T}$ *relative to that base is the diagonal matrix having* $p_1, \ldots, p_n$ *as its diagonal elements.*

This is an immediate corollary of Theorem 5.4.

If the characteristic polynomial of a linear mapping has repeated roots, as in Example 1 above, then the situation is not so simple. A careful analysis is given in Chap. 13. Nevertheless, the last assertion of Theorem 5.5 is valid for *any* endomorphism $\mathbf{T}$ provided that $\mathbf{v}_1, \mathbf{v}_2, \ldots, \mathbf{v}_n$ is a base of eigenvectors of $\mathbf{T}$.

REMARK 3. The problem of computing eigenvectors is in general rather tedious. It is first of all necessary to determine the eigenvalues, i.e., the roots of the characteristic polynomial of the given mapping $\mathbf{T}: U \to U$. If p is an eigenvalue of $\mathbf{T}$, then the eigenvectors that belong to it constitute the kernel of the mapping $p\mathbf{I} - \mathbf{T}$. That kernel can be computed by the method developed in Sec. 9, Chap. 9, for as we have seen in connection with (9.30), Chap. 9, if the matrix of $p\mathbf{I} - \mathbf{T}$ relative to some *base pair* is in diagonal form, then the kernel and image can be read off immediately. But we point out that the reduction process of Sec. 9, Chap. 9, involves at each step a *pair* of bases, one for the first space and another for the second space. Here the two spaces are the same, but nevertheless it is necessary to consider the matrix of $p\mathbf{I} - \mathbf{T}$ relative to a pair of possibly different bases. In general it is not possible to find a single base for which the matrix of an endomorphism is a diagonal matrix. This question will be taken up in Chap. 13.

THEOREM 5.6 *Let* $\mathbf{T}$ *be an endomorphism of a finite-dimensional vector space U, and let W be a subspace (of positive dimension) which is mapped into itself by* $\mathbf{T}$. *Let* $\mathbf{T}'$ *denote the mapping* $\mathbf{T}$ *restricted to elements of W. Then the characteristic polynomial of* $\mathbf{T}'$ *divides the characteristic polynomial of* $\mathbf{T}$.

Proof. Let $\dim U = n$ and $\dim W = r$. Then we can find a base $\mathbf{u}_1, \ldots, \mathbf{u}_n$ of U such that the first r elements form a base for W (Theorem 9.3, Chap. 8). If $\mathbf{a}$ is the matrix of $\mathbf{T}$ relative to the base $\mathbf{u}_1, \ldots, \mathbf{u}_n$, then $\mathbf{a}$ must have the form

$$\mathbf{a} = \begin{pmatrix} \mathbf{a}' & \mathbf{b} \\ \mathbf{0} & \mathbf{c} \end{pmatrix}$$

where $\mathbf{a}'$ is the matrix of $\mathbf{T}'$ relative to $\mathbf{u}_1, \ldots, \mathbf{u}_r$ of W_1. For $\mathbf{T}(\mathbf{u}_i)$ is in W and is equal to $\mathbf{T}'(\mathbf{u}_i)$, for $i = 1, \ldots, r$. Hence $\mathbf{T}(\mathbf{u}_i)$ for $i = 1, \ldots, r$ can be expressed uniquely as a linear combination of $\mathbf{u}_1, \ldots, \mathbf{u}_r$. If now $\varphi(t)$ and $\varphi'(t)$ denote the characteristic polynomials of $\mathbf{T}$ and $\mathbf{T}'$, respectively, then (putting $n - r = s$)

$$\begin{aligned}\varphi(t) &= \det\,(t\mathbf{I}_n - \mathbf{a}) = \det \begin{pmatrix} t\mathbf{I}_r - \mathbf{a}' & -\mathbf{b} \\ \mathbf{0} & t\mathbf{I}_s - \mathbf{c} \end{pmatrix} \\ &= \det\,(t\mathbf{I}_r - \mathbf{a}') \cdot \det\,(t\mathbf{I}_s - \mathbf{c}) \\ &= \varphi'(t) \cdot \det\,(t\mathbf{I}_s - c)\end{aligned}$$

by Theorem 3.4. Q.E.D.

COROLLARY *If p is a k-fold root of the characteristic polynomial of* $\mathbf{T}$, *then the multiplicity of p as eigenvalue cannot exceed k.*

Proof. Let W denote the subspace of U consisting of all the eigenvectors of $\mathbf{T}$ belonging to p. Then $\mathbf{T}$ maps W into itself, clearly. Let $\mathbf{T}'$ denote $\mathbf{T}$ restricted to W. If $\mathbf{w}_1, \ldots, \mathbf{w}_h$ is any base for W, then $\mathbf{T}'(\mathbf{w}_j) = p\mathbf{w}_j$, and so the corresponding matrix of $\mathbf{T}'$ is $p\mathbf{I}_h$. Hence the characteristic polynomial of $\mathbf{T}'$ is $(t - p)^h$, and this must divide the characteristic polynomial of $\mathbf{T}$. Hence $h \leq k$. Q.E.D.

The following theorem is closely related to Theorem 5.6:

THEOREM 5.7 *Let* $\mathbf{T}$ *be an endomorphism of a finite-dimensional vector space U. Suppose that U is the direct sum*† *of subspaces $W_1, W_2, \ldots, W_k$ of positive dimension, and suppose that* $\mathbf{T}$ *maps each W_j into itself ($j = 1, \ldots, k$). Let $\mathbf{T}_j$ denote the mapping* $\mathbf{T}$ *restricted to the elements of W_j, and let $\varphi_j(t)$ be the characteristic polynomial of $\mathbf{T}_j$, $\varphi(t)$ that of* $\mathbf{T}$. *Then $\varphi(t) = \varphi_1(t) \cdots \varphi_k(t)$.*

Proof. Let $B_1, B_2, \ldots, B_k$ be bases for $W_1, W_2, \ldots, W_k$. Our assumption merely means that all the vectors in $B_1, B_2, \ldots, B_k$, taken together, form a base B for U. Now let $\mathbf{a}$ be the matrix of $\mathbf{T}$ relative to B, and let $\mathbf{a}_{(j)}$ be the matrix of $\mathbf{T}_j$ relative to the base B_j ($j = 1, \ldots, k$). Since $\mathbf{T}$ applied to the vectors in B_j is the same as $\mathbf{T}_j$, it follows at once that

$$\mathbf{a} = \begin{pmatrix} \mathbf{a}_{(1)} & & & & \\ & \mathbf{a}_{(2)} & & & \\ & & \cdot & & \\ & & & \cdot & \\ & & & & \cdot \\ & & & & & \mathbf{a}_{(k)} \end{pmatrix}$$

where on the right is indicated a matrix with zero entries except for the square matrices $\mathbf{a}_{(1)}, \ldots, \mathbf{a}_{(k)}$ arranged along the diagonal. Then $t\mathbf{I} - \mathbf{a}$ is a matrix of the same form, and by repeated applications of Theorem 3.3 we find that

$$\det(t\mathbf{T} - \mathbf{a}) = \det(t\mathbf{I} - \mathbf{a}_{(1)}) \cdots \det(t\mathbf{I} - \mathbf{a}_{(k)})$$

where $\mathbf{I}$ always stands for the unit matrix of the proper size. The last equation is what we wanted to prove. Q.E.D.

THEOREM 5.8 *Let* $\mathbf{S}$ *and* $\mathbf{T}$ *be two endomorphisms of a vector space U, and let p be an eigenvalue of* $\mathbf{T}$. *Let W be the subspace consisting of all eigenvectors of* $\mathbf{T}$ *belonging to p. If* $\mathbf{S}$ *and* $\mathbf{T}$ *commute, then* $\mathbf{S}$ *maps W into itself. Furthermore,* $\mathbf{S}$ *maps the kernel and image of* $\mathbf{T}$ *into themselves.*

Proof. Consider first Ker $\mathbf{T}$: If $\mathbf{T}(\mathbf{x}) = \mathbf{0}$, then $\mathbf{T} \circ \mathbf{S}(\mathbf{x}) = \mathbf{S} \circ \mathbf{T}(\mathbf{x}) = \mathbf{0}$, showing that $\mathbf{S}(\mathbf{x})$ is in Ker $\mathbf{T}$. Hence $\mathbf{S}$ maps Ker $\mathbf{T}$ into itself. Now

† See Definition 5.2, Chap. 8.

W is the kernel of $p\mathbf{I} - \mathbf{T}$. $\mathbf{S}$ commutes with this operator if it commutes with $\mathbf{T}$, and therefore, by what was just shown, $\mathbf{S}$ must map W into itself. Finally, if $\mathbf{y}$ is in Im $\mathbf{T}$, then $\mathbf{y} = T(\mathbf{x})$ for some $\mathbf{x}$. But then $\mathbf{S}(\mathbf{y}) = \mathbf{ST}(\mathbf{x}) = \mathbf{T}(\mathbf{S}(\mathbf{x}))$, showing that $\mathbf{S}(\mathbf{y})$ is also in Im $\mathbf{T}$. Q.E.D.

The following theorem connects the eigenvalues of a mapping $\mathbf{T}$ with those of various operators that can be formed from $\mathbf{T}$.

THEOREM 5.9 *Let $\mathbf{T}$ be an endomorphism of an n-dimensional vector space U over a field K, and suppose that the characteristic polynomial $\varphi(t)$ has all its roots in K. That is, suppose that*† $\varphi(t) = (t - p_1) \cdots (t - p_n)$, *where $p_1, \ldots, p_n$ are in K, not necessarily distinct. Let $f(t)$ be any polynomial with coefficients in K, and let $\varphi_f(t)$ be the characteristic polynomial of the operator $f(\mathbf{T})$. Then $\varphi_f(t)$ also has all its roots in K, and the set of roots of $\varphi_f(t)$ is the same as the set of elements $f(p_1), \ldots, f(p_n)$. Furthermore, if $\mathbf{x}$ is an eigenvector of $\mathbf{T}$ belonging to p_j, then $\mathbf{x}$ is also an eigenvector of $f(\mathbf{T})$ belonging to $f(p_j)$. Finally, if* det $\mathbf{T} \neq 0$, *then the characteristic polynomial of $\mathbf{T}^{-1}$ is $(t - p_1^{-1}) \cdots (t - p_n^{-1})$.*

Proof. If $\mathbf{T}(\mathbf{x}) = p\mathbf{x}$, then $\mathbf{T}^2(\mathbf{x}) = \mathbf{T}(\mathbf{T}(\mathbf{x})) = \mathbf{T}(p\mathbf{x}) = p\mathbf{T}(\mathbf{x}) = p^2\mathbf{x}$. By a simple induction, it is easy to see that $\mathbf{T}^k(\mathbf{x}) = p^k\mathbf{x}$ for any positive integer k; and this clearly holds also for $k = 0$, since $\mathbf{T}^0 = \mathbf{I}$.

If now $f(t) = c_0 + c_1t + \cdots + c_rt^r$, then $f(\mathbf{T})(\mathbf{x}) = (c_0\mathbf{I} + c_1\mathbf{T} + \cdots + c_r\mathbf{T}^r)(\mathbf{x}) = c_0\mathbf{x} + c_1\mathbf{T}(\mathbf{x}) + \cdots + c_r\mathbf{T}^r(\mathbf{x}) = c_0\mathbf{x} + c_1p\mathbf{x} + \cdots + c_rp^r\mathbf{x} = f(p) \cdot \mathbf{x}$, still assuming that $\mathbf{T}(\mathbf{x}) = p\mathbf{x}$. Therefore, for each eigenvalue p of $\mathbf{T}$ and eigenvector $\mathbf{x}$ belonging to it, the scalar $f(p)$ is an eigenvalue of $f(\mathbf{T})$ and $\mathbf{x}$ is an eigenvector of $f(\mathbf{T})$ belonging to it.

Now write $\mathbf{S} = f(\mathbf{T})$, and let $\varphi_f(t)$ be its characteristic polynomial. Let $g(t)$ be a monic irreducible factor of $\varphi_f(t)$. We want to show that $g(t)$ has degree 1. To do so, let W be the kernel of the operator $g(\mathbf{S})$. That is, W consists of all vectors $\mathbf{y}$ such that $g(\mathbf{S})(\mathbf{y}) = \mathbf{0}$. Now $\mathbf{T}$ clearly commutes with $\mathbf{S}$, and therefore it commutes with any polynomial in $\mathbf{S}$, in particular with $g(\mathbf{S})$. Therefore $\mathbf{T}$ maps W into itself, by Theorem 5.8. Let $\mathbf{T}'$ denote the mapping $\mathbf{T}$ restricted to W, and let $\varphi'(t)$ be its characteristic polynomial. From the corollary of Theorem 4.6 (applied to any matrix representing $\mathbf{S}$), it follows that dim $W > 0$, and so deg $\varphi'(t) > 0$. Furthermore, $\varphi'(t)$ divides $\varphi(t)$, by Theorem 5.6. Hence, one of the roots of $\varphi(t)$, say p_1, must also be a root of $\varphi'(t)$. There must be a nonzero eigenvector $\mathbf{y}$ of $\mathbf{T}'$ belonging to p_1, by Theorem 5.3. That is, $\mathbf{y} \neq 0$ is in W and $\mathbf{T}(\mathbf{y}) = p_1\mathbf{y}$. But $g(\mathbf{S})(\mathbf{y}) = \mathbf{0}$, or $g(f(\mathbf{T}))(\mathbf{y}) = \mathbf{0}$. By what was shown above, applied to the polynomial $g(f(t))$, we have $g(f(\mathbf{T}))(\mathbf{y}) = g(f(p_1))\mathbf{y}$. Hence, $g(f(p_1)) = 0$, and so $f(p_1)$ is a root of the polynomial $g(t)$. Therefore $g(t) = t - f(p_1)$, since $g(t)$ is monic and irreducible.

† See Sec. 4, Chap. 6. Recall that $\varphi(t)$ is a monic polynomial of degree n.

Hence, the monic irreducible factors of $\varphi_f(t)$ in $K[t]$ must all occur among the polynomials $t - f(p_1), \ldots, t - f(p_n)$.

Finally, the assertion concerning the characteristic polynomial of $\mathbf{T}^{-1}$ follows at once from Exercise 8, Sec. 4. Thus, if $\mathbf{a}$ is the matrix of $\mathbf{T}$ relative to some base, then $\mathbf{a}^{-1}$ is the matrix of $\mathbf{T}^{-1}$, and

$$\det(t\mathbf{I} - \mathbf{a}^{-1}) = \det\left((t\mathbf{a}^{-1}) \cdot \left(\mathbf{a} - \frac{1}{t}\mathbf{I}\right)\right) = \det(t\mathbf{a}^{-1}) \cdot \det\left(\mathbf{a} - \frac{1}{t}\mathbf{I}\right)$$

$$= (-1)^n t^n \cdot (\det \mathbf{a})^{-1} \cdot \varphi\left(\frac{1}{t}\right) \qquad \text{Q.E.D.}$$

EXERCISES

1. Find the eigenvalues and eigenvectors of the mapping $\mathbf{Q}^2 \to \mathbf{Q}^2$ that sends an arbitrary vector $\mathbf{x}$ into $\mathbf{ax}$, where

$$\mathbf{a} = \begin{pmatrix} 11 & 6 \\ -20 & -11 \end{pmatrix}$$

2. Find the eigenvalues and eigenvectors of the mapping $\mathbf{Q}^4 \to \mathbf{Q}^4$ that sends an arbitrary vector $\mathbf{x}$ into $\mathbf{ax}$, where

$$\mathbf{a} = \begin{pmatrix} 0 & -1 & 1 & -1 \\ 0 & -1 & 0 & 0 \\ 0 & 0 & -1 & 0 \\ 1 & -1 & 1 & -2 \end{pmatrix}$$

3. Let P_n denote the vector space of polynomials of degree $<n$ in an indeterminate y with coefficients in the real field. Let $\mathbf{D}$ be the *derivative* mapping of P_n defined by

$$\mathbf{D}\left(\sum_{k=0}^{n-1} a_k y^k\right) = \sum_{k=1}^{n-1} k a_k y^{k-1}$$

Let $\mathbf{T}$ be the endomorphism $\mathbf{D} \cdot (1 - y^2)\mathbf{D}$ of P_n (see Exercise 4, Sec. 4, Chap. 9). Compute the eigenvalues of $\mathbf{T}$ and its eigenvectors of degrees up through 5 (assuming $n > 5$). (These eigenvectors—usually called *eigenfunctions* in this case—are the famous Legendre polynomials, apart from constant factors. They are of importance in many applications.)

4. Find the characteristic polynomial of $\mathbf{I} - 2\mathbf{a} + \mathbf{a}^5 - \mathbf{a}^{10}$, $\mathbf{a}$ being as in Exercise 2.

5. What are the eigenvalues and eigenvectors of $\mathbf{I} - \mathbf{D}^2 + 4\mathbf{D}^{n-2}$ in Exercise 3?

6. Let $\mathbf{T} : U \to U$ be an endomorphism of a finite-dimensional vector space, and let $p_1, p_2, \ldots, p_k$ be distinct eigenvalues of $\mathbf{T}$. Let W_j be the subspace of all the eigenvectors belonging to p_j ($j = 1, \ldots, k$), and let B_j denote a base for W_j. Prove that all the vectors in $B_1, B_2, \ldots, B_k$, taken jointly, are linearly independent. [Hint: The proof is similar to that of Theorem 5.4.]

7. Let **T** be an endomorphism of a space of odd dimension over the real field. Prove that **T** has at least one nonzero eigenvector.

8. Give proofs for the assertions of Remark 1.

9. Let $\mathbf{a} = (a^i{}_j)$ be a real $n \times n$ matrix. Show that the following conditions on **a** are equivalent:

(*a*) $a^i{}_j \geq 0, \sum_{j=1}^{n} a^i{}_j = 1$

(*b*) **a** has the eigenvalue 1 with eigenvector $(1, 1, \ldots, 1)$.

A matrix satisfying either of these conditions is called *stochastic*.

6. *Determinants as volumes*

Theorem 3.1 shows that the determinant of a square matrix gives some measure of the linear dependence or independence of its column (or row) vectors. Here we shall show that, in the case where the field of scalars is the real field **R**, the determinant of a matrix has a natural interpretation in terms of the volume of a certain region.

We deal with a euclidean space E and we denote by $T(E)$ the associated set of mappings (translations) of the set E. Addition of two elements of $T(E)$ is just the operation of composition of those two translations. If p and q are two points of E, then $\overrightarrow{pq}$ denotes the (unique) translation that sends p into q. $T(E)$ is supposed to be a *euclidean* vector space, meaning that there is assigned to every translation **t** a non-negative real number $|\mathbf{t}|$, the *length* of **t**, subject to the requirements of Definition 11.1, Chap. 8. Namely, it is required that there be a base $\mathbf{u}_1, \ldots, \mathbf{u}_n$ in $T(E)$ such that if a translation **x** has components $x^1, x^2, \ldots, x^n$ relative to that base, then

6.1 $$|\mathbf{x}|^2 = \sum_{j=1}^{n} (x^j)^2$$

If **y** is another translation, with components $y^1, \ldots, y^n$, then the inner product of **x** and **y** is the number

6.2 $$(\mathbf{x}, \mathbf{y}) = \sum_{j=1}^{n} x^j y^j = \tfrac{1}{2}[|\mathbf{x} + \mathbf{y}|^2 - |\mathbf{x}|^2 - |\mathbf{y}|^2]$$

A base for which (6.1) holds is called *orthonormal.* An orthonormal base is characterized by

6.3 $$(\mathbf{u}_i, \mathbf{u}_j) = \begin{cases} 0 & \text{if } i \neq j \\ 1 & \text{if } i = j \end{cases}$$

A *hyperplane* H in E consists of all the points obtained by applying all the translations in an $(n-1)$-dimensional subspace of $T(E)$ to some given point of E.

Hence, if the given point is p_0 and if $\mathbf{w}_1, \ldots, \mathbf{w}_{n-1}$ span the $(n-1)$-dimensional subspace, then H consists of all the points p such that

6.4 $$\overrightarrow{p_0p} = s^1\mathbf{w}_1 + \cdots + s^{n-1}\mathbf{w}_{n-1}$$

where $s^1, \ldots, s^{n-1}$ are arbitrary real numbers. For this equation says precisely that p is the result of applying the translation indicated on the right to p_0.

Let us now consider a two-dimensional euclidean space E_2, and let p_0, p_1, p_2 be three noncollinear points in it. If for brevity we write

$$\mathbf{w}_1 = \overrightarrow{p_0p_1} \qquad \mathbf{w}_2 = \overrightarrow{p_0p_2}$$

then our assumption that the points are not collinear means that $\mathbf{w}_1$ and $\mathbf{w}_2$ are linearly independent vectors, hence span the vector space of translations $T(E_2)$.

Let **P** denote the set of all points p such that

6.5 $$\overrightarrow{p_0p} = s^1\mathbf{w}_1 + s^2\mathbf{w}_2 \qquad (0 \leq s^1 \leq 1, 0 \leq s^2 \leq 1)$$

That is, **P** consists of all points p obtained by applying the translation $s^1\mathbf{w}_1 + s^2\mathbf{w}_2$ to p_0, the numbers s^1 and s^2 being confined to the interval from 0 to 1. We shall call **P** the *parallelogram* determined by p_0, p_1, p_2, or by $p_0, \mathbf{w}_1, \mathbf{w}_2$.†

It is not difficult to convince oneself that **P** in fact corresponds precisely to one's intuitive notion of a parallelogram. It is illustrated in Fig. 1. The four vertices are the points obtained by putting 0, 1 for s^1 and s^2 in (6.5). For example, putting $s^1 = 1$, $s^2 = 0$ we get $\overrightarrow{p_0p} = \mathbf{w}_1 = \overrightarrow{p_0p_1}$, whence $p = p_1$. The vertex p_3 is the point obtained by putting $s^1 = 1$ and $s^2 = 1$ in (6.5). Thus $\overrightarrow{p_0p_3} = \overrightarrow{p_0p_1} + \overrightarrow{p_0p_2}$. The edges of **P** consist of the points obtained by putting s^1 or s^2 equal to 0 or 1 in (6.5). For example, the edge joining p_2 and p_3 is obtained by setting $s^2 = 1$ and therefore consists of all points p such that

$$\overrightarrow{p_0p} = s\mathbf{w}_1 + \mathbf{w}_2 \qquad (0 \leq s \leq 1)$$

where we have written simply s for the variable s^2. Since $\overrightarrow{p_0p} - \mathbf{w}_2 = \overrightarrow{p_0p} - \overrightarrow{p_0p_2} = \overrightarrow{p_2p}$, our equation becomes

6.6 $$\overrightarrow{p_2p} = s\mathbf{w}_1 \qquad (0 \leq s \leq 1)$$

That is, the edge in question consists of all points p obtained by applying the translations $s\mathbf{w}_1$ $(0 \leq s \leq 1)$ to p_2. By definition, (6.6) determines a segment of a line—the unique line through p_2 and p_3. [Equation (6.6) is a special case of (6.4), except for the restriction on s.] In a similar way one sees that the other three edges of **P** are segments of lines.

We recall that a euclidean coordinate system in E_2 is obtained by choosing an orthonormal base $\mathbf{u}_1, \mathbf{u}_2$ in the space of translations, along with a point in E_2 as

† **P** depends in general upon the order in which the three points appear.

Figure 1

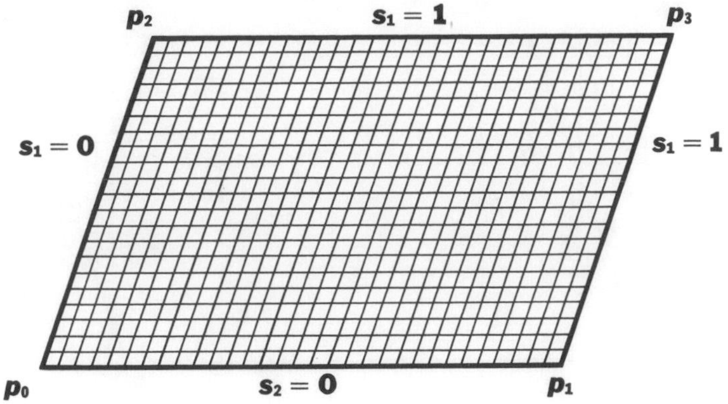

origin. Let us take p_0 as origin. If p is any point, then its coordinates are the unique real numbers x^1, x^2 such that

6.7 $$\overrightarrow{p_0p} = x^1\mathbf{u}_1 + x^2\mathbf{u}_2$$

Let the coordinates of p_1 and p_2 be $a^1{}_1$, $a^2{}_1$ and $a^1{}_2$, $a^2{}_2$, respectively. That is, (6.7) becomes

6.8 $$\mathbf{w}_1 = a^j{}_1\mathbf{u}_j \qquad \mathbf{w}_2 = a^j{}_2\mathbf{u}_j$$

The coordinates of p_1, p_2 are the same as the components of $\mathbf{w}_1$, $\mathbf{w}_2$ (relative to the given orthonormal base). Equation (6.5) becomes

$$x^1\mathbf{u}_1 + x^2\mathbf{u}_2 = s^1 \cdot (a^1{}_1\mathbf{u}_1 + a^2{}_1\mathbf{u}_2) + s^2 \cdot (a^1{}_2\mathbf{u}_1 + a^2{}_2\mathbf{u}_2)$$

Since $\mathbf{u}_1$, $\mathbf{u}_2$ are linearly independent, we can equate coefficients here, getting

6.9 $$\begin{aligned} x^1 &= s^1a^1{}_1 + s^2a^1{}_2 \\ x^2 &= s^1a^2{}_1 + s^2a^2{}_2 \end{aligned} \qquad (0 \leq s^1 \leq 1,\ 0 \leq s^2 \leq 1)$$

This is the coordinate version of the vector equation (6.5).

Our aim is to see how to compute the area of **P**, with the purpose in view of carrying our results over into higher dimensional spaces. Now the first problem that comes up is that of defining *area* to begin with. It is outside our province to go into that question in detail. Indeed, one of the problems solved by calculus is precisely that of giving a workable definition of area for rather arbitrary plane figures (and, more generally, of volumes of figures in spaces of higher dimension). Since we shall deal here only with parallelograms and analogous figures of higher dimension, we shall give a definition of area (or volume) applicable to them, and we shall try to show at the same time that our definition meets reasonable requirements consistent with intuitive prejudices.

We claim that the quantity

6.10 $$\left| \det \begin{pmatrix} a^1{}_1 & a^1{}_2 \\ a^2{}_1 & a^2{}_2 \end{pmatrix} \right| \qquad \text{(absolute value of the determinant!)}$$

Figure 2

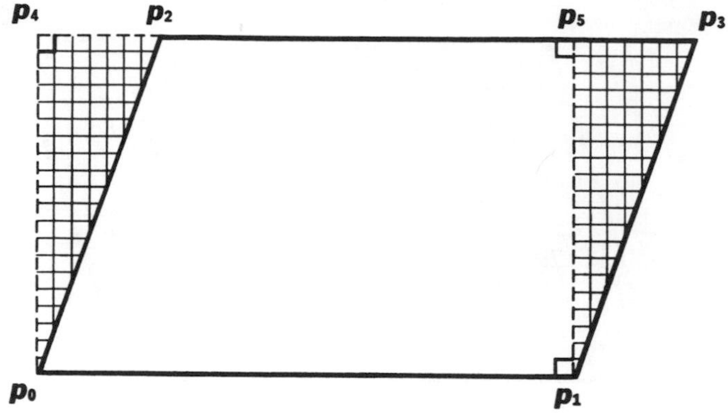

formed from the coordinate vectors $\mathbf{a}_1$, $\mathbf{a}_2$ of $\mathbf{w}_1$, $\mathbf{w}_2$ has all the qualifications entitling it to be called the area of **P**. To see this, consider Fig. 2.

Here we have associated with **P** another parallelogram **P′**, with vertices p_0, p_1, p_4, p_5, such that the angles between its edges are right angles, that is, **P′** is a rectangle. As the diagram shows, **P′** is obtained from **P** by cutting off a triangle on the right and pasting it on the left of the figure.† It is also suggestive to think of **P′** as obtained from **P** by a "shearing motion," causing the upper edge of **P** to slide along itself to the left. It is therefore reasonable to require that our definition of area give the same result for both **P** and **P′**.

Now if the point p_5 has coordinates b^1 and b^2, then the quantity corresponding to (6.10) for **P′** is

6.11 $$\left| \det \begin{pmatrix} a^1{}_1 & b^1 \\ a^2{}_1 & b^2 \end{pmatrix} \right|$$

We calculate this as follows: Since **P′** is by assumption a rectangle, the vectors $\overrightarrow{p_0p_1}$ and $\overrightarrow{p_0p_5}$ are orthogonal. Their components relative to the orthonormal base $\mathbf{u}_1$, $\mathbf{u}_2$ are the elements in the two columns $\mathbf{a}_1$ and $\mathbf{b}$ of (6.11). For the inner product of the two vectors we have then

$$a^1{}_1b^1 + a^2{}_1b^2 = 0$$

Hence to compute (6.11) we have only to use Theorem 6.1, and the result is

6.12 $$[(a^1{}_1)^2 + (a^2{}_1)^2]^{\frac{1}{2}} \cdot [(b^1)^2 + (b^2)^2]^{\frac{1}{2}} = |p_0p_1| \cdot |p_0p_5|$$

by (11.12), Chap. 8. In other words, (6.11) is simply the product of the two sides of the rectangle **P′**, and we naturally define that quantity to be the area of **P′**.

As pointed out above, it is intuitively clear that **P** and **P′** should have the same area, and therefore we take (6.11) as the area of the original parallelogram **P**. Our last step consists of showing that (6.10) and (6.11) are equal. For that purpose

† That is not correct if p_2 and p_3 fall on the same side of p_5. In this case similar considerations still apply.

we must determine the relationship of the column vector **b** in (6.11) to the columns $\mathbf{a}_1$, $\mathbf{a}_2$ in (6.10). Now p_5 is on the line through p_2 and p_3. All points on that line are given by (6.6), with the restriction on s omitted, and so we must have $\overrightarrow{p_2p_5} = s\mathbf{w}_1$ for some value of s. Since $\overrightarrow{p_2p_5} = \overrightarrow{p_0p_5} - \overrightarrow{p_0p_2}$, we have

$$\overrightarrow{p_0p_5} = s\mathbf{w}_1 + \mathbf{w}_2$$

(We do not need to know what s is here.) The corresponding equation for the component vectors of the three vectors in question is

$$\mathbf{b} = s\mathbf{a}_1 + \mathbf{w}_2$$

Therefore (6.10) and (6.11) are equal, by Proposition 2.2.

In particular, it follows that (6.10) does not depend upon the choice of orthonormal base in $T(E_2)$, since the value of (6.11) is independent of that choice, by (6.12). If the three points p_0, p_1, p_2 are collinear, then $\mathbf{w}_1$ and $\mathbf{w}_2$; hence also $\mathbf{a}_1$ and $\mathbf{a}_2$ must be linearly dependent. The parallelogram **P** collapses, and (6.10) vanishes.

We now give the theorem used in getting from (6.11) to (6.12):

THEOREM 6.1 *Let* $\mathbf{a} = (a^j{}_i)$ *be an* $n \times n$ *matrix with coefficients in a field* K, *and suppose that*

6.13 $$\sum_{j=1}^{n} a^j{}_i a^j{}_k = 0 \qquad \text{if } i \neq k$$

then

$$(\det \mathbf{a})^2 = \prod_{i=1}^{n} [(a^1{}_i)^2 + \cdots + (a^n{}_i)^2]$$

Proof. Put $\mathbf{b} = {}^t\mathbf{a} \cdot \mathbf{a}$. Then, by definition,

$$b^k{}_i = \sum_{j=1}^{n} ({}^ta^k{}_j) \cdot a_{\ i} = \sum_{j=1}^{n} a^j{}_k a^j{}_i$$

and so **b** is a diagonal matrix. We have $\det \mathbf{b} = \det ({}^t\mathbf{a} \cdot \mathbf{a}) = (\det {}^t\mathbf{a}) \cdot (\det \mathbf{a}) = (\det \mathbf{a})^2$, and $\det \mathbf{b} = b^1{}_1 \cdot b^2{}_2 \cdots b^n{}_n$, which is what we wanted to prove.

We shall now show briefly how these considerations allow us to define volumes of analogous figures in euclidean spaces of any number of dimensions.

To do so, let $p_0, p_1, \ldots, p_n$ be $n + 1$ points in an n-dimensional euclidean space E_n. For brevity of notation, let us write $\mathbf{w}_i$ for the translation vector $\overrightarrow{p_0p_i}$ in $T(E_n)$. Following (6.5) we define the *parallelotope* **P** determined by the $(n + 1)$-tuple $p_0, p_1, \ldots, p_n$ (or by $p_0, \mathbf{w}_1, \ldots, \mathbf{w}_n$) to be the set of all points p such that

6.14 $$\overrightarrow{p_0p} = s^1\mathbf{w}_1 + s^2\mathbf{w}_2 + \cdots + s^n\mathbf{w}_n \qquad (0 \leq s_j \leq 1 \text{ for } j = 1, \ldots, n)$$

Equation (6.14) sets up a one-to-one correspondence between the points of **P** and the points of the *unit cube* in $\mathbf{R}^n$ consisting of all n-tuples $(s^1, \ldots, s^n)$ for which $0 \leq s^j \leq 1$ $(j = 1, \ldots, n)$, for each index $j = 1, 2, \ldots, n$ the point set **P** has two *faces*, one consisting of all points p for which s^j in (6.14) is equal to zero, the other consisting of all p for which s^j is equal to 1. The 2^n faces of **P** correspond in an obvious way to the four edges of the parallelogram considered above. Each face lies in a hyperplane of E_n, as is easily verified. The *vertices* of **P** are the 2^n points obtained by putting all the s^j in (6.14) equal (independently) to 0 or 1. The given points $p_0, p_1, \ldots, p_n$ are clearly among the vertices. **P** is called *rectangular* if the n vectors $\mathbf{w}_1, \ldots, \mathbf{w}_n$ in (6.14) are mutually orthogonal. If they are moreover all of the same length, then P is called an *n cube*.

Now let $\mathbf{u}_1, \mathbf{u}_2, \ldots, \mathbf{u}_n$ be an orthonormal base for the vector space of translations $T(E_n)$. Let $\mathbf{a}_i$ be the corresponding vector† of $\mathbf{w}_i$. That is,

6.15 $$\mathbf{w}_i = a^k{}_i\mathbf{u}_k \qquad (i = 1, \ldots, n)$$

We now *define* the volume of the parallelotope **P** to the number

6.16 $$\text{vol } \mathbf{P} = |\det \mathbf{a}|$$

where $\mathbf{a} = (\mathbf{a}_1, \ldots, \mathbf{a}_n)$ is the $n \times n$ matrix built from the vectors $\mathbf{a}_i$.

First of all, let us verify that (6.16) does not depend on the particular choice of orthonormal base. If $\mathbf{v}, \ldots, \mathbf{v}_n$ is a second orthonormal base, and if $\mathbf{b}, \ldots, \mathbf{b}_n$ are the component vectors of $\mathbf{w}, \ldots, \mathbf{w}_n$ relative to it, then we have

6.17 $$\mathbf{w}_i = b^k{}_i\mathbf{v}_k \qquad (i = 1, \ldots, n)$$

just as in (6.15). Now let $\mathbf{c} = (c^j{}_i)$ be the matrix from $\{\mathbf{u}_i\}$ to $\{\mathbf{v}_i\}$. Thus,

6.18 $$\mathbf{v}_i = c^j{}_i\mathbf{u}_j \qquad (i = 1, \ldots, n)$$

Then from (6.15), (6.16), (6.17) there follows at once $a^k{}_i = c^k{}_jb^j{}_i$, or $\mathbf{a} = \mathbf{cb}$, where $\mathbf{b} = (\mathbf{b}_1, \ldots, \mathbf{b}_n)$ is the matrix whose columns are the vectors $\mathbf{b}_1, \ldots, \mathbf{b}_n$. Since $\mathbf{v}_1, \ldots, \mathbf{v}_n$ is an orthonormal base, we have

$$(\mathbf{v}_i, \mathbf{v}_k) = \begin{cases} 0 & \text{if } i \neq k \\ 1 & \text{if } i = k \end{cases}$$

by (6.3), and so

$$\sum_{j=1}^{n} c^j{}_ic^j{}_k = \begin{cases} 0 & \text{if } i \neq k \\ 1 & \text{if } i = k \end{cases}$$

by (6.2). Therefore, by Theorem 6.1, $(\det \mathbf{c})^2 = 1$. Then $\det \mathbf{a} = \det (\mathbf{cb}) = (\det \mathbf{c}) \cdot (\det \mathbf{b}) = \pm\det \mathbf{b}$. This shows that (6.16) does not depend upon the choice of orthonormal base.

† The n numbers constituting $\mathbf{a}_i$ are the corresponding coordinates of the point p_i if we take p_0 as origin.

Secondly, let us show that (6.16) gives the "correct" result for a rectangular parallelotope. If **P** is rectangular, then, by definition, $(\mathbf{w}_i, \mathbf{w}_k) = 0$ if $i \neq k$. That is,

$$\sum_{j=1}^{n} a^j{}_i a^j{}_k = \begin{cases} 0 & \text{if } i \neq k \\ |\mathbf{w}_i|^2 & \text{if } i = k \end{cases}$$

by (6.2). Hence, by Theorem 6.1, we have in this case

$$\begin{aligned} \det \mathbf{a} &= \pm |\mathbf{w}_1| \cdot |\mathbf{w}_2| \cdots |\mathbf{w}_n| \\ &= \pm |p_0p_1| \cdot |p_0p_2| \cdots |p_0p_n| \end{aligned}$$

Therefore, (6.16) gives the product of the dimensions of **P** as the volume.

Finally, let us observe that, if **P** is deformed by a shearing motion, its volume as defined by (6.16) does not change. The argument here depends upon a mathematical interpretation of "shearing motion," and we shall appeal to the situation of Fig. 2. Thus, suppose that $\mathbf{w}_n$ is replaced by a new vector $\mathbf{w}'_n$, and let **P**′ denote the new parallelotope (6.14). We shall say that **P**′ is obtained from **P** by a *shear* if the hyperplanes H and H' containing the faces of **P** and **P**′ determined by $s^n = 1$ are identical. Suppose then that p is a point of H. That is, by (6.14), we have

$$\overrightarrow{p_0p} = s^1\mathbf{w}_1 + \cdots + s^{n-1}\mathbf{w}_{n-1} + \mathbf{w}_n$$

Now H and H' are identical if and only if p is also a point of H', and if that is so, there are numbers $t^1, \ldots, t^{n-1}$ such that

$$\overrightarrow{p_0p} = t^1\mathbf{w}_1 + \cdots + t^{n-1}\mathbf{w}_{n-1} + \mathbf{w}'_n$$

Equating these two expressions we find that

$$\mathbf{w}'_n = \mathbf{w}_n + c^1\mathbf{w}_1 + \cdots + c^{n-1}\mathbf{w}_{n-1}$$

for certain numbers $c^1, \ldots, c^{n-1}$. If $\mathbf{a}_n$ is the component vector of $\mathbf{w}'_n$ relative to the base $\mathbf{u}_1, \ldots, \mathbf{u}_n$, then we have

6.19 $$\mathbf{a}'_n = \mathbf{a}_n + c^1\mathbf{a}_1 + \cdots + c^{n-1}\mathbf{a}_{n-1}$$

Now the volume of **P**′, given by (6.16), is $|\det(\mathbf{a}_1, \ldots, \mathbf{a}_{n-1}, \mathbf{a}'_n)|$, and from (6.19) it follows that this is equal to the volume of **P**. In the same way we can treat a shear involving any of the other vectors $\mathbf{w}_1, \ldots, \mathbf{w}_{n-1}$. It is not hard to see that **P** can be deformed into a rectangular parallelotope by a series of appropriate shears. By what was just shown, its volume, as defined by (6.16), is thereby unaltered.

EXERCISES

1. Use (6.10) to show that the area of a parallelogram determined by p_0, p_1, p_2 is equal to $|p_0p_1| \cdot |p_0p_2| \cdot \sin\theta$, where θ is the angle $p_1p_0p_2$.

2. Let p_0, p_1, p_2, p_3 be points of a euclidean 3-space, and let their coordinates relative to some euclidean coordinate system be (2, 0, 3), (0, 1, 2), (−1, −2, 3), (4, 1, 2), respectively. Compute the volume of the parallelotope **P** determined by p_0, p_1, p_2, p_3. Compute the area of the face determined by p_0, p_1, p_2. Which of the following points are in **P**: (½, 0, 2), (5, 4, −2), (−3, −1, 2)? Give the coordinates of the vertices of **P**.

3. Let (2, 1, −1, 0), (4, 1, 0, 3), (2, −2, 0, 0), (0, −1, 2, 3) be the coordinates of four points in E_4 relative to some euclidean coordinate system. Compute the volume of the three-dimensional parallelotope that they determine.

4. Let **P** be a parallelotope in E_n. Prove that the volume of **P** is equal to the product of the volume of a face of **P** times the perpendicular distance to the hyperplane containing the opposite face.

12

Rings of operators and differential equations

1. Introduction

By viewing the differentiation operator d/dx of calculus as an endomorphism of a certain vector space we shall be able to apply some of the results of earlier chapters to prove some important theorems about differential equations. The necessary definitions are given in Sec. 4, and no detailed knowledge of calculus is required. In Secs. 2 and 3 we recall briefly some definitions and simple facts concerning rings and homomorphisms—in particular, homomorphisms resulting from the substitution of operators in polynomials. The reader is referred to Chaps. 1, 2, 6, and 10 for a more elaborate account.

2. Rings and homomorphisms

First of all, a *ring* A is a set of elements equipped with two binary operations, which we call *sum* and *product*, satisfying the following conditions:

(1) *A with the sum operation is an abelian group.*

(2) *The product operation is associative.*

(3) *A contains a unit element (that is, an identity element for the product operation).*†

(4) *The sum and product operations satisfy the distributive law. That is,* $(a + b)c = ac + bc$ *and* $c(a + b) = ca + cb$ *for any elements* a, b, c *of* A.

As usual, we denote the sum of two elements by $a + b$, their product by ab. The first condition requires A to contain a zero element 0 (that is, the identity element for the $+$ operation), and A must contain the negative $-a$ of any element a ($-a$ is the inverse of a for the $+$ operation). We have $0 \cdot a = a \cdot 0 = 0$ for any element of A.

If e is the unit element of A, necessarily unique, then $ea = ae = a$ for any a in A. An element a is called *invertible* if there is an element a' in A such that $aa' = a'a = e$. If that is so, then a' is unique and is called the *inverse* of a (relative to the product operation). It is denoted by a^{-1}. Since a must then be the inverse of a',

† This condition is omitted in some texts.

that is of a^{-1}, we have $(a^{-1})^{-1} = a$. The unit element e is invertible, and $e^{-1} = e$. If a, b are both invertible, then so is ab, and $(ab)^{-1} = b^{-1}a^{-1}$. The zero element 0 of A is not invertible unless it is the only element in A. A is said to be a *commutative* ring if the product operation is commutative ($ab = ba$ for any two elements of A). We recall that a *field* is a commutative ring in which every nonzero element is invertible.

For any element b of a ring A and any positive integer m, the symbol mb denotes the element obtained by adding b to itself m times. Then $(-m)b$ is defined to be the element $m \cdot (-b)$. For the integer 0 we put $0 \cdot b = 0 =$ zero element of A.

In a similar way, b^m denotes the element obtained by forming the product of b with itself m times, m being a positive integer. We put $b^0 = e =$ unit element of A. If b is invertible, then we define b^{-m} by the equation $b^{-m} = (b^{-1})^m$. The usual rules for exponents hold. We refer to Sec. 7, Chap. 2, for a precise account of the operations symbolized by mb and b^m.

EXAMPLE 1 For our purposes we are particularly concerned with the following example, studied in Sec. 4, Chap. 9. Let V be a vector space over a field K, and let E denote the set of all linear mappings of V to itself. We have defined two binary operations in E as follows: Let $\mathbf{S}$ and $\mathbf{T}$ be elements of E. Then $\mathbf{S} + \mathbf{T}$ and $\mathbf{S} \circ \mathbf{T}$ denote the linear mappings of V defined by

2.1
$$\begin{aligned}(\mathbf{S} + \mathbf{T})(\mathbf{x}) &= \mathbf{S}(\mathbf{x}) + \mathbf{T}(\mathbf{x}) \\ (\mathbf{S} \circ \mathbf{T})(\mathbf{x}) &= \mathbf{S}(\mathbf{T}(\mathbf{x}))\end{aligned}$$

for any vector $\mathbf{x}$ in V. E with these two operations is a ring, as is easily verified. Its zero element is the mapping $\mathbf{0}$ that sends every vector of V into the zero vector. The unit element is the identity mapping $\mathbf{I}$. A third operation was defined in Chap. 9. Namely, if c is any element of the field K, and if $\mathbf{T}$ is any element of E, then $c\mathbf{T}$ denotes the linear mapping of V defined by

2.2
$$(c\mathbf{T})(\mathbf{x}) = c \cdot \mathbf{T}(\mathbf{x})$$

for any vector $\mathbf{x}$ in V. E with this operation and the first operation of (2.1) is a vector space over K. The set E with all three operations is an example of what we have called a *K-algebra*. E is called the *algebra* (or *ring*) *of endomorphisms* of V and is sometimes denoted by End (V). Since E is a ring, the exponent notation discussed above is applicable. If $\mathbf{T}$ is any element of E and m a positive integer, then it follows from (2.1) that $\mathbf{T}^m$ is the mapping of V obtained by applying $\mathbf{T}$ m times in succession.

EXAMPLE 2 K being a field, let $K^n{}_n$ be the set of all $n \times n$ matrices with coefficients in K. Then $K^n{}_n$ is a ring with the sum and product operations defined in Sec. 6, Chap. 9, and is a K-algebra with the third operation of scalar multiplication.

A ring B is called a subring of a ring A if the elements of B are all in A and if the sum and product operations of A, applied to elements of B, are the same as the sum and product operations of B.

If A' is a subset of a ring A and if A' contains the unit element e of A, along with the sum, difference, and product of any two of its elements, then A' becomes a subring of A if the sum and product of two elements of A' are defined to be the same as in A. For example, A' must then contain $e - e = 0$ and must also contain $0 - a = -a$ for any a in A'. Condition (1) above is then easy to verify, and the other three conditions are trivial to check.

EXAMPLE 3 Let End (V) be the ring of endomorphisms of a vector space V over a field K, and let K' consist of all the elements $c\mathbf{I}$, c being an arbitrary scalar (the mappings $c\mathbf{I}$ of V to itself are called *scalar mappings*). Then K' is a subring of End (V). Furthermore, the mapping $K \to K'$ defined by $c \to c\mathbf{I}$ is one-to-one, provided that dim $V \neq 0$. K' is then a field, and the mapping just defined is an isomorphism from K to K'.

EXAMPLE 4 $K^n{}_n$ being as in Example 2 above, let K'' consist of all the matrices $c\mathbf{I}$, where c is in K and $\mathbf{I}$ is the $n \times n$ unit matrix (the matrices $c\mathbf{I}$ are called *scalar* matrices). Then K'' is a subring of $K^n{}_n$. It is, in fact, a field, and the mapping $K \to K''$ defined by $c \to c\mathbf{I}$ is an isomorphism.

EXERCISES

1. Referring to Example 3, show that every element of End (V) commutes with every element of K'. Do the same for $K^n{}_n$ and K'' of Example 4.

2. An element a of a ring A is called *nilpotent* if $a^m = 0$ for some positive integer m. Suppose that A is commutative, and let N be the set of all nilpotent elements in A. Prove that the sum, difference, and product of two elements of N is again in N.

3. Let a be a nilpotent element of a ring A, and let e be the unit element. Prove that $e - a$ is invertible. [Hint: Show that $e + a + a^2 + \cdot \cdot \cdot + a^k$ is its inverse if k is large enough.]

4. Let A be a ring, and let S be a subset containing the unit element. Let B consist of all elements of A which can be expressed as (finite) sums of products of the type

$$s_1 s_2 \cdot \cdot \cdot s_r$$

where $s_1, \ldots, s_r$ denote arbitrary elements of S (and r an arbitrary integer). Show that B is a subring of A (called the subring *generated* by S). Show that if an element a of A commutes with every element s of S (that is, $sa = as$), then a commutes with every element of B.

5. Let a, b be elements of a ring A such that $ab = ba = 0$. Prove that $(a + b)^k = a^k + b^k$ for any integer $k \geq 0$

6. An element a of a ring A is called *idempotent* if $a^2 = a$. Let a, b be two idempotent elements such that $ab = ba$. Prove that the subring of A generated by e, a, b consists of all elements $m_0e + m_1a + m_2b + m_3ab$, where $m_0, \ldots, m_3$ are integers.

3. *Homomorphisms of rings*

A homomorphism of two rings A, A' is a mapping $f\colon\ A \to A'$ satisfying the following conditions:

3.1 $$f(a + b) = f(a) + f(b)$$ $$f(ab) = f(a) \cdot f(b)$$

for any two elements a, b of A. From the first equation it follows that $f(0) = 0$ and $f(-a) = -f(a)$ for any a in A (see Sec. 2, Chap. 2). The homomorphism f is called *unitary* if it sends the unit element e of A into the unit element e' of A', $f(e) = e'$. If that is so, then f maps A onto a subring of A', called the *image* of f. For then e' is in the image, by assumption, and if $f(a)$, $f(b)$ are any two elements in the image, then $f(a) \pm f(b)$ and $f(a) \cdot f(b)$ are also in the image, being equal to $f(a \pm b)$ and $f(ab)$, respectively. We shall encounter only unitary homomorphisms in this chapter.

By repeated applications of (3.1) it is easy to verify that if an element a of A is expressed in any way as a (finite) combination

3.2 $$a = (a_1 \cdots a_r) + (b_1 \cdots b_s) + \cdots$$

of sums (or differences) and products, then

3.3 $$f(a) = (f(a_1) \cdots f(a_r)) + (f(b_1) \cdots f(b_s)) + \cdots$$

A homomorphism f is called an isomorphism if it is one-to-one. If that is so, then the inverse mapping f^{-1} is also an isomorphism.

EXAMPLE 1 As already mentioned in Examples 3 and 4 of the preceding section, the mappings $K \to K'$ and $K \to K''$ are isomorphisms.

EXAMPLE 2 Let V be an n-dimensional vector space over a field K $(n > 0)$, and let B be a base for V. Then the mapping End $(V) \to K^n{}_n$ that sends an endomorphism $\mathbf{T}$ of V into its matrix relative to the base B is an isomorphism (Theorem 6.4, Chap. 9).

The applications we have in view in this chapter center round the following situation: Let $g(t)$ be a polynomial in an indeterminate t with coefficients in a field K, and let $\mathbf{T}\colon\ V \to V$ be a linear mapping of a vector space V over K. If $g(t) = b_0 + b_1t + \cdots + b_nt^n$, we recall that $g(\mathbf{T})$ denotes the linear mapping

3.4 $$g(\mathbf{T}) = b_0\mathbf{I} + b_1\mathbf{T} + \cdots + b_n\mathbf{T}^n$$

of V. The operation $g(t) \to g(\mathbf{T})$ defined in this way is a unitary ring-homomorphism $K[t] \to$ End (V) (cf. Theorem 4.4, Chap. 11). The verification is straightforward. If $\mathbf{a}$ denotes an $n \times n$ matrix with coefficients in K, then $g(\mathbf{a})$ denotes the $n \times n$ matrix

3.5 $$g(\mathbf{a}) = b_0\mathbf{I} + b_1\mathbf{a} + \cdots + b_n\mathbf{a}^n$$

where $\mathbf{I}$ here is the $n \times n$ unit matrix. The operation $g(t) \to g(\mathbf{a})$ defined in this way is a unitary ring-homomorphism $K[t] \to K^n{}_n$, and again the verification is straightforward. Homomorphisms obtained in this way by substituting a linear transformation or a matrix for a variable in a polynomial will be called *substitution* homomorphisms. Examples of them have occurred several times in earlier chapters.

It will be convenient to denote the substitution homomorphisms defined by (3.4) and (3.5) by $S_{\mathbf{T}}$ and $S_{\mathbf{a}}$, respectively.

It was pointed out in Sec. 4, Chap. 11, that the substitution homomorphism $S_{\mathbf{T}}$ affords a simple method for computing inverses. We recall the method here.

T being an endomorphism of a vector space V over a field K, suppose that $g(\mathbf{T}) = \mathbf{0}$ for some polynomial $g(t)$ in $K[t]$. For example, $g(t)$ can be taken as the characteristic polynomial of **T**, if V is of finite dimension.† If $f(t)$ is a polynomial which is relatively prime to $g(t)$, *then* $f(\mathbf{T})$ *has an inverse.* For by Theorem 3.4, Chap. 6, there exist polynomials $a(t)$ and $b(t)$ in $K[t]$ such that

3.6 $$a(t)f(t) + b(t)g(t) = 1$$

Applying the substitution homomorphism $S_{\mathbf{T}}$ to this equation we get [cf. (3.2) and (3.3)]

3.7 $$a(\mathbf{T})f(\mathbf{T}) + b(\mathbf{T})g(\mathbf{T}) = \mathbf{I}$$

Since $g(\mathbf{T}) = \mathbf{0}$, by assumption, (3.7) becomes

3.8 $$a(\mathbf{T})f(\mathbf{T}) = \mathbf{I}$$

Now $a(t)f(t) = f(t)a(t)$, and $S_{\mathbf{T}}$ applied to this equation gives $a(\mathbf{T})f(\mathbf{T}) = f(\mathbf{T})a(\mathbf{T})$, whence $f(\mathbf{T})a(\mathbf{T}) = \mathbf{I}$. Therefore $a(\mathbf{T})$ is indeed the inverse of $f(\mathbf{T})$. The polynomial $a(t)$ can be calculated by the methods of Sec. 3, Chap. 6. It is clear that a similar discussion holds for matrices in place of linear operators.

EXAMPLE 3 **T** being an endomorphism of a vector space V, suppose that $\mathbf{T}^r = \mathbf{0}$ for some integer $r > 0$. Here we can take $g(t) = t^r$. From the identity

$$(1 - t)(1 + t + \cdots + t^{r-1}) = 1 - t^r$$

in $K[t]$ we can take $f(t) = 1 - t$, $a(t) = 1 + t + \cdots + t^{r-1}$, $b(t) = 1$, in the notation of (3.7). Therefore,

$$(\mathbf{I} - \mathbf{T})^{-1} = \mathbf{I} + \mathbf{T} + \cdots + \mathbf{T}^{r-1}$$

(This is a special case of Exercise 3 of the preceding section.)

EXAMPLE 4 As in the preceding, let $\mathbf{T}^r = \mathbf{0}$, and let c be any nonzero scalar. From the identity

$$(c - t)\left(\frac{1}{c} + \frac{t}{c^2} + \cdots + \frac{t^{r-1}}{c^r}\right) = 1 - \frac{t^r}{c^r}$$

† By the Cayley-Hamilton theorem, see Sec. 5, Chap. 11.

we conclude, just as in the foregoing, that

$$(c\mathbf{I} - \mathbf{T})^{-1} = \frac{1}{c}\left(\mathbf{I} + \frac{1}{c}\mathbf{T} + \cdots + \frac{1}{c^{r-1}}\mathbf{T}^{r-1}\right)$$

Similarly,

$$\left(\mathbf{I} - \frac{\mathbf{T}}{c}\right)^{-1} = \mathbf{I} + \frac{1}{c}\,\mathbf{T} + \cdots + \frac{1}{c^{r-1}}\,\mathbf{T}^{r-1}$$

EXAMPLE 5 Let V be an n-dimensional vector space over a field K, and let $\mathbf{u}_1, \ldots, \mathbf{u}_n$ be a base. Let $\mathbf{T}$ be the linear mapping from V to itself such that

$$\begin{aligned} \mathbf{T}(\mathbf{u}_i) &= \mathbf{u}_{i-1} \qquad (i = 2, \ldots, n) \\ \mathbf{T}(\mathbf{u}_1) &= \mathbf{0} \end{aligned}$$

The matrix of $\mathbf{T}$ relative to the given base has all entries zero except for a diagonal sequence of 1's above the main diagonal. The characteristic polynomial of $\mathbf{T}$ is therefore t^n. Hence, as in Example 4 above,

$$\left(\mathbf{I} - \frac{1}{c}\,\mathbf{T}\right)^{-1} = \mathbf{I} + \frac{1}{c}\,\mathbf{T} + \cdots + \frac{1}{c^{n-1}}\,\mathbf{T}^{n-1}$$

EXAMPLE 6 Let $\mathbf{T}$ be as in Example 4 above. Then $(\mathbf{T}^2)^{[r/2]+1} = \mathbf{0}$, where $[r/2]$ denotes the greatest integer not exceeding $r/2$. Hence, by the same reasoning,

$$(c\mathbf{I} - \mathbf{T}^2)^{-1} = \frac{1}{c}(\mathbf{I} + \mathbf{T}^2/c + \cdots + (\mathbf{T}^2/c)^{[r/2]})$$

EXAMPLE 7 Let $\mathbf{T}$ be an endomorphism of a vector space V, and let its characteristic polynomial be

$$\varphi(t) = t(t^2 - 1)$$

Compute $(\mathbf{T}^2 + \mathbf{I})^{-1}$. By the Cayley-Hamilton theorem we have $\varphi(\mathbf{T}) = \mathbf{0}$. In the notation of (3.7) we take $g(t) = t(t^2 - 1)$ and $f(t) = t^2 + 1$. Divide $g(t)$ by $f(t)$, obtaining

$$t(t^2 - 1) = t \cdot (t^2 + 1) - 2t$$

Now divide $t^2 + 1$ by the remainder, getting (provided that $2 \neq 0$ in K)

$$t^2 + 1 = -\frac{t}{2}\cdot(-2t) + 1$$

Thus

$$\begin{aligned} 1 &= (t^2 + 1) + \frac{t}{2}(-2t) \\ &= t^2 + 1 + \frac{t}{2}\cdot[t(t^2 - 1) - t(t^2 + 1)] \\ &= (1 - t^2/2)\cdot f(t) + (t/2)\cdot g(t) \end{aligned}$$

This is the method of Sec. 3, Chap. 6; and for $a(t)$ in (3.7) we can take $1 - t^2/2$.

Therefore,

$$(\mathbf{I} + \mathbf{T}^2)^{-1} = \mathbf{I} - \tfrac{1}{2}\mathbf{T}^2$$

EXERCISES

1. Let $\mathbf{T}$ denote an endomorphism of a vector space V, with characteristic polynomial $\varphi(t)$.

(*a*) Express $\mathbf{T}^{-1}$ as a polynomial in $\mathbf{T}$ if $\varphi(t) = (t+1)^2$.

(*b*) Express $(\mathbf{I} + \mathbf{T}^2)^{-1}$ as a polynomial in $\mathbf{T}$ if $\varphi(t) = t_5$. Can you do this for $(\mathbf{T} + \mathbf{T}^3)^{-1}$?

(*c*) Express $(\mathbf{I} + \mathbf{T} + \mathbf{T}^2)^{-1}$ as a polynomial in $\mathbf{T}$ if $\varphi(t) = t^5$.

(*d*) Express $(\mathbf{I} + \mathbf{T} + \mathbf{T}^2)^{-1}$ as a polynomial in $\mathbf{T}$ if $\varphi(t) = t^5(t^2 - 1)$.

(*e*) Find $(\mathbf{I} + 2\mathbf{T} + \mathbf{T}^2)^{-1}$ if $\varphi(t) = t(t^2 + 1)$.

2. Let $\mathbf{a}$ be a square matrix with coefficients in a field K, and let $\varphi(t)$ be its characteristic polynomial. Express $(\mathbf{I} + \mathbf{a} + \mathbf{a}^3)^{-2}$ as a polynomial in $\mathbf{a}$ if $\varphi(t) = (1-t)^2$. Express $(\mathbf{I} - \mathbf{a}^3)^{-1}$ as a polynomial in $\mathbf{a}$ if $\varphi(t) = 1 + t + t^2$, or at least try to.

3. The notation being as in Exercise 2, suppose that $\varphi(t)$ has no roots in K. Prove that $\mathbf{a} - c\mathbf{I}$ has an inverse for any c in K.

4. The differentiation operator

As usual we denote the field of real numbers by **R** and the field of complex numbers by **C**. By a *complex-valued function* on **R** is meant a mapping f from **R** to **C**. If such a function f happens to map **R** into **R**, then it is called *real-valued.* Thus we understand the term "complex-valued function" as including real-valued functions. A simple example is the function that sends an arbitrary real number x into x^2. This function is usually indicated by the symbol x^2. Similarly, the mapping that sends an arbitrary real number x into x^n (n a positive integer) is usually indicated by the symbol x^n. It is real-valued. However, the function $f(x) = (2+i) \cdot x^3$ is not real-valued. If c is any fixed complex number, then the mapping that sends *every* real number into c is a complex-valued function. Such functions are called *constants*, or constant functions.

Let F^* denote the set of all complex-valued functions. If f and g are two of its elements, then we define $f+g$ to be the function that sends an arbitrary real number x into $f(x) + g(x)$. If c is any complex number, then we define cf to be the function that sends any real number x into $c \cdot f(x)$. It is easily verified that F^*, equipped with these two operations, is a vector space over **C**. Its zero element is the constant function 0 that maps all real numbers into 0. We can in fact make F^* into a ring by defining the product fg of two of its elements to be the function that maps an arbitrary real number x into $f(x) \cdot g(x)$.† The three operations just defined can be described briefly by the following equations:

† Not to be confused with the composition of two mappings, which in general here does not make sense.

$$(f + g)(x) = f(x) + g(x)$$

4.1 $$(c \cdot f)(x) = c \cdot f(x)$$

$$(fg)(x) = f(x) \cdot g(x)$$

where x denotes any real number, c denotes any complex number, and where f and g are any complex-valued functions on **R**. As already mentioned, the first two operations make F^* into a vector space over **C**. The first and third operations make F^* into a commutative ring whose unit element is the constant function, denoted simply by 1, that maps all of **R** into the number 1. F^* with all three operations defined above is a **C**-algebra (Sec. 4, Chap. 8). We observe that if c is a complex number, and if we also denote by c the constant function that maps all of **R** into c, then the symbol cf is defined by both the second and third equations of (4.1); the two definitions are clearly the same.

The system F^* is not very interesting for our purposes, and we are now going to define a certain subsystem:

A complex-valued function f on **R** is called *differentiable* if, for every real number x, the limit

4.2 $$\lim_{h \to 0} \frac{f(x+h) - f(x)}{h}$$

exists.† This means that there exists a complex number L for which the following is true: *given any positive real number e, there is a positive real number d such that*

$$\left| \frac{f(x+h) - f(x)}{h} - L \right| < e$$

for all real numbers $h \neq 0$ *with* $-d < h < d$. The number L satisfying this requirement, if it exists, is unique and is denoted by the symbolism of (4.2). Obviously the limit L will in general depend upon x, and we shall sometimes denote it by $f'(x)$. Thus, if f is a differentiable function, then by definition

4.3 $$f'(x) = \lim_{h \to 0} \frac{f(x+h) - f(x)}{h}$$

Since f' assigns a complex number $f'(x)$ to every real number x, f' is again a complex-valued function, that is an element of F^*. The new function f' obtained in this way from a (differentiable) function f is called the *derivative* of f. If f' happens to be differentiable, then we can form its derivative, denoted by f''; f'' is also called the *second* derivative of f. If in turn f'' is differentiable, then its derivative is denoted by f''', called the *third* derivative of f, and so on. If the process can be repeated n times, we obtain the nth derivative $f^{(n)}$ of f.

† The notion of *limit* that arises here is very similar to the one encountered in Chaps. 4 and 5 in connection with Cauchy sequences.

A definition of differentiability, identical in appearance to the foregoing, can also be made for mappings $\mathbf{C} \to \mathbf{C}$ instead of from **R** to **C**, both x and h then being allowed to be complex numbers.

Other commonly used symbols for the derivative f' of a differentiable function f are df/dx and Df. The corresponding symbols for the nth derivative of f (assuming it exists) are d^nf/dx^n and D^nf.

A complex-valued function f is called *indefinitely differentiable* if its successive derivatives f', f'', f''', . . . all exist. We shall be concerned here only with indefinitely differentiable functions. Some examples will be given presently.

Observe that if a differentiable function f is real-valued, then its derivative f' is also real-valued. For the *difference quotient*

4.4 $$\frac{f(x + h) - f(x)}{h}$$

appearing in the definition (4.3) is real for any choice of x and h (they are always supposed to be real), and therefore the limit of that quantity as $h \to 0$ is a real number.

If f is any complex-valued function on **R**, let $u(x)$ denote the real part of $f(x)$ and let $v(x)$ denote the imaginary part of $f(x)$, so that $f(x) = u(x) + iv(x)$. Then u and v are two real-valued functions, and this decomposition of f is unique (Theorem 1.1, Chap. 5). The difference quotient (4.4) can be written as

$$\frac{u(x + h) - u(x)}{h} + i\,\frac{v(x + h) - v(x)}{h}$$

If f is differentiable, then both the real and imaginary parts of its difference quotient must have limits as $h \to 0$, as is easily seen, and therefore both u and v must be differentiable functions, and $f' = u' + iv'$. Hence derivative calculations with complex-valued functions can be reduced in a trivial way to similar calculations with real-valued functions.

EXAMPLE 1 Let c be a complex number, and consider the constant function $f(x) = c$ for all real x. The difference quotient (4.4) for this function is zero for all x and $h \neq 0$ and consequently has the limit zero as $h \to 0$, whatever x. Hence, a constant function is differentiable, and its derivative is the constant function 0. It follows that a constant function is indefinitely differentiable, all its derivatives being zero.

EXAMPLE 2 Consider the function $f(x) = x$ for all real numbers x. The difference quotient (4.4) is equal to $[(x + h) - x]/h = 1$ for all x and for all $h \neq 0$. If follows at once that the derivative of this function is the constant function 1. Hence f' is differentiable, and $f'' = 0$. All the successive derivatives exist and are zero.

EXAMPLE 3 Let $f(x) = x^n$ for all x, n being a positive integer. From the binomial theorem (Theorem 5.2, Chap. 3) we have

$$(x + h)^n = x^n + nx^{n-1}h + \binom{n}{2} x^{n-2}h^2 + \cdots + h^n$$

Therefore the difference quotient (4.4) for this f is

$$nx^{n-1} + \binom{n}{2} x^{n-2}h + \cdots + h^{n-1}$$

The limit of this as $h \to 0$ is nx^{n-1}, and so $f'(x) = nx^{n-1}$. This is again a differentiable function, by the same argument, and its derivative is $f''(x) = n(n-1)x^{n-2}$. If $n = 2$ this is a constant function, with derivative equal to zero. If $n > 2$, the process can be repeated, giving $f'''(x) = n(n-1)(n-2)x^{n-3}$, etc. Starting with x^n we then get the following sequence of derivatives:

$$nx^{n-1}, n(n-1)x^{n-2}, n(n-1)(n-2)x^{n-3}, \ldots, n!, 0, 0, \ldots$$

That is, the nth derivative is the constant function $n!$, and all further derivatives are zero.

EXAMPLE 4 Let $f(x) = a_0 + a_1x + \cdots + a_nx^n$, where $a_0, a_1, \ldots, a_n$ are any complex numbers. Using the results of Example 3 it is easy to see that f is differentiable, and

$$f'(x) = a_1 + 2a_2x + \cdots + na_nx^{n-1}$$

again a polynomial.

EXAMPLE 5 Let $f(x) = e^x = 1 + x + \frac{x^2}{2!} + \frac{x^3}{3!} + \cdots$

(see Sec. 4, Chap. 4). It is a standard theorem of calculus that the infinite series converges for all x and that $f'(x) = f(x)$. This function is equal to its own derivative and is therefore indefinitely differentiable. More generally, putting $f(x) = e^{ax} = 1 + ax + (ax)^2/2! + (ax)^3/3! + \cdots$, where a is any complex number, we have $f'(x) = ae^{ax}$, and this function is also indefinitely differentiable.

If f and g are two differentiable functions, then it is an elementary theorem of calculus, easily proved from the definition above, that $f + g$ is differentiable, and $(f + g)' = f' + g'$. If c is any complex number, then cf is differentiable, and $(cf)' = c \cdot f'$. Furthermore $f \cdot g$ is differentiable, and $(fg)' = f'g + fg'$. In particular, if f and g are infinitely differentiable, then so are $f + g$, cf and fg.

Now let us denote by F the set of all indefinitely differentiable complex-valued functions on $\mathbf{R}$. From the remarks just made, F is a subspace of F^*. Since the product of two elements of F is again in F, it follows that F is also an algebra.

We denote by $\mathbf{D}$ the mapping of F to itself that sends an arbitrary function f into its derivative f'. We shall usually write $\mathbf{D}f$ instead of f'. The rules cited above become

4.5
$$\begin{aligned} \mathbf{D}(f + g) &= \mathbf{D}f + \mathbf{D}g \\ \mathbf{D}(cf) &= c \cdot \mathbf{D}f \\ \mathbf{D}(fg) &= (\mathbf{D}f) \cdot g + f \cdot (\mathbf{D}g) \end{aligned}$$

where f and g are any functions in F and where c is any complex number. The first two rules say that $\mathbf{D}$ is a linear mapping of the vector space F to itself. The third rule ("product rule") contains the second, for $\mathbf{D}c = 0$ for a constant function. $\mathbf{D}$ is called the differentiation operator.

Since $\mathbf{D}$ maps $F \to F$, we can form the composition $\mathbf{D} \circ \mathbf{D} = \mathbf{D}^2$. This means, as usual, $\mathbf{D}$ applied twice. Thus $\mathbf{D}^2 f = \mathbf{D}(\mathbf{D}f) = \mathbf{D}(f') = f''$. That is, $\mathbf{D}^2 f$ is what we have called the second derivative of f. Similarly, $\mathbf{D}^n f = f^{(n)} = n$th derivative of f, for any positive integer n. By $\mathbf{D}^0$ or $\mathbf{I}$ we shall sometimes denote the identity mapping of F. From our examples above we have $\mathbf{D}x^n = nx^{n-1}$, $\mathbf{D}^n x^n = n!$ (n a positive integer), $\mathbf{D}e^{ax} = ae^{ax}$, etc.

Just as with any endomorphism of a vector space, we can form "polynomials" in $\mathbf{D}$ with complex coefficients, any such being again a linear mapping of F to itself.

EXAMPLE 6 For the operator $\mathbf{D}^3 - 2\mathbf{D} + \mathbf{I}$ we have, by definition, $(\mathbf{D}^3 - 2\mathbf{D} + \mathbf{I})f = \mathbf{D}^3 f - 2\mathbf{D} + f = f''' - 2f' + f$. If $f = 3x^3 + x$, then the result is $3x^3 - 18x^2 + x + 16$.

We point out explicitly that our space F contains all polynomials with complex coefficients and all exponentials e^{ax}, where a is any complex number. Since sums and products of elements of F are again in F, it follows that F contains all functions which can be built by a finite number of sum and product operations from polynomials and exponentials.

EXERCISES

1. In the following determine the polynomial $p(t)$ such that the indicated expression is the same as $p(\mathbf{D})f$:

(a) $\dfrac{d^2f}{dx^2} + 3\dfrac{df}{dx} - 2f$

(b) $\dfrac{d^3f}{dx^3} - 4\dfrac{d^2f}{dx^2}$

(c) $f^{(5)} - 16f''' + 2if'' - \sqrt{3}f$

2. Is $\left(\dfrac{df}{dx} + f\right) \cdot \left(\dfrac{df}{dx} - f\right) = (\mathbf{D} + \mathbf{I})(\mathbf{D} - \mathbf{I})f$?

3. Is $\dfrac{d}{dx}\left(\dfrac{df}{dx} - f\right) + \left(\dfrac{df}{dx} - f\right) = [\mathbf{D}(\mathbf{D} - \mathbf{I}) + \mathbf{I}(\mathbf{D} - \mathbf{I})]f$?

4. Is $\dfrac{d^2}{dx^2}\left(\dfrac{d^2f}{dx^2} - f\right) + \left(\dfrac{d^2f}{dx^2} - f\right) = (\mathbf{D}^4 - \mathbf{I})f$?

5. Let f, g be two functions in F, and let n be a positive integer. Prove Leibniz's formula:

$$\mathbf{D}^n(fg) = \sum_{k=0}^{n} \binom{n}{k} (\mathbf{D}^k f) \cdot (\mathbf{D}^{n-k} g)$$

6. If $p(t)$, $q(t)$, $r(t)$ are polynomials in $\mathbf{C}[t]$ such that $p(t) = q(t) \cdot r(t)$, is it true that $p(\mathbf{D}) = q(\mathbf{D}) \circ r(\mathbf{D})$? State your reasons.

7. Compute $(\mathbf{D}^4 + 3\mathbf{D}^2 - \mathbf{D})(4x^5 + 2x^3 - x + 1)$.

8. Let h be an element of F. Show that the mapping $h\mathbf{D}$ of F to itself that sends an arbitrary f into $h \cdot \mathbf{D}f = hf'$ is a linear mapping. Compute the operator $\mathbf{D} \circ (1 - x^2)\mathbf{D}$ and the effect of it applied to a polynomial of 4th degree.

*9. Let $\mathbf{T}$: $F \to F$ be a mapping for which the rules (4.5) are valid. Prove that there is a function h in F such that $\mathbf{T} = h\mathbf{D}$.

5. *Some differentiation formulas*

From (4.5) it is easy to deduce some useful rules for differentiation, and we list a few here, referring to standard calculus texts for more details.

First, if $f(x)$ and $g(x)$ are two differentiable complex-valued functions on $\mathbf{R}$, we cannot in general form either of the two composite mappings $f(g(x))$ or $g(f(x))$. But if one of the functions, say $f(x)$, is real-valued, then the composition $g(f(x))$ makes sense [we do not write this as gf because of the confusion with the product of g and f defined in (4.1)]. This composite function is again differentiable, and we have the "chain rule"

5.1 $$(g(f(x)))' = g'(f(x)) \cdot f'(x)$$

For example, if $f(x) = cx$, c being a real number, and if $g(x) = e^x$, then $g(f(x)) = e^{cx}$, and the rule above gives us

$$(e^{cx})' = ce^{cx}$$

As pointed out earlier, this rule holds for complex c also. We write the rule as†

5.2 $$\mathbf{D}(e^{cx}) = ce^{cx}$$

Combining this with the product rule of (4.5) we get, for any f in F,

5.3 $$\mathbf{D}(e^{cx}f) = (\mathbf{D}e^{cx})f + e^{cx}\mathbf{D}f = ce^{cx}f + e^{cx}\mathbf{D}f$$

or

5.4 $$\mathbf{D}(e^{cx}f) = e^{cx}(c\mathbf{I} + \mathbf{D})f$$

where again $\mathbf{I}$ is the identity mapping of F.

Applying $\mathbf{D}$ to both sides, we get

$$\mathbf{D}^2(e^{cx}f) = \mathbf{D}[e^{cx}(c\mathbf{I} + \mathbf{D})f]$$

and using (5.4) here, with $(c\mathbf{I} + \mathbf{D})f$ in place of f, we get

$$e^{cx}(c\mathbf{I} + \mathbf{D})(c\mathbf{I} + \mathbf{D})f$$

or

5.5 $$\mathbf{D}^2(e^{cx}f) = e^{cx}(c\mathbf{I} + \mathbf{D})^2f$$

† In the language of Chap. 11, e^{cx} is an *eigenfunction* of the operator $\mathbf{D}$.

Applying $\mathbf{D}$ repeatedly in this way, it is easily seen by a simple induction argument that

5.6 $$\mathbf{D}^k(e^{cx}f) = e^{cx}(c\mathbf{I} + \mathbf{D})^k f$$

for any positive integer k.

Now let

5.7 $$p(t) = \sum_{k=0}^{n} a_k t^k$$

be any polynomial with complex coefficients in an indeterminate t. From (5.6) we get

$$\begin{aligned} p(\mathbf{D})(e^{cx}f) &= \left(\sum_{k=0}^{n} a_k \mathbf{D}^k\right)(e^{cx}f) \\ &= \sum_{k=0}^{n} a_k \mathbf{D}^k(e^{cx}f) \\ &= \sum_{k=0}^{n} a_k e^{cx}\,(c\mathbf{I} + \mathbf{D})^k f \end{aligned}$$

or

5.8 $$p(\mathbf{D})(e^{cx}f) = e^{cx}p(c\mathbf{I} + \mathbf{D})\mathrm{f}$$

If we replace c by $-c$ here, then the formula reads

5.9 $$p(\mathbf{D})(e^{-cx}f) = e^{-cx}p(\mathbf{D} - c\mathbf{I})f$$

This formula is basic for the sequel; writing $e^{-cx}f = g$, we get the formula

5.10 $$e^{cx} \cdot p(\mathbf{D})g = p(\mathbf{D} - c\mathbf{I})(e^{cx}g)$$

EXAMPLE Here we have $p(t) = 1 + t + t^2$ and $c = 3$:

$$\begin{aligned} (\mathbf{I} + \mathbf{D} + \mathbf{D}^2)(xe^{3x}) &= e^{3x} \cdot [\mathbf{I} + (3\mathbf{I} + \mathbf{D}) + (3\mathbf{I} + \mathbf{D})^2]x \\ &= e^{3x} \cdot [x + 3x + 1 + (3\mathbf{I} + \mathbf{D}) \cdot (3x + 1)] \\ &= e^{3x} \cdot [x + 3x + 1 + 9x + 3 + 3] \\ &= e^{3x} \cdot (7 + 13x) \end{aligned}$$

EXERCISES

1. Compute $\mathbf{D}^2(e^{3x}x^2)$.
2. Compute $\mathbf{D}^3(x^2e^{3x})$.
3. Compute $(\mathbf{I} + \mathbf{D})^5\ (e^{3x} \cdot x^2)$.

Find functions f satisfying the indicated conditions:

4. $\mathbf{D}f(x) = x^n (n \text{ an integer } \geq 0)$
5. $\mathbf{D}f(x) = e^{cx}$

6. $\mathbf{D}f(x) = xe^{cx}$
7. $\mathbf{D}f(x) = x^2e^{cx}$
8. $\mathbf{D}f(x) = x^ne^{cx}$ (n an integer >0).
9. $\mathbf{D}^3f(x) = 0$ (find more than one answer).
10. $\mathbf{D}^3(e^{-2x}f(x)) = 0$ (find more than one answer).
11. $(\mathbf{D}^2 + \mathbf{I})f = 0$ (find more than one f).
12. Deduce (5.6) from Leibniz's rule (Exercise 5, Sec. 4).

6. Linear differential equations with constant coefficients

A differential equation is, loosely speaking, a relation connecting an unknown function and certain of its derivatives. The problem, of course, is to find the unknown function. A simple example is the equation

$$f' + f = 0$$

A solution of it is $f(x) = e^{-x}$, by (5.2), and in fact any solution must be of the form $f = ce^{-x}$ (c a constant). Another example is

$$f'' + f = 0$$

of which e^{ix} and e^{-ix} are solutions, again by (5.2). Every solution must be of the form $ae^{ix} + be^{-ix}$, with a and b arbitrary constants. The simplest differential equation imaginable is

$$f'(x) = g(x)$$

where $g(x)$ is some given function. The solution of this equation is the chief subject of the integral calculus and is outside our province. We shall not go into the matter except for some rather special choices of $g(x)$. Certain kinds of differential equations, apparently much more complex than the one just mentioned, present algebraic peculiarities which render their solution quite simple, and we shall confine our attention to such equations. The type we propose to study here is of great practical importance.

Sometimes differential equations arise in the form of *systems* consisting of several equations involving several unknown functions and their derivatives. We shall consider some examples in Sec. 9.

Differential equations are of basic importance in most physical applications of mathematics.

A *linear* differential equation is one of the type

$$a_n \frac{d^nf}{dx^n} + a_{n-1} \frac{d^{n-1}f}{dx^{n-1}} + \cdots + a_1 \frac{df}{dx} + a_0f = g$$

where $a_0, a_1, \ldots, a_n, g$ are given functions. We shall consider here only the case in which the coefficients $a_0, \ldots, a_n$ are *constants*. With the $\mathbf{D}$ notation the equation can be written

6.1 $$a_n\mathbf{D}^nf + a_{n-1}\mathbf{D}^{n-1}f + \cdots + a_1\mathbf{D}f + a_0f = g$$

or

6.2 $$(a_n\mathbf{D}^n + a_{n-1}\mathbf{D}^{n-1} + \cdots + a_1\mathbf{D} + a_0\mathbf{I})f = g$$

If we define the polynomial $p(t)$ by

6.3 $$p(t) = \sum_{k=0}^{n} a_kt^k$$

then our equation is

6.4 $$p(\mathbf{D})f = g$$

Since our field of scalars is $\mathbf{C}$, every polynomial in $\mathbf{C}[t]$ can be written as a product of factors of the first degree (Theorem 4.2, Chap. 6), and so $p(t)$ can be put in the form

6.5 $$p(t) = a_n(t - c_1)^{k_1} \cdot (t - c_2)^{k_2} \cdots (t - c_r)^{k_r}$$

where $c_1, \ldots, c_r$ are the distinct roots of $p(t)$, the k's being positive integers. As we have seen, (6.5) remains correct upon substitution of the endomorphism $\mathbf{D}$ for t (see Sec. 3), and so (6.4) is the same as

6.6 $$(\mathbf{D} - c_1\mathbf{I})^{k_1}(\mathbf{D} - c_2\mathbf{I})^{k_2} \cdots (\mathbf{D} - c_r\mathbf{I})^{k_r}f = a_n^{-1} \cdot g$$

It is therefore clear that the study of linear differential equations with constant coefficients is closely connected with the study of operators of the type $(\mathbf{D} - c\mathbf{I})^n$. We now take up that question.

The differentiation operator $\mathbf{D}$ is a linear mapping of the vector space F of indefinitely differentiable functions to itself. $\mathbf{D}$ is not an isomorphism, for $\mathbf{D}$ maps every constant function into 0, as was indicated in Example 1, Sec. 4. Conversely, it can be shown that f must be a constant function if $\mathbf{D}f = 0$ (this is a well-known theorem of calculus). Hence,

6.7 *The kernel of $\mathbf{D}$: $F \to F$ is the one-dimensional subspace consisting of the constant functions.*

If $\mathbf{D}f = \mathbf{D}g$, then $\mathbf{D}(f - g) = 0$, and so $f - g =$ constant. Therefore we see that

6.8 $\mathbf{D}f = \mathbf{D}g$ *if and only if* $f = g + c$, *where c is a constant*

Now let us determine the kernel of $\mathbf{D}^n$. In Sec. 4 we saw that $\mathbf{D}x^m = mx^{m-1}$, and by repeated applications of $\mathbf{D}$ we get $\mathbf{D}^mx^m = m!$. Hence $\mathbf{D}^n\mathrm{x}^m = 0$ if $n > m$. Let us denote by P_k the subspace of F consisting of all polynomials with complex coefficients, of degree *less* than k. Thus in particular P_1 consists of all polynomials of degree zero—hence of all the constant functions. By P_0 we shall denote the subspace of F consisting of the zero function alone.

6.9 *The operator* **D** *maps* P_k *onto* P_{k-1} *for every positive integer* k.

For if f is in P_k, then clearly $\mathbf{D}f$ must have degree 1 less than the degree of f, and so $\mathbf{D}f$ has degree $<k - 1$, since f has degree $<k$. On the other hand, if

6.10 $$g(x) = a_0 + a_1x + \cdots + a_{k-2}x^{k-2}$$

is any element of P_{k-1}, then, putting

6.11 $$h(x) = a_0x + \frac{a_1}{2}x^2 + \cdots + \frac{a_{k-2}}{k-1}x^{k-1}$$

we have $\mathbf{D}h = g$, showing that **D** maps P_k into all of P_{k-1}.

By a very similar argument we prove that

6.12 *If* $\mathbf{D}f$ *is in* P_{k-1}, *then* f *is in* P_k.

For put $\mathbf{D}f = g$, and let $h(x)$ be the polynomial obtained from g as in (6.11). Then $\mathbf{D}h = g$, and so $f = h + c$, where c is a constant, by (6.8), since $\mathbf{D}f = \mathbf{D}g$. Hence f is a polynomial of the same degree as h and is therefore in P_k.

6.13 *The kernel of* $\mathbf{D}^n$ *is* P_n.

This is true for $n = 1$, by (6.1). Suppose it is true for $n - 1$, n being some integer ≥ 2. Now $\mathbf{D}^n f = 0$ if and only if $\mathbf{D}^{n-1}(\mathbf{D}f) = 0$, which is true if and only if $\mathbf{D}f$ is in the kernel of $\mathbf{D}^{n-1}$. By assumption, that kernel is P_{n-1}, and $\mathbf{D}f$ is in P_{n-1} if and only if f is in P_n, by (6.9) and (6.12).

6.14 P_n *is a vector space over* **C** *of dimension* n, *and* $1, x, \ldots, x^{n-1}$ *form a base.*

For if $c_0, c_1, \ldots, c_{n-1}$ are any complex numbers, not all zero, then $c_0 + c_1x + \cdots + c_{n-1}x^{n-1}$ cannot be the zero function, since this polynomial cannot have more than $n - 1$ roots (Theorem 4.1, Chap. 6).

We now introduce the subspace $P_{n,c}$ of F consisting of all the elements of P_n multiplied by e^{cx}.

6.15 $P_{n,c}$ *is a vector space over* C *of dimension* n, *and* $e^{cx}, xe^{cx}, \ldots, x^{n-1}e^{cx}$ *form a base.*

This follows at once from (6.14), since e^{cx} cannot vanish for any x because $e^{-cx}e^{cx} = 1$. Therefore $e^{cx}(c_0 + c_1x + \cdots + c_{n-1}x^{n-1})$ cannot be the zero function unless all the coefficients $c_0, \ldots, c_{n-1}$ are zero.

We can apply formula (5.8) to calculate the kernel of $(\mathbf{D} - c\mathbf{I})^n$. Taking $p(t) = t^n$ in (5.8) we get

6.16 $$\mathbf{D}^n(e^{-cx}f) = e^{-cx}(\mathbf{D} - c\mathbf{I})^n f$$

Since $e^{-cx} \neq 0$ for any x, it follows that $(\mathbf{D} - c\mathbf{I})^n f = 0$ if and only if $\mathbf{D}^n(e^{-cx}f) = 0$. From (6.7) it follows that $e^{-cx}f$ is a polynomial in P_n, and so f is equal to e^{cx} times a polynomial in P_n. That is,

6.17 *The kernel of* $(\mathbf{D} - c\mathbf{I})^n$ *is* $P_{n,c}$.

Consider an element $e^{cx}g(x)$ in $P_{n,c}$ [that is, $g(x)$ is in P_n]. We have [see Eq. (5.4)]

$$\mathbf{D}(e^{cx}g(x)) = e^{cx}(\mathbf{D} + c\mathbf{I})g(x)$$

Since $(\mathbf{D} + c\mathbf{I})g(x)$ is again in P_n, it follows that $\mathbf{D}(e^{cx}g(x))$ is again in $P_{n,c}$. Hence,

6.18 $\mathbf{D}$ *maps* $P_{n,c}$ *into itself.*

6.19 *Denoting by* $\mathbf{T}$ *the operator* $\mathbf{D}$ *restricted*† *to* $P_{n,c}$ (that is, $\mathbf{T}f = \mathbf{D}f$ *for* f *in* $P_{n,c}$), *the characteristic polynomial of* $\mathbf{T}$ *is* $(t - c)^n$.

To show this we observe that the functions

$$u_k = \frac{x^k}{k!}\, e^{cx} \qquad (k = 0, 1, \ldots, n-1)$$

form a base for $P_{n,c}$, by (6.15). We have, using (5.4),

$$\begin{aligned}(\mathbf{D} - c\mathbf{I})\, u_k &= e^{cx}\mathbf{D}(e^{-cx}u_k)\\ &= e^{cx}\mathbf{D}\left(\frac{x^k}{k!}\right)\\ &= \begin{cases} u_{k-1} & \text{for } k > 0\\ 0 & \text{for } k = 0\end{cases}\end{aligned}$$

Recall that $\mathbf{T}u_k = \mathbf{D}u_k$, and so we have

$$\begin{aligned}\mathbf{T}u_k &= cu_k + u_{k-1} \qquad (k = 1, \ldots, n-1)\\ \mathbf{T}u_0 &= cu_0\end{aligned}$$

The matrix of $\mathbf{T}$ with respect to the base $u_0, u_1, \ldots, u_{n-1}$ of $P_{n,c}$ is therefore

$$\begin{pmatrix} c & 1 & 0 & \cdots & & 0\\ 0 & c & 1 & \cdots & & 0\\ 0 & 0 & c & 1 & \cdots & 0\\ \cdot & \cdot & \cdot & \cdot & \cdot & \cdot\\ 0 & 0 & \cdots & & c & 1\\ 0 & 0 & \cdots & & 0 & c\end{pmatrix}$$

and the characteristic polynomial of this matrix, hence of the endomorphism $\mathbf{T}$, is clearly $(t - c)^n$, as claimed.

6.20 *If* b *is a complex number different from* c, *then the operator* $(\mathbf{T} - b\mathbf{I})^m$ *has an inverse for any positive integer* m.

This follows at once from Sec. 3 since the corresponding polynomials $(t - b)^m$ and $(t - c)^n$ are relatively prime.

† We introduce a new letter here because the situation at hand depends strongly on the particular subspace $P_{n,c}$ under consideration. It would not do to use $\mathbf{D}$ indiscriminately.

It is important for us to have an efficient method for computing $(\mathbf{T} - b\mathbf{I})^{-1}$. To do so we have only to find polynomials $p(t)$ and $g(t)$ such that $p(t) \cdot (t - b) + g(t) \cdot (t - c)^n = 1$. As we have had occasion to remark earlier, this can be done by starting from the general identity

6.21 $$(y - 1)(1 + y + y^2 + \cdots + y^{n-1}) = y^n - 1$$

In this we put

6.22 $$y = \frac{t - c}{b - c}$$

(legitimate because $b \neq c$). After a routine simplification, we get

6.23 $$\frac{1}{b - c} \cdot (t - b) \cdot \left[1 + \frac{t - c}{b - c} + \cdots + \left(\frac{t - c}{b - c}\right)^{n-1}\right] = \left(\frac{t - c}{b - c}\right)^n - 1$$

Then indeed we have 1 expressed as a combination of $(t - b)$ and $(t - c)^n$. Now in this polynomial identity we may substitute the operator $\mathbf{T}$ for t, and recalling that $(\mathbf{T} - c\mathbf{I})^n = \mathbf{0}$, by the Cayley-Hamilton theorem, we get

6.24 $$\frac{1}{b - c} \cdot (\mathbf{T} - b\mathbf{I}) \cdot \left[\mathbf{I} + \frac{\mathbf{T} - c\mathbf{I}}{b - c} + \cdots + \left(\frac{\mathbf{T} - c\mathbf{I}}{b - c}\right)^{n-1}\right] = -\mathbf{I}$$

That is,

6.25 $$(\mathbf{T} - b\mathbf{I})^{-1} = -\frac{1}{b - c}\left[\mathbf{I} + \frac{\mathbf{T} - c\mathbf{I}}{b - c} + \cdots + \left(\frac{\mathbf{T} - c\mathbf{I}}{b - c}\right)^{n-1}\right]$$

Recall that $\mathbf{T}$ was used in place of $\mathbf{D}$ to indicate that we are considering only a subspace of F, namely, $P_{n,c}$. The formula just obtained is not true for all of F, because $\mathbf{D} - b\mathbf{I}$ does not have an inverse on F. However, the fact that the formula is limited to the subspace $P_{n,c}$ is sufficiently indicated by the $\mathbf{T}$ on the left, and we may safely write $\mathbf{D}$ on the right. Doing so and raising both sides of (6.25) to the mth power, we get the general formula

6.26 $$(\mathbf{T} - b\mathbf{I})^{-m} = p(\mathbf{D} - c\mathbf{I})$$

where $p(t)$ is the polynomial

6.27 $$p(t) = \left[-\frac{1}{a}\left(1 + \frac{t}{a} + \cdots + \left(\frac{t}{a}\right)^{n-1}\right)\right]^m \qquad (a = b - c)$$

Observe that, since $(\mathbf{T} - c\mathbf{I})^n = \mathbf{0}$, all powers of $\mathbf{D} - c\mathbf{I}$ exceeding the $(n - 1)$th can be omitted.

THEOREM 6.1 *Let $g(x)$ be a polynomial of degree $<n$, and let b, c be two complex numbers, with $b \neq c$. Then every solution of the differential equation*

6.28 $$(\mathbf{D} - b\mathbf{I})^m f = e^{cx} g(x)$$

has the form

6.29 $$f(x) = e^{cx}\left[-\frac{1}{a}\left(\mathbf{I} + \frac{\mathbf{D}}{a} + \cdots + \left(\frac{\mathbf{D}}{a}\right)^{n-1}\right)\right]^m g(x) + h(x)$$

where $h(x)$ is an element of $P_{m,b}$ and where $a = b - c$. Conversely, (6.29) *is a solution of* (6.28) *for any h in $P_{m,b}$.*

Proof. Let $f_1(x)$ stand for the first function on the right of (6.29), so that

$$f_1(x) = e^{cx} \cdot p(\mathbf{D})g(x)$$

where $p(t)$ is the polynomial

$$p(t) = \left[-\frac{1}{a}\left(1 + \frac{t}{a} + \cdots + \left(\frac{t}{a}\right)^{n-1}\right)\right]^m$$

Then

$$f_1(x) = p(\mathbf{D} - c\mathbf{I})(e^{cx}g(x))$$

by (5.10), and $e^{cx}g(x)$ is in $P_{n,c}$. Therefore, by (6.26),

$$(\mathbf{D} - b\mathbf{I})^m f_1 = (\mathbf{T} - b\mathbf{I})^m f_1 = (\mathbf{T} - b\mathbf{I})^m(\mathbf{T} - b\mathbf{I})^{-m}(e^{cx}gx) = e^{cx}g(x)$$

That is, f_1 is a solution of (6.28). If f is another solution, then† $(\mathbf{D} - b\mathbf{I})^m(f - f_1) = 0$, and so $f - f_1$ is in $P_{m,b}$, by (6.17). That is, $f = f_1 + h$, where h is in $P_{m,b}$. Conversely, if h is in $P_{m,b}$, then $(\mathbf{D} - b\mathbf{I})^m h = 0$, and so $f_1 + h$ is a solution of (6.28). Q.E.D.

The following theorem takes care of (6.28) for the case $c = b$.

THEOREM 6.2 *Let $g(x)$ be a polynomial, and let b be a complex number. Then every solution of the differential equation*

6.30 $$(\mathbf{D} - b\mathbf{I})^m f = e^{bx}g(x)$$

is of the form

6.31 $$f = e^{bx}g_1(x) + h(x)$$

where $g_1(x)$ is a polynomial such that $\mathbf{D}^m g_1 = g$ and where h is in $P_{m,b}$. Conversely every such function f is a solution of (6.30).

Proof. Put $f_1 = e^{bx}g_1(x)$, where g_1 is any polynomial such that $\mathbf{D}^m g_1 = g$. We have

† Strictly speaking, we must assume that f is indefinitely differentiable here in order to apply (6.17). But if we assume that f has only as many derivatives as required for (6.28), namely, m, it is easy to deduce that f must be indefinitely differentiable. For the equation can be written

$$f^{(m)} = a_0 f + a_1 f' + \cdots + a_{m-1}f^{(m-1)} + e^{cx}g(x)$$

where $a_0, \ldots, a_{m-1}$ are constants. Since every term on the right is differentiable, it follows that $f^{(m)}$ is differentiable, and so $f^{(m+1)}$ exists. By a simple induction one sees easily that all the derivatives of f exist.

$$(\mathbf{D} - b\mathbf{I})^m f_1 = (\mathbf{D} - b\mathbf{I})^m(e^{bx}g_1) = e^{bx}\mathbf{D}^m g_1 = e^{bx}g(x)$$

by (5.10), showing that f_1 is a solution of (6.30). Now let f be any solution of (6.30). As in the footnote on page 359, f must be indefinitely differentiable. We have $(\mathbf{D} - b\mathbf{I})^m(f - f_1) = 0$, and so $f - f_1$ is in $P_{m,b}$, by (6.17). Thus $f = f_1 + h$, where h is in $P_{m,b}$. Conversely, if h is in that subspace, then $(\mathbf{D} - b\mathbf{I})^m(f_1 + h) = (\mathbf{D} - b\mathbf{I})f_1 = e^{bx}g(x)$.

In the next section we shall show how repeated applications of these two theorems lead to the solution of (6.6) under certain assumptions concerning the right-hand side.

EXAMPLE 1 Solve $(\mathbf{D} + 2\mathbf{I})^3 f = e^{-x}(1 + x^2)$. This case is covered by Theorem 6.1, with $m = 3$, $b = -2$, $c = -1$, $n = 3$. Then $a = b - c = -1$. Hence, the solution is $f = f_1 + h$, where h is any element of $P_{m,b} = P_{3,-2}$, and where

$$\begin{aligned} f_1 &= e^{cx}\left[-\frac{1}{a}\left(\mathbf{I} + \frac{\mathbf{D}}{a} + \cdots + \left(\frac{\mathbf{D}}{a}\right)^{n-1}\right)\right]^m (1 + x^2) \\ &= e^{-x}[\mathbf{I} - \mathbf{D} + \mathbf{D}^2]^3(1 + x^2) \end{aligned}$$

Since $\mathbf{D}^k(1 + x^2) = 0$ if $k > 2$, we can throw out all powers of $\mathbf{D}$ on the right exceeding 2. Then

$$\begin{aligned} f_1 &= e^{-x}[\mathbf{I} - 3\mathbf{D} + 6\mathbf{D}^2]\,(1 + x^2) \\ &= e^{-x}[(1 + x^2) - 3 \cdot (2x) + 6 \cdot (2)] = e^{-x}(13 - 6x + x^2) \end{aligned}$$

The function h in $P_{3,-2}$ must have the form

$$h = e^{-2x}(a_0 + a_1x + a_2x^2)$$

where a_0, a_1, a_2 are arbitrary constants and so the most general solution of our equation is

$$f = e^{-x}(13 - 6x + x^2) + e^{-2x}(a_0 + a_1x + a_2x^2)$$

It is easily verified that this is a solution, as guaranteed by Theorem 6.1.

EXAMPLE 2 Solve $(\mathbf{D} + 2\mathbf{I})^3 f = e^{-2x}(1 + x^2)$. Here we are in the case of Theorem 6.2, with $m = 3$, $b = -2$, $g(x) = 1 + x^2$. We must find a polynomial $g_1(x)$ such that $\mathbf{D}^3 g_1 = g$. That is easily done by the method of (6.10) and (6.11). Namely, by "antidifferentiating" once we get $\mathbf{D}(x + x^3/3) = 1 + x^2$. Repeating, $\mathbf{D}(x^2/2 + x^4/12) = x + x^3/3$. Repeating again, $\mathbf{D}(x^3/6 + x^5/60) = x^2/2 + x^4/12$. Therefore we can take $g_1(x) = x^3/6 + x^5/60$. By Theorem 6.2 the most general solution of our equation is $f = e^{-2x}g_1 + h$, where h is in $P_{3,-2}$.

Hence,

$$f(x) = e^{-2x}(x^3/6 + x^5/60 + a_0 + a_1x + a_2x^2)$$

where a_0, a_1, a_2 are arbitrary constants.

REMARK. The identity $p(\mathbf{D})(e^{cx}f) = e^{cx}p(\mathbf{D} + c\mathbf{I})f$ of (5.8) can often be used to simplify calculations. Consider for example the computation $(\mathbf{D} + 6\mathbf{I})^4(x^3e^{-7x})$. Take $p(t) = (t + 6)^4$. Then our problem is to work out $p(\mathbf{D})(x^3e^{-7x})$. By the identity, this is equal to $e^{-7x}\, p(\mathbf{D} - 7\mathbf{I})x^3$. Since $p(\mathbf{D} - 7\mathbf{I}) = (\mathbf{D} - 7\mathbf{I} + 6\mathbf{I})^4 = (\mathbf{D} - \mathbf{I})^4$, the answer is

$$\begin{aligned} e^{-7x}(\mathbf{D} - \mathbf{I})^4x^3 &= e^{-7x}\left[\mathbf{D}^4 - \binom{4}{1}\mathbf{D}^3 + \binom{4}{2}\mathbf{D}^2 - \binom{4}{3}\mathbf{D} + \mathbf{I}\right](x^3) \\ &= e^{-7x}(-4 \cdot 6 + 6 \cdot 6x - 4 \cdot 3x^2 + x^3) \\ &= e^{-7x}(-24 + 36x - 12x^2 + x^3) \end{aligned}$$

It is worth comparing this method with the method of direct computation.
Another example: Compute $\mathbf{D}^4[e^{6x}(3x^2 + 2x)]$.

Here take $p(t) = t^4$. The identity reads then

$$\begin{aligned} p(\mathbf{D})[e^{6x}(3x^2 + 2x)] &= e^{6x}p(\mathbf{D} + 6\mathbf{I})(3x^2 + 2x) \\ &= e^{6x}(\mathbf{D} + 6\mathbf{I})^4(3x^2 + 2x) \end{aligned}$$

Using the binomial theorem, we get

$$e^{6x}[\mathbf{D}^4 + \binom{4}{1}6\mathbf{D}^3 + \binom{4}{2}6^2\mathbf{D}^2 + \binom{4}{3}6^3\mathbf{D} + 6^4\mathbf{I}](3x^2 + 2x)$$

from which the $\mathbf{D}^4$ and $\mathbf{D}^3$ terms can be dropped. The result is

$$e^{6x}[6^3\mathbf{D}^2 + 4 \cdot 6^3\mathbf{D} + 6^4\mathbf{I}](3x^2 + 2x) = 6^3e^{6x}(14 + 36x + 18x^2)$$

EXERCISES

Compute the following by the method indicated above.

1. $(\mathbf{D} + 2\mathbf{I})(x^4e^{-3x})$
2. $(\mathbf{D} + 2\mathbf{I})(x^8e^{-3x})$
3. $(\mathbf{D} - 2\mathbf{I})(x^4e^{3x})$
4. $(\mathbf{D} + 2\mathbf{I})^3(x^4)$
5. $\mathbf{D}^3[e^{-8x}(4x^5 + 2x^2 - 1)]$
6. $(\mathbf{D} - \mathbf{I})^5(x^4e^{3x} + x^5e^{-2x})$

Find the most general solutions of the following differential equations:

7. $\mathbf{D}^2f = 3x^2 + 2$
8. $(\mathbf{D} + 2\mathbf{I})^2f = xe^{-2x}$
9. $\mathbf{D}^2f = xe^x$
10. $(\mathbf{D} + 2\mathbf{I})^3f = x$
11. $(\mathbf{D} - 4\mathbf{I})^4f = 0$
12. $(\mathbf{D} - 2\mathbf{I})^2f = x^2e^x + (x^3 + 1)e^{2x}$

7. *Finding particular and general solution*

We now turn to the general linear differential equation with constant coefficients. As was remarked at the beginning of Sec. 6, any such equation can be put in the form

7.1 $$p(\mathbf{D})f = g$$

where p stands for a polynomial:

7.2 $$p(t) = a_0 + a_1t + \cdots + a_{n-1}t^{n-1} + t^n$$

[No loss of generality results from assuming that the highest coefficient a_n of $p(t)$ is 1, for, if it were not, we would merely have to divide (7.1) by a_n.] If $b_1, b_2, \ldots, b_r$ are the *distinct* roots of $p(t)$, then

7.3 $$p(t) = (t - b_1)^{m_1} \cdot (t - b_2)^{m_2} \cdots (t - b_r)^{m_r}$$

where $m_1, m_2, \ldots, m_r$ are positive integers [their sum must be $n = \deg p(t)$]. Then (7.1) can also be written

7.4 $$(\mathbf{D} - b_1\mathbf{I})^{m_1}(\mathbf{D} - b_2\mathbf{I})^{m_2} \cdots (\mathbf{D} - b_r\mathbf{I})^{m_r}f = g$$

since the substitution $t \to \mathbf{D}$ produces a homomorphism of the polynomial ring $\mathbf{C}[t]$ into the ring of endomorphisms of the vector space F of indefinitely differentiable functions. We observe that if $g(x)$ in (7.4) is indefinitely differentiable, then any solution f of the equation must also be indefinitely differentiable (see footnote†, page 359).

We shall consider (7.1) or (7.4) only for special types of functions $g(x)$. Namely, we shall assume that $g(x)$ can be expressed as a sum

7.5 $$g(x) = e^{c_1x}g_1(x) + \cdots + e^{c_sx}g_s(x)$$

where each $g_i(x)$ is a polynomial. Any such $g(x)$ is indefinitely differentiable, as we have seen.

The analysis of (7.1) can be broken into a number of simple steps. First of all, if f and f_0 are two solutions of (7.1), then for their difference $h = f - f_0$ we have $p(\mathbf{D})h = p(\mathbf{D})(f - f_0) = p(\mathbf{D})f - p(\mathbf{D})f_0 = g - g = 0$. Hence h is a solution of the so-called homogeneous equation:

7.6 $$p(\mathbf{D})h = 0$$

In other words, h is in the kernel of the operator $p(\mathbf{D})$. Conversely, if h is a solution of (7.6) and if f_0 is a solution of (7.1), then $f = f_0 + h$ is also a solution of (7.1).

All solutions of (7.1) *are obtained from any given solution* f_0 *by adding to* f_0 *a solution of the homogeneous equation* (7.6).

A specific solution of (7.1) is sometimes called a "particular solution."

The next observation is that, if $g(x)$ has the required form (7.5) and if f_i is a solution of

7.7 $$p(\mathbf{D})f_i = e^{c_ix}g_i(x)$$

for $i = 1, 2, \ldots, s$, then the function $f_0 = f_1 + f_2 + \cdots + f_s$ is a solution of (7.1). For then

$$\begin{aligned} p(\mathbf{D})f_0 &= p(\mathbf{D})(f_1 + \cdots + f_s) \\ &= p(\mathbf{D})f_1 + \cdots + p(\mathbf{D})f_s \\ &= e^{c_1x}g_1(x) + \cdots + e^{c_sx}g_s(x) = g(x) \end{aligned}$$

Therefore, to find a solution of (7.1) with $g(x)$ of the form (7.5), we have only to add up solutions of Eq. (7.7). Each such equation is of the type

7.8 $p(\mathbf{D})f = e^{cx}g(x) \qquad (g(x) \text{ a polynomial})$

Write this as

7.9 $(\mathbf{D} - b_1\mathbf{I})^{m_1}(\mathbf{D} - b_2\mathbf{I})^{m_2} \cdots (\mathbf{D} - b_r\mathbf{I})^{m_r}f = e^{cx}g(x)$

The basic observation here is that if we put

$$v(x) = (\mathbf{D} - b_2\mathbf{I})^{m_2} \cdots (\mathbf{D} - b_r\mathbf{I})^{m_r}f$$

then $(\mathbf{D} - b_1\mathbf{I})^{m_1}v(x) = e^{cx}g(x)$, and $v(x)$ can be found from Theorem 6.1 or 6.2. Repeating this process r times, we finally get f. To do this methodically, set

7.10 $v_{k-1} = (\mathbf{D} - b_k\mathbf{I})^{m_k} \cdots (\mathbf{D} - b_r\mathbf{I})^{m_r}f$

for $k = 0, \ldots, r$. In particular, then, $v_0 = p(\mathbf{D})f = e^{cx}g(x)$, and $v_r = f$. Furthermore, $(\mathbf{D} - b_k\mathbf{I})^{m_k}v_k = v_{k-1}$. Writing this out we get the following series of equations:

7.11
$$\begin{aligned}
(\mathbf{D} - b_1\mathbf{I})^{m_1}v_1 &= v_0 = e^{cx}g(x)\\
(\mathbf{D} - b_2\mathbf{I})^{m_2}v_2 &= v_1\\
(\mathbf{D} - b_3\mathbf{I})^{m_3}v_3 &= v_2\\
\cdots\cdots&\cdots\cdots\\
(\mathbf{D} - b_r\mathbf{I})^{m_r}v_r &= v_{r-1} \qquad (v_r = f)
\end{aligned}$$

These equations are all of the same type, and by solving them successively for $v_1, v_2, \ldots, v_{r-1}, v_r = f$, we finally obtain a solution of (7.9). Starting with the first equation we find v_1 from Theorem 6.1 (or else from Theorem 6.2, if $c = b_1$). In either case, the most general solution must have the form

$$v_1(x) = e^{cx}g_0(x) + e^{b_1x}g_1(x)$$

where g_1 and g_2 are polynomials, where the first term is a particular solution of the equation, and where the second term is a solution of the homogeneous equation $(\mathbf{D} - b_1\mathbf{I})^{m_1}h = 0$. Thus, g_1 has degree $< m_1$. And if $g(x) = 0$, we can take $g_0 = 0$. Then the second equation of (7.11) is

$$(\mathbf{D} - b_2\mathbf{I})^{m_2}v_2 = e^{cx}g_0(x) + e^{b_1x}g_1(x)$$

and it can be solved by Theorem 6.1 (or by Theorem 6.2 if $c = b_2$), the two terms on the right being treated separately. It follows then that the most general solution is of the form

$$v_2 = e^{cx}h_0(x) + e^{b_1x}h_1(x) + e^{b_2x}h_2(x)$$

where the $h_i(x)$ are polynomials, with deg $h_1 < m_1$ and deg $h_2 < m_2$. Here the first term stands for a particular solution of the equation

$$(\mathbf{D} - b_2\mathbf{I})^{m_2}v = e^{cx}g_0(x)$$

and may be taken as zero if $g_0 = 0$.

Continuing in this way with the third equation, etc., we finally arrive at $v_r = f$, and we find that f must have the form

7.12 $$f = e^{cx}w_0(x) + e^{b_1x}w_1(x) + \cdots + e^{b_rx}w_r(x)$$

where $w_0, w_1, \ldots, w_r$ are polynomials, with $\deg w_1 < m_1$, $\deg w_2 < m_2, \ldots,$ $\deg w_r < m_r$, and where the first term is a particular solution of the equation $p(\mathbf{D})f = e^{cx}g(x)$. If $g(x) = 0$, then we can assume that $w_0(x) = 0$. Hence we have the following theorem:

THEOREM 7.1 *The most general solution h of the homogeneous equation* (7.6) *has the form*

7.13 $$h = h_1 + h_2 + \cdots + h_r$$

where h_i is an element of P_{m_i,b_i} $(i = 1, \ldots, r)$. That is, $h_i = e^{c_ix} \times$ (polynomial of degree $< m_i$). Any such function is a solution of (7.6).

Collecting our other results above, we can state the theorem as follows:

THEOREM 7.2 *Every solution of the differential equation* (7.1) *is obtained from any particular solution f_0 by adding to it a solution h of the homogeneous equation. If the right member g of* (7.1) *has the form* (7.5), *then* (7.1) *has a solution, and every solution must again be a sum of polynomials multiplied by exponentials. A particular solution can be obtained by repeated applications of Theorems* 6.1 *and* 6.2.

REMARK 1. If c in (7.8) is different from all the b's, then only Theorem 6.1 is used in solving (7.11). It follows from that theorem that one can find a particular solution $e^{cx}w_0(x)$ of (7.8) in which $\deg w_0 = \deg g$. This useful observation is the basis for the method of *undetermined coefficients*, which amounts to writing down a polynomial of the proper degree, with literal coefficients, for w_0 and then determining the coefficients so as to satisfy the differential equation. The same method is available even if c is equal to one of the b's, say, $c = b_1$. In solving the first equation of (7.11) it is necessary to use Theorem 6.2. One can affirm then that only the polynomial called $g_0(x)$ above in v_1 can be taken to have degree equal to $m_1 + \deg g(x)$. The remaining equations in (7.11) will then require only Theorem 6.1 and, as before, we conclude that a particular solution $e^{cx}w_0(x)$ of (7.8) can be found with $\deg w_0 = m_1 + \deg g(x)$. An example of the method of undetermined coefficients is given below. It is often swifter than Theorems 6.1 and 6.2.

REMARK 2. The general solution of (7.1) involves an arbitrary solution h of the homogeneous equation (7.6). From Theorem 7.1 it follows that h contains $m_1 + m_2 + \cdots + m_r = n$ arbitrary constants, namely, the coefficients appearing in the polynomials. Thus the general solution of (7.1) contains n constants which can be specified at will. In most applications of differential equations, those constants, usually called *constants of integration*, must be determined in such a way that the corresponding solution fits other data. An important problem of this type—the initial-value problem—involves determining the constants of integration so that $f(x), f'(x), \ldots, f^{(n-1)}(x)$ will all have prescribed values for some given value of x, say x_0. Then f is required to satisfy n equations $f(x_0) = y_0$, $f'(x_0) = y_1, \ldots, f^{(n-1)}(x_0) = y_{n-1}$, where $y_0, y_1, \ldots, y_{n-1}$ are given numbers. It is not hard to see that these equations enable one to determine the constants of integration uniquely.

EXAMPLE 1 Solve $\dfrac{d^2f}{dx^2} - \dfrac{3df}{dx} + 2f = e^x$. Our equation is $p(\mathbf{D})f = e^x$, with $p(t) = t^2 - 3t + 2 = (t-1)(t-2)$. In the notation of (7.9), $b_1 = 1$, $b_2 = 2$, $c = 1$, $g(x) = 1$. The system (7.11) is

$$(\mathbf{D} - \mathbf{I})v_1 = e^x$$
$$(\mathbf{D} - 2\mathbf{I})v_2 = v_1$$

We need only find particular solutions of these equations, since the general solution of our problem is then obtained by adding on our arbitrary solution of $p(\mathbf{D})h = 0$. To solve the first equation we use Theorem 6.2, which tells us that a solution of it is $e^x \cdot g_1(x)$, where $g_1(x)$ is any polynomial such that $\mathbf{D}g_1 = 1$. We take $g_1 = x$, hence $v_1 = xe^x$. The second equation is $(\mathbf{D} - 2\mathbf{I})v_2 = xe^x$. By Theorem 6.1, Eq. (6.29), a particular solution is $v_2 = e^x[-\mathbf{I} - \mathbf{D}]x = -e^x \cdot (x+1)$. By (7.11), v_2 is a solution of our equation, as is easily verified. By Theorems 7.1 and 7.2, the general solution is

$$f = -e^x(x+1) + ae^x + be^{2x}$$

where a, b are arbitrary constants. Writing $a = a' - 1$, we have

$$f = -xe^x + a'e^x + be^{2x}$$

where a', b are arbitrary.

If f is required to satisfy the initial conditions $f(0) = 1$, $f'(0) = 0$, then we get

$$f(0) = a' + b = 1$$
$$f'(0) = -1 + a' + 2b = 0$$

whence $b = 0$, $a' = 1$. The required solution is $-xe^x + e^x$.

EXAMPLE 2 Solve $f''' - 3f' + 2f = xe^{-x} + x^2$. The equation is $p(\mathbf{D})f = 0$, with $p(t) = t^3 - 3t + 2 = (t-1)^2(t+2)$. According to our general method we first find *particular* solutions of

7.14 $$(\mathbf{D} - \mathbf{I})^2(\mathbf{D} + 2\mathbf{I})f_1 = xe^{-x}$$

and

7.15 $$(\mathbf{D} - \mathbf{I})^2(\mathbf{D} + 2\mathbf{I})f_2 = x^2$$

For the first one we have, in the notation of (7.9), $b_1 = 1$, $b_2 = -2$, $c = -1$. The system (7.11) becomes

$$(\mathbf{D} - \mathbf{I})^2 v_1 = xe^{-x}$$
$$(\mathbf{D} - 2\mathbf{I})v_2 = v_1$$

From (6.29) we can take $v_1 = e^{-x}[-\frac{1}{2}(\mathbf{I} + \mathbf{D}/2)]^2x = \frac{1}{4}e^{-x}[\mathbf{I} + \mathbf{D} + \mathbf{D}^2/4]x = \frac{1}{4}e^{-x}(x+1)$. Applying (6.29) again, we get

$$\begin{aligned} v_2 &= e^{-x}[\mathbf{I} - \mathbf{D}]\left(\frac{x+1}{4}\right) \\ &= \tfrac{1}{4}xe^{-x} \end{aligned}$$

This is a particular solution of (7.14).

For (7.15) we have $b_1 = 1$, $b_2 = -2$, $c = 0$, $g(x) = x^2$, in the notation of (7.9). The system (7.11) is

$$\begin{aligned} (\mathbf{D} - \mathbf{I})^2u_1 &= x^2 \\ (\mathbf{D} + 2\mathbf{I})u_2 &= u \end{aligned}$$

By (6.29) we can take $u_1 = [-(\mathbf{I} + \mathbf{D} + \mathbf{D}^2)]^2(x^2) = [\mathbf{I} + 2\mathbf{D} + 3\mathbf{D}^2](x^2) = x^2 + 4x + 6$. Applying (6.29) to the equation for u_2, we obtain similarly $u_2 = [\frac{1}{2} \cdot (\mathbf{I} - \mathbf{D}/2 + \mathbf{D}^2/4)](x^2 + 4x + 6) = \frac{1}{2}(x^2 + 3x + 9/2)$, which is a particular solution of (7.15). The general solution of the original equation is therefore

$$f(x) = \tfrac{1}{4}xe^{-x} + \tfrac{1}{2}(x^2 + 3x + 9/2) + e^x(ax + b) + ce^{-2x}$$

where a, b, c are arbitrary constants.

To solve the equation by the method of undetermined coefficients, we infer from Remark 1 that the equation $f''' - 3f' + 2f = xe^{-x}$ must have a particular solution of the form $y_1 = (a_0 + a_1x)e^{-x}$. Substituting this in the differential equation one easily finds that $a_0 = 0$, $a_1 = \frac{1}{4}$. Similarly, the equation $f''' - 3f' + 2f = x^2$ must have a particular solution of the form $y_2 = c_0 + c_1x + c_2x^2$. Substituting into the equation one obtains immediately $c_0 = \frac{9}{4}$, $c_1 = \frac{3}{2}$, $c_2 = \frac{1}{2}$.

EXAMPLE 3 Solve $f'' + f = 0$. Our equation is $(\mathbf{D}^2 + \mathbf{I})f = 0$, or $(\mathbf{D} + i\mathbf{I})(\mathbf{D} - i\mathbf{I})f = 0$. By Theorem 7.1 the general solution is $f = ae^{-ix} + be^{ix}$, where a, b are arbitrary constants.

EXERCISES

Find the general solutions of the following differential equations. Use both the method of Theorem 6.1 (or 6.2) and the method of undetermined coefficients to find particular solutions in Exercises 7 to 10.

1. $\dfrac{df}{dx} + 3f = 0$
2. $\dfrac{df}{dx} + 3f = 1$
3. $\dfrac{df}{dx} + 3f = x.$
4. $\dfrac{df}{dx} + 3f = e^{2x}$
5. $\dfrac{df}{dx} + 3f = e^{-3x}$
6. $\dfrac{d^2J}{dx^2} - 2\dfrac{df}{dx} + f = e^{-x}$
7. $\dfrac{d^2f}{dx^2} - 2\dfrac{df}{dx} + f = e^x$
8. $\dfrac{d^2f}{dx^2} - 2\dfrac{df}{dx} - 3f = x^3e^{-x}$

9. $\dfrac{d^3f}{dx^3} + 3\dfrac{d^2f}{dx^2} + 3\dfrac{df}{dx} + f = x^2e^x + xe^{-x}$

10. $\dfrac{d^2f}{dx^2} + f = 1 + 2e^x + ee^{-x}$

11. $f'' + f = 1 + 2e^x + 3e^{-x}$

12. $\dfrac{d^4f}{dx^4} = x^2e^{2x} + e^{ix} + x^4 + x^2 + 1$

13. $f'' - 3f' + 2f = (4x^4 + 3x^2 + 1)e^x + x^7e^{-x} + 2$

Find the solution of this satisfying the initial conditions

$$f(0) = 1, f'(0) = 0, f''(0) = -1$$

14. Find the solution of Exercise 12 satisfying the initial conditions

$$f(0) = 0, f'(0) = 0, f''(0) = 0, f'''(0) = 1$$

8. *Trigonometric functions*

In the preceding section we have seen how to solve any linear differential equation (7.1) with constant coefficients, provided that the function $g(x)$ on the right is a sum of functions

8.1 $$g(x) = e^{c_1x}g_1(x) + \cdots + e^{c_sx}g_s(x)$$

where each $g_1(x)$ is a polynomial. The sum and product of two functions of this type are again of the same type, and it follows easily that all functions of the type (8.1) form a subring E of the ring F of indefinitely differentiable complex-valued functions on **R**. E is also a subspace of F regarded as a vector space over **C**.

We wish to point out here that the ring E contains the functions $\sin ax$, $\cos ax$ (a any complex number); consequently E contains any function which can be built from polynomials and from $\sin ax$, $\cos bx$, e^{cx} by any finite number of additions, subtractions, and products.

We recall (Sec. 4, Chap. 5) that the exponential function is defined by the infinite series

$$e^z = \sum_{n=0}^{\infty} \frac{z^n}{n!} = 1 + z + \frac{z^2}{2!} + \frac{z^3}{3!} + \cdots$$

for any complex number z. Then

$$\begin{aligned} e^{iz} &= 1 + iz + \frac{(iz)^2}{2!} + \frac{(iz)^3}{3!} + \cdots \\ &= \left(1 - \frac{z^2}{2!} + \frac{z^4}{4!} - \frac{z^6}{6!} \pm \cdots\right) + i\left(z - \frac{z^3}{3!} + \frac{z^5}{5!} - \frac{z^7}{7!} \pm \cdots\right) \end{aligned}$$

It is known from calculus† that

† In calculus these formulas are proved for real z. The series converge for all z, real or not, and are used to define $\cos z$ and $\sin z$ for complex z.

$$\cos z = 1 - \frac{z^2}{2!} + \frac{z^4}{4!} - \frac{z^6}{6!} \pm \cdots$$

$$\sin z = z - \frac{z^3}{3!} + \frac{z^5}{5!} - \frac{z^7}{7!} \pm \cdots$$

Comparing the results, we have Euler's formula

$$e^{iz} = \cos z + i \sin z$$

Replacing z by $-z$ and observing that $\cos(-z) = \cos z$ and $\sin(-z) = -\sin z$, we have also

$$e^{-iz} = \cos z - i \sin z$$

Adding the two formulas, we obtain

8.2 $$\cos z = \tfrac{1}{2}(e^{iz} + e^{-iz})$$

Subtracting the two formulas gives us

8.3 $$\sin z = \frac{1}{2i}(e^{iz} - e^{-iz})$$

Putting ax for z, a being any complex numbers:

8.4 $$\cos ax = \frac{1}{2}(e^{iax} + e^{-iax})$$
$$\sin ax = \frac{1}{2i}(e^{iax} - e^{-iax})$$

This shows that $\cos ax$ and $\sin ax$ are indeed in the ring E of all functions of the form (8.1). From (5.2) applied to (8.4) we have the differentiation formulas

8.5 $$\mathbf{D} \cos ax = -a \sin ax$$
$$\mathbf{D} \sin ax = a \cos ax$$

Thus $\mathbf{D}^2 \cos ax = \mathbf{D}(-a \sin ax) = -a^2 \cos ax$. Similarly, $\mathbf{D}^2 \sin ax = a^2 \sin ax$. In particular, $\sin x$ and $\cos x$ are both solutions of the differential equation $f'' + f = 0$. From Example 3, Sec. 7, every solution of this equation must be of the form $ae^{-ix} + be^{ix}$, which we can also write $a(\cos x - i \sin x) + b(\cos x + i \sin x) = a' \cos x + b' \sin x$, where $a' = a + b$ and $b' = i(b - a)$.

Since the differential equation (7.1) can be solved by the methods presented above for any function $g(x)$ in the ring E, it follows in particular that (7.1) can be solved if the right member $g(x)$ is any product of polynomials, sines, cosines, and exponentials.

EXAMPLE 1 Solve $f' - 3f = \sin x$. We can write this as $f' - 3f = (1/2i)e^{ix} - (1/2i)e^{-ix}$. It is obvious by inspection that ae^{ix} should be a particular solution of the equation $f' - 3f = (1/2i)e^{ix}$ for suitable a. Substituting it in we find $a = (-1 + 3i)/20$. Similarly, a particular solution of the equation $f' - 3f = (1/2i)e^{-ix}$ is $[(-1 - 3i)/20]e^{-ix}$. Hence, a particular solution of $f' - 3f = \sin x$ is

$$\frac{-1+3i}{20}e^{ix} - \frac{1+3i}{20}e^{-ix}$$
$$= \tfrac{1}{20}\,[(-1+3i)(\cos x + i\sin x) - (1+3i)(\cos x - i \sin x)]$$
$$= \tfrac{1}{20}\,(-2\cos x - 6\sin x) = -\tfrac{1}{10}\cos x - \tfrac{3}{10}\sin x$$

A result of this form was rather obvious to begin with, in view of the formulas (8.5). It would therefore have been possible to avoid imaginary numbers altogether by trying to find a particular solution of the form $a \cos x + b \sin x$. Substitution in the equation would have led at once to the answer above. The general solution of our equation is

$$f = -\tfrac{1}{10}\cos x - \tfrac{3}{10}\sin x + ce^{3x}$$

c an arbitrary constant.

EXAMPLE 2 Solve $f''' - 8f = x^2 \sin x \cos 2x$. The methodical procedure is to write the equation in the form

8.6
$$(\mathbf{D}^3 - 8\mathbf{I})f = x^2 \cdot \frac{1}{2i}(e^{ix} - e^{-ix}) \cdot \frac{1}{2}(e^{2ix} + e^{-2ix})$$
$$= \frac{1}{4i}[x^2e^{3ix} - x^2e^{-3ix} + x^2e^{-ix} - x^2e^{ix}]$$

The operator on the left factors into

$$(\mathbf{D} - 2\mathbf{I})(\mathbf{D} - \alpha\mathbf{I})(\mathbf{D} - \beta\mathbf{I}) = p(\mathbf{D})$$

where $\alpha = -\sqrt{3} + i$, $\beta = -\sqrt{3} - i$. We can now proceed as in Sec. 7. For example, to find a particular solution of $p(\mathbf{D})f_1 = (1/4i)x^2e^{3ix}$, the system (7.11) becomes

$$(\mathbf{D} - 2\mathbf{I})v_1 = \frac{1}{4i}x^2e^{3ix}$$
$$(\mathbf{D} - \alpha\mathbf{I})v_2 = v_1$$
$$(\mathbf{D} - \beta\mathbf{I})v_3 = v_2$$

A solution $f_1 = v_3$ is obtained by repeated applications of the formula (6.27). Doing the same thing for the other three terms on the right of our Eq. (8.6), we obtain finally a particular solution of (8.6). We omit the details.

EXERCISES

Find the general solution: In all cases express the answer without any imaginary exponentials.

1. $\dfrac{d^2f}{dx^2} - f = \cos x + \sin x$
2. $\dfrac{d^2f}{dx^2} - f = e^x \cos x$
3. $\dfrac{df}{dx} = xe^x \sin x$
4. $\dfrac{df}{dx} - f = e^x \cos 2x$
5. $\dfrac{d^2f}{dx^2} + f = \sin x + \sin^3 x$
6. $\dfrac{df}{dx} = \sin^n x$
7. $\dfrac{df}{dx} = \cos^n x$
8. $\dfrac{d^2f}{dx^2} + f = e^x \cos 3x$
9. $\dfrac{d^2f}{dx^2} + if = e^x$
10. $\dfrac{d^nf}{dx^n} - 2f = 2 \sin x$

9. Systems of equations

Virtually no knowledge of calculus was required in the foregoing sections. Here we shall have to assume that the reader has some acquaintance with differential and integral calculus. In this section we shall take up briefly a topic closely related to the homogeneous equation (7.6), but considerably more general.

Let $a_{ij}(t)$ be complex-valued functions on **R** for $i, j = 1, 2, \ldots, n$ (we use t rather than x as independent variable here), and consider the system of equations

9.1
$$\begin{aligned}
\frac{dx_1}{dt} &= a_{11}x_1 + a_{12}x_2 + \cdots + a_{1n}x_n \\
\frac{dx_2}{dt} &= a_{21}x_1 + a_{22}x_2 + \cdots + a_{2n}x_n \\
&\cdots\cdots\cdots\cdots\cdots\cdots \\
\frac{dx_n}{dt} &= a_{n1}x_1 + a_{n2}x_2 + \cdots + a_{nn}x_n
\end{aligned}$$

By a solution of this system we shall mean an n-tuple of complex-valued differentiable functions $x_1(t), \ldots, x_n(t)$ on **R** such that (9.1) holds for all values t. If $n = 1$, then the system (9.1) reduces to the simple equation

$$\frac{dx}{dt} = ax$$

This can be solved as follows, if $a(t)$ is continuous:

$$\frac{dx}{x} = a\,dt$$

whence

$$\log x = \int a\,dt$$

or

$$x(t) = b \cdot e^{\int a\,dt}$$

b denoting an arbitrary constant. We shall see that an analogous result holds for $n > 1$ under certain assumptions concerning the matrix† $\mathbf{a}(t) = (a_{ij}(t))$ whose coefficients appear in (9.1).

For each real number t, $\mathbf{a}(t)$ is an $n \times n$ matrix with complex coefficients, and so $\mathbf{a}$ is a mapping $\mathbf{R} \to \mathbf{C}_{n,n}$, the set of all $n \times n$ matrices with complex coefficients (we write $\mathbf{C}_{n,n}$ instead of $\mathbf{C}^n{}_n$, since we are using lower indices). Similarly, $\mathbf{x}(t) = (x_1(t), x_2(t), \ldots, x_n(t))$ is a mapping from $\mathbf{R}$ to the vector space of n-tuples of complex numbers. We call $\mathbf{a}(t)$ a matrix-valued function on $\mathbf{R}$, and we call $\mathbf{x}(t)$ a vector-valued function on $\mathbf{R}$.

The matrix-valued function $\mathbf{a}(t)$ is called *differentiable* if all its coefficients $a_{ij}(t)$ are differentiable. We denote by $d\mathbf{a}/dt$ the matrix whose coefficients are da_{ij}/dt.

Similarly, the vector-valued function $\mathbf{x}(t)$ is called *differentiable* if all its coefficients $x_j(t)$ are differentiable, and we write $d\mathbf{x}/dt = (dx/dt, \ldots, dx_n/dt)$. Throughout this section we consider $\mathbf{x}$, $d\mathbf{x}/dt$, etc., as *column* vectors, although we shall often write them as row vectors for compactness of notation. From the definition of matrix multiplication the system (9.1) can be written

9.2 $$d\mathbf{x}/dt = \mathbf{a}\mathbf{x}$$

Just as we can define the derivative of a matrix-valued or vector-valued function, we can define the integral. Namely, we put

$$\int_{t_1}^{t_2} \mathbf{a}(t)\, dt = \left(\int_{t_1}^{t_2} a_{ij}(t)\, dt\right)$$

that is, $\int \mathbf{a}\, dt$ is the matrix whose entries are $\int a_{ij}dt$, this for any continuous matrix-valued function (i.e., whose coefficients are continuous). Similarly if $\mathbf{x}(t)$ is a continuous vector-valued function, we define

$$\int_{t_1}^{t_2} \mathbf{x}\, dt$$

to be the vector whose components are

$$\int_{t_1}^{t_2} x_i\, dt \qquad (i = 1, \ldots, n)$$

It is possible to define the *exponential* of any square *matrix* with complex coefficients. Thus, if $\mathbf{b}$ is such a matrix, then the finite sum

$$\mathbf{I} + \mathbf{b} + \frac{1}{2!}\mathbf{b}^2 + \cdots + \frac{1}{m!}\mathbf{b}^m$$

is certainly defined. It can be shown that the coefficients of this matrix, for $m = 1, 2, 3, \ldots$, form Cauchy sequences and consequently converge as $m \to \infty$

† We shall depart from our index conventions here. Only lower indices will be used, and in the matrix (a_{ij}) the first subscript is the row index, the second subscript is the column index.

to some limit. The matrix having these limiting values as coefficients is denoted by $e^{\mathbf{b}}$. Just as for 1×1 matrices (scalars), we write

9.3 $$e^{\mathbf{b}} = \mathbf{I} + \mathbf{b} + \frac{1}{2!}\mathbf{b}^2 + \cdots + \frac{1}{m!}\mathbf{b}^m + \cdots$$

To sketch how this can be worked out,† consider a 2×2 matrix $\mathbf{b}$ whose eigenvalues (Chap. 11) are α, β. Then the characteristic polynomial $\varphi(y)$ of $\mathbf{b}$ is $(y - \alpha)(y - \beta)$. Divide this polynomial into y^m. From the division algorithm we get a remainder of degree ≤ 1, or else zero. Suppose, say,

9.4 $$y^m = q(y) \cdot (y - \alpha)(y - \beta) + cy + d$$

Putting successively $y = \alpha$, $y = \beta$ in this equation we find

$$\alpha^m = c\alpha + d$$
$$\beta^m = c\beta + d$$

Solving for c and d, we obtain $c = (\alpha^m - \beta^m)/(\alpha - \beta)$ and $d = (\beta\alpha^m - \alpha\beta^m)/(\beta - \alpha)$, assuming $\alpha \neq \beta$, of course. Substituting these values in (9.4) and putting $\mathbf{b}$ for y, there results

9.5 $$\mathbf{b}^m = \frac{\alpha^m - \beta^m}{\alpha - \beta} \cdot \mathbf{b} + \frac{\beta\alpha^m - \alpha\beta^m}{\beta - \alpha}\mathbf{I}$$

by the Cayley-Hamilton theorem.‡ Putting this in (9.3), there results

$$e^{\mathbf{b}} = \sum_{n=0}^{\infty} \frac{\mathbf{b}^m}{m!} = \frac{1}{\alpha - \beta} \cdot \sum_{n=0}^{\infty} \frac{1}{m!}\,[(\alpha^m - \beta^m)\,\mathbf{b} - (\beta\alpha^m - \alpha\beta^m)\,\mathbf{I}]$$
$$= \frac{1}{\alpha - \beta} \cdot (e^{\alpha} - e^{\beta}) \cdot \mathbf{b} - \left(\frac{\beta}{\alpha - \beta}e^{\alpha} - \frac{\alpha}{\alpha - \beta}e^{\beta}\right) \cdot \mathbf{I}$$

For example, for the matrix $\begin{pmatrix} 1 & 2 \\ 0 & -1 \end{pmatrix}$ the eigenvalues are ± 1, and so

$$e^{\mathbf{b}} = \tfrac{1}{2}(e - e^{-1}) \cdot \begin{pmatrix} 1 & 2 \\ 0 & -1 \end{pmatrix} + \tfrac{1}{2}(e + e^{-1})\begin{pmatrix} 1 & 0 \\ 0 & 1 \end{pmatrix}$$
$$= \begin{pmatrix} e & e - \dfrac{1}{e} \\ 0 & \dfrac{1}{e} \end{pmatrix}$$

Returning to the general case of $n \times n$ matrices, from (9.3) we see that $e^{\mathbf{I}} = e \cdot \mathbf{I}$, $e^{\mathbf{0}} = \mathbf{I}$. One can prove (see exercises) that

9.6 $$e^{\mathbf{b}} \cdot e^{\mathbf{c}} = e^{\mathbf{b}+\mathbf{c}} \qquad \text{if } \mathbf{bc} = \mathbf{cb}$$

9.7 $e^{\mathbf{b}}$ *is nonsingular for any* $\mathbf{b}$

† Another method is described in the exercises.
‡ This gives an indication of how to make the computations involved in Theorem 4.5, Chap. 11.

9.8 *If* $\mathbf{b}(t)$ *is a differentiable matrix-valued function on* **R**, *then*

$$\frac{d}{dt}e^{\mathbf{b}(t)} = \frac{d\mathbf{b}}{dt}\cdot e^{\mathbf{b}(t)}$$

provided $\mathbf{b}(t_1)\mathbf{b}(t_2) = \mathbf{b}(t_2)\mathbf{b}(t_1)$ *for every pair of real numbers* t_1, t_2.

9.9 *If* $\mathbf{a}(t)$ *is a continuous matrix-valued function on* **R** *such that* $\mathbf{a}(t_1)\mathbf{a}(t_2) = \mathbf{a}(t_2)\mathbf{a}(t_1)$ *for all* t_1, t_2, *then for the matrix*

$$\mathbf{b}^{(t)} = \int_{t_0}^{t}\mathbf{a}(t)\,dt$$

we have $\mathbf{b}(t_1)\mathbf{b}(t_2) = \mathbf{b}(t_2)\mathbf{b}(t_1)$ *for all* t_1, t_2; *and* $d\mathbf{b}/dt = \mathbf{a}$.

THEOREM 9.1 *Let* $\mathbf{a}(t)$ *be a continuous* $n \times n$ *matrix-valued function on* **R** *such that*

9.10 $$\mathbf{a}(t_1)\mathbf{a}(t_2) = \mathbf{a}(t_2)\mathbf{a}(t_1)$$

for all real numbers t_1, t_2. *Let* $\mathbf{c} = (c_1, \ldots, c_n)$ *be an n-tuple of complex numbers. Then the system of differential equations*

9.11 $$d\mathbf{x}/dt = \mathbf{ax}$$

(where $\mathbf{x}$ *is regarded as a column vector) has as solution the vector-valued function* $\mathbf{x}(t)$ *given by*

9.12 $$\mathbf{x}(t) = \left(e^{\int_{t_0}^{t}\mathbf{a}\,dt}\right)\cdot\mathbf{c}$$

and, moreover, $\mathbf{x}(t_0) = \mathbf{c}$.

For let $\mathbf{u}(t)$ denote the exponential in (9.12), so that

9.13 $$\mathbf{x} = \mathbf{u}\cdot\mathbf{c}$$

Then for the ith component of $\mathbf{x}$ we have

$$x_i = \sum_{j=1}^{n} u_{ij}\cdot c_j$$

whence

$$dx_i/dt = \sum_{j=1}^{n}\left(\frac{du_{ij}}{dt}\right)c_j$$

showing that

9.14 $$d\mathbf{x}/dt = (d\mathbf{u}/dt)\cdot\mathbf{c}$$

By (9.8) we have

$$d\mathbf{u}/dt = \left(\frac{d}{dt}\int_0^t\mathbf{a}\,dt\right)\cdot\mathbf{u}$$

and by (9.9) this is

$$d\mathbf{u}/dt = \mathbf{au}$$

Hence, from (9.13) and (9.14),

$$d\mathbf{x}/dt = \mathbf{auc} = \mathbf{ax}$$

showing that $\mathbf{x}$ is a solution of (9.11). Putting $t = t_0$ in (9.12) gives us $\mathbf{x}(t_0) = e^{\mathbf{o}} \cdot \mathbf{c} = \mathbf{I} \cdot \mathbf{c} = \mathbf{c}$.

EXAMPLE 1 Consider the system (9.10), assuming that the coefficients a_{ij} are constants. That is, the matrix-valued function $\mathbf{a}$ is constant on $\mathbf{R}$. The hypotheses (9.10) are clearly satisfied. The solution (9.12) is very simple. For

$$\int_{t_0}^{t} \mathbf{a}\, dt = (t - t_0) \cdot \mathbf{a}$$

clearly, and so (9.12) reduces to

$$\mathbf{x} = e^{(t-t_0)\mathbf{a}} \cdot \mathbf{c}$$

A somewhat different method is as follows. Suppose that $\mathbf{a}$ has n linearly independent eigenvectors $\mathbf{u}_1, \ldots, \mathbf{u}_n$, with corresponding eigenvalues $p_1, \ldots, p_n$ (this is so if the eigenvalues are distinct, or if $\mathbf{a}$ is symmetric and real, etc.). Expand the (unknown) vector $\mathbf{x}$ in terms of the vectors $\mathbf{u}_i$, say

$$\mathbf{x}(t) = \sum_{i=1}^{n} y_i(t) \cdot \mathbf{u}_i$$

Then

$$\frac{d\mathbf{x}}{dt} = \sum_{i=1}^{n} \frac{dy_i}{dt} \cdot \mathbf{u}_i$$

and

$$\mathbf{ax} = \sum_{i=1}^{n} y_i(t) \cdot \mathbf{au}_i = \sum_{i=1}^{n} p_i y_i \mathbf{u}_i$$

Equating these we obtain

$$\frac{dy_i}{dt} = p_i y_i \qquad (i = 1, \ldots, n)$$

whence

$$y_i = c_i e^{p_i t}$$

the c_i being arbitrary constants. Hence as a solution $\mathbf{x}$ we get

$$\mathbf{x} = \sum_{i=1}^{n} c_i e^{p_i t} \mathbf{u}_i$$

EXAMPLE 2 Consider a homogeneous linear equation

9.15 $$\frac{d^n x}{dt^n} + a_{n-1}\frac{d^{n-1}x}{dt^{n-1}} + \cdots + a_1\frac{dx}{dt} + a_0 x = 0$$

for $x(t)$. Define $x_0, x_1, \ldots, x_{n-1}$ by

$$x_k = \frac{d^k x}{dt^k} \qquad x_0 = x$$

Then we have

9.16 $$\begin{aligned} \frac{dx_0}{dt} &= x_1 \\ \frac{dx_1}{dt} &= x_2 \\ &\cdots\cdots \\ \frac{dx_{n-1}}{dt} &= -a_0x_0 - a_1x_1 - \cdots - a_{n-1}x_{n-1} \end{aligned}$$

A solution of (9.15) gives a solution of the system (9.16). Conversely, as is easily seen, if $\mathbf{x} = (x_0, x_1, \ldots, x_{n-1})$ is a solution of (9.16), then x_0 is a solution of (9.15). If the coefficients of (9.15) are constants, then a solution can be obtained as in Example 1.

EXAMPLE 3 Consider the system

$$\begin{aligned} dx_1/dt &= -x_2 \\ dx_2/dt &= x_1 \end{aligned}$$

Here the matrix $\mathbf{a}$ is

$$\mathbf{a} = \begin{pmatrix} 0 & -1 \\ 1 & 0 \end{pmatrix}$$

We have $\mathbf{a}^2 = -\mathbf{I}$, $\mathbf{a}^3 = -\mathbf{a}$, $\mathbf{a}^4 = \mathbf{I}$, etc. Hence, referring to Example 1,

$$\begin{aligned} e^{t\mathbf{a}} &= \mathbf{I} + t\mathbf{a} + \frac{1}{2!}t^2\mathbf{a}^2 + \frac{1}{3!}t^3\mathbf{a}^3 + \frac{1}{4!}t^4\mathbf{a}^4 + \cdots \\ &= \mathbf{I} + t\mathbf{a} - \frac{1}{2!}t^2\mathbf{I} - \frac{1}{3!}t^3\mathbf{a} + \frac{1}{4!}t^4\mathbf{I} \pm \cdots \\ &= \left(1 - \frac{1}{2!}t^2 + \frac{1}{4!}t^4 - + \cdots\right)\mathbf{I} + \left(t - \frac{1}{3!}t^3 + \frac{1}{5!}t^5 - + \cdots\right)\mathbf{a} \\ &= (\cos t)\mathbf{I} + (\sin t)\mathbf{a} \end{aligned}$$

Hence, as in Example 1, we get a solution $\mathbf{x}(t) = (x_1, x_2)$ satisfying the initial condition $\mathbf{x}(0) = \mathbf{c}$ by putting

$$\mathbf{x} = e^{t\mathbf{a}} \cdot \mathbf{c} = [(\cos t)\mathbf{I} + (\sin t)\mathbf{a}]\,\mathbf{c}$$

or

$$\begin{pmatrix} x_1 \\ x_2 \end{pmatrix} = \begin{pmatrix} \cos t & -\sin t \\ \sin t & \cos t \end{pmatrix} \begin{pmatrix} c_1 \\ c_2 \end{pmatrix}$$

or

$$x_1 = c_1 \cos t - c_2 \sin t$$
$$x_2 = c_1 \sin t + c_2 \cos t$$

where c_1, c_2 are arbitrary constants.

EXERCISES

1. Let E denote the vector space of all $n \times n$ matrices with real coefficients. We make E into a euclidean vector space by defining the "length" of a matrix $\mathbf{a} = (a_{ij})$ in E to be

$$|\mathbf{a}| = \left(\sum_{i,j=1}^{n} a_{ij}^2 \right)^{1/2}$$

Prove that for any two elements $\mathbf{a}$, $\mathbf{b}$ in E,

$$|\mathbf{a} \cdot \mathbf{b}| \leq (2n)^{1/2} \cdot |\mathbf{a}| \cdot |\mathbf{b}|$$

[Hint: If $c_1, \ldots, c_n$ are real numbers with $c_1 \geq c_2 \geq \cdots \geq c_n > 0$, we have $\left(\sum_1^n c_i \right)^2 \leq 2n \sum_1^n c_i^2$, by induction.]

2. Show that

$$|\mathbf{a}^k| \leq (2n)^{k/2} \cdot |\mathbf{a}|^k$$

for any element $\mathbf{a}$ of E and any integer $k \geq 0$.

***3.** For any matrix $\mathbf{a}$ in E show that the sequence $\mathbf{s}_1, \mathbf{s}_2, \mathbf{s}_3, \ldots, \mathbf{s}_k, \ldots$, with

$$\mathbf{s}_k = \mathbf{I} + \mathbf{a} + \frac{1}{2!}\mathbf{a}^2 + \cdots + \frac{1}{k!}\mathbf{a}^k$$

is a Cauchy sequence. That is, show that for any positive real number d there is an integer p such that $|\mathbf{s}_k - \mathbf{s}_h| < d$ for all $h, k > p$.

Prove further that there is a unique matrix $\mathbf{s}$ in E such that for any positive real number d there is an integer p for which $|\mathbf{s}_k - \mathbf{s}| < d$ provided $k > p$. (We naturally *call* $\mathbf{s}$ the *limit* of the sequence $\mathbf{s}_1, \mathbf{s}_2, \ldots$, and it is defined to be $e^{\mathbf{a}}$.)

4. Prove (9.6).

5. Prove (9.7).

6. If $\mathbf{a}(t)$ is a differentiable matrix-valued function on $\mathbf{R}$ [$\mathbf{a}(t)$ being in E for all real numbers t], prove that

$$\frac{d}{dt}\mathbf{a} = \lim_{h \to 0} \frac{1}{h} \cdot [\mathbf{a}(t+h) - \mathbf{a}(t)]$$

limit being defined as in Exercise 3. That is, show that for any real $d > 0$ there exists a number $p > 0$ such that

$$\left| \frac{d}{dt} \mathbf{a} - \frac{1}{h} [\mathbf{a}(t + h) - \mathbf{a}(t)] \right| < d$$

for all nonzero h such that $-p < h < p$.

7. Prove (9.8).

8. Prove (9.9).

9. Find the solution of the system

$$dx_1/dt = x_2$$
$$dx_2/dt = 2x_1 + x_2$$

such that $x_1(0) = c_1$, $x_2(0) = c_2$.

10. Solve the system

$$dx_1/dt = tx_1 + t^2x_2 + t^3x_3$$
$$dx_2/dt = tx_2 + t^2x_3$$
$$dx_3/dt = tx_3$$

11. Solve

$$dx/dt = a(t) \cdot x + b(t) \cdot y$$
$$dy/dt = b(t) \cdot y + a(t) \cdot x$$

where $a(t)$, $b(t)$ denote given functions of t.

12. Compute $e^{\mathbf{a}}$, where

$$\mathbf{a} = \begin{pmatrix} 2 & -12 \\ -1 & 1 \end{pmatrix}$$

10. One-parameter groups and infinitesimal generators

The exponential of a matrix gives an important method of determining commutative subgroups of matrix groups. Indeed, it follows at once from (9.6) that the mapping

10.1 $\quad t \to e^{t\mathbf{a}} \qquad \mathbf{a}$ an $n \times n$ real or complex matrix

is a homomorphism of the additive group of real numbers into the multiplicative group of invertible matrices. For by (10.1) we have

$$s + t \to e^{(s+t)\mathbf{a}} = e^{s\mathbf{a}+t\mathbf{a}} = e^{s\mathbf{a}} \cdot e^{t\mathbf{a}}$$

since $(s\mathbf{a}) \cdot (t\mathbf{a}) = (t\mathbf{a}) \cdot (s\mathbf{a})$.

Conversely, it can be shown that any homomorphism of the additive group of real numbers into the multiplicative group of invertible matrices can be expressed as (10.1) for a suitable matrix **a**. The image of such a homomorphism is called a *one-parameter group*, and the corresponding matrix **a** is called the *infinitesimal generator* of the one-parameter group.

EXAMPLE The rotations about the origin of euclidean two-dimensional vector space form a one-parameter group p. The matrices of the elements of p taken with respect to any orthonormal base $\mathbf{u}_1$, $\mathbf{u}_2$ are

$$\begin{pmatrix} \cos\theta & -\sin\theta \\ \sin\theta & \cos\theta \end{pmatrix}$$

The calculation in Example 3, Sec. 9, shows that

$$e^{\theta\mathbf{a}} = \begin{pmatrix} \cos\theta & -\sin\theta \\ \sin\theta & \cos\theta \end{pmatrix}$$

for all θ, where

$$\mathbf{a} = \begin{pmatrix} 0 & -1 \\ 1 & 0 \end{pmatrix}$$

Thus **a** is the infinitesimal generator of our one-parameter group. The corresponding linear transformation $x \to \mathbf{a}x$ of $\mathbf{R}^2$ is accordingly referred to as an *infinitesimal rotation.*

EXERCISES

1. Define some one-parameter groups geometrically and find their infinitesimal generators.

2. Let E be an n-dimensional euclidean vector space, and let B be an orthonormal base in E. Let **a** be a skew-symmetric matrix.

(*a*) Prove that the linear mappings whose matrices with respect to B are $e^{t\mathbf{a}}$, $-\infty < t < \infty$, form a commutative group of rotations.

*(*b*) Is the homomorphism $t \to e^{\mathbf{a}t}$ a monomorphism for any skew-symmetric **a**?

3. For any matrices **a** and **b**, with **b** invertible, prove

$$\mathbf{b}^{-1}e^{\mathbf{a}}\mathbf{b} = e^{\mathbf{b}^{-1}\mathbf{a}\mathbf{b}}$$

4. Prove: If the eigenvalues of **a** are $\lambda_1, \ldots, \lambda_n$, then the eigenvalues of $e^{\mathbf{a}}$ are $e^{\lambda_1}, \ldots, e^{\lambda_n}$.

5. Using the Jordan normal form (see the following chapter), prove

(*a*) $e^{\mathbf{a}} = \lim_{n\to\infty} \left(\mathbf{I} + \frac{1}{n}\mathbf{a}\right)^n$

(*b*) Can you offer some reason for calling **a** the *infinitesimal generator* of the one-parameter group $e^{t\mathbf{a}}$?

13

The Jordan normal form

1. Introduction

In Sec. 9, Chap. 9, we saw that a linear mapping $\mathbf{T}: U \to V$ of two finite-dimensional vector spaces can be described very simply in terms of bases. Namely, it is always possible to find bases $\{\mathbf{u}_i\}$ and $\{\mathbf{v}_j\}$ for U and V, respectively, such that $\mathbf{T}(\mathbf{u}_i) = \mathbf{v}_i$ $(i = 1, \ldots, r;\ r = \text{rank of } \mathbf{T})$ and $\mathbf{T}(\mathbf{u}_i) = \mathbf{0}$ for i $> r$. In other words, the matrix $\mathbf{t} = (t^j{}_i)$ of $\mathbf{T}$ relative to that base pair is a *diagonal* matrix $(t^j{}_i = 0$ if $i \neq j)$. Moreover, in Chap. 9 we developed an effective method for finding such bases.

These considerations are valid in particular for a mapping $\mathbf{T}$: $U \to U$ of a vector space to itself. But they involve in general the simultaneous use of two different bases $\{\mathbf{u}_i\}$ and $\{\mathbf{v}_j\}$ in U. For many purposes that is very inconvenient. The present chapter is concerned with the problem of finding a single base $\{\mathbf{u}_i\}$ for U which exhibits the action of $\mathbf{T}$ as simply as possible. Or to phrase the problem differently, we wish to find a base for U with respect to which the matrix of $\mathbf{T}$ has the most agreeable form possible. But observe that we have imposed a rather severe restriction in limiting ourselves to a single base for the analysis of $\mathbf{T}$, rather than to a pair of possibly different bases.

A partial answer to this problem has already been pointed out in Sec. 5, Chap. 11 (see Theorem 5.5). We recall that a vector $\mathbf{e} \neq \mathbf{0}$ in U is called an *eigenvector* of $\mathbf{T}$ if

1.1 $$\mathbf{T}(\mathbf{e}) = p\mathbf{e}$$

for some scalar p (p is then called an *eigenvalue* of $\mathbf{T}$, and $\mathbf{e}$ is said to "belong" to p). Now if $\mathbf{T}$ happens to have n linearly independent eigenvectors, say $\mathbf{e}_1, \mathbf{e}_2, \ldots, \mathbf{e}_n$, where $n = \dim U$, with corresponding eigenvalues $p_1, p_2, \ldots, p_n$, then we have

1.2 $$\mathbf{T}(\mathbf{e}_i) = p_i\mathbf{e}_i \qquad (i = 1, \ldots, n)$$

and the $\mathbf{e}_i$ form a base for U. The matrix of $\mathbf{T}$ relative to the base $\{\mathbf{e}_i\}$ is the diagonal matrix whose diagonal elements are $p_1, p_2, \ldots, p_n$. The action of $\mathbf{T}$ in the case at hand can be described very simply as a "stretching" in the n directions determined by $\mathbf{e}_1, \ldots, \mathbf{e}_n$; and the eigenvalues are just the stretching factors.

This situation can be described somewhat differently as follows: Each of the eigenvectors $\mathbf{e}_i$ generates a one-dimensional subspace V_i (consisting of all vectors $x\mathbf{e}_i$, x any scalar), and from (1.2) it is clear that $\mathbf{T}$ maps V_i into itself. Furthermore, U is the *direct sum* of $V_i \oplus \cdots \oplus V_n$ (see Definition 5.2, Chap. 8). For every $\mathbf{x}$ in U can be expressed uniquely as a sum $\mathbf{x} = x^1\mathbf{e}_1 + x^2\mathbf{e}_2 + \cdots + x^n\mathbf{e}_n$, of which each term $x^i\mathbf{e}_i$ (no summation!) is an element of V_i.

In general the situation is not so simple, for a linear operator $\mathbf{T}$ need not have n linearly independent eigenvectors. For example, the mapping $\mathbf{Q}^2 \to \mathbf{Q}^2$ given by the matrix

$$\begin{pmatrix} 1 & 2 \\ 0 & 1 \end{pmatrix}$$

has only the vectors of the form

$$\begin{pmatrix} x \\ 0 \end{pmatrix} \qquad x \text{ any rational number}$$

as eigenvectors. We shall see that the problem we have set for ourselves leads us in general to a decomposition of U into subspaces analogous to the V_i mentioned above, but in general of dimension greater than 1.

2. Elementary linear mappings

Here we shall catalogue some particularly simple types of linear mappings whose actions can easily be "visualized." U denotes an n-dimensional vector space over some field K.

TYPE I Let $\mathbf{T}$ denote the mapping $\mathbf{T} = a\mathbf{I}$ of U, where $\mathbf{I}$ is the identity mapping. Thus $\mathbf{T}(\mathbf{x}) = a\mathbf{x}$ for every $\mathbf{x}$ in U (hence every element of U is an eigenvector of $\mathbf{T}$ belonging to the eigenvalue a). $\mathbf{T}$ operates by stretching each element of U by the factor a. The matrix of $\mathbf{T}$ relative to any base is $a \cdot \mathbf{I}_n$, that is,

$$\begin{pmatrix} a & 0 & \cdots & 0 \\ 0 & a & \cdots & 0 \\ \cdots & \cdots & \cdots & \cdots \\ 0 & 0 & \cdots & a \end{pmatrix}$$

The characteristic polynomial of $\mathbf{T}$ (Definition 5.1, Chap. 11) is $(t - a)^n$. The minimal polynomial† of $\mathbf{T}$ is $t - a$. Mappings of this type are sometimes called *scalar* mappings.

TYPE II Suppose that $\mathbf{T}$: $U \to U$ is a linear mapping for which there is a base $B = \{\mathbf{u}_1, \mathbf{u}_2, \ldots, \mathbf{u}_n\}$ in U such that

2.1
$$\begin{aligned} \mathbf{T}(\mathbf{u}_i) &= \mathbf{u}_{i-1} \qquad (i = 2, 3, \ldots, n) \\ \mathbf{T}(\mathbf{u}_1) &= \mathbf{0} \end{aligned}$$

† That is, the monic polynomial $f(t)$ of least degree with coefficients in K such that $f(\mathbf{T}) = \mathbf{0}$.

We shall call such a $\mathbf{T}$ *nilcyclic of order n*, and a base B for which (2.1) holds will be called a *cyclic base* for $\mathbf{T}$. Taking $n = 4$ for simplicity, the matrix of $\mathbf{T}$ relative to the cyclic base B is

$$\begin{pmatrix} 0 & 1 & 0 & 0 \\ 0 & 0 & 1 & 0 \\ 0 & 0 & 0 & 1 \\ 0 & 0 & 0 & 0 \end{pmatrix}$$

For any n, the matrix of $\mathbf{T}$ has zeros everywhere except for a diagonal sequence of 1's immediately above the main diagonal. The characteristic polynomial of $\mathbf{T}$ is quickly seen to be t^n. The minimal polynomial of $\mathbf{T}$ must divide the characteristic polynomial (Theorem 4.6, Chap. 11) and so must be a power of t. It is not hard to see in fact that the minimal polynomial is also t^n. For, referring to (2.1), we have

$$\begin{aligned} \mathbf{T}^2(\mathbf{u}_i) &= \mathbf{u}_{i-2} \qquad (i = 3, 4, \ldots, n) \\ \mathbf{T}^2(\mathbf{u}_1) &= \mathbf{T}^2(\mathbf{u}_2) = \mathbf{0} \end{aligned}$$

More generally,

2.2
$$\begin{aligned} \mathbf{T}^k(\mathbf{u}_i) &= \mathbf{u}_{i-k} \qquad (i = k + 1, \ldots, n) \\ \mathbf{T}^k(\mathbf{u}_i) &= 0 \qquad (i = 1, \ldots, k) \end{aligned}$$

Hence $\mathbf{T}^n = \mathbf{0}$, but $\mathbf{T}^{n-1} \neq \mathbf{0}$, since $\mathbf{T}^{n-1}(\mathbf{u}_n) = \mathbf{u}_1$.

Observe that the cyclic base B is obtained by applying $\mathbf{T}$ repeatedly to the one element $\mathbf{u}_n$, as follows from (2.2).

TYPE III If $\mathbf{T}$: $U \to U$ is such that there is a base $B = \{\mathbf{e}_1, \ldots, \mathbf{e}_n\}$ of U for which

$$\mathbf{T}(\mathbf{e}_i) = p_i\mathbf{e}_i \qquad (i = 1, \ldots, n; \; p_i \text{ in } K)$$

then we shall call $\mathbf{T}$ a *diagonal* mapping. The equation here is the same as (1.2), and so our requirement is that $\mathbf{T}$ possess n linearly independent eigenvectors. The characteristic polynomial of t is $(t - p_1)(t - p_2) \cdots (t - p_n)$. $\mathbf{T}$, acting on the one-dimensional subspace spanned by $\mathbf{e}_i$, is of Type I, and therefore $\mathbf{T}$ can be thought of as a sum of mappings of Type I, in a sense to be made more precise below. On the other hand, Type III obviously includes Type I.

We shall see that mappings of Types I and II can be used as building blocks out of which we can construct the most general linear mapping.

REMARK. $\mathbf{T}$ being a diagonal mapping, as above, we have $\mathbf{T}^2(\mathbf{e}_i) = \mathbf{T}(p_i\mathbf{e}_i) = p_i\mathbf{T}(\mathbf{e}_i) = p_i^2\mathbf{e}_i$. By a simple induction, $\mathbf{T}^k(\mathbf{e}_i) = p_i^k\mathbf{e}_i$ for $k = 1, 2, 3, \ldots$ (cf. Theorem 5.9, Chap. 11). If $\mathbf{T}^k = \mathbf{0}$, then $p_i^k = 0$ for $i = 1, 2, \ldots, n$, whence $p_1 = p_2 = \cdots = p_n = 0$, since the p_i are elements of a field. Therefore, *no power of a diagonal mapping* $\mathbf{T}$ *can be zero unless* $\mathbf{T} = \mathbf{0}$.

EXERCISES

1. Let $\mathbf{T}$ be a nilcyclic mapping of order n. What are the characteristic and minimal polynomials of $\mathbf{T}^k$? Taking $n = 5$, write down the matrices of $\mathbf{T}^2$, $\mathbf{T}^3$, $\mathbf{T}^4$ relative to a cyclic base B for $\mathbf{T}$.

2. Let $\mathbf{T}: U \to U$ be a linear mapping of an n-dimensional vector space, and suppose that $\mathbf{T} - p\mathbf{I}$ is nilcyclic. Let B be a cyclic base in U for this mapping. Compute the matrix of $\mathbf{T}$ relative to the base B.

3. A linear mapping $\mathbf{T}$ is called *nilpotent* if $\mathbf{T}^m = \mathbf{0}$ for some integer m. Suppose that $\mathbf{S}$, $\mathbf{T}$ are both nilpotent mappings of a vector space U to itself, and suppose that $\mathbf{ST} = \mathbf{TS}$. Prove that $\mathbf{S} + \mathbf{T}$ is nilpotent.

4. Let P_n be the vector space of polynomials of degree $<n$ in a variable t over a field K. Let $\mathbf{D}: P_n \to P_n$ be the differentiation operator. Show that $\mathbf{D}$ is nilcyclic.

5. Let $\mathbf{T}$ be a nilcyclic mapping of order m. Compute the rank and nullity of $\mathbf{T}^k$ ($k = 0, 1, 2,$ etc.).

In the following exercises compute the matrix of $f(\mathbf{T})$ relative to the specified base B:

6. $f(t) = t^2 - 5t + 1$, $\mathbf{T} = c\mathbf{I}$, B any base.

7. $f(t) = t^2 + 1$, $\mathbf{T}$ nilcyclic, B a cyclic base of five elements.

8. $f(t) = t^3 + t$, with $\mathbf{T}$ and B as in Exercise 7.

9. $f(t) = t^6 + 5t^5$, with $\mathbf{T}$ and B as in Exercise 7.

10. $f(t) = t^3 - 5t^2 + t + 7$, $\mathbf{T}$ and B as in Exercise 7.

11. $f(t) = t$, where $\mathbf{T} = c\mathbf{I} + \mathbf{N}$, with $\mathbf{N}$ nilcyclic and B a cyclic base for $\mathbf{N}$.

12. $f(t) = t^2$, $\mathbf{T}$ and B as in Exercise 11.

13. $f(t) = t^3$, $\mathbf{T}$ and B as in Exercise 11.

14. Let $\mathbf{T}$ be a linear mapping of an n-dimensional vector space to itself. Prove that $\mathbf{T}$ is nilpotent if and only if the characteristic polynomial of $\mathbf{T}$ is $\varphi(t) = t^n$.

3. *Direct sum decompositions*

Here we shall recall some things from Sec. 5, Chap. 8, and Sec. 5, Chap. 11 (Theorems 5.6 and 5.7).

DEFINITION 3.1 *Let $W_1, \ldots, W_r$ be subspaces of a vector space U. Then U is said to be the* direct sum *of those subspaces if every element $\mathbf{x}$ of U can be expressed in one and only one way as a sum $\mathbf{x} = \mathbf{x}_1 + \mathbf{x}_2 + \cdots + \mathbf{x}_r$, with $\mathbf{x}_i$ in W_i ($i = 1, \ldots r$).*

If these conditions are fulfilled, then we write

$$U = W_1 \oplus W_2 \oplus \cdots \oplus W_r$$

EXAMPLE 1 Let U have finite dimension n, and let $\mathbf{u}_1, \ldots, \mathbf{u}_n$ be a base. Denote by V_i the one-dimensional subspace consisting of all vectors $a\mathbf{u}_i$ (a an arbitrary scalar). Since every $\mathbf{x}$ in U can be expressed *uniquely* in the form $\mathbf{x} = x^1\mathbf{u}_1 + \cdots + x^n\mathbf{u}_n$, of which the ith term $x^i\mathbf{u}_i$ is in V_i, it follows that $U = V_1 \oplus \cdots \oplus V_n$.

EXAMPLE 2 Let $W_1, \ldots, W_r$ be vector spaces over the same field K. Let U denote the set of all r-tuples $\mathbf{x} = (\mathbf{x}_1, \mathbf{x}_2, \ldots, \mathbf{x}_r)$, with $\mathbf{x}_i$ in W_i $(i = 1, \ldots, r)$. Define addition in U by $(\mathbf{x}_1, \mathbf{x}_2, \ldots, \mathbf{x}_r) + (\mathbf{y}_1, \mathbf{y}_2, \ldots, \mathbf{y}_r) = (\mathbf{x}_1 + \mathbf{y}_1, \mathbf{x}_2 + \mathbf{y}_2, \ldots, \mathbf{x}_r + \mathbf{y}_r)$. Define scalar multiplication by $c(\mathbf{x}_1, \mathbf{x}_2, \ldots, \mathbf{x}_r) = (c\mathbf{x}_1, c\mathbf{x}_2, \ldots, c\mathbf{x}_r)$. With these definitions, U is a vector space over K (trivial verification). For fixed i, all elements of U of the type $(\mathbf{0}, \ldots, \mathbf{x}_i, \ldots, \mathbf{0})$, with zeros except in the ith place, form a subspace W_i' of U. U is the direct sum of $W_1', \ldots, W_r'$, and W_i' is isomorphic to W_i.

THEOREM 3.1 *Let the vector space U be a direct sum of subspaces $W_1, W_2, \ldots, W_r$. If $\mathbf{w}_1, \mathbf{w}_2, \ldots, \mathbf{w}_r$ are nonzero elements of $W_1, W_2, \ldots, W_r$, respectively, then they are linearly independent. Furthermore, if an arbitrary $\mathbf{x}$ in U is expressed as a sum $\mathbf{x} = \mathbf{x}_1 + \mathbf{x}_2 + \cdots + \mathbf{x}_r$, with $\mathbf{x}_i$ in W_i for $i = 1, \ldots, r$, then each $\mathbf{x}_i$ is uniquely determined by $\mathbf{x}$, and the mapping $\mathbf{x} \to \mathbf{x}_i$ is a linear mapping of U onto W_i, called the* projection *onto W_i.*

Proof. For the first assertion, each W_i contains $\mathbf{0}$, and therefore Definition 3.1, applied to the zero element, says that if we express $\mathbf{0}$ as a sum $\mathbf{0} = \mathbf{a}_1 + \mathbf{a}_2 + \cdots + \mathbf{a}_r$, with $\mathbf{a}_i$ in W_i for each i, then the $\mathbf{a}$'s must all be zero. Now if $c_1\mathbf{w}_1 + \cdots + c_r\mathbf{w}_r = \mathbf{0}$ for certain scalars c_i, then, by what was just said, each term $c_i\mathbf{w}_i$ is zero, and so each c_i is zero, because $\mathbf{w}_i \neq 0$.

For the second assertion, the fact that $\mathbf{x}_i$ is uniquely determined by $\mathbf{x}$ is just the requirement of Definition 3.1. Hence the operation that assigns $\mathbf{x}_i$ to $\mathbf{x}$ is well defined. That is, $\mathbf{x} \to \mathbf{x}_i$ is really a mapping of U to W_i. It is routine to verify that it is a linear mapping. Q.E.D.

Let $\mathbf{P}_i$: $U \to U$ be the ith projection, as defined in the theorem above, but considered as a mapping from U to itself rather than to the subspace W_i. We can form the composition $\mathbf{P}_j \circ \mathbf{P}_i$ of any two of these mappings, and the result is easy to calculate. Thus, let $\mathbf{x}$ be an arbitrary element of U, and write it in the form $\mathbf{x} = \mathbf{x}_1 + \cdots + \mathbf{x}_i + \cdots + \mathbf{x}_r$, with each $\mathbf{x}_i$ in W_i. Doing the same thing for any one of the $\mathbf{x}_i$, we get $\mathbf{x}_i = \mathbf{0} + \cdots + \mathbf{x}_i + \cdots + \mathbf{0}$ (all terms zero except the ith), by Definition 3.1. Then by definition we have $\mathbf{P}_j(\mathbf{x}_i) = \mathbf{0}$ if $j \neq i$, and $\mathbf{P}_i(\mathbf{x}) = \mathbf{P}_i(\mathbf{x}_i) = \mathbf{x}_i$. Hence, $\mathbf{P}_j \circ \mathbf{P}_i(\mathbf{x}) = \mathbf{P}_j(\mathbf{x}_i) = \mathbf{0}$ or $\mathbf{x}_i$, according as $j \neq i$ or $j = i$. Thus

3.1 $$\mathbf{P}_i \circ \mathbf{P}_j = \begin{cases} \mathbf{0} & \text{if } j \neq i \\ \mathbf{P}_i & \text{if } j = i \end{cases}$$

In particular, $\mathbf{P}_i^2 = \mathbf{P}_i$. (In general, an endomorphism $\mathbf{T}$ such that $\mathbf{T}^2 = \mathbf{T}$ is called *idempotent*. It follows that $\mathbf{T}^3 = \mathbf{T}$, etc.)

The following proposition gives a useful criterion for a space to be the direct sum of two subspaces.

PROPOSITION 3.2 *Let W_1 and W_2 be subspaces of a vector space U, and suppose that every vector in U can be expressed in at least one way as a sum of an element of W_1 and an element of W_2. Then U is the direct sum of W_1 and W_2 if and only if* $\mathbf{0}$ *is the only element common to both W_1 and W_2.*

Proof. By assumption, an arbitrary $\mathbf{x}$ in U can be expressed as a sum $\mathbf{x} = \mathbf{x}_1 + \mathbf{x}_2$, with $\mathbf{x}_1$ in W_1 and $\mathbf{x}_2$ in W_2. Suppose that $\mathbf{x} = \mathbf{x}_1' + \mathbf{x}_2'$ is a second expression of the same type for $\mathbf{x}$. Then $\mathbf{0} = \mathbf{x}_1 - \mathbf{x}_1' + \mathbf{x}_2 - \mathbf{x}_2'$, or $\mathbf{x}_1 - \mathbf{x}_1' = \mathbf{x}_2' - \mathbf{x}_2$. By assumption, $\mathbf{x}_1$ and $\mathbf{x}_1'$ are in W_1, and so $\mathbf{x}_1 - \mathbf{x}_1'$ is in W_1. Similarly, $\mathbf{x}_2' - \mathbf{x}_2$ is in W_2. Therefore, the element $\mathbf{y} = \mathbf{x}_1 - \mathbf{x}_1' = \mathbf{x}_2' - \mathbf{x}_2$ is in both W_1 and W_2. If W_1 and W_2 have only the zero element in common, then $\mathbf{y} = \mathbf{0}$, and consequently the two expressions for $\mathbf{x}$ must be identical. Hence $U = W_1 \oplus W_2$. Suppose, conversely, that U is the direct sum $W_1 \oplus W_2$, and let $\mathbf{v}$ be a nonzero element in both W_1 and W_2. Then $\mathbf{v} = \mathbf{0} + \mathbf{v} = \mathbf{v} + \mathbf{0}$, and these are two different expressions for $\mathbf{v}$ of the type $\mathbf{v} = \mathbf{v}_1 + \mathbf{v}_2$ ($\mathbf{v}_1$ in W_1, $\mathbf{v}_2$ in W_2), contradicting Definition 3.1.

COROLLARY *Let* $\mathbf{T}: U \to U$ *be an idempotent endomorphism of a vector space. That is,* $\mathbf{T}^2 = \mathbf{T}$. *Then U is the direct sum of the kernel of* $\mathbf{T}$ *and of the image of* $\mathbf{T}$.

Proof. Put $W_1 = \text{Im } \mathbf{T}$ and $W_2 = \text{Ker } \mathbf{T}$. If $\mathbf{y}$ is in both W_1 and W_2, then $\mathbf{y} = \mathbf{T}(\mathbf{x})$ for some $\mathbf{x}$ and also $\mathbf{T}(\mathbf{y}) = \mathbf{0}$. Hence $\mathbf{T}^2(\mathbf{x}) = \mathbf{0}$. But $\mathbf{T}^2(\mathbf{x}) = \mathbf{T}(\mathbf{x}) = \mathbf{y}$; so $\mathbf{y} = \mathbf{0}$. Hence W_1, W_2 have only the zero in common. For an arbitrary $\mathbf{x}$ in U, put $\mathbf{x}_1 = \mathbf{T}(\mathbf{x})$ and $\mathbf{x}_2 = \mathbf{x} - \mathbf{T}(\mathbf{x}) = \mathbf{x} - \mathbf{x}_1$. Then $\mathbf{x} = \mathbf{x}_1 + \mathbf{x}_2$, and $\mathbf{x}_1$ is in W_1, $\mathbf{x}_2$ is in W_2. For in fact $\mathbf{T}(\mathbf{x}_2) = \mathbf{T}(\mathbf{x}) - \mathbf{T}^2(\mathbf{x}) = \mathbf{T}(\mathbf{x}) - \mathbf{T}(\mathbf{x}) = \mathbf{0}$. The assertion follows by Proposition 3.2 above. Q.E.D.

PROPOSITION 3.3 *Let U be the direct sum of finite-dimensional subspaces $W_1, W_2, \ldots, W_r$. Let B_i denote a base for W_i $(i = 1, \ldots, r)$. Then $B_1, B_2, \ldots, B_r$, taken jointly, constitute a base for U. In particular,* $\dim U = \dim W_1 + \cdots + \dim W_r$.

Proof. The elements of $B_1, \ldots, B_r$, taken jointly, are linearly independent. For let $B_1 = \{\mathbf{u}_1, \ldots, \mathbf{u}_h\}$, $B_2 = \{\mathbf{v}_1, \ldots, \mathbf{v}_k\}$, etc. If these elements were linearly dependent, then there would exist a linear relation

3.2 $$a_1\mathbf{u}_1 + \cdots + a_h\mathbf{u}_h + b_1\mathbf{v}_1 + \cdots + b_k\mathbf{v}_k + \cdots = \mathbf{0}$$

Put $\mathbf{w}_1 = a_1\mathbf{u}_1 + \cdots + a_h\mathbf{u}_h$, $\mathbf{w}_2 = b_1\mathbf{v}_1 + \cdots + b_k\mathbf{v}_k$, etc. Then the equation above is

$$\mathbf{w}_1 + \mathbf{w}_2 + \cdots + \mathbf{w}_r = \mathbf{0}$$

From Theorem 3.1 we must have $\mathbf{w}_1 = \mathbf{0}$, $\mathbf{w}_2 = \mathbf{0}, \ldots, \mathbf{w}_r = \mathbf{0}$. Since $\mathbf{u}_1, \ldots, \mathbf{u}_h$ are linearly independent, $\mathbf{w}_1 = \mathbf{0}$ is only possible if $a_1 = 0$,

$\ldots, a_h = 0$. Similarly, from $\mathbf{w}_2 = \mathbf{0}$ there follows $b_1 = 0, \ldots, b_k = 0$, etc. Hence all the coefficients in (3.2) must be zero.

Then to show that all the elements in the bases B_i form a base for U, we have only to show that they span U. If we write an arbitrary $\mathbf{x}$ in U in the form $\mathbf{x} = \mathbf{x}_1 + \cdots + \mathbf{x}_r$, with $\mathbf{x}_i$ in W_i, then $\mathbf{x}_i$ can be expressed in terms of the base B_i $(i = 1, \ldots, r)$. Hence $\mathbf{x}$ itself can be expressed as a linear combination of all the elements in $B_1, \ldots, B_r$.

Q.E.D.

We now tie up the notion of *direct sum* with linear mappings.

DEFINITION 3.2 *Let $\mathbf{T}: U \to U$ be an endomorphism of a vector space U. A subspace V of U is called* **T**-*stable if* **T** *maps V to V.*

For example, the subspace of U consisting of the zero element alone is **T**-stable for any **T**.

If V is a **T**-stable subspace of U, then we denote by $\mathbf{T}_V$ the *restriction* of **T** to V. That is, $\mathbf{T}_V : V \to V$ is the mapping defined by $\mathbf{T}_V(\mathbf{x}) = \mathbf{T}(\mathbf{x})$ for $\mathbf{x}$ in V. It is clearly a linear mapping.

DEFINITION 3.3 *Let $\mathbf{T}_1, \mathbf{T}_2, \ldots, \mathbf{T}_r$ be endomorphisms of a vector space U. Then* **T** *will be called the* direct sum *of $\mathbf{T}_1, \ldots, \mathbf{T}_r$ if*

3.3
$$\mathbf{T} = \mathbf{T}_1 + \cdots + \mathbf{T}_r$$
$$\mathbf{T}_i \circ \mathbf{T}_j = 0 \qquad \text{for } i \neq j$$

To indicate this situation we shall sometimes write

$$\mathbf{T} = \mathbf{T}_1 \oplus \cdots \oplus \mathbf{T}_r$$

EXAMPLE Let $U = W_1 \oplus \cdots \oplus W_r$ and let $\mathbf{P}_1, \ldots, \mathbf{P}_r$ be the projection operators of (3.1). From (3.1) it follows readily that

$$\mathbf{I} = \mathbf{P}_1 \oplus \cdots \oplus \mathbf{P}_r$$

The following theorem shows how linear mappings can be built up from mappings defined on subspaces.

PROPOSITION 3.4 *Let a vector space U be a direct sum $U = W_1 \oplus \cdots \oplus W_r$ of certain subspaces. For given i let $\mathbf{T}_i: W_i \to W_i$ be a linear mapping. Then there is a uniquely determined linear mapping $\mathbf{T}'_i: U \to U$ such that $\mathbf{T}'_i(\mathbf{x}) = \mathbf{T}_i(\mathbf{x})$ for $\mathbf{x}$ in W_i and $\mathbf{T}'_i(\mathbf{x}) = \mathbf{0}$ for $\mathbf{x}$ in W_j $(j \neq i)$. If $\mathbf{T}_i$ is given for each i, then $\mathbf{T} = \mathbf{T}'_1 + \cdots + \mathbf{T}'_r$ is a direct sum; the subspaces W_i are* **T**-*stable, and* **T** *is the unique linear mapping of U to itself whose restriction to W_i is the same as $\mathbf{T}_i$ for $i = 1, \ldots, r$. We denote* **T** *by the symbol $\mathbf{T}_1 \oplus \cdots \oplus \mathbf{T}_r$.*

Proof. Let $\mathbf{P}_i: U \to U$ be the projection of (3.1). Define $\mathbf{T}'_i$ by $\mathbf{T}'_i(\mathbf{x}) = \mathbf{T}_i(\mathbf{P}_i(\mathbf{x}))$ for any $\mathbf{x}$ in U. It is clear that $\mathbf{T}'_i$ thus defined has the required properties and is uniquely determined by them. Furthermore, it is evident that $\mathbf{P}_i\mathbf{T}'_i = \mathbf{T}'_i\mathbf{P}_i = \mathbf{T}'_i$. Hence

$$\mathbf{T}'_i \circ \mathbf{T}'_j = (\mathbf{T}'_i \circ \mathbf{P}'_i) \circ (\mathbf{P}'_j \circ \mathbf{T}'_j) = \mathbf{T}'_i \circ (\mathbf{P}'_i \circ \mathbf{P}'_j) \circ \mathbf{T}'_j = \mathbf{0} \qquad \text{if } i \neq j$$

by (3.1). This shows that $\mathbf{T} = \mathbf{T}'_1 + \cdots + \mathbf{T}'_r$ satisfies the conditions of Definition 3.3. The remaining assertions are trivial to verify. Q.E.D.

REMARK. The mapping $\mathbf{T}$ of the theorem can be denoted by any of the three symbols $\mathbf{T}_1 \oplus \cdots \oplus \mathbf{T}_r$, $\mathbf{T}'_1 \oplus \cdots \oplus \mathbf{T}'_r$, $\mathbf{T}'_1 + \cdots + \mathbf{T}'_r$ in accordance with our conventions.

The following theorem is a kind of converse to the preceding:

PROPOSITION 3.5 *Let $\mathbf{T}: U \to U$ be an endomorphism of a vector space, and let U be a direct sum $U = W_1 \oplus \cdots \oplus W_r$ of $\mathbf{T}$-stable subspaces. Then for each i there is a unique linear mapping $\mathbf{T}_i: U \to U$ such that $\mathbf{T}_i(\mathbf{x}) = \mathbf{T}(\mathbf{x})$ for $\mathbf{x}$ in W_i and $\mathbf{T}_i(\mathbf{x}) = \mathbf{0}$ for $\mathbf{x}$ in W_j $(j \neq i)$. Furthermore $\mathbf{T}$ is the direct sum $\mathbf{T} = \mathbf{T}_1 \oplus \cdots \oplus \mathbf{T}_r$. We call $\mathbf{T}_i$ the W_i* part *of $\mathbf{T}$.*

Proof. Let $\mathbf{P}_1, \ldots, \mathbf{P}_r$ be the projection mappings of (3.1). Define $\mathbf{T}_i$ by $\mathbf{T}_i = \mathbf{T} \circ \mathbf{P}_i$. Since W_i is $\mathbf{T}$-stable, we have $\mathbf{T} \circ \mathbf{P}_i = \mathbf{P}_i \circ \mathbf{T}$. Therefore

$$\mathbf{T}_i \circ \mathbf{T}_j = (\mathbf{T} \circ \mathbf{P}_i) \circ (\mathbf{T} \circ \mathbf{P}_j) = \mathbf{T} \circ \mathbf{T} \circ \mathbf{P}_i \circ \mathbf{P}_j = \mathbf{0} \qquad \text{if } i \neq j$$

The other assertions are trivial to verify. Q.E.D.

EXAMPLE 3 Let $\mathbf{T}$ be a diagonal mapping of an n-dimensional vector space U (Sec. 2, Type III). Let $B = \{\mathbf{e}_1, \ldots, \mathbf{e}_n\}$ be a base for which the matrix of $\mathbf{T}$ is a diagonal matrix, say $\mathbf{T}(\mathbf{e}_i) = p_i\mathbf{e}_i$ $(i = 1, \ldots, n)$. Let V_i denote the subspace of U generated by $\mathbf{e}_i$. Then V_i is $\mathbf{T}$-stable. Denoting by $\mathbf{T}_i: V_i \to V_i$ the restriction of $\mathbf{T}$ to the elements of V_i, then $\mathbf{T} = \mathbf{T}_1 \oplus \cdots \oplus \mathbf{T}_n$, by Theorem 3.4. We can equally well write $\mathbf{T} = \mathbf{T}'_1 \oplus \cdots \oplus \mathbf{T}'_n$, where $\mathbf{T}'_i$ is the V_i part of $\mathbf{T}$ (cf. Theorem 3.4). That is, $\mathbf{T}'_i(\mathbf{x}) = \mathbf{T}(\mathbf{x})$ for $\mathbf{x}$ in W_i, and $\mathbf{T}'_i(\mathbf{x}) = \mathbf{0}$ for $\mathbf{x}$ in W_j with $j \neq i$.

Hence, a diagonal mapping is a direct sum of mappings of Type I. This gives a precise meaning to the observation at the end of the paragraph of Sec. 2 concerning mappings of Type III.

The following proposition has occurred as a part of Theorem 5.7, Chap. 11.

PROPOSITION 3.6 *Let $\mathbf{T}: U \to U$ be a linear mapping of a finite-dimensional vector space U, and let U be a direct sum of $\mathbf{T}$-stable subspaces $W_1, \ldots, W_r$. Let B_i denote a base for W_i $(i = 1, \ldots, r)$, and let $B = \{B_1, B_2, \ldots, B_r\}$ be the base for U consisting of all the vectors in the B_i, in the indicated order. Let $\mathbf{T}_i$ be the restriction of $\mathbf{T}$ to W_i, so that $\mathbf{T} = \mathbf{T}_1 \oplus \cdots \oplus \mathbf{T}_r$, and let $\mathbf{a}_i$ denote its matrix relative to the base B_i. If $\mathbf{a}$ denotes the matrix of $\mathbf{T}$ relative to the base B then*

3.4 $$\mathbf{a} = \begin{pmatrix} \mathbf{a}_1 & & & \\ & \mathbf{a}_2 & & \\ & & \ddots & \\ & & & \mathbf{a}_r \end{pmatrix}$$

(This symbolism means that $\mathbf{a}$ consists of the square matrices $\mathbf{a}_1, \ldots, \mathbf{a}_r$, arranged along the diagonal, with zeros elsewhere.)

Proof. Recall first from Proposition 3.3 that B is in fact a base for U. If $B_i = \{\mathbf{u}_1, \ldots, \mathbf{u}_h\}$, say, then the effect of $\mathbf{T}$ on these elements is the same as the effect of $\mathbf{T}_i$. Thus $\mathbf{T}(\mathbf{u}_1), \ldots, \mathbf{T}(\mathbf{u}_h)$ can all be expressed as linear combinations of $\mathbf{u}_1, \ldots, \mathbf{u}_h$ by means of the matrix $\mathbf{a}_i$. Consequently, the column of $\mathbf{a}$ in (3.4) corresponding to $\mathbf{u}_1$ (for example) will have nonzero entries only in those rows corresponding to $\mathbf{u}_1, \ldots, \mathbf{u}_h$, and in those entries it will have the same elements as in the first column of $\mathbf{a}_1$. The same is true for the other columns. Q.E.D.

EXAMPLE 4 Let U be a vector space with base $B = \{\mathbf{e}_1, \mathbf{e}_2, \mathbf{e}_3, \mathbf{e}_4\}$, and let $\mathbf{T}$ be the linear mapping of U determined by

$$\mathbf{T}(\mathbf{e}_1) = 3\mathbf{e}_1$$
$$\mathbf{T}(\mathbf{e}_2) = -2\mathbf{e}_2$$
$$\mathbf{T}(\mathbf{e}_3) = \mathbf{e}_4$$
$$\mathbf{T}(\mathbf{e}_4) = \mathbf{e}_3$$

Let V_1 be the subspace generated by $B_1 = \{\mathbf{e}_1\}$, let V_2 be the subspace generated by $B_2 = \{\mathbf{e}_2\}$, and let V_3 be the subspace generated by $B_3 = \{\mathbf{e}_3, \mathbf{e}_4\}$. Plainly we have $U = V_1 \oplus V_2 \oplus V_3$, and the three subspaces are $\mathbf{T}$-stable. Letting $\mathbf{T}_i$ denote the restriction of $\mathbf{T}$ to V_i, we have $\mathbf{T} = \mathbf{T}_1 \oplus \mathbf{T}_2 \oplus \mathbf{T}_3$. The matrix $\mathbf{a}$ of $\mathbf{T}$ relative to B is

$$\mathbf{a} = \begin{pmatrix} \mathbf{a}_1 & & \\ & \mathbf{a}_2 & \\ & & \mathbf{a}_3 \end{pmatrix} = \left(\begin{array}{c|c|cc} 3 & 0 & 0 & 0 \\ \hline 0 & -2 & 0 & 0 \\ \hline 0 & 0 & 0 & 1 \\ 0 & 0 & 1 & 0 \end{array}\right)$$

where

$$\mathbf{a}_1 = (3) \qquad \mathbf{a}_2 = (-2) \qquad \mathbf{a}_3 = \begin{pmatrix} 0 & 1 \\ 1 & 0 \end{pmatrix}$$

are the matrices of $\mathbf{T}_1, \mathbf{T}_2, \mathbf{T}_3$ relative to B_1, B_2, B_3, respectively.

EXAMPLE 5 Referring to Example 3, the matrix of $\mathbf{T}_i$ relative to the base $B_i = \{\mathbf{e}_i\}$ of V_i is the 1×1 matrix (p_i). The matrix of $\mathbf{T} = \mathbf{T}_1 \oplus \cdots \oplus \mathbf{T}_n$ relative to the joint base B is the diagonal matrix

$$\begin{pmatrix} p_1 & & & & & \\ & p_2 & & & & \\ & & \cdot & & & \\ & & & \cdot & & \\ & & & & \cdot & \\ & & & & & p_n \end{pmatrix}$$

in conformity with Theorem 3.6.

EXERCISES

1. Let $\mathbf{T}$ be an endomorphism of a vector space U, and let U be the direct sum of $\mathbf{T}$-stable subspaces $W_1, \ldots, W_r$. Let $\mathbf{T}_i$ denote the restriction of $\mathbf{T}$ to W_i. Prove that

$$\text{Ker } \mathbf{T} = \text{Ker } \mathbf{T}_1 \oplus \cdots \oplus \text{Ker } \mathbf{T}_r$$

and

$$\text{Im } \mathbf{T} = \text{Im } \mathbf{T}_1 \oplus \cdots \oplus \text{Im } \mathbf{T}_r$$

2. Let $\mathbf{T}, \mathbf{T}_1, \ldots, \mathbf{T}_r$ be endomorphisms of a vector space, and suppose that $\mathbf{T} = \mathbf{T}_1 \oplus \cdots \oplus \mathbf{T}_r$ (direct sum). Prove that $\mathbf{T}^k = \mathbf{T}_1{}^k \oplus \cdots \oplus \mathbf{T}_r{}^k$ for $k = 1, 2, 3$, etc.

3. Let U be a vector space with base $\{\mathbf{e}_1, \mathbf{e}_2\}$, and let $\mathbf{T}$ be the nilcyclic mapping such that $\mathbf{T}(\mathbf{e}_1) = \mathbf{0}$ and $\mathbf{T}(\mathbf{e}_2) = \mathbf{e}_1$. Let V be the subspace generated by $\mathbf{e}_1$. Is V a $\mathbf{T}$-stable subspace? Does there exist a $\mathbf{T}$-stable subspace W such that $U = V \oplus W$?

4. Let $\mathbf{T}: U \to U$ be an endomorphism of an n-dimensional vector space, and let V be an r-dimensional subspace. Let $B = \{\mathbf{e}_1, \ldots, \mathbf{e}_n\}$ be a base for U, and suppose that $A = \{\mathbf{e}_1, \ldots, \mathbf{e}_r\}$ is a base for V. Prove that V is a $\mathbf{T}$-stable subspace if and only if the matrix of $\mathbf{T}$ relative to B has the form

$$\left(\begin{array}{c|c} \cdot\ \cdot\ \cdot & \cdot\ \cdot\ \cdot \\ \hline \mathbf{0} & \cdot\ \cdot\ \cdot \end{array}\right)$$

That is, the lower left-hand corner is the $(n - r) \times r$ zero matrix.

5. Let $\mathbf{T}: U \to U$ be an endomorphism of a vector space, and let V be a $\mathbf{T}$-stable subspace. If $\mathbf{T}$ has an inverse, show that V is stable for $\mathbf{T}^{-1}$ and that $(\mathbf{T}^{-1})_V = (\mathbf{T}_V)^{-1}$ (restrictions to V).

6. Let $\mathbf{T}: U \to U$ be an endomorphism of a vector space which is a direct sum of $\mathbf{T}$-stable subspaces $W_1, \ldots, W_r$. Let $\mathbf{T}_i$ denote the restriction of $\mathbf{T}$ to W_i. Show that $\mathbf{T}$ has an inverse if and only if each $\mathbf{T}_i: W_i \to W_i$ is an isomorphism. If that is so, show that

$$\mathbf{T}^{-1} = \mathbf{T}_1{}^{-1} \oplus \cdots \oplus \mathbf{T}_r{}^{-1}$$

7. Let $\mathbf{T}, \mathbf{T}_1, \ldots, \mathbf{T}_r$ be as in Exercise 6, and assume that U is of finite dimension. Prove that

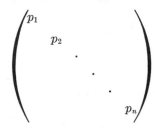

$$\det \mathbf{T} = (\det \mathbf{T}_1) \cdots (\det \mathbf{T}_r)$$

8. The mappings $\mathbf{T}, \mathbf{T}_1, \ldots, \mathbf{T}_r$ being as in Exercise 6, let $f(t)$ be a polynomial in a variable t with coefficients in the field of scalars. Prove that

$$f(\mathbf{T}) = f(\mathbf{T}_1) \oplus \cdots \oplus f(\mathbf{T}_n)$$

if $f(0) = 0$.

9. The mappings being as in Exercise 7, let $\varphi(t), \varphi_1(t), \ldots, \varphi_r(t)$ be their respective characteristic polynomials. Prove that

$$\varphi(t) = \varphi_1(t) \cdots \varphi_r(t)$$

10. Let $\mathbf{T}$ be an endomorphism of a finite-dimensional vector space U, and let $\mathbf{x}$ be a nonzero vector in U. Let k be the largest integer such that $\mathbf{x}, \mathbf{T}(\mathbf{x}), \ldots, \mathbf{T}^{k-1}(\mathbf{x})$ are linearly independent. Show that they generate a k-dimensional $\mathbf{T}$-stable subspace V of U. Show that there are uniquely determined scalars $a_0, \ldots, a_{k-1}$ such that $\mathbf{T}^k(\mathbf{x}) = a_0\mathbf{x} + \cdots + a_{k-1}\mathbf{T}^{k-1}(\mathbf{x})$, and prove that the characteristic polynomial of $\mathbf{T}_V$ is $t^k - a_{k-1}t^{k-1} - \cdots - a_1t - a_0$.

4. Nilpotent mappings

An endomorphism $\mathbf{T}: U \to U$ of a vector space is called *nilpotent* if $\mathbf{T}^k = \mathbf{0}$ for some integer k. For example, nilcyclic mappings are nilpotent (Type II, Sec. 2). But a nonzero diagonal mapping is not nilpotent (see the Remark at the end of Sec. 2).

A direct sum of nilpotent mappings is nilpotent—in particular, a direct sum of nilcyclic mappings is nilpotent. For let $\mathbf{T}: U \to U$ be the direct sum $\mathbf{T} = \mathbf{T}_1 \oplus \cdots \oplus \mathbf{T}_r$ of endomorphisms of subspaces $W_1, \ldots, W_r$, respectively, where $U = W_1 \oplus \cdots \oplus W_r$. Suppose that $\mathbf{T}_i^{k_i} = \mathbf{0}$ for $i = 1, \ldots, n$, the k_i being certain integers. Let k be the greatest of these integers k_i. Then $\mathbf{T}_i^k = \mathbf{0}$ for $i = 1, \ldots, r$, plainly. We claim that $\mathbf{T}^k = \mathbf{0}$.

To show this, let $\mathbf{T}_i'$ $(i = 1, \ldots, r)$ be the W_i part of $\mathbf{T}$ (cf. Proposition 3.5). Thus, $\mathbf{T}_i'(\mathbf{x}) = \mathbf{T}_i(\mathbf{x})$ for $\mathbf{x}$ in W_i and $\mathbf{T}_i'(\mathbf{x}) = \mathbf{0}$ for $\mathbf{x}$ in W_j with $j \neq i$. Clearly $\mathbf{T}_i'^k = \mathbf{0}$, since $\mathbf{T}_i^k = \mathbf{0}$. From (3.3) we have

$$\mathbf{T}^2 = (\mathbf{T}_1' + \cdots + \mathbf{T}_r')^2 = \sum_{i,j=1}^{r} \mathbf{T}_i'\mathbf{T}_j' = \mathbf{T}_1'^2 + \cdots + \mathbf{T}_r'^2$$

since the terms $\mathbf{T}_i'\mathbf{T}_j'$ with $i \neq j$ disappear. By a simple induction we find similarly that

$$\mathbf{T}^k = \mathbf{T}_1'^k + \cdots + \mathbf{T}_r'^k = \mathbf{0}$$

as claimed.

A direct sum of nilcyclic mappings is nilpotent, as was just shown. The main purpose of this paragraph is to show that a nilpotent mapping of a finite-dimensional vector space is the direct sum of nilcyclic parts. We require the following result:

THEOREM 4.1 *Let* $\mathbf{T}$ *be a linear mapping of a vector space* U, *and let* V *be a* $\mathbf{T}$-*stable subspace. Then there exists a vector space* U^0 *and two linear mappings* $\mathbf{S}: U \to U^0$ *and* $\mathbf{T}_0: U^0 \to U^0$ *such that*

$$\text{Ker } \mathbf{S} = V \qquad \mathbf{I}_m \mathbf{S} = U^0 \qquad \text{and} \qquad \mathbf{ST} = \mathbf{T}_0 \mathbf{S}$$

This theorem has already been proved in Sec. 10, Chap. 9. The desired U^0, $\mathbf{S}$, and $\mathbf{T}_0$ are given by

4.1 $$U^0 = U/V$$

4.2 $$\mathbf{T}_0 = \mathbf{T}_{U/V}$$

where U/V is the quotient module whose elements are all the different cosets $\mathbf{x} + V$. $\mathbf{S}: U \to U/V$ is the *projection*

4.3 $$\mathbf{x} \to \mathbf{x} + V$$

and $\mathbf{T}_{U/V}$, the U/V part of $\mathbf{T}$, is defined by

4.4 $$\mathbf{T}_{U/V}: \mathbf{x} + V \to T(\mathbf{x}) + V$$

for any coset $\mathbf{x} + V$.

The relation $\mathbf{ST} = \mathbf{T}_0\mathbf{S}$ can be depicted by the diagram

$$\begin{array}{ccc} & \mathbf{T} & \\ U & \longrightarrow & U \\ \mathbf{S} \downarrow & & \downarrow \mathbf{S} \\ U^0 & \longrightarrow & U^0 \\ & \mathbf{T}_0 & \end{array}$$

We now come to the main result of this section.

THEOREM 4.2 *Every nilpotent mapping of a finite-dimensional vector space* U *is the direct sum of nilcyclic mappings of certain subspaces, and* U *is the direct sum of those subspaces.*

Proof. We prove the theorem by induction on dim U. If the dimension is 1, then the assertion is plainly true. For let $\mathbf{e}$ be a base for U (that is, any nonzero vector). Then $\mathbf{T}(\mathbf{e}) = a\mathbf{e}$ for some scalar a. If $\mathbf{T}$ is nilpotent, say $\mathbf{T}^m = \mathbf{0}$, then $a^m = 0$, and so $a = 0$, $\mathbf{T} = \mathbf{0}$. The base $\mathbf{e}$ is a cyclic base for $\mathbf{T}$.

Suppose then that the theorem holds for vector spaces of dimension $<n$, where n is an integer greater than 1, and let dim $U = n$. Further, let m be the smallest integer such that $\mathbf{T}^m = \mathbf{0}$. Then $\mathbf{T}^{m-1} \neq \mathbf{0}$, and so there is a vector $\mathbf{x}$ in U such that $\mathbf{T}^{m-1}(\mathbf{x}) \neq \mathbf{0}$. Set $\mathbf{e}_1 = \mathbf{T}^{m-1}(\mathbf{x})$, $\mathbf{e}_2 = \mathbf{T}^{m-2}(\mathbf{x})$, . . . , $\mathbf{e}_{m-1} = \mathbf{T}(\mathbf{x})$, $\mathbf{e}_m = \mathbf{x}$. The vectors in the set $B = \{\mathbf{e}_1, \ldots, \mathbf{e}_m\}$ are linearly independent. For suppose that $a_1\mathbf{e}_1 + \cdots + a_m\mathbf{e}_m = 0$ for certain scalars $a_1, \ldots, a_m$. That is,

$$a_1\mathbf{T}^{m-1}(\mathbf{x}) + \cdots + a_{m-1}\mathbf{T}(\mathbf{x}) + a_m\mathbf{x} = \mathbf{0}$$

Applying $\mathbf{T}^{m-1}$ to this and keeping in mind that $\mathbf{T}^m = \mathbf{0}$, we get $a_m\mathbf{T}^{m-1}(\mathbf{x}) = \mathbf{0}$, whence $a_m = 0$. The equation is therefore

$$a_1\mathbf{T}^{m-1}(\mathbf{x}) + \cdots + a_{m-1}\mathbf{T}(\mathbf{x}) = \mathbf{0}$$

Applying $\mathbf{T}^{m-2}$ to this equation, we obtain $a_{m-1}\mathbf{T}^{m-1}(\mathbf{x}) = \mathbf{0}$, and so $a_{m-1} = 0$. Continuing in this way by a simple induction, we conclude that all the a's are zero. Let V denote the subspace of U generated by the set B. Then V is clearly **T**-stable, and the restriction of **T** to V is nilcyclic; B is a cyclic base for V. The following observation is important: (A). *If* $\mathbf{T}^k(\mathbf{y})$ *is in* V *for some element* $\mathbf{y}$ *of* U, *where* $0 \le k \le m$, *then there is an element* $\mathbf{y}'$ *in* U *such that* $\mathbf{T}^k(\mathbf{y}') = \mathbf{0}$ *and such that* $\mathbf{y}' - \mathbf{y}$ *is in* V.

To see this put $\mathbf{z} = \mathbf{T}^k(\mathbf{y})$. Then $\mathbf{z}$ is in V and $\mathbf{T}^{m-k}(\mathbf{z}) = \mathbf{0}$, since $\mathbf{T}^m(\mathbf{y}) = \mathbf{0}$. Expand $\mathbf{z}$ in terms of the cyclic base B in V, say, $\mathbf{z} = c_1\mathbf{e}_1 + \cdots + c_m\mathbf{e}_m$. Now $\mathbf{T}^{m-k}$ sends $\mathbf{e}_j$ into zero if $j \le m - k$, and it sends $\mathbf{e}_j$ into $\mathbf{e}_{j-(m-k)}$ if $j > m - k$. Applying $\mathbf{T}^{m-k}$ to both sides of the equation we obtain

$$\mathbf{0} = \mathbf{T}^{m-k}(\mathbf{z}) = c_{m-k+1}\mathbf{e}_1 + \cdots + c_m\mathbf{e}_k$$

from which it follows that $c_{m-k+1}, \ldots, c_m$ must all be zero. Hence $\mathbf{z} = c_1\mathbf{e}_1 + \cdots + c_{m-k}\mathbf{e}_{m-k}$. Define $\mathbf{z}'$ by the formula $\mathbf{z}' = c_1\mathbf{e}_{k+1} + \cdots + c_{m-k}\mathbf{e}_m$. Then clearly $\mathbf{T}^k(\mathbf{z}') = \mathbf{z}$. Putting $\mathbf{y}' = \mathbf{y} - \mathbf{z}'$ we have finally $\mathbf{T}^k(\mathbf{y}') = \mathbf{T}^k(\mathbf{y}) - T^k(\mathbf{z}') = \mathbf{z} - \mathbf{z} = \mathbf{0}$, and $\mathbf{y}' - \mathbf{y} = -\mathbf{z}'$ is an element of V, as desired.

Since V is **T**-stable, we can apply Theorem 4.1 to the situation at hand. The theorem guarantees the existence of a vector space U^0 and of linear mappings S and $\mathbf{T}_0$ such that Ker S $= V$, Im S $= U^0$, and $\mathbf{S}\mathbf{T} = \mathbf{T}_0\mathbf{S}$. From this last equation we have

$$\mathbf{S} \circ \mathbf{T}^2 = (\mathbf{S} \circ \mathbf{T}) \circ \mathbf{T} = (\mathbf{T}_0 \circ \mathbf{S}) \circ \mathbf{T} = \mathbf{T}_0 \circ (\mathbf{S} \circ \mathbf{T}) = \mathbf{T}_0 \circ (\mathbf{T}_0 \circ \mathbf{S}) = \mathbf{T}_0^2 \circ \mathbf{S}$$

Similarly, by a simple induction, we have

$$\mathbf{S} \circ \mathbf{T}^k = \mathbf{T}_0^k \circ \mathbf{S}$$

for $k = 0, 1, 2, 3$, etc. Putting $k = m$ here, we see that $\mathbf{T}_0^m \circ \mathbf{S} = \mathbf{0}$, since $\mathbf{T}^m = \mathbf{0}$. But S maps U *onto* all of U^0, and it follows at once from $\mathbf{T}_0^m\mathbf{S} = \mathbf{0}$ that $\mathbf{T}_0^m = \mathbf{0}$.

Now dim U = dim Ker S + dim Im S = dim V + dim U^0. Since dim $V = m > 0$, we must have dim $U^0 <$ dim V. If $V = U$, then **T** itself is nilcyclic, and we are done. If $V \ne U$, then dim $U^0 > 0$. As just observed, the mapping $\mathbf{T}_0$ of U^0 is nilpotent. Therefore, by our induction assumption, U^0 is the direct sum $U^0 = W_1{}^0 \oplus \cdots \oplus W_r{}^0$ of $\mathbf{T}_0$-stable subspaces such that the restriction of $\mathbf{T}_0$ to each $W_i{}^0$ is nilcyclic. Consequently each $W_i{}^0$ has a cyclic base $B_i{}^0$, obtained by applying $\mathbf{T}_0$ repeatedly to a single element $\mathbf{u}_i{}^0$. That is, if $m_i = \dim W_i{}^0$, then $B_i{}^0$ consists of the elements

4.5 $$\mathbf{T}_0{}^j(\mathbf{u}_i{}^0) \qquad (j = 0, 1, \ldots, m_i - 1)$$

(taken in the order of decreasing j); and $\mathbf{T}_0{}^{m_i}(\mathbf{u}_i{}^0) = \mathbf{0}$. Since $\mathbf{S}$ maps U onto U^0, for each i there is an element $\mathbf{u}_i$ in U such that $\mathbf{S}(\mathbf{u}_i) = \mathbf{u}_i{}^0$. Since $\mathbf{S} \circ \mathbf{T}^{m_i}(\mathbf{u}_i) = \mathbf{T}_0{}^{m_i}(\mathbf{S}(\mathbf{u}_i)) = \mathbf{T}_0{}^{m_i}(\mathbf{u}_i{}^0) = \mathbf{0}$, it follows that $\mathbf{T}^{m_i}(\mathbf{u}_i)$ is in the kernel of $\mathbf{S}$, namely, in V. Moreover, $\mathbf{u}_i$ can be altered at will by adding to it any element of V. We conclude from (A) above that $\mathbf{u}_i$ can be chosen in such a way that

4.6 $$\mathbf{T}^{m_i}(\mathbf{u}_i) = \mathbf{0} \qquad (i = 1, \ldots, r)$$

Now let B_i be the set of elements

4.7 $$\mathbf{T}^j(\mathbf{u}_i) \qquad (j = 0, 1, \ldots, m_i - 1)$$

taken in the order of decreasing j, and let W_i be the subspace of U generated by B_i. From (4.6) and (4.7) it is clear that W_i is $\mathbf{T}$-stable. We must show that $U = W_1 \oplus \cdots \oplus W_r \oplus V$, and to do so we have only to show that $B_1, \ldots, B_r, B$, taken jointly, form a base for U. Then let $\mathbf{y}$ be an arbitrary element of U. By assumption and Proposition 3.3, the element $S(\mathbf{y})$ in U_0 can be expressed as a linear combination of elements in $B_1{}^0, \ldots, B_r{}^0$. In that linear combination let us replace the elements (4.5) of $B_i{}^0$ by the corresponding elements (4.7) of B_i. The result is an element $\mathbf{y}'$ of U such that $\mathbf{S}(\mathbf{y}') = \mathbf{S}(\mathbf{y})$, clearly, since $\mathbf{S}$ maps B_i into $B_i{}^0$. Thus $S(\mathbf{y}' - \mathbf{y}) = \mathbf{0}$, and so $\mathbf{v} = \mathbf{y}' - \mathbf{y}$ is an element of V and can therefore be expressed as a linear combination of the elements of the base B. Hence $\mathbf{y} = \mathbf{y}' + \mathbf{v}$ is a linear combination of elements in $B_1, \ldots, B_r, B$. The latter elements are linearly independent, as follows easily from similar reasoning (that is, by applying $\mathbf{S}$ to any nontrivial relation among them).

Writing W_{r+1} for V and denoting by $\mathbf{T}_i$ the restriction of $\mathbf{T}$ to W_i $(i = 1, \ldots, r + 1)$, we have

$$\mathbf{T} = \mathbf{T}_1 \oplus \cdots \oplus \mathbf{T}_{r+1}$$

Furthermore, each $\mathbf{T}_i$ is nilcyclic, and B_i (or B in the case of W_{r+1}) is a cyclic base for W_i. Q.E.D.

EXAMPLE Let $\mathbf{T}$ be an endomorphism of U whose matrix with respect to the base $A = \{\mathbf{u}_1, \mathbf{u}_2, \mathbf{u}_3, \mathbf{u}_4\}$ is

$$\begin{pmatrix} 2 & -8 & 12 & -60 \\ 2 & -5 & 9 & -48 \\ 6 & -17 & 29 & -152 \\ 1 & -3 & 5 & -26 \end{pmatrix}$$

By direct calculation the characteristic polynomial of $\mathbf{T}$ is found to be t^4. Hence $\mathbf{T}^4 = \mathbf{0}$, and so $\mathbf{T}$ is nilpotent. It is easily verified, using the matrix, that $\mathbf{T}^2 = \mathbf{0}$. In the notation of the proof of Theorem 4.2, the integer m here is then 2. Following the proof of Theorem 4.2, we take any vector $\mathbf{x}$ such that $\mathbf{T}(\mathbf{x}) \neq \mathbf{0}$, and consider the subspace generated by $\mathbf{x}$ and $\mathbf{T}(\mathbf{x})$. Let us take $\mathbf{x}$ to be $\mathbf{u}_1$, and write $\mathbf{e}_2 = \mathbf{u}_1$ and $\mathbf{e}_1 = \mathbf{T}(\mathbf{u}_1)$. That is,

4.8
$$\begin{aligned} \mathbf{e}_2 &= \mathbf{u}_1 \\ \mathbf{e}_1 &= 2\mathbf{u}_1 + 2\mathbf{u}_2 + 6\mathbf{u}_3 + \mathbf{u}_4 = \mathbf{T}(\mathbf{e}_2) \end{aligned}$$

This pair of vectors generates a two-dimensional $\mathbf{T}$-stable subspace V_1, and they form a cyclic base for $\mathbf{T}$ restricted to V_1.

If we can find another vector $\mathbf{y}$ such that $\mathbf{y}$, $\mathbf{T}(\mathbf{y})$ and $\mathbf{e}_1$, $\mathbf{e}_2$ are all linearly independent, then we shall have the desired decomposition of $\mathbf{T}$. Let us try $\mathbf{u}_3$. Write

4.9
$$\begin{aligned} \mathbf{e}_4 &= \mathbf{u}_3 \\ \mathbf{e}_3 &= -60\mathbf{u}_1 - 48\mathbf{u}_2 - 152\mathbf{u}_3 - 26\mathbf{u}_4 = \mathbf{T}(\mathbf{e}_4) \end{aligned}$$

It is easy to see that (4.8) and (4.9) can be solved for $\mathbf{u}_1, \ldots, \mathbf{u}_4$ in terms of $B = \{\mathbf{e}_1, \ldots, \mathbf{e}_4\}$, so that the latter is a base of U. The matrix of $\mathbf{T}$ relative to B is

$$\left(\begin{array}{cc|cc} 0 & 1 & 0 & 0 \\ 0 & 0 & 0 & 0 \\ \hline 0 & 0 & 0 & 1 \\ 0 & 0 & 0 & 0 \end{array}\right)$$

Denoting by V_2 the subspace spanned by $\mathbf{e}_3$ and $\mathbf{e}_4$, we have $U = V_1 \oplus V_2$. Denoting by $\mathbf{T}_i$ the restriction of $\mathbf{T}$ to V_i, we have $\mathbf{T} = \mathbf{T}_1 \oplus \mathbf{T}_2$, and $\mathbf{T}_1$ and $\mathbf{T}_2$ are nilcyclic.

We shall abstain from giving an example exhibiting the various complications arising in the computations connected with Theorem 4.2. Since the proof of Theorem 4.2 is inductive in nature, it carries with it more or less explicit instructions for performing the calculations. In the notation of the proof, starting from U we obtain an m-dimensional subspace V generated by $\mathbf{x}, \mathbf{T}(\mathbf{x}), \ldots, \mathbf{T}^{m-1}(\mathbf{x})$. If $V = U$, then we are done. Otherwise, the induction step required involves replacing U by a lower dimensional subspace U^0 equipped with two linear mappings $\mathbf{S}: U \to U^0$ and $\mathbf{T}_0: U^0 \to U^0$ such that $\operatorname{Ker} \mathbf{S} = V$ and $\mathbf{S} \circ \mathbf{T} = \mathbf{T}_0 \circ \mathbf{S}$. Then $\mathbf{T}_0$ is again nilpotent (assuming $\mathbf{T}$ is), and we can start afresh with $\mathbf{T}_0$ and

U_0, repeating the same argument for them. Only a finite number of reduction steps of this type are necessary, since the dimension drops at each step.

EXERCISES

1. Let **T** be a linear mapping whose matrix with respect to a base $\{\mathbf{e}_1, \mathbf{e}_2\}$ is

$$\begin{pmatrix} 0 & 2 \\ 0 & 0 \end{pmatrix}$$

Prove that **T** is nilcyclic, and find a cyclic base.

2. Let **T** be a linear mapping whose matrix with respect to a base $\{\mathbf{e}_1, \mathbf{e}_2, \mathbf{e}_3\}$ is

$$\begin{pmatrix} 0 & a & b \\ 0 & 0 & c \\ 0 & 0 & 0 \end{pmatrix}$$

Prove that **T** is nilpotent. Under what circumstances is it nilcyclic?

3. Let a linear mapping **T** have a triangular matrix with respect to some base $\{\mathbf{e}_1, \ldots, \mathbf{e}_n\}$, and suppose that the diagonal entries are all zero. Prove that **T** is nilpotent.

4. Prove the converse of Exercise 3. That is, if **T** is a nilpotent mapping of a finite-dimensional vector space, then there is a base relative to which the matrix of **T** has the desired form.

5. Let **T** be a nilpotent endomorphism of an n-dimensional space U, and let $U = W_1 \oplus \cdots \oplus W_r$ be a direct sum decomposition into **T**-stable subspaces, on each of which **T** is nilcyclic. Prove that

$$r = \dim \operatorname{Ker} \mathbf{T}$$

[Hint: What is the dimension of Ker $\mathbf{T}_i$, where $\mathbf{T}_i$ is the restriction of **T** to W_i?]

6. Let **T** be nilcyclic of order m. What is dim Ker **T**?

7. Hypotheses as in Exercise 5. Let $n_1, n_2, \ldots, n_r$ be the dimensions of $W_1, \ldots, W_r$. Prove that for any integer $h \geq 1$ the number of integers in the set $n_1, \ldots, n_r$ which are $\geq h$ is equal to

$$\dim \operatorname{Ker} \mathbf{T}^h - \dim \operatorname{Ker} \mathbf{T}^{h-1}$$

[Hint: Use Exercise 6 above and Exercise 1, Sec. 3.] (Taking $h = 1$ here we get the result of Exercise 5.) Conclude from the result above that r as well as the set of integers $n_1, \ldots, n_r$ are uniquely determined by **T** and do not depend upon the particular decomposition into nilcyclic parts.

8. Let U, V, U^0, **T**, **S**, $\mathbf{T}_0$ be as in Theorem 4.1. Prove that if $\{\mathbf{u}_1, \ldots, \mathbf{u}_n\}$ is a base for U, then there is a subset of them which is carried by **S** into a base for U^0.

Taking $n = 5$, let V have the vectors

$$\mathbf{e}_1 = \mathbf{u}_1 - 2\mathbf{u}_2 + \mathbf{u}_4 + \mathbf{u}_5$$
$$\mathbf{e}_2 = 2\mathbf{u}_1 - \mathbf{u}_3 + 4\mathbf{u}_5$$
$$\mathbf{e}_3 = \mathbf{u}_2 - \mathbf{u}_4 + \mathbf{u}_5$$

as base. Show that $\mathbf{S}(\mathbf{u}_4)$ and $\mathbf{S}(\mathbf{u}_5)$ form a base for U^0. If **T** has matrix

$$\begin{pmatrix} -5 & -1 & 1 & 0 & 3 \\ 1 & 1 & 4 & 1 & 0 \\ -2 & -1 & -4 & 0 & 0 \\ -1 & 1 & 1 & 2 & 1 \\ 5 & 3 & 13 & 0 & 1 \end{pmatrix}$$

relative to the given base $\{\mathbf{u}_1, \ldots, \mathbf{u}_5\}$, show that V is $\mathbf{T}$-stable, and compute the matrix of $\mathbf{T}^0$ relative to the base $\{\mathbf{S}(\mathbf{u}_4), \mathbf{S}(\mathbf{u}_5)\}$.

5. *Characteristic subspaces*

Let $\mathbf{T}$: $U \to U$ be a linear mapping of an n-dimensional vector space over a field K; and let $\varphi(t)$ be the characteristic polynomial of $\mathbf{T}$ (cf. Sec. 5, Chap. 11). We recall that if $\mathbf{a}$ is the matrix of $\mathbf{T}$ relative to any base in U, then

$$\varphi(t) = \det (t\mathbf{I} - \mathbf{a})$$

and $\varphi(t)$ is a monic polynomial of degree $n = \dim U$ (see Theorem 4.2, Chap. 11).

Throughout Secs. 5, 6, 7 we shall assume that all the roots of $\varphi(t)$ are in K. More precisely, we shall assume that $\varphi(t)$ splits into a product of factors of degree 1, say

5.1 $$\varphi(t) = (t - p_1)(t - p_2) \cdots (t - p_n)$$

all the p_j being in K. If our field of scalars is the complex field, then the assumption is automatically verified, by virtue of Theorem 4.2, Chap. 6. Naturally some of the p_i in (5.1) may be repeated several times. Suppose then that $p_1, p_2, \ldots, p_r$ are the *distinct* roots of $\varphi(t)$. Gathering repeated factors in (5.1) together, we can write it as

5.2 $$\varphi(t) = (t - p_1)^{n_1} \cdot (t - p_2)^{n_2} \cdots (t - p_r)^{n_r}$$

where $n_1, n_2, \ldots, n_r$ are positive integers such that $n_1 + \cdots + n_r = n$. We recall that the roots p_i are called the *eigenvalues* of $\mathbf{T}$.

DEFINITION 5.1 *The kernel of the operator $(p_i\mathbf{I} - \mathbf{T})^{n_i}$ is called the* characteristic subspace *of U belonging to the eigenvalue p_i. We denote it by V_i. Hence, $\mathbf{x}$ is in V_i if and only if*

$$(\mathbf{T} - p_i\mathbf{I})^{n_i}(\mathbf{x}) = \mathbf{0}$$

V_i is indeed a subspace of U, for the kernel of any linear mapping is a subspace. Moreover, V_i is $\mathbf{T}$-stable. To see this we observe that

5.3 $$\mathbf{T} \circ (\mathbf{T} - p_i\mathbf{I})^{n_i} = (\mathbf{T} - p_i\mathbf{I})^{n_i} \circ \mathbf{T}$$

which follows at once from the polynomial identity

$$t(t - p_i)^{n_i} = (t - p_i)^{n_i}t$$

and the fact that the substitution $t \to \mathbf{T}$ preserves polynomial identities (see Theorem 4.4, Chap. 11). Then if $\mathbf{x}$ is in V_i, we have $(\mathbf{T} - p_i\,\mathbf{I})^{n_i}(\mathbf{x}) = \mathbf{0}$, by definition, and so $\mathbf{T}(\mathbf{T} - p_i\,\mathbf{I})^{n_i}(\mathbf{x}) = \mathbf{T}(\mathbf{0}) = \mathbf{0}$. From (5.3) there follows

$$(\mathbf{T} - p_i\,\mathbf{I})^{n_i}\mathbf{T}(\mathbf{x}) = \mathbf{0}$$

showing that $\mathbf{T}(\mathbf{x})$ is in V_i. Hence $\mathbf{T}$ maps V_i to itself.

It is convenient to associate with $\varphi(t)$ the polynomial $f_i(t)$ $(i = 1, \ldots, r)$ defined by

5.4 $$f_i(t) = (t - p_1)^{n_1} \cdots (t - p_{i-1})^{n_{i-1}}(t - p_{i+1})^{n_{i+1}} \cdots (t - p_r)^{n_r}$$

Then clearly

5.5 $$\varphi(t) = (t - p_i)^{n_i}f_i(t)$$

and $f_1(t), f_2(t), \ldots, f_r(t)$ have no common factors other than constants. That is, their greatest common divisor is 1. Therefore there exist polynomials $a_1(t), \ldots, a_r(t)$ with coefficients in K such that

5.6 $$1 = f_1(t)a_1(t) + \cdots + f_r(t)a_r(t)$$

(See Theorem 3.4 and Exercise 3, Sec. 3, Chap 6.)

The main result of this section is the following theorem:

THEOREM 5.1 *Let* $\mathbf{T}$ *be a linear mapping of an n-dimensional vector space* U *to itself, and suppose that the characteristic polynomial of* $\mathbf{T}$ *is* $\varphi(t) = (t - p_1)^{n_1} \cdots (t - p_r)^{n_r}$ *where* $p_1, \ldots, p_r$ *are the distinct eigenvalues of* $\mathbf{T}$*. Then* U *is the direct sum* $U = V_1 \oplus \cdots \oplus V_r$ *of the characteristic subspaces. These subspaces are* $\mathbf{T}$*-stable; and if* $\mathbf{T}_i$ *denotes the restriction of* $\mathbf{T}$ *to* V_i*, then the characteristic polynomial of* $\mathbf{T}_i$ *is* $(t - p_i)^{n_i}$*. Finally,* $\dim V_i = n_i$.

Proof. We have already shown that the characteristic subspaces U_i are $\mathbf{T}$-stable. Now let $\mathbf{x}$ be any vector in U. To (5.6) let us apply the substitution homomorphism that replaces t by $\mathbf{T}$. The result is

5.7 $$\mathbf{I} = f_1(\mathbf{T}) \circ a_1(\mathbf{T}) + \cdots + f_r(\mathbf{T}) \circ a_r(\mathbf{T}) \qquad \text{(Theorem 4.4, Chap. 11)}$$

Hence

$$\mathbf{x} = \mathbf{I}(\mathbf{x}) = f_1(\mathbf{T}) \circ a_1(\mathbf{T})(\mathbf{x}) + \cdots + f_r(\mathbf{T}) \circ a_r(\mathbf{T})(\mathbf{x})$$

Write

5.8 $$\mathbf{x}_i = f_i(\mathbf{T}) \circ a_i(\mathbf{T})(\mathbf{x})$$

so that the preceding equation is

5.9 $$\mathbf{x} = \mathbf{x}_1 + \cdots + \mathbf{x}_r$$

Now apply operator $(\mathbf{T} - p_i\mathbf{I})^{n_i}$ to (5.9). From (5.5),

$$\varphi(\mathbf{T}) = (\mathbf{T} - p_i\mathbf{I})^{n_i} \circ f_i(\mathbf{T})$$

whence, by (5.8),

$$(\mathbf{T} - p_i\mathbf{I})^{n_i}(\mathbf{x}_i) = \varphi(\mathbf{T}) \circ a_i(\mathbf{T})(\mathbf{x}) = \mathbf{0}$$

by the Cayley-Hamilton theorem (Theorem 5.2, Chap. 11). Therefore $\mathbf{x}_i$ is in the characteristic subspace V_i. We have shown that every vector $\mathbf{x}$ in U can be expressed in at least one way as a sum (5.8) of elements in the V_i. We must show now that the expression is unique. Let $\mathbf{x} = \mathbf{x}_1' + \cdots + \mathbf{x}_r'$ be another expression of the same type, that is, with $\mathbf{x}_i'$ in V_i. Subtracting the two we get

$$\mathbf{0} = \mathbf{y}_1 + \cdots + \mathbf{y}_r$$

where $\mathbf{y}_i = \mathbf{x}_i' - \mathbf{x}_i$ is again in V_i. We have only to show that the $\mathbf{y}_i$ are all zero.

If $\mathbf{v}$ is any vector in V_i, then $(\mathbf{T} - p_i\mathbf{I})^{n_i}(\mathbf{v}) = 0$, by definition. Now the polynomial $f_j(t)$ contains the factor $(t - p_i)^{n_i}$ if $j \neq i$, and so

5.10 $$f_j(\mathbf{T})(\mathbf{v}) = \mathbf{0} \qquad \text{if } \mathbf{v} \text{ is in } V_i \text{ and } i \neq j$$

Then from the identity (5.7) we find that

5.11 $$\mathbf{v} = f_i(\mathbf{T}) \circ a_i(\mathbf{T})(\mathbf{v}) \qquad \text{for } \mathbf{v} \text{ in } V_i$$

since $f_j(\mathbf{T}) \circ a_j(\mathbf{T})(\mathbf{v}) = \mathbf{0} \qquad \text{for } j \neq i$

by (5.10).

Now apply the operator $f_i(\mathbf{T}) \circ a_i(\mathbf{T})$ to the equation

$$\mathbf{0} = \mathbf{y}_1 + \cdots + \mathbf{y}_r$$

From (5.10) we obtain

$$\mathbf{0} = f_i(\mathbf{T}) \circ a_i(\mathbf{T})(\mathbf{y}_i)$$

and the right-hand side is equal to $\mathbf{y}_i$, by (5.11). Thus $\mathbf{y}_i = 0$, and we have proved that $U = V_1 \oplus \cdots \oplus V_r$, and therefore

$$\mathbf{T} = \mathbf{T}_1 \oplus \cdots \oplus \mathbf{T}_r$$

by Proposition 3.5, where $\mathbf{T}_i\colon V_i \to V_i$ is the restriction of $\mathbf{T}$ to V_i. Observe that (5.11) says that $a_i(\mathbf{T})$ is the inverse of $f_i(\mathbf{T})$ on the subspace V_i. That is,

$$a_i(\mathbf{T}_i) = f_i(\mathbf{T}_i)^{-1}$$

The operators

$$f_i(\mathbf{T}) \circ a_i(\mathbf{T})$$

are precisely the projection operators $\mathbf{P}_i$ discussed in connection with (3.1).

To complete the proof of our theorem, we start with the fact that $(\mathbf{T}_i - p_i\mathbf{I})^{n_i} = \mathbf{0}$ on V_i (here $\mathbf{I}$ denotes the identity on V_i). Hence the characteristic polynomial of $\mathbf{T}_i$ must be $(t - p_i)^{k_i}$ for some integer k_i. This follows at once from Theorem 4.6, Chap. 4. For the minimal polynomial of $\mathbf{T}_i$ must divide $(t - p_i)^{n_i}$ and must therefore be a power of $t - p_i$. The minimal and characteristic polynomials of $\mathbf{T}_i$ have the same irreducible factors—namely, $t - p_i$—and so the characteristic polynomial of $\mathbf{T}_i$ is also a power of $t - p_i$. By Theorem 5.7, Chap. 11, we have

$$\varphi(t) = (t - p_1)^{k_1} \cdots (t - p_r)^{k_r}$$

the product of the characteristic polynomials of the $\mathbf{T}_i$. Comparing this with (5.2) we conclude that $k_1 = n_1, \ldots, k_r = n_r$. Q.E.D.

EXERCISES

In the following exercises $\mathbf{T}$ denotes a linear mapping of a vector space to itself, and $\text{mat}_B\,\mathbf{T}$ denotes the matrix of $\mathbf{T}$ relative to some base B.

1. Find the characteristic subspaces of $\mathbf{T}$ if

$$\text{mat}_B\,\mathbf{T} = \begin{pmatrix} -1 & 0 \\ 0 & -2 \end{pmatrix}$$

where $B = \{\mathbf{e}_1, \mathbf{e}_2\}$.

2. Find the characteristic subspaces if

$$\text{mat}_B\,\mathbf{T} = \begin{pmatrix} 3 & 5 \\ 0 & 3 \end{pmatrix}$$

3. Find the characteristic subspaces if

$$\text{mat}_B\,\mathbf{T} = \begin{pmatrix} 0 & 1 \\ -1 & 0 \end{pmatrix}$$

4. Find the characteristic subspaces if

$$\text{mat}_B\,\mathbf{T} = \begin{pmatrix} 3 & 5 & 0 \\ 0 & 3 & 0 \\ 0 & 0 & 2 \end{pmatrix}$$

5. Find the characteristic subspaces if

$$\text{mat}_B\,\mathbf{T} = \begin{pmatrix} 3 & 5 & 0 \\ 0 & 3 & 0 \\ 0 & 0 & 3 \end{pmatrix}$$

6. Find the characteristic subspaces if

$$\text{mat}_B\,\mathbf{T} = \begin{pmatrix} 5 & 1 & -1 \\ 0 & 2 & 1 \\ 0 & 3 & 1 \end{pmatrix}$$

7. What are the characteristic subspaces of a nilpotent mapping?

8. Let $\mathbf{T}$ be a linear mapping of an n-dimensional vector space U over a field K, and let p be an element of K. Let V_p denote the kernel of $(\mathbf{T} - p\mathbf{I})^n$.

(*a*) Prove that $V_p \neq \mathbf{0}$ if and only if p is an eigenvalue of $\mathbf{T}$.

(*b*) Prove that $V_p = \text{Ker}\ (\mathbf{T} - p\mathbf{I})^m$, where m is the highest power of $t - p$ that divides the characteristic polynomial of $\mathbf{T}$.

(*c*) Prove that $\dim V_p = m$.

(*d*) Let $\mathbf{T}'$ denote the restriction of $\mathbf{T}$ to V_p. Prove that the characteristic polynomial of $\mathbf{T}'$ is $(t - p)^m$.

6. The Jordan normal form

Again let $\mathbf{T}: U \to U$ be a linear mapping of an n-dimensional vector space U over a field K, and assume that the characteristic polynomial $\varphi(t)$ can be factored completely:

6.1 $$\varphi(t) = (t - p_1)^{n_1} \cdot (t - p_2)^{n_2} \cdots (t - p_r)^{n_r}$$

where $p_1, p_2, \ldots, p_r$ are the distinct eigenvalues of $\mathbf{T}$, all in the field K. Again let

6.2 $$V_i = \text{Ker}\ (\mathbf{T} - p_i\mathbf{I})^{n_i}$$

be the characteristic subspace belonging to p_i. By Theorem 5.1 we have

6.3 $$U = V_1 \oplus \cdots \oplus V_r$$

and

6.4 $$\mathbf{T} = \mathbf{T}_1 \oplus \cdots \oplus \mathbf{T}_r$$

where $\mathbf{T}_i: V_i \to V_i$ is the restriction of $\mathbf{T}$ to the stable subspace V_i.

By (6.2) we have $(\mathbf{T}_i - p_i\mathbf{I})^{n_i} = \mathbf{0}$ on V_i, and therefore we can apply the results of Sec. 4 to the nilpotent operator $\mathbf{T}_i - p_i\mathbf{I}$. By Theorem 4.2 the subspace V_i can in turn be split into a direct sum of subspaces

6.5 $$V_i = W_{i1} \oplus \cdots \oplus W_{ik_i}$$

of a certain number k_i of $(\mathbf{T}_i - p_i\mathbf{I})$-stable subspaces, on each of which $\mathbf{T}_i - p_i\mathbf{I}$ is nilcyclic. The W_{ij} are in fact $\mathbf{T}$-stable, for let $\mathbf{x}$ be in W_{ij}. Then $(\mathbf{T} - p_i\mathbf{I})(\mathbf{x}) = \mathbf{T}_i(\mathbf{x}) - p_i\mathbf{x}$ is in W_{ij}, since W_{ij} is stable for $\mathbf{T}_i - p_i\mathbf{I}$. But $p_i\mathbf{x}$ is certainly in W_{ij}, and therefore $\mathbf{T}(\mathbf{x})$ must also be in W_{ij}, being equal to $p_i\mathbf{x}$ plus an element of W_{ij}. Thus, denoting by $\mathbf{T}_{ij}$ the restriction of $\mathbf{T}$ to W_{ij}, we have

6.6 $$\mathbf{T}_i = \mathbf{T}_{i1} \oplus \cdots \oplus \mathbf{T}_{ik_i}$$

by Proposition 3.5.

Now let us determine the matrix of the mapping $\mathbf{T}_{ij}$ of W_{ij}. Since $\mathbf{T}_{ij} - p_i\mathbf{I}$ is nilcyclic, there is a cyclic base B_{ij} for W_{ij}. For simplicity of notation, suppose that

$B_{ij} = \{\mathbf{e}_1, \mathbf{e}_2, \ldots, \mathbf{e}_q\}$. This is a cyclic base for the operator $\mathbf{T}_{ij} - p_i\mathbf{I}$, and therefore (cf. Sec. 2, Type II) the matrix of $\mathbf{T}_{ij} - p_i\mathbf{I}$ relative to that base must be the $q \times q$ matrix

$$\begin{pmatrix} 0 & 1 & 0 & \cdots & 0 \\ 0 & 0 & 1 & \cdots & 0 \\ \cdot & \cdot & \cdot & \cdots & \cdot \\ 0 & 0 & 0 & \cdots & 1 \\ 0 & 0 & 0 & \cdots & 0 \end{pmatrix} \tag{6.7}$$

Now

$$\mathbf{T}_{ij} = p_i\mathbf{I} + (\mathbf{T}_{ij} - p_i\mathbf{I})$$

and consequently the matrix of $\mathbf{T}_{ij}$ relative to the base in question is equal to $p_i \times$ identity matrix plus the matrix (6.7). That is, denoting by $\text{mat}_{B_{ij}}\mathbf{T}_{ij}$ the matrix of $\mathbf{T}_{ij}$, we have

$$\text{mat}_{B_{ij}}\,\mathbf{T}_{ij} = \begin{pmatrix} p_i & 1 & 0 & \cdots & 0 \\ 0 & p_i & 1 & \cdots & 0 \\ \cdot & \cdot & \cdot & \cdots & \cdot \\ 0 & 0 & 0 & \cdots\; p_i & 1 \\ 0 & 0 & 0 & \cdots\; 0 & p_i \end{pmatrix} \tag{6.8}$$

consisting of p_i along the main diagonal and 1's on the diagonal just above the main diagonal.

For each W_{ij} we have a cyclic base B_{ij} (for $\mathbf{T}_i - p_i\mathbf{I}$). Let $B_i = \{B_{i1}, \ldots, B_{ik_i}\}$ be the joint base for V_i obtained from the bases of the various subspaces $W_{i1}, \ldots, W_{ik_i}$ (Proposition 3.3). Similarly, let $B = \{B_1, \ldots, B_r\}$ be the base for U obtained by joining the bases B_i of the characteristic subspaces V_i. Then by Proposition 3.6 we have

$$\text{mat}_B\,\mathbf{T} = \begin{pmatrix} \boxed{\text{mat}_{B_1}\,\mathbf{T}_1} & & & \\ & \boxed{\text{mat}_{B_2}\,\mathbf{T}_2} & & \\ & & \ddots & \\ & & & \boxed{\text{mat}_{B_r}\,\mathbf{T}_r} \end{pmatrix} \tag{6.9}$$

where $\text{mat}_B\,\mathbf{T}$ stands for the matrix of $\mathbf{T}$ relative to the base B, etc., and where the entries in (6.9) off of the diagonal blocks are all zero.

In turn, from (6.6) we have

$$\text{mat}_{B_i}\,\mathbf{T}_i = \begin{pmatrix} \boxed{\text{mat}_{B_{i1}}\,\mathbf{T}_{i1}} & & \\ & \ddots & \\ & & \boxed{\text{mat}_{B_{ik_i}}\,\mathbf{T}_{ik_i}} \end{pmatrix} \tag{6.10}$$

with zeros off the diagonal blocks.

We summarize our findings in the following theorem:

THEOREM 6.1 **(Jordan normal form theorem)** *Let* **T** *be a linear mapping of a finite-dimensional vector space* U *to itself, and assume that the characteristic polynomial of* **T** *has all its roots in the field of scalars. Then there is a base* B *in* U *with respect to which the matrix of* **T** *has a diagonal block form in which each block is of the type* (6.8).

As might be expected, the process of determining the promised base B for which the matrix of **T** is in Jordan normal form is rather tedious. However, the procedure is reasonably straightforward.

Suppose, as is usually the case, that **T** is specified by means of its matrix relative to some base A in the vector space U. The first step is to compute the characteristic polynomial $\varphi(t)$ of **T** from that matrix and to determine the roots of $\varphi(t)$. Suppose that has been done, so that we have $\varphi(t)$ in the form (6.1).

The next task, rather arduous, is to compute the characteristic subspaces V_i. Recall that $V_i = \text{Ker } \mathbf{S}_i$, where $\mathbf{S}_i$ stands for $(\mathbf{T} - p_i\mathbf{I})^{n_i}$. To do this we proceed as follows: First compute the matrix of $\mathbf{S}_i$ relative to the given base A. It is

$$\text{mat}_A\ \mathbf{S}_i = (\text{mat}_A\ \mathbf{T} - p_i\mathbf{I})^{ni}$$

Only simple matrix operations are required for this step. To determine Ker $\mathbf{S}_i$ we use the method of Sec. 9, Chap. 9. Thus by a series of elementary row and column operations on $\text{mat}_A\ \mathbf{S}_i$ we can determine a *pair* of bases A'_i and A''_i in U with respect to which $\mathbf{S}_i$ has a diagonal matrix. The kernel of $\mathbf{S}_i$ can then be read off immediately: V_i is generated by the elements of A'_i which are mapped by $\mathbf{S}_i$ into zero, and they are the elements that correspond to zero diagonal elements in the matrix of $\mathbf{S}_i$ relative to the base pair A'_i, A''_i.

The subset of A'_i just described is a base for V_i, call it A_i. It is easy to compute how **T** operates on the elements of A_i, and doing so we obtain the matrix of $\mathbf{T}_i$ relative to A_i, where $\mathbf{T}_i$ is the restriction of **T** to the stable subspace V_i.

The last step is the decomposition of the nilpotent operators $\mathbf{T}_i - p_i\mathbf{I}$ into nilcyclic parts by the method described in Sec. 4.

EXAMPLE Let $\mathbf{T}: U \to U$ have the following matrix with respect to a given base $A = \{\mathbf{u}_1, \mathbf{u}_2, \mathbf{u}_3, \mathbf{u}_4\}$:

$$\text{mat}_A\ \mathbf{T} = \begin{pmatrix} 2 & 1 & -6 & -6 \\ 0 & 2 & 0 & 0 \\ -3 & -1 & 5 & 6 \\ 3 & 1 & -6 & -7 \end{pmatrix}$$

A simple calculation gives us the characteristic polynomial:

$$\varphi(t) = (t+1)^2(t-2)^2$$

The characteristic subspaces are therefore

$$V_1 = \text{Ker } (\mathbf{T} + \mathbf{I})^2 \qquad V_2 = \text{Ker } (\mathbf{T} - 2\mathbf{I})^2$$

For the first operator we have

$$\operatorname{mat}_A (\mathbf{T} + \mathbf{I})^2 = \begin{pmatrix} 9 & 6 & -18 & -18 \\ 0 & 9 & 0 & 0 \\ -9 & -6 & 18 & 18 \\ 9 & 6 & -18 & -18 \end{pmatrix}$$

obviously of rank 2. It is a trivial matter to reduce it to diagonal form by the method of Sec. 9, Chap. 9. Thus, following (9.1), Chap. 9, introduce the base $A'' = \{\mathbf{v}_1, \ldots, \mathbf{v}_4\}$ defined by

$$\mathbf{v}_1 = \mathbf{u}_1 - \mathbf{u}_3 + \mathbf{u}_4$$
$$\mathbf{v}_j = \mathbf{u}_j \qquad (j = 2, 3, 4)$$

It is quickly seen that the matrix of $(\mathbf{T} + \mathbf{I})^2$ relative to the base pair A, A'' [that is, $\mathbf{T}(\mathbf{u}_i)$ expressed in terms of the $\mathbf{v}_j$] is

$$\begin{pmatrix} 9 & 6 & -18 & -18 \\ 0 & 9 & 0 & 0 \\ 0 & 0 & 0 & 0 \\ 0 & 0 & 0 & 0 \end{pmatrix}$$

in conformity with the general rules of Sec. 9, Chap. 9. Now following (9.6), Chap. 9, define the base $A' = \{\mathbf{u}_1', \ldots, \mathbf{u}_4'\}$ by

$$\mathbf{u}_1' = \mathbf{u}_1, \ \mathbf{u}_2' = -\tfrac{2}{3}\mathbf{u}_1 + \mathbf{u}_2, \ \mathbf{u}_3' = 2\mathbf{u}_1 + \mathbf{u}_3, \ \mathbf{u}_4' = 2\mathbf{u}_1 + \mathbf{u}_4.$$

Then the matrix of $(\mathbf{T} + \mathbf{I})^2$ relative to the base pair A', A'' is

$$\begin{pmatrix} 9 & 0 & 0 & 0 \\ 0 & 9 & 0 & 0 \\ 0 & 0 & 0 & 0 \\ 0 & 0 & 0 & 0 \end{pmatrix}$$

It is immediate that Ker $(\mathbf{T} + \mathbf{I})^2$ is generated by $\mathbf{u}_3', \mathbf{u}_4'$. Thus

$$V_1 \text{ has the base } \begin{cases} 2\mathbf{u}_1 + \mathbf{u}_3 \\ 2\mathbf{u}_1 + \mathbf{u}_4 \end{cases}$$

In an entirely analogous way we calculate

$$\operatorname{mat}_A (\mathbf{T} - 2\mathbf{I})^2 = \begin{pmatrix} 0 & 0 & 18 & 18 \\ 0 & 0 & 0 & 0 \\ 9 & 0 & -9 & -18 \\ -9 & 0 & 18 & 27 \end{pmatrix}$$

and from this

$$V_2 \text{ has the base } \begin{cases} \mathbf{u}_1 - \mathbf{u}_3 + \mathbf{u}_4 \\ \mathbf{u}_2 \end{cases}$$

Denote the four vectors just obtained by $\mathbf{e}_1, \ldots, \mathbf{e}_4$. Thus

$$\mathbf{e}_1 = 2\mathbf{u}_1 + \mathbf{u}_3 \qquad \mathbf{e}_2 = 2\mathbf{u}_1 + \mathbf{u}_4 \qquad \mathbf{e}_3 = \mathbf{u}_1 - \mathbf{u}_3 + \mathbf{u}_4 \qquad \mathbf{e}_4 = \mathbf{u}_2$$

A simple calculation shows that $\mathbf{T} + \mathbf{I}$ maps $\mathbf{e}_1$ and $\mathbf{e}_2$ into zero. That is, $\mathbf{T}(\mathbf{e}_1) = -\mathbf{e}_1$ and $\mathbf{T}(\mathbf{e}_2) = -\mathbf{e}_2$, and $\mathbf{e}_1$, $\mathbf{e}_2$ are eigenvectors belonging to the characteristic root -1. Again a trivial calculation shows that $\mathbf{T} - 2\mathbf{I}$ maps $\mathbf{e}_4 \to \mathbf{e}_3$ and $\mathbf{e}_3 \to \mathbf{0}$. Hence the matrix of $\mathbf{T}$ relative to the new base $B = \{\mathbf{e}_1, \mathbf{e}_2, \mathbf{e}_3, \mathbf{e}_4\}$ is

$$\text{mat}_B\, \mathbf{T} = \begin{pmatrix} -1 & 0 & 0 & 0 \\ 0 & -1 & 0 & 0 \\ 0 & 0 & 2 & 1 \\ 0 & 0 & 0 & 2 \end{pmatrix}$$

This matrix is indeed in Jordan normal form.

We now require the following result:

THEOREM 6.2 *Let $\mathbf{T}: U \to U$ be a linear mapping of a finite-dimensional vector space over a field K. A necessary and sufficient condition for $\mathbf{T}$ to be a diagonal mapping is that there exist distinct elements in K, say $p_1, \ldots, p_r$, such that*

6.11 $$(\mathbf{T} - p_i\mathbf{I})(\mathbf{T} - p_2\mathbf{I}) \cdots (\mathbf{T} - p_r\mathbf{I}) = \mathbf{0}$$

Proof. If $\mathbf{T}$ is diagonal, then by definition (Sec. 2, Type III) there is a base $\{\mathbf{e}_1, \ldots, \mathbf{e}_n\}$ of U such that $\mathbf{T}(\mathbf{e}_i) = p_i\mathbf{e}_i$ for $i = 1, \ldots, n$, where each p_i is in K. Let $p_1, \ldots, p_r$ be the distinct p's. Then the operator $(\mathbf{T} - p_1\mathbf{I}) \cdots (\mathbf{T} - p_r\mathbf{I})$ clearly maps each $\mathbf{e}_i$ into zero and consequently maps all of U into zero. Hence (6.11) holds.

Conversely, let (6.11) hold for $\mathbf{T}$. If a factor $\mathbf{T} - p_i\mathbf{I}$ has an inverse on U, then it can simply be omitted from (6.11), and we suppose that is done. Then the spaces

6.12 $$U_i = \text{Ker}\,(\mathbf{T} - p_i\mathbf{I}) \qquad (i = 1, \ldots, r)$$

all have positive dimension. Now reasoning just as in the proof of Theorem 5.1, with the U_i in place of the characteristic subspaces and with $f(t) = (t - p_1) \cdots (t - p_r)$ in place of the characteristic polynomial $\varphi(t)$, we conclude that $U = U_1 \oplus \cdots \oplus U_r$. On U_i the mapping $\mathbf{T} - p_i\mathbf{I}$ is zero. That is, $\mathbf{T}$ restricted to U_i is the same as $p_i\mathbf{I}$. If B_i is any base for U_i, and if $B = \{B_1, \ldots, B_r\}$ is the joint base in U, then it follows at once that $\text{mat}_B\, \mathbf{T}$ is diagonal. Q.E.D.

COROLLARY *Let $\mathbf{T}$ be a diagonal mapping of a finite-dimensional vector space U to itself, and let W be a $\mathbf{T}$-stable subspace. Then the restriction $\mathbf{T}_W$ of $\mathbf{T}$ to W is also a diagonal mapping.*

Proof. By Theorem 6.2, $\mathbf{T}$ satisfies an equation of type (6.11). But then $\mathbf{T}_W$ plainly satisfies the same equation, and therefore $\mathbf{T}_W$ is diagonal, by Theorem 6.2 again. Q.E.D.

THEOREM 6.3 *Let* $\mathbf{T}: U \to U$ *be a linear mapping of a finite-dimensional vector space over a field K, and suppose that the characteristic polynomial of* $\mathbf{T}$ *has all its roots in K. Then there are mappings* $\mathbf{S}$ *and* $\mathbf{N}$ *of U to itself such that*

6.13
$$\begin{aligned}&\mathbf{S} \text{ is a diagonal mapping}\\&\mathbf{N} \text{ is nilpotent}\\&\mathbf{SN} = \mathbf{NS}\\&\mathbf{T} = \mathbf{S} + \mathbf{N}\end{aligned}$$

Moreover, $\mathbf{S}$ *and* $\mathbf{N}$ *are uniquely determined by these conditions.*

Proof. The existence of $\mathbf{S}$ and $\mathbf{N}$ is rather obvious from the Jordan normal form. For if the matrix of $\mathbf{T}$ is in Jordan normal form, then it has the eigenvalues of $\mathbf{T}$ along its diagonal and a certain number of 1's just above the diagonal, all other entries being zero. Therefore the matrix of $\mathbf{T}$ can be written as the sum of a diagonal matrix and another matrix having as its only nonzero entries a certain number of 1's just above the diagonal. It is not hard to verify that the two matrices commute and define endomorphisms of U satisfying (6.13).

To write this out more systematically, let V_i be the characteristic subspace of U corresponding to the eigenvalue p_i (notation as earlier in this section). Thus

6.14
$$V_i = \text{Ker}\,(\mathbf{T} - p_i\mathbf{I})^{n_i} \qquad (i = 1, \ldots, r)$$

Let $\mathbf{T}_i$ and $\mathbf{I}_i$ denote the restrictions of $\mathbf{T}$ and $\mathbf{I}$ to V_i, and put

6.15
$$\mathbf{N}_i = \mathbf{T}_i - p_i\mathbf{I}_i \qquad \mathbf{S}_i = p_i\mathbf{I}_i$$

The operator $\mathbf{N}_i$ is nilpotent, by (6.14), and $\mathbf{S}_i$ is a diagonal mapping, clearly. We have

$$\mathbf{T}_i = \mathbf{S}_i + \mathbf{N}_i$$

and it is clear that $\mathbf{S}_i \circ \mathbf{N}_i = \mathbf{N}_i \circ \mathbf{S}_i$. Set

6.16
$$\mathbf{S} = \mathbf{S}_1 \oplus \cdots \oplus \mathbf{S}_r \qquad \mathbf{N} = \mathbf{N}_1 \oplus \cdots \oplus \mathbf{N}_r$$

(see Proposition 3.4). A direct sum of nilpotent mappings is again nilpotent, as we have had occasion to observe at the beginning of Sec. 4. Hence $\mathbf{N}$ is nilpotent. $\mathbf{S}$ is clearly a diagonal mapping. For let B_i be any base in V_i. The matrix of $\mathbf{S}_i$ for that base is just $p_i \times$ identity. Hence the matrix of $\mathbf{S}$ relative to the joint base $B = \{B_1, \ldots, B_r\}$ in U is a diagonal matrix. Furthermore $\mathbf{S} \circ \mathbf{N} = \mathbf{N} \circ \mathbf{S}$, and it quickly follows that $\mathbf{S}$ and $\mathbf{N}$ as just defined satisfy (6.13).

To show uniqueness, let $\mathbf{S}'$, $\mathbf{N}'$ be another pair of mappings satisfying (6.13). We observe that we have then $\mathbf{S}' \circ \mathbf{T} = \mathbf{S}' \circ (\mathbf{S}' + \mathbf{N}') =$

$\mathbf{S}' \circ \mathbf{S}' + \mathbf{S}' \circ \mathbf{N}' = \mathbf{S}' \circ \mathbf{S}' + \mathbf{N}' \circ \mathbf{S}' = (\mathbf{S}' + \mathbf{N}') \circ \mathbf{S}' = \mathbf{T} \circ \mathbf{S}'$; $\mathbf{S}'$ commutes with $\mathbf{T}$.

Let $\mathbf{x}$ be an element of the characteristic subspace V_i. Then $\mathbf{S}'(\mathbf{x})$ is also in V_i. Indeed,

$$(\mathbf{T} - p_i\mathbf{I})^{n_i}\mathbf{S}'(\mathbf{x}) = \mathbf{S}'(\mathbf{T} - p_i\mathbf{I})^{n_i}(\mathbf{x}) = \mathbf{0}$$

since $\mathbf{S}'$ commutes with $\mathbf{T}$, hence also with any polynomial in $\mathbf{T}$. Therefore the subspaces V_i are all $\mathbf{S}'$-stable.

Denote by $\mathbf{S}'_i$ the restriction of $\mathbf{S}'$ to V_i. By assumption, $\mathbf{S}'$ is a diagonal mapping, and consequently so is $\mathbf{S}'_i$, by the corollary to Theorem 6.2. Then there is a base B'_i in V_i such that the matrix of $\mathbf{S}'_i$ relative to it is diagonal. Referring to (6.15), the matrix of $\mathbf{S}_i$ relative to B'_i is also diagonal, namely, $p_i \times$ identity. It follows at once that $\mathbf{S}_i \circ \mathbf{S}'_i = \mathbf{S}'_i \circ \mathbf{S}_i$ and that $\mathbf{S}_i - \mathbf{S}'_i$ is a diagonal mapping. $\mathbf{S} - \mathbf{S}'$ is therefore diagonal, because its matrix relative to the joint base $B' = \{B'_1, \ldots, B'_r\}$ is diagonal. Furthermore, $\mathbf{S} \circ \mathbf{S}' = \mathbf{S}' \circ \mathbf{S}$.

We have now $\mathbf{T} = \mathbf{S} + \mathbf{N} = \mathbf{S}' + \mathbf{N}'$. Hence

$$\mathbf{N} \circ \mathbf{N}' = (\mathbf{T} - \mathbf{S}) \circ (\mathbf{T} - \mathbf{S}')$$
$$\mathbf{N}' \circ \mathbf{N} = (\mathbf{T} - \mathbf{S}') \circ (\mathbf{T} - \mathbf{S})$$

Since $\mathbf{S}$, $\mathbf{T}$, $\mathbf{S}'$ all commute, it follows that $\mathbf{N} \circ \mathbf{N}' = \mathbf{N}' \circ \mathbf{N}$.

Now $\mathbf{N}$ and $\mathbf{N}'$ are nilpotent, and so $\mathbf{N}^m = \mathbf{N}'^m = \mathbf{0}$ for some integer m. From the binomial theorem (valid here because $\mathbf{N}'$ and $\mathbf{N}$ commute; see Theorem 5.2, Chap. 3), we get

$$(\mathbf{N}' - \mathbf{N})^{2m} = \sum_{k=0}^{2m} \binom{2m}{k} (-1)^k\, \mathbf{N}'^k \circ \mathbf{N}^{2m-k} = \mathbf{0}$$

for in each term at least one of the two exponents k, $2m - k$ must be $\geq m$. Consider now the equation

$$\mathbf{S} - \mathbf{S}' = \mathbf{N}' - \mathbf{N}$$

As we have just seen, the left side is a diagonal mapping, and the right side is nilpotent. But, as was remarked in Sec. 2, a diagonal mapping cannot be nilpotent unless it is zero. Therefore from the last equation we conclude that $\mathbf{S} - \mathbf{S}' = \mathbf{0}$. Hence $\mathbf{S} = \mathbf{S}'$, $\mathbf{N} = \mathbf{N}'$. Q.E.D.

EXERCISES

The following problems refer to vector spaces over the complex field. In each of them is given the matrix of a linear mapping $\mathbf{T}$ relative to some base A in the space. In each case find a new base relative to which the matrix of $\mathbf{T}$ is in Jordan normal form, and write down that form.

1. $\begin{pmatrix} 1 & 2 \\ 0 & 3 \end{pmatrix}$

2. $\begin{pmatrix} 1 & 2 \\ 0 & 1 \end{pmatrix}$

3. $\begin{pmatrix} 3 & 2 \\ 0 & 3 \end{pmatrix}$

4. $\begin{pmatrix} 3 & 2 \\ -2 & 0 \end{pmatrix}$

5. $\begin{pmatrix} 1 & 1 \\ -1 & 1 \end{pmatrix}$

6. $\begin{pmatrix} -1 & a & b \\ 0 & 3 & 2 \\ 0 & -2 & 0 \end{pmatrix}$

(for various a, b)

7. $\begin{pmatrix} -1 & 6 & 1 & 6 \\ 4 & -6 & -1 & -9 \\ 0 & 0 & -1 & 0 \\ -2 & 8 & 1 & 10 \end{pmatrix}$

8. $\begin{pmatrix} -3 & 1 & 10 & 12 \\ 0 & -1 & 0 & 0 \\ 3 & -1 & -4 & -6 \\ -3 & 1 & 6 & 8 \end{pmatrix}$

9. $\begin{pmatrix} -1 & 0 & 6 & 6 \\ 0 & -1 & 0 & 0 \\ 3 & 0 & -4 & -6 \\ -3 & 0 & 6 & 8 \end{pmatrix}$

10. $\begin{pmatrix} -2 & 1 & 0 & 0 & 0 \\ 0 & -2 & 0 & 0 & 0 \\ 0 & 0 & 0 & 0 & 0 \\ 0 & 0 & 0 & 2 & 1 \\ 0 & 0 & 0 & 0 & 2 \end{pmatrix}$

11. $\begin{pmatrix} 1 & 1 & 2 & 1 & 2 \\ 0 & 2 & 3 & -1 & 0 \\ 0 & 0 & -1 & 4 & -2 \\ 0 & 0 & 0 & 3 & 1 \\ 0 & 0 & 0 & 0 & 4 \end{pmatrix}$

12. Find a 4×4 matrix which is not triangular and which has integral eigenvalues. Reduce it to Jordan normal form.

7. *Uniqueness of the Jordan normal form*

To what extent is the Jordan normal form of the matrix of a linear mapping unique? The diagonal blocks in the Jordan normal form correspond to the **T**-stable subspaces $W_{i,j}$ of (6.5). By rearranging the order of the latter, we effect permutations of the blocks (6.8) that make up the Jordan normal form. *But apart from such permutations, the Jordan normal form is unique,* as we now proceed to prove. We continue with the notation of Sec. 6.

Ignoring permutations of the blocks of type (6.8) that constitute a matrix in Jordan normal form, the only data necessary to determine it are the following:

(1) The distinct diagonal entries $p_1, \ldots, p_r$ occurring in the blocks of type (6.8)

(2) The number k_i of blocks of the type (6.8) which belong to p_i

(3) The size of each of the blocks of type (6.8)

Our task is to prove that, for any two matrices in Jordan normal form representing the same linear mapping **T**, the data listed above are the same. It will follow then that the matrices are the same, apart from permutations of the order in which the blocks occur.

The strategy here is quite simple. We have only to show that the data above are completely determined by **T**.

1. Let B' be a base for U with respect to which the matrix of **T** is in Jordan normal form. Let **a** be that matrix, and let $p_1, \ldots, p_r$ be its distinct diagonal elements, p_i occurring n_i times, say. Since **a** is a *triangular* matrix, we have then

$$\det (t\mathbf{I} - \mathbf{a}) = (t - p_i)^{n_1} \cdots (t - p_r)^{n_r}$$

and this must be the characteristic polynomial $\varphi(t)$ of **T**, hence depends only on **T**. Therefore $p_1, \ldots, p_r$ must be the distinct eigenvalues of **T**.

2. The matrix **a** being as above, let $\mathbf{a}_{(i)}$ be the $n_i \times n_i$ block having p_i along the diagonal. Then $\mathbf{a}_{(i)}$ corresponds to a subset B'_i of the base B', and B'_i contains n_i vectors. Let V'_i be the subspace of U spanned by B'_i. Then V'_i is **T**-stable, clearly, and the characteristic polynomial of the restriction of **T** to V'_i is $(t - p_i)^{n_i}$. Hence $(\mathbf{T} - p_i\mathbf{I})^{n_i}$ maps V'_i into zero. Therefore V'_i is contained in the characteristic subspace of V_i belonging to p_i. It has the same dimension n_i, and so $V'_i = V_i$.

Since the matrix **a** was supposed to be in Jordan normal form, the block $\mathbf{a}_{(i)}$ has a certain number k_i of smaller blocks $\mathbf{a}_{(ij)}$ arranged along its diagonal, each of the form (6.8). And each such block corresponds to a certain subset B'_{ij} of the base B'_i of $V_i (= V'_i)$. Let W'_{ij} be the subspace of V_i generated by B'_{ij}. Then W'_{ij} is **T**-stable, and $(\mathbf{T} - p_i\mathbf{I})$ must be nilcyclic on W'_{ij} because of the form of $\mathbf{a}_{(ij)}$, which is the matrix of **T** restricted to W'_{ij}. We claim now that the number k_i in question here is

7.1 $$k_i = \dim \operatorname{Ker} (\mathbf{T} - p_i\mathbf{I})$$

To see this, we note first that $\operatorname{Ker} (\mathbf{T} - p_i\mathbf{I})$ is a subspace of $V_i = \operatorname{Ker} (\mathbf{T} - p_i\mathbf{I})^{n_i}$, as is obvious. From just above we have

7.2 $$V_i = W'_{i1} \oplus \cdots \oplus W'_{ik_i}$$

Now $\mathbf{T} - p_i\mathbf{I}$ is nilcyclic on each W'_{ij} here, and a nilcyclic mapping necessarily has a kernel of dimension 1. It follows easily that each term of (7.2) produces a contribution of 1 to $\dim \operatorname{Ker} (\mathbf{T} - p_i\mathbf{I})$, from which (7.1) follows. (See Exercise 6, Sec. 4.)

From (7.1) it is clear that k_i depends only on **T** (and i) and consequently must be the same for all Jordan matrices representing **T**.

3. Finally we must occupy ourselves with the sizes of the various blocks $\mathbf{a}_{(ij)}$ that form $\mathbf{a}_{(i)}$. In other words, we must deal with the dimensions of the W'_{ij} above. These dimensions are the orders of the various nilcyclic parts into which $\mathbf{T} - p_i\mathbf{I}$ is decomposed in V_i. Then let

7.3 $$n_{i1}, n_{i2}, \ldots, n_{ik_i}$$

be the dimensions of $W'_{i1}, \ldots, W'_{ik_i}$, respectively. We want to show that the set of integers (7.3) depends only on $\mathbf{T}$ (and i). Observe that we do not claim that the subspaces W'_{ij} are the same for all Jordan matrices representing $\mathbf{T}$.

Now if $\mathbf{L}$ is any nilcyclic mapping, of order s, say, then

7.4 $$\dim \operatorname{Ker} L^h - \dim \operatorname{Ker} L^{h-1} = \begin{cases} 1 & \text{for } 1 \le h \le s \\ 0 & \text{for } h > s \end{cases}$$

as follows at once from Sec. 2. From this we shall deduce that

7.5 *The number of integers n_{ij} in* (7.3) *such that $n_{ij} \ge h$ is equal to*

$$\dim \operatorname{Ker} (\mathbf{T} - p_i\mathbf{I})^h - \dim \operatorname{Ker} (\mathbf{T} - p_i\mathbf{I})^{h-1} \qquad \textit{for } h = 1, 2, 3, \textit{etc.}$$

In fact, $\operatorname{Ker} (\mathbf{T} - p_i\mathbf{I})^h$ is contained in the characteristic subspace V_i for $h = 0$, 1, 2, etc. Denote by $\mathbf{L}_{ij}$ the restriction of $\mathbf{T} - p_i\mathbf{I}$ to W'_{ij}. Then $\mathbf{L}_{ij}$ is nilcyclic of order n_{ij} [because $\mathbf{a}_{(ij)}$ is of the type (6.8)]. It is easily seen that $\operatorname{Ker} (\mathbf{T} - p_i\mathbf{I})^h$ is the direct sum

$$\operatorname{Ker} \mathbf{L}_{i1}{}^h \oplus \cdots \oplus \operatorname{Ker} \mathbf{L}_{ik_i}{}^h$$

because of (7.2). Thus

$$\dim \operatorname{Ker} (\mathbf{T} - p_i\mathbf{I})^h = \sum_{j=1}^{k_i} \dim \operatorname{Ker} \mathbf{L}_{ij}{}^h$$

Then (7.5) follows easily from (7.4) applied to the $\mathbf{L}_{ij}$. Formula (7.5) shows that the set of numbers (7.3) depends only on $\mathbf{T}$ and i and not upon the particular choice of W'_{ij}. (See Exercise 7, Sec. 4.)

This completes the proof of the uniqueness of the Jordan normal form.

8. *The problem of similarity*

Let U be a vector space over a field K. Two linear mappings $\mathbf{T}_1 : U \to U$ and $\mathbf{T}_2 : U \to U$ are called *similar* (notation: $\mathbf{T}_1 \sim \mathbf{T}_2$) if there is an isomorphism $\mathbf{S} : U \to U$ such that

8.1 $$\mathbf{T}_1 \circ \mathbf{S} = \mathbf{S} \circ \mathbf{T}_2$$

or equivalently if

8.2 $$\mathbf{T}_2 = \mathbf{S}^{-1} \circ \mathbf{T}_1 \circ \mathbf{S}$$

If we represent our mappings by arrows, then the situation at hand can be described by the following diagram:

$$\begin{array}{ccc} U & \xrightarrow{\mathbf{T}_1} & U \\ \mathbf{S}\uparrow & & \uparrow\mathbf{S} \\ U & \xrightarrow[\mathbf{T}_2]{} & U \end{array}$$

Condition (8.1) requires that the result of following the upper circuit ($\mathbf{T}_1 \circ \mathbf{S}$) be the same as that of following the lower circuit ($\mathbf{S} \circ \mathbf{T}_2$). Note that $\mathbf{S}$ here is required to be one-to-one.

Suppose that $\dim U = n$ (finite), and let $B_1 = \{\mathbf{u}_1, \ldots, \mathbf{u}_n\}$ and $B_2 = \{\mathbf{v}_1, \ldots, \mathbf{v}_n\}$ be two bases for U. Let $\mathbf{S}$ be the isomorphism that maps $\mathbf{v}_i$ to $\mathbf{u}_i$ for $i = 1, \ldots, n$. Write $\text{mat}_{B_i}\, \mathbf{T}_j$ for the matrix of $\mathbf{T}_j$ with respect to B_i (i, $j = 1, 2$), etc. From Theorem 7.2, Chap. 9, there follows

8.3 $$\begin{aligned} \text{mat}_{B_1}\, \mathbf{T}_1 &= (\text{mat}_{B_2}\, \mathbf{S})^{-1}(\text{mat}_{B_2}\, \mathbf{T}_1)(\text{mat}_{B_2}\, \mathbf{S}) \\ &= \text{mat}_{B_2}\, (\mathbf{S}^{-1}\mathbf{T}_1\mathbf{S}) \end{aligned}$$

If (8.2) holds—and only then—the right-hand side here is $\text{mat}_{B_2}\mathbf{T}_2$.

Therefore $\mathbf{T}_1 \sim \mathbf{T}_2$ *if and only if there exist bases in* U *for which* $\mathbf{T}_1$ *and* $\mathbf{T}_2$ *have identical matrices.*

Let B be a base for U and put

$$\mathbf{a} = \text{mat}_B\, \mathbf{T}_1 \qquad \mathbf{b} = \text{mat}_B\, \mathbf{T}_2 \qquad \mathbf{c} = \text{mat}_B\, \mathbf{S}$$

Then (8.2) holds if and only if

8.4 $$\mathbf{b} = \mathbf{c}^{-1}\mathbf{a}\mathbf{c}$$

Accordingly, we define two (square) matrices $\mathbf{a}$, $\mathbf{b}$ to be *similar* if and only if there is a nonsingular matrix $\mathbf{c}$ for which (8.4) holds. It is easily seen from Theorem 7.2, Chap. 9, that (8.4) holds if and only if $\mathbf{a}$ and $\mathbf{b}$ both represent the same linear mapping with respect to (possibly) different bases, $\mathbf{c}$ then being the matrix of the base change.

We pose the following problem: *Give reasonable conditions, necessary and sufficient, for two linear mappings (or two matrices) to be similar.*

One answer to this problem can be based on the uniqueness of the Jordan normal form (Sec. 7).

First of all, suppose that $\mathbf{T}_1 \sim \mathbf{T}_2$, and let B_1 be a base in U for which the matrix of $\mathbf{T}_1$ is in Jordan normal form. Let $\mathbf{S}$ be an isomorphism for which (8.2) holds, and let B_2 be the base in U obtained by applying $\mathbf{S}^{-1}$ to the elements of B_1. By (8.3) we have

$$\text{mat}_{B_1}\, \mathbf{T}_1 = \text{mat}_{B_2}\, \mathbf{T}_2$$

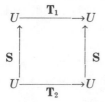

and so $\mathbf{T}_2$ has the same Jordan normal form as $\mathbf{T}_1$. Conversely, if $\mathbf{T}_1$ and $\mathbf{T}_2$ have the same Jordan normal form with respect to certain bases B_1, B_2, and if $\mathbf{S}$ denotes the isomorphism that transforms B_2 into B_1, then (8.2) holds, and so $\mathbf{T}_1 \sim \mathbf{T}_2$.

Referring now to the data of (1), (2), (3) in Sec. 7, and to the subsequent analysis of them, we derive the following alternative formulation of the criterion for $\mathbf{T}_1 \sim \mathbf{T}_2$ just given. That is, $\mathbf{T}_1 \sim \mathbf{T}_2$ if and only if the conditions below are satisfied (assuming that the eigenvalues of $\mathbf{T}_1$ and $\mathbf{T}_2$ are all in the field of scalars K):

8.5 (1) $\mathbf{T}_1$ *and* $\mathbf{T}_2$ *have identical characteristic polynomials.*

(2) $\dim \operatorname{Ker} (\mathbf{T}_1 - p_i\mathbf{I})^h = \dim \operatorname{Ker} (\mathbf{T}_2 - p_i\mathbf{I})^h$ *for each eigenvalue* p_i *and for* $h = 1, \ldots, n_i$, *where* n_i *is the power of* $(t - p_i)$ *in the characteristic polynomial.*

Condition (2) just enunciated is the necessary and sufficient condition for the numbers k_i and n_{ij} to be the same (apart from permutations) for $\mathbf{T}_1$ and $\mathbf{T}_2$, according to (7.1) and (7.5). Thus (1) and (2) hold if and only if $\operatorname{mat}_{B_1} \mathbf{T}_1 = \operatorname{mat}_{B_2} \mathbf{T}_2$ for suitable bases which yield the Jordan normal form for $\mathbf{T}_1$ and $\mathbf{T}_2$.

The criterion given by (1) and (2) above apply equally well to matrices, for any $n \times n$ matrix with coefficients in K can be regarded as a linear mapping of the vector space K^n of column vectors.

EXAMPLE 1 Take $\mathbf{T}_1 = \begin{pmatrix} 0 & 1 \\ -1 & 0 \end{pmatrix}$ and $\mathbf{T}_2 = \begin{pmatrix} i & 0 \\ 0 & -i \end{pmatrix}$, where $i = \sqrt{-1}$, $\mathbf{T}_1$ and $\mathbf{T}_2$ being regarded as linear mappings of the vector space $\mathbf{C}^2$ of complex column vectors. We shall show that $\mathbf{T}_1 \sim \mathbf{T}_2$.

The characteristic polynomials are

$$\det (t\,\mathbf{I} - \mathbf{T}_1) = \det \begin{pmatrix} t & -1 \\ 1 & t \end{pmatrix} = t^2 + 1$$

$$\det (t\,\mathbf{I} - \mathbf{T}_2) = \det \begin{pmatrix} t - i & 0 \\ 0 & t + i \end{pmatrix} = t^2 + 1$$

The characteristic polynomials are identical and the eigenvalues are i, $-i$. The equality (2) of (8.5) has to be checked only for $h = 1$, and it is easily seen that $\dim \operatorname{Ker} (\mathbf{T}_j - p\mathbf{I}) = 1$ for $p = \pm i$ and $j = 1, 2$.

Therefore $\mathbf{T}_1 \sim \mathbf{T}_2$. It is easily verified that $\mathbf{T}_2 = \mathbf{S}^{-1}\mathbf{T}_1\mathbf{S}$, where

$$\mathbf{S} = \begin{pmatrix} 1 & 1 \\ i & -i \end{pmatrix}$$

EXAMPLE 2 Let $\mathbf{T}_1$ be a linear mapping of an n-dimensional vector space. U over a field K, and suppose that $\mathbf{T}_1$ has n distinct eigenvalues $p_1, \ldots, p_n$. Choose a base $A = \{\mathbf{u}_i\}$ in U, and let $\mathbf{T}_2$ be the linear mapping defined by $\mathbf{T}_2(\mathbf{u}_i) = p_i\mathbf{u}_i$ $(i = 1, \ldots, n)$. Then $\mathbf{T}_1$ and $\mathbf{T}_2$ are similar. According to the discussion above, this merely means that there is a base $B = \{\mathbf{v}_i\}$ in U such that $\operatorname{mat}_B \mathbf{T}_1 = \operatorname{mat}_A \mathbf{T}_2$, and the latter is a diagonal matrix. That is, $\mathbf{T}_1 \sim \mathbf{T}_2$ here simply means that $\mathbf{T}_1$ is a diagonal mapping. This has already been shown in Sec. 1.

To see how the criterion (8.5) applies here, it is clear that $\mathbf{T}_1$ and $\mathbf{T}_2$ have the same characteristic polynomial, namely, $(t - p_1) \cdots (t - p_n)$.

For the second part (2) of (8.5), we know that in general, if $V_i = \text{Ker}\,(\mathbf{T} - p_i\mathbf{I})^{n_i}$, n_i being the power of $(t - p_i)$ in the characteristic polynomial, then dim $V_i = n_i$ and $n_1 + \cdots + n_n = n$. In the case at hand, $n_1 = 1, \ldots, n_n = 1$. It is only necessary to check (2) for $h = 1$ here, and, as just observed, dim $(\mathbf{T}_j - p_i\mathbf{I}) = 1$ for $j = 1, 2$ and $i = 1, \ldots, n$. Hence, condition (2) is satisfied here.

EXERCISES

Test the following matrices for similarity (for both general and special values of a, b, c):

1. $\begin{pmatrix} 0 & 2 \\ 0 & 0 \end{pmatrix}$ and $\begin{pmatrix} 0 & 1 \\ 0 & 0 \end{pmatrix}$ **2.** $\begin{pmatrix} 2 & 0 \\ 0 & 0 \end{pmatrix}$ and $\begin{pmatrix} 1 & 0 \\ 0 & 0 \end{pmatrix}$

3. $\begin{pmatrix} 0 & 0 \\ 1 & 0 \end{pmatrix}$ and $\begin{pmatrix} 0 & 1 \\ 0 & 0 \end{pmatrix}$ **4.** $\begin{pmatrix} 0 & a & 0 \\ 0 & 0 & b \\ 0 & 0 & 0 \end{pmatrix}$ and $\begin{pmatrix} 0 & 1 & 0 \\ 0 & 0 & 1 \\ 0 & 0 & 0 \end{pmatrix}$

5. $\begin{pmatrix} 0 & a & c \\ 0 & 0 & b \\ 0 & 0 & 0 \end{pmatrix}$ and $\begin{pmatrix} 0 & 1 & 0 \\ 0 & 0 & 1 \\ 0 & 0 & 0 \end{pmatrix}$ **6.** $\begin{pmatrix} 3 & 5 & 2 \\ 0 & 1 & 0 \\ 0 & 0 & 3 \end{pmatrix}$ and $\begin{pmatrix} 3 & a & 0 \\ 0 & 3 & 0 \\ 0 & 0 & 1 \end{pmatrix}$

7. $\begin{pmatrix} a & -b \\ b & a \end{pmatrix}$ and $\begin{pmatrix} c & 0 \\ 0 & -c \end{pmatrix}$

9. *Elementary divisors*

Criterion (8.5) for similarity of linear mappings (or matrices) has two drawbacks:

(1) It is usually impossible to solve a polynomial equation of degree greater than 4 exactly, and therefore it is usually impossible to determine the eigenvalues of an endomorphism exactly.

(2) The criterion applies only in the important but rather special case in which the mappings have all their eigenvalues in the field of scalars K. That is no restriction if the field is the complex field; but in general the characteristic polynomial will not have all its roots in K.

We shall therefore give another criterion for similarity which is not subject to the foregoing objections.

We commence with some preparatory observations. Here K denotes a field. We shall consider the polynomial domain $K[t]$ of polynomials in an indeterminate t with coefficients in K.

Let $f_1, \ldots, f_r$ be polynomials in $K[t]$, and let us denote by $(f_1, \ldots, f_r)$ the set consisting of all polynomials f which can be expressed in the form

9.1 $$f = a_1f_1 + \cdots + a_rf_r$$

the a_i being also in $K[t]$. If $f' = b_1f_1 + \cdots + b_rf_r$ is another polynomial of the same type, then clearly $f + f'$ is also of the form (9.1). Let g be any polynomial in $K[t]$, and let f be as in (9.1). Then

$$gf = (ga_1)f_1 + \cdots + (ga_r)f_r$$

which is again of the type (9.1). Therefore the system $(f_1, \ldots, f_r)$ contains the sum and difference of any two of its elements, and it contains the product of any of its elements by an arbitrary polynomial in $K[t]$. In particular, $(f_1, \ldots, f_r)$ contains the product of any two of its elements. It is plain that $(f_1, \ldots, f_r)$ contains $f_1, \ldots, f_r$.

We call this system of polynomials the *ideal* generated by the f_i. As a special case, the ideal (f) generated by a single polynomial f simply consists of all products $a \cdot f$, where a is an arbitrary polynomial in $K[t]$.

Let $h = \text{g.c.d. } \{f_1, \ldots, f_r\}$ denote the greatest common divisor of $f_1, \ldots, f_r$. From Sec. 3, Chap. 6, we know that h can be expressed in the form (9.1). Therefore h is in the ideal $(f_1, \ldots, f_r)$. On the other hand, h divides each f_i, say $f_i = g_i \cdot h$. Therefore each f_i is in the ideal generated by h. It follows that the two ideals are identical:

9.2 $$(f_1, \ldots, f_r) = (h) \qquad \text{if } h = \text{g.c.d. } \{f_1, \ldots, f_r\}$$

From this it follows that

9.3 $$(f_1, \ldots, f_r) = (g_1, \ldots, g_s) \qquad \text{if and only if}$$
$$\text{g.c.d. } \{f_1, \ldots, f_r\} = \text{g.c.d. } \{g_1, \ldots, g_r\}$$

Let $\mathbf{a} = (a^j{}_i)$ be a matrix with coefficients in an integral domain. Now form the matrix made up of those elements of $\mathbf{a}$ which are in columns $i_1, \ldots, i_p$ and rows $j_1, \ldots, j_p$. The determinant of this $p \times p$ matrix is denoted by $a^{j_1 \cdots j_p}_{i_1 \cdots i_p}$. Thus

9.4 $$a^{j_1 \cdots j_p}_{i_1 \cdots i_p} = \det \begin{pmatrix} a^{j_1}_{i_1} & \cdots & a^{j_1}_{i_p} \\ \cdots & \cdots & \cdots \\ a^{j_p}_{i_1} & \cdots & a^{j_p}_{i_p} \end{pmatrix}$$

These quantities are called the $p \times p$ *minors* of $\mathbf{a}$. The 1×1 minors are simply the entries $a^j{}_i$ in $\mathbf{a}$. If $\mathbf{a}$ is square, say $n \times n$, then the minor $a^{1 \cdots n}_{1 \cdots n}$ is none other than $\det \mathbf{a}$.

We now consider matrices with coefficients in the polynomial domain $K[t]$.

THEOREM 9.1 *Let* $\mathbf{f} = (f^j{}_i)$ *and* $\mathbf{g} = (g^j{}_i)$ *be two matrices with coefficients in the polynomial ring* $K[t]$. *If there is a third matrix* $\mathbf{a}$, *also with polynomial coefficients, such that* $\mathbf{f} = \mathbf{ag}$ *or else* $\mathbf{f} = \mathbf{ga}$, *then the* $p \times p$ *minors of* $\mathbf{f}$ *are all in the ideal generated by the* $p \times p$ *minors of* $\mathbf{g}$.

Proof. Suppose that $\mathbf{f} = \mathbf{ga}$. For simplicity of notation consider the minor $f_{1\ldots p}^{1\ldots p}$ of $\mathbf{f}$. We have by (9.4) and the formula (2.7), Chap. 11,

$$f_{1\ldots p}^{1\ldots p} = \sum_s e(s) \cdot f_1^{s(1)} \cdots f_p^{s(p)}$$

where s denotes an arbitrary permutation of $1, \ldots, p$ and where $e(s)$ denotes its sign. Since $f^j{}_i = g^j{}_k a^k{}_i$ (Einstein summation convention on k here), we obtain

$$\begin{aligned} f_{1\ldots p}^{1\ldots p} &= \sum_s e(s) \cdot \left(g_{k_1}^{s(1)} a_1^{k_1}\right) \cdots \left(g_{k_p}^{s(p)} a_p^{k_p}\right) \\ &= \sum_s e(s) \cdot g_{k_1}^{s(1)} \cdots g_{k_p}^{s(p)} a_1^{k_1} \cdots a_p^{k_p} \\ &= g_{k_1\ldots k_p}^{1\ldots p} \cdot a_1^{k_1} \cdots a_p^{k_p} \end{aligned}$$

This is an expression of the type (9.1) for $f_{1\ldots p}^{1\ldots p}$ in terms of the $g_{k_1\ldots k_p}^{1\ldots p}$, showing that $f_{1\ldots p}^{1\ldots p}$ is in the ideal generated by the $p \times p$ minors of the matrix $(g^j{}_i)$. The same argument holds for any minor $f_{i_1\ldots i_p}^{j_1\ldots j_p}$, and, with trivial modification, for the case $\mathbf{f} = \mathbf{ag}$. Q.E.D.

THEOREM 9.2 *Let* **a**, **b**, **f**, **g** *be matrices with coefficients in* $K[t]$. *Suppose that* **a** *and* **b** *are square and that* det **a** *and* det **b** *are nonzero constants (that is, nonzero elements of* K*). If*

9.5 $\mathbf{f} = \mathbf{agb}$

then the $p \times p$ *minors of* **f** *have the same g.c.d. as the* $p \times p$ *minors of* **g**.†

Proof. First of all, the inverses $\mathbf{a}^{-1}$ and $\mathbf{b}^{-1}$ have all their coefficients in $K[t]$. This follows from the fact that the coefficients of $\mathbf{a}^{-1}$, say, are —except for sign—the $(n-1) \times (n-1)$ minors of $\mathbf{a}$, divided by det $\mathbf{a}$. We have assumed that det $\mathbf{a}$ is a nonzero constant.

Now Theorem 9.1 says that the $p \times p$ minors of $\mathbf{f} = (\mathbf{ag})\mathbf{b}$ are in the ideal generated by the $p \times p$ minors of $\mathbf{ag}$; and these $p \times p$ minors are in turn in the ideal generated by $\mathbf{g}$. Hence, the $p \times p$ minors of $\mathbf{f}$ are in the ideal generated by the $p \times p$ minors of $\mathbf{g}$. From (9.5) we have

$$\mathbf{g} = \mathbf{a}^{-1}\mathbf{f}\mathbf{b}^{-1}$$

and from the remarks above we conclude similarly that the $p \times p$ minors of $\mathbf{g}$ are in the ideal generated by those of $\mathbf{f}$. The assertion then follows from (9.3). Q.E.D.

† We understand this to mean that if all the $p \times p$ minors of **g** are zero (the g.c.d. is not defined) then so are all the $p \times p$ minors of **f**, and vice versa.

9.6 *For any $n \times n$ matrix* $\mathbf{a}$ *with coefficients in* $K[t]$, *we denote by* $d_p[\mathbf{a}]$ *the monic g.c.d. of all the* $p \times p$ *minors of* $\mathbf{a}$, *provided they are not all zero. For* $p = 0$ *we set* $d_0[\mathbf{a}] = 1$.

THEOREM 9.3 *For any matrix with coefficients in* $K[t]$, $d_{p-1}[\mathbf{a}]$ *divides* $d_p[\mathbf{a}]$ *for* $p = 1, 2, \ldots, r$, *where r is the largest integer for which the* $r \times r$ *minors are not all zero.*†

Proof. Consider a nonzero $p \times p$ minor of $\mathbf{a}$ ($p > 1$). Expand the determinant that defines it by some row or column. The result is a sum of $(p-1) \times (p-1)$ minors multiplied by coefficients of $\mathbf{a}$ (and by ± 1). Since $d_{p-1}[\mathbf{a}]$ divides all the $(p-1) \times (p-1)$ minors in the sum, it must divide the given $p \times p$ minor. The assertion follows at once from the definition of $d_p[\mathbf{a}]$. Q.E.D.

We can indicate the assertion of the theorem by writing

9.7 $$d_0[\mathbf{a}] \,|\, d_1[\mathbf{a}] \,|\, d_2[\mathbf{a}] \,|\, \cdots \,|\, d_r[\mathbf{a}]$$

DEFINITION 9.1 *Let* $\mathbf{a}$ *be a matrix with coefficients in* $K[t]$, *and let r be its rank. Let* $d_p[\mathbf{a}]$ $(p = 0, 1, \ldots, r)$ *be the polynomials defined in* (9.6). We denote the *quotient of* $d_p[\mathbf{a}]$ *by* $d_{p-1}[\mathbf{a}]$ *by* $q_p[\mathbf{a}]$. *That is,*

9.8 $$d_p[\mathbf{a}] = q_p[\mathbf{a}] \cdot d_{p-1}[\mathbf{a}] \qquad (p = 1, \ldots, r)$$

The polynomial $q_p[\mathbf{a}]$ *is called the pth* torsion order *of* $\mathbf{a}$. *We define* $q_p[\mathbf{a}]$ *to be zero for* $p > r$. *If* $\mathbf{a}$ *has coefficients in the field K, then the pth torsion order of the matrix* $t\,\mathbf{I} - \mathbf{a}$ *is called the pth* elementary divisor *of* $\mathbf{a}$.

EXAMPLE 1 For a diagonal matrix the calculations are not difficult:

$$\begin{pmatrix} 1 & 0 & 0 & 0 \\ 0 & t & 0 & 0 \\ 0 & 0 & -1 & 0 \\ 0 & 0 & 0 & t^2+1 \end{pmatrix}$$

The nonzero 1×1 minors are $1, -1, t, t^2 + 1$. Their g.c.d. is 1. The nonzero 2×2 minors are (apart from sign) $1, t, (t^2+1), t(t^2+1)$. Their g.c.d. is 1. The nonzero 3×3 minors (omitting signs) are $t, t^2+1, t \cdot (t^2+1)$. Their g.c.d. is 1. The nonzero 4×4 minor is $t(t^2+1)$. Hence the torsion orders are $1, 1, 1, t(t^2+1)$.

EXAMPLE 2

$$\begin{pmatrix} 1 & 0 & 0 & 0 \\ 0 & t & 0 & 0 \\ 0 & 0 & t(t-1) & 0 \\ 0 & 0 & 0 & 0 \end{pmatrix}$$

† r is simply the rank of the matrix $\mathbf{a}$. See Corollary 2 of Theorem 3.1, Chap. 11.

Here $d_1 = 1$, clearly. The nonzero 2×2 minors (omitting signs) are t, $t(t-1)$, $t^2(t-1)$. Hence $d_2 = t$. The nonzero 3×3 minor (omitting signs) is $t^2(t-1) = d_3$. The torsion orders are $1, t, t(t-1)$.

We now look into the problem of computing torsion orders. The procedure we are about to develop is based upon the method explained in Sec. 9, Chap. 9. Theorem 7.3, Chap. 9, together with Eq. (7.3), states that if **a** is any matrix with coefficients in a field L, then there exist nonsingular matrices **b**, **c** with coefficients in L such that

bac *is a diagonal matrix*

The matrices **b**, **c** here correspond to certain base changes in the vector spaces in question. In Sec. 9, Chap. 9, it was shown how to make the required base changes by a series of elementary row and column operations on the given matrix **a**. It is easily seen from Sec. 9, Chap. 9, that the matrices **b**, **c** can be determined in such a way that

$$\det \mathbf{b} = \pm 1 \qquad \det \mathbf{c} = \pm 1$$

The foregoing applies in particular to matrices with coefficients in the field $K(t)$ of rational functions in t. However we are interested in matrices with coefficients in the smaller system $K[t]$ of polynomials in t. Let us see how much of the method of Sec. 9, Chap. 9, survives if we confine our elements to $K[t]$, so that unrestricted division is prohibited.

The basic operation of Sec. 9, Chap. 9, is the rather trivial one of subtracting suitable multiples of a given row in a matrix from the other rows in order to kill off all the elements in a specified column—save that element in the given row, of course. (Similar operation for columns.) The only modification of the process necessitated here is the following:

Let $\mathbf{a}^h = (a^h{}_1, \ldots, a^h{}_n)$ and $\mathbf{a}^j = (a^j{}_1, \ldots, a^j{}_n)$ be two rows of our matrix, and suppose we want to subtract some multiple of $\mathbf{a}^j$ from $\mathbf{a}^h$ in order to get 0 in the kth position of row h. If we confine ourselves to polynomials, that is not possible unless $a^j{}_k$ divides $a^h{}_k$, clearly. Therefore we do the next best thing: we subtract from $\mathbf{a}^h$ the multiple of $\mathbf{a}^j$ that leaves a polynomial of lowest possible degree in the kth place of row h. More specifically, applying the division algorithm to the polynomials $a^j{}_k$ and $a^h{}_k$, we can write

9.9 $$a^h{}_k = q \cdot a^j{}_k + r$$

where $r = 0$ or else $\deg r < \deg a^j{}_k$. Then, subtracting $q\mathbf{a}^j$ from $\mathbf{a}^h$, we obtain the remainder r in the kth place of the new hth row. A similar modification applies to elementary column operations, naturally.

The central point here is the following: Let $a^j{}_i$ and $a^l{}_k$ be two nonzero elements of a matrix **a** with coefficients in $K[t]$. If neither of these two elements divides the other, then **a** can be transformed by elementary row and column operations (i.e., using only polynomials) into a new matrix **a**′ which contains a nonzero element of lower degree than either $a^j{}_i$ or $a^h{}_k$. The argument is very simple. If $a^j{}_i$ and $a^h{}_k$ are in the same column ($i = k$), and if $\deg a^j{}_k \leq \deg a^h{}_k$, say, then we subtract $q\mathbf{a}^j$ from $\mathbf{a}^h$, where q is as in (9.9). By our assumption the remainder r in (9.9) cannot be zero and it has lower degree than $a^j{}_k$ and $a^h{}_k$; r appears, as pointed out above, in the (h, k) position in the new matrix. A similar procedure is valid if $a^j{}_i$, $a^h{}_k$ are in the same row ($j = h$). If $i \neq k$ and $j \neq h$, the same conclusion can be arrived at easily by comparing both $a^j{}_i$ and $a^h{}_k$ with $a^h{}_i$.

Thus, if $a^j{}_i$ is the element of least degree in **a**, and if it does not divide *every* element of **a**, then elementary row and column operations of the kind just considered lead to a new matrix **a**′ containing an element of lower degree. Starting afresh with **a**′, if an element of least degree does not divide every element of **a**′, then in the same way we obtain a new matrix **a**″ containing an element of yet lower degree. Since degrees of polynomials cannot be negative, the process must terminate after a finite number of steps, say with a matrix **b**. By permuting rows and columns in **b** we can assume that $b^1{}_1$ is a nonzero element of least degree. By what was just said, $b^1{}_1$ must divide every element of **b**. Therefore, by subtracting suitable polynomial multiples of the first row (or first column) of **b** from the other rows (or columns), we get a matrix **b**′ having zeros everywhere in the first row and first column, except for $b^1{}_1$. Hence **b**′ will have the form

$$\left(\begin{array}{c|ccc} b^1{}_1 & 0 & \cdots & 0 \\ \hline 0 & & & \\ \cdot & & & \\ \cdot & & \mathbf{c} & \\ \cdot & & & \\ 0 & & & \end{array}\right) \tag{9.10}$$

We can now repeat the same argument with the smaller matrix **c**, without disturbing the first row or column of the larger matrix. The following theorem is then evident:

THEOREM 9.4 *If* **a** *is any matrix with coefficients in the polynomial ring* $K[t]$, *then it is possible to transform* **a** *into a diagonal matrix* **a**′ *by a series of elementary row and column operations,*† *using only polynomials. This can be done in such a way that if* $q_1(t), \ldots, q_r(t)$ *are the nonzero diagonal terms in* **a**′, *then* $q_1|q_2| \cdots |q_r$.

For the last assertion, recall that $b^1{}_1$ in (9.10) divides every element in the matrix. If we transform the submatrix **c** into the same form (9.10) and denote the corner element by $c^2{}_2$, then $b^1{}_1$ must divide $c^2{}_2$, etc.

EXAMPLE 3 For the matrix

† Including permutations of rows or of columns.

$$\begin{pmatrix} t & 0 & 0 \\ 0 & 0 & t+1 \\ 0 & t^2 & 0 \end{pmatrix}$$

we first add row 1 to row 2 and then subtract column 1 from column 3 in the result, obtaining

$$\begin{pmatrix} t & 0 & -t \\ t & 0 & 1 \\ 0 & t^2 & 0 \end{pmatrix}$$

Here we have an element of degree zero. Interchange column 1, column 3 and row 1, row 2:

$$\begin{pmatrix} 1 & 0 & t \\ -t & 0 & t \\ 0 & t^2 & 0 \end{pmatrix}$$

Add $t \times$ row 1 to row 2:

$$\begin{pmatrix} 1 & 0 & t \\ 0 & 0 & t+t^2 \\ 0 & t^2 & 0 \end{pmatrix}$$

Subtract $t \times$ column 1 from column 3:

$$\begin{pmatrix} 1 & 0 & 0 \\ 0 & 0 & t+t^2 \\ 0 & t^2 & 0 \end{pmatrix}$$

This has the form (9.10). We continue with the 2×2 matrix

$$\begin{pmatrix} 0 & t+t^2 \\ t^2 & 0 \end{pmatrix}$$

Add row 2 to row 1 and then, in the result, subtract column 1 from column 2:

$$\begin{pmatrix} t^2 & t \\ t^2 & -t^2 \end{pmatrix}$$

Subtract $t \times$ column 2 from column 1 and then interchange column 1 and column 2:

$$\begin{pmatrix} t & 0 \\ 0 & t^2+t^3 \end{pmatrix}$$

Thus the diagonal form of the 3×3 matrix is

$$\begin{pmatrix} 1 & 0 & 0 \\ 0 & t & 0 \\ 0 & 0 & t^2+t^3 \end{pmatrix}$$

Clearly $1|t|(t^2 + t^3)$ as promised in the theorem.

Let R denote an elementary row operation on matrices with coefficients in $K[t]$. It is easily verified that

$$R(\mathbf{ab}) = R(\mathbf{a}) \cdot \mathbf{b}$$

That is, the same result is obtained by either applying R to the product **ab** or by applying R to **a** and then multiplying by **b**. Similarly, if C denotes an elementary column operation, then

$$C(\mathbf{ab}) = \mathbf{a} \cdot C(\mathbf{b})$$

In particular, taking either **a** or **b** to be the identity matrix, we obtain the following rules:

9.11
$$R(\mathbf{a}) = R(\mathbf{I}) \cdot \mathbf{a}$$
$$C(\mathbf{a}) = \mathbf{a} \cdot C(\mathbf{I})$$

Now let $R_1, \ldots, R_p$ and $C_1, \ldots, C_q$ denote the series of row and column operations required to reduce a matrix **a** to diagonal form **a′** according to Theorem 9.4. Set

$$\mathbf{b}_i = R_i(\mathbf{I})$$

and

$$\mathbf{c}_i = C_i(\mathbf{I})$$

By repeated applications of (9.11) we get

9.12 $$\mathbf{a}' = \mathbf{b}_p \cdot \mathbf{b}_{p-1} \cdots \mathbf{b}_1 \cdot \mathbf{a} \cdot \mathbf{c}_1 \cdot \mathbf{c}_2 \cdots \mathbf{c}_q$$

Consider one of the matrices $\mathbf{b}_i$: It is obtained from the unit matrix by an elementary row operation, which does not alter the determinant, or by a permutation, which at most changes the sign. Therefore, $\det \mathbf{b}_i = \pm 1$. Similarly, $\det \mathbf{c}_i = \pm 1$. Write

$$\mathbf{b} = \mathbf{b}_p \cdots \mathbf{b}_1$$

and

$$\mathbf{c} = \mathbf{c}_1 \cdots \mathbf{c}_q$$

We have then

9.13 $$\mathbf{a}' = \mathbf{bac} \qquad \det \mathbf{b} = \pm 1 \qquad \det \mathbf{c} = \pm 1$$

From Theorem 9.2 it follows that **a** and **a′** have the same torsion orders. But for the diagonal matrix **a′** it is very easily seen that the nonzero torsion orders are (apart from constant factors) just the nonzero diagonal elements $q_1(t), \ldots, q_r(t)$ This follows at once from the definitions and the fact that $q_1|q_2| \cdots |q_r$. We have thus proved the following theorem:

THEOREM 9.5 *Let* **a** *be a matrix of rank r with coefficients in the polynomial ring* $K[t]$. *Then the torsion orders* $q_1, \ldots, q_r$ of **a** *satisfy* $q_1 | q_2 | \cdots | q_r$. *Moreover, the torsion orders are, except for constant factors, the same as the nonzero diagonal elements obtained when* **a** *is put into diagonal form by elementary row and column operations according to Theorem* 9.4.

(The nonzero torsion orders are monic polynomials, as follows from the definition.)

Recall that the elementary divisors of a square matrix **a** with coefficients in the field K are by definition the torsion orders of the matrix $t\,\mathbf{I} - \mathbf{a}$. Hence, the following is true:

COROLLARY *The nonzero elementary divisors of a square matrix with coefficients in K satisfy* $q_1(t) | q_2(t) | \cdots | q_r(t)$. *Moreover they can be computed by a definite procedure involving only a finite number of additions and multiplications.*

EXAMPLE 4 Compute the elementary divisors of

$$\mathbf{a} = \begin{pmatrix} 3 & 0 & 1 \\ 2 & -1 & 0 \\ 0 & 2 & -1 \end{pmatrix}$$

We have

$$t\,\mathbf{I} - \mathbf{a} = \begin{pmatrix} t-3 & 0 & -1 \\ -2 & t+1 & 0 \\ 0 & -2 & t+1 \end{pmatrix} \to \begin{pmatrix} -1 & 0 & t-3 \\ 0 & t+1 & -2 \\ t+1 & -2 & 0 \end{pmatrix}$$

permuting columns 1 and 3. Add $(t+1) \times$ row 1 to row 3; and then add $(t-3) \times$ column 1 to column 3. The result:

$$\begin{pmatrix} -1 & 0 & 0 \\ 0 & t+1 & -2 \\ 0 & -2 & t^2 - 2t - 3 \end{pmatrix}$$

Exchange rows 2 and 3:

$$\begin{pmatrix} -1 & 0 & 0 \\ 0 & -2 & t^2 - 2t - 3 \\ 0 & t+1 & -2 \end{pmatrix}$$

Add $\frac{1}{2}(t+1) \times$ row 2 to row 3:

$$\begin{pmatrix} -1 & 0 & 0 \\ 0 & -2 & t^2 - 2t - 3 \\ 0 & 0 & \frac{1}{2}(t^3 - t^2 - 5t - 7) \end{pmatrix}$$

Add $\frac{1}{2}(t^2 - 2t - 3) \times$ column 2 to column 3:

$$\begin{pmatrix} -1 & 0 & 0 \\ 0 & -2 & 0 \\ 0 & 0 & \frac{1}{2}(t^3 - t^2 - 5t - 7) \end{pmatrix}$$

The elementary divisors of **a** (that is, the torsion orders of $t\mathbf{I} - \mathbf{a}$) are 1, 1, $t^3 - t^2 - 5t - 7$, since they are monic polynomials. The last one is the characteristic polynomial of **a**.

REMARK. We had occasion to remark in Chap. 6 the very close parallel between the theory of the g.c.d. for integers and the analogous theory for polynomials. It is easy to see that all the foregoing material, with the obvious modifications of terminology, holds equally well for matrices with integral coefficients. That is, one simply replaces the integral domain $K[t]$ by $\mathbf{Z}$.

EXERCISES

Find the torsion orders of the following matrices:

1. $\begin{pmatrix} t & 0 \\ 0 & t+1 \end{pmatrix}$

2. $\begin{pmatrix} t & 0 & 3 \\ 0 & t+1 & 0 \end{pmatrix}$

3. $\begin{pmatrix} t & 0 & 0 \\ 0 & t+1 & 0 \\ 0 & 0 & t+2 \end{pmatrix}$

4. $\begin{pmatrix} t & 1 \\ 0 & t \end{pmatrix}$

5. $\begin{pmatrix} t & 1 & 0 \\ 0 & t & 0 \\ 0 & 0 & t \end{pmatrix}$

6. $\begin{pmatrix} t & 1 & 0 \\ 0 & t & 0 \\ 0 & 0 & t+1 \end{pmatrix}$

7. The diagonal matrix with diagonal terms $t - \beta_1, t - \beta_2, \ldots, t - \beta_n$ with $\beta_1, \ldots, \beta_n$ all distinct.

8. The matrix $(tI - \mathbf{a})$ where $\mathbf{a}$ is the matrix given in Exercise 6, Sec. 5.

9. $\mathbf{a} = \begin{pmatrix} \beta_1 & 1 & 0 & 0 \\ 0 & \beta_1 & 0 & 0 \\ 0 & 0 & \beta_2 & 1 \\ 0 & 0 & 0 & \beta_2 \end{pmatrix}$ with $\beta_1 \neq \beta_2$

10. $\mathbf{a}$ as in Exercise 9 with $\beta_1 = \beta_2$.

10. Elementary divisors and similarity

It follows at once from Theorem 9.2 that the elementary divisors of similar matrices are identical [cf. Eq. (8.4)]. Therefore one can define the *elementary divisors of a linear mapping* **T** of a finite-dimensional vector space to be the elementary divisors of the matrix of **T** with respect to any base for **T**. In fact, any two such matrices are similar.

In (8.5) we have given a criterion for two linear mappings to be similar—in the special case where all the eigenvalues are in the field of scalars. We shall now give another criterion.

THEOREM 10.1 *Let U be a vector space of finite dimension over a field K. Let $\mathbf{T}_1$ and $\mathbf{T}_2$ be two linear mappings of U to U. A necessary and sufficient condition for $\mathbf{T}_1$ and $\mathbf{T}_2$ to be similar is that they have the same elementary divisors.*

We shall give two proofs for Theorem 10.1. Our first proof is for the illuminating special case that all the eigenvalues of the mappings are in the field K. Our proof for the general case is given in Sec. 11.

Proof. First of all, if $\mathbf{T}_1$ and $\mathbf{T}_2$ are similar, then their matrices relative to any base in U are similar. Since similar matrices have the same elementary divisors, it follows that $\mathbf{T}_1$ and $\mathbf{T}_2$ have the same elementary divisors.

To prove the converse, we assume that the eigenvalues of $\mathbf{T}_1$ and $\mathbf{T}_2$ are all in K, and we assume that $\mathbf{T}_1$ and $\mathbf{T}_2$ have the same elementary divisors. We have only to prove that $\mathbf{T}_1$ and $\mathbf{T}_2$ have the same Jordan normal form, and then it follows from Sec. 8 that $\mathbf{T}_1 \sim \mathbf{T}_2$.

Consider first the computation of the elementary divisors of a linear mapping $\mathbf{T}$ such that $\mathbf{T} - p\mathbf{I}$ is nilcyclic of order n. Let B be a cyclic base with respect to $\mathbf{T} - p\mathbf{I}$, and let $\mathbf{a}$ denote the matrix of $\mathbf{T}$ relative to that base. To compute the elementary divisors we must consider the matrix $t\,\mathbf{I} - \mathbf{a}$. Below are listed a series of elementary column operations on $t\,\mathbf{I} - \mathbf{a}$:

10.1
$$\begin{pmatrix} t-p & -1 & 0 & \cdots & 0 \\ 0 & t-p & -1 & \cdots & 0 \\ 0 & 0 & t-p & \cdots & 0 \\ \cdots & \cdots & \cdots & \cdots & \cdots \\ 0 & 0 & \cdots & \cdots & t-p \end{pmatrix} \to \begin{pmatrix} 0 & -1 & 0 & \cdots & 0 \\ (t-p)^2 & t-p & -1 & \cdots & 0 \\ 0 & 0 & t-p & \cdots & 0 \\ \cdots & \cdots & \cdots & \cdots & \cdots \\ 0 & 0 & \cdots & \cdots & t-p \end{pmatrix}$$

$$\to \begin{pmatrix} 0 & -1 & 0 & \cdots & 0 \\ 0 & 0 & -1 & \cdots & 0 \\ (t-p)^3 & (t-p)^2 & (t-p) & \cdots & 0 \\ \cdots & \cdots & \cdots & \cdots & \cdots \\ 0 & \cdots & \cdots & \cdots & t-p \end{pmatrix} \to$$

$$\begin{pmatrix} 0 & -1 & 0 & \cdots & 0 \\ 0 & 0 & -1 & \cdots & 0 \\ \cdots & \cdots & \cdots & \cdots & \cdots \\ \cdots & \cdots & \cdots & \cdots & \cdots \\ (t-p)^{n-1} & (t-p)^{n-2} & & \cdots & -1 \\ 0 & 0 & & \cdots & t-p \end{pmatrix} \to$$

$$\begin{pmatrix} 0 & -1 & 0 & \cdots & 0 \\ 0 & 0 & -1 & \cdots & 0 \\ \cdots & \cdots & \cdots & \cdots & \cdots \\ \cdots & \cdots & \cdots & \cdots & -1 \\ (t-p)^n & 0 & 0 & & 0 \end{pmatrix} \to$$

$$\begin{pmatrix} -1 & & & & & 0 \\ & -1 & & & & \\ & & \cdot & & & \\ & & & \cdot & & \\ 0 & & & & \cdot & \\ & & & & -1 & \\ & & & & & (t-p)^n \end{pmatrix}$$

Thus the elementary divisors are 1, 1, . . . , $(t - p)^n$.

Next consider the Jordan normal form of a linear mapping **T** whose eigenvalues are all in the field K. Let **a** be its matrix relative to some base. Since **a** is similar to a matrix in Jordan normal form, $t\,\mathbf{I} - \mathbf{a}$ has the same torsion orders as a matrix of diagonal blocks, each block of the form (10.1) above. Now the torsion orders of a diagonal matrix of this sort, having diagonal elements either -1 or else of the type $(t - p)^n$, are easily computed, and it is quickly seen that the matrix can be reconstructed from the knowledge of its torsion orders, apart from a permutation of the blocks. Therefore from the elementary divisors we can reconstruct a Jordan normal form for a linear mapping **T**. If $\mathbf{T}_1$ and $\mathbf{T}_2$ have the same elementary divisors, they therefore have identical Jordan normal forms, whence $\mathbf{T}_1 \sim \mathbf{T}_2$.

EXAMPLE 1 Let the torsion orders be 1, 1, 1, $(t - 5)^2$, $(t - 5)^3$. For a matrix of the type just discussed, we must have a 2×2 block and a 3×3 block. The following diagonal matrix meets the requirements:

$$\begin{pmatrix} -1 & & & & \\ & -1 & & & \\ & & (t-5)^3 & & \\ & & & -1 & \\ & & & & (t-5)^2 \end{pmatrix}$$

EXAMPLE 2 Let the torsion orders be 1, 1, 1, $(t - 2)^2$ $(t + 1)^3$. Again we need a 2×2 block and a 3×3 block:

$$\begin{pmatrix} -1 & & & & \\ & (t-2)^2 & & & \\ & & -1 & & \\ & & & -1 & \\ & & & & (t+1)^3 \end{pmatrix}$$

EXERCISES

Reconstruct the Jordan normal form from the given elementary divisors.

1. 1, 1, t^3
2. 1, 1, 1, 1, t, t^4

3. 1, 1, 1, $t(t+1)(t-1)(t-2)$
4. 1, 1, 1, $t^2(t+1)(t-1)$
5. 1, 1, 1, $t^2(t+1)^2$

6–10. Given that **T** has the elementary divisors above, find the elementary divisors of $\mathbf{T}^2$.

11. Modules, torsion orders, and the rational canonical form

By definition, the elementary divisors of an $n \times n$ matrix **a** are the torsion orders of the matrix $t\mathbf{I} - \mathbf{a}$, where t is an indeterminate and **I** is the $n \times n$ identity matrix. In this section we shall interpret the significance of the matrix $t\mathbf{I} - \mathbf{a}$. Thereafter, Theorem 10.1 will become transparent.

Let U be a finite-dimensional vector space over a field K, and let **T** be an endomorphism of U. We shall define, strange as it may seem, a $K[t]$-module structure on U. (See Sec. 11, Chap. 9.) The definition is as follows:

For any polynomial $p(t)$ in $K[t]$, we define the scalar multiplication by

11.1 $p(t) \cdot \mathbf{x} = p(\mathbf{T})(\mathbf{x})$

for any **x** in U. Inasmuch as the mapping $p(t) \to p(\mathbf{T})$ is a ring homomorphism of $K[t]$ into the ring of endomorphisms of the vector space U, it is readily seen that (11.1) defines U as a module over the ring $K[t]$, and we denote it by $U^{\mathbf{T}}$.

Although the module U, considered as a module over the field K has a base, the module $U^{\mathbf{T}}$, as a module over $K[t]$, *does not have a base.* For if **e** were a base element of $U^{\mathbf{T}}$, it would be true that $p(t)\mathbf{e} \neq \mathbf{0}$ for any nonzero polynomial $p(t)$—which is impossible since $\varphi(t)\mathbf{e} = \varphi(\mathbf{T}) \cdot \mathbf{e} = \mathbf{0}$ if we take $\varphi(t)$ to be the characteristic polynomial of **T**. Given two endomorphisms $\mathbf{T}_1$ and $\mathbf{T}_2$ of the vector space U, we obtain two $K[t]$-modules $U^{\mathbf{T}_1}$ and $U^{\mathbf{T}_2}$, respectively.

11.2 *The endomorphisms* $\mathbf{T}_1$ *and* $\mathbf{T}_2$ *are similar if and only if the modules* $U^{\mathbf{T}_1}$ *and* $U^{\mathbf{T}_2}$ *are isomorphic.*

Proof. By definition, $\mathbf{T}_1$ and $\mathbf{T}_2$ are similar if and only if there is a vector-space isomorphism $\mathbf{S}: U \to U$ such that

11.3 $\mathbf{T}_1\mathbf{S} = \mathbf{S}\mathbf{T}_2$

By definition of the modules $U^{\mathbf{T}_1}$ and $U^{\mathbf{T}_2}$, we have

$$t\mathbf{x} = \mathbf{T}_1\mathbf{x} \qquad \text{for all } \mathbf{x} \text{ in } U^{\mathbf{T}_1}$$
$$t\mathbf{x} = \mathbf{T}_2\mathbf{x} \qquad \text{for all } \mathbf{x} \text{ in } U^{\mathbf{T}_2}$$

Hence, if **S** is a vector-space isomorphism satisfying (11.3)

$$\mathbf{S}(t\mathbf{x}) = \mathbf{S}\mathbf{T}_2(\mathbf{x}) = \mathbf{T}_1\mathbf{S}(\mathbf{x}) = t\mathbf{S}(\mathbf{x})$$

for all **x** in $U^{\mathbf{T}_2}$. It follows in turn that

$$\mathbf{S}(t^2\mathbf{x}) = \mathbf{S}(t(t\mathbf{x})) = t\mathbf{S}(t\mathbf{x}) = t^2\mathbf{S}(\mathbf{x})$$

and more generally that

11.4 $$\mathbf{S}(p(t)\mathbf{x}) = p(t)\mathbf{S}(\mathbf{x})$$

for all $\mathbf{x}$ in the module $U^{\mathbf{T}_2}$ and for all polynomials $p(t)$. Equation (11.4) shows that $\mathbf{S}$ is not merely an isomorphism of the vector space U (over the field K) but is in addition a module isomorphism over the ring $K[t]$, of $U^{\mathbf{T}_2}$ onto $U^{\mathbf{T}_1}$. The converse can be proved by retracing steps. Thereby, assertion (11.2) is proved.

Our strategy for proving Theorem 10.1 can now be revealed. We shall show that if $\mathbf{T}$ is an endomorphism of the vector space U over the field K, then we can construct a module over the ring $K[t]$ isomorphic to the above-defined module $U^{\mathbf{T}}$, from *merely* a knowledge of the *elementary divisors* of $\mathbf{T}$. An immediate consequence of such a construction is: if two endomorphisms $\mathbf{T}_1$ and $\mathbf{T}_2$ have the same elementary divisors, then $U^{\mathbf{T}_1}$ and $U^{\mathbf{T}_2}$ are isomorphic; hence $\mathbf{T}_1$ and $\mathbf{T}_2$ are similar.

Our construction will come in two steps. Throughout the discussion below, $\mathbf{T}$ denotes a fixed endomorphism $U \to U$, where U is an n-dimensional vector space over the field K; $U^{\mathbf{T}}$ denotes the corresponding module over the ring $K[t]$.

STEP 1 Construct a free module M over the ring $K[t]$ and a submodule N such that

11.5 $$M/N \approx U^{\mathbf{T}}$$

where $\approx$ denotes "is isomorphic to as a module over the ring $K[t]$."

The construction is as follows. Let $B = \{\mathbf{e}_1, \ldots, \mathbf{e}_n\}$ be a base of the vector space U over the field K. The mapping

$$\varphi: K^n \to U$$

given by

$$\varphi(c_1, \ldots, c_n) = c_1\mathbf{e}_1 + \cdots + c_n\mathbf{e}_n \qquad (c_i \text{ in } K)$$

is a vector-space isomorphism. Set

$$\mathbf{e}_i^* = \varphi^{-1}(\mathbf{e}_i)$$

Set

$$M = K[t]^n$$

that is, M is the $K[t]$-module of all n-tuples $(r_1, \ldots, r_n)$ where each r_i belongs to the ring $K[t]$.

Let $\mathbf{a} = (a^j{}_i)$ denote the matrix of the endomorphism $\mathbf{T}$ with respect to $\mathbf{B}$; that is,

11.6 $$\mathbf{T}\mathbf{e}_i = \sum_{j=1}^{n} a^j{}_i\mathbf{e}_j \qquad (i = 1, 2, \ldots, n)$$

We may regard each element $\mathbf{x}$ in K^n as an element in the larger module $M = K[t]^n$. In particular, $B^* = \{\mathbf{e}_1^*, \ldots, \mathbf{e}_n^*\}$ is a base of the module M. Let $\mathbf{T}^*$ denote the endomorphism of M whose matrix with respect to the base B^* is $\mathbf{a}$; that is,

11.7 $$\mathbf{T}^*\mathbf{e}_i^* = \sum_{j=1}^{n} a^j{}_i \mathbf{e}_j^*$$

We may at last specify the desired submodule N. Set

11.8 $$N = \text{image } (t\,\mathbf{I}^* - \mathbf{T}^*) = (t\,\mathbf{I}^* - \mathbf{T}^*)M$$

where $\mathbf{I}^*$ denotes the identity mapping of M onto M. More explicitly, N is the submodule of M generated by the n-tuples

11.8′ $$\begin{array}{l} (t - a^1{}_1, -a^2{}_1, -a^3{}_1, \ldots, -a^n{}_1) \\ (-a^1{}_2, t - a^2{}_2, -a^3{}_2, \ldots, -a^n{}_2) \\ \cdots\cdots\cdots\cdots\cdots\cdots \\ (-a^1{}_n, -a^2{}_n, -a^3{}_n, \ldots, t - a^n{}_n) \end{array}$$

in other words, the columns of the matrix

11.8″ $$t\,\mathbf{I} - \mathbf{a}$$

We now prove that $M/N \approx U^{\mathbf{T}}$. Let $\mathbf{f}$: $M \to U^{\mathbf{T}}$ be the $K[t]$-module homomorphism such that

11.9 $$\mathbf{f}(\mathbf{e}_i^*) = \mathbf{e}_i \qquad (i = 1, 2, \ldots, n)$$

The existence and uniqueness of $\mathbf{f}$ is assured by the result in Sec. 11, Chap. 9. Moreover,

11.10 $$\mathbf{f}(\mathbf{T}^*(\mathbf{e}_i^*)) = \mathbf{f} \circ \mathbf{T}^* \circ \varphi^{-1}(\mathbf{e}_i) = \mathbf{f} \circ \varphi^{-1} \circ \mathbf{T}(\mathbf{e}_i) = \mathbf{T}(\mathbf{e}_i)$$

for $(i = 1, \ldots, n)$, since $\mathbf{T} \circ \varphi(\mathbf{x}) = \varphi \circ \mathbf{T}^*(\mathbf{x})$ for all $\mathbf{x}$ in the subset K^n of the module M by (11.7), and $\mathbf{f}$ coincides with φ on K^n by (11.9). Hence

11.11 $$\mathbf{f} \circ \mathbf{T}^* = \mathbf{T} \circ \mathbf{f}$$

On the other hand, since f is a $K[t]$-module homomorphism,

$$\mathbf{f}(t\mathbf{x}) = t\mathbf{f}(\mathbf{x}) = \mathbf{T}\mathbf{f}(\mathbf{x})$$

for all $\mathbf{x}$ in M. Hence

$$\mathbf{f} \circ tI^* = \mathbf{T} \circ \mathbf{f} = \mathbf{f} \circ \mathbf{T}^*$$

and consequently

11.12 $$\mathbf{f} \circ (t\mathbf{I}^* - \mathbf{T}^*) = 0$$

In other words, $N = (t\mathbf{I}^* - \mathbf{T}^*)\,M$ is in the kernel of $\mathbf{f}$.

It follows from Sec. 11, Chap. 9, that there is a homomorphism $\mathbf{f}''$: $M/N \to U^{\mathbf{T}}$ such that $\mathbf{f}'' \circ \pi = \mathbf{f}$, where π is the projection of M onto M/N; in a diagram,

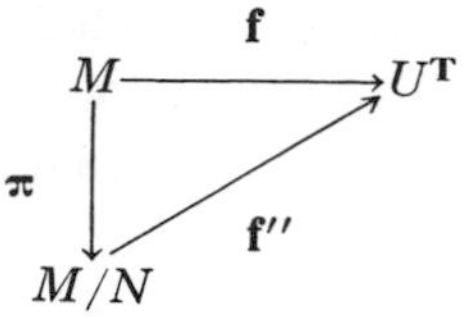

We shall prove that $\mathbf{f}''$ is an isomorphism by showing that it has an inverse. Let $g\colon U^{\mathbf{T}} \to M/N$ be the mapping given by $U^{\mathbf{T}} \xrightarrow{\varphi^{-1}} K^n \to M \xrightarrow{\boldsymbol{\pi}} M/N$, that is,

$$\mathbf{g} = \boldsymbol{\pi} \circ \varphi^{-1}$$

We have $\mathbf{f}'' \circ \mathbf{g} = \mathbf{f}'' \circ \boldsymbol{\pi} \circ \varphi^{-1} = \mathbf{f} \circ \varphi^{-1} =$ the identity mapping of $U^{\mathbf{T}}$. It follows at once that $\mathbf{g}$ is a $K[t]$-module monomorphism. In order to prove that $\mathbf{g}$ is an epimorphism, we note that

$$t\,\mathbf{I}^*(\mathbf{x}) \equiv \mathbf{T}^*(\mathbf{x}) \qquad \text{mod } N$$

for any $\mathbf{x}$ in M, where "$\mathbf{x} \equiv \mathbf{y}$ mod N" means "$\mathbf{x} - \mathbf{y}$ is in N." Hence, mod N, we get

$$t\mathbf{x} \equiv \mathbf{T}^*(\mathbf{x})$$
$$t^2(\mathbf{x}) = t \cdot t(\mathbf{x}) \equiv t\,\mathbf{T}^*(\mathbf{x}) = \mathbf{T}^*(t\mathbf{x}) \equiv \mathbf{T}^*(\mathbf{T}^*(\mathbf{x}))$$

inasmuch as $\mathbf{T}^*$ is a $K[t]$-module endomorphism and $\mathbf{T}^*(\mathbf{x}) \equiv \mathbf{T}^*(\mathbf{y})$ mod N if $\mathbf{x} \equiv \mathbf{y}$ mod N. It follows similarly that

$$t^k\mathbf{x} \equiv \mathbf{T}^{*k}(\mathbf{x}) \text{ mod } N$$

and

$$p(t)\mathbf{x} \equiv p(\mathbf{T}^*)(\mathbf{x}) \text{ mod } N$$

for any polynomial $p(t)$ in the ring $K[t]$. Given now any element $\mathbf{x}$ in M, we may write

$$\mathbf{x} = p_1(t)\mathbf{e}_1^* + \cdots + p_n(t)\mathbf{e}_n^*$$

with $p_1(t), \ldots, p_n(t)$ elements of the ring $K[t]$. Consequently,

$$\mathbf{x} \equiv p_1(\mathbf{T}^*)\mathbf{e}_1^* + p_2(\mathbf{T}^*)\mathbf{e}_2^* + \cdots + p_n(\mathbf{T}^*)\mathbf{e}_n^* \text{ mod } N$$

From (11.7) we see that $\mathbf{T}^*$ sends K^n into K^n. Hence the right-hand term of the above equation is in K^n and each element of M can be expressed in the form

$$\mathbf{y} + \mathbf{z}$$

$\mathbf{y}$ in the subset K^n and z in the submodule N; in other words, we can write $M = K^n + N$. Now

$$\mathbf{g}(U^{\mathbf{T}}) = \boldsymbol{\pi} \circ \varphi^{-1}(U^{\mathbf{T}}) = \boldsymbol{\pi}(K^n) = \boldsymbol{\pi}(K^n + N)$$
$$= \boldsymbol{\pi}(M) = M/N$$

Consequently $\mathbf{g}$ is an epimorphism. It follows at once that $\mathbf{g}$ is an isomorphism and that $\mathbf{f}''$ is an isomorphism too. We sum up our result in the following theorem.

THEOREM 11.1 *Let* $\mathbf{T}$ *be an endomorphism of an n-dimensional vector space* U *over a field* K*, and let* $U^{\mathbf{T}}$ *be the corresponding* $K[t]$*-module formed from* U *upon defining* $p(t)\mathbf{x} = p(\mathbf{T})\mathbf{x}$ *for any* $p(t)$ *in the ring of polynomials in an indeterminate* t*. Let* M *be the free* $K[t]$*-module* $K[t]^n$*, and let* $\mathbf{T}^*$ *be the endomorphism of* M *defined by* (11.7). *Let* N *denote the image of the endomorphism* $(t\mathbf{I}^* - \mathbf{T}^*)$*, where* $\mathbf{I}^*$ *is the identity mapping of* M*. Then as* $K[t]$*-module,* M/N *is isomorphic to* $U^{\mathbf{T}}$.

STEP 2 We now relate the elementary divisors of the endomorphism $\mathbf{T}$ to the $K[t]$-submodule N.

By definition, the elementary divisors of the endomorphism $\mathbf{T}$ are the torsion orders of the matrix $t\,\mathbf{I} - \mathbf{a}$, where $\mathbf{a}$ is the matrix of $\mathbf{T}$ with respect to any base. By (9.13), we have

11.13 $$t\mathbf{I} - \mathbf{a} = \mathbf{b}\,\boldsymbol{\Delta}\,\mathbf{c}$$

where $\boldsymbol{\Delta}$, $\mathbf{b}$, and $\mathbf{c}$ are matrices with coefficients in $K[t]$ with $\det \mathbf{b} = \pm\det \mathbf{c} = \pm 1$, and $\boldsymbol{\Delta}$ is a diagonal matrix,

$$\boldsymbol{\Delta} = \begin{pmatrix} q_1(t) & & & & \\ & q_2(t) & & & \\ & & \cdot & & \\ & & & \cdot & \\ & & & & \cdot \\ & & & & & q_n(t) \end{pmatrix}$$

with $q_1(t) \mid q_2(t) \mid \cdots \mid q_n(t)$.

Let $\mathbf{S}^*$, $\boldsymbol{\Delta}^*$, and $\mathbf{R}^*$ denote the endomorphisms of M whose matrices with respect to the base $B^* = \{\mathbf{e}_1^*, \ldots, \mathbf{e}_n^*\}$ are $\mathbf{b}$, $\boldsymbol{\Delta}$, and $\mathbf{c}$. Inasmuch as $\det \mathbf{b} = \pm 1$, the inverse matrix $\mathbf{b}^{-1}$ has its coefficients in the ring $K[t]$, and consequently the endomorphism $\mathbf{S}^*$ of the module M is an invertible automorphism of M. Similarly, the module endomorphism $\mathbf{R}^*$ is an invertible automorphism. Since the left side of Eq. (11.13) is the matrix of $t\,\mathbf{I}^* - \mathbf{T}^*$ with respect to B^*, we have

11.14 $$t\,\mathbf{I}^* - \mathbf{T}^* = \mathbf{S}^*\boldsymbol{\Delta}^*\mathbf{R}^*$$

Hence $N = (t\,\mathbf{I}^* - \mathbf{T}^*)(M) = \mathbf{S}^*\boldsymbol{\Delta}^*\mathbf{R}^*(M) = \mathbf{S}^*\boldsymbol{\Delta}^*(M)$, and so

11.15 $$\mathbf{S}^{*-1}(N) = \boldsymbol{\Delta}^*(M)$$

Equation (11.15) implies that the automorphism $\mathbf{S}^{*-1}$ of M sends N onto the submodule $\boldsymbol{\Delta}^*(M)$. Hence, by Sec. 11, Chap. 9, the M/N part of $\mathbf{S}^{*-1}$ induces an isomorphism of the quotient module M/N onto the quotient module $M/\boldsymbol{\Delta}^*(M)$. Now the matrix $\boldsymbol{\Delta}$ is obviously determined by the elementary divisors $q_1(t), \ldots,$ $q_n(t)$. Hence the quotient module $M/\boldsymbol{\Delta}^*(M)$ is determined by the elementary divisors. Since

$$M/\boldsymbol{\Delta}^*(M) \approx M/N \approx U^{\mathbf{T}}$$

we find that, to within an isomorphism, the $K[t]$-module $U^{\mathbf{T}}$ is uniquely determined by the elementary divisors of $\mathbf{T}$. In view of remark (11.2), Theorem 10.1 is now proved.

However, our proof gives much more information than Theorem 10.1. For the module $U^{\mathbf{T}}$ can be described quite explicitly in terms of the elementary divisors. The module $M = K[t]^n$ is the *direct sum* of n copies of $K[t]$:

11.16′
$$\begin{aligned} M &= K[t] \oplus \cdots \oplus K[t] \\ \mathbf{\Delta}^*(M) &= (q_1(t)) \oplus \cdots \oplus (q_n(t)) \end{aligned}$$

where $(q_i(t))$ denotes the *principal ideal* in $K[t]$ generated by $q_i(t)$, that is, the submodule of $K[t]$ with the single base element $q_i(t)$. The quotient module has the form

11.16″
$$M/N = K[t]/(q_1(t)) \oplus \cdots \oplus K[t]/(q_n(t))$$

It remains to say some words about a $K[t]$-module of the form $K[t]/(q(t))$, where we may assume that $q(t)$ is a monic polynomial. We have seen that a vector space U over the field K together with an endomorphism of U defines a module over the ring $K[t]$. Conversely, a $K[t]$-module L defines a vector space over the field K together with an endomorphism $\mathbf{T}$ defined by $\mathbf{Tx} = t\mathbf{x}$ for all $\mathbf{x}$ in L. Considering $U = K[t]/(q(t))$ as a vector space over the field K, what is the nature of the corresponding endomorphism $\mathbf{T}$?

Let $q(t) = a_0 + a_1t + \cdots + t^r$ be a monic polynomial of degree r. Then as a vector space over K, $K[t]/(q(t))$ has as a base the r elements $\pi(1), \pi(t), \ldots, \pi(t^{r-1})$, where $\pi\colon K[t] \to K[t]/(q(t))$ is the projection (cf. Exercise 11, Sec. 11, Chap. 9). Moreover the projection π is a *ring* homomorphism (cf. Exercise 9, Sec. 11, Chap. 9). Consequently we have

$$\begin{aligned} \mathbf{T}\pi(1) &= t\pi(1) = \pi(t) \\ \mathbf{T}\pi(t^k) &= t\pi(t^k) = \pi(t^{k+1}) \\ \mathbf{T}\pi(t^{r-1}) &= t\pi(t^{r-1}) = \pi(t^r) \end{aligned}$$

However $\pi(a_0 + a_1t + \cdots + t^r) = 0$ implies

$$\pi(t^r) = -(a_0\pi(1) + a_1\pi(t) + \cdots + a_{r-1}\pi(t^{r-1}))$$

In short, relative to the base $\pi(1), \ldots, \pi(t^{r-1})$, the matrix of the endomorphism $\mathbf{T}$ of the vector space U is

11.17
$$\begin{pmatrix} 0 & 0 & \cdots & 0 & -a_0 \\ 1 & 0 & \cdots & 0 & -a_1 \\ 0 & 1 & \cdots & 0 & -a_2 \\ \cdot & \cdot & \cdots & \cdot & \cdot \\ 0 & 0 & \cdots & 1 & -a_{r-1} \end{pmatrix}$$

We have $q(\mathbf{T}) = \mathbf{0}$ since

$$q(\mathbf{T})(U) = q(t)\pi(K[t]) = \pi(q(t)K[t]) = \mathbf{0}$$

Moreover, for any polynomial $p(t)$ of degree less than r, $p(\mathbf{T}) \neq 0$, since

$$p(\mathbf{T})\pi(1) = p(t)\pi(1) = \pi(p(t)) \neq \mathbf{0}$$

Consequently,

11.18 *$q(t)$ is the minimal polynomial of the endomorphism* $\mathbf{T}$.

We can sum up our conclusions in the following way:

THEOREM 11.2 (**The theorem on the rational canonical form**) *Let* $\mathbf{T}$ *be an endomorphism of an n-dimensional vector space* U *over a field* K, *and let* $q_1(t) \mid q_2(t) \mid \cdots \mid q_r(t)$ *be the elementary divisors of* $\mathbf{T}$ *that are distinct from* 1. *Then there is a base for* U *with respect to which the matrix of* T *has the block form*

11.19
$$\begin{pmatrix} \mathbf{0} & \mathbf{0} & \cdots & \mathbf{0} \\ \mathbf{0} & \mathbf{a}_1 & \cdots & \mathbf{0} \\ \cdot & & & \\ \cdot & & & \\ \cdot & & & \cdot \quad \cdot \\ \mathbf{0} & \mathbf{0} & \cdots & \mathbf{a}_r \end{pmatrix}$$

where the first $\mathbf{0}$ *is an* $(n - r)x(n - r)0$ *matrix and where the ith block is determined from the i-th elementary divisor* $q_i(t)$ *by the formula* (11.17). *Moreover, the minimal polynomial of* $\mathbf{T}$ *is* $q_r(t)$.

The block form (11.19) comes from the direct sum (11.16′), and that is why we can ignore the $n - r$ elementary divisors which are equal to 1—for they yield a summand $K[t]/(1)$ which is the zero subspace.

Note 1. There can be no zero elementary divisors since the product of the elementary divisors is the characteristic polynomial $\varphi(t) = \det(t\mathbf{I} - \mathbf{T})$. Also, $\varphi(t)|q_r(t)^r$, where r is the number of elementary divisors different from 1. Thus the characteristic polynomial is the minimal polynomial if and only if $r = 1$.

Note 2. Assertion (11.16) can be regarded as an interpretation of the matrix equation (11.13). On the other hand equation (11.13) is a special instance of Eq. (9.13):

9.13 $$\mathbf{\Delta} = \mathbf{bac} \qquad \det \mathbf{b} = \pm 1 \qquad \det \mathbf{c} = \pm 1$$

where $\mathbf{a}$ is an $m \times n$ matrix with coefficients in $K[t]$, and $\mathbf{\Delta}$ is the diagonal $m \times n$ matrix of rank r:

$$\begin{pmatrix} q_1(t) & \cdots & 0 & 0 & \cdots & 0 \\ \cdot & \cdot & \cdot & \cdot & \cdot & \cdot \\ 0 & \cdots & q_r(t) & 0 & \cdots & 0 \\ 0 & \cdots & 0 & 0 & \cdots & 0 \\ \cdot & \cdot & \cdot & \cdot & \cdot & \cdot \\ 0 & \cdots & 0 & 0 & \cdots & 0 \end{pmatrix}$$

and **b**, **c** are square $m \times m$ and $n \times n$ matrices with coefficients in $K[t]$. Equation (9.13) has an interpretation similar to (11.16). Namely, let M denote the free $K[t]$-module $K[t]^n$, and let N denote the submodule generated by the n columns of the matrix **a**.

11.20
$$\begin{aligned} \mathbf{a}_1 &= (a^1{}_1, a^2{}_1, \ldots, a^n{}_1) \\ &\cdots\cdots\cdots \\ \mathbf{a}_n &= (a^1{}_n, a^2{}_n, \ldots, a^m{}_n) \end{aligned}$$

Equation (9.13) means in effect: upon replacing the base $\{\mathbf{e}_1^*, \ldots, \mathbf{e}_m^*\}$ of M by the base $\{\mathbf{b}_1^*, \ldots, \mathbf{b}_m^*\}$ consisting of the column vectors of the inverse matrix $\mathbf{b}^{-1}$, and upon replacing the submodule generators $\mathbf{a}_1, \ldots, \mathbf{a}_n$ by the linear combinations made up of the column vectors of the matrix **ac**, the submodule N becomes simply generated by

11.21 $$q_1\mathbf{b}_1^*, q_2\mathbf{b}_2^*, \ldots, q_r\mathbf{b}_r^*$$

where $q_1|q_2| \cdots |q_r$ are the torsion orders of the matrix **a**.

The proof consists of introducing the free module $M_1 = K[t]^m$, the module homomorphisms

$$\mathbf{T}^* \text{ and } \mathbf{\Delta}^*: K[t]^n \to K[t]^m$$

and the module automorphisms

$$\begin{aligned} &\mathbf{S}^*: K[t]^m \to K[t]^m \\ &\mathbf{R}^*: K[t]^n \to K[t]^n \end{aligned}$$

whose matrices are, respectively,

a and **Δ**	with respect to $\{e_1^*, \ldots, e_n^*\}, \{e_1^*, \ldots, e_m^*\}$
b	with respect to $\{e_1^*, \ldots, e_m^*\}$
c	with respect to $\{e_1^*, \ldots, e_n^*\}$

The submodule N is the image of $\mathbf{T}^*$, and the base (11.21) is found from the relation

$$\begin{aligned} \{q_1\mathbf{e}_1^*, \ldots, q_r\mathbf{e}_r^*, \mathbf{0}, \ldots, \mathbf{0}\} &= \{\mathbf{\Delta}^*(\mathbf{e}_1^*), \ldots, \mathbf{\Delta}^*(\mathbf{e}_n^*)\} \\ &= \{\mathbf{S}^* \cdot (\mathbf{T}^*\mathbf{R}^*)(\mathbf{e}_1^*), \ldots, \mathbf{S}^* \cdot (\mathbf{T}^*\mathbf{R}^*)(\mathbf{e}_m^*)\} \end{aligned}$$

EXERCISES

1. Deduce from the rational canonical form theorem that every nilpotent endomorphism of a finite-dimensional vector space is a direct sum of nilcyclic parts.

2. Carry out a discussion of matrix equation (9.13), replacing the ring $K[t]$ by the ring of integers **Z**. As a consequence prove

(*a*) Every submodule of a finitely generated free **Z**-module has a base of the type (11.21).

(*b*) Every finite abelian group is a direct sum of cyclic groups of orders $q_1, q_2, \ldots, q_r$ with $q_1|q_2| \cdots |q_r$. These numbers are called the *torsion orders* of G. Prove that the torsion orders of G are unique.

3. Let **T** be an endomorphism of a finite-dimensional vector space U of a field K, and let q denote the product of all the irreducible factors in the minimal polynomial of **T**. Assume that q and its derivative q' have g.c.d. 1. (This is automatically satisfied if K is of characteristic zero or is finite.)

(*a*) Prove that $q(\mathbf{T})^r = \mathbf{0}$ for some r.

(*b*) Find a polynomial $f(t)$ such that

$$[q(\mathbf{T} - f(\mathbf{T}))]^{r/2} = \mathbf{0}$$

[Hint: Expanding in Taylor's series,

$$q(t - f(t)q(t)) = q(t) - q'(t)(f(t)q(t)) + \cdots$$

and substituting $t = \mathbf{T}$, the problem reduces to finding $f(t)$ so that $q(t)|(1 - q'(t)f(t)$.]

4. Continuing the notation of Exercise 3, let θ denote the ring-endomorphism of $K[t]$ given by

$$t \to t - f(t)q(t)$$

Prove the following:

(*a*) $q(\theta(t)) \equiv q(t)^2 f_1(t) \pmod{q(t)^r}$

(*b*) $q(\theta^2(t)) \equiv q(t)^4 f_2(t) \pmod{q(t)^r}$

($\theta^2(t)$ denoting $\theta(\theta(t))$; and $f_1(t)$, $f_2(t)$ in $K[t]$)

(*c*) $q(\theta^k(\mathbf{T})) = 0$ for $2^k > r$.

5. Set $\mathbf{S} = \theta^k(\mathbf{T})$, $\mathbf{N} = \mathbf{T} - \mathbf{S}$. Assuming that all the roots of $q(t)$ are in the field K, prove that **S** and **N** are the endomorphisms described in Theorem 6.3.

6. Let **S** be an endomorphism of a vector space U over a field K, and let $q(t)$ be the minimal polynomial of **S**. Assume that $q(t)$ has no repeated factors. (Such an endomorphism is called *semisimple*.) Prove: Any **S**-stable subspace V admits an **S**-stable complement W such that $U = V \oplus W$ (direct).

12. Finitely generated abelian groups

We have already remarked that a module over the ring of integers $\mathbf{Z}$ is equivalent to an abelian group. On the other hand, one may note (cf. Exercise 2, Sec. 11) that the diagonalization process of Sec. 9 carries over bodily for matrices with integer coefficients if we replace the ring $K[t]$ by the ring $\mathbf{Z}$. As a result, one can assert the analogue of Note 2 above for the case of abelian groups. Thus, given a free abelian group (i.e., a free $\mathbf{Z}$-module) having a base of n elements, and given a subgroup N, one can find a base

$$x_1, x_2, \ldots, x_n$$

for M, and unique positive integers $q_1, q_2, \ldots, q_r$ such that N has a base

$$q_1x_1, q_2x_2, \ldots, q_rx_r$$

with $q_1|q_2| \cdots |q_r$.

As a consequence, we have for the quotient group

12.1 $$M/N \cong \mathbf{Z}_{q_1} + \mathbf{Z}_{q_2} + \cdots + \mathbf{Z}_{q_r} + \underbrace{\mathbf{Z} + \cdots + \mathbf{Z}}_{n-r}$$

Given now any abelian group G with n generators, $y_1, \ldots, y_n$, we take a free abelian group M with n generators $z_1, \ldots, z_n$, and we map the free **Z**-module M onto the **Z**-module G by the mapping f:

$$f\colon z_i \to y_i \qquad (i = 1, \ldots, n)$$

The kernel of f is some submodule N, and we have $M/N = G$. Applying the result (12.1), we find unique positive integers $q_1, q_2, \ldots, q_r$ such that

$$G = \mathbf{Z}_{q_1} + \cdots + \mathbf{Z}_{q_r} + \underbrace{\mathbf{Z} + \cdots + \mathbf{Z}}_{n-r}$$

and $q_1|q_2| \cdots |q_r$.

For finite abelian groups we must have $r = n$ here. For this case our result, in slightly different form, is given in Sec. 7, Chap. 10. (See Exercise 7 of that section.)

The subgroup $\mathbf{Z}_{q_1} + \cdots + \mathbf{Z}_{q_r}$ is called the *torsion* subgroup of G—it may be characterized as the subgroup of G which consists of all the elements of finite order. The numbers $q_1, \ldots, q_n$ which are greater than 1 are called the *torsion orders* of G. The number $n - r$ of summands isomorphic to **Z** is called the *rank* of G.

EXERCISES

1. Prove that two finite abelian groups are isomorphic if and only if they have the same torsion orders. [Hint: Use induction after characterizing the largest torsion order.]

2. Prove that two finitely generated abelian groups are isomorphic if and only if they have the same torsion orders and the same rank.

14

Quadratic and Hermitian forms

1. Introduction

In Sec. 11, Chap. 8, we took up briefly the question of defining lengths of vectors and angles between vectors. In the present chapter we shall go into this question more methodically.

It was pointed out in Chap. 8 that in general it does not make sense to try to define *length* and *angle* in a vector space. Vector-space axioms deal only with addition of vectors and with scalar multiplication. In order to define length of vectors it is necessary to impose an additional structure upon a vector space. We begin with some considerations which are closely related to the *inner product* of Eq. (11.4), Chap. 8.

2. Linear functions; dual spaces

Let V be a vector space over a field K. By a *linear function* on V is meant a linear mapping $\mathbf{f}\colon V \to K$. That is, $\mathbf{f}$ is required to satisfy

2.1 $$\begin{cases} \mathbf{f}(\mathbf{x} + \mathbf{y}) = \mathbf{f}(\mathbf{x}) + \mathbf{f}(\mathbf{y}) & \text{for all } \mathbf{x}, \mathbf{y} \text{ in } V \\ \mathbf{f}(a\mathbf{x}) = a\mathbf{f}(\mathbf{x}) & \text{for all } \mathbf{x} \text{ in } V,\ a \text{ in } K \end{cases}$$

From this it follows that $\mathbf{f}(\mathbf{0}) = 0$ and $\mathbf{f}(-\mathbf{x}) = -\mathbf{f}(\mathbf{x})$ for any $\mathbf{x}$ in V (Sec. 3, Chap. 9).

Denoting by V^* the set of all such linear functions, we make V^* into a vector space over K by defining $\mathbf{f} + \mathbf{g}$ and $a\mathbf{f}$ by the rules

2.2 $$\begin{aligned} (\mathbf{f} + \mathbf{g})(\mathbf{x}) &= \mathbf{f}(\mathbf{x}) + \mathbf{g}(\mathbf{x}) && \mathbf{f} \text{ and } \mathbf{g} \text{ in } V^*,\ \mathbf{x} \text{ in } V \\ (a\mathbf{f})(\mathbf{x}) &= a \cdot \mathbf{f}(\mathbf{x}) && \mathbf{f} \text{ in } V^*,\ a \text{ in } K,\ \mathbf{x} \text{ in } V \end{aligned}$$

It is trivial to check that $\mathbf{f} + \mathbf{g}$ and $a\mathbf{f}$ are again linear functions on V, hence elements of V^*. We recall that V^* is called the dual vector space of V (Sec. 4, Chap. 9).

If $B = \{\mathbf{e}_1, \ldots, \mathbf{e}_n\}$ is a base for V, supposed of dimension n, and if $\mathbf{x} = x^i\mathbf{e}_i$ is any vector in V, then for a linear function $\mathbf{f}$ we have

$$\mathbf{f}(\mathbf{x}) = \mathbf{f}(x^i\mathbf{e}_i) = x^i\mathbf{f}(\mathbf{e}_i)$$

by (2.2). Write

2.3 $$f_i = \mathbf{f}(\mathbf{e}_i)$$

so that

2.4 $$\mathbf{f}(\mathbf{x}) = x^i f_i$$

Thus $\mathbf{f}$ is completely determined by the n scalars $f_1, \ldots, f_n$. Conversely, given any n-tuple of scalars $(f_1, \ldots, f_n)$, the formula (2.3) defines a linear function $\mathbf{f}$, plainly. In particular, taking $f_i = 0$ for $i \neq j$ and $f_j = 1$, we get a linear function, call it $\mathbf{e}^j$, for which (2.4) becomes

2.5 $$\mathbf{e}^j(\mathbf{x}) = x^j$$

Thus $\mathbf{e}^j$ is none other than the mapping $V \to K$ that sends $\mathbf{x}$ into its jth component relative to B. In particular,

2.6 $$\mathbf{e}^j(\mathbf{e}_i) = \begin{cases} 0 & \text{if } i \neq j \\ 1 & \text{if } i = j \end{cases}$$

The n linear functions $\mathbf{e}^j$ so defined form a base $B^* = \{\mathbf{e}^1, \ldots, \mathbf{e}^n\}$ of V^*. For if $f_1, \ldots, f_n$ are scalars, then $(f_i\mathbf{e}^i)(\mathbf{x}) = f_i\mathbf{e}^i(\mathbf{x}) = f_i x^i$, by (2.2) and (2.5). Therefore, if the f_i are defined by (2.3), starting from any linear function $\mathbf{f}$, it follows that both $\mathbf{f}$ and $f_i\mathbf{e}^i$ send any $\mathbf{x}$ in V into the same element of K. Hence

2.7 $$\mathbf{f} = f_i\mathbf{e}^i$$

On the other hand, the $\mathbf{e}^i$ are linearly independent, as follows at once from (2.6). The base B^* is called the *dual base* associated with B. In particular, dim V^* = dim V.

From Sec. 4, Chap. 9, we recall the notation

2.8 $$\langle \mathbf{f}, \mathbf{x} \rangle = \mathbf{f}(\mathbf{x})$$

introduced in order to put elements of V and V^* on a kind of equal footing in formulas. In this notation, formulas (2.3) to (2.7) become

2.9
$$\begin{aligned} \mathbf{x} &= x^i\mathbf{e}_i & \mathbf{f} &= f_i\mathbf{e}^i \\ x^i &= \langle \mathbf{e}^i, \mathbf{x} \rangle & f_i &= \langle \mathbf{f}, \mathbf{e}_i \rangle \\ \langle \mathbf{f}, \mathbf{x} \rangle &= f_i x^i \\ \langle \mathbf{e}^j, \mathbf{e}_i \rangle &= \begin{cases} 0 & i \neq j \\ 1 & i = j \end{cases} \end{aligned}$$

We recall the easily verified formulas (4.9), Chap. 9:

2.10
$$\begin{aligned} \langle \mathbf{f}, \mathbf{x} + \mathbf{y} \rangle &= \langle \mathbf{f}, \mathbf{x} \rangle + \langle \mathbf{f}, \mathbf{y} \rangle \\ \langle \mathbf{f} + \mathbf{g}, \mathbf{x} \rangle &= \langle \mathbf{f}, \mathbf{x} \rangle + \langle \mathbf{g}, \mathbf{x} \rangle \\ \langle a\mathbf{f}, \mathbf{x} \rangle &= \langle \mathbf{f}, a\mathbf{x} \rangle = a\langle \mathbf{f}, \mathbf{x} \rangle \end{aligned}$$

for any $\mathbf{f}$, $\mathbf{g}$ in V^*, $\mathbf{x}$, $\mathbf{y}$ in V, and a in K. These are simply (2.1) and (2.2).

Let us denote by $\langle\ ,\mathbf{x}\rangle$ the mapping that sends $\mathbf{f}$ in V^* into the scalar $\langle\mathbf{f},\mathbf{x}\rangle$. From the second and third equations above it is clear that the creature $\langle\ ,\mathbf{x}\rangle$ is a linear mapping $V^* \to K$, hence is an element of the dual space V^{**} of V^*. The correspondence $\mathbf{x} \to \langle\ ,\mathbf{x}\rangle$ therefore gives as a mapping $V \to V^{**}$. It is a linear-mapping, as is plain from the first and third equations above. If an element $\mathbf{x}$ is sent into zero by our mapping, that means $\langle\mathbf{f},\mathbf{x}\rangle = 0$ for all $\mathbf{f}$, which is possible only for $\mathbf{x} = \mathbf{0}$. Now if V has finite dimension n, then we know that $\dim V^* = n$, whence in turn $\dim V^{**} = n$. As was just pointed out, the kernel of $V \to V^{**}$ is zero, and it follows that our mapping must be an isomorphism. Hence, $\mathbf{V}$ *and the dual of* V^* *are isomorphic in a natural way* (if $\dim V \neq \infty$). For this reason we can simply abolish V^{**} in order to minimize the number of vector spaces at hand; every element of V^{**} can be unambiguously represented by an element of V, and vice versa.

But in general the dual space V^* cannot be swept under the carpet so easily. Of course V and V^*, having equal dimension, must be isomorphic. However it is an important fact that in general there is no *naturally* determined isomorphism $V \to V^*$. If we choose a base $\mathbf{e}_1, \ldots, \mathbf{e}_n$ in V, then we can define an isomorphism $\mathbf{T}$ by the requirement $\mathbf{T}(\mathbf{e}_i) = \mathbf{e}^i$ (dual base), for example. But it is easily seen that $\mathbf{T}$ so defined depends strongly on the choice of base in V.† Some vector spaces have a distinguished base, and if we agree in that case to define $\mathbf{T}$ by means of the distinguished base, then it becomes fixed once for all, and V^* becomes superfluous in the same way as V^{**} above.

This situation arises in particular with the space K^n of $n \times 1$ matrices (that is, column vectors), which has the distinguished base $\mathbf{e}_1, \ldots, \mathbf{e}_n$ in which $\mathbf{e}_i$ is the ith column of the unit matrix $\mathbf{I}_n$. Any linear function $\mathbf{f}$ on K^n is completely determined by the scalars $f_i = \mathbf{f}(\mathbf{e}_i)$, according to (2.3), and $\mathbf{f}$ can be unambiguously represented by the n-tuple

$$\begin{pmatrix} f_1 \\ \cdot \\ \cdot \\ \cdot \\ f_n \end{pmatrix}$$

which is an element of K^n. Because of our index conventions, however, it is convenient to think of this n-tuple as a row vector $(f_1, \ldots, f_n)$, consequently as an element of K_n (we point out again that K^n and K_n differ only in notation). Thus K_n can be thought of as the dual of K^n, and vice versa.

As was already pointed out in Chap. 9, the index convention in V (lower indices on base vectors, upper indices on components) leads in a compelling way to the

† For example, if $\dim V = 1$ and if we define $\mathbf{T}: V \to V^*$ by $\mathbf{T}(\mathbf{e}) = \mathbf{e}^*$ (dual base of $\mathbf{e}$ in V), then replacing $\mathbf{e}$ by a new base $c\mathbf{e}$ (and $\mathbf{e}^*$ by $(1/c)\mathbf{e}^*$) changes $\mathbf{T}$ to $(1/c^2)\mathbf{T}$.

opposite convention in the dual space V^*. These conventions are natural and convenient. Moreover, they are the well-established conventions of tensor calculus. Various other index systems are in common use—for example (as in Chap. 8), keeping all indices as subscripts. But all index conventions have at some point or other a minor flaw, the result of which is to force the user to employ the transpose of a matrix where he did not expect to. We shall point out the difficulty in our system. It is one which will not cause us much concern.

Let U, V be vector spaces over a field K, with dim $U = m$ and dim $V = n$, and let $\mathbf{T}\colon U \to V$ be a linear mapping. If $B_1 = \{\mathbf{u}_i\}$ and $B_2 = \{\mathbf{v}_j\}$ are bases for U, V, then the corresponding matrix of $\mathbf{T}$ is $\mathbf{a} = (a^j{}_i)$, where $\mathbf{T}(\mathbf{u}_i) = a^j{}_i\mathbf{v}_j$. By Definition 5.1, Chap. 9, the components $a^1{}_i, \ldots, a^n{}_i$ of $\mathbf{T}(\mathbf{u}_i)$ form the ith column of $\mathbf{a}$, which is therefore $n \times m$.

Now if $\mathbf{f}$ is an element of V^*, then $\mathbf{f} \circ \mathbf{T}$ is an element of U^*, being a linear mapping $U \to K$. Thus the correspondence $\mathbf{f} \to \mathbf{f} \circ \mathbf{T}$ maps V^* to U^*. This mapping, denoted by $\mathbf{T}^*$, is linear and is called the *transpose* of $\mathbf{T}$. It is characterized by the relation

2.11 $$\langle \mathbf{T}^*(\mathbf{f}), \mathbf{x}\rangle = \langle \mathbf{f}, \mathbf{T}(\mathbf{x})\rangle \qquad \mathbf{x} \text{ in } U, \mathbf{f} \text{ in } V^*$$

(See Theorem 4.4, Chap. 9.)

What is the matrix of $\mathbf{T}^*$? Let $B_1^* = \{\mathbf{u}^i\}$ and $B_2^* = \{\mathbf{v}^j\}$ be the dual bases of B_1, B_2. We must compute the components of $\mathbf{T}^*(\mathbf{v}^j)$ relative to the base B_1^* in U^*. According to (2.9) those components are the quantities

$$\langle \mathbf{T}^*(\mathbf{v}^j), \mathbf{u}_i\rangle$$

By (2.11), this is the same as

$$\begin{aligned} \langle \mathbf{v}^j, \mathbf{T}(\mathbf{u}_i)\rangle &= \langle \mathbf{v}^j, a^k{}_i\mathbf{v}_k\rangle \\ &= a^k{}_i\langle \mathbf{v}^j, \mathbf{v}_k\rangle = a^j{}_i \end{aligned}$$

using (2.9). Therefore,

2.12 $$\mathbf{T}^*(\mathbf{v}^j) = a^j{}_i\mathbf{u}^i$$

It would therefore seem natural to take $(a^j{}_i) = \mathbf{a}$ as the matrix of $\mathbf{T}^*$ relative to the base pair B_2^*, B_1^*. But that violates the convention of Definition 5.1, Chap. 9, according to which the matrix of $\mathbf{T}^*$ relative to B_2^*, B_1^* must have $a^j{}_1, a^j{}_2, \ldots, a^j{}_m$ in its jth column. That is, the matrix of $\mathbf{T}^*$ relative to B_2^*, B_1^* is the transpose ${}^t\mathbf{a}$. We state this as the following proposition:

PROPOSITION 2.1 *Let U and V be finite-dimensional vector spaces over a field K, and let $\mathbf{T}$ be a linear mapping $U \to V$. Let $\mathbf{a}$ be the matrix of $\mathbf{T}$ relative to a base pair B_1, B_2 in U, V, respectively. Then the transpose $\mathbf{T}^*\colon V^* \to U^*$* of $\mathbf{T}$, *mapping $\mathbf{g}$ in V^* into $\mathbf{g} \circ \mathbf{T}$, has ${}^t\mathbf{a}$ as its matrix relative to the dual base pair B_2^*, B_1^*.*

EXERCISES

1. Let $B = \{\mathbf{e}_i\}$ and $B_1 = \{\mathbf{v}_i\}$ be two bases in $V (i = 1, \ldots, n)$. Let $\mathbf{p}$ be the matrix from B to B_1. That is, $\mathbf{v}_i = p^j{}_i \mathbf{e}_j$. Prove that ${}^t\mathbf{p}^{-1}$ is the matrix from the dual base B^* to the dual base B_1^*.

2. Let V be a vector space of dimension n, and let B^* be a base in the dual space V^*. Prove that B^* is the dual of some base in V.

3. Let V be an n-dimensional vector space, and let V^* be its dual. Let W^* be an r-dimensional subspace of V^*. Prove that all $\mathbf{x}$ in V such that $\langle \mathbf{f}, \mathbf{x} \rangle = 0$ for every $\mathbf{f}$ in W^* form an $(n - r)$-dimensional subspace U of V. Conversely, given such a U, show that all $\mathbf{f}$ in V^* such that $\langle \mathbf{f}, \mathbf{x} \rangle = 0$ for every $\mathbf{x}$ in U form an r-dimensional subspace W^* of V^*. (U is called the *orthogonal complement* of W^*, and vice versa.)

4. V being a vector space of dimension n, let $\mathbf{f}_1, \ldots, \mathbf{f}_k$ be k linear functions on V. Let V^1 consist of all $\mathbf{x}$ in V such that $\langle \mathbf{f}_j, \mathbf{x} \rangle = 0$ for $j = 1, \ldots, k$. Show that V^1 is a subspace of V of dimension $\geq n - k$, equality holding if and only if $\mathbf{f}_1, \ldots, \mathbf{f}_k$ are linearly independent. Show that every subspace V^1 of V can be obtained in this way.

5. Let $B = \{\mathbf{e}_1, \mathbf{e}_2\}$ be a base for a vector space V, and put $B_1 = \{\mathbf{e}_1 - \mathbf{e}_2, 2\mathbf{e}_1 + \mathbf{e}_2\}$. Show that B_1 is a base in V provided that $1 + 1 + 1 \neq 0$ in the field of scalars, and determine the dual base B_1^* in terms of B^*.

6. Let $B = \{\mathbf{e}_1, \ldots, \mathbf{e}_n\}$ be a base for a vector space V, and let $B^* = \{\mathbf{e}^1, \ldots, \mathbf{e}^n\}$ be its dual base. Set $\mathbf{g} = \mathbf{e}^1 + c_2\mathbf{e}^2 + \cdots + c_n\mathbf{e}^n$. Show that $\{\mathbf{g}, \mathbf{e}^2, \ldots, \mathbf{e}^n\}$ is a base for V^*, for any scalars c_i. Find the base in V of which it is the dual.

7. $\mathbf{Q}$ being the rational field, let $\mathbf{T}\colon\ \mathbf{Q}^3 \to \mathbf{Q}^3$ be the linear mapping that sends a column vector $\mathbf{x}$ into $\mathbf{ax}$, where

$$\mathbf{a} = \begin{pmatrix} 2 & -1 & 0 \\ -3 & 4 & 2 \\ 1 & 1 & 5 \end{pmatrix}$$

Where does the transpose $\mathbf{T}^*$ of $\mathbf{T}$ map the vectors $(4, 0, 3)$ and $(1, 1, 1)$?

8. Let U, V be finite-dimensional vector spaces over a field K, and let $\mathbf{S}\colon V^* \to U^*$ be a linear mapping of their duals. Prove the following:

(*a*) There is a unique linear mapping $\mathbf{T}\colon U \to V$ such that $\mathbf{S} = \mathbf{T}^*$.

(*b*) $\mathbf{T}$ is a monomorphism if and only if $\mathbf{S}$ is an epimorphism.

(*c*) $\mathbf{T}$ is an epimorphism if and only if $\mathbf{S}$ is a monomorphism.

(*d*) rank $\mathbf{T}$ = rank $\mathbf{S}$.

9. Show that $\mathbf{e}_i$ spans the orthogonal complement of the subspace of V^* spanned by $\mathbf{e}^1, \ldots, \mathbf{e}^{i-1}, \mathbf{e}^{i+1}, \ldots, \mathbf{e}^n$.

10. If $\mathbf{x}$ is a vector in V such that $\langle \mathbf{f}, \mathbf{x} \rangle = 0$ for all $\mathbf{f}$ in V^*, prove that $\mathbf{x} = \mathbf{0}$ if $\dim V \neq \infty$.

11. Let $B = \{\mathbf{e}_1, \mathbf{e}_2, \mathbf{e}_3\}$ be a base for a vector space V over $\mathbf{Q}$, and let $B^* = \{\mathbf{e}^1, \mathbf{e}^2, \mathbf{e}^3\}$ be the dual base. Set $\mathbf{v}^1 = \mathbf{e}^1 + 2\mathbf{e}^2 + \mathbf{e}^3$, $\mathbf{v}^2 = -\mathbf{e}^2 + 3\mathbf{e}^3$, $\mathbf{v}^3 = \mathbf{e}^1 + 2\mathbf{e}^2$. Find the base in V of which $\{\mathbf{v}^1, \mathbf{v}^2, \mathbf{v}^3\}$ is the dual.

3. Bilinear functions

Again let V denote a vector space over a field K. By a *bilinear function* (or *form*) $\mathbf{f}$ on V is meant a mapping which assigns to every ordered pair of vectors $\mathbf{x}$, $\mathbf{y}$ in V an element $\mathbf{f}(\mathbf{x}, \mathbf{y})$ in K and which is linear in both $\mathbf{x}$, $\mathbf{y}$. In other words, denoting by $V \times V$ the set of all ordered pairs of vectors $\mathbf{x}$, $\mathbf{y}$ in V, $\mathbf{f}$ is a mapping $V \times V \to K$ satisfying the following conditions:

3.1
$$\begin{aligned} \mathbf{f}(\mathbf{x}, \mathbf{y} + \mathbf{z}) &= \mathbf{f}(\mathbf{x}, \mathbf{y}) + \mathbf{f}(\mathbf{x}, \mathbf{z}) \\ \mathbf{f}(\mathbf{x} + \mathbf{z}, \mathbf{y}) &= \mathbf{f}(\mathbf{x}, \mathbf{y}) + \mathbf{f}(\mathbf{z}, \mathbf{y}) \\ \mathbf{f}(a\mathbf{x}, \mathbf{y}) &= \mathbf{f}(\mathbf{x}, a\mathbf{y}) = a \cdot \mathbf{f}(\mathbf{x}, \mathbf{y}) \end{aligned}$$

for any $\mathbf{x}$, $\mathbf{y}$, $\mathbf{z}$ in V and any a in K.

Such a function is called *symmetric* if $\mathbf{f}(\mathbf{x}, \mathbf{y}) = \mathbf{f}(\mathbf{y}, \mathbf{x})$ for any $\mathbf{x}$, $\mathbf{y}$; $\mathbf{f}$ is *skew-symmetric* if $\mathbf{f}(\mathbf{x}, \mathbf{y}) = -\mathbf{f}(\mathbf{y}, \mathbf{x})$ for any $\mathbf{x}$, $\mathbf{y}$.

EXAMPLE 1 Let $\mathbf{f}$ be any bilinear function on V. Define $\mathbf{g}$ and $\mathbf{h}$ by $\mathbf{g}(\mathbf{x}, \mathbf{y}) = \mathbf{f}(\mathbf{x}, \mathbf{y}) + \mathbf{f}(\mathbf{y}, \mathbf{x})$ and $\mathbf{h}(\mathbf{x}, \mathbf{y}) = \mathbf{f}(\mathbf{x}, \mathbf{y}) - \mathbf{f}(\mathbf{y}, \mathbf{x})$. Then $\mathbf{g}$ is a symmetric bilinear function on V, and $\mathbf{h}$ is a skew-symmetric bilinear function.

EXAMPLE 2 Define $\mathbf{f}$ on K^n as follows: if $\mathbf{x}$ and $\mathbf{y}$ are any two vectors in K^n, put

$$\mathbf{f}(\mathbf{x}, \mathbf{y}) = x^1y^1 + \cdots + x^ny^n = \sum_{i=1}^{n} x^iy^i$$

It is quickly seen that this $\mathbf{f}$ is a bilinear function on K_n. For $\mathbf{R}^n$ we have already encountered it in (11.4), Chap. 8.

The following definition shows how to construct bilinear functions from linear functions:

DEFINITION 3.1 *Let* $\mathbf{f}_1$ *and* $\mathbf{f}_2$ *be two linear functions on a vector space* V. *Then* $\mathbf{f}_1 \otimes \mathbf{f}_2$ *will denote the bilinear function defined by*

3.2
$$(\mathbf{f}_1 \otimes \mathbf{f}_2)(\mathbf{x}, \mathbf{y}) = \mathbf{f}_1(\mathbf{x}) \cdot \mathbf{f}_2(\mathbf{y}) = \langle \mathbf{f}_1, \mathbf{x} \rangle \cdot \langle \mathbf{f}_2, \mathbf{y} \rangle$$

On the right is indicated a product of two scalars. It is trivial to verify that $\mathbf{f}_1 \otimes \mathbf{f}_2$ is a bilinear function.

We denote the set of all bilinear functions on V by V_2^*. Just as with V^* of Sec. 2, we can make V_2^* into a vector space over the field of scalars K by the following definitions of sum $\mathbf{f} + \mathbf{g}$ and scalar product $a\mathbf{f}$:

3.3
$$\begin{aligned} (\mathbf{f} + \mathbf{g})(\mathbf{x}, \mathbf{y}) &= \mathbf{f}(\mathbf{x}, \mathbf{y}) + \mathbf{g}(\mathbf{x}, \mathbf{y}) \\ (a\mathbf{f})(\mathbf{x}, \mathbf{y}) &= a \cdot \mathbf{f}(\mathbf{x}, \mathbf{y}) \end{aligned}$$

for any bilinear functions **f**, **g**, for any **x**, **y** in V, and any a in K. It is quickly verified that $\mathbf{f} + \mathbf{g}$ and $a\mathbf{f}$ defined in this manner are bilinear functions and that V_2^* thereby becomes a vector space over K.

In particular, if $\mathbf{f}_1, \ldots, \mathbf{f}_r, \mathbf{g}_1, \ldots, \mathbf{g}_r$ are *linear* functions on V, we can form sums of the type

$$a_1(\mathbf{f}_1 \otimes \mathbf{g}_1) + a_2(\mathbf{f}_2 \otimes \mathbf{g}_2) + \cdots + a_r(\mathbf{f}_r \otimes \mathbf{g}_r)$$

to obtain bilinear functions on V. We shall soon see that, if $\dim V < \infty$, then any bilinear function can be expressed in this way.

Now let V be a vector space of dimension n over K, and let $B = \{\mathbf{e}_1, \ldots, \mathbf{e}_n\}$ be a base for V. For any bilinear function **f** on V, consider the scalars

3.4 $$a_{ij} = \mathbf{f}(\mathbf{e}_i, \mathbf{e}_j) \qquad (i, j = 1, \ldots, n)$$

The a_{ij} form an $n \times n$ matrix $\mathbf{a} = (a_{ij})$ in which the first index is understood to be the row index.

DEFINITION 3.2 *The $n \times n$ matrix* **a** *of* (3.4) *is called the matrix of* **f** *relative to the base B.*

If $\mathbf{x} = x^i\mathbf{e}_i$ and $\mathbf{y} = y^j\mathbf{e}_j$ are any two elements of V, then using (3.1) repeatedly we get

3.5 $$\mathbf{f}(\mathbf{x}, \mathbf{y}) = \mathbf{f}(x^i\mathbf{e}_i, y^j\mathbf{e}_j) = x^iy^j\mathbf{f}(\mathbf{e}_i, \mathbf{e}_j) = a_{ij}x^iy^j$$

Conversely it is clear that if **a** is any $n \times n$ matrix with coefficients in K, then formula (3.5) defines a bilinear function **f** on V. From the definition of matrix multiplication we can write (3.5) in the form

3.5′ $$\mathbf{f}(\mathbf{x}, \mathbf{y}) = {}^t\hat{\mathbf{x}}\mathbf{a}\hat{\mathbf{y}}$$

where $\hat{\mathbf{x}}$ denotes the column vector made up of $x^1, \ldots, x^n$, and similarly for $\hat{\mathbf{y}}$.

EXAMPLE 3 Let $B = \{\mathbf{e}_1, \ldots, \mathbf{e}_n\}$ be the canonical base in K^n. That is, $\mathbf{e}_i$ is the ith column of the unit matrix. Referring to Example 2, the matrix of the bilinear form $x^1y^1 + \cdots + x^ny^n$ relative to B is the unit matrix $\mathbf{I}_n$.

It follows at once from (3.4) and (3.5) that **f** is symmetric if and only if its matrix **a** is symmetric, that is, $a_{ij} = a_{ji}$, or ${}^t\mathbf{a} = \mathbf{a}$; **f** is skew-symmetric if and only if its matrix **a** is skew-symmetric, that is, $a_{ij} = -a_{ji}$, or ${}^t\mathbf{a} = -\mathbf{a}$.

Equation (3.5) can be put in slightly different form as follows:

PROPOSITION 3.1 *Let* **a** *be the matrix of a bilinear function* **f** *relative to a base $B = \{\mathbf{e}_1, \ldots, \mathbf{e}_n\}$ of the vector space V. Let $B^* = \{\mathbf{e}^1, \ldots, \mathbf{e}^n\}$ be the dual base in V^*. Then*

3.6 $$\mathbf{f} = a_{ij}\mathbf{e}^i \otimes \mathbf{e}^j$$

Conversely, if (3.6) *holds, then $\mathbf{a} = (a_{ij})$ is the matrix of* **f** *relative to B.*

Proof. From (3.2) and (3.3) we have

$$(a_{ij}\mathbf{e}^i \otimes \mathbf{e}^j)(\mathbf{x}, \mathbf{y}) = a_{ij} \langle \mathbf{e}^i, \mathbf{x}\rangle \cdot \langle \mathbf{e}^j, \mathbf{y}\rangle = a_{ij}x^iy^j$$

the latter by (2.9). The assertion follows from (3.5). Q.E.D.

Let us now see how the matrix of a bilinear function $\mathbf{f}$ changes with a change of base. Let $B' = \{\mathbf{e}'_1, \ldots, \mathbf{e}'_n\}$ be another base in V, and let $\mathbf{a}'$ be the corresponding matrix of $\mathbf{f}$. That is, $a'_{ij} = \mathbf{f}(\mathbf{e}'_i, \mathbf{e}'_j)$. Let $\mathbf{p} = (p^h{}_i)$ be the matrix from B to B'. That is,

3.7 $$\mathbf{e}'_i = p^h{}_i\mathbf{e}_h$$

Then

$$\mathbf{f}(\mathbf{e}'_i, \mathbf{e}'_j) = \mathbf{f}(p^h{}_i\mathbf{e}_h, p^k{}_j\mathbf{e}_k) = p^h{}_ip^k{}_j\mathbf{f}(\mathbf{e}_h, \mathbf{e}_k)$$

using (3.5), and so

3.8 $$a'_{ij} = p^h{}_ia_{hk}p^k{}_j$$

As a matrix product this is

3.9 $$\mathbf{a}' = {}^t\mathbf{pap}$$

(Recall that h is the *row* index in $p^h{}_i$, and in a_{hk}, which accounts for the transpose in the first factor.) Observe that (3.9) is not the same as the rule for the change of the matrix of a linear mapping $V \to V$.

Since both $\mathbf{p}$ and ${}^t\mathbf{p}$ must be nonsingular, it follows from Sec. 8, Chap. 9, that $\mathbf{a}$ and $\mathbf{a}'$ have the same rank. Therefore we can define the rank of $\mathbf{f}$ as follows:

DEFINITION 3.3 *Let* $\mathbf{f}$ *be a bilinear function on an n-dimensional vector space V. Then the rank of* $\mathbf{f}$ *is defined to be the same as the rank of the matrix of* $\mathbf{f}$ *relative to any base in V.*

Another interpretation of the rank of $\mathbf{f}$ can be given as follows: Let $\mathbf{f}(\mathbf{x},\ \ )$ denote the operation that sends any $\mathbf{y}$ in V into the scalar $\mathbf{f}(\mathbf{x}, \mathbf{y})$. Then $\mathbf{f}(\mathbf{x},\ \ )$ is a linear mapping $V \to K$, by (3.1), hence is an element of V^*. We have therefore a mapping $\mathbf{T}_1\colon V \to V^*$ sending $\mathbf{x}$ into $\mathbf{f}(\mathbf{x},\ \ )$, easily seen to be linear. Let us compute its matrix relative to the base pair B, B^*. By definition, $\mathbf{T}_1(\mathbf{e}_i) = \mathbf{f}(\mathbf{e}_i,\ \ )$, and this sends $\mathbf{e}_j$ into $\mathbf{f}(\mathbf{e}_i, \mathbf{e}_j) = a_{ij}$. Therefore, by (2.9),

3.10 $$\mathbf{T}_1(\mathbf{e}_i) = \mathbf{f}(\mathbf{e}_i,\ \ ) = a_{ij}\mathbf{e}^j$$

From Definition 5.1, Chap. 9, the matrix of $\mathbf{T}_1$ relative to the base pair B, B^* is precisely ${}^t\mathbf{a}$.

In a similar way we obtain a second mapping $\mathbf{T}_2\colon V \to V^*$, sending $\mathbf{x}$ into $\mathbf{f}(\ \ , \mathbf{x})$, where this symbol denotes the operation that maps any $\mathbf{y}$ in V into $\mathbf{f}(\mathbf{y}, \mathbf{x})$. Then

3.11 $$\mathbf{T}_2(\mathbf{e}_i) = \mathbf{f}(\ \ , \mathbf{e}_i) = a_{ji}\mathbf{e}^j$$

The matrix of $\mathbf{T}_2$ relative to B, B^* is $\mathbf{a}$. The rank of $\mathbf{f}$ is therefore none other than the rank of $\mathbf{T}_1$ or $\mathbf{T}_2$, by Theorem 8.2, Chap. 9. Observe that $\mathbf{T}_1 = \mathbf{T}_2$ if $\mathbf{f}$ is symmetric.

REMARK. In Secs. 2 and 3 we have defined linear functions $\mathbf{f}(\mathbf{x})$ and bilinear functions $\mathbf{f}(\mathbf{x}, \mathbf{y})$ on a vector space. There is no reason for stopping at 2; in a similar way we can define 3-linear functions $\mathbf{f}(\mathbf{x}, \mathbf{y}, \mathbf{z})$ of ordered triples of vectors in V, and so on. This is indeed the subject of Chap. 16. Bilinear functions are examples of *tensors* on V. They are sometimes called *dyadic* tensors.

EXERCISES

1. Let V be a vector space of dimension n, and let $\mathbf{f}^1, \ldots, \mathbf{f}^n$ be a base for its dual space V^*. Prove that the elements $\mathbf{f}^i \otimes \mathbf{f}^j (i, j = 1, \ldots, n)$ form a base of the space of bilinear functions V_2^*. Prove that $\dim V_2^* = n^2$.

2. Let $\mathbf{f}$ be a bilinear function on a vector space V over a field K, and suppose that $1 + 1 \neq 0$ in K. Prove that $\mathbf{f}$ can be written uniquely as a sum $\mathbf{f}' + \mathbf{f}''$, where $\mathbf{f}'$ is a symmetric bilinear function and where $\mathbf{f}''$ is a skew-symmetric bilinear function.

3. Let V be a vector space of dimension n. Let V_2^* be the space of bilinear functions on V. Show that the symmetric elements of V_2^* form a subspace U_1, and show that the skew-symmetric elements form a subspace U_2. Compute $\dim U_1$ and $\dim U_2$. If $1 + 1 \neq 0$ in the field of scalars, prove that V_2^* is the direct sum of U_1 and U_2.

4. Let $B = \{\mathbf{e}_1, \mathbf{e}_2\}$ be a base for a vector space V over the real field $\mathbf{R}$. Let $\mathbf{f}$ be the bilinear function on V whose matrix with respect to B is

$$\begin{pmatrix} 1 & 2 \\ 2 & -1 \end{pmatrix}$$

Find a new base in V with respect to which the matrix of $\mathbf{f}$ is the unit matrix. Compute $\mathbf{f}(\mathbf{x}, \mathbf{x})$, $f(\mathbf{y}, \mathbf{y})$, and $f(\mathbf{x}, \mathbf{y})$, where $\mathbf{x} = 3\mathbf{e}_1 + \mathbf{e}_2$ and $\mathbf{y} = \mathbf{e}_1 - 2\mathbf{e}_2$.

5. Let $\mathbf{g}^1, \ldots, \mathbf{g}^r$ be linear functions on an n-dimensional vector space V. Set

$$\mathbf{f} = c_1 \mathbf{g}^1 \otimes \mathbf{g}^1 + \cdots + c_r \mathbf{g}^r \otimes \mathbf{g}^r$$

Prove that the rank of $\mathbf{f}$ is $\leq r$, and give a reasonable condition for equality to hold.

6. Referring to Definition 3.1, under what circumstances is $\mathbf{f}_1 \otimes \mathbf{f}_2 = \mathbf{f}_2 \otimes \mathbf{f}_1$?

7. Let $\mathbf{f}$ be a bilinear function of rank n on a vector space V of dimension n ($\mathbf{f}$ is then called nondegenerate). Let U be an r-dimensional subspace of V. Let W consist of all $\mathbf{x}$ in V such that $\mathbf{f}(\mathbf{x}, \mathbf{u}) = 0$ for every $\mathbf{u}$ in U. Show that W is a subspace of dimension $n - r$.

4. *Quadratic forms*

Let V denote a vector space of dimension n over a field K. If $\mathbf{f}$ is a bilinear function on V, then we get a mapping $Q: V \to K$ defined by $Q(\mathbf{x}) = \mathbf{f}(\mathbf{x}, \mathbf{x})$. Such mappings are of considerable importance and are the subject of this section.

DEFINITION 4.1 *A mapping $Q: V \to K$ is called a* quadratic form *on V if there is a symmetric bilinear function $\mathbf{f}$ on V such that $Q(\mathbf{x}) = \mathbf{f}(\mathbf{x}, \mathbf{x})$. We call Q the quadratic form associated with $\mathbf{f}$.*

Let us work out some simple properties of such a Q. First of all, $Q(a\mathbf{x}) = f(a\mathbf{x}, a\mathbf{x}) = a^2\mathbf{f}(\mathbf{x}, \mathbf{x})$, by (3.1). Hence

4.1 $$Q(a\mathbf{x}) = a^2Q(\mathbf{x})$$

In particular,

4.2 $$Q(-\mathbf{x}) = Q(\mathbf{x})$$

Further, using (3.1) again,

$$\begin{aligned} Q(\mathbf{x} + \mathbf{y}) = \mathbf{f}(\mathbf{x} + \mathbf{y}, \mathbf{x} + \mathbf{y}) &= \mathbf{f}(\mathbf{x}, \mathbf{x} + \mathbf{y}) + \mathbf{f}(\mathbf{y}, \mathbf{x} + \mathbf{y}) \\ &= \mathbf{f}(\mathbf{x}, \mathbf{x}) + \mathbf{f}(\mathbf{x}, \mathbf{y}) + \mathbf{f}(\mathbf{y}, \mathbf{x}) + \mathbf{f}(\mathbf{y}, \mathbf{y}) \end{aligned}$$

Since $\mathbf{f}$ is assumed to be symmetric, there results

4.3 $$Q(\mathbf{x} + \mathbf{y}) = Q(\mathbf{x}) + 2 \cdot \mathbf{f}(\mathbf{x}, \mathbf{y}) + Q(\mathbf{y})$$

where 2 denotes the element $1 + 1$ of K. This equation shows that if $1 + 1 \neq 0$ (that is, if K is not of characteristic 2), then $\mathbf{f}$ is completely determined by Q. Sometimes $\mathbf{f}$ is called the *polar form* of Q.

Replacing $\mathbf{y}$ by $-\mathbf{y}$ above, we obtain

$$Q(\mathbf{x} - \mathbf{y}) = Q(\mathbf{x}) - 2\mathbf{f}(\mathbf{x}, \mathbf{y}) + Q(\mathbf{y})$$

Therefore

4.4 $$Q(\mathbf{x} + \mathbf{y}) - Q(\mathbf{x} - \mathbf{y}) = 4\mathbf{f}(\mathbf{x}, \mathbf{y})$$

PROPOSITION 4.1 *If Q is a quadratic form on a vector space V, then the function $\mathbf{h}$ defined by*

4.5 $$\mathbf{h}(\mathbf{x}, \mathbf{y}) = Q(\mathbf{x} + \mathbf{y}) - Q(\mathbf{x} - \mathbf{y})$$

is a symmetric bilinear function on V. Conversely, if Q is a mapping $V \to K$ for which (4.5) holds, if $Q(\mathbf{0}) = 0$, and if $1 + 1 \neq 0$ in K, then Q is a quadratic form on V. It is associated with a uniquely determined symmetric bilinear function on V, namely, $\frac{1}{4}\mathbf{h}$.

Proof. The first assertion follows from (4.4). For the converse, if $1 + 1 \neq 0$ in K, then $(1 + 1)^2 \neq 0$. This element is denoted above by 4. We have

$$\tfrac{1}{4}\mathbf{h}(x, x) = \mathbf{h}(\tfrac{1}{2}\mathbf{x}, \tfrac{1}{2}\mathbf{x}) = Q(\tfrac{1}{2}\mathbf{x} + \tfrac{1}{2}\mathbf{x}) - Q(\mathbf{0})$$

by (4.1) and (4.5). Since $Q(\mathbf{0}) = 0$, by assumption, we get $\frac{1}{4}\mathbf{h}(\mathbf{x}, \mathbf{x}) = Q(\mathbf{x})$. Q cannot be associated with any other symmetric bilinear function, by (4.4). Q.E.D.

EXAMPLE 1 Consider the vector space K^n of $n \times 1$ matrices (column vectors). Let $\mathbf{a} = (a_{ij})$ be any symmetric $n \times n$ matrix with coefficients in K. Define Q by

$$Q(\mathbf{x}) = a_{ij}x^ix^j$$

where $\mathbf{x}$ is the column vector with entries $x^1, \ldots, x^n$. Then

$$\begin{aligned} Q(\mathbf{x} + \mathbf{y}) - Q(\mathbf{x} - \mathbf{y}) &= a_{ij}(x^i + y^i)(x^j + y^j) - a_{ij}(x^i - y^i)(x^j - y^j) \\ &= 2a_{ij}x^iy^j + 2a_{ij}y^ix^j \\ &= 4a_{ij}x^iy^j \end{aligned}$$

since $a_{ij} = a_{ji}$. Q is the quadratic form associated with the bilinear function $\mathbf{f}$ defined by

$$\mathbf{f}(\mathbf{x}, \mathbf{y}) = a_{ij}x^iy^j$$

From the definition of matrix multiplication, we have

$$\mathbf{f}(\mathbf{x}, \mathbf{y}) = {}^t\mathbf{x}\mathbf{a}\mathbf{y} = {}^t\mathbf{y}\mathbf{a}\mathbf{x}$$

and

$$Q(\mathbf{x}) = {}^t\mathbf{x}\mathbf{a}\mathbf{x}$$

In particular, if $\mathbf{a}$ is the unit matrix, then this reduces to

$$\mathbf{f}(\mathbf{x}, \mathbf{y}) = {}^t\mathbf{x}\mathbf{y} = {}^t\mathbf{y}\mathbf{x} = \sum_{i=1}^{n} x^iy^i$$

and

$$Q(\mathbf{x}) = {}^t\mathbf{x}\mathbf{x} = \sum_{i=1}^{n} (x^i)^2$$

We have already encountered these in Sec. 11, Chap. 8.

EXAMPLE 2 Consider the mapping Q of $\mathbf{R}^2$ to $\mathbf{R}$ defined by

$$Q(\mathbf{v}) = 4x^2 + 6xy + 9y^2 \qquad \text{where } \mathbf{v} = \begin{pmatrix} x \\ y \end{pmatrix}$$

This is the special case of the foregoing corresponding to the matrix

$$a = \begin{pmatrix} 4 & 3 \\ 3 & 9 \end{pmatrix}$$

The bilinear function associated with Q is given by

$$\mathbf{f}(\mathbf{v}, \mathbf{v}') = 4xx' + 3(xy' + x'y) + 9yy'$$

where

$$\mathbf{v}' = \begin{pmatrix} x' \\ y' \end{pmatrix}$$

If we define addition and scalar multiplication of quadratic forms on V by

4.6
$$(Q + Q')(\mathbf{x}) = Q(\mathbf{x}) + Q'(\mathbf{x})$$
$$(aQ)(\mathbf{x}) = a \cdot Q(\mathbf{x})$$

then it follows easily from Definition 4.1 that $Q + Q'$ and aQ are again quadratic forms on V. In this way we make the set of all quadratic forms on V into a vector space over K.

The following definition shows how quadratic forms can be built from linear functions on V.

DEFINITION 4.2 *Let $\mathbf{f}_1$ and $\mathbf{f}_2$ be two linear functions on a vector space V over K. Then by $\mathbf{f}_1\mathbf{f}_2$ we denote the mapping $V \to K$ defined by*

4.7 $$(\mathbf{f}_1\mathbf{f}_2)(\mathbf{x}) = \mathbf{f}_1(\mathbf{x}) \cdot \mathbf{f}_2(\mathbf{x}) = \langle \mathbf{f}_1, \mathbf{x}\rangle\langle \mathbf{f}_2, \mathbf{x}\rangle$$

If $1 + 1 \neq 0$ in K, then $\mathbf{f}_1\mathbf{f}_2$ is a quadratic form on V. If $\mathbf{f}_1 = \mathbf{f}_2$, then that is so for any K.

In fact, $\mathbf{f}_1\mathbf{f}_2$ is none other than the quadratic form associated with the symmetric bilinear function $\frac{1}{2}(\mathbf{f}_1 \otimes \mathbf{f}_2 + \mathbf{f}_2 \otimes \mathbf{f}_1)$, assuming that $2 \neq 0$ (see Definition 3.1); $\mathbf{f}_1\mathbf{f}_1$ is the quadratic form associated with $\mathbf{f}_1 \otimes \mathbf{f}_1$.

Observe that $\mathbf{f}_1\mathbf{f}_2 = \mathbf{f}_2\mathbf{f}_1$, as follows at once from (4.7). For $\mathbf{f}_1\mathbf{f}_1$ we naturally write $\mathbf{f}_1^2$, etc. Using the definitions of (4.6), we can build arbitrary linear combinations of such quadratic forms $\mathbf{f}_1\mathbf{f}_2$ (assuming that $1 + 1 \neq 0$ in K) to obtain other quadratic forms on V.

Corresponding to Proposition 3.1 we have the simple result below. We recall that the matrix of a symmetric bilinear function on a vector space (of finite dimension), relative to any base, is symmetric.

PROPOSITION 4.2 *Let $\mathbf{f}$ be a symmetric bilinear function on a vector space V, and let $\mathbf{a}$ be its matrix relative to a base $B = \{\mathbf{e}_1, \ldots, \mathbf{e}_n\}$ in V.* If $B^* = \{\mathbf{e}^1, \ldots, \mathbf{e}^n\}$ *denotes the dual base in the space of linear functions on V, then for the quadratic form Q associated with $\mathbf{f}$ we have*

4.8 $$Q = a_{ij}\mathbf{e}^i\mathbf{e}^j$$

Conversely, given any symmetric $n \times n$ matrix $\mathbf{a}$ with coefficients in the field of scalars K, then (4.8) *defines a quadratic form on V. If $1 + 1 \neq 0$ in K, then $\mathbf{a}$ is uniquely determined by Q and is also called the matrix of Q relative to B.*

Proof. Equation (4.8) follows at once from (3.6) and Definition 4.2 above. For the converse, given a matrix $\mathbf{a}$ of the type stated, (3.6) defines a symmetric bilinear function $\mathbf{f}$ having Q as its associated quadratic form. Now no other matrix $\mathbf{a}'$ can give the same $\mathbf{f}$, by Proposition 3.1, and no other $\mathbf{f}$ can give the same Q, if $1 + 1 \neq 0$ in K, by Proposition 4.1. Therefore no two different matrices can give the same Q, if $1 + 1 \neq 0$. Q.E.D.

Equation (4.8) can be expressed in different ways. If $\mathbf{x}$ is any vector in V, and if its components with respect to B are $x^1, \ldots, x^n$, then $\langle \mathbf{e}^i, \mathbf{x} \rangle = x^i$, by (2.9). According to (4.6), (4.7), and (4.8) we have then

$$Q(x) = a_{ij} \langle \mathbf{e}^i, \mathbf{x} \rangle \cdot \langle \mathbf{e}^j, \mathbf{x} \rangle$$

or

4.9 $$Q(x) = a_{ij} x^i x^j$$

which is of course just (3.5) with $\mathbf{x} = \mathbf{y}$. Denoting by $\hat{\mathbf{x}}$ the column vector whose elements are $x^1, \ldots, x^n$, we have the matrix form of (4.9),

4.10 $$Q(\mathbf{x}) = {}^t\hat{\mathbf{x}}\mathbf{a}\hat{\mathbf{x}}$$

a special case of (3.5′).

REMARK 1. If $1 + 1 = 0$ in K, then (4.8) reduces to

4.11 $$Q = \sum_{i=1}^{n} a_{ii} (\mathbf{e}^i)^2$$

For the mixed terms appear in pairs. For example,

$$a_{12}\mathbf{e}^1\mathbf{e}^2 + a_{21}\mathbf{e}^2\mathbf{e}^1 = (1 + 1)a_{12}\mathbf{e}^1\mathbf{e}^2 = \mathbf{0}$$

since $a_{12} = a_{21}$ and $\mathbf{e}^1\mathbf{e}^2 = \mathbf{e}^2\mathbf{e}^1$. Hence, all the mixed terms in (4.8) add up to zero. It follows that the uniqueness assertion of Proposition 4.2 is false in this case.

EXAMPLE 3 If $1 + 1 = 0$ in K, then we have

$$(x, y)\begin{pmatrix} 1 & 1 \\ 1 & 1 \end{pmatrix}\begin{pmatrix} x \\ y \end{pmatrix} = x^2 + (1 + 1)xy + y^2 = x^2 + y^2$$

and

$$(x, y)\begin{pmatrix} 1 & 0 \\ 0 & 1 \end{pmatrix}\begin{pmatrix} x \\ y \end{pmatrix} = x^2 + y^2$$

for any vector $\begin{pmatrix} x \\ y \end{pmatrix}$ in K^2. Thus the quadratic form $x^2 + y^2$ is given by two different matrices.

REMARK 2. Let $\mathbf{f}$ be any bilinear function on V, and assume that $1 + 1 \neq 0$ in K. By Example 1, Sec. 3, we can write $\mathbf{f} = \mathbf{g} + \mathbf{h}$, where $\mathbf{g}$ is symmetric and $\mathbf{h}$ is skew-symmetric. Then $\mathbf{f}(\mathbf{x}, \mathbf{x}) = \mathbf{g}(\mathbf{x}, \mathbf{x}) + \mathbf{h}(\mathbf{x}, \mathbf{x})$. But $\mathbf{h}(\mathbf{x}, \mathbf{y}) = -\mathbf{h}(\mathbf{y}, \mathbf{x})$, whence $\mathbf{h}(\mathbf{x}, \mathbf{x}) = -\mathbf{h}(\mathbf{x}, \mathbf{x})$, or $(1 + 1)\mathbf{h}(\mathbf{x}, \mathbf{x}) = 0$. Therefore $\mathbf{h}(\mathbf{x}, \mathbf{x}) = 0$. This shows why we deal only with symmetric bilinear functions in the context of quadratic forms.

EXERCISES

1. Let Q be the quadratic form on K^n defined by $Q(\mathbf{x}) = x_1^2 + \cdots + x_n^2$ for $\mathbf{x} = {}^t(x_1, \ldots, x_n)$. Find the matrix of Q relative to each of the following bases, assuming $1 + 1 \neq 0$ in K.

   (*a*) $\mathbf{e}_i = (0, \ldots, 1, \ldots, 0)$ (1 in the ith place)
   (*b*) $\mathbf{f}_i = (0, \ldots, 2, \ldots, 0)$ (2 in the ith place)
   (*c*) $\mathbf{g}_i = (0, \ldots, i, \ldots, 0)$ (i in the ith place)
   (*d*) $\mathbf{h}_1 = \mathbf{e}_1 + \mathbf{e}_2$, $\mathbf{h}_2 = \mathbf{e}_1 - \mathbf{e}_2$, $\mathbf{h}_i = \mathbf{e}_i$ for $i > 2$.
   (*e*) Taking $n = 2$, the base $\mathbf{e}_1' = 3\mathbf{e}_1 - \mathbf{e}_2$, $\mathbf{e}_2' = \mathbf{e}_1 + 4\mathbf{e}_2$.

   Verify (3.9) for case (*e*).

2. Let $\mathbf{R}$ denote the real field and define

$$Q: \mathbf{R}^2 \to \mathbf{R} \qquad \text{by } Q(\mathbf{v}) = ax^2 + 2bxy + cy^2$$

where $\mathbf{v} = \begin{pmatrix} x \\ y \end{pmatrix}$, and where a, b, c are given real numbers. Find the matrix of Q relative to the canonical base B of $\mathbf{R}^2$.

3. With Q as in Exercise 2, suppose there are vectors $\mathbf{v}$, $\mathbf{w}$ in $\mathbf{R}^2$ such that $Q(\mathbf{v}) > 0$ and $Q(\mathbf{w}) < 0$. Prove that there is a nonzero vector $\mathbf{u}$ in $\mathbf{R}^2$ such that $Q(\mathbf{u}) = 0$. Prove that there is a base $B' = \{\mathbf{e}_1', \mathbf{e}_2'\}$ such that $Q(\mathbf{v}) = x'^2 - y'^2$ if $\mathbf{v} = x'\mathbf{e}_1' + y'\mathbf{e}_2'$.

4. With Q as in Exercise 2, find necessary and sufficient conditions on a, b, c such that $Q(\mathbf{v}) > 0$ whenever $\mathbf{v} \neq 0$.

5. Let Q be a nonzero quadratic form on a vector space over the complex field. Prove that there exist vectors $\mathbf{x}$, $\mathbf{y}$ in the space such that $Q(\mathbf{x})$ is a negative real number and $Q(\mathbf{y})$ is a pure imaginary number $\neq 0$.

6. Let Q be a quadratic form on a vector space V, and let $\mathbf{T}: V \to V$ be a linear mapping. Define Q' by $Q'(\mathbf{x}) = Q(\mathbf{T}(\mathbf{x}))$. Show that Q' is a quadratic form on V, and if $\dim V \neq \infty$ show how to compute the matrix of Q' from those of Q and $\mathbf{T}$.

5. *Reduction to diagonal form*

Let V be an n-dimensional vector space over a field K, and let $\mathbf{f}$ be a symmetric bilinear function on V, with associated quadratic form Q. That is, $Q(\mathbf{x}) = \mathbf{f}(\mathbf{x}, \mathbf{x})$. In general the matrix of $\mathbf{f}$ (or Q) relative to a base B in V will contain nonzero terms off the diagonal, giving rise to mixed terms in (3.6) or (4.8). In view of Remark 1 of the preceding section the mixed terms can be omitted from (4.8) if $1 + 1 = 0$ in K.

Then, assuming $1 + 1 \neq 0$ in K, we propose to show that it is possible to find a base in B for which the matrix of $\mathbf{f}$ and Q is a diagonal matrix. The method that we use comes from the ancient Babylonian algebraists and amounts to "completing the square."

Start with any base $B = \{\mathbf{e}_1, \ldots, \mathbf{e}_n\}$ in V, and let $\mathbf{a}$ be the matrix of $\mathbf{f}$ and Q

relative to B. We naturally assume that $\mathbf{f} \neq 0$, so that $\mathbf{a}$ contains at least one nonzero element.

To achieve our goal we are going to make a series of base changes, and for our purposes it will be most convenient to do that in the dual space V^* of V. Our first step is to show that we can assume $a_{11} \neq 0$, after a possible preliminary base change.

Suppose first of all that all the diagonal elements a_{ii} of $\mathbf{a}$ are zero. That situation can be remedied as follows: Let a_{hk} be a nonzero element of $\mathbf{a}$ $(h \neq k)$, and define a new base $B' = \{\mathbf{e}'_1, \ldots, \mathbf{e}'_n\}$ in V by

5.1
$$\begin{aligned} \mathbf{e}'_i &= \mathbf{e}_i \qquad \text{for } i \neq k \\ \mathbf{e}'_k &= \mathbf{e}_k + \mathbf{e}_h \end{aligned}$$

We note that the dual bases $B^* = \{\mathbf{e}^1, \ldots, \mathbf{e}^n\}$ and $B'^* = \{\mathbf{e}'^1, \ldots, \mathbf{e}'^n\}$ are related by

5.2
$$\begin{aligned} \mathbf{e}'^i &= \mathbf{e}^i \qquad \text{for } i \neq h \\ \mathbf{e}'^h &= \mathbf{e}^h - \mathbf{e}^k \end{aligned}$$

for it is easily checked that (2.9) holds for B' and B'^*. For the matrix $\mathbf{a}'$ of $\mathbf{f}$ relative to B' we have

$$\begin{aligned} a'_{kk} &= \mathbf{f}(\mathbf{e}'_k, \mathbf{e}'_k) = \mathbf{f}(\mathbf{e}_k + \mathbf{e}_h, \mathbf{e}_k + \mathbf{e}_h) \\ &= \mathbf{f}(\mathbf{e}_k, \mathbf{e}_k) + 2\mathbf{f}(\mathbf{e}_k, \mathbf{e}_h) + \mathbf{f}(\mathbf{e}_h, \mathbf{e}_h) \\ &= a_{kk} + 2a_{kh} + a_{hh} = 2a_{kh} \neq 0 \end{aligned}$$

since we have assumed $a_{kk} = a_{hh} = 0$ and $a_{kh} \neq 0$.

We shall assume that this preliminary base change has been made, if necessary, so that $\mathbf{a}$ itself has a nonzero diagonal element a_{kk}. By interchanging $\mathbf{e}_1$ and $\mathbf{e}_k$ in the base B, we put that element in the 1, 1 location of the matrix. Therefore we shall assume that $a_{11} \neq 0$.

We begin with (4.8) and we shall make a series of base changes in the dual space V^* of V. Separating out all the terms in (4.8) containing $\mathbf{e}^1$ we obtain

$$\begin{aligned} Q &= \sum_{i,j=1}^{n} a_{ij}\mathbf{e}^i\mathbf{e}^j \\ &= a_{11}(\mathbf{e}^1)^2 + 2(a_{12}\mathbf{e}^1\mathbf{e}^2 + \cdots + a_{1n}\mathbf{e}^1\mathbf{e}^n) + \sum_{i,j=2}^{n} a_{ij}\mathbf{e}^i\mathbf{e}^j \end{aligned}$$

using the fact that $a_{12} = a_{21}$, etc. We can rewrite this as

$$Q = a_{11}(\mathbf{e}^1 + c_2\mathbf{e}^2 + \cdots + c_n\mathbf{e}^n)^2 - a_{11}(c_2\mathbf{e}^2 + \cdots + c_n\mathbf{e}^n)^2 + \sum_{i,j=2}^{n} a_{ij}\mathbf{e}^i\mathbf{e}^j$$

where

5.3
$$c_j = a_{1j}/a_{11} \qquad (j = 2, \ldots, n)$$

Put

5.4 $$a'_{ij} = a_{ij} - a_{11}c_ic_j \qquad (i, j = 2, \ldots, n)$$

and

5.5 $$\mathbf{v}^1 = \mathbf{e}^1 + c_2\mathbf{e}^2 + \cdots + c_n\mathbf{e}^n$$

Then it is quickly seen that

$$Q = a_{11}(\mathbf{v}^1)^2 + \sum_{i,j=2}^{n} a'_{ij}\mathbf{e}^i\mathbf{e}^j$$

Since the linear functions $\mathbf{e}^1, \ldots, \mathbf{e}^n$ on V form a base for V^*, it is clear that the set $\{\mathbf{v}^1, \mathbf{e}^2, \ldots, \mathbf{e}^n\}$ is also a base for V^*.

If not all the a_{ij} are zero, then we can repeat the same procedure for the quadratic form

$$Q' = \sum_{i,j=2}^{n} a'_{ij}\mathbf{e}^i\mathbf{e}^j$$

Thus, assuming that $a'_{22} \neq 0$ [otherwise a preliminary change of base as described above in connection with (5.1) and (5.2) is necessary] we can put Q' in the form

$$Q' = a'_{22}(\mathbf{v}^2)^2 + \sum_{i,j=3}^{n} a''_{ij}\, e^ie^j$$

where $\mathbf{v}^2$ is given by an expression of the type

5.6 $$\mathbf{v}^2 = \mathbf{e}^2 + c_3\mathbf{e}^3 + \cdots + c_n\mathbf{e}^n$$

analogous to (4.5) but involving only $\mathbf{e}^2, \ldots, \mathbf{e}^n$. The elements $\{\mathbf{v}^1, \mathbf{v}^2, \mathbf{e}^3, \ldots, \mathbf{e}^n\}$ form a base for V^*.

Continuing in this way, it is plain that after at most $n - 1$ steps we shall arrive at a new base $B_1^* = \{\mathbf{v}^1, \mathbf{v}^2, \ldots, \mathbf{v}^n\}$ for V^* for which Q has the form

5.7 $$Q = d_1(\mathbf{v}^1)^2 + d_2(\mathbf{v}^2)^2 + \cdots + d_n(\mathbf{v}^n)^2$$

Moreover it is clear from the steps above that if some d_k is zero, then so are d_{k+1}, d_{k+2}, etc.

THEOREM 5.1 *Let* **f** *be a symmetric bilinear form on an n-dimensional vector space V over a field K in which* $1 + 1 \neq 0$. *Let Q be the quadratic form associated with* **f**. *Then there exists a base* $B_1 = \{\mathbf{v}_1, \ldots, \mathbf{v}_n\}$ *for V with respect to which the matrix of* **f** *and Q is a diagonal matrix. If* **f** *has rank r, then* B_1 *can be so chosen that its first r diagonal elements* $d_1, d_2, \ldots, d_r$ *are nonzero, and then*

5.8 $$\mathbf{f} = d_1(\mathbf{v}^1 \otimes \mathbf{v}^1) + \cdots + d_r(\mathbf{v}^r \otimes \mathbf{v}^r)$$

and

5.9 $$Q = d_1(\mathbf{v}^1)^2 + \cdots + d_r(\mathbf{v}^r)^2$$

where

$B_1^* = \{\mathbf{v}^1, \ldots, \mathbf{v}^n\}$ *is the dual base of* B_1

Proof. Let $B_1^* = \{\mathbf{v}^1, \ldots, \mathbf{v}^n\}$ be the base for V^* appearing in (5.7). Now B_1^* is certainly the dual of a base $B_1 = \{\mathbf{v}_1, \ldots, \mathbf{v}_n\}$ in V (see Exercise 2, Sec. 2). Applying Theorem 3.1 to (5.7) above, we see that the matrix of $\mathbf{f}$ relative to B_1 must be the diagonal matrix with $d_1, d_2, \ldots, d_n$ as diagonal elements. From Definition 3.3 and the remark following (5.7) it is clear that $d_j = 0$ for $j > r$. Finally, (5.9) is just (5.7) with the zero terms omitted; (5.8) follows from (3.6). Q.E.D.

If $\mathbf{x}$, $\mathbf{y}$ in V have components $x^1, \ldots, x^n$ and $y^1, \ldots, y^n$, respectively, relative to the base B_1, then from (3.5) and (4.9), applied to B_1, we have

5.10 $$\mathbf{f}(\mathbf{x}, \mathbf{y}) = d_1x^1y^1 + \cdots + d_rx^ry^r$$

5.11 $$Q(\mathbf{x}) = d_1(x^1)^2 + \cdots + d_r(x^r)^2$$

Determination of a base in V having the properties stated is usually called *diagonalization* of the quadratic form Q, or reduction of Q to *diagonal form.*

COROLLARY 1 *If K is the real number field* $\mathbf{R}$, *then the base B_1 can be chosen so that $d_i = 1$ for $i = 1, \ldots, s$ and $d_i = -1$ for $i = s + 1, \ldots, r$, where $0 \leqslant s \leqslant r$.*† In particular, (5.9) becomes

5.12 $$Q = (\mathbf{v}^1)^2 + \cdots + (\mathbf{v}^s)^2 - (\mathbf{v}^{s+1})^2 - \cdots - (\mathbf{v}^r)^2$$

Proof. If $d_i > 0$ we simply replace the base vector $\mathbf{v}_i$ by $d_i^{-\frac{1}{2}}\mathbf{v}_i$ (and $\mathbf{v}^i$ by $d_i^{\frac{1}{2}}\mathbf{v}^i$). If $d_i < 0$, we replace $\mathbf{v}_i$ by $(-d_i)^{-\frac{1}{2}}\mathbf{v}_i$ and $\mathbf{v}^i$ by $(-d_i)^{\frac{1}{2}}\mathbf{v}^i$. By suitably renumbering these vectors if necessary, we achieve the desired form (5.12). Q.E.D.

COROLLARY 2 *If K is the complex field* $\mathbf{C}$, *then the base B_1 can be chosen so that $d_i = 1$ for $i = 1, \ldots, r$.*

Proof. There is a complex number h_i such that $h_i^2 = d_i$. (Theorem 3.3, Chap. 5). Replace $\mathbf{v}_i$ by $h_i^{-1}\mathbf{v}_i$ for $i = 1, \ldots, r$, and $\mathbf{v}^i$ by $h_i\mathbf{v}_i$. Q.E.D.

COROLLARY 3 *Let* $\mathbf{a}$ *be a symmetric $n \times n$ matrix with coefficients in a field K in which $1 + 1 \neq 0$. Then there exists a nonsingular $n \times n$ matrix* $\mathbf{p}$ *with coefficients in K such that*

5.13 $${}^t\mathbf{pap}$$

is a diagonal matrix.

Proof. We have only to take any base $B = \{\mathbf{e}_1, \ldots, \mathbf{e}_n\}$ in an n-dimensional vector space over K and then define $\mathbf{f} = a_{ij}\mathbf{e}^i \otimes \mathbf{e}^j$. Apply-

† If $s = 0$ we understand that none of the d_i is equal to $+1$; if $s = r$ we understand that none of the d_i is equal to -1.

ing Theorem 5.1, we can find a new base B_1 for which $\mathbf{f}$ has a diagonal matrix. If $\mathbf{p}$ is the matrix from B to B_1, then (5.13) is that diagonal matrix, by (3.9). Q.E.D.

EXAMPLE 1 Let V be a three-dimensional vector space over $\mathbf{R}$, and let Q be the quadratic form on V whose matrix with respect to a given base $B = \{\mathbf{e}_1, \mathbf{e}_2, \mathbf{e}_3\}$ is

$$\begin{pmatrix} 1 & 2 & -3 \\ 2 & 1 & 0 \\ -3 & 0 & 0 \end{pmatrix}$$

Then, by (4.8),

$$Q = (\mathbf{e}^1)^2 + 4\mathbf{e}^1\mathbf{e}^2 - 6\mathbf{e}^1\mathbf{e}^3 + (\mathbf{e}^2)^2$$

which we rewrite as

$$\begin{aligned} Q &= (\mathbf{e}^1 + 2\mathbf{e}^2 - 3\mathbf{e}^3)^2 - (2\mathbf{e}^2 - 3\mathbf{e}^3)^2 + (\mathbf{e}^2)^2 \\ &= (\mathbf{e}^1 + 2\mathbf{e}^2 - 3\mathbf{e}^3)^2 - 3(\mathbf{e}^2)^2 + 12\mathbf{e}^2\mathbf{e}^3 - 9(\mathbf{e}^3)^2 \end{aligned}$$

Set

5.14 $$\mathbf{v}^1 = \mathbf{e}^1 + 2\mathbf{e}^2 - 3\mathbf{e}^3$$

Then

$$Q = (\mathbf{v}^1)^2 - 3(\mathbf{e}^2)^2 + 12\mathbf{e}^2\mathbf{e}^3 - 9(\mathbf{e}^3)^2$$

Repeating the process,

$$-3(\mathbf{e}^2)^2 + 12\mathbf{e}^2\mathbf{e}^3 - 9(\mathbf{e}^3)^2 = -3(\mathbf{e}^2 - 2\mathbf{e}^3)^2 + 4(\mathbf{e}^3)^2 - 9(\mathbf{e}^3)^2$$

Put

5.15 $$\mathbf{v}^2 = \sqrt{3}(\mathbf{e}^2 - 2\mathbf{e}^3) \qquad \mathbf{v}^3 = \sqrt{5}\mathbf{e}^3$$

The result is

$$Q = (\mathbf{v}^1)^2 - (\mathbf{v}^2)^2 - (\mathbf{v}^3)^2$$

the form promised by Corollary 1. The matrix from $B^* = \{\mathbf{e}^1, \mathbf{e}^2, \mathbf{e}^3\}$ to $B_1^* = \{\mathbf{v}^1, \mathbf{v}^2, \mathbf{v}^3\}$ is

5.16 $$\begin{pmatrix} 1 & 0 & 0 \\ 2 & \sqrt{3} & 0 \\ -3 & -2\sqrt{3} & \sqrt{5} \end{pmatrix}$$

The inverse of this matrix transforms from B to the base in V of which B_1^* is the dual.

DEFINITION 5.1 *Let Q be a quadratic form on a finite-dimensional vector space over a field K in which* $1 + 1 \neq 0$. *Then the* rank *of Q is defined to be the same as the rank of the symmetric bilinear function associated with Q (see Definition* 3.3).

Thus the integer r in Theorem 5.1 is also the rank of Q. If the matrix of Q with respect to some base in V is diagonal, then r is precisely the number of nonzero diagonal terms, for by definition the rank of Q is the same as the rank of the matrix of Q relative to any base in V.

DEFINITION 5.2 *Let* $\mathbf{f}$ *be a symmetric bilinear function on an* n*-dimensional vector space* V *over a field* K *in which* $1 + 1 \neq 0$. *Let* Q *be the quadratic form associated with* $\mathbf{f}$. *The set of all vectors* $\mathbf{x}$ *in* V *such that* $\mathbf{f}(\mathbf{x}, \mathbf{y}) = 0$ *for every* $\mathbf{y}$ *in* V *is a subspace* N *of* V, *called the nullspace of* $\mathbf{f}$ *or* Q.

Clearly N is precisely the kernel of the mapping $\mathbf{T}_1$ of (3.10). We have therefore, by Theorem 3.2, Chap. 9, the following theorem:

THEOREM 5.2 *The dimension of the nullspace of* Q *is equal to* $n - r$, r *being the rank of* Q.

If $\mathbf{x}$ is in the nullspace of Q, then $Q(\mathbf{x}) = \mathbf{f}(\mathbf{x}, \mathbf{x}) = 0$, clearly. But there may be vectors $\mathbf{x}$ not in N for which $Q(\mathbf{x}) = 0$.

We now look into the integer s appearing in Corollary 1 of Theorem 5.1 above. Let $B_1 = \{\mathbf{v}_1, \ldots, \mathbf{v}_n\}$ and $B_2 = \{\mathbf{w}_1, \ldots, \mathbf{w}_n\}$ be two bases, for each of which the matrix of Q is diagonal, consisting of ± 1 or 0. Let $d_1, \ldots, d_n$ be the diagonal elements in the matrix of Q relative to B_1, and let $d'_1, \ldots, d'_n$ be the diagonal elements in the matrix of Q relative to B_2. Both sets contain exactly r nonzero elements, r being the rank of Q. By suitably numbering the base elements we can assume that $d_i = d'_i = 0$ for $i > r$ and that

$$d_i = \begin{cases} 1 & \text{for } i = 1, \ldots, s \\ -1 & \text{for } i = s + 1, \ldots, r \end{cases}$$

$$d'_i \quad \begin{cases} 1 & \text{for } i = 1, \ldots, t \\ -1 & \text{for } i = t + 1, \ldots, r \end{cases}$$

We want to show that $s = t$. Suppose then that $s > t$. If $\mathbf{x} = x^1\mathbf{v}_1 + \cdots + x^s\mathbf{v}_s$, then $Q(\mathbf{x}) = (x^1)^2 + \cdots + (x^s)^2$. Hence $Q(\mathbf{x}) > 0$ if $\mathbf{x}$ is a nonzero element in the subspace L spanned by $\mathbf{v}_1, \ldots, \mathbf{v}_s$. Similarly, $Q(\mathbf{y}) \leq 0$ for any $\mathbf{y}$ in the subspace M spanned by $\mathbf{w}_{t+1}, \ldots, \mathbf{w}_n$. Since $\dim L = s$, $\dim M = n - t$ it follows that L and M must have a nonzero vector in common if $s > t$, a contradiction. We therefore have the following result, known as Sylvester's law of inertia:

THEOREM 5.3 *Let* Q *be a quadratic form on an* n*-dimensional vector space over the real field* $\mathbf{R}$. *If* Q *is reduced to diagonal form in any manner, then the number of positive diagonal elements and the number of negative diagonal elements depend only on* Q, *not on the particular base.*

In the notation of Corollary 1 of Theorem 5.1, the number s (or sometimes $r - s$) is called the *signature* of Q.

EXERCISES

1. Let $B = \{\mathbf{e}_1, \mathbf{e}_2, \mathbf{e}_3\}$ be a base for a vector space V over $\mathbf{R}$. Define Q by

$$Q(\mathbf{x}) = 2x^2 - 4xy + 2xz + 3y^2 - 2yz + 4z^2$$

if $\mathbf{x} = x\mathbf{e}_1 + y\mathbf{e}_2 + z\mathbf{e}_3$. Find a base in V for which Q has the diagonal form (5.12). What is the signature?

2. Find a nonsingular matrix $\mathbf{a}$ such that ${}^t\mathbf{aba}$ is a diagonal matrix, where

$$\mathbf{b} = \begin{pmatrix} 2 & -1 \\ -1 & 0 \end{pmatrix}$$

3. Work Exercise 2 with

$$\mathbf{b} = \begin{pmatrix} 1 & -1 & 2 \\ -1 & 3 & 0 \\ 2 & 0 & 4 \end{pmatrix}$$

In the following exercises, $\mathbf{x}_i$ denotes the linear functions on $\mathbf{R}^n$ that sends any column vector into its ith entry ($i = 1, \ldots, n$).

4. Describe the locus of $\mathbf{x}_1\mathbf{x}_2 = 1$ in $\mathbf{R}^2$. That is, describe the set of elements of $\mathbf{R}^2$ which are mapped into 1 by the quadratic function $\mathbf{x}_1\mathbf{x}_2$.

5. Describe the locus of $\mathbf{x}_1\mathbf{x}_2 - \mathbf{x}_3^2 = 1$ in $\mathbf{R}^3$.

6. Describe the locus of $\mathbf{x}_1^2 + 2\mathbf{x}_1\mathbf{x}_2 + 2\mathbf{x}_1\mathbf{x}_3 + 2\mathbf{x}_2^2 + 2\mathbf{x}_3^2 = 1$ in $\mathbf{R}^3$.

In the following exercises determine whether there is a nonzero vector $\mathbf{v}$ in $\mathbf{R}^n$ such that $Q(\mathbf{v}) = 0$.

7. $Q = \mathbf{x}_1^2 + \mathbf{x}_2^2 + \mathbf{x}_3^2 + \mathbf{x}_4^2$ in $\mathbf{R}^5$.

8. $Q = \mathbf{x}_1^2 + \mathbf{x}_2^2 - \mathbf{x}_3^2$ in $\mathbf{R}^3$.

9. $Q = \mathbf{x}_1^2 + 2\mathbf{x}_1\mathbf{x}_2 + 2\mathbf{x}_1\mathbf{x}_3 + 2\mathbf{x}_2^2 + 2\mathbf{x}_3^2$ in $\mathbf{R}^3$.

10. $Q = \mathbf{x}_1^2 + 2\mathbf{x}_1\mathbf{x}_2 + 2\mathbf{x}_1\mathbf{x}_3 + 2\mathbf{x}_2^2$ in $\mathbf{R}^3$.

11. Find the nullspace of Q in Exercise 8.

12. Find the nullspace of Q in Exercise 10.

6. *Hermitian forms; unitary mappings*

Throughout the rest of this chapter we deal *exclusively* with two special fields K:

$K = \mathbf{R}$, the field of real numbers
$K = \mathbf{C}$, the field of complex numbers

For any element a in K (hence a is a complex number, possibly real) we denote by $\bar{a}$ the complex conjugate of a. The mapping $a \to \bar{a}$ is an isomorphism of K to itself sending real numbers, and only those, into themselves (see Sec. 1, Chap. 5).

As we have seen in Sec. 11, Chap. 8, a quadratic form of a certain type on a vector space over $\mathbf{R}$ gives a means of defining lengths and angles. A quadratic form on a vector space over $\mathbf{C}$ is not suitable for this purpose. For if Q is such a form and if $Q(\mathbf{x})$ is a nonzero real number for some $\mathbf{x}$, then $Q\left(\frac{1 + \sqrt{-1}}{\sqrt{2}}\,\mathbf{x}\right) =$

$\sqrt{-1}\, Q(\mathbf{x})$, which is a pure imaginary number. Therefore if $Q \neq 0$, then $Q(\mathbf{x})$ cannot possibly be a real number for *all* vectors in the space. We therefore make a small modification.

Let V be a vector space over K (where $K = \mathbf{R}$ or $K = \mathbf{C}$). Denote by $V \times V$ the set of all ordered pairs of vectors $\mathbf{x}$, $\mathbf{y}$ in V. By a *Hermitian form*† H on V is meant a mapping $V \times V \to K$ such that

6.1 $\quad H(\mathbf{x}, \mathbf{y})$ is linear in $\mathbf{x}$ for any fixed $\mathbf{y}$

6.2 $\quad H(\mathbf{y}, \mathbf{x}) = \overline{H(\mathbf{x}, \mathbf{y})} \qquad$ (complex conjugate)

More explicitly, (6.1) means

6.3
$$\begin{aligned} H(\mathbf{x} + \mathbf{v}, \mathbf{y}) &= H(\mathbf{x}, \mathbf{y}) + H(\mathbf{v}, \mathbf{y}) \\ H(a\mathbf{x}, \mathbf{y}) &= a \cdot H(\mathbf{x}, \mathbf{y}) \end{aligned}$$

for any $\mathbf{x}$, $\mathbf{v}$, $\mathbf{y}$ in V and a in K. Using (6.2) and (6.3) we have

$$\begin{aligned} H(\mathbf{x}, \mathbf{y} + \mathbf{w}) &= \overline{H(\mathbf{y} + \mathbf{w}, \mathbf{x})} = \overline{H(\mathbf{y}, \mathbf{x})} + \overline{H(\mathbf{w}, \mathbf{x})} \\ &= H(\mathbf{x}, \mathbf{y}) + H(\mathbf{x}, \mathbf{w}) \end{aligned}$$

Thus

6.4 $\quad H(\mathbf{x}, \mathbf{y} + \mathbf{w}) = H(\mathbf{x}, \mathbf{y}) + H(\mathbf{x}, \mathbf{w})$

Further,

$$\begin{aligned} H(\mathbf{x}, a\mathbf{y}) &= \overline{H(a\mathbf{y}, \mathbf{x})} = \overline{a \cdot H(\mathbf{y}, \mathbf{x})} \\ &= \bar{a} \cdot \overline{H(\mathbf{y}, \mathbf{x})} \end{aligned}$$

whence

6.5 $\quad H(\mathbf{x}, a\mathbf{y}) = \bar{a} \cdot H(\mathbf{x}, \mathbf{y})$

If $K = \mathbf{R}$, it is clear that H is simply a symmetric bilinear function. If $K = \mathbf{C}$, it differs from a bilinear symmetric function only by (6.2) and (6.5).

EXAMPLE 1 Let $\mathbf{x}$, $\mathbf{y}$ denote elements of K^n (column vectors). Then

$$H(\mathbf{x}, \mathbf{y}) = x^1\bar{y}^1 + x^2\bar{y}^2 + \cdots + x^n\bar{y}^n$$

is a Hermitian form. We call it the *cartesian* Hermitian form for K^n. If $K = \mathbf{R}$, this is the same as the bilinear form of Example 2, Sec. 3.

The point of Hermitian forms is the following:

6.6 $\quad H(\mathbf{x}, \mathbf{x})$ *is a real number for any* $\mathbf{x}$.

For by (6.2) we have $H(\mathbf{x}, \mathbf{x}) = \overline{H(\mathbf{x}, \mathbf{x})}$. H is called *positive definite* if $H(\mathbf{x}, \mathbf{x}) > 0$ for all $\mathbf{x} \neq \mathbf{0}$.

It should be apparent that most of the things worked out in the foregoing sections for symmetric bilinear forms will hold, with minor modifications, for Hermitian

† After the French mathematician Charles Hermite (1822–1902).

forms. We shall point out the main facts briefly, mentioning again that, for $K = \mathbf{R}$, they are merely repetitions of the corresponding statements in the preceding sections. Most proofs are left to the reader.

If H is a Hermitian form on an n-dimensional vector space V, and if $B = \{\mathbf{e}_1, \ldots, \mathbf{e}_n\}$ is a base for V, then the matrix $\mathbf{a} = (a_{ij})$ of H relative to B is defined by

6.7 $$a_{ij} = H(\mathbf{e}_i, \mathbf{e}_j)$$

From (6.2) we have

6.8 $$a_{ji} = \bar{a}_{ij} \qquad \text{or} \qquad {}^t\mathbf{a} = \bar{\mathbf{a}}$$

A matrix with this property is called *Hermitian*. If $K = \mathbf{R}$, this is just the condition for $\mathbf{a}$ to be symmetric.

If $\mathbf{x} = x^i\mathbf{e}_i$ and $\mathbf{y} = y^j\mathbf{e}_j$, then

6.9 $$H(\mathbf{x}, \mathbf{y}) = a_{ij}x^i\bar{y}^j$$

If $\mathbf{e}'_i = p^j{}_i\mathbf{e}_j$ $(i = 1, \ldots, n)$ form a new base B' for V, then the matrix $\mathbf{a}'$ of H relative to B' is obtained from $\mathbf{a}$ by

6.10 $$\mathbf{a}' = {}^t\mathbf{p}\mathbf{a}\bar{\mathbf{p}}$$

We define the *rank* of H to be the rank of its matrix relative to any base in V. Thus H has rank n if and only if $\det \mathbf{a} \neq 0$.

If H is positive definite, then its rank must be equal to $\dim V$. For if $\det \mathbf{a} = 0$, then there exist nonzero numbers $x^1, \ldots, x^n$ such that $a_{ij}x^i = 0$. But then $H(\mathbf{x}, \mathbf{x}) = 0$, by (6.9), for the vector $\mathbf{x} = x^i\mathbf{e}_i$.

Now let $\mathbf{g}$ be a linear function on V. By $\bar{\mathbf{g}}$ we denote the mapping $V \to K$ defined by

6.11 $$\bar{\mathbf{g}}(\mathbf{x}) = \overline{\mathbf{g}(\mathbf{x})}$$

If $\mathbf{f}$ is another linear function on V, then by $\mathbf{f}\bar{\mathbf{g}}$ we denote the mapping $V \to K$ defined by

6.12 $$(\mathbf{f}\bar{\mathbf{g}})(\mathbf{x}) = \mathbf{f}(\mathbf{x}) \cdot \bar{\mathbf{g}}(\mathbf{x}) = \mathbf{f}(\mathbf{x}) \cdot \overline{\mathbf{g}(\mathbf{x})}$$

With this notation we have

6.13 $$H = a_{ij}\mathbf{e}^i\bar{\mathbf{e}}^j$$

where $B^* = \{\mathbf{e}^1, \ldots, \mathbf{e}^n\}$ is the dual base of B above.

EXAMPLE 2 Let $\mathbf{e}^i$ denote the linear function on K^n sending a column vector $\mathbf{x}$ into its ith component x^i. Then the cartesian form of Example 1 can be written

6.14 $$H = \mathbf{e}^1\bar{\mathbf{e}}^1 + \cdots + \mathbf{e}^n\bar{\mathbf{e}}^n$$

The matrix of this form with respect to the canonical base $B = \{\mathbf{e}_1, \ldots, \mathbf{e}_n\}$ of K^n is the unit matrix $\mathbf{I}_n$. This form is visibly positive definite.

A Hermitian form H on an n-dimensional space V can be reduced to diagonal form by essentially the same argument used in Sec. 5 for bilinear forms. For example, take the case $n = 2$, for which (6.13) is

$$H = a_{11}\mathbf{e}^1\bar{\mathbf{e}}^1 + a_{12}\mathbf{e}^1\bar{\mathbf{e}}^2 + a_{21}\mathbf{e}^2\bar{\mathbf{e}}^1 + a_{22}\mathbf{e}^2\bar{\mathbf{e}}^2$$

By a preliminary change of base in V, as described in Sec. 5, we can arrange things so that $a_{11} \neq 0$. Recall that $a_{ij} = \bar{a}_{ji}$; in particular, a_{11} and a_{22} are *real*. Now put

$$\mathbf{v}^1 = \mathbf{e}^1 + c\mathbf{e}^2 \qquad \text{with } c = a_{21}/a_{11}$$

Then

$$\begin{aligned} a_{11}\mathbf{v}^1\bar{\mathbf{v}}^1 &= a_{11}(\mathbf{e}^1 + c\mathbf{e}^2)(\bar{\mathbf{e}}^1 + \bar{c}\bar{\mathbf{e}}^2) \\ &= a_{11}\mathbf{e}^1\bar{\mathbf{e}}^1 + a_{11}c\mathbf{e}^2\bar{\mathbf{e}}^1 + a_{11}\bar{c}\mathbf{e}^1\bar{\mathbf{e}}^2 + a_{11}c\bar{c}\mathbf{e}^2\bar{\mathbf{e}}^2 \end{aligned}$$

By definition, $a_{11}c = a_{21}$, and we have $a_{11}\bar{c} = \overline{a_{11}c} = \bar{a}_{21} = a_{12}$ (since a_{11} is real). Hence,

$$a_{11}\mathbf{v}^1\bar{\mathbf{v}}^1 = a_{11}\mathbf{e}^1\bar{\mathbf{e}}^1 + a_{21}\mathbf{e}^2\bar{\mathbf{e}}^1 + a_{12}\mathbf{e}^1\bar{\mathbf{e}}^2 + a^{11}c\bar{c}\mathbf{e}^2\bar{\mathbf{e}}^2$$

Hence,

$$H = a_{11}\mathbf{v}^1\bar{\mathbf{v}}^1 + (a_{22} - a_{11}c\bar{c})\mathbf{e}^2\bar{\mathbf{e}}^2$$

A similar argument holds for $n > 2$, and it is easily seen that one can find a base $\mathbf{v}^1, \ldots, \mathbf{v}^n$ in the dual space of V such that

$$H = d_1\mathbf{v}^1\bar{\mathbf{v}}^1 + \cdots + d_r\mathbf{v}^r\bar{\mathbf{v}}^r$$

where r is the rank of H, and where $d_1, \ldots, d_r$ are nonzero real numbers. Putting $\mathbf{u}^i = \sqrt{d_k}\mathbf{v}^i$ if $d_i > 0$ and $\mathbf{u}^i = \sqrt{-d_i}\mathbf{v}^i$ if $d_i < 0$, we then obtain (after a suitable renumbering, if necessary)

6.15 $$H = \mathbf{u}^1\bar{\mathbf{u}}^1 + \cdots + \mathbf{u}^s\bar{\mathbf{u}}^s - \mathbf{u}^{s+1}\bar{\mathbf{u}}^{s+1} - \cdots - \mathbf{u}^r\bar{\mathbf{u}}^r$$

The number s is called the *signature* of H (or of the matrix of H relative to any base); and s does not depend on the particular base change used to put H in the *diagonal form* (6.15).

H again denoting a Hermitian form on an n-dimensional vector space V over K ($= \mathbf{R}$ or $= \mathbf{C}$), a linear mapping $\mathbf{T}\colon V \to V$ is called *H-unitary* if

6.16 $$H(\mathbf{Tx}, \mathbf{Ty}) = H(\mathbf{x}, \mathbf{y})$$

for all $\mathbf{x}, \mathbf{y}$ in V, where we have written simply $\mathbf{Tx}$ for $\mathbf{T}(\mathbf{x})$, etc. (For the case $K = \mathbf{R}$ the term *H-orthogonal* is often used instead of *H-unitary.*)

Let $B = \{\mathbf{e}_1, \ldots, \mathbf{e}_n\}$ be a base for V, and let $\mathbf{a}$ be the corresponding matrix of H. Further, let $\mathbf{c} = (c^k{}_i)$ be the matrix of $\mathbf{T}$ relative to B, so that $\mathbf{Te}_i = c^k{}_i\mathbf{e}_k$ Putting $\mathbf{x} = \mathbf{e}_i$ and $\mathbf{y} = \mathbf{e}_j$ in (6.16) we obtain

$$H(c^k{}_i\mathbf{e}_k, c^h{}_j\mathbf{e}_h) = H(\mathbf{e}_i, \mathbf{e}_j)$$

or

6.17 $$c^k{}_i a_{kh} \bar{c}^h{}_j = a_{ij}$$

or

6.18 $${}^t\mathbf{c}\mathbf{a}\bar{\mathbf{c}} = \mathbf{a}$$

It is easy to verify conversely that if (6.18) holds, then $\mathbf{T}$ is H-unitary. If H has rank n, that is, if det $\mathbf{a} \neq 0$, then from (6.18) we conclude that det $\mathbf{c} \neq 0$, and so $\mathbf{T}$ must be a one-to-one mapping, that is, an isomorphism of V. Then $\mathbf{T}^{-1}$ is defined, and from (6.16) applied to $\mathbf{T}^{-1}\mathbf{x}$ and $\mathbf{T}^{-1}\mathbf{y}$ in place of $\mathbf{x}$ and $\mathbf{y}$, one sees immediately that $\mathbf{T}^{-1}$ is also H-unitary. Furthermore, if $\mathbf{S}$ and $\mathbf{T}$ are both H-unitary, then so is $\mathbf{S} \circ \mathbf{T}$. For

$$H(\mathbf{S} \circ \mathbf{T}\mathbf{x}, \mathbf{S} \circ \mathbf{T}\mathbf{y}) = H(\mathbf{T}\mathbf{x}, \mathbf{T}\mathbf{y}) = H(\mathbf{x}, \mathbf{y})$$

by (6.16), applied twice.

Therefore, if H is nondegenerate (i.e., if its rank is equal to dim V), then all the H-unitary mappings of V to itself form a group, with composition of mappings as group operation. That group is called the *unitary group* of H.†

As a particularly important special case, suppose that the matrix of H relative to the given base in V is the unit matrix, as in Example 2 above (if H is positive definite, then such a base can always be found by the diagonalization procedure outlined above). Then (6.18) boils down to

6.19 $${}^t\mathbf{c}\bar{\mathbf{c}} = \mathbf{I}$$

Taking complex conjugates of both sides, we have

$${}^t\bar{\mathbf{c}}\mathbf{c} = \mathbf{I}$$

since $\mathbf{I}$ is a real matrix. Thus (6.19) can also be written as

6.20 $$\mathbf{c}^{-1} = {}^t\bar{\mathbf{c}}$$

A complex matrix satisfying this condition is called a *unitary* matrix (or sometimes an *orthogonal* matrix, if $\mathbf{c}$ is real).

EXAMPLE 3 The matrix

$$\begin{pmatrix} \cos\alpha & -\sin\alpha \\ \sin\alpha & \cos\alpha \end{pmatrix}$$

is an orthogonal matrix for any real number α.

Since a matrix and its inverse commute, (6.19) gives us

$${}^t\mathbf{c}\bar{\mathbf{c}} = \bar{\mathbf{c}}{}^t\mathbf{c} = \mathbf{I}$$

Written out these equations become

† If $K = \mathbf{R}$, it is also called the *orthogonal group* of H.

6.21 $$\sum_{j=1}^{n} c^i{}_i \bar{c}^i{}_k = \begin{cases} 1 & \text{if } i = k \\ 0 & \text{if } i \neq k \end{cases}$$

and

6.22 $$\sum_{j=1}^{n} \bar{c}^i{}_j c^k{}_j = \begin{cases} 1 & \text{if } i = k \\ 0 & \text{if } i = k \end{cases}$$

These relations are sometimes described by saying that the columns (or the rows) of $\mathbf{c}$ are *mutually orthogonal unit vectors.* We shall go into this terminology in the next section.

THEOREM 6.1 *Let H be a Hermitian form on a vector space V. A linear mapping* $\mathbf{T}$ *of V to itself is H-unitary if and only if*

6.23 $$H(\mathbf{T}x, \mathbf{T}x) = H(\mathbf{x}, \mathbf{x})$$

for all $\mathbf{x}$ *in V.*

Proof. From (6.16) it is clear that (6.23) must hold if $\mathbf{T}$ is H-unitary. Suppose now that (6.23) holds. Apply (6.23) to $\mathbf{x} + \mathbf{y}$. Using (6.1) to (6.5) we have

$$H(\mathbf{T}(\mathbf{x} + \mathbf{y}), \mathbf{T}(\mathbf{x} + \mathbf{y})) = H(\mathbf{Tx}, \mathbf{Tx}) + H(\mathbf{Tx}, \mathbf{Ty}) + H(\mathbf{Ty}, \mathbf{Tx}) + H(\mathbf{Ty}, \mathbf{Ty})$$

The left side here is equal to $H(\mathbf{x} + \mathbf{y}, \mathbf{x} + \mathbf{y})$, by (6.23). Expanding this out and using (6.23) on the right of the expression above, one gets

6.24 $$H(\mathbf{x}, \mathbf{y}) + H(\mathbf{y}, \mathbf{x}) = H(\mathbf{Tx}, \mathbf{Ty}) + H(\mathbf{Ty}, \mathbf{Tx})$$

In the case of the real field, H is symmetric, and the last equation reduces to

$$2H(\mathbf{x}, \mathbf{y}) = 2H(\mathbf{Tx}, \mathbf{Ty})$$

from which (6.16) follows at once. For the case of the complex field, replace $\mathbf{x}$ in (6.24) by $i\mathbf{x}$, where $i = \sqrt{-1}$. Using (6.3) and (6.5) one obtains easily

$$H(\mathbf{x}, \mathbf{y}) - H(\mathbf{y}, \mathbf{x}) = H(\mathbf{Tx}, \mathbf{Ty}) - H(\mathbf{Ty}, \mathbf{Tx})$$

Adding to (6.24) we obtain (6.16). Q.E.D.

EXAMPLE 4 Let H be the Hermitian (or quadratic) form on the vector space $\mathbf{R}^2$ defined by

$$H(\mathbf{v}, \mathbf{v}) = x^2 + y^2 \qquad \text{for } \mathbf{v} = \begin{pmatrix} x \\ y \end{pmatrix}$$

Let $\mathbf{T}$ be the linear mapping defined by

$$\mathbf{T}\mathbf{v} = \begin{pmatrix} a & b \\ c & d \end{pmatrix}\begin{pmatrix} x \\ y \end{pmatrix} = \begin{pmatrix} ax + by \\ cx + dy \end{pmatrix}$$

Then

$$\begin{aligned} H(\mathbf{T}\mathbf{v}, \mathbf{T}\mathbf{v}) &= (ax + by)^2 + (cx + dy)^2 \\ &= (a^2 + c^2)x^2 + 2(ab + cd)xy + (b^2 + d^2)y^2 \end{aligned}$$

For $\mathbf{T}$ to be H-unitary (or orthogonal) it is necessary and sufficient that

$$\begin{aligned} a^2 + c^2 &= 1 \\ ab + cd &= 0 \\ b^2 + d^2 &= 1 \end{aligned}$$

[These are just Eq. (6.22) for this special case.] From the first equation $a^2 + c^2 = 1$ it follows that $-1 \leq a \leq 1$, since a, c are real. We can then find a number α such that $a = \cos \alpha$, $c = \sin \alpha$. From the other equations it is easy to deduce that $b = -\sin \alpha$, $d = \cos \alpha$. Hence, the matrix of $\mathbf{T}$ is of the type of Example 3. The H-unitary mappings can be thought of as rotations about a point in the euclidean plane.

EXAMPLE 5 Let H be the Hermitian form

$$H(\mathbf{x}, \mathbf{y}) = x^1y^1 + x^2y^2 + x^3y^3$$

on the vector space $\mathbf{R}^3$. The H-unitary transformations can be thought of as rigid motions about a fixed point in euclidean 3-space.

EXAMPLE 6 Let H be the Hermitian form on $\mathbf{R}^4$ defined by

$$H(\mathbf{x}, \mathbf{y}) = x^1y^1 - x^2y^2 - x^3y^3 - x^4y^4$$

The unitary group of H is called the *Lorentz group*. It is of great importance in relativity theory.

EXERCISES

1. Let H be a Hermitian form of rank r on a vector space V of dimension n over the field of complex numbers. Prove that there is a base $\{\mathbf{x}^1, \mathbf{x}^2, \ldots, \mathbf{x}^n\}$ in V^* such that

$$H(\mathbf{v}, \mathbf{w}) = a_1\mathbf{x}^1(\mathbf{v})\overline{\mathbf{x}^1(\mathbf{w})} + \cdots + a_r\mathbf{x}^r(\mathbf{v})\overline{\mathbf{x}^r(\mathbf{w})}$$

where

$$a_i = \pm 1$$

2. In Exercise 1 prove that the number of a_i equal to $+1$ is independent of the particular base.

3. Let $B = \{\mathbf{e}_1, \mathbf{e}_2, \mathbf{e}_3\}$ be a base for a vector space V over $\mathbf{C}$, and let H be a Hermitian form on V. Let its matrix relative to B be

$$\begin{pmatrix} 1 & 0 & i \\ 0 & 2 & 3+i \\ -i & 3-i & -1 \end{pmatrix}$$

Find a new base in V for which the matrix of H is diagonal.

7. Euclidean vector spaces

In this section we shall go briefly into matters discussed in Sec. 11, Chap. 8. By a *euclidean vector space E* we mean a vector space over the field K of real or complex numbers on which there is prescribed a positive definite Hermitian form H. The scalar $H(\mathbf{x}, \mathbf{y})$ is called the *inner product* of the vectors $\mathbf{x}$ and $\mathbf{y}$ in E. Instead of writing $H(\mathbf{x}, \mathbf{y})$ we shall often use the simpler notation $(\mathbf{x}, \mathbf{y})$. We recall the definition:

7.1 $(\mathbf{x}, \mathbf{y})$ *is linear in* $\mathbf{x}$.

7.2 $(\mathbf{x}, \mathbf{y}) = \overline{(\mathbf{y}, \mathbf{x})}$

7.3 $(\mathbf{x}, \mathbf{x}) \geq 0$ *and* $(\mathbf{x}, \mathbf{x}) = 0$ *if and only if* $\mathbf{x} = \mathbf{0}$.

For any element $\mathbf{x}$ in E we define the *length* $|\mathbf{x}|$ of $\mathbf{x}$ by

7.4 $|\mathbf{x}| = \sqrt{(\mathbf{x}, \mathbf{x})}$

By (7.3) we have $|\mathbf{x}| > 0$ unless $\mathbf{x} = \mathbf{0}$.

EXAMPLE 1 The vector space $\mathbf{R}_n$ becomes a euclidean vector space if we define the inner product $(\mathbf{x}, \mathbf{y})$ of two row vectors $\mathbf{x} = (x_1, \ldots, x_n)$ and $\mathbf{y} = (y_1, \ldots, y_n)$ by

$$(\mathbf{x}, \mathbf{y}) = x_1y_1 + \cdots + x_ny_n$$

EXAMPLE 2 The vector space $\mathbf{C}_n$ becomes a euclidean vector space if we define the inner product $(\mathbf{x}, \mathbf{y})$ of two row vectors by

$$(x, y) = x_1\bar{y}_1 + \cdots + x_n\bar{y}_n$$

If $\mathbf{x}$ and $\mathbf{y}$ are real, then this is the same as in the foregoing example.

We shall refer to these inner products in $\mathbf{R}_n$ and $\mathbf{C}_n$ as the *standard* inner products.

A linear mapping $\mathbf{T}$: $E \to E$ of a euclidean vector space is called *unitary* if

$$(\mathbf{Tx}, \mathbf{Ty}) = (\mathbf{x}, \mathbf{y})$$

for all $\mathbf{x}$, $\mathbf{y}$ in E. (The term *orthogonal* is often used if the scalar field is $\mathbf{R}$.) If E is infinite-dimensional, one adds the condition that $\mathbf{T}$ maps E onto E.

THEOREM 7.1 **(Schwarz inequality)** *For any two vectors* $\mathbf{x}$, $\mathbf{y}$ *in* E,

7.5 $|(\mathbf{x}, \mathbf{y})| \leq |\mathbf{x}| \cdot |\mathbf{y}|$

equality holding if and only if one vector is a scalar multiple of the other.

Proof. The argument is essentially the same as that for Theorem 11.1, Chap. 8, except that $(\mathbf{x}, \mathbf{y})$ may not be a real number here. First of all, if $(\mathbf{x}, \mathbf{y}) = 0$, (7.5) clearly holds. Assume then that $p = (\mathbf{x}, \mathbf{y})$ is not zero, and set $\mathbf{x}' = q\mathbf{x}$, where $q = \frac{|p|}{p}$. We have $|q| = \frac{|p|}{|p|} = 1$, clearly. Then, using (7.1)

$$|(\mathbf{x}', \mathbf{y})| = |(q\mathbf{x}, \mathbf{y})| = |\mathrm{q} \cdot (\mathbf{x}, \mathbf{y})| = |q| \cdot |(\mathbf{x}, \mathbf{y})| = |(\mathbf{x}, \mathbf{y})|$$

From (7.1) and (7.2) we have

$$|\mathbf{x}'|^2 = (\mathbf{x}', \mathbf{x}') = (q\mathbf{x}, q\mathbf{x}) = q\bar{q}(\mathbf{x}, \mathbf{x}) = |q|^2 \cdot |\mathbf{x}|^2$$

and so $|\mathbf{x}'|^2 = |\mathbf{x}|^2$. Therefore the right and left members of (7.5) remain unchanged if we replace $\mathbf{x}$ by $\mathbf{x}'$. The advantage of this is that $(\mathbf{x}', \mathbf{y})$ is *real*. For

$$(\mathbf{x}', \mathbf{y}) = (q\mathbf{x}, \mathbf{y}) = q \cdot (\mathbf{x}, \mathbf{y}) = qp = |p|$$

by definition of p and q. Hence $(\mathbf{x}', \mathbf{y}) = (\mathbf{y}, \mathbf{x}')$. Now let t be any *real* number. We have

$$(\mathbf{x}' + t\mathbf{y}, \mathbf{x}' + t\mathbf{y}) \geq 0$$

by (7.3). Expanding out the expression by use of (7.1) and (7.2) we obtain

$$(\mathbf{x}', \mathbf{x}') + t(\mathbf{x}', \mathbf{y}) + t(\mathbf{y}, \mathbf{x}') + t^2(\mathbf{y}, \mathbf{y}) \geq 0$$

By what was just said, this is the same as

$$(\mathbf{x}', \mathbf{x}') + 2t(\mathbf{x}', \mathbf{y}') + t^2(\mathbf{y}, \mathbf{y}) \geq 0$$

or

$$|\mathbf{x}'|^2 + 2t(\mathbf{x}', \mathbf{y}') + t^2 \cdot |\mathbf{y}|^2 \geq 0$$

Set

$$a = |\mathbf{y}|^2 \qquad b = 2(\mathbf{x}', \mathbf{y}) \qquad c = |\mathbf{x}'|^2$$

These are real numbers, and we have

$$at^2 + bt + c \geq 0$$

for all real numbers t. Therefore the quadratic on the left cannot have two distinct real roots. From the quadratic formula it follows that

$$b^2 - 4ac \leq 0$$

or

$$4(\mathbf{x}', \mathbf{y})^2 - 4|\mathbf{x}'|^2 \cdot |\mathbf{y}|^2 \leq 0$$

or

$$(\mathbf{x}', \mathbf{y})^2 \leq |\mathbf{x}'|^2 \cdot |\mathbf{y}|^2$$

whence

$$|(\mathbf{x}', \mathbf{y})| \leq |\mathbf{x}'| \cdot |\mathbf{y}|$$

which is what we wanted to prove. Suppose now that equality holds in (7.5). If $p = (\mathbf{x}, \mathbf{y}) = 0$, then $|\mathbf{x}| \cdot |\mathbf{y}| = 0$, and so either $\mathbf{x}$ or $\mathbf{y}$ is the zero vector. If $p \neq 0$, then by our calculations above we have $b^2 - 4ac = 0$. In this case $at^2 + bt + c$ has two equal real roots t_0, and so $(\mathbf{x}' - t_0\mathbf{y}, \mathbf{x}' - t_0\mathbf{y}) = |\mathbf{x}' - t_0\mathbf{y}|^2 = 0$, whence $\mathbf{x}' - t_0\mathbf{y} = \mathbf{0}$, or $\mathbf{x} = \frac{t_0}{p}\mathbf{y}$. The converse is trivial to prove. Q.E.D.

As an immediate consequence of Schwarz's inequality we have the following theorem:

THEOREM 7.2 (Triangle inequality) *For any vectors* $\mathbf{x}$, $\mathbf{y}$ *in the euclidean vector space* E,

7.6 $$|\mathbf{x} + \mathbf{y}| \leq |\mathbf{x}| + |\mathbf{y}|$$

Proof. We have from (7.1), (7.2), (7.4),

$$\begin{aligned}
|\mathbf{x} + \mathbf{y}|^2 &= (\mathbf{x} + \mathbf{y}, \mathbf{x} + \mathbf{y}) \\
&= (\mathbf{x}, \mathbf{x}) + (\mathbf{x}, \mathbf{y}) + (\mathbf{y}, \mathbf{x}) + (\mathbf{y}, \mathbf{y}) \\
&\leq (\mathbf{x}, \mathbf{x}) + |(\mathbf{x}, \mathbf{y})| + |(\mathbf{y}, \mathbf{x})| + (\mathbf{y}, \mathbf{y}) \\
&= |\mathbf{x}|^2 + 2|(\mathbf{x}, \mathbf{y})| + |\mathbf{y}|^2 \\
&\leq |\mathbf{x}|^2 + 2|\mathbf{x}| \cdot |\mathbf{y}| + |\mathbf{y}|^2 \qquad \text{(Schwarz inequality)} \\
&= (|\mathbf{x}| + |\mathbf{y}|)^2
\end{aligned}$$

Taking square roots we obtain the conclusion. Q.E.D.

Just as in Sec. 11, Chap. 8, we can use the Schwarz inequality to define angles between two vectors in a euclidean space E. Thus, let $\mathbf{x}$, $\mathbf{y}$ be two *nonzero* vectors. Then the number

$$a = \tfrac{1}{2}\,\frac{(\mathbf{x}, \mathbf{y}) + (\mathbf{y}, \mathbf{x})}{|\mathbf{x}|\,|\mathbf{y}|} = \text{real part of } \frac{(\mathbf{x}, \mathbf{y})}{|\mathbf{x}|\,|\mathbf{y}|}$$

is real, and $-1 \leq a \leq 1$, by the Schwarz inequality. Therefore there is a uniquely determined number θ such that $0 \leq \theta \leq \pi$ and

$$\cos\theta = a$$

This number θ is defined to be the angle between $\mathbf{x}$ and $\mathbf{y}$ and will sometimes be denoted by $\measuredangle(\mathbf{x}, \mathbf{y})$.

In the case of a euclidean vector space E over the *real* field, it follows at once from the definition that

7.7 $$(\mathbf{x}, \mathbf{y}) = |\mathbf{x}| \cdot |\mathbf{y}| \cdot \cos\measuredangle(\mathbf{x}, \mathbf{y})$$

For a vector space over the complex field one has

7.8 $$\tfrac{1}{2}((\mathbf{x}, \mathbf{y}) + (\mathbf{y}, \mathbf{x})) = |\mathbf{x}| \cdot |\mathbf{y}| \cdot \cos \measuredangle (\mathbf{x}, \mathbf{y})$$

For any euclidean vector space it is easy to deduce the *law of cosines:*

7.9 $$|\mathbf{x} + \mathbf{y}|^2 = |\mathbf{x}|^2 + |\mathbf{y}|^2 + 2|\mathbf{x}| \cdot |\mathbf{y}| \cdot \cos \measuredangle (\mathbf{x}, \mathbf{y})$$

This is equivalent to the following identity, which holds for any three vectors $\mathbf{u}$, $\mathbf{x}$, $\mathbf{y}$ such that $\mathbf{u} \neq \mathbf{x}$ and $\mathbf{u} \neq \mathbf{y}$:

7.10 $$|\mathbf{x} - \mathbf{y}|^2 = |\mathbf{x} - \mathbf{u}|^2 + |\mathbf{y} - \mathbf{u}|^2 - 2 \cdot |\mathbf{x} - \mathbf{u}| \cdot |\mathbf{y} - \mathbf{u}| \cdot \cos \measuredangle (\mathbf{x} - \mathbf{u}, \mathbf{y} - \mathbf{u})$$

The number $|\mathbf{x} - \mathbf{y}|$ is called the *distance* between $\mathbf{x}$ and $\mathbf{y}$.

EXERCISES

1. For any vectors $\mathbf{v}$ and $\mathbf{w}$ in a euclidean vector space E, prove: $|\mathbf{v}| - |\mathbf{w}| \leq |\mathbf{v} - \mathbf{w}|$.

2. Prove the law of cosines identity (7.9).

3. Prove identity (7.10).

4. In a euclidean vector space, the notion of angle can be defined explicitly in terms of length. What is this definition?

5. Let $\mathbf{v}$ be a unit vector in a euclidean space E, that is, $|\mathbf{v}| = 1$. For any vector $\mathbf{u}$ in E, we set

$$\text{Proj}_{\mathbf{v}}\, \mathbf{u} = (\mathbf{u}, \mathbf{v})\mathbf{v}$$

(called the *projection* of $\mathbf{u}$ on $\mathbf{v}$). Prove

$$\text{Proj}_{\mathbf{v}}\, (\mathbf{u}_1 + \mathbf{u}_2 + \cdots + \mathbf{u}_n) = \text{Proj}_{\mathbf{v}}\, \mathbf{u}_1 + \text{Proj}_{\mathbf{v}}\, \mathbf{u}_2 + \cdots + \text{Proj}_{\mathbf{v}}\, \mathbf{u}_n$$

Interpret this geometrically.

6. Let E be a euclidean space, and let $\mathbf{T}: E \to E$ be a mapping such that

$$|\mathbf{T}\mathbf{v}| = |\mathbf{v}|$$

for all $\mathbf{v}$ in E. Prove that $\mathbf{T}$ is linear and hence unitary.

8. Orthonormal bases

Throughout this section we deal with a euclidean vector space over the field K, where either $K = \mathbf{R}$ or $K = \mathbf{C}$. The inner product of two vectors $\mathbf{x}$, $\mathbf{y}$ of E will be denoted by $(\mathbf{x}, \mathbf{y})$.

DEFINITION 8.1 *Two vectors* $\mathbf{x}$, $\mathbf{y}$ *of* E *are called* orthogonal *if* $(\mathbf{x}, \mathbf{y}) = 0$; *they are called* perpendicular *if*

$$\textit{Real part of } (\mathbf{x}, \mathbf{y}) = 0$$

If K is the real field, then these two notions are clearly the same. But if K is the complex field, they are different. For orthogonal vectors are certainly perpendicular, but perpendicular vectors need not be orthogonal. For example, cos $\measuredangle$

$(\sqrt{-1}\mathbf{v}, \mathbf{v}) = 0$ if $\mathbf{v} \neq \mathbf{0}$, so that $\measuredangle (\sqrt{-1}\mathbf{v}, \mathbf{v}) = \pi/2$. But $(\sqrt{-1}\mathbf{v}, \mathbf{v}) = \sqrt{-1}\,|\mathbf{v}|^2 \neq 0$.

DEFINITION 8.2 *Two subspaces U, V of E are said to be* orthogonal *if $(\mathbf{u}, \mathbf{v}) = 0$ for all $\mathbf{u}$ in U and $\mathbf{v}$ in V.*

For any subspace U of E we denote by $U^\perp$ the set of all vectors in E which are orthogonal to every element of U. It is quickly verified that $U^\perp$ is a subspace of E. It is called the *orthogonal complement* of U.

DEFINITION 8.3 *A set of vectors $\mathbf{u}_1$, $\mathbf{u}_2$, $\mathbf{u}_3$, etc., is called* orthonormal *if*

8.1
$$\begin{aligned} (\mathbf{u}_i, \mathbf{u}_j) &= 0 \qquad \text{for } i \neq j \\ (\mathbf{u}_i, \mathbf{u}_i) &= 1 \qquad \textit{for each } i \textit{ and } j \end{aligned}$$

In particular, if E has finite dimension n, then a base $\{\mathbf{e}_1, \ldots, \mathbf{e}_n\}$ is called *orthonormal* if (8.1) holds for these vectors.

PROPOSITION 8.1 *Orthonormal vectors are linearly independent.*

Proof. Suppose that $a_1\mathbf{u}_1 + \cdots + a_r\mathbf{u}_r = \mathbf{0}$, the $\mathbf{u}_i$ being orthonormal. Take the inner product of the left side with $\mathbf{u}_1$:

$$(a_1\mathbf{u}_1 + \cdots + a_r\mathbf{u}_r, \mathbf{u}_1) = (\mathbf{0}, \mathbf{u}_1) = 0$$

or

$$a_1(\mathbf{u}_1, \mathbf{u}_1) + a_2(\mathbf{u}_2, \mathbf{u}_1) + \cdots + a_r(\mathbf{u}_r, \mathbf{u}_1) = 0$$

By (8.1) this reduces to $a_1 = 0$. Similarly, replacing $\mathbf{u}$ on the right by $\mathbf{u}_k$, we get $a_k = 0$ $(k = 1, \ldots, r)$. Q.E.D.

PROPOSITION 8.2 *If $\mathbf{u}$ is a nonzero vector in E, then*

$$\mathbf{v} = \frac{1}{|\mathbf{u}|} \cdot \mathbf{u}$$

is a unit vector; that is, $|\mathbf{v}| = 1$.

Proof. $$(\mathbf{v}, \mathbf{v}) = \left(\frac{1}{|\mathbf{u}|} \cdot \mathbf{u}, \frac{1}{|\mathbf{u}|} \cdot \mathbf{u}\right) = \frac{1}{|\mathbf{u}|^2} \cdot (\mathbf{u}, \mathbf{u}) = 1.$$

We say that $\mathbf{v}$ is obtained from $\mathbf{u}$ by *normalization*.

THEOREM 8.3 *If $\mathbf{v}_1, \ldots, \mathbf{v}_r$ are orthonormal vectors in E and if $\mathbf{x}$ lies in the subspace which they span, then*

8.2
$$\mathbf{x} = (\mathbf{x}, \mathbf{v}_1) \cdot \mathbf{v}_1 + \cdots + (\mathbf{x}, \mathbf{v}_r) \cdot \mathbf{v}_r$$

Proof. By assumption, $\mathbf{x} = c_1\mathbf{v}_1 + \cdots + c_r\mathbf{v}_r$ for certain scalars c_i. Then

$$\begin{aligned} (\mathbf{x}, \mathbf{v}_k) &= (c_1\mathbf{v}_1 + \cdots + c_r\mathbf{v}_r, \mathbf{v}_k) \\ &= c_1(\mathbf{v}_1, \mathbf{v}_k) + \cdots + c_k(\mathbf{v}_k, \mathbf{v}_k) + \cdots + c_r(\mathbf{v}_r, \mathbf{v}_k) \\ &= c_k \end{aligned}$$

Q.E.D.

THEOREM 8.4 *If* $\mathbf{u}_1, \mathbf{u}_2, \mathbf{u}_3, \ldots$ *are linearly independent vectors in* E, *then the vectors* $\mathbf{v}_1, \mathbf{v}_2, \mathbf{v}_3, \ldots$ *given by the formulas below form an orthonormal set which spans the same subspace of* E *as the* $\mathbf{u}_i$:

$$\mathbf{v}_1 = \frac{\mathbf{u}_1}{|\mathbf{u}_1|}$$

$$\mathbf{v}_2 = \frac{\mathbf{u}_2 - (\mathbf{u}_2, \mathbf{v}_1) \cdot \mathbf{v}_1}{|\mathbf{u}_2 - (\mathbf{u}_2, \mathbf{v}_1) \cdot \mathbf{v}_1|}$$

$$\mathbf{v}_3 = \frac{\mathbf{u}_3 - (\mathbf{u}_3, \mathbf{v}_1) \cdot \mathbf{v}_1 - (\mathbf{u}_3, \mathbf{v}_2) \cdot \mathbf{v}_2}{|\mathbf{u}_3 - (\mathbf{u}_3, \mathbf{v}_1) \cdot \mathbf{v}_1 - (\mathbf{u}_3, \mathbf{v}_2) \cdot \mathbf{v}_2|}$$

$$\cdots\cdots\cdots$$

$$\mathbf{v}_k = \frac{\mathbf{u}_k - (\mathbf{u}_k, \mathbf{v}_1)\mathbf{v}_1 - (\mathbf{u}_k, \mathbf{v}_2)\mathbf{v}_2 - \cdots - (\mathbf{u}_k, \mathbf{v}_{k-1})\mathbf{v}_{k-1}}{|\mathbf{u}_k - (\mathbf{u}_k, \mathbf{v}_1)\mathbf{v}_1 - (\mathbf{u}_k, \mathbf{v}_2)\mathbf{v}_2 - \cdots - (\mathbf{u}_k, \mathbf{v}_{k-1})\mathbf{v}_{k-1}|}$$

etc.

Proof. In each denominator stands the length of the vector in the numerator. Therefore, by Proposition 8.2, the v's will all be unit vectors, provided that the numerators are not zero. Consider $\mathbf{v}_k$. From the formula, it is a linear combination of $\mathbf{u}_k$ and $\mathbf{v}_1, \mathbf{v}_2, \ldots, \mathbf{v}_{k-1}$. By a simple induction it follows that the numerator in $\mathbf{v}_k$ is a linear combination of $\mathbf{u}_1, \mathbf{u}_2, \ldots, \mathbf{u}_k$, hence cannot be zero because of the assumed linear independence of the latter. Therefore the formulas above all make sense; their denominators cannot be zero. It is also clear that $\mathbf{u}_k$ is a linear combination of $\mathbf{v}_1, \ldots, \mathbf{v}_k$, showing that $\{\mathbf{u}_1, \ldots, \mathbf{u}_k\}$ and $\{\mathbf{v}_1, \ldots, \mathbf{v}_k\}$ span the same subspace of E, for any k. To show that the v's are orthonormal we use induction. We show that the set $\mathbf{v}_1, \mathbf{v}_2, \ldots, \mathbf{v}_k$ is orthonormal for any k (that is, any k not exceeding the number of $\mathbf{u}_i$ given to start with). For $k = 1$ the assertion is trivial. Suppose it holds for $k - 1$, so that $\mathbf{v}_1, \mathbf{v}_2, \ldots, \mathbf{v}_{k-1}$ are orthonormal. Denoting the denominator in the formula for $\mathbf{v}_k$ by a_k, we have

$$a_k\mathbf{v}_k = \mathbf{u}_k - c_1\mathbf{v}_1 - c_2\mathbf{v}_2 - \cdots - c_{k-1}\mathbf{v}_{k-1}$$

where $c_j = (\mathbf{u}_k, \mathbf{v}_j)$. Then, for $j < k$,

$$a_k(\mathbf{v}_k, \mathbf{v}_j) = (\mathbf{u}_k, \mathbf{v}_j) - c_1(\mathbf{v}_1, \mathbf{v}_j) - \cdots - c_{k-1}(\mathbf{v}_{k-1}, \mathbf{v}_j)$$

By assumption, the only nonzero term on the right, after the first, is

$$-c_j(\mathbf{v}_j, \mathbf{v}_j) = -c_j = -(\mathbf{u}_k, \mathbf{v}_j)$$

Hence $(a_k\mathbf{v}_k, \mathbf{v}_j) = 0$, and so $(\mathbf{v}_k, \mathbf{v}_j) = 0$ for $j < k$. As already noted, $(\mathbf{v}_k, \mathbf{v}_k) = 1$. Hence $\mathbf{v}_1, \ldots, \mathbf{v}_k$ form an orthonormal set, and by induction this is true for any k. Q.E.D.

REMARK. This procedure for obtaining an orthonormal set from any linearly independent set of vectors is called the *Schmidt orthonormalization process*.

As an immediate corollary we have the following theorem:

THEOREM 8.5 *If the euclidean vector space E has finite dimension, then E has an orthonormal base.*

Proof. One has only to apply the Schmidt process to any base for E.

Suppose then that $\dim E = n$, and let $\{\mathbf{e}_1, \ldots, \mathbf{e}_n\}$ be an orthonormal base. Let

$$\mathbf{x} = x^i \mathbf{e}_i \qquad \mathbf{y} = y^j \mathbf{e}_j$$

be two vectors in E. We have

$$(\mathbf{x}, \mathbf{y}) = (x^i \mathbf{e}_i, \mathbf{y}) = x^i (\mathbf{e}_i, \mathbf{y})$$

But

$$\begin{aligned}(\mathbf{e}_i, \mathbf{y}) = \overline{(\mathbf{y}, \mathbf{e}_i)} = \overline{(y^j \mathbf{e}_j, \mathbf{e}_i)} &= \overline{y^j (\mathbf{e}_j, \mathbf{e}_i)} \\ &= \bar{y}^j (\mathbf{e}_i, \mathbf{e}_j)\end{aligned}$$

Therefore,

8.3 $$(\mathbf{x}, \mathbf{y}) = x^1 \bar{y}^1 + \cdots + x^n \bar{y}^n$$

It follows that if E' is another euclidean vector space over the same field (**R** or **C**), and if $\mathbf{e}'_1, \ldots, \mathbf{e}'_n$ is an orthonormal base, then the mapping $T: E \to E'$ defined by

$$\mathbf{T}(x^i \mathbf{e}_i) = x^i \mathbf{e}'_i$$

is an isomorphism compatible with inner products. That is,

8.4 $$(x, y) = (T(x), T(y))$$

the right-hand side being the inner product in E' of the image vectors $\mathbf{T}(\mathbf{x})$, $\mathbf{T}(\mathbf{y})$. *We conclude that any two euclidean vector spaces of the same dimension and with the same field of scalars are isomorphic*, in the sense that there is an isomorphism from one to the other which preserves vector lengths and inner products.

THEOREM 8.6 *Let U be a finite-dimensional subspace of a euclidean vector space E. Then $E = U \oplus U^\perp$, the direct sum of U and its orthogonal complement.*

Proof. Let $\{\mathbf{e}_1, \ldots, \mathbf{e}_r\}$ be an orthonormal base for U (one exists, by Theorem 8.4). For any $\mathbf{x}$ in E set

8.5 $$\begin{aligned}\mathbf{x}' &= (\mathbf{x}, \mathbf{e}_1)\mathbf{e}_1 + \cdots + (\mathbf{x}, \mathbf{e}_r)\mathbf{e}_r \\ \mathbf{x}'' &= \mathbf{x} - \mathbf{x}'\end{aligned}$$

Then $\mathbf{x}'$ is in U, and

$$\begin{aligned}(\mathbf{x}'', \mathbf{e}_j) &= (\mathbf{x} - \mathbf{x}', \mathbf{e}_j) \\ &= (\mathbf{x}, \mathbf{e}_j) - (\mathbf{x}'\mathbf{e}_j) \\ &= (\mathbf{x}, \mathbf{e}_j) - \sum_{k=1}^{r} (\mathbf{x}, \mathbf{e}_k)\ (\mathbf{e}_k, \mathbf{e}_j) \\ &= (\mathbf{x}, \mathbf{e}_j) - (\mathbf{x}, \mathbf{e}_j)(\mathbf{e}_j, \mathbf{e}_j) = 0\end{aligned}$$

Therefore $\mathbf{x}''$ is orthogonal to $\mathbf{e}_1, \ldots, \mathbf{e}_r$, hence to every vector in U. That is, $\mathbf{x}''$ is in $U^\perp$. It follows that every $\mathbf{x}$ in E can be expressed as a sum of a vector in U and a vector in $U^\perp$. But U and $U^\perp$ have only the zero vector in common. For if $\mathbf{x}$ is in both U and $U^\perp$, it must be orthogonal to itself. That is, $(\mathbf{x}, \mathbf{x}) = 0$, or $|\mathbf{x}| = 0$; hence $\mathbf{x} = \mathbf{0}$. Therefore, by definition (see Sec. 5, Chap. 8) E is the direct sum of U and $U^\perp$. Q.E.D.

The theorem says that each element $\mathbf{x}$ of E can be expressed *uniquely* as a sum $\mathbf{x} = \mathbf{x}' + \mathbf{x}''$, with $\mathbf{x}'$ in U and $\mathbf{x}''$ in $U^\perp$. The element $\mathbf{x}'$ is called the *projection* of $\mathbf{x}$ on U. The element $\mathbf{x}''$ is called the *perpendicular* from $\mathbf{x}$ to U. Equation (8.5) gives explicit formulas. Since $(\mathbf{x}', \mathbf{x}'') = 0$, we have

$$\begin{aligned}(\mathbf{x}, \mathbf{x}) &= (\mathbf{x}' + \mathbf{x}'', \mathbf{x}' + \mathbf{x}'') \\ &= (\mathbf{x}', \mathbf{x}') + (\mathbf{x}', \mathbf{x}'') + \overline{(\mathbf{x}', \mathbf{x}'')} + (\mathbf{x}'', \mathbf{x}'') \\ &= (\mathbf{x}', \mathbf{x}') + (\mathbf{x}'', \mathbf{x}'')\end{aligned}$$

and so

8.6 $$|\mathbf{x}|^2 = |\mathbf{x}'|^2 + |\mathbf{x}''|^2$$

Furthermore, $\mathbf{x}'$ *is the element of* U *that is nearest to* $\mathbf{x}$. For if $\mathbf{y}$ is any element of U, then by the law of cosines,

$$\begin{aligned}|\mathbf{x} - \mathbf{y}|^2 &= |(\mathbf{x} - \mathbf{x}') + (\mathbf{x}' - \mathbf{y})|^2 \\ &= |\mathbf{x} - \mathbf{x}'|^2 + |\mathbf{x}' - \mathbf{y}|^2 + 2|\mathbf{x} - \mathbf{x}'|\,|\mathbf{x}' - \mathbf{y}| \cos \measuredangle(\mathbf{x} - \mathbf{x}', \mathbf{x}' - \mathbf{y}) \\ &= |\mathbf{x} - \mathbf{x}'|^2 + |\mathbf{x}' - \mathbf{y}|^2\end{aligned}$$

since $\cos \measuredangle(\mathbf{x} - \mathbf{x}', \mathbf{x}' - \mathbf{y}) = 0$ ($\mathbf{x} - \mathbf{x}'$ is in $U^\perp$ and $\mathbf{x}' - \mathbf{y}$ is in U).

Hence, $|\mathbf{x} - \mathbf{y}|^2 \geq |\mathbf{x} - \mathbf{x}'|^2$ and so $|\mathbf{x} - \mathbf{y}| \geq |\mathbf{x} - \mathbf{x}'|$.

EXERCISES

Here K denotes either the real or complex field, and $\mathbf{e}_1, \ldots, \mathbf{e}_n$ denote the columns of the $n \times n$ unit matrix. K^n is to be given its standard inner product.

1. Show that $\{\mathbf{e}_1, \ldots, \mathbf{e}_n\}$ is an orthonormal base.

2. Taking $n = 3$, let $B = \{\mathbf{e}_1 + \mathbf{e}_2 + \mathbf{e}_3, \mathbf{e}_2 + \mathbf{e}_3, \mathbf{e}_3\}$. Compute the base that is obtained from B by the Schmidt orthonormalization process.

3. Solve Exercise 2 for the base $B = \{5\mathbf{e}_1, 4\mathbf{e}_1 + 3\mathbf{e}_2, 2\mathbf{e}_1 + 3\mathbf{e}_2 + 17\mathbf{e}_3\}$.

4. Let $n = 3$ and $K = \mathbf{R}$. Find the element $\mathbf{x}$ in the plane spanned by

$$\begin{pmatrix}1\\0\\0\end{pmatrix} \quad \text{and} \quad \begin{pmatrix}3\\2\\1\end{pmatrix}$$

that is nearest to the element $\begin{pmatrix}3\\2\\1\end{pmatrix}$. Compute the distance between them.

5. In $\mathbf{R}_3$ find a nonzero vector which is perpendicular to both (a_1, a_2, a_3) and (b_1, b_2, b_3). Hint: Expand the following two determinants by their first columns:

$$\begin{vmatrix} a_1 & a_1 & b_1 \\ a_2 & a_2 & b_2 \\ a_3 & a_3 & b_3 \end{vmatrix} \quad \text{and} \quad \begin{vmatrix} b_1 & a_1 & b_1 \\ b_2 & a_2 & b_2 \\ b_3 & a_3 & b_3 \end{vmatrix}$$

6. In $\mathbf{R}_3$, prove that the shortest distance from an element (u, v, w) to the plane with equation $ax + by + cz = 0$ is given by

$$\frac{au + bv + cw}{\sqrt{a^2 + b^2 + c^2}}$$

7. Let $B = \{\mathbf{u}_1, \ldots, \mathbf{u}_n\}$ be an orthonormal base in an n-dimensional euclidean space, and let $B' = \{\mathbf{v}_1, \ldots, \mathbf{v}_n\}$ be another base. Prove that B' is orthonormal if and only if the matrix from B to B$'$ is unitary.

8. Prove that if the column vectors of an $n \times n$ matrix form an orthonormal set in K^n, then so do the row vectors, in K_n.

9. Fourier series, Bessel's inequality

Here we shall look briefly into some questions of importance in connection with infinite-dimensional spaces.

First of all, let E be any euclidean vector space, and let $\mathbf{u}_1$, $\mathbf{u}_2$, $\mathbf{u}_3$, etc., be an orthonormal set of vectors in E. As usual we denote the inner product in E by $(\mathbf{x}, \mathbf{y})$. For an $\mathbf{x}$ in E the numbers

$$x_i = (\mathbf{x}, \mathbf{u}_i)$$

are often called the *Fourier coefficients* of $\mathbf{x}$ relative to the set $\{\mathbf{u}_1, \mathbf{u}_2, \ldots\}$. The reason for this terminology will be explained presently. We first state the following theorem.

THEOREM 9.1 *The quantity* $|\mathbf{x} - (c_1\mathbf{u}_1 + \cdots + c_n\mathbf{u}_n)|$ has its smallest value when $c_1, \ldots, c_n$ *are the Fourier coefficients of* $\mathbf{x}$: $c_i = (\mathbf{x}, \mathbf{u}_i)$.

Proof. This has been proved in the previous section. For let U be the subspace of E spanned by $\mathbf{u}_1, \ldots, \mathbf{u}_n$. Then $E = U \oplus U^\perp$. The vector $\mathbf{y} = c_1\mathbf{u}_1 + \cdots + c_n\mathbf{u}_n$ is in U for any scalars c_i, of course, and we are seeking to determine the c_i in such a way as to minimize the distance $|\mathbf{x} - \mathbf{y}|$. We saw in Sec. 8 that this is minimum if and only if $\mathbf{y} = (\mathbf{x}, \mathbf{u}_1) \cdot \mathbf{u}_1 + \cdots + (\mathbf{x}, \mathbf{u}_n) \cdot \mathbf{u}_n$. Q.E.D.

THEOREM 9.2 **(Bessel's inequality)** *The Fourier coefficients* x_i *of* $\mathbf{x}$ *satisfy*

$$\sum_{i=1}^{n} |x_i|^2 \leq |\mathbf{x}|^2$$

Proof. We have clearly

$$(\mathbf{x} - x_1\mathbf{u}_1 - \cdots - x_n\mathbf{u}_n, \mathbf{x} - x_1\mathbf{u}_1 - \cdots - x_n\mathbf{u}_n) \geq 0$$

Expanding out the left side, we get

$$(\mathbf{x}, \mathbf{x}) - \sum_1^n x_i (\mathbf{u}_i, \mathbf{x}) - \sum_1^n \bar{x}_i (\mathbf{x}, \mathbf{u}_i) + \sum_1^n x_i\bar{x}_j (\mathbf{u}_i, \mathbf{u}_j) \geq 0$$

Now $(\mathbf{u}_i, \mathbf{x}) = \overline{(\mathbf{x}, \mathbf{u}_i)} = x_i$. Using the orthonormal property of the $\mathbf{u}_i$, our expression above becomes

$$(\mathbf{x}, \mathbf{x}) - \sum_1^n x_i\bar{x}_i - \sum_1^n \bar{x}_i x_i + \sum_1^n x_i\bar{x}_i \geq 0$$

or

$$(\mathbf{x}, \mathbf{x}) \geq \sum_1^n |x_i|^2$$

This holds for any value of n, from which the assertion follows. Q.E.D.

Now let F denote the set of all continuous real-valued functions on the interval $-\pi \leq x \leq \pi$ of real numbers. We make F into a vector space over **R** by defining addition and scalar multiplication in the usual way. That is, $(f + g)(x) = f(x) + g(x)$ and $(cf)(x) = c \cdot f(x)$ for any f, g in F and c in **R**. Furthermore we make F into a euclidean vector space by introducing the following symmetric bilinear form on F:

9.1 $$(f, g) = \frac{1}{\pi} \int_{-\pi}^{\pi} f(x) \cdot g(x)\, dx$$

The associated quadratic function (f, f) is positive definite, since

$$\frac{1}{\pi} \int_{-\pi}^{\pi} f(x)^2\, dx > 0$$

for any continuous function except the constant function 0. Therefore the form (f, g) makes F into a euclidean space. The functions in the set

$$B = \left\{\frac{1}{\sqrt{2}}, \cos x, \sin x, \cos 2x, \sin 2x, \ldots, \cos nx, \sin nx, \ldots\right\}$$

are all in F, and from the rules of integral calculus it is quickly verified that they form an orthonormal set.

Let U_n denote the subspace of F spanned by $B_n = \left\{\frac{1}{\sqrt{2}}, \cos x, \sin x, \ldots, \right.$ $\left.\cos nx, \sin nx\right\}$. Thus $\dim U = 2n + 1$. By Theorem 9.1 the element f_n of U_n which is *nearest* to a given element f of F, that is, for which the distance

$$\begin{aligned}|f - f_n| &= \sqrt{(f - f_n, f - f_n)} \\ &= \sqrt{\frac{1}{\pi} \int_{-\pi}^{\pi} (f - f_n)^2\, dx}\end{aligned}$$

is a minimum, is the function

9.2 $$f_n = a_0 \cdot \frac{1}{\sqrt{2}} + a_1 \cos x + b_1 \sin x + \cdots + a_n \cos nx + b_n \sin nx$$

where the a's and b's are the Fourier coefficients of f. That is,

9.3 $$\begin{aligned} a_0 &= \left(f, \frac{1}{\sqrt{2}}\right) = \frac{1}{\pi}\int_{-\pi}^{\pi} \frac{1}{\sqrt{2}} f(x)\, dx \\ a_k &= (f, \cos kx) = \frac{1}{\pi}\int_{-\pi}^{\pi} f(x) \cos kx\, dx \\ b_k &= (f, \sin kx) = \frac{1}{\pi}\int_{-\pi}^{\pi} f(x) \sin kx\, dx \end{aligned}$$

Bessel's inequality says that

9.4 $$|f|^2 = \frac{1}{\pi}\int_{-\pi}^{\pi} f(x)^2\, dx \geq \sum_{k=0}^{\infty} a_k^2 + \sum_{k=1}^{\infty} b_k^2$$

Now in general, a sequence of elements $\mathbf{v}_1$, $\mathbf{v}_2$, $\mathbf{v}_3$, etc., in a euclidean vector space E is called a *Cauchy sequence*† if for any positive real number e there is an integer p such that

$$|\mathbf{v}_n - \mathbf{v}_m| < e \qquad \text{for all } m,\ n > p$$

A sequence $\mathbf{v}_1, \mathbf{v}_2, \mathbf{v}_2, \ldots$ in E is said to have an element $\mathbf{v}$ of E as a *limit* if for any positive number e there is an integer p such that $|\mathbf{v} - \mathbf{v}_n| < e$ for all $n > p$. The sequence is said to converge to $\mathbf{v}$. It is easily shown that any sequence in E which has a limit must be a Cauchy sequence, and the limit is unique. The space E is said to be *complete* if every Cauchy sequence in E has a limit.

Let us apply these remarks to our function space F. First of all, it is not hard to show that F is *not* a complete space. However, if f is an element of F, and if f_n is the function (9.2), then it is a standard result that the sequence $f_0, f_1, f_2, \ldots,$ $f_n, \ldots$ is a Cauchy sequence in F having f as its limit. Under certain circumstances (for example, if f is continuously differentiable) it is possible to write

$$f(x) = a_0 + \sum_{n=1}^{\infty} a_n \cos nx + b_n \sin nx$$

the infinite series on the right converging in the sense defined in Chap. 4. The series is called the *Fourier series* for f. The f_n above are simply the partial sums of the Fourier series.

Without entering into details we mention that F can be "completed." That is, by allowing functions f from a more extensive class, one obtains a complete euclidean vector space H containing F as a subspace. The space H in question is

† Compare this definition of a Cauchy sequence with those in Chaps. 4, 5. Note that "distance" is the determining factor here.

an example of a *Hilbert space*. Such euclidean vector spaces are of great importance in many applications of mathematics, for example to quantum theory.

Let G denote the set of continuous real-valued functions on the interval $-1 \leq x \leq 1$. We can make G into a euclidean vector space, just as with F above, by defining the inner product of two elements of G by

$$(f, g) = \int_{-1}^{1} f(x)g(x)\, dx$$

By applying the Schmidt orthonormalization process to the functions

9.5 $\quad 1, x, x^2, x^3, \ldots, x^n, \ldots$

one obtains a sequence of polynomials $P_0(x), P_1(x), P_2(x), \ldots$ which play a role in G analogous to that of the system B in F. The $P_n(x)$, apart from some numerical factors, are the *Legendre polynomials*.

EXERCISES

1. Prove that a finite-dimensional euclidean space is complete.
2. Prove that if a sequence of elements in a euclidean space has a limit, then it is a Cauchy sequence.
3. Let a_0, a_1, b_1, a_2, b_2, etc., be real numbers, and define f_n by the formula (9.2). Prove that the f_n form a Cauchy sequence if and only if the series $\sum_{k=1}^{\infty} (a_k^2 + b_k^2)$ converges.
4. Compute the first four polynomials P_0, P_1, P_2, P_3 described above. Prove that $P_n(x)$ is a polynomial of degree n for every $n = 0, 1, 2$, etc.

10. The eigenvalues of a Hermitian matrix

Let $\mathbf{a} = (a_{ij})$ be an $n \times n$ Hermitian matrix. We recall that this means that

10.1 $\quad a_{ji} = \bar{a}_{ij} \qquad (i, j = 1, \ldots, n)$

In particular, $a_{ii} = \bar{a}_{ii}$, so the diagonal elements are real. Equation (10.1) can be written as ${}^t\mathbf{a} = \bar{\mathbf{a}}$.

THEOREM 10.1 *The eigenvalues of a Hermitian matrix are real.*

Proof. Let p be an eigenvalue of $\mathbf{a}$. That is, p is a root of the polynomial $\varphi(t) = \det(t\mathbf{I} - \mathbf{a})$. By assumption, $\det(p\mathbf{I} - \mathbf{a}) = 0$, and so there is a nonzero vector $\mathbf{u}$ in $\mathbf{C}^n$ such that $(p\mathbf{I} - \mathbf{a})\mathbf{u} = \mathbf{0}$, or

10.2 $\quad \mathbf{au} = p\mathbf{u}$

(See corollary, Theorem 5.3, Chap. 11). Now for any $\mathbf{x}, \mathbf{y}$ in $\mathbf{C}^n$ define

$$A(\mathbf{x}, \mathbf{y}) = {}^t\bar{\mathbf{y}}\mathbf{a}\mathbf{x} = \sum_{j,k=1}^{n} a_{jk}\bar{y}^j x^k$$

This is a Hermitian form on $\mathbf{C}^n$, as is quickly verified, using (10.1). Therefore $A(\mathbf{x}, \mathbf{x})$ is real. Now multiply (10.2) on the left by the row vector ${}^t\bar{\mathbf{u}}$, getting

$$ {}^t\bar{\mathbf{u}}\mathbf{a}\mathbf{u} = p \cdot {}^t\bar{\mathbf{u}}\mathbf{u} $$

or

$$ A(\mathbf{u}, \mathbf{u}) = p \cdot {}^t\bar{\mathbf{u}}\mathbf{u} = p \cdot \sum_{i=1}^{n} \bar{u}^j u^j = p \sum_{i=1}^{n} |u^j|^2 $$

or

10.3 $$ p = \frac{A(\mathbf{u}, \mathbf{u})}{|\mathbf{u}|^2} $$

This shows that p is real. Q.E.D.

COROLLARY *The eigenvalues of a real symmetric $n \times n$ matrix are real numbers.*

For such a matrix is a special case of a Hermitian matrix.

We recall that an endomorphism $\mathbf{T}$ of a euclidean vector space E is called *self-adjoint* if

10.4 $$ (\mathbf{T}\mathbf{x}, \mathbf{y}) = (\mathbf{x}, \mathbf{T}\mathbf{y}) $$

for all $\mathbf{x}$, $\mathbf{y}$ in E. Assume now that E has dimension n, and let $B = \{\mathbf{e}_1, \ldots, \mathbf{e}_n\}$ be an orthonormal base in E. Let $\mathbf{a} = (a^j{}_i)$ be the matrix of $\mathbf{T}$ relative to the base B. Then by definition $\mathbf{T}(\mathbf{e}_i) = a^j{}_i\mathbf{e}_j$. By (8.2) we have

10.5 $$ a^j{}_i = (\mathbf{T}\mathbf{e}_i, \mathbf{e}_j) $$

Similarly,

$$ \begin{aligned} a^i{}_j &= (\mathbf{T}\mathbf{e}_j, \mathbf{e}_i) \\ &= \overline{(\mathbf{e}_i, \mathbf{T}\mathbf{e}_j)} && \text{using } (\mathbf{y}, \mathbf{x}) = \overline{(\mathbf{x}, \mathbf{y})} \\ &= \overline{(\mathbf{T}\mathbf{e}_i, \mathbf{e}_j)} && \text{by (10.4)} \\ &= \bar{a}^j{}_i && \text{by (10.5)} \end{aligned} $$

Hence *the matrix of a self-adjoint endomorphism relative to an orthonormal base is a Hermitian matrix.*

THEOREM 10.2 *Let $\mathbf{T}$ be a self-adjoint linear mapping of a finite-dimensional euclidean vector space E over the field of real or of complex numbers. Then there is an orthonormal base in E consisting entirely of eigenvectors of $\mathbf{T}$. Moreover, the eigenvalues of $\mathbf{T}$ are real.*

Proof. According to Definitions 5.1, 5.2, Chap. 11, the eigenvalues of $\mathbf{T}$ are the same as the eigenvalues of the matrix of $\mathbf{T}$ relative to any base in E. As we have just seen, the matrix of $\mathbf{T}$ relative to an orthonormal base is Hermitian, therefore has real eigenvalues, by Theorem 10.1. This proves the last assertion of the theorem.

To prove the rest of the theorem, let $p_1, p_2, \ldots, p_r$ be the *distinct* eigenvalues of $\mathbf{T}$. Denoting by $\mathbf{I}$ the identity mapping of E, the operator $p_j\mathbf{I}$ also maps E to itself, whether the field of scalars is $\mathbf{R}$ or $\mathbf{C}$, since p_j is real. Let V_j denote the kernel of the operator $p_j\mathbf{I} - \mathbf{T}$. That is V_j consists of all vectors $\mathbf{x}$ such that $(p_j\mathbf{I} - \mathbf{T})(\mathbf{x}) = \mathbf{0}$, or $\mathbf{T}(\mathbf{x}) = p_j\mathbf{x}$. In other words, V_j consists of all eigenvectors belonging to the eigenvalue p_j; V_j is a subspace of E. First of all we show that

10.6 *V_j and V_k are orthogonal subspaces if $j \neq k$.*

We must show that the inner product $(\mathbf{x}, \mathbf{y})$ is zero if $\mathbf{x}$ is in V_j and $\mathbf{y}$ is in V_k. This is very easy. First of all, by definition we have $\mathbf{Tx} = p_j\mathbf{x}$ and $\mathbf{Ty} = p_k\mathbf{y}$, and $p_j \neq p_k$. By (10.4),

$$(\mathbf{Tx}, \mathbf{y}) = (\mathbf{x}, \mathbf{Ty})$$

whence

$$(p_j\mathbf{x}, \mathbf{y}) = (\mathbf{x}, p_k\mathbf{y})$$

or

$$p_j(\mathbf{x}, \mathbf{y}) = p_k(\mathbf{x}, \mathbf{y})$$

where on the right we have used the fact that p_k is real. The last equation can be written

$$(p_j - p_k)(\mathbf{x}, \mathbf{y}) = 0$$

and so

$$(\mathbf{x}, \mathbf{y}) = 0$$

Now set

10.7 $$V = V_1 + \cdots + V_r$$

That is, V consists of all vectors $\mathbf{v}$ in E such that $\mathbf{v}$ can be expressed as a sum

10.8 $$\mathbf{v} = \mathbf{v}_1 + \cdots + \mathbf{v}_r \qquad \text{with } \mathbf{v}_j \text{ in } V_j \qquad (j = 1, \ldots, r)$$

It is clear that V is a subspace of E. Furthermore it is $\mathbf{T}$-stable. For applying $\mathbf{T}$ to (10.8) gives us

$$\mathbf{T}(\mathbf{v}) = \mathbf{T}(\mathbf{v}_1) + \cdots + \mathbf{T}(\mathbf{v}_r) = p_1\mathbf{v}_1 + \cdots + p_r\mathbf{v}_r$$

Since each $p_i\mathbf{v}_i$ is in V_i, it follows that $\mathbf{T}(\mathbf{v})$ is in V.

Now let E' denote the orthogonal complement of V. By Theorem 8.6, E is the direct sum

10.9 $$E = V \oplus E'$$

From this it follows that E' is also **T**-stable. For let **w** be an element of E'. By definition, $(\mathbf{v}, \mathbf{w}) = 0$ for every **v** in V. By (10.4), $(\mathbf{v}, \mathbf{Tw}) = (\mathbf{Tv}, \mathbf{w})$. Since **Tv** is in V, we have $(\mathbf{Tv}, \mathbf{w}) = 0$, whence $(\mathbf{v}, \mathbf{Tw}) = 0$, showing that **Tw** is orthogonal to all vectors in V, hence is in E'.

We next show that E' consists of the zero vector alone. For let $\mathbf{T}'$ denote the restriction of **T** to E'. If $\dim E' > 0$, then $\mathbf{T}'$ must have at least one eigenvalue q; and accordingly there is a nonzero vector **w** in E' such that $\mathbf{T}'\mathbf{w} = q\mathbf{w}$. But $\mathbf{T}'$ is the same as **T** on E', and so $\mathbf{Tw} = q\mathbf{w}$. Hence, **w** is an eigenvector for **T**, and so q is an eigenvalue for **T**, therefore must be the same as one of the p_j, say p_1. But then **w** is in V_1, hence in V, which contradicts (10.9). It follows that $\dim E'$ cannot be greater than zero.

Hence, from (10.9) and (10.7) we now have

10.10 $$E = V_1 + \cdots + V_r$$

Finally, let B_j be an orthonormal base for $V_j (j = 1, \ldots, r)$, and let $B = \{B_1, \ldots, B_r\}$ be the combined set of vectors obtained by putting all the B_j together. From (10.6) it is immediate that B is an orthonormal set; from (10.10), B must span E; from Proposition 8.1, the vectors in B are linearly independent. Therefore B is an orthonormal base for E, and each vector in B is an eigenvector of **T** since each vector of B is in one of the V_j. Q.E.D.

COROLLARY 1 *Let $\varphi(t)$ be the characteristic polynomial of* **T**, *and let*

10.11 $$\varphi(t) = (t - p_1)^{n_1}(t - p_2)^{n_2} \cdots (t - p_r)^{n_r}$$

be its factorization, where $p_1, p_2, \ldots, p_r$ are the distinct eigenvalues of **T**. *Then E is the direct sum of the subspaces $V_j = \operatorname{Ker}(p_j\mathbf{I} - \mathbf{T})$, $j = 1, \ldots, r$; and $\dim V_j = n_j$.*

Proof. The fact that $E = V_1 \oplus \cdots \oplus V_r$ follows at once from the observation that the joint base $B = \{B_1, \ldots, B_r\}$ is a base for E, where B_j is a base for $V_j (j = 1, \ldots, r)$. We have then $\dim E = \dim V_1 + \cdots + \dim V_r$ and also $\dim E = n_1 + \cdots + n_r$. But $\dim V_j \leq n_j$, by the corollary to Theorem 5.6, Chap. 11. From these relations it is clear that $\dim V_j = n_j$. Q.E.D.

COROLLARY 2 *Let* **a** *be a Hermitian $n \times n$ matrix. Then there is a unitary matrix* **c** *such that*

$$\mathbf{c}^{-1}\mathbf{a}\mathbf{c} = \mathbf{p}$$

where **p** *is a diagonal matrix with real coefficients.*

Proof. Let $\mathbf{T}: \mathbf{C}^n \to \mathbf{C}^n$ be the mapping that sends a column vector **x** into **ax**, $\mathbf{C}^n$ being equipped with its standard inner product

10.12 $$(\mathbf{x}, \mathbf{y}) = x^1\bar{y}^1 + \cdots + x^n\bar{y}^n$$

Then $\mathbf{a}$ is the matrix of $\mathbf{T}$ relative to the canonical base $B_0 = \{\mathbf{e}_1, \ldots, \mathbf{e}_n\}$, where $\mathbf{e}_j$ denotes the jth column of the $n \times n$ unit matrix; and $\mathbf{T}$ is self-adjoint for the inner product (10.12). Furthermore, B_0 is an orthonormal base in $\mathbf{C}^n$ for (10.12). By Theorem 10.2, there is an orthonormal base $B = \{\mathbf{u}_1, \ldots, \mathbf{u}_n\}$ in $\mathbf{C}^n$ such that each $\mathbf{u}_i$ is an eigenvector of $\mathbf{T}$. The matrix of $\mathbf{T}$ relative to B is therefore a diagonal matrix $\mathbf{p}$ with real entries. Let $\mathbf{c}$ be the matrix from B_0 to B. Then $\mathbf{p} = \mathbf{c}^{-1}\mathbf{a}\mathbf{c}$. Q.E.D.

REMARK 1. Applying (6.20) we see that the equation $\mathbf{c}^{-1}\mathbf{a}\mathbf{c} = \mathbf{p}$ can also be written ${}^t\bar{\mathbf{c}}\mathbf{a}\mathbf{c} = \mathbf{p}$. Furthermore, if $\mathbf{a}$ happens to be real, hence symmetric, we can replace $\mathbf{C}^n$ in the argument above by $\mathbf{R}^n$, and it is then clear that the matrix $\mathbf{c}$ will be *real*, hence orthogonal.

REMARK 2. It should be noted that the column vectors of the matrix $\mathbf{c}$ form an orthonormal set of eigenvectors for the Hermitian matrix $\mathbf{a}$.

11. Simultaneous diagonalization of two Hermitian forms

From the results of the preceding section we can easily deduce an important theorem concerning Hermitian forms. We begin with an auxiliary result.

THEOREM 11.1 *Let F and H be Hermitian forms on a finite-dimensional vector space V over $\mathbf{R}$ or $\mathbf{C}$, with H nondegenerate. Then there exists a linear transformation $\mathbf{T}$ of V to itself such that $F(\mathbf{x}, \mathbf{y}) = H(\mathbf{T}\mathbf{x}, \mathbf{y})$ for all $\mathbf{x}$ and $\mathbf{y}$. Furthermore, $\mathbf{T}$ is self-adjoint for H; that is,*

$$H(\mathbf{T}\mathbf{x}, \mathbf{y}) = H(\mathbf{x}, \mathbf{T}\mathbf{y})$$

Proof. Let $B = \{\mathbf{u}_1, \ldots, \mathbf{u}_n\}$ be a base in V. The matrices of F and H relative to B are then given by

11.1 $$a_{ij} = F(\mathbf{u}_i, \mathbf{u}_j) \qquad \text{and} \qquad b_{ij} = H(\mathbf{u}_i, \mathbf{u}_j)$$

as in Sec. 6. By assumption, the matrix $\mathbf{b} = (b_{ij})$ is nonsingular. That is, $\det \mathbf{b} \neq 0$. Write $\mathbf{a} = (a_{ij})$ for the matrix of F, and define $\mathbf{c}$ by $\mathbf{c} = {}^t(\mathbf{a}\mathbf{b}^{-1})$, or

$$\mathbf{a} = {}^t\mathbf{c}\mathbf{b}$$

If we write the elements of $\mathbf{c}$ as $c^k{}_i$, then according to our row and column conventions the last equation is the same as

11.2 $$a_{ij} = c^k{}_i b_{kj}$$

Define $\mathbf{T}$ to be the linear transformation such that

$$\mathbf{T}\mathbf{u}_i = c^k{}_i \mathbf{u}_k$$

Then, for $\mathbf{x} = x^i\mathbf{u}_i$ and $\mathbf{y} = y^i\mathbf{u}_j$ we have

$$\begin{aligned} H(\mathbf{Tx}, \mathbf{y}) &= H(x^i c^k{}_i \mathbf{u}_k, y^j \mathbf{u}_j) \\ &= x^i c^k{}_i \bar{y}^j \cdot H(\mathbf{u}_k, \mathbf{u}_j) \\ &= x^i c^k{}_i b_{kj} \bar{y}^j = x^i a_{ij} \bar{y}^j = F(\mathbf{x}, \mathbf{y}) \end{aligned}$$

using the Hermitian property of H, along with (11.1) and (11.2). Finally, for any $\mathbf{x}$, $\mathbf{y}$, $H(\mathbf{x}, \mathbf{Ty}) = \overline{H(\mathbf{Ty}, \mathbf{x})} = \overline{F(\mathbf{y}, \mathbf{x})} = F(\mathbf{x}, \mathbf{y}) = H(\mathbf{Tx}, \mathbf{y})$, showing that $\mathbf{T}$ is self-adjoint for H. Q.E.D.

THEOREM 11.2 (Principal-axis theorem) *Let F and H be Hermitian forms on a finite-dimensional vector space V over* **R** *or* **C**, *with H positive definite. Then there is a base in V for which the matrices of both F and H are diagonal matrices with real entries, and in fact such a base can be found for which the matrix of H is the unit matrix.*

Proof. V with the form H is a euclidean vector space, since H is a positive definite Hermitian form. Let $\mathbf{T}: V \to V$ be the linear mapping of the preceding theorem, so that $F(\mathbf{x}, \mathbf{y}) = H(\mathbf{Tx}, \mathbf{y})$. Since $\mathbf{T}$ is self-adjoint, it follows from Theorem 10.2 that there is an *orthonormal* base $B = \{\mathbf{u}_1, \ldots, \mathbf{u}_n\}$ in V consisting entirely of eigenvectors of $\mathbf{T}$, say $\mathbf{Tu}_i = p_i \mathbf{u}_i$ $(i = 1, \ldots, n)$. For the matrix of H relative to B we have

$$H(\mathbf{u}_i, \mathbf{u}_j) = \delta_{ij} = \begin{cases} 1 & \text{if } i = j \\ 0 & \text{if } i \neq j \end{cases}$$

since B is orthonormal. For the matrix of F we get

$$\begin{aligned} F(\mathbf{u}_i, \mathbf{u}_j) &= H(\mathbf{Tu}_i, \mathbf{u}_j) \\ &= H(p_i \mathbf{u}_i, \mathbf{u}_j) \\ &= p_i H(\mathbf{u}_i, \mathbf{u}_j) = p_i \delta_{ij} \end{aligned}$$

Hence the matrix of H relative to B is the unit matrix $\mathbf{I} = (\delta_{ij})$, and the matrix of F relative to B is the diagonal matrix whose entries are the eigenvalues $p_1, \ldots, p_n$ of $\mathbf{T}$, necessarily real numbers. Q.E.D.

For the base B just described, if $\mathbf{x} = x^i \mathbf{u}_i$ and $\mathbf{y} = y^j \mathbf{u}_j$, we have $H(\mathbf{x}, \mathbf{y}) = H(x^i \mathbf{u}_i, y^j \mathbf{u}_j) = x^i \bar{y}^j H(\mathbf{u}_i, \mathbf{u}_j) = \delta_{ij} x^i \bar{y}^j$ or

11.3 $$H(x, y) = x^1 \bar{y}^1 + \cdots + x^n \bar{y}^n$$

Similarly,

11.4 $$F(x, y) = p_1 x^1 \bar{y}^1 + \cdots + p_n x^n \bar{y}^n$$

To illustrate the geometrical meaning of Theorem 11.2, consider the vector space $\mathbf{R}_n$ of real row vectors. As we have seen in Sec. 4, a *quadratic form* on Q is a mapping $\mathbf{R}_n \to \mathbf{R}$ given by an expression

11.5 $$Q(\mathbf{x}) = \sum_{i,j=1}^{n} a_{ij} x_i x_j$$

where $\mathbf{x} = (x_1, \ldots, x_n)$ and where $\mathbf{a} = (a_{ij})$ is a symmetric real matrix. With Q is associated the symmetric bilinear form

11.6 $$F(\mathbf{x},\mathbf{y}) = \sum_{i,j=1}^{n} a_{ij}x_iy_j$$

Introduce the standard inner product

11.7 $$(\mathbf{x}, \mathbf{y}) = \sum_{i=1}^{n} x_iy_i$$

From the results of Sec. 5 we know that there is a base in $\mathbf{R}_n$ for which (11.6) reduces to a diagonal form (see Fig. 1). Theorem 11.2 adds the information that

Figure 1 The locus of the equation $Q = 1$ with Q the quadratic form (11.5) is called a *quadric* surface. One can choose orthogonal coordinate axes along principal axes so as to reduce the equation of a quadric surface to

$$\frac{x_1^2}{a_1^2} \pm \frac{x_2^2}{a_2^2} \pm \cdots \pm \frac{x_n^2}{a_n^2} = 1$$

(*A*) Ellipsoid: $\frac{x_1^2}{a_1^2} + \frac{x_2^2}{a_2^2} + \frac{x_3^2}{a_3^2} = 1$

(*B*) One-sheeted hyperboloid: $\frac{x_1^2}{a_1^2} + \frac{x_2^2}{a_2^2} - \frac{x_3^2}{a_3^2} = 1$

(*C*) Two-sheeted hyperboloid: $\frac{x_1^2}{a_1^2} - \frac{x_2^2}{a_2^2} - \frac{x_3^2}{a_3^2} = 1$

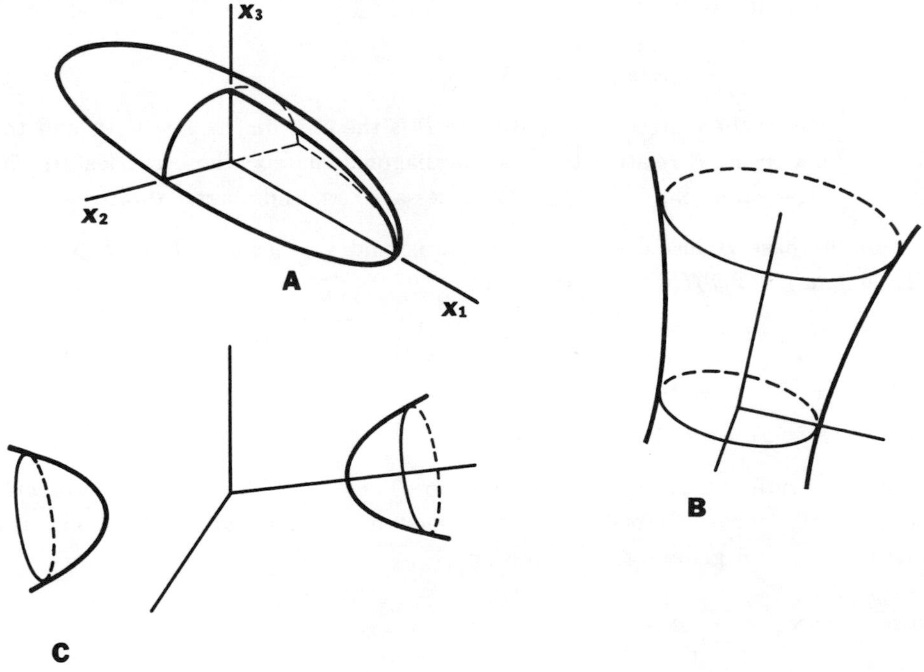

such a base can be found which is orthonormal. If $B = \{\mathbf{u}_1, \ldots, \mathbf{u}_n\}$ is a base with this property, and if we denote the components of a vector $\mathbf{x} = (x_1, \ldots, x_n)$ relative to B by $x_1', \ldots, x_n'$, so that $\mathbf{x} = x_1'\mathbf{u}_1 + \cdots + y_n'\mathbf{u}_n$, then (11.6) reduces to the form (11.4), and

$$Q(\mathbf{x}) = p_i x_1'^2 + \cdots + p_n x_n'^2$$

Since the base is orthonormal, we have

$$|\mathbf{x}|^2 = x_1^2 + \cdots + x_n^2 = x_1'^2 + \cdots + x_n'^2$$

Let us consider the locus defined by $Q(\mathbf{x}) = 1$ for the case $n = 3$. Then our equation can be written

$$Q(\mathbf{x}) = p_1 x_1'^2 + p_2 x_2'^2 + p_3 x_3'^2 = 1$$

For purposes of illustration suppose that the p_i are positive (so that Q is positive definite). We can then write $p_i = 1/a_i^2$, where a_i is a positive real number, and our equation becomes

$$\left(\frac{x_1'}{a_1}\right)^2 + \left(\frac{x_2'}{a_2}\right)^2 + \left(\frac{x_3'}{a_3}\right)^2 = 1$$

This is the equation of an ellipsoid, with semi-axes equal to a_1, a_2, a_3. The base vectors $\mathbf{u}_1$, $\mathbf{u}_2$, $\mathbf{u}_3$ give the directions of the *principal axes* of the ellipsoid. (If the three eigenvalues p_1, p_2, p_3 are different, then the principal axes are uniquely determined. If two or more of them coincide, then that is no longer the case. For example, if they are all equal, then our equation above is the equation of a sphere.) Observe that the line in $\mathbf{R}_3$ determined by the vector $\mathbf{u}_1$ is the same as the locus $x_2' = 0$, $x_3' = 0$. The same is true for the other two axes of the ellipsoid.

EXERCISES

1. Let Q be the quadratic form on $\mathbf{R}_3$ defined by (11.5), with matrix

$$\begin{pmatrix} 1 & 2 & 0 \\ 2 & 1 & -3 \\ 0 & -3 & 2 \end{pmatrix}$$

Describe the locus $Q(\mathbf{x}) = 1$ in $\mathbf{R}_3$.

2. Let $\mathbf{a}$ be a symmetric $n \times n$ matrix with real coefficients. Let $\mathbf{u}_1, \ldots, \mathbf{u}_n$ be a set of orthonormal eigenvectors of $\mathbf{a}$ (why does such a set exist?), and let $\mathbf{q} = (\mathbf{u}_1, \ldots, \mathbf{u}_n)$ be the matrix having these vectors as its columns. Prove that $\mathbf{q}$ is an orthogonal matrix and that ${}^t\mathbf{qaq}$ is a diagonal matrix whose entries are the eigenvalues of $\mathbf{a}$. (The matrix $\mathbf{q}$ is sometimes called the *modal* matrix of $\mathbf{a}$.)

***3.** Let $\mathbf{a}$ be as in the preceding exercise. Show that the largest eigenvalue of $\mathbf{a}$ is equal to the greatest value of ${}^t\mathbf{xax}$ for all *unit* vectors $\mathbf{x}$ in $\mathbf{R}^n$.

12. Unitary matrices

We mention here a few useful facts concerning unitary matrices. Recall first that a matrix $\mathbf{a}$ with complex coefficients is called unitary if

12.1 $\quad {}^t\bar{\mathbf{a}} = \mathbf{a}^{-1}$

(A real matrix with this property, that is, ${}^t\mathbf{a} = \mathbf{a}^{-1}$, is called *orthogonal.*)

By a discussion which closely parallels the proofs of Theorems 10.1 and 10.2 one can easily demonstrate the following facts:

12.2 *The eigenvalues of a unitary matrix are complex numbers of absolute value* 1.

12.3 *If* $\mathbf{T}$ *is a unitary mapping of a finite-dimensional euclidean space* E *over the field of complex numbers, then there is an orthonormal base in* E *consisting entirely of eigenvectors of* $\mathbf{T}$. *Moreover, the eigenvalues of* $\mathbf{T}$ *have absolute value* 1.

12.4 *If* $\mathbf{a}$ *is a unitary matrix, then there is a unitary matrix* $\mathbf{u}$ *such that*

$$\mathbf{u}^{-1}\mathbf{a}\mathbf{u} = \mathbf{d}$$

where $\mathbf{d}$ *is a diagonal matrix whose diagonal entries have absolute value* 1.

The proofs of these assertions are left as exercises.

EXAMPLE Let $\mathbf{T}$ be a unitary mapping of a finite-dimensional euclidean vector space E over $\mathbf{C}$. Consider the sequence of linear mappings

12.5 $\quad \mathbf{T}_1, \mathbf{T}_2, \ldots, \mathbf{T}_k, \ldots$

where

$$\mathbf{T}_k = \frac{1}{k}(\mathbf{I} + \mathbf{T} + \cdots + \mathbf{T}^{k-1})$$

Does the sequence (12.5) converge to some limiting linear mapping? We can answer in the affirmative as follows: According to (12.3) we can find an orthonormal base B in E for which the matrix of $\mathbf{T}$ is a diagonal matrix $\mathbf{d}$ with diagonal elements $p_1, p_2, \ldots, p_n$ such that $|p_i| = 1$. It follows that the matrix of $\mathbf{T}_k$ relative to the base B is the sum

$$\frac{1}{k}(\mathbf{I} + \mathbf{d} + \cdots + \mathbf{d}^{k-1})$$

This is again a diagonal matrix, the ith diagonal element being

$$\begin{aligned} \frac{1}{k}(1 + p_i + \cdots + p_i^{k-1}) &= \frac{1}{k}\cdot\frac{1 - p_i^k}{1 - p_i} && \text{if } p_i \neq 1 \\ &= 1 && \text{if } p_i = 1 \end{aligned}$$

Hence, since $|p_i| = 1$, we have

$$\lim_{k\to\infty} \frac{1}{k} (1 + p_i + \cdots + p_i^{k-1}) = \begin{cases} 1 & \text{if } p_i = 1 \\ 0 & \text{if } p_i \neq 1 \end{cases}$$

It follows that

$$\lim_{k\to\infty} \frac{1}{k} (\mathbf{I} + \mathbf{T} + \cdots + \mathbf{T}^{k-1})$$

exists, its matrix relative to B being a diagonal matrix with ith entry equal to 1 or 0 according to whether

$$p_i = 1 \qquad \text{or} \qquad p_i \neq 1$$

This same result, in the case of a complete infinite-dimensional euclidean space, is a celebrated theorem known as the mean ergodic theorem. It has important applications in statistical mechanics. The proof involves some increased technical difficulties but is based on essentially the same idea as the foregoing argument.

EXERCISES

1. Write out a proof of (12.2).
2. Prove (12.3).
3. Prove (12.4).
4. Let M_n denote the set of all $n \times n$ matrices with complex coefficients. Define an inner product in M_n by $(\mathbf{a}, \mathbf{b}) = Tr(\mathbf{a}{}^t\bar{\mathbf{b}})$, where Tr is the mapping that sends any matrix in M_n into the sum of its diagonal elements. Prove that M_n is a euclidean space of dimension n^2 over **C**.
5. With M_n as in the preceding exercise, consider the sum

$$\mathbf{a}_k = \mathbf{I} + \mathbf{a} + \frac{1}{2!}\mathbf{a}^2 + \cdots + \frac{1}{k!}\mathbf{a}^k$$

for any $\mathbf{a}$ in M_n. Prove that $\mathbf{a}_1, \mathbf{a}_2, \mathbf{a}_3, \ldots$ so defined form a Cauchy sequence in M_n: Since M_n, being finite-dimensional, is complete, this Cauchy sequence has a limit, denoted by $\exp \mathbf{a}$.

6. Let $\mathbf{b}$ be a nonsingular matrix in M_n. Show that
$\exp(\mathbf{bab}^{-1}) = \mathbf{b}(\exp \mathbf{a})\mathbf{b}^{-1}$
7. Show that if $\mathbf{a}$ is a Hermitian matrix in M_n, then $\exp \mathbf{a}$ is a positive definite Hermitian matrix.
8. Let $\mathbf{a}$ be a skew-Hermitian matrix in M_n. That is, ${}^t\mathbf{a} = -\bar{\mathbf{a}}$. Prove that $\exp \mathbf{a}$ is unitary.

13. Vector products in oriented 3-space

The present section deals with some observations which are important for many physical applications. We deal here exclusively with vector spaces over the real field **R**. The questions to be discussed here are taken up in a more general form in Chap. 16.

First of all, everyone is familiar with the notion of *orientation* in the plane or in 3-space. For example, by common convention, a coordinate system (x, y, z) in physical 3-space is called *right-handed* if a right-handed screw placed along the z axis, and rotated through 90 deg in the sense from the x axis to the y axis, moves in the positive direction along the z axis.

The question of orientation is very important for many purposes, and we now show how the concept may be transcribed into mathematical terms for any finite-dimensional vector space V over **R**.

Let $B = \{\mathbf{u}_1, \ldots, \mathbf{u}_n\}$ and $B' = \{\mathbf{v}_1, \ldots, \mathbf{v}_n\}$ be two bases for V.

Then they are connected by a certain $n \times n$ matrix $\mathbf{a} = (a^j{}_i)$:

13.1 $$\mathbf{v}_i = a^j{}_i \mathbf{u}_j$$

The inverse relation

13.2 $$\mathbf{u}_i = b^j{}_i \mathbf{v}_j$$

is given by another matrix $\mathbf{b} = (b^j{}_i)$, and the two matrices are inverses of each other: $\mathbf{ab} = \mathbf{ba} = \mathbf{I}$. From general rules for determinants we have

$$(\det \mathbf{a})(\det \mathbf{b}) = 1$$

Hence either det **a** and det **b** are both positive or are both negative.

DEFINITION 13.1 *Let V be a finite-dimensional vector space over* **R**. *By an* orientation *of V is meant a mapping h which assigns to each base B of V a number $h(B)$, either $+1$ or -1, in such a way that if* **a** *is the matrix from B to B', then*

13.3 $$h(B) \cdot h(B') \cdot \det \mathbf{a} > 0$$

It is easy to see that there are exactly two orientations of V and that if h is one of them, then $-h$ is the other. For select a fixed base B_0 in V, and start off by defining $h(B_0) = +1$, say. We claim that this determines $h(B)$ uniquely for any base B in such a way as to satisfy (13.3). For if **c** is the matrix from B_0 to B, then (13.3) requires us to have $h(B_0) \cdot h(B) \cdot \det \mathbf{c} > 0$, or $h(B) \cdot \det \mathbf{c} > 0$, since we have put $h(B_0) = 1$. Hence we set $h(B) = 1$ if $\det \mathbf{c} > 0$ and $h(B) = -1$ if $\det \mathbf{c} < 0$. In this way $h(B)$ is determined for all bases. To show that (13.3) holds, let B, B' be two bases, and let $\mathbf{c}, \mathbf{c}'$ be the matrices from B_0 to B and from B_0 to B', respectively. As just observed, we must have $h(B) \cdot \det \mathbf{c} > 0$ and $h(B') \cdot \det \mathbf{c}' > 0$. Therefore $h(B) \cdot h(B')\,(\det \mathbf{c})\,(\det \mathbf{c}') > 0$. Now the matrix **a** from B to B' is easily seen to be equal to $\mathbf{c}^{-1}\mathbf{c}'$. Hence

$$\begin{aligned} h(B) \cdot h(B') \cdot \det \mathbf{a} &= h(B) \cdot h(B')(\det \mathbf{c}^{-1})(\det \mathbf{c}') \\ &= h(B) \cdot h(B')(\det \mathbf{c})^{-1}(\det \mathbf{c}') \\ &= h(B) \cdot h(B')\,\frac{(\det \mathbf{c})(\det \mathbf{c}')}{(\det \mathbf{c}^2)} > 0 \end{aligned}$$

If we had started off with $h(B_0) = -1$, then all the signs $h(B)$ would have been reversed. This proves the statements made above.

By an *oriented* vector space V we mean a finite-dimensional space over $\mathbf{R}$ equipped with one of the two possible orientations. In general there is no reason for preferring one orientation to the other. But we observe that for the space $\mathbf{R}^n$ there is a natural orientation, namely, that one which assigns $+1$ to the canonical base $\{\mathbf{e}_1, \ldots, \mathbf{e}_n\}$, where as usual $\mathbf{e}_j$ denotes the jth column of the $n \times n$ unit matrix.

$B = \{\mathbf{u}_1, \ldots, \mathbf{u}_n\}$ being any base in V, if we set $B' = \{-\mathbf{u}_1, \mathbf{u}_2, \ldots, \mathbf{u}_n\}$, then the matrix from B to B' has determinant -1, and so from (13.3) we see that $h(B)$ and $h(B')$ must have opposite signs. If $n \geq 2$ and we set $B' = \{\mathbf{u}_2, \mathbf{u}_1, \mathbf{u}_3, \ldots, \mathbf{u}_n\}$, then again $h(B)$ and $h(B')$ must have opposite signs.

An orientation h on a vector space splits the bases into two classes, one class consisting of bases B for which $h(B) = +1$, and the other class consisting of bases B for which $h(B) = -1$. Equation (13.3) says that the matrix connecting two bases in the same class has a positive determinant. The bases for which $h(B) = +1$ can be thought of as analogous to right-handed coordinate systems in physical 3-space. But as we have remarked above, there is in general no way of singling out a preferred orientation in a vector space, and therefore there is no way of deciding which class of bases should be called right- or left-handed.

Now let E be an oriented two-dimensional euclidean vector space over $\mathbf{R}$. We shall see that the orientation, denote it by h, enables us to define the notion of positive and negative angles. Namely, let $\mathbf{u}$ and $\mathbf{v}$ be two nonzero vectors in E. In Sec. 11, Chap. 8, and again in Sec. 7 of the present chapter we defined the angle θ between $\mathbf{u}$ and $\mathbf{v}$ by

13.4 $$\cos\theta = \frac{(\mathbf{u}, \mathbf{v})}{|\mathbf{u}||\mathbf{v}|} \qquad (0 \leq \theta \leq \pi)$$

where $(\mathbf{u}, \mathbf{v})$ denotes the inner product in E.

We can now attach a sign to θ as follows. If $\mathbf{v}$ is not a multiple of $\mathbf{u}$ (otherwise $\theta = 0$ or $\theta = \pi$), then $\{\mathbf{u}, \mathbf{v}\}$ is a base for E. We now define the oriented angle $\measuredangle(\mathbf{u}, \mathbf{v})$ by

13.5 $$\measuredangle(\mathbf{u}, \mathbf{v}) = h(\{\mathbf{u}, \mathbf{v}\}) \cdot \theta$$

where θ is as in (13.4) and where $h(\{\mathbf{u}, \mathbf{v}\})$ is the number $+1$ or -1 which the orientation h assigns to the base $\{\mathbf{u}, \mathbf{v}\}$. If we reverse $\mathbf{u}$ and $\mathbf{v}$, then h changes sign, and therefore

13.6 $$\measuredangle(\mathbf{v}, \mathbf{u}) = -\measuredangle(\mathbf{u}, \mathbf{v})$$

One can easily verify that the oriented angle obeys the usual elementary rules of calculation, namely,

13.7 $$\measuredangle(\mathbf{u}, \mathbf{w}) = \measuredangle(\mathbf{u}, \mathbf{v}) + \measuredangle(\mathbf{v}, \mathbf{w})$$

provided of course that angles differing by multiples of 2π are identified. (Clearly angles should be regarded as elements of the factor group $\mathbf{R}/P$, where P is the subgroup of the additive group of $\mathbf{R}$ consisting of all integral multiples of 2π.)

Now let us consider a three-dimensional oriented euclidean vector space E over $\mathbf{R}$, the orientation being denoted by h, as before. We are now going to define a very useful binary operation $\times$ in E.

DEFINITION 13.2 *If* $\mathbf{u}$ *and* $\mathbf{v}$ *are linearly independent vectors in* E, *then* $\mathbf{u} \times \mathbf{v}$ *denotes the vector defined by the conditions*

13.8
$$\begin{aligned}(\mathbf{u}, \mathbf{u} \times \mathbf{v}) &= (\mathbf{v}, \mathbf{u} \times \mathbf{v}) = 0\\ |\mathbf{u} \times \mathbf{v}| &= |\mathbf{u}| \cdot |\mathbf{v}| \sin \theta\\ h(\{\mathbf{u}, \mathbf{v}, \mathbf{u} \times \mathbf{v}\}) &= 1\end{aligned}$$

where $(\mathbf{x}, \mathbf{y})$ *denotes the inner product in* E *and where* θ *is the angle between* $\mathbf{u}$ *and* $\mathbf{v}$, *with* $0 < \theta < \pi$. *If* $\mathbf{u}, \mathbf{v}$ *are linearly dependent, then* $\mathbf{u} \times \mathbf{v}$ *is defined to be the zero vector in* E (see Fig. 2).

The first condition says that $\mathbf{u} \times \mathbf{v}$ is orthogonal to both $\mathbf{u}$ and $\mathbf{v}$. The set of all vectors $\mathbf{x}$ such that $(\mathbf{u}, \mathbf{x}) = (\mathbf{v}, \mathbf{x}) = 0$ is a one-dimensional subspace L of E (assuming that $\mathbf{u}$ and $\mathbf{v}$ are linearly independent.) Let $\mathbf{w}$ be a unit vector in L. Then $\mathbf{w}$ spans L, and since $\mathbf{u} \times \mathbf{v}$ must be in L, we shall have $\mathbf{u} \times \mathbf{v} = c\mathbf{w}$, for some number c. Then $|\mathbf{u} \times \mathbf{v}| = |c\mathbf{w}| = |c| \cdot |\mathbf{w}| = |c|$, and so $c = \pm|\mathbf{u}| \cdot |\mathbf{v}| \sin \theta$, by the second condition of (13.8). It remains only to fix the sign of c. The third condition of (13.8) requires that h assign the value $+1$ to the base $\{\mathbf{u}, \mathbf{v}, c\mathbf{w}\}$, and this determines the sign of c. Hence (13.8) defines $\mathbf{u} \times \mathbf{v}$ uniquely. We observe that the second condition of (13.8) can be rewritten slightly as follows:

$$|\mathbf{u} \times \mathbf{v}|^2 = |\mathbf{u}|^2|\mathbf{v}|^2 \sin^2 \theta = |\mathbf{u}|^2|\mathbf{v}|^2(1 - \cos^2 \theta)$$

Figure 2 $|u|\ |v| \sin \theta$ is the area of the parallelogram formed by **u** and **v**. The direction of **u × v** depends on the orientation selected for 3-space. Thus the outer product of two vectors is preserved by any unitary transformation **T**, provided that **T** preserves orientation.

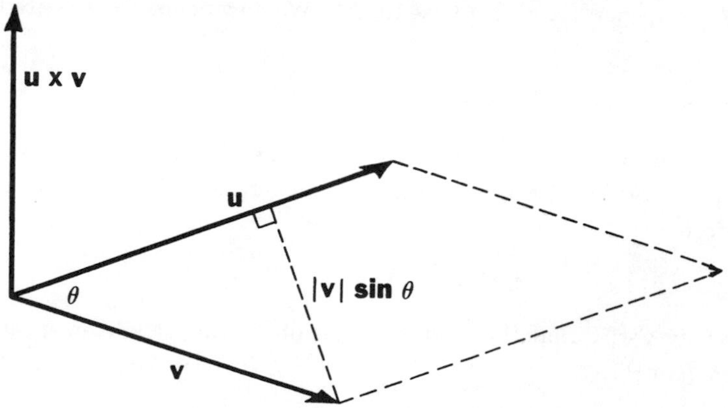

Using (13.4) we get

13.9 $$|\mathbf{u} \times \mathbf{v}|^2 = |\mathbf{u}|^2|\mathbf{v}|^2 - (\mathbf{u}, \mathbf{v})^2$$

We now show how to compute $\mathbf{u} \times \mathbf{v}$: Let $B = \{\mathbf{e}_1, \mathbf{e}_2, \mathbf{e}_3\}$ be an orthonormal base in E, and put

$$\mathbf{u} = u^i\mathbf{e}_i \qquad \mathbf{v} = v^i\mathbf{e}_i$$

For a vector $\mathbf{x} = x^i\mathbf{e}_i$ the condition $(\mathbf{u}, \mathbf{x}) = (\mathbf{v}, \mathbf{x}) = 0$ becomes

13.10 $$u^1x^1 + u^2x^2 + u^3x^3 = 0 \qquad v^1x^1 + v^2x^2 + v^3x^3 = 0$$

since B is orthonormal. We can easily solve these equations as follows: We have

13.11 $$\begin{vmatrix} u^1 & u^1 & v^1 \\ u^2 & u^2 & v^2 \\ u^3 & u^3 & v^3 \end{vmatrix} = 0$$

since two columns are identical. Expanding by the first column we get

$$u^1t^1 + u^2t^2 + u^3t^3 = 0$$

where

$$t^1 = \begin{vmatrix} u^2 & v^2 \\ u^3 & v^3 \end{vmatrix} = u^2v^3 - u^3v^2$$

13.12 $$t^2 = -\begin{vmatrix} u^1 & v^1 \\ u^3 & v^3 \end{vmatrix} = u^3v^1 - u^1v^3$$

$$t^3 = \begin{vmatrix} u^1 & v^1 \\ u^2 & v^2 \end{vmatrix} = u^1v^2 - u^2v^1$$

Replacing the first column by the v^i gives similarly

$$v^1t^1 + v^2t^2 + v^3t^3 = 0$$

Furthermore, if $\mathbf{u}$ and $\mathbf{v}$ are linearly independent, then t^1, t^2, t^3 cannot all be zero. For the matrix consisting of the last two columns of (13.11) must have rank 2, and so at least one of the 2×2 determinants (13.12) is nonzero. But in fact it is a straightforward matter to check that

13.13 $$(t^1)^2 + (t^2)^2 + (t^3)^2 = |\mathbf{u}|^2|\mathbf{v}|^2 - (\mathbf{u}, \mathbf{v})^2$$

Hence, by (13.9), the vector

13.14 $$\mathbf{t} = t^i\mathbf{e}_i$$

satisfies the first two conditions of (13.8). Therefore $\mathbf{u} \times \mathbf{v} = \pm\mathbf{t}$. To determine the sign, let us now suppose that the orthonormal base B is such that $h(B) = 1$. Since $h(\{\mathbf{u}, \mathbf{v}, \mathbf{u} \times \mathbf{v}\}) = 1$ also, it follows from Definition 13.1 that the matrix from B to $\{\mathbf{u}, \mathbf{v}, \mathbf{u} \times \mathbf{v}\}$ must have positive determinant. Now the matrix $\mathbf{a}$ from B to $\{\mathbf{u}, \mathbf{v}, \mathbf{t}\}$ is simply

13.15 $$a = \begin{pmatrix} u^1 & v^1 & t^1 \\ u^2 & v^2 & t^2 \\ u^3 & v^3 & t^3 \end{pmatrix}$$

To calculate its determinant expand by the third column. Taking account of (13.12) one obtains

13.16 $$\det \mathbf{a} = (t^1)^2 + (t^2)^2 + (t^3)^2 = |\mathbf{t}|^2$$

This is positive, of course, and it follows that we must take

13.17 $$\mathbf{u} \times \mathbf{v} = \mathbf{t} = (u^2v^3 - u^3v^2)\mathbf{e}_1 + (u^3v^1 - u^1v^3)\mathbf{e}_2 + (u^1v^2 - u^2v^1)\mathbf{e}_3$$

Hence we have achieved our aim of computing $\mathbf{u} \times \mathbf{v}$. Observe that the quantities t^1, t^2, t^3 are all zero if $\mathbf{u}$ and $\mathbf{v}$ are linearly dependent. Therefore the formula above gives the correct result in this case, too.

It is plain from (13.17) that

13.18 $$\mathbf{v} \times \mathbf{u} = -\mathbf{u} \times \mathbf{v} \qquad \mathbf{u} \times \mathbf{u} = \mathbf{0}$$

a result which also follows directly from Definition 13.2.

The operation $\times$ is variously referred to as the *outer product*, or the *cross product*, or the *vector product*. It is *anticommutative*, as the preceding equation shows. From the formula (13.17) it is simple to verify that $\times$ is *bilinear*, i.e., that it satisfies the following distributive laws:

13.19 $$\begin{aligned} (a\mathbf{u} + b\mathbf{w}) \times \mathbf{v} &= a(\mathbf{u} \times \mathbf{v}) + b(\mathbf{w} \times \mathbf{v}) \\ \mathbf{u} \times (c\mathbf{v} + d\mathbf{w}) &= c(\mathbf{u} \times \mathbf{v}) + d(\mathbf{u} \times \mathbf{w}) \end{aligned}$$

However, $\times$ is *not* an associative operation.

Using (13.17) one can easily show that $\times$ satisfies the following modified associative law, known as the *Jacobi identity:*†

13.20 $$\mathbf{u} \times (\mathbf{v} \times \mathbf{w}) + \mathbf{w} \times (\mathbf{u} \times \mathbf{v}) + \mathbf{v} \times (\mathbf{w} \times \mathbf{u}) = \mathbf{0}$$

We recall from Sec. 6, Chap. 11, that $|\mathbf{u}| \cdot |\mathbf{v}| \sin\theta$ is the area of the parallelogram spanned by $\mathbf{u}$ and $\mathbf{v}$. From (13.8) it follows that the length of $\mathbf{u} \times \mathbf{v}$ is defined to be equal to that area. According to Sec. 6, Chap. 11, again, the volume of the parallelepiped spanned by $\mathbf{u}$, $\mathbf{v}$, $\mathbf{u} \times \mathbf{v}$ is equal to the determinant of (13.15), hence to $|\mathbf{u}|^2\,|\mathbf{v}|^2 \sin^2\theta$, by (13.16).

We mention the following formulas:

13.21 $$\mathbf{e}_1 \times \mathbf{e}_2 = \mathbf{e}_3 \qquad \mathbf{e}_1 \times \mathbf{e}_3 = -\mathbf{e}_2 \qquad \mathbf{e}_2 \times \mathbf{e}_3 = \mathbf{e}_1$$

† After Karl G. J. Jacobi (1804–1851).

where $\{e_1, e_2, e_3\}$ is any orthonormal base for which $h = +1$. These follow at once from Definition 13.2. Further, if $\mathbf{u} = u^i\mathbf{e}_i$, $\mathbf{v} = v^i\mathbf{e}_i$, $\mathbf{w} = w^i\mathbf{e}_i$, then

$$(\mathbf{u} \times \mathbf{v}, \mathbf{w}) = t^1w^1 + t^2w^2 + t^3w^3$$

where the t^i are as in (13.12). We have then

13.22
$$(\mathbf{u} \times \mathbf{v}, \mathbf{w}) = \begin{vmatrix} u^1 & v^1 & w^1 \\ u^2 & v^2 & w^2 \\ u^3 & v^3 & w^3 \end{vmatrix}$$

as follows at once by expanding by the third column.

EXAMPLE Consider $\mathbf{R}_3$, with its standard inner product, its natural orientation, and its canonical base B: $\mathbf{e}_1 = (1, 0, 0)$, $\mathbf{e}_2 = (0, 1, 0)$, $\mathbf{e}_3 = (0, 0, 1)$. We recall that the natural orientation h is that for which $h(B) = 1$. Let $\mathbf{u} = (1, 2, -1)$, $\mathbf{v} = (3, 0, 4)$. Then, by (13.17),

$$\mathbf{u} \times \mathbf{v} = 8\mathbf{e}_1 - 7\mathbf{e}_2 - 6\mathbf{e}_3 = (8, -7, -6)$$

REMARK 1. E above with its vector-space operations and the cross product $\times$ is an example of a Lie algebra.† In general, a Lie algebra is a finite-dimensional vector space equipped with a product operation satisfying (13.18), (13.19), (13.20). Such systems are very important in the study of *continuous* groups.

REMARK 2. An operation generalizing the cross product for spaces of dimension greater than 3 is studied in Chap. 16.

EXERCISES

1. Prove the formula (13.7) for oriented angles.
2. Prove Eq. (13.13).
3. Given linearly independent vectors $\mathbf{u}$ and $\mathbf{v}$ in an oriented three-dimensional euclidean vector space, describe a simple way of obtaining from them an orthonormal base $\{\mathbf{e}_1, \mathbf{e}_2, \mathbf{e}_3\}$ such that $\mathbf{e}_1 = c\mathbf{u}$, where $c > 0$.
4. Prove the following formula for any vectors $\mathbf{a}$, $\mathbf{b}$, $\mathbf{c}$ in an oriented euclidean 3-space:
$$\mathbf{a} \times (\mathbf{b} \times \mathbf{c}) = (\mathbf{c},\mathbf{a}) \cdot \mathbf{b} - (\mathbf{b},\mathbf{a}) \cdot \mathbf{c}$$
5. Calculate the area of the parallelogram P in $\mathbf{R}_3$ spanned by the vectors $\mathbf{u} = (3, 0, -1)$ and $\mathbf{v} = (1, 2, -2)$.
6. Let $\{\mathbf{e}_1, \mathbf{e}_2, \mathbf{e}_3\}$ be an orthonormal base in an oriented euclidean 3-space. Assuming that the base is positive, calculate
   (*a*) $(\mathbf{e}_1 \times \mathbf{e}_2) \cdot \mathbf{e}_3$
   (*b*) $(\mathbf{e}_1 \times \mathbf{e}_2) \times \mathbf{e}_3$
   (*c*) $(\mathbf{e}_1 - \mathbf{e}_2 + 3\mathbf{e}_3) \times (2\mathbf{e}_1 + \mathbf{e}_2)$
7. Find the volume of the tetrahedron in $\mathbf{R}_3$ whose vertices are $(0, 0, 0)$, $(1, -1, 3)$, $(2, 1, 1)$, $(3, 4, 5)$.

† After Sophus Lie (1842–1899).

8. Prove the identity

$$((\mathbf{u} \times \mathbf{v}), (\mathbf{w} \times \mathbf{z})) = (\mathbf{u}, \mathbf{w})(\mathbf{v}, \mathbf{z}) - (\mathbf{u}, \mathbf{z})(\mathbf{v}, \mathbf{w})$$

for the cross product.

9. Prove that

$$\begin{vmatrix} (\mathbf{u}, \mathbf{u}) & (\mathbf{u}, \mathbf{v}) \\ (\mathbf{v}, \mathbf{u}) & (\mathbf{v}, \mathbf{v}) \end{vmatrix} = |\mathbf{u} \times \mathbf{v}|^2$$

in an oriented euclidean 3-space.

10. Using the cross product, prove the law of sines

$$\frac{a}{\sin \alpha} = \frac{b}{\sin \beta} = \frac{c}{\sin \gamma}$$

for a triangle in $\mathbf{R}_3$.

11. Prove the Jacobi identity (13.20).

14. Analytic geometry in n dimensions

In this section we generalize the considerations of Sec. 12, Chap. 8, to study certain geometric questions in n-dimensional affine space. Our aim here is merely to indicate how linear algebra can be applied to such problems. We refer the reader to Secs. 10 and 11, Chap. 8, for definitions of affine and euclidean space. Recall that one obtains a coordinate system in E_n by selecting a point p_0 as the origin and a base $\mathbf{e}_1, \mathbf{e}_2, \ldots, \mathbf{e}_n$ for the vector space of translations $T(E_n)$. Then for any point q the translation vector $\overrightarrow{p_0q}$ can be expressed uniquely as

$$\overrightarrow{p_0q} = x^1\mathbf{e}_1 + \cdots + x^n\mathbf{e}_n$$

We write $q = (x^1, \ldots, x^n)$ with respect to p_0; $\mathbf{e}_1, \ldots, \mathbf{e}_n$ or simply $q = (x^1, \ldots, x^n)$ when there is no risk of misunderstanding. If the base is orthonormal, we call the coordinate system *euclidean*.

Let us first discuss k-dimensional affine subspaces Γ of E_n (see Sec. 10, Chap. 8, for a slightly different point of view). Such a subspace Γ is, by definition, the set of all points obtained from a fixed point q_0 by a translation in a k-dimensional subspace $T(\Gamma)$ of $T(E_n)$. Let $\mathbf{u}_1, \ldots, \mathbf{u}_k$ be a base for $T(\Gamma)$, and suppose that

$$\mathbf{u}_j = \sum_{i=1}^{n} a^i{}_j\mathbf{e}_i \qquad (j = 1, 2, \ldots, k)$$

Then, if q is any point of Γ, $\overrightarrow{q_0q} \in T(\Gamma)$ and so there exist scalars $\lambda_1, \lambda_2, \ldots, \lambda_k$ such that

$$\overrightarrow{q_0q} = \sum_{j=1}^{k} \lambda_j\mathbf{u}_j = \sum_{j=1}^{k}\sum_{i=1}^{n} \lambda_j a^i{}_j\mathbf{e}_i$$

Thus, if $q_0 = (x_0^1, \ldots, x_0^n)$, $q = (x^1, \ldots, x^n)$, then

14.1 $$x^i = x_0^i + \sum_{j=1}^{k} \lambda_j a^i{}_j \qquad (i = 1, 2, \ldots, n)$$

These are the *parametric equations of* Γ, the "parameters" being $\lambda_1, \ldots, \lambda_k$, and as they range over all possible elements of the field $\mathbf{R}$, the point $(x^1, \ldots, x^n)$ ranges over all points of Γ.

To obtain another form of these equations, let us write them in matrix notation as

14.2 $$\mathbf{X} = \mathbf{\Lambda A}$$

where $\mathbf{X} = (x^1 - x_0^1, \ldots, x^n - x_0^n)$, $\mathbf{\Lambda} = (\lambda_1, \ldots, \lambda_k)$, $\mathbf{A} = (a^i{}_j)$ are $1 \times n$, $1 \times k$, and $k \times n$ matrices, respectively. Note that rank $\mathbf{A} = k$ since $\mathbf{u}_1, \ldots, \mathbf{u}_k$ are linearly independent. Interpreting $\mathbf{A}$ as the matrix of a linear transformation $F: V^n \to W^k$ of an n-dimensional vector space V^n to a k-dimensional vector space W^k (with respect to some bases), we see that the dimension of the kernel of F is $n - k$ (Theorem 3.2, Chap. 9). If we denote this kernel by U^{n-k} and pick a base in it, we obtain a matrix $\mathbf{B}$ representing the inclusion map $G: U^{n-k} \to V^n$; clearly the composition FG is the zero map and so $\mathbf{AB} = \mathbf{0}$. In other words, we have found an $n \times (n - k)$ matrix $\mathbf{B}$ of rank $n - k$ such that $\mathbf{AB} = \mathbf{0}$, and so multiplying (14.2) on the right by $\mathbf{B}$, we obtain

$$\mathbf{XB} = \mathbf{0}$$

This may be written as a system of $n - k$ equations:

14.3 $$\sum_{i=1}^{n} b_{ij}(x^i - x_0^i) = 0 \qquad (j = 1, 2, \ldots, n - k)$$

or, finally, as

14.4 $$\sum_{i=1}^{n} b_{ij}x^i = c_j \qquad (j = 1, 2, \ldots, n - k)$$

where $c_j = \sum_{i=1}^{n} b_{jk}x_0^i$. Conversely such a system of equations represents a k-dimensional affine subspace, as follows from Theorem 8.5, Chap. 9.

THEOREM 14.1 *If* $\mathbf{B} = (b_{ij})$ *is a matrix of rank* $n - k$, *the set of all points* $(x^1, \ldots, x^n)$ *in* E_n *satisfying the system of equations*

$$\sum_{i=1}^{n} b_{ij}x^i = c_j \qquad (j = 1, 2, \ldots, n - k)$$

is a k-dimensional affine subspace of E_n, and conversely, any k-dimensional subspace may be described in this fashion.

In particular, if dim $(\Gamma) = n - 1$, then $n - k = 1$ and the single equation

14.5 $$b_1x^1 + \cdots + b_nx^n = c$$

represents the *hyperplane* Γ. If $p_0 = (x^1, \ldots, x^n)$, $p_1 = (y^1, \ldots, y^n)$ are two distinct points of Γ, then $b_i x^i = b_i y^i = c$, and so

$$b_1(x^1 - y^1) + \cdots + b_n(x^n - y^n) = 0$$

Thus the vector $\mathbf{b} = (b_1, \ldots, b_n)$ is orthogonal to the translation vector $\overrightarrow{p_0p_1}$, where p_0, p_1 are arbitrary points of Γ. This provides a geometric interpretation of the coefficients $b_1, \ldots, b_n$.

As a sample of the type of question easily answered using the properties of (euclidean) affine spaces, let us ask, What is the shortest distance from a point q (not on Γ) to the hyperplane Γ?

From what we have just seen, an orthonormal basis for $T(E_n)$ may be obtained by adjoining to an orthonormal basis of $T(\Gamma)$ the *unit* vector $\mathbf{b}/|\mathbf{b}|$, which we denote by $\mathbf{n}$. Clearly

$$\mathbf{n} = \left(\frac{b_1}{c}, \ldots, \frac{b_n}{c}\right) \qquad \text{where } c = \sqrt{b_i^2 + \cdots b_n^2}$$

It is now a consequence of the discussion following the proof of Theorem 8.6 that the required shortest distance is

$$D = (\overrightarrow{pq}, \mathbf{n})$$

where p is an arbitrary point of Γ (see Fig. 3).

Taking $q = (q^1, \ldots, q^n)$, $p = (p^1, \ldots, p^n)$, a straightforward computation yields the following theorem.

THEOREM 14.2 *The shortest distance D from the point $q = (q^1, \ldots, q^n)$ to the hyperplane $b_1x^1 + \cdots + b_nx^n = c$ is given by*

14.6 $$D = \frac{b^1q^1 + \cdots + b_nq^n - c}{\sqrt{b_1^2 + \cdots + b_n^2}}$$

So far we have studied affine subspaces which are described in terms of linear equations. Let us now consider *quadrics*, the sets of points $(x^1, \ldots, x^n)$ in E_n which satisfy a quadratic equation:

14.7 $$\sum_{i,j=1}^{n} a_{ij}x^ix^j + \sum_{i=1}^{n} 2b_ix^i + c = 0$$

Figure 3

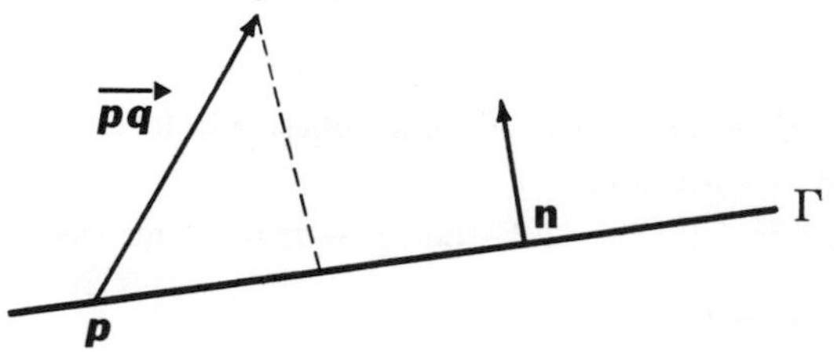

We may assume that $a_{ij} = a_{ji}$, $1 \leq i, j \leq n$, (why?) and so apply Corollary 2, Sec. 10, which tells us that there is an orthogonal change of basis in $T(E_n)$, transforming the euclidean coordinate system $(x^1, \ldots, x^n)$ to another $(y^1, \ldots, y^n)$ and such that (14.7) in the new system reads as

14.8 $$\sum_{i=1}^{n} p_i(y^i)^2 + \sum_{i=1}^{n} q_i y^i + r = 0$$

By a permutation of the base elements, we may assume that $p_i \neq 0$, $i = 1, 2, \ldots, k$ $(k \leq n)$ and $p_i = 0$, $k < i \leq n$. We can eliminate the linear terms in $y^1, y^2, \ldots, y^k$ as in Sec. 12, Chap. 8, by a translation of the coordinate system given by

$$z^i = y^i + q_i/2p_i \qquad (i = 1, 2, \ldots, k)$$
$$z^i = y^i \qquad (i > k)$$

and (14.8) becomes

14.9 $$\sum_{i=1}^{k} p_i(z^i)^2 + \sum_{i=k+1}^{n} q_i z^i + s = 0$$

If all q_i vanish, we obtain an equation of the form

14.10 $$\sum_{i=1}^{k} p_i(z^i)^2 + s = 0$$

On the other hand, if not all q_i vanish, we make a change of coordinate system:

$$w^i = z^i \qquad (i = 1, 2, \ldots, k)$$
$$w^{k+1} = \frac{1}{Q}\left(\sum_{i=k+1}^{n} q_i z^i\right)$$

where Q and $w^{k+2}, \ldots, w^n$ are so chosen that the transformation is orthogonal (see Exercise 8). A final translation enables us to eliminate the constant term and we obtain the equation

14.11 $$\sum_{i=1}^{k} p_i(w^i)^2 + Qw^{k+1} = 0$$

Thus we have *two possible types of equations:* (14.10) and (14.11). Some of the possibilities for $n = 3$ are illustrated below. Note that the original polynomial of (14.7) was reduced to that of (14.10) and (14.11) by a succession of translations and orthogonal transformations of $T(E_n)$. The various transformations we have used act in $T(E_n)$, *not* in E_n, so that the geometric figure represented by Eq. (14.7) is left unchanged but the equation describing it is successively simplified by changing coordinate systems. Exactly the same manipulations can also be interpreted

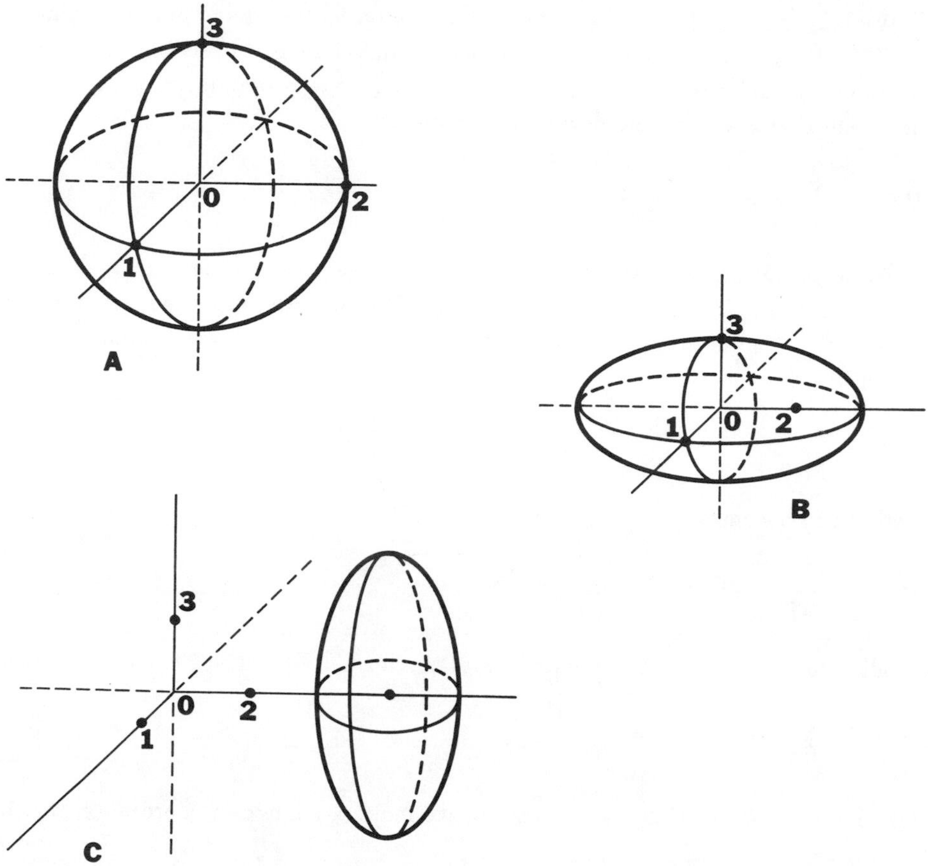

Figure 4† (*A*) The sphere: $(x^1)^2 + (x^2)^2 + (x^3)^2 = 1$. (*B*) Its image under T_1, $T_1(x^1, x^2, x^3) = (x^1, \frac{1}{2}x^2, x^3)$. (*C*) Its image under T_2, $T_2(x^1, x^2, x^3) = (x^1, x^2 - 3, \frac{1}{2}x^3)$.

from a different point of view, which leans on our geometric intuition. In this view, the coordinate system is fixed once and for all, and the transformations, acting now on E_n, transform the points $(x^1, \ldots, x^n)$ satisfying (14.7) into $(z^1, \ldots, z^n)$ satisfying (14.10) or $(w^1, \ldots, w^n)$ satisfying (14.11). In other words the geometric figure represented by Eq. (14.7) is mapped onto one given by (14.10) or (14.11) (see Fig 4). The point in either approach is to study the original quadric by replacing it with one whose equation is more perspicuous. However, we must be careful that the geometric properties in which we are interested are preserved by the transformations employed. This leads us to a point of view first clearly expressed by F. Klein in his celebrated and extremely influential "Erlangen program" (1872),‡ according to which geometry is the study of properties of geometric entities invariant under certain groups of transformations. Thus,

† The points 1, 2, 3 denote $\mathbf{e}_1(0)$, $\mathbf{e}_2(0)$, $\mathbf{e}_3(0)$, respectively, where 0 is the origin and $\mathbf{e}_1$, $\mathbf{e}_2$, $\mathbf{e}_3$ an orthonormal basis for $T(E_3)$.

‡ English translation in *Bulletin of New York Mathematical Society*, vol. 2, 1892.

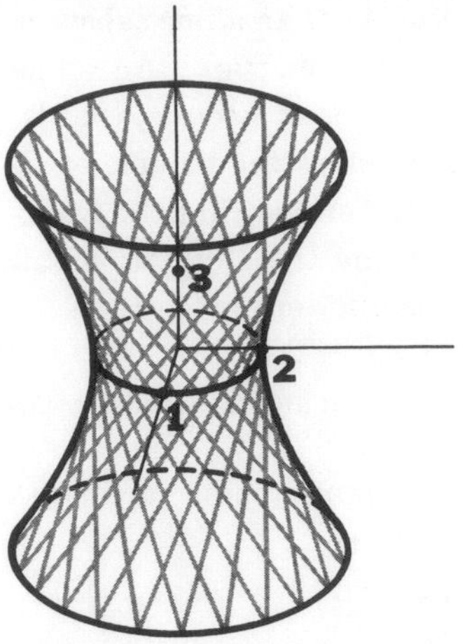

Figure 5

The hyperboloid of one sheet $(x^1)^2 + (x^2)^2 - (x^3)^2 = 1$.

different groups of transformations yield different geometries. It is not our intention here to develop these considerations at length; let us merely indicate their connection with the preceding discussion of affine subspaces and quadrics.

Let E_n denote a euclidean vector space, which we regard as an affine space (cf. page 191, Example 1). The transformations we have been using are *affine transformations* of E_n, namely, compositions of linear transformations and translations. If we consider only nonsingular linear mappings, the resulting set is a group (why?) called the *affine group*, A_n. If $f \in A_n$, its action on E_n is given by the equation

$$f(\mathbf{x}) = \mathbf{A}\mathbf{x} + \mathbf{v}$$

where $\mathbf{A}$ is a nonsingular linear mapping of E_n and $\mathbf{v}$ is a fixed (that is, independent of $\mathbf{x}$) element of E_n. Its inverse is clearly given by $f^{-1}(\mathbf{y}) = \mathbf{A}^{-1}(\mathbf{y} - \mathbf{v})$, and its product with g, $g(\mathbf{x}) = \mathbf{B}\mathbf{x} + \mathbf{w}$ is given by $(g \cdot f)(\mathbf{x}) = g(f(\mathbf{x})) = \mathbf{BA}(\mathbf{x}) + (\mathbf{B}\mathbf{v} + \mathbf{w})$. The affine group A_n preserves k-dimensional affine subspaces and

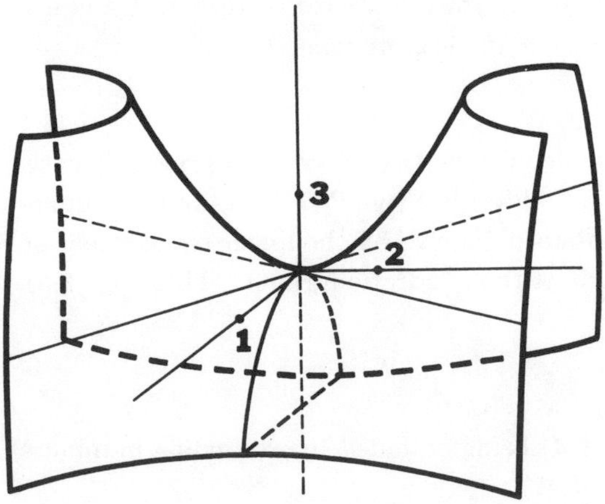

Figure 6

The hyperbolic paraboloid $(x^1)^2 - (x^2)^2 + x^3 = 0$.

quadrics, in the sense that the image under any element of A_n of an affine subspace (a quadric) is an affine subspace of the same dimension (a quadric). An affine transformation f is called a *rigid motion* if it preserves lengths of vectors, that is, if $|f(\mathbf{x})| = |\mathbf{x}|$ for every $\mathbf{x} \in E_n$; it is *volume-preserving* if it leaves the volume of all parallelotopes invariant (cf. Sec. 6, Chap. 11). It is easily verified that the translations, the rigid motions, and the volume-preserving affine transformations all constitute subgroups of A_n, the first one normal (what is quotient group?).

We have proved above:

Any quadric can be transformed by a rigid motion into a quadric whose equation has the form (14.10) *or* (14.11)

We conclude this brief section by studying a certain quantity associated with every quadric and its invariance under affine transformations.

Referring to equation (14.7), we set $c = a_{n+1,\,n+1}$ and $b_i = a_{i,n+1} = a_{n+1,i}$ $(i = 1, \ldots, n)$

DEFINITION The *discriminant* of the quadric of (14.7) is the $(n + 1) \times (n + 1)$ determinant $|(a_{ij})|$. It will be denoted by $\Delta(P)$ where P is the polynomial in (14.7).

Thus the discriminant of the quadric $\sum_1^n a_{ij}x^ix^j + 1 = 0$ equals the determinant $|(a_{ij})|$ $\quad (i, j = 1, \ldots, n)$

THEOREM 14.3 *Let* $\mathbf{T}$ *denote the affine transformation* $\mathbf{T}(\mathbf{x}) = \mathbf{Ax} + \mathbf{v}$ *of* E_n, *and* $\mathbf{T}P$ *the polynomial* $P(\mathbf{T}(\mathbf{x}))$. *Then*

$$\Delta(\mathbf{T}P) = \det^2(\mathbf{A}) \cdot \Delta(P)$$

Proof. To a point $\mathbf{x} = (x^1, \ldots, x^n)$ of E^n let us associate the point $\mathbf{x}' = (x^1, \ldots, x^n, 1)$ of E^{n+1}. Introduce the polynomial $P'(x^1, \ldots, x^{n+1})$ in $n + 1$ variables by the equation

$$P'(x^1, \ldots, x^{n+1}) = \sum_{i,j=1}^{n+1} a_{ij}x^ix^j \qquad (a_{ij} = a_{ji})$$

Note that this is a quadratic form on E_{n+1} and that it is uniquely determined by the condition $\mathbf{P}'(\mathbf{x}') = \mathbf{P}(\mathbf{x})$. Associate, finally, to the *affine* transformation $\mathbf{T}$ on E_n the *linear* transformation $\mathbf{T}'$ on E_{n+1} as follows: if $\mathbf{M}$ and $\mathbf{r}$ denote the $n \times n$ matrix and the row vector representing $\mathbf{A}$ and $\mathbf{v}$, $\mathbf{T}'$ is represented by the $(n + 1) \times (n + 1)$ matrix

$$\mathbf{M}' = \begin{pmatrix} \mathbf{M} & 0 \\ \mathbf{r} & 1 \end{pmatrix}$$

It is immediate from these definitions that $\mathbf{T}'(\mathbf{x}') = (\mathbf{T}(\mathbf{x}))'$. Hence, $(\mathbf{T}P)'(\mathbf{x}') = \mathbf{T}P(\mathbf{x}) = P(\mathbf{T}(\mathbf{x})) = P'[(\mathbf{T}(\mathbf{x}))'] = P'[\mathbf{T}'(\mathbf{x}')]$, and the quadratic form $(\mathbf{T}P)'$ on E_{n+1} is obtained from P' by the linear transformation $\mathbf{T}'$. Denote by $\mu(Q)$ the matrix of the quadratic form Q. Then, by (3.9),

$$\mu((\mathbf{T}P)') = {}^t\mathbf{M}'\mu(P')\mathbf{M}' \quad \text{and}$$

$$\Delta(\mathbf{T}P) = \det \mu((\mathbf{T}P)') = \det^2(\mathbf{M}') \cdot \det \mu(P') = \det^2(\mathbf{M}) \cdot \Delta(P)$$

the identity $\det^2(\mathbf{M}') = \det^2(\mathbf{M})$ being obtained by expanding in minors according to the last column of $\mathbf{M}'$.

It follows from the preceding theorem that the *sign* of the discriminant of a quadric is preserved by A_n and that the discriminant itself is preserved by the subgroup of volume-preserving affine transformations (cf. Exercise 9).

EXERCISES

1. Find the equations of the hyperplane in E_n passing through the points $(1, 0, \ldots, 0), (0, 1, 0, \ldots, 0), \ldots, (0, 0, \ldots, 0, 1)$.

2. Find the shortest distance from the origin to the hyperplane of Exercise 1.

3. Can one generalize the discussion leading to Theorem 14.2 to obtain the shortest distance from a point in E_n to a k-dimensional affine subspace?

4. Describe the surfaces in E_3 whose equations are

(*a*) $y = xz$ (*b*) $z = x^2 + y^2$

(*c*) $\dfrac{x^2}{25} - \dfrac{y^2}{1} - \dfrac{z^2}{4} = 1$ (*d*) $\dfrac{x^2}{4} + \dfrac{y^2}{9} - \dfrac{z^2}{16} = -1$

5. Under what conditions will surfaces in E_3 given by the equations below have the property that through every point of the surface there passes a straight line contained entirely in the surface?

$$\lambda_1 x_1^2 + \lambda_2 x_2^2 + \lambda_3 x_3^2 = 1$$
$$\lambda_1 x_1^2 + \lambda_2 x_2^2 + \mu x_3 = 0$$

***6.** Generalize Exercise 5 to E_n.

7. Prove that surfaces whose equation is given by (14.10) have "central symmetry," i.e., if a point lies on the surface, so does its "reflection" through the origin. Conversely, show that if a quadric surface possesses a center of symmetry as above, then its equation may be reduced to the form (14.10).

8. If $\mathbf{v}$ is a nonzero row (or column) vector, then an orthogonal matrix can always be found containing a multiple of $\mathbf{v}$ as a row (or column).

9. Find necessary and sufficient conditions in order that the affine transformation f, $f(\mathbf{x}) = \mathbf{A}\mathbf{x} + \mathbf{v}$, be volume-preserving. Show that these transformations form a group. Show that for any $f \in A_n$, the ratio volume $(\mathbf{P})/$volume $(f(\mathbf{P}))$ is constant for all parallelotopes $\mathbf{P}$ in E_n.

10. Let A be an affine space over an arbitrary field K. Let $p_1, \ldots, p_n$ be points of A.

(a) Prove $\sum_1^n \lambda_i \overrightarrow{p_0 p_i}(p_0) = \sum_1^n \lambda_i \overrightarrow{q_0 p_i}(q_0)$ for any points p_0, q_0 in A, provided that $\lambda_1 + \cdots + \lambda_n = 1$.

(b) *Define* $\lambda_1 p_1 + \cdots + \lambda_n p_n$ where $\lambda_1 + \cdots + \lambda_n = 1$ by the expression in (a). *Define* a mapping $f: A \to A$ to be *affine* if and only if $f(\Sigma \lambda_i p_i) = \Sigma \lambda_i f(p_i)$ whenever $\lambda_1 + \cdots + \lambda_n = 1$. *Define* an affine mapping to be *linear* with respect to p_0 if $f(p_0) = p_0$.

(c) Prove that an affine map f is a translation if and only if $f(p) \neq p$ for all p in A.

(d) Prove that an affine mapping is a composition of a linear mapping and a translation.

15

Quotient structures

In this chapter we shall describe the fundamental notion of *quotient set*, and we shall illustrate its importance by numerous mathematical constructions. Several of the topics presented here have already been encountered in previous chapters, but they are treated in this chapter from a more advanced point of view.

1. Mappings

Let A and B be sets. We wish to give a definition of *a mapping from A to B*. In Chap. 1, we defined a mapping from A to B as a *rule* which *assigns* to each element of A an element of B. While this definition has served us up to this point, the authors must confess that the notion of a *rule* has been left vague—indeed, too vague for the standards of precision that we impose on ourselves. We wish therefore to give a more precise definition of a mapping.

Before presenting the definition, we call to the reader's attention the role that mappings play in mathematics: simply to let us know which elements of A correspond to which elements of B. Put another way, a mapping serves only to provide the information for any ordered pair (x, y) with x in A and y in B: Is y assigned to x?

In a pragmatic spirit, therefore, we bypass the difficult problem of defining a *rule* and we adopt the following definition of a mapping.

DEFINITION 1.1 *Let A and B be sets.* $A \times B$ *is the set of all ordered pairs* (x, y) *with* x *in* A *and* y *in* B.

DEFINITION 1.2 *A* mapping f *from* A *to* B *is a subset of* $A \times B$ *satisfying the following condition:*

For each element x in A, there is one and only one element y in B such that (x, y) is in f; this element y is denoted by $f(x)$. We say that "f assigns to x the element $f(x)$" or "f sends x into $f(x)$." If f is a mapping of A to B, we sometimes write $f\colon A \rightarrow B$.

Thus, to specify a mapping f is equivalent to specifying, for each x in A, the element $f(x)$ in B. A mapping of A to B is sometimes called a *function* from A to B.

EXAMPLE 1 Let $\mathbf{Z}$ be the system of integers, and let f be the subset of $\mathbf{Z} \times \mathbf{Z}$ consisting of all ordered pairs

$$(x, 2x)$$

with x in $\mathbf{Z}$. This f is a mapping. An equivalent description of this mapping f is:

f is the mapping of $\mathbf{Z}$ to $\mathbf{Z}$ given by
$f(x) = 2x$
for all x in $\mathbf{Z}$

EXAMPLE 2 Let K be a field, and let f be the subset of $K \times K$ consisting of all ordered pairs (x, x^2), with x in K. Here $f(x) = x^2$ for all x in K.

It may be noted that what we are calling "the mapping f from A to B" is precisely what some textbooks call "the graph of the function f." Our definition of mapping is inspired by the observation that the graph of a function f gives the value of $f(x)$ for each x and therefore yields a perfectly adequate definition of "function."

EXAMPLE 3 A *binary operation* on a set A is a mapping of $A \times A$ into A. In the usual multiplicative notation, the binary operation assigns to the ordered pair (a, b) the element $a \cdot b$.

Given a mapping f from a set A to a set B, we call A the *domain* of f and B the *range* of f. The subset of B consisting of all elements $f(x)$ with x in A is called the *image* of f, or the *image* of A *under* f; it is denoted by $f(A)$. If $B = f(A)$, the mapping f is called *surjective*. If $f(x) = f(x')$ implies $x = x'$, the mapping f is called *injective*. A mapping f is called *bijective* if it is both injective and surjective. A bijective mapping is frequently called a *one-to-one* mapping.

For any mapping f of A to B, one denotes by f^{-1} the subset of all (y, x) in $B \times A$ such that (x, y) is in f. The subset f^{-1} is *not* a mapping of B to A unless f is a bijective mapping. In case f is a bijective mapping, we call f^{-1} the *inverse* of f. For any mapping f of A to B and for any y in B, we denote by $f^{-1}(y)$ the subset of all elements x in A such that $f(x) = y$; the subset $f^{-1}(y)$ is called the *inverse image of* y.

In Example 1, the mapping f is injective but not surjective; the inverse image $f^{-1}(y)$ is $y/2$ if y is an even integer and is the empty subset of $\mathbf{Z}$ if y is odd. In Example 2, the mapping f is not injective if $1 \neq -1$ in K, since $f(-x) = x^2 = f(x)$ for all x, but $-1 \neq 1$.

The mapping f of A to A such that $f(x) = x$ for all x in A is called the *identity* mapping of A. Given a mapping $f\colon A \to B$ and a mapping $g\colon B \to C$, we define the *composition* $g \circ f\colon A \to C$ as the mapping of A to C given by

$$g \circ f(x) = g(f(x))$$

for all x in A. If f is a bijective mapping of A to B, then clearly

$$f^{-1} \circ f = \text{identity mapping of } A$$
$$f \circ f^{-1} = \text{identity mapping of } B$$

If f is a mapping of a set A to a set B, and A' is a subset of A, the mapping of A' to B given by $x \rightarrow f(x)$ for x in A' is called the *restriction of f to A'*.

EXERCISES

1. Let A be a set. Let G denote the set of all bijective mappings of A to A. Prove that G becomes a group if composition is taken as the binary operation of G.

2. Let A and B be sets. Let $f\colon A \rightarrow B$ and $g\colon B \rightarrow A$ be mappings.

(*a*) If $f \circ g$ = identity mapping of B, f is surjective.

(*b*) If $g \circ f$ = identity mapping of A, f is injective.

(*c*) Let A' be a subset of A, and let I denote the identity mapping of A'. Is the composition $f \circ I$ the same as the restriction of f to A'?

2. Relations

The considerations which led to the definition of mapping lead to the following definition of a *relation.*

DEFINITION *A relation R on a set A is a subset of $A \times A$. We say that the elements x and y of A are in the relation R if and only if (x, y) is in R.*

Notation. Let R be a relation on a set A. We write xRy if and only if (x, y) is in R.

Thus a relation R is the totality of ordered pairs (x, y) such that xRy.

EXAMPLE 1 Let $\mathbf{Z}$ be the system of integers. The relation $<$ is the subset of all elements (x, y) in $\mathbf{Z} \times \mathbf{Z}$ such that $y - x$ is positive.

A relation R on a set A is called *reflexive* if xRx for all x in A. A relation R is called *symmetric* if yRx whenever xRy, for any x and y in A. A relation R is called *transitive* if, for any x, y, z in the set A such that xRy and yRz, we have xRz.

The relation $<$ in Example 1 is transitive, but not reflexive and not symmetric.

EXAMPLE 2 Let $\mathbf{Z}$ be the system of integers, and let $\leq$ be the relation defined by $x \leq y$ if and only if $x < y$ or $x = y$. The relation $\leq$ is reflexive and transitive, but not symmetric.

A relation R on a set A is called an *equivalence relation* if and only if R is reflexive, symmetric, and transitive.

EXAMPLE 3 Let A be a set, and let R be the set $A \times A$. Then R is the relation on A such that xRy for all x and y in A. Obviously R is reflexive, symmetric, and transitive. Thus R is an equivalence relation.

EXAMPLE 4 Let A be a set, and let R be the subset of all elements (x, x) in $A \times A$ with x in A. R is the relation such that xRy if and only if $x = y$. This relation is clearly reflexive, symmetric, and transitive.

EXAMPLE 5 Let $\mathbf{J}$ be the system of positive integers, or whole numbers as they are sometimes called. Let $A = \mathbf{J} \times \mathbf{J}$. Let Δ be the relation on A given by

$$(x, y) \,\Delta\, (x', y') \text{ if and only if } x + y' = x' + y$$

for any x, y, x', y' in $\mathbf{J}$. Then Δ is an equivalence relation.

EXAMPLE 6 Let $\mathbf{Z}$ be the system of integers. Let $\mathbf{Z}^*$ denote the subset of all nonzero integers. Let $A = \mathbf{Z} \times \mathbf{Z}^*$. Let F be the relation on A given by

$$(x, y)F(x', y') \text{ if and only if } xy' = x'y$$

for any x, x' in $\mathbf{Z}$ and y, y' in $\mathbf{Z}^*$. The relation F is an equivalence relation.

EXERCISES

1. Prove that the relation Δ in Example 5 is an equivalence relation on $\mathbf{J} \times \mathbf{J}$.
2. Prove that the relation F in Example 6 is an equivalence relation on $\mathbf{Z} \times \mathbf{Z}^*$.

3. *Quotient set*

Let R be an equivalence relation on a set A. For any element x in A, we denote by xR the set of all elements y in A such that xRy. The various subsets xR as x varies over A satisfy the following two conditions:

$R1$. *x is in xR for every x in A.*

$R2$. *If xR and yR have a common element, then $xR = yR$.*

The first condition comes from the fact that an equivalence relation is reflexive. The second condition is proved as follows. Suppose xR and yR each contain the element z of A. Then xRz and yRz. By the symmetry of equivalence relations, zRy. By transitivity, xRz and zRy imply xRy. Now if t is in xR, then we obtain in turn

$$\begin{aligned} &xRt \\ &tRx \\ &tRy \\ &yRt \end{aligned}$$

and thus t is in yR. Therefore xR is a subset of yR. By the same argument, yR is a subset of xR. Hence $xR = yR$.

The subset xR is called "the R-equivalence class of x." Conditions $R1$ and $R2$ assert in effect that each element of A lies in one and only one R-equivalence class. Thus the R-equivalence classes cover A and partition A into mutually disjoint subsets.

We now take a conceptual leap forward: we consider the collection of equivalence classes and denote this set (or collection) by A/R. That is, *each element of the set* A/R *is a subset of* A, namely, an R-equivalence class. The set A/R is called the *quotient set of* A mod R.

The mapping $\pi\colon A \to A/R$ which assigns to each x in A its R-equivalence class xR is called the *projection* of A onto A/R. Clearly $\pi^{-1}(\pi(x))$ is the R-equivalence class containing x, for any x in A.

EXAMPLE 1† Let G be a group, and let H be a subgroup. We define the relation R on G as follows:

$$xRy \text{ if and only if } x^{-1}y \text{ is in } H.$$

It is a simple exercise to prove that R is an equivalence relation. Moreover, the R-equivalence class containing an element x is the totality of elements y such that

$$x^{-1}y \text{ is in } H.$$

Multiplying on the left by x, we see that this condition is equivalent to

$$y \text{ is in } xH,$$

where xH denotes the set of all elements xh with h in H.

$$xR = xH$$

We call the subset xH the left *H-coset* of x. We denote by G/R the quotient set of G mod R by the symbol G/H also, and we call it "G mod H." In case the binary operation of G is denoted by $+$, we denote the left H-coset by $x + H$.

EXAMPLE 2 Let $\mathbf{Z}$ be the group of integers with addition as the binary operation. The even integers $2\mathbf{Z}$ form a subgroup. The quotient set $\mathbf{Z}/2\mathbf{Z}$ consists of only two cosets $0 + 2\mathbf{Z}$ and $1 + 2\mathbf{Z}$, since for any integer n, either n or $n - 1$ is even (prove this by the division algorithm!).

EXAMPLE 3 Let $\mathbf{Z}$ be the group of integers with addition as the binary operation. Let n be a positive integer, and let $n\mathbf{Z}$ denote the multiples of n. The quotient space $\mathbf{Z}/n\mathbf{Z}$ consists of exactly n elements

$$n\mathbf{Z},\ 1 + n\mathbf{Z},\ 2 + n\mathbf{Z},\ \ldots,\ (n-1) + n\mathbf{Z}$$

The proof of this assertion is left as an exercise. In Chap. 2, these cosets were called "residue classes modulo n," and the set of integers $0, 1, 2, \ldots, n - 1$ were called "a complete set of residues mod n."

EXERCISES

1. Prove that the relation of Example 1 is an equivalence relation.
2. Prove that the quotient space $\mathbf{Z}/n\mathbf{Z}$ has exactly n elements.

† See Sec. 10, Chap. 2, and Sec. 4, Chap. 10, for additional examples.

3. Let G be a group having n elements, and let H be a subgroup having r elements.

(*a*) Prove that each right H coset has exactly r elements.

(*b*) Prove that $r|n$.

(*c*) Prove that $r \cdot s = n$, where s is the number of elements in G/H.

4. In a group G having n elements, prove that x^n = identity for any x in G.

4. Binary operations on quotient sets

Let G be a group, let H be a subgroup, and let π denote the projection $x \to xH$ of G onto the quotient set G/H. *Is it possible to define a binary operation on G/H so that G/H becomes a group and π becomes a homomorphism of groups?*

Suppose that indeed there is such a binary operation in G/H. Since a homomorphism of groups sends the identity into the identity, $\pi(1) = 1'$: where 1 and $1'$ denote the identity elements of G and G/H, respectively. Since $\pi^{-1}(\pi(1))$ is the right H-coset containing 1, we have $\pi^{-1}(1') = H$. Now for any x in G,

$$\pi(xHx^{-1}) = \pi(x)\pi(H)\pi(x)^{-1} = \pi(x)1'\pi(x)^{-1} = 1'$$

Hence

4.1 $\quad xHx^{-1}$ is a subset of H, for each x in G.

Condition (4.1) is thus a necessary condition for the existence of a desired binary operation on G/H.

DEFINITION 4.1 *A* subgroup *H of a group G is called normal if and only if xhx^{-1} is in H for each x in G and h in H (this concept has been introduced in Chap. 10).*

THEOREM 4.1 *Let G be a group, let H be a normal subgroup of G, and let π be the projection of G onto G/H. There is one and only one binary operation on G/H with respect to which G/H is a group and π a homomorphism of groups.*

Proof. For any elements x and y in G, we consider the set of all elements in G of the form $xHyH$. Inasmuch as H is a *normal* subgroup, we have

$$Hy = yH$$

for all y in G. Thus

$$xHyH = xyHH = xyH$$

That is, the product of two cosets is a coset. Accordingly,

$$\theta\colon (xH, yH) \to xyH$$

is a mapping of $G/H \times G/H$ into G/H, and we take θ as the binary operation in G/H. Obviously, for all x and y in G, we have

4.2 $$\pi(x) \cdot \pi(y) = \pi(xy)$$

when we write the binary operation θ as multiplication. From Eq. (4.2) it may be verified directly that the binary operation of G/H satisfies the conditions imposed by the axioms of a group. Thus, G/H is a group and π is a homomorphism of groups. The uniqueness of the binary operation on G/H follows from the formula

4.3 $$u \cdot v = \pi(\pi^{-1}(u) \cdot \pi^{-1}(v)) \qquad \text{all } u, v \text{ in } G/H$$

which is a restatement of Eq. (4.2).

DEFINITION 4.2 *Let G be a group and H a normal subgroup. The* quotient group *G/H is the quotient set G/H with the binary operation taken as in Theorem* 4.1.

EXAMPLE 1 Let **Z** denote the group of integers with addition as the binary operation. Since **Z** is abelian, every subgroup of **Z** is normal. Hence we may speak of the quotient *group* $\mathbf{Z}/n\mathbf{Z}$. It is a group with exactly n elements.

EXAMPLE 2 Let G denote the permutation group of $\{1, 2, \ldots, n\}$. Let H denote the subgroup of elements of G which keep n fixed. Then two elements x and y of G lie in the same coset if and only if $x^{-1}y$ is in H, that is,

$$y \text{ is in } xH$$

This condition is equivalent to

$$y(n) = x(n)$$

That is, the permutations x and y send n into the same integer. Since there are n possible integers into which n can be sent, we see that G/H has exactly n elements. Hence by Exercise 3, Sec. 3, we see that

$$(\text{number of elements in } G) = n \times (\text{number of elements in } H)$$

Clearly H is isomorphic to the permutation group of $\{1, \ldots, n-1\}$. Letting σ_n denote the number of elements in the permutation group of $\{1, \ldots, n\}$, we have

$$\begin{aligned}\sigma_n &= n \cdot \sigma_{n-1} \\ &= n \cdot (n-1)\sigma_{n-2} \\ &\quad \cdots\cdots\cdots \\ &= n \cdot (n-1)(n-2) \cdots 2 \cdot \sigma_1 \\ &= n!\end{aligned}$$

It should be noted that H is not a normal subgroup of G and that G/H cannot be made into a group in such a way that π is a homomorphism of groups.

We now pose for rings the same question that was posed above for groups: Given a ring A, and an additive subgroup B (that is, a subgroup with respect to the binary operation of addition in A), *is it possible to define binary operations on the* *quotient set A/B so that the projection $\pi: A \to A/B$ becomes a ring homomorphism?* The problem of defining addition has already been solved in the affirmative. For with respect to addition, A is a commutative group and H is a normal subgroup, and addition can be defined as in Theorem 4.1. The definition of multiplication is possible only in a special circumstance.

DEFINITION 4.3 *Let A be a ring, and let B be an additive subgroup. B is called an* ideal *in A if and only if xb and bx are in B for all x in A and b in B.*

EXAMPLE 3 Let $\mathbf{Z}$ be the ring of integers, and let n be any integer. Then $n\mathbf{Z}$ is an ideal in $\mathbf{Z}$.

EXAMPLE 4 Let A be any commutative ring, and let x be any element in A. Then xA is an ideal in A for any x in A; xA is called the *principal ideal generated by x.*

EXAMPLE 5 Let A be a ring, and let B be a subset of A. We consider the intersection J of all the ideals of A which contain B. Then J is clearly an ideal. We call J the *ideal generated by the subset B.* One must not confuse the *ideal* generated by B and the *subring* of A generated by B. The latter is the intersection of all the subrings of A which contain B.

Additive examples of ideals may be found in Exercise 3, Sec. 9, Chap. 2; Exercise 2, Sec. 3, Chap. 6; and Exercise 7, Sec. 4.

THEOREM 4.2 *Let A be a ring, let B be an ideal, and let π denote the projection of A onto A/B. There is one and only one way of defining addition and multiplication in A/B so that π becomes a ring homomorphism. Conversely, if B is an additive subgroup of A such that binary operations can be defined in A/B so that π is a ring homomorphism, then the subgroup B is an ideal.*

The proof of Theorem 4.2 is similar to the proof of Theorem 4.1 and is left as an exercise for the reader.

DEFINITION 4.4 *Let A be a ring, and let B be an ideal in A. The ring obtained by taking on A/B the binary operations described in Theorem 4.2 is called the* quotient ring A mod B *and is denoted by A/B.*

EXAMPLE 6 Let $\mathbf{Z}$ be the ring of integers, and let n be an element of $\mathbf{Z}$. Then $n\mathbf{Z}$ is an ideal. Let $\mathbf{Z}_n$ denote the quotient ring $\mathbf{Z}/n\mathbf{Z}$. $\mathbf{Z}_n$ is a ring with n elements. The zero element of $\mathbf{Z}_n$ is the coset $n\mathbf{Z}$. The unit element is the coset $1 + n\mathbf{Z}$. *An element $r + n\mathbf{Z}$ of $\mathbf{Z}_n$ has a multiplicative inverse if and only if g.c.d.$(r, n) = 1$.* For if g.c.d. $(r, n) = 1$, there are integers a and b such that $ar + bn = 1$. Applying the ring homomorphism $\pi: \mathbf{Z} \to \mathbf{Z}_n$, we have

$$\pi(a)\pi(r) = \pi(1)$$

Since $\pi(r) = r + n\mathbf{Z}$, we see that $r + n\mathbf{Z}$ has a multiplicative inverse.

Conversely, if $r + n\mathbf{Z}$ has a multiplicative inverse, there is a coset $s + n\mathbf{Z}$ such that

$$\pi(s)\pi(r) = \pi(1)$$

This implies that

$$\pi(sr - 1) = \pi(0)$$

or

$$sr - 1 \text{ is in } \pi^{-1}(\pi(0)) = n\mathbf{Z}$$

that is, there is a z in $\mathbf{Z}$ such that

$$sr - 1 = nz$$

From this equation it is immediate that any integer dividing both r and n also divides 1. Consequently,

$$\text{g.c.d. } (r, n) = 1$$

In particular, if p is a prime integer, every nonzero element of the ring $\mathbf{Z}_r$ has a multiplicative inverse. Hence $\mathbf{Z}_p$ is a *field*, for every prime p.

EXERCISES

1. A subgroup H of a group G is normal if and only if each left H-coset is a right H-coset, that is, $xH = Hx$ for all x in G.

2. Deduce from Eq. (4.2) that the binary operation of G/H is associative.

3. Deduce from Eq. (4.2) that the equation $ax = b$ has a unique solution x for each a and b in G/H.

4. Let G be a group of permutations of a set X, let x be an element of the set X, and let G_x denote the set of all permutations in G such that $g(x) = x$.

(*a*) Prove that G_x is a subgroup of G. It is called the *stabilizer* of x.

(*b*) Let $G(x)$ denote the set of all elements in X of the form $g(x)$ with g in G. The subset $G(x)$ is called the *orbit* of x. Prove that there is a bijective mapping of the quotient space G/G_x onto the orbit $G(x)$. [Hint: Map the coset gG_x into the element $g(x)$.]

5. Prove Theorem 4.2.

6. Let K be a field, and let x be an indeterminate over the field K. Let A denote the ring of polynomials $K[x]$. Let p be a prime element (i.e., irreducible polynomial) in A, and let B denote the principal ideal pA. Prove that the quotient ring A/B is a field.

7. Let A be a commutative ring. An ideal P in A with $P \neq A$ is called a *prime ideal* if and only if for any x and y in A whose product xy is in P, either x is in P or y is in P. Prove: Let A be a commutative ring and B an ideal in A. Then A/B is an integral domain if and only if B is a prime ideal in A.

8. Let A be a commutative ring, and let B be an ideal in A, with $B \neq A$. The quotient A/B is a field if and only if B is a *maximal* ideal, that is, if B is not contained in a larger ideal, other than A itself.

9. Prove that every prime ideal in the ring of integers is maximal.

10. Let K be a field, and let x be an indeterminate over K. Prove that every prime ideal in $K[x]$ is maximal.

11. Let V be a vector space over a field K, let U be a subspace of V, and let π denote the projection of V onto V/U. Prove that operations can be so defined on V/U that π becomes a linear mapping.

12. Let V and U be as in Exercise 11. Prove $\dim U + \dim V/U = \dim V$.

13. Let T be a linear mapping of V to V such that T carries U into U. Prove that

(*a*) The rule

$$x + U \to Tx + U$$

defines a mapping of V/U into V/U which is linear. This mapping is called the V/U part of T and is denoted by $T_{V/U}$.

(*b*) $\det T = \det T_U \cdot \det T_{V/U}$, where $T_U\colon U \to U$ is the U part of T.

14. Let G be a group, and let f be a homomorphism of G into a group G'. Let H be a normal subgroup of G lying in the kernel of f. Prove that there is one and only one homomorphism $\bar{f}\colon G/H \to G'$ such that

$$\bar{f} \circ \pi = f$$

where π is the projection of G onto the quotient group G/H.

15. State and prove the analogue of Exercise 14 for rings.

16. Prove: The only ideals in a field K are (0) and K.

17. Prove: A homomorphism of a field is either a monomorphism or maps the field into zero.

18. Prove: The ideal generated by a nonzero element in the ring A of $n \times n$ matrices with coefficients in a field F is the entire ring A.

5. *The construction of the field of quotients of an integral domain*

Let D be an integral domain (cf. Chap. 2). We wish to construct a field K satisfying the following conditions:

(1) K contains a subring D' isomorphic to D.

(2) Each element of K is a quotient of elements of D'.

Our construction is as follows. Let D^* be the set of nonzero elements in D. Let $A = D \times D^*$. Let F be the relation on A given by $(x, y)\,F(x', y')$ if and only if $xy' = x'y$ for any (x, y) and (x', y') in A. By Exercise 2, Sec. 2, the relation F is an equivalence relation in $D \times D^*$. (F is modeled after the equality relation between fractions.) Set $K = A/F$. We shall now define addition and multiplication in K.

Define for any elements (x, y) and (x', y') in A

$$(x, y) + (x', y') = (xy' + x'y, yy')$$
$$(x, y) \cdot (x', y') = (xx', yy')$$

It is readily verified that for any elements a and b in A, $\pi^{-1}(\pi(a) + \pi(b))$ are each F-equivalence classes, where π denotes the projection of A onto A/F. Thereby, one can define addition and multiplication on K by the formula

$$q_1 + q_2 = \pi(\pi^{-1}(q_1) + \pi^{-1}(q_2))$$
$$q_1 \cdot q_2 = \pi(\pi^{-1}(q_1) \cdot \pi^{-1}(q_2))$$

for any q_1 and q_2 in K. One can check, axiom by axiom, that K is a field. The mapping

$$\varphi\colon z \to \pi((z, 1))$$

is a monomorphism of the integral domain D into K. Set $D' = \varphi(D)$. Since

$$(a, b) = (a, 1) \cdot (1, b)$$

and

$$\pi((1, b)) \cdot \pi((b, 1)) = \pi((b, b)) = \text{the unity in } K$$

we have

$$\pi((1, b)) = (\pi[(b, 1)])^{-1}$$

and

$$\pi(a, b) = \pi((a, 1)) \cdot (\pi[(b, 1)])^{-1}$$

that is, each element of K is a quotient of elements in D'.

EXERCISE

Check, axiom by axiom, that K is a field.

6. The construction of the field of real numbers from the field of rational numbers

Let **J** be the set of positive integers. Let A be a set. By a *sequence* of elements of A we mean a function from **J** to A. If f is a sequence of elements of A we call $f(1)$ the first element of the sequence, $f(2)$ the second element of the sequence, $f(3)$ the third element of the sequence, and $f(n)$ the nth element of the sequence for any positive integer n. It is customary to write f_n for $f(n)$ and to write $(a_1, a_2, a_3, \ldots, a_n, \ldots)$ for the sequence f with $f(1) = a_1$, $f(2) = a_2$, $f(3) = a_3$, and more generally $f(n) = a_n$ for each positive integer n.

EXAMPLE 1 The sequence of digits in the decimal expansion .333 · · · for $\frac{1}{3}$ is the constant function $f(n) = 3$ for all n in **J**.

EXAMPLE 2 The sequence of rational numbers

$$1, \frac{1}{2}, \frac{1}{4}, \ . \ . \ . \ , \frac{1}{2^{n-1}}, \ . \ . \ .$$

is the function $f: \mathbf{J} \to \mathbf{Q}$ such that

$$f(n) = \frac{1}{2^{n-1}}$$

EXAMPLE 3 The sequence of rational numbers

$$\frac{1}{3}, \frac{1}{4}, \frac{1}{5}, \ . \ . \ . \ , \frac{1}{n+2}$$

is the function $f: \mathbf{J} \to \mathbf{Q}$ such that

$$f(n) = \frac{1}{n+2}$$

A sequence of rational numbers $(a_1, a_2, \ldots, a_n, \ldots)$ is called a *Cauchy sequence* if and only if:

Given any positive rational number e, there is an integer p such that

$$|a_n - a_m| < e$$

for all $m, n > p$.

We denote by $\mathbf{Q}^{\mathbf{J}}$ the set of all sequences of rational numbers. In $\mathbf{Q}^{\mathbf{J}}$ we define addition and multiplication by the usual rule for the addition and multiplication of functions:

$$(f + g)(n) = f(n) + g(n)$$
$$(f \cdot g)(n) = f(n) \cdot g(n)$$

for all n in **J**. The set $\mathbf{Q}^{\mathbf{J}}$ is clearly a commutative ring with these operations.

Let A denote the subset of Cauchy sequences in $\mathbf{Q}^{\mathbf{J}}$. It is easily checked that A is a subring in $\mathbf{Q}^{\mathbf{J}}$.

Let N denote the subset of A consisting of Cauchy sequences $(a_1, a_2, \ldots, a_n, \ldots)$ with $\lim_{n\to\infty} a_n = 0$. It is easily checked that N is an ideal in A. Set

$$\mathbf{R} = A/N$$

Let π denote the projection of A onto **R**. One can easily verify the following:

(1) Any nonzero element in **R** has a multiplicative inverse. Thus the commutative ring **R** is a field.

(2) For any rational number q, let q^* denote the constant sequence whose nth term is q for each positive integer n. Let φ denote the mapping

$$q \to \pi(q^*)$$

of $\mathbf{Q}$ into $\mathbf{R}$. Then φ is a field monomorphism of $\mathbf{Q}$ into $\mathbf{R}$. We set $\mathbf{Q}' = \varphi(\mathbf{Q})$.

(3) Let $\mathbf{R}^+$ denote the subset of $\mathbf{R}$ defined as follows:
$\pi(f)$ belongs to $\mathbf{R}^+$ if and only if there is a positive rational number r and a positive integer p such that

$$f(n) \geq r$$

for all $n > p$.

It is not difficult to prove that

(i) If r and s are in $\mathbf{R}^+$, then $r + s$ and $r \cdot s$ are in $\mathbf{R}^+$.

(ii) If r is in $\mathbf{R}^+$, then $-r$ is not in r^+.

(iii) If r is not the zero element of the field $\mathbf{R}$, then either r or $-r$ is in $\mathbf{R}^+$.

Upon declaring $\mathbf{R}^+$ to be the set of positive elements in $\mathbf{R}$, we make $\mathbf{R}$ into an ordered field. It is clear that

(iv) Given any element c in $\mathbf{R}$, there is an element q in the subfield $\mathbf{Q}'$ such that $q > c$.

The main purpose of our construction of $\mathbf{R}$ can now be stated at last. The ordered field $\mathbf{R}$ has the property

(v) $\mathbf{R}$ is a *complete* ordered field.

Proof. Let $r_1, r_2, \ldots, r_n, \ldots$ be a Cauchy sequence of elements in $\mathbf{R}$. Each element r_i is by definition $\pi(a_i)$, where a_i is an element of A; that is, a_i is a Cauchy sequence of rational numbers

$$a_{i,1}, a_{i,2}, \ldots, a_{i,h}, \ldots$$

For each i, there is an integer p_i such that

$$|a_{i,m} - a_{i,n}| < \frac{1}{2^i} \qquad \text{for } m, n > p_i$$

Now consider the sequence of rational numbers

$$b_1, b_2, \ldots, b_n, \ldots$$

with

$$b_n = a_{n,p_n}$$

We show that $b_1, b_2, \ldots, b_n, \ldots$ is a Cauchy sequence in $\mathbf{Q}$. For given any positive rational e, we select the integer p so that

$$|r_n - r_m| < \frac{e'}{3} \text{ for } m, n > p$$

Next select the integer q so that $\frac{1}{2^q} < \frac{e}{3}$. Then we have

$$\begin{aligned}|b_n - b_m| = |a_{n,p_n} - a_{m,p_m}| &= |(a_{n,p_n} - a_{n,i}) + (a_{n,i} - a_{m,i}) \\ &\qquad + (a_{m,i} - a_{m,p_m})| \\ &\leq |a_{n,p_n} - a_{n,i}| + |a_{n,i} - a_{m,i}| + |a_{m,i} - a_{m,p_m}|\end{aligned}$$

for any subscript i. Now by definition of the order in **R**, we deduce from

$$|r_m - r_n| < \frac{e'}{3} \text{ that}$$

$$|a_{n,i} - a_{m,i}| < \frac{e}{3}$$

for all $i > q$, for some integer q. Hence for $m, n, i > p + q$ we have

$$|b_n - b_m| < \frac{1}{2^q} + \frac{e}{3} + \frac{1}{2^q} < \frac{e}{3} + \frac{e}{3} + \frac{e}{3} = e$$

That is,

$$|b_n - b_m| < e$$

for all $m, n > p + q$. Therefore $b_1, b_2, b_3, \ldots$ is a Cauchy sequence.

Let r denote the element of **R** that is represented by the sequence $b_1, b_2, \ldots, b_n, \ldots$. It follows directly from definitions that $\lim_{n\to\infty} r_i = r$. Therefore **R** is a complete ordered field.

It follows now from Exercise 4, Sec. 3, Chap. 4, that **R** satisfies the axioms for the field of real numbers.

Note. The constructions of Secs. 5 and 6 reveal that the system of real numbers can be constructed from the system of integers. Consequently, the assumptions made about the system of real numbers cannot lead to an inconsistency or contradiction unless the assumptions about the system of integers likewise lead to a contradiction—for any assertion about real numbers ultimately can be reformulated as a statement about integers.

It is for this reason that the mathematician takes the trouble to construct the real-number system.

The question of whether the assumptions imposed on the system of integers can lead to a contradiction has received intensive study by mathematicians and logicians. By far the most important investigation of this question was made by Kurt Gödel, in a celebrated memoir published in 1930 in the *Monatshefte für Mathematik und Physik.*

Suffice it to say that the question of the consistency of the assumptions concerning the integers leads to the question of the consistency of logic itself, since the system of integers can be constructed from the basic terms of logic alone. Such a construction is given for example in Russell and Whitehead's "Principia Mathematica."

The construction of the integers from the terms of logic comes in three stages. First one defines the system **J** of whole numbers. Then one defines in **J** the binary operations of addition and multiplication. Finally one extends the system **J** to the system of integers (negative as well as positive). Indeed, one can obtain **Z** as $(\mathbf{J} \times \mathbf{J})/\Delta$, where Δ is the equivalence relation defined in Example 5, Sec. 2.

EXERCISES

1. Prove, in detail, assertions (1), (2), and (3) above.
2. Prove (i), (ii), (iii), and (iv) above.
3. Exhibit the bijective mapping of **Z** onto $(\mathbf{J} \times \mathbf{J})/\Delta$, and derive the binary operations of **Z** from the corresponding operations of **J**.

7. The construction of a field containing a root of a polynomial

Let K be a field, let x be an indeterminate over K, and let $K[x]$ denote the ring of polynomials in x with coefficients in K. By definition, for any elements c_0, c_1, $\ldots, c_n$ in K, the polynomial $c_0 + c_1x + c_2x^2 + \cdots + c_nx^n = 0$ (in $K[x]$) if and only if $c_0 = c_1 = c_2 = \cdots = c_n = 0$. If L is a field containing K, and b is an element of L, then the mapping θ_b: $K[x] \to L$ given by

$$\theta_b\colon c_0 + c_1x + \cdots + c_nx^n \to c_0 + c_1b + \cdots + c_nb^h$$

is a ring homomorphism of $K[x]$ into L called the "b-substitution homomorphism." An element b in L is called a *zero* or *root* of the polynomial $f(x) = c_0 + c_1b + \cdots + c_nb^n = 0$ in L, that is, $\theta_b(f(x)) = 0$. We know that an element b in K is a zero of a polynomial $f(x)$ with coefficients in K if and only if $x - b$ divides $f(x)$ in the ring $K[x]$; for upon applying the division algorithm, we obtain

$$f(x) = (x - b)q(x) + r$$

with r a constant, and the constant $r = 0$ since

$$0 = f(b) = 0 \cdot q(b) + r$$

Hence, if $f(x)$ is an irreducible polynomial of degree greater than 1, $f(x)$ has no roots in K, and $f(b) \neq 0$ in K for all b in K.

We pose the problem: *Given an irreducible polynomial $f(x)$ in $K[x]$, construct a field L containing K such that for some b in L,*

7.1 $\quad f(b) = 0$

The solution of this problem is quite simple. Let B denote the ideal $f(x) \cdot K[x]$ of the ring $K[x]$ consisting of all the polynomials in $K[x]$ that are divisible by the irreducible polynomial $f(x)$. From the unique factorization theorem† in $K[x]$, one

† Theorem 3.6, Chap. 6.

sees at once that if $g(x)$ and $h(x)$ are in $K[x]$ and the product $g(x) \cdot h(x)$ is in B, then either $g(x)$ is in B or $h(x)$ is in B; that is, B is a *prime* ideal (cf., Exercise 7, Sec. 4). It follows by Exercises 10 and 8, Sec. 4, that the quotient ring $K[x]/B$ is a *field*. Let π denote the projection of $K[x]$ onto $K[x]/B$. Then π yields a ring homomorphism of the subfield K in $K[x]$. Hence, by Exercise 17, Sec. 4, π maps K monomorphically or $\pi(K) = (0)$. The latter possibility is excluded since 1 is not in the kernel of π. Hence, the field $K[x]/B$ contains a subfield $\pi(K)$ isomorphic to K. Set $L' = K[x]/B$, $K' = \pi(K)$, and $c' = \pi(c)$ for any c in K. Set $b = \pi(x)$. Then we have $L' = \pi(K[x])$, and L' consists of all expressions of the form

$$a_0' + a_1'b + a_2'b^2 + \cdots + a_n'b^n$$

with $a_0', a_1', \ldots, a_n'$ arbitrary elements of K'. Since B is the kernel of the homomorphism π, we have

$$\begin{aligned} 0 = \pi(f(x)) &= \pi(c_0 + c_1x + c_2x^2 + \cdots + c_nx^n) \\ &= c_0' + c_1'\pi(x) + \cdots + c_n'\pi(x^n) \\ &= c_0' + c_1'b + \cdots + c_n'b^n \\ &= f'(b) \end{aligned}$$

that is,

7.2 $$f'(b) = 0$$

where

$$f(x) = c_0 + cx + c_2x^2 + \cdots + c_nx^n$$

and

$$f'(x') = c_0' + c_1'x' + c_2'x^2 + \cdots + c_n'x'^n$$

It is clear that any polynomial $f(x)$ in $K[x]$ is irreducible in $K[x]$ if and only if the corresponding polynomial $f'(x')$ in $K'[x']$ is irreducible in $K'[x']$, where x is an indeterminate over K and x' an indeterminate over K'. Thus Eq. (7.2) reveals that our problem is solved for the field K', which is isomorphic to K.

In order to solve the problem for the original field K, one can resort to a standard trick of logic. Let L be any set containing K which can be put in a one-to-one correspondence φ with L' in such a way that each element c of K corresponds with $\pi(c)$ in K'; that is, φ: $L \to L'$ is a bijective mapping and $\varphi(c) = \pi(c)$ for all c in K. (The existence of such a set L, while intuitively obvious, can be proved only after digging into the foundations of logic). Define the binary operations in L to correspond to those in L; that is, define

$$\begin{aligned} u + v &= \varphi^{-1}(\varphi(u) + \varphi(v)) \\ u \cdot v &= \varphi^{-1}(\varphi(u) \cdot \varphi(v)) \end{aligned}$$

Then L is the desired field.†

† The reader may find it profitable to consult Exercise 9, Sec. 4, Chap. 6, for a slightly different description of L.

By repeating the construction above, one can find a field L which contains all the roots of any given polynomial $f(x)$ in $K[x]$. By repeating the construction infinitely many times, one can find a field $\bar{K}$ which contains the roots of all the polynomials in $K[x]$, the field obtained in this way is *algebraically closed;* that is, any polynomial $\bar{K}[x]$ has a root in $\bar{K}$.

8. *A paradox to avoid*

Given sets A and B, we employ the notation $A \sim B$ to mean that there is a bijective mapping from A to B. Clearly

$A \sim A.$
8.1 If $A \sim B$, then $B \sim A$.
If $A \sim B$ and $B \sim C$, then $A \sim C$.

The assertions (8.1) seem to say that $\sim$ is an equivalence relation. However, we must be very careful to specify on *which* set $\sim$ is a relation. One is tempted to say: $\sim$ is a relation on the *set* X of *all* sets. Our reason for not treating $\sim$ as a relation on this X is that it is advisable to avoid all mention of X. The reason for this self-imposed taboo is:

The usual rules of logic lead to a self-contradiction if one applies them to X.

We give a celebrated example due to Bertrand Russell. Let Y be the set of *all* elements of X satisfying the condition:

y is not an element of y.

If Y is not an element of Y, then Y is an element of Y by definition of Y—a contradiction. If Y is an element of Y, then Y is not an element of Y—again a contradiction. Thus, in any case, we are stuck with a contradiction.

This logical paradox can be avoided by adopting additional rules of logic which would make the foregoing paradox impossible to formulate.

The rule that is most often adopted by mathematicians is to declare that the totality of sets is *not* a set. Even more, one never uses "*all* the sets such that . . . ," but rather "all the subsets of the *set* A such that . . . ." With such conventions, the Russell paradox cannot be formulated, and we escape, as far as we know at present, the spectre of contradictions in logic.

9. *Bernstein's theorem on cardinal numbers*

Two sets A and B are said to have the same *cardinal number* if and only if $A \sim B$, that is, there is a bijective mapping from A to B.

Let $\mathbf{J}$ denote the set of positive integers and let $\mathbf{J}_n$ then denote the subset of elements z in $\mathbf{J}$ with $z \leq n$. We say that the cardinal number of a set A is n if and only if $A \sim \mathbf{J}_n$. One can prove (by induction) that if $\mathbf{J}_m \sim \mathbf{J}_n$, then $m = n$.

Thus if a set has the same cardinal number as some $\mathbf{J}_m$, then the cardinal number of A is a unique integer. A set is called *finite* if $A \sim \mathbf{J}_n$, for some n. A set is called *infinite* if it is not finite. It can be proved (cf., Exercise 8 below) that a set A is infinite if and only if there is a subset A' in A with $A' \neq A$ and $A' \sim A$. For example, the set of integers $\mathbf{Z}$ and the set of even integers $2\mathbf{Z}$ have the same cardinal number, since the mapping $z \to 2z$ is a bijective mapping of $\mathbf{Z}$ to $2\mathbf{Z}$.

One of the most important observations about cardinal numbers is given by the following theorem of F. Bernstein.

THEOREM 9.1 *Let $f: A \to B$ and $g: B \to A$ be injective mappings. Then there is a bijective mapping $\phi: A \to B$.*

Proof. Set

$$s = g \circ f$$
$$t = f \circ g$$

The mappings s and t are injective and $f \circ s = f \circ (g \circ f) = (f \circ g) \circ f = t \circ f$, that is

9.1 $$f \circ s = t \circ f$$

For each non-negative integer n, we denote by s^n the composition $s \circ s \cdot \cdot \cdot \circ s$ taken n times, s^0 denoting the identity mapping of A.

We define the relation S on A by

$$xSy \text{ if } y = s^n(x) \text{ or } x' = s^n(y) \text{ for some } n$$

The relation S is an equivalence relation on A. (Prove this!) Similarly, define the equivalence relation T on the set B by

$$xTy \text{ if } y = t^n(x) \text{ or } x = t^n(y)$$

for some non-negative integer n.

We observe that there are two kinds of S-equivalence classes:

(i) One in which each element x can be expressed as $s(y)$.

(ii) One which is not of type (i).

An S-equivalence class of type (i) which contains an element x consists of the elements

$$\ldots, s^{-1}(s^{-1}(x)), s^{-1}(x), x, s(x), s^2(x), \ldots, s^n(x), \ldots$$

An equivalence class of type (ii) must have an element x_0 such that $x_0 \neq s(y)$ for any y in A; it is clear, therefore, that the infinite sequence

$$x_0, s(x_0), s^2(x_0), \ldots$$

makes up such an S-equivalence class. We call x_0 the *generator* of this equivalence class. Clearly an equivalence class of type (ii) has a unique generator.

By virtue of (9.1), one sees that the mapping f maps any S-equivalence class of type (i) into a T-equivalence class of type (i). (Verify this!) Therefore f maps each S-equivalence class of type (ii) into a T-equivalence class of type (ii).

Let x_0S be an S-equivalence class of type (ii) with generator x_0. The image $f(x_0S)$ is contained in a T-equivalence class of type (ii), and this latter class therefore has a generator y_0. We assert: Either

9.2 $$f(x_0) = y_0 \qquad \text{or} \qquad g(y_0) = x_0$$

For if $f(x_0) \neq y_0$, we know that $f(x_0)$ is not a generator of its T-equivalence class, and therefore

$$f(x_0) = t^n(y_0) \qquad (n > 0)$$

Hence

$$f(x_0) = (f \circ g) \circ (f \circ g)^{n-1}(y_0) = f(g(f \circ g)^{n-1}(y_0))$$

Since f is injective,

$$\begin{aligned} x_0 &= g \circ (f \circ g)^{n-1}(y_0) \\ &= (g \circ f)^{n-1} \circ g(y_0) \end{aligned}$$

since

$$\begin{aligned} g \circ (f \circ g)^{n-1} &= g \circ (f \circ g) \circ \cdots \circ (f \circ g) = (g \circ f) \circ (g \circ f) \circ \cdots \circ g \\ &= (g \circ f)^{n-1} \circ g \end{aligned}$$

Thus $n = 1$, $f(x_0) = f \circ g(y_0)$, and

$$x_0 = g(y_0)$$

As a consequence of assertion (9.2), we can find a bijective mapping between any S-equivalence class of type (ii) and its corresponding T-equivalence class. Namely, let x_0S be an equivalence class of type (ii) with generator x_0, and let y_0 be the generator of the equivalence class containing $f(x_0S)$. The mapping

9.3 $$s^n(x_0) \to t^n(y_0) \qquad (n = 0, 1, 2, \ldots)$$

is a bijective mapping of the equivalence classes.

On the other hand, if x belongs to an S-equivalence class of type (i), the mapping

9.4 $$x \to f(x)$$

is a bijective mapping of the S-equivalence class xS to the T-equivalence class $f(x)T$.

Let φ be the mapping of A to B that is defined by (9.3) and (9.4) for elements in equivalence classes of type (ii) and type (i), respectively. Then φ is the desired bijective mapping.

EXERCISES

Let **J**, **Z**, **Q**, and **R** be as in Sec. 6.

1. Prove $\mathbf{J} \sim \mathbf{Z}$.

2. Prove $\mathbf{J} \sim \mathbf{Q}$.

3. Let A be a set, let $P(A)$ denote the set of all subsets of A, and let 2^A denote the set of all functions from A to the set of two elements $\{0, 1\}$. Prove $P(A) \sim 2^A$. [Hint: Consider the mapping $f \to f^{-1}(0)$.]

4. For any set A, prove that $A \sim 2^A$ is impossible. [Hint: Given a mapping $\theta: A \to 2^A$, let g be an element of 2^A such that $g(a) \neq \theta(a)(a)$ for each a in A. Show that g is not in the image of θ.]

5. Prove that the relation S defined in Sec. 9 is an equivalence relation.

6. Prove $\mathbf{R} \sim 2\mathbf{J}$.

7. Deduce from Exercises 4, 5, and 6 that $\mathbf{J} \sim \mathbf{R}$ is false (cf. corollary to Theorem 4.2, Chap. 4).

8. A set A is infinite if and only if $A \sim A'$ for some proper subset A' of A with $A' \neq A$.

9. Let A be a set, and let R be the relation on $P(A)$: BRC if and only if $B \sim C$. Prove that $P(A)/R$ has a relation $\leqslant$ such that:

(*a*) $\pi(b) \leqslant \pi(c)$ if B is a subset of C, where $\pi: P(A) \to P(A)/R$ is the projection associated with R.

(*b*) For any elements a and b in $P(A)/R$, either $a \leqslant b$ or $b \leqslant a$.

(*c*) If $a \leqslant b$ and $b < a$, then $a = b$.

10. Does each non-empty subset of $P(A)/R$ have a least element?

16

Tensors

1. *Introduction*

This chapter is concerned with some important systems associated with a vector space. First we define the tensor product $U \otimes V$ of two vector spaces over a field K. Roughly speaking, $U \otimes V$ is the nearest we can come to making the set $U \times V$ of all pairs (u, v) into a vector space satisfying

$$(u_1 + u_2, v) = (u_1, v) + (u_2, v) \qquad \text{and} \qquad (u, v_1 + v_2) = (u, v_1) + (u, v_2)$$

With this operation we then form spaces $U_0^{\,p} = U \otimes U \otimes \cdots \otimes U$ (p times). Roughly speaking, again, $U_0^{\,p}$ is the smallest vector space which contains all p-tuples of vectors in U. Using the dual space U^* of U we also form spaces $U_q^{\,0} = U^* \otimes U^* \otimes \cdots \otimes U^*$ (q times). The elements of $U_q^{\,0}$ can be considered as q-linear functions on U; the elements of $U_0^{\,p}$ can be considered as p-linear functions on U^*. In this way the study of multilinear operations can be reduced to the study of linear operations. Further, we form the spaces $U_q^{\,p} = U_0^{\,p} \otimes U_q^{\,0}$, and finally we put these all together into a single gigantic system called the *tensor algebra* of U. It can be thought of as consisting of all multilinear operators on U and U^*.

Each nonsingular linear transformation of U induces a transformation on each $U_q^{\,p}$, and the resulting transformations characterize the *type* of the tensor spaces. From the tensor algebra of U we shall derive another system called the *exterior algebra* of U. It has important connections with subspaces of U.

2. *Tensor products*

In this section we define an important operation on vector spaces. We first state two preliminary definitions which will be used frequently in this chapter.

DEFINITION 2.1 *Let* $S_1, \ldots, S_r$ *be arbitrary sets. Then* $S_1 \times S_2 \times \cdots \times S_r$ *will denote the set of all ordered r-tuples* $(s_1, s_2, \ldots, s_r)$, *with* s_i *in* S_i *for* $i = 1, \ldots, r$.

The set thus defined is called the *cartesian product* of $S_1, \ldots, S_r$.

DEFINITION 2.2 *Let* $U_1, \ldots, U_r$, W *be vector spaces over a field* K. *A mapping* $f: U_1 \times \cdots \times U_r \to W$ *is called r-linear*† *if* $\mathbf{f}(\mathbf{x}_1, \mathbf{x}_2, \ldots, \mathbf{x}_r)$ *is linear in each of the r entries, that is, if*

2.1
$$\mathbf{f}(\ldots, \mathbf{x}_i + \mathbf{x}'_i, \ldots) = \mathbf{f}(\ldots, \mathbf{x}_i, \ldots) + \mathbf{f}(\ldots, \mathbf{x}'_i, \ldots)$$
$$\mathbf{f}(\ldots, c\mathbf{x}_i, \ldots) = c \cdot \mathbf{f}(\ldots, \mathbf{x}_i, \ldots)$$

for any $\mathbf{x}_i$, $\mathbf{x}'_i$ *in* U_i *and any c in K, the entries in the places* $1, \ldots, i-1, i+1, \ldots, r$ *being arbitrary (but the same on both sides of* (2.1)*, naturally).*

For $r = 1$ this is simply the definition of a linear mapping $U_1 \to W$. For $r = 2$ such a mapping $\mathbf{f}$ is called *bilinear*. For example, a bilinear function on a vector space U, as defined in Chap. 14, is a bilinear mapping $U \times U \to K$, as defined above. All r-linear mappings $U_1 \times \cdots \times U_r \to W$ form a vector space over K, with the usual definitions of addition and scalar product of mappings.

Now let U and V be finite-dimensional vector spaces over the same field of scalars K and choose bases $\{\mathbf{u}_1, \ldots, \mathbf{u}_m\}$ in U and $\{\mathbf{v}_1, \ldots, \mathbf{v}_n\}$ in V, so that we assume $\dim U = m$ and $\dim V = n$. Let P be a vector space of dimension $m \cdot n$ over K. Since there are $m \cdot n$ index pairs (i, j) with $i = 1, \ldots, m$ and $j = 1, \ldots, n$, we can use these pairs to index the elements of a base $\{\mathbf{p}_{ij}\}$ in P. That being done, we define a mapping $\mathbf{f}: U \times V \to P$ as follows:

2.2
$$\mathbf{f}(\mathbf{x}, \mathbf{y}) = x^i y^j \mathbf{p}_{ij} \qquad \textit{where } \mathbf{x} = x^i\mathbf{u}_i \textit{ and } \mathbf{y} = y^j\mathbf{v}_j$$

It is easily verified that $\mathbf{f}$ is bilinear, and (2.2) gives $\mathbf{f}(\mathbf{u}_i, \mathbf{v}_j) = \mathbf{p}_{ij}$. The *image* of $\mathbf{f}$, that is, the set $\mathbf{f}(U \times V)$ in P, contains the base $\{\mathbf{p}_{ij}\}$ and therefore spans P. Furthermore, $\mathbf{f}$ has the following important property: Let $\mathbf{g}: U \times V \to L$ be any bilinear mapping into a vector space L. Define a *linear* mapping $\mathbf{g}_1: P \to L$ by the rule

2.3
$$\mathbf{g}_1(\mathbf{p}_{ij}) = \mathbf{g}(\mathbf{u}_i, \mathbf{v}_j)$$

This defines $\mathbf{g}_1$ on the base $\{\mathbf{p}_{ij}\}$ in P and therefore determines $\mathbf{g}_1$ uniquely by linearity. *For this mapping* $\mathbf{g}$, *we have* $\mathbf{g} = \mathbf{g}_1 \circ \mathbf{f}$. For

$$(\mathbf{g}_1 \circ \mathbf{f})(\mathbf{x}, \mathbf{y}) = \mathbf{g}_1(\mathbf{f}(\mathbf{x}, \mathbf{y}))$$
$$\mathbf{g}_1(x^i y^j \mathbf{p}_{ij}) = x^i y^j \mathbf{g}_1(\mathbf{p}_{ij}) = x^i y^j \mathbf{g}(\mathbf{u}_i, \mathbf{v}_j)$$

using (2.2), (2.3) and the linearity of $\mathbf{g}_1$. On the other hand

$$\mathbf{g}(\mathbf{x}, \mathbf{y}) = \mathbf{g}(x^i\mathbf{u}_i, y^j\mathbf{v}_j) = x^i y^j \cdot \mathbf{g}(\mathbf{u}_i, \mathbf{v}_j)$$

from the bilinearity of $\mathbf{g}$ [that is, from Eq. (2.1)]. Hence we have shown that any bilinear mapping $\mathbf{g}$ of $U \times V$ can be "factored" into the composition of a linear mapping $\mathbf{g}_1$ of P and of the fixed bilinear mapping $\mathbf{f}$.

The space P with the mapping $\mathbf{f}$ is called a *tensor product* of U and V. The description we have just given of it suffers from the disagreeable drawback of being

† Or it is called simply *multilinear* if there is no need to specify r.

tied to bases in the vector spaces. We can overcome this by simply taking the properties of $\mathbf{f}$ cited above as the basis for an axiomatic definition, which we now state.

DEFINITION 2.3 *By a* tensor product *of two vector spaces U, V over a field K is meant a vector space P over K equipped with a fixed bilinear mapping $\mathbf{f}: U \times V \to P$ having the following properties: The image $\mathbf{f}(U \times V)$ spans P; and if $\mathbf{g}: U \times V \to L$ is any bilinear mapping into a vector space L, then there exists a linear mapping $\mathbf{g}_1: P \to L$ such that $\mathbf{g} = \mathbf{g}_1 \circ \mathbf{f}$.*

The existence of a tensor product of two finite-dimensional vector spaces is assured by the discussion above. We observe that Definition 2.3 makes sense for infinite-dimensional spaces, too, and the existence of tensor products in general can be demonstrated by a similar argument. We shall be concerned almost exclusively with finite-dimensional spaces in this chapter, and we shall therefore not go into the infinite-dimensional case.

REMARK 1. The tensor-product operation is of great importance in many parts of mathematics. With minor modifications Definition 2.3 can be applied to other kinds of algebraic structures. For example, if U and V denote any additive abelian groups, and if we replace K above by the ring of integers $\mathbf{Z}$, then Definition 2.3 becomes the definition of the tensor product of two abelian groups (for this modification the terms *linear* and *bilinear* are still to be taken in the sense of Definition 2.2, with "vector space" replaced by "additive abelian group" and with K replaced by $\mathbf{Z}$).

We start with a very simple proposition which is of use in analyzing Definition 2.3.

PROPOSITION 2.1 *Let U be a vector space over a field K, and let S be a subset which spans U. If $\mathbf{h}_1$ and $\mathbf{h}_2$ are linear mappings of U to another vector space, and if $\mathbf{h}_1$ and $\mathbf{h}_2$ have the same effect on elements of S, then $\mathbf{h}_1 = \mathbf{h}_2$.*

Proof. By assumption (cf. Exercise 5, Sec. 5, Chap. 8) every vector $\mathbf{x}$ in U can be expressed as a linear combination $\mathbf{x} = c_1\mathbf{s}_1 + \cdots + c_r\mathbf{s}_r$ of elements in S with coefficients c_i in K. Since $\mathbf{h}_1$ is linear, $\mathbf{h}_1(\mathbf{x}) = c_1\mathbf{h}_1(\mathbf{s}_1) + \cdots + c_r\mathbf{h}_1(\mathbf{s}_r)$, and similarly for $\mathbf{h}_2$. By assumption, $\mathbf{h}_1(\mathbf{s}_i) = \mathbf{h}_2(\mathbf{s}_i)$ for $i = 1, \ldots, r$, whence $\mathbf{h}_1(\mathbf{x}) = \mathbf{h}_2(\mathbf{x})$. Q.E.D.

PROPOSITION 2.2 *The linear mapping $\mathbf{g}_1: P \to L$ of Definition 2.3 is uniquely determined by the bilinear mapping $\mathbf{g}$.*

Proof. We have $\mathbf{g} = \mathbf{g}_1 \circ \mathbf{f}$. Let $\mathbf{g}_2$ be another linear mapping $P \to L$ such that $\mathbf{g} = \mathbf{g}_2 \circ \mathbf{f}$, so that $\mathbf{g}_1 \circ \mathbf{f} = \mathbf{g}_2 \circ \mathbf{f}$. Then $\mathbf{g}_1$ and $\mathbf{g}_2$ have the same effect on all elements in the image $\mathbf{f}(U \times V)$ in P. By assumption, this image spans P, and therefore $\mathbf{g}_1 = \mathbf{g}_2$, by Proposition 2.1. Q.E.D.

According to Definition 2.3, a tensor product of U and V consists of a vector space P and a certain bilinear mapping $\mathbf{f}$. We shall sometimes indicate a tensor product by the notation $\{P, \mathbf{f}\}$.

THEOREM 2.3 *Let $\{P, \mathbf{f}\}$ and $\{P', \mathbf{f}'\}$ be two tensor products of vector spaces U and V. Then there is one and only one linear mapping $\mathbf{h}: P \to P'$ such that $\mathbf{f}' = \mathbf{h} \circ \mathbf{f}$, and $\mathbf{h}$ is an isomorphism.*

Proof. By Definition 2.3, $\mathbf{f}$ and $\mathbf{f}'$ are bilinear mappings of $U \times V$ into P and P', respectively. Taking $\mathbf{g}$ in Definition 2.3 to be $\mathbf{f}'$, we see from the definition that there is a linear mapping $\mathbf{h}: P \to P'$ such that $\mathbf{f}' = \mathbf{h} \circ \mathbf{f}$; and $\mathbf{h}$ is unique, by the preceding theorem. Similarly, there is a unique linear mapping $\mathbf{h}': P' \to P$ such that $\mathbf{f} = \mathbf{h}' \circ \mathbf{f}'$. Hence, $\mathbf{f} = \mathbf{h}' \circ (\mathbf{h} \circ \mathbf{f}) = (\mathbf{h}' \circ \mathbf{h}) \circ \mathbf{f}$, and therefore, for any element $\mathbf{t}$ in the image $\mathbf{f}(U \times V)$ of $\mathbf{f}$, we must have $\mathbf{t} = (\mathbf{h}' \circ \mathbf{h})(\mathbf{t})$. Thus $\mathbf{h}' \circ \mathbf{h}$ has the same effect on elements $\mathbf{f}(U \times V)$ as the identity mapping of P. By assumption, $\mathbf{f}(U \times V)$ spans P, and so $\mathbf{h}' \circ \mathbf{h}$ must be the identity mapping of P, by Proposition 2.1. By a similar argument, $\mathbf{h} \circ \mathbf{h}'$ is the identity mapping of P'. Therefore $\mathbf{h}$ and $\mathbf{h}'$ are inverse mappings and must consequently be one-to-one. Q.E.D.

The theorem just established shows that any two tensor products of U and V are *canonically* isomorphic, that is, in a specific way. Thus any two tensor products are interchangeable, and for this reason we shall usually not distinguish between different tensor products of U and V. Any one of them $\{P, \mathbf{f}\}$ will be denoted by $U \otimes V$, called simply *the* tensor product of U and V, and for the given bilinear mapping $\mathbf{f}$ of $U \times V$ to P, that is, to $U \otimes V$, we shall use the notation

2.4 $$\mathbf{f}(\mathbf{x}, \mathbf{y}) = \mathbf{x} \otimes \mathbf{y}$$

With this notation the bilinearity of $\mathbf{f}$ is expressed by the following rules, which are just restatements of (2.1):

2.5 $$\begin{aligned} (\mathbf{x} + \mathbf{x}') \otimes \mathbf{y} &= \mathbf{x} \otimes \mathbf{y} + \mathbf{x}' \otimes \mathbf{y} \\ \mathbf{x} \otimes (\mathbf{y} + \mathbf{y}') &= \mathbf{x} \otimes \mathbf{y} + \mathbf{x} \otimes \mathbf{y}' \\ (c\mathbf{x}) \otimes \mathbf{y} &= \mathbf{x} \otimes (c\mathbf{y}) = c \cdot (\mathbf{x} \otimes \mathbf{y}) \end{aligned}$$

for any $\mathbf{x}$, $\mathbf{x}'$ in U, any $\mathbf{y}$, $\mathbf{y}'$ in V, and any c in K. Definition 2.3 says that, given any bilinear mapping $\mathbf{g}: U \times V \to L$, there is a linear mapping $\mathbf{g}_1: U \otimes V \to L$, necessarily unique (Proposition 2.2), such that $\mathbf{g} = \mathbf{g}_1 \circ \mathbf{f}$. That is, $\mathbf{g}(\mathbf{x}, \mathbf{y}) = \mathbf{g}_1(\mathbf{f}(\mathbf{x}, \mathbf{y}))$, or, using (2.4),

2.6 $$\mathbf{g}(\mathbf{x}, \mathbf{y}) = \mathbf{g}_1(\mathbf{x} \otimes \mathbf{y})$$

PROPOSITION 2.4 *Let $U \otimes V$ be the tensor product of two vector spaces U, V over K. Then every element of $U \otimes V$ can be expressed in at least one way as a sum*

$$\sum_{i=1}^{s} \mathbf{x}_i \otimes \mathbf{y}_i$$

with $\mathbf{x}_i$ in U and $\mathbf{y}_i$ in V $(i = 1, \ldots, s)$.

Proof. Let $U \otimes V$ be the tensor product $\{P, \mathbf{f}\}$. By Definition 2.3 the image $\mathbf{f}(U \times V)$ in P spans P. Therefore any element $\mathbf{t}$ of P can be expressed as a linear combination $\mathbf{t} = c_1\mathbf{u}_1 + \cdots + c_s\mathbf{u}_s$, where each $\mathbf{u}_i$ is in $\mathbf{f}(U \times V)$. That is, each $\mathbf{u}_i$ can be written $\mathbf{u}_i = \mathbf{f}(\mathbf{x}_i, \mathbf{y}_i)$. Now $c_i\mathbf{u}_i = c_i\mathbf{f}(\mathbf{x}_i, \mathbf{y}_i) = \mathbf{f}(c_i\mathbf{x}_i, \mathbf{y}_i)$, since $\mathbf{f}$ is bilinear. Writing $\mathbf{x}'_i = c_i\mathbf{x}_i$, we have

$$\mathbf{t} = \mathbf{f}(\mathbf{x}'_1, \mathbf{y}_1) + \cdots + \mathbf{f}(\mathbf{x}'_s, \mathbf{y}_s), \qquad \text{or} \qquad \mathbf{t} = \mathbf{x}'_1 \otimes \mathbf{y}_1 + \cdots + \mathbf{x}'_s \otimes \mathbf{y}_s$$

in the notation of (2.4). This proves our contention. Q.E.D.

THEOREM 2.5 *Let U and V be vector spaces over a field K, of dimensions m and n, respectively. Then their tensor product $U \otimes V$ has dimension mn. If $\{\mathbf{u}_1, \ldots, \mathbf{u}_m\}$ and $\{\mathbf{v}_1, \ldots, \mathbf{v}_n\}$ are bases for U resp. V, then the elements $\mathbf{u}_i \otimes \mathbf{v}_j$ in $U \otimes V$ $(i = 1, \ldots, m;\ \ j = 1, \ldots, n)$ form a base for $U \otimes V$.*

Proof. Let $\mathbf{f}: U \times V \to P$ be the bilinear mapping defined in (2.2). Then $\{P, \mathbf{f}\}$ satisfies Definition 2.3 and can therefore be taken as the tensor product $U \otimes V$. Now P has as base the elements $\{\mathbf{p}_{ij}\}$ and therefore has dimension mn. From (2.2) and (2.4) we have $\mathbf{p}_{ij} = \mathbf{u}_i \otimes \mathbf{u}_j$. Q.E.D.

THEOREM 2.6 *Let U and V be two vector spaces over a field K. Then there is a unique isomorphism from $U \otimes V$ to $V \otimes U$ sending $\mathbf{x} \otimes \mathbf{y}$ into $\mathbf{y} \otimes \mathbf{x}$ for any $\mathbf{x}$ in U and $\mathbf{y}$ in V.*

Proof. Let $U \otimes V$ be the tensor product $\{P, \mathbf{f},\}$, and let $V \otimes U$ be the tensor product $\{Q, \mathbf{f}'\}$, so that $\mathbf{f}'$ is a bilinear mapping of $V \times U$ to Q. Now the mapping $\mathbf{g}: V \times U \to P$ defined by $\mathbf{g}(\mathbf{y}, \mathbf{x}) = \mathbf{f}(\mathbf{x}, \mathbf{y})$ obviously satisfies Definition 2.3, with U and V interchanged. Hence $\{P, \mathbf{g}\}$ is also a tensor product of V and U, in that order. By Theorem 2.3 there is a unique linear mapping $\mathbf{h}: P \to Q$, necessarily an isomorphism, such that $\mathbf{h} \circ \mathbf{g} = \mathbf{f}'$. Using the notation $\mathbf{f}(\mathbf{x}, \mathbf{y}) = \mathbf{x} \otimes \mathbf{y}$ and $\mathbf{f}'(\mathbf{y}, \mathbf{x}) = \mathbf{y} \otimes \mathbf{x}$, this last equation gives us $(\mathbf{h} \circ \mathbf{g})(\mathbf{y}, \mathbf{x}) = \mathbf{f}'(\mathbf{y}, \mathbf{x})$, or $\mathbf{h}(\mathbf{g}(\mathbf{y}, \mathbf{x})) = \mathbf{y} \otimes \mathbf{x}$, or finally $\mathbf{h}(\mathbf{x} \otimes \mathbf{y}) = \mathbf{y} \otimes \mathbf{x}$. Q.E.D.

The theorem just proved is a kind of "commutative" law for the tensor product of two vector spaces. In the following paragraph we establish an analogous "associative law."

EXERCISES

1. U being a vector space over K, show that there is a unique linear mapping $\mathbf{h}: K \otimes U \to U$ such that $\mathbf{h}(1 \otimes \mathbf{x}) = \mathbf{x}$ for all $\mathbf{x}$ in U, and show that $\mathbf{h}$ is an isomorphism.

2. If $\mathbf{f}: U_1 \times \cdots \times U_r \to L$ and $\mathbf{g}: V_1 \times \cdots \times V_s \to M$ are multilinear mappings, prove that the mapping $\mathbf{h}$ of $U_1 \times \cdots \times U_r \times V_1 \times \cdots \times V_s$ into $L \otimes M$ defined by

$$\mathbf{h}(\mathbf{u}_1, \ldots, \mathbf{u}_r, \mathbf{v}_1, \ldots, \mathbf{v}_s) = \mathbf{f}(\mathbf{u}_1, \ldots, \mathbf{u}_r) \otimes \mathbf{g}(\mathbf{v}_1, \ldots, \mathbf{v}_s)$$

is $(r + s)$-linear.

3. Let U, V be vector spaces over K, and suppose that V is the direct sum of subspaces V_1 and V_2. Show that $U \otimes V$ can be regarded as the direct sum of $U \otimes V_1$ and $U \otimes V_2$.

4. If $\mathbf{f}: U \to U'$ and $\mathbf{g}: V \to V'$ are linear mappings of vector spaces over K, show that there is a unique linear mapping $\mathbf{h}: U \otimes V \to U' \otimes V'$ such that $\mathbf{h}(\mathbf{x} \otimes \mathbf{y}) = \mathbf{f}(\mathbf{x}) \otimes \mathbf{g}(\mathbf{y})$ for all $\mathbf{x}$ in U and $\mathbf{y}$ in V.

5. Let $\mathbf{f}: U \times V \to P$ be a bilinear mapping of finite-dimensional vector spaces over K such that $\mathbf{f}(U \times V)$ spans P. Suppose that for every bilinear mapping $\mathbf{g}: U \times V \to K$ there exists a linear mapping $\mathbf{g}_1: P \to K$ such that $\mathbf{g} = \mathbf{g}_1 \circ \mathbf{f}$. Show that $\{P, \mathbf{f}\}$ is a tensor product of U and V.

6. Write out in detail the definition of the tensor product $G_1 \otimes G_2$ of additive abelian groups.

***7.** For any additive abelian group G prove that there is a unique homomorphism $G \otimes \mathbf{Z} \to G$ mapping $a \otimes 1$ into a for any a in G, and show that the mapping is an isomorphism.

***8.** Let G_1 be a group of order 3, and let G_2 be a group of order 5. Prove that $G_1 \otimes G_2$ consists of the zero element alone.

***9.** Let U, V be vector spaces over K, and let W consist of all mappings $f: U \times V \to K$ such that f maps all but a finite number of pairs $(\mathbf{x}, \mathbf{y})$ into zero. Make W into a vector space by the usual definitions of addition of mappings and of scalar multiplication. We use the following notation: If f in W maps all pairs $(\mathbf{x}, \mathbf{y})$ into zero except, say, $(\mathbf{x}_1, \mathbf{y}_1), \ldots, (\mathbf{x}_r, \mathbf{y}_r)$, and if f maps the ith one of these into the scalar a_i, then denote f by the symbol

$$a_1(\mathbf{x}_1, \mathbf{y}_1) + a_2(\mathbf{x}_2, \mathbf{y}_2) + \cdots + a_r(\mathbf{x}_r, \mathbf{y}_r)$$

With this notation let J denote the subspace of W generated by all elements represented by symbols of the following types:

$$(\mathbf{x} + \mathbf{x}', \mathbf{y}) - (\mathbf{x}, \mathbf{y}) - (\mathbf{x}', \mathbf{y})$$
$$(\mathbf{x}, \mathbf{y} + \mathbf{y}') - (\mathbf{x}, \mathbf{y}) - (\mathbf{x}, \mathbf{y}')$$
$$(a\mathbf{x}, y) - (\mathbf{x}, a\mathbf{y})$$
$$(a\mathbf{x}, y) - a(\mathbf{x}, \mathbf{y})$$

Prove that the quotient space W/J is a tensor product of U and V (see Sec. 10, Chap. 9).

3. *Tensor products of more than two factors*

Given vector spaces U, V, W over a field K, we can apply the tensor-product operation twice, forming, for example, $(U \otimes V) \otimes W$, etc. In a similar way we can form repeated tensor products with any number of factors. In this section we shall prove the basic facts. The most important applications in this chapter will involve repeated tensor products $(U \otimes U) \otimes U$, etc., of a single space. We start with an auxiliary result.

THEOREM 3.1 *Let U, V, W, L be vector spaces over a field K, and let $\mathbf{g}: U \times V \times W \to L$ be a 3-linear mapping. Then there is a unique linear mapping $\mathbf{g}': (U \otimes V) \otimes W \to L$ such that $\mathbf{g}(\mathbf{x}, \mathbf{y}, \mathbf{z}) = \mathbf{g}'((\mathbf{x} \otimes \mathbf{y}) \otimes \mathbf{z})$ for any $\mathbf{x}$ in U, $\mathbf{y}$ in V, $\mathbf{z}$ in W.*

Proof. For fixed $\mathbf{z}$ in W the mapping $U \times V \to L$ defined by $(\mathbf{x}, \mathbf{y}) \to \mathbf{g}(\mathbf{x}, \mathbf{y}, \mathbf{z})$ is clearly bilinear. Therefore, by definition of $U \otimes V$ and by Proposition 2.2, we have

3.1 $$\mathbf{g}(\mathbf{x}, \mathbf{y}, \mathbf{z}) = \mathbf{g}_1(\mathbf{x} \otimes \mathbf{y}, \mathbf{z})$$

where $\mathbf{g}_1$ is a *unique* linear mapping, depending on $\mathbf{z}$, of $U \otimes V \to L$. We claim that $\mathbf{g}_1$ depends linearly on $\mathbf{z}$, that is, that

3.2 $$\begin{aligned} \mathbf{g}_1(\mathbf{t}, \mathbf{z} + \mathbf{z}') &= \mathbf{g}_1(\mathbf{t}, \mathbf{z}) + \mathbf{g}_1(\mathbf{t}, \mathbf{z}') \\ \mathbf{g}_1(\mathbf{t}, c\mathbf{z}) &= c \cdot \mathbf{g}_1(\mathbf{t}, \mathbf{z}) \end{aligned}$$

for any $\mathbf{t}$ in $U \otimes V$, any $\mathbf{z}, \mathbf{z}'$ in W, and any c in K. To prove this we start with

$$\mathbf{g}(\mathbf{x}, \mathbf{y}, \mathbf{z} + \mathbf{z}') = \mathbf{g}(\mathbf{x}, \mathbf{y}, \mathbf{z}) + \mathbf{g}(\mathbf{x}, \mathbf{y}, \mathbf{z}')$$

which follows from the fact that $\mathbf{g}$ is multilinear. Using (3.1) on each of the three terms, we obtain

3.3 $$\mathbf{g}_1(\mathbf{x} \otimes \mathbf{y}, \mathbf{z} + \mathbf{z}') = \mathbf{g}_1(\mathbf{x} \otimes \mathbf{y}, \mathbf{z}) + \mathbf{g}_1(\mathbf{x} \otimes \mathbf{y}, \mathbf{z}')$$

Similarly, from the equation $\mathbf{g}(\mathbf{x}, \mathbf{y}, c\mathbf{z}) = c \cdot \mathbf{g}(\mathbf{x}, \mathbf{y}, \mathbf{z})$, we get

3.4 $$\mathbf{g}_1(\mathbf{x} \otimes \mathbf{y}, c\mathbf{z}) = c \cdot \mathbf{g}_1(\mathbf{x} \otimes \mathbf{y}, \mathbf{z})$$

These equations show that (3.2) holds for elements of the type $\mathbf{x} \otimes \mathbf{y}$ in $U \otimes V$. But from Proposition 2.4 we can write any $\mathbf{t}$ in $U \otimes V$ as a sum of such elements, say $\mathbf{t} = \Sigma\, \mathbf{x}_i \otimes \mathbf{y}_i$. Replacing $\mathbf{x} \otimes \mathbf{y}$ in (3.3) by $\mathbf{x}_i \otimes \mathbf{y}_i$ and summing, we have

$$\Sigma_i\, \mathbf{g}_1(\mathbf{x}_i \otimes \mathbf{y}_i, \mathbf{z} + \mathbf{z}') = \Sigma_i\, \mathbf{g}_1(\mathbf{x}_i \otimes \mathbf{y}_i, \mathbf{z}) + \Sigma_i\, \mathbf{g}_1(\mathbf{x}_i \otimes \mathbf{y}_i, \mathbf{z}')$$

Since $\mathbf{g}_1$ is linear in its first entry, we obtain for the left member

$$\Sigma_i\, \mathbf{g}_1(\mathbf{x}_i \otimes \mathbf{y}_i, \mathbf{z} + \mathbf{z}') = \mathbf{g}_1(\Sigma_i\, \mathbf{x}_i \otimes \mathbf{y}_i, \mathbf{z} + \mathbf{z}') = \mathbf{g}_1(\mathbf{t}, \mathbf{z} + \mathbf{z}')$$

Doing the same thing for the other two sums above, we obtain the first equation of (3.2). The second equation follows similarly from (3.4).

Thus we now know that $\mathbf{g}_1(\mathbf{t}, \mathbf{z})$ is linear in both entries. In other words, it is a bilinear mapping of $(U \otimes V) \times W$ to L. Hence, by definition of $(U \otimes V) \otimes W$, there is a linear mapping $\mathbf{g}': (U \otimes V) \otimes W \to L$ such that

3.5 $$\mathbf{g}_1(\mathbf{t}, \mathbf{z}) = \mathbf{g}'(\mathbf{t} \otimes \mathbf{z})$$

Combining this with (3.1), we obtain $\mathbf{g}(\mathbf{x}, \mathbf{y}, \mathbf{z}) = \mathbf{g}_1(\mathbf{x} \otimes \mathbf{y}, \mathbf{z}) = \mathbf{g}'((\mathbf{x} \otimes \mathbf{y}) \otimes \mathbf{z})$. Moreover, this last equation determines the linear mapping $\mathbf{g}'$

uniquely. For one easily sees from Proposition 2.4 applied twice that $(U \otimes V) \otimes W$ is spanned by elements of the form $(\mathbf{x} \otimes \mathbf{y}) \otimes \mathbf{z}$. The last equation above specifies $\mathbf{g}'$ for all elements of that form, hence determines $\mathbf{g}'$ uniquely, by Proposition 2.1. Q.E.D.

COROLLARY *Under the same hypotheses, there is a unique linear mapping* $\mathbf{g}': U \otimes (V \otimes W) \to L$ *such that* $\mathbf{g}(\mathbf{x}, \mathbf{y}, \mathbf{z}) = \mathbf{g}'(\mathbf{x} \otimes (\mathbf{y} \otimes \mathbf{z}))$.

REMARK 1. One must be wary of trying to define linear mappings of tensor products by specifying them on the tensor product of elements. The equation $\mathbf{g}(\mathbf{x}, \mathbf{y}, \mathbf{z}) = \mathbf{g}'(\mathbf{x} \otimes (\mathbf{y} \otimes \mathbf{z}))$ determines the linear mapping $\mathbf{g}'$ uniquely, as we have just seen. But it does not by any means guarantee that $\mathbf{g}'$ exists. The trouble is that the element $\mathbf{x} \otimes (\mathbf{y} \otimes \mathbf{z})$ can be written in many different ways, for example, $\frac{1}{2}\mathbf{x} \otimes (2\mathbf{y} \otimes \mathbf{z})$, or $9\mathbf{x} \otimes (\frac{1}{3}\mathbf{y} \otimes \frac{1}{3}\mathbf{z})$, etc., and consequently one must guard against plausible-looking definitions which are in fact inconsistent. For example, we cannot define a linear mapping $\mathbf{f}: U \otimes U \to U$ by setting $\mathbf{f}(\mathbf{x} \otimes \mathbf{y}) = \mathbf{x} + \mathbf{y}$. For $\mathbf{x} \otimes \mathbf{y} = (-\mathbf{x}) \otimes (-\mathbf{y})$, and the same prescription would give $\mathbf{f}(\mathbf{x} \otimes \mathbf{y}) = \mathbf{f}((-\mathbf{x}) \otimes (-\mathbf{y})) = -\mathbf{x} - \mathbf{y}$, which is nonsense.

We now prove the "associative law" for tensor products.

THEOREM 3.2 *Let* U, V, W *be vector spaces over a field* K. *Then there is a unique linear mapping* $\mathbf{h}: (U \otimes V) \otimes W \to U \otimes (V \otimes W)$ *such that* $\mathbf{h}((\mathbf{x} \otimes \mathbf{y}) \otimes \mathbf{z}) = \mathbf{x} \otimes (\mathbf{y} \otimes \mathbf{z})$ *for any* $\mathbf{x}$ *in* U, $\mathbf{y}$ *in* V, $\mathbf{z}$ *in* W. *Furthermore,* $\mathbf{h}$ *is an isomorphism.*

Proof. It is trivial to check that the mapping $\mathbf{g}: U \times V \times W \to U \otimes (V \otimes W)$ defined by

3.6 $$\mathbf{g}(\mathbf{x}, \mathbf{y}, \mathbf{z}) = \mathbf{x} \otimes (\mathbf{y} \otimes \mathbf{z})$$

is 3-linear. Hence, by Theorem 3.1 (with $L = U \otimes (V \otimes W)$), there is a unique linear mapping $\mathbf{h}: (U \otimes V) \otimes W \to U \otimes (V \otimes W)$ satisfying $\mathbf{g}(\mathbf{x}, \mathbf{y}, \mathbf{z}) = \mathbf{h}((\mathbf{x} \otimes \mathbf{y}) \otimes \mathbf{z})$. Thus, by (3.6), we have $\mathbf{h}((\mathbf{x} \otimes \mathbf{y}) \otimes \mathbf{z}) = \mathbf{x} \otimes (\mathbf{y} \otimes \mathbf{z})$.

To show that $\mathbf{h}$ is an isomorphism, one proves by a similar argument, using the corollary to Theorem 3.1, that there is a unique linear mapping $\mathbf{h}': U \otimes (V \otimes W) \to (U \otimes V) \otimes W$ such that $\mathbf{h}'(\mathbf{x} \otimes (\mathbf{y} \otimes \mathbf{z})) = (\mathbf{x} \otimes \mathbf{y}) \otimes \mathbf{z}$. Then $\mathbf{h}' \circ \mathbf{h}$ is a linear mapping of $(U \otimes V) \otimes W$ to itself which maps each element $(\mathbf{x} \otimes \mathbf{y}) \otimes \mathbf{z}$ into itself. From Proposition 2.1 it follows that $\mathbf{h}' \circ \mathbf{h}$ is the identity mapping of $(U \otimes V) \otimes W$ to itself, since the elements of the form $(\mathbf{x} \otimes \mathbf{y}) \otimes \mathbf{z}$ span $(U \otimes V) \otimes W$, by Proposition 2.4. Similarly, $\mathbf{h} \circ \mathbf{h}'$ is the identity mapping of $U \otimes (V \otimes W)$, and so both $\mathbf{h}$ and $\mathbf{h}'$ must be one-to-one, hence are isomorphisms. Q.E.D.

In view of Theorem 3.2 we shall usually not distinguish in our notation between $(U \otimes V) \otimes W$ and $U \otimes (V \otimes W)$, writing simply $U \otimes V \otimes W$. An element $(\mathbf{x} \otimes \mathbf{y}) \otimes \mathbf{z}$, or $\mathbf{x} \otimes (\mathbf{y} \otimes \mathbf{z})$, will be written as $\mathbf{x} \otimes \mathbf{y} \otimes \mathbf{z}$. Similar simplifications of notation will be made for products of more than three factors. Thus, if $U_1, \ldots, U_r$ are vector spaces over K, we denote their tensor product by $U_1 \otimes \cdots \otimes U_r$, and so on.

The following theorem shows that multiple tensor products satisfy conditions analogous to those of Definition 2.3:

THEOREM 3.3 *Let $U_1, \ldots, U_r$ be vector spaces over K. The mapping $\mathbf{f}: U_1 \times \cdots \times U_r \to U_1 \otimes \cdots \otimes U_r$ defined by*

3.7 $$\mathbf{f}(\mathbf{x}_1, \ldots, \mathbf{x}_r) = \mathbf{x}_1 \otimes \cdots \otimes \mathbf{x}_r$$

(x_i in U_1) is r-linear, and its image spans $U_1 \otimes \cdots \otimes U_r$. If $\mathbf{g}: U_1 \times \cdots \times U_r \to L$ is any r-linear mapping into a vector space L, then there is a unique linear mapping $\mathbf{g}': U_1 \otimes \cdots \otimes U_r \to L$ such that

3.8 $$\mathbf{g}(\mathbf{x}_1, \ldots, \mathbf{x}_r) = \mathbf{g}'(\mathbf{x}_1 \otimes \cdots \otimes \mathbf{x}_r)$$

Proof. This follows easily by induction on r. For $r = 1$ it is trivial, and for $r = 2$ it is merely a restatement of Definition 2.3.

We suppose then that the theorem holds for k factors, $k < r$, and we deduce that it must also hold for r factors. By assumption, the mapping $\mathbf{f}': U_1 \times \cdots \times U_{r-1} \to U_1 \otimes \cdots \otimes U_{r-1}$ defined by $\mathbf{f}'(\mathbf{x}_1, \ldots, \mathbf{x}_{r-1}) = \mathbf{x}_1 \otimes \cdots \otimes \mathbf{x}_{r-1}$ is multilinear. The mapping $\mathbf{f}$ of (3.7) can be written $\mathbf{f}(\mathbf{x}_1, \ldots, \mathbf{x}_r) = \mathbf{f}'(\mathbf{x}_1, \ldots, \mathbf{x}_{r-1}) \otimes \mathbf{x}_r$. Using the multilinearity of $\mathbf{f}'$ and the bilinearity of $\otimes$ [i.e., the rules (2.5)] one very easily sees that $\mathbf{f}$ is r-linear.

Now the image of $\mathbf{f}'$ consists of all elements $\mathbf{x}_1 \otimes \cdots \otimes \mathbf{x}_{r-1}$ in $U_1 \otimes \cdots \otimes U_{r-1}$. By assumption, the image of $\mathbf{f}'$ generates $U_1 \otimes \cdots \otimes U_{r-1}$. That is, every element of this vector space can be written in at least one way as a linear combination of elements of the type $\mathbf{x}_1 \otimes \cdots \otimes \mathbf{x}_{r-1}$. Now by Proposition 2.4, every element of $U_1 \otimes \cdots \otimes U_r = (U_1 \otimes \cdots \otimes U_{r-1}) \otimes U_r$ can be expressed in at least one way as a finite sum of elements of the type $\mathbf{w} \otimes \mathbf{x}_r$, with $\mathbf{w}$ in $U_1 \otimes \cdots \otimes U_{r-1}$ and $\mathbf{x}_r$ in U_r. Writing each such $\mathbf{w}$ as a linear combination of elements of the form $\mathbf{x}_1 \otimes \cdots \otimes \mathbf{x}_{r-1}$ and using the bilinearity of $\otimes$, one easily sees that every element of $U_1 \otimes \cdots \otimes U_r$ can be expressed as a linear combination of elements of the type $\mathbf{x}_1 \otimes \cdots \otimes \mathbf{x}_r$. Hence, the image of $\mathbf{f}$ spans $U_1 \otimes \cdots \otimes U_r$.

Finally, let $\mathbf{g}$ be an r-linear mapping $U_1 \otimes \cdots \otimes U_r \to L$. For each $\mathbf{x}_r$ in U_r, the mapping $U_1 \times \cdots \times U_{r-1} \to L$ defined by $(\mathbf{x}_1, \ldots, \mathbf{x}_{r-1}) \to \mathbf{g}(\mathbf{x}_1, \ldots, \mathbf{x}_r)$ is an $(r - 1)$-linear mapping. By induction assumption, there is a *unique* linear mapping $\mathbf{g}_1: U_1 \otimes \cdots \otimes U_{r-1} \to L$, depending upon x_r, such that

3.9 $\mathbf{g}(\mathbf{x}_1, \ldots, \mathbf{x}_r) = \mathbf{g}_1(\mathbf{x}_1 \otimes \cdots \otimes \mathbf{x}_{r-1}, \mathbf{x}_r)$

Just as in the proof of Theorem 3.1 above, one shows that $\mathbf{g}_1$ is a bilinear mapping of $(U_1 \otimes \cdots \otimes U_{r-1}) \times U_r \to L$. Therefore, by Definition 2.3, there is a linear mapping $\mathbf{g}'$ of $(U_1 \otimes \cdots \otimes U_{r-1}) \otimes U_r = U_1 \otimes \cdots \otimes U_r$ to L such that $\mathbf{g}_1(\mathbf{t}, \mathbf{x}_r) = \mathbf{g}'(\mathbf{t} \otimes \mathbf{x}_r)$ for any $\mathbf{t}$ in $U_1 \otimes \cdots \otimes U_{r-1}$ and any $\mathbf{x}_r$ in U_r. Hence, using (3.9), we see that $\mathbf{g}'$ satisfies Eq. (3.8). Furthermore, (3.8) determines the linear mapping $\mathbf{g}'$ uniquely, by Proposition 2.1 and the fact, established above, that the elements of the form $\mathbf{x}_1 \otimes \cdots \otimes \mathbf{x}_r$ span $U_1 \otimes \cdots \otimes U_r$. Hence, by assuming the theorem for $k < r$ factors, we have proved that it holds for r factors. By mathematical induction, it follows that Theorem 3.3 holds for all values of r. Q.E.D.

COROLLARY *Any element in $U_1 \otimes \cdots \otimes U_r$ can be expressed in at least one way as a finite sum of elements of the form $\mathbf{x}_1 \otimes \cdots \otimes \mathbf{x}_r$, with $\mathbf{x}_i$ in U_i $(i = 1, \ldots, r)$.*

Proof. Since elements of this form span $U_1 \otimes \cdots \otimes U_r$, by Theorem 3.3, any element of this vector space can be written as a linear combination of such elements. That is, any $\mathbf{t}$ in $U_1 \otimes \cdots \otimes U_r$ can be written as a sum of elements of the type $c(\mathbf{x}_1 \otimes \cdots \otimes \mathbf{x}_r)$, with c in K. But $c(\mathbf{x}_1 \otimes \cdots \otimes \mathbf{x}_r) = (c\mathbf{x}_1) \otimes \mathbf{x}_2 \otimes \cdots \otimes \mathbf{x}_r$, by multilinearity, and $c\mathbf{x}_1$ is again in U_1. The assertion follows at once. Q.E.D.

THEOREM 3.4 *Let $U_1, \ldots, U_r$ be vector spaces over a field K, and let k be an integer with $1 < k < r$. Then there is a unique bilinear mapping $\mathbf{g}$ from $(U_1 \otimes \cdots \otimes U_k) \times (U_{k+1} \otimes \cdots \otimes U_r)$ to $U_1 \otimes \cdots \otimes U_r$ such that*

$$\mathbf{g}(\mathbf{x}_1 \otimes \cdots \otimes \mathbf{x}_k, \mathbf{x}_{k+1} \otimes \cdots \otimes \mathbf{x}_r) = \mathbf{x}_1 \otimes \cdots \otimes \mathbf{x}_r$$

Proof. By definition, the mapping of $(U_1 \otimes \cdots \otimes U_k) \times (U_{k+1} \otimes \cdots \otimes U_r \to (U_1 \otimes \cdots \otimes U_k) \otimes (U_{k+1} \otimes \cdots \otimes U_r)$ defined by $(\mathbf{u}, \mathbf{v}) \to \mathbf{u} \otimes \mathbf{v}$ for $\mathbf{u}$ in $U_1 \otimes \cdots \otimes U_k$ and $\mathbf{v}$ in $U_{k+1} \otimes \cdots \otimes U_r$ is bilinear, and it has the required property. The uniqueness follows from Proposition 2.1 and the fact that $U_1 \otimes \cdots \otimes U_k$ is spanned by elements of the type $\mathbf{x}_1 \otimes \cdots \otimes \mathbf{x}_k$, and similarly for $U_{k+1} \otimes \cdots \otimes U_r$. Q.E.D.

The simple theorem above is a special case of a much more general theorem of the same type, whose main difficulty lies in the awkwardness of its statement. Let us suppose that the index set $\{1, \ldots, r\}$ is divided into p non-overlapping subsets $J_1, \ldots, J_p$, all of them ordered in some way. If J_i consists of the integers $i_1, \ldots, i_k$, let us set

$$V_i = U_{i_1} \otimes \cdots \otimes U_{i_k}$$

In this way we get p vector spaces. Let us call a *simple vector* in V_i one of the type $\mathbf{x}_{i_1} \otimes \cdots \otimes \mathbf{x}_{i_k}$, with $\mathbf{x}_{i_1}$ in U_{i_1}, etc.

THEOREM 3.5 *There is a unique p-linear mapping* $\mathbf{g}: V_1 \times \cdots \times V_p \to U_1 \otimes \cdots \otimes U_r$ *such that*

$$\mathbf{g}(\mathbf{s}_1, \ldots, \mathbf{s}_p) = \mathbf{x}_1 \otimes \cdots \otimes \mathbf{x}_r$$

if $\mathbf{s}_i$ *is the simple vector in* V_i *composed of those* $\mathbf{x}_j$ *on the right corresponding to the indices in* J_i.

The proof is easily obtained from Theorem 3.3 and Proposition 2.1 in essentially the same way as the proof of Theorem 3.4 above.

EXERCISES

1. Let $U_i (i = 1, \ldots, r)$ be finite-dimensional vector spaces over K, and let $B_i = \{\mathbf{u}_j^{(i)}\}$ be a base for U_i. Prove that the elements

$$\mathbf{u}_{j_1 \cdots j_r} = \mathbf{u}_{j_1}^{(1)} \otimes \mathbf{u}_{j_2}^{(2)} \otimes \cdots \otimes \mathbf{u}_{j_r}^{(r)}$$

form a base for $U_1 \otimes \cdots \otimes U_r$. If $\mathbf{x}_i = x_i{}^j \mathbf{u}_j^{(i)}$ is a vector in U_i, show that

$$\mathbf{x}_1 \otimes \cdots \otimes \mathbf{x}_r = x_1{}^{j_1} \cdots x_r{}^{j_r} \mathbf{u}_{j_1 \ldots j_r}$$

2. Write out a proof of Theorem 3.5 in the special case $r = 5$, with $J_1 = \{2, 3\}$, $J_2 = \{4, 1\}$, $J_3 = \{5\}$.

3. Let $U_1, \ldots, U_r$ be vector spaces over K. Let $\mathbf{f}$ be an r-linear mapping of $U_1 \times \cdots \times U_r$ to a vector space P such that the image of $\mathbf{f}$ spans P. Suppose furthermore that, for any r-linear mapping $\mathbf{g}$ *of* $U_1 \times \cdots \times U_r$ to a vector space L, there is a linear mapping $\mathbf{g}_1: P \to L$ such that $\mathbf{g} = \mathbf{g}_1 \circ \mathbf{f}$. Prove that there is a unique linear mapping $\mathbf{h}: P \to U_1 \otimes \cdots \otimes U_r$ such that $\mathbf{h} \circ \mathbf{f}(\mathbf{x}_1, \ldots, \mathbf{x}_r) = \mathbf{x}_1 \otimes \cdots \otimes \mathbf{x}_r$, and show that $\mathbf{h}$ is an isomorphism.

4. Tensor products of mappings

In this section we show that the tensor-product operation on vector spaces leads to a corresponding operation for linear mappings.

THEOREM 4.1 *Let* $\mathbf{f}_i: U_i \to V_i$ *be a linear mapping of vector spaces over a field* K, *for* $i = 1, \ldots, r$. *Then there is a unique linear mapping* $\mathbf{f}: U_1 \otimes \cdots \otimes U_r \to V_1 \otimes \cdots \otimes V_r$ *such that*

4.1 $$\mathbf{f}(\mathbf{x}_1 \otimes \cdots \otimes \mathbf{x}_r) = \mathbf{f}_1(\mathbf{x}_1) \otimes \cdots \otimes \mathbf{f}_r(\mathbf{x}_r)$$

for any $\mathbf{x}_i$ *in* U_i $(i = 1, \ldots, r)$.

Proof. It is trivial to verify that the mapping $\mathbf{h}: U_1 \times \cdots \times U_r \to V_1 \otimes \cdot \otimes V_r$ defined by $\mathbf{h}(\mathbf{x}_1, \ldots, \mathbf{x}_r) = \mathbf{f}_1(\mathbf{x}_1) \otimes \cdots \otimes \mathbf{f}_r(\mathbf{x}_r)$ is r-linear. By Theorem 3.3 there exists a unique linear mapping $\mathbf{f}: U_1 \otimes \cdots \otimes U_r \to V_1 \otimes \cdots \otimes V_r$ such that $\mathbf{h}(\mathbf{x}_1, \ldots, \mathbf{x}_r) = \mathbf{f}(\mathbf{x}_1 \otimes \cdots \otimes \mathbf{x}_r)$. Q.E.D.

DEFINITION 4.1 *The linear mapping* $\mathbf{f}$ *of the preceding theorem is called the* tensor product *of* $\mathbf{f}_1, \ldots, \mathbf{f}_r$ *and is denoted by* $\mathbf{f}_1 \otimes \cdots \otimes \mathbf{f}_r$.

With this notation, Eq. (4.1) reads

4.2 $$(\mathbf{f}_1 \otimes \cdots \otimes \mathbf{f}_r)(\mathbf{x}_1 \otimes \cdots \otimes \mathbf{x}_r) = \mathbf{f}_1(\mathbf{x}_1) \otimes \cdots \otimes \mathbf{f}_r(\mathbf{x}_r)$$

This operation on mappings obeys several simple laws. For example, it is associative:

4.3 $$(\mathbf{f}_1 \otimes \mathbf{f}_2) \otimes \mathbf{f}_3 = \mathbf{f}_1 \otimes (\mathbf{f}_2 \otimes \mathbf{f}_3)$$

For the left side sends an element $\mathbf{t} \otimes \mathbf{x}_3$ in $(U_1 \otimes U_2) \otimes U_3$ into $(\mathbf{f}_1 \otimes \mathbf{f}_2)(\mathbf{t}) \otimes \mathbf{f}_3(\mathbf{x}_3)$, by (4.2). Taking $\mathbf{t} = \mathbf{x}_1 \otimes \mathbf{x}_2$, we have $(\mathbf{f}_1 \otimes \mathbf{f}_2)(\mathbf{x}_1 \otimes \mathbf{x}_2) = \mathbf{f}_1(\mathbf{x}_1) \otimes \mathbf{f}_2(\mathbf{x}_2)$, by (4.2) again, and so $(\mathbf{f}_1 \otimes \mathbf{f}_2) \otimes \mathbf{f}_3$ sends $(\mathbf{x}_1 \otimes \mathbf{x}_2) \otimes \mathbf{x}_3$ into the element $(\mathbf{f}_1(\mathbf{x}_1) \otimes \mathbf{f}_2(\mathbf{x}_2)) \otimes \mathbf{f}_3(\mathbf{x}_3)$ in $(V_1 \otimes V_2) \otimes V_3$. Similarly, the right side of (4.3) sends $\mathbf{x}_1 \otimes (\mathbf{x}_2 \otimes \mathbf{x}_3)$ in $U_1 \otimes (U_2 \otimes U_3)$ into the element $\mathbf{f}_1(\mathbf{x}_1) \otimes (\mathbf{f}_2(\mathbf{x}_2) \otimes \mathbf{f}_3(\mathbf{x}_3))$ in $V_1 \otimes (V_2 \otimes V_3)$. If we now identify $(U_1 \otimes U_2) \otimes U_3$ and $U_1 \otimes (U_2 \otimes U_3)$ according to the conventions made following Theorem 3.2, and similarly for the V's; then our assertion follows.

Thus the equality sign in (4.3) is not really correct, since it depends upon our willingness to replace one vector space $(U_1 \otimes U_2) \otimes U_3$ by another one $U_1 \otimes (U_2 \otimes U_3)$ which is isomorphic to it in a fixed way (and similarly for the V's). In principle one could develop a rigorously correct notation which would maintain the distinction† between $(U_1 \otimes U_2) \otimes U_3$ and $U_1 \otimes (U_2 \otimes U_3)$, etc. But the satisfaction of having such an impeccable notation would be far outweighed by its ungainly complexity. We shall therefore go ahead and write = when we really mean something else.

One easily verifies the following rule, which is a kind of extension of (4.3):

4.4 $$(\mathbf{f}_1 \otimes \cdots \otimes \mathbf{f}_k) \otimes (\mathbf{f}_{k+1} \otimes \cdots \otimes \mathbf{f}_r) = \mathbf{f}_1 \otimes \cdots \otimes \mathbf{f}_r$$

The rule is a simple consequence of the uniqueness of the indicated linear mappings. Another important property of the tensor product is expressed in the following theorem.

THEOREM 4.2 *The tensor product* $\mathbf{f}_1 \otimes \cdots \otimes \mathbf{f}_r$ *of mappings is a multilinear operation.*

Proof. We recall that the vector space of all linear mappings $U_i \to V_i$ is devoted by Hom (U_i, V_i) (see Sec. 4, Chap. 9). A more precise statement of the theorem is as follows: The mapping

4.5 $$\text{Hom }(U_1, V_1) \times \cdots \times \text{Hom }(U_r, V_r) \to \text{Hom }(U_1 \otimes \cdots \otimes U_r, V_1 \otimes \cdots \otimes V_r)$$

defined by

† We recall that even the symbol $U_1 \otimes U_2$ itself does not denote a fixed vector space, denoting as it does any of the infinite number of isomorphic tensor products.

4.6 $$(\mathbf{f}_1, \ldots, \mathbf{f}_r) \to \mathbf{f}_1 \otimes \cdots \otimes \mathbf{f}_r$$

is an r-linear mapping.

We must prove that

4.7 $$\begin{aligned} \mathbf{f}_1 \otimes \cdots \otimes (\mathbf{f}_k + \mathbf{f}'_k) \otimes \cdots \otimes \mathbf{f}_r &= \mathbf{f}_1 \otimes \cdots \otimes \mathbf{f}_k \otimes \cdots \otimes \mathbf{f}_r \\ &\quad + \mathbf{f}_1 \otimes \cdots \otimes \mathbf{f}'_k \otimes \cdots \otimes \mathbf{f}_r \\ \mathbf{f}_1 \otimes \cdots \otimes (c\mathbf{f}_k) \otimes \cdots \otimes \mathbf{f}_r &= c \cdot (\mathbf{f}_1 \otimes \cdots \otimes \mathbf{f}_k \otimes \cdots \otimes \mathbf{f}_r) \end{aligned}$$

By (4.2) the mapping on the left of the first equation sends $\mathbf{x}_1 \otimes \cdots \otimes \mathbf{x}_r$ into

4.8 $$\mathbf{f}_1(\mathbf{x}_1) \otimes \cdots \otimes (\mathbf{f}_k + \mathbf{f}'_k)(\mathbf{x}_k) \otimes \cdots \otimes \mathbf{f}_r(\mathbf{x}_r)$$

By definition, $(\mathbf{f}_k + \mathbf{f}'_k)(\mathbf{x}_k) = \mathbf{f}_k(\mathbf{x}_k) + \mathbf{f}'_k(\mathbf{x}_k)$. Putting this in (4.8) and using the multilinearity of the tensor product in $V_1 \otimes \cdots \otimes V_r$ (Theorem 3.3), we find that (4.8) is equal to

$$\mathbf{f}_1(\mathbf{x}_1) \otimes \cdots \otimes \mathbf{f}_k(\mathbf{x}_k) \otimes \cdots \otimes \mathbf{f}_r(\mathbf{x}_r) + \mathbf{f}_1(\mathbf{x}_1) \otimes \cdots \otimes \mathbf{f}'_k(\mathbf{x}_k) \otimes \cdots \otimes \mathbf{f}_r(\mathbf{x}_r)$$

Now the right side of the first equation in (4.7) has exactly the same effect on $\mathbf{x}_1 \otimes \cdots \otimes \mathbf{x}_r$, as is quickly seen. The correctness of the first equation of (4.7) then follows from the uniqueness part of Theorem 4.1. The second equation is proved similarly. Q.E.D.

THEOREM 4.3 *Let $U_1, \ldots, U_r$ be vector spaces over K, and let $\mathbf{g}_i\colon U_i \to K$ be a linear mapping ($i = 1, \ldots, r$). Then there is a unique linear mapping $\mathbf{g}\colon U_1 \otimes \cdots \otimes U_r \to K$ such that*

$$\mathbf{g}(\mathbf{x}_1 \otimes \cdots \otimes \mathbf{x}_r) = \mathbf{g}_1(\mathbf{x}_1) \cdots \mathbf{g}_r(\mathbf{x}_r)$$

for any $\mathbf{x}_i$ in U_i ($i = 1, \ldots, r$).

Proof. The mapping $U_1 \times \ldots \times U_r \to K$ sending $(\mathbf{x}_1, \ldots, \mathbf{x}_r)$ into $\mathbf{g}_1(\mathbf{x}_1) \cdots \mathbf{g}_r(\mathbf{x}_r)$ is easily seen to be r-linear. The assertion follows at once from Theorem 3.3. Q.E.D.

The foregoing theorem can be connected with Theorem 4.1 as follows: The tensor product $\mathbf{g}_1 \otimes \cdots \otimes \mathbf{g}_r$ is a linear mapping of $U_1 \otimes \cdots \otimes U_r$ to $K \otimes \cdots \otimes K$ (r times). The mapping $\mathbf{h}\colon K \otimes \cdots \otimes K \to K$ defined by $c_1 \otimes \cdots \otimes c_r \to c_1 \cdots c_r$ is an isomorphism of these systems regarded as vector spaces over K. The mapping $\mathbf{g}$ of Theorem 4.3 is simply the composition of $\mathbf{g}_1 \otimes \cdots \otimes \mathbf{g}_r$ and $\mathbf{h}$.

EXERCISES

1. Prove that $\mathbf{h}\colon K \otimes \cdots \otimes K \to K$ as just defined is a vector-space isomorphism.

2. Let $\mathbf{f}_i\colon U_i \to V_i$ and $\mathbf{g}_i\colon V_i \to W_i$ be linear mappings of vector spaces over K. Prove that

$$(\mathbf{g}_1 \otimes \cdots \otimes \mathbf{g}_r) \circ (\mathbf{f}_1 \otimes \cdots \otimes \mathbf{f}_r) = (\mathbf{g}_1 \circ \mathbf{f}_1) \otimes \cdots \otimes (\mathbf{g}_r \circ \mathbf{f}_r)$$

3. Let $\mathbf{u}_1, \ldots, \mathbf{u}_r$ be linearly independent elements of U, and let $\mathbf{v}_1, \ldots, \mathbf{v}_s$ be linearly independent elements of V, where both U and V are finite-dimensional vector spaces over a field K. Prove that the rs elements $\mathbf{u}_i \otimes \mathbf{v}_j$ in $U \otimes V$ are linearly independent.

***4.** Let $\mathbf{f}\colon U \to U'$ and $\mathbf{g}\colon V \to V'$ be linear mappings of finite-dimensional vector spaces over K. Prove that

$$\text{Ker } (\mathbf{f} \otimes \mathbf{g}) = (\text{Ker } \mathbf{f}) \otimes V + U \otimes (\text{Ker } \mathbf{g})$$

and

$$\text{Im } (\mathbf{f} \otimes \mathbf{g}) = (\text{Im } \mathbf{f}) \otimes (\text{Im } \mathbf{g})$$

5. Let $\mathbf{T}\colon U \to U$ and $\mathbf{S}\colon V \to V$ be endomorphisms of vector spaces over K. Let $\mathbf{x}$ be an eigenvector of $\mathbf{T}$, and let $\mathbf{y}$ be an eigenvector of $\mathbf{S}$. Prove that $\mathbf{x} \otimes \mathbf{y}$ is an eigenvector of $\mathbf{T} \otimes \mathbf{S}$.

5. *The tensor algebra of a vector space*

We start with a preliminary definition which allows us to embed any given vector spaces over a field K in a larger vector space.

Let J denote an arbitrary set, and suppose that there is assigned to each element j in J a vector space U_j over K. Let S denote the set of all mappings f which assign to each j in J a vector $f(j)$ in U_j in such a way that

5.1 *$f(j)$ is the zero vector in U_j for all but a finite number of j in J.*

We make S into a vector space over K as follows:

5.2
$$(f + f')(j) = f(j) + f'(j)$$
$$(cf)(j) = c \cdot f(j)$$

for any f, f' in S, any j in J, and any c in K. It is quickly seen that $f + f'$ and cf so defined are again elements of S, and it is a routine matter to verify that S equipped with these operations is a vector space.

DEFINITION 5.1 *The space S is called the* direct sum *of the family* $\{U_j\}$.

Suppose for example that J is the finite set $J = \{1, 2, \ldots, n\}$. Condition (5.1) is superfluous in this case. An element f of S assigns to each integer j from 1 to n a vector $\mathbf{x}_j$ in U_j. Thus f is simply the n-tuple $(\mathbf{x}_1, \ldots, \mathbf{x}_n)$. With this notation, (5.2) becomes

5.3
$$(\mathbf{x}_1, \ldots, \mathbf{x}_n) + (\mathbf{y}_1, \ldots, \mathbf{y}_n) = (\mathbf{x}_1 + \mathbf{y}_1, \ldots, \mathbf{x}_n + \mathbf{y}_n)$$
$$c(\mathbf{x}_1, \ldots, \mathbf{x}_n) = (c\mathbf{x}_1, \ldots, c\mathbf{x}_n)$$

Hence, for finite sets J, the definition of the direct sum coincides with that given earlier (Exercise 3, Sec. 3, Chap. 8, and Exercise 2, Sec. 3, Chap. 13).

REMARK 1. If condition (5.1) is omitted, the resulting vector space is called the *direct product* of the U_j. If J is finite, then there is no distinction between direct sum and direct product.

Returning to the general case, let $\mathbf{x}_j$ be an element of U_j. Denote by $\mathbf{x}'_j$ the element of S defined by

5.4 $$\mathbf{x}'_j(i) = \begin{cases} \mathbf{x}_j & \text{if } i = j \\ \mathbf{0} & \text{if } i \neq j \end{cases}$$

It follows at once that the mapping $U_j \to S$ defined by $\mathbf{x}_j \to \mathbf{x}'_j$ is a linear mapping which maps U_j isomorphically onto a subspace U'_j of S. Now let f be any element of S and write $f(j) = \mathbf{x}_j$, so that $\mathbf{x}_j$ is in U_j. By condition (5.1), all but a finite number of the $\mathbf{x}_j$ are zero. Let $\mathbf{x}_{j_1}, \ldots, \mathbf{x}_{j_r}$ be those which are not zero. From (5.4) and (5.2) it follows at once that

5.5 $$f = \mathbf{x}'_{j_1} + \cdots + \mathbf{x}'_{j_r}$$

Conversely, given any elements $\mathbf{x}_{j_1}, \ldots, \mathbf{x}_{j_r}$ in $U_{j_1}, \ldots, U_{j_r}$, (5.5) defines an element f in S.

Finally, we simplify our notation by writing $\mathbf{x}_j$ instead of $\mathbf{x}'_j$. With this step forward we have the following:

5.6 *Any element of the direct sum S can be expressed as a finite sum*

$$\mathbf{x}_{j_1} + \mathbf{x}_{j_2} + \cdots + \mathbf{x}_{j_r}$$

with $\mathbf{x}_{j_1}$ in $U_{j_1}, \ldots, \mathbf{x}_{j_r}$ in U_{j_r}. Furthermore, the expression is unique, provided the **x**'s *are nonzero and provided the elements $j_1, \ldots, j_r$ of J are distinct.*

Now let U be an n-dimensional vector space over a field K. We recall that the *dual* vector space U^* of U is the vector space of all linear mappings $U \to K$; U^* also has dimension n (see Sec. 4, Chap. 9, and Sec. 2, Chap. 14). We introduce the following notation:

5.7 $$U^p{}_q = \underbrace{U \otimes \cdots \otimes U}_{p} \otimes \underbrace{U^* \otimes \cdots \otimes U^*}_{q}$$

In particular, $U^p{}_0$ is the tensor product of U with itself p times, and $U^0{}_q$ is the tensor product of U^* with itself q times. Thus $U^1{}_0 = U$ and $U^0{}_1 = U^*$. We further define

5.8 $$U^0{}_0 = K$$

From all these vector spaces we now build a giant vector space $T(U)$, namely, their direct sum:

5.9 $$T(U) = \text{direct sum of all } U^p{}_q \qquad (p, q = 0, 1, 2 \ldots)$$

The elements of $T(U)$ are called *tensors* on U. As we have just seen, each $U^p{}_q$ can be regarded as a subspace of $T(U)$. The elements of $U^p{}_0$ are called *contra-*

variant† tensors of rank p; elements of $U^0{}_q$ are called *covariant*† tensors of rank q; elements of $U^p{}_q$ with $p, q > 0$ are called *mixed* tensors of type (p, q).

From (5.7) we have

5.10 $$U^p{}_q = U^p{}_0 \otimes U^0{}_q$$

provided $p > 0$ and $q > 0$. This formula can still be regarded as correct even if p or q is zero. For example, if $q = 0$, the right-hand side is $U^p{}_0 \otimes U^0{}_0 = U^p{}_0 \otimes K$. But there is a unique isomorphism from this space to $U^p{}_0$ mapping $\mathbf{x} \otimes c$ into $c\mathbf{x}$ for any $\mathbf{x}$ in $U^p{}_0$ and c in K. Therefore $U^p{}_0 \otimes U^0{}_0$ can be unambiguously identified with $U^p{}_0$. The same is true for $U^0{}_q$.

$T(U)$ is a vector space over K, and we now show that it can be made into a *ring*. That is, we define a product in $T(U)$. First we define the product of elements $\mathbf{t}$ and $\mathbf{t}'$ in the subspaces $U^p{}_q$ and $U^r{}_s$, respectively, and their product will be in U^{p+r}_{q+s}. Thus we require a bilinear mapping

5.11 $$U^p{}_q \times U^r{}_s \to U^{p+r}_{q+s}$$

It is easily obtained as follows: the mapping

5.12 $$U^p{}_q \times U^r{}_s \to U^p{}_q \otimes U^r{}_s$$

given by

5.13 $$(\mathbf{t}, \mathbf{t}') \to \mathbf{t} \otimes \mathbf{t}'$$

is bilinear, by definition of the tensor product. Using (5.10) we have $U^p{}_q \otimes U^r{}_s = U^p{}_0 \otimes U^0{}_q \otimes U^r{}_0 \otimes U^0{}_s$, provided we make the appropriate identifications required in (5.10) if any of the indices p, q, r, s are zero. From Theorem 2.6 one easily shows that there is a unique isomorphism

5.14 $$U^p{}_q \otimes U^r{}_s \to U^p{}_0 \otimes U^r{}_0 \otimes U^0{}_q \otimes U^0{}_s = U^{p+r}_{q+s}$$

such that

5.15 $$\mathbf{x} \otimes \mathbf{y}^* \otimes \mathbf{z} \otimes \mathbf{w}^* \to \mathbf{x} \otimes \mathbf{z} \otimes \mathbf{y}^* \otimes \mathbf{w}^*$$

for any $\mathbf{x}$ in $U^p{}_0$, $\mathbf{y}^*$ in $U^0{}_q$, $\mathbf{z}$ in $U^r{}_0$, and $\mathbf{w}^*$ in $U^0{}_s$.

We now define (5.11) to be the composition of (5.12) and (5.14), and we shall continue to denote it by the tensor-product symbol, even though that will conflict slightly with our earlier notation because of the interchange of factors involved in (5.14). Hence, for $\mathbf{t}$ in $U^p{}_q$ and $\mathbf{t}'$ in $U^r{}_s$ we denote the element in U^{p+r}_{q+s} obtained from (5.12) and (5.14) by $\mathbf{t} \otimes \mathbf{t}'$. Thus, for $\mathbf{t} = \mathbf{x} \otimes \mathbf{y}^*$ and $\mathbf{t}' = \mathbf{z} \otimes \mathbf{w}^*$ we have

† These are purely conventional terms borrowed from differential geometry. We observe that, since the dual of U^* can be identified with U (Sec. 2, Chap. 13), the space $T(U^*)$ can be identified with $T(U)$ in a specific way. Which tensors are called contravariant and which are called covariant depends upon whether one starts with U or U^*.

5.16 $(\mathbf{x} \otimes \mathbf{y}^*) \otimes (\mathbf{z} \otimes \mathbf{w}^*) = \mathbf{x} \otimes \mathbf{z} \otimes \mathbf{y}^* \otimes \mathbf{w}^*$

If any of the indices p, q, r, s are zero, this formula is to be interpreted as follows: *A tensor product of a scalar and any tensor is understood to be ordinary scalar multiplication.* For the identification of $U^p{}_0 \otimes U^0{}_0$ with $U^p{}_0$ required to make (5.10) valid when $q = 0$ amounts to replacing $\mathbf{x} \otimes c$ by $c\mathbf{x}$; similarly, if $p = 0$, the identification of $U^0{}_0 \otimes U^0{}_q$ with $U^0{}_q$ is achieved by replacing $c \otimes \mathbf{y}^*$ by $c\mathbf{y}^*$, etc.

To complete the definition of the product in $T(U)$ we use (5.6): Any element $\mathbf{t}$ in $T(U)$ can be expressed as a finite sum $\mathbf{t} = \mathbf{t}_1 + \cdots + \mathbf{t}_k$ of *homogeneous* elements, i.e., elements in various of the subspaces $U_q{}^p$. If $\mathbf{t}' = \mathbf{t}_1' + \cdots + \mathbf{t}_l'$ is another element of $T(U)$, also expressed as a sum of elements in the subspaces $U^p{}_q$, then we define

5.17 $$\mathbf{t} \otimes \mathbf{t}' = \sum_{i,j} \mathbf{t}_i \otimes \mathbf{t}_j'$$

each term on the right being given by (5.16). From the uniqueness part of (5.6) one shows easily that (5.17) does not depend upon the particular expressions for $\mathbf{t}$ and $\mathbf{t}'$ as sums of homogeneous elements.

THEOREM 5.1 *The system $T(U)$, with product defined by (5.16) and (5.17), is a K-algebra. Every element of $T(U)$ can be expressed as a finite sum of elements of the type*

5.18 $$\mathbf{x}_1 \otimes \cdots \otimes \mathbf{x}_p \otimes \mathbf{y}_1^* \otimes \cdots \otimes \mathbf{y}_q^* \qquad (\mathbf{x}_i \text{ in } U^i{}_0,\ \mathbf{y}^*{}_j \text{ in } U^0{}_j)$$

and the product in $T(P)$ of two such elements is given by

5.19 $$\begin{aligned}(\mathbf{x}_1 \otimes \cdots \otimes \mathbf{x}_p \otimes \mathbf{y}_1^* \otimes \cdots \otimes \mathbf{y}_q^*) \otimes (\mathbf{z}_1 \otimes \cdots \otimes \mathbf{z}_r \otimes \mathbf{w}_1^* \otimes \cdots \otimes \mathbf{w}_s^*) \\ = \mathbf{x}_1 \otimes \cdots \otimes \mathbf{x}_p \otimes \mathbf{z}_1 \otimes \cdots \otimes \mathbf{z}_r \otimes \mathbf{y}_1^* \otimes \cdots \otimes \mathbf{y}_q^* \otimes \mathbf{w}_1^* \otimes \cdots \otimes \mathbf{w}_s^*\end{aligned}$$

Furthermore, the contravariant tensors in $T(U)$ form a subalgebra

5.20 $T_0(U)$ = *direct sum of* $U^p{}_0$ $(p = 0, 1, 2, \ldots)$ *of* $T(U)$

and the covariant tensors form a subalgebra

5.21 $T^0(U)$ = *direct sum of* $U^0{}_q$ $(q = 0, 1, 2, \ldots)$ *of* $T(U)$

We recall that a K-algebra is a vector space over K with a product operation which makes it a ring and which satisfies the associative law (4.3) of Sec. 4, Chap. 8. It is a routine matter to verify that the product $\otimes$ in $T(U)$ meets these requirements. The fact that any element in $T(U)$ can be expressed as a sum of elements (5.18) follows at once from the corollary of Theorem 3.3 and from (5.6). The formula (5.19) is an expanded version of (5.16). It is clear that $T_0(U)$ defined by (5.20) is a subspace of $T(U)$, and that the product of any two elements of $T_0(U)$ is again in $T_0(U)$. The same is true for $T^0(U)$.

DEFINITION 5.2 $T_0(U)$ *is called the* contravariant tensor algebra *over* U, *and* $T^0(U)$ *is called the* covariant tensor algebra *over* U; $T(U)$ *is called simply the* tensor algebra *over* U.

THEOREM 5.2 *Let* U *and* V *be finite-dimensional vector spaces over a field* K, *and let* $\mathbf{f}: U \to V$ *be a linear mapping. Then there is a uniquely determined homomorphism* $\mathbf{f}_0: T_0(U) \to T_0(V)$ *of the contravariant tensor algebras such that*

5.22 $$\mathbf{f}_0(\mathbf{x}) = \mathbf{f}(\mathbf{x}) \qquad \text{for any } \mathbf{x} \text{ in } U = U_0^1$$

Furthermore, there is a uniquely determined homomorphism $\mathbf{f}^0: T^0(V) \to T^0(U)$ *of the covariant tensor algebras such that*

5.23 $$\mathbf{f}^0(\mathbf{y}^*) = {}^t\mathbf{f}(\mathbf{y}^*) \qquad \text{for any } \mathbf{y}^* \text{ in } V^* = V^0{}_1$$

where ${}^t\mathbf{f}$ *denotes the transpose of* $\mathbf{f}$.†

Proof. First of all, a homomorphism of *algebras* is a mapping which is compatible with all three of the operations in sight—namely, sum, scalar multiplication, and product. In particular, $\mathbf{f}^0$ and $\mathbf{f}_0$ must be linear mappings.

Consider first $\mathbf{f}_0$: For it to be compatible with the product operation we must have $\mathbf{f}_0(\mathbf{x}_1 \otimes \mathbf{x}_2) = \mathbf{f}_0(\mathbf{x}_1) \otimes \mathbf{f}_0(\mathbf{x}_2)$ for any $\mathbf{x}_1$, $\mathbf{x}_2$ in U, and from (5.22) we get $\mathbf{f}_0(\mathbf{x}_1 \otimes \mathbf{x}_2) = \mathbf{f}(\mathbf{x}_1) \otimes \mathbf{f}(\mathbf{x}_2)$. By a simple induction, one finds similarly the requirement

5.24 $$\begin{aligned} \mathbf{f}_0(\mathbf{x}_1 \otimes \cdots \otimes \mathbf{x}_p) &= \mathbf{f}_0(\mathbf{x}_1) \otimes \cdots \otimes \mathbf{f}_0(\mathbf{x}_p) \\ &= \mathbf{f}(\mathbf{x}_1) \otimes \cdots \otimes \mathbf{f}(\mathbf{x}_p) \end{aligned}$$

for any $\mathbf{x}_1, \ldots, \mathbf{x}_p$ in U. By Theorem 4.1 there is a unique linear mapping $U_0{}^p \to V_0{}^p$ satisfying this condition, namely, $\mathbf{f} \otimes \cdots \otimes \mathbf{f}$ (p times). Since $\mathbf{f}_0$ is also linear, it follows at once that

5.25 $$\mathbf{f}_0 = \underbrace{\mathbf{f} \otimes \cdots \otimes \mathbf{f}}_{p} \qquad \text{on } U^p{}_0$$

This shows at once that $\mathbf{f}_0$ is uniquely determined. Conversely it shows us how to construct $\mathbf{f}_0$. Namely, any $\mathbf{t}$ in $T_0(U)$ can be expressed as a sum $\mathbf{t} = \mathbf{t}_1 + \cdots + \mathbf{t}_k$ of elements in the various subspaces $U^p{}_0$, say $\mathbf{t}_i$ in $U_0^{p_i}$. We then *define*

5.26 $$\mathbf{f}_0(\mathbf{t}) = \mathbf{f}_0(\mathbf{t}_1) + \cdots + \mathbf{f}_0(\mathbf{t}_k)$$

with

† We denote the transpose here by ${}^t\mathbf{f}$ instead of $\mathbf{f}^*$. The latter symbol is used below for another purpose.

5.27 $$\mathbf{f}_0(\mathbf{t}_i) = \underbrace{(\mathbf{f} \otimes \cdots \otimes \mathbf{f})}_{p_i}(\mathbf{t}_i)$$

This defines $\mathbf{f}_0$ uniquely, and it is easily verified that $\mathbf{f}_0$ is a homomorphism as claimed. The assertion concerning $\mathbf{f}^0$ is proved similarly; the mapping ${}^t\mathbf{f}$ involved is discussed in Sec. 4, Chap. 9, and Sec. 2, Chap. 13.

Q.E.D.

The preceding theorem leads to an important element of structure underlying the tensor spaces associated with a vector space U. Let us denote by $GL(U)$ the group of all invertible linear mappings of U to itself (this group is called the *general linear group* on U). Then $GL(U)$ operates on U as a group of transformations, in the sense of Definition 5.1, Chap. 10. We show now that $GL(U)$ acts in a natural way as a group of transformations on the entire tensor algebra $T(U)$. According to Sec. 5, Chap. 10, we must produce a homomorphism λ of $GL(U)$ to the group of all one-to-one mappings of $T(U)$ to itself.

First of all, for any invertible linear mapping $\mathbf{f}$ of U to itself we define

5.28 $$\mathbf{f}^* = {}^t(\mathbf{f}^{-1})$$

We claim that $\mathbf{f}^*$ is an invertible linear mapping of U^* to itself (U^* denotes the dual space of U), and that

5.29 $$(\mathbf{fg})^* = \mathbf{f}^*\mathbf{g}^*$$

for any $\mathbf{f}$, $\mathbf{g}$ in $GL(U)$.

To show this, recall that the transpose ${}^t\mathbf{f}$ of any linear mapping $\mathbf{f}$ of U to itself is the unique linear mapping of the dual U^* to itself such that

5.30 $$\langle {}^t\mathbf{f}(\mathbf{x}^*), \mathbf{y}\rangle = \langle \mathbf{x}^*, \mathbf{f}(\mathbf{y})\rangle$$

for any $\mathbf{x}^*$ in U^* and any $\mathbf{y}$ in U. In particular, for the identity mapping $\mathbf{I}$ of U we have $\langle {}^t\mathbf{I}(\mathbf{x}^*), \mathbf{y}\rangle = \langle \mathbf{x}^*, \mathbf{I}(\mathbf{y})\rangle = \langle \mathbf{x}^*, \mathbf{y}\rangle$, and it follows that ${}^t\mathbf{I}$ is the identity mapping of U^*. Now replace $\mathbf{x}^*$ in (5.30) by ${}^t\mathbf{g}(\mathbf{x}^*)$. Since $({}^t\mathbf{f}\,{}^t\mathbf{g})(\mathbf{x}^*) = {}^t\mathbf{f}({}^t\mathbf{g}(\mathbf{x}^*))$, by definition of composition, Eq. (5.30) gives us $\langle ({}^t\mathbf{f}\,{}^t\mathbf{g})(\mathbf{x}^*), \mathbf{y}\rangle = \langle {}^t\mathbf{f}({}^t\mathbf{g}(\mathbf{x}^*)), \mathbf{y}\rangle = \langle {}^t\mathbf{g}(\mathbf{x}^*), \mathbf{f}(\mathbf{y})\rangle = \langle \mathbf{x}^*, \mathbf{g}(\mathbf{f}(\mathbf{y}))\rangle = \langle \mathbf{x}^*, (\mathbf{gf})(\mathbf{y})\rangle = \langle {}^t(\mathbf{gf})(\mathbf{x}^*), \mathbf{y}\rangle$, this holding for all $\mathbf{x}^*$ in U^* and all $\mathbf{y}$ in U. From this we conclude that

5.31 $${}^t(\mathbf{gf}) = {}^t\mathbf{f}\,{}^t\mathbf{g}.$$

Replace $\mathbf{g}$ here by $\mathbf{f}^{-1}$. The result is ${}^t\mathbf{I} = {}^t\mathbf{f}\,{}^t(\mathbf{f}^{-1})$. But ${}^t\mathbf{I}$ is the identity mapping of U^*, and therefore ${}^t(\mathbf{f}^{-1})$ is the inverse of ${}^t\mathbf{f}$. That is, ${}^t(\mathbf{f}^{-1}) = ({}^t\mathbf{f})^{-1}$. In particular, ${}^t\mathbf{f}$ is invertible if $\mathbf{f}$ is invertible. Referring now to (5.30), we have $(\mathbf{fg})^* = {}^t(\mathbf{fg})^{-1} = {}^t(\mathbf{g}^{-1}\mathbf{f}^{-1})$, by the general rule for inverses; from (5.31) there results $(\mathbf{fg})^* = {}^t(\mathbf{f}^{-1})\,{}^t(\mathbf{g}^{-1})$, which proves (5.29).

Now write $\mathbf{f}^p{}_0$ for the restriction of $\mathbf{f}_0$ of Theorem 5.2 to elements of $U^p{}_0$. Thus, by (5.25),

5.32 $$\mathbf{f}^p{}_0 = \underbrace{\mathbf{f} \otimes \cdots \otimes \mathbf{f}}_{p} \quad \text{on } U^p{}_0$$

The second part of Theorem 5.2, applied to a mapping $\mathbf{g}\colon U \to U$, asserts the existence of a unique ring-homomorphism $\mathbf{g}^0$ of $T^0(U)$ to itself such that $\mathbf{g}^0 = {}^t\mathbf{g}$ on $U^0{}_1 = U^*$. By simple considerations analogous to those leading to (5.25), we have

5.33 $$\mathbf{g}^0 = \underbrace{{}^t\mathbf{g} \otimes \cdots \otimes {}^t\mathbf{g}}_{q} \quad \text{on } U^0{}_q$$

For $\mathbf{g}$ here take $\mathbf{f}^{-1}$ and denote the restriction of the resulting $\mathbf{g}^0 = (\mathbf{f}^{-1})^0$ to $U^0{}_q$ by $\mathbf{f}^0{}_q$. According to (5.28) and (5.33) we have

5.34 $$\mathbf{f}^0{}_q = \underbrace{\mathbf{f}^* \otimes \cdots \otimes \mathbf{f}^*}_{q} \quad \text{on } U^0{}_q$$

We now define

5.35 $$\mathbf{f}^p{}_q = \mathbf{f}^p{}_0 \otimes \mathbf{f}^0{}_q$$

for any $\mathbf{f}$ in $GL(U)$. This is an isomorphism from $U^p{}_q$ to itself, and

5.36 $$\mathbf{f}^p{}_q = \underbrace{\mathbf{f} \otimes \cdots \otimes \mathbf{f}}_{p} \otimes \underbrace{\mathbf{f}^* \otimes \cdots \otimes \mathbf{f}^*}_{q}$$

Using (5.29) one shows easily that

5.37 $$(\mathbf{fg})^p{}_q = \mathbf{f}^p{}_q \mathbf{g}^p{}_q$$

For any $\mathbf{f}$, $\mathbf{g}$ in $GL(U)$. Hence we have $GL(U)$ operating as a group of linear transformations on $U^p{}_q$.

Finally, define a linear mapping $\lambda(\mathbf{f})$ of $T(U)$ to itself as follows: If $\mathbf{t}$ is any tensor in $T(U)$ and if we write it in the form $\mathbf{t} = \mathbf{t}_1 + \cdots + \mathbf{t}_r$, where each $\mathbf{t}_i$ is an element of some $U^{p_i}{}_{q_i}$, then we define

$$\lambda(\mathbf{f})(\mathbf{t}) = \sum_{i=1}^{r} \mathbf{f}^{p_i}{}_{q_i}(\mathbf{t}_i)$$

(the mapping $\lambda(\mathbf{f})$ is simply the *direct sum* of the $\mathbf{f}^p{}_q$). From (5.37) there follows

$$\lambda(\mathbf{fg}) = \lambda(\mathbf{f})\,\lambda(\mathbf{g})$$

for any $\mathbf{f}$, $\mathbf{g}$ in $GL(U)$, and the correspondence $\mathbf{f} \to \lambda(\mathbf{f})$ establishes the operation of $GL(U)$ as a group of linear transformations on $T(U)$. Moreover it is easily seen, using Theorem 5.2, that each $\lambda(\mathbf{f})$ is in fact an isomorphism of the tensor algebra $T(U)$ to itself.

DEFINITION 5.3 *Let U and W be vector spaces over the same field, and let there be given a fixed operation h of $GL(U)$ as a group of linear transformations of W to itself (that is, h is a homomorphism from $GL(U)$ to $GL(W)$). We call W, with the* *operation h, a space of tensors of type (p, q) on U if and only if there is a linear mapping* φ: $W \to U^p{}_q$ *whose kernel is zero and for which*

5.38 $$\varphi(h(\mathbf{f})\mathbf{w}) = \mathbf{f}^p{}_q(\varphi(\mathbf{w}))$$

for all $\mathbf{w}$ *in* W *and all* $\mathbf{f}$ *in* $GL(U)$.

This last condition states that φ is compatible with the operation of $GL(U)$ in W and $U^p{}_q$.

EXAMPLE Let A_r denote the space of all r-linear functions on a vector space U over a field K. That is, A_r is the space of all r-linear mappings

$$\underbrace{U \times \cdots \times U}_{r} \to K$$

In Theorem 7.1 below it is shown that any r-linear function $\mathbf{w}$ on U determines a unique element $\mathbf{w}'$ in $U^0{}_r$ and that the mapping φ_r: $A_r \to U^0{}_r$ that sends $\mathbf{w}$ into $\mathbf{w}'$ is an isomorphism.

We define an operation h of $GL(U)$ on A_r as follows, writing simply $\mathbf{f}_r$ for $h(\mathbf{f})$. Thus $\mathbf{f}_r$ denotes the action of $\mathbf{f}$ on A_r, and it is given by the formula

5.39 $$\mathbf{f}_r\mathbf{w}(\mathbf{x}_1, \ldots, \mathbf{x}_r) = \mathbf{w}(\mathbf{f}^{-1}(\mathbf{x}_1), \ldots, \mathbf{f}^{-1}(\mathbf{x}_r))$$

for any $\mathbf{f}$ in $GL(U)$, any $\mathbf{w}$ in A_r, and any $\mathbf{x}_1, \ldots, \mathbf{x}_r$ in U. One verifies easily that $(\mathbf{fg})_r = \mathbf{f}_r\mathbf{g}_r$ for $\mathbf{f}$ and $\mathbf{g}$ in $GL(U)$, and it is easy to show furthermore that

$$\varphi_r(\mathbf{f}_r(\mathbf{w})) = \mathbf{f}^0{}_r(\varphi_r(\mathbf{w}))$$

which is just condition (5.38). Therefore A_r is a space of tensors of type $(0, r)$ on U.

EXERCISES

1. Let U be a one-dimensional vector space over K. Prove that the contravariant tensor algebra $T_0(U)$ is isomorphic to the polynomial algebra $K[t]$ in one variable t over K.
2. If $\mathbf{f}$: $U \to V$ is injective (i.e., has kernel zero), prove that $\mathbf{f}_0$ of Theorem 5.2 is injective. If $\mathbf{f}$ is surjective, prove that $\mathbf{f}_0$ is surjective and that $\mathbf{f}^0$ is injective. ("$\mathbf{f}$ is surjective" means that $\mathrm{Im}(\mathbf{f}) = V$, and similarly for $\mathbf{f}_0$.)
3. If $\dim U = n$, prove that $\dim U^p{}_q = n^{p+q}$.
4. Let $GL(U)$ operate on Hom (U, U) by: $\mathbf{x} \to \mathbf{g}^{-1}\mathbf{x}\mathbf{g}$. Show that Hom (U, U) is thereby a space of tensors of type (1,1).

6. *Bases and components*

Again let U denote a finite-dimensional vector space over a field K, say $\dim U = n$, and let $T(U)$ be its tensor algebra, as defined in the preceding section. We shall show that a base in U gives rise to a base in each of the subspaces $U^p{}_q$ of $T(U)$.

Let $B = \{\mathbf{e}_1, \ldots, \mathbf{e}_n\}$ be a base in U. Associated with B is the so-called dual base $B^* = \{\mathbf{e}^1, \ldots, \mathbf{e}^n\}$ in the dual space U^*. We recall that B^* is defined by the conditions

6.1 $$\langle \mathbf{e}^j, \mathbf{e}_i \rangle = \delta^j{}_i = \begin{cases} 1 & \text{if } i = j \\ 0 & \text{if } i \neq j \end{cases}$$

where in general $\langle \mathbf{f}, \mathbf{x} \rangle$ denotes the element $\mathbf{f}(\mathbf{x})$ in K into which a linear function $\mathbf{f}$ on U maps a vector $\mathbf{x}$ (see Sec. 4, Chap. 9, and Sec. 2, Chap. 14).

By repeated application of Theorem 2.5 one easily shows that the elements

6.2 $$\mathbf{e}^{j_1 \cdots j_q}_{i_1 \cdots i_p} = \mathbf{e}_{i_1} \otimes \cdots \otimes \mathbf{e}_{i_p} \otimes \mathbf{e}^{j_1} \otimes \cdots \otimes \mathbf{e}^{j_q}$$

form a base for $U^p{}_q$, where the i's and j's range independently from 1 to n. Thus $\dim U^p{}_q = n^{p+q}$. Therefore any element $\mathbf{t}$ in $U^p{}_q$ can be written uniquely as

6.3 $$\mathbf{t} = t^{i_1 \cdots i_p}_{j_1 \cdots j_q} \mathbf{e}^{j_1 \cdots j_q}_{i_1 \cdots i_p}$$

where the $t^{i_1 \cdots i_p}_{j_1 \cdots j_q}$ are elements of K. They are the *components* of $\mathbf{t}$ relative to the base (6.2). Since the base (6.2) is uniquely determined by the base B in U, we also call the $t^{i_1 \cdots i_p}_{j_1 \cdots j_q}$ the *components of* $\mathbf{t}$ *relative to* B.

To give an example, let $\mathbf{x}_1, \ldots, \mathbf{x}_p$ be elements of U, and let $\mathbf{y}^*_1, \ldots, \mathbf{y}^*_q$ be elements of U^*. Let

$$\mathbf{x}_a = x^i{}_a \mathbf{e}_i \qquad \mathbf{y}^*_b = y^b{}_j \mathbf{e}^j$$

Then

$$\mathbf{x}_1 \otimes \cdots \otimes \mathbf{x}_p \otimes \mathbf{y}^*_1 \otimes \cdots \otimes \mathbf{y}^*_q = (x^{i_1}_1 \mathbf{e}_{i_1}) \otimes \cdots \otimes (x^{i_p}_p \mathbf{e}_{i_p}) \otimes (y^1_{j_1} \mathbf{e}^{j_1}) \otimes \cdots \otimes (y^q_{j_q} \mathbf{e}^{j_q})$$

Using the multilinearity of the product on the right (Theorem 3.3), we obtain the expression

6.4 $$x^{i_1}_1 \cdots x^{i_p}_p y^1_{j_1} \cdots y^q_{j_q} \mathbf{e}^{j_1 \cdots j_q}_{i_1 \cdots i_p}$$

showing that the components of $\mathbf{x}_1 \otimes \cdots \otimes \mathbf{x}_p \otimes \mathbf{y}^*_1 \otimes \cdots \otimes \mathbf{y}^*_q$ relative to B are the quantities $x^{i_1}_1 \cdots x^{i_p}_p y^1_{j_1} \cdots y^p_{j_q}$ formed from the components of the vectors.

Let us now compute the components of a tensor product $\mathbf{t} \otimes \mathbf{t}'$, where $\mathbf{t}$ is in $U^p{}_q$ and $\mathbf{t}'$ is in $U^r{}_s$. Suppose then that

6.5 $$\mathbf{t} = t^{i_1 \cdots i_p}_{j_1 \cdots j_q} \mathbf{e}^{j_1 \cdots j_q}_{i_1 \cdots i_p} \qquad \mathbf{t}' = t'^{h_1 \cdots h_r}_{k_1 \cdots k_s} \mathbf{e}^{k_1 \cdots k_s}_{h_1 \cdots h_r}$$

From the fact that the product in $T(U)$ is bilinear,

$$\mathbf{t} \otimes \mathbf{t}' = t^{i_1 \cdots i_p}_{j_1 \cdots j_q} t'^{h_1 \cdots h_r}_{k_1 \cdots k_s} \mathbf{e}^{j_1 \cdots j_q}_{i_1 \cdots i_p} \otimes \mathbf{e}^{k_1 \cdots k_s}_{h_1 \cdots h_r}$$

From (6.2) and (5.19), this becomes

$$\mathbf{t} \otimes \mathbf{t}' = t^{i_1 \cdots i_p}_{j_1 \cdots j_q} t'^{h_1 \cdots h_r}_{k_1 \cdots k_s} \mathbf{e}^{j_1 \cdots j_q k_1 \cdots k_s}_{i_1 \cdots i_p h_1 \cdots h_r} \tag{6.6}$$

In other words, if we write

$$\mathbf{t} \otimes \mathbf{t}' = t''^{i_1 \cdots i_{p+r}}_{j_1 \cdots j_{q+s}} \mathbf{e}^{j_1 \cdots j_{q+s}}_{i_1 \cdots i_{p+r}} \tag{6.7}$$

then

$$t''^{i_1 \cdots i_{p+r}}_{j_1 \cdots j_{q+s}} = t^{i_1 \cdots i_p}_{j_1 \cdots j_q} t'^{i_{p+1} \cdots i_{p+r}}_{j_{q+1} \cdots j_{q+s}} \tag{6.8}$$

Therefore, the components of $\mathbf{t} \otimes \mathbf{t}'$ are obtained by simply multiplying the appropriate components of $\mathbf{t}$ and $\mathbf{t}'$, all relative to the given base B.

The effect of a change of base in U on tensor components is easily computed. Let $B_1 = \{\mathbf{u}_1, \ldots, \mathbf{u}_n\}$ be another base, and let $B_1^* = \{\mathbf{u}^1, \ldots, \mathbf{u}^n\}$ be its dual base. Let

$$\mathbf{e}_i = a^h{}_i \mathbf{u}_h \qquad \mathbf{e}^j = b^j{}_k \mathbf{u}^k \tag{6.9}$$

be the equations connecting B and B_1 and the dual bases. From (6.1) we have

$$\begin{aligned} \delta^j{}_i = \langle b^j{}_k \mathbf{u}^k, a^h{}_i \mathbf{u}_h \rangle &= b^j{}_k a^h{}_i \langle \mathbf{u}^k, \mathbf{u}_h \rangle \\ &= b^j{}_k a^h{}_i \delta^k{}_h = b^j{}_k a^k{}_i \end{aligned}$$

showing that $(a^h{}_i)$ and $(b^j{}_k)$ are *inverse* matrices.

Substituting (6.9) in (6.2) and using the multilinearity of the tensor product, we obtain

$$\mathbf{e}^{j_1 \cdots j_q}_{i_1 \cdots i_p} = a^{h_1}_{i_1} \cdots a^{h_p}_{i_p} b^{j_1}_{k_1} \cdots b^{j_q}_{k_q} \mathbf{u}^{k_1 \cdots k_q}_{h_1 \cdots h_p} \tag{6.10}$$

where

$$\mathbf{u}^{k_1 \cdots k_q}_{h_1 \cdots h_p} = \mathbf{u}_{h_1} \otimes \cdots \otimes \mathbf{u}_{h_p} \otimes \mathbf{u}^{k_1} \otimes \cdots \otimes \mathbf{u}^{k_q} \tag{6.11}$$

Referring now to (6.3), if $\mathbf{t}$ has components $\bar{t}^{h_1 \cdots h_p}_{k_1 \cdots k_q}$ relative to the new base B_1, then from (6.10) and (6.3) there follows readily

$$\bar{t}^{h_1 \cdots h_p}_{k_1 \cdots k_q} = t^{i_1 \cdots i_p}_{j_1 \cdots j_q} a^{h_1}_{i_1} \cdots a^{h_p}_{i_p} b^{j_1}_{k_1} \cdots b^{j_q}_{k_q} \tag{6.12}$$

(See Exercise 2 below for an interpretation of this equation.)

Finally we compute the mappings $\mathbf{f}_0$ and $\mathbf{f}^0$ of Theorem 5.2 in terms of components. Let $\mathbf{f}: U \to V$ be a mapping of finite-dimensional vector spaces, and let $B = \{\mathbf{e}_1, \ldots, \mathbf{e}_n\}$ and $B' = \{\mathbf{v}_1, \ldots, \mathbf{v}_m\}$ be bases for U and V, respectively. Let

$$\mathbf{f}(\mathbf{e}_i) = c^h{}_i \mathbf{v}_h \tag{6.13}$$

By (5.23) we have

$$\begin{aligned}\mathbf{f}_0(\mathbf{e}_{i_1} \otimes \cdots \otimes \mathbf{e}_{i_p}) &= \mathbf{f}(\mathbf{e}_{i_1}) \otimes \cdots \otimes \mathbf{f}(\mathbf{e}_{i_p}) \\ &= (c^{h_1}_{i_1}\mathbf{v}_{h_1}) \otimes \cdots \otimes (c^{h_p}_{i_p}\mathbf{v}_{h_p}) \\ &= c^{h_1}_{i_1} \cdots c^{h_p}_{i_p}\mathbf{v}_{h_1} \otimes \cdots \otimes \mathbf{v}_{h_p}\end{aligned}$$

or

6.14 $$\mathbf{f}_0(\mathbf{e}_{i_1 \ldots i_p}) = c^{h_1}{}_{i_1} \cdots c^{h_p}{}_{i_p}\mathbf{v}_{h_1 \ldots h_p}$$

where

6.15 $$\mathbf{e}_{i_1 \ldots i_p} = \mathbf{e}_{i_1} \otimes \cdots \otimes \mathbf{e}_{i_p}$$

and similarly for $\mathbf{v}_{h_1 \ldots h_p}$. If $\mathbf{t} = t^{i_1 \cdots i_p}\mathbf{e}_{i_1 \ldots i_p}$ is an element of $U^p{}_0$, then by linearity there follows

6.16 $$\mathbf{f}_0(\mathbf{t}) = t^{i_1 \cdots i_p}\mathbf{f}_0(\mathbf{e}_{i_1 \ldots i_p}) = t^{i_1 \cdots i_p}c^{h_1}_{i_1} \cdots c^{h_p}_{i_p}\mathbf{v}_{h_1 \ldots j_p}$$

showing how to compute the components of $\mathbf{f}_0(\mathbf{t})$ relative to the base B' in V.

To compute $\mathbf{f}^0$ we recall from Theorem 4.4, Chap. 9, that

$$\langle {}^t\mathbf{f}(\mathbf{y}^*), \mathbf{x}\rangle = \langle \mathbf{y}^*, \mathbf{f}(\mathbf{x})\rangle$$

for $\mathbf{x}$ in U and $\mathbf{y}^*$ in V^*. Let $B^* = \{\mathbf{e}^1, \ldots, \mathbf{e}^n\}$ and $B'^* = \{\mathbf{v}^1, \ldots, \mathbf{v}^m\}$ be the bases dual to B and B'. We have

$$\begin{aligned}\langle {}^t\mathbf{f}(\mathbf{v}^j), \mathbf{e}_i\rangle &= \langle \mathbf{v}^j, \mathbf{f}(\mathbf{e}_i)\rangle \\ &= \langle \mathbf{v}^j, c^h{}_i\mathbf{v}_h\rangle = c^h{}_i\langle \mathbf{v}^j, \mathbf{v}_h\rangle = c^j{}_i\end{aligned}$$

whence

6.17 $${}^t\mathbf{f}(\mathbf{v}^j) = c^j{}_i\mathbf{e}^i$$

Then, writing

6.18 $$\begin{aligned}\mathbf{v}^{j_1 \cdots j_q} &= \mathbf{v}^{j_1} \otimes \cdots \otimes \mathbf{v}^{j_q} \\ \mathbf{e}^{i_1 \cdots i_q} &= \mathbf{e}^{i_1} \otimes \cdots \otimes e^{i_q}\end{aligned}$$

we have

$$\begin{aligned}\mathbf{f}^0(\mathbf{v}^{j_1 \cdots j_q}) &= {}^t\mathbf{f}(\mathbf{v}^{j_1}) \otimes \cdots \otimes {}^t\mathbf{f}(\mathbf{v}^{j_q}) \\ &= (c^{j_1}_{i_1}\mathbf{e}^{i_1}) \otimes \cdots \otimes (c^{j_q}_{i_q}\mathbf{e}^{i_q})\end{aligned}$$

by (5.23), and so

6.19 $$\mathbf{f}^0(\mathbf{v}^{j_1 \cdots j_q}) = c^{j_1}_{i_1} \cdots c^{j_q}_{i_q}\mathbf{e}^{i_1 \cdots i_q}$$

which shows the effect of $\mathbf{f}^0$ on the base elements $\mathbf{v}^{j_1 \cdots j_q}$ in $V^0{}_q$. If

$$\mathbf{t} = t_{j_1 \ldots j_q}\mathbf{v}^{j_1 \cdots j_q}$$

is an element of $V^0{}_q$, then, by linearity of $\mathbf{f}^0$,

6.20 $$\mathbf{f}^0(\mathbf{t}) = t_{j_1 \ldots j_q}c^{j_1}_{i_1} \cdots c^{j_q}_{i_q}\mathbf{e}^{i_1 \cdots i_q}$$

which shows that the components of $\mathbf{f}^0(t)$ relative to B are the quantities

6.21 $$t_{j_1 \ldots j_q} c^{j_1}_{i_1} \cdots c^{j_q}_{i_q}$$

EXERCISES

1. Let $\mathbf{f}^0$ be as above, let $\mathbf{t}_1$ be in $V^0{}_q$ and let $\mathbf{t}_2$ be in $V^0{}_r$. Show how to compute the components of $\mathbf{f}^0(\mathbf{t}_1 \otimes \mathbf{t}_2)$ in U^0_{q+r}.

2. Let $\mathbf{g}$ denote the automorphism of U given by formula (6.9). Prove that (6.12) is the operation $\mathbf{g}^p{}_q$ of $\mathbf{g}$ on $U^p{}_q$.

7. *Contraction of tensors*

Let U be an n-dimensional vector space over a field K, and as usual let U^* denote its dual space. An element $\mathbf{y}^*$ of U^* is a linear mapping $U \to K$, and for any $\mathbf{x}$ in U we denote the scalar $\mathbf{y}^*(\mathbf{x})$ by the symbol $\langle \mathbf{y}^*, \mathbf{x} \rangle$. The mapping $U \times U^* \to K$ defined by

7.1 $$(\mathbf{x}, \mathbf{y}^*) \to \langle \mathbf{y}^*, \mathbf{x} \rangle$$

is a bilinear mapping. By definition of $U \otimes U^* = U^1{}_1$ there is a unique linear mapping $U^1{}_1 \to K$ such that

7.2 $$\mathbf{x} \otimes \mathbf{y}^* \to \langle \mathbf{y}^*, \mathbf{x} \rangle$$

This mapping is called *contraction*. Now let $B = \{\mathbf{e}_1, \ldots, \mathbf{e}_n\}$ be a base in U, and let $B^* = \{\mathbf{e}^1, \ldots, \mathbf{e}^n\}$ be the dual base in U^*. If

7.3 $$\mathbf{x} = x^i \mathbf{e}_i \qquad \mathbf{y}^* = y_j \mathbf{e}^j$$

then from (6.1) we have

7.4 $$\langle \mathbf{y}^*, \mathbf{x} \rangle = x^i y_i$$

Thus (7.2) can be written

7.5 $$x^i y_j \, \mathbf{e}_i \otimes \mathbf{e}^j \to x^i y_j \langle \mathbf{e}^j, \mathbf{e}_i \rangle = x^i y_i$$

More generally, if $\mathbf{t} = t^i{}_j \mathbf{e}_i \otimes \mathbf{e}^j$ is any tensor in $U^1{}_1$, then the mapping $U^1{}_1 \to K$ determined by (7.2) sends $\mathbf{t}$ into the scalar

7.6 $$t^i{}_j \langle \mathbf{e}^j, \mathbf{e}_i \rangle = t^i{}_i$$

by linearity. (We note that the components of $\mathbf{t}$ form an $n \times n$ matrix $(t^i{}_j)$, and the quantity on the right is the sum of its diagonal elements, i.e., the *trace* of the matrix.)

In this section we show how to extend the operation of contraction to other tensors. Consider now the space $U^p{}_q$ defined in (5.7). We assume here that $p > 0$

and $q > 0$. Fix two integers h, k, with $1 \leq h \leq p$ and $1 \leq k \leq q$, and consider the mapping

$$\text{7.7} \qquad \underbrace{U \times \cdots \times U}_{p} \times \underbrace{U^* \times \cdots \times U^*}_{q} \to U^{p-1}_{q-1}$$

defined by

$$\text{7.8} \qquad (\mathbf{x}_1, \ldots, \mathbf{x}_p, \mathbf{y}_1^*, \ldots, \mathbf{y}_q^*) \to \langle \mathbf{y}_k^*, \mathbf{x}_h \rangle \cdot \mathbf{x}_1 \otimes \cdots \hat{\mathbf{x}}_h \cdots \otimes \mathbf{x}_p \otimes \mathbf{y}_1^* \otimes \cdots \hat{\mathbf{y}}_k^* \cdots \otimes \mathbf{y}_q^*)$$

where the symbols $\hat{\mathbf{x}}_h$ and $\hat{\mathbf{y}}_k^*$ indicate that those factors are to be omitted. Thus the $\mathbf{x}$ part of the tensor product written above stands for

$$\mathbf{x}_1 \otimes \cdots \otimes \mathbf{x}_{h-1} \otimes \mathbf{x}_{h+1} \otimes \cdots \otimes \mathbf{x}_p$$

and similarly for the $\mathbf{y}^*$ part. One verifies without difficulty that the mapping (7.7) so defined is multilinear. Therefore, by Theorem 3.3, there is a unique linear mapping

$$\text{7.9} \qquad C^h{}_k \colon U^p{}_q \to U^{p-1}_{q-1}$$

such that

$$\text{7.10} \qquad C^h{}_k(\mathbf{x}_1 \otimes \cdots \otimes \mathbf{x}_p \otimes \mathbf{y}_1^* \otimes \cdots \otimes \mathbf{y}_q^*) = \langle \mathbf{y}_k^*, \mathbf{x}_h \rangle \cdot \mathbf{x}_1 \otimes \cdots \hat{\mathbf{x}}_h \cdots \otimes \mathbf{x}_p \otimes \mathbf{y}_1^* \cdots \hat{\mathbf{y}}_k^* \cdots \otimes y_q^*$$

for any $\mathbf{x}_i$ in U and $\mathbf{y}_j^*$ in U^*. In particular, for the base elements

$$\text{7.11} \qquad \mathbf{e}^{j_1 \cdots j_q}_{i_1 \cdots i_p} = \mathbf{e}_{i_1} \otimes \cdots \otimes \mathbf{e}_{i_p} \otimes \mathbf{e}^{j_i} \otimes \cdots \otimes \mathbf{e}^{j_q}$$

in $U^p{}_q$ we have

$$\text{7.12} \qquad C^h{}_k\left(\mathbf{e}^{j_1 \cdots j_q}_{k_1 \cdots i_p}\right) = \langle \mathbf{e}^{j_k}, \mathbf{e}_{i_h} \rangle \cdot \mathbf{e}^{j_1 \cdots \hat{j}_k \cdots j_p}_{i_1 \cdots \hat{i}_h \cdots i_p} = \delta^{j_k}{}_{i_h} \cdot \mathbf{e}^{j_1 \cdots \hat{j}_k \cdots j_p}_{i_1 \cdots \hat{i}_h \cdots i_p}$$

where again $\hat{j}_k$, $\hat{i}_h$ denote omission of those indices. Now let

$$\text{7.13} \qquad \mathbf{t} = t^{i_1 \cdots i_p}_{j_1 \cdots j_q} \mathbf{e}^{j_1 \cdots j_p}_{i_1 \cdots i_q}$$

be any tensor in $U^p{}_q$. Applying $C^h{}_k$ to $\mathbf{t}$ and using linearity and (7.12), we obtain

$$C^h{}_k(\mathbf{t}) = t^{i_1 \cdots i_{h-1} i\, i_{h+1} \cdots i_p}_{j_1 \cdots j_{k-1} i\, j_{k+1} \cdots j_q} \mathbf{e}^{j_1 \cdots \hat{j}_k \cdots j_q}_{i_1 \cdots \hat{i}_h \cdots i_p}$$

changing the names of the indices, we can rewrite this as

$$\text{7.14} \qquad C^h{}_k(\mathbf{t}) = t^{i_1 \cdots i_{h-1} i\, i_h \cdots i_{p-1}}_{j_1 \cdots j_{k-1} i\, j_k \cdots j_{q-1}} \mathbf{e}^{j_1 \cdots j_{q-1}}_{i_1 \cdots i_{p-1}}$$

Hence, the components of $C^h{}_k(\mathbf{t})$ are obtained from those of $\mathbf{t}$ by summing over the hth upper index and the kth lower index. In particular, we have, for $\mathbf{t} = t^i{}_j\mathbf{e}^j{}_i$ in $U^1{}_1$,

$$C^1{}_1(\mathbf{t}) = t^i{}_i$$

as in (7.6). Another important example of this operation is as follows. Take

7.15 $$\mathbf{t} = t^i{}_j\mathbf{e}^j{}_i \quad \text{in } U^1{}_1 \quad \text{and} \quad \mathbf{x} = x^i\mathbf{e}_i \quad \text{in } U$$

Apply the contraction operation $C^2{}_1$ to the element

$$\mathbf{t} \otimes \mathbf{x} = t^i{}_jx^k\mathbf{e}^j{}_{ik} \qquad \text{in } U^2{}_1$$

The result is

$$C^2{}_1(\mathbf{t} \otimes \mathbf{x}) = t^i{}_jx^j\mathbf{e}_i \qquad \text{in } U^1{}_0 = U$$

Therefore the operation

7.16 $$\mathbf{x} \to C^2{}_1(\mathbf{t} \otimes \mathbf{x})$$

is the linear mapping $U \to U$ whose matrix relative to the base B is $(t^i{}_j)$, and in this way one can regard the tensors in $U^1{}_1$ as endomorphisms $U \to U$. Similarly, taking $\mathbf{y}^* = y_i\mathbf{e}^i$ in U^*, we have

$$C^1{}_2(\mathbf{t} \otimes \mathbf{y}^*) = t^i{}_jy_i\mathbf{e}^j$$

and consequently

7.17 $$\mathbf{y}^* \to C^1{}_2(\mathbf{t} \otimes \mathbf{y}^*)$$

is the linear mapping $U^* \to U^*$ whose matrix is the transpose of $(t^i{}_j)$. In fact, the mapping (7.17) is the transpose of the mapping (7.16).

The contraction operations $C^h{}_k$ can be applied in a wide variety of ways, clearly. In particular, they can be repeated. Consider an element $\mathbf{u} = u^{ij}_{kh}\mathbf{e}^{kh}_{ij}$ of $U^2{}_2$. We have

$$C^1{}_1(\mathbf{u}) = u^{ij}_{ih}\mathbf{e}^h{}_j$$

an element of $U^1{}_1$. Applying $C^1{}_1$ again (it affects only the two free indices j, h) we get

$$C^1{}_1 \circ C^1{}_1(\mathbf{u}) = u^{ij}_{ij}$$

This is easily seen to be the same as $C^1{}_1 \circ C^2{}_2(\mathbf{u})$. Similarly,

$$C^1{}_2(\mathbf{u}) = u^{ij}_{ki}\mathbf{e}^k{}_j$$

and so

$$C^1{}_1 \circ C^1{}_2(\mathbf{u}) = u^{ij}_{ji}$$

Similar considerations apply to any $U^r{}_r$. Thus, let

7.18 $$\mathbf{u} = u^{i_1 \cdots i_r}_{j_1 \cdots j_r}\, \mathbf{e}^{j_1 \cdots j_r}_{i_1 \cdots i_r}$$

be any tensor in $U^r{}_r$. The contraction $C^1{}_1$ results in summation over the first upper and lower indices, so that $C^1{}_1(\mathbf{u})$ has components

7.19 $$u^{i_1 i_2 \cdots i_r}_{i_1 j_2 \cdots j_r} = u'^{i_2 \cdots i_r}_{j_2 \cdots j_r}$$

$C^1{}_1$ applied to this causes summation over the first upper and lower indices, and $C^1{}_1(C^1{}_1(\mathbf{u}))$ has components

7.20 $$u^{i_1 i_2 i_3 \cdots i_r}_{i_1 i_2 j_3 \cdots j_r} = u''^{i_3 \cdots i_r}_{j_3 \cdots j_r}$$

Continuing in this way, one finds at once that application r times of $C^1{}_1$ to $\mathbf{u}$ yields the scalar

7.21 $$\underbrace{C^1{}_1 \circ C^1{}_1 \circ \cdots \circ C^1{}_1}_{r}(\mathbf{u}) = u^{i_1 \cdots i_r}_{i_1 \cdots i_r}$$

The mapping $\mathbf{u} \to u^{i_1 \cdots i_r}_{i_1 \cdots i_r}$ is a linear mapping $U^r{}_r \to K$, since each $C^1{}_1$ is linear.

Now take a tensor $\mathbf{t} = t^{i_1 \cdots i_r}\, \mathbf{e}_{i_1 \cdots i_r}$ in $U^r{}_0$ and a tensor $\mathbf{t}' = t'_{j_1 \cdots j_r}\, \mathbf{e}^{j_1 \cdots j_r}$ in $U^0{}_r$. Their product $\mathbf{t} \otimes \mathbf{t}'$ is in $U^r{}_r$ and its components are $t^{i_1 \cdots i_r}\, t'_{j_1 \cdots j_r}$. Then (7.21) applied to $\mathbf{t} \otimes \mathbf{t}'$ yields a scalar which we shall denote by $\langle \mathbf{t}', \mathbf{t} \rangle$. Thus, in terms of the components,

7.22 $$\langle \mathbf{t}', \mathbf{t} \rangle = t^{i_1 \cdots i_r}\, t'_{i_1 \cdots i_r}$$

For $\mathbf{t} = \mathbf{x}_1 \otimes \cdots \otimes \mathbf{x}_r$ and $\mathbf{t}' = \mathbf{y}^*_1 \otimes \cdots \otimes \mathbf{y}^*_r$, this reduces to

7.23 $$\langle \mathbf{y}^*_1 \otimes \cdots \otimes \mathbf{y}^*_r, \mathbf{x}_1 \otimes \cdots \otimes \mathbf{x}_r \rangle = \langle \mathbf{y}^*_1, \mathbf{x}_1 \rangle \cdots \langle \mathbf{y}^*_r, \mathbf{x}_r \rangle$$

Referring to (7.22), the mapping $(\mathbf{t}, \mathbf{t}') \to \mathbf{t} \otimes \mathbf{t}'$ is bilinear; the mapping (7.21) is linear; hence

7.24 $$(\mathbf{t}, \mathbf{t}') \to \langle \mathbf{t}', \mathbf{t} \rangle$$

is a bilinear mapping $U^r{}_0 \times U^0{}_r \to K$. For $r = 1$ it is the same as (7.1). For fixed $\mathbf{t}'$, the mapping $\mathbf{t} \to \langle \mathbf{t}', \mathbf{t} \rangle$ is a linear mapping $U^r{}_0 \to K$, hence is an element of the dual space of $U^r{}_0$. In this way we can regard $U^0{}_r$ as the dual space of $U^r{}_0$, and vice versa.

Let us make the following definition:

DEFINITION 7.1 *An r-linear function* $\mathbf{f}$ *on a vector space* U *over* K *is an r-linear mapping*

$$\underbrace{U \times \cdots \times U}_{r} \to K$$

The latter notion is defined in Definition 2.2.

As a final observation here, let $\mathbf{t}'$ be a fixed element in $U^0{}_r$. Then the entity $\mathbf{t}''$ defined by

7.25 $$\mathbf{t}''(\mathbf{x}_1, \ldots, \mathbf{x}_r) = \langle \mathbf{t}', \mathbf{x}_1 \otimes \cdots \otimes \mathbf{x}_r \rangle$$

is clearly an r-linear function on U.

THEOREM 7.1 *The correspondence* $\mathbf{t}' \to \mathbf{t}''$ *defined by* (7.25) *is an isomorphism from* $U^0{}_r$ *to the vector space of r-linear functions on* U *compatible with the operation of* $GL(U)$ *on each.*

Proof. Let $\mathbf{t}''$ be an r-linear function on U, and define $\mathbf{t}'$ by

$$\mathbf{t}' = \mathbf{t}''(\mathbf{e}_{i_1}, \ldots, \mathbf{e}_{i_r}) \cdot \mathbf{e}^{i_1 \cdots i_r}$$

Then $\mathbf{t}'$ is an element of $U^0{}_r$, and it is easily seen that $\mathbf{t}'$ does not depend on the particular choice of base $B = \{\mathbf{e}_1, \ldots, \mathbf{e}_n\}$. Moreover, (7.25) holds for this $\mathbf{t}'$. Therefore the mapping $\mathbf{t}' \to \mathbf{t}''$ is a one-to-one mapping of $U^0{}_r$ to the space of r-linear functions, and it is trivial to verify that it is a linear mapping compatible with the operation of $GL(U)$. Q.E.D.

This theorem gives a rather concrete meaning to $U^0{}_r$, showing that its elements can be identified with r-linear functions on U. In particular, the elements of $U^0{}_2$ can be regarded as bilinear functions on U. In a similar way one shows that elements of $U^r{}_0$ can be considered as r-linear functions on U^*.

REMARK. Tensors which arise in physics often occur as multilinear functions on vectors. Most tensors in physical applications are so-called *dyadic* tensors, that is, elements of $U_0{}^2$, $U^1{}_1$, or $U^0{}_2$ in our terminology. We recall that elements of $U^1{}_1$ can be interpreted as linear transformations $U \to U$, as in (7.16). We note that elements of $U^0{}_2$ can be thought of as linear mappings $U \to U^*$. Namely, for $\mathbf{t}$ in $U^0{}_2$, the mappings

$$\mathbf{x} \to C^1{}_1(\mathbf{t} \otimes \mathbf{x})$$

and

$$\mathbf{x} \to C^1{}_2(\mathbf{t} \otimes \mathbf{x})$$

are both linear mappings $U \to U^*$. Similarly, elements of $U^2{}_0$ can be interpreted (in two ways) as linear mappings $U^* \to U$.

EXERCISES

1. Let $\mathbf{f}$: $U \to V$ be a linear mapping of finite-dimensional vector spaces over K. Let $\mathbf{f}_0$ and $\mathbf{f}^0$ be the mappings of Theorem 5.2. Prove that $\mathbf{f}^0$, restricted to elements of $V^0{}_p$, is the transpose of $\mathbf{f}_0$ restricted to elements of $U^p{}_0$.

2. Show that elements of $U^1{}_3$ can be interpreted as linear mappings $U^3{}_0 \to U$ and as linear mappings $U^* \to U^0{}_3$.

3. Given a linear mapping $U^p{}_q \to U^r{}_s$, show how it can be represented by a tensor in $T(U)$.

4. Let $\mathbf{f}$ be an r-linear function on U, and let $\mathbf{g}$ be an s-linear function on U. Let $\mathbf{h}$ be the $(r + s)$-linear function defined by $\mathbf{h}(\mathbf{x}_1, \ldots, \mathbf{x}_{r+s}) = \mathbf{f}(\mathbf{x}_1, \ldots, \mathbf{x}_r) \cdot \mathbf{g}(\mathbf{x}_{r+1}, \ldots, \mathbf{x}_s)$. Let $\mathbf{u}$, $\mathbf{v}$, $\mathbf{w}$ be the tensors in $U^0{}_r$, $U^0{}_s$, U^0_{r+s} corresponding to $\mathbf{f}$, $\mathbf{g}$, $\mathbf{h}$, respectively, according to Theorem 7.1. Prove that $\mathbf{w} = \mathbf{u} \otimes \mathbf{v}$.

5. Prove that the mapping (7.8) is compatible with the operations of $GL(U)$ on $U^p{}_q$ and U^{p-1}_{q-1}.

8. *Symmetry properties*

Again we let U denote an n-dimensional vector space over a field K. However, we now impose a condition on K: we assume that no multiple of the unit element 1 in K is equal to zero. That is, we assume that the elements $1 + 1$, $1 + 1 + 1$, etc., in K are nonzero. In particular we exclude finite fields. The fields **Q**, **R**, **C** certainly fulfill the requirement, and in later sections we shall be concerned solely with vector spaces over the real field **R**. The reason for our present restriction will soon be apparent.

As usual we denote by $U^p{}_q$ the space defined in (5.7). In particular,

8.1 $$U^p{}_0 = \underbrace{U \otimes \cdots \otimes U}_{p}$$

Let h and k be integers with $1 \leq h \leq k \leq p$. The mapping

$$\underbrace{U \times \cdots \times U}_{p} \to U^p{}_0$$

defined by

8.2 $$(\mathbf{x}_1, \ldots, \mathbf{x}_p) \to \mathbf{x}_1 \otimes \cdots \otimes \mathbf{x}_k \otimes \cdots \otimes \mathbf{x}_h \otimes \cdots \otimes \mathbf{x}_p$$

(interchanging $\mathbf{x}_h$ and $\mathbf{x}_k$) is certainly multilinear. Consequently (Theorem 3.3) there is a unique linear mapping $S_{h,k}$: $U^p{}_0 \to U^p{}_0$ such that

8.3 $$S_{h,k}(\mathbf{x}_1 \otimes \cdots \otimes \mathbf{x}_h \otimes \cdots \otimes \mathbf{x}_k \otimes \cdots \otimes \mathbf{x}_p) = \mathbf{x}_1 \otimes \cdots \otimes \mathbf{x}_k \otimes \cdots \otimes \mathbf{x}_h \otimes \cdots \otimes \mathbf{x}_p$$

and it is easily seen that $S_{h,k}$ is an isomorphism. In particular, if $B = \{\mathbf{e}_1, \ldots, \mathbf{e}_n\}$ is a base for U, and if as usual we put

8.4 $$\mathbf{e}_{i_1 \ldots i_p} = \mathbf{e}_{i_1} \otimes \cdots \otimes \mathbf{e}_{i_p}$$

then

8.5 $$S_{h,k}(\mathbf{e}_{i_1 \ldots i_p}) = \mathbf{e}_{i_1 \ldots i_k \ldots i_h \ldots i_p}$$

A tensor $\mathbf{t}$ in $U^p{}_0$ is said to be *symmetric* in the h and k places, or in the h and k indices, if

8.6 $$S_{h,k}(\mathbf{t}) = \mathbf{t}$$

and $\mathbf{t}$ is said to be *skew-symmetric*, or *alternating*, in the h and k places, or indices, if

8.7 $$S_{h,k}(\mathbf{t}) = -\mathbf{t}$$

These conditions are easily transcribed for the components of $\mathbf{t}$ relative to the base B as follows: Let

8.8 $$\mathbf{t} = t^{i_1 \cdots i_p}\mathbf{e}_{i_1 \cdots i_p}$$

From (8.5) and the linearity of $S_{h,k}$ we have

$$S_{h,k}(\mathbf{t}) = t^{i_1 \cdots i_p}\mathbf{e}_{i_1 \cdots i_k \cdots i_h \cdots i_p}$$

From this and (8.8) it is immediate that (8.6) is equivalent to

8.9 $$t^{i_1 \cdots i_k \cdots i_h \cdots i_p} = t^{i_1 \cdots i_h \cdots i_k \cdots i_p}$$

for all sets of indices $i_\nu = 1, 2, \ldots, n$. Similarly, (8.7) is equivalent to

8.10 $$t^{i_1 \cdots i_k \cdots i_h \cdots i_p} = -t^{i_1 \cdots i_h \cdots i_k \cdots i_p}$$

More generally, if σ denotes any permutation of the integers $1, \ldots, p$, then there is a unique isomorphism S_σ: $U^p{}_0 \to U^p{}_0$ such that

8.11 $$S_\sigma(\mathbf{x}_1 \otimes \cdots \otimes \mathbf{x}_p) = \mathbf{x}_{\sigma(1)} \otimes \cdots \otimes \mathbf{x}_{\sigma(p)}$$

for any $\mathbf{x}_i$ in U, the argument being the same as with $S_{h,k}$ above. A tensor $\mathbf{t}$ in $U^p{}_0$ is said to be *symmetric* with respect to σ if

8.12 $$S_\sigma(\mathbf{t}) = \mathbf{t}$$

The equivalent condition on the components of $\mathbf{t}$ is easily found to be

8.13 $$t^{i_1 \cdots i_p} = t^{i_{\sigma(1)} \cdots i_{\sigma(p)}}$$

Similarly, $\mathbf{t}$ is said to be *alternating*, or *skew-symmetric*, with respect to σ if

8.14 $$S_\sigma(\mathbf{t}) = -\mathbf{t} \qquad \textit{and } \sigma \textit{ odd}$$

For the components of $\mathbf{t}$ in this case one only has to put a minus sign on one side of (8.13).

Now any permutation σ of $\{1, \ldots, p\}$ can be expressed as a product

$$\sigma = \sigma_1\sigma_2 \cdots \sigma_m$$

of transpositions (Theorem 3.4, Chap. 10). For the corresponding mappings $S_\sigma, S_{\sigma_1}, \ldots, S_{\sigma_m}$ of $U^p{}_0$ to itself one easily finds that

8.15 $$S_\sigma = S_{\sigma_1} \cdots S_{\sigma_m}$$

and therefore problems of symmetry can be reduced to questions involving mappings of the type $S_{h,k}$ considered at the beginning of this section.

A tensor $\mathbf{t}$ in $U^p{}_0$ is called symmetric if (8.12) holds for every permutation σ o $\{1, \ldots, p\}$. From the remarks just made it is clear that $\mathbf{t}$ is symmetric if and only if (8.12) holds for every transposition σ of two elements of $\{1, \ldots, p\}$.

Given any tensor $\mathbf{t}$ in $U^p{}_0$ it is easy to construct from it a new tensor having given symmetry properties. For example, suppose we want to obtain from $\mathbf{t}$ a symmetric tensor, as just defined. Form the sum

8.16 $$S(\mathbf{t}) = \sum_\sigma S_\sigma(\mathbf{t})$$

where on the right σ runs through all permutations of $\{1, \ldots, p\}$. If σ_1 is any permutation of this set, then

$$S_{\sigma_1}(S(\mathbf{t})) = \sum_\sigma S_{\sigma_1}(S_\sigma(\mathbf{t})) = \sum_\sigma S_{\sigma_1\sigma}(\mathbf{t})$$

Since the permutations of $\{1, \ldots, p\}$ form a group, it follows that, as σ runs through all its elements, so does $\sigma_1\sigma$. Therefore the expression on the right above is the same as the right member of (8.16). That is, $S_{\sigma_1}(S(\mathbf{t})) = S(\mathbf{t})$, and so $S(\mathbf{t})$ is a *symmetric* tensor. Now if $\mathbf{t}$ happened to be symmetric to begin with, then every term $S_\sigma(\mathbf{t})$ in (8.16) is equal to $\mathbf{t}$. There are $p!$ terms, and so

8.17 $$S(\mathbf{t}) = p!\mathbf{t} \qquad \text{if } \mathbf{t} \text{ is symmetric}$$

If some multiple of the unit 1 in K were zero, then (8.17) would be zero for large enough p. This unsatisfactory situation is precluded by our assumption concerning K. The element $p! = p! \times 1$ in K is not zero, hence has an inverse. We can then form the operator $\frac{1}{p!} S$, and it has the property that it is a linear mapping $U^p{}_0 \to U^p{}_0$ which carries every tensor $\mathbf{t}$ into a symmetric tensor, mapping symmetric tensors into themselves.

For the components of $\frac{1}{p!} S(\mathbf{t})$ it is easily seen from (8.16) that they are the elements $t'^{i_1 \cdots i_p}$ given by

8.18 $$t'^{i_1 \cdots i_p} = \frac{1}{p!} \sum_\sigma t^{i_{\sigma(1)} \cdots i_{\sigma(p)}}$$

For $p = 2$ this reduces to

8.19 $$t'^{ij} = \tfrac{1}{2}(t^{ij} + t^{ji})$$

A tensor $\mathbf{t}$ in $U^p{}_0$ is called *skew-symmetric*, or *alternating*, if (8.14) holds for every odd permutation σ of the set $\{1, \ldots, p\}$. From the remarks above concerning

(8.15), and from Theorem 3.5, Chap. 10, it is clear that **t** is alternating if and only if (8.7) holds for every pair of integers h, k with $1 \leq h \leq k \leq p$.

Just as with S above, we can build an operator A which produces an alternating tensor from any tensor **t** in $U^p{}_0$. Namely, we put

8.20 $$A(\mathbf{t}) = \frac{1}{p!} \sum_\sigma \operatorname{sign}(\sigma) \cdot S_\sigma(\mathbf{t})$$

the sum being over all permutations σ of $\{1, \ldots, p\}$, with $\operatorname{sign}(\sigma) = +1$ or -1 according as σ is even or odd. If σ' is any transposition of two elements of $\{1, \ldots, p\}$, then

$$\begin{aligned} S_{\sigma'}(A(t)) &= \frac{1}{p!} \sum_\sigma \operatorname{sign}(\sigma) \cdot S_{\sigma'}(S_\sigma(\mathbf{t})) \\ &= \frac{1}{p!} \sum_\sigma \operatorname{sign}(\sigma) \cdot S_{\sigma'\sigma}(\mathbf{t}) \\ &= -\frac{1}{p!} \sum_\sigma \operatorname{sign}(\sigma'\sigma) \cdot S_{\sigma'\sigma}(\mathbf{t}) \end{aligned}$$

since σ' is odd. As σ runs through all permutations of $\{1, \ldots, p\}$, so does $\sigma'\sigma$, and so there follows

$$S_{\sigma'}(A(\mathbf{t})) = -A(\mathbf{t})$$

showing that $A(\mathbf{t})$ is an alternating tensor. If **t** itself is alternating, then from (8.14) it follows easily that $\operatorname{sign}(\sigma) \cdot S_\sigma(\mathbf{t}) = \mathbf{t}$, whence

8.21 $$A(\mathbf{t}) = \mathbf{t} \qquad \text{if } \mathbf{t} \text{ is alternating}$$

As with (8.18) it is quickly seen that $A(t)$ has as components the elements

8.22 $$t''^{i_1 \cdots i_p} = \frac{1}{p!} \sum_\sigma \operatorname{sign}(\sigma) \cdot t^{i_{\sigma(1)} \cdots i_{\sigma(p)}}$$

For $p = 2$ this reduces to

8.23 $$t''^{ij} = \tfrac{1}{2}(t^{ij} - t^{ji})$$

Alternating tensors will play an important role later in this chapter. We observe that for the base vectors (8.4) the formula (8.20) gives

8.24 $$A(\mathbf{e}_{i_1 \cdots i_p}) = \frac{1}{p!} \sum_\sigma \operatorname{sign}(\sigma) \cdot \mathbf{e}_{i_{\sigma(1)}} \otimes \cdots \otimes \mathbf{e}_{i_{\sigma(p)}}$$

The components of $\mathbf{e}_{a_1 \cdots a_p}$ relative to that same base are clearly the elements $\delta^{i_1}_{a_1} \cdots \delta^{i_p}_{a_p}$, since

$$\mathbf{e}_{a_1 \cdots a_p} = \delta^{i_1}_{a_1} \cdots \delta^{i_p}_{a_p} \mathbf{e}_{i_1 \cdots i_p}$$

Putting these in (8.22) we find that the components of $A(\mathbf{e}_{a_1 \ldots a_p})$ are the elements

8.25 $$\delta^{i_1 \ldots i_p}_{a_1 \ldots a_p} = \frac{1}{p!} \sum_\sigma \operatorname{sign}(\sigma) \cdot \delta^{i_{\sigma(1)}}_{a_1} \cdots \delta^{i_{\sigma(p)}}_{a_p} = \frac{1}{p!} \cdot \begin{vmatrix} \delta^{i_1}_{a_1} & \cdots & \delta^{i_1}_{a_p} \\ \cdots & \cdots & \cdots \\ \delta^{i_p}_{a_1} & \cdots & \delta^{i_p}_{a_p} \end{vmatrix}$$

by (2.7) of Chap. 11.

It is clear that an entirely analogous discussion can be carried through for the covariant tensor space $U^0{}_p$. We shall not bother to write out the corresponding formulas, which are essentially the same as the foregoing, with upper and lower indices interchanged. Putting the results together with those above, one obtains similar results for mixed tensors in $U^p{}_q = U^p{}_0 \otimes U^0{}_q$.

EXERCISES

1. Exhibit a linear mapping $Y\colon U^p{}_0 \to U^p{}_0$ such that $Y(\mathbf{t})$ is skew-symmetric in the first three places, assuming $p \geq 3$, and such that $Y(\mathbf{t}) = \mathbf{t}$ if $\mathbf{t}$ already has that property.
2. Exhibit a linear mapping $W\colon U^1{}_3 \to U^1{}_3$ such that $W(\mathbf{t})$ is skew-symmetric in its first two covariant places and such that $W(\mathbf{t}) = \mathbf{t}$ if $\mathbf{t}$ already has that property.
3. Prove that the operators $\frac{1}{p!} S$ and A defined above are idempotent. What are their eigenvalues and eigenvectors?
4. Prove that the skew-symmetric tensors in $U^p{}_0$ form a subspace. Compute its dimension. Do the same for the symmetric tensors.
5. The operator A can be represented as a tensor in $U^p{}_p$. Show how that can be done. Do the same for $\frac{1}{p!} S$.

9. *The metric*

Let U be an n-dimensional euclidean vector space over the real field $\mathbf{R}$. We recall from Sec. 11, Chap. 8, and Sec. 7, Chap. 14, that U must be equipped with a symmetric bilinear form, denoted here simply by parenthesis (,), such that $(\mathbf{x}, \mathbf{x}) > 0$ unless $\mathbf{x} = 0$. The length of a vector $\mathbf{x}$ is defined by

9.1 $$|\mathbf{x}| = \sqrt{(\mathbf{x}, \mathbf{x})}$$

From Theorem 7.1, the form (,) can be considered as an element of $U^0{}_2$. If $B_1 = \{\mathbf{u}_1, \ldots, \mathbf{u}_n\}$ is any base in U, then the *matrix* of the form relative to that base, call it (g_{ij}), is given by

9.2 $$g_{ij} = (\mathbf{u}_i, \mathbf{u}_j)$$

The element

9.3 $$\mathbf{g}^* = g_{ij}\,\mathbf{u}^i \otimes \mathbf{u}^j$$

in $U^0{}_2$ is precisely the one that can be identified with the given form according to Theorem 7.1, since the contraction

$$C^1{}_1 \cdot C^1{}_1(\mathbf{g}^* \otimes \mathbf{x} \otimes \mathbf{y}) = g_{ij}x^iy^j \qquad (\mathbf{x} = x^i\mathbf{u}_i,\ \mathbf{y} = y^i\mathbf{u}_i)$$

is precisely the inner product $(\mathbf{x}, \mathbf{y})$. We observe that $\mathbf{g}^*$ is a symmetric tensor, as defined in the preceding section. A base $B = \{\mathbf{e}_1, \ldots, \mathbf{e}_n\}$ in U is called *orthonormal* if

$$(\mathbf{e}_i, \mathbf{e}_j) = \begin{cases} 0 & \text{if } i \neq j \\ 1 & \text{if } i = j \end{cases}$$

Such bases always exist, and (9.3) reduces to

9.4 $$\mathbf{g}^* = \sum_{i=1}^{n} \mathbf{e}^i \otimes \mathbf{e}^i$$

The bilinear form (,), or the equivalent tensor **g**, is sometimes called a *metric* on U. Our purpose here is to show that all the subspaces $U^p{}_q$ of the tensor algebra inherit metrics from the given one on U, hence become euclidean vector spaces.

First of all, consider the linear mapping $L: U \to U^*$ defined by

9.5 $$\mathbf{L}(\mathbf{x}) = (\mathbf{x},\ \ )$$

That is, $\mathbf{L}(\mathbf{x})$ denotes the element of U^* that maps an arbitrary $\mathbf{y}$ into $(\mathbf{x}, \mathbf{y})$. In other words,

9.6 $$\langle \mathbf{L}(\mathbf{x}), \mathbf{y}\rangle = (\mathbf{x}, \mathbf{y})$$

For the base $B_1 = \{\mathbf{u}_1, \ldots, \mathbf{u}_n\}$ we have

$$\langle \mathbf{L}(\mathbf{u}_i), \mathbf{u}_j\rangle = (\mathbf{u}_i, \mathbf{u}_j) = g_{ij}$$

whence

9.7 $$\mathbf{L}(\mathbf{u}_i) = g_{ij}\mathbf{u}^j$$

since both sides are elements of U^* which have the same effect on any vector in U. Since (g_{ij}) is positive definite, its determinant is nonzero, and therefore $\mathbf{L}$ is an isomorphism. Consequently the inverse mapping $\mathbf{L}^{-1}$ exists and is given by a certain matrix

9.8 $$\mathbf{L}^{-1}(\mathbf{u}^j) = g^{jk}\mathbf{u}_k$$

relative to the base B_1 and its dual. From (9.7),

$$\mathbf{u}_i = \mathbf{L}^{-1}(\mathbf{L}\mathbf{u}_i) = \mathbf{L}^{-1}(g_{ij}\mathbf{u}^j) = g_{ij}\mathbf{L}^{-1}(\mathbf{u}^j) = g_{ij}g^{jk}\mathbf{u}_k$$

showing that

9.9 $$g_{ij}g^{jk} = \delta^k{}_i = \begin{cases} 1 & \text{if } i = k \\ 0 & \text{if } i \neq k \end{cases}$$

That is, (g_{ij}) and (g^{ij}) are inverse matrices. Since a matrix and its inverse commute, (9.9) implies the equations

9.10 $$g^{ik}g_{kh} = \delta^i{}_h$$

We use the mapping $\mathbf{L}^{-1}$ to define an inner product on U^*, denoted also by parentheses. Thus, for two elements $\mathbf{x}^*$ and $\mathbf{y}^*$ of U^* we set

9.11 $$(\mathbf{x}^*, \mathbf{y}^*) = (\mathbf{L}^{-1}\mathbf{x}^*, \mathbf{L}^{-1}\mathbf{y}^*)$$

the right-hand side being the given inner product in U. It is obvious that (9.11) defines a symmetric bilinear function on U^*, and it is positive definite, since the right-hand side of (9.11) is positive definite. We define the *length* of a vector $\mathbf{x}^*$ in U^* as usual by

9.12 $$|\mathbf{x}^*| = \sqrt{(\mathbf{x}^*, \mathbf{x}^*)} = |\mathbf{L}^{-1}(\mathbf{x}^*)|$$

Thus we have simply defined the length in U^* in such a way that $\mathbf{L}$ (and $\mathbf{L}^{-1}$) are *length-preserving* mappings.

To compute the inner product in U^* we have, for the dual base elements $\mathbf{u}^i$,

$$\begin{aligned}(\mathbf{u}^i, \mathbf{u}^j) &= (\mathbf{L}^{-1}\mathbf{u}^i, \mathbf{L}^{-1}\mathbf{u}^j) = (g^{ih}\mathbf{u}_h, g^{jk}\mathbf{u}_k) \\ &= g^{ih}g^{jk}(\mathbf{u}_h, \mathbf{u}_k) = g^{ih}g^{jk}g_{hk}\end{aligned}$$

by (9.8) and (9.2). From (9.10), $g^{ih}g_{hk} = \delta^i{}_k$, and so $(\mathbf{u}^i, \mathbf{u}^j) = g^{ji}$. Since $(\mathbf{u}^i, \mathbf{u}^j) = (\mathbf{u}^j, \mathbf{u}^i)$, we have $g^{ji} = g^{ij}$, and so we can write

9.13 $$(\mathbf{u}^i, \mathbf{u}^j) = g^{ij}$$

For vectors

$$\mathbf{x}^* = x_i\mathbf{u}^i \qquad \mathbf{y}^* = y_i\mathbf{u}^i$$

in U^* there results $(\mathbf{x}^*, \mathbf{y}^*) = (x_i\mathbf{u}^i, y_i, \mathbf{u}^j) = x_iy_j(\mathbf{u}^i, \mathbf{u}^j)$, whence

9.14 $$(\mathbf{x}^*, \mathbf{y}^*) = g^{ij}x_iy_j$$

Consider now the special case of an orthonormal base $B = \{\mathbf{e}_1, \ldots, \mathbf{e}_n\}$, and as usual let $B^* = \{\mathbf{e}^1, \ldots, \mathbf{e}^n\}$ be the dual base in U^*. For this base the elements g_{ij} of (9.2) become

$$(\mathbf{e}_i, \mathbf{e}_j) = \delta_{ij} = \begin{cases} 1 & \text{if } i = j \\ 0 & \text{if } i \neq j \end{cases}$$

Therefore (9.7) becomes

$$\mathbf{L}(\mathbf{e}_i) = \delta_{ij}\mathbf{e}^j = \mathbf{e}^i$$

and similarly (9.8) reduces to

$$\mathbf{L}^{-1}(\mathbf{e}^i) = \mathbf{e}_i$$

Then (9.11) gives us

9.15 $$(\mathbf{e}^i, \mathbf{e}^j) = (\mathbf{e}_i, \mathbf{e}_j) = \delta_{ij}$$

showing that the dual base B^* is also an orthonormal base.

We now use the inner products on U and U^* to define an inner product on $U^p{}_q$ for any p, q. Let $\mathbf{w}$ be an element of $U^{2q}{}_{2p}$, and let $\mathbf{t}$ and $\mathbf{t}'$ be elements of $U^p{}_q$. Then the tensor $\mathbf{w} \otimes \mathbf{t} \otimes \mathbf{t}'$ is in $U^{2(p+q)}_{2(p+q)}$. By performing a suitable series of $2(p + q)$ contractions, denoted simply by C, we shall obtain from $\mathbf{w} \otimes \mathbf{t} \otimes \mathbf{t}'$ a scalar $C(\mathbf{w} \otimes \mathbf{t} \otimes \mathbf{t}')$, as in (7.21). The mapping

9.16 $$(\mathbf{t}, \mathbf{t}') \to C(\mathbf{w} \otimes \mathbf{t} \otimes \mathbf{t}')$$

will then be a bilinear mapping $U^p{}_q \times U^p{}_q \to K$. With a suitable choice of $\mathbf{w}$ and C we can hope to get in this way a symmetric, positive definite bilinear form on $U^p{}_q$. To carry this out we start with

9.17 $$\mathbf{g} = g^{ij}\,\mathbf{u}_i \otimes \mathbf{u}_j \qquad \mathbf{g}^* = g_{ij}\,\mathbf{u}^i \otimes \mathbf{u}^j$$

These are symmetric elements of $U^2{}_0$ and $U^0{}_2$, respectively, and they do not depend upon the particular choice of base $B_1 = \{\mathbf{u}_1, \ldots, \mathbf{u}_n\}$, as is easily verified. We now set

9.18 $$\mathbf{w} = \underbrace{\mathbf{g} \otimes \cdots \otimes \mathbf{g}}_{q} \otimes \underbrace{\mathbf{g}^* \otimes \cdots \otimes \mathbf{g}^*}_{p}$$

which is indeed an element in $U^{2q}{}_{2p}$. We must now specify the contraction operator C. The notation used in Sec. 7 is rather cumbersome, and C can be more simply described as follows: The components of $\mathbf{w}$ with respect to the base $B_1 = \{\mathbf{u}_1, \ldots, \mathbf{u}_n\}$ are

$$g^{i_1j_1} \cdots g^{i_qj_q} g_{h_1k_1} \cdots g_{h_pk_p}$$

with suitable choice of indices. We choose C to be the contraction that gives

9.19 $$C(\mathbf{w} \otimes \mathbf{t} \otimes \mathbf{t}') = g^{i_1j_1} \cdots g^{i_qj_q} g_{h_1k_1} \cdots g_{h_pk_p}\, t^{h_1 \cdots h_p}_{i_1 \cdots i_p}\, t'^{k_1 \cdots k_p}_{j_1 \cdots j_q}$$

where $t^{h_1 \cdots h_p}_{i_1 \cdots i_q}$ are the components of $\mathbf{t}$ relative to the base B, and similarly for $\mathbf{t}'$. The inner product in $U^p{}_q$ is then defined to be

9.20 $$(\mathbf{t}, \mathbf{t}') = C(\mathbf{w} \otimes \mathbf{t} \otimes \mathbf{t}')$$

From (9.19) it is easily seen to be symmetric. For an orthonormal base $B = \{\mathbf{e}_1, \ldots, \mathbf{e}_n\}$ in U, (9.19) reduces to

9.21 $$(\mathbf{t}, \mathbf{t}') = \sum t^{h_1 \cdots h_p}_{i_1 \cdots i_q}\, t'^{h_1 \cdots h_p}_{i_1 \cdots i_q}$$

the sum being over all sets of indices i_μ, $h_\nu = 1, \ldots, n$. In particular, (9.21) gives

9.22 $$(\mathbf{t}, \mathbf{t}) = \sum \left(t^{h_1 \ldots h_p}_{i_1 \ldots i_q} \right)^2$$

showing that $(\mathbf{t}, \mathbf{t}) > 0$ unless $\mathbf{t} = \mathbf{0}$. Thus the bilinear function (9.20) gives $U^p{}_q$ the structure of a euclidean vector space. We define the *magnitude*, or *length*, of an element $\mathbf{t}$ by

9.23 $$|\mathbf{t}| = \sqrt{(\mathbf{t}, \mathbf{t})}$$

Furthermore, the elements

9.24 $$\mathbf{e}^{b_1 \ldots b_q}_{a_1 \ldots a_p} = \mathbf{e}_{a_1} \otimes \cdots \otimes \mathbf{e}_{a_p} \otimes \mathbf{e}^{b_1} \otimes \cdots \otimes \mathbf{e}^{b_q}$$

form an orthonormal base in $U^p{}_q$, if the $\mathbf{e}_i$ form an orthonormal base in U. This follows at once from (9.21) since the components of (9.23) relative to that base are

$$\delta^{h_1}_{a_1} \cdots \delta^{h_p}_{a_p} \delta^{b_1}_{i_1} \cdots \delta^{b_q}_{i_q}$$

Finally, if $\mathbf{t} = \mathbf{x}_1 \otimes \cdots \otimes \mathbf{x}_p \otimes \mathbf{y}^*_1 \otimes \cdots \otimes \mathbf{y}^*_q$, then (9.19) gives

9.25 $$(\mathbf{t}, \mathbf{t}) = (\mathbf{x}_1, \mathbf{x}_1) \cdots (\mathbf{x}_p, \mathbf{x}_p)(\mathbf{y}^*_1, \mathbf{y}^*_1) \cdots (\mathbf{y}^*_q, \mathbf{y}^*_q)$$

and a similar expression holds for the inner product $(\mathbf{t}, \mathbf{t}')$ of two tensors of this type.

EXERCISES

1. Describe the contraction operation C used above in the notation of Sec. 7 for the case $p = 2$, $q = 1$.

2. Prove in detail that the elements (9.23) form an orthonormal base in $U^p{}_q$.

3. Show how to make $T(U)$ into a euclidean vector space.

4. Let $\mathbf{t}$ be in $U^p{}_q$, and let $\mathbf{t}'$ be in $U^r{}_s$. Prove that $|\mathbf{t} \otimes \mathbf{t}'| = |\mathbf{t}| \cdot |\mathbf{t}'|$, and show that the definition of $|\mathbf{t}|$ given above is the only one for which this holds for all values of p, q, r, s.

5. Prove: If one considers the operations on only the unitary group on a euclidean vector space U, then $U^p{}_q$, U^0_{p+q}, and U^{p+q}_0 are all canonically isomorphic. [Hint: Use the canonical isomorphism $U \to U^*$ of the euclidean space U.]

10. *The exterior algebra*

Starting with a vector space U over a field K, we now describe an important algebraic system called the *exterior algebra* of U.

As usual let $T_0(U)$ denote the contravariant tensor algebra of U. Thus $T_0(U)$ is the direct sum of the subspaces

10.1 $$U^p{}_0 = U \otimes \cdots \otimes U \qquad (p \text{ factors})$$

and $T_0(U)$ has the product operation $\otimes$. Let S denote the *ideal* of $T_0(U)$ generated by all elements of the type

$$\mathbf{x} \otimes \mathbf{x} \qquad (\mathbf{x} \text{ in } U) \tag{10.2}$$

That is, S consists of all elements in $T_0(U)$ which can be obtained from elements of the type (10.2) by a finite number of the three operations in $T_0(U)$, that is, addition, scalar multiplication, and products by *arbitrary* elements in $T_0(U)$.

It is clear first of all that the sum and difference of any two elements of S are again in S. Hence S is a subgroup of $T_0(U)$, regarded simply as an abelian group, and we can therefore form the quotient group $T_0(U)/S$, consisting of all the cosets of S (see Sec. 4, Chap. 10). Every coset of S can be written (in many ways) in the form $\mathbf{t} + S$, $\mathbf{t}$ being any element of $T_0(U)$ in the coset. We recall that addition in $T_0(U)/S$ is given by

$$(\mathbf{t}_1 + S) + (\mathbf{t}_2 + S) = (\mathbf{t}_1 + \mathbf{t}_2) + S \tag{10.3}$$

We make $T_0(U)/S$ into an algebra by defining two other operations. First, if c is a scalar, we set

$$c \cdot (\mathbf{t} + S) = c\mathbf{t} + S \tag{10.4}$$

If $\mathbf{t}' + S = \mathbf{t} + S$, then $\mathbf{t}' - \mathbf{t}$ is in S. From the definition of S it is clear that $c(\mathbf{t}' - \mathbf{t})$ is also in S, whence $c\mathbf{t}' + S = c\mathbf{t} + S$, showing that (10.4) depends only on the coset, not upon the particular element $\mathbf{t}$ in it. Operations (10.3) and (10.4) make $T_0(U)/S$ into a vector space over K.

Finally we define a product operation $\wedge$ in $T_0(U)/S$ by the rule

$$(\mathbf{t}_1 + S) \wedge (\mathbf{t}_2 + S) = (\mathbf{t}_1 \otimes \mathbf{t}_2) + S \tag{10.5}$$

The right-hand side depends only on the cosets. For if $\mathbf{t}_1'$ is in $\mathbf{t}_1 + S$ and if $\mathbf{t}^2$ is in $\mathbf{t}_2 + S$, then both $\mathbf{t}_1' - \mathbf{t}_1$ and $\mathbf{t}_2' - \mathbf{t}_2$ are in S. From the definition of S it is clear that the products $(\mathbf{t}_1' - \mathbf{t}_1) \otimes \mathbf{t}_2'$ and $\mathbf{t}_1 \otimes (\mathbf{t}_2' - \mathbf{t}_2)$ must also be in S. Hence so is their sum $\mathbf{t}_1' \otimes \mathbf{t}_2' - \mathbf{t}_1 \otimes \mathbf{t}_2$, and therefore $(\mathbf{t}_1' \otimes \mathbf{t}_2') + S = (\mathbf{t}_1 \otimes \mathbf{t}_2) + S$.

It follows at once from (10.5) that this new product operation, called *exterior* multiplication, is associative.

The *quotient algebra*† $T_0(U)/S$ just defined is called the exterior algebra of U. We shall denote it by $\wedge U$. It has a very simple structure, which we now examine.

Let $\mathbf{P}\colon T_0(U) \to \wedge U$ be the *canonical* mapping, sending each element $\mathbf{t}$ of $T_0(U)$ into the coset containing it:

$$\mathbf{P}(\mathbf{t}) = \mathbf{t} + S \tag{10.6}$$

From (10.3) and (10.4) it follows immediately that $\mathbf{P}$ is a linear mapping with kernel S; (10.5) is simply the equation

$$\mathbf{P}(\mathbf{t}_1 \otimes \mathbf{t}_2) = \mathbf{P}(\mathbf{t}_1) \wedge \mathbf{P}(\mathbf{t}_2) \tag{10.7}$$

† This construction is described in detail in Chap. 15.

showing that **P** is compatible with the product operations in $T_0(U)$ and $\wedge U$. Hence, **P** is a homomorphism of K-algebras.

P maps the subspace $U^p{}_0$ of $T_0(U)$ onto a certain subspace of $\wedge U$. We denote that subspace by $\wedge^p U$. Thus

10.8 $$\wedge^p U = \mathbf{P}(U_0{}^p)$$

From its definition it is clear that $S = \text{Ker } \mathbf{P}$ contains no elements of $U^0{}_0 = K$ or of $U^1{}_0 = U$, and consequently **P** maps K *isomorphically* onto $\wedge^0 U$ and it maps U *isomorphically* onto $\wedge^1 U$. For this reason we shall simply identify $\wedge^0 U$ with K and $\wedge^1 U$ with U. Thus we have

10.9 $$\mathbf{P}(c) = c \quad \text{for } c \text{ in } K; \qquad \mathbf{P}(\mathbf{x}) = \mathbf{x} \quad \text{for } \mathbf{x} \text{ in } U$$

Now $U^p{}_0$ is spanned by elements of the type $\mathbf{x}_1 \otimes \cdots \otimes \mathbf{x}_p$ ($\mathbf{x}_i$ in U). From (10.7), $\mathbf{P}(\mathbf{x}_1 \otimes \cdots \otimes \mathbf{x}_p) = \mathbf{P}(\mathbf{x}_1) \wedge \cdots \wedge \mathbf{P}(\mathbf{x}_p)$, which can be written as $\mathbf{x}_1 \wedge \cdots \wedge \mathbf{x}_p$ by (10.9). Since **P** maps $U^p{}_0$ onto $\wedge^p U$, we conclude that

10.10 *$\wedge^p U$ is spanned by elements of the type*
$$\mathbf{x}_1 \wedge \cdots \wedge \mathbf{x}_p \quad \textit{with } \mathbf{x}_i \textit{ in } U \qquad (p > 0)$$

Elements of $\wedge^p U$ are said to have *degree p*.

From (10.2) it is clear that $\mathbf{x} \otimes \mathbf{x}$ is in S for any vector $\mathbf{x}$ in U. Hence $\mathbf{P}(\mathbf{x} \otimes \mathbf{x}) = \mathbf{0}$, or $\mathbf{P}(\mathbf{x}) \wedge \mathbf{P}(\mathbf{x}) = \mathbf{0}$, by (10.7). Writing simply $\mathbf{x}$ for $\mathbf{P}(\mathbf{x})$, as in (10.9), we obtain the rule

10.11 $$\mathbf{x} \wedge \mathbf{x} = \mathbf{0} \qquad \text{for all } \mathbf{x} \text{ in } U$$

The idea behind the definition of $\wedge U$ begins to emerge at this point. The ideal S contains all elements of $T_0(U)$ which have any sort of symmetry. Such elements go into zero in the quotient space $T_0(U)/S$. Equation (10.11) is a particular instance of this.

10.12 *The mapping* $\underbrace{U \times \cdots \times U}_{p} \to \wedge^p U$

defined by $(\mathbf{x}_1, \ldots, \mathbf{x}_p) \to \mathbf{x}_1 \wedge \cdots \wedge \mathbf{x}_p$ *is p-linear.*

This follows from the fact that the mapping in question is the composition of the multilinear mapping $(\mathbf{x}_1, \ldots, \mathbf{x}_p) \to \mathbf{x}_1 \otimes \cdots \otimes \mathbf{x}_p$ and of the linear mapping **P**.

If $\mathbf{x}$ and $\mathbf{y}$ are vectors in U, then

$$(\mathbf{x} + \mathbf{y}) \wedge (\mathbf{x} + \mathbf{y}) = \mathbf{x} \wedge \mathbf{x} + \mathbf{x} \wedge \mathbf{y} + \mathbf{y} \wedge \mathbf{x} + \mathbf{y} \wedge \mathbf{y} \qquad \text{by (10.12)}$$

From (10.11), $(\mathbf{x} + \mathbf{y}) \wedge (\mathbf{x} + \mathbf{y}) = \mathbf{0}$, $\mathbf{x} \wedge \mathbf{x} = \mathbf{0}$, $\mathbf{y} \wedge \mathbf{y} = \mathbf{0}$, and there follows $\mathbf{x} \wedge \mathbf{y} + \mathbf{y} \wedge \mathbf{x} = \mathbf{0}$, or

10.13 $$\mathbf{x} \wedge \mathbf{y} = -\mathbf{y} \wedge \mathbf{x} \qquad (\mathbf{x}, \mathbf{y} \text{ in } U)$$

From these there results at once

10.14 $$\mathbf{x}_{i_1} \wedge \cdots \wedge \mathbf{x}_{i_p} = \operatorname{sign} \begin{pmatrix} 1 & \cdots & p \\ i_1 & \cdots & i_p \end{pmatrix} \cdot \mathbf{x}_1 \wedge \cdots \wedge \mathbf{x}_p \qquad (\mathbf{x}_i \text{ in } U)$$

showing that the expression $\mathbf{x}_1 \wedge \cdots \wedge \mathbf{x}_p$ is *skew-symmetric* in its entries. We have further

10.15 $$\mathbf{x}_1 \wedge \cdots \wedge \mathbf{x}_p = \mathbf{0} \qquad \textit{if any two of the } \mathbf{x}_i \textit{ are identical } (\mathbf{x}_i \text{ in } U)$$

For suppose $\mathbf{x}_j = \mathbf{x}_k$. By a suitable permutation we can put $\mathbf{x}_j$ and $\mathbf{x}_k$ next to each other. If $\mathbf{x}_j = \mathbf{x}_k$, then $\mathbf{x}_j \wedge \mathbf{x}_k = \mathbf{0}$, by (10.11). The permutation can at most change the sign, by (10.14), from which the assertion follows.

Applying (10.13) repeatedly, or else using (10.14), we have

10.16 $$\mathbf{x}_1 \wedge \cdots \wedge \mathbf{x}_p \wedge \mathbf{y}_1 \wedge \cdots \wedge \mathbf{y}_q = (-1)^{pq}\mathbf{y}_1 \wedge \cdots \wedge \mathbf{y}_q \wedge \mathbf{x}_1 \wedge \cdots \wedge \mathbf{x}_p$$

for any $\mathbf{x}_i$, $\mathbf{y}_i$ in U. From (10.10), any element $\mathbf{u}$ in $\Lambda^p U$ can be written as a linear combination of elements $\mathbf{x}_1 \wedge \cdots \wedge \mathbf{x}_p$. Similarly, for any $\mathbf{v}$ in $\Lambda^q U$. Hence from (10.16) we have

10.17 $$\mathbf{u} \wedge \mathbf{v} = (-1)^{pq}\, \mathbf{v} \wedge \mathbf{u} \qquad \text{for } \mathbf{u} \text{ in } \Lambda^p U,\ \mathbf{v} \text{ in } \Lambda^q U$$

[Observe that (10.11) does not necessarily hold for an element $\mathbf{x}$ in $\Lambda^p U$ with $p > 1$.] The following fact is of basic importance:

10.18 $$\mathbf{x}_1 \wedge \cdots \wedge \mathbf{x}_p = \mathbf{0} \qquad \textit{if and only if } \mathbf{x}_1, \ldots, \mathbf{x}_p \textit{ are linearly dependent} \qquad (\mathbf{x}_i \textit{ in } U)$$

First of all, if the vectors are linearly dependent, then one of them can be expressed as a linear combination of the others, say, $\mathbf{x}_p = c_1\mathbf{x}_1 + \cdots + c_{p-1}\mathbf{x}_{p-1}$. Then from (10.12) we obtain

$$\begin{aligned} \mathbf{x}_1 \wedge \cdots \wedge \mathbf{x}_p &= \mathbf{x}_1 \wedge \cdots \wedge \mathbf{x}_{p-1} \wedge (c_1\mathbf{x}_1 + \cdots + c_{p-1}\mathbf{x}_{p-1}) \\ &= \sum_{j=1}^{p-1} c_j \cdot \mathbf{x}_1 \wedge \cdots \wedge \mathbf{x}_{p-1} \wedge \mathbf{x}_j \end{aligned}$$

Each term on the right is zero, by (10.15). A similar argument holds in general, clearly.

The converse proposition is not quite so easy. We shall prove it for the case of a finite-dimensional space U, dim $U = n$, say. Let us first look at the ingredients of the ideal S. By definition S consists of all finite sums of elements of the type $\mathbf{t} \otimes \mathbf{y} \otimes \mathbf{y} \otimes \mathbf{t}'$, with $\mathbf{y}$ in U and $\mathbf{t}$, $\mathbf{t}'$ arbitrary elements of $T_0(U)$. Since $\mathbf{t}$ and $\mathbf{t}'$ can be expressed as sums of elements of the type $\mathbf{w}_1 \otimes \cdots \otimes \mathbf{w}_k (\mathbf{w}_i$ in $U)$, it follows that every element of S can be expressed as a sum of elements of the type

10.19 $$\mathbf{w}_1 \otimes \cdots \otimes \mathbf{w}_k \otimes \mathbf{y} \otimes \mathbf{y} \otimes \mathbf{z}_1 \otimes \cdots \otimes \mathbf{z}_h$$

with $\mathbf{w}_i$, $\mathbf{y}$, and $\mathbf{z}_j$ all in U.

Let $\mathbf{x}_1, \ldots, \mathbf{x}_p$ be linearly independent elements of U. We can find elements $\mathbf{x}_{p+1}, \ldots, \mathbf{x}_n$ in U such that $\mathbf{x}_1, \ldots, \mathbf{x}_n$ form a base for U. If $\mathbf{x}_1 \wedge \cdots \wedge \mathbf{x}_n = \mathbf{0}$, then from (10.14) and (10.15) we have

$$\mathbf{x}_{i_1} \wedge \cdots \wedge \mathbf{x}_{i_n} = \mathbf{0}$$

for any indices $i_\nu = 1, \ldots, n$. The left member is equal to $\mathbf{P}(\mathbf{x}_{i_1} \otimes \cdots \otimes \mathbf{x}_{i_n})$, and thus $\mathbf{x}_{i_1} \otimes \cdots \otimes \mathbf{x}_{i_n}$ must be in the kernel of $\mathbf{P}$, that is, in the ideal S. But the n^n elements $\mathbf{x}_{i_1} \otimes \cdots \otimes \mathbf{x}_{i_n}$ span $U^n{}_0$, and so every element of $U^n{}_0$ is in S. We shall show that this is impossible.

If $\mathbf{t}$ is an element of $U^n{}_0$, and if $\mathbf{t}$ is in S, then $\mathbf{t}$ can be written as a sum of elements of the type (10.19). Since $T_0(U)$ is a direct sum of $U^0{}_0$, $U^1{}_0$, etc., it follows that, in the resulting expression for $\mathbf{t}$, all terms (10.19) which do not have exactly n factors must add up to zero, hence can be omitted. Therefore $\mathbf{t}$ can be expressed as a sum of terms (10.19), with $k + h + 2 = n$. Since $\mathbf{x}_1, \ldots, \mathbf{x}_n$ span U, we can write

$$\mathbf{w}_i = a^j{}_i\mathbf{x}_j, \qquad \mathbf{y} = b^j\mathbf{x}_j, \qquad \mathbf{z}_i = c^j{}_i\mathbf{x}_j$$

Putting this in (10.19), we obtain

$$a_1^{j_1} \cdots a_k^{j_k} b^{j_{k+1}} b^{j_{k+2}} c_1^{j_{k+3}} \cdots c_h^{j_n} \cdot \mathbf{x}_{j_1} \otimes \cdots \otimes \mathbf{x}_{j_n}$$

If we put

10.20 $$\mathbf{u}_{j_1 \ldots j_n} = \mathbf{x}_{j_1} \otimes \cdots \otimes \mathbf{x}_{j_{k+1}} \otimes \mathbf{x}_{j_{k+2}} \otimes \cdots \otimes \mathbf{x}_{j_n} + \mathbf{x}_{j_1} \otimes \cdots \otimes \mathbf{x}_{j_{k+2}} \otimes \mathbf{x}_{j_{k+1}} \otimes \cdots \otimes \mathbf{x}_{j_n}$$

then the expression above can be written as

$$\sum_{j_{k+1} \leq j_{k+2}} a_1^{j_1} \cdots a_k^{j_k} b^{j_{k+1}} b^{j_{k+2}} c_1^{j_{k+3}} \cdots c_h^{j_n} \mathbf{u}_{j_1 \ldots j_n}$$

Hence, if every element of $U^n{}_0$ is in S, then $U^n{}_0$ is spanned by elements of the type (10.20) with $j_{k+1} \leq j_{k+2}$. The number of such elements is manifestly less than $n^n = \dim U^n{}_0$, a contradiction. Therefore we must have $\mathbf{x}_1 \wedge \cdots \wedge \mathbf{x}_n \neq \mathbf{0}$. But then

$$(\mathbf{x}_1 \wedge \cdots \wedge \mathbf{x}_p) \wedge (\mathbf{x}_{p+1} \wedge \cdots \wedge \mathbf{x}_n) \neq \mathbf{0}$$

from which $\mathbf{x}_1 \wedge \cdots \wedge \mathbf{x}_p \neq \mathbf{0}$. Q.E.D.

From (10.18) we have the immediate corollary

10.21 $$\Lambda^p U = 0 \qquad \text{if } p > n = \dim U$$

For $\Lambda^p U$ is spanned by elements of the type $\mathbf{x}_1 \wedge \cdots \wedge \mathbf{x}_p$ ($\mathbf{x}_i$ in U), and every such element is zero if $p > n$, by (10.18).

It follows easily that ΛU is the direct sum of the subspaces $\Lambda^p U$ ($p = 0, \ldots, n$). That is,

10.22 $$\Lambda U = \Lambda^0 U \oplus \Lambda^1 U \oplus \cdots \oplus \Lambda^n U$$

We now compute the dimensions of the $\Lambda^p U$. Let $B = \{\mathbf{e}_1, \ldots, \mathbf{e}_n\}$ be a base for U. If $\mathbf{x}_i = x^j{}_i \mathbf{e}_j$ $(i = 1, \ldots, p)$, then

$$\begin{aligned} \mathbf{x}_1 \wedge \cdots \wedge \mathbf{x}_p &= (x_1^{j_1} \mathbf{e}_{j_1}) \wedge \cdots \wedge (x_p^{j_p} \mathbf{e}_{j_p}) \\ &= x_1^{j_1} \cdots x_p^{j_p} \cdot \mathbf{e}_{j_1} \wedge \cdots \wedge \mathbf{e}_{j_p} \end{aligned}$$

by (10.12). From this and (10.10) it is clear that $\Lambda^p U$ is spanned by the elements $\mathbf{e}_{j_1} \wedge \cdots \wedge \mathbf{e}_{j_n}$. But from (10.14) and (10.15) we see at once that $\Lambda^p U$ is in fact spanned by the elements $\mathbf{e}_{j_1} \wedge \cdots \wedge \mathbf{e}_{j_p}$ with $1 \leq j_1 < \cdots < j_p \leq n$. There are $\binom{n}{p}$ choices of distinct indices $j_1, \ldots, j_p$ from 1 to n, and they can be arranged uniquely in increasing order. Hence, there are $\binom{n}{p}$ elements $\mathbf{e}_{j_1} \wedge \cdots \wedge \mathbf{e}_{j_r}$ such that $1 \leq j_1 < \cdots < j_p \leq n$. These elements are linearly independent in $\Lambda^p U$. For suppose that

10.23 $$\sum_{j_1 < \cdots < j_p} c^{j_1 \cdots j_p} \cdot \mathbf{e}_{j_1} \wedge \cdots \wedge \mathbf{e}_{j_p} = 0$$

for some scalars $c^{j_1 \cdots j_p}$. Let $k_{p+1}, \ldots, k_n$ be distinct integers from 1 to n, and form the exterior product of the left member above with the element $\mathbf{e}_{k_{p+1}} \wedge \cdots \wedge \mathbf{e}_{k_n}$. All terms

$$\mathbf{e}_{j_1} \wedge \cdots \wedge \mathbf{e}_{j_p} \wedge \mathbf{e}_{k_{p+1}} \wedge \cdots \wedge \mathbf{e}_{k_n} \qquad (j_1 < \cdots < j_p)$$

vanish except the one for which $j_1, \ldots, j_p$ is the complementary set of indices $k_1, \ldots, k_p$ corresponding to $k_{p+1}, \ldots, k_n$, so that $k_1, \ldots, k_n$ is a permutation of $1, \ldots, n$. Thus the product of the left side of (10.23) and $\mathbf{e}_{k+1} \wedge \cdots \wedge \mathbf{e}_n$ reduces to the single term

$$c^{k_1 \cdots k_p} \mathbf{e}_{k_1} \wedge \cdots \wedge \mathbf{e}_{k_n} \qquad \text{(no summation)}$$

and this must be zero, by (10.23). But $\mathbf{e}_{k_1} \wedge \cdots \wedge \mathbf{e}_{k_n}$ is not zero, by (10.18), showing that $c^{k_1 \cdots k_p} = 0$. We have therefore proved that

10.24 $$\dim \Lambda^p U = \binom{n}{p} \qquad (p = 0, 1, \ldots, n)$$

and that

10.25 *the elements* $\mathbf{e}_{j_1} \wedge \cdots \wedge \mathbf{e}_{j_p}$ *with* $1 \leq j_1 < \cdots < j_p \leq n$ *form a base in* $\Lambda^p U$ *if* $\{\mathbf{e}_1, \ldots, \mathbf{e}_n\}$ *is a base in* U *(for* $p > 0$*)*

From (10.22), (10.24)

10.26 $$\dim \Lambda U = \binom{n}{0} + \binom{n}{1} + \cdots + \binom{n}{n} = (1 + 1)^n = 2^n$$

Hence we have exhibited the structure of the exterior algebra ΛU.

THEOREM 10.1 *Let* $\mathbf{f}: U \times \cdots \times U \to W$ *be a p-linear mapping such that* $\mathbf{f}(\mathbf{x}_1, \ldots, \mathbf{x}_p) = \mathbf{0}$ *whenever two adjacent* **x**'s *are equal. Then there exists a unique linear mapping* $\mathbf{f}': \Lambda^p U \to W$ *such that* $\mathbf{f}(\mathbf{x}_1, \ldots, \mathbf{x}_p) = \mathbf{f}'(\mathbf{x}_1 \wedge \cdots \wedge \mathbf{x}_p)$ *for any* $\mathbf{x}_i$ *in* U.

Proof. By Theorem 3.3 there is a linear mapping $\mathbf{f}'': U^p{}_0 \to W$ such that $\mathbf{f}(\mathbf{x}_1, \ldots, \mathbf{x}_p) = \mathbf{f}''(\mathbf{x}_1 \otimes \cdots \otimes \mathbf{x}_p)$. If $\mathbf{x}_1 \otimes \cdots \otimes \mathbf{x}_p$ is an element of the type (10.19), then $\mathbf{f}(\mathbf{x}_1 \otimes \cdots \otimes \mathbf{x}_p) = \mathbf{0}$, by the assumption on **f**. By linearity it follows that every element of S which is in $U^p{}_0$ is mapped into zero by $\mathbf{f}''$. Therefore, if **t** and **t**′ are elements of $U^p{}_0$ such that $\mathbf{t} - \mathbf{t}'$ is in S, then $\mathbf{f}''(\mathbf{t}) = \mathbf{f}''(\mathbf{t}')$. It follows that $\mathbf{f}''$ maps every element of $U^p{}_0$ in a coset of S into the same element of W. Then, for any element **u** of $\Lambda^p U$ we simply define $\mathbf{f}'(\mathbf{u}) = \mathbf{f}''(\mathbf{t})$, where **t** is any element of $U^p{}_0$ in the coset **u**. It is quickly verified that $\mathbf{f}'$ has the desired properties. Q.E.D.

The following theorem is of some importance.

THEOREM 10.2 *Let* U *and* V *be finite-dimensional vector spaces over a field* K, *and let* $\mathbf{f}: U \to V$ *be a linear mapping. Then there is a unique homomorphism* $\hat{\mathbf{f}}: \Lambda U \to \Lambda V$ *of the exterior algebras such that* $\hat{\mathbf{f}}(\mathbf{x}) = \mathbf{f}(\mathbf{x})$ *for any* **x** *in* U. $\hat{\mathbf{f}}$ *maps* $\Lambda^p U$ *to* $\Lambda^p V$ *for all* p.

Proof. $\hat{\mathbf{f}}$ is required to be a homomorphism of algebras and must therefore be compatible with the three operations in ΛU and ΛV, namely addition, scalar multiplication, and exterior product. In particular, $\hat{\mathbf{f}}$ must be a linear mapping.

To show that $\hat{\mathbf{f}}$ exists, let $\mathbf{f}_0: T_0(U) \to T_0(V)$ be the homomorphism of the tensor algebras described in Theorem 5.2. As above, let $\mathbf{P}: T_0(U) \to \Lambda U$ be the canonical mapping, and let $\mathbf{P}': T_0(V) \to \Lambda V$ be the similar mapping for V. Put $S = \text{Ker } \mathbf{P}$ and $S' = \text{Ker } \mathbf{P}'$. As we have seen, every element of S can be written as a sum of terms of the form (10.19). Applying $\mathbf{f}_0$ to (10.19), we obtain the element

10.27 $$\mathbf{f}(\mathbf{w}_1) \otimes \cdots \otimes \mathbf{f}(\mathbf{w}_k) \otimes \mathbf{f}(\mathbf{y}) \otimes \mathbf{f}(\mathbf{y}) \otimes \mathbf{f}(\mathbf{z}_1) \otimes \cdots \otimes \mathbf{f}(\mathbf{z}_h)$$

since $\mathbf{f}_0$ is compatible with $\otimes$ and since $\mathbf{f}_0(\mathbf{x}) = \mathbf{f}(\mathbf{x})$ for any **x** in U. The element $\mathbf{f}(\mathbf{y})$ is in V, of course, and therefore (10.27) is an element of the ideal S', by definition of $\Lambda V = T_0(V)/S'$.

Therefore $\mathbf{f}_0$ maps S to S'. If $\mathbf{t} + S$ is a coset of S, that is, an element of ΛU, we define

10.28 $$\hat{\mathbf{f}}(\mathbf{t} + S) = \mathbf{f}_0(\mathbf{t}) + S'$$

If $\mathbf{t} + S = \mathbf{t}_1 + S$, then $\mathbf{t} - \mathbf{t}_1$ is in S, and so $\mathbf{f}_0(\mathbf{t} - \mathbf{t}_1) = \mathbf{f}_0(\mathbf{t}) - \mathbf{f}_0(\mathbf{t}_1)$ is in S'. Therefore $\mathbf{f}_0(\mathbf{t}) + S' = \mathbf{f}_0(\mathbf{t}_1) + S'$, showing that (10.28) depends only on the coset and not upon the particular representative **t**. Hence

(10.28) defines a mapping $\hat{\mathbf{f}}$ from ΛU to ΛV.† Since $\mathbf{P}(\mathbf{t}) = \mathbf{t} + S$ and $\mathbf{P}'(\mathbf{f}_0(\mathbf{t})) = \mathbf{f}_0(\mathbf{t}) + S'$, Eq. (10.28) can be written

10.29 $$\hat{\mathbf{f}}(\mathbf{P}(\mathbf{t})) = \mathbf{P}'(\mathbf{f}_0(\mathbf{t}))$$

It is a straightforward matter to check that $\hat{\mathbf{f}}$ has the required properties. For example, if $\mathbf{u}$ and $\mathbf{v}$ are elements of ΛU, say, $\mathbf{u} = \mathbf{t}_1 + S$ and $\mathbf{v} = \mathbf{t}_2 + S$, then $\mathbf{u} = \mathbf{P}(\mathbf{t}_1)$ and $\mathbf{v} = \mathbf{P}(\mathbf{t}_2)$. Hence,

$$\mathbf{u} \wedge \mathbf{v} = \mathbf{P}(\mathbf{t}_1 \otimes \mathbf{t}_2)$$

by (10.7). By (10.29) we have

$$\begin{aligned}\hat{\mathbf{f}}(\mathbf{u} \wedge \mathbf{v}) &= \hat{\mathbf{f}}(\mathbf{P}(\mathbf{t}_1 \otimes \mathbf{t}_2))\\ &= \mathbf{P}'(\mathbf{f}_0(\mathbf{t}_1 \otimes \mathbf{t}_2))\\ &= \mathbf{P}'(\mathbf{f}_0(\mathbf{t}_1) \otimes \mathbf{f}_0(\mathbf{t}_2))\\ &= \mathbf{P}'(\mathbf{f}_0(\mathbf{t}_1)) \wedge \mathbf{P}'(\mathbf{f}_0(\mathbf{t}_2))\\ &= \hat{\mathbf{f}}(\mathbf{u}) \wedge \hat{\mathbf{f}}(\mathbf{v})\end{aligned}$$

The linearity of $\hat{\mathbf{f}}$ follows in a similar way. For $\mathbf{x}$ in U we have $\mathbf{P}(\mathbf{x}) = \mathbf{x}$, by (10.9), and (10.29) gives us $\hat{\mathbf{f}}(\mathbf{x}) = \mathbf{P}'(\mathbf{f}(\mathbf{x})) = \mathbf{f}(\mathbf{x})$, since $\mathbf{f}_0(\mathbf{x}) = \mathbf{f}(\mathbf{x})$ and since $\mathbf{P}'(\mathbf{y}) = \mathbf{y}$ for any element in V. The uniqueness of $\hat{\mathbf{f}}$ is easily demonstrated. For linearity implies that $\hat{\mathbf{f}}$ is uniquely determined by its effect on a base in ΛU. Such a base is exhibited in (10.25) (the base element in $\Lambda^0 U = K$ is simply the unit 1). Now

10.30 $$\begin{aligned}\hat{\mathbf{f}}(\mathbf{e}_{j_1} \wedge \cdots \wedge \mathbf{e}_{j_p}) &= \hat{\mathbf{f}}(\mathbf{e}_{j_1}) \wedge \cdots \wedge \hat{\mathbf{f}}(\mathbf{e}_{j_p})\\ &= \mathbf{f}(\mathbf{e}_{j_1}) \wedge \cdots \wedge \mathbf{f}(\mathbf{e}_{j_p})\end{aligned}$$

since $\hat{\mathbf{f}}$ is compatible with Λ and since $\hat{\mathbf{f}}(\mathbf{x}) = \mathbf{f}(\mathbf{x})$ for $\mathbf{x}$ in U. Therefore the left member of (10.30) is completely determined by $\mathbf{f}$, and consequently $\hat{\mathbf{f}}$ is determined by $\mathbf{f}$. Q.E.D.

COROLLARY *Let* $\mathbf{f}: U \to V$ *and* $\mathbf{g}: V \to W$ *be linear mappings of finite-dimensional vector spaces over* K. *Set* $\mathbf{h} = \mathbf{g} \circ \mathbf{f}$. *Then for the mappings of Theorem* 10.1 *we have* $\hat{\mathbf{h}} = \hat{\mathbf{g}} \circ \hat{\mathbf{f}}$.

Proof. It is easily verified that $\hat{\mathbf{g}} \circ \hat{\mathbf{f}}$ is a homomorphism from ΛU to ΛW and that $\hat{\mathbf{h}}(\mathbf{x}) = \hat{\mathbf{g}} \circ \hat{\mathbf{f}}(\mathbf{x})$ for $\mathbf{x}$ in U. Therefore $\hat{\mathbf{h}} = \hat{\mathbf{g}} \circ \hat{\mathbf{f}}$, by uniqueness. Q.E.D.

The theorem has an important application. Namely, let $\mathbf{f}: U \to U$ be a linear mapping of an n-dimensional vector space over K. Then, by the theorem, $\mathbf{f}$ determines an endomorphism $\hat{\mathbf{f}}$ of ΛU, and $\hat{\mathbf{f}}$ maps the one-dimensional vector space $\Lambda^n U$ to itself. But an endomorphism of a one-dimensional vector space is completely determined by a single scalar. Thus, if $\mathbf{u}$ is any nonzero element of $\Lambda^n U$, then $\hat{\mathbf{f}}(\mathbf{u})$ must be a multiple of $\mathbf{u}$, say

10.31 $$\hat{\mathbf{f}}(\mathbf{u}) = c\mathbf{u} \qquad (c \text{ in } K)$$

† See Exercise 2, Sec. 4, Chap. 10. $\hat{\mathbf{f}}$ is simply the *induced* mapping of the quotients.

since $\mathbf{f}(\mathbf{u})$ is in the space spanned by $\mathbf{u}$. The scalar c does not depend upon the particular choice of $\mathbf{u} \neq \mathbf{0}$ in $\Lambda^n U$.

DEFINITION 10.1 *The scalar c of* (10.31) *determined by the mapping* $\mathbf{f}$ *of U is called the* determinant *of* $\mathbf{f}$, *denoted by* det $\mathbf{f}$.

It is easy to show that this definition coincides with our earlier definition (Definition 5.1, Chap. 11). To do so we show how to compute $\hat{\mathbf{f}}$ in terms of bases. Let $B = \{\mathbf{e}_1, \ldots, \mathbf{e}_n\}$ be a base in U, and let $\mathbf{f}$ be given by

10.32 $$\mathbf{f}(\mathbf{e}_i) = c^j{}_i \mathbf{e}_j$$

Then

10.33 $$\begin{aligned} \hat{\mathbf{f}}(\mathbf{e}_{i_1} \wedge \cdots \wedge \mathbf{e}_{i_p}) &= \mathbf{f}(\mathbf{e}_{i_1}) \wedge \cdots \wedge \mathbf{f}(\mathbf{e}_{i_p}) \\ &= (c^{j_1}_{i_1}\mathbf{e}_{j_1}) \wedge \cdots \wedge (c^{j_p}_{i_p}\mathbf{e}_{j_p}) \\ &= c^{j_1}_{i_1} \cdots c^{j_p}_{i_p}\, \mathbf{e}_{j_1} \wedge \cdots \wedge \mathbf{e}_{j_p} \end{aligned}$$

by (10.30). If any of the indices $i_1, \ldots, i_p$ are equal, then both sides must be zero. We therefore assume that $1 \leq i_1 < \cdots < i_p \leq n$. The sum on the right runs over all p-tuples $j_1, \ldots, j_p$ from 1 to n. Since $\mathbf{e}_{j_1} \wedge \cdots \wedge \mathbf{e}_{j_p} = \mathbf{0}$ if two indices are repeated, we can restrict the summation to p-tuples of distinct indices. Now let $1 \leq k_1 < \cdots < k_p \leq n$ be a p-tuple arranged in increasing order. If $j_1, \ldots, j_p$ is a permutation of it, then

$$\mathbf{e}_{j_1} \wedge \cdots \wedge \mathbf{e}_{j_p} = \operatorname{sign}\begin{pmatrix} k_1 & \cdots & k_p \\ j_1 & \cdots & j_p \end{pmatrix} \cdot \mathbf{e}_{k_1} \wedge \cdots \wedge \mathbf{e}_{k_p}$$

where *no* summation is understood on the right. Collecting together all terms in (10.33) which are permutations of $k_1, \ldots, k_p$, one easily sees that they add up to

$$\Sigma \operatorname{sign}\begin{pmatrix} k_1 & \cdots & k_p \\ j_1 & \cdots & j_p \end{pmatrix} \cdot c^{j_1}_{i_1} \cdots c^{j_p}_{i_p} \cdot \mathbf{e}_{k_1} \wedge \cdots \wedge \mathbf{e}_{k_p} \qquad \text{(no summation on } k_1, \ldots, k_p)$$

the sum being over all permutations of $k_1, \ldots, k_p$. From (2.7), Chap. 11, the total coefficient of $\mathbf{e}_{k_1} \wedge \cdots \wedge \mathbf{e}_{k_p}$ is the quantity

10.34 $$c^{k_1 \ldots k_p}_{i_1 \ldots i_p} = \begin{vmatrix} c^{k_1}_{i_1} & \cdots & c^{k_1}_{i_p} \\ \cdots & \cdots & \cdots \\ c^{k_p}_{i_1} & \cdots & c^{k_p}_{i_p} \end{vmatrix}$$

Hence, for the base (10.25), we have

10.35 $$\hat{\mathbf{f}}(\mathbf{e}_{i_1} \wedge \cdots \wedge \mathbf{e}_{i_p}) = \sum_{k_1 < \cdots < k_p} c^{k_1 \ldots k_p}_{i_1 \ldots i_p}\, \mathbf{e}_{k_1} \wedge \cdots \wedge \mathbf{e}_{k_p}$$

The quantities (10.34) therefore give the "matrix" of $\hat{\mathbf{f}}$ on $\Lambda^p U$ relative to the base consisting of the elements $\mathbf{e}_{i_1} \wedge \cdots \wedge \mathbf{e}_{i_p}$, with $i_1 < \cdots < i_p$.

For $p = n$, (10.35) becomes

10.36 $$\mathbf{f}(\mathbf{e}_1 \wedge \cdots \wedge \mathbf{e}_n) = c^{1 \cdots n}_{1 \cdots n}\, \mathbf{e}_1 \wedge \cdots \wedge \mathbf{e}_n$$

and by (10.34), $c^{1 \cdots n}_{1 \cdots n} = \det (c^j{}_i)$. Hence the determinant of $\mathbf{f}$ in Definition 10.1 is the same as that defined in Chap. 11.

Observe that for the special case of the identity mapping of U, (10.32) becomes $\mathbf{f}(\mathbf{e}_i) = \delta^j{}_i \mathbf{e}_j$, and the corresponding quantities (10.34) are

10.37 $$\delta^{k_1 \cdots k_p}_{i_1 \cdots i_p} = \begin{vmatrix} \delta^{k_1}_{i_1} & \cdots & \delta^{k_1}_{k_p} \\ \cdots & \cdots & \cdots \\ \delta^{k_p}_{i_1} & \cdots & \delta^{k_p}_{i_p} \end{vmatrix}$$

We have

10.38 $$\delta^{k_1 \cdots k_p}_{i_1 \cdots i_p} = \begin{cases} 1 & \text{if } k_1, \ldots, k_p \text{ is an even permutation of } i_1, \ldots, i_p; \\ -1 & \text{if } k_1, \ldots, k_p \text{ is an odd permutation of } i_1, \ldots, i_p; \\ 0 & \text{otherwise.} \end{cases}$$

These are the generalized *Kronecker symbols.*

Using Definition 10.1 it is possible to write out a theory of determinants without writing any matrices. As a simple example, it follows at once from the corollary of Theorem 10.2 that

10.39 $$\det (\mathbf{g} \circ \mathbf{f}) = \det \mathbf{g} \cdot \det \mathbf{f}$$

for two endomorphisms $\mathbf{f}$ and $\mathbf{g}$ of U. Hence we have the product rule for determinants. One easily concludes that $\mathbf{f}\colon U \to U$ is an isomorphism if and only if $\det \mathbf{f} \neq 0$.

EXERCISES

1. Let $B = \{\mathbf{e}_1, \ldots, \mathbf{e}_n\}$ and $B' = \{\mathbf{u}_1, \ldots, \mathbf{u}_n\}$ be two bases in U. Work out the connection between the corresponding bases (10.25) in $\Lambda^p U$. What is the result if B' is obtained from B by simply permuting the $\mathbf{e}_i$?

2. Let $\mathbf{f}\colon U \to V$ be a linear mapping of finite-dimensional vector spaces, and suppose that $\mathbf{f}$ maps U isomorphically onto a subspace of V. Prove that the homomorphism $\mathbf{f}$ of Theorem 10.1 maps ΛU isomorphically onto a subalgebra of ΛV.

3. Let $\mathbf{x}$ be an element of an n-dimensional vector space U. Compute the dimension of the kernel of the mapping $\Lambda^p U \to \Lambda^{p+1} U$ defined by $\mathbf{u} \to \mathbf{x} \wedge \mathbf{u}$.

4. Let $\mathbf{u}$ be an element of $\Lambda^p U$, and let $\mathbf{v}$ be an element of $\Lambda^q U$, U being an n-dimensional vector space. Show how to compute the components of $\mathbf{u} \wedge \mathbf{v}$ from the components of $\mathbf{u}$ and $\mathbf{v}$ relative to some base in U.

*5. Let the vector space U be the direct sum $V \oplus W$ of two finite-dimensional subspaces. Show that $\Lambda^p U$ is isomorphic in a natural way to the direct sum

$$(\Lambda^p V \otimes \Lambda^0 W) \oplus (\Lambda^{p-1} V \otimes \Lambda^1 W) \oplus \cdots \oplus (\Lambda^0 V \otimes \Lambda^p W)$$

If $\mathbf{f}$ is an endomorphism of U for which V and W are both $\mathbf{f}$-stable, show that $\det \mathbf{f} = \det \mathbf{f}' \cdot \det \mathbf{f}''$, using Definition 10.1, where $\mathbf{f}'$ is the restriction of $\mathbf{f}$ to V and where $\mathbf{f}''$ is the restriction of $\mathbf{f}$ to W.

6. Let $\mathbf{f}\colon U \to U$ be an endomorphism of the linear space U. Let V be a subspace with base $\mathbf{x}_1, \ldots, \mathbf{x}_n$. Prove that $\mathbf{f}$ sends V into V if and only if $\mathbf{x}_1 \wedge \cdots \wedge \mathbf{x}_n$ is an eigenvector of the induced mapping $\hat{\mathbf{f}}$ of $\mathbf{f}$ on the exterior algebra.

11. *Plücker coordinates; duality*

Let V be a subspace of an n-dimensional vector space U over a field K. The mapping $\mathbf{f}\colon V \to U$ defined by $\mathbf{f}(\mathbf{x}) = \mathbf{x}$ ($\mathbf{x}$ in V) is a linear mapping, and by Theorem 10.1 there is associated with it a homomorphism $\hat{\mathbf{f}}\colon \Lambda V \to \Lambda U$. If $\dim V = p$, then $\Lambda^p V$ is a one-dimensional space, and it is mapped by $\hat{\mathbf{f}}$ onto a one-dimensional subspace L_V of $\Lambda^p U$. Thus, if $\{\mathbf{v}_1, \ldots, \mathbf{v}_p\}$ is any base for V, then $\Lambda^p V$ is spanned by the element $\mathbf{v}_1 \wedge \cdots \wedge \mathbf{v}_p$, and $\hat{\mathbf{f}}$ maps this element into

11.1 $$\hat{\mathbf{f}}(\mathbf{v}_1 \wedge \cdots \wedge \mathbf{v}_p) = \mathbf{f}(\mathbf{v}_1) \wedge \cdots \wedge \mathbf{f}(\mathbf{v}_p) = \mathbf{v}_1 \wedge \cdots \wedge \mathbf{v}_p$$

in $\Lambda^p U$. Strictly speaking, we should use different symbols for the exterior product in ΛV and ΛU, since the symbol $\mathbf{v}_1 \wedge \cdots \wedge \mathbf{v}_p$ has two different meanings here—on the left side of (11.1) it designates an element of $\Lambda^p V$, on the right it designates an element of $\Lambda^p U$. In any case, $\mathbf{v}_1, \ldots, \mathbf{v}_p$ are linearly independent elements of U, and therefore the right-hand side of (11.1) is a nonzero element in $\Lambda^p U$, by (10.18). It spans a one-dimensional subspace which depends only on V, and we have called that space L_V.

Now let $B = \{\mathbf{e}_1, \ldots, \mathbf{e}_n\}$ be a base in U. L_V is spanned by any nonzero element in it, for example $\mathbf{v}_1 \wedge \cdots \wedge \mathbf{v}_p$, and by (10.25) any such element $\mathbf{t}$ can be written uniquely in the form

11.2 $$\mathbf{t} = \sum_{i_1 < \cdots < i_p} t^{i_1 \cdots i_p}\, \mathbf{e}_{i_1} \wedge \cdots \wedge \mathbf{e}_{i_p}$$

Any two nonzero elements $\mathbf{t}$ and $\mathbf{t}'$ in L_V are multiples of each other: $\mathbf{t}' = c\mathbf{t}$ and $\mathbf{t} = c^{-1}\mathbf{t}'$. Hence, if

$$\mathbf{t}' = \sum_{i_1 < \cdots < i_p} t'^{i_1 \cdots i_p}\, \mathbf{e}_{i_1} \wedge \cdots \wedge \mathbf{e}_{i_p}$$

then

11.3 $$t'^{i_1 \cdots i_p} = c \cdot t^{i_1 \cdots i_p}$$

DEFINITION 11.1 *The scalars $t^{i_1 \cdots i_p}$ of (11.2) are called* Plücker coordinates *of the subspace V (relative to the base B in U).*

Equation (11.3) shows that any two sets of Plücker coordinates of V differ by a scalar factor. Hence the ratios of the $t^{i_1 \cdots i_p}$ are the same as the corresponding ratios of the $t'^{i_1 \cdots i_p}$. The ratios are therefore uniquely determined by V. Sometimes the ratios of the $t^{i_1 \cdots i_p}$, rather than t's themselves, are called the Plücker coordinates of V.

Consider the vector space K_{r+1} of $(r+1)$-tuples $\mathbf{x} = (x_0, \ldots, x_r)$, x_i in K. Let us call two such vectors $\mathbf{x}$ and $\mathbf{y}$ *equivalent* if they are both nonzero and if $\mathbf{x} = c\mathbf{y}$ for some scalar $c \neq 0$. This relation of equivalence splits the nonzero vectors of K_{r+1} into equivalence classes, and clearly each equivalence class consists of all nonzero elements in a one-dimensional subspace of K_{r+1}. Thus the equivalence classes are in one-to-one correspondence with the lines through the origin in K_{r+1}.

DEFINITION 11.2 *The set of all equivalence classes of nonzero vectors in K_{r+1}, as defined above, is called the* projective space *of dimension r over K, denoted by $\mathbf{P}_r(K)$. If Q is any point (that is, element) of $\mathbf{P}_r(K)$, and if $\mathbf{x} = (x_0, \ldots, x_r)$ is any vector in the equivalence class of which Q consists, then the x_i are called* homogeneous coordinates *of Q.*

If we take $r = \binom{n}{p} - 1 = \dim \Lambda^p U - 1$, then we see that the Plücker coordinates of V, enumerated in some fixed order, can be considered as the homogeneous coordinates of a point in $\mathbf{P}_r(K)$. However, not every point in $\mathbf{P}_r(K)$ represents a p-dimensional subspace of U. For every element of L_V is a multiple of $\mathbf{v}_1 \wedge \cdots \wedge \mathbf{v}_p$. Elements of this type are called *simple*, or *decomposable*, p-vectors. If $\mathbf{t}$ is in L_V, then

$$\mathbf{t} \wedge \mathbf{t} = \mathbf{0} \qquad \text{since} \qquad (\mathbf{v}_1 \wedge \cdots \wedge \mathbf{v}_p) \wedge (\mathbf{v}_1 \wedge \cdots \wedge \mathbf{v}_p) = \mathbf{0}$$

by (10.15). This imposes certain relations upon the Plücker coordinates. For example, take $n = 4$, $p = 2$, so that (11.2) becomes

$$\mathbf{t} = \sum_{i<j} t^{ij}\, \mathbf{e}_i \wedge \mathbf{e}_j$$

Then

$$\begin{aligned}
\mathbf{t} \wedge \mathbf{t} &= \Big(\sum_{i<j} t^{ij}\, \mathbf{e}_i \wedge \mathbf{e}_j\Big) \wedge \Big(\sum_{h<k} t^{hk}\, \mathbf{e}_h \wedge \mathbf{e}_k\Big) \\
&= \sum_{i<j} \sum_{h<k} t^{ij} t^{hk}\, \mathbf{e}_i \wedge \mathbf{e}_j \wedge \mathbf{e}_h \wedge \mathbf{e}_k \\
&= 2(t^{12}t^{34} - t^{13}t^{24} + t^{14}t^{23})\mathbf{e}_1 \wedge \mathbf{e}_2 \wedge \mathbf{e}_3 \wedge \mathbf{e}_4
\end{aligned}$$

Since $\mathbf{t} \wedge \mathbf{t} = \mathbf{0}$ if $\mathbf{t}$ is in L_V, we find that the Plücker coordinates must satisfy the equation

11.4 $\qquad t^{12}t^{34} - t^{13}t^{24} + t^{14}t^{23} = 0$

if $1 + 1 \neq 0$ in K.

In general, those points of $\mathbf{P}_r(K)$ which correspond to p-dimensional subspaces of U must satisfy certain conditions which can be expressed as algebraic conditions of the type (11.4) on their homogeneous coordinates. The points of the projective space which do correspond to p-dimensional subspaces of U constitute a subset called the *Grassmann variety* of p-dimensional subspaces in U.

Now consider the special case of an *oriented* euclidean vector space U of dimension n over $\mathbf{R}$. We recall (Sec. 13, Chap. 14) that the orientation simply divides the bases in U into positive and negative classes, two bases in the same class being related by a matrix with positive determinant.

Denote by $(\mathbf{x}, \mathbf{y})$ the inner product of two vectors in U. That same operation makes every subspace V of U into a euclidean vector space, of course, and V can be oriented in two ways (if $\dim V > 0$).

Let $\{\mathbf{e}_1, \ldots, \mathbf{e}_n\}$ be a *positive* orthonormal base in U, and let $\mathbf{u}_1, \ldots, \mathbf{u}_n$ be arbitrary vectors, say, $\mathbf{u}_i = c^j{}_i\mathbf{e}_j$. Let $\mathbf{f}$ be the endomorphism of U such that $\mathbf{f}(\mathbf{e}_1) = \mathbf{u}_i$ $(i = 1, \ldots, n)$. We make the following definition:

11.5 $$\det(\mathbf{u}_1, \ldots, \mathbf{u}_n) = \det \mathbf{f}$$

By Theorem 10.2, $\hat{\mathbf{f}}(\mathbf{e}_1 \wedge \cdots \wedge e_n) = \mathbf{f}(\mathbf{e}_1) \wedge \cdots \wedge \mathbf{f}(\mathbf{e}_n) = \mathbf{u}_1 \wedge \cdots \wedge \mathbf{u}_n$. By Definition 10.1, $\hat{\mathbf{f}}(\mathbf{e}_1 \wedge \cdots \wedge \mathbf{e}_n) = (\det \mathbf{f}) \cdot \mathbf{e}_1 \wedge \cdots \wedge \mathbf{e}_n$. Hence

11.6 $$\mathbf{u}_1 \wedge \cdots \wedge \mathbf{u}_n = \det(\mathbf{u}_1, \ldots, \mathbf{u}_n) \cdot \mathbf{e}_1 \wedge \cdots \wedge \mathbf{e}_n$$

By (10.33), (10.34),

11.7 $$\det(\mathbf{u}_1, \ldots, \mathbf{u}_n) = \det(c^j{}_i)$$

If $\{\mathbf{u}_1, \ldots, \mathbf{u}_n\}$ is also an orthonormal base, then $\mathbf{c} = (c^j{}_i)$ is an orthogonal matrix, ${}^t\mathbf{c}\mathbf{c} = \mathbf{I}$, whence $(\det \mathbf{c})^2 = 1$, or $\det \mathbf{c} = \pm 1$. If $\{\mathbf{e}_1, \ldots, \mathbf{e}_n\}$, $\{\mathbf{u}_1, \ldots, \mathbf{u}_n\}$ are both positive orthonormal bases (or both negative), then $\det \mathbf{c} = +1$, and (11.6) becomes

$$\mathbf{u}_1 \wedge \cdots \wedge \mathbf{u}_n = \mathbf{e}_1 \wedge \cdots \wedge \mathbf{e}_n$$

We define

11.8 $$\Omega = \mathbf{e}_1 \wedge \cdots \wedge \mathbf{e}_n$$

where $\{\mathbf{e}_1, \ldots, \mathbf{e}_n\}$ is any positive orthonormal base. The preceding equation shows that Ω does not depend upon the choice of base. Equation (11.6) can be written

11.9 $$\mathbf{u}_1 \wedge \cdots \wedge \mathbf{u}_n = \det(\mathbf{u}_1, \ldots, \mathbf{u}_n) \cdot \Omega$$

It is clear that $\det(\mathbf{u}_1, \ldots, \mathbf{u}_n)$ does not depend on the positive orthonormal base involved in (11.5). From Sec. 6, Chap. 11, the number $|\det(\mathbf{u}_1, \ldots, \mathbf{u}_n)|$ can be interpreted as the volume of the parallelepiped determined in U by the vectors $\mathbf{u}_1, \ldots, \mathbf{u}_n$. It is easily verified that $\det(\mathbf{u}_1, \ldots, \mathbf{u}_n)$ is an n-linear function.

Now let $\mathbf{v}_1, \ldots, \mathbf{v}_p$ be linearly independent vectors in U. They span a p-dimensional subspace V, and the foregoing considerations can be applied to V, once an orientation has been chosen for V. The quantity

11.10 $$\det(\mathbf{v}_1, \ldots, \mathbf{v}_p)$$

is then defined by (11.5) applied to V. (We define this quantity to be zero if $\mathbf{v}_1, \ldots, \mathbf{v}_p$ are linearly dependent.) Reversing the orientation in V changes the sign of (11.10). Thus the absolute value

11.11 $$|\det(\mathbf{v}_1, \ldots, \mathbf{v}_p)|$$

depends only on $\mathbf{v}_1, \ldots, \mathbf{v}_p$ and not on the orientation of V.

It is clear that

11.12 $$\det(\mathbf{v}_1, \ldots, c\mathbf{v}_j, \ldots, \mathbf{v}_p) = c \cdot \det(\mathbf{v}_1, \ldots, \mathbf{v}_j, \ldots, \mathbf{v}_p)$$

However, the function $\det(\mathbf{v}_1, \ldots, \mathbf{v}_p)$ is not multilinear, since it involves orienting p-dimensional subspaces of U, and there is no consistent way of orienting them all at once except for $p = 0$, $p = n$.

If $\mathbf{v}_1 \wedge \cdots \wedge \mathbf{v}_p = \mathbf{v}'_1 \wedge \cdots \wedge \mathbf{v}'_p$, then $\det(\mathbf{v}_1, \ldots, \mathbf{v}_p) = \det(\mathbf{v}'_1, \ldots, \mathbf{v}'_p)$. For if $\mathbf{v}_1 \wedge \cdots \wedge \mathbf{v}_p = \mathbf{0}$, then the $\mathbf{v}_i$, hence also the $\mathbf{v}'_i$, are linearly dependent, and the determinants are zero, by definition. If $\mathbf{v}_1 \wedge \cdots \wedge \mathbf{v}_p \neq \mathbf{0}$, we have $\mathbf{v}_1 \wedge \cdots \wedge \mathbf{v}_p \wedge \mathbf{v}'_j = \mathbf{v}'_1 \wedge \cdots \wedge \mathbf{v}'_p \wedge \mathbf{v}'_j = \mathbf{0}$, from which it follows that $\mathbf{v}_1, \ldots, \mathbf{v}_p, \mathbf{v}'_j$ are linearly dependent, but $\mathbf{v}_1, \ldots, \mathbf{v}_p$ are not, by (10.18). Hence $\mathbf{v}'_j$ is in the subspace spanned by $\mathbf{v}_1, \ldots, \mathbf{v}_p$. We conclude at once that $\mathbf{v}_1, \ldots, \mathbf{v}_p$ and $\mathbf{v}'_1, \ldots, \mathbf{v}'_p$ span precisely the same subspace V. (This amounts to saying that two different subspaces of U cannot have the same Plücker coordinates.) An orientation of V being fixed, the equality of the two determinants above follows from (11.9) applied to V rather than U.

Let $\mathbf{v}$ be a *decomposable* element in $\Lambda^p U$. That is, $\mathbf{v}$ can be expressed in at least one way as a product $\mathbf{v} = \mathbf{v}_1 \wedge \cdots \wedge \mathbf{v}_p$ of vectors in U. If $\mathbf{v} \neq 0$, then those vectors span a p-dimensional subspace V. As we have just seen, if also $\mathbf{v} = \mathbf{v}'_1 \wedge \cdots \wedge \mathbf{v}'_p$, then $\mathbf{v}'_1, \ldots, \mathbf{v}'_p$ span the same subspace, and $\det(\mathbf{v}_1, \ldots, \mathbf{v}_p) = \det(\mathbf{v}'_1, \ldots, \mathbf{v}'_p)$. This number therefore depends only on $\mathbf{v}$ (and the orientation of V). Accordingly we define

11.13 $$\det \mathbf{v} = \det(\mathbf{v}_1, \ldots, \mathbf{v}_p) \qquad \text{if } \mathbf{v} = \mathbf{v}_1 \wedge \cdots \wedge \mathbf{v}_p$$

The absolute value $|\det \mathbf{v}|$ depends only on the element $\mathbf{v}$.

Let $\mathbf{v} = \mathbf{v}_1 \wedge \cdots \wedge \mathbf{v}_p$ and $\mathbf{w} = \mathbf{w}_1 \wedge \cdots \wedge \mathbf{w}_q$ be nonzero elements of $\Lambda^p U$ and $\Lambda^q U$. and suppose that the p-dimensional subspace V determined by $\mathbf{v}$ is orthogonal to the q-dimensional subspace W determined by $\mathbf{w}$. We say then that $\mathbf{v}$, $\mathbf{w}$ are orthogonal. Let $\{\mathbf{e}_1, \ldots, \mathbf{e}_p\}$ be an orthonormal base in V, and let $\{\mathbf{e}_{p+1}, \ldots, \mathbf{e}_{p+q}\}$ be an orthonormal base in W. Then $\{\mathbf{e}_1, \ldots, \mathbf{e}_{p+q}\}$ is an orthonormal base in the $(p+q)$-dimensional subspace Y determined by $\mathbf{v} \wedge \mathbf{w}$. By (11.6), (11.13) we have

$$\begin{aligned} \mathbf{v} &= \pm |\det \mathbf{v}| \cdot \mathbf{e}_1 \wedge \cdots \wedge \mathbf{e}_p && \text{in } V \\ \mathbf{w} &= \pm |\det \mathbf{w}| \cdot \mathbf{e}_{p+1} \wedge \cdots \wedge \mathbf{e}_{p+q} && \text{in } W \\ \mathbf{v} \wedge \mathbf{w} &= \pm |\det (\mathbf{v} \wedge \mathbf{w})| \cdot \mathbf{e}_1 \wedge \cdots \wedge \mathbf{e}_{p+q} && \text{in } Y \end{aligned}$$

Hence

11.14 $$|\det \mathbf{v}| \cdot |\det \mathbf{w}| = \det |\mathbf{v} \wedge \mathbf{w}| \qquad \text{if } \mathbf{v}, \mathbf{w} \textit{ are orthogonal}$$

Now let $\mathbf{v}$ be a nonzero *decomposable* element in $\Lambda^p U$. As we have just seen, $\mathbf{v}$ determines a unique p-dimensional subspace V in U. Let $V^\perp$ denote its *orthogonal complement*, consisting of all vectors $\mathbf{x}$ in U such that $(\mathbf{x}, \mathbf{y}) = 0$ for every $\mathbf{y}$ in V. $V^\perp$ is an $(n-p)$-dimensional subspace, hence corresponds to a one-dimensional subspace $L_{V^\perp}$ in $\Lambda^{n-p}U$. If $\{\mathbf{w}_1, \ldots, \mathbf{w}_{n-p}\}$ is a base in $V^\perp$, then $L_{V^\perp}$ is spanned by the element $\mathbf{w} = \mathbf{w}_1 \wedge \cdots \wedge \mathbf{w}_{n-p}$. We now choose the base to satisfy the condition

11.15 $$\begin{aligned} &|\det \mathbf{w}| = |\det \mathbf{v}| \\ &\det \mathbf{v} \wedge \mathbf{w} > 0 \end{aligned}$$

The second condition here merely requires that, if $\mathbf{v} = \mathbf{v}_1 \wedge \cdots \wedge \mathbf{v}_p$, then $\{\mathbf{v}_1, \ldots, \mathbf{v}_p, \mathbf{w}_1, \ldots, \mathbf{w}_{n-p}\}$ must be a positive base in U. Starting with any base $\{\mathbf{w}_1, \ldots, \mathbf{w}_{n-p}\}$ one obtains a base meeting the conditions by simply replacing $\mathbf{w}_1$ by a suitable multiple $c\mathbf{w}_1$, as is easily seen (assuming $n - p > 0$).

The base $\{\mathbf{w}_1, \ldots, \mathbf{w}_{n-p}\}$ in $V^\perp$ is not uniquely determined by these conditions, but the element $\mathbf{w} = \mathbf{w}_1 \wedge \cdots \wedge \mathbf{w}_{n-p}$ in $\Lambda^{n-p}U$ is uniquely determined. For if $\{\mathbf{w}'_1, \ldots, \mathbf{w}'_{n-p}\}$ is another base in $V^\perp$, then $\mathbf{w}$ and $\mathbf{w}' = \mathbf{w}'_1 \wedge \cdots \wedge \mathbf{w}'_{n-p}$ are both in the same one-dimensional subspace $L_{V^\perp}$, and so $\mathbf{w}' = a\mathbf{w}$, for some number a. If $\mathbf{w}'$ satisfies (11.15), then $a = 1$, clearly. The element $\mathbf{w}$, uniquely determined by $\mathbf{v}$, is called the *dual* of $\mathbf{v}$ and is denoted by $*\mathbf{v}$. Equation (11.15) then reads

11.16 $$\begin{cases} |\det (*\mathbf{v})| = |\det \mathbf{v}| \\ \det (\mathbf{v} \wedge *\mathbf{v}) > 0 \end{cases}$$

For $\mathbf{v} = \mathbf{0}$ we define $*\mathbf{v} = \mathbf{0}$, naturally.

For any positive orthonormal base $\{\mathbf{e}_1, \ldots, \mathbf{e}_n\}$ in U it follows at once that that $*(\mathbf{e}_1 \wedge \cdots \wedge \mathbf{e}_p) = \mathbf{e}_{p+1} \wedge \cdots \wedge \mathbf{e}_n$. More generally, if $\mathbf{e}_{i_1} \wedge \cdots \wedge \mathbf{e}_{i_p} \neq 0$, that is, if the indices are distinct, then

11.17 $$*(\mathbf{e}_{i_1} \wedge \cdots \wedge \mathbf{e}_{i_p}) = \pm \mathbf{e}_{i_{p+1}} \wedge \cdots \wedge \mathbf{e}_{i_n}$$

where $i_{p+1}, \ldots, i_n$ are indices such that $i_1, \ldots, i_n$ is a permutation of $1, \ldots, n$, the sign $\pm$ in (11.17) being the sign of that permutation. For example, if $n = 3$, we have

11.18 $$*(\mathbf{e}_1 \wedge \mathbf{e}_2) = \mathbf{e}_3 \qquad *(\mathbf{e}_1 \wedge \mathbf{e}_3) = -\mathbf{e}_2 \qquad *(\mathbf{e}_2 \wedge \mathbf{e}_3) = \mathbf{e}_1$$

The operation $*$ assigns to every nonzero *decomposable* element $\mathbf{v}$ in $\Lambda^p U$ a certain nonzero decomposable element $*\mathbf{v}$ in $\Lambda^{n-p} U$. We naturally define $*\mathbf{v} = \mathbf{0}$ if $\mathbf{v} = \mathbf{0}$, and we now show that $*$ can be uniquely extended, by the requirement of linearity, to a mapping $\Lambda^p U \to \Lambda^{n-p} U$.

We first observe that the mapping

$$g\colon \underbrace{U \times \cdots \times U}_{p} \to \Lambda^{n-p} U$$

defined by

11.19 $$\mathbf{g}(\mathbf{v}_1, \ldots, \mathbf{v}_p) = *(\mathbf{v}_1 \wedge \cdots \wedge \mathbf{v}_p)$$

is p-linear. We shall prove this for the first entry $\mathbf{v}_1$.

The equation $\mathbf{g}(c\mathbf{v}_1, \mathbf{v}_2, \ldots, \mathbf{v}_p) = c \cdot \mathbf{g}(\mathbf{v}_1, \ldots, \mathbf{v}_p)$ is the same as

11.20 $$*(c\mathbf{v}_1 \wedge \mathbf{v}_2 \wedge \cdots \wedge \mathbf{v}_p) = c \cdot *(\mathbf{v}_1 \wedge \cdots \wedge \mathbf{v}_p)$$

Write $\mathbf{v} = \mathbf{v}_1 \wedge \cdots \wedge \mathbf{v}_p$. The equation is trivial if $c = 0$ or if $\mathbf{v} = \mathbf{0}$, and we therefore assume that they are nonzero. We have $(c\mathbf{v}_1) \wedge \mathbf{v}_2 \wedge \cdots \wedge \mathbf{v}_p = c \cdot (\mathbf{v}_1 \wedge \cdots \wedge \mathbf{v}_p) = c\mathbf{v}$, and $\det (c\mathbf{v}) = c \cdot \det \mathbf{v}$, by (11.12). Since $\mathbf{v}$ and $c\mathbf{v}$ determine the same p-dimensional subspace of U, it follows that $*\mathbf{v}$ and $*(c\mathbf{v})$ can differ only by a scalar factor. We want to show that $*(c\mathbf{v}) = c \cdot (*\mathbf{v})$. Just as with $c\mathbf{v}$, we have $\det c(*\mathbf{v}) = c \cdot \det (*\mathbf{v})$. It is trivial to verify that $c(*\mathbf{v})$ fulfills the requirements (11.16) for $*(c\mathbf{v})$.

Next we must show that $g(\mathbf{v}_1 + \mathbf{v}_1', \mathbf{v}_2, \ldots, \mathbf{v}_p) = \mathbf{g}(\mathbf{v}_1, \mathbf{v}_2, \ldots, \mathbf{v}_p) + \mathbf{g}(\mathbf{v}_1', \mathbf{v}_2, \ldots, \mathbf{v}_p)$. That is, we must prove

11.21 $$*[(\mathbf{v}_1 + \mathbf{v}_1') \wedge \mathbf{v}_2 \wedge \cdots \wedge \mathbf{v}_p] = *(\mathbf{v}_1 \wedge \mathbf{v}_2 \wedge \cdots \wedge \mathbf{v}_p) + *(\mathbf{v}_1' \wedge \mathbf{v}_2 \wedge \cdots \wedge \mathbf{v}_p)$$

The equation is trivial if $\mathbf{v}_2 \wedge \cdots \wedge \mathbf{v}_p = \mathbf{0}$, and we therefore assume that $\mathbf{v}_2 \wedge \cdots \wedge \mathbf{v}_p \neq \mathbf{0}$. Let $\mathbf{u}_2, \ldots, \mathbf{u}_p$ be an orthonormal base in the space spanned by $\mathbf{v}_2, \ldots, \mathbf{v}_p$. Then we shall have $\mathbf{v}_2 \wedge \cdots \wedge \mathbf{v}_p = c \cdot \mathbf{u}_2 \wedge \cdots \wedge \mathbf{u}_p$ for some number $c \neq 0$. Set $\mathbf{u}_1 = \mathbf{v}_1 - (a_2\mathbf{u}_2 + \cdots + a_p\mathbf{u}_p)$, where $a_j = (\mathbf{v}_1, \mathbf{u}_j)$. That is, $\mathbf{u}_1$ is obtained by subtracting from $\mathbf{v}_1$ its orthogonal projection on the subspace spanned by $\mathbf{u}_2, \ldots, \mathbf{u}_p$, so that $\mathbf{u}_1$ is orthogonal to $\mathbf{u}_2, \ldots, \mathbf{u}_p$. We have

$$\begin{aligned}\mathbf{v}_1 \wedge \mathbf{v}_2 \wedge \cdots \wedge \mathbf{v}_p &= c \cdot \mathbf{v}_1 \wedge \mathbf{u}_2 \wedge \cdots \wedge \mathbf{u}_p \\ &= c \cdot (\mathbf{u}_1 + a_2\mathbf{u}_2 + \cdots + a_p\mathbf{u}_p) \wedge \mathbf{u}_2 \wedge \cdots \wedge \mathbf{u}_p \\ &= c \cdot \mathbf{u}_1 \wedge \mathbf{u}_2 \wedge \cdots \wedge \mathbf{u}_p\end{aligned}$$

Similarly, put $\mathbf{u}_1' = \mathbf{v}_1' - (a_2'\mathbf{u}_2 + \cdots + a_p'\mathbf{u}_p)$, where $a_j' = (\mathbf{v}_1', \mathbf{u}_j)$. Then

$$\mathbf{v}_1' \wedge \mathbf{v}_2 \wedge \cdots \wedge \mathbf{v}_p = c\mathbf{u}_1' \wedge \mathbf{u}_2 \wedge \cdots \wedge \mathbf{u}_p$$

and

$$(\mathbf{v}_1 + \mathbf{v}_1') \wedge \mathbf{v}_2 \wedge \cdots \wedge \mathbf{v}_p = c \cdot (\mathbf{u}_1 + \mathbf{u}_1') \wedge \mathbf{u}_2 \wedge \cdots \wedge \mathbf{u}_p$$

Putting these expressions in (11.21) and using (11.20) to get rid of the factor c, we find that (11.21) is equivalent to

11.22 $$*[(\mathbf{u}_1 + \mathbf{u}_1') \wedge \mathbf{u}_2 \wedge \cdots \wedge \mathbf{u}_p] = *(\mathbf{u}_1 \wedge \mathbf{u}_2 \wedge \cdots \wedge \mathbf{u}_p) + *(\mathbf{u}_1' \wedge \mathbf{u}_2 \wedge \cdots \wedge \mathbf{u}_p)$$

This is trivial if $\mathbf{u}_1 = \mathbf{0}$, and we assume $\mathbf{u}_1 \neq \mathbf{0}$. Set $\mathbf{u}_1'' = \mathbf{u}_1' - a\mathbf{u}_1$, where $a = (\mathbf{u}_1', \mathbf{u}_1)/(\mathbf{u}_1, \mathbf{u}_1)$, so that $\mathbf{u}_1''$ is orthogonal to $\mathbf{u}_1$ (as well as to $\mathbf{u}_2, \ldots, \mathbf{u}_p$). Writing $\mathbf{x} = \mathbf{u}_2 \wedge \cdots \wedge \mathbf{u}_p$, our equation above then becomes

11.23 $$*[(b\mathbf{u}_1 + \mathbf{u}_1'') \wedge \mathbf{x}] = *(\mathbf{u}_1 \wedge \mathbf{x}) + *[(a\mathbf{u}_1 + \mathbf{u}_1'') \wedge \mathbf{x}]$$

where $b = 1 + a$. To prove this equation we show first that

11.24 $$*[(a\mathbf{u}_1 + \mathbf{u}_1'') \wedge \mathbf{x}] = a \cdot *(\mathbf{u}_1 \wedge \mathbf{x}) + *(\mathbf{u}_1'' \wedge \mathbf{x})$$

This is trivial if $a = 0$ or $\mathbf{u}_1'' = \mathbf{0}$, and we therefore assume that they are not zero. The vectors $\mathbf{u}_1, \mathbf{u}_1'', \cdots, \mathbf{u}_p$ are then mutually orthogonal and nonzero. Let $\mathbf{w}_2, \ldots, \mathbf{w}_{n-p}$ be an orthonormal base in the orthogonal complement of the $(p + 1)$-dimensional space that they span. Then $\mathbf{u}_1'', \mathbf{w}_2, \ldots, \mathbf{w}_{n-p}$ span the space orthogonal to $\mathbf{u}_1, \mathbf{u}_2, \ldots, \mathbf{u}_p$, and so

11.25 $$*(\mathbf{u}_1 \wedge \mathbf{x}) = r\mathbf{u}_1'' \wedge \mathbf{w}_2 \wedge \cdots \wedge \mathbf{w}_{n-p}$$

for some scalar r. Since $\mathbf{v}_2, \ldots, \mathbf{v}_p$ are orthonormal, $|\det \mathbf{x}| = 1$. Clearly $|\det \mathbf{u}_1| = |\mathbf{u}_1|$. From (11.14), $|\det (\mathbf{u}_1 \wedge \mathbf{x})| = |\mathbf{u}_1|$; similarly, $\det (r\mathbf{u}_1'' \wedge \mathbf{w}_2 \wedge \cdots \wedge \mathbf{w}_{n-p}) = |r| \cdot |\mathbf{u}_1''|$. From (11.16) there follows $|\mathbf{u}_1| = |r| \cdot |\mathbf{u}_1''|$.

By similar reasoning,

11.26 $$*(\mathbf{u}_1'' \wedge \mathbf{x}) = s\mathbf{u}_1 \wedge \mathbf{w}_2 \wedge \cdots \wedge \mathbf{w}_{n-p}$$

and

$$|\mathbf{u}_1''| = |s| \cdot |\mathbf{u}_1|$$

From (11.25), (11.14)

$$\begin{aligned}(\mathbf{u}_1 \wedge \mathbf{x}) \wedge *(\mathbf{u}_1 \wedge \mathbf{x}) &= r \cdot \mathbf{u}_1 \wedge \mathbf{x} \wedge \mathbf{u}_1'' \wedge \mathbf{w}_2 \wedge \cdots \wedge \mathbf{w}_{n-p} \\ &= (-1)^{p-1} r \cdot \mathbf{u}_1 \wedge \mathbf{u}_1'' \wedge \mathbf{x} \wedge \mathbf{w}_2 \wedge \cdots \wedge \mathbf{w}_{n-p} \\ &= (-1)^{p-1} r \cdot |\mathbf{u}_1| \cdot |\mathbf{u}_1''| \cdot t \cdot \Omega\end{aligned}$$

where $t = +1$ if $\{\mathbf{u}_1, \mathbf{u}_1'', \mathbf{u}_2, \ldots, \mathbf{u}_p, \mathbf{w}_2, \ldots, \mathbf{w}_{n-p}\}$ is a positive base, and $t = -1$ if it is a negative base. By (11.16), $(-1)^{p-1}rt > 0$. In a similar way we obtain

$$(\mathbf{u}_1'' \wedge \mathbf{x}) \wedge *(\mathbf{u}_1'' \wedge \mathbf{x}) = (-1)^p s|\mathbf{u}_1||\mathbf{u}_1''| \cdot t\Omega$$

and $-(-1)^{p-1}st > 0$. Hence $r \cdot s < 0$.

The right-hand side of (11.24) is

11.27 $$(ar\mathbf{u}_1'' + s\mathbf{u}_1) \wedge \mathbf{w}_2 \wedge \cdots \wedge \mathbf{w}_{n-p}$$

To show that this is equal to the left member of (11.24), we first observe that $ar\mathbf{u}_1'' + s\mathbf{u}_1$ is orthogonal to $a\mathbf{u}_1 + \mathbf{u}_1''$. For

$$(ar\mathbf{u}_1'' + s\mathbf{u}_1, a\mathbf{u}_1 + \mathbf{u}_1'') = a^2r(\mathbf{u}_1'', \mathbf{u}_1) + ar(\mathbf{u}_1'', \mathbf{u}_1'') + as(\mathbf{u}_1, \mathbf{u}_1) + s(\mathbf{u}_1, \mathbf{u}_1'')$$

Now $(\mathbf{u}_1'', \mathbf{u}_1) = 0$. The expression reduces to

$$ar \cdot |\mathbf{u}_1''|^2 + as|\mathbf{u}_1|^2$$

Either r or s must be positive. If $r < 0$, then $r \cdot |\mathbf{u}_1''| = |\mathbf{u}_1|$, from above, and $s \cdot |\mathbf{u}_1| = -|\mathbf{u}_1|''$. Then (11.27) reduces to $a \cdot (|\mathbf{u}_1| \cdot |\mathbf{u}_1''| - |\mathbf{u}_1| \cdot |\mathbf{u}_1''|) = 0$. The same argument holds if $s > 0$ and $r < 0$.

It follows that $ar\mathbf{u}_1'' + s\mathbf{u}_1, \mathbf{w}_2, \ldots, \mathbf{w}_{n-p}$ span the space orthogonal to the space spanned by $a\mathbf{u}_1 + \mathbf{u}_1'', \mathbf{u}_2, \ldots, \mathbf{u}_p$. Hence (11.27) is equal to the left member of (11.24), apart from a possible constant factor. From (11.14),

$$\det [(a\mathbf{u}_1 + \mathbf{u}_1'') \wedge \mathbf{u}_2 \wedge \cdots \wedge \mathbf{u}_p] = |a\mathbf{u}_1 + \mathbf{u}_1''|$$

Since $\mathbf{u}_1, \mathbf{u}_1''$ are orthogonal, this is equal to $\sqrt{a^2|\mathbf{u}_1|^2 + |\mathbf{u}_1''|^2}$. Similarly, the determinant of (11.27) is equal to

$$|ar\mathbf{u}_1'' + s\mathbf{u}_1| = \sqrt{a^2r^2|\mathbf{u}_1''|^2 + s^2|\mathbf{u}_1|^2}$$

Using the fact that $r^2|\mathbf{u}_1''|^2 = |\mathbf{u}_1|^2$ and $s^2|\mathbf{u}_1|^2 = |\mathbf{u}_1''|^2$, we have

$$|ar\mathbf{u}_1'' + s\mathbf{u}_1| = |a\mathbf{u}_1 + \mathbf{u}_1''|$$

Therefore (11.27) is equal to the left member of (11.24) apart from the sign. To check that point, we have

$$\begin{aligned}[(a\mathbf{u}_1 + \mathbf{u}_1'') \wedge \mathbf{x}] \wedge (ar\mathbf{u}_1'' + s\mathbf{u}_1) \wedge \mathbf{w}_2 \wedge \cdots \wedge \mathbf{w}_{n-p} \\ = a^2r\mathbf{u}_1 \wedge \mathbf{x} \wedge \mathbf{u}_1'' \wedge \mathbf{w}_2 \wedge \cdots \wedge \mathbf{w}_{n-p} \\ + s\mathbf{u}_1'' \wedge \mathbf{x} \wedge \mathbf{u}_1 \wedge \mathbf{w}_2 \wedge \cdots \wedge \mathbf{w}_{n-p} \\ = (-1)^{p-1}(a^2r - s) \cdot \mathbf{u}_1 \wedge \mathbf{u}_1'' \wedge \mathbf{x} \wedge \mathbf{w}_2 \wedge \cdots \wedge \mathbf{w}_{n-p} \\ = (-1)^{p-1}(a^2r - s) \cdot t \cdot |\mathbf{u}_1| \cdot |\mathbf{u}_1|'' \cdot \Omega\end{aligned}$$

and $(-1)^{p-1}(a^2r - s)t > 0$, from above. This shows that (11.27) is equal to the left member of (11.24), verifying (11.24).

To show that (11.23) holds, we apply (11.24) to the left member with b in place of a. The left side of (11.23) is then equal to

$$b \cdot *(\mathbf{u}_1 \wedge \mathbf{x}) + *(\mathbf{u}_1'' \wedge \mathbf{x})$$

The right member of (11.23) is, by (11.24),

$$*(\mathbf{u}_1 \wedge \mathbf{x}) + a \cdot *(\mathbf{u}_1 \wedge \mathbf{x}) + *(\mathbf{u}_1'' \wedge \mathbf{x}) = (1 + a) \cdot *(\mathbf{u}_1 \wedge \mathbf{x}) + *(\mathbf{u}_1'' \wedge \mathbf{x})$$

Since $1 + a = b$, this proves (11.23), hence also (11.21).

This shows that $\mathbf{g}$ of (11.19) is linear in the first entry. Since $\mathbf{v}_2 \wedge \mathbf{v}_1 \wedge \mathbf{v}_3 \wedge \cdots \wedge \mathbf{v}_p = -\mathbf{v}_1 \wedge \cdots \wedge \mathbf{v}_p$, we have $*(\mathbf{v}_2 \wedge \mathbf{v}_1 \wedge \mathbf{v}_3 \wedge \cdots \wedge \mathbf{v}_p) = -*(\mathbf{v}_1 \wedge \mathbf{v}_2 \wedge$

$\cdots \wedge \mathbf{v}_p)$, by (11.20). Thus $\mathbf{g}(\mathbf{v}_1, \mathbf{v}_2, \ldots, \mathbf{v}_p) = -\mathbf{g}(\mathbf{v}_2, \mathbf{v}_1, \mathbf{v}_3, \ldots, \mathbf{v}_p)$, from which it follows that $\mathbf{g}$ is linear in the second entry $\mathbf{v}_2$. The same is true for the others.

Thus $\mathbf{g}$ is a p-linear mapping, and clearly $\mathbf{g}(\mathbf{v}_1, \mathbf{v}_2, \ldots, \mathbf{v}_p) = \mathbf{0}$ if any two entries are equal. Therefore, by Theorem 10.1, there is a unique linear mapping $\mathbf{g}'$: $\Lambda^p U \to \Lambda^{n-p} U$ such that $\mathbf{g}(\mathbf{v}_1, \ldots, \mathbf{v}_p) = \mathbf{g}'(\mathbf{v}_1 \wedge \cdots \wedge \mathbf{v}_p)$. That is,

$$\mathbf{g}'(\mathbf{v}_1 \wedge \cdots \wedge \mathbf{v}_p) = *(\mathbf{v}_1 \wedge \cdots \wedge \mathbf{v}_p)$$

For an arbitrary element $\mathbf{v}$ in $\Lambda^p U$ we denote the element $\mathbf{g}'(\mathbf{v})$ by $*\mathbf{v}$. Finally, for $p = 0$, we define $*c = c\Omega$ for any scalar c, Ω being as in (11.8); for $p = n$, we define $*(c\Omega) = c$. We have proved the following result:

THEOREM 11.1 *Let U be an oriented n-dimensional euclidean vector space over* $\mathbf{R}$. *For each $p = 0, 1, \ldots, n$ there is a linear mapping $*$ from $\Lambda^p U$ to $\Lambda^{n-p} U$ such that $*\mathbf{v}$ is given by the following conditions if $\mathbf{v}$ is decomposable: $*\mathbf{v}$ is orthogonal to $\mathbf{v}$,* $|\det \mathbf{v}| = |\det (*\mathbf{v})|$, *and* $\det (\mathbf{v} \wedge *\mathbf{v}) > 0$.

It is easily verified, using (11.16), that

11.28 $$*(*\mathbf{v}) = (-1)^{p(n-p)}\mathbf{v} \qquad \text{for } \mathbf{v} \text{ in } \Lambda^p U$$

Hence $*$ is an isomorphism. Further, $*$ can be computed from its effect on a positive orthonormal base $\{\mathbf{e}_1, \ldots, \mathbf{e}_n\}$ by (11.17), since $*$ is linear.

From (11.17) we have at once

11.29 $$(\mathbf{e}_{i_1} \wedge \cdots \wedge \mathbf{e}_{i_p}) \wedge *(\mathbf{e}_{j_1} \wedge \cdots \wedge \mathbf{e}_{j_p}) = \delta^{j_1 \ldots j_p}_{i_1 \ldots i_p} \cdot \Omega$$

where $\delta^{j_1 \ldots j_p}_{i_1 \ldots i_p}$ is the generalized Kronecker symbol introduced in Sec. 10. Let us define $(\mathbf{u}, \mathbf{v})$ by the formula

11.30 $$\mathbf{u} \wedge *\mathbf{v} = (\mathbf{u}, \mathbf{v}) \cdot \Omega \qquad \text{for } \mathbf{u}, \mathbf{v} \text{ in } \Lambda^p U$$

Hence $(\mathbf{u}, \mathbf{v}) = \det (\mathbf{u} \wedge *\mathbf{v})$, and $(\mathbf{u}, \mathbf{v})$ is a bilinear function on $\Lambda^p U$. Equation (11.29) becomes

11.31 $$(\mathbf{e}_{i_1} \wedge \cdots \wedge \mathbf{e}_{i_p}, \mathbf{e}_{j_1} \wedge \cdots \wedge \mathbf{e}_{j_p}) = \delta^{j_1 \ldots j_p}_{i_1 \ldots i_p}$$

If

$$\mathbf{u} = \sum_{i_1 < \cdots < i_p} u^{i_1 \ldots i_p} \mathbf{e}_{i_1} \wedge \cdots \wedge \mathbf{e}_{i_p}$$

and

$$\mathbf{v} = \sum_{i_1 < \cdots < i_p} v^{i_1 \ldots i_p} \mathbf{e}_{i_1} \wedge \cdots \wedge \mathbf{e}_{i_p}$$

then there follows, from (11.31),

11.32 $$(\mathbf{u}, \mathbf{v}) = \sum_{i_1 < \cdots < i_p} u^{i_1 \ldots i_p} v^{i_1 \ldots i_p}$$

Hence $(\mathbf{u}, \mathbf{v})$ is a symmetric bilinear function on $\Lambda^p U$, and $(\mathbf{u}, \mathbf{u}) > 0$ unless $\mathbf{u} = \mathbf{0}$. This form therefore gives $\Lambda^p U$ the structure of a euclidean vector space.

For $n = 3$ it is clear from (11.18) that

11.33 $$\mathbf{x} \times \mathbf{y} = *(\mathbf{x} \wedge \mathbf{y})$$

for any $\mathbf{x}$ and $\mathbf{y}$ in U, the left side of (11.33) being as defined in Sec. 13, Chap. 14.

The euclidean structure of U therefore defines a euclidean structure in each $\Lambda^p U$. In general, a bilinear function on a vector space U defines a bilinear function in $\Lambda^p U$, as we now show.

Then let U be an n-dimensional vector space over a field K, and let H denote a bilinear function on U, that is, a bilinear mapping $H\colon U \times U \to K$. Consider the mapping

$$\mathbf{f}\colon \underbrace{U \times \cdots \times U}_{2p} \to K$$

defined by

11.34 $$\mathbf{f}(\mathbf{x}_1, \ldots, \mathbf{x}_p; \mathbf{y}_1, \ldots, \mathbf{y}_p) = \Sigma \operatorname{sign} \begin{pmatrix} 1 & \cdots & p \\ i_1 & \cdots & i_p \end{pmatrix} \cdot H(\mathbf{x}_1, \mathbf{y}_{i_1}) \cdots H(\mathbf{x}_p, \mathbf{y}_{i_p})$$

the sum being over all permutations of $1, \ldots, p$. The mapping is visibly a multilinear mapping. If two adjacent $\mathbf{x}_j$ are equal, then the right-hand side is zero. For example, if $\mathbf{x}_1 = \mathbf{x}_2$, then the terms

$$H(\mathbf{x}_1, \mathbf{y}_{i_1}) \cdot H(\mathbf{x}_2, \mathbf{y}_{i_2}) \cdots H(\mathbf{x}_1, \mathbf{y}_{i_p})$$

and

$$H(\mathbf{x}_1, \mathbf{y}_{i_2}) \cdot H(\mathbf{x}_2, \mathbf{y}_{i_1}) \cdots H(\mathbf{x}_p, \mathbf{y}_{i_p})$$

are equal but occur in (11.34) with opposite signs. In a similar way one shows that (11.34) is zero of two adjacent $\mathbf{y}$'s are equal.

For fixed elements $\mathbf{y}_1, \ldots, \mathbf{y}_p$, (11.34) defines a p-linear mapping, sending a p-tuple $\mathbf{x}_1, \ldots, \mathbf{x}_p$ into $\mathbf{f}(\mathbf{x}_1, \ldots, \mathbf{x}_p; \mathbf{y}_1, \ldots, \mathbf{y}_p)$. By Theorem 10.1, there is a unique mapping

$$\mathbf{f}'\colon \Lambda^p U \times \underbrace{U \times \cdots \times U}_{p} \to K$$

which is linear in its first entry and satisfies

$$\mathbf{f}(\mathbf{x}_1, \ldots, \mathbf{x}_p; \mathbf{y}_1, \ldots, \mathbf{y}_p) = \mathbf{f}'(\mathbf{x}_1 \wedge \cdots \wedge \mathbf{x}_p; \mathbf{y}_1, \ldots, \mathbf{y}_p)$$

Since $\Lambda^p U$ is spanned by decomposable elements, one verifies easily that, for any fixed element $\mathbf{u}$ in $\Lambda^p U$, the quantity

$$\mathbf{f}'(\mathbf{u}; \mathbf{y}_1, \ldots, \mathbf{y}_p)$$

is linear in the p entries $\mathbf{y}_1, \ldots, \mathbf{y}_p$ and is zero if any two adjacent $\mathbf{y}$'s are equal. By Theorem 10.1 again, there is a unique mapping

$$H^{(p)}: \Lambda^p U \times \Lambda^p U \to K$$

such that

$$\mathbf{f}'(\mathbf{u}; \mathbf{y}_1, \ldots, \mathbf{y}_p) = H^{(p)}(\mathbf{u}, \mathbf{y}_1 \wedge \cdots \wedge \mathbf{y}_p)$$

It follows easily that $H^{(p)}$ is bilinear. In short, $H^{(p)}$ is the unique bilinear function on $\Lambda^p U$ such that

11.35 $$H^{(p)}(\mathbf{x}_1 \wedge \cdots \wedge \mathbf{x}_p; \mathbf{y}_1 \wedge \cdots \wedge \mathbf{y}_p) = \Sigma \operatorname{sign} \begin{pmatrix} 1 & \cdots & p \\ i_1 & \cdots & i_p \end{pmatrix} \cdot H(\mathbf{x}_1, \mathbf{y}_{i_1}) \cdots H(\mathbf{x}_p, \mathbf{y}_{i_p})$$

If H is symmetric, so is $H^{(p)}$, as is easily verified.

To compute $H^{(p)}$ in terms of bases, let $\{\mathbf{e}_1, \ldots, \mathbf{e}_n\}$ be a base in U, and put

11.36 $$H(\mathbf{e}_i, \mathbf{e}_j) = g_{ij}$$

From (11.35) we obtain

$$H^{(p)}(\mathbf{e}_{i_1} \wedge \cdots \wedge \mathbf{e}_{i_p}, \mathbf{e}_{j_1} \wedge \cdots \wedge \mathbf{e}_{j_p}) = \Sigma \operatorname{sign}(s) \cdot g_{i_1 j_{s1}} \cdots g_{i_p j_{sp}}$$

the sum being over all permutations s of $1, \ldots, p$ (in the sum $s1, \ldots, sp$ denote the effects of s on $1, \ldots, p$). From (2.7), Chap. 11, we see that

11.37 $$H^{(p)}(\mathbf{e}_{i_1} \wedge \cdots \wedge \mathbf{e}_{i_p}, \mathbf{e}_{j_1} \wedge \cdots \wedge \mathbf{e}_{j_p}) = \begin{vmatrix} g_{i_1 j_1} & \cdots & g_{i_1 j_p} \\ \cdots & \cdots & \cdots \\ g_{i_p j_1} & \cdots & g_{i_p j_p} \end{vmatrix}$$

Suppose now that U is a euclidean vector space over **R**, with inner product $H(\mathbf{x}, \mathbf{y})$. If $\{\mathbf{e}_1, \ldots, \mathbf{e}_n\}$ is an orthonormal base, then $g_{ij} = 1$ if $i = j$ and $g_{ij} = 0$ otherwise. If $i_1 < \cdots < i_p$ and $j_1 < \cdots < j_p$, then (11.37) is clearly equal to zero unless $i_1 = j_1, \ldots, i_p = j_p$, in which case it is equal to 1. Therefore we see that the p-vectors $\mathbf{e}_{i_1} \wedge \cdots \wedge \mathbf{e}_{i_p}$ with $i_1 < \cdots < i_p$ form an orthonormal base in $\Lambda^p U$ for the inner product $H^{(p)}$. From (11.31) it follows that $H^{(p)}$ in this case is the same as the inner product defined in (11.30) by means of the dual operator $*$.

EXERCISES

1. Let $\{\mathbf{e}_1, \ldots, \mathbf{e}_n\}$ be an orthonormal base in an oriented euclidean vector space U over **R**. Let $\mathbf{x} = 3\mathbf{e}_1 - \mathbf{e}_2 + \mathbf{e}_3$ and let $\mathbf{y} = \mathbf{e}_1 + \mathbf{e}_2 - \mathbf{e}_3$. Compute $*(\mathbf{x} \wedge \mathbf{y})$.

2. Let $\{\mathbf{e}_1, \ldots, \mathbf{e}_4\}$ be as above, with $n = 4$. Find the Plücker coordinates of the two-dimensional space spanned by $\mathbf{u} = \mathbf{e}_1 - \mathbf{e}_3 + 4\mathbf{e}_4$ and $\mathbf{v} = \mathbf{e}_1 + \mathbf{e}_2 - 3\mathbf{e}_3$. Compute $\det \mathbf{u} \wedge \mathbf{v}$.

3. Let $\{\mathbf{e}_1, \ldots, \mathbf{e}_4\}$ be as above. The quantities $t^{12} = 4$, $t^{13} = -1$, $t^{14} = 2$, $t^{23} = -6$, $t^{24} = 4$, $t^{34} = 2$ are Plücker coordinates of a two-dimensional subspace. Find a base for that subspace.

4. Let V_1 and V_2 be p-dimensional subspaces of an oriented n-dimensional euclidean vector space U. Prove that $V_1 = V_2$ if they have the same Plücker coordinates.

5. Let U be as above, and let $\mathbf{v}_1, \ldots, \mathbf{v}_p$ be vectors in U, with $\mathbf{v}_1$ orthogonal to $\mathbf{v}_2, \ldots, \mathbf{v}_p$. Prove that

$$|\mathbf{v}_1|^2 \cdot *(\mathbf{v}_2 \wedge \cdots \wedge \mathbf{v}_p) = (-1)^{p-1} \cdot \mathbf{v}_1 \wedge *(\mathbf{v}_1 \wedge \mathbf{v}_2 \wedge \cdots \wedge \mathbf{v}_p).$$

6. Prove that there is a natural isomorphism from $\Lambda^p U^*$ to the dual space of $\Lambda^p U$, U being a finite dimensional vector space over any field.

12. Skew-symmetric tensors

We consider here an n-dimensional vector space U over a field K of *characteristic zero.* That is, we assume that no multiple of the unit element 1 in K is zero. The fields $\mathbf{Q}$, $\mathbf{R}$, $\mathbf{C}$ are fields of characteristic zero.

Consider now the tensor space

12.1 $$U^p{}_0 = U \otimes \cdots \otimes U \qquad (p \text{ times})$$

In Sec. 8 we defined the notion of an *alternating*, or *skew-symmetric*, element of $U^p{}_0$. Let us denote by $A^p(U)$ the set of all alternating elements of $U^p{}_0$. $A^p(U)$ is a subspace of $U^p{}_0$.† We shall show here that $A^p(U)$ can be identified with the exterior product $\Lambda^p U$:

Let A_p denote the alternation operator defined in (8.20). Thus A_p is a linear mapping $U^p{}_0 \to A^p(U)$, and $A_p(\mathbf{t}) = \mathbf{t}$ for any $\mathbf{t}$ in $A^p U$. It follows at once that $A^p(U)$ is spanned by the elements

12.2 $$A_p(\mathbf{e}_{i_1} \otimes \cdots \otimes \mathbf{e}_{i_p}) \qquad (i_1 < i_2 < \cdots < i_p)$$

and they form a base in $A^p(U)$, as follows easily from the fact that all the elements $\mathbf{e}_{j_1} \otimes \cdots \otimes \mathbf{e}_{j_p}$ form a base in $U^p{}_0$.

The mapping

$$\mathbf{h}_p\colon \underbrace{U \times \cdots \times U}_{p} \to A^p(U)$$

defined by

12.3 $$\mathbf{h}_p(\mathbf{x}_1, \ldots, \mathbf{x}_p) = A_p(\mathbf{x}_1 \otimes \cdots \otimes \mathbf{x}_p)$$

is a p-linear mapping, obviously, and $\mathbf{h}(\mathbf{x}_1, \ldots, \mathbf{x}_p) = \mathbf{0}$ if any two adjacent $\mathbf{x}_j$ are equal. Therefore (Theorem 10.1) there is a unique linear mapping $\mathbf{h}'_p\colon \Lambda^p U \to A^p(U)$ such that

12.4 $$\mathbf{h}'_p(\mathbf{x}_1 \wedge \cdots \wedge \mathbf{x}_p) = A_p(\mathbf{x}_1 \otimes \cdots \otimes \mathbf{x}_p)$$

for any $\mathbf{x}_j$ in U.‡ In particular

$$\mathbf{h}'_p(\mathbf{e}_{i_1} \wedge \cdots \wedge \mathbf{e}_{i_p}) = A_p(\mathbf{e}_{i_1} \otimes \cdots \otimes \mathbf{e}_{i_p})$$

† By $A^0(U)$ we understand $U^0{}_0 = K$. Similarly, $A^1(U)$ is U itself.
‡ For $p = 0$, $\mathbf{h}'_0 = \mathbf{h}_0$ is just the identity mapping of $\Lambda^0 U = K$ to $U^0{}_0 = K$.

From this we conclude that $\mathbf{h}'_p$ is an isomorphism. Furthermore, if $\mathbf{u}$ is in $\Lambda^p U$ and if $\mathbf{v}$ is in $\Lambda^q U$, then

12.5 $$\mathbf{h}'_{p+q}(\mathbf{u} \wedge \mathbf{v}) = A_{p+q}(\mathbf{h}'_p(\mathbf{u}) \otimes \mathbf{h}'_q(\mathbf{v}))$$

By linearity it suffices to check this for decomposable elements $\mathbf{u} = \mathbf{x}_1 \wedge \cdots \wedge \mathbf{x}_p$ and $\mathbf{v} = \mathbf{y}_1 \wedge \cdots \wedge \mathbf{y}_q$. The right-hand side of (12.5) is then equal to

12.6 $$A_{p+q}(A_p(\mathbf{x}_1 \otimes \cdots \otimes \mathbf{x}_p) \otimes A_q(\mathbf{y}_1 \otimes \cdots \otimes \mathbf{y}_q))$$

By (8.20),

$$A_p(\mathbf{x}_1 \otimes \cdots \otimes \mathbf{x}_p) = \frac{1}{p!} \sum_{\sigma} \operatorname{sign}(\sigma) \cdot \mathbf{x}_{\sigma(1)} \otimes \cdots \otimes \mathbf{x}_{\sigma(p)}$$

where σ runs over all permutations of $1, \ldots, p$. Similarly, if we write $\mathbf{y}_1 = \mathbf{x}_{p+1}, \ldots, \mathbf{y}_q = \mathbf{x}_{p+q}$, then

$$A_q(\mathbf{y}_1 \otimes \cdots \otimes \mathbf{y}_q) = \frac{1}{q!} \sum_{\sigma'} \operatorname{sign} \sigma' \cdot \mathbf{x}_{\sigma'(p+1)} \otimes \cdots \otimes \mathbf{x}_{\sigma'(p+q)}$$

where σ' runs over all permutations of $p + 1, \ldots, p + q$. For σ and σ' as above denote by $\sigma\sigma'$ the permutation of $1, \ldots, p + q$ defined by

$$\sigma\sigma'(j) = \begin{cases} \sigma(j) & (j = 1, \ldots, p) \\ \sigma'(j) & (j = p + 1, \ldots, q) \end{cases}$$

Then (12.6) can be written as

$$\frac{1}{p!q!(p+q)!} \sum_{\tau,\sigma,\sigma'} \operatorname{sign}(\tau\sigma\sigma')\mathbf{x}_{\tau\sigma\sigma'(1)} \otimes \cdots \otimes \mathbf{x}_{\tau\sigma\sigma'(p+q)}$$

using the fact that $\operatorname{sign}(\tau) \operatorname{sign}(\sigma) \operatorname{sign}(\sigma') = \operatorname{sign}(\tau\sigma\sigma')$, τ here running through all permutations of $1, \ldots, p + q$. As it does so, the element $\tau\sigma\sigma'$ also runs through all permutations of $1, \ldots, p + q$, and there are $p!q!$ pairs σ, σ'. Hence the sum above is the same as

$$\begin{aligned} \frac{1}{(p+q)!} \cdot \sum \operatorname{sign}(\tau) \cdot \mathbf{x}_{\tau(1)} \otimes \cdots \otimes \mathbf{x}_{\tau(p+q)} \\ = A_{p+q}(\mathbf{x}_1 \otimes \cdots \otimes \mathbf{x}_{p+q}) \\ = A_{p+q}(\mathbf{x}_1 \otimes \cdots \otimes \mathbf{x}_p \otimes \mathbf{y}_1 \otimes \cdots \otimes \mathbf{y}_q) \\ = \mathbf{h}'_{p+q}(\mathbf{x}_1 \wedge \cdots \wedge \mathbf{x}_p \wedge \mathbf{y}_1 \wedge \cdots \wedge \mathbf{y}_q) \end{aligned}$$

and this is equal to the left side of (12.5) for $\mathbf{u} = \mathbf{x}_1 \wedge \cdots \wedge \mathbf{x}_p$ and $\mathbf{v} = \mathbf{y}_1 \wedge \cdots \wedge \mathbf{y}_q$.

If we define a product $\mathbf{t}_p \wedge \mathbf{t}'_q$ of an element $\mathbf{t}_p$ in $A^p(U)$ and an element $\mathbf{t}'_q$ in $A^q(U)$ by

12.7 $$\mathbf{t}_p \wedge \mathbf{t}_q = A_{p+q}(\mathbf{t}_p \otimes \mathbf{t}'_q)$$

then (12.5) becomes

12.8 $$\mathbf{h}'_{p+q}(\mathbf{u} \wedge \mathbf{v}) = \mathbf{h}'_p(\mathbf{u}) \wedge \mathbf{h}'_q(\mathbf{v})$$

Now put

12.9 $$A(U) = A^0(U) \oplus A^1(U) \oplus \cdots \oplus A^n(U)$$

where we understand $A^0(U) = K$ and $A^1(U) = U$. If $\mathbf{t}$ and $\mathbf{t}'$ are any two elements of (12.9), then we can write uniquely

$$\mathbf{t} = \mathbf{t}_0 + \mathbf{t}_1 + \cdots + \mathbf{t}_n$$
$$\mathbf{t}' = \mathbf{t}'_0 + \mathbf{t}'_1 + \cdots + \mathbf{t}'_n$$

with $\mathbf{t}_p$ and $\mathbf{t}'_p$ in $A^p(U)$. We define the product of $\mathbf{t}$ and $\mathbf{t}'$ by the obvious rule

12.10 $$\mathbf{t} \wedge \mathbf{t}' = \sum_{p,q} \mathbf{t}_p \wedge \mathbf{t}'_q$$

each term on the right being defined by (12.7). Furthermore any $\mathbf{u}$ in $\bigwedge U$ can be written uniquely as a sum

$$\mathbf{u} = \mathbf{u}_0 + \mathbf{u}_1 + \cdots + \mathbf{u}_n$$

with $\mathbf{u}_p$ in $\bigwedge^p U$. We define

12.11 $$\mathbf{h}(\mathbf{u}) = \sum_1^n \mathbf{h}'_p(\mathbf{u}_p)$$

It is clear that $\mathbf{h}$ is a linear mapping $\mathbf{h}\colon \bigwedge U \to AU$, and

12.12 $$\mathbf{h}(\mathbf{u} \wedge \mathbf{v}) = \mathbf{h}(\mathbf{u}) \wedge \mathbf{h}(\mathbf{v})$$

for any two elements $\mathbf{u}$, $\mathbf{v}$ of $\bigwedge U$, and that $\mathbf{h}$ is compatible with the operation of $GL(U)$.

We have proved the following theorem:

THEOREM 12.1 *Let U be an n-dimensional vector space over a field K of characteristic zero. Let $A(U)$ denote the algebra of alternating tensors* (12.9) *with product defined by* (12.7). *Then there is a natural isomorphism* $\mathbf{h}\colon \bigwedge U \to A(U)$ *of the exterior algebra of U to $A(U)$.*

For this reason the exterior algebra of a vector space over the real field is quite often defined to be what we have here called $A(U)$. According to Theorem 7.1, an element in $A^p(U)$ can be unambiguously identified with a skew-symmetric p-linear function on U^*.

Index

Numbers in italic type indicate the reference is in an exercise